NORDIC PROTECTORATE

• Stockholm

• Riga

BALTIC SEA

DIS...

——— National Border

- - - - - - - Autonomous or Semi-Autonomous Region

Areas Under German Civil or Military Law

Danzig

NEW REICH

Hamburg

OLD REICH

Berlin • Posen

Vistula

Göringstadt

□ *Ruins*

SOVIET UNION

Oder

Breslau •

GENERAL GOVERNMENT

Cracow •

Hitlerstadt •

• Neu Sandez

Danube

//// *Szaflary*

• Vienna

Munich •

• Budapest

RUMANIAN REICHSKOMMISARIAT

Belgrade •

BLACK SEA

ITALIAN AUTONOMOUS REGION

• Rome

SOUTHEASTERN REICHSKOMMISARIAT

TURKEY

THE
Children's
War

THE
Children's
War

J.N. STROYAR

POCKET BOOKS

New York   London   Toronto   Sydney   Singapore

POCKET BOOKS, a division of Simon & Schuster, Inc.
1230 Avenue of the Americas, New York, NY 10020

Copyright © 2001 by J. N. Stroyar

Library of Congress Cataloging-in-Publication Data

Stroyar, J. N.
   The children's war / J. N. Stroyar.
    p. cm.
   ISBN 0-7434-0739-3
    1. World War, 1939–1945—Influence—Fiction.   2. National socialism—Fiction.
  3. Europe—Fiction. 4. Nazis—Fiction. I. Title.

PS3569.T7366 C48 2001
813'.6—dc21   00-068683

First Pocket Books hardcover printing June 2001

10 9 8 7 6 5 4 3 2 1

Maps by Paul Pugliese

Printed in the U.S.A.

To Genia
(1930–1945)
slave laborer
(1940–45)
You have not been forgotten.

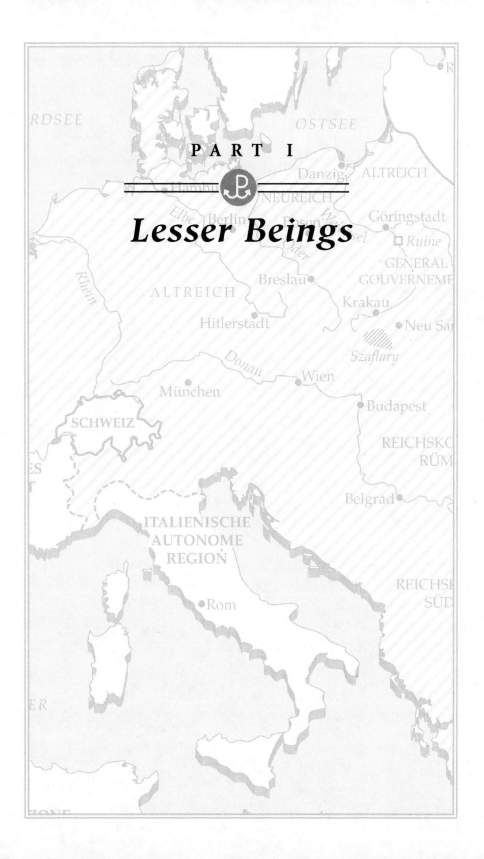

PART I

Lesser Beings

———————————— 1 ————————————

"**A**S THE LONDON DIVISIONS of the glorious troops of the Fatherland march proudly past the gauleiter's podium, they salute the Thousand Year Reich!" the announcer intoned pompously. "Following them, in impressive formation, are the noble soldiers of our great allies, the Red Army! Together our victorious armies will defeat the evil empire of capitalist gangsters across the Atlantic and claim our rightful place as the only superpower of the millennium!"

It was enough to make him get up and turn the television off. The room went dark, illuminated only by the thin strip of orange light that scattered off the night fog to find its way through the gap between the shade and the window frame. The ominous thump, thump, thump of a police helicopter flying low overhead rattled the thin glass of the windowpane. Neither of them took any notice of it.

Allison slumped onto the pillow on his bed and took a deep drag off the cigarette he had momentarily abandoned. "Did you go?" she asked, waving her hand at the television to indicate the parade that they had just seen on the news.

"Of course! You know me, always the patriot!"

"Yes, our little blond-haired, blue-eyed Aryan boy!" she enthused comically.

"There's more brown than blond," he sniffed, "and my eyes are gray!"

"It has always bugged you, hasn't it, looking like one of their poster boys?" she guessed with an indulgent smile.

"No. Other people have always bugged me, trying to convert me, trying to get me . . ." He stopped, suddenly aware that she had been teasing. He smiled sheepishly at his folly and she laughed in response.

"So why did you go to the parade?" she asked.

"It ran right past the restaurant, so I didn't get much choice. We all stepped outside, waving our little flags. Look." He pointed at the bedside table. "I brought one of each back for you."

She glanced at the two flags lying intimately one on top of the other, the hammer and sickle obscuring most of the swastika. "Ah, yes, so we're allies again," she observed.

"Seems so."

"They did the switch rather fast this time."

"That's because nobody gives a fuck anymore," he guessed as he returned to the bed and gently removed the cigarette from her fingers. He stubbed it out, then turned to look at her suggestively. "I certainly don't, do you?"

"What's this?" She picked up an official-looking piece of paper that was lying underneath the little flags.

"Ach, a notice from the neighborhood committee. I've missed three meetings this month. Don't worry, I'll get the restaurant to say I was on the evening shift."

"I do worry," she countered. "You should go to these things. It doesn't look good to miss so many."

He waved his hand in exasperation. "Every time I go, the local matrons swoop down on me like vultures so they can introduce me to eligible and near-eligible women. 'Not married! How are you ever going to get a flat?' " he mimicked. "Sooner or later they're going to march me and some other poor unfortunate to the registry office and we'll be married before we can sober up enough to object."

"Maybe you should get married. Find someone you could trust, you know, from the organization."

He sat next to her on the bed and gently curled one of her dark locks around his finger. "Then there'd be two divorces necessary, wouldn't there?"

She smiled wanly. "Isn't it about time we go pick up those papers?"

He shook his head. "No, I was warned off our contact this morning. May be tainted."

"So there's no work for tonight?" she sniffed. "I canceled going to a concert with . . ."

"Your husband?" he asked as he leaned into her and kissed her neck, then her cheek, then her lips.

"Why didn't you tell me earlier?"

"I'm sorry. I didn't mean to mislead you, I only just found out this morning. There's still time if you want to go." His hand slid down her arm to clasp her hand.

Her fingers wove into his. "I'd like to stay," she murmured.

"Do you have any idea how much I love you?" he whispered, choking back the intensity of his need for her.

She reached out and pulled him onto her, and there, in the darkness, in the privacy of the simple room he rented under an assumed name, there, where no one would find them, he made love to her, to the woman he loved, to the woman he loved more than life.

To a woman who was dead. Dead for four years.

His thoughts choked on this paradox, and gasping at the inconsistency, he opened his eyes. There was nothing but darkness surrounding. He frantically searched for a meaning to this part of his dream, but he could see nothing, not a hint of light. Jarring memories swept through him: fighting for his life, crashing noises, dizzying pain. Blackness. A nothingness as horrible and irremediable as Allison's death. With a slow, burning terror, he realized he was not dreaming.

He blinked his eyes and forced them to focus. Still nothing. Something was pressing against his eyes, and he tried reaching for his face but could not locate his arms. He finally found them by shaking them a bit, and as they awoke, he reached for his face again but they would still not move. He tried moving his legs, but they were frozen into place, numb from inaction. He tried to shake himself free and became aware that he was constrained in every direction.

Was he dead? Is this what death felt like? Dark, silent, immobile. He knew though that he was alive: a splitting pain in his skull made him feel certain of that. Not dead. Just surrounded by silent darkness. Maybe he was in a coffin. Maybe they thought he was dead. Maybe they had buried him. Or maybe they knew he was alive and had buried him anyway.

Oh, God.

The muscles of his chest tightened; he could not breathe! He panted uselessly, his throat constricted in panic. He licked his lips but his mouth was dry, and he choked on the dust he imagined surrounded him. He struggled to gain control of himself, swallowed hard, and nearly retched. Something was in his mouth! Cautiously, he concentrated one step at a time on determining what was going on. His tongue probed forward and tasted cloth: he was gagged. He moved the muscles of his face and recognized that he was blindfolded, too.

He explored further, concentrating on his arms. With an effort, he was able to move his hands a fraction of an inch—enough to determine that his wrists were bound together and tied to something else. He pulled sharply upward, and sharp pains shot through his arms and back. Clearly he had been in this position for some time. As his nerves awoke and he rediscovered each bit of his body, he ascertained that he was sitting with his arms wrapped around his legs and his wrists bound by a short length of cord to his ankles. If he dropped his head forward slightly, it could rest on his knees.

So, he wasn't in a coffin, not unless it had a very odd shape. As he calmed down, he began to wonder how he had remained upright for so long in such an awkward position. He rocked from side to side gently and felt something brush his shoulder on either side. He tried rocking back and forth, and he felt something supporting his back and could just scrape something with his feet. With growing dread, he raised his head as high as he could and felt his hair brush against something rough. It smelled like wood.

He swallowed hard several times before he allowed himself to realize that he was inside a crate just large enough to accommodate his curled-up body. He focused on breathing slowly, deeply, and tried not to notice how stale the air was. Tried not to think about the weight of earth that must be pressing down on him. Tried not to think about death by asphyxiation. Tried not to think about his lonely body moldering away to an unidentified skeleton.

Sunshine! Yes, he would think about sunshine. A bright, sunny, breezy day in the distant future. A desert, in fact. Endless sand cliffs and sunshine. For some reason, the distant future was sun-swept and barren with red dust and a cloudless, crystal blue sky. The sun beat down mercilessly on an empty landscape of ravines and canyons. There was no sign of life, or was there? The scurry of a rat, the cry of a distant hawk circling high above, two children playing, poking into the sand, digging up odds and ends. By a ravine. And what's that? A bit of wood sticking out from the cliff edge. *No.* An investigation, people standing around, curious. *No, stop this!* A box. Careful, don't break it! *No, no!* Look! A crumpled skeleton! *No, it doesn't have to be like that!* Poor bastard must have died in torment, wonder why. Perhaps religious significance? *No!* And so alone, some voice intones.

No, no, no, no, NO!

Despite his efforts, his breaths came in shorter and shorter gasps and he began to tremble. Not here. Not alone. Not now. Not like this! Oh God, oh God, oh God, they had buried him alive! Bound and gagged and blindfolded in a crate. Oh, God, not like this, not like this! He threw his head wildly backward, struck the wood hard. The shock brought him up short. Had it given slightly? As if the crate were not packed in earth? And where was the smell of dirt? He stifled his breathing and listened carefully. Were those sounds? Industrial noises? A train?

If they had wanted to strike terror in his heart, they were succeeding. But who were they? Clearly, somewhere along the line, he had been betrayed back into the hands of the Reich. "Time to go home, boy." That's what those thugs had said. The very last words he had heard: "Time to go home." Home to endless uniforms, to the stomp of boots, to ranting propaganda. Home to snooping neighbors, to droning officials, to permits and permissions. Home to fluttering flags, to ubiquitous swastikas, to gray and lifeless cities. Home to prison.

He listened intently, heard no sound over the pounding of his heart. Had his ears deceived him? Had they just left him somewhere to die horribly in a wooden crate? Was this their revenge, their sentence of death? If they had wanted to kill him, why not just do it? Why suffocate him or starve him or whatever? Surely, he had not been left to die; it was just too bizarre. As bizarre as quicklime-laden railway carriages, as bizarre as gas chambers . . .

The blackness closed in on him. Impotent surges of energy tormented his limbs. He needed to move! He needed to see! He did not want to die like this! Alone, ignorant, abandoned. He began to struggle mindlessly against his bonds, threw himself against the walls of the crate, attempted to scream through the cloth that choked him. After an unmeasurable time, he stopped, exhausted. Sweat streamed down his face, bright flashes danced before his eyes with each pound of his heart, his wrists were raw and slick with blood, and no one had come to him.

He struggled to keep his panic at bay, searching his past for something to fill the blankness. His grandmother's flat, sitting on the floor, his head resting on his knees, eyes shut tight against the sight of the dingy, moldy concrete of the walls and the leaden skies outside. The phonograph's volume so low he had to listen with his entire being. Music drifting around him: *There'll be bluebirds over, the white cliffs of Dover . . .* As the old, illegal song ran through his mind, he worked quietly on removing his blindfold. By scraping his face against his knees, he managed to work the cloth off his eyes and over his forehead. *There'll be love and laughter . . .* Next he forced the gag from his mouth, down his face, and let it settle around his neck. Elated by his progress, he began working on the knots that held his wrists in place. . . . *when the world is free.* As he contorted his wrists in his struggle to untie himself, the words ran out and silence closed in. He could not remember any more of the song! The melody became garbled with his confused effort to remember. The darkness pressed against him, seeping like a cloud of death into his ears and eyes and mouth, working its way into the depths of his being, seeking out his soul and destroying the music. He tried to divert the pressing blackness with other thoughts, with laughter and light and fresh air, but the effort of untying his hands broke his concentration, and time and again the darkness threatened to envelop his being.

There'll be bluebirds over . . . He pushed his terror back. . . . *the white cliffs of Dover.* He could see them now, could hear the sound of the waves pounding against the seawall. He felt the sting of the bitter salt air as he had awaited the ferry those four years ago. It had been a dark day, a "terminal day" was what Allison would have called it. "It's a terminal day," she would state, indicating that the mood of the weather was like some sort of ending. It was never clear whether terminal days were good or bad; they just were. He remembered the impenetrable barrier of gray on the horizon and had nodded his head in agreement. Yes, it had been a terminal day.

The wind had been high, or at least so it seemed to someone who had lived his life in the confines of a city. Seagulls mewed incessantly, and he had looked up at them to try to determine if Allison's spirit animated one of them. It had been only a month since her murder, and he still did things like that: he still looked for signs. There was nothing though; the birds were just birds. Flags slapped and banged noisily against their poles as the wind whipped around them, their clanging competing with the normal din of an industrial port. The ferry terminal was surrounded by flags, one on each post of the barbed-wire fence, the familiar red with its white circle around a black swastika—the flag of his country, the flag that had, so many decades ago, before he was even born, won its right to dominate his island home.

Hundreds of boys were around him, shifting uneasily, cold and anxious to get under way. He remembered feeling distinctly out of place among all those kids. There were some other men, but the vast majority were sixteen-year-olds; that was the age when every able-bodied male from the conquered nation was required to serve his Reich. They received their notices with their sixteenth birthday and were marshaled once a week at the local train station. From there, hours of travel and even more hours of organization brought them tired, hungry, and cowed to the docks at Dover.

A few cold drops of rain were carried on the wind. They slapped into his face and he closed his eyes to savor the salt breeze, but it felt hot and the salty taste trickled into his mouth. He opened his eyes to the terrifying blackness and the enforced paralysis of his bonds. He had known it was there, but the reality nevertheless shocked him. It could have been hours later; hunger gnawed at his thoughts, thirst was driving him mad. The knots refused to budge. He could not work his fingers around far enough to get a good grasp on the ropes. Finally, he stopped, tasted the sweat that dripped into his mouth, and wondered what he should do next.

He closed his eyes against the darkness and tried to hear something. There was nothing though, nothing at all. Before the insanity of silence claimed him, he let his thoughts slip back into his memory. He heard the buzz of conversation around him: boys making friends, telling where they had come from, exchanging insights. Most of them had probably never left their native district, and now they were to be sent away for six years to work somewhere on the Continent as *Pflichtarbeiter.* For some it was like a great adventure, a welcome break from the crowding, the shortages, the tedious routine of their homes. For others, the ones who had an intuitive understanding of just how long six years was, it was a painful separation from all they knew and loved.

It had been different for him. Instead of a birthday notice, he had been pulled out of his London prison cell early in the morning and shoved into the last carriage of a troop train heading south. There, along with a few other men, he had remained, manacled, until they had arrived at the docks. Then, somewhat inexplicably, the handcuffs had been removed and they were integrated into the general population of arriving boys, and there he stood, a convicted criminal with twenty years of forced labor to look forward to, guilty of that most basic and heinous of crimes in a police state: the possession of bad papers. A conscription dodger with insufficient and incomplete identity documents had been the best he could manage: a fake name, a fake history, inadequate papers, and a twenty-year sentence were still preferable to death by firing squad.

The wind caught at his hair and he impatiently brushed it out of his eyes. A few more drops of rain splattered heavily. After a time, the great doors of the ferry were opened and they were herded into the hold, divided into groups of about twenty and shoved into small, smelly compartments. The only light was from the hallway, and as the doors were shut, only a narrow beam from the tiny window cut its swath through the thick air.

He began to gasp as the foul air choked him. The dim light of the hold was swallowed by the darkness surrounding, and his dreamlike memories evaporated like wisps of hope. His muscles ached fiercely and he longed to stretch. Timidly he pushed against his bonds but they did not give, so he stopped before his lack of mobility could provoke panic. Again he tried to undo the knots on his wrist.

He worked feverishly, his fingers aching with the effort at pulling. Then he heard it, the clear, unmistakable sound of a train. So, he wasn't underground; he was near a rail line, or maybe even on a slowly moving train. He tried to determine if there was any movement, but he was shaking so violently from fear and exhaustion that he could not tell. At least now he felt sure he was being sent back. Whether they intended for him to survive the trip, whether they would kill him at the other end, he could not know, but at least now there was an end in sight. Whatever it was.

2

*T*HERE WAS NO END in sight, Richard Traugutt thought as he tapped his fingers lightly on the arm of his chair and hummed a waltz under his breath. He was a tall, lean man with dark brown eyes and dark, almost black, wavy hair that was streaked through with gray here and there. Not the prototype of an Aryan Nazi, admittedly, but he had done well within the system and was moving rapidly upward—rewarded for his brains and devotion if not his looks. He took a sip of his coffee and blinked slowly as he sat in his uncomfortable chair, savoring that precious moment that he did not have to look at the speaker or his interminable slides.

He wondered if he could make some excuse and leave the room or if he had tried that gambit once too often. He lit a cigarette and decided to stay, since the presentation was almost entirely for his benefit. Besides, it would soon be over and it would do well for him to sit all the way through one of these things once in a while. He did not want to get a reputation for being rude, after all.

The cloud of smoke he exhaled obscured his vision for a few seconds, but when it cleared, the room and its tedious occupants came into focus once again. The speaker was a handsome young man with an aristocratic demeanor and a fine mustache that he fussed over incessantly.

"Here we have an overview of the organization's structure as determined so far," the speaker explained. "It was difficult extracting this information from our prisoner, but we convinced him to cooperate!"

The small audience chuckled appropriately.

"Unfortunately, it seems our suspicions have been confirmed. The bombings carried out in the center of Krakau were done by a small group of terrorists who are not in any way connected with the Home Army. Desirable as it is, our total annihilation of this little group will not in any way impinge on that other organization."

There were scattered groans of disappointment from around the room.

Richard's thoughts turned to that other organization, the Armia Krajowa, the

Home Army: a Mafia, some said; a terrorist army according to others. Whatever it was, it was the bogeyman for the Nazi *Ordnung* enforced upon the subject peoples of the land. It lived and breathed among the occupiers, its heartbeat thumped ominously beneath the city streets, its breath hissed out of dark alleys and struck fear into any who crossed its path. It was everywhere and nowhere, powerful and impotent; its very real threats of retaliations affected the actions of each and every officer posted to the eastern Reich, yet it did not even exist. Their enemies were defeated, subjugated, annihilated, they were told, so it could not exist.

A murmur of approval penetrated Richard's consciousness. The speaker was showing before and after photographs of the prisoner whom he had personally interrogated. Richard glanced at the pictures, then back at the speaker, and could not stifle the word *arsehole* as it slipped in a whisper past his lips. Always the same thing, always the most brutal, least effective approach. The man should be transferred, Richard decided, and he began to plot. There was a new installation near Breslau, a reeducation center being established inside a large military complex. They could lose this idiot by sending him there—he would no longer be under Richard's direction and it would almost look like a promotion. The arsehole would do well there with his clubs and his chains and his penchant for inflicting pain with mindless abandon. Yes, Breslau, that would get him out of their hair.

Richard's assistant, Til, walked over to him and crouched down so he could whisper something in Richard's ear. Richard leaned in attentively.

"There have been a lot of complaints from Party officials," Til whispered earnestly.

Richard nodded his head to show he was listening but kept his eyes on the proceedings.

"It seems after the sixth or seventh child, they say their wives don't feel, um, to put it delicately, don't feel quite as snug."

"Um-huh." Richard maintained a look of concerned interest. His wife was only pregnant with their fifth, but still he recognized the problem.

"So the health ministry has been studying the situation," Til continued to whisper. "And it seems they finally have a solution."

"Really?" Richard asked, and sipped his coffee as the speaker showed another gruesome photograph.

"Yes, quite simple, actually. They recommend one buy a large ham, shove it in, and pull out the bone."

Richard sputtered, spitting coffee in the process. The speaker turned around to glance questioningly at him. Richard motioned that it was nothing.

The speaker continued to proudly explain his techniques. Til smirked and went back to stand where he had been before. Richard glanced at his watch and wondered if he would be late getting home that evening. It was not really important, since his wife was away visiting relatives. It would be difficult for her. She was *Volksdeutsch*, a woman who had declared herself German after discovering appropriate blood relations long in the past. One of the many curious cases of people discovering lost Germanic roots decades after the establishment of the Reich. Even more curious, but not atypical, none of her family had found this connection or decided to use it.

Richard's own past was pristine: a father who had served the Reich well, living in London and raising his child there, a bloodline that had been documented pure as far back as his great-great-great-grandparents, active service in the military, Party membership, a brilliant career in government that was advancing quickly; only his wife, Katrin, or as he called her at home, Kasia, was a weak link in this otherwise impeccable background. Though, by all legal measures, she should have been using the language since she was born, she still spoke German with a noticeable accent, and even worse, her relatives insisted on retaining their Polish identity. Richard sighed and wondered how things were going for her. Conceivably, listening to an arsehole drone on ad nauseam about his prowess with a truncheon was preferable to what his poor wife was encountering at the hands of her family.

Kasia paced up and down the platform. The train screamed its warning and slowly chugged its way out of the station. Fifteen more minutes, she thought. Fifteen more minutes. Maybe they've encountered difficulty finding transportation, or maybe there is a roadblock and their papers are being checked. But it was none of those things, she knew. No one was coming for her. They did not welcome her visit and they would not greet her at the station—no matter how many advance messages she sent. She checked her watch and paced a bit more. Ten minutes, she thought. If they don't come in ten minutes, I'll go on my own. She paced a bit more and absently wiped the tears from her cheek as she checked her watch yet again. Five minutes. Five minutes more. Surely they would come to the station to meet the daughter and sister they had not seen for years? Surely they would not shun her in this manner. She checked her watch again and went to the taxi stand.

When she stated the destination, the driver shook his head. She tried the next cab and received the same response. When the third driver asserted that he would not drive into the neighborhood, she asked to be dropped off as close as possible and she would walk the rest of the way. The cabdriver whistled derisively but took the fare anyway.

Kasia stepped out of the cab at the edge of the township and looked across the vast array of hovels that her people now called home. Each and every resident could at one time have claimed another home: some hailed back to mansions and great estates, others to one-room tenements. All the residents had only two things in common: they had not cooperated with the regime and they had somehow survived. Every now and then the neighborhood withstood a purge as the Germans marched in and seized various people guilty of political crimes or

Jewish ancestry or whatever. Every now and then the neighborhood withstood mass kidnappings as soldiers took the children of illegal marriages for use as slaves or for adoption by good German families. Every now and then the neighborhood withstood roundups, where able-bodied men and women were seized as *Zwangsarbeiter,* forced labor, to work without wages or even the most minimal rights in the Reich's factories and farms or as domestic slaves for the Reich's overworked *Hausfrauen.* Every now and then the population of the slum dropped precipitously either through the intervention of their overlords or through disease or hunger. Still, despite all the purges and winnowing of the population, they survived, scrabbling for life on the edge, reproducing and hoping for the future, teaching their children a forbidden culture and a forbidden language. Teaching stubbornness and determination and history. Teaching hate.

Gathering her courage, Kasia pulled her shawl more tightly around herself and stepped off the road and into the dirt alley that led to the stinking piles of garbage and staring faces of her brethren. She had dressed as inconspicuously as possible, but her presence drew attention as if she were wearing a sign saying INTERLOPER. She walked with a knowledgeable stride down the paths, afraid of showing even the slightest hesitation. She took a left at an unfamiliar junction and realized that she had probably taken a wrong turn somewhere. Nothing looked familiar.

Kasia decided not to turn around, fearing that if she showed she was lost, she might invite trouble. She continued to walk purposefully, picking her way through the debris, agilely leaping over the sewage ditches, holding her head high with a look of calmness that belied the tumult of fear inside her. She turned a corner and was in a central square. A small fountain in the center was no longer running, but someone had neatly planted flowers around the base. A group of youths played a boisterous game of soccer with a battered old ball that they kicked with reckless abandon. Someone sent the ball flying toward the flowers, and to Kasia's surprise one of the boys thrust out an arm and batted it back with his hand into the field of play. No one chided him for his action, and Kasia guessed the flowers were sufficiently off-limits to merit violation of the most sacred rules of the ball game.

She walked over to the flowers and read the little hand-printed card that lay buried among them. In Polish was written: "These flowers are planted in memory of those who died fighting for our freedom." Kasia picked up the card and saw that on the back was written in German: "This card was placed here by A. Mandartschik, who takes sole responsibility for it. No hostages need be shot." It was signed using a non-Germanized spelling, and below the signature was an address and a tiny map that would help the Gestapo arrest the culprit if need be.

Kasia raised her eyebrows, wondering what Richard would think of such a bold gesture. Carefully she replaced the card and continued on her way, asking directions from one of the old men who lounged in a group near the door of a bar. They explained where she should go, and within a few minutes she was back on familiar turf.

The door to her parents' hovel was missing, and now only a heavy woolen blanket hung over the entrance. Kasia knocked forcefully on the wooden frame and waited. When she had been a young girl, her family had been evicted from its tenement apartment and had taken refuge here on the outskirts of the town now called Tschenstochau. In the distance the ruins of the ancient monastery loomed, its miraculous history insufficient to repel these modern invaders, its famous Black Madonna missing and no longer able to protect it from the vindictive destructiveness of the new occupiers. Around her were the squalid shanties of the dispossessed. They lived here illegally, unable to obtain legal residence anywhere, and as squatters, they did not merit even the most basic city services and were open to arrest and deportation without notice.

Kasia pounded on the wooden beam again and waited. The move into the squatters' suburb had nearly broken her parents. They had found living in the tenement wretched enough and had at that time talked longingly of the old days when their families had owned town houses in Poznań. Their home city was now called Posen and the territory had completely and ruthlessly been denuded of all its Polish inhabitants as they had been murdered or forced to flee eastward when the area was incorporated into the Reich proper. Only one family member had shamed them in those terrible times. Kasia's mother's uncle had chosen to declare himself and his family *Volksdeutsch* and had been obliged to deny his heritage and adopt the German language and culture, but had in return been able to maintain his property and his family's lives.

Kasia pounded on the doorframe a third time, then pulled the heavy curtain aside and walked in. The front room was completely different from what she remembered, but she did not hesitate long enough to wonder why; instead she marched through to the back room, since she thought she heard someone in there. Hiding from me! she thought angrily as she stormed in.

She stopped and blushed a shade of bright red. On the thin mattress on the floor was a couple having sex. Not just sex, but the most contorted version of the sport that she had ever seen! The man was bent over the woman, his head somewhere down near her thighs. He was older, his brown hair streaked with gray; his fleshy body was red and sweaty from his efforts, and in his panting determination to achieve his goal, he did not even notice her intrusion. His partner did. She looked up at Kasia and giggled in execrable German, "If you could see your face right now!"

Kasia blushed even redder.

The woman's thin, wan face was framed quite nicely by the thick, hairy, sweaty thighs of her companion. With the casual disdain of a prostitute who had done enough for her money, she thrust her arms between the man's legs as if swimming through a cave and somehow managed to pull herself up even as her client reached in confused lust for the disappearing parts of her body.

She stood and pulled on a robe as the man hugged himself and moaned, "Oh, oh, oh, don't leave me now. Not now!"

The woman threw him a look of practiced pity, then asked Kasia, "May I help you, *gnädige Frau?*"

"I speak Polish," Kasia shot back angrily, forgetting for the moment her own embarrassment.

The woman turned to a rough wooden table on which sat a bottle of vodka and a couple of dirty glasses. She poured herself some vodka and then, turning to Kasia, asked, "You want some?"

Kasia stared at the filthy glasses and shook her head.

Rolling on the mattress as if in pain, the customer continued to moan drunkenly, "Oh, oh, oh, I love you. Come back to bed, *Schatzi*. Don't leave me like this!"

"He won't get it up tonight, that's for sure," the woman commented, casting a glance at the man. She drank her vodka down in several gulps, then said, "So, you're not from the Morality Ministry. What do you want?"

"My family lived here, I thought they still did. I'm sorry for intruding," Kasia answered apologetically, regaining some of her civility. She knew it was pointless asking for information and so she turned to leave.

As she reached the threshold, the woman called out, "Are you Frau Traugutt?"

Shocked by the question, Kasia turned back. "What makes you ask that?"

The woman went over to a shelf in a dark corner of the room and extracted a small bundle of letters. She thrust them at Kasia, saying, "They didn't get these. I don't know where they've gone. No forwarding address," she added, using the typical euphemism for "vanished without a trace."

Kasia grasped the small bundle of letters, each addressed in her own careful handwriting. Fearing that she would burst into tears, she fled the hovel without saying a word.

3

*I*T WASN'T TEARS THAT streamed down his face, it was his eyes melting in the blazing inferno into which he had been thrown. That's why he could see nothing, that's why it was so dark. He writhed in agony as the flames consumed him, but he could not move. He was stiff and lifeless. Immobile. Dead.

He suddenly realized that the roaring of the flames was the thundering of his heart in his ears, that his blindness was the darkness of the box, that his immobility was the ropes that held him bound. He was drenched in sweat, his hands frozen into place with his fingers clawing uselessly at the knots. His breath came back at him hot and fetid, his sobs of despair echoed noisily in the impenetrable blackness. He tried to lick his lips but his mouth was dry. He was gasping but still his lungs ached for want of air. God, he was going to die!

A huge door slammed into place, and the faintest whiff of fresh air reached him. He heard workmen clambering around, heard boxes being moved. He heard them approach and he struggled to find his voice. Like in some terrible nightmare, he found he could hardly make a noise. Eventually, he rasped for help.

"Shut up!" a rough voice called out as the crate was lifted up. "Shut up, or we'll put you down on your head."

The threat sounded real enough. The crate was carried some distance and then dropped unceremoniously. He heard them retreating and then heard the sound of a much smaller door being shut. Darkness and silence closed in on him again, and in self-defense he retreated into himself, moaning softly like a lost child, allowing the hallucinations of slow suffocation to claim him again.

Later the sound of the door opening brought him back to his senses. There was the familiar buzz of fluorescent lights, and the faintest glimmer penetrated the cracks of the box. Several people approached, and one inserted a crowbar into a crevice between the crate's lid and side. Light and fresh air streamed in through the tiny opening. Light! Air! He felt a huge surge of joy and relief.

As the side of the crate was pried off, a million suns exploded into view. He squeezed his eyes shut against the flood of light and drank in deep gulps of air. Somebody reached in and grabbed his shoulder and jerked him out of the crate. He landed heavily on his side on the floor. The rough concrete curved gently to a drain in the center: the floor of a prison cell.

"Phew! Put the hose on him!"

"Look, he's lost his blindfold, and the gag!"

"Those damn morons can't do anything right."

A heavy jet of water pummeled his body. It felt glorious and he slurped at the water running down his face as he lay trussed on the floor. He coughed and sputtered and tried to turn away when the hose was aimed at his face, but still it felt wonderful to be alive and free of his coffin.

"Okay, that's enough. Let's start the interrogation."

He was enjoying the sensations of life too much to be as terrified by that sentence as he should have been. A knife was used to saw off his bonds, then he was dragged to his feet. He could not stand on his own though, and someone had to hold him up. They fired questions at him rapidly, hoping to get information from him while he was still groggy and disoriented. He did not answer then; he could not, even if he had wanted to.

They kept at him over the next several hours, or perhaps it was days, incessantly questioning him and beating him to elicit the truth. They knew plenty already. They knew the name he had been using, they knew that he had been arrested with inadequate documentation. They knew he had been sentenced to twenty years and had served four. They knew he had escaped from his work camp to Switzerland, but they did not know how.

Over time he answered their questions, concocting a story about his escape that was essentially the truth. He gave it to them piecemeal, so they would be further convinced of its veracity. He left out only a few essential bits of information to protect his friends: there was no blackmail of the *Kommandant,* no damning pieces of paper held in reserve by them. Rather, to explain the *Kommandant's* cooperation in his escape, he claimed they were lovers and the *Kommandant* had engineered his escape in order to join him later in Switzerland. The details of the escape were essentially the same after that: the uniform, the papers, the driver, being dumped on the other side of the formidable border, returning everything but a set of civilian clothes to the driver. Standing alone, free for the first time in years, surrounded by a profusion of promiscuous autumn flowers.

He told them of his first days of freedom. He left out the kindly old couple who had taken him in and fed him, he left out that they had kept him for three days to build up his strength. Instead of mentioning how they had borrowed a car to drive him into town, he told his interrogators that he had wandered into the town hall on his own. He recounted the great, noisy hall with its clattering typewriters and ringing phones. He told them about the prim young woman who had given him numerous forms to fill out in his bid for asylum. He explained how he had been diverted from one overfull waiting room to another, on the top floor. "But you know about that, don't you?" he asked. "That part was all yours, wasn't it?"

They didn't answer him, they just pressed for more details and he went on, because there was no harm in telling them what they already knew. "The door locked behind me, I was alone in this so-called waiting room. It looked like a storage room. By the time I had decided not to try and scale the roof, your henchmen came in. They had clubs, I was unarmed. I don't really remember the rest."

Once he told them his story, he kept his silence, but they continued to question him, demanding details that did not exist, wanting names of accomplices and scapegoats. He refused to implicate his friends, had no names he would give them, so they kept at him, day after day until he lost all track of what they were even asking, until they lost track of why they were asking it, until it became nothing more than part of the routine.

His stoic courage, his brave determination to remain human in the face of such inhumane treatment, rapidly gave way to an obliviousness born of overwhelming pain, fear, and boredom. He lost track of his name, forgot his legend. He stood when pulled to his feet, sat when pushed into a chair. He swallowed blood as it filled his mouth. He stared mindlessly at his tormentors as they carried out their mindless rituals. Their act centered around him, yet he was no longer a part of it; he remained an object in their hands, sometimes questioned, sometimes beaten, sometimes ignored.

Sometimes they would even take a tea break in the middle of an interrogation. Others would wander into the room and he would listen through the pain fog as they talked about what their children were doing, about sports teams or office politics. Sometimes one of them would offer him some tea, unfastening his hands so he could hold the cup, wiping away a bit of blood from his mouth so the taste would not be spoiled. Once in a while someone would even give him a cigarette, and he would sit there trembling and smoking, unable to answer their jovial questions about who he thought would win the league title that year.

They laughed at him, teased him for being slow to answer or confused by their questions. Once, when his head had fallen to the table, someone pulled it up by his hair and pushed a doughnut at him so that he could have a bite and join in their tea-break conversation. They all laughed at the cream and sugar smeared over his mouth. The blood that dripped onto the pastry looked like raspberry jam, someone remarked. Don't waste good food like that, someone else chided. Then the break ended, the extra bodies filtered out, and they began their work on him again.

Finally a week passed when nobody came to get him. A local purge had occurred and the prison had suddenly filled with suspects, all of whom had to be interrogated so that they could implicate their comrades and coworkers. Compared to such ripe targets full of names and ideology, he was rather boring. In due course, he was presented with a neatly typed confession and asked to sign it. He did so without even bothering to read the document. The single sheet of paper was added to his file indicating that his questioning had been completed and he was to be bound over for trial.

4

"**O**W!" ZOSIA YELPED. She lay on a high pile of hay under the dark beams of an ancient barn, young and beautiful, naked and covered with a light sheen of sweat in the chill autumnal air. She had untamably curly, golden blond hair, blue eyes, and an athletically muscled, exquisitely curvaceous body.

Adam licked his lips in anticipation just looking at her. He was also naked and even more sweaty. His hair was blond as well, but it was paler than Zosia's, straight and strangely streaked with dark brown, as if it were changing color. The two of them had exuberantly abandoned their cross-country run and taken refuge in the barn to have a private last-minute encounter. He leaned over the slight bulge of Zosia's belly and gently kissed the exposed skin.

"What's the matter?" Adam asked. "The little one kicking you?"

"No, it's this damned hay," Zosia grumbled. "Who in God's name suggested we make love in a haystack?"

"You did, my dear," Adam murmured as he continued to plant little kisses in a line along her stomach. A faint, dark stripe, caused by her pregnancy, extended from her navel down between her legs, and he intended to follow its guidance.

"Well, I want to be on top," Zosia interrupted him, sitting up abruptly. "I keep getting poked by this damned straw!"

Adam leaned back, stretched, and yawned. "Fine with me, you can do the work!"

"Do you call it work?" Zosia asked, easily miffed.

Adam observed her wryly. "With you, sometimes." The look of disappointment turning to anger on Zosia's face warned him that she was in no mood for jokes, but he was tired of her moods, so he crawled off her and over to his clothes. He rooted around until he found a cigarette and lit himself one.

"Are you nuts?" Zosia screeched. "This is a haystack! You could burn the whole barn down!"

Adam shrugged. "Ah, the peasants will rebuild it. They have nothing better to do now that the harvest is in."

"That is exactly the sort of attitude that causes them to resent us," Zosia warned, shivering in the October chill. Without Adam's body heat, it was quite cold in the hay.

"It was a joke, my dear. Besides, the little ingrates have no idea how good they have it. They should be kissing our feet in gratitude for defending their freedom."

"If you're into feet-kissing . . ." Zosia pointed suggestively at her toes.

Adam smiled at her. "Not now, pumpkin." He reached into the pocket of his trousers and extracted his watch. "It's nearly time, we should go."

"Just like that," Zosia grumbled. "First you get me all excited, then you decide we're running late."

"As talented as I am, I can't change the heavens, love." He held up the watch. "Look, we're supposed to be getting married in two hours. Our friends will be waiting for us."

"Ah, let them wait, we can do it some other time," Zosia suggested, stretching languorously in the straw.

"No, no, no. You're not getting out of it that easily, you little minx. I've got your word, now you're coming to the ceremony and we're making it official. I've done my part, you're knocked up, now it's time you do yours!"

"Ah, you're no fun! Already acting like an old married man!"

"Come on, we should get back to the bunker and get dressed up."

"I still haven't decided what to wear," Zosia protested.

Adam took one last puff from his cigarette then carefully stubbed out the end on the heel of his foot. "I think you should wear that sleazy prostitute's dress. All the makeup, too. The priest will love that!"

Zosia picked up a handful of straw and threw it at him.

"Is that any way to treat your husband-to-be? You should show some respect!" Adam teased.

Zosia picked up a bigger handful, crawled over to Adam, and ceremoniously dumped it on his lap. "Here's your respect, O lord of the manor." She reached down into the neat little pile and Adam smiled with anticipation, but Zosia fooled him. Instead of fondling him as he expected, she picked out a long, sturdy piece of straw and poked him with it. "Time to get going!" she ordered. "Move it! Up and at 'em!"

It was not the sexiest gesture on earth, but it had its effect, and Adam lunged at her and together they tumbled back into the straw.

Zosia's preparations for the marriage ceremony were rushed at best. She hurriedly showered and combed the last of the straw from her hair, then she grabbed the white dress that Adam's mother, Marysia, had offered her and threw it over her head. From the cupboard, she took out a large lace curtain that had hung on a balcony window of her grandmother's town house before the place had been confiscated; she wrapped that around the dress and draped the end of it over her head like a veil. She used a belt to cinch the whole ensemble securely into place, grabbed a bunch of flowers out of a vase, and squeezed her feet into a pair of nice shoes that her sister owned.

Zosia's mother, Anna, shook her head in dismay as her daughter rushed around knocking over things and spreading mayhem throughout their tiny, underground, concrete flat. "I'm sure Adam has been preparing all morning," her mother chided.

Zosia smiled at the image of Adam on his knees, straddling her in the straw, his muscular body glinting with sweat, his red-blond pubic hair reflecting the light that had come in shafts through the gaps in the barn wall. "Naturally," she replied. "In fact, I'm sure he's been to confession. Probably been on his knees all morning, but that's only because he knows how lucky he is to finally get me!"

"Speaking of being gotten, or begetting, are you going to announce your pregnancy after the wedding?"

"Naw, I'll just let them all count on their fingers when I give birth. It will give the gossips something to do."

Anna was momentarily silent, and Zosia knew it was out of an old-fashioned sense of embarrassment. Finally Anna managed to overcome her hesitation and said, "Zosiu, there are certain things . . ."

Zosia stopped her frenzied activity and gave her mother her full attention. Not because she was interested in hearing what her mother had to say, rather because she was intrigued by her mother's attempt to say anything at all.

"I mean," Anna continued unsteadily, "I know you must have already . . . Well, it's obvious you don't need my advice about . . . It's just that . . ."

"Yes, Mamusiu?" Zosia asked with sickening sweetness.

"Marriage is serious," Anna plunged in. "So is parenthood. Why didn't you wait until after the wedding to get pregnant?"

"Wait? Hell, this is the reason I'm getting married! Do you think I'd tie myself down for any other reason?"

"It's an accident? You don't want the child?"

"No, it's not an accident and of course I want the child! It's a husband I'm not keen on, but Adam refused to make a baby unless I promised to marry him. I guess he thinks it will settle me down," Zosia said laughingly.

"I thought you loved Adam."

"I do. Really and truly. I'm just not ready to be married to him, or anyone else for that matter. But time marches on and I want to have babies, and this seems the best way. Anyway, kids need fathers. Especially my kids, especially with my schedule."

"But why before the wedding?" Anna moaned.

"I had to be sure Adam was up to the job of making babies before I tied myself down with him. That's all."

"That's hardly romantic," Anna commented sourly.

"Romance? What did that get you, Ma? Six children, the love of a thoughtless man, your goals and aspirations on permanent hold?" Zosia snorted. "You've worked like a slave for him all his life and now he's shooting up the political ladder and you have to struggle to find time to keep a seat on the Council! Romance! Ha!"

"Your father is not thoughtless," Anna protested weakly.

"I can't wear these shoes!" Zosia wailed suddenly. "They hurt my feet, I can hardly walk in them!"

"Why don't you borrow a pair from Julia? She has a lot of nice things and her feet are your size, aren't they?"

"My size!" Zosia squeaked. "Impossible!" Julia was Adam's elder sister. Unlike her brother she was dark-haired and dark-eyed, but like Adam, Julia was tall and accordingly well-proportioned, and next to her Amazonian sister-in-law-to-be, Zosia felt rather small and delicate.

Zosia took another step in the painfully tight shoes and relented. "Oh, all right, if they don't fit, I can stuff something inside them." She slipped off her sister's shoes and went to Julia's flat.

Julia and her son lived in a tiny two-room apartment on the same wing as Anna and her family, so Zosia did not have far to tread down the dimly lit underground corridors. As she padded barefoot along the concrete floors, she did not smell the damp or hear the quiet hiss of the ventilation fans, nor did she think about the overwhelming weight of earth that shielded them all in their tunnels, for she, like Adam and Julia and many others, had been raised from birth in this strange military complex that existed as an outlaw outpost of the Home Army in the deep forests of the Carpathian Mountains and in the expanded bunkers and tunnels left over from the active warfare of decades ago.

They were the elite, the ad hoc Underground government of the entire southern region of their now invisible country and the military staff of a headquarters for scattered partisan encampments that defended their small piece of free land in the middle of the Thousand Year Reich. They regularly moved from one society to another using faked documents, faked histories, entire faked lives, to support their activities among the German occupiers. They continued a resistance movement dedicated more to cultural survival than active warfare, and as the decades had gone by they had turned more and more from guns and bombs and sabotage to education and economics and politics. Still, they were at war, and as they struggled to maintain contact with their thousand-year-old history and to keep the local population from sinking completely into the mire of ignorance and semistarved slavery, they did not lose sight of their need to remain a military outpost, defending their borders and preparing for the inevitably violent uprising that would overthrow their brutal oppressors and resurrect their ancient, beloved homeland.

Though it was not completely shut, Zosia knocked at the door of Julia's flat. Olek greeted her with a broad smile. Eighteen years ago, when she was only eighteen, Julia had been assigned to infiltrate a government office in Berlin. She worked in the Security Ministry as a secretary, moving up from the typing pool to a trusted position handling an entire department's files. She carefully maneuvered herself into advantageous personal relationships, including having a torrid affair with a young and handsome Party official, and after two years of patiently feeding information back to her people, she had an opportunity to complete her mission and plant a deterrent bomb in a suitable location. She returned not only having successfully completed her assignment but with a bulging belly. Though she refused to name the father, she decided to keep the baby, and the gangly, brown-haired, sixteen-year-old youth who greeted Zosia was the happy result.

"Colonel Król!" Olek snapped to attention and saluted Zosia with comic seriousness.

"Cut the crap," Zosia snapped, fed up by all the teasing her new commission had earned her.

"Just showing proper respect for our youngest female colonel, and, of course, the soon-to-be wife of a powerful Council member!" Olek remarked with military precision. "Not even thirty yet." Olek whistled his admiration.

"I've been on active duty for sixteen years," Zosia retorted, "and it's well past time I get proper recognition. I should be on that Council!"

Olek winked to try to ease Zosia's irritation. "I just figured that if they tolerate you and Uncle Adam, then they'll tolerate anybody and there's hope for me!"

Sometimes her reputation as spoiled-brat-cum-golden-girl, the brave, talented, impetuous, and adored youngest daughter of powerful parents, annoyed Zosia. At other times, she used her position to exquisite effect. Right now, she simply ignored Olek's gibes. "Where's your mother?"

Olek shrugged. "Out."

"Drinking?"

"Probably."

"I hope she makes it to the wedding. She's my maid of honor, after all," Zosia fretted, but not very convincingly.

"What do you need her for?"

"I don't, I just need her closet," Zosia answered as she tromped past Olek into the apartment. "Fashion emergency."

With a bit of stuffing the shoes fit well enough, and Zosia did not suffer unduly as she marched forward to take Adam's hand. Adam looked quite dashing in the uniform he had chosen to wear. The uniform matched his most commonly assumed identity, that of an SS major, but he had carefully removed the obnoxious Nazi paraphernalia that was usually attached and had covered the German insignia with the shields and decorations of his own rank in the Home Army. Or rather, his mother probably had. Adam was not particularly handy with needle and thread or, in fact, any other domestic object. Nor was Zosia, and the pair's combined gross domestic incompetence was the source of many jokes and wagers among their friends and comrades.

The ceremony was held outside in the crisp October air, and with the inspiration of the wind rustling the leaves and the bright sunshine glinting through the pines, Zosia and Adam quieted their natural exuberance and solemnly pledged themselves to each other. After the ceremony, the touching display of solemnity did not last very long, and the wedding party soon became raucous. Adam and Zosia joined in the dancing and drinking and merrymaking until early the following morning and then absconded quietly, mounting a horse and disappearing into the predawn mist that covered the pine woods in an ethereal cloak of gray.

5

Gray. Grayness everywhere. Gray walls, gray floor, gray ceiling. Even the wooden door had a gray patina. His clothes were gray from dirt, his skin, sallow and gray from imprisonment. As the gray fluorescent bulb flickered day in and day out, he thought he would go mad if he did not see the sun soon. He didn't though. He just waited, aching, hungry, scared, and bored in a demihell of gray.

While he waited, a routine of sorts developed. They continued to feed him, delivering food in the morning and the evening; he was able to visit the toilet twice a day, just after breakfast and just after his dinner, but otherwise he never left his cell. His new cellmates, two friends from the same factory, had no reason to trust him, and their conversation was somewhat limited as he did not trust them either. By virtue of his seniority, he claimed one of the two cots for himself. They could have ganged up on him and seized it, but they did not, opting instead to share the other cot between them. The two were taken out and interrogated regularly, and his heart went out to each as he heard their cries of pain, but when they returned, he did not bother being solicitous. Let them offer each other comfort. In any case, they were Germans—union organizers, he gathered from their occasional conversations—and for that reason alone he was not much inclined to like them. Let *them* enjoy the bestiality their master race had inflicted on its subject peoples. Let *them* understand what it felt like to be labeled as somehow inferior.

Monique. That was the word his eyes settled on. The writer had used blood to draw a heart and inscribe the name across it. His eyes wandered further, searching out the next graffito in a familiar routine. *Dona eis requiem.* He heard the words sung, whispered almost, in his mind. It was the funeral of a friend, and a stranger stood next to him in the church singing quietly, mourning her loss. He had not looked at her face, his eyes had been too intent on Allison and her husband, only a few pews away. He remembered how, unaware that she was being observed, she discreetly made the sign of the cross. It was then that he had realized how very little he knew about her. His eyes returned to the wall and the word *Freiheit* scratched near his cot. Freedom. Then there was the long polemic near the door. Each day he managed to decipher a bit more of the rambling sentences. Each line was more incoherent than the last, as the writer had slowly succumbed to daily torture.

Done with reading the graffiti, he lay on his cot, exhausted and bored, and watched as his two companions wrote furtive notes with pens and paper they had somehow managed to acquire.

"What are you staring at?" one of them asked accusingly.

He shook his head at his faux pas. "Sorry," he muttered.

"Do you want a bit of paper?" the second one asked, rather more helpfully. "We'll see that the note gets out."

He shook his head again, then rolled onto his back and stared up at the ceiling. "There's no one out there," he said as if talking about God. "No one at all."

The second one stood and walked over to his cot. "No one?"

A series of faces passed through his mind: his little sister, his mother, his father, his friends, Allison. He felt an urge to confide in his cellmate but blinked the deadly impulse away with the faces. "No one," he repeated in a voice that indicated further questions would be unwelcome. There was an awkward silence, and then the union organizer pursed his lips as if preparing to ask another question. He decided to preempt it, and taking in the two with his eyes, he asked, "So what have you two lads been up to that has gotten the local cops so riled?"

That's all it took. The union organizer was an idealist and talked freely of his traitorous beliefs, smiling with pleasure at the rare opportunity to have an interested audience. Only the sound of the door being opened interrupted his long monologue. All three prisoners looked with trepidation at the two men who entered. One was their usual guard, the other an officer. As the guard herded the two union organizers to the far side of the room to bar their exit, the officer beckoned imperiously to him. He smiled at his two comrades as they cowered in the corner. "I guess you won't need to share the cot anymore," he quipped as he obediently rose to his feet. He submitted to having his hands bound behind his back, and then he was shoved toward the door.

Rather pointlessly, one of the union organizers called out, "Good luck," as he disappeared down the hall.

The court was a modest affair: a simple wooden table with two chairs, one occupied by a harried-looking military official sitting in judgment and the other by a prosecutor who presided over stacks of documents. Off to the side a private sat at a small table and took notes. It was late afternoon and everyone in the courtroom was obviously tired.

He approached the bench as ordered; there was no defense attorney, no cross-examination; he stood helpless and alone as his guard retreated to the far wall to light a cigarette. Sighing heavily, the prosecutor set down his cigarette and began impatiently searching through a stack of files. Finally finding the right one, the prosecutor pulled it out, slumped back into his chair, and finished the cigarette, fussily waving away the cloud of smoke it had produced.

It took about five minutes for the charges to be read. Crossing the border turned into a litany of crimes: escape from imprisonment, unauthorized departure from his place of work, falsifying documents, resisting arrest, corruption and bribery, deception, fraud, besmirching the reputation of the Reich, violation of national borders, smuggling . . . He stopped listening. They were throwing the book at him. It was, quite literally, overkill since his escape attempt—his second criminal conviction!—was in and of itself sufficient to get him the death penalty. As the prosecutor concluded by summarizing the evidence and reading out his confession, the judge stirred and prepared to pass sentence.

"I want counsel," he demanded into the momentary silence.

The bald statement stunned them all, then finally the judge found the where-withal to answer, "You have abrogated that right."

"That's impossible. I demand a defense."

"Be silent. You will not speak out of turn," the judge responded coldly, trying to hide his irritation.

"I want a defense."

"You have no right to an attorney. Now be silent!"

"Then I want my turn to speak. I demand an opportunity to defend myself."

"You will not make demands of this court!" the judge snapped angrily.

"I demand—"

"Shut up!"

He refused to stay quiet. He shouted out his opinions over the objections of the court and the senseless pounding of the judge's gavel. As it degenerated into a shouting match, his guard threw down his cigarette, carefully ground it out with his boot, and approached his prisoner. Assuming the guard would try to drag him away, he rushed to vent his years of outrage and anger, but the guard was in no mood for such physical exertion. The guard swung the butt of his pistol at the back of his prisoner's head and watched impassively as the defendant crumpled to the floor, thus restoring silence and dignity to the courtroom.

"Guilty," muttered the judge, ticking a box on a sheet of paper. "Sentence: death," he added, checking another little box on the form. He carefully placed the sheet on a stack of papers, and as the prisoner was dragged out of the room, the judge sighed, rubbed his forehead, then called out, "Next!"

6

"**H**ERE'S YOUR ADDRESS," Richard snorted as he let the slip of paper float down to Kasia's lap. "It seems they're moving up in the world," he added sarcastically.

Kasia grasped the slip of paper and read the address. "Poznań? Are they registered there?"

"Posen," Richard snapped testily. "No, but your sister was granted a work permit and a temporary, foreign-employee residence permit. I assume your parents are living with her since they wouldn't be able to resist going 'home' as they would call it."

Kasia suppressed a bitter reply. Richard had only met her parents once, and their unremitting hostility toward him had left its impression. Fascist murderer, her father had called him. Baby thief, her mother had said, tears in her eyes. Pigheaded ignoramuses, Richard had called them, deliberately sacrificing their children's future to a chimerical nonsense. Kasia held the paper tightly in her hand and asked imploringly, "Do you think I could try another visit?"

Richard motioned to the servant to light him a cigarette. "You know, in my position, these things are not easy," he replied coldly.

"I know, darling."

Richard smoked in silence for a moment. Kasia stared wide-eyed at him, wordlessly pleading. With each puff of the cigarette he felt a little more mellow, and finally relenting, he said, "I'll check with the authorities."

The building had been constructed sometime in the sixties or seventies: a massive tower of moldering concrete, misfitted windows, and dangling electrical wires. The concrete steps that led around and around, up innumerable flights, had huge chunks chipped away from overuse, poor maintenance, and vandalism. Here and there in the walls the slabs had chipped down to the rusting metal bars that threaded their way through as structural supports.

Kasia stopped on the eleventh floor, and once she had caught her breath, she turned into the hallway and began inspecting the doors. The numbers indicated that she had miscounted and had one more stairway to climb, so she returned to the steps and dragged herself up another flight. When she finally achieved the eleventh floor, she walked down the gloomy hallway peering at the faded numbers on each door until she found the appropriate one. There was a small nameplate next to the door and in tiny handwriting was written her sister's name.

Kasia rang the bell and waited. She had not warned anyone she was coming, and she had deliberately chosen the dinner hours so that she would have the best chance of finding someone at home.

"Who's there?" a voice asked in German.

"I have news of Kasia," she answered.

The door opened a tiny width and a young woman peered out. "Who are you?"

Kasia looked into the face of her younger sister and was ready to reveal herself, but her sister recognized her and slammed the door shut before she could say a word. A muffled "Go away!" came at her like a knife through the door.

Kasia rang the bell again and pressed her ear to the door. Inside she could hear an argument, and she continued to ring the bell insistently. Again the door opened, this time held by Kasia's father. He motioned her inside, but even as she stepped through, her sister pushed past her and left the apartment. A man whom Kasia did not know approached and stared at her with undisguised curiosity, then dutifully followed Kasia's sister out the door and down the hall.

"Your brother-in-law," her father explained. "They're married, though of course they never got official permission." He led her to the dinner table where her mother and brother were seated but did not offer her a seat. Kasia seated herself, and grabbing one of the glasses on the table, poured herself some water from a pitcher.

"It's tap water," her brother warned. "It will make a fine lady like you quite sick if you're not used to it."

Kasia already felt so sick from her pregnancy that she found herself pushing the glass away, even though she had not meant to.

"What do you want from us?" her mother asked wearily. "Does your husband need our winter coats for his dog? Or maybe he would like to steal your sister's child to clean his toilet?"

"Mama . . . ," Kasia began, but stopped as her mother raised a hand in warning.

"Do not call me mother! They stole two children from me, Kasia! Two innocents taken as babes from my arms. Your brothers! Stolen so that they could become some other couple's adopted children or so that they could slave in some carpet factory weaving their fine carpets. Torn from my arms because I did not have a legal marriage, a legal marriage which they would not grant to me! They were stolen, but you, you harlot, you go voluntarily into their homes, you sleep with that man you call a husband, you produce children for him! You carry some piece of paper they've given you to prove your worth, but in here"—Kasia's mother tapped her chest dramatically—"in here, you are hollow. You are no daughter of mine."

"I've brought pictures of the children. Your grandchildren, Mama."

"I am not your mother!"

"Darling," Kasia's father soothed his wife, "let her speak."

"My husband does not steal children," Kasia stated. "Your sons were taken decades ago, before I was born, before Richard was born. If only you would get to know him, you would see, he is a good man."

"A good man! There is no such thing as a good German! The only good German is a dead German!" Kasia's brother inserted angrily.

"Hatred gets us nowhere," Kasia replied quietly. "I have my reasons for what I do, for what I have done . . ."

"What reasons could explain such a betrayal?" Kasia's father asked pointedly.

"I can't explain, Papa. You must have faith in me. We do not need to discuss our differences. I just wanted to tell you about the children, to show you their pictures, to see if we can offer you any help—"

"Help? *Help?*" Kasia's brother interjected. "They steal everything, they destroy everything. They slaughter people for this reason and that reason and for no reason at all, and then they want to know if they can offer us help?"

"Kasia, how can you be so naive?" her father asked plaintively. "They only keep us alive to produce cheap agricultural goods, to slave in their factories and in their homes. They have destroyed our universities and schools, they have slaughtered our political and religious leaders, they continue to use terror to suppress even the tiniest glimmerings of freedom or hope. How can you leave your people and become one of them?"

"I have not become 'one of them'! I married Richard, that's all. I've made a life and a family with a man who represents all the wrong things to you. But he was not born a symbol, he is just a person, and it's unfair of you to shun me just because I love the wrong person."

"He's no innocent bystander! He works in the Security Ministry!" Kasia's brother scolded.

"Please leave." Kasia's father stood and moved around to her seat. He placed his hands on the back of her chair as if he would pull it out from under her if she did not stand up. "Leave and do not return. It is not safe for you to come here, and your presence could make difficulties for us. Leave now."

Kasia looked desperately from her mother to her brother and then up at her father, but none of them betrayed the slightest emotion. She stood slowly, gathering the photos that she had laid in front of her on the table, tidying them into a neat little pile. "I've marked their names and a little about them on the back," she said, tears invading her voice. "I'll leave them for you."

"Take your photographs and go. We cannot afford such fancy things," Kasia's mother stated coldly, pushing the pile roughly toward her daughter. "We do not want you here. You do not belong to us. Go."

Kasia walked slowly toward the door. On the threshold she stopped and turned to confront her family one last time. They did not even look up at her. Drawing up every last ounce of self-discipline that she had, Kasia suppressed a bitter tirade and left in silence. By the time she reached the street, she found the photographs, torn into tiny bits, scattered on the ground and lifted by the wind along the dirty, treeless street.

"I told you so," Richard said, and indeed he had.

Kasia did not say a word in reply, just stared up at him with those beautiful, wide, brown eyes of hers. He kissed her forehead, then put his arms around her, and she buried her head in his chest. He bent his head down to kiss her hair. "I'm sorry, darling," he said with uncharacteristic tenderness. "I wish it could be otherwise."

He felt her body trembling as she finally gave way to the tears she had held back for so long.

"Do you know, both your sister and her husband are in the Underground?" he asked, casually trying to change the subject to cheer her up.

Kasia looked up in alarm at her husband. He smiled a reassurance. "Don't worry, no one at the Ministry knows. They're safe."

"What do they do?" Kasia asked unsteadily.

"They're quite low down. Obviously," he added smugly. "They're involved in printing and distributing illegal textbooks. Or so I've been told."

Kasia nodded, proud of her sister but unwilling to say so to her husband.

"You know, I have to go to Breslau. Inspection tour," Richard reminded her.

"Breslau? You don't have any connection with anything there, do you?"

"No, but I have a personal invitation from my erstwhile subordinate. I've accepted it because I want to keep tabs on what is going on there. I'm catching the midnight train."

"Midnight?" Kasia asked, confused. "Won't that get you in too early?"

Richard sighed. "My host has asked if I could come early, so I could see an entire day's routine." He stroked Kasia's hair worriedly. "Are you going to be all right on your own?"

Collecting herself, Kasia nodded. "Yes, I have the children and the servants and my fine house, after all."

7

RICHARD HUDDLED in the back of the taxi and yawned yet again. He turned his head to look out the window into the cold, dark November morning. Not even a glimmer of dawn on the horizon. Distant bells chimed. One, two, three, four, he counted, then yawned again. God in heaven, what a stupid life he led!

The taxi turned onto a road that Richard thought he recognized. A barbed-wire fence on the right finally gave way to a blank brick wall. "How far?" he asked the driver.

"About two kilometers, *mein Herr*."

Richard let a few hundred meters speed by, then he said, "Let me out here. I'll walk the rest of the way."

By the time he and Lederman were pacing through the prison, he had stopped yawning, but the salubrious effects of his walk were overwhelmed by the stifling air of the cells. He was led up a staircase and into a separate section of the prison. They passed through a door and entered onto a walkway overlooking a darkened room that, Richard realized, had once been a large gymnasium. The balcony circled the entire gymnasium, and beneath them the floor had been divided with concrete blocks into a maze of individual cells, each covered by a protective net of chicken wire at the level of the walkway. In each cell was a single prisoner, all of them apparently asleep, though the prison was alive with their varied moans and sighs.

"These are for the new recruits and our problem cases," Lederman confided. "We keep them in isolation to better observe their responses to our stimuli."

"Why white?" Richard asked as he scanned the walls and floor and ceilings. Everything was white.

"It's supposed to be quite disorienting to them," Lederman explained.

"To me, too," Richard admitted. He felt nauseous and he wondered if it was the stench or the incongruous whiteness.

A loud thunk and a sudden blaze of fluorescent lights caused him to wince. The prisoners immediately began to rise as shouts, curses, and orders from the guards echoed throughout the room. The two of them continued their inspection of the room and its contents, stopping here and there for Lederman to make an observation or so that Richard could ask a question. Eventually they came to a stop over a small section of cells.

"These are the new ones. I wanted you to see their orientation, but most of them have already been dealt with. All but him." Lederman pointed to a prisoner who remained prone. He had been thrown onto a straw mattress without a blanket or clothing, and Richard shuddered with vicarious cold. Like the other new recruits, the prisoner's head had been shaved, on his right wrist was a metal band, and on his left forearm a tattooed number. The metal band, which was welded into place, contained all the information anyone could want about the prisoner, including his number, so the tattoo was redundant, and Richard wondered why it had not been dispensed with yet. Tradition, he supposed, or more precisely, inertia.

Lederman turned to the nearest guard and ordered, "Wake him up!"

The guard glanced down at the prisoner. "He's out cold, *mein Herr*."

"I saw him twitch. Wake him up!" Lederman repeated angrily. "And fetch whoever's on call."

As the guard disappeared to carry out his tasks, Richard decided to explore Lederman's opinions and asked, "Why do we still use tattoos? Aren't they somewhat redundant?"

Lederman smiled knowledgeably. "No, no. You see, we've really got the dyes down perfect—they're essentially irremovable! You see, knowing that, the prisoner is aware that his status is for life! These are all convicts, condemned prisoners, and we want them to be aware this is it—there is no other life for them. None but abject service to the Fatherland."

"I see," Richard agreed tiredly.

"It's more than that, though," his companion explained pompously. "Not only does it mark them for life, it gives them an accurate sense of their worth—they are now like cattle, no longer human. That is, if they ever were."

"So you reclassify people?"

"No, never! We just correct previous misclassifications."

"I see," Richard said, as he watched a bucket of water being thrown onto the unconscious prisoner. The man stirred and moaned. Two guards approached him. "I notice you have everything here: Belgians, Dutch, Frenchmen, Poles, even some Russians. What about condemned Germans? Those with unquestionable pedigrees?"

Lederman shook his head. "For our few German miscreants, I'm afraid we must carry out their sentences. We cannot allow them to mix back in with the population. They are like an infection. It would not only be confusing, but dangerous."

"I see." Richard turned his attention back down to the prisoner. He noticed that though the man's body bore a number of injuries, none of them looked recent except for a nasty welt on the back of his head. "What is this one?" he asked as the guards dragged the man to his feet and then pushed him down onto his knees.

"Common criminal," Lederman explained. "English."

Richard watched the criminal look around in confusion as he tried to take in his situation. He looked at the walls of his cell, at his lack of clothes, at the cold water that trickled down his skin. He had the frantic, terrified eyes of a wild animal caught in an incomprehensible trap. His hand reached up to his head, and an expression of horror came over his face when he discovered his lack of hair. He noticed his manacle and brought his left hand up to touch it. As he did so, he saw the tattoo on his forearm and his attention was diverted from the wristband to a savage attempt to rub the numbers off. The two guards standing over him exchanged a look of amusement.

"Not only criminal," Lederman continued, "but a pervert as well."

"Was he convicted for that?" Richard asked as the prisoner began a panicked attempt to free himself from the hold of his guards.

"No." Lederman sounded sad. "Rules of evidence wouldn't allow it."

With a sudden effort the prisoner rose from his knees, but was immediately forced back down. "Why not?"

"They only had his word and it would have impugned the reputation of a German officer to accept his testimony."

"Ah. So, a homosexual," Richard said. Again the prisoner made a wild attempt to climb to his feet. "Lucky for him he wasn't so labeled."

The prisoner was slammed back down, and he yelped with pain as his knees hit the concrete. His struggling ceased momentarily as he seemed to be gaining control of his panic. "Yes," Lederman agreed. "I can't even tell the guards. At least not formally—so he'll escape the special attention his sort usually gets."

The prisoner looked up at them, noticing his audience for the first time. He opened his mouth as if he were going to say something, but then his attention was diverted by the door of his cell swinging open. A middle-aged man, mildly overweight, dressed as a bureaucrat would, entered, followed by a guard with a chair. The guard set the chair down, and then all three of the guards withdrew from the room. The bureaucrat calmly sat down and observed his subject for a moment as he lit a cigarette. His face was bland, almost expressionless, his hair thin and, on the top, balding. To Richard, he looked the perfect part of the anonymous official.

With the suddenness of an opening line in a theatrical production, the official spoke. "You are under an execution order. You are as good as dead now."

The criminal stared at his visitor as if waiting for him to disappear along with the rest of his nightmare.

"Did you hear me?" the official asked.

The criminal turned his head from side to side as if looking for somebody to whom these words might be addressed. He looked upward at his audience, almost pleadingly. Richard bestowed a sympathetic smile on him, and that, for some odd reason, seemed to calm him. His eyes bored into Richard's as if he could will a knowledge of his humanity into Richard's head. Then he looked back down at the official, apparently ready to deal with his situation.

"Did you hear me?" the official repeated almost angrily. "You are under a sentence of death!"

"So why all this fuss?" the criminal answered with disarming, quiet logic. "Why not just kill me and get it over with?"

Richard raised his eyebrows in surprise. He had expected a low-class and highly accented German, but the man spoke as though he were an educated, fluent speaker. Richard tilted his head with interest. Perhaps this second-rate opera might be worth watching after all.

The official grinned as though he had predicted exactly such a response and was pleased by his acumen. "Shall we?" he asked, and moved to stand next to the prisoner, pulling a gun out from his jacket as he did so. He placed the gun against the prisoner's temple. "Do you wish to die?"

Richard realized that the prisoner had been coerced by his disorientation and the theaterlike atmosphere to respond in a histrionic and, in retrospect, rather stupid manner. His bold attempt at preserving his dignity had not only been pointless, it had left him in the absurd position of having to argue, naked and on his knees, with a man who had a gun pointed at his skull. Richard imagined that with the cold reality of imminent death, the man was already regretting his bravado and perhaps rethinking his next response.

Indeed there was no immediate answer, and all the prisoner did was instinctively try to lean away from the gun, but for each millimeter that he tilted his head, the gun followed. Someone in the distance coughed; the ash on the tip of the official's cigarette grew long. The prisoner glanced upward, as if seeking answers from his disinterested observers. Richard stifled another yawn and noticed that Lederman was fondling his mustache and smirking.

"Answer me," the official repeated calmly. "Do you wish to die?"

A glimmer of defiance appeared in the criminal's eyes and then disappeared. Richard knew that in his mind's eye the prisoner was shouting his denunciation of the system, or saying something stupid about the coming revolution, but the man was smart enough to keep his mouth shut. The official pressed the gun even closer. Almost imperceptibly his fingers twitched.

"No!" the prisoner gasped without meaning to.

"What? What was that? Shall I kill you?"

"No. Please don't shoot me." The prisoner glanced up at his audience again, as if asking their forgiveness for his unwillingness to provide them with a fine show. Richard did feel rather disappointed.

"So you want to live?" the official asked, shoving the gun abruptly forward as if stabbing with a knife.

The prisoner winced. "Yes, I want to live."

"Whatever it takes?"

"Whatever it takes," the prisoner agreed reluctantly.

Lederman leaned in toward Richard. "So he's passed stage one. Now begins stage two."

Richard nodded and hid another yawn behind his hand.

The official replaced the pistol in his jacket, sat back down in his chair. "Then we can deal with you." He nodded his head toward the mattress.

Choosing a spot that was not water-soaked, the prisoner sat as directed, crossing his arms defensively in front of himself.

The official paused to blow a stream of smoke into the air, then asked, "Do you understand your position here?"

"I think so."

"It is my job to see that you do. I am a staff psychiatrist for this institution." The man announced this so proudly that Richard had to cover his mouth to hide his laughter. The psychiatrist continued, "I have evaluated your records and determined that you may be suitable for our purposes. Your answer to my question confirms that belief."

"I'm overwhelmed by your astute observations," the prisoner responded.

The doctor smiled at his success and Lederman nodded approvingly, both missing the prisoner's sarcasm. Richard took his eyes off the scene only long enough to glance disdainfully at his companion.

"Now I will begin your orientation," the doctor announced. "It is important that you understand your stay of execution. You have been diagnosed as having sluggish schizophrenia, and as such you are useless to society. We may be able to reverse your condition and make you a productive member of society, but first you will need to undergo extensive therapy and reeducation."

"Aha," the prisoner agreed as though truly enlightened.

"Not only is your mental condition degenerate, but you are a criminal and through your criminal activities you have forfeited everything; you have no right to anything in this society—"

"When did I ever?"

"—your life belongs to the state."

"Whose doesn't? Aren't all our lives intended for the glorification of the state? Isn't that what we're taught in school? 'Loyal subjects of a glorious empire, proud children of a benevolent Fatherland,' " the prisoner quoted, " 'ancient tribes reunited: naturally bound by the laws of the Thousand Year Reich, bonded in brotherhood—' "

"Shut up!" the psychiatrist snapped. "You will speak only when required and always with due respect!"

Richard could barely contain his laughter; he leaned forward against the railing to get a better view. Suddenly, the second-rate opera had turned into a first-class farce.

The psychiatrist glared at his prisoner a moment but then seemed to regret his outburst, as if it were beneath his dignity. He closed his eyes, inhaled deeply from his cigarette, then once he was sufficiently calmed, continued, "You are the property of the state, and as such you are valuable to the state only so long as you work. All the laws and regulations pertaining to *Untermensch* pertain to you. You will learn them and obey them. As long as you work, as long as you obey each and every law and each and every command put to you, you may be permitted to live. Is that clear?"

"Yes."

"If you cease to work or refuse a command or in any way threaten any citizen or structure of the state, your sentence will be carried out immediately. Is that clear?"

"Yes."

"The price of disobedience is death. Is that clear?"

"It's clear," the prisoner murmured.

Exasperated, the psychiatrist exclaimed, "You will *always* refer to your betters with the appropriate degree of respect! Now, have I made myself clear?"

"Yes, *Herr Doktor*, you've made yourself clear."

"That's better. You are being given a second chance, and you will be appropriately thankful."

"Of course, *Herr Doktor,* I am truly grateful," the prisoner responded in a voice that was a study of pious gratitude. Richard coughed into a handkerchief to hide his smile.

"Good, I see that you can learn fast," the doctor congratulated himself. "You'll begin within the hour. You will join a group of other recruits then. You are never to speak to any of them, nor are you to speak to anyone else unless required to do so."

Despite this last command, the prisoner asked, "Could you just tell me one thing?"

He asked it in such a conversational tone that the doctor was taken off guard and responded without thinking, "What?"

Richard and Lederman had begun to leave, but upon hearing the prisoner's question, Richard turned back to listen. Lederman, noticing that his guest hesitated, waited respectfully.

"I'm now an *Untermensch,* right?" the prisoner asked, then without waiting for an answer continued, "However, if I understand your"—he hesitated as if searching for a polite word—"ideology correctly, that's a matter of genes rather than jurisprudence."

The psychiatrist nodded reluctantly

"So how is it that I can go from being a non-Germanic Aryan, *id est,* inferior, but not an *Untermensch,* to being an *Untermensch?*"

"Your actions have shown your true blood."

Richard had to smile at that logic. Lederman came forward and whispered in his ear, "This one will truly need special attention." Richard nodded without taking his eyes off the scene below.

"So, I have been an *Untermensch* all along?" the prisoner persisted.

"Yes, clearly. You were an orphan, were you not?"

"Yes."

"There you have it. You must have some Jewish or other foul blood in you, as do so many of you English."

"But what about my hair? It was blond, sort of," the prisoner explained. "And look, I have blue eyes." He pointed at them in a gesture of helpfulness that once again, and rather fortunately, the psychiatrist did not recognize as sarcastic.

"Doesn't matter. It's in the blood."

"I see. But why wasn't it obvious before?"

The psychiatrist hesitated. "I shan't debate with you, that would be folly. Nevertheless, I am intrigued by your question. You see, I believe your entire race is corrupt, so you had no trouble hiding your true nature among your own kind—it was just so much filth among garbage."

"But the English are part of the *Volk.* That's what I learned in school. One people, one master race, born to rule, reunited after a tragic separation, reaffirming their common bonds of brotherhood and natural right to—"

"Stop your blathering!" the psychiatrist snapped angrily.

"Just quoting doctrine," the prisoner apologized innocently, "about the English."

"Traitors, all of them."

"Nevertheless, still a part of the *Volk*."

"Some are, others are trash—mixed race, like you. Loathsome, vile, filthy!" The psychiatrist became incensed and began to yell. "You may arrogantly try to mimic us and use our language with your educated vocabulary, but you're still inferior and your efforts are repugnant: like watching a monkey use fine china. You think you're clever enough to know our ways and hide among us, but sooner or later we always ferret you rats out! You're polluted and your very existence defiles our culture. You were born a subhuman and you will always be a lesser being; your endeavors to pass for a true Aryan have been fruitless. We will now teach you to behave in a manner appropriate to your status."

The prisoner looked unimpressed. "So, it's all in the blood, eh?"

"All in the blood," the psychiatrist solemnly echoed.

"Heavens, isn't it about time you guys developed a blood test for this? Wouldn't it make your lives so much simpler?" the prisoner asked.

Richard turned his laugh into a cough. Lederman blinked slowly as he considered the suggestion.

"Yes, it would," the psychiatrist agreed all too seriously, "and I'm sure one day we will."

8

Zosia sipped her tea nervously in the little tearoom across the street from where Stefi stood in the chill dawn air. She looked at her sixteen-year-old apprentice in her provocative clothing with her overmade face and her sultry stance and nodded her head approvingly. A man approached Stefi, a farmer to judge from his clothes, but she said something that caused him to walk away shaking his head. As the night gave way to morning, Zosia became frustrated at their lack of success. She tapped her teacup nervously. Another twenty minutes, she thought, then they'd give it up for today as well. Their target was known to frequent this corner, and they had bribed the usual denizens away so that Stefi would be the natural choice, but now the third morning was upon them without success. Zosia was just beginning to mutter an imprecation under her breath when she spotted the uniform that she wanted. Black from head to toe with a nifty cap and nice death-head insignia. She squinted her eyes and studied the face. Success at last!

Zosia paid for her tea and left the shop in time to follow Stefi and her client down the street. She ducked into a seedy alley and from there watched the two disappear into the entrance of the inn. She strolled down the dark, narrow passage, ducked behind a pile of crates and garbage, and slipped into a door that took her up a back stairway so that she would be in the bedroom when Stefi and her client arrived. She settled herself into the only chair in the room and, picking up the yarn that she had left in a basket, waited patiently, crocheting a blanket for her baby.

The man opened the door and started when he saw Zosia. He drew his gun, but she waved her hand impatiently and said in a thickly accented German, "There is no need for that."

"What's this about?" the man demanded, turning toward Stefi as if ready to hit her.

"I am her sister," Zosia explained. "This is her first time. If you let me stay, I give you her for half the agreed price."

Stefi looked appropriately terrified. Zosia wondered how much of it was an act.

The man studied Zosia, wondering if he might work a better deal with two for one. "Stand up," he ordered.

Zosia obeyed as if it were second nature, standing with her back swayed and her stomach pushed out. The man sneered at her large belly and shook his head. More little Slavic trash running around, fouling the streets and committing crimes. Why didn't they just round up these pregnant cows and abort their monstrosities? It wasn't like they could hide their condition!

"She'll do it for free," he suggested. "And you'll be grateful for that."

"One quarter price," Zosia countered. "We need to eat."

"You both look fat enough," the man sneered.

"Please, *mein Herr*," Zosia begged.

"Take off your coat," the man told Stefi. She did so, and he looked her up and down and grudgingly agreed. "All right. Thirty marks. That's a loaf of bread for you, isn't it?"

One-tenth her street worth. "Yes, *mein Herr*. Thank you for your kind generosity," Zosia replied grovelingly.

He put his gun in the holster and removed it with his coat, uniform jacket, and tie. "Now come here, little princess," he called to Stefi, beckoning with his finger. Stefi approached timidly. He began undoing her buttons and reached inside her blouse. Zosia had placed herself back into the chair so she could see Stefi's face and was behind the man's back. She saw her apprentice cringe as the man's hands caressed her, and she gave her a smile and an encouraging nod. He would have been long dead in her hands, but she let Stefi find her own technique, in her own time. Stefi attempted to hug him, her hands dancing nervously around the man's back as she tried to ascertain his size and physique. Her fingers wandered up to his neck and teased at the bristly hair at the base of his skull.

One of his hands tore at the button and zipper on the back of her skirt and eventually managed to open it. Helpfully Stefi reached down to push the tight skirt over her hips. She then discreetly reached behind her neck and undid the necklace she wore—Zosia's necklace. Her fingers curled around the necklace and held it in a tight little fist. She reached up to embrace her lover, but he disconcertingly stepped back to survey his treasure.

Zosia saw Stefi's panicked look as her plan fell apart and nodded knowingly to her apprentice to reassure her. She did not pause in her crocheting as she commented quietly, "Turn around for your man, dearie. He wants to see you."

"Yes, yes," the man agreed amiably as Stefi stepped out of her skirt and turned around in front of him. This one was really quite good-looking. She looked vibrant and healthy and her curves were full. He was used to weak muscles and pallid flesh draped over bony hips. Of course, she was too poor to afford stockings, so all she had on was a worn slip and underwear, but perhaps if he made an investment, took her on as a mistress, he could outfit her appropriately. He reached forward and pushed her blouse off so that he could survey her just in her slip. He motioned with his finger that she should turn around again. Black stockings, high heels, and lace—yes, he should cover her in lace. And wash her hair, too.

He reached forward and grasped her hands in his. Stefi's eyes widened with fear as his fist closed around hers. Surely he must have noticed the necklace she was holding. She looked at Zosia to leap up and save her but Zosia continued to crochet calmly.

"You know," he propositioned, "I could make something out of you." He was oblivious to the way she held her hand in a fist—far too many other things were on his mind. He let her hands drop, and he reached toward her breasts and began fondling them roughly. Then his hands moved to the straps of her slip and pulled each off her shoulder. His hands returned to her breasts as they began to emerge from beneath the material. Stefi realized with a surge of horror that her arms were pinned down by the straps of her slip. She either had to move the straps back up—a move that was sure to ignite his anger, or she had to pull the slip off her arms—a move that would expose her completely to his lecherous gaze.

She glanced again at Zosia, gathered her courage, and shook her shoulder so that the slip slid farther down, off her breasts. Without further hesitation, she extricated her arms from the straps, and as the slip slid onto her hips and hung there precariously, she threw her arms enthusiastically about the man's shoulders and dove into his embrace. She could feel how hard he was, could feel her nipples pressed against the fabric of his shirt. She felt the strength of his muscles and understood intuitively how easily he could crush her in his arms. Her fingers uncurled enough to find the catch hidden in the filigree of Zosia's pendant, and the blade leapt out. His left hand closed around her breast in a possessive hold while his other hand moved downward. With one movement, she brought her hand up and into his neck even as his hand was clumsily probing into her underwear and finding its way between her legs.

Perhaps because he was reaching down to thrust his fingers into her, perhaps because she was nervous—whatever the reason, she placed the blade badly. His head jerked back and he glared at her angrily, the hand on her breast digging convulsively into her. Blood spurted from the wound, soaking her hand and his shirt. Zosia continued to crochet, unperturbed. Stefi pulled the knife out, and even as he reached up to strangle her, she plunged it into his skull again. He gurgled at her, his eyes wide with the realization that he was no longer controlling the situation. Zosia glanced up to ascertain the effectiveness of Stefi's second blow, nodded approvingly, then turned her attention back to the blanket before she lost count on the number of single crochets she had made. The man dropped down, twitching and jerking at Stefi's feet. Zosia reached a natural break point in the pattern, tucked the blanket into the basket, and stood up.

"Well done," she congratulated a stunned Stefi. "Very good for a first try."

Stefi stared down at the man who had collapsed at her feet. She held her bloody hand out and away from herself, but the knife remained in the man's neck.

"Always remove the knife immediately," Zosia advised. "You don't want them grabbing it." She waited to see if Stefi understood, hoping that the girl was not too traumatized. Stefi shuddered as if waking up and then mechanically stooped down and removed the knife from her victim's neck.

As Stefi stood again, still holding her hand out and away from herself, Zosia put her arm around her and whispered, "Good girl," kissing her gently on the cheek. She looked at the spasming man and decided he was probably not going to die soon enough. What a mess!

She waited a moment until Stefi's breathing had eased, and then said softly, "I'm afraid he's not quite dead yet. Do you want me to finish him for you?"

"No." Stefi's voice came from a distance. "No, I'll do it. Just tell me how."

"Anyway you want to, dear. He's already made a mess."

"But how should I have done it?" Stefi asked plaintively.

Zosia placed her hand around Stefi's so they were holding the knife together. "Here," she said as she guided her apprentice down to the body, "I'll show you." Together the two women brought the knife to the base of his skull. Zosia corrected the angle, then, when she was sure it was right, she said, "Now," and together they shoved the blade up and into their victim's brain.

They stood together and Zosia waited patiently, holding Stefi's shoulders as she recovered herself.

"Phew, what's that smell?" Stefi asked suddenly.

"He's defecated. His hard-on probably prevented him from urinating, but I wouldn't be surprised if he's come as well."

"Yuck!" Stefi commented, sounding not unlike the teenager she was.

Zosia was all business. "Wipe off the knife with your slip and throw the slip into the fireplace." She went over to her basket and removed some kerosene. She glanced up the chimney, and then when Stefi had placed her bloody slip in the fireplace, Zosia sprayed it with the fuel.

"What about the rug?" Stefi asked as Zosia lit the fire.

"We'll need it. They're used to messes here—hence all the throw rugs."

Stefi nodded noncommittally.

As the fire burned, Zosia picked up the victim's jacket and holster, checked to see his documents were in the jacket, and grabbing the cap as well, she shoved it all into her basket. She removed his watch and frisked the body, taking anything of value, however remote, and placed it all in her basket. "Wash yourself," she told Stefi, pointing at the sink, "then put your clothes back on. We don't have all day."

"Sorry." Stefi stepped gingerly past the dead man on the floor and carefully washed and inspected herself for blood. When she was finished, she pulled on her skirt and blouse and inspected them as well.

When Stefi was ready and the fire had died out, Zosia tucked away her necklace, gave the room a quick inspection, and then together they wrapped the throw rug around the body and hauled it to the door. The floor underneath was unmarked: the rug had been thick enough.

They put on their coats, then Zosia tied a rope around the rug and the man's ankles and showed Stefi how she could haul the body down the steps on her own if necessary using the rug as a sledge. "We don't usually need to do such things," Zosia added, "but in this case, a cover-up has been ordered."

"I understand." Stefi nodded. Funny, it had all been explained to her in advance, but her mind had gone completely blank after she had stuck the knife in the man's neck.

They pulled the body down the stairs and out the door into a lightly falling rain. There behind the crates and the garbage they were well hidden from the street. Zosia locked the door, and then, after glancing past the stack of debris to check that the alley was empty, she returned to the body.

Together they unrolled the rug and Zosia carefully folded it into a small square. She unpacked a sack from her basket and shoved the rug into it. Then, rolling the body over, she said, "Now we'll make sure it looks like he was attacked here. By robbers. Or perhaps by a rival." She glanced up at Stefi and, making a quick decision, said, "Watch the street. I'll do it."

"No. I'll do it," Stefi insisted. "I can handle it."

"Okay." Zosia handed her apprentice a nasty-looking knife. "Make a mess of it—we don't want them to notice those pretty little neck wounds."

Stefi nodded. For a moment she hesitated, then she felt his hands pulling at her breast, felt his fingers groping between her legs, and with a sudden resolve she raised the knife and brought it down with a brutal strength into his back. She repeated the motion over and over, in a frenzied surge of anger.

Suddenly Zosia reached out and grasped her wrist. "That's enough, dear," she said quietly. "Just get the neck now."

Stefi brushed the rain from her face, then carefully placed the knife on her victim's neck. She plunged the blade in and dragged downward, cutting across his shoulder, tearing the skin and obscuring the tiny punctures.

"Well done," Zosia congratulated her. She gently removed the knife from Stefi's shaking hands, dropped the blade into its scabbard, and buried the thing in her basket. "Let's go. You carry the potatoes, and I'll haul the basket of cabbages."

Stefi nodded mechanically.

Zosia smiled at her apprentice and said sympathetically, "Relax, sweetie. You've done really well. Two or three more times and your technique will be perfect."

"I feel sick," Stefi said, her body beginning to tremble violently.

"See if you can't hold it until we get home," Zosia advised as she surveyed the sky. "This rain is only going to get worse."

9

IT WAS ONLY GOING to get worse, he thought as he stood in the doorway and looked up. A cold drizzle emanated from the leaden skies, falling lightly into the courtyard. The faint gray stretch of clouds on the horizon was the first daylight he had seen in weeks, and he shook like a leaf as he finally allowed himself a moment to think about what had just happened. Only an hour or so ago, he had been doused with water, had awakened in such bizarre circumstances that he could not credit their reality. He had been interviewed, or interrogated, or at least threatened. And he had capitulated entirely. Uncertain what his words had meant, he had accepted life at their behest over death.

Immediately afterward he had been taken out of his cell and, along with others, ranted at. He had responded to the prompts, had denounced himself as worthless, had agreed that obedience was the only option. He had been warned, in screeching tones, that the price of disobedience was death. And now, he was obeying the first direct command. Still naked, with nothing but a number on his arm, a manacle on his wrist, and a tattered rag in his hand, he had been sent outside, told to cross the courtyard and enter the barracks on the far side so that he could scrub the latrines there.

He shuddered with cold and a relentless fear. He was so hungry he kept convulsively trying to chew something. He gathered his courage and took a few tentative steps across the slippery stones toward his destination, but again he hesitated. They had taken everything from him! His clothes, his hair, his name! He was so utterly alone and so completely at their mercy that terror was the only rational response. How, in God's name, could he possibly continue? He looked up at the sky as if begging for a sign, something that would tell him how to proceed in this grotesque nightmare. A snowflake landed by his nose, melted, and ran down his cheek. He brought his gaze back down to the ground and the pockets of frost that nestled between the cobblestones. He was nearly frozen, but still he could not bring himself to move. He was a prisoner, a nameless, faceless prisoner, and he had given his life to them in the hopes of preserving it for a few more months. Oh, God, what had he done? He looked down at the number on his arm and recited it mentally. It was, for now, his only name.

With a monumental effort of will, he forced himself forward, crossed the courtyard, and grasped the door handle. A quiet sob escaped his lips as he rotated his head to view where he had come from, then, determined to face whatever awaited him before he completely lost his composure, he opened the door. He was surprised to find the barracks relatively empty. A few soldiers lounged about, and one or two were changing clothes or organizing their kit, but most of the cots were empty. As he proceeded down the aisle between the cots, somebody nudged his friend and muttered, "Look, another poor, dumb shit sent over by those loonies." He got a few incurious glances, and someone tossed a towel at him, possibly to be helpful, but he did not know what was permitted, so he ignored it as it dropped to the floor.

He found his way to the latrines and surveyed them with resigned despair. They were filthy. He began with the cleaner parts—the sinks and benches, but inevitably he was forced to undertake the cleaning of the showers and toilets. Hunger aggravated the nausea inspired by the filth, and he retched repeatedly, but did not vomit. With only the now sodden cloth to aid him, he was forced to scratch at the filth with his fingers; nevertheless, he persevered, hoping that this first test of his resolve would be the worst and that if he did well, he would be moved up to the next stage, which would be less repugnant.

After a time he became inured to the smell and the dirt and was able to scrape mold, matted hair, and other detritus out of the shower sewers with equanimity. Several times soldiers entered and used the latrine, but they generally avoided him and left him to his work. One or two felt the need to kick him out of the way as he scrubbed near the door, but then he learned to scuttle quickly away whenever he heard anyone coming in.

Later in the morning, when his job was nearing completion, he heard a squad return to the main room of the barracks. Within moments several of them had entered the latrine and, upon spotting him, decided to have some fun. He continued to scrape away some rust-colored mold from the tiling near a sewer even as they began to surround him.

Some of them were preparing to shower and were naked or clad only in towels; others still wore their full uniforms, and one of these nudged him with the toe of his boot and asked, "Hey, boy, whatcha doing? Hmm?"

Before he could even conceive of answering, this question was followed by others.

"Getting on with your work, boy?"

"Hey there, what happened to all your hair?"

"Whatcha doing there?"

"Hey! Look at your betters when they address you!"

He looked at the speaker. He was a young, smiling boy of no more than seventeen. "How come you ain't doing useful work?"

"How come you here, boy?"

"Hey, check his wrist, see what it says!"

Someone grabbed at his right arm, hauled it upward and twisted it around so they could read his identification band. "A criminal! Tell us, what did you do bad, huh?"

"You touch any of our women?" The speaker was a powerfully built, brown-haired young man clad only in a towel.

"No, I didn't. No . . ."

"What did you do, huh? Come on, you can trust us."

"Leave him alone. Come on."

"Bet he laid his filthy hands on one of our women."

"No, I didn't . . ."

"Come on, guys, leave him alone," someone suggested, tugging on an arm.

"What then, you filthy pig!" the brown-haired speaker persisted.

"I . . . ," he stammered.

"You what?"

"Hey, I got an idea!"

"You all crave our women, you shit dog! He's raped one of our women!"

"No, no . . . ," he almost begged.

"Shut up, you're all liars."

"Calm down, Georg, you don't know what he's done."

"Let's teach him a lesson anyway!" the smiling boy suggested. A few of the group followed his inspired lead and dragged him to one of the sinks, filling it with water. His head was forced into the water, and even as he struggled to squirm free of his captors and come up for air, someone pounded on him mercilessly.

Suddenly he was released. He flung his head upward, gasping, prepared to be resubmerged, but no one forced him back down. He sank to the floor and it took a moment for the pounding of his heart in his ears to subside enough for him to hear the now rather subdued background conversation.

". . . wasn't hurting him, Sergeant."

"Honest, Sergeant, we was just having some fun."

"Enough. Go about your business."

Mumbled "yes, sir's" indicated that the small crowd was dispersing rather sheepishly. After a moment he heard the approach of the sergeant. Cowering on the floor, dripping wet, shaven, naked, and beaten, he could hardly imagine less dignified circumstances, but he summoned his pride and looked the man directly in the eyes. The sergeant looked him up and down, decided he was sufficiently unharmed, and left without saying a word, rather as if he were a machine incapable of understanding speech.

He stared after the lumbering form, wanting to say something, but the words *I am human* stuck in his throat.

The job assigned to him for the afternoon was no less unpleasant, but he managed to complete it without incident. Afterward, he and the other recruits were provided with potatoes and some gristly gravy for dinner, and then they were marched to the latrine to empty their buckets and wash. In the evening they endured hours of indoctrination, and then, numb with weariness, they were marched back. As he entered his cell, he was handed a blanket: it was rough and worn and smelled, but it was beautiful to him and he felt a wave of gratitude to his captors for this unforeseen luxury.

The next day, upon returning to his cell, he discovered he had been awarded clothing and footwear. The shoes were short, black lace-up boots with worn heels and cracks along the seams. He put them to one side and pensively fingered the roughly woven gray-blue material of the trousers. The material was rather worn, and he could not help but wonder what had become of the previous wearer. The long-sleeved, collarless shirt he had been given was made of a similarly worn material but had brand-new identifying patches sewn with a careful hand onto the shoulders.

He dressed quickly, then glanced down at himself, trying to imagine what he looked like to the rest of the world. Pretty pathetic, he guessed. The cut and colors of his uniform betrayed his status to all; the shoulder patches summarized everything that was considered relevant: a white strip of cloth on which his identification number had been printed, a patch with the cross of Saint George to identify him as English, a black stripe with a green triangle to show he was a criminal, and finally a red strip of cloth with a yellow inset to indicate, if he remembered correctly, that he was a *Zwangsarbeiter,* a forced laborer, further categorized as *Untermensch,* that is, subhuman.

He grasped the material of his sleeve in his hand and stared at the insignia. Quite a load of shit to carry around, he thought, all the hierarchies and divisions, the ethnicities and classifications of his society, summarized there, on his sleeves. It was an appalling indictment of the entire culture that his worth could be summarized so cavalierly, that his identity was a number, that his legal rights had been reduced to nothing. An appalling indictment, yet he could feel no bitterness. He was simply too elated that he finally had clothes.

10

"THAT WAS THE NEWS for this November evening. You have been listening to Julianna and the Voice of Freedom. Keep the faith." Julia signed off the broadcast and poured herself a tumbler of vodka as the strains of the national anthem filled the air. She did not have to hear it to broadcast it, but she liked to listen to the words anyway.

"Good job, as usual," the technician assured her from the doorway.

"Any jamming today?"

"No, we're doing a lot better with the multiple-source broadcasting. It will take them a while to work that one out."

"Well, let's get out of here while the going's good," Julia said, downing the vodka in a gulp.

"There's no hurry," the technician assured her, "they haven't even found the relay stations yet."

Julia shook her head. With each year she had grown more rather than less nervous, and any unnecessary delays or risks bothered her. "Fine. You stay and put up a welcome sign. I'm going."

She packed her bag and walked out into the damp evening air. Maybe it's time to quit, she thought. This was, after all, only a sideline, one of the less specialized of her assignments. It would be silly to be arrested or shot for doing something that almost any volunteer off the street could do. Collect impartial and foreign news reports and read them to the populace. Who couldn't do that? Her specialization was in planting and maintaining a series of deterrent bombs throughout Nazi government buildings. That required skill and training that was, to say the least, rare. She should save herself for that, she should not expose herself to other unnecessary risks. That's how she should present her case to the Council. She would not tell them of her growing anxiety, of her war weariness, of her need to drink more and more vodka to steady her nerves. It would be a simple case of protecting a valuable and rare resource: her bomb skills.

She thought about this as she glared impatiently out the window of her first-class train compartment. The train seemed to move so slowly! The sooner she got to Berlin, the sooner she could implant the upgraded remote-control detonators they had just received from the North American Union into their deterrents, and the sooner she would be done!

She thought about the location of the devices that she maintained in that city and about the identities she would adopt to gain access to each. It was difficult for her, there were so few excuses available for the presence of a woman in an unusual location: cleaning lady, secretary, prostitute. That about covered the career options in the Reich. Of course, this wasn't strictly true, but anything else drew notice, and that, when one was infiltrating, was bad. On the other hand, there were advantages as well: women were so typically unimportant that nobody took notice of them. As a secretary she could walk into an office, remove files, and walk off with them without anyone even being aware that she had been there, and prostitutes counted as virtual nonpersons and could attend social functions and conferences without drawing the slightest suspicion. She was also in much less danger of being denounced, for the usual path to information was through a man, and it never drew suspicion if an attractive woman tried to become friendly with a powerful man—everyone knew her motives: money and power. In that way, she might or might not succeed, but she rarely put herself in any danger.

There was, Julia thought, only one group in society that drew even less attention to themselves and that was the nameless, faceless multitude of forced laborers who scurried around with their heads bowed and their shoulders slumped as they carried out the commands of their bosses and obeyed the whims of their masters. With the right uniform and papers, a person could go anywhere—walking mindlessly into the middle of a firing range or into the core of a reactor—and nobody would raise an eyebrow for, after all, what would be the point in having a brutalized and submissive pool of workers if one could not give out insane orders now and then? Still, despite the perfect cover such anonymity might afford, she had never chosen that route and was unaware of anyone else who had; doubtless the fear of being trapped in that caste was just too great.

The train's whistle sounded lonely and cold through the dark night. A leaden rain began slapping at the windows, drawing slanted streaks that glinted with reflected light. Berlin was hours away, it was dark and she was tired, yet she had no desire to sleep. Julia lit a cigarette and watched as the smoke clouded the window. In the patterns she saw a map of her future, and everywhere she looked she saw only one answer: America. She needed to get herself and Olek out of the Reich and to that strange land overseas. America. She could stop looking over her shoulders there. America. Olek wouldn't have to carry a rifle. In America she could enroll him in a decent school and he could live a normal life. America, the train's wheels chanted to her. America, the whistle screamed. No Gestapo in America, no fear of torture, no nightly tremors as she woke up from a dream of being shot. She had to leave this madness, she had to get there, with her son. She needed a way out, she needed a plan. America, she thought. It would solve the fears, ease the worries, soothe the anxieties. In America she would sleep through the night. In America her hands would stop trembling. Go to the Council, she thought, resign, get out, leave. Then go to America. That's what she would do.

Julia reached into her bag and pulled out the bottle of vodka. Only one other person was in the compartment, a sleeping young man, so she had no need to be discreet. She removed the cap, put the bottle to her lips, and drank. It was unflavored; the sweetness of the flavored vodkas made her sick if she drank too much, so she drank the unflavored variety, the stuff they called clean water.

Only one more job, she thought. Complete this mission in Berlin, it would be the last, and then she would take Olek and they would leave. Abandon the madness and the madmen to their guns and their bombs and their bombs and their guns. Leave the murderers with their corpses, leave the torturers and the tortured behind. Leave the prisons and the camps, the conscription and the forced labor. Leave behind the identity cards and bloodline proofs, the documents and the endless mounds of paper. She would go to America and be free. As she heard the word repeated over and over in the clacking of the wheels, she drifted off to sleep.

By late morning, she arrived at the pension that was one of their safe houses in Berlin and greeted with profuse kisses the old couple who ran the inn. They showed her to her room and handed over the extra items that she had requested. She sorted through the papers and clothes, prepared herself for that evening's task, then stressed by the travel and worry, drank some more vodka and collapsed exhausted into bed.

Hours later, a soft knock at the door woke her. The old woman came into the room bearing a tray of food. "I thought you would need something to eat," she explained sheepishly. "We worry about you, Julia."

Julia shook her head. "There's no need to worry, I'm fine." She looked at the tray and smiled. "Thanks for the soup; nobody makes better soup than you!"

The old woman blushed at the compliment. "And how is your family? How is your son? And how is my favorite nephew, Cyprian?"

"Olek is well, growing fast. I'm very proud of him. My father is also well, he sends his love."

"And Marysia?"

"My mother is busy, as usual. Have you heard that Zosia Król and Adam have married? She's pregnant, too."

"Ah, Adam and my goddaughter! They will make a fine pair!"

"I suppose," Julia replied noncommittally. "At least now Adam will have some competition from somebody as arrogant and self-obsessed as himself."

The old woman wagged her head gently and clucked softly. "Do not be so hard on them, they are fine children and both are very selfless when it comes to the important things."

Julia shrugged. "If you say so."

"Is Adam still teaching?"

"Yes, he goes into Kraków and stays for several weeks at a time so that he can cover a course. When he's there, I guess he sometimes works with Zosia's brother. He's stationed there, you know—"

The old woman nodded.

"—and carries out some other assignments, so I guess it's forgivable, the extra risk he takes."

"Adam loves teaching, he loves passing on our culture. He doesn't need excuses to do it."

Julia shrugged again. "It's an unnecessary risk. He should confine himself to his specialization."

"I think his field of work is depressing if there is no counterpoint," the old woman suggested. "We all live under stress, dear child. Don't begrudge your brother the right to do something positive like teaching our poor benighted people."

"It's not like he's teaching children how to read! These are university-level subjects. Obscure shit."

"We need to maintain our culture. They closed the universities, shot the professors, arrested the students—all for a reason! They know how important education is to a free people, and so do we. You should know that."

"I guess so."

"Oh, Julia, my beloved Julia. You have always been my favorite and I know you well. What is wrong, child?" The old woman had switched to Polish, whispering to avoid being overheard. She spoke German stiffly, with an excruciatingly formal propriety, but when she spoke her native language, she did so with a singsong accent that sounded as if she hailed from much farther east.

"I need to quit," Julia sighed. "I need to take Olek away from all this and just go somewhere safe."

The old woman tilted her head and contemplated Julia. "Have you asked about this?"

"Not yet. I'm afraid of what the answer might be. But after I finish this assignment, I'm . . . That's it, I'm finished. I can't handle it anymore."

The old woman nodded her sympathy. "You've done good work, Julia. Don't worry, they'll help you retire to the countryside, if that's what you want."

Julia shook her head. "No. I want out. Completely. Out of here. I want to go to America. I want money to start a new life. I need money, dollars, American dollars."

The old woman didn't say anything to that. She blinked slowly, then pointed at the soup. "It's getting cold, you should eat. If you want to nap, I'll wake you up in plenty of time." She left without waiting for an answer and closed the door quietly after herself, as if leaving the room of a very sick person.

Several hours later, Julia rose from her nap and began to don her first persona. She dressed as a cleaning woman, fixed her hair and makeup, checked her papers, and packed her equipment into a handbag that had a separate bottom compartment discreetly hidden inside. Assuming an appropriate accent, she practiced a few typical sentences, and when she was satisfied with herself, she drank a glass of vodka, rinsed her mouth, and made her way out into the early evening.

The department store was already closed, it being well past the time shops could legally stay open. It was ten minutes before the normal cleaning staff was supposed to arrive when Julia reached the side door and presented her papers to the security guard who stood there.

"New?" he asked as he scanned the papers.

"Yes, sir." Julia felt herself trembling, so to steady herself, she studied the customers still inside the shop. Almost exclusively men, they were allowed in after hours as a "personal favor" by the store management. Of course, the prices of the merchandise might be a bit higher in the evening, but the convenience of being able to shop after work was more than worth the expense. Gifts for the wife, gifts for the mistress, they were men who could afford the added cost of tapping on the closed shop window with a handful of marks but could not afford to disappear from work for hours on end during the middle of the day, as so many of the truly influential did.

"Figures," the guard replied. "Nobody else shows up on time!" He directed her toward the cleaning cupboard and suggested she make a cup of tea before starting, since "the others will make sure you do more than your fair share, once they get here."

Julia nodded her appreciation of his advice and disappeared into the store. She went straight down the stairs into the bowels of the building and proceeded knowledgeably along a corridor that led to a boiler room. She unlocked the door with a passkey and went inside. She scanned around for the attendant, but he was nowhere in sight. Once she was sure the room was empty, she ducked behind one of the massive furnaces and crawled along a narrow space between a huge duct and the wall. As the duct bent upward, she scrabbled underneath it and came to a sewer grate in the floor. Julia pulled a wrench out of her bag and undid the bolts, then carefully moving the heavy grate to the side, she slipped down and out of sight.

She landed in about a foot of water and sludge and swore angrily. The old passage had been disconnected from the city's system years before, after massive construction on the street, and she had not expected there to be more than a few inches of seepage in the tunnel. The mud had splashed her uniform and seeped into her boots, and now she would spend the rest of the time freezing cold and miserably wet. She trudged for a short distance along the sewer, swearing the entire time, until she came to the opening that she was seeking. It let her up and into the subbasement of another building, a government records office. As far as she knew, there was no direct access from that building into its cellar, and the little room was entirely cut off from the city above. That, however, was not the room's attraction. It's advantage lay in its location: directly next to and below an annex of the *Reichssicherheitshauptamt*—the headquarters of the Reich's security apparatus.

In the tiny, abandoned subbasement had been placed a large wooden crate, securely locked and labeled with dire government warnings that it must not be touched or disturbed in any way whatsoever. Julia went to the box, checked the seal, and then unlocked it. Inside, it waited quietly for her gentle touch. She stroked the cold metal, breathing a sigh of relief as she did so. She inspected the data recorder, noted the readings, and then with the tenderness of a lover, began to remove the cover plate and replace the detonator with the upgraded model that she had brought with her.

As she worked, her hands were steady, her thoughts calm. There was something so satisfying in tending her terrible machines of death, or as she thought of them, her guarantors of life, that only when she was working with them did she feel at peace and unafraid.

She finished the exchange, changed a few settings, and after replacing everything, returned the way she had come. In the boiler room, she brushed off her uniform, wiped the mud from her boots, and headed back into the store. She went to a back exit, unhooked the alarm, and walked out the door without anyone noticing. Back on the street, she breathed deeply, sending out a little cloud of steam into the night sky. One down, six to go.

The next three caused no difficulty, and she accomplished them in a matter of days. After that she went to work at the *Reichsuniversität*. She presented her papers to the secretary in charge of the library and indicated that she had been told to start work that morning helping out with the filing of archives. The university was sufficiently hierarchical that nobody thought to question the largesse, and grateful for the extra help, the secretary put her to work immediately. Julia planned to stay long enough to establish a presence, and then, when she had completed her work, she would be properly reassigned, thus leaving without causing any awkward questions to be raised.

The university itself was not a target, at least not one that Julia was assigned to, but there were laboratories in an institute associated with the university in which weapons research was carried out, and those were. For the quick work that Julia wanted to do, there was no point going through the mess of getting herself vetted and assigned directly to the laboratories. It was sufficient to be an accepted presence at the university and to await an appropriate opportunity.

Over the next several weeks, Julia finished the last two jobs and finally had an opportunity to enter the institute and access the deterrents that were hidden there. Everything went smoothly, and when she presented the library secretary with her transfer papers, she could smile with genuine pleasure as she expressed her sorrow at leaving such a friendly workplace and said that she hoped to return soon.

She was still smiling as she boarded the train leaving Berlin. Hours later, changing trains in Breslau, she shivered in the cold night air as she hustled from one platform to the next. She climbed aboard the train to Krakau and found a comfortable seat near a window. As the train sped off, she stared out into the night, watching the city as it unfolded past her. Darkness returned as they headed into the surrounding countryside, but then on the outskirts of the town the night was illuminated by the sprawling mass of a huge military installation. Julia was unable to stop herself from expertly scanning the complex for useful information, but of course there was nothing in sight of the train, just residences and the prison. She wondered briefly what was going on inside those walls, but then they were gone from view and her mind turned to other thoughts. She snuggled into her seat, opened a book and read, but she did not really pay attention to the words; rather she let them drift past her in a meaningless jumble of images.

11

*T*HE WORDS WERE MEANINGLESS. They came at him in tidal waves, slamming violently into his brain, but he ignored them and let them wash past. His thoughts remained undamaged by the propaganda, by the idiocy they ranted at him. He heard the train whistle and he felt a surge of joy; it gave him a chance to be distracted by thoughts of that other world, the world where normal people rode on trains. He had looked forward to hearing it and was pleased that he had not miscalculated the time.

They were commanded to repeat something, and he let his voice join the others as they shouted slogans and praise for the Reich. He bore the tedious humiliation stoically, letting his mind wander freely, sure that his demeanor and shouting would not betray the fact that he was not mentally present to even hear the words pounded into his brain. Sometimes at night, though, the words would come back to him and he knew then that they were making progress in the battle of his will against theirs.

The evening indoctrination was part of a routine. The days were spent working: from early in the morning until late in the evening he worked. Whether it was shoveling gravel or breaking stones or polishing someone's silverware, he worked. There were manufactories on the site, and sometimes he was assigned to those. Sometimes not. The only pattern was that each day, whatever he did, he worked, sometimes alone, always in silence.

He saw the other prisoners only at certain times of the day: when they were permitted to empty their buckets, when they stripped and were searched for lice or whatever, when they received their work orders. They were not permitted to talk to or even look at each other, and so they remained in a cowed silence, only ever daring to speak when commanded to at the indoctrinating lectures. These were held in the evenings, after a long day's work, and consisted of hours of rants and forced chants. They stood together in straight lines—men and women, but no children—in a small auditorium, staring forward, never looking either to their right or their left, never speaking a word except to shout slogans on command.

Once in a while the evening lecture routine was interrupted by a one-on-one visit with a staff psychiatrist. They seemed keen to look into his mind and study his responses, and he was put through a battery of psychological tests, drug therapies, and interviews. He did not know if this was usual or if he had been singled out, but in any case he lied consistently and outrageously. He did not know whether they noticed or expected such behavior, nor did he care: it amused him to play games with them just as they did with him, and that reason alone sufficed.

Besides the work and the interviews, there were punishments: for misbehavior, for showing independent thought, for speaking, for stepping out of line, for showing disrespect, for not working sufficiently hard, for any number of things and for nothing at all. It was part of the indoctrination of worthlessness. The punishments varied from being slapped or hit or kicked or punched to being tortured, but he was fairly adept at avoiding them.

"You've always been good at putting on an act," Allison said, and he smiled in response. He did not know for sure how she had meant it, but he took it as a compliment. It had certainly helped to get him and his friends out of trouble more than once. He lingered on that thought, on Allison, on his friends, on their good times as they had walked arm in arm through the street singing rowdy, illegal songs on their way home from the pub. At times like those, when they had brazenly snubbed the authorities, when he had constructed outrageous excuses with a straight face and managed to placate an irate patrolman, when they had had to cover their mouths to contain their laughter—at times like those, it had felt as if they ruled the night.

A whistling sound snapped his attention back to the auditorium. For the briefest moment he thought it was the train again, but then he felt the sharp pain of braided leather tearing through his shirt and cutting his skin. He swallowed a cry of pain, and suppressing an instinct to turn and confront his attacker, he immediately joined in the chant of praise for the Reich that he had so carelessly failed to shout.

He waited tensely for the next stroke, but to his great relief there was none. He had only just mentally sighed his relief when a baton was tapped against the back of his neck, pulling him out of line. He followed the wordless directions that, with taps and jabs, sent him out of the auditorium, down a hallway, and into an empty room. The entire room was white: floor, ceiling, walls. There were no windows and no furniture; the only relief from the stark whiteness was that somebody's blood was spattered on the floor and on the walls. He looked up and was relieved to see that none was on the ceiling. He stood alone there, waiting and wondering at the severity of his punishment for such a minor offense as daydreaming.

After a long time, the officer who seemed to be responsible for his reeducation entered the room. The officer brought a handkerchief to his nose, holding it there, as if in defense against the smell, and studied him. Suddenly, the officer pulled away his handkerchief and snapped, "Eyes down! You're in the presence of a superior! You know that!"

He dropped his gaze to the floor.

"The psychiatrists have observed you over this past month," the officer informed him as he pulled a sheet of paper out of his breast pocket and unfolded it. "Their summary tells me that you have consistently exhibited appropriate responses to stimuli, that you have rapidly learned all that has been put to you, that you have had a minimal failure rate, and that on the rare occasions of inappropriate behavior, you have accepted punishment without protest."

He felt a glimmer of hope.

"In other words," the officer sneered, "they think you're ready."

He looked up with interest, holding his breath in anticipation.

The officer looked at him for a long moment, then said quite casually, "They're fools. I know you're not."

He let his breath out slowly. He had to swallow as the meaning of the officer's words sank in.

The officer began pacing. "You think you can fool everyone, you think that by playing along, we'll figure you've learned your lessons. But I know; I can tell. You're not ready, not at all. You still think it's a game, don't you?"

An image of Allison's shattered body came to mind and he shook his head, replied ruefully, "No, I know it's for real."

The young man walked up to him and reached out to touch his monthlong growth of hair. "You think this makes you different, this blond hair."

"No," he said in response to the officer's touch.

The officer misunderstood. "Oh, yes, you do. Your blue eyes, your blond hair, your fancy language—you think you're one of us! You think you're special! But you're just as foul as any long-nosed Jew. Worse even, because you're a traitor and you choose to be what you are."

He did not respond and the young man spun away to continue his lament, more to the walls than to his captive audience. "Four years! Good God, nearly four years in a labor camp and look what they managed to come up with. They haven't a clue about discipline! How in God's name do we let such things happen?"

Still he could think of no cogent response, so he remained silent. His trainer walked back up to him, grabbed his sleeve, crumpling the insignia in his fist. "Look at this profanity! Criminal, ha! Whatever they had to hide with you, we all know what you are, you pervert. You may have escaped being marked for what you are, but I've read your file, I know, and I don't want you alive in the same world with my children."

Knowing that it was his own words that had condemned him to this man's judgment, he did not debate the charge; instead he said, "I've done you no harm."

The officer sputtered, "Harm! Your very existence fouls this planet, and we'd all be better off with you dead. You disgust me!"

He considered for a moment telling the truth to the officer. He regretted his cover story now and he doubted that revealing the existence of blackmail information against the *Kommandant* would have caused his comrades too much difficulty, but it was too late. The officer would not believe him and would certainly not change his opinion even if he did. Indeed, if he revealed that he had convincingly lied under interrogation, then he might never win his freedom from this hellhole. With that in mind, he tried a different approach. Summoning up every bit of acting ability that he had, he said, "I admit my actions in the past have been evil, but I can change. Please give me a chance."

"Change!" his trainer mocked. "A snake remains a snake and a pig remains a pig. You're a swine. You have these misleading physical traits, your hair, your eyes, but I'm not that naive, I've handled your type before. Many of you have had to be crushed." He closed his fist as if crushing something. "You are not the first nor will you be the last. You have ideas about yourself and therefore it will take a little longer to beat some respect into you, but believe me, we will do it, because it's your natural place to serve at our feet. We are the master race, we are the

Übermensch! You are born to serve and we are born to rule and you will only attain true peace and happiness when you realize that. It is written—"

"You know," he interrupted impatiently, "you could at least read what you are wont to quote. You do know how to read, don't you?" Even as he said it, he regretted his reckless outburst. When, he wondered, would he ever learn to keep his mouth shut?

The officer walked right up to him and struck him. "So you cannot help but show your true colors! I've known it all along! I was right! They've gone easy on you because they like you, because they thought you were civilized, but that's going to change. They're not in control, I am. You *Engländer*, I have no respect for you or your people! Their methods have failed and now it is my turn. You see, I know there is a type of person, snakes like you, who learn early in life to lie and camouflage themselves and to get by in any situation. Over and over again they deceive everyone with their acts, but as soon as the pressure is off, they return to their native habits. They never learn. They can't learn. There is nothing to do but remove them entirely."

He looked at his tormentor questioningly.

The officer laughed. "No, I don't mean that I have to kill you. I have better methods than that. I'm going to remove every trace of your personality. You're going to feel so much pain, you will be so disoriented, that you're just going to leave and there will be nothing left but a very well-trained body. By the time I am through with you, you will truly regret your behavior, or rather, you won't even be capable of such behavior."

"*Mein Herr,* I'm not like that. I can learn. Forgive my mistakes, please . . ."

"Ha! Good try!" the officer scoffed. Then tapping him gently on the skull, the officer explained, "You see, you're still in there. That won't do. As long as you're in there, you will stay in here."

The intelligent and cultured young man then turned on his heel and headed toward the door. He opened it and two men entered. One carried shackles, the other a heavily laden burlap bag. As the two men tromped in, the young officer hissed a warning to them under his breath, then turning to smile at him, said, "You like games, see how you like this one."

12

"SEE HOW YOU LIKE this one!" Til announced gleefully. "Two Haitians walked into a shop owned by a Jew in Manhattan—"

"Is your supply of jokes endless?" Richard asked.

"This isn't a joke. Look, it's here in this American newspaper." Til held up the page and tapped the relevant story.

"I thought I told you to look for information on American technology. You shouldn't even be reading that section," Richard grumbled.

"What, your wife said no last night? You should beat her, pregnancy is no excuse."

Richard scowled at him. His underling's familiarity was getting irksome.

"Anyway, I am doing my job," Til offered in expiation. "You get much more information from advertisements than from the articles. See?" He held up the paper again. "There's an ad right here. The article next to it just caught my attention."

Richard grabbed the paper and looked at the advertisement Til had indicated. It did indeed announce, for all to see, the latest trend in computer technology. Richard shook his head at the stupidity of the Americans. Why, in heaven's name, did they publish what should be classified information? Well, their idiocy was his department's gain. With a little knowledge of English, they had no need for espionage; all they had to do was buy some newspapers and magazines either in the North American Union itself or in some convenient neutral country, then ship the information back into the Reich. A few hours of reading gave them invaluable economic, political, and technical information as well as a wealth of anti-American propaganda in the form of stories about crime, disorder, degeneracy, and the general disintegration of American society.

With that last thought, Richard scanned the story Til had indicated. It was quite amusing, and the misunderstandings and violence involved clearly showed the danger of allowing races to mix freely. "Thank God we live in an orderly society," Richard commented as he finished the article. "You ought to send this over to propaganda. They could make good use of it."

"Quite a story, isn't it? What a hellhole that city must be with all its dark-skinned people, and its immigrants with their turbans and their strange rituals, and all the criminals skulking in every alley!"

Richard nodded his agreement. "Speaking of hellholes . . ."

"Ah, yes, you've got a train to catch. That explains the mood!" Til chuckled.

"Yes, time to visit our little sadist and see what he's up to. And there's no point you gloating, I'm taking you with me."

"What? I . . . ," Til stammered.

"Yep." Richard stretched in his seat. "I need some backup. Last time he didn't give me a minute's peace while I was there, he was so busy trying to impress me, so this time I want you to go through the files while that little shit amuses me with whatever he's been up to. Plucking wings off flies, or whatever."

"Ah, it's a dirty job, but somebody's got to do it," Til joked.

"Yes. Anyway, call your wife and tell her to send a suitcase—we'll need to spend the night."

"Don't have a phone. I'll just go home and pack."

"No, we're too busy. Send one of the lads around with a message," Richard said, taking his revenge for Til's earlier comment. "I want you digging out technical information. And no more Jew stories!"

Til sneered behind Richard's back, but did as his boss had ordered.

Their little sadist had indeed been quite busy. Til carefully searched through the files to get some meaningful statistics on drug usage, prisoner makeup, and mortality rates, as Lederman enthusiastically dragged Richard around on a tour of the facility, showing him his own separate complex of offices, cells, lecture halls, and workshops.

They stopped to observe a group of women sewing uniforms. Richard looked disinterestedly at the rows of bowed heads and hunched shoulders as Lederman continued a lecture on his techniques.

"It's one of the more effective ones. No observable injuries, so quick, too!" Lederman enthused.

"Huh?"

"The muscle relaxant. The prisoner just sits there, then all of a sudden they realize they can't breathe!"

"Then what?"

"Depends. If we want to keep them, we inject a stimulant. If not, well . . . Anyway, after they've been through that just once, they are absolutely terrified of any needle brought near them. Absolute terror," Lederman repeated cheerfully, leading Richard to another room to inspect some electronic devices that had just been imported.

"I've found, by experimenting," Lederman explained as he fondled one of the devices, "that shoving this stun gun into their mouths is singularly effective. Brutally painful. They collapse to the ground immediately." He replaced the device on its shelf. "Of course, you have to be careful not to break their teeth, and the side effects are somewhat unpleasant."

"Side effects?" Richard asked, wondering what could be more unpleasant than having a jolt of electricity wash directly through one's body.

"Muscle spasms, so . . . Well, as you might guess, it makes quite a mess."

"Where does this stuff come from?" Richard asked, looking at the rows of devices.

"America. They use it in their prisons. Supposed to be humane!" Lederman said, laughing.

After that they stepped outside to see the execution grounds. En route, they stopped at a work crew and watched them breaking up stones in preparation for construction at the site. Richard looked on dispassionately as the men slaved away. Though at his high rank, he could expect never to be exposed to anything similar, the fickleness of the Reich toward its highest political officers was such that he could not feel entirely at ease.

It had been that way all along, he thought. Certainly political rivalries had taken their toll as early as the thirties with its "blood purges," and Hitler had made it clear that the Führer would not be above torturing his own men if they stepped too far out of line. There were, for example, the piano-wire hangings of the forties for the traitors who had too loudly questioned the Führer's continuing appeasement of the Soviet Union and his change of heart about attacking their unwieldy Communist ally. Those, it was said, had been filmed so that Hitler could watch their gruesome deaths over and over.

The men worked unceasingly, sweat dripping from them, even in the damp early-March chill. Though they were trembling with exhaustion and it was obvious some were having difficulty even lifting their tools, they continued to swing their sledgehammers and pickaxes at the stone. Whenever one of them paused, even for a few seconds, the entire crew was punished.

This must be why they were standing there so long, Richard thought. To prove his toughness, his host was waiting for one of them to collapse. As he observed the wretched theater, Richard wondered what his own fate would be if he ever fell on the wrong side of that fine line. Certainly not reeducation, he would be spared this nonsense, but would it be a pistol placed discreetly on his desk or would it be worse? He supposed it depended on the nature of his as-yet-unknown offense, and on the politics and personalities of the time.

After Hitler's death things had calmed down a bit with those who were out of favor simply being disgraced and kicked out of the Party, only occasionally to be quietly murdered afterward. It had continued that way, working toward a normalization of the politics, well into the sixties, but then things had begun to go wrong. Strikes, riots, and uprisings had spread throughout the Reich; there had been confusion in the hierarchy about how to handle such things, and the response had oscillated between repression and appeasement. The result of such confusion had been disastrous, and it had looked for a time as though the entire Reich would collapse into anarchy under the strain, but then a strong-arm faction took control, put their man into power, and regained the upper hand.

That Führer's peaceful demise in '81 had occasioned a renaissance of sorts. There was a period of "openness" and "restructuring." Those repositories for all who were considered unfit to live within the Reich, the concentration camps, were downsized, and some of them were even closed altogether. It had looked as though the Reich might bumble its way into a limited democracy or a benevolent dictatorship, but in the late eighties, a series of Freedom Movements, coupled with rampant inflation and unemployment, led to yet another period of crisis, which ended with heavy-handed repression, a reopening of the camps, and a "return to the old values." The racial laws and strict discipline were applied with renewed vigor, and state employment was expanded to the extent that there was now a labor shortage. The vast resources thrown into keeping a lid on the unrest had absorbed a huge number of young men into the services, taxes had to be raised, and the repression had to be stepped up even further to maintain order. It was a vicious cycle of overemployment in parasitic government services, taxation to support the expenditures, and repression to support the taxation.

The government had calcified, the Führer had surrounded himself with a series of yes-men who belonged to either his first or second "ring" of advisers, and the entire system was creaking its way toward another crisis.

Dangerous times, Richard thought, but dangerous times also meant opportunities. He and all the other men waiting to take over the reins of power walked a tightrope, never knowing which way the wind would blow, never sure when a purge would be necessary to "encourage the others," never knowing if now was the moment to grab that brass ring. Still, Richard did not feel as exposed as many of his fellows, for he lacked the vices that caused most of their downfalls. He was not interested in mistresses or money, he had no desire to spend or show off. He was not addicted to anything: not alcohol, nor gambling, nor sadism. He did not believe a word of the Nazi mythology and so was unencumbered by any idiotic ideology, and he was willing to lie, to cheat, to smile, and to charm his way to his goal. He was intelligent, charming, handsome, and fit; he was perfectly placed to obtain whatever he wanted, and what he wanted was power, pure and simple.

One of the prisoners stopped working. He did not collapse, he simply stood still, leaning on his sledgehammer, ignoring the commands shouted at him. Richard and his host watched as the guards flailed wildly at the entire group. The guilty prisoner remained unmoved, so the guards changed tactics and beat at him alone. Richard suggested that they continue the tour. Lederman seemed disappointed that they were not going to wait to see the man die, but he did not object and they continued on their way, eventually returning to Lederman's office. There they discussed the effectiveness of various drugs and therapies, assessed the success rate of different members of the staff, and ended up chatting about Lederman's youth and his sports achievements.

". . . the knees ended it all," Lederman explained. "Just as well, it is hardly a fit career for a gentleman."

"Indeed," Richard agreed.

Suddenly Lederman glanced at his watch and exclaimed, "Goodness, I almost forgot! I have someone to show you."

They left the office and paced rapidly down the hall and out the door. Richard's shoulders slumped as he realized they were heading back toward the prison. He was led down a series of hallways containing heavy metal doors set into the uniformly gray concrete walls. Lederman came to a stop in front of one of the doors and had it opened.

Semidarkness and an unidentifiable stench greeted them. The room had concrete walls and a tiny window that provided the dim light; it was completely empty except for a prisoner who stood in the middle of the room as if placed there and told to stay put. He had an air of having been there a long time, standing an eternity, waiting for them.

The prisoner wore chains: a short length across his ankles, another binding his wrists, and another that led from his wrists down to his feet so that he could not lift his hands much above his waist while standing. A length of rope was also tied around his neck, the end of which dangled a few feet and was not attached to anything. Since there was nothing else in the cell Richard could conceivably observe, he approached the prisoner and looked him over, trying to determine what had made Lederman single him out. Though the prisoner was reasonably tall and well-built, he was emaciated and filthy with hair that was caked with dirt, or worse.

The man kept his head and eyes down and did not return Richard's curious stare, nor did he turn or in any other way react as Richard paced pensively around him. The identification on the man's arm indicated that he was English and a common criminal. Gingerly, Richard plucked a bit of something from the man's hair. He sniffed it and then crumpled it to a coarse black powder—it was dried blood, and obviously not the source of the stench that emanated from the man and his clothing. The smell was rather overpowering, and Richard finished his inspection quickly so that he could put some distance between them.

As Richard paced back toward the door, Lederman, who had politely waited there, gave him a slight bow, clicking his heels as he did so. "What's the rope for?" Richard asked.

Lederman looked over at the prisoner as if noticing him for the first time. "I don't know," he admitted. Both he and Richard turned to the guard for an explanation.

"Don't know, sir," the guard answered.

"Take it off," Richard ordered.

"Take it off," Lederman parroted. The guard attempted to untie the rope, but the knot was too filthy. After a few minutes, he used a knife and cut the rope off. The entire time, even when the knife was slipped between the rope and his throat, the prisoner stood passively disinterested.

"He was one of the ones I saw in November, isn't he?" Richard asked as he carefully inspected his fingers to make sure none of the dried blood had adhered to them.

"Yes, yes!" Lederman sounded excited. "I'm glad you remember. Just watch. I want to show you the progress we've made."

"That will be fascinating. I can tell already, you've made some changes in him."

Lederman smiled at the compliment, then turning his attention to the prisoner, snarled, "Down!"

The prisoner apparently understood this to mean he should immediately drop to his knees, crouching with his shoulders hunched and his head bent forward. Lederman stepped forward and pressed his hand into the prisoner's forehead, pushing it upward a bit so the prisoner looked forward. As Lederman removed his hand, the prisoner's head stayed exactly where he had placed it. Lederman turned and grabbed a truncheon from the guard and approached the prisoner again.

"Remain still," Lederman commanded. He theatrically touched the club to the prisoner's cheek to align it, then raised it threateningly. The prisoner did not move, his expression did not change in the slightest. Lederman whistled a warning then violently swung the club toward the prisoner's head. Though his eyes closed in fear, the prisoner remained still. At the last instant, the club swerved to pass over his head, just grazing his hair. Richard could see the man wince as he felt the breeze over his head, but still he did not move.

Lederman turned to Richard and grinned. "See?" he trumpeted. "Didn't move an inch! Now, watch this." He turned his attention back to the prisoner and commanded, "Move!" and as he said that word, he swung again. This time the prisoner scuttled backward, just managing to avoid the blow that would have impacted his head. Lederman swung again and again, driving the prisoner backward until he was against a wall, forcing him to change direction and scrabble desperately along the wall until he was trapped in a corner, shielding his head as best he could with his fettered arms, cringing expectantly.

Lederman stopped then and turned to look at Richard.

Richard wasn't sure what that demonstration was supposed to have proved, but he smiled encouragingly anyway.

"Would you care to have a go?" Lederman asked, offering Richard the club.

Richard shook his head. "No thanks. Don't want to spoil my polo swing," he joked.

Lederman laughed and spun back around, in the same movement swinging the truncheon forcefully, hitting the prisoner's upraised arm and the side of his head. The man moaned with pain.

Richard glanced again at the green triangle and ethnic identification. He felt absurdly relieved that the man was not only a criminal but also a foreigner—the former meant he could dismiss the prisoner's suffering as probably well-deserved, and the latter put a comfortable distance between them, the sort of safety-net distance one used when looking at the bloated bellies of starving, but faraway, children.

After that first blow, Lederman paused as if deciding whether to continue the beating. By all measures the prisoner had performed admirably, and he decided to reward him by not punishing him further. He hung the truncheon on his belt, then turned to the guard and asked, "Have you kept my orders with regard to food and water?"

The guard replied enthusiastically, "Yes, sir! Not a crumb of food nor a drop of water since you gave the order, sir!"

Lederman paced back to the center of the room. "Come here!" he snapped.

The prisoner began to rise, but Lederman ordered, "No! Crawl!" Obediently, the prisoner returned to his hands and knees and crawled toward the center of the room. His chains scraped noisily across the floor, and he favored the arm that had just been hit. When he reached the center, he was ordered to stand and he immediately struggled back to his feet. Richard could now see the unnaturally thin, cracked, dry lips, the bones that jutted painfully out of the sunken flesh of his face.

"Are you thirsty?" Lederman asked him.

The prisoner seemed stunned by the question. Bewildered, he raised his gaze from the floor and looked at his tormentors with unfocused, bloodshot eyes. His mouth lolled open and a swollen tongue touched the lips as if wetting them in preparation to say something, but his lips remained dry and he remained silent.

Completely mad, Richard thought, as he listened to the rasp of the prisoner's labored breathing.

"I asked you a question!" Lederman screeched at him.

"I am sorry, *mein Herr*," the prisoner apologized in a hoarse whisper, mechanically, as though he had said the phrase countless times. He seemed to collect himself and added carefully, "Yes, I am thirsty. Very thirsty."

"Get me a cup of water," Lederman ordered one of the guards. He motioned for the other guard to stand behind the prisoner, and Richard wondered at this maneuver. A slight smile played across the guard's face as he assumed a position with which he was obviously familiar.

The cup of water was brought in and handed to Lederman. Richard watched with detached curiosity as the prisoner's eyes lighted on the precious fluid. His face assumed a look not unlike lust, and again the tongue tried to wet the lips. The prisoner's hands twitched but did not move to reach for the cup; instead he waited, quivering with anticipation, like the well-trained animal that he was.

They stood like that a moment, a tableau of thirst about to be quenched, then Lederman began waving the cup back and forth, carelessly letting water spill over the sides and splash noisily to the floor. The prisoner's eyes widened at the cruel waste, his body jerked convulsively with aborted attempts to snatch at the water. Then suddenly he realized what was expected, and he went arduously down on his knees and in the most abject tones began begging for the water.

Lederman smiled benevolently at the performance, glancing up at Richard to invite him to share the triumph of their explicit superiority. Richard stifled a yawn and wondered if he could get a cup of coffee somewhere. The prisoner continued to beg, his words emerging hesitantly, sticking in the dryness of his throat. As he pleaded, he raised his chained hands in supplication. Lederman brought the cup nearer so that the prisoner could smell the water, putting it within his grasp.

As the prisoner thankfully reached for the cup, Lederman's indulgent smile turned to an angry scowl and he motioned to the guard behind the prisoner. The guard responded by agilely raising his leg and kicking the prisoner brutally in the back, just below the neck. The prisoner was slammed forward, the water went flying; the cup clattered noisily to the floor even as the prisoner landed with a heavy thump, his face crashing painfully into his arms and his chains.

Richard watched as the man desperately wet his lips on his arms and then moved his face to the floor to try to lap up the spilled water before it had all seeped away. Lederman's laughter filled the cell, the two guards joined in, and Richard added his own weak chuckle of approval to the humiliating performance.

The others were so involved in their merrymaking that they did not see the way the prisoner interrupted his efforts to look up at them, but Richard saw it, and the expression of pure hatred that greeted him told him that the prisoner was not completely mad, that someone was hiding deep inside that wretched exterior, and that one day, if that person ever escaped, they should all fear for their lives.

Unnerved, Richard glanced at his oblivious companions. By the time he looked back down at the prisoner, the expression was gone, and the man was busily trying to suck water from stone. Lederman indicated that the guards should return the man to his work crew, then suggested to Richard that they take a break and have a cup of coffee and a pastry in the lounge. "Made right here in our own bakery on the premises," Lederman enthused as he described their pastries, "absolutely fresh and simply delicious!"

He was right, the pastries were delicious, but the coffee was even better. Real coffee, freshly brewed. Richard savored a mouthful, then asked, "Why that man?"

"Man?" Lederman repeated, confused. "Oh, the prisoner!" he corrected.

"Why him?" Richard repeated, bored by the pedantry.

Lederman sipped his coffee and tasted his cherry tart before answering, "I chose him deliberately because he's a tough case; I wanted you to see that I'm not afraid of challenges."

"Indeed," Richard commented ambiguously. "What makes him so difficult?"

"Oh, you saw him! He thinks he's part of the master race because of his looks. Even worse is the way he speaks—like he's somebody. That from a common criminal!"

"What exactly was his crime?"

"Now this is interesting." Lederman dropped his voice as if revealing secrets. "His file says draft-dodging and an unauthorized exit from the Reich with the usual fraud and deception that involves."

"So?"

"But I know he was involved in homosexual activities. Not only that, but he has no record before being arrested for draft-dodging, about four years ago."

"No record? What's wrong with that?" Richard asked, betraying some confusion.

"You misunderstand. I mean no record at all! His file has all the normal stuff—orphanage, school, work—up to when he was sixteen, then poof! He vanishes from the face of the earth. No work record, no residences, no ration coupons, nothing for years and years."

"Hmm, that is strange. Was he prosecuted along those lines?"

"No! Well, he got five years for having his papers out of order and fifteen for not being able to prove he had done his conscription, but what I want to know is, what was he doing all those years?"

"Good question," Richard agreed.

"You can imagine the crimes he must have committed! And he wasn't prosecuted for any of them!"

"Maybe he was just a beggar."

"Does he look like a beggar to you?" Lederman asked with a touch of derision.

Richard raised an eyebrow at the tone. "We must not exclude any possibility," he answered dryly.

"I guess not. But he doesn't talk like a beggar either. There's something there, mark my words! He thinks he's somebody, he even tried to match wits with me!"

"Yes, I remember how he made fun of that psychiatrist, too."

"Huh?"

"The first day, when we watched from above. Remember?"

"Oh, yeah, yeah, even then," Lederman agreed uneasily. "Anyway, he had ideas about himself, and that always takes a bit of time to break. What I want to do is find the quickest way to let his sort know their place. You could say I'm looking for the fastest way to drill through their thick skulls and suck out all the unnecessary dross. He's one of my test cases."

"What does that mean?"

"Well, as you know, when we want to break a prisoner, but keep him physically intact, we tend to use drugs," Lederman explained, clearly relishing his role as expert.

"Um-huh."

"The problem is, the drugs tend to leave them in a very unsuitable condition."

"Unsuitable?" Richard asked.

"Psychotic. All well and good if you plan to keep them locked up, but it becomes problematic if there is any intention of releasing them into a more complex work situation."

"I see. So, what are you doing instead?"

"I'm testing out various combinations of torture and drugs. Rather than simply beating them into submission or drugging them into insanity, I'm developing a technique of changing their personalities. Or rather, erasing them. The brutal punishments keep them reacting in an acceptable manner, the drugs secure that their thoughts flow in one direction only: mindless obedience. No other thoughts allowed, none at all."

"Impressive."

"All I have to do is get the mix just right, then we can put them to work in any capacity for the Fatherland!"

"Ah, yes. You are a true patriot." Richard ran his finger around the edge of his coffee cup, watching the ripples that his action created.

"I've worked on the one you saw for three months, and I must admit," Lederman confessed, "I hardly expected he would survive this long, but as you can see, he's not only still alive, he's essentially presentable—no broken teeth, no significant facial scarring . . ."

"I noticed. It is quite remarkable. How did you manage it?"

"With difficulty. Frankly, I have trouble keeping the staff under control. We lose about fifty percent of our prisoners through their carelessness."

"What do you mean by *lose?*"

"Ach, when they get too damaged, we have to carry out their sentences. But with this case, we've been lucky. No unfortunate accidents, and as far as modifying his behavior, we've had some success."

"*Some* success?" Richard asked. "I'd say complete success! He behaved himself admirably during your demonstration."

"Oh, that!" Lederman waved away the compliment. As no further assertion of his expertise followed, he cocked his head to the side and said, "You may be right. He does seem truly subdued."

"No doubt the prisoners recognize your natural superiority and respond to it."

"Do you think?" Lederman asked, stroking his mustache.

"Oh, yes, definitely. I'm sure of it. You can be proud of your accomplishments, you have a real talent. I'll tell you what." Richard was now on a roll and he only stopped long enough to light a cigarette. "Give that fellow some food and water, clean him up, let him recuperate for a week or so, and I bet you will be amazed at the product you have."

"You don't think he'll just slip right back into his old ways?"

"With your handling? No way! As you said, you've erased his personality. Nothing left but a drone. Don't underestimate yourself!"

Lederman looked pensive. "What about the way he grabbed for that water so presumptuously?"

Richard shook his head vigorously. "No, no! You misinterpreted. He was pleading, not grabbing." He raised his hands in mock supplication. "You see? Prayer! To a superior being."

Lederman nodded. "I see, I see. Hmm. Maybe I have underestimated myself."

"Put him in a household."

"A household?"

"Yes, right in the midst of society! With somebody important. That will impress everyone."

"Oh, I couldn't do that! At least not right away." Lederman stroked his chin.

"You must show him off. He's such an accomplishment!"

"Well, perhaps I could find something . . ." Lederman paused, then asked again, "You really think he's ready? So soon?"

Richard thought of that look of pure hatred and he grinned. "I'm sure of it!"

13

THE FOG THINNED AND the features of a man slowly coalesced into view: a pale, thin face; half-closed, gray-blue eyes; blond hair, streaked here and there with brown. He looked down, leaned forward, and brought both hands up to his face in a mechanical, well-trained way. Something scraped against his skin and he pulled his hands away to inspect the razor for blood. Again the ghostly image caught his eye. Who was this person? What in God's name was happening?

The thoughts scared him and he immediately ducked back down to repeat his well-practiced maneuver. Water was running slowly from a tap in front of him and he used it to rinse the razor. Though he was not thirsty, he felt a pressing need to drink and bent down and let some of the water into his mouth. He savored its taste and swallowed reluctantly. He raised himself and was again greeted by the eerily familiar face. With both hands he reached toward it and was not surprised to feel a cold, glassy surface. His attention was diverted from his reflection to his wrists—there were no chains binding them. He brought his hands down and very carefully separated them. They moved freely apart, and he stared at his left hand as it hovered independent and distant from his right. He glanced up from his hand, along the row of sinks, then, reassured by the lack of imminent danger, he allowed himself the incredible bravery of free thought.

His brow furrowed with the effort of remembering. It had been some time now, days at least, since they had removed his chains. Water, food, those things, too, had been provided. His work had been tolerable, the time allowed for sleep . . . Dare he think it? Longer than usual? Adequate even? He rotated his head, looking nervously all around. He was alone at a row of sinks, there was a mirror in front of him and a sharp razor in his hand. The last command he could recall was that he should shower, shave, and dress in a new uniform. What the hell were they up to? Everything was so different, so impermissible! His body ached, he was awash with pain, there was no doubt about that, but as he did a slow inventory, he realized that he had not recently been hurt. Not for days at least.

He finished shaving and glanced down the long row of empty sinks and located his guard, sitting on a bench against the far wall casually reaming out his left ear with his little finger. The guard noticed his prisoner's look and interrupted his efforts long enough to ask, "What's your problem?"

He froze at those words, casting his eyes down to stare at the floor. There could be no clearer sign that punishment was due, yet in the time it took the thought to pass through his mind, nothing happened. Slowly he raised his eyes and looked carefully back down the line of sinks. No reaction. The guard had proceeded to clean his right ear as thoroughly as he had reamed out the left.

With a confusion of fear and hope, he returned to his cell and collected his belongings in a bag he was given for that purpose. Despite the myriad crimes he committed—hesitating, looking around, thinking—nobody came to take him away. The usual guard who paced the hall had opened his cell door incuriously and did not comment when he stepped back out with his meager supplies. The guard who had watched him in the showers led him away, taking him out of the building and to an office in a section of the complex in which he had never been.

Three other men were already there. Behind the desk sat a young bureaucrat with a well-honed expression of disinterest, and behind him and off to one side stood the officer who had overseen his reeducation. The third man was old with wispy white hair. He wore the medals of a pensioner, a minor Party official, and a veteran and looked the sort who had earned some level of gratitude from his society. The three did not interrupt their conversation as he was brought in and left standing to one side of the desk, although the old man did give him a curious glance.

". . . in lieu of the usual payment and with regards to the sum exchanged for the aforementioned official fees," the bureaucrat finished droning.

"Whatever, whatever," the old man agreed, waving his hand impatiently. "Just show me where to sign. No money, or for that matter"—he glanced pointedly around—"body is going to replace my son." The old man sighed as the two men behind the desk looked at him with a mixture of pity and annoyance, then continued quietly, almost to himself, "But I need somebody to help out now that . . ." He sighed again, looked to the bureaucrat. "Where do I sign?"

"Here."

"There, is that all?"

"Yes, except of course for the follow-up formalities I already explained. You did understand that—"

"Yes, yes, yes." The old man stood up with surprising alacrity. Upon closer inspection it was clear he was not really all that old, rather more worn-out.

The officer finally spoke. "Well, Herr Reusch, we wish you luck. He has been thoroughly trained, and if you follow the simple instructions I gave to you, then you should have no problems. If, however, you do have any trouble with him, no matter how trivial, don't hesitate to contact me. I'll see to it personally."

Outside in the cold sunshine, once they were entirely alone, the old man turned to him and extended his hand saying, "My name is Reusch. Ernst Reusch."

He stared in panic at the hand. Herr Reusch seemed oblivious to his dilemma but eventually withdrew his hand as he continued, "Don't be misled by *them*. We're not as bad as all that. Anyway, all I want is a helper, and this is the only way they could find a . . . find, er, someone to, uh, find a replacement for my son." A note of sadness crept into Herr Reusch's voice. "He died, uh, tragically, in an, er, accident, I guess." There was a moment of silence, then Herr Reusch added in a markedly different tone, "Don't worry. We'll treat you well. My wife and I, that is. She's waiting at home. With supper."

He nodded, astounded by the words. Was he hallucinating? Was this all a drug-induced fantasy? Had he, at long last, stepped over that invisible line into insanity? But it felt like reality—some core part of himself still knew the difference. He turned around and looked at the outside of the military complex for the very first time. The huge flags with their swastikas hung limply over the gates. A motto was mounted over the entrance, but he could not read it from his distance. The brick of the walls looked no more or less terrible than any other brick walls. He turned his gaze upward to stare into the sun.

"Are you all right?" Herr Reusch asked suddenly, concerned by his silence.

"Getting better by the minute," he whispered, looking back to earth and wincing at his momentary blindness.

"Somewhere in these papers . . ." Herr Reusch stopped.

He looked at Herr Reusch expectantly.

"I'm sure that . . ." Again Herr Reusch stopped, apparently embarrassed, then with a sudden resolve, he blurted out, "You, um, you have a name. Don't you?"

He stared at the old man, this man who apparently now owned him. His name. His name? His lips moved but no sound emerged. He heard a number being shouted out, he heard Allison whisper something, he heard his father's voice, but none of those were right.

"Your name?" Herr Reusch repeated. "Certainly you don't want me to use this stupid number, do you?"

It was an invitation to rejoin the world, but what was the answer? What was it? He sifted through his memories, through aliases and legends, and with an effort focused on one. That was it, the one written on his papers the day of his arrest. "Peter," he said quietly, fascinated by the sound.

"Peter?" Herr Reusch repeated, overemphasizing the English vowels.

Peter nodded. "Yes, Peter."

"Good. Let's use that, then. Is that okay?"

"As you wish, *mein Herr,*" he heard himself reply. He was adrift in a sea of confusion. Too many things were going on in his mind: thoughts, memories, perceptions he had not had for . . . How long? An eternity. "Could you tell me just one thing, *mein Herr?*"

Herr Reusch nodded agreeably.

"What's the date?"

"March." Herr Reusch sounded momentarily confused as he summoned up the exact date. "The twelfth of March. Why, did you forget?"

"Yes," he answered distractedly, "yes, I forgot."

That afternoon, he was registered with the local police and the district police. He watched with detached fascination as his old wristband was removed and another indicating his new status was affixed to his arm. He noticed that, though his number and Reusch's name was on the band, his own name was not. He was also issued identification papers, which duplicated the information on the band but included his photograph and the details of his current life.

After that, Herr Reusch introduced him to his new home. Everything he had gone through left him thoroughly unprepared for the Reusch household. They did, indeed, simply need someone to help out. Herr Reusch ran a small shop near a huge housing complex, and he needed someone to mind the store while he took care of the accounts or other business. Peter's job consisted of serving the customers by helping them locate items, stocking the shelves, unloading and unpacking deliveries, taking inventory, and even occasionally using the cash register. At night he slept in a back room of the shop and served as a guard against crime, which, of course, did not officially exist. He found it strange that Herr Reusch could trust him in such a capacity and even stranger that he wanted to be worthy of that trust.

The shop was in an ugly, squat building constructed of gray cinder blocks; it had a flat gravel roof and tiny, useless windows along the sides. A huge window at the front of the shop was permanently darkened by posters, banners, displays, and the inescapable red-and-black flags. Around the shop loomed giant residential towers, blocking out most of the sun. The estate seemed to stretch endlessly with identical towers scattered at odd angles in some absurd attempt at *Gemütlichkeit,* the monstrous forms interrupted only by the shop, an elementary school, a bakery, and a few service buildings. The surrounding grounds were landscaped with packed mud, weeds, and a few hardy patches of unmown grass. Nearby was a highway, and a sheet-metal bus stop seemingly provided the only contact with the outside world.

Despite their frightful ugliness, the apartments were in fairly good shape, and he was not too surprised to learn that their residents were considered to be rather well-off. Most tenants had apartments with two bedrooms, so the living room did not have to convert into a bedroom, and some even owned cars, which were kept in a storage parking lot on the other side of the complex awaiting the rare days their owners had enough petrol ration coupons to take them out for a drive.

There was a bakery on the far side, but other than that, the shop was the only one in the complex and was consequently constantly busy. Herr Reusch even, occasionally, kept it open after normal shop-closing hours in order to provide his customers with essentials. This bit of illegal courtesy made him well-beloved and respected, and because he treated his worker with respect, his customers followed suit and did likewise.

In the back room of the shop, Frau Reusch had prepared a private space for Peter with basic furnishings, and after expressing surprise at the paucity of his worldly goods, she immediately set about providing him with various personal possessions. He ate his breakfast alone in the shop, but was usually invited up to the Reusch apartment for dinner and was provided with a nicely packed supper by Frau Reusch before he returned to the store to reopen for the afternoon. She also provided him with books and magazines to keep him amused during his off hours and placed a small television in his room so that he could watch that as well.

The shop could only be locked with a key from the outside, and so initially, when Herr Reusch had closed for the evening, Peter had effectively been locked inside. This apparently did not seem strange to Herr Reusch, and Peter hesitated to mention how disconcerting it was. Within days, he solved the problem for himself by disabling the alarm and the lock on the emergency exit and using that to come and go freely in the evening. In his spare time, he wandered about the housing estate and even enjoyed the tiny duck pond he found near its edge. He had no reason to leave the estate—it was essentially surrounded on three sides by industry and on the fourth by a highway—so the legal hindrances to his movements off the estate did not really impinge on his sense of freedom. Also, the local patrols knew him, and although they occasionally issued the usual dire threats about walking around without a pass or a purpose, they generally left him alone. He strolled along the residential paths, watched the children playing near the school, chatted to the customers in the shop, and conversed at length with the Reusches, Frau Reusch in particular.

She was a remarkable woman, intelligent, well-read, and full of fascinating stories and insights. She had a wonderful collection of books, even some prewar tomes in English, and she let him borrow them and gave several to him as gifts. After he had worked his way through her personal library, she began to take books out of the town library for him to read. Their discussions ranged over a wide variety of topics from ancient history to personal anecdotes; they only avoided politics, recent history, and the exact details of his past. Over time, their friendship developed further and they began to confide more and more in each other.

"You know, there's no one here I feel really comfortable talking to," she said one day, waving her hand around her to indicate the residents of the apartment block. "You never know when someone has an ax to grind or something. You just can't trust anyone."

He nodded. It was a familiar theme, and he knew she was simply working up the courage to tell him something. He did not press; she would tell him if and when she felt ready.

She pulled out her cigarette case and offered him one. He accepted it, but put it in his pocket, saving it for later or as barter material.

Frau Reusch removed one for herself, lit it, and sat silently smoking for a moment.

"Peter"—she dropped her voice—"I never did tell you about my son."

"No, you never did. What was his name?"

"Ernst. Just like his father. Maybe it was a bit silly of us, but we really wanted him to feel as though he belonged with us."

"Was there any doubt?"

She set down her cigarette and sipped her tea. Suddenly, as if she had only just noticed it, she waved at the television and snapped, "Would you turn that damn thing off!"

He went over to the set and found the off switch; it was the first time he had been in the apartment while the television was off, and he found it extraordinarily quiet. She continued to sip her tea as he sat back down.

Another moment passed; she glanced at the mantel clock. It ticked loudly—

the only noise in the room. "We couldn't have children. There is so much pressure to have children and we couldn't produce even one! You can imagine what that is like."

Actually in England it had been rather the reverse situation. When young couples generally set up house in a parents' living room, it was not surprising that few thought about large broods of children. Life was so unpleasant and the future so bleak that most families were hard-pressed to want to produce even one child, and the paperwork needed for a birth permit was both cumbersome and expensive. It was debated whether there was a deliberate government policy to discourage the birth of English children, but whether or not there was, that was the overall effect. The English birthrate, already rather low, had fallen dramatically after the hostilities ceased and continued to decline, for in the long run, economic hardship won out over patriotic fervor. But these things did not seem appropriate to Frau Reusch's story, so he simply nodded.

"So, we adopted a child. That is not all that easy, I'll have you know, but Ernst was a veteran, decorated at that, and we had some friends in high places, and eventually a child was found for us. He was wonderful! He had the blondest hair and the most beautiful blue eyes. But that wasn't why we loved him." She paused, wrapped in memories.

"He came to us when he was two or so. A scared little boy; some terrible accident had taken his parents, or so we were told. He soon learned to call us Mom and Dad, and to answer to Ernst, and to treat this place as his home. He had a wonderful personality. So kind. So loving.

"The trouble started later, when he was about sixteen. Long before then, I began to have my doubts about where he had come from. After he first arrived, he had nightmares and would scream, 'Don't go, don't go!' and sometimes he asked us if we were going to go, or if we were going to be taken away.

"At first I tried to believe it was simply confusion on his part. That *going* meant 'dying' or something like that. But then I also heard stories, whispered tales, about how some children were stolen from their parents. Even so, I thought, if his parents were arrested or guilty of some crime, perhaps it was better for a little boy to be raised by a good family, people who would take care of him, people who would provide him with opportunities, people who would care about him.

"I figured, if the official story wasn't true—and I had, have, no idea whether or not it is—well, if it wasn't true, then perhaps I had saved him from some terrible life with drug addicts or criminals."

The words had come out in a rush, but suddenly she stopped and stared absently out the window. Her fingers brushed against her lips as though trying to coax words from them. Peter waited silently, remembering a quote from Himmler he had once read: *We must not endow these people with decent German thoughts and logical conclusions of which they are not capable, but we must take them as they really are . . . I think it is our duty to take their children with us. . . . We either win over the good blood we can use for ourselves . . . or else we destroy that blood.*

Frau Reusch picked her cigarette back up, smoked silently for a moment, then stubbed it out with single-minded intensity. When she was satisfied that every spark had been extinguished, she spoke.

"So I left it at that. Eventually, it was necessary to tell him that he had been adopted. I didn't want him to find out accidentally, some other way. You know people, they do talk! So, when he was fifteen, I told him. At first there wasn't any problem. He said that we were his parents and that was that. But a year later, he began to ask questions. He wanted to know more about his birth parents. Where did he come from? What had happened to them? What had they named him?

"Well, although I had no official information, I was able to answer one question. Maybe I shouldn't have. But I did. I told him that he used to answer, when asked, that his name was Jan, and that he used to say some words that I simply did not recognize. I don't know, they could have been anything. You know how hard it is to understand children, and at the time I didn't want to hear anything other than German. I know Jan is a Dutch name, and I think it is Czech or Polish as well. But I wanted him to be like us, so I told myself that he was German and his name had been Johann. I even thought we should use that name, but Ernst argued that it would confuse the boy to be renamed yet again."

She sighed, refilled the teacups, and offered him more cake.

"Did he hear the same rumors that you had, about adopted children?" Peter inquired gently.

"Oh, yes, and more. He heard that sometimes children were simply taken for no reason at all. That they were taken from perfectly good, perfectly loving families. He heard that villages were sometimes destroyed in retaliation for terrorist acts, that the adults were sent to their deaths in concentration camps, and that the children, especially the ones with Aryan features, were given to good German families for adoption.

"I don't know where he got such stories, maybe from some cleaning lady at school—those Slavs, they will tell such tales! But I couldn't tell him whether or not they were true." She turned away from him to look out the window and began to sob. "God knows, I had no intention of stealing somebody's baby!"

No, he thought, but you did accept a nameless child without a history, and you carefully avoided asking the right questions.

She seemed to sense his unease. "You must think I'm a monster. But honestly, at the time, I had never heard of such a thing. I never suspected! I still don't know for sure. All I knew at the time was I wanted a child, and there was a little boy who needed me."

She looked at him, her eyes begging him for forgiveness. "We were good to him, we loved him. We really did."

"I know you did. You did what you thought was right—you can't ask more than that of yourself," he said, trying to console her, but his words felt empty. It wasn't his place to offer forgiveness.

"Well, Ernst, our son, wasn't satisfied. He wanted to know for sure. Of course, there was no hope of an official response. He tried and tried. We tried to help. Pulled strings, asked friends. Eventually it was clear that we were annoying people and that if we kept pressing for information, there could be trouble. So we tried to talk him out of finding out anything, but he became obsessed."

"A past is a precious thing," Peter offered obscurely.

Frau Reusch studied him for a moment, a question on her lips, but then she decided better of it and continued with her story. "It occupied all his free time. He took trips, tried to track sources, tried to find any scrap of information. Eventually—he was twenty already, my how the time went by—eventually, he tried to break into a registry office. He was shot dead as an intruder."

Frau Reusch stopped, a hard look in her eyes. "I sometimes wonder . . ."

He did not get to find out what she was wondering, for at that moment Herr Reusch returned from his after-dinner stroll and they returned to the shop to reopen it for the afternoon. He thought about Frau Reusch and her son throughout the afternoon, but he could not conceive of any consolation he could offer her nor could he work out the implications of her revelations for himself. No wonder they were so unusually kind to him, he was taking the dead boy's place! It should have made him feel more secure, but instead he felt uneasy. He knew intuitively that their loyalty to him was a figment of their needs and that they would abandon him to his fate as soon as he became a liability. The question that remained unanswered was, Did that really matter?

14

"**P**USH!" ADAM NEARLY SCREAMED in her ear. "*Push!*"

"I have an idea," Zosia said dryly between gasps. "How about one of you people push for a little while and I'll just take a break?"

No one laughed. They all seemed so serious! Here she was, the one who was in pain, sweating, gasping, and groaning; straining with all her might to push that little head out of her body, and they were so serious they could not even laugh at her little joke. She felt like berating them, but then she felt another wave of pain and someone stupidly yelled in her ear to push again.

She tried again to no avail, then she heard Marysia whisper soothingly in her ear that she should simply rest for a few moments. "Gather your strength and ignore the contractions," she said softly.

Zosia looked up into her mother-in-law's round, dark eyes, looked at the lines on her face and the silver sprinkled throughout her black hair, and she felt comforted. If Adam's mother said everything was okay, then it was all okay. Her own mother flapped her arms in a near frenzy in the background. Judging from her nervous antics, one would never guess that she herself had borne six children, but that was typical of Anna—if it had anything to do with her children, she fretted extravagantly, perhaps making up for her husband's famed British reserve.

Zosia turned her thoughts to her father and wondered if his dispassion was genuine or a calculated exhibition of his determinedly English character. "Anything to stay above the fray," her father would say, as if simply existing among so many "foreigners" was an accomplishment he could be congratulated for or as if emotion were something that could be caught from them, like a disease.

"Okay, now," counseled Marysia.

Zosia threw her will into pushing, and slowly the recalcitrant head of her child emerged. She felt the sudden easing of pressure, telling her that she had succeeded, and she gasped for breath.

"Marvelous!" Adam praised. "You're doing great!"

Adam held Zosia up and she peeked at the head nestled between her legs.

"The rest will be easy," Marysia assured her, and indeed it was.

Only a moment later, Adam held their daughter while Marysia gently washed away the birth debris and cut the cord. The little girl squeaked and gasped and finally wheezed her way into a full-bodied cry. As Marysia cleaned the child, Adam regarded her adoringly and Anna fussed over her, stroking her hands and touching her feet. No one seemed to notice that Zosia lay exhausted on her pillow regarding the four of them as though from a distance.

"Do you have a name for her?" Marysia asked, stroking the infant's face with her finger.

"Joanna," Adam answered proudly. "After Grandmother."

They continued to admire and fuss over the infant, each taking a turn at holding her until finally Zosia panted, "May I hold her?"

They all looked up at her as if surprised. "But of course!" Marysia said, and placed the baby on Zosia's breast.

Adam grinned at Zosia. "Since you got her, I'll go have a cigarette. I've been dying to have one. I'm beat from all that!"

Zosia, Marysia, and Anna all burst out laughing, but Adam was already gone. "Shall I try and feed her?" Zosia asked.

"You can try," Marysia said, "but I doubt she'll be ready to eat."

Zosia held the baby to her breast and crooned over her little miracle of creation whilst Marysia and Anna began cleaning up. Another series of contractions began about the time Adam returned, and he took Joanna into his arms as the placenta was delivered.

Marysia and Anna were still busy making Zosia and the room presentable when her first visitor arrived. "Is anyone home?" Alex asked in his peculiar accent as he tapped lightly on the doorjamb.

"Dad!" Zosia exclaimed.

Alex grinned benevolently at his youngest daughter. He was a stocky man with hair that had gone completely and somewhat prematurely gray. "Silver" he called it with his usual authoritative and all-knowing manner. "So, where's my grandchild?" Alex asked as he bustled over to Joanna. "Can this little bundle possibly be her? My goodness, what a little cabbage!" he said as he whisked her into his arms. He stroked the tiny fingers and asked, "So, how did it go, sweetheart?"

"Whew!" Zosia sighed. "I think I'll revise the number of kids I'll have downward a bit."

"Oh, that wasn't so bad!" Adam assured her breezily.

"How would you know?" Alex asked pointedly.

"I think I'll go have another smoke," Adam said by way of an answer, and left the room.

"Dad!" Zosia pretended to chide.

"He doesn't appreciate you," Alex grumbled.

Zosia glanced guiltily toward Marysia and said, "Well, he was worth marrying just to have Marysia and Cyprian as my in-laws!"

Alex looked back at Marysia and smiled his agreement. "Yes, your mother and I are glad, too. All the more so now."

"Now? Why now?" Zosia asked, suddenly suspicious.

"Alex!" Anna hissed. "This is hardly the time!"

"What, what's going on?" Zosia asked, looking from one to the other.

"It's not bad news, don't worry," Alex explained. "We're just getting transferred. We asked for it, and it's come through."

"You want to leave?" Zosia asked, incensed. "You asked for it? You didn't tell me!"

"Calm down, little one. You know your brother's been transferred to Göringstadt."

"Yes, quite a coup for him."

"Well, we've decided to go there as well and help out. He's been having a very hard time of it, and with yet another baby due . . . Anyway, they can use the help, and besides, it will be a move up for both me and your mother."

"Mother?"

"I've been elected to join the Warszawa Council once I'm there," Anna replied.

Zosia raised her eyebrows in surprise and wondered if either her brother or her father had something to do with that.

"Yes, and I've been put forward as a candidate for the government-in-exile. I need to be up there to coordinate my campaign and to get to know the leadership a bit better."

"You!" Zosia exclaimed.

"I can't imagine why they want me. I guess they think my English fluency is a boon." Alex had grown up in England and had only learned Polish when he was deported back to his father's homeland by the new Nazi government.

"Oh, don't be modest," Marysia chided. "Everybody knows you're a natural for politics."

"Maybe. Anyway, there's no rush. We won't be leaving for some time, but once we're gone, Marysia and Cyprian have promised to take care of you, so you won't be alone."

Zosia was hardly a child, but at the moment she did not feel like pointing that out to her father; instead she reminded him, "I'll have Adam, too."

"Ah, yes, your husband, too," Alex conceded.

Zosia furrowed her brow, then asked, "If you're leaving, Dad, there will be an empty seat on the Council here, won't there?"

Alex smiled at his daughter. "Yes, good thinking. I'll talk to Katerina and see what we can do for you." Katerina chaired the Council and was, by virtue of her position, her vast experience, and most of all her unyielding personality, a woman of considerable influence.

"Won't it seem a little stacked if you, Adam, and my mother all have Council seats?" Julia asked from the doorway.

"Julia! Look at my little girl!" Zosia enthused. "Isn't she gorgeous?"

Julia came into the room, greeted everyone with kisses, and then taking the baby into her arms, declared, "A niece! I've waited so long for a little girl in this family!"

"Just like I've waited for a son-in-law," Marysia commented somewhat sourly, having noted the smell of alcohol that accompanied her daughter into the room.

Julia shot her a contemptuous look and said, "When one is deserving of me."

"Olek—" Marysia began.

"Has turned out to be a fine lad," Zosia interjected. "And I'm sure he'll welcome his little cousin with open arms."

"Indeed he will," Julia agreed. She turned her attention back to the baby and cooed at her. "She's beautiful, Zosiu. Absolutely marvelous! Congratulations to both of you. How do you feel? How did it go?"

The others drifted out as Julia and Zosia chatted. Adam joined them after a time, and then their mutual friend Tadek stopped by. Tadek was a tall, lank man with dark brown hair and icy gray eyes. Only six years prior, he had joined their group from the outside as a rather unusual recruit, having first attempted suicide by walking, unescorted and uninvited, directly into the no-man's-zone that surrounded their mountainous retreat. Zosia had been out and about that day and had decided to disobey orders and bring the interloper in alive. They learned he had just lost his wife to a street roundup, that she had been put in an SS brothel, and that he had, in desperation, sought them out to gain their help in rescuing her. Of course, they did no such thing—with all the criminal depravity that was perpetrated in the name of the Reich, they could not afford the resources to single out and save one lone woman from a life of sexual slavery.

Despite that, Tadek offered them his services and was accepted into their ranks. He moved up rapidly in the hierarchy and was valued for his cool analyticity and his ability to make decisions unemotionally. Only once had he screwed up, in an unapproved and bungled attempt to rescue his wife. It had cost a number of his comrades their lives, and only with great difficulty had he come to terms with that failure. Since then he had been exemplary in obeying the rules, and since then it was said that the only thing that could rile his temper was the irrationality of his fellow conspirators and their willingness to take useless risks.

Tadek greeted both Julia and Zosia with a kiss on the lips.

Adam cleared his throat. "Ahem. If I might remind my dear comrade," he joked, "the lady is now a married woman." He tapped his cheek to indicate where Tadek should have planted the kiss for Zosia.

"Sorry," Tadek responded, and he bent down to Zosia and kissed first the left cheek, then the right, then the left again. He held the last kiss, running his tongue over her skin and creeping upward in a line of little kisses to nuzzle her ear. Zosia giggled in response, and Julia giggled as she saw Adam turn bright red.

"Is that better?" Tadek asked his friend. He did not wait for an answer, instead turning his attention to the newborn. He cooed and fussed over the sleeping baby now in Julia's arms, and they discussed the birth and Joanna's future and then news and local gossip, and at length, the conversation turned to Julia's work.

"It has just gotten to be too much," Julia conceded after she had described her efforts in Berlin several months earlier. She did not look up as she spoke; rather, she stared entranced at the infant, stroking her nose repeatedly as if to invoke magic.

"But it all went well?" Zosia asked. "Didn't it?"

"Oh, yes. Every time it goes well until it doesn't; then you're dead, end of story. I'm tired of it."

"We all have to die sooner or later," Adam commented. "No one gets out of this life alive."

"Well, I'd rather not die sooner."

"Don't you want to contribute anything? Do you just want to retire?" Adam asked pointedly.

"I *have* contributed!" Julia snapped.

"So did you talk with the Council?" Zosia asked before Adam and Julia started sniping at each other.

"Yeah, they'll assign me to work on-site. If I don't want to, I never have to leave here again."

"Great!" Zosia enthused. Maybe it was the relief of having the birth over with, but for some reason she was feeling munificent toward the entire world, and though, like Adam, she could not understand Julia's gnawing fears, she did recognize that they were real.

"So why are you looking so glum?" Tadek asked Julia.

"It's Olek. I asked them to remove him from active duty as well, but they say that I don't have the right to make that sort of decision for him. They want him to keep patrolling."

"Well, everyone does. Why shouldn't he?" Adam asked.

"I don't want him to take that risk. I don't want him involved in all this." Julia waved her hand expansively. "Why can't he have a normal youth?"

"Big question," Zosia said. "How does Olek feel about it?"

"Oh, he wants to do it all. He wants to be like . . ." Julia threw an angry look at her brother. "You know, always out there, right in their face, killing the enemy. Our angel of vengeance."

"It's not vengeance," Adam retorted. "Each and every one is a judicial execution, ordered by our courts."

"Julia, you know better than that," Zosia chided gently.

Julia shrugged. "Whatever they are, it involves being out there among *them*. That's what Olek wants. Nothing subtle like propaganda work or organization. No, he admires his uncle!"

"And his mother, I would guess," Tadek said. "I know you've grown weary, but you are one of our best and your son knows that."

"Was," Julia corrected. "I've lost my nerve. Not only for me, but for him. He means too much to me." She handed the baby back to Zosia.

Zosia beheld her infant for a few moments thinking about what Julia had said. "I have plans for my child," she said at last, though she did not reveal what they were.

"So did I," Julia said with a wan smile. She stretched and shook her head and with it her mood. "But that's neither here nor there. Now I have different plans. All I have to do is train my replacement and that's it, I'll be free!"

Tadek knocked discreetly on the wooden arm of Julia's chair as Julia emphatically repeated, "I will be free!"

15

I WILL BE FREE, Peter thought as he wandered the grounds of the housing estate contemplating yet again the possibility of escape. Rather than go through tedious and useless planning, he gave in to his urge to daydream and imagined what it would be like to live as a free man again. Since he was daydreaming, he allowed himself to cobble together a fantastic scenario where Allison was still alive as well. She had not, after all, been dead when they brought her out of her flat, or better yet, it had been a double agent who had been in her apartment that night. Allison had not even been there; she had gone into hiding and had waited these four and a half years for him to return so they could start their life together.

He shook his head in faint disgust. In that direction lay madness. Better to base his plans on reality, and the reality was, it was not as easy as he had thought it would be. After his release into Herr Reusch's hands, he had wisely given himself several months to let his injuries heal, to rebuild his strength and regain lost weight. The time had passed quickly, and though he felt better, he did not feel as well or as strong as he had hoped.

His initial, straightforward plan to simply leave at the first opportunity was complicated by two things. The first was that he knew if he was recaptured, he would be sent back to torture, and he did not feel he was ready to stomach that risk. The second complication was the Reusches' trust in him. Logically, of course, it should not have had any effect; yet, strangely, he felt a loyalty to this couple who had, in effect, rescued him from hell. He did not know if they would be held responsible if he escaped, but he feared their leniency toward him might well cause them to be suspect.

He had also learned a number of things over the months that he had been with them. Most did not bode well for his chances. For one thing, patrols were frequent and intrusive. Those that recognized him usually left him alone, but the several times he had wandered more than a few hundred meters along the highway had unnerved him. Each time he quickly drew the attention of a passing patrol, his papers were checked, and he was sent back to his home base with a stern warning not to wander too far without an appropriate pass.

He also ascertained that as long as he wore his uniform, a pass that took him more than a few kilometers from his home would immediately be suspect. So, he would need to wear civilian clothes, but that would require a completely different set of papers, and then there were his permanent identifications. How could he hope to hide the metal wristband and the tattoo on his arm? Perhaps he could remove the band somehow, but with the slightest suspicion, his arm could be inspected and he would be caught.

He scratched absentmindedly at the number as he leaned against the side of a building and thought about his options. In the distance, he saw two young boys walking along, playing with a toy bow and arrow. They shot the arrow into the air, chased it, reloaded, and then repeated the exercise. Suddenly they stopped their game—one boy shoved the arrow up his sleeve, the other hid the bow under his shirt. Peter repositioned himself to look around the corner of the building to see what they were watching and was surprised to see that it was only a normal patrol. The guards strutted past the boys, who watched them solemnly as they passed, and then, only when the patrol was well past them, did the boys resume their play. He was struck by how odd the scene was: there was nothing wrong with the toy, the patrol would never even have noticed it, yet the boys, out of habit, assumed that if they were having fun, then they should be careful not to show it when the police were around. And the boys were Germans!

Such observations of civic stress, he felt certain, would be useful to the Underground, if only he could report them. But such observations also brought home just how daunting a challenge escape was: when even the citizenry, the beneficiaries of the system, were afraid of their police, what hope did he have of avoiding their scrutiny long enough to reach and cross a safe border?

He wandered farther, to the edge of the complex near the bakery. He had noticed about a month ago that a new worker—a *Zwangsarbeiterin*—had arrived, and he was hoping to get a chance to meet her. Since Frau Reusch usually did all the shopping, he had no reason, and therefore no permission, to visit the bakery, so he simply made a point of regularly strolling past whenever he had a chance. Every time he had walked past since his initial sighting, she had either been busy or nowhere in sight, but this evening he was in luck for she was sitting outside on the ground, shelling peas.

She watched suspiciously as he approached but did not make a move to leave.

"May I help you?" he asked.

She glanced at the door of the bakery, then shrugged. "I guess they won't object."

He sat down next to her, leaning against the rough concrete of the bakery wall. The midday heat had passed, but the heavy gray blocks still radiated warmth. The woman continued her work without bothering even to look at him. Peter studied her. She wore the woman's equivalent of his uniform: a dark blue, sleeveless dress with a pale blue blouse underneath. She had long, curly, black hair that hung in an unruly mass and heavy eyebrows over small, dark eyes. She had full lips and a rounded face that made her look as though she had a double chin, even though she was not heavy enough to actually have one. She looked healthy enough, not emaciated or pale like some, and he guessed she was in her late twenties.

He grabbed a handful of the pods and began working on them, diverting his attention from her face and staring out across the expanse of sandy dirt that led right up to the ground-floor balconies of the nearest tower block. As he absently emptied the peas and discarded the husks, the woman gave him a curious glance. She laboriously worked on splitting a hull as he did several more in rapid succession. Finally she opened the hull and painstakingly extracted the peas one at a time. He cleaned a few more, looking now at the clouds as his hands worked mechanically.

"Where'd you get so good at that?" she asked almost accusingly.

It was, he thought, not so much a matter of his being good at shelling the peas, rather it was more a question of how she managed to be quite so incompetent, but he did not say that; instead he replied, "Don't worry, it's easy, you'll soon get the hang of it."

"Why should I?"

He brought his attention down from the clouds to look at her. It was a fair point and he replied somewhat apologetically, "No reason. No reason at all."

They worked in silence for a few moments, then he asked, "What's your name?"

"Maria."

"That's pretty." He waited a moment, but she didn't ask, so he offered, "I'm Peter." He extended his hand but she ignored it.

Again they fell silent. He wondered at her unfriendliness but knew it could have many sources, so he decided to wait patiently, reasonably comfortable with the silence and her company. They were nearly at the bottom of the bowl when she suddenly broke her silence.

"Do you want to sleep with me?"

"What?"

As if a dam had broken, she suddenly became loquacious. "I'm about to explode! I haven't had a good fuck since I got here!"

"How long have you been here?"

"Oh, I guess it's been four or five weeks. I came from the city." She jerked her head in the direction of the highway that led into Breslau. "I had a good setup there. Reasonable work, no beatings—at least not many—and a closet to myself."

"What happened?"

"Oh, they suspected their stupid son was getting romantically involved with me. Hah!" she snorted. "I mean, I was fucking him, okay, but involved? Christ! He's a kid! Fourteen!"

"Fourteen?"

"Yeah. The brat. Though I must admit, he wasn't bad in bed once I taught him what to do."

"How old are you?"

"Eighteen," she announced proudly. "So, they cleared me out quietly before there could be any scandal, and here I am! Exiled to nowhere!"

"Where are you from?"

"Weren't you listening?"

"No, I mean originally."

"Oh, that . . . I was told Forino." At his blank look, she explained without patience, "It's supposed to be near Napoli."

"Naples? You're Italian? I thought you were allies. I thought they left you alone."

She shrugged disinterestedly; the world was what it was. "So you wanna do it?"

"Maybe after I get to know you a bit first."

She rolled her eyes in disgust, then scrunching her face up so she could see the details of his shoulder patch, she said suddenly, "English?"

"Yeah."

"Oh! Do you prefer boys?"

"No!" he answered, too surprised to be anything other than amused.

"What's the green mean?"

"Criminal," he stated dryly.

"Oh." She seemed refreshingly unperturbed.

"Maria!" a harsh voice bellowed from within.

"Got to go," she said, getting to her feet. "If you want to see me, come back at midnight. I'll meet you over there." She pointed to the stand of glass cases that displayed the day's newspaper and, grabbing her bowls, disappeared through the door.

Peter came at midnight, but she did not show up. He returned the following night. She appeared within ten minutes. When she did not say anything, he suggested they take a stroll. He was hoping to get her to talk. It was odd, but his intellectual needs, his hunger for friendship, quite overwhelmed any other desire. As they walked, he looked at her and tried to work up something like lust for her. It wasn't easy: she was not particularly attractive to him.

"Sorry I couldn't make it last night."

He knew by her tone that she was lying: clearly she thought she needed to tease his interest. Perhaps she was right. If he had been fifteen or sixteen, well, at that time of his life, almost any human female was enough to provoke urgent physical needs. Later, as he matured, he began to enjoy having relationships, and then after that came genuine love. Once he had sex coupled with love, he was not so sure he could so easily drop back to mindless physical pleasure. Plus there was the other consideration—his enforced abstinence of the past years had left him doubting that he could simply jump into bed with the first woman who came along. Perhaps if he had felt that Maria would have shown any degree of patience, he might have been willing to try, but he knew instinctively that she would be merciless in humiliating him if things did not go as planned, so he hesitated.

"So, you want to have sex tonight? It's a good night. I'm safe," she broke into his thoughts.

By safe, he knew she meant that she was unlikely to get pregnant. It was the only form of birth control accessible to them: a mix of abstinence, rhythm, and withdrawal. Since *Zwangsarbeiter* were forbidden by law to have intercourse, they obviously had no need for contraceptives, and since Germans were supposed to produce as many children as possible, they obviously had no need for any either. The situation was quite different in England; there the government was all too happy to discourage births, but since the state could never organize efficient distribution of contraceptive pills or condoms, the populace had to rely on the freely provided sterilizations and abortions.

"Well?" she prompted.

"Not right now."

In the dark it was hard to see, but he knew she had wrinkled her nose in a mixture of disbelief and exasperation. "Do you have any cigarettes?" she asked suddenly.

"No. But if you like, I'll try and get you some."

"Yeah. I'd like that."

"It'll cost you," he warned.

"Huh? Look, just pick the place and I'm all yours!"

"No, that's not what I meant."

"What did you mean?"

"I want you to tell me about yourself. About what you think and feel and about your history."

"What, are you an informer?" Maria asked suspiciously.

"No, just curious," he answered, trying not to laugh.

"Man, you're weird."

"Maybe, but indulge me."

So she did. She chatted amiably enough about her life but did not seem to offer much in the way of thoughts or philosophy. It had never really occurred to her to question the status quo, and for that she was a happier person than he could ever be. She did not seem to have any interest in his history or his opinions, and he did not bother to offer up anything unsolicited. She only seemed interested in one piece of information.

"Do you have a girlfriend already?" she asked.

"No."

"Then what's the problem?"

"Just be patient for a day or two. Okay?" He kissed her affectionately on the forehead and they parted.

They met the following night and he gave her the cigarettes—whole cigarettes, not just ends—that he had acquired from Frau Reusch. Her delight was genuinely charming and he felt some of his reserve slip a bit. Still, it was not so much chatting to her—her conversation was limited and already rather repetitive—as his thoughts during the day that let him warm to the idea of having sex with her. He really wanted to establish some contact with the world independent of the Reusches, and he wanted to experience something like normal life again. Yet, it was not easy to be enthusiastic about sex with a woman whom he did not love, hardly even liked, and who was not particularly physically attractive to him either.

It was, in the end, her own desires that swayed him. If nothing else, it would clearly give her pleasure; so, he allowed himself to daydream, to desire, to anticipate, and by their third meeting he was ready to end her interminable abstinence. They returned to his room and he made love to her. And it was lovemaking, for the entire time his mind was elsewhere, with someone else. He knew that she would not notice, or if she did, she would not mind for she had made it abundantly clear that she longed for the physical act, not impossible emotional complications.

Afterward she smoked one of the cigarettes he had given her and surprised him by saying, "I knew you'd be good."

He allowed himself to enjoy the compliment—she may even have meant it seriously. He murmured something appropriately complimentary to her in return.

"What's her name?" she asked suddenly.

He looked up at her, startled by the question. Then he realized she was not accusing him of having another girlfriend, she just wanted to know whom he was thinking about. "Allison," he replied.

"She's dead?"

"Yeah. Some years now. How'd you know?"

"Oh, you're not the sort to cheat."

He felt a sudden tightening in his chest. If only you knew, he thought.

She finished the cigarette and with it, her afterglow. She allowed herself to notice her surroundings. "Gee, you've got it good here."

"I guess so."

"I'd kill for a place like this."

He smiled noncommittally.

"Do they hit you much?" she asked while playing with the controls on the television.

"Not at all."

"Shit. You don't know how lucky you are."

"I guess not."

"Can you get me more cigarettes?" she asked, still enamored with the television.

"I'll see what I can do."

"Why don't you just take them from the shop?" she suggested, obviously convinced he was too simple to have thought of such a solution himself.

He shook his head without bothering to explain.

Over the weeks that followed, they met fairly regularly. Maria was virtually insatiable and he had no real problem with keeping their relationship almost entirely sexual—for one thing, when they were fucking, he had no need to think about how tedious her company was otherwise. He tried on numerous occasions to get her to talk about anything that required thought, but she brushed off his attempts with an air of impatient contempt. When he tried to tell her anything about his own thoughts and feelings, she would rapidly cut him off by yawning expansively or interrupting him with the single word *boring* drawn out in a singsong voice. So, he surrendered to the inevitable and withdrew to a level of interaction with which she could be comfortable. He satisfied her needs by providing a continuous supply of cigarettes, and she returned the favor by never commenting that he was making love to a ghost.

Usually he would meet her at night by the newspaper stand and they would stroll a bit and then return to his room. Afterward, he always insisted on walking her back home. She assumed he accompanied her because of some old-fashioned concept of chivalry, and she was, at least in part, correct. He knew that any patrolling policeman coming across a lone woman might be liable to take advantage of the situation, and he hoped his presence would deter such an ugly possibility. A more pressing motive, however, was that he wanted to prevent trouble for both of them. He felt that her careless attitude would inevitably cause her to be caught if she were to walk back alone and that she would immediately implicate him. On the other hand, if he accompanied her, he could both help prevent them from being detected and come up with reasonable excuses if they were caught.

As they returned to her residence one humid night, he wondered if she would be offended to know that he did not really trust her to handle the journey on her own. He doubted it; she seemed completely oblivious to any such subtleties. Indeed, he had to remind her repeatedly to keep her voice down as they walked along, and he noticed, even now, she was heading straight into the light of a security lamp because—as she so often explained—it was shorter than going around. Automatically, he reached for her arm to pull her back into the safety of the shadows, but it was too late—a passing patrol had noticed.

"Halt!"

He froze, his heart pounding. He felt Maria push herself up against him as if she could melt into his shadow. The patrol approached—two boys who wore the uniform of the youth league, and a man wearing the uniform of the regular district security police. The dark green of his shirt was stained with sweat under the arms.

The policeman, aware of his responsible role, was extremely businesslike. "Your papers."

Peter and Maria handed over their documents. The policeman perused them, then handed them to the boys to look at. They scanned the papers eagerly.

"Where are your passes?"

"We have none, *mein Herr*," Peter answered. Maria remained in terrified silence.

"You are not permitted out without passes. Certainly not past curfew!" the policeman scolded.

"We're sorry, *mein Herr*. We just wanted to get a breath of air. It's so hot inside."

As if reminded of the heat, the policeman wiped his brow with the back of his hand. "You're Reusch's boy, aren't you?"

"Yes, *mein Herr*." Though *boy* was hardly appropriate given that he was older than any of them, it was, nevertheless, the accepted term.

"And you"—the policeman indicated Maria—"you work at the bakery, don't you?"

She nodded.

"I've given both of you warnings before, haven't I?" He sounded parental in his disapproval and exasperation. Since Peter had received numerous warnings while wandering around in the daytime, he presumed that the man was correct in his case, and he assumed that the same was true for Maria. Somehow, in broad daylight, the warnings had never seemed serious, and he was therefore quite surprised that the patrolman remembered such infractions. But he had, and he narrowed his eyes and continued, "Such blatant disregard for the law cannot go unpunished."

Peter noticed the boys had stopped looking at the papers and were staring avidly at Maria. At the promise of punishment, their faces had lit up with anticipation. He took a calculated risk, and drawing the attention of the patrolman to the two boys with his eyes, Peter then looked directly at him and said, "Please let her return home, *mein Herr*. She's new here and I've misled her. It's my fault, punish me."

The policeman had not failed to notice the looks in the boys' eyes and, with ill-disguised contempt for his young charges, agreed. "All right. Go home."

Maria stared at him wide-eyed.

"I said scram!"

She took off at a run toward the bakery. Peter watched her disappear into the darkness, then turned his attention to his own predicament.

"Now, boy, we can lock you up and bring Herr Reusch in to bail you out in the morning. Course, can't guarantee your safety overnight," the policeman warned him. "Or we can deal with you tonight, unofficially."

"I know the rules of the game," Peter agreed, then sighing, added, "Let's get it over with now."

The two youths were assigned to hold his arms, and then the policeman began the attack. As it progressed and Peter folded beneath the blows, the boys released his arms to join in. They did not beat him up too badly—clearly the policeman wanted to keep his apprentices under control; they mostly pummeled his stomach and jabbed their knees into his groin for good measure. As he collapsed onto the ground, they followed up with a few halfhearted kicks and then stopped.

He lay still, as his and Maria's papers were tossed onto the ground near him, and then the patrol left, satisfied with their dispensation of justice. After a few moments, he found the strength to rise, collect the documents, and stagger home. He let himself into his room, wiped his face with a cold, wet cloth, and then curled up into his bed to try to sleep off the effects of the justice system.

The next morning, Herr Reusch failed to notice anything was amiss, but at lunchtime, as Peter lowered himself painfully into his chair, Frau Reusch was immediately suspicious.

"What's the matter? Are you in pain?"

He shook his head. "It's nothing."

"What's happened? Did you get beat up?"

He looked at her, somewhat surprised that that would be her first guess. What about stomach flu or a hangover or any other normal event? But then, beating people was normal—why should she pretend otherwise? What had started in the thirties with the public humiliation and harassment of Jews and other "enemies" had spread throughout society into a sometimes deadly, but completely normal, way of life.

In answer to her questioning look, he nodded, then looked away.

"What happened?"

"I went out for a walk at night. A patrol objected to the fact I did not have a pass."

"Oh, my! They aren't supposed to do that!" Frau Reusch objected. Herr Reusch maintained an interested silence.

"From my position, that's a little difficult to explain to them," Peter answered.

"Why were you out?" A strong implication of disapproval was in Frau Reusch's voice. "Was it to see your girlfriend?"

"How did you know I had a girlfriend?"

"Oh, it was obvious. After all, you weren't smoking all those cigarettes."

He nodded. He felt oddly embarrassed by the whole incident; somehow this society had confined him to a position not unlike that of a child, and he was helpless to prevent it.

"Look," Herr Reusch finally spoke up, "if you need to see your lady friend at night, let me know, I'll write some sort of pass for you."

"That's very kind of you," he responded, hoping he sounded more thankful than he felt, "but you must understand how demeaning that would be for me."

"Why?" they asked in concert.

"Whatever our political masters say, I am an independent and fully human adult. To essentially have to ask for your permission to see a woman . . ." He opened his hands. Certainly it would be clear to them now.

They were perplexed. "Whatever is the problem with having us write you a pass?" Herr Reusch asked, his voice carrying a hint of sourness at Peter's ingratitude. He apparently had not considered the impracticalities involved: what sort of excuse would suffice after curfew, how Peter would explain Maria's presence, and so on. Herr Reusch only wanted to know why his offer to help had been so rudely rejected.

Peter looked into the two faces of convention: good people, kind people, totally oblivious people. He felt the task was beyond him and he settled for an easy way out. "There's no problem. Don't mind me, I'm just a bit unnerved by what happened. Anyway, there's no need anymore, we broke up last night."

That was, of course, a lie. That evening Peter went to see Maria again. The relationship had grown tedious for him and he had, until his conversation with the Reusches, contemplated ending it, but now he felt more determined than ever to continue seeing her. In any case, he needed to return her papers to her before they were missed.

She saw him waiting by the newsstand and met him within a few minutes. When he handed her the documents, she breathed, "Oh, thank God!" but did not venture further comment on the night before. She tucked the documents into the pouch she wore around her neck, tucked it back under her blouse, and then began talking, too loudly, about some incident in the bakery.

Peter interrupted her. "I'm fine thanks."

"What?"

"And you're welcome."

"Huh?"

"Never mind," he sighed, exasperated by his own idiotic attempt at sarcasm. "Just from now on, two rules, if you want to continue our meetings."

Something in the tone of his voice penetrated enough for her to ask, "What?" with a little more seriousness than usual.

"No more talking outside of my room—not one word! And while we're walking back and forth, you hold on to my arm and stay next to me. No wandering into the light. Got that?"

"Yeah," she agreed sullenly.

For good measure, he grabbed her arm and held it tightly as they walked back to his room. Several times she began to interrupt the silence, but he clapped his hand over her mouth each time, and eventually she got the subtle hint, and in this way they managed to continue their clandestine liaisons without again being harassed by the local constabulary or any other officious sort of night prowler.

16

JULIA STOPPED PROWLING the street near the entrance of the club and rifled through her purse. She found her lipstick and a small mirror and took a moment to apply another layer of deep red to her lips. Nothing seemed to be going right, not this stupid job, not her stupid life. Though she had spent the past months secure in their mountain retreat, Olek had, despite her pleas, continued patrolling. Even worse, he had begun training as an infiltrator, studying to perfect his accent and his mannerisms, making forays into the towns to do observational work, accompanying senior members of the Underground on their missions in order to gain experience and confidence. He had even spent two months with Zosia's eldest brother, Ryszard, living at his house, working in his office as a gofer, learning the ways of the enemy, learning to fit in without drawing attention to himself. Olek had returned full of ideas and enthusiasm, convinced of his invincibility. He had also fallen in what he called "love" with Ryszard's eldest daughter, a girl whose warm good looks belied an icy soul. Julia whistled her anger through clenched teeth. It was too much, the boy was only sixteen!

Julia blamed Adam and Zosia for a good portion of Olek's behavior. They were so breezy about the dangers, so jovial about the risks! When it came to their work, they acted half their ages. They disappeared into the morning mist with their stilettos and their guns and emerged days later with grins and anecdotes about their accomplishments. Zosia even took the baby along with her so that she could continue nursing! She enticed Olek with gruesome tales of evil men writhing as they died in her arms, of traitors and blackmailers begging in vain for mercy, of having to wash blood off her chest before she could put the baby to her breast; it was exactly the sort of nonsense that would appeal to a teenage boy.

Mindless of the risk that any student faced by attending, Adam took Olek into Krakau to visit the illegal class that he taught there; he helped Olek with his weapons instruction; he encouraged him into strenuous physical training. Did Zosia teach Olek her computer skills so that he could work from within the bunker? No! She encouraged him to enroll in her self-defense classes, she taught him her knife-fighting skills! Adam and Zosia, the terrible twosome! They held court in their luxurious two-room flat, the one Zosia had wrangled to keep after her parents had vacated it to go to Göringstadt; they both held seats on the Council now, they both were ridiculously decorated and promoted to ranks that were inappropriate to their youth. They were the blond-haired, blue-eyed golden couple with their precious little golden-girl daughter . . .

With the thought of Joanna, Julia stopped her mental diatribe. Joanna was a wonderful baby, a four-month-old bundle of toothless smiles and irresistible belly laughs, and Adam and Zosia obviously loved her dearly. Julia sighed. It was pointless chiding them or anyone else for the fact that Olek did not want to live his life safely cosseted by the mountains. He was a healthy young lad surrounded by suffering and injustice and felt that he could do something about it. She herself had once felt that way, why should her own son be any different?

Like herself, he had never seen what peace was like, he had never had the opportunity to live a normal life. Like herself, he was a child of their interminable war. A war that ebbed and flowed, that sucked their lives from their very bodies, that sucked their souls and their consciences into a void. A war that left nothing of those it touched except empty shells of suffering or mindless perpetrators of the brutal order it had established. Only a core resistance remained, flickering with its faint light of hope in the future. Was it any wonder her son wanted to be part of that small hope? He would not voluntarily avoid the dangers involved, she would simply have to remove him from the situation. America was the answer. If she could take him to America, then he could live a normal life and he could understand that one did not need to kill or risk death and torture just to maintain one's honor. In America there was that elusive creature: peace. He would learn what the word meant there. All she needed was money. Dollars. American dollars.

Julia ignored the passersby who shot contemptuous glances at her tight skirt and low-cut blouse, and she looked up at the glowering Berlin sky. Soon another August storm would be upon them. How the time had flown since her last visit to Berlin! She had spent the months training a replacement and doing other mundane work. The Council had kept their word, when this job was complete, when her replacement felt comfortable with his duties, then she would be done with this nonsense. That, however, would not solve her problem. It was not enough for her to be safe, she wanted her son to be safe as well. Was it really such an awful thing for a mother to want?

She flung the lipstick back into her purse and rummaged until she found her hip flask. Casting a quick glance around, she took a clandestine swig and put the bottle back into her purse. She noticed that her hands were shaking as she pulled the zipper shut. Things had not been going well. She and her apprentice had already successfully covered all their other target sites, but each had been difficult, and each had left her both emotionally and physically drained. This last target had been particularly problematic. They had had three setbacks, the first being nothing more than an intrusive patrol, but Julia had felt spooked and had abandoned their attempt for that evening. Their next try was frustrated by a bomb scare that saw the entire area they were trying to enter cordoned off. On the third attempt, they finally reached the house that abutted a private club that was favored by high-level officials, but there was construction at the site and the house was being torn down. Julia had stood across the street from the house, her fists clenched in frustrated rage, as she saw her plans go awry yet again.

She checked her watch and swore. Another five minutes to kill before the club opened. Other prostitutes were gathering, waiting to bribe the staff when they opened the door so that they could be let inside. Rather than concentrate on the details of the job ahead, Julia's mind strayed yet again to her long-term plans. First, she would need papers, tickets, and money to get into Switzerland—that would not be terribly difficult. A few favors could be called in, or she could just ask the Council for that sort of largesse or she could fabricate some reason for the travel. Whatever. It was once she was in Switzerland that things would be difficult. A direct application to the Americans for permission to immigrate was unlikely to be granted: their record on refugees was chaotic at best, and they were growing increasingly touchy about letting foreigners in, for whatever reason. She could, of course, apply to visit, but a traveler's visa for a Reich citizen would be next to impossible to obtain. So, she would need papers for her and Olek indicating they were from some neutral land, and she would probably have to arrange travel to the American Union from that land. That would require some forward planning and considerable bribes. Once they were in America, they needed to get a lawyer and seek asylum, and that, she presumed, also cost money. Or maybe living underground for a few years and applying for legal status later, during an amnesty, would be the safest course? She could imagine what would happen to them if they failed in their bid for asylum and were deported back into the Reich—if they survived interrogation and did not betray themselves as members of the Underground, Olek would probably be inducted into a punishment battalion and she would be sold to some industrialist to slave out the remainder of her days in some airless factory.

The doors to the club were opened and Julia pressed forward with the other women to gain admittance. Technically no women were allowed inside, but the rules were bent when a sufficiently pretty woman offered a sufficiently substantial bribe at the door. The club was an attractive location—all the highest-ranking members of the local government offices belonged to it, and once a lady arranged a liaison with one of those men, she could be set up for years, even life. Anecdotal tales abounded of this or that lady who had not only been taken on as a mistress but who had ended up married and had settled into society as a proper wife of a high-ranking Party member. Even foreign women stood a chance of gaining an entrée into society in this manner, and Julia noticed a few around her who spoke accented German. She did not; she spoke high German without a discernible accent and carried papers that indicated she had been born in Hannover.

When it came her turn, the doorman sized her up rather critically. She was attractive, but perhaps he noticed her relative maturity compared to the girls who pressed themselves determinedly forward against her. Julia smiled knowingly, winked at the man, and indicated with a glance at her hand that the bribe was conveniently predivided into two piles—the one he could split with his fellows and the other he could keep for himself. He was already studying the next prospective entrant as he grabbed the money into his left hand and gestured her into the bar with his right. Julia ducked into the dim room, took a few steps away from the door, and waited patiently as her papers were examined, she was frisked, and her bag was searched. As she waited, she pulled out her metal cigarette case, took a cigarette out for herself, and offered one to the security guard. He accepted and smiled broadly when she lit it for him. He finished his inspection and motioned her onward. She threw the cigarette case back into her purse and, entering into the public bar at the front of the club, took in her surroundings. She had some time to kill before her partner would show up—they had decided late evening was the best time to try to approach their target, and he did not need to be there until then. Julia, however, had decided to come in early so she could inconspicuously join the crowd at the door and so she could scout the premises and the clientele at her leisure.

The evening passed amusingly enough. She placed herself in an advantageous location and allowed the men to initiate the conversations. Halfway through the evening, having been treated to a substantial amount of fine cognac, she agreed to join a table of revelers as they celebrated the retirement of one of their comrades. The guest of honor was a well-kept man with silver hair and a ready smile. By virtue of her age relative to that of the other girls at the table, Julia fell naturally into the role of his companion, and as the evening progressed, she ended up sitting on his lap and nuzzling his ear playfully. His hands hovered near her without actually touching her, and finally she decided to help him overcome his shyness and gently grabbed one of his hands and placed it boldly on her breast. He blushed but did not remove it. She laughed good-naturedly, and the rest of his companions joined in teasing him for his old-fashioned manners.

"We'll miss you, Heiner. I've been told your replacement is nowhere near as subtle," one of them remarked.

"Do you know who it'll be?" Heiner asked.

"A fellow named Vogel."

"Andreas Vogel? He's older than I am!"

"No, Karl Vogel. No relation. He's in Paris now, but he's Berlin by career."

Julia stopped nuzzling. Dreamily, she pressed her face close to her companion's, but her mind was whirling. They continued to talk about Heiner's replacement and then about his plans for the future, all the while drinking toasts, all the while moving their hands over their playful, willing companions. Julia enjoyed being touched, she enjoyed the physical sensation despite the emotional barriers that she necessarily kept in place. She had learned her host had been working in the Security Ministry, she had learned he was relatively well-placed. Given that information, she knew that in his work he could be neither gentle nor shy. He was involved in some of the dirtiest work for one of the dirtiest governments on the planet, and despite his old-fashioned manners and his blushing timidity, he was, no doubt, a swine.

She ran her fingers along his neck, stopping momentarily to feel the place where one could sink a stiletto directly into the cerebral cortex. A quick, almost painless death. It was better than he deserved. She felt herself growing excited and was surprised by that. It had been years since she had felt anything other than dread, and here she was, sitting on the lap of an irredeemable pig, feeling aroused! It was, she realized, the mention of Karl's name. He was a pig as well: selfish, vain, brutal to subordinates, groveling to superiors, but he had been a passionate lover in his day and the thought of him, Olek's father, had brought back a flood of memories.

It also brought a brilliant idea to mind. Karl was moving up in the world—that was obvious. He was still fairly young, only forty, and he was moving into the position being vacated by this fossil; that was a good sign that his career was progressing well. He probably had money by now, probably a lot if his father-in-law was finally dead or if they had come to terms at last. He also had power and access. He could get his hands on hard currency, and through him she could arrange her and Olek's ticket out of the country!

Heiner turned his attention to her suddenly. "I, er, what if, um, well, do you think we could move to one of the private rooms, young lady?"

Julia could feel how hard he was against her thigh. She glanced at the clock: there was plenty of time. "I'd love to," she answered. The party broke up with various couples disappearing to the private "apartments" made available to club members. These were little more than tiny rooms used for private dinners, important discussions, and clandestine meetings. Each had a large, comfortably wide couch, a small table, and several chairs.

Once Heiner had closed the door and they were alone, he wasted no time on old-fashioned manners or shyness. He almost lunged at Julia, pulling at her buttons as he kissed her passionately and rolled her onto the couch. Soon they were both gasping and panting and grasping at each other, but for all the noise and bother, not much was accomplished. Heiner had simply had too much to drink. Even Julia was feeling slightly woozy, and soon they both gave up on the idea and ended up clasped in each other's sweaty arms, passionately sleepy and verging on hungover.

Once Heiner was fast asleep, Julia extricated herself from his arms. She dressed quickly, then took a moment to extract his wallet from his pants. She took what would be considered a typical, hefty fee and left the rest. It was the best way to avoid either suspicion of her motives or a police report of theft, and besides, the money would come in handy. She crept quietly out of the room only to meet one of Heiner's comrades in the hallway.

"Hey, I know you!" he shouted.

Julia cringed at his loudness. "Shh!" she advised, waving her hand wildly. Was it possible he recognized her from her years working in the RSHA? It was long in the past, but his accusation sent shudders down her spine.

"You're that pickpocket," he said artfully.

Oh, it was only a ploy to get free sex in exchange for not turning her in to the police. Naturally, no one wanted to undergo an investigation, and any prostitute was a ripe target for such blackmail. Julia smiled her relief. She eyed her good-looking blackmailer from head to toe and her smile broadened. "Look," she said, "let's skip the nonsense. I'll make you a deal. You let me enjoy it, no tough stuff, and I'll happily give you a good fuck, gratis."

"You've got it!" he agreed, and together they went off and satisfied each other.

"Where the hell have you been?" her partner, Romek, hissed at her from the hallway near the women's toilet.

A women's toilet—ha!—and women weren't even supposed to be admitted to the club! Fucking typical, Julia thought. The hypocrisy was transparent; all one had to do was never question the world order. "Got delayed," she answered tersely. "And just because I'm playing this role does not mean you can forget that I am your commanding officer. Got that?"

"Sorry, ma'am," her apprentice apologized sheepishly. "I was just worried."

"Where's your equipment?"

"I left it near the basement entrance." He had gained access to the club via the service entrance, presenting credentials that had convinced the staff he was attending to a possible gas leak deep in the bowels of the building. "There has been a slight but unexpected drop in pressure detected at our distribution junction," he had told them. "We're checking out all the buildings in the neighborhood. Probably due to the construction. Not an emergency, yet, but I'll let you know if the building needs to be evacuated."

They collected the tools and descended into the basement together. "Where is it?" Romek asked.

Julia paced around, mentally measuring the room and matching it to the plans she had studied. "I'm not sure," she answered, then indicating a spot on the floor, she said, "Move those boxes and cut into the floor there."

She retreated to a corner of the room, swiped the dirt away from a box, and sat down as her companion began his work. Reaching into her purse, she pulled out a file and began working on her nails. Romek glanced at her but did not comment. Once he had cut out the floorboards and pried them up, they surveyed the hole together. About a meter beneath them was another floor. They both climbed into the crawl space and snooped around. Finally they found what they were looking for: an ancient trapdoor that led into the cistern hidden below.

Side by side, on their hands and knees, they peered downward into the damp gloom of the empty cistern. "Don't they know this is here?" Romek asked.

Julia shook her head. "It's not centered under this building, so I think it's from an earlier building that was renovated down to ground level. I usually got into there from the house next door, the one they're demolishing, then I'd crawl along until I was under this building." She shined her flashlight into the cistern, illuminating a nondescript box in a dark corner. "See? There it is!"

Her partner nodded. "Do you think they'll find it now that they've torn down the other house?"

Julia shrugged. "Maybe. They seem to be stopping at the foundation, but if they do find it, well, it's just one of many." She laughed lightly. "We plant two for every one they uncover. This whole city is full of our little weeds just waiting to grow!"

"And how many of our people do we lose keeping it that way?" Romek asked, apparently irked by her lack of seriousness.

Julia laughed again and looked down at the deterrent. "Oh, over the years they've been here, I'd say each one has cost us about three lives. Pretty expensive blackmail, isn't it?"

"Especially since we haven't really used them yet," he said, shuddering and looking over his shoulder to the hole in the floor above them.

"Not really. Just a few samples to show we mean business." Julia smiled at her companion's nervousness and then said impishly, "Interestingly, this bomb hasn't cost us anyone yet—so by the law of averages, it's due, isn't it?"

Romek looked at her in alarm and she laughed. "Don't worry, if they find us here and drag us out, they won't kill you right away. I'm sure they'll manage to prolong your life for days, weeks even."

"Shall we get to work?" he asked, deadpan.

Julia reached into her bag and extracted the cigarette case. She pried off the bottom and handed the metallic card to her companion. Then she lit a cigarette and lowered herself so that she was lounging on the floor next to the trapdoor, languidly holding the flashlight so that it illuminated the cistern. "Sure. You know what to do."

Using a rope, Romek climbed down into the cistern and approached the bomb. He worked in silence with Julia occasionally offering advice and reminders. He installed the new detonator, checked and corrected some of the settings, recorded some data, cleaned the contacts, and replaced a bit of rotted wire. "Done," he announced quietly.

"Shh!" Julia hissed as she switched off the light. They remained silently in the darkness, listening to the sound of someone opening the door to the room above them.

"Bugger," Julia whispered, extinguishing her cigarette hurriedly.

"Who's down there?" a voice called through the hole in the floor.

"It's me. I'm checking a gas line," Romek called out.

"In the dark?" A face stared blindly into the darkness.

Julia turned on the flashlight and shined it in the direction of the hole. "I've got a light," her partner explained.

"Are you okay down there?" It sounded like one of the waiters rather than a security guard.

"Sure. Just doing my job. I'll be out in a few minutes."

"Is that smoke? Are you smoking? I thought there was a gas leak!" the voice nearly shrieked.

"No, everything's okay. Don't worry," Romek answered.

"All right. Make sure you put these boxes back—they're in the way here."

"Will do!"

As Romek made appropriate banging noises, Julia remained very still. The sounds from above indicated their visitor had left. They waited a moment, then Julia cautiously poked her head out the hole. She glanced around the room and then popped back under. "All clear," she announced as she went to help Romek up the rope.

Back in the little cellar room, they replaced the floorboards, cleaned up the sawdust, and stacked the boxes on top of the hole they had made. "It's going to have to do," Julia announced. "We didn't come prepared to build secret entrances, after all."

Julia cleaned herself up and the two of them parted company. She climbed the stairs back to the main floor, wincing as she stepped into the glare of the hallway lights.

"What have you been up to?" a voice accused. "You're not supposed to be down there."

Julia cursed silently, stumbled, and fell into a drunken stupor on the floor. She heard the voice moan, "Oh, God, not another one," as hands reached under her arms and lifted her up. She was half-carried, half-dragged to a lounge and laid out on one of the couches. Whoever had discovered her lost interest and walked away as soon as she was safely tucked onto the couch. Julia waited a few minutes, then blearily pried an eye open and scanned her surroundings. There were a few more besotted souls, several people conversing in a corner, and another two sitting in chairs smoking. She climbed unsteadily to her feet, made a quiet retching noise, and staggered to the door. Although her steps steadied the farther she got from the lounge, she maintained a rather drunken walk until she was several blocks from the club. There she stopped to light a cigarette and turn discreetly around to inspect the trail behind her. She was alone.

It was well past curfew and she knew she should move on quickly; nevertheless, she stood there for several moments deciding what to do. Shower first, change clothes, send Romek on his way, then Paris. With that decided, she headed back to her hotel.

The city looked even grittier than the last time. Julia felt a pang of sorrow and yearning for a place she had never known. Her father talked about Paris though he also did not remember it any more than he remembered what the smoldering ruin of Warsaw had once looked like. In both instances though, he had stories from his parents and he had passed on their impressions to his daughter. In the case of Warsaw, there was nothing to return to—it was gone, ruined, completely leveled, but with Paris there was still the shell of the city that her grandparents had loved. Beautiful, lively, welcoming, the City of Lights. Julia walked along its streets noting that the lights were a lot more red than the last time she had visited. Prostitutes paced and their clients prowled as Paris bowed to the needs of its masters. Having lost all political and economic power, it was now nothing more than the entertainment center for a hypocritical and sexually frustrated Reich.

Julia reached an intersection and consulted the hand-drawn map that she clutched in her fist. With only a bit of subterfuge, she had managed to ferret out Karl's address, and with her standard German papers, it had not taken much to arrange a legitimate trip to the city as a tourist. Now came the hard part. She entered the hallway of the apartment block and ascended the steps without being stopped or questioned. She rapped lightly at the door of Karl's apartment and waited.

Karl himself opened the door. He was dressed in a dark satin robe. His hair was still blond, still thick. His blue eyes were still clear, but he had gained weight and he was considerably less attractive than he had once been. "Yes?" he asked, eyeing Julia from head to toe.

Julia glanced past him into the apartment and saw that it was empty. She looked back at Karl and smiling enticingly said, "Don't you recognize me?"

Karl frowned, stared at her a moment longer, than said, "Julia? My God, you look good!"

"So do you," she lied. The lack of a servant worried her. Was Karl broke?

"Come in. What brings you to Paris?"

"I was visiting," Julia explained as she took a seat on the couch, "and I spotted you walking. I'm afraid I followed you home that evening, but didn't have the courage to knock at your door until now."

Karl accepted the explanation without comment. He offered his guest a cognac, then poured one for himself.

"I've missed you," Julia said, sipping her drink. She kicked off her shoes and tucked her legs up onto the cushion.

"You just disappeared from my life. What happened?"

"You know, you were married, I was pregnant—there was no future in it."

"Did you keep the baby?" Karl asked almost without interest. His eyes were fixed on Julia's breasts.

"Yes. You have a son, a fine young man now."

Karl nodded as if listening to a long speech.

"He's missed having a father though," Julia said, laying a foundation upon which she would build later. "It's easy for a boy to get into trouble, especially at his age."

"I'd soon put a stop to that," Karl bragged. "You can't be too soft on them. Got to beat sense into them, that's what my father did, that's what I've done. Uwe and Geerd, well, I didn't spare the strap, and they've turned out to be real men."

"Yes, well, without you around, I need something else, some—"

"Just look at that!" Karl interrupted to point excitedly at the television. "Our boy's got one in on that nigger!"

"What are you watching?" Julia asked, turning her head to notice for the first time that the television was on. Two men, one white, one black, were boxing.

"Ach, a title fight. That's our boy there beating the crap out of that Angolan. Those niggers might be strong, but they have no brains, no brains at all. Can't think, so they can't fight well."

"Yes, of course." Julia swirled her cognac and wondered how long she should wait to pick up the conversation.

"Would you like a cigarette?" Karl asked as he lit one for himself.

"How is it you're lighting your own cigarettes?" Julia asked, glancing around the room for traces of another presence. "Is it the servant's night off?"

"You know I prefer tied help," Karl said, referring to his unwillingness to pay for waged labor. "One lump sum and you get a lease for months." He gave Julia a cigarette and lit it for her.

"Ah, yes. Always the clever businessman!" Julia agreed, exhaling a stream of smoke heavenward. "But then, where is he, or is it she?"

"Back in Berlin. Elspeth shrieked when I said I wanted to bring the girl with me. Said she couldn't do without help for two months, not with five kids at home."

"You have five children now?"

"Seven, but Uwe went off to the SS and Geerd's in the army."

"Ah. Your sons are not only fine men, but true patriots, just like you. The Fatherland certainly appreciates such loyalty."

"Tell that to the damn Labor Ministry," Karl mumbled. He went to the side table and refilled his glass. "Here's to getting what one deserves!" he toasted somewhat sourly.

"What's the matter?" Julia asked, a look of sympathetic concern on her face. She moved her hand slowly up her thigh, absently pulling her skirt a few inches upward with it.

It took some time and some drinks to get the entire story out of Karl, but eventually he confided that one of the laborers he had leased from the government had met with an unfortunate demise. The Labor Ministry had assessed a fine that had eaten into his salary and was only recently completely paid off. "The goddamned bastards! It's not like it was a person. He was subhuman scum, from a race of pigs, what did they expect? These lesser beings, you've got to keep them disciplined and in line, but just make a little mistake and those bureaucrats are on your arse talking about replacement costs and lost services!"

"Oh, that is unfortunate!" Julia agreed with heartfelt sympathy, leaning her head against Karl's chest as he sat next to her. "So how do you have a girl now?"

"A subordinate of mine loaned her to me for a few months. I've been tucking away some sums." Karl's arm was around her shoulder; his other hand reached up cautiously to finger the material of her dress just below the neckline. "I'm fed up with these bureaucrats—I'm going to purchase a contract, then they can't harass me about my treatment of my own property!"

"Good idea!" Julia enthused, raising herself slightly so that Karl's hand slipped down naturally to her breast. She quickly ran through the typical cost in fees and bribes for purchasing a lifetime contract on a forced laborer, then converted it to dollars at the preferential rate that Karl would be able to get using his position in government. It would be enough. It would be enough!

= **17** =

"**I**T'S MORE THAN ENOUGH!" Maria assured him with quite surprising civility. "Such gifts! No one has ever celebrated my birthday before! I didn't even know it was in September until you read it in my papers!"

"There are some advantages to education," Peter agreed quietly.

They sat on his bed, side by side, and sipped wine as she opened each little gift and squealed her delight. He accepted her thanks with as much enthusiasm as he could muster, but he did not feel particularly cheerful. Of all the days in the year, her birthday would have to be the same day that Allison had been murdered! He did not tell Maria about that and she did not detect his grim mood as he commemorated the sad fifth anniversary in lonely silence. In fact, she was sufficiently unaware of his frame of mind that she decided it was time to present him with a proposition.

"I have a wonderful surprise to give you in return," she said while lighting one of the cigarettes he had acquired for her.

"What's that?" he asked as he picked up and lit one of the cigarettes he had just given her.

"Hey!" Maria protested. "You gave those to me!"

Peter raised his eyebrows in contemptuous disbelief.

Maria decided not to push the point. She continued with her original intent. "There's a new worker at the bakery—a French girl . . ."

"Uh-huh." He had, by this time, acquired a habit of nodding and agreeing without really listening. He enjoyed the cigarette. It was his first in a long time— since one of his torturers had given him one. Maybe he could afford to start smoking again. Maybe Frau Reusch was sufficiently dependable that he would not be left readdicted and stranded without a supply.

". . . I want you to break her in."

That, at least, got his attention. "What are you talking about?"

"She's not had a man yet. I told her you'd do it."

"Are you nuts?"

"No, don't worry, I won't be jealous."

He shook his head at her misinterpretation, but she did not notice, instead continuing unabated, "You'll be perfect for the job."

"I don't think it's a good idea," he finally managed to say.

"Why not?"

"I don't want to sleep with a girl, and I doubt she wants to sleep with me."

"Oh, she wants to—believe me!"

"How old is she?"

Maria hesitated. "Sixteen."

"That's too young." He laughed with mild self-deprecation. "At least for me."

"No, you've got to! She needs to be taught!"

"Why? Why not wait until she finds somebody she likes?" He wanted to say that sex should be more than fucking, but he realized how hollow that would sound given their relationship. He tried changing tack. "We're not . . . ," but he realized he could not think of any way to finish that phrase without sounding like some Nazi pamphlet denouncing the corrupt habits of *Untermensch*.

"Look—what are her alternatives? She's going to be noticed by some man— or boy—sooner or later. Do you want her first experience, maybe her only experience, to be that?"

Peter lowered his head into his hands. Of course, a lifetime of rape. And it wasn't even a crime. For a German woman to have sex with an inferior was criminal—possibly a death sentence for the inferior-race man, but for a German man to force sex on an inferior woman was nothing at all.

He looked up at Maria: Was her near addiction to mindless sex rather more an addiction to voluntary sex? Was it a reasonable compensation for the continuous threat of rape? It would explain why she had risked seducing the young boy at her previous employer's—it gave her a measure of control over her fate: seduce him while he was still too young to coerce or force her into sex. Once again, he found himself wishing that she had been more forthcoming in her thoughts about the world—but perhaps it was not a thought-out strategy on her part. Perhaps it was the instinctive response of a little girl who had been thrown into a terrifying and brutal world with nothing but her own determination to survive to guide her.

"All right," he sighed, "let me meet her."

Maria kissed him happily. "I knew you'd say yes, and I know you'll be gentle and teach her well."

"I only said I'd meet her," he replied dejectedly.

The next night a slight young girl, her shift hanging loosely from her tiny form, awaited him at the newspaper display case. In the dim light, he could barely discern that the uniform was quite different from Maria's. It was a gray pinafore dress over a simply cut, pale yellow blouse; it looked like a tasteless school uniform and was meant to indicate that she was an apprentice. So, they were instituting the rumored change: the apprenticeships were to start at a young age and require a tuition that could then be paid off via a lifetime of service—in other words, the system had not changed at all but the words had.

It was a step toward normalcy; during the years of perpetual war, forced labor conscription was no more barbaric than forced military obligations and could in fact be viewed as a sort of conscientious objection to soldiering, but now there was an acknowledgment that the world recognized this class of workers as nothing more than slaves, and this was the latest effort to combat that. There would still be criminal convictions and other reasons for the life-sentence forced labor, especially of adults, and all those who already wore gray-blue would probably continue to do so as they aged and died in their jobs, but now the ranks of the servant class would also be filled with these apprentices and indentured servants. It would dilute his number with different uniforms, different attitudes, and different rules; perhaps they would even gain some civil rights. It would also bring the Reich into line with all the other countries of the world where debt, rather than legal standing, kept people bound.

The girl stepped back as he approached, pressing her back into the plate glass. Above her head, behind the glass, he could read the headline: "1,000 Partisans Hanged in District of Neustadt!" He did not know where this Neustadt was; he presumed it was in the eastern colonial region—there nearly everything had been renamed from the original Slavic to a "Neu-this" or a "Neu-that." The German frustration at not having been able to press farther east, into the great open expanses of the Soviet empire, had relieved itself in a brutal occupation of the lands that they had conquered: the Central European countries that had lain between them and their ultimate and unachieved goal. Previous inhabitants of these lands had been driven from their homes into "townships" of forced labor pools or had systematically been murdered to make way for the new colonists. By all accounts, the slaughter there was still continuing.

He looked down into the ashen face of the frightened young girl. He smiled at her, but her expression did not waver. It was not a safe place to stand for any length of time, so without saying anything, he gently grasped her hand and led her back to the store. Once they were inside his room, he guided her into a chair and then asked if she wanted a cup of tea. She shook her head.

"Well, I'm going to have one, so I'll put the kettle on."

She watched his every move, her mouth set in determined silence. Only one chair was in the room, so he sat on the edge of the bed, across from her.

"My name's Peter. What's your name?"

"Emma," she whispered. She was gaunt and pale and looked younger than her sixteen years.

"Pleased to meet you, Emma."

"It's not my real name. That's just what they call me. They said my own name was too fancy."

"What is your real name?"

"Jacqueline."

"That's a beautiful name."

She nodded sadly as though its loss weighed heavily on her.

"How old are you?" he asked.

"Thirteen, *mein Herr.*"

He smiled at her honorific as well as at Maria's deception. Thirteen—that looked more like the right age.

"You don't want to do this, do you?" he asked gently.

"Maria says I have to."

He shook his head. "No, you don't."

"She says that it'd be better for me to get it over with—with someone who won't hurt me too much."

"You don't have to do anything, little one. And I think it's better that you don't." He did not mention that at this point it was probably moot: her scared, wan, thirteen-year-old face was more effective than a freezing-cold shower at dousing whatever desire he might have had. "I'll make you a cup of tea, and we can just chat a bit. Okay?"

"Maria will yell at me."

"She doesn't have the right to tell you what to do."

"I can't go back and tell her that nothing happened. She'll kill me!"

"Then lie to her. I'll tell you what to say."

She looked relieved, and for the first time a small smile appeared on her face. "Would you do that?"

"Sure. Someday, when you're ready, the information might be useful to you." He hoped that it would be when she was ready, not when somebody else decided she was ripe, but he could do nothing to protect her for the rest of her life, and there seemed no point in dwelling on unpleasant future possibilities.

So, they drank tea and he told her what men and women did together and how it could be a beautiful and loving thing. She listened, intrigued, her eyes dancing with possibilities. At one point she got up from the chair to sit next to him on the bed. He kissed her hair and told her she was beautiful and intelligent and that someday she would make someone very happy, but that as long as she had a choice, she must not do anything she did not want to do.

He wanted to stop there, with the vague superstitious belief that if he did not mention rape, then perhaps she would be spared, but he felt almost a fatherly responsibility toward her and decided that he should at least discuss the grim realities of her life. But he did not know what to say. He did not understand the mind-set of the type of man who would do such a thing, and his own experiences with violence offered no reassuring insights. In the end, he decided to say very little. "Finally, if someone attacks you—whatever form their violence takes—remember to love yourself and don't blame yourself. If they commit indignities, it reflects on them, not you."

Emma nodded solemnly as she listened to his words and put them in a safe place in her heart, but she was more intrigued by what he was doing as he spoke. She noticed that the fingers of his left hand clawed at his identification band as if trying in vain to shift its position. She grinned impishly at him, and saying, "Watch this!" she folded her thumb against her palm and gently slid her band over her hand and off her wrist.

Peter stared, stunned by envy, at the loose metal circle that she held triumphantly in the air. Wasn't it enough that she did not have to wear a permanent tattoo on her arm?

"I guess they made it loose so I could grow into it," she explained. "But they don't know I can take it off."

He nodded, unable to say a word. The extent of his sudden jealous rage horrified him. Where had it come from? What had he become?

"Yours looks tight—is it uncomfortable?" Emma asked innocently.

With an effort he turned his attention away from the band she so casually flipped from one hand into the other and answered her question evenly. "Yes, very. It was put on after months of near-starvation rations. Since then I've had a much more normal diet and so I've regained the lost weight. Unfortunately, that has made this thing uncomfortably tight."

"It bothers you to see mine off?"

He did not want to admit to being so petty, but since it was undeniable, he nodded.

"Yeah, it bothers Maria, too."

Though it was unintended, he did not miss the irony in that.

"I'll put it back on," she said without rancor, and deftly slipped the bracelet back onto her wrist.

Furious with himself, he could only manage to mutter, "Thanks."

She nodded and smiled and hugged him, her thin little arms unable to reach around him. He stroked her hair and held her for a moment. If he had had a normal life, had married young and had a daughter, she could be this age. He could be teaching her about life, comforting her when she felt sad. Instead . . . He sighed and pulled away to make another cup of tea for them both. They talked about other topics for about another hour, then he walked her back to the bakery.

*　　*　　*

"So did you enjoy her?" Maria had only managed to contain her curiosity with the greatest difficulty.

Peter shut the door to his room and put the kettle on as she plunked herself down on his bed. She lay on her stomach, her chin cupped in her hands, her legs casually sprawled.

"Well?"

"She's a nice girl," he finally answered, "but get off her back—give her time to grow up."

"She doesn't have time."

The seriousness of Maria's reply was unusual and unexpected. "Perhaps she does," he said, "nothing's happened yet, has it?"

"But did you enjoy her?"

"Well enough," he answered obscurely. Even pretending to have slept with a thirteen-year-old girl was repulsive to him.

"Good! Then you can keep her."

"Maria!" he felt a surge of revulsion at her implication. "I know this may be hard for you to believe, but you just can't go giving other people away!"

"But you said you liked her." She sounded hurt. She rolled to a sitting position.

"That's not the point. It's just not right!" How could he hope to explain to her a morality that no one had ever exhibited? He wondered what would happen if the regime were finally overthrown. Where would all these children—raised without respect for themselves or anyone else—where would they fit into a normal society?

She looked at him perplexed, chewing her thumbnail.

"I know this is not . . ." He sighed, tried to be more direct. "Slavery is wrong, Maria. It's wrong for you and it's wrong for me, and it's wrong for you to treat Jacqueline as if she were yours to do with as you please."

"Her name's Emma."

He accepted that with a wave of his hand. "We have to put up with our situation because we have no choice, but you can't—"

"Who says?"

He hesitated and she jumped at this sign of weakness. Pointing toward the window, she hissed, "Everybody out there says it's okay, everyone but you! Where would I go if I wasn't here? Huh? Answer that! What would I do? You can't answer that, can you! You want me to give up everything I have. For what? For nothing!" She moved her finger to point it at him. "You're the only one who's dissatisfied, and you want to make me unhappy, too!"

He considered her for a moment, then deciding not to argue, said, "I don't want Emma. I want you." That, he assumed, would put an end to the messy issue.

"I'm busy."

"Busy?"

"Yeah, there's a German lad—he's interested."

"Is that what you want?"

"Oh, yeah, he's got much better access to food and cigarettes and stuff. And you know . . ." She scrunched her face a bit to indicate a well-known truth.

"Know what?"

"He's a German!"

"Ah, yes." Superhuman, aristocratic, nearly magical. Could he blame her? He weighed his options, then offered, "I won't mind if you see us both."

"He would. He'd have you shot if he found out. Probably me, too!" She sounded proud of his imputed jealousy and power.

Not shot, beaten to death, Peter thought bitterly. Whereas a shooting could introduce legal complications, an overzealous beating would not be so unusual, especially if her boyfriend and his friends found him doing something illegal, such as sleeping with her. And they would, because sooner or later she would tell them. Yes, beaten to death; they could get away with that.

"As you wish." He sighed, wondering why he felt so lonely.

"You're not going to cause problems?" She looked at him suspiciously; obviously she had not expected him to capitulate so easily.

"No. No, I won't cause you trouble. I promise."

"He thinks I'm a virgin."

"He'll never hear otherwise. But, Maria, please be careful!"

"So, you want Emma?"

Oh, so that was it. Emma was supposed to buy his cooperation and silence. She was a nice girl, pretty, bright, she liked him. Sooner or later somebody else would . . . It'd be best if it were someone *she* wanted, someone she could trust. She'd be fourteen soon. He'd be gentle, patient, they could talk, be friends, maybe after a few months . . .

"Well?" Maria pressed.

Peter shook his head angrily. "No, I don't want to even see her!" Regretting the harshness of his tone, he added gently, "Just give her my regards; I wish her a good life."

Maria kissed him and turned to leave.

"Maria?" he knew she could not miss the plea in his voice.

She looked back at him expectantly, enjoying her power.

"Will you stay the night? Just this one last time? Please."

"Sure," she conceded nobly, "for old times."

18

"IT JUST KEEPS GETTING better and better, Herr Traugutt, doesn't it?" the organizer enthused. "The Reich goes from strength to strength!"

"Yes," Richard agreed, placing a protective arm around his wife's shoulders to ward off the evening chill, "we are truly the envy of the world with our organization, our cultural cohesiveness, and our proud and noble master race!"

The organizer grinned. "Especially now, especially with the Americans all tied in knots."

"This current American fiasco is just—oh, what can I say—a gift from the gods!" Richard let his fingers stray along the delicate fabric of Kasia's dress. It was new, he had insisted that she buy something special for the occasion, aware of how many people would be observing them, and even though Kasia was still carrying extra weight left over from her pregnancy, she had chosen well and she looked exquisite.

Kasia looked up at her husband and smiled, but was then distracted by the fireworks that exploded magnificently across the river, over the sky of Göringstadt. So, this was to be their new home. It was a huge, sprawling colossus of a city—the administrative center for the region, the place of refuge for tired German colonists, the transportation nexus, and the location of wage-paying industrial jobs. The Traugutt family would move from Krakau to Göringstadt, following Richard's magnificent career progression. Richard's promotion was big news and he was already being treated with greater respect. Even she was treated more delicately. Gone were the sneering references to her improper accent, gone were the penetrating stares as the other wives searched for faults in her manner or her words or the way she dressed. Richard had achieved a position of significant power, and that meant he could hurt people, and so now everyone was more careful, more respectful, more civil.

Kasia looked around at the heroic expanse of concrete that made up the central square and felt a wave of nostalgia for something she had never seen. Just a few miles upstream, on the Weichsel before its confluence with the Bug River, were the ruins of Warschau, or as her people had called it, Warszawa. Images of the medieval old town, the royal palace, the Barbican, and the palaces of the *Szlachta* came to mind. She had seen none of these things, they no longer existed, but the images were part of her youth and they remained burned into her soul as they were into the souls of all her people.

Warsaw, the capital, the seat of their resistance. The city had been demolished, completely leveled, in retaliation for an uprising long ago. The entire population had been destroyed: arrested and shot or deported to concentration camps and starved. The order from Hitler had been to burn, bomb, and raze everything and, to fulfill a boast, to build an airstrip over the historic center. When their train had passed through the ruins earlier in the day, she had seen mile upon mile of charred rubble, had gazed sorrowfully at the ashes that blew in the wind. Wildflowers and trees sprouted here and there, but none were very old—they were regularly bulldozed, doused in oil, and set on fire in a senseless act of ongoing vandalism; salt on an ancient and terrible wound. The Poles would not be allowed to forget the price of resistance—their capital was to lay in ruins for as long as one of them was alive to see it. For as long as she was alive. Kasia looked down at the river and noticed, even in the darkness, that a scattering of ash floated on the surface.

"Vandalism," their host was saying as if he had read her thoughts. "Apparently vandalism is on the rise there as well."

"Fortunate that we don't have such things here," Kasia commented sourly.

The host smiled at her, though Richard threw her a warning glance.

"It's all evidence of their incredible decadence," Richard commented. "The financial scandals, that fag for a vice president, all of it, just food for the fires of revolution. That culture won't last long. They have no morality, no direction. They need leadership, true leadership."

"Like what we could offer."

"Exactly. Aryan purity." A barrage of fireworks kept Richard from saying more. Kasia watched entranced as the beautiful bursts of color filled the sky. Red, black, and white exploded in a finale of dizzying sound and light, and there, in the sky, was formed a giant, glowing flag. The crowd roared its approval and there was a surge of energy as a chorus of the national anthem was raised. Around her voices rose and fell with the hypnotic tones of glory and power to *Deutschland über alles.*

The extravaganza finished and the crowds were ushered into the new Party Congress Hall. The general public thronged into the massive marble lobby; those with invitations were led into the main reception hall. Richard and Kasia were pressed from all sides, and Richard complained to the organizer about the lack of order and security.

The organizer begged their patience and boldly forced his way through the crowd to make a path for them. At the door, their passes were inspected and they were released from the swarm into a light and airy hall with only several hundred other guests. The organizer showed them to their reserved seats, then made his excuses to go handle the mess created by security.

The hall buzzed with conversation, the women's laughter tinkled lightly, the men guffawed and slapped each other's back. Champagne was served in glistening glasses, music from a string quartet floated around them, the chandeliers sparkled magically, a feeling of gaiety and happiness was everywhere. Kasia and Richard were seated at a round table with eight other distinguished visitors to the city. They quickly introduced themselves and fell into a lively conversation about the city's architecture, cultural life, and livability.

As they spoke, there was a muffled boom and the sound of distant panicked screams. They all looked up in alarm but nobody moved. After a moment of intense silence in the hall, excited whispers began spreading like a swarm of bees through the room.

"Not another idiotic bombing!" Richard commented as he waved to a waiter to light him a cigarette. "Can't we keep these damn people in line?"

"Do you think we should go?" Kasia asked softly as she fingered the intricate pattern on the pewter plate in front of her.

"No, no, it will all be sorted out soon," Richard assured her, and indeed it was. The bomb had been in a wing in which nobody had yet entered; it had done minor damage and had caused no injuries. The political fallout would be immense, but for now, they could enjoy their meal.

"This is good luck for you, isn't it?" the man next to Kasia commented to Richard. He had introduced himself as visiting from the Security Divisional Headquarters in Paris, and he was already aware of Richard's impending move.

"Ah, Herr Bloch, whatever do you mean?" Kasia asked, smiling sweetly.

Herr Bloch smiled in return. "Dear lady! Women are so naive! Minor damage, timed so there are no injuries, but located inside the building! Doesn't that tell you anything!"

Kasia shook her head.

"It was a warning. It was thoroughly professional. They're saying, 'Look what we can do!' I'm sure your husband is aware that an embarrassing bombing like this will disgrace local security."

"So?" Kasia pressed.

Richard answered for Herr Bloch. "He's trying to say that as an outsider moving into a new location, the disadvantages I would have faced, of not being on the inside loop here, have now been more than offset by the fact that they will all be hanging their heads in shame."

"If they're lucky enough to get away with that!" Herr Bloch agreed.

"Meanwhile, I can come in with a clean slate, and if one or two heads must roll, well . . ." Richard opened his hands expressively. "I'm here to serve!"

"So, it couldn't have been better than if you ordered it yourself," Kasia commented slyly.

Richard's eyes narrowed in warning, but he smiled as he said, "Except that these things happen all the time here. Göringstadt's crime rates are phenomenal. Most of it is for the criminal police to deal with, but still, I'll have my work cut out for me."

"Is it unsafe?" Kasia asked.

"We like to say it isn't, but I'm afraid, darling, just between you and me and our friends here, the city is a mess. If they were to put any more police on the street, they'd be tripping over each other, but still there's all sorts of depravity going on."

"And why is that?" Kasia asked as if making a political point.

"Corruption?" Herr Bloch suggested.

Richard shrugged. "Desperation. You can't take everything from a people—you've got to leave them with something, otherwise they have no reason to obey the laws, and frankly with desperate people, brute force is not really enough. It holds them down, but there is always that seething hatred, seeping out from under the boot heel. Ask Herr Bloch, I'm sure he'll tell you things are much more civilized in Paris. There, our approach was different, and if you ask me, much more sensible."

"Brave words," Herr Bloch said nervously. "But even in my fair city we have our share of crime. Too many non-Aryans. They live like . . . well, they have a different set of standards." He then started to detail recent cases that had come to his attention and had piqued his interest. Kasia and Richard listened politely to the tales of kidnappings, shootings, stabbings, and other acts of criminality as they worked through their appetizer, their soup, their entrée, and their salad. Only once did Kasia interrupt Herr Bloch's seemingly endless supply of grotesque tales to ask for more details, then as the dessert arrived, Kasia explained that she had an infant back at the hotel who would be in dire need of her and that, unfortunately, the delay caused by the bombing was forcing her to leave the festivities early.

Richard groaned, but dutifully rose to accompany his wife out of the hall and back to their hotel.

19

"**A**NY WORD OF JULIA?" Cyprian asked as he entered their apartment.

"Hello to you," Marysia replied somewhat miffed. Her cat, Siwa, shifted uneasily in her lap.

"Well?"

"You know I would tell you as soon as we heard anything. Maybe just once you could greet me with something other than that question." Marysia ran her fingers over Siwa's soft, gray fur and breathed deeply.

"Has the Council assigned anyone to track her yet?"

"I told you, that's not going to happen. Zosia's been using her spare time to comb through the Berlin police files, but she hasn't found anything yet."

"Spare time?"

"She's using every minute she has. She says she's having trouble getting access to some of the files—some of their data has been misentered, plus it seems the computers in Berlin have been crashing with some regularity, and for once that has worked to our disadvantage."

"Shit. We should have someone there. This is ridiculous!"

"So far Julia's papers haven't turned up, nor is there a body matching her description. There was one female floater from the Spree with long, dark hair, but the estimate of how long she'd been in the water makes it unlikely to be Julia. Though, I suppose they could be wrong."

Cyprian glowered at his wife's callous wording.

"We're going to have to conclude that she just ran off," Marysia suggested glumly.

"Never! She wouldn't do that! And she would never leave Olek!"

Marysia shrugged. "Maybe she's on a bender."

"If she has left, it's your harping on her that's driven her away!" Cyprian fumed.

"Don't try and blame me! If you hadn't always defended her, maybe she would have brought her behavior under control!" Marysia retorted angrily. "I'm fed up with your insinuations, I'm fed up with—" A knock on the door interrupted them.

Nonplussed, both stared at the door, then Cyprian went to open it. Olek came in looking dejected.

"Olek, you don't have to knock! Our place is yours!" Marysia soothed.

"I heard you from the hall. It was about Mama, wasn't it?"

Cyprian sighed. "We're sorry, son. I'm sure your mom will be back soon."

"Come have some dinner," Marysia insisted as she let Siwa down and stood. "I have duck for you."

Olek smiled his appreciation. "And what are you two having?"

Marysia and Cyprian both waved their hands impatiently. "Don't you worry about us," Cyprian assured him. "We have some cabbage and noodles that are just right for us."

"You can't keep wasting your meat rations on me."

"Who says it's a waste?" Marysia chided. "We never used it up before. We're old, we really don't need all that much. You're growing. Now come, I've made a nice sauce for the duck. Come on, sit, eat!"

They were at the table eating when Zosia poked her head in the door. "Knock, knock, anyone here?" She bustled into the room carrying Joanna and a bag of baby supplies. "Can you watch Joanna for me? Adam's out and I want to spend some time . . ." Zosia threw a glance at Olek as Marysia accepted the baby from her arms. "You know."

"Have you found anything, Aunt Zosia?" Olek asked plaintively.

Zosia shook her head. "No. I've accessed everything I could in the police files. I thought I might look at the Travel Bureau's records next."

"What?" Cyprian asked.

"She kept a good set of papers; maybe she got a passport to somewhere."

"Are you saying you think she left the country?" Cyprian accused. "That's stupid! She left everything at the pension! Why would anyone travel like that!"

"She left her equipment and all but one identification—exactly the sort of things one is better off not carrying around the countryside. Besides, I was thinking she may have applied for an internal passport. I didn't figure she could get an external one that quickly."

"Which name did she keep, Auntie Zosia?" Olek asked.

"Hoffmeier, honey. Julia Hoffmeier."

"She left all her clothes!" Cyprian yelled.

"We don't know that," Zosia answered coolly. "All we know is she left some clothes there. She sent Romek on his way saying she had some business to take care of. To me that sounds like she was planning something."

"But what?" Marysia asked. "Do you really think she'd leave without saying anything?"

Zosia shook her head. "If you have any better ideas . . ."

A light rap at the door caused them all to turn their heads. Zosia was closest, so she went to answer it. She disappeared into the hall, a quiet, young voice said something to her indiscernible to the others, and then she returned holding a note. "This just came through from Communications," she explained, clutching the note. "It suggests we look into the Paris police files."

Two days later Olek bid his grandparents farewell, shouldered his pack, and left for patrol. Within five minutes of his departure Zosia showed up at Cyprian and Marysia's door. "Is Olek gone?" she asked.

Cyprian glanced down at the sheaf of paper that Zosia was holding and turned white. "What is it?" Marysia asked.

"I wanted you to see this first so you could break the news to him," Zosia said as she held out the papers. "I'm sorry."

Cyprian took the papers from her and Zosia left. He looked down at the words, but could not bring himself to read them so he handed them to his wife and went to sit on the couch. Marysia found her reading glasses and sat down, then began to read the police report from Paris.

The nearly naked body of an unidentified woman in her thirties had been found in the Bois de Boulogne early in the morning about two weeks after Julia's disappearance. Investigators estimated that she had been killed sometime the night before, probably between 2 and 5 A.M. The woman had sustained severe injuries to her head, wounds on her wrists were consistent with her having been handcuffed. While still alive, she had been sexually assaulted with extreme brutality, beaten, and stabbed with a shallow knife—the sort carried by boys in the Hitler Youth. Cause of death was strangulation. The body had been dragged, but not a great distance, and the investigator assumed her murder had happened within the park.

The report noted the physical characteristics of the corpse, and Marysia recognized each and every one of her daughter's traits. The report also noted that the victim had been intoxicated, and based upon that and the fact that her disappearance had not been reported, it was assumed that she was a prostitute. The report conjectured that she had attempted to rob her client and had been attacked in retaliation. No identity papers or any other personal effects were found. Inquiries were made in the red-light district, but no one recognized the victim nor was any information forthcoming. There were no suspects and no further action had been taken on the investigation.

Marysia finished the brief, gruesome document. She covered her mouth with her hand and closed her eyes as a wave of nausea spread through her. When she had gathered her courage, she opened her eyes and turned the page. The following report was from the coroner and detailed the damage done to the victim's body. Marysia scanned it quickly, looking only for clues and refusing to think about what the words meant otherwise. Like a detective story, she told herself. She started to retch before she had finished and turned the page, deciding that she could search for clues later.

She turned to the next document and read a completely different report of an attempted break-in at a hotel in the area just south of the Gare du Nord. Using the key to the street doors, a man had entered the hotel without ringing the bell after the night staff had retired and had attempted to remove a room key from its hook. The night manager, who had been resting in an adjacent room, heard noise and preempted the thief in his attempt. The man fled without taking anything. The night manager was unable to describe the intruder other than to say it had been a well-built man. The night manager reported that only one guest was absent that evening and that she had not picked up her key in more than three days. He was afraid that the guest had skipped out without paying her bill, although her room still contained all her belongings. Police decided to investigate and had the room opened. Within the room they found clothing, the usual personal effects of a traveler, and some travel documents indicating she had come from Berlin. They also discovered a large stash of American dollars. Reports varied as to how much money was there, but the amount turned in was over six thousand American dollars. A separate investigation was initiated to determine if that was the entire amount of money found at the scene.

Marysia grunted and rubbed her forehead. She could just imagine the intense negotiations that had been carried out in that hotel room by the staff and the investigators.

"What's so funny?" Cyprian accused.

"Nothing." Marysia turned her attention back to the report. The room had been registered to a Julia Hoffmeier, who had traveled there from Berlin and was a resident of Göringstadt. Using the photograph on the travel documents, the investigators were able to identify the body they had discovered three days prior as hers. The police attempted to locate someone to identify and claim the body, but they discovered that the victim's Berlin address was a complete fake and that nobody claimed to know of her at the Göringstadt address given in her papers.

With the combined information of the body and the break-in, police theorized that the victim had been attacked by someone who knew of the money in the victim's possession. He had apparently assaulted her with a blunt object, inflicting the head injuries, then when the victim was helpless, had bound her hands. He then tried to beat her into handing over the money. When that failed, the victim was murdered, possibly accidentally, since many of the injuries inflicted on the victim were consistent with frustrated rage. The assailant then rifled through the victim's clothes and purse looking for either a room key or an indication of where the money might be and, finding the street-door key to the hotel, decided to attempt a robbery of her room. Caught in the act, he had fled empty-handed.

A few more documents were attached, follow-up reports and other useless details. Marysia scanned them quickly, then dropped the pile onto the floor. She closed her eyes and saw the image of her little daughter bringing her flowers from the field, her clothes covered in mud, her hair in a tangle, a wide grin on her face. Her little Julia.

"What's the report say?" Cyprian's voice came out of the distance.

"Julia's dead." Marysia bent down and picked up the papers and put them on the coffee table in front of her husband. "If you want the details, read it yourself. I can't repeat it." She got up from her seat and left the room. She emerged from the bunker into the autumnal chill and went for a long walk in the woods.

20

"**Y**OU CAME FROM SOME sort of training camp before you arrived here, didn't you?" Frau Reusch inquired of Peter one day out of the blue.

Still holding the cup of tea she had given him, he stood and walked over to the apartment window. A cold spring rain slapped against the glass, and the air was so misty he could barely make out the roof of the shop far below.

"Peter?"

He sipped his tea, then decided to answer. "Yes, your husband was there, perhaps he'll describe it to you."

"I'm not interested in the externals. Was it"—she paused, searching for the right word—"was it unpleasant?"

He sniffed at her choice of words. "You could say that."

"How so?"

He shrugged. "It just was."

"Was there"—she paused again, as if the word itself were painful—"torture?"

The rain was coming down in sheets now. Everything disappeared into a blinding grayness.

"Were you tortured?" she asked more explicitly and a bit louder.

The sheets moved like curtains in the wind, up and away and then back, pounding violently against the window. Water dripped down the edges and puddled on the narrow metal sill.

"I said . . ."

"I heard you," he answered.

There was a long pause, then she asked quietly, "Why did they do it?"

"Why indeed," he echoed. He thought about how obvious it had seemed then; one was tortured, what else was there to it? It was another world, contained within and tolerated by the one he and Frau Reusch now lived in. Frau Reusch looked hurt by his reluctance, as if she believed he did not trust her, so finally he answered, "To teach me to view the world with fear."

She cocked her head as if confused. "But why?"

"So I can be easily controlled. As I let you control me now."

She ignored the implications of that, asking instead, "Do you think that was unusual?"

"Unusual?"

"I mean, do you think you were just unlucky, or was this sort of thing to be expected?"

"The latter. Look, could we just change the subject?"

She persisted. "What about, well, if you hadn't come here, what kind of place might you have expected? I mean, what other sort of jobs were possible?"

"I really don't know."

"Surely you must have had some idea."

"Yes, I suppose so," he admitted. "I really was rather surprised that I ended up in a place like this—I mean a household. Usually one would have expected an able-bodied man to be assigned to some industry. Who knows, maybe there was a shortage of domestic laborers at the time. Maybe it was somebody's idea of a joke. I've never been able to find any logic in your system."

"My system?"

"The system, I meant."

"What were the industrial jobs like?"

"They vary considerably. There are the worst sort—one doesn't last long in those."

"What do you mean by 'last long'? Do you mean you get reassigned?"

He laughed at that. "No, no." He spent a moment bringing his laughter under control, then suddenly deadly serious, he said, "No. People die. Worked to death, radiation sickness, killed in industrial accidents, beaten to death: you name it."

"Oh."

"I really didn't think I was in for much of a reprieve from my death sentence. I should thank you for making my life so tolerable." Should, but couldn't, he thought. He was, after all, still a prisoner.

"So working in a household is the best you could have hoped for?"

"Yes, as long as I didn't hope for my freedom."

She suddenly changed tack. "I'm going to visit my sister, the one who lives near München, for a few weeks."

"When are you leaving?"

"Tomorrow."

He nodded.

"I'll miss you, Peter," she said, standing up and coming over to him. Something in her stance seemed odd. Suddenly she surged forward and threw her arms around him; it was the first time they had ever touched and he was stunned by her action. "You've been like a son to me. I'll miss you."

"I'll miss you, too," he responded awkwardly.

The next morning he saw her waiting for the bus and watched from the door of the shop as she climbed in. She glanced at him but he did not wave for fear the neighbors might notice and wonder at such familiarity. As the bus' drove off toward the city, he turned back into the shop to continue his work stocking the shelves.

Later that day they took their meal as usual, in the apartment. Peter politely chewed his way through the unidentifiable concoction set before him and then magnanimously offered to make the following day's meal. Herr Reusch sheepishly accepted, and after that they ate fairly well. On the third day, as Peter was preparing to open the shop, Herr Reusch appeared and asked him to come up to the apartment.

Wondering if he was going to be enlisted into making breakfast as well, Peter followed Herr Reusch up the steps. The door to the apartment was ajar and he was surprised to see a man inside. As they entered the apartment, he took a closer look and recognized the visitor as a stranger who had come to the shop about a month back.

"Here we are," Herr Reusch announced. "Peter, this is Herr Vogel and—"

"This isn't a garden party, and I don't do introductions with an *Untermensch!*" the man snapped. He was in his forties and roughly the same height as Peter, perhaps a bit shorter. He was a heavy man with dark blond hair that looked to be natural and clear blue eyes. In his youth he was probably well built, but now he was clearly tending toward fat.

Herr Vogel turned to Peter and ordered, "On your knees. Hands on your head."

Peter glared at him. He was just deciding to refuse when Herr Reusch pleaded, "Peter, do as he says. Please." So Peter relented and carefully went down on his knees and clasped his hands on his head.

The man got up from the couch and walked around as if inspecting him. "Please," Herr Vogel whined, mocking Herr Reusch. "Please?" He stopped his circuit behind Peter, stood there silently for a moment. Peter felt a wisp of his hair being lifted; he shuddered but managed not to move otherwise. The strand of hair was dropped, but still the man remained silent behind him.

"I guess he'll do," Herr Vogel finally pronounced.

Do for what?

"Get up," Herr Vogel commanded. He came around to face Peter once he was standing and said, "You're coming with me."

"What? Where?" Peter did not even attempt to keep the incredulity out of his tone. He looked to Herr Reusch to put the man straight, but Herr Reusch had wandered over to his desk.

"What are you talking about?" Peter finally asked the man directly.

Herr Vogel backhanded him. "Don't you dare use that tone with me!" he snarled.

Before Peter could overcome his surprise, Herr Vogel had walked over to Herr Reusch. Herr Reusch was grimacing, but he said nothing about Herr Vogel's violent outburst. Instead he handed Herr Vogel the packet of documents that Peter recognized as his papers.

"You have to go with this man now." Herr Reusch spoke quietly, but his voice conveyed a sense of urgency that Peter was unused to.

"I don't understand. What's going on?"

"Silence!" the man hissed at him.

"*What is going on?*" Peter insisted, ignoring the angry glance from the man.

"Herr Vogel here has purchased your indenture," Herr Reusch finally explained. He must have seen a look of total incomprehension on Peter's face because he felt the need to explain slowly, "I'm afraid you've been sold."

Sold? *Sold?* Peter found himself still questioning the concept even as he was led down the stairs of the apartment to the shop to collect his things, then out into the street and over to the man's car. He had stood in numb silence as the last bits of paper had been exchanged and signed; he could not read them from where he stood and had not even tried. He had silently obeyed when told to gather his things, painfully aware that they stood right outside the door to his room, giving him no privacy, no time to think, and now he was walking out of one life and into another. Just like that. He threw several questioning glances at Herr Reusch, but they were determinedly ignored. Sold?

He remained at a loss, standing by the door of the car, as Herr Vogel went to the back of the car, opened it, tossed Peter's belongings in, and removed handcuffs and a long piece of black cloth.

"Oh, I don't think that will be necessary," Herr Reusch opined naively.

"It's the law," Herr Vogel asserted. "Certainly, you don't violate the law, do you?"

"No, of course not. I only meant—oh, never mind."

Peter gave Herr Reusch a look bordering on panic. *What have you done to me?*

Herr Reusch shrugged guiltily. He looked confused, as if things were different than he had expected. As Herr Vogel snapped one of the rings around Peter's wrist, Herr Reusch ventured, "If you have any problems, just let me know. I'm . . . uh, maybe we can arrange something else."

Herr Vogel had already twisted Peter's arm behind his back and roughly pulled the other arm back to meet it. Without pausing, he stated, "There won't be any problems," and snapped the second ring shut. Using one hand to guide Peter's head, Herr Vogel pushed him into the backseat of the car. Peter climbed in, looked back at Herr Reusch again. This time he had abandoned any attempt to get an explanation; he just wanted to convey as much anger and disgust as he could through his expression. Still holding the cloth, Herr Vogel went to the back of his car, to close it. Herr Reusch grabbed the opportunity to lean inside the car and say, "Peter, I—"

"Go to hell," Peter hissed.

Herr Vogel returned to Peter. "I almost forgot!" he laughed, waving the black cloth. He reached inside the car, pushed Peter's chin to face away from them, draped the blindfold over his face, and tied it behind his head. Peter felt the cloth press against his eyes and fought back an inchoate fear. Herr Vogel nudged his shoulder to indicate he should lie across the seat, saying almost jovially, "Be a good boy, nice and quiet, and I won't have to put you in the trunk."

Peter immediately slumped down as Herr Vogel had indicated. He lay in obedient silence as Herr Vogel started the car, letting nothing more than a small sob of fear escape his lips. In the time it took for him to be shoved into a car, he had lost everything and everyone. The whole thing had taken so little time, Herr Reusch would not even be late opening the shop.

"Get out!" Herr Vogel ordered, tugging on his arm. The handcuffs were removed, and without asking permission, Peter immediately reached up and pushed the blindfold off his eyes. He stood unsteadily, blinking at the painful glare of daylight, and surveyed his surroundings.

He stood on the curb of a well-kept, tree-lined street of detached houses each with its own fenced-in garden and many with garages. The street was quiet, but there were cars parked along its length. And such cars! Not the small, cheap, domestically produced machines available to the ordinary German working class after a twenty-year wait on the priority list. No! These were expensive, new, imported models, sleek and shiny, with polished chrome gleaming in the sunlight.

Herr Vogel opened the trunk and Peter removed his belongings, and when Herr Vogel indicated, he removed a largish sack as well. Laden with his life's possessions, and it would seem, some food, he followed Herr Vogel toward one of the houses. It was a huge, two-story brick house, with a stylish, steeply pitched roof, surrounded by a high fence and a somewhat unkempt garden, and though Herr Vogel had parked on the street, it had a driveway, garage, and garden shed as well. As they passed through the gate into the yard, Herr Vogel gestured toward the garden, saying, "This will be one of your responsibilities."

They approached the massive wooden door at the front of the house, and Herr Vogel rang the bell. The door was opened by a woman who Peter guessed was Frau Vogel. She looked to be in her late thirties, although she wore a soured expression that made her look, at first glance, somewhat older. Her bleached-blond hair was braided and pinned on top of her head, in the traditional fashion favored by the wives of Party officials, and she wore a flower-print dress that did nothing to flatter her figure. She had a pudgy face that looked as though it could at any moment give way to a kind expression, if only she allowed it, and her demeanor conveyed a one-word impression: proper. She was the picture of Aryan propriety.

She greeted her husband and stepped back to let them in. Peter twisted his head to scan the hall of his new home. Fine wallpaper, rich paneling, a small table with delicate figurines, plush wool carpet running up the stairway.

"So, is this what you got us, Karl?" Frau Vogel asked. "I thought you were getting a boy. He's not very young."

"No, but he's strong enough," Herr Vogel replied.

Peter turned from one to the other as they spoke, but they ignored him.

"I suppose so. Too bad we must make do with only one . . ." Frau Vogel fingered the insignia on his uniform. He glanced down at her hand in vague disapproval, but his action went unnoticed. "English," she muttered, then her eyes narrowed and she asked, "Green? Is he a criminal?"

Discreetly, he pulled away from her grasp.

"Technically. You know how things are, you take what comes. Better than a political."

"Yes, at least he won't be spouting propaganda all the time. But should we really let him into the house?"

Wondering what the alternative was, Peter looked questioningly at her, but she did not see him.

"Don't worry, he's quite safe, gone through a rigid training program. Besides, he's been working for more than a year with no problems at all. His previous owners swear by him." At this, Herr Vogel's eyes gleamed mischievously as if he were privy to some joke. "Here are his papers and those are his first month's rations. You'll need to get an identity card for him tomorrow; his old one had to be turned in. Give me a call at work if there's a problem."

She nodded, scanned the papers Herr Vogel had handed her, murmuring, "What should we call him?"

"*Peter*," Herr Vogel answered, emphasizing the English pronunciation. "That's what he's been called up to now. I see no point in changing that. It'd only confuse him."

Peter sputtered, but still they simply ignored him.

Frau Vogel nodded. "How long do we have him for?"

He shifted uncomfortably.

"Lifelong, darling. Completely ours."

"Really!" Frau Vogel's eyes lit up. "Oh, that's wonderful! How did you manage it?"

"Trade secret, love. I thought you'd like the surprise."

Peter set down the bundles he was carrying and crossed his arms. Enough already! He did not like being a "surprise" for someone else, and he wanted their ridiculous conversation to end.

For the first time, Frau Vogel addressed him directly. "You will not stand like that—uncross your arms immediately. It looks disrespectful."

He hesitated; his eyes narrowed as he debated whether he should obey. Sudden dark memories fluttered at the edge of his perception; voices echoed into a pandemonium inside his head: *the price of disobedience . . .*

"I said—" Frau Vogel began.

Disconcerted by the clamor in his head, he uncrossed his arms. "Sorry, *gnädige Frau,*" he said reflexively. *A rigid training program*—so that was what they called it. To him it had been torture and the continual threat of death.

Frau Vogel accepted his apology with a brusque nod. Drawing herself up to her full height, she indicated his belongings. "Let's see what's in there."

They went into the kitchen and opened the bundle on the table.

"Books!" Herr Vogel howled, looking at the three books Peter had dared to bring. "What are you doing with books? What is this trash?"

"Poems, by William Blake. Songs of innocence and experience," Peter said, translating the title for them.

"Songs?" Frau Vogel asked. "I thought you said poems!"

"It's in that illogical, polluted pig-language," Herr Vogel remarked, paging through the book. "The Americans speak that crap. A gangster language, that's what it is."

"Is it pornography?" Frau Vogel asked, glancing at one of the reprinted plates.

"It's trash," Herr Vogel asserted, and set it aside. "He can throw it in the fireplace tonight." He set the other English-language book, a set of short stories, on the same pile. He then picked up the third book and opened its cover. "At least this is in German!" he said, then squinting his eyes at the pages, he asked, "Mathematics? Do you understand this?"

Sensing danger, Peter answered, "No, *mein Herr.* I just noticed it among some junk in the stockroom and asked if I could have it."

"Why?"

"I liked the funny-looking characters."

Herr Vogel sniffed. "You shouldn't have such things. I'll put it in my office."

Once they had finished picking through his meager possessions, discarding or confiscating this and that, Frau Vogel ordered him to follow her. "Bring that stuff with you," she added, indicating the depleted pile and his rations, and they began a tour of the house. They went through each floor and for each room she listed daily and weekly tasks she expected to be carried out. The house consisted of three floors and a cellar. The ground floor had a reception area near the front door with a wardrobe for coats and a stairway off to the left. Behind the stairs was Herr Vogel's study. On the right was a sitting room—the television was in that room; currently the title sequence for a documentary about crime in America was playing. Next to the sitting room was the dining room, and across the back of the house was the kitchen, with a large pantry that contained all the food cupboards as well as the refrigerator. Peter noticed that all the cabinets and doors had locks and that Frau Vogel, in keeping with tradition, carried the keys. A back door in the kitchen led outside to the back garden, and beyond that was an alley where the garbage was put.

A stairway led from the kitchen into the cellar. The cellar contained two rooms: the one with the stairway was used almost exclusively for storage and a workbench. The other room, at the front of the house, was divided in two: to the right was the furnace and the coal bin with a chute leading up to street level; to the left were storage cupboards, a toilet, and a laundry area including wash-basins. He was told to leave his rations in this area; presumably, none of his food was fresh enough to need refrigeration, though Frau Vogel did advise him to store it in the cupboard and not on the floor, to discourage rats. As Frau Vogel continued to detail his work assignments, Peter opened the cupboard. Inside he found a single electric coil for cooking, several utensils, a chipped plate, a bowl, a tin cup, and a couple of dented tin pans. If his mood had been a little less bleak, he might have laughed. It was so predictable: Where in the world did they get these things? He realized that since a washbasin was down here as well, he would have no need to use the kitchen at all. So, not only his food would be separate, but every aspect of his life would be kept scrupulously apart from theirs. Clearly, though he was clean enough to work for them, he was too filthy to live his life in their presence.

They worked their way back upstairs. Already the numerous jobs he had been assigned were swimming in his head. He doubted that he would remember everything and was hard-pressed to care. The first floor consisted of bed-rooms. There was a family bathroom and a separate room for the toilet, and the master bedroom had its own bathroom suite. Frau Vogel mentioned repeatedly how important it was to keep the bathrooms and toilets scrupu-lously clean, implying that this would be no once-a-day task, rather more like a vocation.

They continued up to the second floor, under the roof, which was split in two. There were two more bedrooms for the younger children in one half, and the attic occupied the other half. As they looked into the attic storage area, Frau Vogel spoke for the first time without enumerating a job or a restriction. "You can sleep in there. I think there are some rags about which you can use to make a bed. You really shouldn't be under the same roof with us," she fretted aloud, "but there isn't anywhere else right now."

As she spoke, he wondered idly if she was referring to some sort of manual, thinking that it would be amusing, but not surprising. Even with the mild weather he noticed that the attic was considerably colder than the rest of the house. It obviously was not insulated and would be an uncomfortable residence at the best of times.

He set his bundle down inside the attic as Frau Vogel consulted her watch. "The children will be home shortly. We have to get dinner prepared. Come on." She turned on her heel and strode away without looking back. Peter fought back a crushing sense of despair and, after giving the attic room one last glance, followed her down the stairs.

══════════ 21 ══════════

Mᴀʀʏsɪᴀ sᴀᴛ ʙᴏʟᴛ ᴜᴘʀɪɢʜᴛ in bed. Julia, her poor Julia. Always the same dream, always the faceless assailant attacking her little girl. She turned to look at her husband, hoping to gain some comfort from him, even as he slept, but in the dim light she could just barely make out that his side of the bed was empty.

She cursed quietly, climbed out of bed, and crept silently into the other room of the small apartment. Olek was asleep on their couch; no one else was in sight. She spent a moment contemplating her grandson as Siwa purred and rubbed herself against her legs. Marysia decided against waking Olek; it was better they kept as much from him as possible. He already knew too much for one so young.

After pulling on some clothes, a coat, and a pair of boots, she headed outside. After about an hour of tromping through the woods, along a difficult path that ran next to a rivulet, she began to hear the sounds of the waterfall. A sentry greeted her and, without her asking, pointed out where her husband sat.

"It's always the same," she acknowledged wearily. "Could you give us some privacy?"

The sentry withdrew some distance and Marysia approached her husband. He was sitting on a rock, staring into the pounding water, holding his knees and rocking slowly back and forth. Marysia sat next to him and waited silently. She could hear his moaning, a soft, rhythmic sobbing, like the weak cry of a child inured to long suffering.

"Cyprian," she said at long last, "please come back to the flat."

He did not answer her.

"Cyprian. This has got to stop. I miss her, too, but we have a life to lead here. You have two grandchildren, a son who needs you . . ."

"None of you cared about her. You drove her to it."

"You know that's not true."

"Always harping on her. You could never accept her the way she was."

"Cyprian. It wasn't my fault!"

"And Adam! Always making her feel worthless."

"He didn't do that. Don't lay this on him. God knows, it's difficult enough without you—"

"He and that harlot wife of his, leading Olek astray . . ."

"Stop this! I know Julia was your favorite, but for God sakes, don't destroy everything else because you've lost her! Adam is your son, don't do this to him. He doesn't need your accusations. None of us do."

"None of you cared."

"Well, then, show that you care. Snap out of this! Care for her son! Olek needs you!"

"He doesn't need me. He's his father's son."

"What? His father? We don't even know who his father is!"

"But we know his father killed her."

"We don't know that. We don't know who she saw in Paris."

"The boy has his father's blood. He's a Nazi."

"Cyprian! Have you gone mad?" Marysia asked, horrified. She was going to say more, but then she wondered if her question should be taken seriously. Had her husband gone mad? Very carefully, as if handling a poisonous snake, she asked, "What is it you want?"

"I want out of here."

"We've discussed that. I'm not leaving," she stated firmly.

"I want out of here."

"How are we going to do without a cryptographer?" she asked, hoping to ignite his sense of loyalty.

"I want out of here," he said as if he had not heard her.

"Would you train someone to take your place? Before you go?" she asked, turning to the practical difficulties of his demands.

"I want out of here," he chanted.

"Where would you go?"

"I want out of here."

"Do you care?"

"I want out of here."

"Okay. I'm staying, but I guess that doesn't matter to you . . ."

"I want out of here."

"I'll take it up with the Council." Timidly she placed a hand on her husband's back. "We'll take care of you. We'll find you a place, far away from here."

Cyprian stopped his chant. They sat in silence for a moment listening to the waterfall, then suddenly he said quite calmly, "I'm not mad, my dear Marysiu. I just want out. I can't stand any of you anymore."

"None of us?"

Cyprian shook his head.

"Not me? After all these years together?"

Cyprian continued to shake his head.

"Not your son? He's done you no wrong."

Cyprian shook his head.

"What about Olek or Joanna?"

"No! Neither of them!"

"Your friends?"

"I have no friends here. I have nothing here. I want to go. Let me out."

Marysia stood. "I'll do what I can." She was going to leave, but stopped. "I just want to tell you one thing, dear."

Cyprian looked up at her as if he were listening.

"I loved her, too." Marysia walked off thoroughly disgusted.

22

*P*ETER WALKED AN APPROPRIATELY respectful distance behind Frau Vogel as she led the way. Ahead lay a small, nondescript building: the local police station. Today it would be made official—his life had changed hands. The officer on duty knew Frau Vogel personally and greeted her respectfully, asking after the children by name. After the pro forma pleasantries were completed, Frau Vogel explained Peter's presence. The officer scrutinized him carefully, trying to commit his features to memory, then took his fingerprints and photo for the files, filled out a number of forms, and finally entered his number and place of work into the local registry.

After the local registration was finished, they were sent to the main building of the district security police in Berlin to complete the formalities. Only then did he realize he now lived in a suburb of the capital. Just approaching the bland building in the center of the city caused a cold sweat to appear on his brow. The sensation of raw power was overwhelming. His right hand ached, and without realizing what he was doing, he tried to slide the band on his wrist up and down to try to relieve the tension. Finally Frau Vogel was driven to snap, "Stop that! They'll think you're guilty of something, then we'll be here forever." Obviously, even she felt somewhat daunted by the aura of authority.

Inside, they joined a long queue for the reception desk. After a short wait, Frau Vogel ordered him to stay in line and walked off. Fear gripped him as he watched her disappear around a corner: she had taken all the documents with her! In police headquarters, wearing the uniform of a criminal, undocumented! Unregistered! His heart thundered as he forced himself to keep his gaze lowered, trying to remain as insignificant as possible. After an eternity Frau Vogel reappeared with Herr Vogel and motioned to him to leave the queue and follow them as they turned to go down another corridor. He rushed after them and caught up as Herr Vogel stopped to show his identification to a guard. Peter continued to follow a few steps behind as Herr and Frau Vogel were escorted to an unmarked door and shown into a large office with twenty or so desks. They walked through that and into a small private office at the back. Herr and Frau · Vogel confidently approached the desk as Peter slipped in and stood unnoticed near the wall.

A heavily built man with thin brown hair sat behind the desk poring over some documents. He immediately snapped to attention and saluted when he saw Herr Vogel, then added, rather incongruously, "Herr Vogel! What an unexpected pleasure!"

Herr Vogel waved his hand upward with a casual *"Heil,"* then said, "Herr Franz, you remember my wife, don't you?"

"Of course, always a pleasure, Frau Vogel!" Herr Franz replied, giving Frau Vogel a crisp bow. Herr Franz seemed genuinely pleased to see them, although he betrayed a certain anxiety by repeatedly eyeing his cigarette as it burned in the ashtray. Suddenly he snatched it up to take a puff. He made a motion as if to sit back down, but changed his mind and instead shuffled his weight uneasily from one leg to the other. "So, what can I do for you?" he asked, directing his attention back to Herr Vogel.

"We have to register him," Herr Vogel replied as he indicated Peter, "and the wait seemed horrendous. Would you mind handling it for us now?" Despite the politeness of the request, something in Herr Vogel's tone told Peter that it was an order.

The man behind the desk certainly reacted as though it were. "Of course, of course, just leave it to me. No problem at all!"

"Good. Well, I really should get back to the ministry." Herr Vogel turned toward Frau Vogel. "Do you mind if I leave you to handle it from here?"

"No, not at all. I'll see you back at home this evening."

"Frau Vogel, if I may interrupt," Herr Franz interjected obsequiously, "there's no reason for you to stay. I can take care of everything and bring your boy to your house this evening after work."

"Oh, that would be wonderful of you. Are you sure you don't mind?" Frau Vogel cooed.

Peter shifted his gaze from one to the other, wondering if any of them would even acknowledge his presence.

"No, of course not. It's on my way home. It will be my pleasure!"

"Yes, okay. You have our address in Schönwalde?"

"Yes, I'll see you this evening."

"Thank you." Frau Vogel handed over Peter's docket and she and Herr Vogel left together.

Herr Franz followed them with his eyes. As the door shut behind them, the smile dropped from his face and he muttered to himself, "Shit. As if I don't have enough to do today."

Peter cocked his head slightly at the faux pas and was mildly pleased to see a startled response as Herr Franz took notice of him for the first time. Herr Franz glared a warning at him, then walked to the door, opened it, and called out to one of his staff to come into his office.

A young woman appeared at the door. Her hair, bleached to the standard platinum blond, was neatly pinned up. She wore a conservatively cut, dark brown suit and a serious expression. She snapped a curt *"Heil, Hitler!"* complete with hand gesture, then added in a normal voice, "Yes, *mein Herr?"*

It was, Peter thought, one of the few small mercies of his place in society that no one expected him to indulge in the *Heil* nonsense, and when the secretary glanced curiously at him, he took advantage of this one liberty and winked at her in return. Her look of shock was rewarding, and she immediately turned her attention back to her boss.

After the situation was explained to her, the young woman led him away to her desk. She spent about an hour typing up forms and cross-checking references and numbers while he stood, shifting his weight from one leg to the other, in the narrow space between the desks. Finally, she pulled the last sheet out of her typewriter with a flourish, gathered together a stack of documents, and led him through the labyrinth of desks to a door near the back of the room.

The door led to a stairwell, and as they descended the steps to a floor well below ground level, he felt his pulse quicken. They went down a corridor, passing a number of heavy, closed doors. The light tapping of the secretary's heels sounded incongruously ordinary in the oppressive atmosphere. As they turned a corner, he espied their destination and relaxed a bit. At the end of the hallway was a workroom door, the top half open to reveal a mechanic's shop.

A radio was playing inside the shop, and he could see various tools and machines lining the greasy shelves. The young woman stopped at the half-open door and, disdaining to go farther, called inside for the mechanic on duty. An older man appeared; he had wispy gray hair and wore a pair of heavy glasses. A mischievous grin appeared on his face as he noticed the young woman, and he made a fuss about wiping his hands on a greasy cloth to clean them.

"So, you couldn't resist coming to see me again!" he teased.

She smiled indulgently at him, then said, "We have a rush order. Can you replace his identity band right now?"

"For you, anything." The mechanic took the papers and looked at the information on them. "Yeah, come back in about forty minutes, maybe an hour." Then he looked up at her and winked. "Unless you want to stay here and watch a master at work."

"Love to, but I'm absolutely swamped with work."

"Okay, okay. You bureaucrats aren't happy unless you're pushing paper."

"Don't let him get lost," she admonished as she walked off. "I'll be back." Her heels made tapping sounds as she retreated back down the hall.

"You all right?"

It took Peter a moment to realize he was being spoken to. He jerked his head up, stunned.

"You don't look so well. Are you all right?"

"I'm fine," he finally stammered.

The fellow kept up a continuous jovial patter as he led Peter into the shop and seated him in a chair next to a workbench. He placed Peter's right arm on the bench and inspected the metal band. "Bad workmanship. These things require skill, but any old cobbler is allowed to put them on. Look at this." He twisted Peter's wrist around, showed him the seam. "That causes irritation. It's too tight, doesn't move around enough. I can't get under it with proper metal cutters. Maybe that's why they did it that way. Hmm?"

He brought over a heavy board with leather straps affixed to it. Sticking the board under Peter's arm, he buckled the straps at his wrist and elbow, explaining, "This will help you keep your arm still. We don't want you losing your hand, do we? It'd be more stable attached to the table, but we can't have everything." He shoved a thin piece of metal between the band and Peter's skin and then slid a mounted saw across the bench and positioned it over his arm. "Here, use this," he said, handing Peter a piece of heavy cloth. "Turn your head away and hold this over your ear to protect your hearing. I only have one set of these," he continued, tapping the ear protectors he wore around his neck. "Bought them myself," he added as he put them on and set about adjusting the saw.

He continued to speak even after he started the saw and began cutting the metal. Peter could not hear most of the monologue, something about precision cutting and bad equipment; nevertheless, he felt comforted by it. He concentrated on remaining perfectly still as he felt the whir of the blade just above his wrist.

At long last, the whining of the saw stopped. Peter looked to see a neat slice cut out of the metal band. The mechanic released the leather straps and then used two sets of pliers to pull the crescent shape flat enough to slide off.

With poignant memories of freedom, Peter rotated his arm and ran his fingers gently over its surface. The skin of his wrist was tender, the area under the band paler than the rest, and the balance felt wrong without the familiar weight, but for those few minutes at least he was rid of the damn thing. The old man watched him in silence, then said almost wistfully, "It's my experience that everyone prefers to have the old one off first thing, before I make the new one. We can have a little break before I start on it. You want some tea?"

Peter nodded and the old man turned to put on a little coil on which a kettle stood. "Not supposed to have this, you know, but none of the bigwigs ever come down here, so, I get to keep my little kitchen." He laughed, turning toward Peter to encourage him to join in.

Peter smiled wanly in return.

"Ach, you're relatively new at this, aren't you?" the old man asked.

"Just over a year."

"Heh. You must have really offended someone! A nice-looking Aryan-type like you, you should be upstairs making other people's lives miserable!"

Peter nodded. The old man turned his back to pour the tea, saying as he did so, "Ach, look, we all work for someone. I wear a badge, see!" He pointed to the badge that was pinned to his shirt. "And a uniform. We all got bosses. That's what it's like in an orderly society."

"I want to be free," Peter mouthed in case anyone was listening in.

The old man waved a hand dismissively. "Don't we all! If it's not bosses, it's wives and kids. Then, just when you figure you can't stand it anymore, they up and leave you all alone and . . ." His voice trailed off and his eyes took on a distant look. They were both silent for a moment, then, as if speaking to himself, the old man said, "None of us get to do what we want in this world. Just put on an act. Survive. It's what we all do."

By the time Peter was returned to Herr Vogel's friend, he had another identity band affixed to his wrist and an identity card complete with photo. "All finished, *mein Herr*," the young woman informed her boss as she deposited the documentation on his desk.

"All right. I'll take it from here." As she left the room, Herr Franz consulted his watch, then finally addressed Peter directly: "Sit down over there and don't say a word."

There was no chair where Herr Franz had indicated, so he sat on the floor, his back resting against the wall, his arms supported on his knees. He sat very still and stared at the wall opposite. The shadows cast by the afternoon sun suggested unfathomable secrets in their patterns, but he did not even attempt to interpret them. He waited in silence, sitting on the floor of an office of a man he didn't even know in the headquarters of Reich Security in Berlin, waited while Herr Franz worked, waited patiently like a package to be delivered back to his prison. A pang of homesickness swept through him, made all the more poignant by the fact that he did not even know where home was anymore.

He wondered why exchanging one prison for another bothered him so much, but he already knew the reason. He had fooled himself into believing in his virtual freedom with the Reusches. It had not been much worse than living as a worker in London. There were curfews and district borders and random violence, but otherwise they pretty much left one alone to live one's life. It had been stupid to be lured into such a false sense of liberty; stupid, but also sanity preserving. Now, things would be different. Much different. He knew already that not one day would pass without his being constantly reminded by the Vogels that he was a prisoner. Not only a prisoner, but *their* prisoner.

He sighed heavily and Herr Franz looked up at him in annoyance. He apologized, then rested his head on his hands and thought about Allison, what a lovely woman she was, how much happiness she had brought into his life. He closed his eyes and remembered the years they had spent together, years that had passed wonderfully in a shared sense of purpose, in an intellectual exchange that brightened every day, in warm embraces and tender words. Her image had grown dim with time; he could no longer see the exact curve of her face or the arch of her eyebrows, but the smile, the look of compassion and love in her eyes—that was still vivid. After all these years, he thought, after all these years, she was still dead and he still missed her. Missed her terribly.

"Wake up," Herr Franz ordered, nudging him with his foot. "Get up, it's time to go."

Peter nearly fell as he tried to stand—his legs were asleep and his joints ached. He hobbled stiffly across the floor as blood returned to his limbs, but Herr Franz did not even notice as he headed out the door. When they reached the front lobby, Herr Franz told him, "I have to take the tram. I don't want any trouble from you." He pulled out a pair of handcuffs, locking Peter's wrists behind his back. "Understood?"

Peter nodded, idly wondering what sort of trouble was expected from him. Was he supposed to go berserk at the thought of riding a tram? Did Herr Franz expect him to try to escape? Where to? The entire country was a prison to him. Without good papers, there was no need for locked doors or chains.

Herr Franz grabbed his arm and pulled him along to the tram stop as if he were a backward child. When the tram arrived, they climbed on. Herr Franz showed his season ticket and asked the conductor what the fare was for Peter.

The conductor looked at him, saw his clothing, and bellowed, "He's not allowed on here!"

Herr Franz cursed under his breath, pulled out a badge, and grated, "Official business." Snapping the leather wallet of the identification shut, he did not wait for the conductor's reaction, just dragged Peter down the aisle of recoiling passengers. Every eye followed them as they made their way to an open space. The tram was initially crowded, but a space cleared around Peter as if he carried the plague.

Many of the passengers continued to watch him, some curious, others contemptuous. A balding man a few rows in front of them pointed at him surreptitiously and whispered something into his son's ear. The boy stared at him, incredulous—his eyes never straying until his father pulled him to get off several stops later.

Peter ignored them all. This was his first chance to get a good look at the city and the surrounding residential areas. The center of the town had been a showpiece of monumental sculptures, marble façades, and well-kept, albeit somewhat drab, buildings. However, the shoddiness of the outlying housing blocks was amazing. The Berlin workers' housing was no better than that found around London. In general, it looked tidier; there was less garbage strewn about, but the concrete structures had the same cracked, damp look, and panes of broken glass and dangling electrical wires could be seen.

Here and there he spotted a playground, some occupied by children, others empty, and a few pedestrians were walking about, but, other than for the ubiquitous patrols, the areas looked nearly abandoned. Posters exhorting the people to work harder and encouraging ever greater acts of patriotism were everywhere; none of them looked weather-beaten: they must have been constantly maintained, in sharp contrast to the grim apartment blocks.

Peter looked around the tram and assessed the passengers. Most wore stylish clothing, but upon closer inspection, he realized that the cut and quality of the cloth was almost uniformly low. A few, like his companion, wore finely tailored apparel, but the rest were arrayed in ill-fitting garments. And they stank as badly as any workers' bus in London. The smell of old sweat in polyester was almost overwhelming. Clearly, the soap ration was as meager and the water supply as unpredictable here as in London.

After several stops, Herr Franz found a free seat and sat down with a grunt to light a cigarette. Peter remained standing near him—he knew better than to even think of sitting down. Without a free hand he had difficulty keeping his balance, and he swayed precariously at every curve in the track. After a while, Herr Franz reached out and grabbed his arm to hold him steady.

From his vantage point, Peter watched out the windows as they passed through an industrial region. The tram was apparently an express through this region. It hurried without stopping past long, orderly queues of tired-looking workers in uniforms of various shades of gray. Whatever superior attitude they had assumed inside the factories when he had been assigned to work there, they obviously lost it once they exited the grounds and were faced with the commute to their dismal homes.

It gave him a perspective on their attitudes he had never had before. Conceivably, the propaganda of a lifetime had not succeeded in making them feel naturally superior to the forced laborers they worked beside; rather, it was possible they had feigned a cruel and dominant attitude to bolster their own abysmal self-esteem. With a sudden pang Peter realized how little he actually knew about the society he and his comrades had spent their lives opposing. Perhaps with a bit more information, they could have been more effective in their efforts.

The tram arrived at the end of the line. It disgorged its passengers into a large plaza containing a confusing assortment of bus stops, taxi stands, tram shelters, and kiosks. Peter had never seen anything quite like it. Transport in London was rather limited, and other than walking, most people never did anything other than take a company-provided bus to their place of work. He spun around, trying to take it all in and organize it mentally so he could memorize useful details for future reference.

"Don't get any bright ideas," Herr Franz growled, grabbing his arm and pulling him roughly toward some bus timetables. Herr Franz spent some time checking the tables, and it became obvious, despite what he had said, that the Vogel household was not on his usual route home. They spent sufficient time loitering around the posters to draw the attention of a suspicious patrolman, who wandered over and politely asked to see their papers. Herr Franz complied with his request and the patrolman promptly apologized for the inconvenience and asked if he could be of help.

The patrolman explained to Herr Franz the best bus to take and where to transfer and added that they had just missed the bus and the next would not be leaving for another half hour. Herr Franz thanked him and, his patience exhausted, headed toward the taxi stand. He dragged Peter along, forcing him to walk sideways with a stumbling, twisted gait, then pushed him inside a waiting taxi and climbed in. The driver twisted around to stare at them and opened his mouth to say something, but when he saw Herr Franz's face, he changed his mind and asked instead, "Where to, *mein Herr?*"

At their destination, as Peter climbed out of the car, Herr Franz grabbed his arm and flung him toward the house. Fed up, Peter turned to confront him. "Damn it! Don't take your anger out on me!"

Herr Franz walked up to him, grasped the chain between his wrists, and wrenched upward, asking, "Why not?"

Peter gasped at the pain in his shoulder and elbows. Having no quick answer to this demonstration of modern ethics, he agreed, "All right, all right." Herr Franz released him and they continued to the house.

At the door a transformation came over Herr Franz, and by the time Frau Vogel greeted him, he was smiling and relaxed. He gave her the papers and they exchanged pleasantries. Remembering what the mechanic had said to him, Peter watched the act with grim satisfaction.

=== **23** ===

"**S**O THEN THE MOTHER SAYS, 'Maria, you stay here and stir the pasta. This is a job for Mama!' "

Everyone was still laughing as Richard walked into the room. Til grinned and launched into another joke. "There were these two Englishmen and a Frenchman . . ."

Richard sat down at the head of the table and listened. He laughed with the others at the end, then raised his hand to preempt further entertainment. "Sorry to interrupt, but we have business to conduct."

The men at the table groaned subtly, and though it was a measure of his popularity that they felt free to do so, it nevertheless annoyed him. They worked their way through the agenda, finally coming to the seventh point: the treatment of prisoners on remand.

"Now I realize," Richard explained, "that once we have a confession out of them, it's clear they are guilty. Nevertheless, we must carry out procedure and see that they get to trial. This habit of turning guilty prisoners over to the more brutish elements in our security services as some sort of toys for them must stop. We're losing far too many prisoners that way, and the cover-ups are wearing thin. You may not realize this, but an accretion of unconvicted corpses in our jails *does* affect government negotiations. Among others, we've got the damn Nigerians fussing at us about human rights, and we're right in the middle of sensitive oil negotiations. I'm sure the pressure there is coming from the North American Union; nevertheless, we must give them some solid assurances in order for these negotiations to go forward.

"Til has drawn up an executive order which will be sent out—top secret, naturally—which, in effect, will explain this situation and require some controls within our prisons on the disposal of confessed prisoners. As section heads, it is your responsibility to see that these orders are carried out and to institute the oversight programs which will contain the situation. I'll expect a report on the controls that you plan to put into place in each of your sections within the week. Four months from now, you will submit a follow-up report with *documented* statistics on prisoner mortality and the effectiveness of your control program. Understood?"

"No invented statistics," Til reiterated to the group. "We will check."

Richard nodded.

"Is this Reich-wide?"

"No," Richard answered. "It's an initiative to be carried out in several test regions, the area around Göringstadt being one of them. Off the record"— Richard glanced at the secretary to indicate she should stop writing—"we're having some problems which we hope this will solve."

"Problems?"

"Crime. Terrorism," Til answered. "You see, we've made a study of other caste cultures, and though the level of violence among the lower castes is always much higher than that of the upper strata, in most cultures it is directed inward—that is, the scumbags tend to attack each other. As, for instance, in the American inner cities.

"Here, there is a difference. Our crime victims are most often good, upstanding German colonists. We think there is a message being sent, and though we will never acknowledge it, we must do something about it. The numbers of colonizers who return to the Alt Reich is intolerable. Our people are being driven out of what should be their own lands."

"We also have," Richard continued, "an inordinate number of terrorist episodes, such as that explosion in the Congress Hall on its opening day. That was before I arrived, and I've been ordered to clean things up here. This will be our first move."

"Isn't that conceding defeat?" one of the section heads asked.

"Only if we call it that. What I am suggesting is strict enforcement of the law. No more extrajudicial executions—and that means no more careless torture. Understood?"

"Why only this region?"

"It's not just this region. It's being implemented in several regions, and in each, crime rates and terrorism will be monitored and compared to control regions. I will be making periodic reports to Berlin on the effectiveness of the new rules on prisoner mortality and popular morale. Once they have had time to be effective, I will report again on the overall effect of the program, and based on my evidence and that of the other test areas, a ruling will be made as to whether or not to institute these changes Reich-wide. We are on display, gentlemen, and it's up to you to make sure we do the job right."

One of the group raised a tentative hand. "What about convicted prisoners? I mean, the ones convicted of capital crimes. Sometimes they go astray in our system before we get a chance to carry out their sentences."

Another piped up, "Yeah, the boys need something! If you take this away from them—"

"Enough!" Richard grated. "If 'the boys' need to vent their aggressions, they can always transfer to a camp assignment or work in interrogation. There will be no more extracurricular executions in our prisons, understood?"

"I understand about the ones on remand, but I don't understand why we should exert ourselves to keep the convicted ones in good health."

"There's a policy shift there as well," Til answered for his boss. "There are many jobs which are obviously beneath German dignity, but the alternative of importing foreign waged workers is considered destabilizing. Witness the riots in Leipzig last year or the dark-skinned areas of Hamburg with all their strange smells. These foreigners bring too many weird ideas with them, and we're better off without them polluting our culture.

"If we use our own people, we can keep them under control. With the labor shortage such as it is, however, this puts pressure on our workforce—for instance, we can't afford to recruit domestic workers at the expense of our industrial workforce. There's a program to alleviate the problem by retraining condemned, nonviolent convicts. We're having fairly good success with the program, so except in unusual cases, those convicted of capital crimes will be given the opportunity to be recycled into the workforce.

"This has an added advantage," Til continued. "For if unemployment ever shoots up again, these people can be easily removed from the labor pool, simply by terminating their contracts and carrying out their original sentences."

After a minor amount of debate about the advisability of the program, the meeting moved on to the next point and finally, after two more hours, concluded. Til, told a few more jokes, lightening everyone's mood, and then the group broke up, leaving only Richard, Til, and the secretary. Til and Richard conferred with her for a few minutes to clarify what should appear in the minutes, and then the two of them walked back to Richard's office together. There Richard sorted through some papers, while Til went over to the liquor cabinet.

"Want a drink?" he offered while pouring himself one.

"Yeah, the usual," Richard replied, distracted because he seemed to have lost a sheet of paper. He sat at his desk and methodically checked the drawers.

"Your wife is *Volksdeutsch,* isn't she?" Til asked, setting the drink he had poured down on Richard's desk.

"You know she is," Richard answered, looking up from his paper shuffling.

"Funny, isn't it?" Til said, swilling his drink around pensively.

"No. There are many Germans who were outside the old Reich boundaries, and we've welcomed each and every one into the fold. *Heim ins Reich,* you know."

"There is this interesting thing, though," Til intimated. He spotted a piece of paper on the floor and casually picked it up and handed it to his boss. "Is this what you're looking for?"

"Yes, thanks," Richard answered, shoving it into his briefcase.

"Her family isn't."

"Whose family isn't what?"

"Your wife's. They're not *Volksdeutsch.* Isn't that odd?"

"I wouldn't know. I've only met them once and then very briefly." Richard stared at his desk for a moment before adding, "We don't exactly get along."

"Ah, then you wouldn't know that several members of her family are in the Underground."

"No. If that were true, I wouldn't know about it," Richard answered without looking up.

"And it wouldn't affect you. Wouldn't even hold up your brilliant career?"

"Probably not," Richard grated. "After all, I have no contact with them whatsoever. Neither does my wife."

"So you wouldn't care if they were arrested and brought up on charges of terrorism?"

Richard lowered his head farther and rubbed the back of his neck.

"Because, after all," Til continued, "that would be the patriotic thing to do."

Still looking at his desktop, Richard said, "You know, arresting innocent people can be very . . . It's not—"

"Oh, don't worry!" Til rushed to assure him. "They're not innocent. The evidence is very strong. Very strong."

Finally Richard looked up. "What do you want, Til?"

Seating himself on the corner of Richard's desk, Til smiled. "I'm not a rich man, you see. There's the house, and the children. And my wife, she has expensive tastes . . ."

Richard closed his eyes as he listened.

". . . the salary of someone in my position. It's low, you know. It doesn't reflect my true usefulness. I try to get ahead, but you know, it's a jungle out there, and the opportunities for one such as me, are, well, rather limited. As a loyal lieutenant, you understand, I don't have the freedom of movement you do, I can't take advantage of the opportunities that arise, I—"

Richard opened his eyes. "Would a bonus of five hundred thousand be of help?"

Til smiled broadly. "Initially."

"Initially?"

"I've been your right-hand man for years, Richard. I can call you that, can't I?" Til asked, then without waiting for an answer, he continued, "And I've learned from the best. Don't worry, I won't ruin you. Take your time." Til stood and, after carefully downing his drink and setting the dirty glass down on Richard's desk, walked toward the door.

"I really wish you hadn't done that, Til," Richard whispered to the departing figure of his amusing subordinate. He rested his forehead on his hand and closed his eyes in sorrow.

<hr>

24

RELUCTANTLY, PETER OPENED his eyes. It was still dark in the attic, but he could see a glow of orange on the droplets of dew that had condensed on the window. Judging by the sun, and he was surprisingly good at that now, it was time to start his day. He groaned, rolled over in the uncomfortable bed of old rugs and rags that he had made for himself, and began to fall back asleep. He had been dreaming of Allison, of how she would wake him by running her hands over his body, how she would grab hold of him and stroke him until he was wild with desire for her before he was even truly awake. The dream had left him with a pointless erection, and he thought that maybe he should do something about it, but then he remembered how viciously Frau Vogel had kicked his ribs the last time he overslept, and with an expressive sigh he abandoned his dreams, rose, and pulled on his clothing.

He emerged from the attic and descended the steps to the ground floor. There he paused to open the drapes and shutters in each room before descending farther, into the cellar. Though it was late April, it was still quite chilly, and he took several minutes to stoke the furnace so that the house would be warm by the time the family rose. He stood a moment watching the glow of the flames, then turned to take care of his personal needs. After washing, he ran his hand over his face to feel the stubble of his beard. Though his hair was light, no doubt the growth would be visible, so with a resigned grunt, he pulled out his miserably dull razor and began painstakingly scraping at his face. When he had finished, he ran his fingers over his face again to be sure he had not missed anywhere, then he turned to his food cupboard and surveyed the wretched collection contained therein.

He had been provided with a month's worth of food when he had first arrived, and after surveying the paltry, rotting foodstuffs, he had dutifully stored them in the cupboard, mentally dividing the quantities into daily allotments. It had not worked. He had not had the self-control to eat only a thirtieth of his food each day, and much of it had started to spoil, so he had been obliged to eat it quickly. Now there was hardly anything left and there were still eight days left in the month. It wasn't fair, he had arrived a week before the first of the month and had not been given anything extra for that week, and the food had been old and insufficient and he had been used to much better, and now, now it looked as if he was going to go hungry for days!

Meanwhile, he prepared and served and cleaned up obscene quantities of food for the family, none of which he was permitted to touch—not even the leftovers, not even when they were thrown away. Of course, that had not stopped him from plucking them out of the garbage late at night, but by then the food was often inedible. Even the ducks took priority over him! He had once asked Frau Vogel if she would let him have the old bread instead of taking it to the duck pond in the park, and she had looked at him as though he had just asked her if he could strangle those adorable little ducklings and pull off their wings with his teeth.

He chewed at his thumb and looked at the food. God, he was hungry! His stomach kept cramping and he had a headache from the pain. Of course, the headache was probably not due to hunger—more likely it was from Frau Vogel's habit of hitting him at every opportunity. Always a slam with the hand, or some handy object, right into his face. The temple, the ear, his cheek, jaw, chin—it didn't matter where, just some part of his face. Everything that displeased her, anytime she needed to draw his attention to something—wham!—into his face. They were weak blows usually, especially when she used her bare hand, but the accumulated effect of her incessant pounding throughout the day was jarring, and by evening the bones of his face ached from the continuous abuse, and a dull roar of pain filled his head.

"Stop hitting me!" he had exclaimed once in exasperation. She had reported the insubordination to her husband, who had then dutifully reminded him of what real pain was. Since then he had learned to apologize more often, to address them both with excruciating deference and formality, to back away such that he kept a physical distance between himself and Frau Vogel to discourage her sudden temper, and since then the abuse had decreased. Nevertheless, it had not disappeared entirely, and he not only cringed anytime he heard his name screeched out, but he had acquired a despicable, jumpy nervousness anytime either of them were anywhere nearby.

He reached into the cupboard and pulled out a carrot. It had grown soft and wrinkled with age, but it was still edible and would divert his attention away from his hunger for at least a few minutes. He ground it between his teeth as he climbed the steps up to the back door. There on a peg was his jacket, but he ignored it, deciding that it was not cold enough to bother. He grabbed the packet of documents he needed for his morning tasks and went out into the brisk dawn.

He trod a pedestrian path that he knew was *nur für Deutsche,* that is, it was only for Germans. In his youth, the *nur für Deutsche* signs had been ubiquitous, but here they were unnecessary. Everyone knew that *Gastarbeiter*, as foreign workers, including forced laborers, were so genteelly called, walked along the roads; the pristine parks and pedestrian paths were for Germans to enjoy. Strolling, relaxing, sitting on a bench—all of it, all of it was illegal for him. He had no right to leave the house except to perform work. He had no right to free time and therefore no need for any comforts. Who needed signs?

The path passed by a duck pond, and for that reason alone he often risked taking it. He liked watching them, and he used the time he gained by walking the shorter albeit forbidden path to spend a moment contemplating the still water and the quiet forms of the awakening ducks. It would be nice, he thought, to throw them some bread crumbs, but instead he found himself scanning the surrounding grass and the nearby trash bins for unused bread or any other edible refuse.

There was nothing today. He crossed the little stone bridge over the stream and skirted around the monument to Hitler. Somebody had lain some flowers—forget-me-nots?—at the base, beneath the dates. A faint impression could just be discerned on the pavement where the pedestal had stood in earlier times before it was removed and then replaced according to the political fashion of the day. Currently, political orthodoxy was "in" and the old regulations were being reintroduced and more zealously enforced than in recent years. The "war effort" explained away anything that ideology missed.

He passed two gardeners—*Zwangsarbeiter*, naturally—carefully trimming the grass from the edge of the path. The one had been muttering something to the other, but they stopped when they heard him approach. They eyed his uniform suspiciously, deciding to remain silent as long as he was near. Once he was several yards past, he heard the muttering resume.

When he reached the bakery, no one was in line. He went up to the window and was greeted by Roman, the baker's assistant. Roman had been forced labor since early childhood and barely remembered any other life. His uniform carried a similar set of badges to Peter's, giving his number, identifying his nationality, and indicating that he was a *Zwangsarbeiter*. Unlike Peter, however, there was no green triangle, so he was not labeled criminal, and the yellow inset on the red stripe was missing, indicating that, though he was of an inferior race, he had not formally lost his Aryan status. Indeed, he was not being punished, he was simply working under the guidance and at the direction of his superiors to achieve a more perfect society.

"So, how's it going?" Roman asked.

"Eh, the usual. I'm hungry." Peter handed over the ration book. The Vogels received first-class rations, a rarity even in their well-to-do neighborhood, and their ration book was appropriately impressive.

"The usual?" Roman asked as he paged through the leatherbound book to remove the requisite number of coupons.

"What else?" Peter grunted.

Roman looked behind himself to see if any of his bosses were nearby. "If you wait a few minutes, we'll have some fresh out of the oven." It was an invitation to converse.

Peter glanced behind himself to be sure no police were around. "Sure. How are things?"

"Oh, not much new. We got a new worker about three days ago. I've been showing him the ropes. How are things there? Have you asked Frau Vogel about your rations?"

"Yeah. I pointed out to her that they were running low and it wasn't my fault since I had come into the house before the first of the month."

"And?"

"And she said it'd do me some good to learn some self-discipline."

"Ouch! She's a hard case. Do they keep the food locked up there?"

"Yeah." Peter glanced behind himself again, then said in a low voice, "Once I get the right sort of tool, I'll solve that problem."

"Don't you think they'll notice?" Roman asked, quite concerned.

"If I were to take what I wanted, definitely. Frau Vogel's not the trusting sort. You're right, I won't be able to abscond with much, but even a little will help. I could really use some fresh food!"

"Yeah, you look like hell." Roman brought his hand out from under the counter and keeping it cupped over something reached forward. Peter pressed his hand around the offered roll and shoved it immediately into his mouth. As he struggled to chew it, Roman explained, "There's always some clumsy clod who drops a tray here. We take it in turns, on account of the punishment."

"Thanks," Peter murmured, trying not to spit food as he spoke. He swallowed the last of the bread and added, "My mother would have been appalled to see me wolf down food like this."

"I thought you were an orphan."

"Oh, yeah. Whatever."

"So, you're still settling in there?" Roman asked, indicating that he had no interest in prying.

Peter sputtered. "Ach, it's just nonstop shit: Do this, do that, why haven't you done such and such, why can't you read our minds!" he whined in imitation. "The kids, too. They all think I'm their personal slave."

"How many of the kids are at home now?"

"Five. Uwe and Geerd are off to the military. I've not even met them. The oldest one at home is Horst. He's the worst of the lot."

"Is he the tall, blond kid?"

"Yeah, skinny as a rail, pale blond, pale blue eyes. He's only sixteen, I think, but he already wants me to use *Sie* with him."

"And he uses *du* with you?"

"Of course! He's sure he's destined for leadership. Too bad he's as thick as a brick, dumber than his father even."

Roman laughed. "I've heard Herr Vogel is quite sharp."

Peter screwed up his face in thought. "You know, I really can't tell. Sometimes he seems reasonably bright, and at other times . . . Well, maybe it's just that he's so brainwashed."

"I've also heard he can be quite violent."

"You're not the first person to tell me that." Peter sighed. "Certainly the children are scared of him. They seem to use me as a buffer. Lucky me."

"Well, be careful."

Peter began to say something, but he stopped as he saw Roman's boss approaching.

"What the hell are you doing?" the boss demanded.

"I was waiting to give our valued customers a fresh batch of rolls, *mein Herr*," Roman replied crisply.

"All our rolls are fresh!" the baker snarled. "Fill his order now!"

Out of sight of his boss, Roman made a slight face and packed a bag of rolls and croissants. "The freshest for our most valued family," he said with a wink as he handed the bag over.

Peter nodded his farewell and headed back to the house. He started to head down the pedestrian path, but he spotted an older couple walking along, heading toward the duck pond. They were exactly the stodgy, pious sort who would fuss about his presence, and he decided to walk back along the road to avoid the possibility of trouble.

Traffic was beginning to pick up. The pavement along the street's edge was easily wide enough for two people, but as a businessman approached from the opposite direction, Peter was obliged by law to step into the gutter to let the man pass; so, he stood among the wet and decaying leaves and waited rather than walk on through the mud. They studiously avoided looking at each other—the man with his head held high and his gaze fixed forward, Peter with his attention focused on something on the other side of the road, his eyes lowered enough so as not to incite trouble but not so low as to make him feel cowed: it was a delicate balance, a compromise contrived to preserve his sanity. He had to make a point of not actually noticing the man, for if he did, he was obliged to greet him with a sign of respect—a simple bow of the head, a touch on the forehead, would do it. It was an old-fashioned gesture of courtesy, a remnant of tipping one's hat, but the element of coercion had replaced all pretense of civility, and he loathed the gesture with his entire being and did whatever he could to avoid performing what was to him a thoroughly sinister ritual.

When the man had passed, Peter stepped back onto the pavement, pointedly wiping his feet as he did so. Before he took a step, a patrol of three young guards approached. They demanded to see his papers and managed to spend nearly five minutes inspecting them. First they thumbed through his identity papers, finally satisfying themselves that those were in order, then they inspected his pass.

He carried the same pass each day on his trip to the bakery. It allowed him freedom of movement during certain morning hours within the administrative district. The exact boundaries of the district had never been clarified, but he knew that the local bakery and shops were within the borders. Judging from what he knew about the administration of local government, he guessed he could wander about two kilometers before violating the confines of his invisible prison. In any case, he was, he knew, well within those boundaries and he did not expect trouble from the youths on account of his papers; nevertheless, he felt a growing nausea as he stood with his head and eyes lowered.

Finally, they decided all was in order. He walked on rapidly. When he got back to the house, he set down the documents and went into the kitchen to put on the kettle. He arranged the rolls nicely in a basket, dumping the crumbs into his hand so that he could eat them, then he set the table and prepared the coffeepot using the exactly measured amount that Frau Vogel allowed him to put out the night before. He turned off the kettle just as the water boiled so that it would be nice and hot and ready to boil when he needed it later, checked the time, and headed toward the stairs.

At the base of the steps he hesitated. This was the worst part of the day and it took some effort of will for him to force himself through the routine. Finally, he compelled himself to ascend and approach the master-bedroom door. He knocked lightly and the sleepy voice of Frau Vogel told him he could come in.

He entered and greeted the two of them as cheerfully as he could manage using the order he had determined was essential: Herr Vogel first, then Frau Vogel. Herr Vogel did not even reply; Frau Vogel grunted something about the worklist for the day. He ignored her and opened the drapes, then went into the bathroom and quickly whisked out the tub, cleaned the toilet, arranged the towels, and started the water for a bath. "Shall I open the window a bit for *meine Gnädige?*" he asked as he returned to the bedroom.

"Is it cold out?" Frau Vogel replied, sitting up in bed.

He carried her robe over to her and helped her into it as she stood. "It will be warm soon."

"But is it cold now?" she asked impatiently.

That was a matter of opinion, he thought, but he did not dare say that. Instead he replied, "No, *gnädige Frau.*"

"Then open it."

He opened the window and returned to check the bath. Frau Vogel usually preferred to bathe in private, and as she shut the bathroom door, he went about using the time wisely, preparing the clothing she had indicated that she wanted laid out and making his rounds of the children's rooms, rousing them and opening their blinds.

The youngest, a shy little girl of five named Gisela, asked for a glass of water and wanted him to stay with her as she sat up in bed and drank it. She told him that she had had bad dreams, and she held his hand tightly as he stooped down next to her. When she had finished, he kissed her forehead and told her it was time to get up and so she did not need to worry about her dreams anymore, then he rushed back to Frau Vogel's side.

Once he had finished helping Frau Vogel, he returned to the bathroom to clean it and begin Herr Vogel's bath. Herr Vogel had drunk too much the night before and was truly averse to getting up. Peter tried several times to wake him with quiet words, finally resorting to gently shaking his shoulder.

Herr Vogel opened one eye and looked up at him. "Remove your hand from me this instant," he said threateningly.

"Sorry, *mein Herr.* Your bath is ready."

The routine was repeated except that he had to attend to Herr Vogel as he bathed, shaved, and otherwise prepared himself. Peter was allowed only a brief respite to go to Herr Vogel's closet and fetch the clothing needed for that morning. Herr Vogel called out to him from the bathroom like an admiral aboard a great ship instructing him on each piece of clothing as he made the bed, searched through the closet and drawers, and laid out the suit on the bed as instructed.

When Herr Vogel emerged, he surveyed the clothing with a scowl. "I said the *dark* brown tie."

"That isn't it?" Peter asked as he gestured toward the tie.

Without answering, Herr Vogel pointed imperiously toward his belt.

Cursing his own stupidity, Peter reached for the belt. He carefully folded it in two and handed it to Herr Vogel so he would be inclined to grab the end with the buckle. Peter stared at the floor and stood stock-still then, knowing it would be quicker that way. About twice a week, he thought, as Herr Vogel swung the belt into his upper arm. His eyes squeezed shut against the sharp pain. The belt was swung at him a few more times: his head, his neck, his arm again. Suddenly, Herr Vogel flung the belt to the floor. Peter opened his eyes, contemplated it, then stooped down and picked it up. He held it briefly before he could bring himself to offer it back to Herr Vogel.

"Get the correct tie," Herr Vogel commanded, neglecting to accept the belt.

Peter thanked him, set the belt on the bed, and went to the closet to locate the tie.

Once Herr Vogel was satisfactorily dressed, Peter left him to return to the kitchen. Frau Vogel was already there; she unlocked the pantry and directed him to bring out the usual items. It was nearly always the same, but she insisted on the ceremony of directing him. As he reemerged with the desired items, the pantry door closed behind him with a reassuring click. Frau Vogel nodded her approval and went into the dining room to join her family as he stocked the table with the jams and butter and the cheeses and sausages, then went back to get the coffee as the family began their morning meal.

After breakfast was served, Herr Vogel left for work and the children were sent to their various schools. Peter cleared the dishes, prepared Frau Vogel a cup of tea, then returned upstairs to clean the bathrooms, make the beds, and pick up after the children. The first room he tackled was Horst's. It was, actually, quite clean, but the military precision upon which Horst insisted meant that his room involved the most work of all. Peter made the bed to the required specifications, picked up the dirty boots that had been left out for him to polish, and made a mental note to return and repair the frayed drapery cord that had been pointed out to him earlier. He then went to Ulrike's room; she was the eldest daughter, a quiet, studious girl of nearly fifteen. He made her bed, tidied her books and papers, swept and dusted, and cleaned the hair out of her brush. He looked at the brittle, damaged strands and felt rather sorry for the poor girl—not even fifteen and she felt obliged to bleach her hair to a horribly unnatural whitish blond. Ah, the price of Aryan blood!

He then went up the flight of stairs to the two bedrooms that were on the second floor. The youngest son, Rudi, had one of them. His room was complete pandemonium, and as Peter picked up the endless stacks of debris, he wondered if Rudi's chaos was a deliberate signal of contempt or just typical for an undisciplined seven-year-old. The other room was shared by little Gisela and her twelve-year-old sister, Teresa. Teresa was clearly the brightest of the children and he liked her the best. She was loud and self-confident and friendly. She joked with and teased him and stuck her tongue out at her mother's back when chided for doing so. There was not much work to do in their room, and he finished quickly and headed back downstairs before Frau Vogel grew upset at his interminable absence.

Not surprisingly, Frau Vogel managed to keep him busy with an endless series of tasks well into the afternoon. When it was time for Rudi and Gisela to return from their school, he was sent to pick them up with explicit instructions to take them to the park so that they would not be underfoot at home.

He met them at the school gate. Gisela ran to him, but Rudi ignored him and walked toward his home.

"Your mother wants you to go to the park," he explained as he grabbed Rudi's arm and tried to change his direction.

"I don't have to listen to you!" Rudi spat in reply.

"I like the park!" Gisela enthused.

Peter pulled the boy, perhaps a little more forcefully than was advisable. "Your mother wants you to go to the park. I'll give you something when you get there."

Rudi relented and changed direction. "Did you bring us a snack?"

Peter nodded. "Yes. Something for you and your sister."

Rudi giggled. "None for you!"

"No, nothing for me," he agreed tiredly.

After they had their snack, the children finally settled into playing without fighting or making any other sort of trouble, and Peter took a moment to catch his breath from the day's endeavors. He was hungry and he was tired. He looked longingly at the park benches, but they were forbidden to him and he was already pushing the limits of disrespect by leaning against a tree to relax as he watched the children.

Rudi began showing off on the climbing frame and was in his element with the other children. Gisela, as usual, was alone. She motioned to Peter to come and push her on the swings, and he ungrudgingly obliged.

As he pushed Gisela on the swing, the happy shouts of the other children melted into an undifferentiated confusion of his past. The raucous noise of boys playing football in the street, his name being called out as they invited him to join them. "No," he yelled back at his friends, "I'm carrying groceries for my grandmother!"

"You can join them, Niklaus," he heard his grandmother's voice saying. "I'll carry the sacks up to my flat."

"No, Nanna," he had replied with the earnestness of a nine-year-old. "I'll carry them. You wait here while I take these, and then I'll come back for the rest."

When he had carried everything in for her and put the groceries away, he had not left to join the game, rather he had put on a phonograph record and sat on the floor with his head on his knees listening to the old, scratchy songs.

"Did your mother say you could stay the night?" his grandmother had asked. He had nodded.

"What's wrong, dear?" she had asked. "Why are you crying?"

He had looked up at her, embarrassed that she had noticed. "They want to send me away," he had answered, "to some horrible boarding school for German boys!"

"It's supposed to be a good school," his grandmother had explained.

"Then why doesn't my brother have to go? Why don't they send Erich, he'd love to go!"

"I know. They wanted him to, but your mother told me it was your scores that stood out. You're the bright one, you did so well on your school exams, the private school agreed to take you."

"I don't want to go!"

"They've already spent a lot of money buying a place there for you. You should take advantage of it. Your parents just want what's best for you, dear."

"You don't think it's for the best!"

"No, I don't," his grandmother admitted. "We're *Nichtdeutsch* and no amount of collaborating is going to change that. As they say, the English are *Gemischt*, we've polluted our blood with mixing. We'll always be treated as second-class."

"They want me to speak German, they want me to be one of them!" He had tossed his head in the direction of Gestapo headquarters in a contemptuous reference to the Nazi administration of London.

"Your mother and your father think you'll have the best future that way. Look at your father, he's managed a good job in government."

"Do you like what he does?" he had asked her, knowing full well the answer.

"You know I don't. You know your grandfather died fighting these bastards, you know what I think of them." But then she gestured around the pathetic little one-room flat she rented. "But look at this. I'm an old woman with no future, with grown children. I don't have to live with this for much longer. You do. Maybe you should try to make your way in their world."

He had shaken his head vehemently. "It's all because Anna died in that epidemic. Mum thinks I brought it into the house and so she wants to send me away!"

"No, no, it's not that. She's worried by how badly you took Anna's death. She knows how special your little sister was to you. She worries about you, honey, about the way you speak, about the children you play with. She thinks you're in a street gang, and she wants you out of this neighborhood before you get into bad trouble. She cares about you, she really does."

"I don't care. I don't want to go and I won't!"

"You won't have any choice. Try, dear. Just try to fit in," she had advised.

She was right, he had not had any choice. When he was sent away to school, his instinct for survival, his youth, his loneliness, allowed him to be swayed. He tried to fit in. He was an excellent student; gifted and motivated, he excelled in everything except modern history, where rather than write essays containing the lies he was taught, he left page after page blank on his exams. One or two teachers even said he could make something of himself if only he were not so defiant, and they deplored that such a fine mind, especially in science and mathematics, was essentially wasted. But it was with the other students that he really wanted to belong. He longed to have friends he could talk to and trust. Several other English boys were at the school, but they wanted nothing to do with him or each other—they wanted to forget their common ancestry and blend into the ruling elite. And so did he. He erased the last vestiges of an accent, he joined the sports teams, he struggled to be like the others: anything to assuage his awful loneliness. But they would have none of it: to them he was a born traitor and could never be anything more. He was excluded by birth from their ruling class, and they used every opportunity possible to remind him of it.

Near the end of his third year at the school, his brother, Erich, attained the fateful age of sixteen and dutifully went off to serve in the labor draft. It was a relief to have that Nazi zealot out of his life, but it was the only positive change that year. As he turned twelve, he moved from being one of the eldest in the lower school to one of the youngest in the upper school, and the bullying intensified accordingly. During that year his grandmother died and he lost the only person in the world he trusted. By the end of the school year, he was exhausted by the harassment and the continuous need to defend his place in the ridiculous pecking order. He came home for the summer holiday worn and despairing. Only with the greatest effort of will and the most dire threats from his father was he able to drag himself back to begin his second year at the upper school. It was no better. When he visited home for a short break, he remained silent and depressed, too tired even to yell at his parents about it; he simply wondered aloud as he slumped into an armchair what they could possibly have intended by sending him into such a hell. His mother came over to him and sat on the arm of the chair and stroked his hair, saying, "It's all right, it will be all right, everything will be okay, trust me."

He pulled angrily away; forcing himself not to shout, he said, "I *don't* trust you!"

She answered softly, "Everything has a reason. I know how much you're hurt." There was pain in her voice as she added, "Be patient. Trust us."

All he could say was "I don't."

The incident was perfectly clear in his mind. He had replayed it so many times trying to work out what she had meant. He had never found out. He had stormed out of the flat and gone for a long walk. After he had cooled down a bit, he had walked back home. Where else could he go? As he had turned the corner to his street, he had seen the Gestapo van. He stood horrified, watching from a distance as his parents were thrown into the back. He fled then. He never learned what happened to them. Years of inquiries through numerous sources had turned up nothing. They had simply disappeared like so many others into *Nacht und Nebel,* into the night and fog.

Their disappearance left him wondering to this day if they had planned to work him into the system for some purpose other than what they had told him. Had they left him in ignorance to protect him until he was old enough to join a conspiracy? Or had his mother's words simply meant that in the end he would see that collaborating would be for the best? The pain of their abrupt separation was only made worse by his unanswered questions. After all these years, he still wondered.

"It's too high!" Gisela wailed, bringing him sharply back to the present. "It's too much!"

He brought the swing rapidly under control. "I'm sorry, little one." He glanced around to see if Rudi had overheard them, but fortunately he was involved in playing a war game. "I'm sorry. Are you all right?"

Gisela shook her head. "I'm going to tell Mama."

"Please don't," he breathed. "I said I was sorry."

"You scared me. You're a bad man!"

"I know," he sighed. "I'm sorry. I'm really, really sorry. It was an accident. We all make mistakes, don't we?"

"The Führer doesn't!" Gisela corrected.

"No, the Führer doesn't make mistakes. I meant everybody else does."

"I want to climb the castle!" Gisela said, pointing toward the pile of rocks that formed the centerpiece of the park. Relieved, Peter took her hand and led her to them. He helped her climb up and together they stood triumphantly at the top.

"I'm a princess!" Gisela pointed regally toward the children playing below. "And those are all my slaves!"

He followed her gesture with his eyes and then surveyed the surrounding area. The park was on a hill, and in the valley around were a series of residential areas, each similar to his own in their arrangement around a small shopping area, but each decreasing in wealth. The last of these, almost invisible on the horizon, was almost shabby—the houses were small, single-story, flat-roofed dwellings of concrete block packed in one against the other.

To his right a thick yellow smog hung low in the sky, shrouding most of the buildings in a permanent haze. The grimy houses of that region gave way to the high, gray walls of an industrial park. Behind the walls, he knew, were the barracks of workers and the factories that kept the Reich supplied with such necessities as tractors and bombs. He had often wondered as a child if his parents had ended their days behind such walls. Or had they simply been killed? He felt a painful jab of conscience as he thought back to the day he had stood and watched them being taken away. How could he have just stood there? Paralyzed with fear, he had not tried to fight for their lives or follow the van or even ask the neighbors afterward what they knew. Instead he had fled back the way he had come. He had run away without looking back.

Lost and alone, he had stopped running far from home, gasping for breath, and realized that he had nowhere to go. He remembered standing under a bridge over the Temms with the fetid water lapping quietly against the crumbling concrete base as he had sobbed silently, too frightened to cry aloud. He had lived rough for days, sheltering among piles of garbage in dark alleys—places where even the patrols did not bother to look, stealing what food he could. Every day he returned to his neighborhood and observed his parents' flat, but there was no sign of life. He checked the hostage lists and the lists of executed prisoners, but again, nothing. He wandered as if haunted from prison to prison, from one courtroom to the next, searching for a sign of what had happened, but there was no trace of them.

After a number of days, he returned to watch his home and saw shadows moving behind the curtains. He entered the housing estate and climbed the stairs to the sixth floor. When he put his ear against the door of the flat, he heard the sounds of normal living. Someone else had moved in. The state had sold the property, and probably everything inside as well. For the first time he had an idea of how alone and dispossessed he really was.

Gisela was tugging at his hand. "I want to go home."

He glanced at the sky and nodded. "Okay, we've been out long enough."

He herded the children home and took up where he had left off on his endless list of jobs. As dinnertime approached, he was called into the kitchen to chop vegetables and help Frau Vogel prepare the dinner. Herr Vogel arrived home around half past six, and Peter was expected to be at the door to open it for him. It was a rather awkward time as he could not stray far from his post as doorman and yet was expected to see to everyone else's needs as they arrived home and settled in for the evening. Herr Vogel finally arrived, and after Peter had taken his coat and hat, lit his cigarette, and served him a drink, Peter went into the dining room and laid the table, then into the kitchen to finish the meal preparation.

He served the evening meal to his betters, cleaned up the dishes, served them their drinks, and then set about finishing some of his chores from earlier in the day. Herr and Frau Vogel settled down in front of the television, the children dispersed to their rooms, and after everything had grown quiet, he crept into the cellar and surveyed his abject stash of food. He was so unbelievably hungry!

He grabbed a limp quarter cabbage and began chopping it up. It looked fairly tainted, so he decided to boil it in water and swore quietly when he realized he had run out of salt. Unsalted, half-rotted, boiled cabbage! God, he was hungry!

"Peter!" Frau Vogel's voice penetrated into the depths of the cellar.

He turned off the electric coil and headed up the stairs. Waterlogged, unsalted, half-rotted, *half*-boiled cabbage, he corrected. Great.

He found her in the dining room. "Yes, *gnä' Frau?*"

"Oh, for heaven's sake! Can't you ever say that correctly!"

"My apologies, *gnädige Frau*," he responded, carefully pronouncing each syllable of her title.

"Your sleeves are rolled up again. How many times do I have to tell you, it's untidy!"

He rolled his sleeves down and apologized.

"And your collar button!" she added angrily.

He buttoned the top buttons of his shirt and apologized again.

"What's with these windows?" Frau Vogel asked, pointing at the dining room windows.

"*Gnädige Frau?*" he answered, unable even to guess what she meant.

She walked right up to him and hit him. "Don't act stupid."

"I'm sorry, *gnädige Frau*," he said through gritted teeth, "but I really don't understand what you want. I cleaned them yesterday."

Frau Vogel pointed at one of them. "The blind doesn't open right!"

"I know, *gnädige Frau*." he quickly took a small step back as he saw Frau Vogel raise her hand. "Wait, wait!" he pleaded, then explained hurriedly, "I plan to repair it, but it's a major job—the mechanism is jammed and I have to take the window apart."

Frau Vogel relented. "Can you do that?" she asked, suddenly interested.

"I think so. I'll need some tools."

"All right, you can use Herr Vogel's. Do it tomorrow."

He nodded. "Yes, *Gnädigste*. Is that all?"

"For now," she said, and left the room. He rolled up his sleeves and unbuttoned the top buttons of his shirt en route back to the cellar. Just another three or four hours, he thought wearily, then he could climb into his bed in the attic and go to sleep for a few hours until it began all over again.

25

"**A**RE YOU ABSOLUTELY SURE no one knows you're here?" Stefi asked yet again as she peered out the hotel room window to the street below. "My father would kill me if he found out."

"Don't worry, sweetpea, I would never tell a soul," Til whispered as he nuzzled her ear. "After all, it's not *you* your father would kill if he found out about us. Besides, my wife would certainly do me in even if your father didn't!"

Stefi sighed. "Good," she purred. Til began kissing the back of her neck and she wriggled with pleasure. "Ooh, that feels good!" He gently undid the little button at the top of her blouse, then the next, then the one after that. He pulled her blouse back a bit and kissed her shoulder, while letting his hand drift seductively downward under the fabric.

Stefi wriggled her shoulders and stepped out of his grasp. "Would you like a drink?" she asked, walking over to the bottle and glasses that she had brought along and set on a bedside table. She uncapped the bottle, poured herself a drink, and sat down on the bed without touching the glass.

Til sat down in the armchair and indulgently asked, "Is this your first time?"

"Would you think less of me if I said it wasn't?"

Til shook his head. "No, I wouldn't. You're young, but very attractive. I imagine you've had to fight the boys off for years now."

"Well, it is."

"It is? The first time?"

Stefi nodded. "You're right about the boys, but I haven't liked any of them. I like men. Kind, gentle, intelligent men, like you."

Til smiled weakly at the compliment.

"Strong, handsome, sexy," she added dreamily, as if reading Til's thoughts, or his face. "You're all those things. A real man, not some boy."

Til's smile broadened. "This is the third time we've gotten together."

Stefi glanced guiltily at the bed, "I know, I'm sorry. I . . ."

Til followed her glance. "Oh, I didn't mean that! Look, if you're not ready for that, don't worry. We can just chat, cuddle a bit, who knows. I like you, Stefi, I really do. This isn't just some gambit for me to get a cheap thrill, I think we have something special going for us."

"I like you too, Til," she said almost sadly. "I really do."

"Why the long face then?"

"Oh, no reason," she answered, picking her mood up perceptibly. "Girls get this way when it's a special moment."

Til got up from the chair and sat next to her on the bed. He put a fatherly arm around her shoulder, then leaned in and brushed his face against her hair. Stefi lowered her head as if deep in thought or undecided about something. Til placed his hand under her chin and gently lifted it so that she was looking into his eyes. "You are very, very beautiful," he whispered.

They held each other's eyes for a moment and then slowly their lips came together in a long and passionate kiss.

Til stared up at the ceiling and smiled with pleasure. So easy, it had been so easy to assuage her fears, and despite her claim to be inexperienced, she was very good in bed—almost as if she were going out of her way to please him, perhaps even neglecting her own pleasure. That thing she did with her mouth . . . Intuition, she had said. "Do you like it?" she had innocently asked. Did he like it? Wow! Either the girl had had a really good teacher or she had phenomenal intuition.

Stefi stirred and awoke from her brief nap. She turned toward Til and smiled seductively. "Oh, that was marvelous," she cooed. She pulled herself closer to him and wrapped her body around his.

He stroked her hair and held her close. "I love you." As soon as he said it, he wished he hadn't.

Stefi pulled her face away so she could look at him. "You don't have to say that, Til. I love you, but I know you have a family and things. It's enough that you want to be with me now and then. Don't love me, it will just complicate everything."

She climbed out of bed and went to the bathroom. When she emerged, she had washed and dressed, so he decided to do likewise. As he came out of the bathroom, she handed him a drink. "A toast," she said, "to a beautiful, uncomplicated relationship."

"You are amazingly understanding." Til drank the shot of whiskey. He made a face at the taste but decided not to comment on her youthful ignorance of good liquor.

"I know," Stefi agreed. Again she seemed quite sad.

"What's the matter, sweetpea? Didn't you enjoy your first time?"

"Oh, I did. That's the problem. I've got to go now and I don't want to."

He noticed there were tears in her eyes. "It'll be okay. We'll get together again, soon."

"Will you stay here, like you promised? If anyone sees me leave, I don't want them to link me and you. It would be disastrous." Stefi picked up the glasses and went into the bathroom to wash them.

"Your father and mother are out of town, honey," Til called out to her. "Who's going to see you?"

"Will you stay?" she insisted as she tucked away the glasses and the bottle in her bag.

"Of course, I promised. I even brought a book. See? I'll stay an hour before I go back to work, and I'll come and check out tomorrow morning. Just like I promised."

The following morning, when Richard returned to work, he noticed Til was not in yet. As he sat at his desk and began reading his mail, the secretary stepped into his office.

"Excuse me, Herr Traugutt."

"Yes?" he asked, still busy perusing a letter.

"It's about Til."

Something in the secretary's voice made Richard look up. "What's the matter, what is it?"

"He's had a heart attack."

"A heart attack? Where is he, is he okay?"

"No, he's dead."

"Dead? A heart attack? He's so young!" Richard exclaimed, truly shocked. "How did it happen? Where?"

"He was found in a hotel room, *mein Herr*. The police think he must have gone in there with a prostitute or a mistress, but nobody saw the woman and she wasn't there when he was found. She probably panicked and left."

"Probably."

"The odd thing was, he was fully dressed, lying on the bed, with a book."

"Hmm. That is odd. Did they look for fingerprints?"

"No sir. The death was not suspicious. Should I send an order down for them to look?"

Richard shook his head. "No, there's no point causing his widow any further grief. The most we'd locate is a woman she'd rather not know about."

"Is there anything I can get you, Herr Traugutt?" the secretary asked, respectful of Richard's obvious distress.

"His family doesn't have a phone, do they?"

"No, *mein Herr*."

"Ach, I'll visit later. Could you send my condolences, some flowers or something?"

"I've already done that, Herr Traugutt." The secretary came forward and handed him a note. "Here's what your card said."

Richard read the brief message. "Thank you." He sighed heavily. "I think I'd just like to be alone for a few minutes."

The secretary nodded sympathetically and left.

Richard rested his chin on his fists and stared at the desk. He remained that way, silent and unmoving, a long time.

26

"AND DID THOSE FEET in ancient time, walk upon England's mountains green?" His hands worked deftly in the pungent earth as he sang softly under his breath. Even though he was outside and she was not, he kept his voice low so that Frau Vogel, or rather Elspeth, would not overhear him singing in English. She did not understand the language and was therefore sure to assume there was something obscene or inappropriate in the words.

The song, the twittering of the birds, the warm, June sunshine on his back, all conspired to make him think he was elsewhere—perhaps England's mountains green, wherever they might be. He glanced down at his left wrist to find out the time and was vaguely surprised that no watch was there. Shaking his head at his idiotic lapse of memory, he squinted up at the sun and decided it was time to leave the virtual freedom of the yard and return to the prison of the house to prepare the coffee for Elspeth's coffee circle. As was a tradition among German ladies of her class, she and a small circle of friends met regularly at each other's house to drink coffee, eat cake, and discuss household affairs and gossip. This week, it was Elspeth's turn to be hostess and was the second time that Peter would serve them.

He had accomplished much in the intervening weeks. He had settled into a routine that was acceptable to Elspeth: he did many tasks without explicit instructions and even took over the scheduling of some of his work. In particular, he learned about gardening simply by observing the actions of the next-door neighbor and, when possible, asking him questions surreptitiously over the fence.

Today, at the neighbor's instigation, he had decided to thin the flower beds, removing the dead and dying flowers and even cutting a few of the full blooms to make way for the coming blossoms. The small pile of flowers lay in the sun, ready to be discarded. On an impulse, he picked out the best flowers before discarding the pile and brought them indoors. He intended to place them in a vase somewhere discreet to cheer up the house, but as he came in the back door, Elspeth was already in the kitchen and observed them in his hand.

"What's that?" she asked accusingly.

"Flowers, *gnä' Frau.*" Aware that such an answer was sure to be interpreted as sarcasm, he added quickly, "For you," as he extended them toward her. He was well aware that she was unlikely to view the gesture favorably. He expected anything from a neutral shrug to indignation that he should be so insolent as to present *her* flowers as though they were *his* to present.

He was shocked by her response. "Flowers? For me?" She sounded almost coquettish. "Oh, how sweet! I'll put them in a vase. How lovely. Yes, yes." She took the bunch and went to fetch a vase herself, mumbling, "Flowers. For me."

Later, during her coffee klatch, she even pointed out the vase and the source of the flowers to her friends.

"Oh, my dear Frau Vogel! How cute!" her friend, Frau Widerhausen, acknowledged agreeably.

"He *is* handsome," Frau Meissner said unexpectedly and to no one in particular.

None of the others seemed to have heard her as Frau Schindler said almost simultaneously, "I don't know, my dear, I don't think it's wise."

"Nonsense, my dear Frau Schindler, there's no harm in it."

"You shouldn't encourage such behavior," Frau Schindler insisted dictatorially. Though she was probably the youngest of the group, and quite pretty as well, she outranked them all by virtue of her much older and very powerful husband.

"What behavior?" Frau Widerhausen asked.

"Familiar behavior."

"Nonsense. He was simply pruning the flower bed."

"Still, it's the implication."

"What implication?" Frau Widerhausen persisted.

"Of intimacy," Frau Schindler replied ominously.

"Intimacy! Oh, my dear Frau Schindler, you do read too much into things. It was just a nice gesture," Elspeth retorted.

"See, it already has you thinking wrongly," Frau Schindler trumpeted.

"What's wrong with niceness?" Elspeth asked innocently.

"Next he'll be expecting you to reciprocate, and then where will discipline be?"

"Our discipline is very strict here," Elspeth protested.

"No, it isn't," Frau Schindler asserted. "The very last time I was here, I heard him humming to himself."

"No! Not in front of you?" Elspeth asked, rather afraid of the answer.

"No, in the garden. Nevertheless, my dear, you never know what words go with those tunes! They sing rude songs, with words like Hitler had only one big . . . well, you know," Frau Schindler explained, suddenly flustered. She tapped her chest to calm herself and continued solemnly, "He must keep silent. It's the only way to retain order!"

Frau Vogel seemed ready to debate this point as well, but then considered better of it. "Well, my dear Frau Schindler, you are so much wiser in the ways of the world. You must be right. I'll have a word with him about it later—make sure he understands that it was inappropriate. Yes. Yes, I see now—you're quite right. Yes, I'll speak to him later. Firmly. Yes." Elspeth would probably have continued to mutter in this vein if Frau Meissner had not indicated, with a frown of disappointment, that the coffeepot was empty.

Peter was called to refill it, and after counting down an appropriate delay, he launched himself from his eavesdropping position near the door and came into the room. He threw an evaluative glance at Frau Meissner. So, she thought he was handsome, eh? Then he risked glaring briefly at Frau Schindler and finally completed his act with a deferential nod toward Frau Vogel as he removed the empty coffeepot.

Despite Frau Schindler's dire warnings, Frau Vogel never did bother to speak to him about the flowers; instead, once the women had been hustled out the door, she rushed to the shops with Peter in tow to try to buy something special for her husband. "He's feeling a bit stressed of late," she intimated as they walked along, apparently forgetting that this was exactly the sort of thing Frau Schindler had warned against. "Everything is changing at his work, and he just doesn't know who's going to come out on top."

Elspeth stopped by the statue of Hitler and stared at it as if in adoring sorrow.

"If only I could handle things directly," she sighed, "it would be so much easier." Peter remained silent a respectful distance behind her. He also looked at the statue as if contemplating the world's great loss. "Well, I guess we should get moving. The last thing we need is for my husband to get home before us. Not in his present mood!"

They did some shopping and then went to the butcher shop, where Elspeth picked her way through the expensive, unrationed sausages hoping to find something that Karl liked so that she could surprise him and conceivably soothe him for yet another evening. Peter waited patiently, unable to indulge in any higher-level thinking as he was overwhelmed by the pungent smell of the meat. Perhaps the butcher noticed how he gazed hungrily at the nearby links, for he interrupted his work to approach Frau Vogel and ask if he could provide her with anything specific. She had been so distracted by her thoughts that she looked up vaguely surprised by his question. As she began to answer, she noticed the clock on the wall and gasped, "That can't be the time!"

The butcher turned to look at the clock, then consulted his watch. "Yes, that clock is correct, *gnädige Frau.*"

"Oh, I have to go!" She rushed out the door. Peter followed and almost stumbled over her as she came to a dead stop only steps outside the shop. He heard her swear quietly under her breath. The cause of her frustration was obvious: the square had temporarily been closed due to a bomb scare, and the only way to leave or enter was by waiting in a queue to go through a security check.

There were only two official exits and the queues at both were long. Frau Vogel hesitated a moment before choosing the slightly shorter queue. After only a few moments, she lost patience though, and telling Peter to wait in line, she approached the officer in command. Try as she might though, he would not look up from his work—he knew from experience that if he heard the plea of one rushed shopper, then he would immediately be inundated. Exasperated, Elspeth finally returned to her place in line, but she was not so easily defeated.

"Come with me," she said, and pulled Peter out of the queue and over to a barricade on the far side of the square. It was a simple police barrier blocking the gap between two buildings. On the far side of the narrow alley created by the two shops was a similar barrier.

They stood there and Elspeth glanced expectantly down the alley, but there was nothing to see. When a moment had passed and no one approached or seemed to notice her, she turned to Peter. "Go down the alley and get someone's attention from the other side."

"I can't do that!" he protested in utter astonishment.

"Nonsense! Don't be such a coward. Go!"

"Frau Vogel!"

"That's an order! Now go!" She pointed adamantly at the passage between the two buildings.

Well aware that he could be shot for what he was going to do, he handed her the packages he was carrying and ducked under the barrier. He walked down the alley, approached the far barrier, and looked across. "There's no one here," he stated, and turned to come back.

"Well, crawl underneath!" Elspeth ordered, waving him back away from her. "Get someone!"

He went back to the far barrier and glanced around. Still no one. Frau Vogel waved at him to go ahead, and reluctantly he lowered himself to the ground to clamber underneath.

"Hands up! What the hell do you think you're doing, boy?" a voice asked. Peter only had time to notice the rifle pointed at his face. He automatically placed his hands on his head as a pair of arms tugged at him, pulling him through to the other side.

"What do you think you're doing?"

"Following orders." Peter threw his head back down the alley. "She's the one you want to talk to."

He heard the private mutter a curse.

"What's up?" a sergeant asked as he approached the two of them.

"The lady there," the soldier explained, pointing down the alley to Frau Vogel as she waited haughtily.

"Check him out," the sergeant ordered, then moved the first barrier and went down the alley to open the path for Frau Vogel. She followed him down the passage, a look of regal annoyance on her face. The private finished frisking Peter, then checked the packages that Frau Vogel had brought with her. As he finished, he turned toward Frau Vogel expectantly.

"Just what do you think you are doing?" Frau Vogel asked as the young man reached toward her.

"I have to search everyone, *gnädige Frau*," he explained politely.

"Oh, no, you don't!"

"*Gnädige Frau*," the sergeant interrupted rather brusquely, "not only will you be searched, but I will have to write out a fine for the way you have attempted to violate a secured area."

"You will do nothing of the sort!" Elspeth snorted.

Peter watched with some amusement as Frau Vogel debated with the two men about their duty. Despite her rush, Elspeth was managing to turn a ten-second frisk into a major waste of time. Another security officer was brought over, the debate continued, the possibility of having a woman do the search was mooted and rejected, then finally the ranking officer was found and brought over.

"What's the problem, *gnädige Frau*?" the ranking officer asked.

"These rude young men want to touch me!" Elspeth huffed.

The ranking officer inspected her papers. He stiffened, then sheepishly returned her papers to her. "My humblest apologies, Frau Vogel. Of course there is no reason for you to be searched! Please accept our sincerest apologies." He bowed slightly and motioned for her to continue on her way. The security officers looked at him, utterly astounded.

Elspeth harrumphed and stormed off, but Peter lingered long enough to hear the ranking officer hiss at his men, "You idiots! Didn't you see who her husband is? God, I hope she didn't get my name." Peter laughed to himself, then hurried to catch up with Elspeth, or rather, the noble Frau Vogel.

When they reached the house, Karl was not home yet, so Frau Vogel ordered Peter to unpack the purchases and make her some tea, but before he could do either, they heard the slam of the car door. Karl usually took the train in to work since the center of Berlin was no place for his beloved car to sit virtually unattended, but recently he had preferred to drive in, perhaps hoping that the status symbol of his Russian-made Zil would impress anyone watching him during the current crisis.

Peter went to the door and opened it. His salutation and brief nod were met with a sullen stare. Obviously Karl was still suffering through the agony of not knowing whom to flatter at work.

"Shall I bring you a drink?" Peter asked as he handed Karl a cigarette from the box that was kept by the door and lit it with the crystal lighter that sat next to the box.

Karl sucked greedily on the cigarette, then blew the smoke back into Peter's face. As Peter blinked away the smoke, Karl smiled slightly, clearly relieved of some of his monumental burden of stress. "Yeah, bring some vodka. I'll be in my study."

Peter got the keys to the liquor cabinet from Elspeth, took Karl the drink, returned the keys, and then went into the sitting room to tackle the job he had delayed doing since early morning. Elspeth wanted the rug cleaned; not only that, she wanted it cleaned by hand because it was, as she put it, "so very valuable and so delicate." He had hoped to vacuum it while she was out, but the day had slipped by without his having had an opportunity, so he finally swallowed his pride, got down on his hands and knees, and picked lint off the carpet. It took ages. As his fingers worked through the fine wool, he thought of the hands that had woven the exquisite pattern. Small hands, probably. Probably a child, most likely a child who would never earn enough to do anything more than condemn his or her own child to work in an airless factory, weaving carpets. Elspeth was right, he thought, the carpet merited some care. Now, if only she'd be so enlightened about human beings!

"Now, I'm not an expert, but I thought we had a vacuum cleaner," Karl teased from the doorway.

Peter sat back on his heels and looked at Karl in exactly the manner he knew he wasn't supposed to. "*Meine gnädige Herrin* feels that this carpet is too easily damaged and too valuable and wants it cleaned by hand, *m'n'err*. Thus, I am cleaning it by hand."

"That's idiotic."

Peter bit his tongue and resumed working.

"Do that later, I have a job for you."

"I'll be done with this job in just two minutes, *m'n'err*," Peter answered as he worked a tiny dead bug out from one of the wool strands. Out of the corner of his eye he noticed Karl walk across the carpet toward him. Clearly he had angered Karl, and cursing his foolishness, he cringed expectantly.

However, Karl carefully stepped around him and over to the ashtray, where he took a few more puffs from his cigarette and then ground it out. Then, carefully lifting the cover off the ashtray, he casually flung the contents onto the rug.

Stunned, Peter could do little more than stare at him with his mouth open.

"Now you have more than two minutes' work, so the job will be worth returning to." Karl smiled. He looked almost happy, completely relieved of the day's worries. He walked back across the carpet, grinding the ashes in as he did so. He stopped next to Peter, a promise of violence in his stance. "I'm taking my car out tonight. I want it scrubbed inside and out. Now. Understood?"

"Immediately, *mein Herr*," Peter agreed as Karl walked out of the room. Peter stood, threw a resigned glance at the rug and the hours of work it now represented, then quickly left the room to carry out Karl's command.

The sleek black Zil was Karl's pride and joy. It was the same one Peter had been forced to ride in when he'd made his journey from the Reusches' and he had trouble looking at it without feeling a slight nausea. It was kept scrupulously clean at all times, but on certain days, Karl wanted it particularly shined and polished. Those were the days when he was going "out." Peter did not know where "out" was, but he suspected that Karl kept a mistress. It would certainly not be unusual, despite the Party's shrill insistence on family values; in fact, in some social circles, it seemed to be almost obligatory. Still, the outings were relatively infrequent; so either Elspeth had put her foot down about their frequency, or they were explained by something other than another woman.

In any case, it was left to Peter to make the car gleam. He was still polishing the chrome when he heard Karl bellow his name from inside the house. Exasperated, he threw down his cloth and went inside. Now what the hell does he want, he fumed silently as he asked politely, "*Mein Herr?*"

"It's time for our tea. Haven't you prepared it?"

Peter glanced at the clock as he apologized. He turned to go into the kitchen and almost ran into Elspeth entering the room. He apologized even as she asked, "Where's our tea?" and then, seeing the rug, exclaimed, "Aren't you done with this yet? My God, how long does it take you to do something?"

He ground his teeth and looked back at Karl to see if he would offer an explanation, but he was wrapped up in reading the Party newspaper. Peter apologized for the rug and turned to go to make the tea. Before he reached the door, Elspeth added, "And look at those damn windows! They're filthy! Do I have to tell you every single thing to do? Why can't you just take care of things! Why do I have to notice everything?"

He stopped in the doorway and held on to the frame. As he was apologizing yet again, he watched Ulrike come into the hall from outside. She kicked her shoes into a corner, dropped her coat on the floor, and tossed her hat toward a table, but missed; then she ran up the stairs. He pushed himself out the door, but before he reached the kitchen, he heard Horst yelling for him from his bedroom. He put on the kettle, then headed for the stairs. En route he picked up Ulrike's things and hung them in the closet, even as Horst yelled for him a third time.

Horst wanted his boots polished and another award sewn onto his uniform; Peter tromped down the steps with Horst's things, assured Elspeth that her tea was coming, and headed directly back to the kitchen. He set the things down and stood there for a moment, staring blindly out the kitchen window, waiting for the water to boil.

"No wonder you never get anything done," Elspeth chided angrily from the doorway, then added, "Fix the latch on the dining room window. It doesn't close right anymore."

It never had. It was one of those innumerable repairs that had apparently accumulated over the decades. "Yes, *gnä' Frau*," he replied, and added it to his mental list.

"The hall is muddy again."

"I noticed. I'll give it another swipe as soon as I get a chance, *gnä' Frau*."

Elspeth glanced downward and commented, "This floor needs to be swept as well."

"Of course, *gnä' Frau*."

"And the armchair in the sitting room—the arm is loose. I noticed it when Herr Schindler leaned against it the other night. Why haven't you fixed it?"

Though probably rhetorical, he answered the question anyway: "I didn't notice it." Surprisingly, it was the truth.

"Fix it today."

"I'll need to take it apart." Or at least get Karl's fat carcass out of it. Actually, Peter had no idea what needed doing, but it was best not to let Elspeth know that, otherwise she would probably try to direct him, and then he'd never be able to sort out what was wrong.

"Then do it tomorrow. I don't want you disturbing us."

"I'll need tools," he said, finally forcing his attention away from the window.

Elspeth clicked her tongue in exasperation. "All right, I'll get Herr Vogel to leave me the key to the tool cabinet." With that settled, she returned to her original reason for coming into the kitchen. "Now, why is the rug not done?"

He sighed. He knew if he told her the truth, she would have him punished for lying or lack of respect or something, so he simply shrugged. Elspeth took a step toward him, casting about for a likely weapon. He took half a step back but was otherwise resigned to whatever expression her anger would take. Elspeth stopped and looked around in confusion; there was nothing to hand! She snorted angrily, spun on her heel, and left the room. He stared at the empty space where she had been. He did not move. He felt a pressure in his head, behind his eyes. It felt like a dam beginning to burst. This was his life? This was his life. He squinted his eyes slightly, as if trying to focus on a distant object, but there was nothing to look at. The kettle shrieked, and mechanically he turned to pour the tea.

The next morning Roman listened to Peter's brief description of the idiotic behavior he had endured the previous day. "Ach, it's been the same throughout history, there's always some sort of nobility pushing us peasants around," Roman said.

"They're insane," Peter countered.

"Naw, he's just a bully."

"And she's a spoiled brat."

"Ach, she just wants someone to love her," Roman suggested humorously.

Peter snorted. "Well, it ain't gonna be me."

Roman laughed. "Better knock on wood when you say something like that."

Peter scanned around, then tapped his fist against the building. "Concrete will have to do."

Several other workers joined the queue, so with that their conversation had to end. Roman handed Peter the bag of rolls and advised, "Unpack it yourself."

Intrigued, Peter stopped outside the house and rummaged through the bag. In the bottom was a slender, sturdy piece of metal. He pulled out his treasure and grinned. It would be perfect! He silently thanked his friend, hid his new treasure, and entered the house.

The first job he tackled after breakfast was the armchair. It was the sort of work he preferred: Elspeth had no idea what needed to be done; so, if he managed to advertise the job as sufficiently complicated, she would leave him alone for quite a long time as long as he looked busy. He also had no idea what needed to be done, but that was neither here nor there. With a bit of patience and common sense, he knew he would be able to figure something out.

First he went to Karl's tool cabinet in the cellar and selected a few likely tools. Elspeth watched him do this so that she could be sure he did not steal anything. He was careful not to let her see him smile at the thought that he would now be able to pick the lock anytime he wanted. Besides the tools, hanging in orderly rows on their little racks, several pairs of handcuffs were in the cabinet. He felt a slight chill as his eyes settled on them, and the smile vanished from his face.

Elspeth duly noted what he decided to remove and grumbled, "Why so much? Don't think I'll lose track!"

"I'm not sure what I'll need, *gnä' Frau*. This will save me making trips up and down."

"Goodness, you're so lazy!"

"And it will prevent me from having to disturb *meine gnädige Herrin* unduly each time I realize I need something."

"Ah, well. Okay then."

They went up the stairs together, but then she left him alone. He located the loose arm, and after reaching down between the arm and the seat, he quickly decided that was the wrong approach. He turned the heavy chair upside down and carefully began removing the fabric that covered the bottom. It had been fixed to the wood with brass studs, and he removed each of them and set them aside in a little dish. Beneath the fabric were springs and upholstery material, padding and support struts.

It did not take much looking, or rather feeling, to locate the source of the problem. The arm was affixed to the main body of the chair with several heavy bolts—most of which had been stripped out of the wood by overuse.

He stood for a moment thinking about what he could do to remedy the problem. He could try to fill in the holes, but he doubted it would hold for long given the way both Karl and Herr Schindler threw their weight against the arm. And Ulrike had a habit of perching on it and pressing her legs against the arm opposite. Or he could use bigger bolts and hope they would hold in the gouged wood. But where would he get some? The ones in the chair were already quite large. It was in fact a rather well-made piece of furniture. Old, almost antique.

He thought about drilling new holes and moving the bolts, but the thought of explaining all that to Elspeth to get her permission and the necessary equipment was rather off-putting. He stared at the chair for a moment longer. Funny, he wasn't even allowed to sit in it. All of the furniture was off-limits to him. It meant that if he ever had a spare moment, there was nowhere he was legitimately allowed to rest. It really was quite ludicrous. Even more ridiculous was the con-straints this rule put on his performing simple tasks such as sewing the endless lit-tle honor badges that the children earned onto their uniforms or repairing some small household device. Sometimes, he simply waited until everyone was tucked up in bed to finish such jobs; then he could use a table and chair with impunity. Also, whenever they were all out of the house, he would throw himself into the armchair or onto the sofa just for the sake of enjoying the forbidden luxury, but those occasions were rare. His only determined and obvious use of their furniture was that he would use the step stool in the kitchen, mainly to eat his meals, even when Elspeth was in the house. If she came into the kitchen, he simply stood up immediately. Of course she noticed, and once or twice she had reminded him that it was not his chair, but she had never punished him for using it. At least not yet.

"Why aren't you doing anything?" Elspeth asked, checking up on him earlier than usual.

Deciding on his course of action, he explained, "Here's what I need to do, *gnä' Frau.*" He explained how he needed to put in an extra piece of wood along the arms to support the bolts and how he would have to dismantle the chair a bit further to reach all the relevant points.

"I don't see what you mean." Elspeth was, for once, perplexed rather than accusing.

"Here." He shoved both hands in and pulled the padding back to show her how the arm was connected farther up, under the cushion. As he pressed forcefully against the ancient upholstery, his fingers broke through an already existing tear in the fabric. The stuffing felt odd to him and he pulled a bit out as he extracted his fingers. He held it in his hand and they both looked at it.

"Horsehair," Frau Vogel announced as though he had asked.

He shook his head, disconcerted. "No, it's too soft."

"Nonsense. Put it back in."

He rolled the hair around in his fingers. "It's human," he said, mostly to himself. He realized that this was something he had not wanted to know. He looked at Frau Vogel, hoping she would offer an alternate explanation.

"Nonsense. It's horsehair. Now put it back!"

"No, it's too soft. Feel it."

"I said put it back. Don't make me have to say it again!"

"*It's human hair!*"

"Peter! Do as you're told!" She spun on her heel and left the room.

He continued to roll the hair in his hand. Black and brown and gold and gray strands tangled together in an irremediable knot. Finally, without knowing exactly what he planned to do with it, he put the selection of hair in his pocket and tried to concentrate on finishing his work.

27

ALEX STUDIED THE PAPERS on his lap, but he just could not concentrate on his work. He glanced down the aisle of the airliner, but no stewards were in sight. He leaned forward slightly so that he could see past his neighbor out the window. The Manhattan skyline was just visible on the horizon, and Alex smiled. Something about the Free City always appealed to him. He remembered how his father had talked about New York, back when it was still an integral part of the United States. New York was his second Vienna—the only other possible destination in his father's abruptly terminated musical career. What would his father think of the teeming metropolis now? He would probably be pleased. Still a center for art and music, still the capital of the free world, and now a Free City in its own right, the home of numerous exiles, the seat of their temporary governments, the nexus of resistance to the Third Reich's stranglehold on Europe. Only Britain had chosen a different location for its government in exile, choosing Toronto as its base of operations.

His father would have laughed at that. He would have guessed that Manhattan was too lively for them, and so they had fled to the stultifying atmosphere of Toronto. He had hated the English—not his wife, she was different, but the English as a group. "Cold people," he would snort. "Think that showing affection to their children is a sign of weakness." He had said that at Paddington, when Alex had pulled away too quickly from his embrace. "No soul!" his father had snapped, waving his hands in an embarrassing display of emotion. Alex had winced, hoping that nobody in the busy train station would notice them. True to form, none of them did.

Alex had never understood his father's rantings, never understood his desire to return to Vienna, never understood his father's speaking German to him at home. "Didn't you grow up speaking Polish?" he had once asked his father.

"Yes, and Yiddish, too! So why do you moan so much learning just one other language, huh? Speak German. When you can do that, I'll teach you Polish." He never did teach his son, though; events overtook him.

The plane dropped and Alex's stomach grew queasy. He was nervous about this trip—it was so important to stir things up, yet so difficult to arouse any interest anymore. He tapped his fingers on the notes he had prepared and wondered, not for the first time, if this would at last do the trick.

The airport weapon scanners were even less obtrusive than last time, and this time there were no bomb-sniffing dogs. Automated, Alex guessed. He greedily eyed the computerized scanner that examined his documents. The surly immigration official removed the documents from the machine, opened them by hand, and compared Alex's face with his picture.

"Swiss?"

"That's what it says," Alex answered.

"You're all fucking Swiss, aren't you?" The official seemed to object to the whole hypocritical procedure, but that did not stop him from stamping the word *admitted* on Alex's documents.

"Thank you," Alex said with distinct courtesy. He caught a cab and headed to the home of a friend.

"Pay him," Alex ordered as he greeted his friend. "I don't have any money."

The friend shook his head and paid the fare. By midafternoon Alex was on the fourteenth floor of a midtown building, trying to convince a disinterested young man to take a closer look at the materials he had smuggled in.

"I don't know why they sent you to me," the youth admitted while his eyes scanned the ceiling of his office as if looking for fairies. "I'm sure there must be someone else who has a better grasp of this, uh, history stuff."

"It's not history!" Alex harrumphed. "Look here, young man, this is footage of executions that take place nowadays in the camps! They've claimed those places have been sanitized, but I have proof to the contrary!"

"I don't know . . ."

"People risked their lives—paid with their lives!—to get this footage."

The young man touched the film canister. "Is this stuff even compatible with our machines?"

Alex sighed. "Yes, it can be translated . . ."

"Are there any, you know, like sex scenes?"

*　　*　　*

Three days later Alex was having no better luck with a wizened old producer. "I'm sorry, old boy, this stuff is just old hat. I mean, we can show it, and all that happens is we get a protest from the German delegations that we're defaming their culture. Everybody else is not interested. They've seen it all. Much worse in fact. I mean, how many times can you watch someone getting shot? Hmm?"

"But this is politically important. The government is trying to normalize relations! Don't you think the people should know the cover-ups going on?"

"The people couldn't give a shit about cover-ups. Hey, the U.S. has an election coming up, and have you heard about the sexual shenanigans of the vice presidential candidate?"

"Yes, I know, he's supposed to be a closet homosexual," Alex agreed tiredly.

"Not just! Now we have the hate groups organizing against him, we have denials from the candidate, we have his wife describing their 'luscious' sex life, we have queer groups asserting that he should be proud of his leanings . . .'"

"How, in the end, will this affect world policy or the standing of the United States as a world power?"

"Huh? Oh! Not at all, but that's not the point. The point is, we're in this business to make money, and that"—the producer pointed at the film—"won't make a cent. End of story."

"What about your commitment to public service?" Alex indicated the plaque on the wall behind the producer's desk. "Won't this help fulfill your quota of public-interest, not-for-profit stories?"

The producer leaned forward and lowered his voice. "Just between you and me, old boy, in theory it would, but"—and here he lowered his voice even further—"it seems there has been some pressure from the government to put a lid on this sort of stuff. Seems it fouls up negotiations on certain key things."

"They're selling them arms and equipment, huh?"

The producer waved his hands and pursed his lips in determined silence.

"Better the Nazis than the Communists, huh?"

The producer shrugged.

"I thought this was a free and independent city, beholden to no national government."

"Yes, in theory, but we have many legal ties with the continent. It's complicated."

"I thought you had freedom of the press enshrined in your Constitution."

"We do," the producer sighed. "We could run with this, or anything else for that matter. But it won't make money, it won't make the government happy. . . . What's the point? I mean, we have to get our license renewed, we have strong competition out there. Have you seen the sort of stuff that's aired nowadays? Sex, violence . . ."

"This is violent," Alex tried one last time.

The producer laughed. "That's a good one. Wrong sort of violence, old boy. Not personal enough."

"It was for the people who died."

"Ah, well, they don't subscribe to our channel, now, do they?"

Alex stood. "Thanks for your time. Sorry it was wasted."

"Ah, no problem! Hey, take your film directly to Congress, maybe you'll find a subcommittee that's interested."

"I have an appointment in D.C. tomorrow."

The producer laughed.

"It's not that the congressman is not sympathetic to your concerns," the suave young woman assured him, "it's just that he really does not have much power on the committee. We've tried several times to introduce this sort of evidence into the record, and each time we've been stymied."

"People are dying," Alex said.

"People are dying everywhere. If we took time to fixate on every detail of the internal runnings of every podunk country, I'm afraid we wouldn't have time to conduct our own affairs."

"How can you be so callous?"

"I'm not." The woman stood and closed the door of the office before reseating herself. "Personally, this is one that bothers me. But I work with other people who are worried by famines or crime or child abuse. Each and every one of them has the right to think his or her problem is the most important. We try our best to steer the government in a direction that would be beneficial to your people, but we are a large country, with many interests. It's difficult making a case for the importance of a bunch of foreigners who have been at each other's throat for centuries. Among some of our colleagues, it's even said that we should be glad that the Europeans are only slaughtering each other currently, and if we were to free them from their current predicament, they'd go off and create mayhem in some innocent corner of the world."

"Innocent?"

"I'm quoting. Look, we'll make a copy of the film, and I'll do what I can to see that it is used as evidence in some committee or other, but the prospects aren't good right now."

"Why not?"

"Politics. The current majority wants to dispense with this whole human rights stuff. Caring about foreigners is a vote-loser, and nobody wants to lose votes."

"What do you suggest I do?" Alex asked in desperation.

"Make it a vote-winner," she said simply.

"How?"

She shook her head. "I haven't a clue."

28

"**Y**OU'LL NEVER GUESS WHAT!" Elspeth bubbled as soon as Karl came through the door. She surged forward to hug her husband, nearly tripping on Peter as he took Karl's things and handed him a cigarette.

"You're right," Karl said without interest, "I haven't a clue." He looked tired.

"Mother's coming to visit! For two weeks. Isn't that wonderful?"

"Ach, is it that time of year again?" After his cigarette was lit, Karl moved toward the sitting room, with the obvious intent that Elspeth would join him, but she waved her hand at him.

"Can't rest now, there's so much to do. Peter, come! There's more cleaning upstairs. Hurry up."

As Elspeth rushed off, Karl caught Peter's eye and muttered, "Better you than me," with something like bemused pity.

On the morning of Elspeth's mother's arrival, Peter carried her bags into the guest room that had been so meticulously prepared for her and, as ordered, unpacked their contents. As he unfolded her clothes and placed them into a drawer, Frau von dem Bach came into the room. She was somewhat taller than average for her age, and she carried herself with an aristocratic arrogance that her daughter could never hope to achieve. Her hair was a natural chestnut with streaks of gray, and she wore it on top of her head as if to emphasize her height. She looked around appreciatively at the neatly made bed, the fresh flowers in the vase, the odor of cleanliness. Everything and everyone had been rearranged to make sure she had a suitably furnished guest room, and as a result the room sparkled.

She complimented the room, then turned to watch what he was doing. "No, no, that goes down there," she said, indicating that she wanted some clothes in the bottom drawer, "and those go in there." She pointed to the wardrobe.

He nodded, finished unpacking her luggage, and turning to leave, asked, "Will there be anything else, *gnädige Frau?*"

"Come here." Frau von dem Bach beckoned with a finger. "I didn't get a good chance to look at you in the station."

She had seated herself in the chair near the bed, and he came to stand by her. She eyed him for a long moment, then regally ordered him to turn around for her. After he had complied, she observed, "You're as tall as a German, that's unusual. Most of the working English I've seen are little runts. Why's that?"

It wasn't clear whether she was asking why he was tall or why most English weren't. He didn't even agree with her observation, but he chose to answer, "Malnutrition can do terrible things to people."

"So you think they're malnourished?"

"I think the island produces too much for export," he answered obscurely.

"You don't think your people are treated fairly?" It was less a question than a statement.

He hesitated, then said simply, "No."

"I wonder what the people in India would have to say about that."

"I have no idea."

"Alas, it is the age-old complaint of all colonial regions. I suppose your British

Empire would have known about that; you know, like when Ireland was export-ing food during the potato famine," she commented slyly.

"Yes, that was emphasized in history class."

"The invincible British Empire! Ach, and now the tide has turned against you." She raised her eyebrows expectantly.

"Apparently," he answered, unsure of what she wanted from him.

"So where do you think all that food goes?" she asked with no obvious intent.

He hesitated, then deciding to throw caution to the wind, stated dryly, "Your son-in-law seems to manage to consume a fair amount of it."

She released a controlled little titter. "Yes, he has grown in recent years! He used to be quite trim—handsome, even. I think his work is less strenuous than it used to be. I gather, from what I hear, he used to keep in shape by beating people up. Now"—she studied her fingernails—"he uses his brain, so he does absolutely nothing at all."

Peter did not smile.

"Ah, yes"—she noticed his lack of response—"but I don't suppose you find that very humorous, do you?"

"No, *gnädige Frau*. Is that all, *gnädige Frau*?"

"Not quite. Let me see your papers."

He handed them to her and watched as she perused them.

"Your history begins with your criminal conviction?"

"Yes, *gnädige Frau*."

"But you existed before that."

"One would assume so, *gnädige Frau*," he answered with subdued humor.

"So where is the rest of your documentation?"

"With Herr Vogel, *gnädige Frau*. In his study."

"Ah, yes, of course. Well, tell me, what does it say? Do your parents know what you've been up to?"

"I was a foundling."

"An orphan?"

"Yes, *gnädige Frau*." He stopped himself from saying that at least that was his current story.

"I'm surprised you weren't adopted, what with your hair and eyes and all."

He shrugged. It was not up to him to explain the machinations of the SS Lebensborn, the SS division that abducted and Germanized suitable children from inferior races.

"But they certainly taught you good German in any case."

"All the orphanages use only German, *gnädige Frau*."

She continued to study the pages. "Still, they had no intention of you ending up like this, did they?"

"We were raised to serve the Fatherland, *Gnädigste*. I can only hope I am doing that now," he replied ironically.

Frau von dem Bach sniffed her amusement, then tapping the documents, said, "It's not in here. What's your name?"

"Peter, *gnädige Frau.*"

"I meant your last name—and I don't mean Vogel."

"I used to be called Halifax."

"Halifax? As in *Lord* Halifax?"

A little laugh broke free at that. He shook his head and bit his lower lip to try to control his expression. "No, as in Manchester, Coventry, Leeds, Halifax."

"Cities?"

"Nuclear cities."

She cocked her head in confusion.

"They named foundlings after the nearest city. I guess I was found near Halifax."

"I see, so you're the product of a nuclear dump. Hmm." She dropped his papers onto her lap as if they were useless and studied his face as if searching for traces of his history. "Working class?" she asked suddenly.

"I don't know. As I said, I was found abandoned."

"That'd be my guess, despite your height," she continued as if talking about the lineage of a racehorse. "Just my daughter's type. She has a weakness for peasant strength, just like that husband of hers."

He did not know what to say to that.

"You know what the problem was," she said as if he had asked a question, "the British got rather untidy about keeping track. So many upstarts from the lower classes! Democracy—what a mistake it was! It started this whole messy business. Now, everything's turned around, the leaders follow and the followers lead!"

He remained silent.

"Tell me," she said, suddenly changing tack, "you were convicted for a relatively minor offense. What was it, leaving the Reich without proper authorization?"

"Yes, *gnädige Frau.* That was my second criminal conviction."

"Ah. What was the first?" she asked, her head tilted with interest.

"Draft-dodging."

"What did that get you?"

"Twenty years," he answered without betraying his bitterness.

"And this second conviction merited a death sentence?"

"Yes, *gnädige Frau.*"

"And the permanent markings." She nodded at his arm.

Realizing that he was in violation of Elspeth's rules, he rolled down his sleeves. In answer to Frau von dem Bach, he said, "Yes, they indicate I live under a stay of execution."

"Interesting. So no retirement for you?" she asked, referring to the tendency to release forced laborers into society to fend for themselves when they were no longer able to work.

"No. When I cease to be useful, I will be shot, *gnädige Frau,*" he stated with calculated bluntness.

"A rather draconian punishment," Frau von dem Bach commented as she fanned herself with his papers.

"People have been killed for less, *gnädige Frau*. Much less."

Frau von dem Bach smiled at his brazen innuendo. "I don't think we bothered to convict *them* of anything."

"I guess not, *gnädige Frau*."

"Anyway, we don't talk about that, do we," she intimated, taking yet another step in their intricate pas de deux.

"Apparently not, *gnädige Frau*."

Frau von dem Bach shifted in her seat. "So rather than kill you, they reinvent you. What a very efficient use of bodies."

"If you think my labor is being used efficiently, yes."

"You don't think lighting my son-in-law's cigarettes is gainful employment?"

"I wouldn't dare to comment on the methods of my superiors."

"Wisely so." She glanced back at his papers. "Not only a condemned convict, but also, quite conveniently, of inferior blood. Don't you find it odd that they can magically discover after all those years that you are, and presumably always have been, subhuman?"

"I have never attempted to understand your justice system. Or whatever you want to call it."

She sighed, signaling that she had finished amusing herself. "Neither have I," she admitted, handing the documents back to him, "neither have I."

"May I go now, *gnädige Frau*?"

"Yes, of course." She winked at him. "I think I'll nap a bit. Come and get me for dinner."

29

"T WO WEEKS, YOU SAID?" Karl moaned. "Hasn't it been two weeks yet?" He set down his empty glass and pointed toward it meaningfully. Peter refilled it with whiskey, then resumed standing by the wall.

"She's not leaving until Sunday, dear," Elspeth answered patiently. "Do try and be polite until then."

Karl sputtered, "She's an arrogant old cow with stupid, old-fashioned, and impractical ideas! Her and her stupid society!"

"You thought highly of our connections when you wanted to marry me."

"Lot of good that did. They cut us off completely. Investigating me like that!"

"I know," Elspeth soothed. "But they couldn't understand us. They thought I was deceived by your blond hair and pretty black uniform."

"They were angry I was landless. Called me a nobody!" Karl snarled. "As if my political background was worthless!"

"Well, to them it was, dear. Anyway, it was a long time ago. They were just concerned for my welfare."

"That's not what you said at the time!"

Elspeth eyed Peter as if wondering whether she should continue their conversation in front of him. He ignored her, staring blankly at the minute hand on the mantel clock as it slowly approached twelve. It would chime then and their inanity would be drowned out for a few blessed seconds.

"I was angry, yes," Elspeth admitted to Karl, clearly deciding that Peter was sufficiently inanimate to not merit further consideration. "But now that Daddy is long dead, and we are married, isn't it time to let bygones be bygones?"

"Dying like that! He cheated me out of my revenge!" Karl fumed. "He was so bitter at our marriage, I bet even the damn maggots can't stomach eating his sticky white remains."

"Karl! That's disgusting! Whatever you thought then, it's time to let it go. Mother has tried to rebuild the bridges—can't we work with her?"

Karl sputtered again. "Why should we?"

"Mother likes hearing about your promotions. Maybe you could tell her more about your work."

"She just likes to keep an eye on my career because she's afraid one of these days, I'll be powerful enough to get her back for her meddling."

"Karl! You wouldn't!"

"Of course not, darling," Karl replied smoothly. "Of course not."

Elspeth gave Karl a baleful look, then stood and walked over to the door. "She said she'd join us for a drink. I wonder . . . Oh, there you are!"

Frau von dem Bach swept down the steps and into the sitting room as if into a grand reception. She kissed Elspeth on the cheek, gestured toward Peter for a cognac, then seated herself, saying, "Don't bother to stand, Karl."

"Didn't even cross my mind," Karl replied, settling deeper into his armchair, and gesturing to Peter to get him another cigarette. "In fact, that is just one more positive benefit of our revolution, no more of this silly class nonsense."

"Oh," Frau von dem Bach replied, eyeing Peter smugly.

"Peter, lower the shutters!" Elspeth snapped testily. "Do I have to tell you everything?"

"Yes," Karl continued, "we've recognized the superiority of all Germans as the Aryan nobility and we no longer look down on those who work. It did not go far enough though. We really need even more fundamental changes."

"How so?" Frau von dem Bach asked without interest.

"We should have cleaned house more efficiently. We got rid of the damn Jews and all those other troublesome types—the Communists, the religious zealots, the foreigners, you know . . ."

"Uh-huh."

"But we should have cleaned out the aristocrats as well. Wiped out the god-damned gentry and the intelligentsia! Just like we did in Poland."

Both Elspeth and her mother looked at him aghast. "Karl! What are you say-ing?" Elspeth asked in horror.

"I think, dear, he's forgotten that we are all good Germans as well," Frau von dem Bach commented as she accepted the cognac from Peter.

"Oh, I only meant the troublesome ones," Karl soothed unconvincingly. He downed his whiskey in a gulp.

"No, you clearly said 'like in Poland,'" Frau von dem Bach reminded him, sipping her cognac. "If I remember correctly, it was decided that they were all troublesome—the Polish gentry was exterminated nearly without exception."

"That's because they thought they were noble, but there is only one *Herrenvolk,* and that is the Germans!"

"If *all* Germans are the natural nobility of the Aryan races, then how can there be a German nobility?" Frau von dem Bach asked pointedly.

"There can't!" Karl sneered. "We should have followed Stalin's lead on that. He purged Soviet society of its disloyal elements very efficiently. The kulaks cer-tainly learned their lesson." Karl smiled to himself and added quite admiringly, "Seven million disloyal Ruthenians in one single terror famine. Seven million and the world hardly blinked! You've got to admire the guy. Now that's a way to keep order!"

"Since when do we take lessons from the Communists?" Frau von dem Bach asked archly.

"Since they have the right idea!" Karl slammed his fist on the end table.

Elspeth interrupted, "Peter—refill our drinks! Can't you see Herr Vogel's is empty? And top mine up."

"Ah, I do so like Mozart," Frau von dem Bach commented, obviously follow-ing Elspeth's lead and trying to change the subject.

"I don't care for all that highfalutin crap music. Who wants to hear it any-way?" Karl snarled, then gulped down the whiskey Peter had just poured and motioned for another.

"Karl, dear," Elspeth soothed, "it's what's playing on the television now. Don't you hear it? Don't you like it? I thought you liked this station in the evening."

"Oh, that, yeah, yeah. What I meant was . . . Yeah, I like it, I just don't know the stupid names. Isn't it enough to listen? Who needs the names of this stuff."

"Yes, that's quite observant of you," Frau von dem Bach cooed, "certainly one can enjoy the essential beauty of the music without knowing the composer."

"Damn right!" Karl snapped. "After all, knowing the names of all those com-posers and that sort of crap didn't help that traitor down the street, now did it?"

"What?" Frau von dem Bach looked to Elspeth for clarification.

"I think my husband is referring to our neighbor. He was a very cultured man. A real gentleman. Loved his books, had a vast collection of music. Anyway, last month, his son turned him in for listening to illegal broadcasts. He's in prison now. Or at least that's the last we heard."

"His son? *His very own son?*"

"Yes, sad, isn't it?" Elspeth agreed reluctantly.

"I can't imagine one's own child doing something so horrid!"

"Mother, it was for the state."

"Still, children owe their parents loyalty."

"I suppose . . ." Elspeth fell uncomfortably silent.

"There's even a famous quote about ungrateful children," Frau von dem Bach remarked pointedly.

"You mean, 'A disloyal child is sharper than a serpent's tooth,' " Karl asserted pompously. "It's Goethe!"

Frau von dem Bach looked at Karl as if deciding what to say. Elspeth bit her lip nervously.

" 'How sharper than a serpent's tooth it is, to have a thankless child,' " Peter quoted quietly in English from where he was standing. He realized, too late, that he had spoken aloud. Frau von dem Bach nodded slightly; Karl and Elspeth stared at him nonplussed. He translated for them, then added, "It's from Shakespeare. *King Lear*."

The silence was deafening. Elspeth sat stock-still. Frau von dem Bach glanced curiously from Peter to Karl and back again as if, heretically, comparing their intellectual capabilities. Karl ground out his cigarette, stood, and walked over to Peter.

Peter met Karl's glare with an even expression. "I just thought *mein Herr* might like to know," he said, aware that Karl was already so furious that there was no point in apologizing.

"You self-satisfied, arrogant little worm!" Karl hissed in a cloud of alcohol. "You think you're so damn intelligent, don't you! You think you're better than me, don't you, you swine. Well, I'll show you how useful all that learning is. I'll show you who's better here. You'll regret those words!"

"I already do," Peter replied truthfully.

"Karl, Karl," Frau von dem Bach interrupted. "Your class is showing, Karl. Leave him alone. Come, sit down, join civilization. He *was* right, after all."

Karl spun to face her, nearly losing his balance. He glowered at the women, but was unable to summon up any appropriate words.

"Darling," Elspeth interjected softly, "please. We're having a nice chat. Just forget it. Please?"

Karl took a deep breath. He looked from one woman to the other. Finally he said, "I'm going out." He turned back toward Peter and mouthed, so that the women could not see him, *Later*.

After he left the room, Elspeth sighed and shook her head. There was a moment of awkward silence, then Elspeth ventured, "Perhaps you'd like some tea?"

"Child, how in the world—"

"Mother, he is my husband. I will not hear a word against him in this house!"

"I'm not trying to break up your marriage, dear. God knows with seven children you don't need that! But really, Elspeth, how do you put up with such nonsense!"

"Oh, he didn't mean anything by that." Elspeth nodded her head toward Peter. "He wasn't going to hurt him."

"That's not what I meant!"

"What then?"

"His comments about our people."

"*Our* people? I left that all behind when I married Karl. You and Daddy saw to that," Elspeth retorted bitterly.

"Elspeth! He was talking about murder! Haven't you any idea?"

"He was exaggerating."

"He said 'wipe them all out'!"

"Oh, that was referring to the Poles."

"Elspeth," Frau von dem Bach's voice grew soft, "you don't know much about what went on then. Maybe we should have told you more, but we were afraid."

"What are you talking about?"

"Don't you know—we lost friends. Relatives even!"

"Relatives? How could we lose relatives? They were Slavs! They're not like us! They are a different race, an inferior race!"

"Borders, child, are lines drawn on a map. As a class, most of us mixed freely, visited each other's estates, married. Our names reflected chance histories; our language . . . well, we preferred French." Frau von dem Bach glanced at Peter and muttered, "And now it is the servants who speak more than one language."

"Decadence," Elspeth declared.

Frau von dem Bach chose to ignore her. "I can still remember my mother and father finding out about all that went on there. They were horrified to learn that belonging to a landowning, educated class was equivalent to a death sentence in German-occupied Poland!"

"It was always part of Germany," Elspeth corrected. "We took back what was ours."

Frau von dem Bach was undeterred. "Of course, some saved themselves by proving they were, after all, ethnically German—*Volksdeutsch*—but still there were those brave, romantic souls who refused on principle, or those who had uncooperative officials handling their case, or those who were swept away in the firestorm before they could even react. Oh, it was terrible! Whole noble families wiped out! Those whom the Nazis didn't kill, the Soviets liquidated by executing en masse in their anonymous forests or by sending to their deaths in Siberia."

"You are not comparing us with those Communist beasts are you?"

"For my parents, your grandparents, it was rather too close for comfort, but then it was too late for them to withdraw their support from the regime—you see, they had made quite a profit out of it. So they were obliged to accept the slaughter as an unfortunate fait accompli."

Elspeth yawned.

"Don't you see?" Frau von dem Bach pleaded. "But for an arbitrary border, barely twenty years old, it could have been us!"

"Nonsense."

"They were destroyed for their class! It was class that mattered. It still does. Your husband and his ilk despise us as a class! You watch, they're going to try and destroy us!"

"Oh, Mother, don't fret. Germans are the natural master race; the Führer won't ever allow harm to come to us. Now that we've purified the land, we can live in everlasting peace."

Frau von dem Bach grimaced with frustration. Patiently she said, "The question, Elspeth, is who will be considered polluted next? You don't realize how many *Germans* were slaughtered to make way for your New Order. Look at how many Jews fought for the Fatherland in the Great War. Look at how many ran industries which kept our economy on the cutting edge!"

"They weren't proper Germans."

"One day, my dear, you might wake up to find you're not a 'proper German' either."

"Nonsense, I'm completely loyal! I do wish you'd stop talking such rot. Especially in front of . . ." Elspeth nodded her head at Peter as though not invoking his name would be sufficient to prevent him from understanding all that had gone before.

Frau von dem Bach said something in French, which he guessed, using what little he knew, meant that they could always speak in a language he did not understand. Elspeth looked completely blank and he bit his lip to keep from laughing.

Frau von dem Bach rolled her eyes in exasperation, then she addressed him directly in German: "Get me another cognac—a really large one."

After the women retired for the night, Peter cleared up the drink glasses and finished his other work from the day. He then went into the cellar and looked at his supplies. There was a bit of sausage left; he sniffed it and wrinkled his nose in distaste. It was hard keeping meat during the summer months: even the coolness of the cellar was insufficient to prevent rot. He wiped off the mold and decided to boil the meat for a while. He knew he had plenty of time since Karl would not be back until very late and he was obliged to stay up until then.

Once the meat had boiled, he inspected the greasy water and decided it would serve as a reasonable base for soup the next day. No point wasting all those wonderful globs of fat—the calories were precious. He decided to prepare the soup then and there since he had the time, and he chopped some onions, a carrot, and a bit of cabbage and even diced up some of the meat to add to it. He was running low on salt and decided to pilfer some from Elspeth's pantry. While he was at it, he decided to borrow a few spices and a bit of barley as well. That would give the soup some flavor and body. It was a good time to pilfer—what with Frau von dem Bach in the house, Elspeth was too distracted to notice such things.

After he had added the extra ingredients, he set the coil to its lowest setting and went upstairs to eat his meal in the relative comfort of the kitchen. When he was finished, he returned to the cellar, turned off the coil, and covered the soup. A rat ventured out from the shadows, and without thinking, he killed it by slamming the edge of his heel on its neck. Grasping it by the tail, he picked it up and spent a moment contemplating it. They must be edible, he thought; certainly cats eat them. The rat swung unappetizingly back and forth, blood filling its mouth. Of course, it would have to be cooked thoroughly. Really thoroughly. Some sort of recipe was lurking in the back of his head—something he had heard in his youth. Scald it, then use cold water, then defur and gut the thing. Then something about soaking it in brine and spices. Hammer the muscles into steaks, dry for a day, and then cook.

The rat continued to swing, ticktock, ticktock. Probably his method of execution had sprayed the rodent's guts throughout its body: it was probably totally inedible. And, he decided with a smile, he wasn't that hungry yet. Maybe in a year or so he would establish a rodent-meat assembly line: little rat steaks hanging out to dry in the cellar. Wouldn't Elspeth be horrified! It would be worth doing just to see her expression. He went up the steps and tossed the cadaver into the back garden. It was too risky stepping outside at night; he would bury it tomorrow. He returned to the cellar, spent a few minutes washing and shaving, and then decided he should probably return to the ground floor. It was one o'clock in the morning—Karl might well be back soon. He rubbed his face in irritation: he was tired and had to get up in a few hours to fetch the morning bread, but he could not go to sleep until Karl returned home.

Upstairs, he opened the front door and looked out into the well-lit night. Still no sign of Karl. The air was warm and humid, and the division between inside and outside seemed obscured; it all looked so normal, so peaceful. It struck him as odd that if he walked out the door and into the street, he could be arrested or shot; it was past curfew, and nothing but an emergency could explain his presence out of doors. It had been that way all his life: always some boundary, always some curfew. He closed the door and went to the drinks cabinet. He had carefully obscured Elspeth's view when he had put the whiskey away so she would not know how low the bottle was, at least not until she had a chance to check when her mother was not around. Since she was a great believer in the power of locks, he could usually pull out a shot or two with no problem; now, with her mother visiting, he estimated that he could easily pour a tumbler without her noticing. He pulled out his pick and opened the lock and, pouring some whiskey into a glass, drank it down in several gulps. It felt good going down, burning him with the sensation of a genuine life. He poured more and, keeping his ears open for Karl, savored it. When he finished, he rinsed and replaced the glass, then went into the hall and sat down on the floor near the door so he could hear Karl arrive.

He felt quite worried about what Karl would do to him since their little interchange that evening. He wished that the ladies had let Karl take whatever revenge he needed then and there, in the sure knowledge that Karl would have controlled himself in their presence. Now, however, he was not sure what to expect. From his position on the floor, he reached up to the little hall table, the one with all of Elspeth's stupid glass figurines, the ones that needed to be cleaned all the time, and opened the cigarette box and grabbed one. She usually counted them, but again, with her mother in the house, he doubted she would be able to keep track of each and every one. He grabbed the little crystal lighter that sat next to the box and lit the cigarette.

He inhaled deeply, listening carefully for Karl as he took what pleasure he could from the cigarette, but he need not have worried as Karl did not return until nearly four. He awoke from a deep sleep when he heard the car door slam and only managed to get up just in time to open the door. Karl staggered in, nodded toward the cigarettes, and Peter nervously lit one for him. Karl blew a stream of smoke into Peter's face and then told him to fetch some whiskey.

"Frau Vogel is asleep, *mein Herr*," he protested gently.

Karl did not reply, rather just looked at him with that don't-make-me-repeat-myself look.

Resigned, he climbed the steps to Elspeth's bedroom, rapped lightly on the door, and went in when she responded.

"What is it? What time is it?"

"Four o'clock."

"Where's my husband? What do you want?" She sounded dazed.

"Herr Vogel is in the sitting room; he wants the keys to the drinks cabinet."

Elspeth sighed heavily. For a moment she seemed about to engage in a long-distance debate using him as the go-between, but then decided better of it. She removed the small key she wore on a ribbon around her neck and opened the drawer of her bedside table.

"Here," she said, flinging the entire ring of keys at him. "Tell him to serve himself; you should be in bed already."

He raised an eyebrow at the ludicrousness of her suggestion, but did not comment. He returned with the keys to the drinks cabinet and poured the whiskey. He waited, standing tiredly, as Karl drank that, and then Peter poured another and waited some more. Karl smoked and drank and stared at him but did not say a word. Eventually, Karl had enough and, checking that the cabinet was locked, took the keys and headed toward the bedroom. Peter followed, helped Karl prepare for bed, and then, utterly dispirited, climbed the next flight of steps to his own attic room.

30

THE ATMOSPHERE IN THE room was stultifying. Not so much that there were too many bodies in too small a space, nor that the windows had not been opened despite the oppressive summer heat—that, after all, was impossible given the security considerations—nor was it even due to the ubiquitous presence of black, brown, and gray uniforms and suits. The air was simply thick with inappropriate metaphors, sleazy compliments, innuendos, and veiled threats. It was, needless to say, another useless, time-wasting, and obligatory Party political meeting.

Richard stretched as much as he dared and discreetly yawned behind his hand. A young woman entered the room and tapped the shoulder of the man in front of him, conveying an important message that gave the lucky fellow a well-earned break from the tedium. Richard scanned the room and noticed how nearly every eye had covertly watched the woman as she walked up the aisle, bent over the rows of bored men, and talked to her boss. Even the speaker seemed momentarily distracted from his stale pronouncements, but then he found his wind and continued to drone on.

Eventually he finished and the obedient audience applauded. At this point all eyes moved to the Führer and awaited that subtle moment when his hands approached each other to rest rather than clap. Nearly everyone caught the moment, and the applause dropped off precipitously to near silence. The one or two laggards stopped clapping and glanced around embarrassed.

The next speaker was introduced, a Herr Schacht. Finally! Richard sat up to listen closely. Schacht introduced the prison-reform concepts that Richard had outlined only months earlier to his own staff. Richard listened as Schacht explained how there had been trials in various locations around the Reich and that preliminary results were filtering in. "It seems that given the preliminary results of these initiatives, which were introduced by . . ." Schacht's eyes strayed into the audience, settling briefly on Richard before moving on. Richard leaned in to hear his name invoked. He had worked so hard to get someone in Berlin to listen to him, and now here was his moment! ". . . myself," Schacht concluded, "to the Führer only several months ago, we can feel confident that things are moving in the right direction."

Richard grimaced. It was probably good news that Schacht felt it necessary to steal his applause; nevertheless, he grit his teeth in irritation. He continued to listen as Schacht presented the Göringstadt results, which had been handed to him only the day before. At no point did he mention Richard's name, at no point was there any indication that anyone else was involved in the program. It was exactly what Richard had expected, and he was perversely gratified, since he had planned accordingly. He had banked a great deal on the success of this venture and had risked a lot by publicizing his involvement in advance of the results. Furthermore, he had already organized his own minor publicity stunt for this meeting, which would get the attention he needed from the high command and make his name known and his presence desired. He glanced at his watch and counted down the minutes.

Precisely on time a beautiful young woman stepped onto the stage from a side entrance. She took several doelike steps toward the speaker, then paused, as if stunned by the sudden glare of eyes that rested on her. She threw a heartbreakingly vulnerable glance into the audience; her eyes rested momentarily on the Führer, and a surge of sexual energy charged the auditorium. Then her eyes moved languorously across the room and settled on her father. Everyone turned in their seats to see who was the beneficiary of this glorious creature's attention. Richard graced his daughter with a questioning half-smile, and she turned back toward the speaker and approached the podium, whispering something into his ear.

The Führer watched Richard's daughter intently, his chest heaving. He licked his lips and leaned toward his companion as if asking a question.

"That is not how these things are handled!" Schacht snapped at the young woman.

The Führer turned his attention to the speaker and frowned. The young woman apologized in an undertone and the word "emergency" escaped into the microphone.

Schacht scowled and then announced, "Traugutt, you have an emergency and are needed at the hospital!"

Richard rose, made his way out to the aisle, approached the stage, and extended an arm to his daughter as she descended the steps. He listened as she whispered what had brought her to interrupt the conference and saw, out of the corner of his eye, how the Führer stared at his daughter, how his gaze dropped down from her glistening brown hair to her long, sensuous legs, taking in every detail in between. Richard turned to the Führer and bowed, beginning an apology, which was preempted by the Führer's rising to his feet and extending his hand.

"And just how did such a lovely creature escape the attention of our security?" the Führer asked, holding her hand in both of his.

"Oh, I was thoroughly searched," the lovely creature replied. Richard watched how the Führer's lips twitched. "And I had to prove my identity, I mean, my relationship to one of the attendees."

"And just what relationship is that?" the Führer asked, breathless with anticipation.

"This is my daughter," Richard explained to the Führer's obvious relief. Richard continued by introducing himself and explaining that he currently resided in Göringstadt, that his wife had remained behind, and so his daughter had had no one else to turn to when his young son had taken ill.

"But of course, you must tend to your family!" the Führer responded understandingly. "The family is the backbone of our Reich! By all means, don't hesitate, your child needs you! Go sign whatever forms the hospital needs, but I do hope we get a chance to meet again later."

"Yes, later," Richard agreed.

"Yes, later," his daughter echoed with an alluring smile.

31

"IT'S *LATER*," KARL HISSED at Peter as the carriage doors of Frau von dem Bach's train slammed shut. Whistles shrilled along the platform, the train began to roll, and Elspeth waved cheerily at her mother's carriage, hoping that she would take the time to look back to see her and know she would be missed.

No sooner had they stepped through the door of the house than Karl turned to Peter and ordered, "Into my study, now."

"Karl, now? There's lots of cleaning up to do, I need him," Elspeth protested.

"Now!" Karl snarled as he marched off. Peter glanced at Elspeth before following obediently.

Karl sat at his desk, put his feet up on it, and indicated with a wag of his finger that he wanted a cigarette lit. Peter placed one between Karl's lips, lit it for him, and then retreated to the far side of the desk.

Karl motioned for him to shut the door, then smoked philosophically for a moment as he surveyed his visitor. "You know, you confuse me," he said suddenly. "You have such a bad attitude. Why?"

Surreptitiously Peter scanned the room, trying to find a clue as to what lay in store for him.

"I've asked you a question! Answer me!" Karl snapped.

"Sorry, *mein Herr.* I thought it was rhetorical."

"Rhetorical," Karl repeated as if annoyed. He removed his feet from the desk and leaned forward to speak intensely. "I don't like your attitude, boy. It's going to change."

Peter remained worriedly silent as Karl stood up, walked out from behind the desk, and strolled around the room. He approached Peter from behind and said to the back of his neck, "I planned to beat the shit out of you. But you already knew that, didn't you?"

"Yes, *m'n'err,*" Peter acknowledged grimly.

"In fact, I even thought of taking you down to the Ministry—let the boys have a go at you. They need practice, you know."

Ludicrously, Peter nodded his agreement.

"But they can be so careless, hmm?"

"Yes, *mein Herr.*" Peter felt sick with apprehension.

Karl strolled to the bookcase. "You seem surprisingly well educated," he said, suddenly conversational, his finger running across the volumes of pristine books on the shelves. "Where did you go to school?"

"The Horst Wesel Academy near Slau, *m'n'err,*" Peter answered, then grimaced with self-disgust at his own stupidity. Whatever had possessed him to say that? He squeezed his eyes shut as he tried to work out the implications of the inconsistencies between his words and his documents.

"Well?" Karl asked, still studying his bookshelf.

"Forgive me, *mein Herr.* What did you say?"

"What the hell is wrong with you? I said, that was my old school. Eton," Karl barked. He used the old name for the upper school, flaunting the laws of his own government in an uncontrollable display of snobbery. "Why don't I remember you being there?"

"I don't know, *mein Herr.* Maybe we weren't contemporaries. So you grew up there? In England I mean?" Peter asked, trying to change the direction of the conversation.

"Yes, I spent some time in London. My father was posted there."

"Do you speak any English, *mein Herr?*"

"I didn't own a dog." Karl laughed, pleased by the wit of his rejoinder.

It wasn't an original. Peter had heard it numerous times before. Indeed, it was the style among the local population of Germans to speak to their dogs in English. Thus, for many of them, the extent of their English consisted of such words as *sit, stay, beg, good boy,* and *shut up.* Peter thought about the quote he had heard attributed to Charles V about only speaking German to his horse, but he decided not to repeat it. Rather, he asked, "How long did you live in London?"

"Too long. Barren place, no trees, no parks."

"It didn't used to be like that."

"How would you know?"

"I had heard," Peter replied steadily. The casual tone of their interchange was reassuring—maybe he could avoid being beat up after all. "Is your family still there?"

"I'm asking the questions here."

"Sorry, *mein Herr.*"

"The question is, why were you at my school? How did you get in?"

"I don't know. It was . . ." He had almost said that it was his parents' fault. "I didn't really attend," he admitted on a sudden inspiration. "I worked in the kitchens. The orphanage arranged that for me. I used to just listen in to the lectures."

"So a liar as well as a thief."

"A thief, *mein Herr?*"

"Stealing knowledge. It was clearly a mistake. It gave you ideas above your station. Well, we can remedy that. We'll start with a simple lesson." Karl chose a book from the shelf and returned to his seat at the desk. He took another deep draw from his cigarette, then looked at it as if it had somehow surprised him. He ground it out before continuing.

"Here," he said, leaning back and shaking the volume in his hand, "is knowledge." He placed the book carefully on the desk and, leaning forward again, reached into his jacket and removed his gun. "And here," he continued, holding the gun in the palm of his hand, "is power. The question is, which is stronger?"

Peter read the title of the book—it was a series of readings on the development of civilization compiled by the Boys' League for the Preservation of Fatherland Values. He swallowed a laugh.

"Answer me!"

"It took knowledge to construct the gun, *m'n'err.*"

"But very little to use it."

"If you say so, *m'n'err.*"

Karl did not notice the insult. "Put your hands flat on the desk."

Peter did as he was told. He had to lean forward to place his hands on the surface of the desk, and he stood there awkwardly, wondering what Karl was up to.

"Now you tell me which is stronger!" Karl said, picking up the book and slamming it down on Peter's right hand. Peter winced more from surprise than pain. Karl stood up, held the gun by the barrel, and raised it over Peter's left hand. Peter watched in horror as the butt of the gun came crashing down toward his hand. Instinctively, he pulled his hand away. The gun smashed into the desk, denting the fine wood.

"You swine! I did not give you permission to move your hand! Look what you've done to my desk!" Karl screamed. "Put your hand back there. Put your hand back on the desk!"

Peter hesitated, weighing his options and his instincts. Finally he placed his left hand, palm down, flat on the desk and said quietly, "Please, *mein Herr,* please don't do this."

"Oh, so you don't want me to test which is stronger?"

"No, *mein Herr.*"

Surprisingly, Karl did not push the point. "So, you are not completely devoid of reason," he stated dryly as he set the pistol down.

Peter stared at it, relieved, but still he did not dare move his hand.

"You recognize that power is what's important, and you know, instinctively, that I have it and you don't. That's not the problem, is it?" Karl asked, surprisingly conversational again.

"*Mein Herr?*" Peter asked, confused.

"They taught you well enough not to disobey direct commands, and you're clever, you learned your lessons." Karl eyed his gun, then smiling amiably said, "If I broke your hand, it would prove nothing, nothing at all. All that would happen is I would end up shorthanded!" He giggled at his joke.

Cautiously, Peter removed his hand from the desk. He did not know what to say, so he said nothing.

Karl circled around the desk to him. "It's not direct commands that are the problem, it's your entire attitude. Sullen and insubordinate. You just don't appreciate how good you have it here, do you, boy?"

Clearly an answer was required, but Peter was stymied as to what he could say.

"See"—Karl seemed to be speaking to someone else—"you can't even answer." He leaned close to Peter and hissed into his ear, "You're meant to be useful to me, do you understand? You've failed our society once"—he tapped the green triangle on Peter's sleeve with two fingers—"but you've been given a second chance. You're a very lucky boy."

Karl backed away, assuming a conversational tone again. "But you don't appreciate your luck, do you? You have a job in this life, but you don't want to do it. You think you're too good for it, don't you?"

Karl did not pause long enough for Peter to answer. "If you can't do this job, then we'll get you another. I can replace you, and you can do something else to serve the Fatherland. How about working in a mine? You're strong, I'd give you six whole months there. Or how about a submarine base? There's a lot of nuclear crap that needs cleaning up. You'd last longer and you could watch yourself dying. Lose your hair, excrete blood from every orifice. How would that suit you?"

Peter could think of nothing less absurd to say than, "It wouldn't, *mein Herr.*"

"You're right. You don't really want a different job, you want to learn how to do this one right, don't you?" Karl snapped his fingers theatrically. "I have it! I'll send you back for further reeducation! I'm sure they'd be interested in improving your shortcomings. They could make a study of you. How about that?"

Peter stared at the gun on the desk. He had given his answer ages ago, to that psychiatrist.

"It's up to you," Karl said. "You have a straightforward choice: you can be well-behaved, courteous, and grateful and serve me here, or you can go back there. Which is it?"

Peter swallowed, then answered, "Here, *mein Herr.*"

"You *want* to serve me?"

"Yes, *mein Herr*," Peter whispered.

Karl shook his head in mock sadness. "I'm sorry, you're just not very convincing."

"I don't understand, *mein Herr.* What do you want from me?"

"Convince me," Karl answered innocently.

Peter resorted to feigning further confusion. "*Mein Herr?*"

"I'm losing patience. I need proof that your attitude is going to improve. Either you convince me now, or I will hand you back over to them. Understood?" Karl pointed imperiously toward the floor.

Peter understood all too well. He knew what could be done to a human and he knew he would not face a second time. So, slowly, reluctantly, painfully, he went down onto his knees.

32

ADAM ROSE FROM HIS KNEES, making the sign of the cross as he did so. The candle flickered in a breeze, almost died, but then the weak flame recovered and burned steadily. "Don't worry about Olek. We'll take care of him," he whispered into the gloom of the chapel.

As was his habit, he had visited the chapel in preparation for venturing out on another mission. The job was a rather straightforward bit of sabotage that would serve little more than propaganda purposes, and he looked forward to the outing. The groundwork had been done, the villagers notified; all he had to do was lead the team that would hold up a train and then help distribute the foodstuffs to the local denizens. There was, naturally, a minor amount of danger, but that was all part of the game and it made him feel tense and alive.

He turned to leave, but someone was in the doorway. It took a moment to recognize the silhouette as Zosia.

"I thought I'd find you in here," she said. "Thinking about Julia?"

Adam nodded. "And Olek. He was so precious to her."

Zosia stepped forward into the gloom to give her husband a hug. "She loved her child, as you love yours."

Adam looked over her shoulder into the almost blinding light of the corridor. "If anything should happen to me—"

"Oh, Adam, don't say such things!"

"Zosiu, it's time we grow up and face realities. Something could happen to either one of us. What would you do if something happened to me? What about Joanna?"

"You know she'll be taken care of. There's me, there's Marysia, even Tadek would help."

Adam shook his head. "He hates children!"

"He'd still help," Zosia soothed.

"You wouldn't let him adopt her, would you?"

Zosia cocked her head in confusion. "Why would I do that?"

"What if you married him?"

"I'd never marry anyone else."

"You're still young, I wouldn't mind, you might change your mind. There's no reason you should be alone for the rest of your life."

"Adam! You're the only man in my life. Forever!"

"But if you did—just promise me this. Promise me that Joanna will remain my daughter! Promise!"

Zosia felt confused by the intensity of his concerns. "She'll always be your daughter. No matter what happens, no one can take that away. I won't let anyone take that away, Adam. She'll always know you're her father, her only father."

"You promise?"

"Solemnly."

Adam hugged Zosia and then, kissing her cheek, whispered, "I've got to go now." He slipped out of the chapel, leaving Zosia to contemplate the flickering candle he had lit for his sister.

The soft moss provided a nice mat for their cards. Adam sat cross-legged on the ground in front of the small pile, scanning his hand, as Tadek leaned back against the trunk of a tree and surveyed in the distance to see how the setting up of the railroad barriers was progressing.

"Why didn't Zosia come?" Tadek asked.

"You know Katerina objects to us being top-heavy when we do these things," Adam answered without looking up.

"She's objected for years. You've suddenly become obedient?"

"No. It's Joanna. We've decided, since we're parents now, not to double-team anymore. Pity, I miss the celebration afterwards."

"So do I," Tadek said.

Adam threw such a sharp look in his direction that Tadek burst out laughing. "I knew that'd get you!" he snorted.

Adam turned back to his cards, struggling to look disinterested. He laid a card down and casually asked, "Did you visit my wife during my last absence?"

"Her name is Zosia," Tadek said playfully.

"Well?" Adam pressed.

"They're almost done," Tadek informed him.

"That wasn't my question," Adam persisted.

Tadek smiled at his friend. "What did Zosia tell you?"

"She said you were very helpful."

"That's me all right, always ready to offer a hand."

"You hate children," Adam pointed out.

"Not hate, just find them irksome," Tadek corrected.

"Any long walks?"

"Don't remember."

"Zosia said you went for one of your walks."

"Then I guess we did," Tadek said agreeably.

Adam folded his cards into his hand and gave his full attention to his friend. "I know you and—"

"Dearest comrade, is this why you insisted I come along?"

"Yes," Adam said with a forced grin, "so I can keep an eye on you!"

"Hey!" a young voice interrupted them. "The train's coming!"

Tadek and Adam stood, donned their equipment, and joined the other members of the team. The job went smoothly, the engineer and conductor and the maintenance crew were all too willing to obey the team's commands. Only four soldiers were guarding the train, and they were quickly disarmed and held at gunpoint a few yards away.

The partisans began unloading the train, organizing the food into discrete units for easy pickup by the locals. Someone called to Adam that he had found some files as well, and Adam and Tadek went over to the boxcar to inspect the crates.

Adam looked at the outside of the crate, reading the delivery label. "It doesn't seem like they were hiding these. It's clearly labeled for an office."

"Hmm. But they are encrypted," Tadek commented as he paged through a notebook.

"They encrypt everything," Adam said.

"Do you think they're of any value?" Tadek asked as he surveyed the three crates of paper files.

"Doubt it." Adam picked up another notebook and scanned the documents. "I wish I had a clue how to look at these things."

"Should we leave them?" Tadek asked.

"I don't know. It's a lot to carry back, but there could be something here. Trouble is, with my dad gone, there's no one left to sort through this junk."

"How's he doing?"

"Pff. Who knows. Once he got his new identity, he cut us off completely. Not a word. I tried to talk to him before he left, but he just stared at me like I was the devil incarnate."

"You used to get on well with him," Tadek remarked.

"Used to. Now he can't stand the sight of me." Adam stared off into the distance, trying not to show Tadek how much his father's rejection had hurt him. Under his breath he explained, "He blames me for Julia's death."

"What? How?"

"Oh, I think in his mind, he's angry I didn't follow in his footsteps and become a cryptographer. Then I would have stayed in camp and played it safe, then Olek wouldn't have been inspired to go out and do dangerous things, and so Julia wouldn't have felt driven to find an escape, so she wouldn't have gone off to Paris to get money. . . . Something like that."

Tadek whistled. "Quite a convoluted argument for blaming you."

"He's not—" Adam was interrupted by the sound of gunfire. He threw himself to the ground even as he searched for the source and aimed his pistol. Tadek fired off a shot, hitting the German guard who was firing wildly at them. The guard collapsed to the ground, and a local girl scurried over to him and kicked his gun away. She turned him over and searched him as others hurriedly frisked the other three terrified prisoners.

"What the hell happened!" Adam demanded.

A young boy looked up from the body of the lad who had been guarding the four. "He's killed my brother!"

"Edek's badly wounded," someone else reported.

"Fuck," Adam swore. He directed several of the group to frisk the train crew and another couple to carry the bodies a safe distance away and to try to tend to Edek.

"The bastard's not dead, sir," the girl reported, looking up from the German guard who had caused the mayhem.

"Let me see." Adam approached the man. He was lying on the ground, staring up with eyes full of hate. Adam dropped on one knee next to him, aimed his pistol, and shot him through the head.

Adam looked up into the stunned face of the girl who stood over them. "How old are you?"

"Fourteen, sir," she answered, her eyes glued to the executed soldier's head.

"Fourteen," Adam repeated, wiping his hand and his pistol on the grass to clean them. He stood. "Those three, up against the train. Now!"

The other three guards were herded toward the train. They were made to face the train with their hands held high. Adam approached the first of them, his pistol drawn. He pointed the gun at the back of the man's head.

"It wasn't me," the man whispered. Adam could see his entire body trembling.

• "Adam," Tadek spoke into his ear. "They're not a security risk."

"Neither was the one who had the hidden gun."

"The one who shot our boys is dead. It wasn't these three."

"They shouldn't even be here!" Adam hissed. "Stealing food from starving people! It *is* them!"

"Don't be what you hate." Tadek stepped away to let his friend make his own decisions.

Adam hesitated, stepped back, and waving his pistol to indicate a gully, said, "Take them over there and tie each up to a tree. Get them out of my sight!"

Though the three prisoners could not understand his orders, they heaved a sigh of relief as they were led away.

Adam called over two young partisans. "You two, walk the train crew a few miles into the woods. Hold them an hour, then release them."

"What are you going to do about the guards?" Tadek asked.

"After the food is distributed, we can inform someone of their location."

"Shall we get the distribution under way?"

Adam nodded.

"What about the files?" Tadek asked.

"Burn them!" Adam ordered.

"Okay."

"Can you handle it from here? I want to check on Edek; we'll have to carry him into the village."

"Send someone else—you shouldn't take that sort of risk," Tadek advised.

"No, I'll go. It's my fault, I fucked up. After I get Edek tended to, I'll talk to the dead boy's parents."

"Okay. Good luck. Meet you back at the encampment."

Adam nodded. He kept seeing the chaotic seconds in his mind. The way the boy twisted in pain and fell clutching his throat. His brother's look of anguish as he realized what had happened. Adam closed his eyes to try to blot out the images, but then he opened them again, swore quietly, and went to see how the injured boy was faring.

33

"**Y**ARDLEY!" A VOICE YELLED. "Alan! Slow down! Hey, wait up!"

He stopped and turned to see Graham forcing his way through the crowd gathered at the entrance of the new government superstore. "What are you doing here?" Graham gasped as he finally caught up with his friend.

"I'm meeting some friends, at Göbbel's Ball."

"Where?"

He tossed his head in the direction of a pub. "I forgot, you're not a native Londoner. It's the Goose and Bull, over there. What's up?"

"I have some news!" Graham answered excitedly. "I've been promoted!"

"What?"

"Yeah, I'm your boss now!" Graham grinned at him.

"*What?*"

"Well, you didn't want the job."

"What job? Sherwood's?"

"Yes, didn't you know? Sherwood's off to America and I'm taking over as the liaison. I assumed they asked you first, didn't they?"

He shook his head, disconcerted by the slight. "No, no. I guess they figured I wouldn't want it."

"Guess so. We know you like being here on the ground, in the thick of it."

Yes, on the ground, in the thick of it, near Allison. He had turned down other promotions, it was no big deal that this time they hadn't even asked. He opened his mouth to say something, but he felt a sudden sharp stabbing pain in his ribs. "Ow!" he yelped, and rolled away.

Elspeth kicked him again. "Get up, you lazy swine! You're late, our breakfast will be late!"

He rolled to his knees and climbed to his feet, apologizing as he did so. Elspeth stomped out of the attic, and Peter took a moment to gather himself. What did he need to do today? he wondered as he rubbed the sleep from his face. What day was it? Oh, yes, Sunday. A week since Frau von dem Bach had left. A week since he had gone down on his knees, begging to be allowed to stay, to be allowed to serve them. A week of feeling sick to his stomach that he had *pleaded* to stay.

He paced to the window and glanced out. Sunshine! At long last, after endless days of rain. He closed his eyes to enjoy the thought: sunshine on a Sunday, blessed Sunday. Not only would the family leave the house today to go to their silly political rally, but there was sunshine! They would follow the rally with a long, *gemütlich,* and nearly obligatory walk in the woods, and the sunshine would keep them out for hours. Hours of rallies, hours of strolling, hours of drinking coffee and eating cake in a woodland café. Hours of being away from him!

It was with an irrepressibly cheerful respect that he served up their morning breakfast and helped them prepare for their day. He held the door open for them as they filed out and closed it gently behind Gisela as she was the last in the long line to tromp across the threshold. He paused in the sudden stillness and listened to the beautiful silence that reigned in the house, then, unable to suppress his joy any longer, he squeezed his eyes shut, raised both fists into the air, and whispered, "Yes!"

"Hey, lads, look who's showed up," Josef called out.

"Long time no see," Martin chimed in, moving over to make a place for him.

"Been busy," Peter explained as he seated himself on the packed dirt. He leaned his back against the wall of the warehouse, scanned the surroundings to make sure he had not brought any trouble with him, and added, "Deal me in."

"Did you bring an ante?" Roman asked, scratching determinedly at his ankle.

"And some." Peter pulled the bottle of wine out from the sack he carried.

"Hey, ho! How'd you manage that?" Josef asked.

"With the mother-in-law around, it was easy. They were so busy sniping at each other."

"Oh, yeah, that's right. Is the old crone gone then?" Vasil wondered.

"Ach, she wasn't so bad. She got her daughter to promise to buy me a mattress, though I doubt Elspeth will do it."

"You shouldn't call her that," Martin warned. "Sounds disrespectful."

"She calls me Peter. Don't see why I shouldn't use her first name."

"There you go again with your egalitarian bullshit. Where'd you get that stuff?"

"My grandmother," Peter answered, smiling fondly at her memory. "She'd quote the American Declaration of Independence to me, read me 'Common Sense,' taught me about England's proud, democratic history."

"And that's exactly why you're always in trouble," Martin said. "You should forget all that nonsense and learn your place." Like Roman, Martin had not lost his Aryan status. He pointed a finger at the yellow inset of Peter's red stripe and added, "Learn to show respect for your betters!"

"Or at least fake it," Roman amended. He cursed quietly and began scratching farther up his leg.

"I do a reasonable act," Peter said as he studied his cards. "I've gotten pretty good at handling them."

"Acts are hard to keep up," Martin warned.

"Not for me," Peter countered. "I've had lots of practice. That's at least one positive thing that I can say for my youth."

"You can't keep it up forever. If you don't drop your highfalutin attitude, you're gonna end up in trouble, mark my words."

"I'll be gone before then. I'm just biding my time until the right opportunity arises."

His friends laughed good-naturedly. "You'll be saying that twenty years from now," Josef guessed.

"Yeah, and he'll be explaining how his dear Frau Vogel couldn't manage without him," Vasil added.

Peter didn't respond. A sudden, dizzying darkness had settled over him, turning their jovial teasing into a cacophony of unpleasant sounds and terrifying sights. Shuddering with fear, he blinked away the images. Just the thought of escape . . . What in God's name had they done to him?

"Are you going to play?" Martin pressed.

"Hmm? Oh, yes, I'll take two." Peter laid down two cards.

Roman had begun scratching his back, struggling to reach between his shoulders.

"What's up with you?" Vasil asked. "Fleas?"

"Must be ants here," Roman muttered, scratching maniacally. He stood and inspected the ground. "Oh, shit! Just look at this, there's grease here! It's all over my uniform. I'll never get it out!"

"So?" Vasil asked.

"So, you numskull, I work in a bakery! How the hell am I going to explain grease on my clothes?"

"Wear them inside out and tell your boss it's a fashion statement," Peter suggested.

"Use some vinegar," Josef offered somewhat more helpfully. "My wife swears by it."

"Now where the hell would I get vinegar?"

"Your wife?" Peter asked Josef in surprise. "You're married?"

"Yep. Don't get to see her much, though. Not since she has to stay in all the time."

"That's the best way to have a marriage," Vasil opined. "Long distance."

"Like you would know," Roman commented, scrubbing uselessly at his uniform with the palm of his hand. "Shit, shit, shit!"

"I hope I get to see her before the baby comes," Josef added, ignoring Roman's antics.

"Baby? Is your marriage legal?" Peter asked.

"Of course not," Josef scoffed. "Naw, she's having it for the lady of the house. They've reached an agreement."

"How did they decide to work it?" Roman asked, now using his fingernail to scrape away as much of the grease as possible.

"My wife is staying out of sight while her lady is faking a pregnancy. They have an agreeable doctor, so it should all go smoothly."

"Then your wife gets to care for the kid?"

"Sure. She's going to be the nanny. Her people even agreed to try and get hold of my contract, though we don't know if they'll manage it."

"Or will even try to." Roman sighed his exasperation and, shifting to a clean patch of dirt, sat back down.

"Do they know you're the father?" Peter asked.

"Heavens no!" Josef breathed. "It's his! It really is his."

Peter noticed the way Josef had nervously glanced at Martin as he said that, so he decided to change the subject and, turning to Roman, offered, "There's grease remover at the house. I'll stop by the bakery on the way back. Put the trousers in a bag near the waste bins, and I'll get them back to you as soon as I can. Unless, of course, that's your only pair!"

The others laughed. "Maybe that's what he always does—after all, we only see his upper half through the window!" Vasil joked.

"Is anyone here playing cards?" Martin asked.

They hadn't played long, but Peter was already up by two packets of tea and a half tin of ersatz coffee when he saw Elda approaching. She stopped at the edge of their circle and smiled nervously at him.

"Sorry to disappoint you, gentlemen," he apologized as he gathered his prizes into his sack and stood up, "but you'll have to make up your losses some other time. The lady awaits me."

"Ho, ho! Isn't she just a bit old for you?" Vasil asked. Elda bit her lip and looked away, embarrassed.

"You're just jealous," Peter replied. He gave the lady a slight bow and then gently took her arm and they walked away together.

They skirted the warehouse, stopping at the loading dock. Peter jumped down to the tracks and then helped Elda down. He glanced at the ground, but there had been an oil spill, so they decided to walk farther along the tracks, back toward the suburban residences. They scanned the tracks nervously as they walked along; when they reached the first suburban platform, they stopped, carefully surveyed their surroundings, then quickly ducked down under it. The concrete arch gave them about a meter of headroom, which rapidly decreased to only a few inches, so they decided to arrange themselves lying flat on their stomachs with their heads facing outward, toward the tracks and sunlight.

"Did you bring it with you?" he asked.

In response, she reached into the folds of her skirt and pulled out a book. She opened it to a page with a picture of children playing with a ball under a bright yellow sun. A simple sentence was written beneath the picture.

"Okay, now," Peter began, "can you find the word *ball* in that sentence? Remember, it will start with a *b*. You can hear the sound, right?"

Elda nodded and pointed at the word. "Ball," she read.

"Very good! Now, do you think you can find the word *sun?* What letter does it start with?"

"Ess," Elda answered proudly. She pointed to a word. "Is it that one?"

They continued to meet regularly, but after several weeks Elda's schedule changed so that it became impossible for her to meet with him during the day, so they agreed to try to meet once a week, at night. The rearrangement left Peter with some unexpected free time during the day, and as he heard Elspeth leave to go to a neighborhood committee meeting, he paused in his work and wondered how he should make use of it. His hand rested on the smooth wood of the piano, which he was polishing, and he found his eyes were drawn downward to the sparkling row of white and black keys.

Rather unusually, his parents had owned a piano. Their tiny apartment could ill afford the space a piano cost, but his mother had bought an upright second-hand and shoved it into the living room between the armchair and the television. She had offered to teach him how to play, and his willingness to learn had been one of the few joys that he had given her. Her method had been to teach him to play various pieces by heart; he had learned a bit about reading music, but mostly he had let his fingers learn a song and let his mind wander as his hands worked their way along the keys.

His mother had started him off with a few simple pieces but had rapidly grown bored with that and moved to what she called "real music." She was partial to Chopin and he had seen the incredible compositions as a challenge. By the time his parents were arrested, he could adequately play some rather complicated pieces. His mother even told him he played well, but it was never clear whether that was a genuine assessment of his skill or just parental encouragement. In any case, he had enjoyed playing the piano, and even more so he had enjoyed being able to accept his mother's guidance. He might well have rejected everything else his parents had to offer, but that was a gift he had thought he could keep.

He stroked the polished wood, paralyzed by indecision. He knew he could never reconstruct the music in his head, but conceivably his hands might remember. The problem was if he tried to play something, he might discover that it had all been lost. Glancing at the clock, he sat down and let his fingers rest on the keys. They felt considerably different. Of course, he had a man's hands now. Tentatively, he played a few notes. It felt different, too, but he did not know if that was because his fingers had a different strength or because it was a different piano. In any case, it sounded nice. Elspeth kept the piano tuned although no one played it anymore, not since Geerd, the second son, had moved out; doubtless she kept it ready for his return.

He tried to think of a song, but nothing came to mind; he drew a complete blank. He let his fingers rest on the keys as his mind wandered back to those days in the London apartment block, to the little concerts he would give. His mother and father and both his grandmothers were in attendance, and there he was, the center of attention, able to produce music that they all claimed was beautiful. He had felt so proud of himself at those times, so successful. The adults drank gin and chatted quietly as he played the same few songs over and over, and the room grew warm with their boisterous applause and their happy laughter. His fingers now began moving and the first few bars of a nocturne emerged. Stunned, he stopped and realized he did not know how to continue. He tried the bars again but they were lost.

He tried relaxing and thinking about his old home. He heard Nanna's voice as she spoke in a whisper to her daughter, saying something about what a fine lad he had turned out to be. Again he was able to play a phrase. Warning himself not to panic, he kept going, but eventually his surprise caused him to focus on what he was doing and he stopped again. In this way, over two hours, he managed to reconstruct parts of the nocturne, and he smiled to himself with the knowledge that somewhere deep inside, the music had survived.

Thereafter, whenever he could, he returned to the piano to try to remember what he had once known. Over time, he managed to reconstruct Beethoven's "Für Elise," which was one of the first songs he had ever learned, and a polonaise by Chopin, which had been one of his proudest achievements. The nocturne remained a shadow and he was unable to grasp it in its entirety, but that did not bother him. It was enough to play the few songs he could remember, to enjoy the sensation of creating the sounds with his fingers and to lose himself in the feeling of freedom and choice it gave him.

"Well done. What was that?" a voice asked.

He jumped up so quickly he knocked the bench over, then stared at Elspeth in speechless horror. He had not even heard her return, and there she stood calmly in the doorway. How long had she been there? he wondered.

"I said, what was that?"

Finally, he managed to collect himself enough to stammer, 'Für Elise' by Beethoven, *gnä' Frau.*"

"Play something else," Elspeth commanded.

"*What?*"

"I said, I want to hear another song."

"Another song?"

"As I said." It was not clear why, but it almost sounded like a threat.

He righted the bench and sat down. The gleaming row of white and black keys mocked him with their repetitious complexity. There were so many of them! How could he ever choose the right ones? He took a deep breath and began playing the only other song he knew through to the end: the Chopin polonaise.

When he finished, Elspeth said, "That was beautiful. What was it?"

"Schubert," he lied. Who knew whether a Polish nationalist from the nineteenth century was offensive or proscribed?

"Very good." Elspeth was speaking in a stilted manner, as though completing a ritual. She continued in that vein, "Now, stand up and close the piano."

He did as she commanded. Her voice was chilling, and as he slid the cover back into place, he felt as though he were placing the lid on a coffin.

"Now," Elspeth spoke as to a child, "put the bench back where it belongs."

He did so, then turned to face her. There was something more, and he knew it.

"Now," Elspeth said distinctly, as though he would have trouble understanding, or as if what she had to say was serious, "if you ever touch my piano again to do anything other than clean it, I will have my husband break your fingers. Do you understand?"

He nodded. He believed her, too. The transition from the woman who could enjoy listening to him play to the woman who threatened to destroy his hands was seamless and all the more believable because of that.

That evening, as he huddled with Elda under the platform, he found himself stroking his fingers, wondering if Elspeth would really ever do such a thing. Probably not, but he wasn't about to try to find out.

"Are you going to tell me what this word is?" Elda asked, obviously not for the first time.

"Huh? Oh, I'm sorry." He squinted his eyes and tried to read the word she was pointing at.

"What's on your mind?" Elda asked, closing the book before he could make the word out in the dim light.

He told her about Elspeth and the piano.

"But she didn't hurt you, did she?"

He shook his head. "No, not at all."

"So what's the problem? I mean, it is *her* piano, isn't it?"

He struggled to find the words to explain without sounding like some sort of rabble-rousing Communist agitator.

"I mean, look at it from her point of view," Elda offered helpfully. "Would you want your worker messing around with your valuable stuff rather than doing his job? Wouldn't that tick you off?"

"What are you doing under there?" an angry voice demanded, startling them both. Peter and Elda pressed themselves deeper into the shadows, but it was too late, they had been too careless.

"I said, what are you doing under there?" Someone jumped down from the platform above, and then a face peered at them. "That's not a good place to hide." The face disappeared briefly, the legs turned this way and that, then the face reappeared. "Come on out, I'll show you a better place, further up the tracks."

====================== 34 ======================

*R*ICHARD LEANED BACK, closed his eyes, and let the music wash over him. The concerto came to an end and the announcer's dulcet tones filled the silence. Richard sighed and opened his eyes to the harsh fluorescent lights of his office. Reluctantly, he reached over and turned off the radio, then sighing again, he checked the time. Only ten minutes late. It was probably long enough. He buzzed his secretary and asked, "Are the candidates ready?"

"Yes, *mein Herr,* they are waiting in the small conference room, as you requested," her crisp voice answered through the intercom.

As he strode down the hall toward the small conference room, he thought about Til. The competent aide with his irrepressible jokes would be hard to replace, and Richard sorely missed Til's wicked sense of humor. Nevertheless, he already knew which candidate he would choose; it was only a formality that he was obliged to interview all three.

He entered the room and the three young men snapped to attention. Richard scanned them, trying to guess which was his man: one tall with close-cropped brown hair, one short with brown hair that was already perilously thin, and a pale, dark-haired young man with an intense, worried expression. It would be the worried one, he decided with some regret—there would no longer be any jokes in the office.

"Welcome, gentlemen, I'm glad you could make it here," Richard greeted them.

They looked somewhat confused by this, and it took a moment before each managed to stammer a reply.

"I wanted to address the three of you together to save myself some repetition. Afterwards, I'll talk to you individually to learn more about you so that I can make my decision on which of you would be best suited to work as my aide," Richard explained, then added, "But first, please introduce yourselves." He turned to the tall one to start.

"I'm Geerd Vogel."

"And you're from . . . ?" Richard prompted.

"Berlin, *mein Herr*," Geerd answered. "I mean, originally. Now I'm stationed—"

"Yes, yes, I know all that," Richard interrupted impatiently. "What's your father do?"

Geerd cast his eyes down for a moment as if searching for the correct answer, then reluctantly answered, "He works for the Reichssicherheitshauptamt."

"Interesting." Turning toward the short, balding one, Richard asked, "And you?"

"Wolf-Dietrich Schindler, *mein Herr*," the young man announced crisply. "From Berlin as well," he added before Richard could prompt him.

"Ah, and your father?"

"RSHA as well, *mein Herr*."

Richard turned to the intense young man. "And you?"

"Stefan Oldemeier, *mein Herr*. From Danzig, *mein Herr*. My father was a dockworker."

"Ach, a genuine worker for the National Socialist German Worker's Party!" Richard added as the three young men exchanged confused glances. "How unique!"

Richard turned from them and started pacing, then brusquely ordered, "Sit down, sit down!"

Once the candidates had seated themselves, he began, "Your applications were vetted through several layers of bureaucracy, both military and civilian. You are all Party members, you are all military, and two of you have connections in Berlin as well. I am aware of the expectations that will be placed upon you in this position, but perhaps you are not; so allow me to enlighten you.

"Your job will be to serve as my aide, and if necessary, my bodyguard. You will gather information for me, provide assistance at meetings and during my travels, and as your career progresses, oversee some projects. You will also be expected to spy on me and report to your superiors on my activities. This oversight of our activities by both the Party and the military is . . . ." Richard paused and scanned each face in turn. "Unavoidable," he said at last.

"Nevertheless, beyond those constraints, I expect absolute loyalty from my subordinates. I will make no attempt to hinder you from carrying out your duties, I have nothing to hide.

"However, I do not expect, nor will I tolerate, any extracurricular investigative efforts on your part. Your position here is not to be used as a springboard to military success at my expense! In return, when I make my report on you to my superiors, as I must, I will also limit myself to relevant facts. We will both feign ignorance of each other's necessary activities in this respect, and in this manner we will be able to have a comfortable working relationship without the petty infighting and corruption which so often makes our jobs difficult."

There was a murmur and Richard raised his eyebrows, inviting a response.

"Herr Traugutt," Geerd objected, "no one has made any attempt to subvert my loyalty to you!"

Richard laughed. "I haven't hired you yet." He surveyed Geerd and Wolf-Dietrich, pointedly ignoring Stefan. "You two will be under special pressure, given your fathers' positions in Berlin. It would be remiss of them not to try and take advantage of your position as my aide to learn more about me and my activities, and it would be similarly remiss of me not to use you to extend my knowledge base. Clearly you will need to make some decisions about where your loyalties lie if you come to work for me."

Wolf-Dietrich opened his mouth to speak, but Richard raised a warning finger. "And you will need to learn to consider your words carefully. This is not a battlefield, gentlemen; here, words are weapons."

Richard stopped and considered his little audience. "I'll talk with you first," he said, motioning peremptorily toward Stefan, and then walked out of the room without looking back. Stefan rose and hurriedly followed him.

"Shit," Wolf-Dietrich swore quietly under his breath. "He's scary."

"I think he's just honest."

"Damn! I thought my father's position would be an advantage, but it's clear he doesn't want us."

"You think? I was rather encouraged."

"Can't imagine why. He nearly said it to our faces—he doesn't want us spying on him for our fathers."

"But why would he say that unless he wants us to convince him that wouldn't be the case?" Geerd asked.

"Because he wants to discourage us. That way, we won't make trouble if we're not selected."

"Oh. Hmm. I still think he's open to being convinced. He didn't seem to like how sour that other guy was. I think that's why he took him first, to get rid of him."

"Well, do you still want the job?" Wolf-Dietrich asked as if proving his point.

"Yes! And believe me, I'd be loyal. I have no interest in helping out my father's career!"

"Me neither. In fact, that's why I applied for this job—my father wants to have me reassigned to one of his pet projects. I'd get to be somebody's lackey and spy on him at the same time. I'd do anything to be outside my father's direct line of command."

"Me, too," Geerd agreed. "God knows it was a blessing being able to join the military. It was the only thing that saved me and my brother. My father used to beat the shit out of us all the time. All in the name of discipline!"

"Yeah, they're big on that—when they're in control!" Wolf-Dietrich agreed. He cocked his head at Geerd. "I guess I know you: your brother is Uwe, isn't he?"

"That's him all right."

"What's he up to?"

"Military. Ran away from my father as well, only with Uwe, I think it happened too late."

"Eh?"

"He's mad, I swear. Completely deranged."

"Why? What's your father do?"

"Oh, nothing really unusual. Just likes to control people. He ran me and Uwe like we were two soldiers." Geerd paused and scratched the back of his neck. "The only respite was when we had a man working in the house; then my father seemed to take out all his frustrations on him. My father would get so angry, so uncontrolled, he'd . . ." Geerd sighed. "After Uwe left, I got the special attention. Now I guess it's my brother, although he's the favored one, so maybe not. Plus Mom says we have another *Zwangsarbeiter,* so I guess Horst gets to be spared all the fun and games . . ."

"What happened to the first servant?" Wolf-Dietrich asked.

"He died," Geerd answered. "He just . . . He died."

"You have sisters, don't you?" Wolf-Dietrich asked.

"Yeah. Luckily for them, my father seems to consider females too unimportant to worry about. My mother handles them. Any women servants, too."

"My father doesn't give a shit what I turn out like. He thinks I'm just one of his career tools," Wolf-Dietrich moaned.

They sat in silence a moment, then Geerd ventured, "I wonder if things would have been better if we had lost."

"Lost what?"

"The war. I wonder what it would have been like."

"Shit," Wolf-Dietrich swore, glancing nervously around the room. "Are you nuts?"

"I'm allowed to wonder."

"Pff. Well, by our own philosophy, losers get stomped on, so I suppose . . ."

"Yeah, but if they'd won, it'd be their philosophy that would matter. I wonder what drives them?"

"Money," Wolf-Dietrich stated categorically. "Look what happened to us after the First World War. Shit, if they had won, we'd have been reparationed back into serfdom. There'd have been show trials to get rid of the leaders, and the rest of us would be doffing our caps to our Anglo-French capitalist lords."

"Yeah, probably."

They both fell silent again; the minutes dragged on.

"Shit, I hope I get this job, I really don't want to go to Hamburg," Wolf-Dietrich intimated.

"I don't want to go home," Geerd replied. "But I really have to visit. I need to see my mom and my sisters."

"You have leave?"

"Yes, starting Monday."

"First time back?"

"Uh-huh. First time since I left. I wonder what it'll be like."

"Good luck."

"I hope I don't need it," Geerd answered.

====================================== 35 ======================================

"**Y**OU'RE HOME!" his mother said, smothering him with a big hug.

"Ah, Ma!" Geerd responded almost shyly. He hated to admit how much he had missed her hugs.

His mother turned to the servant who stood patiently waiting a few feet away. He wore an ugly, bluish gray uniform, and Geerd guessed that he was the *Zwangsarbeiter* his mother had written to him about. Unusually then, for his status, he looked Geerd directly in the eyes and his lips curled ever so slightly, as if in disdainful judgment.

"Take the luggage upstairs!" his mother ordered, then turning to Geerd, she added in a much softer tone, "We've put Horst back in with Rudi, so you can have a room to yourself!"

Geerd thanked her and, kissing her once more on the cheeks, bounded up the steps to his room. He grunted happily at the servant, who was already unpacking his bags, and removed his jacket, cap, and gun and turned to leave. At the door he stopped and reconsidered. He looked back at the pistol on the dresser and then at the servant as he removed the clothes from a bag and placed them into the drawers. He returned to the dresser, picked up the gun, and took it back downstairs without noticing the scornful smile that his action provoked.

As he reached the bottom of the steps, he suddenly remembered something and bounded back up the stairs. "Hey, you," he called out to the servant. "Do you know how to read?"

The man shook his head.

"Ah." Geerd waited in the doorway. As soon as he saw the Underground newspaper emerge from underneath the clothing in his bag, he ordered, "Put that in the bottom drawer, under the clothes. It's military."

Geerd watched as the servant obediently buried the paper, then with a happy little grunt, he left again, returning to the sitting room to chat with his mother. He had a nice long conversation with her, interrupted only by some tea and cakes that were brought in for them. When he noticed the hour getting near to the time his father would be home, he made his excuses, explaining that he had friends who simply had to be seen, and fled the house.

The days progressed in that manner. Despite having been away a long time, he spent little time at the house. He visited old friends during the days and prowled the bars at night. His mother expressed mild disappointment, his father scowled but did not interfere: the military, it seemed, had conferred upon him a complete immunity from parental authority. Despite the uniforms and the salutes and the military hierarchy, he could say he was free for the first time in his life.

His freedom, though, had its limits. He discovered this on Sunday morning when he had naturally assumed that he could spend the time sleeping off his hangover. Instead he was awakened by somebody gently shaking his shoulder. He looked up and saw the *Zwangsarbeiter* looking down at him.

"What the hell are you doing here?" he grunted.

"You must get up, *mein Herr,*" came the terse but polite reply.

Geerd was not feeling well, and he was affronted by this presumptuousness. "Get the hell out of my room."

"I'm sorry, *mein Herr,* but I must wake you up. Your mother insists that you get up," the man explained as he picked up Geerd's robe and held it ready for him.

"Oh, fuck her. Get out of here. That's an order." Geerd paused, then asked in a confused tone, "You know what that means, don't you?"

"You must get up. She insists, *mein Herr.*"

"Didn't you hear me? Scram! Do I have to hit you?" he asked irritably.

"If you must," the man replied contemptuously.

Geerd groaned and stretched. "Oh, well." He succumbed to the inevitable. "What's this all about?"

"I believe you must attend a rally."

"Oh, fuck. I forgot about that shit." Geerd yawned. "Okay, I'm up, tell Mother I'll be down in a few minutes." Noticing a look of distaste and indecision on the *Zwangsarbeiter*'s face, he asked, "What is it now?"

"I'm afraid, *mein Herr,* I'm supposed to make sure you get out of bed and then help you prepare."

"Really? What in the world is my mother playing at?" Then not giving the man time to reply, Geerd sighed, "Oh, all right." He climbed out of bed, put on the offered robe, and stretched again. "Your smiling face has more than prepared me—I'll manage to shave and dress on my own." He waved his hand in a frivolous gesture and finished with a military "Dismissed!"

The *Zwangsarbeiter* turned to leave, but Geerd called out, "Hey, you. Wait, wait! Do you have a light?" Somehow, somewhere last night he had lost his lighter. The servant obliged and Geerd said between desperate draws off his first cigarette of the day, "Now, there, ah, yes, by all means . . ."

Again the man turned to leave.

"Hold on. Wait," Geerd ordered. "Rub my back, that bed has made it sore."

Geerd leaned back into the massage, and as the rough hands worked his muscles, he wondered why he always had a sore back when he was home. Every muscle was tense and stiff. "Ow!" he shouted. "That hurt!"

"Sorry, *mein Herr.*"

Geerd rolled his eyes. Can't even get a decent backrub nowadays. "All right, that's enough," he sighed, exasperated. "You can go."

Geerd did not go out that evening. There really was nowhere to go on a Sunday evening, and he had worn out his welcome with the few friends he had who were still in town. No, Sunday was an evening for families, and he had to spend it wholesomely, in the bosom of his beloved family. That night he lay in bed thinking about his unit and wondering if he would still be with them or if he would be working in Göringstadt. Maybe it would be better to stay with them. They were due to move south of Hitlerstadt soon—more trouble with some locals there. Too many settlers being attacked, their farms burned. It would be good to go with them, to do something useful, to protect good German folk—people who, unlike his father, made an honest living from the land. The terrorists, or partisans, or whatever they called themselves, would be hunted down, arrested, and suitably punished. Order would be restored. He would be bringing peace to a troubled land. He did not even mind the danger to himself that it would involve.

He felt restless and decided to get up. At the base of the stairs he noticed the *Zwangsarbeiter* sitting morosely on the floor in the hallway, staring at nothing.

"How come you're still up?" Geerd asked.

The man continued to stare tiredly at the wall opposite. It took ages before he deigned to reply, "Your brother is still out."

"So?"

"So I wait up to see to any needs he might have when he returns."

"Why?"

The man glanced up the stairway, toward Geerd's parents' room. "Orders," he sighed.

"But I was out late every night this week. And you were . . ."

"There to greet you every time," the *Zwangsarbeiter* finished. He finally brought himself to look at Geerd directly. "Did you think I was an insomniac?"

Geerd shifted uneasily. "No, I just didn't think about . . . I . . . It wasn't . . ." He stopped, confused. Somehow the man had made him feel guilty for doing nothing more than having a good time. He resented the man's rudeness, yet, on the other hand, he felt kind of bad that he had not noticed the unintended consequences of his actions. "Do you want a cigarette?" he asked suddenly, reaching into the pocket of his robe to find his pack.

The *Zwangsarbeiter* glanced up the stairway again. "Sure, why not." He stood, accepted the proffered cigarette, then grabbing the crystal lighter that stood on the hall table, he lit Geerd's and then his own. They continued to stand there, smoking in silence, Geerd leaning casually against the banister, the *Zwangsarbeiter* staring nervously up the stairway.

When they had finished, Geerd pulled out the pack of cigarettes again. He looked at it for a moment, then on a sudden impulse, he held it out to his companion, saying, "Here, you keep it."

The *Zwangsarbeiter* gave Geerd an inscrutable look as he reached for the gift. "Thanks," he muttered.

Geerd heaved a disappointed sigh. Somehow he had expected more enthusiasm at his largesse. "Well, I guess I'll go back to bed," he said, but as he turned to climb back up the steps, he somehow felt that something more needed to be said. He hesitated a long time. The *Zwangsarbeiter* had already reseated himself and was back to staring at the same point on the wall directly across. Still Geerd hesitated. Why did he feel the need to say something? It was stupid, weak even. The man had been quite surly, hardly even thankful for the cigarettes. He should just climb the stairs and go back to bed. Yet he couldn't.

This was exactly the sort of thing his father harangued him about all the time. "Weak!" his father would call him. "Manipulable! Emotional! Soft!" The insults would follow him the rest of his life. "Spineless, indecisive, pathetic, inferior." He knew them by heart. He looked at the *Zwangsarbeiter*. Would anything he said make a difference anyway?

"You know," he began, trying to decide what he should say, "I didn't know . . . I'm sorry about keeping you up all week."

The man cut him off with a sharp look, his eyes narrowed as if he considered Geerd beneath contempt, and those lips curled in that familiar look of disdain, but then, slowly his look softened and a resigned smile replaced the sneer. "It wasn't your fault," he finally said, switching, disconcertingly, to familiar speech. "It's your father's orders." He turned his attention back to the wall, adding, "Children are not responsible for the actions of their parents."

Geerd was so shocked by the man's sudden lack of deference that he barely heard what had been said. He opened his mouth several times to say something like *I'm a full-grown man! I'm not a servant! I'm an officer!* He finally decided on "Good night."

"Good night," the *Zwangsarbeiter* replied without looking up. "Sleep well, child."

Only on the train back to his unit did Geerd really hear what had been said to him. He replayed the words over and over in his mind and wished that he had said something more in return.

36

SHORTLY AFTER GEERD'S DEPARTURE, the family went on their summer holiday to a Baltic resort town that had been built by the government as a spa for Party officials. Peter accompanied Elspeth and the children on the train while Karl drove down and met them there. The spa was a miserable affair of well-ordered *gemütlich* shops and neat rows of concrete-block cottages, all a short walk from the sea. Little flags, strung along lines that stretched from one building to another, fluttered incessantly in the wind, and each cottage had a concrete swastika, done in relief and then painted black, on its peak.

Peter found himself sleeping on the floor of their cottage, keeping everything in order and tending to the needs, wishes, and whims of the entire family. They were depressingly ever-present in the small house, and their petty desires seemed to multiply with the sea breezes. It was made abundantly clear that he was not on holiday—he was present solely to see to their needs—and so he was never taken with them on their walks along the beach nor was he permitted to explore on his own. Elspeth had him accompany her into the town to shop once or twice, but the cold waters of the Baltic remained unseen.

Driven by the maddening scent of salt, he tried, several times, to leave the confines of the cottage's fenced-in yard but each time was immediately turned back. On his fourth attempt, the patrolman recognized him and threatened to arrest him. He pleaded to be let off with a warning. By this time he knew how to restrict himself to simple words, how to accent his voice, how to shuffle and flinch and avert his gaze, and the young patrolman took pity on the poor, ignorant, inferior being and, tossing his papers onto the ground, let him go. As Peter scrambled after the valuable scraps before they scattered in the breeze, he decided not to press his luck any further and thereafter confined himself to fulfilling his duties and remaining at the house.

At the end of the family's stay, he was ordered to scrub the cottage from top to bottom to make sure it was clean, orderly, and welcoming for the next family that would arrive shortly after the inspection. As they returned to Berlin, it was, he realized, the first time that their suburban house looked welcoming. Anything to get away from the terrible claustrophobia and unending demands of that horrible seaside resort!

And back to his school, for that's almost what it was now. Elda was progressing marvelously, and his newfound friend, Konstantin, had asked if he could bring a young coworker along the next time they met. After enthusiastically agreeing, it had especially irked Peter that he himself had then missed every possible meeting since. First Geerd's late nights out, then the family holiday. But now, at last, he could try to meet them. If only they haven't given up on my ever coming back, he thought.

They hadn't. In fact, Roman was there as well. Having ferried messages of cancellations and apologies to the students, he had become intrigued and wondered if he, too, could attend.

Peter paced the small storage room that Konstantin had shown him and Elda after discovering them under the train platform. He scanned the faces of his four eager students, cleared his throat, and began. "With all of you at different levels, and with, I gather, different expectations, I think we're going to have to organize this a bit." He stopped and studied the laden shelves of the room. "What exactly is all this stuff?" he asked Konstantin.

"Oh, it's some of the equipment we use to fix tracks when we find something wrong with them."

Peter made an appreciative face. It was rather more complicated than he would ever have expected, if he had ever given it any thought. "They trust you with a lot of stuff here."

"Ah, that's just because of my exalted status as a *Pflichtarbeiter!*" Konstantin joked.

"Not like us true lowlifes," Roman inserted.

"Yes, maybe my first course will be on caste systems throughout the centuries," Peter suggested with a little laugh. "And how they are almost always supported by the people just above the bottom rung." He stopped to light a cigarette and noticed how the boy whom Konstantin had brought along stared at the insignia on his shoulder. "It was a joke," he explained to the boy, then added somewhat sourly, "And no, I'm not really a criminal."

"Then what *did* you do?" the boy dared to ask.

"I hacked some guy to death," Peter answered deadpan. Then, into the boy's astonished silence, he added, "For staring at me."

The boy immediately looked away, his eyes nervously settling on Konstantin.

"That, also, was a joke," Konstantin reassured him. "My friend here has a rather weird sense of humor."

Peter laughed good-naturedly. "He's right. Don't worry, kid, I was guilty of nothing. Now, let's begin."

After about an hour Elda had to leave. The boy and Roman left shortly after that, and as Konstantin secured the door behind them, Peter returned to his pacing, musing, "I think I can steal sufficient paper from Herr Vogel's office, but I don't see how I'm going to take four or five pens without him noticing."

"I could buy two or three," Konstantin offered. "I am, after all, paid something."

Peter nodded. "That would help." He continued to pace worriedly.

"What's the matter?"

"The boy. Are you sure we can trust him?"

Konstantin nodded. "Yeah, I'm sure. He's a good kid."

"Why did he act so strangely?"

"I think he's in awe of you. I don't think he's ever met anyone—I mean, one of us—who's so obviously educated."

"Ah."

"How do you know so much? I thought you said you never went to school."

"I lied," Peter answered. He sighed. "I have my reasons for not being entirely honest with everyone."

"You were in an Underground?"

Peter stopped pacing and studied Konstantin for a moment. An Underground press had gotten Konstantin into his current predicament. He had done nothing more than live in the same building in which the illegal newspaper was printed. He had claimed, as had all the other residents, that he had known nothing about the activities of the terrorists in the cellar. He had, nonetheless, been found guilty of conspiracy and sentenced to ten years labor. So, now he served out his time as a track inspector, walking the lengths of rails from early morning until sunset, inspecting them and keeping them clean. He only had four more years until he'd be free. Did he resent Underground movements? Peter wondered.

"I take it that means yes," Konstantin said laughingly. "Is that what you plan to go back to? I mean, once you get out of here?"

Peter nodded. "Sort of. I mean, I can't go back to where I was, but maybe I can find somewhere where I can carry on my work."

"And what work is that?"

"Fighting for freedom," Peter answered, wondering why it wasn't obvious.

Konstantin laughed again. "Why don't you do that here?"

"Here? *Here?* I'm powerless here! You can't fight for equal rights from a situation like this! It's all I can do to keep myself from getting sent back to, to . . ." His voice faltered. He had *pleaded* with Karl.

Konstantin cocked his head to the side. "What's the matter? You're as pale as a ghost."

Peter leaned against the only bit of bare wall in the room and rubbed his forehead. "I wasn't sent straight here. I was sent . . . I was reeducated first, you see." He smiled wanly at his friend. "It was so bad, I can't even remember most of what happened. I don't want to remember. I just know, well, it left me . . ." He stopped to gather himself. "I'm too afraid to do anything like that. I couldn't possibly organize anything."

"But you have already!" Konstantin assured him. "Good God! You've taught Elda to read! You can teach these people! You know what they're like. Most of them are ignorant of freedom. Teach them! Change their attitudes!"

"Real change tends to come from above. Emancipation of slaves, suffrage for women, the extension of the vote to nonpropertied men—those sorts of things were usually granted by the rulers," Peter argued.

"Even if that's true, each and every one of these people is in contact with one of our rulers. Don't you think they might have an influence? Don't you think they should be prepared to know what to demand, what to do if their demands are met? Don't you think they should know why there is a revolution if there ever is one? You don't want them freed into an ignorance that lets them be resuppressed with Jim Crow–style laws, now do you?"

Peter laughed lightly, shaking his head in amusement at how his friend had cleverly deceived him. "You were involved in that press, weren't you?"

Konstantin shrugged. "So, it's agreed? I can recruit a few more students?"

37

"**H**OW WOULD YOU LIKE to take a little vacation, darling?" Adam asked as he kissed Zosia hello.

Joanna came toddling across the room to him squealing, "Da da da da!" and he hefted her up and began nuzzling her tummy. She giggled uproariously in reply.

"Oh, yes! What's up? Where to?" Zosia asked, poking Adam in the ribs to get his attention away from his daughter.

"What? Oh. Berlin."

"Berlin? That's not a break, it's business! What are you doing there?"

"Got to hang around and wait for a knock at the door. Wanda's told me your brother's getting vetted for another security clearance, and I'm supposed to be an old school roommate, or something like that."

"What about the age differences?"

"Okay, not a school roommate—maybe I fagged for him. Better?"

"Um."

"If you and Joanna are there with me, it will make it all the more believable that we're a reliable, German family vouching for an old family friend."

"Hmm. What do we get, a house?"

"Yeah. We'll have just moved in, so the neighbors won't be expected to know us—if they check that far, which I doubt."

"This is quite some production."

"They're pulling out all the stops, getting everybody out and about to try and make his story stick, placing relatives, friends, old schoolmates, all sorts of history all over the bloody Reich. This is big. If we can get Ryszard past this hurdle, then he'll really be well placed."

"It's a lot of expense," Zosia commented.

"But worth it," Adam countered. "Once Ryszard is in high enough, he can pull in all sorts of people, access all sorts of files, arrange things for us. It'll be worth every penny. Besides, a few bank heists will cover the costs."

"Bank heists!" Zosia laughed. "That dates you!"

"I'm sorry, my dear. I know you and your magic fingers can pull in the readies straight out of Reich accounts, but it's just hard for an old-timer like me to accept these newfangled thingies."

"You mean computer fraud, O wizened old man?"

"Yeah. Somehow it just doesn't seem right doing it that way. Too easy."

"You old fart!"

"Hey, I'm exactly your age!"

"You'd never guess it. But I'll have you know, I work my fingers to the bone pulling in the pfennigs."

"I know, sweetie. I wasn't denigrating your work. Honest," Adam soothed. "I know it takes a lot of skill."

"And work."

"And work," Adam agreed. "But know your money is well spent. Look, we'll have a beautiful place in Berlin for a month or so, we'll wheedle invitations to parties and spread Ryszard's good name about, we can meet fine people, and—"

"Fine people?"

"All right, Nazi shits, but powerful ones. A few good words here and there, a few dinner parties, let Joanna practice her *Deutsch* in situ—"

Zosia sucked her breath in through her teeth. "I don't know about that."

"All right. We'll not drag her out. We'll take a nanny. How about Ludwik's girl, Barbara?"

"Fine. Hey, if Ryszard gets this promotion, what about my mom and dad?" Zosia asked, glancing toward Joanna, who had wandered off toward the kitchen area of their flat.

Adam followed Zosia's glance and strode after Joanna, picking her up before she reached the oven. "Hey, it's on!" he exclaimed. "Are you cooking?"

"No, Marysia's borrowing it. Hers isn't working, and I could hardly say no since she always offers us some of her cooking."

"Just as well, or we'd all starve."

"You're quite welcome to cook anytime you want to," Zosia offered huffily.

"Me? What do I know about cooking?"

Zosia shrugged. "What do I? Anyway, what about Mom and Dad?"

"They're still going to play Ryszard's parents. Unless, of course, your dad gets elected to the government in exile. Then it's off to America!"

"That's what Julia should have done."

"What?"

"Run for office. Then she could have gone to America with Olek."

"She would have never made it in politics. Not her style."

"No, I guess not," Zosia agreed sadly. "Hey, why don't we include Olek in the family? It would be a good experience for him to get out and about, and maybe he and Barbara—"

"No way! He's hooked on your brother's daughter."

"It would be funny if Julia's son and Ryszard's daughter ended up together."

"How come?"

"Don't you remember? Ryszard used to be keen on Julia."

Adam shook his head.

"Ah, you were probably too young to notice," Zosia said condescendingly.

Adam grinned broadly.

"Or too busy with your own lusty teenage thoughts," Zosia amended.

"Only about you."

"Um-hmm. Anyway, first she was too young, then their work separated them, and then Ryszard got married, Julia got knocked up, and that was it."

"That might explain why he made the effort to come to her funeral. I thought he looked rather hurt," Adam remarked.

"Yes, well, did you notice he came alone?" Zosia pointed out.

"I thought that was because it's too hard for them all to get away."

"I think it was because he never told his little wifey that he carried a torch for Julia."

"Why do you call her that? She's all right."

"She's a doormat. My brother will use anybody who lets him, and she lets him!"

"Maybe," Adam agreed reluctantly. "It's hard to tell the difference between usury and love sometimes."

"So, what about Olek?" Zosia asked, bored with the subject of domesticated wives.

"I think it's a good idea. He could use the practice, but I don't think he should be family. He should come as our servant. After all, we'll have an entire house and he can keep our nanny company."

"Oh, he won't like that."

"*Zwangsarbeiter,*" Adam suggested, chuckling at his vision of Olek's reaction.

"No, seriously, Adam."

"I am serious! You know these people spend most of their money on keeping their jobs—you know, gifts, bribes, parties, *Zwangsarbeiter.* They have to prove their position in society! And the only people who bother with waged labor are those who are unsure of their position. For people as high in the hierarchy as we're supposed to be, hiring waged labor is like renting furniture: you would only do it if you felt you weren't going to be around for long!"

"I know, I know," Zosia agreed. "But think of poor Olek! He's been through so much. You don't want to ask that of him!"

"All right. Live-in, waged labor. It'll lower our prestige, you know."

"I know, but he'll appreciate it."

Zosia shuffled through the invitations, laying them out on the fine wooden table of their beautiful dining room so that she could sort them by importance and date. "How in the world did you manage to get invited to so many parties? I mean, you don't work anywhere, you don't belong to any clubs, you don't have relatives, you don't even exist!"

Adam smiled. "All my native charm, darling!"

"No, really."

"Ryszard introduced me at the officers' club as a visitor. He was taken in there by some friend he's managed to acquire here in Berlin. Some official he visited earlier. Anyway, I spent some money, let on my importance, handed out my card, and voilà! Suddenly everyone knows us!" Adam gestured magnificently toward the stack of envelopes. "Besides, it's *Winterfest*, everyone is looking for someone to impress with their fine houses and their overstuffed larders."

"Yeah, even I managed to acquire a few personal invitations," Zosia agreed. "The neighbor saw me out and about with Barbara and Joanna and she invited us—you and me—to her house for a party. Wanted to welcome us as a new neighbor, she said."

"How very polite."

Zosia grunted. "Pillage our country, murder millions of people, but heaven forbid, can't be rude to a new neighbor."

"Probably kind to her dog, as well."

"Doesn't have one. We talked about that. What she does have is a *Zwangsarbeiter*. Proud of that, she is."

"That proves my point—we lost prestige not forcing Olek to play that part."

"Yeah. She talked about him as if he wasn't even there. And he just stood there, a few feet behind her, staring at the ground. I couldn't see his face, but I thought he looked a bit like you!" Zosia teased.

"Pff! You're obviously suffering from stress-induced hallucinations, my dear."

"Maybe. So, here's the game plan." She gestured toward the carefully organized invitations. "I'm afraid we have a lot of smiling ahead of us."

"All part of the job, dear. All part of the job."

38

"**Y**OU'RE BOOKED FOR the Meissners' on Wednesday," Elspeth explained.

"I don't know where that is," Peter said.

"Yes, you do. You've driven me there."

"I don't know how to get there on foot," he amended, hoping she'd take the hint.

"I'll tell you when I write your pass. It'll take about an hour to walk."

"Will I come back that night?"

"Of course, I'll need you in the morning." Elspeth shuffled through some invitations trying to find a specific one. "Then on Thursday, you'll be working an official gig in the Reichstag Annex."

"How will I get there?"

"We're going, so you'll be driving us in. We'll take the car when we leave, but I guess there'll be some sort of bus for the workers."

He nodded. Two more late nights. Yet another cancellation for his students.

"You'll have to handle the children in the morning. I'm sure my husband and I will want to sleep in."

"So would I," he muttered.

"Huh?" Elspeth looked up.

"And Friday, *gnädige Frau?*"

"Here, of course. Ach!" Elspeth spat, slapping her forehead in exasperation. "I forgot you're supposed to work at the Schindlers' that night. What am I supposed to do!"

"I guess you'll have to reschedule your party, *gnädige Frau*," he suggested, pleased that she had hit her own face and not his.

"Nonsense! The invitations have been sent! People I don't even know. These parties are getting out of hand. . . . Oh, well, I'll just have to rearrange your schedule. I guess we'll need extra help as well. How was that girl who worked here last week, the Meissners' girl?"

"The twelve-year-old?" he asked, remembering the solemn, silent young thing who had shown up at their door and worked obediently throughout the night. "She was fine. A good worker." Late in the evening when everyone was drunk, he had tried to ask her where she had come from, but even then she had refused to say or do anything that might be considered insubordinate. Even answering his questions.

"I'll get her then. Or maybe the Hoffman girl. They owe me a favor."

Peter nodded. He had been used as the payback for a favor often enough already that he did not even mentally protest the idea of trading people around like so many poker chips.

The Hoffmans' girl arrived on the appointed evening. She looked to be around eighteen and wore the gray and yellow of an indentured servant. She had walked the eight kilometers or so from her residence and stood now at the back door, her mousy brown hair hanging loosely about her face, looking somewhat bedraggled and confused. Peter welcomed her, generously offered her some of his tea and bread, then went to inform Elspeth of her arrival.

They worked together through the evening serving the canapés, offering drinks, and tending the kitchen. She had pulled her hair back and straightened her clothing, and Peter watched in fascination as he saw a miraculous transformation come over her as she stepped among the guests. She smiled demurely, her eyes sparkled with implied flattery, and she evinced an air of genuine respect and almost awe as she carried out her duties. In the kitchen, though, her demeanor was sullen and she treated him with a disdain bordering on contempt. He assumed her arrogance was born of their different uniforms, for although the conditions of her life were essentially identical to his, she had been given a higher social rank, which, though arbitrary and imaginary, was taken quite seriously by those whom it benefited.

Despite her exalted position, she was, however, not above indulging in the favorite sport of domestic staff during this season. Because of all the parties and the attendant confusion, the established tradition among domestic staff was to stuff themselves silly on food from the kitchen, and the Hoffmans' girl not only grabbed at the spare food, she seemed to assume her superior status gave her precedence. As Peter was already feeling rather sated, he let her have her little victories over him and amused himself instead with grabbing food directly from the party. It was certainly riskier, but a lot more entertaining as well.

As the evening wore on and the guests became more inebriated, the risks diminished considerably, and it was almost without a thought that he swiped a bit of leberwurst on a corner of bread that someone had bit into and then left on a side table. He popped it whole into his mouth and was endeavoring to chew it discreetly when Elspeth summoned him. He made his way to her side of the room, struggling to dissolve the food so that he could swallow it without being seen to chew. He nearly choked as he forced half of it down his throat. The other half got shoved into a corner of his mouth so he could murmur, *"Gnädige Frau?"*

"See, you can see it if you look at him." Elspeth did not deign to address him, rather she was pointing out something to her guests.

They hovered around him, scrutinizing his face in particular. Eventually one confused onlooker said, "But he does have blue eyes."

"Yes, and his hair isn't really dark."

"In fact, he looks just like one of us," a woman opined impishly. Peter looked at her; she was achingly beautiful. Her hair was a dark blond, darker than the other women's but only because it was not bleached. Her eyes darted quickly around, and then, when she decided she was unobserved, she winked at him.

He was taken aback. He looked for a hint of explanation in her expression, but there was none, as if it had not even happened.

"That doesn't matter," Elspeth assured them knowledgeably. "You can see it in their faces: they're just not as intelligent, they lack honesty, and they don't have our good German character."

He scanned the faces surrounding him. For whom was this performance? Did Elspeth really believe what she was saying? The women around him looked dutifully impressed by her words, but then they would, it was only polite.

"They really aren't the same as us, are they?" someone ventured.

"Not at all!" the dark blond woman agreed heartily. None of the surrounding women heard the sarcasm in her voice, but Peter was sure it was there. Again he could not stop himself from looking at her face. He thought he saw a glimmer of camaraderie in her eyes, but there was no way he could react to it.

"It's not hard to see their innate inferiority," someone else was saying.

"They're like children."

"Except they lack the innocence."

"You're right, of course."

"Can you imagine that some people hold we are all created equal!"

"Utter nonsense."

He noticed that Elspeth's eyes left him and strayed to the servant girl as she nodded her agreement.

"The Americans even put it in one of their documents. It's so obviously untrue!"

"Goes against history."

"And common sense."

"They're idiots! It's so obvious there are classes of people! Only race-mixing ever makes it unclear."

"Yes, and look what mixing does. Such a shame to pollute the pure blood." This was followed by a moan, as if the thought caused genuine pain.

"Like the English," Elspeth agreed. "*Gemischt*, like him."

There was a general murmur of agreement. As if also agreeing, the woman with the dark blond hair reached out to touch him. She stroked his cheek and he felt the skin tingle at her touch. He felt his heart would break from longing, and he determinedly pulled his gaze away from her and in so doing caught Elspeth's eye; she scowled in return, clearly indicating that he should not be so brazen as to look directly at any of them.

He focused his eyes on her midriff, and that seemed to placate her. As the ladies' conversation swam around him, he studied the intricate pattern of multicolored swastikas worked into her dress; here and there, where the seams gathered the material together, the four arms of the *Hakenkreuz* collapsed into three, or sprouted a fifth. Why exactly were other races so different? he heard someone ask. The little swastika mutants marched dutifully down the length of Elspeth's dress, disappearing into the pleats, without providing an answer. Another empty glass was set on his tray, and the last full glass of *Sekt* was plucked off it.

With the tray emptied, he was released from the clutch of women to return to the kitchen. Elspeth discreetly extricated herself as well and followed him in. He heard her behind him just as he was reaching for something to eat, and he awkwardly set the bread and cheese back down on the serving board.

"What is your problem?" she demanded angrily.

"*Gnädige Frau?*" he responded, genuinely confused.

"You! Out there! You're so grim. Damn it, you're spoiling the mood of my party!"

Grim was hardly the right word, more like *bewitched*, but that hardly seemed a sensible thing to say to her, so he said, "My apologies, *gnä' Frau*."

"Just get that miserable look off your face. Look at her," Elspeth said, pointing at the girl who had just returned to the kitchen with a cheerful grin, "she knows how to serve!"

"Yes, *gnä' Frau*."

"Smile!" Elspeth demanded.

"As you insist, *gnä' Frau*." He let his eyes drop down along her tasteless dress. A sardonic smile appeared without effort. It was all he could do to keep from snorting his derision.

She slapped him. "How dare you mock my orders!"

"I beg your forgiveness, *gnädige Frau,*" he heard himself say as he pulled the smile back into a reasonably serious look.

Elspeth snorted. "Just don't let me see you looking miserable again. You understand?" She did not wait for an answer as she swung out into the hall, her face lightening into a charming and happy expression as she went.

Afterward, when they were cleaning up, Peter and the girl gathered the abandoned food and drink into the kitchen for later disposal. As soon as Elspeth grew tired of watching them and went to bed, they both immediately returned to the kitchen and ate and drank everything that should, technically, have been thrown away. The girl then returned to the sitting room, inspected every ashtray, and secreted any unused cigarette ends in her pockets. Peter decided to let her keep all the little treasures since he already had a reasonable supply, but he was annoyed when the next thing she did was to throw herself down on the couch and promptly fall asleep.

He glared at her for a moment, but then decided to let her sleep and finish the work himself. Hours later, when he was done, he nudged her.

"Get up. You can't stay there."

"Why not?" she mumbled sleepily.

"If Frau Vogel finds you, I'll get the shit kicked out of me."

"How likely is it that someone will notice?" she responded, unimpressed.

"Likely enough. Come on, you can sleep upstairs."

She groaned and reluctantly stood up. "Where's the toilet?"

"In the cellar."

"Oh, lucky you. Indoor plumbing." With that, she promptly headed to the guest toilet off the hallway. He grimaced in annoyance but said nothing. He paced the hall, nervously glancing upstairs to be sure no one had observed her breach of discipline. Although it had never explicitly been stated, he was sure he would be held responsible for her actions.

When she finally emerged, he grasped her arm and led her up the stairs to the attic.

"Christ! It's freezing in here!" she exclaimed.

"I know. We'll have to sleep together. There's not enough bedding. Anyway it will be warmer." It was not necessary to add that if they wanted, this was also a good time to indulge in personal relations. He had managed a few one-night stands in this manner, but he suspected that this girl was not going to be one of them.

She gave him a critical look, and he added, "Don't worry, you'll be safe. I'm not going to do anything you don't want me to do." That did not seem to satisfy her, and he realized it was probably the thought of bedding with a lower class that bothered her. Tough, he thought, and without bothering further with her, he lay down fully dressed and wrapped himself in his blankets. He awoke later in the night to find her huddled against his body; she felt so cold that he pulled the covers up over her and wrapped his arm around her, then fell back asleep.

In the morning he carefully extricated himself from her and left to carry out his usual morning duties. By the time he had returned, she was in the kitchen standing with cheerful respect by the table where Elspeth was sitting, writing out the pass that would allow the girl to walk back home. As she left, Elspeth sighed, "They're lucky to have such a well-behaved servant." She looked critically at him and added, "You should be more like her."

"Yes," he agreed tiredly, "I should."

He had a pounding headache—probably caused by the wild mixture of alcohols and foods he had consumed the night before—and he wished Elspeth would leave the kitchen so he could get on with his work.

"Where are the leftovers from last night?" Elspeth's voice grated on his headache.

"They were locked away, *gnä' Frau*. Before you went to bed. Remember?" he answered between throbs, wondering if he could continue to suppress the urge to vomit.

"Not those! The others, the food that had been left lying around."

"There wasn't much of that, *gnä' Frau*. What there was, was composted," he said, moving closer to the sink, just in case.

Elspeth walked over to the pot used to gather compostable foods. When Peter had initially suggested creating a compost pile for the garden, she had had her suspicions even then. Now she looked into the collection of wilted carrot shavings, coffee grounds, and eggshells with a growing conviction that her suspicions had been right. "I don't see anything in here."

"They're outside, *gnädige Frau*," he answered as he eyed the drain.

"You took them out last night? In the freezing cold?" she asked, forcing him to dig himself in deeper.

"Yes, *gnädige Frau*."

"But you left this?" She indicated the pot.

"Yes, *gnädige Frau*. I'm afraid I forgot about that."

"You're lying."

"No, *gnädige Frau*."

"You know we can go outside and check the compost heap."

"Yes, *gnädige Frau*."

"The more you lie, the worse it will be for you."

"Forgive me, *gnädige Frau*." It was not as much of an admission as it sounded. They had carried out this routine before, and whether or not he was telling the truth, he invariably apologized at this point. Determining the truth was rarely Elspeth's goal; rather, she was simply asserting her authority over him and the reason for his apology was generally irrelevant.

Unusually, Elspeth pursued the subject. "I talked to the girl before she left. She said she saw you steal the food that was left out. Is that true?"

Despite a surge of anger at the girl, he knew it was pointless implicating her as well. Reluctantly, he replied, "Yes, *gnädige Frau*."

"You realize, this can't go unpunished."

The hangover wasn't enough? he wanted to ask, but all he said was, "I understand, *gnädige Frau.*"

The eldest son, Uwe, was unable to be at home—this was the first time he had missed the *Winterfest,* and Elspeth carried off the nearly obligatory worried-mother act admirably. That afternoon, Geerd arrived home on leave, and she made up for Uwe's absence by absolutely inundating her second son with kisses and hugs. Geerd accepted the attention with good-natured impatience, greeted his father cordially, and kissed and hugged all his sisters enthusiastically. Gisela, in particular, absolutely bubbled over upon his arrival, and Peter found himself smiling, quite naturally, at her happiness.

The following evening was the *Bescherung,* the traditional exchange of presents. It was a quiet affair—no guests, just the family itself. After dinner, everyone retired to the sitting room to munch pastries and sip *Glühwein* or, for the three youngest children, hot cocoa. The television carried a series of heartwarming messages from the Party leadership and an occasional "Hi, Mom, and hail to the Fatherland" from one of the troops who could not be at home. Elspeth kept an eye on the screen during these short intermissions, sure that Uwe would be waving his hello at any moment. Peter stood uneasily near the door, regularly returning to the cauldrons in the kitchen to refill their glasses, and watched silently as the elder members of the family slipped into drunkenness. His feeling of isolation was amplified by their boisterous good humor, and he found his eyes wandering time and again to the flames that leapt up the chimney in the fireplace. If only she had lived. If only it had been different . . .

Horst told an off-color joke about *Rassenmischung*—he had finally returned from visiting friends just a few minutes before dinner, much to Elspeth's annoyance—and Ulrike giggled uproariously and promptly spilled the remainder of her wine. It was the first time she had been permitted to join the adults in drinking, and she was flushed with excitement.

Elspeth broke into Peter's reverie, snapping at him to clean up the mess. He looked around, vaguely shocked by his surroundings, then gathering himself, responded to her order before she could get angry. After the spilled *Glühwein* was cleaned and everybody's glasses refilled, Karl announced it was time to open the presents. It was somehow quite clear that Peter should not leave the room even though there was no real reason for him to be there; so he remained, uselessly standing by the door. There had been no time since breakfast for him to eat, and unlike the previous parties, it had been almost impossible to snag food at this gathering; he stood, hunger cramping his stomach, an intense loneliness preying on his soul, watching as if from a remote distance as each member of the family gave and received gifts. There were presents from absent relatives, from friends, from colleagues, and especially underlings. There were the happy shrieks from the children, the disappointed sighs, the quizzical expressions. All of it slipped into a general background roar as his eyes were drawn, once again, to the flames.

The fire required another log, and he absently attended to that as the exchange continued. He prodded and poked at the wood somewhat longer than necessary, taking a private enjoyment in the warmth that buffeted his face as he built up the flames. Not until Teresa tapped his shoulder was he aware that she had approached.

"It's for you," she said, holding out a small package.

His mouth fell open in surprise; he hesitated to take the package, noticing instead that Karl was beginning to rise from his seat, a look of suffused anger on his face. Karl begin to snarl, "What the hell—" but Elspeth, who was sitting on the arm of his chair, placed a restraining hand on his shoulder and said something in a low voice. She nodded at Teresa, who had looked back questioningly, to reassure her.

"As long as it's not too much," Karl conceded, and sat back in his chair with an avid look on his face.

"It's from all of us," Teresa assured Peter rather improbably.

Peter had remained throughout in the crouched position he had used to tend the fire, and now he looked up into Teresa's sincere face and smiled slightly. He took the package and opened it quickly. Inside was a box with three white hand-kerchiefs. They had a white, embroidered pattern of artistically linked swastikas worked into the material, but were otherwise unadorned.

After they had seen the gift, everyone's eyes turned expectantly toward Karl. He motioned imperially for Peter to bring the box to him. He rubbed his chin as he inspected its contents, looked meaningfully at Peter as if to indicate just how gracious he was being, then finally muttered, "All right."

Peter turned and smiled broadly at Teresa, took in the other children with his eyes, then again looked at her directly to say, almost in a whisper, "Thank you." His voice nearly broke with emotion as he repeated, "Thank you."

39

*L*IGHT SPLINTERED OFF the crystals of the chandelier and danced, fairylike, on the flowers of the flocked wallpaper. The huge, spotlessly clean windows looking out into the cold winter night reflected the merrymakers in their finery. The strains of the string quartet mingled with the rustle of dresses, the clink of glasses, and the low murmur of conversation.

"Is this really and truly the last of these things?" Zosia whispered into Adam's ear. "If I hear one more stupid joke about—"

"Calm down, sweetheart. Smile. We'll be through soon enough," Adam said, smiling into the crowd of partygoers, his head tilted ever so slightly toward Zosia.

Zosia sipped her drink and scanned the crowd milling around the large hall with its marble columns and period furniture set discreetly against the walls. Huge heroic works of art filled one wall entirely; another was taken up by the floor-to-ceiling windows hung with heavy velvet drapes. Servants scurried around offering drinks and hors d'oeuvres. Women chatted in gowns that glittered, men smoked pensively wearing uniforms and ceremonial swords. Zosia herself was clad in an emerald green, formfitting, off-the-shoulder dress that bespoke wealth and power sufficient to allow her to stand out in a crowd. "Poor Ryszard. I don't know how he does this year in and year out!" she whispered gloomily.

"Neither do I," Adam agreed. "But we've done really good work. I swear everyone in Berlin is now my great good friend and everyone knows about my father's naval career, my mother's wealth, and my lifelong friendship with your brother."

"Just don't overdo it," Zosia advised.

Adam laughed and blew a stream of smoke into the air. "Ninety percent of the histories told here are false. Why should mine be any different? Naw, Wanda's consulted extensively with Ryszard, and she and I discussed this ad nauseam. The only important thing is for them to know he's connected and he existed long before his sudden appearance in Krakau twenty years ago. All the rest is window dressing."

Zosia nodded. She felt somewhat left out by her brother's working through Adam, but that was typical. Ryszard had been immersed in the male-dominated, hierarchical Nazi culture for so long, it was second nature to him and he had probably not meant to slight his sister. His *little* sister. Their age differences were such that he would probably never take her seriously. Doubtless that had a part in it as well.

Zosia threw a tiny kiss in Adam's direction. "I'm going to wander."

"Good idea, we're not here to talk to each other, after all."

She walked over to a servant holding a tray of champagne, deposited her glass, picked up a new one, then looked around for someone to talk to. She decided to make her way toward a collection of older-looking men in uniforms. As she approached, she expected a slight parting of the group, but their shoulders stayed determinedly close together, and at the last minute Zosia veered away to save herself embarrassment. She ended up in a group of women discussing local affairs.

"... but the new government store will have all that!" one was enthusing.

"I like the local shops. They're *gemütlich*. These huge stores, they're horrible," another said, shuddering in response.

"They destroy the fabric of our culture. The government should not allow them!"

"But it is nice to get imported items. You can't get those in the local stores."

"What, in heaven's name, do we need imports for? We produce what we need here!"

"What about fresh fruit in winter?" Zosia suggested. "From the south?"

"Our grandmothers made do without fancy fruits from Lebanon!"

The conversation dragged on. Zosia perceived the pecking order of the husbands' jobs or wealth by virtue of each woman's willingness to bully her companions. Though relatively young for the group, Zosia decided that she would insert herself quite high into that hierarchy and aggressively debated every point that came up.

Eventually one of the ladies was sufficiently annoyed to turn to her and ask, "I'm sorry, I don't believe we've ever met!"

Zosia drew herself up and haughtily announced her own and her husband's name. She threw in a terse biography, emphasizing important names with such vigor that all the ladies nodded their familiarity, though each and every one of them was a complete invention. Then, when she was convinced they were all sufficiently impressed, so much so that none dared admit her own ignorance, Zosia casually threw in her brother's alias. One or two of the women seemed to genuinely recognize Ryszard's name, and they smiled with their knowledge of being comfortably close to power.

"But you are new to Berlin?" one of the more confident women asked.

"Yes, I'm used to sunnier climes," Zosia hinted. "My husband is here temporarily, working with . . . Oh, I guess I'm not supposed to say."

The confident woman was understanding and tactfully ignored the faux pas. "How do you find our fair city?"

"The air stinks," Zosia declared undiplomatically.

"Where do you live?" one of the ladies asked sympathetically.

"Schönwalde. Supposed to be a favorite with Party members, but I think the name is misleading!"

"Oh, I bet it's the canal near there. It needs to be dredged."

"I think the problem is that factory they've put nearby."

"Factory?"

"Yes, the fertilizer plant."

Zosia's ears pricked up. "When did that get opened?"

Half an hour later she had wrung all the information she could out of the women and she went in search of the husband who had provided most of it. With only a minor effort she managed to shoulder her way into the group he was in. She stood among the men, demurely sipping her drink, looking entranced by their intelligence and masculinity, charming them with her smile. It took another hour to subtly insert herself into their company and change the direction of the conversation, but finally she felt happy with the quality of the information she had picked up, and she returned to Adam flushed with success.

"What are you looking so smug about?" he asked as they walked hand in hand through the bitter night air from the train stop to their house.

"I not only spread Ryszard's good name, I have some information my father might be able to use," Zosia replied, kicking a bit of snow into the air with her toe.

"About what?" Adam asked, dropping her hand so he could place his arm around her shoulder. He leaned down and affectionately placed his face close to hers.

"Chemical weapons," Zosia whispered proudly. "If we can track down the details, I'm sure that will impress the Americans!"

She felt Adam pull himself in closer, and he whispered in return, "My beautiful Zosiu, I love you so."

"Did you hear me?"

"Yes. I'm proud of you." He let his lips brush against her cheek.

"It will take some time to track down all the details."

"Months, I would guess," he murmured, kissing her ear.

"And then we might need to organize getting someone inside."

"You know where I'd like to get inside of?"

"You and Tadek could do it. We'll send directives from two different offices. . . . Mmm, what are you doing?"

"Joanna will be asleep by the time we get back," Adam pointed out suggestively.

"Adam!"

"Months, Zosia. We have months. We'll go back, we'll gather information, we'll organize everything in due course. There's plenty of time. Let's take just a few minutes to ourselves." He unlocked the door of their house and led her inside. In the hallway he helped her remove her coat, then he took off his coat and boots. He lifted her into his arms and set her down in a chair. He knelt down and removed her boots, then reached up under her dress to find the top of her stockings. With a bit of difficulty, he managed to unhook the stockings, then he rolled each down her leg, kissing her thigh as he did so.

Zosia began to squirm with delectable discomfort. "We're in the hallway. Olek or Barbara might discover us," she protested weakly.

Adam finished removing her stockings, and sweeping her into his arms, he carried her into the sitting room, closing the door with his foot as he went past. While still holding her, he bent his hand upward and unhooked the little button at the back of her dress and began sliding the zipper down.

"Zippers are marvelous things," he commented as he set her down on the fine wool carpet. He lowered himself next to her and gently pushed the folds of fine emerald green fabric off her shoulders. He bent into her and kissed her shoulders, then her neck, and worked his way up to her lips, all the while letting his hands stray over her soft, exposed skin.

"Months," Zosia murmured dreamily. "Months. Yes, we'll get all the work done. We have months."

= **40** =

"**H**OW WILL THE HOUSEWORK get done? And the garden? For the first time in years it looks presentable!" Elspeth fumed. She stopped her angry pacing in front of the window and looked out at the emerging greenery. Spring! Planting, weeding, trimming, cleaning! There was so much work to do! "I simply will not go back to doing without adequate help!" she huffed.

"You don't have to. It's all arranged: he'll only be on an eight-hour shift, so he'll still be available to you eighteen hours a day," Karl answered.

"Sixteen."

"What?"

"Sixteen. Eight and sixteen makes twenty-four," Elspeth explained patiently.

"Oh, yeah. Of course. Anyway, you know what I mean. He'll start at eight in the evening and finish at four in the morning. So, there will be plenty of time to finish the supper dishes, serve up our drinks, then out to the Krupp factory. He won't be around in the evening, but he doesn't do much then anyway."

Elspeth disagreed. "He finishes up a lot of the day work then."

"Well, he'll just have to work faster during the day. I'm not here, and I suspect you just don't push hard enough," Karl responded with growing irritation.

"I don't let him slack off," Elspeth retorted.

"Hmm."

"What about when we have guests? It will look bad if we have to do everything ourselves in the evening!"

"If they're important, he can stay here that evening; if not, well, those guests don't pay the bills!" Karl replied sharply.

"Is it really worth it?"

"Definitely. If he starts immediately, we can get a jump on the price increases. They're not slated to be instituted until May first. His wages will not only make up for the extra cost of his rations, we'll even make a tidy little profit. About time, too." Karl's tone indicated that the debate had concluded.

Elspeth nodded, concerned but unwilling to carry the argument further.

So it was the next day Peter was informed of his new responsibilities. He listened with growing dismay to the brief description of his schedule. His precious nights! His clandestine meetings! His sanity! All would be lost. Quietly, hoping Elspeth might intervene, he said, "But, *mein Herr,* there won't be any time for . . ."

Karl raised his eyebrows and pursed his lips in a gesture of exaggerated interest. Peter recognized the violence implicit in the expression, but he was desperate. "If I leave work at four in the morning, I won't have any time to sleep!"

"Ach, you'll manage," Karl growled.

"*Mein Herr*, please . . ."

Karl stood and Peter fell silent. Karl walked up to him to ask, "Are you questioning my orders?"

"No, of course not, *mein Herr*. Just please, please reconsider," Peter begged.

Karl slugged him for that. "Nobody questions my orders!" he growled, then walked away to return to his armchair. "Get me a cigarette."

Swallowing blood, Peter glanced at Elspeth, furious at her silence. His eyes strayed to Karl, but there was no point in saying anything more, so he went to get the cigarette.

At half past seven, he made his way to the industrial estate that he passed whenever he went to get his rations. Because it was evening and he did not regularly walk this route, his papers were checked three separate times en route. Karl had flung a special permit at him, grunting that he'd need it to get to and from work. Indeed, it permitted exactly that: to be on the precise route between the house and the factory just before and just after his shift for the duration of one calendar month. That and nothing more.

He arrived at the plant a few minutes past eight, his papers were checked, he was given some coveralls, an identification tag was pinned to his uniform, and he was promptly led to a work site. The foreman there casually pointed to a sawed-off broomstick that rested in the corner by his chair and said tersely, "Don't be late again." That was his entire introduction and initiation to the plant.

His job involved unloading large drums that were filled with a foul-smelling chemical—fertilizer, it was said—off a production line and loading them onto a small truck that carried them to some unspecified destination. That was it, nonstop, for eight backbreaking hours.

Within the first half hour, any novelty value in the new job had been completely eroded. He had studied every strut of the warehouselike roof, estimated the number of rivets in each steel I-beam, memorized the pattern of stains and cracks on the concrete floor, and ascertained that no other worker ever came within speaking distance. As he worked, he tried to amuse himself by remembering the work he used to do, the analyses that had at one time been second nature to him, but somewhere along the way he had lost crucial facts, had let slip the fine connections. He scoured his brain but they seemed to be missing. Maybe it was hunger or exhaustion or the utter desolation of his existence, but something interfered with his ability to think clearly.

As the night passed, the growing ache in his muscles, the weariness creeping into his bones, slowed his thoughts further and he began to daydream about simpler and simpler concepts. About food, about rest. How the rough wool of his blanket would feel when he drew it up to his face, how that potato would taste when it had been boiled and generously salted. A persistent, sharp pain in his right temple began to make even those musings difficult to pursue, and as he let himself slip into a robotic semisleep, he spared one last thought for what this job would eventually do to his brain: the work was quite literally mind-numbing.

There was one minor break in the routine: when he had finished loading the small automatic trolley, the foreman informed him he should throw a lever to send it forward and allow the next empty cart to approach. He fixated on that simple action as his last connection to a human decision-making process. A machine would not get to decide when to pull that lever! A machine would not enjoy the sensation of the sudden rest for some muscles, the sudden use of others. A machine . . . He stopped that line of insane thought—what had begun in the evening as a joke had by early morning taken on a grotesque seriousness.

By the end of the first shift, he felt he had been assigned to a slow death by overwork. Every muscle in his legs, back, and arms ached, and his hands cramped from the awkward grip he was forced to use on the slippery, dirty drums. Whatever leaked from the seams of the drums not only had a foul, caustic odor, but it irritated his bare hands, and by the end of the night they felt as though they were on fire. At four in the morning, a whistle blew, he turned in his tag and the filthy coveralls, and then, along with all the other nonresident workers, he was free to leave and return home.

As he walked the long path home along the quiet streets, his head echoed with the continuous ringing and pounding of the factory. His papers were checked several times, but the special permit seemed to satisfy all inquiries. Finally, he reached the relative safety of the house and quietly entered through the back door. They had been obliged to give him a key to this door as Elspeth had not wanted to keep it unlocked for the night, and clearly, no one would be up to let him in.

From what she had said when he left, he knew Elspeth apparently harbored some insane belief that he would clean up the evening's mess before retiring for the night. He took time only to wash his burning hands in the kitchen sink; the cool water relieved the pain a bit, but the sensation did not disappear altogether. He realized that he was staring at his hands, unable to recall what he had just been thinking. The water was running so he turned it off. No, that was not it, something else. Oh, yes, Allison. She might have known what the chemicals were; maybe she could have guessed what they were used for. He was clueless. All he knew was that they hurt him. And he missed her. That hurt, too.

He dried his hands carefully and gave a short laugh as he looked around at the dishes and spills and detritus that had accumulated. He left it all and went into the hall. Ignoring the drinks glasses in the sitting room with their hardening glaze of sickly sweet liquid, he pointedly stepped over the toys strewn about the hall and the stairs. It would all have to wait. In this instance at least, he would simply have to disappoint Elspeth. Dimly aware that he had just over an hour to sleep, he climbed the steps to the attic and collapsed into his bed thoroughly exhausted.

An hour or so later he awoke. His muscles were so sore, it was actually a relief to get up from the hard floor. As he stood up, he retched and spat up a handful of foul-smelling, rust-colored mucus. Disgusted, he wiped his hand on a rag and threw it into a corner. Since he had not eaten, he assumed it was hunger that had inspired his brief nausea. He yawned expansively and stretched to try to wake himself. Though he was tired, it was more the aching soreness of his muscles that bothered him, and he gave himself a rudimentary neck rub before venturing out to purchase the family's breakfast.

At the best of times, he never felt thoroughly rested, and with this, his first night of near sleeplessness, he felt slightly stunned. It was as though he were almost drunk. He had energy enough to carry out his work—clearly he was drawing on his reserves—but he felt oddly detached from everything around him. It was as though he were inhabiting someone else's body, and though he was somewhat unfamiliar with it, it worked well enough.

The daytime routine was tedious but not particularly taxing. Now and then he realized that he had simply stopped whatever he was doing quite without meaning to; he would wake from his daze to find himself standing, staring sightlessly, his hand resting on a bookshelf or a piece of furniture. He would blink, look around, and then with a sigh, remember what he had been doing and continue doing it. As the day wore on, the realization that he would return to the factory in the evening gained reality, and he began to dread the night.

His second night at work was worse than the first. By the time he staggered home in the early-morning chill, he was barely able to do more than mindlessly put one foot in front of the other. His muscles felt like lead; each move required a concentrated effort of will, and as he climbed the steps to his bed, he grabbed for air in painful little gasps. He collapsed into his bed aware of the pounding of his heart, aware that even closed, his eyes ached, but aware of little else.

Elspeth had to wake him in the morning and she was furious. She knew that this stupid idea of Karl's would mean nothing but trouble for her, and she vented her anger with well-placed kicks and a stream of incomprehensible invective. He rolled away from her kicks, struggled to his feet, and began offering apologies he barely understood when he was interrupted by a fit of coughing that ended in him spitting up a handful of rust-colored mucus. Horrified, he stared at it. It was the same color as the chemical he carried. Was he ingesting it somehow? Or was it blood giving the vomit that strange color?

Elspeth was equally horrified, but for different reasons. "That's disgusting! Clean it up!" she ordered.

He found the rag he had used the day before and wiped his hand on it.

"You're filthy and you stink. You're utterly revolting," Elspeth added by way of commiseration.

He nodded, apologized, and promised to clean himself up. Elspeth stomped off and he began another grueling day. He muddled his way through his routine as if in a sleepwalk: all the muscles in his body hurt—they were stiff and sore and responded with a disturbing clumsiness. His hands felt as if they were on fire, the cramping in them had spread to his arms, and there were painful spasms in his back as well. His eyes burned as though he were looking into a furnace, and he could barely fight the urge to close them.

He felt sure that he would drop dead that very evening, but when he returned to his job that night, he found his body already beginning to adapt. It had been more than two years since he had been required to do strenuous physical labor, but his body recognized the work, and over the next several days, his muscles strengthened, his hands hardened, and he ceased to feel like death was stalking him. He also worked at coping with his new schedule: he noticed that the bakeries were open by the time he was let off, so he began taking the morning ration card with him to work and purchasing the family's breakfast on his way home. This allowed him some extra time to sleep in, and with the children beginning to go on their summer schedules, he was able to add a few more precious minutes to his night's sleep.

Still, no matter how much he adapted, his day inevitably began just two hours after it had ended. The day's work was rarely strenuous, and he knew the routine well enough that it involved little thought, but sleep deprivation and the exhausting labor of his evenings rapidly took their toll. Eventually, he lost his ability to concentrate; his mind seemed to shut down all but the most basic functions, and he wandered from day to day without even the energy to observe his own decline. Too tired to protest, he stumbled through his work, snatching at sleep whenever he could. Outside, he could kneel by the flower beds to weed them and close his eyes for a few precious moments; inside, he submerged his hands in soapy water and shut his eyes as he scrubbed the dishes mechanically, dreams obscuring his vision, factory noises drowning out commands until someone yelled at or hit him.

After several weeks, he noticed as he walked home in the chill dawn air that his eyes bled tears. He did not know their source—whether it was irritation or exhaustion or emotion—nor did he know how long it had been occurring. They continued to stream down his face as he lay down to sleep, but by the morning they had stopped—he was completely dehydrated. When he awoke, it was all he could do to remember to drink some water and eat some food before he began his day.

It became more and more difficult to do his work in the house, and if he had been conscious enough to make decisions, he might have decided to sleep and accept the consequences, whatever they were. But he had thrown himself into a completely automatic state, and he rolled out of his bed most mornings without prompting, and on the mornings he missed, Elspeth was sure to help him awaken with curses and kicks. Finally, though, his body made the decision that he could not make, and he slept so soundly one morning that Elspeth thought that perhaps he was dead. She prodded him with her foot, but he did not move. Then she kicked and he did not respond. She went to put on the light and have a closer look, a slight chill creeping down her spine at the thought of discovering a corpse.

In the light, she could clearly see he was breathing; in fact, he was nearly gasping. He lay curled as if in pain, and his face, even in sleep, grimaced. She noticed that he had not washed the dirt from the factory off his face, and she felt revolted and angered. So typical of his race! So unclean! As she looked at him, she realized, too that tears had cut channels in the dirt and had left salt stains on his face. Just what one would expect of his sort, she thought, so weak they can't control their emotions. Crying! A full-grown man, he should be ashamed! She tried again to wake him, but he did not move.

She felt thoroughly fed up. This whole business was Karl's doing, yet she was the one who had to get Peter up in the morning, she was the one who had to rearrange their evenings and handle the jobs that he simply could not do. She was tired of sewing and mending and cooking, and she was tired of the garden falling into ruin and repairs going undone. He moved so slowly, he barely accomplished anything before he was obliged to leave for the factory, and then each job was pushed into the next day and the next and the next.

Karl should see this, she thought, and left to get him. Karl did not take well to being pulled out of bed and up to the attic, but he accepted Elspeth's explanation that she was not strong enough to shake Peter hard enough to wake him, and so, doing his manly duty, he stomped up the steps to sort out the problem. He surveyed the sleeping form with undisguised disgust, then aimed a good kick with his slippered foot to a point between the shoulder blades. Peter rolled and groaned but did not awaken. Karl bent down, grasped Peter's arms, and hauled him to his feet. It was harder than he expected and he was terribly off-balance, but he managed to pull the body up far enough so that he could throw it against the wall.

Being thrown against the wall was enough to wake Peter, and his first conscious moment was a realization that he was sliding down a wall into an awkward sort of sitting position. The next realization was that Karl and Elspeth were staring at him.

This can't be good, he thought, and immediately began to try to climb to his feet. A spasm of coughing prevented him, and he coughed and gasped and finally, as usual, ended it by spitting something out of his throat. He did not even bother to look; he just wiped his hand on his pants and tried again to stand.

Karl gave Elspeth a satisfied smirk and left the attic. Elspeth, shuddering her revulsion, told him he was late and to hurry, and then she followed after her husband.

What a civilized and cultured pair, Peter thought with a remnant of his old humor. Then he realized where he was and what he had to do and that there was no end in sight. He had an urge to weep, but he was too dehydrated.

<hr />

41

ADAM GRINNED as he was shown through the door of the office. A paunchy, balding man in a brown suit stood to greet him enthusiastically. "Ah, *Herr Major,* so glad you could come, so glad you could visit us!"

Adam shook his hand and accepted a drink from a pretty, smiling young woman. She gave him a sidelong glance and then blushed quite becomingly before turning away. Adam scanned the fine office with its large oak desk, its plush furnishings, and its exquisite decorations and then turned his attention to the other man, who sat waiting in an armchair, smoking a cigarette.

"Ach, I see you've noticed Herr Steinbach. I take it you two know of each other?" the manager asked.

Adam nodded. "Yes, Herr Steinbach's and my office have been in communication for some time, though we've never met." He extended his hand to shake Herr Steinbach's.

Tadek stood reluctantly and accepted the proffered hand. "Ah, *Herr Major,* it's always a pleasure to meet with the military arm of security," he commented snidely.

"Likewise for your branch," Adam responded jovially. He downed his drink in a gulp, handed it to the secretary for a refill, and walked over to the large picture window and looked out at the gentle landscape of suburban Berlin. "You have a nice view."

The manager stood next to him and nodded. "Yes, it is a nice view. But it's in the other direction that you'll see the business end of this place. Shall we begin our tour?"

Tadek and Adam dutifully followed their tour guide as he led them into the bowels of the chemical factory. "I know you're interested in the security of our storage facilities here," the manager explained, "and I want to assure you that we have the most secure arrangements imaginable."

"Just as well," Adam commented. "We pay through the nose to get these chemicals."

"Not only that," Tadek added, "we don't want our enemies knowing that they're here in volume."

"Oh, don't worry about that! It's a fertilizer plant as far as the public is concerned."

"I'm concerned about the electronics," Adam commented. "Where are those kept? You realize that we have to smuggle some of the more complicated mechanisms in from America, don't you?"

"I thought these things were brought in through India," the manager said.

"Oh, no," Tadek explained. "They had an election in August and since then the supply has dried up."

"Until we find out who we have to bribe in the current government," Adam added.

"Yes. Of course. Until then we're dependent on American connections run through Argentina. That's why these things must be so carefully guarded!" Tadek emphasized.

"Oh, yes, yes. I'm aware of all that," the manager explained. "You'll notice that I'm conducting the tour personally and that no one else is accompanying us! I understand how important this is, and I want to assure you, gentlemen, you have nothing to worry about!"

Adam grinned at their host, though Tadek looked unconvinced. They walked through a huge open area and then turned down a narrow corridor and ducked into a small room. "Here are the circuits you were wondering about," the manager assured Adam. "You'll notice the guards near the entrance, the lock on the door, and the fact that this room, though convenient to the work area, is totally isolated from it."

Adam nodded absently as he inspected the shelves with their unidentifiable gadgets laid out in neat rows, carefully labeled and numbered. Tadek returned abruptly into the hall and demanded, "What about that?" as he pointed upward at a videocamera discreetly located in a crevice in the ceiling.

The manager hurried after him and answered obsequiously, "That watches everyone who enters or leaves."

"And who views the film?" Tadek asked.

The manager began to reply but was interrupted by a violent sneeze and the sound of crashing objects from within the tiny room. They both rushed back inside to find Adam standing somewhat sheepishly among a pile of the delicate electronic mechanisms. He shrugged expressively. "Sorry!"

The manager shook his head in dismay, but said, "No problem, no problem. I'll have someone sort it all out."

Adam smiled his appreciation as he fingered the tiny devices in his pocket. They proceeded from there to a balcony overlooking another large work area where barrels of chemicals were being shipped off to various subunits of the factory. They watched the workers for a few minutes, and then Tadek suggested, "Let's go down there so we can see things up close."

The manager made a face. "It's quite dirty. I'm not sure we want to do that."

"No problem!" Adam assured him. "If you want to see dirt, you should walk into one of our concentration camps! Utter pigsties. Why, this is immaculate in comparison!" He gestured broadly toward the shop floor. "Don't you agree, Herr Steinbach!"

"I'm afraid I haven't made a habit of tromping through any camps, so I can't say. Nevertheless, I am interested in seeing what's going on. It looks like you have *Zwangsarbeiter* down there. Isn't it rather dangerous to have nonloyal workers?"

"No, no, no! It's no problem," the manager assured them as they tromped down the metal steps together. "We keep them under very tight control, and they work only in nonsensitive areas."

"It seems an unnecessary risk," Adam commented. "Why not just hire workers?"

"Nobody else wants to do the dirty work; we get complaints and illnesses if we put waged labor on this stuff. Besides, they're cheaper, much cheaper," the manager finished, gesturing toward one worker who was loading the barrels from a line onto a trolley.

Tadek studied the inefficiencies of the system and the moronic waste of labor. "Do these workers live on-site?" he asked the manager as Adam turned away from them and casually wandered over to some barrels standing nearby.

"Don't touch it, it's pretty nasty stuff!" the manager warned Adam.

"But your worker is covered in this stuff," Adam pointed out.

The manager shrugged. "That sort! They're used to it."

"Do they live on-site?" Tadek asked more forcefully, miffed that he was being ignored.

"Most do. We hire in some local labor now and then, when there's a shortfall of workers. They wear a special tag—like this one has." The manager gestured.

Tadek continued to quiz him on the advisability of such a system and approached the laborer they were watching to get a closer look. The manager hurried to keep up with him to defend his workforce selection, and they both left Adam behind as he mindlessly poked among the barrels, dabbing at a spill and wiping the accumulated chemicals onto his handkerchief.

Eventually he joined the other two as Tadek was saying, "If you can't place the trolleys closer, some sort of slide would make sense."

"Oh, it works well enough like this," the manager assured him as the laborer flung his arms around another drum and lifted it off the conveyor, carried it a few meters across the floor, and dropped it onto the trolley. He did not look at them as he worked, and Tadek had the impression he was a cleverly disguised robot. In fact, he looked like a mindless version of his companion and he said as much. "*Herr Major*, this one looks like you," he teased.

"Nonsense!" Adam admonished. "Don't be stupid! He doesn't look anything like me."

The manager looked from one to the other as if comparing the subhuman with his superhuman counterpart, but decided not to voice his opinion.

"No, really," Tadek insisted, just to annoy his friend. "I bet if you threw that one in a shower and dressed him up—"

"Don't talk rot!" Adam snapped. "Are these things sealed well?" he asked suddenly as the worker approached the barrel he had been toying with.

"Oh, yes! No problems there!" the manager assured them.

"Really?" Tadek asked, surging forward to look more closely. He bumped into the laborer and managed to trip him just as he was dragging the barrel off the conveyor. The worker stumbled backward, the drum fell to the ground, the cap popped off, and an orangish sludge spilled onto the factory floor.

Tadek sputtered his disgust at the droplets that had sprayed onto his suit, and the manager rushed forward to calm Tadek and berate the laborer while Adam stooped down to inspect the spill and discreetly scoop some of the sludge into a glass vial he held in the palm of his hand. He pressed the cap onto the vial and deftly pocketed it as he stood and went to join his companions.

"Are you all right?" Adam asked Tadek as the two of them walked away from the scene. The manager rushed to join them, leaving the foreman to deal with the mess. He apologized profusely, offering to return to the offices immediately so Tadek could wash.

"That's all right. I don't think I got much of it on me," Tadek assured him. "It was my fault really."

"Nonsense!" the manager argued. "It was that worker. That is a problem with the forced labor, they're so unreliable. But don't worry, he'll be punished."

There was a sickening thud of wood on flesh and a pained groan from behind them. Adam glanced back at the worker. "Indeed."

Tadek followed his glance. "That isn't necessary," he protested to the manager. "It really was my fault."

"Oh, it's not good for discipline to make exceptions."

"Besides, they're used to that sort of thing," Adam agreed breezily. "He won't even really feel it."

"Better than I had hoped!" Adam beamed at Tadek over his beer. "I think we have everything we need."

"I can't believe you got a vialful. The chemists will be pleased."

"Yeah, I thought the handkerchief was going to have to do, but then I had that inspiration to loosen the cap."

"Sheer genius," Tadek praised.

"Glad you followed my lead there. It was brilliant the way you got that guy to drop the drum."

Tadek shrugged. "I felt a bit sorry for him."

"I noticed. What were you thinking, telling the manager it wasn't his fault?"

"I don't know. It was stupid. You did a nice job covering. You can really pull off the callous act."

"Who says it's an act?" At Tadek's disbelieving look, Adam explained, "No, really. Neither of us have a clue what happened to him yesterday or what will happen to him tomorrow. I think it's rather hypocritical to pretend to care for the three minutes he's within our sight."

"I guess so."

"His life is already wasted; what we have to think about are the people who still have a chance."

"You're right, you're right. Still . . ."

"And what was that nonsense about saying he looked like me? I thought you'd gone mad!" Adam chided.

"Sorry, I couldn't resist. He did, you know."

Adam snorted. "There I am, supposed to be one of the elite among the *Herrenvolk,* and you point at some godforsaken, half-dead *Untermensch* and say I look like him!"

"Eh, the manager knew I was kidding you. Don't sweat it."

"I'm not sweating it!"

Tadek rested his mouth on his hand but was unable to hide his laughter.

They traveled together to Göringstadt and met up with Alex there. "Good job, boys," he praised, holding the vial in the air as if he were an expert on chemical analysis. "Is this all you got?"

"All! Of course it's all!" Adam sputtered. "What the hell did you expect?" he asked his father-in-law.

"Calmly now. Calm down, boy," Alex soothed irritatingly. "I was just hoping to have a good amount to analyze here as well as an untouched sample to send off to the NAU."

"We have your handkerchief," Tadek reminded Adam.

Adam pulled out the small plastic bag that held his damp handkerchief. "This was all you were going to get before we had a stroke of luck," he chided Alex.

Alex looked at the bag and sighed. "Well, I suppose it will help," he said, accepting it reluctantly. "Did you get any information about what they're up to?"

"Chemical weapons, like we thought," Tadek answered.

"I meant," Alex said patiently, "any new information?"

Adam rolled his eyes and muttered something.

"Neither of us are experts in that field," Tadek reminded Alex. "All I can say is that this seemed to be the only important ingredient. I don't know if it becomes deadly in combination with something simple, but it certainly isn't deadly in this form. At least not immediately so."

"How do you know?" Alex asked.

"I touched it," Adam volunteered, "and the manager warned me it might burn, nothing worse than that."

"Besides, some of the workers were covered in it. I'm sure it affected their health in the long term, but obviously they were able to continue functioning in the short run."

Alex looked pensive. "Maybe it needs to be exploded."

"Ah, that reminds me," Adam said, reaching into his pocket. "Here are some electronic thingies they seemed to think were truly important to the process. I think I got one of each, but I'm not sure."

"Great!" Alex responded. "Maybe with these and the vial, we can work out what the hell they're making. With luck, it will be a nerve gas or something good for terrorist attacks."

"Why would that be lucky?" Tadek asked.

"Oh, it's the Americans. They keep losing interest in us. If they find out that the Reich is producing nerve gas for terrorist export—say to poison the Manhattan subway or something—then that will perk their ideas up a bit."

"But if it's just to kill people over here, they won't care," Adam guessed.

"Afraid not. It's hard to keep their interest in people they can't see. They need a good scare now and then, and maybe with this"—Alex held the vial up to the light again—"we can give them one."

42

"**H**ERR TRAUGUTT, how good of you to visit us here in Berlin. And how are things going in . . . uh, which city was it again?" Karl asked with sly disinterest. As he spoke, he had a difficult time pulling his attention away from the American magazine that lay open on his desk.

"Göringstadt," Richard answered dryly. "We in the provinces are aware that here in Berlin you are extremely busy and don't have much time for tedious reports, but I have been instructed to inform you of my results since, as I understand it, you are involved in counterterrorism efforts?"

"Yes, but I'm afraid I don't understand what your prisoner statistics have to do with terrorism." Karl's eyes never left the magazine, and Richard was drawn to half stand to get a glimpse of what Karl was reading.

Karl noticed Richard's action and quickly said, "It's smut—obviously. I'm researching the decadence of the American culture and how this affects them. I feel that in these photographs of"—Karl shuddered his distaste—"women conducting themselves so immorally, we have proof of the entire corruption of that society. Exactly the sort of corruption that would lead to their state-sponsored terrorism within our lands!"

"I agree completely," Richard said smoothly. "They are a filthy people, and it behooves us to be informed of exactly how decadent that culture is. In fact, I've made a study of this, and if you're interested, I could probably supply you with further information—magazines and the like—along these lines."

"Really?"

"Oh, yes. I have amassed quite a collection, even videotapes, and I would be honored to share it with you. You wouldn't believe what they depict. Lesbian sex, interracial couplings, oral sex, ach! It is absolutely disgusting."

"Disgusting?" Karl repeated.

"But enlightening," Richard assured him. "It would not do for us to be uninformed, now would it?"

"No, no, not at all," Karl agreed, suddenly happy in his discovery of a new friend and useful colleague. "You know what, Richard—I may call you that?"

"Of course."

"I think we'll need to discuss this in greater depth. Maybe I'll even manage a trip out to Göringstadt."

"We'd be honored. Perhaps we could . . ." Richard stopped speaking as a man walked unannounced into Karl's office. Karl stood immediately to greet his visitor, and Richard followed his lead.

"Herr Schindler! How good of you to visit!" Karl enthused, clicking his heels and bowing slightly.

Richard read the signals and delved into the names and life summaries that Kasia had compiled for him and that he had so arduously memorized. Schindler, Schindler—ah, yes! Silently thanking Kasia for her tireless work, he was prepared with a gracious smile when Schindler turned to him in confusion.

"Who's this?" Schindler asked Karl.

"This is Richard Traugutt. He's here from Göringstadt to make a report."

"Treugott, Treugott . . . ," Schindler repeated distractedly.

"And this—" Karl attempted to conclude the introduction.

"Oh, Herr Schindler needs no introduction to me!" Richard grinned. At Schindler's confused look, he explained, "Your methods on the London riots are quite famous! We studied your techniques and have applied them successfully in many situations. In fact, I was just telling Herr Vogel how it was your inspiration which caused me to initiate the changes I'm reporting on here in Berlin."

"Treugott, Treugott . . . ," Schindler repeated. "Yes, of course, your report. Ah, yes, I've heard. Um, so what have you been up to?"

Richard managed to talk to Schindler for nearly twenty minutes, praising his famous work and his marvelous career. Schindler invited him to dinner for the next day, and Richard happily accepted. By the time Schindler remembered what he had come to Karl's office for, he and Richard were like old friends.

"Ah, yes, to get back to business," Schindler said, turning to Karl and waving a report that he had clutched the entire time. "Your report miscalculated the numbers! Here's the proposal and it's way over budget! That isn't what you told me! How are we supposed to pay for these things?"

Karl timidly took the report from Schindler's hands and paged through until he found the numbers. He stared at them disconsolately, shaking his head in disbelief. "This isn't what they told me," he muttered. "The bastards are trying to screw us."

Richard waited patiently for a few minutes, listening to Schindler and Vogel worry about the prices set forth in the proposal, then, when the moment seemed right, he asked, "May I have a look? Perhaps an unfamiliar eye will spot the problem."

Both Schindler and Karl looked at him in surprise.

"You gentlemen are both experts here," Richard explained, "but your very expertise may make it difficult for you to notice an irrational mistake in the presentation."

"What's your clearance?" Schindler asked.

"Top secret, *mein Herr.*"

"Well, that will certainly suffice." Schindler handed the report to Richard. "If you can work out what's wrong here . . ."

Richard scanned the report. "So the arms are manufactured in the North American Union and are given to the Mexican government to aid in their fight against drug smuggling?"

"That's right. We get them from there via Spain," Karl added.

"And it's these prices which are the problem?" Richard asked, indicating an accounts page. He noticed that the page seemed to be computer-generated. That, in and of itself, was interesting.

"Yes, they're outrageous!"

"Of course, since the point of origin for the arms is Mexico City, the prices are in pesos," Richard commented to himself.

There was silence from his two companions.

"It's always difficult for me to remember things like that," Richard continued, mostly to himself. "You know, the symbol for the peso is the same as that for the dollar. Confusing for someone like me, but I'm sure you gentlemen are used to such subtleties."

Both Karl and Schindler nodded.

"And, let me see, I'm not an expert, so I have trouble converting, but I think the mark is running at three and a half to the dollar on export trades, and the peso is, oh, something like seven to the dollar, so that would make each of these prices—oh, that is quite simple! Divide by two and the prices are in the equivalent marks. But you knew that, of course."

Karl peered at the page. "Yes, of course, if you divide by two, the prices . . ."

Schindler looked at the page. "Yes, divide by two . . . Oh, look at the time." He snatched the report from Richard's hands. "We'll handle this later. I think I have a meeting."

He was gone before either Richard or Karl could say a word.

Karl looked in the direction Schindler had gone and laughed silently. Richard laughed as well, just happy in the camaraderie of a close-knit, well-organized, competent ministry. Karl rubbed his face and then asked, "What are you doing this evening? Do you have plans? My wife and I would enjoy having you and your wife to dinner."

"Dinner? That sounds wonderful," Richard said agreeably. "Unfortunately, I am here alone. My wife remained in Göringstadt with the children."

"Ah, pity. Perhaps I could invite a suitable companion for you. Just for the evening?"

Richard nodded. "What about the archivist. Is she married?"

"The archivist? Hmm. Don't know. I'll have my secretary find out and issue her an invitation if it's appropriate."

"Oh, thanks, but no. She might view it as a summons. I'll go down there and ask her myself. I'd like to meet a few people in this building anyway. After all, I might be working here one day."

In your dreams, Karl thought.

Richard and the archivist, a young woman named Beate, arrived a few minutes late. A servant took their raincoats and umbrellas, showed them into the sitting room, and offered them cigarettes, sherry, and appetizers.

Richard relaxed in his seat and discreetly scanned the room. The house was smaller than his own back in Göringstadt, but he had learned that was typical for Berlin housing. The prices in the city were higher and the competition for good housing was more intense.

They chatted for only a brief while and then were relocated to the dining room—there seemed to be a slight rush to have dinner. It was just as well. Richard was quite hungry, and he wondered if it was his hunger that made the food taste so good or if it was genuinely delicious. He complimented Frau Vogel on her cooking, then seeing the slightly guilty look on her face added, "Or should I compliment you on your choice of cooks?"

Frau Vogel glanced at the servant as she answered, "Oh, it's all my own doing." She paused, then added, "It was just a bit of a rush this afternoon, my husband didn't give me much notice. I hope that everything is up to standard?"

"It is absolutely delicious!" Richard enthused. Beate nodded her head in agreement.

The dinner plates were removed, and a few minutes later desserts were set in front of them. The servant's arm brushed against Beate's shoulder, and he apologized for disturbing her.

Frau Vogel scowled at him, but Beate graciously replied, "Oh, that's quite all right!"

It was the first time Richard had truly noticed the servant, and he found himself oddly perplexed by the blond man who served the dinner so mechanically. His ashen complexion was eerily emphasized by the candlelight, and beneath his vacantly staring eyes were the blue shadows of exhaustion.

As Richard watched him, he noticed how the man's whole body shook periodically with some great effort at restraint. Richard realized the man was suppressing a violent cough, and this was what had made him bump into Beate. Something about the man looked vaguely familiar. Richard tilted his head so he could get a glance at the insignia on the uniform. An English criminal. Well, that would narrow it down to only several hundred men, none of whom would have been important enough to remember. Probably someone he had seen in that notorious prison in Exeter. Still, it would be amusing to see what the man had to say for himself.

"Do you speak English?" he said in English to the servant.

The man looked up at him, perplexed.

"Yes, I'm talking to you. Do you speak English?" Richard pressed. Again he used English. The others at the table looked at him with curiosity.

Finally, the servant managed to nod.

"Were you born there?" Richard asked, still in English.

Again the servant nodded.

"Where?"

"London, *mein Herr.*" The servant winced as he said the words as though he had said something wrong.

"Ah, London, that's where I was born," Richard explained in English. He still could not work out why the man seemed familiar. London certainly didn't narrow down the possibilities.

His thoughts were interrupted by the archivist asking, "What are you saying to him?"

"Oh, I asked if he spoke English and if he was born there."

Karl laughed. "He was found in a trash bin near Halifax and raised in an orphanage. Even his mother knew he was worthless!"

Beate gasped.

"Yes, the English are abominable, even toward their own. But don't fret for him, *Fräulein.* His bad blood showed up early enough when he turned criminal. He's lucky we've given him a home and a purpose. Isn't that right?" Karl finished by addressing the servant.

The servant looked at Karl in confusion.

Karl turned to his guests and apologized. "He's slow-witted, I'm sorry. But they all are. It's the impure blood." He turned back toward the servant and said very slowly, "We've given you a place in this society, isn't that right?"

The servant nodded. "Yes. I am very grateful to Herr and Frau Vogel for providing me with meaningful employment."

"And for keeping you on the path of righteousness," Frau Vogel added.

"Yes," the servant agreed. "And for keeping me on a righteous path."

Beate nodded, satisfied.

"I grew up in England as well," Karl said, turning the conversation back to a topic with which he was comfortable. "Though, of course, I'm pure German!"

"You did?" Richard asked. Chiding himself for wasting time on trivialities, he dismissed the servant from his mind and focused on Karl. "Where?"

"London of course! My father was in the colonial government. What about you?"

"I was raised there as well," Richard admitted reluctantly. "That's why I can speak a bit of English."

"I can't," Karl bragged. "Not a word! Stupid language. Idiotic spellings. Totally illogical structure."

Richard nodded. "So, you grew up there. Where did you go to school?"

From that point on, the discussion centered around Karl's youth. Richard was the truly interested guest, asking questions and refraining from offering too many of his own opinions. Karl was in his element. Eventually the conversation turned to other topics, and they relocated to the sitting room. They were served drinks, and then Karl motioned to the servant. "Clean up the dishes, then you can leave."

"Where's he going?" Richard asked as the servant left the room.

"Oh, he's working the night shift at a local factory. I get some money out of his worthless hide that way. Clever, isn't it?"

Richard nodded. "Yes, very. Be careful though."

"Why?"

"Well, certainly you know, if you rent out one of your laborers for more than a week or two, the Labor Ministry is likely to reevaluate your need for that laborer. It has been known to happen that a contracted laborer is seized and reassigned to someone with a greater need."

"I didn't know that!" Karl breathed in horror.

Elspeth cast a worried look toward the kitchen. "Stop him!" she whispered.

"A few weeks, you say?" Karl asked.

Richard nodded. "It's in the regulations. I can show you tomorrow if you wish. It's also, no doubt, among all the papers you signed."

Karl stood suddenly. "Excuse me. I have to make a phone call."

Ten minutes later he emerged from his study and went into the kitchen. "You are not to go to the factory tonight. That's finished."

Peter was standing at the back door, his pass in hand, ready to leave. He looked down at the pass, at the month stamped onto it. September. It used to say May, he thought.

"Do you understand?" Karl asked in clearly pronounced syllables.

Whatever happened to June? July? August?

"I said, do you understand?"

"I am not to go to the factory tonight," Peter repeated numbly. "That's finished."

"That's right," Karl said almost gently. "That's right."

Karl turned to leave.

"*Mein Herr.*"

"What?"

"Thank you, *mein Herr*," Peter said with heartfelt sincerity. "Thank you."

Karl nodded his head curtly in acknowledgment.

43

THERE WAS A COLD, driving rain. Richard had his arm protectively wrapped around Beate's shoulders, and she huddled against him to shelter under his umbrella as they stood in the doorway to ring the Schindlers' bell. Richard had spent some considerable time in her presence, and they had become quite close. During the day, with a charming, boyish grin, he had explained how he sometimes inadvertently made insensitive remarks and he would dearly like to avoid such mistakes with his new acquaintance Schindler. Beate was understanding, she often had the same trouble, she admitted, and she had helpfully opened the personnel file for Herr Schindler just to ease their evening's conversation.

They had learned much about his career. They had also learned he was on his third wife. His first wife had given him two daughters, both in their midthirties, both married and living in the Western Reich. After being divorced, his first wife had moved back to Bavaria. With his second wife, he had one, unmarried son, who was twenty-five and worked in a special branch of the army. "That boy applied to be my aide," Richard had confided to Beate.

Schindler's current wife was named Greta, and she was only a few years older than his daughters. She had been born in Switzerland of a German diplomat and his Swiss wife, and judging from the fact that their marriage papers were filed the day after Schindler's second divorce was finalized, Richard and Beate surmised that she had schemed long and hard to reach her current position. "I've heard about her," Beate had whispered. "She's mean as hell if she thinks you're her inferior—and that's what she thinks of all us working gals, but for the men in the office, she's always charming."

"Maybe she's looking for someone with more promise than her husband," Richard had suggested.

"Well," Beate had replied, wrapping her arm around him, "tell her you're taken!"

A young lad opened the door for them. He had pale skin, brown hair, and the slack mouth and vacant stare common to peoples who have lived isolated in the hills for too long. He announced their presence and, after taking their coats and umbrella, led them into the parlor.

When the two of them stepped into the parlor, they were greeted not only by Herr Schindler and his wife but by Karl and Elspeth as well. "What a wonderful surprise!" Richard remarked, and turning toward Frau Vogel, added, "Always a pleasure!"

He greeted Frau Schindler with charming deference, kissing her hand and adding, "You know, in Göringstadt, it is the custom to greet women by kissing them on the cheeks, but I'm afraid, here in Berlin, my greeting might be misinterpreted!"

"Nonsense!" Frau Schindler argued. "I insist we honor your customs." She leaned forward and extended her cheek expectantly.

Richard obliged, bestowing three light kisses.

"They've just gone native, if you ask me," Herr Schindler opined somewhat huffily.

"Ah, yes, that is a very perceptive observation," Richard agreed, "but I would have expected nothing less from you! Your ability to analyze situations in colonial territory is, of course, why you have been so successful in your administration of southeast England. Certainly we could use someone of your talent in Göringstadt!"

While Herr Schindler grinned his agreement, Richard smiled discreetly at Frau Schindler.

"But that would be a step down," Karl observed rather sullenly.

"Yes, it's true there is no place that compares with Berlin," Richard replied. "But we do have our compensations. For one thing, I can greet beautiful women with kisses, and there are so many in Berlin!" As he said that, his eyes took in each woman in turn, convincing each his words were intended solely for her. Frau Vogel, blushing slightly, approached expectantly, and Richard greeted her as well.

"But you're not from the East," Karl noted. "You said you were from London."

"Yes, that's right."

"Ach, that explains why you don't have that lousy Eastern accent!" Herr Schindler remarked. "Like saying *Ratusch* instead of *Rathaus,* God in heaven!"

"Indeed, I was raised in London," Richard explained, "but the past twenty years of my career have been spent east of Berlin, and it's with that region that I feel the most familiar, though I have not, as far as I know, picked up the dialect."

They began to discuss Richard's background and the coincidences that Karl was raised in London and that Schindler currently held overall responsibility for security in the area. Karl noted that Richard even spoke some English, as evinced by his brief and one-sided conversation the previous night.

"Yes, it's been a long time, but I thought I'd try out a few words. Your fellow wasn't very responsive though, was he?"

"They're not very bright, these people. It's unfair to expect much of them," Frau Schindler commented.

"Indeed," Herr Schindler agreed, "Karl's boy more than proves their inferiority."

Karl nodded vigorously, though Elspeth looked somewhat dubious. "But he's English, you know, and they are of the blood," she reminded them all.

"Pff!" Herr Schindler sputtered. "I've had to deal with these people, and whatever pure blood they once had, it's gone! They're a bunch of thugs and reprobates. Hopeless, absolutely hopeless, and the sooner we recognize that, the better!"

"But how can we change the fact that they are part of the *Volk?*" Elspeth asked.

"Hah! We all know that pollution ruins the blood, that's why we had to clean up our own society first. It's been obvious from the first," Herr Schindler lectured. "We try to deal with these people in a civilized manner, then, if that doesn't work, we know they need special handling! That's the way it was with the Poles, and—"

"With the Poles?" Elspeth asked.

"It's not generally known," Richard answered, "but Hitler's government wanted to form an alliance with them against the Communists. At that point they were considered worthy of being our allies."

"Why didn't they? Weren't they anticommunist?"

"Yes, they were, but they were uncomfortable with us as well. They had certain problems with our determination to handle some of their internal affairs. Their Jewish problem for instance. They said that Polish Jews would remain Polish citizens and as such were off-limits to German policy."

"Of course, that just proved they were corrupt to the core," Herr Schindler said. "Then the English, declaring war on us, what a letdown! The Norwegians resisting us, who would have expected that from a Nordic tribe! Ach! So many betrayals. Clearly our movement to purify Europe came not one minute too soon!"

"My father had to work with them, with the English," Karl added, "back when we were still trying to coax them into cooperating. What a shambles! We pushed a few into government, but none of them really made it. They were incompetent and sooner or later dropped out of the Party or disappeared altogether."

"What about now?" Richard asked. "Some of them still hold key positions."

"A mistake, if you ask me," Herr Schindler said. "I think they should be barred outright. It was an experiment that didn't work. They're corrupted, and the only thing they're fit for is something like what you have, Karl."

"The problem is they lack discipline," Frau Schindler added. "That whole culture is decadent. It leads to lax behavior and that leads to problems. Like with your boy."

"Problems?" Elspeth asked somewhat worriedly.

"Yes, I've already told you what I think of your indulging him like you do," Frau Schindler admonished.

"Indulging?" Elspeth repeated helplessly.

Beate smiled wanly at her, Richard busied himself by pulling out a pack of cigarettes and offering them around.

"Yes, you indulge him," Frau Schindler insisted.

"That lad of yours does act uppity, Karl," Herr Schindler agreed as he accepted one of Richard's cigarettes. "You've been too lenient with him. I think he could do with a sound thrashing."

"Ach," Karl disagreed, "he's all right. We've got him well in hand."

Richard thought of the man he had seen the night before. There had been nothing in his behavior to suggest anything other than a weary obedience; yet, judging from the level of discomfort the Schindlers were provoking in the Vogels, it was clear there was more history to the conversation than he understood. He decided to keep a discreet silence or perhaps offer a change of subject. As he was still contemplating the various segues that were on hand, a second servant boy came and stood expectantly in the doorway. This boy looked only marginally older than the first and had a sufficiently similar face that Richard thought the two might be brothers. Frau Schindler acknowledged him, and he announced that dinner was ready to be served.

They moved to the dining room, and the conversation flowed naturally along political lines, finally settling on an exchange of office gossip between Karl and Herr Schindler, and an exchange of neighborhood gossip between Frau Schindler and Elspeth. Beate remained grimly mute with the unfamiliar conversation imposed on her, but Richard was intrigued by the insights provided by the men. The meal itself was a rather bland affair of overcooked meat served with two styles of potatoes. When Richard complimented it, Frau Schindler admitted that she had a cook who came in during the day to prepare the evening meal.

"Yesterday, Frau Vogel cooked the meal herself," Beate informed her hosts. It was her first attempt at entering into the conversation, and the sudden cold look she received from Frau Schindler caused her to fall into bewildered silence.

Richard stepped in to rescue his companion, saying, "Both meals have shown me the wonders of Berlin cooking."

"Or is it English cooking?" Herr Schindler asked jovially, directing his comment toward Karl.

Elspeth stiffened; Karl looked wary.

"Your boy has many talents, doesn't he?" Herr Schindler pressed.

"He does what he's told to do," Karl answered at last.

"I'd keep my eye on that one," Herr Schindler advised.

"He's harmless enough," Karl assured him wearily.

"I don't know, I don't think so," Herr Schindler said. "I don't trust any of them," he added, apparently oblivious to the presence of his own two servants in the room.

"I think it's worse when there is only one of them. Like with you, Elspeth," Frau Schindler interjected.

"One suffices," Elspeth responded quickly.

"Of course. I just meant that you have so much work there, with the children and the house, you really could use more help. Still, I suppose the house isn't that big." Frau Schindler added the final jab quite smoothly.

"One is enough, even for a large house, if everything is properly organized," Karl grated. "There is a labor shortage, and we're just doing our patriotic duty to minimize our use of the labor pool."

"But it does mean that he's everywhere in the house, doing everything. That could be dangerous," Herr Schindler said, then added rather casually, "I think they should all be castrated. We'd all be safer then."

Richard noticed a fleeting expression on the face of the boy opposite him. So they weren't so oblivious!

"It isn't current policy," Karl answered slowly, shifting uncomfortably. Unconsciously he had clasped his hands protectively in front of himself.

"I think it should be," Herr Schindler pressed. "Do you have any idea how they breed? Like vermin. We'll be inundated soon."

"We'll be smothered!" Frau Schindler added tartly.

At that comment, Richard scrutinized her with keen interest. Here might be the ally he was seeking! Clearly the long-suffering Frau Schindler was frustrated by her husband's slow and stuttering climb to power and was advertising her disdain for him and his policies. She was proving her cleverness as well, for a glance at Herr Schindler showed that he accepted her comment as dutiful, wifely support of his position, and he did not hesitate to add, "In fact, I think it should not only be offered, it should be mandatory for all of them; especially in domestic situations."

"But then, darling, who would we blame for getting the maids pregnant?" Frau Schindler interjected with a pointed glance at her husband.

"They should be fixed as well!" Herr Schindler snarled.

Frau Schindler smiled graciously. "Or simply remove the women altogether. That's the trend, isn't it?"

"Why?" Beate asked.

"They offer too much temptation to our German manhood," Frau Schindler answered.

"And the men servants?" Beate asked.

"Aryan women aren't tempted by such things," Elspeth explained rather piously. Richard noted the strange look her husband gave her.

"We could solve the problem by having them all fixed," Herr Schindler reiterated.

"I believe the Labor Ministry has weighed these things carefully," Richard said calmly, "and they've come to the conclusion that it would be unwise, under current conditions, to do any such thing to the forced labor."

"Why?" Beate asked.

"Besides the expense, it would be a public relations nightmare," Richard explained. "Every state kills people, but not many permanently maim their subjects—at least not in the civilized world."

"What do we care about public relations?" Herr Schindler asked somewhat belligerently. "Mass sterilization was there in the original plans, and we backed away from it and never have had the courage to follow through. Public relations are for weaklings!" He motioned toward his empty wineglass and muttered a curse at the boy who had failed to refill it quickly enough.

"International relations are important for us," Richard asserted. "Our economy is faltering without sufficient trade, and besides, we are the master race, we should set an example of civilized behavior."

"Pah!" Herr Schindler disagreed.

"But wasn't it common before for civilized societies to castrate slaves, say, in harems?" Beate argued rather more cogently. "I mean, if it's viewed as normal, would people object? After all, these people aren't planning on having families anyway. They can hardly manage to take care of themselves, not to mention children. It would be doing them a favor."

"You're right," Richard agreed. "Of course, that has its own problems." He sipped the last of his wine. The boy behind him refilled his glass as soon as he set it back on the table.

"How so?" Frau Schindler asked.

"Seems it was not uncommon for Roman women, for example, to use castrated slaves for their sexual pleasure. Since the women could not be impregnated, they had nothing to fear."

"But that's impossible!" Karl scoffed.

"No, only if it's done before puberty," Beate answered. "You see, if it's done to a fully adult male, then all it prevents is pregnancies, not . . ." She blushed rather than finish the sentence.

"Now that is intriguing," Elspeth commented. Karl glared at her.

"Yes," Frau Schindler added.

"Perhaps it could be done so that the men, at least, are rendered, er . . . ineffective," Karl suggested.

Again the boy opposite Richard allowed an expression to darken his face.

"That would have to be rather brutal," Richard said. "And there would be the possibility that the subject would feel irrationally vengeful. He would, remember, still be physically fit and quite capable of violence."

"Ah, that would be a problem," Elspeth Vogel murmured.

"It could be done before they are even released into society," Karl suggested. "Slam some anesthesia into their face and the next thing they know, they wake up altered, not knowing who to blame. Imagine the look on their faces!" He snickered. "Like those Italians the Ethiopians got their hands on!"

"I hate to spoil your fun, but I was thinking of something which they would not even know about," Herr Schindler said. "Something which we could use against inferior populations wholesale, to clear out lands and keep their numbers under control. Let the lowlifes have their sordid little sex lives, I just don't want them polluting our world with their monstrous little creations."

"I thought we already had a handle on the indigenous populations in the colonial territories," Elspeth commented. "There's been a steady decline, and I thought we were keeping the rest for labor purposes . . ."

"Out East, yes! That's the way we should have done it all!" Schindler howled. "It's the West that needs control. Do you know, taken together, they outnumber us? They breed filth and corruption right into our society! We must do something!"

"Yes, it is clear that we do need some method of keeping the lower castes under control," Richard conceded.

"Perhaps an education campaign," Beate suggested.

"Hah!" Herr Schindler scoffed. "They're too stupid to learn. That's obvious! If you knew the statistics on illicit births, the squalling bundles that turn up in Dumpsters and on doorsteps. God knows how many are kept by their mothers, running around, undocumented, unclassified, not serving any purpose, draining our coffers."

"Is there any way to do that?" Beate asked.

"Do what?" Elspeth asked, confused.

"Sterilize people without their realizing it," Richard explained.

"Is there?" Elspeth asked Richard.

He shrugged. "Radiation, perhaps."

"No, no, no," Herr Schindler disagreed. "We'd want to be more selective than that! Wouldn't want to get our own after all!"

"Well, then, is there a way?" Richard asked.

Herr Schindler smiled. He turned toward the elder boy and said, "You two, go into the cellar and pull out a crate of the Bordeaux '87. I want you to carefully remove each bottle and clean the dust off each. Remember, like I taught you! Then, when you've done that, decant one bottle and bring it to us. And don't you dare disturb the sediment or it will be your hides! Understood?" As he finished, he reached into his pocket and pulled out a small ring of keys and threw them at the feet of the boy.

Without his expression changing in the slightest, the boy stooped to pick up the keys as he said, "Understood, *mein Herr.*"

After he and his companion left the room, Herr Schindler paced to the door, checked they were gone, and said, "That will keep them busy for a few minutes." He sat back down at the table, enjoying the atmosphere of mystery he had created, and then, leaning forward over his plate and lowering his voice conspiratorially, said, "The Führer has plans . . ."

44

"Y OU COME HERE OFTEN?" Stefi asked the young officer. She sipped her drink, demurely peering over the glass at him. He was a short fellow with thin brown hair that was already, prematurely, receding.

"What? Oh, I'm sorry, I didn't notice you there." The young man seemed nervous and somewhat out of place in the large hall.

"I asked if you come to these official parties very often," Stefi repeated, rephrasing the question toward something she hoped he could handle.

"Only when my father makes me."

"Which one is he?" Stefi asked, indicating the dignitaries, officials, and officers standing around, munching on appetizers and chatting.

"That one." The young man pointed toward an older man.

"Oh! Isn't that Herr Schindler?"

"Yes. That's him all right."

"My name's Stefi."

"Oh."

"What's your name?"

"Me? Oh, I'm Wolf-Dietrich."

"Pleased to meet you." There was an awkward silence, then Stefi added, "I really hate these things. I feel so out of place here."

"You, too?"

"Yeah. Do you mind if we just chat a bit? That way I can say I socialized."

"I don't think that's wise. I have a girlfriend."

"Is she here?"

"No, but . . ."

"Oh! I'm sure she wouldn't mind if you are friendly to a poor lost soul. I'm just visiting Berlin, and I don't know anybody here, and I was hoping we might be friends." Stefi paused, waited an appropriate few seconds, then added in a carefully provocative voice, "Just for the time I'm here. Only temporary, you see."

Wolf-Dietrich suddenly lost interest in the chandelier that he had been studying and turned his full attention to her. He let his eyes stray down her body, noting the deep cut of her dress, the curve of her waist, the long legs just barely visible through a demure cut in her gown. "Temporary, you say?"

"Yes. I'm just looking to have fun," Stefi answered with a winning smile. "How about you?"

"I'm only in town for a few weeks. I have a girlfriend here, but we don't get to see each other that often. It's sort of a leftover relationship."

"So, where you are, there are no women?"

"No. It's a research lab located way out in the middle of the heath. Nothing around for miles. Of course, I could go into town, but, well, it's not really my style to just meet women in bars."

"Which town?" Stefi asked.

"Hamburg," Wolf-Dietrich answered. "Oh, I'm not supposed to . . . oh, I'm sure, no harm done. Just don't tell anyone I told you that."

"Of course not. You know, I think that's really nice, that you don't go barhopping. A handsome young officer like you would have, I'm sure, no trouble picking up all sorts of women."

"You think?"

Stefi nodded solemnly. "In fact, I'm sure the village girls are all over you."

"We're not even close to a village."

"Nothing?"

"For miles. The area was cleared out years ago for some reason or another."

"Where does the help come from?"

"Oh, most of them are army and live there. Some locals come in, but they're all men or old and haggard."

"Too bad! I had heard the girls in that region were especially beautiful."

"Well, if they are, they are kept well-hidden."

"Have you ever been into the village?"

"Which one?"

"Any of them."

"Well, I haven't seen Undeloh, but everyone assures me there's nothing there. As for Döhle, it's a dump."

"Pity." Stefi sipped her drink and waited for Wolf-Dietrich to say something. When it became apparent he was incapable of initiating a conversation, she asked, "If you don't get to see her often, why isn't your girlfriend here?"

"Her Women's League is off somewhere improving the world," Wolf-Dietrich answered grumpily.

"That is a pity," Stefi sighed. "I think a girl should be around for her man. If you're not here most of the time, she should make a point of being here when you are."

"You think?"

"Yes."

"I said something like that, and she said, since I'm never around, I shouldn't begrudge her a few days away."

"Sounds like she has her priorities wrong."

"You think?"

"Yes. Or maybe, she has somebody else who takes greater priority?"

"I doubt it."

"Oh?" Stefi asked, intrigued by his self-confidence.

"Yeah, she's not going to let me go *that* easily!" Wolf-Dietrich declared bitterly.

"You think she only likes you for your father's position?"

"I know she does! Worse than that, it's her father who tells her to like me."

"Then why do you stick with her?"

"Have to. Dad would kill me if I broke it off."

"He's using you?" Stefi asked with genuine sympathy.

Wolf-Dietrich looked across the room at his father, then at Stefi. He considered her for a moment, then looked back at his father. He looked rather sad but did not say anything.

"I won't quote you," Stefi said softly.

" 'We are all loyal tools of the state,' " Wolf-Dietrich quoted. " 'We all serve the Fatherland in whatever capacity we can.' "

"But we can choose our form of service," Stefi suggested.

"See that man there?" Wolf-Dietrich pointed to one of the waiters.

"Yes. What about him?" Stefi asked, lowering her voice.

"They have them in special uniforms for tonight, so you can't tell, but I know, he's a *Zwangsarbeiter*. If you look closely, you can see the manacle on his wrist."

"So?"

"So, he's serving the Fatherland."

Stefi furrowed her brow, then remembering that made her unattractive, she raised her eyebrows and smiled questioningly.

"He's lucky. He knows exactly what to do and exactly when to do it. He just does whatever he's told to do, and he serves the Fatherland. No second-guessing, no screwing up, no father constantly trying to manipulate others through him," Wolf-Dietrich whined.

Stefi looked closely at the man Wolf-Dietrich was talking about. He was probably close enough to overhear their conversation, but Wolf-Dietrich spoke as if he were deaf, and the servant betrayed no sign of having heard a word. "You can still make choices about what you do," she suggested.

"Choices! Hah! It's all been chosen for me! I'm a conduit, nothing more!"

"A conduit, yes," Stefi repeated sympathetically. "It must be horrible for you." She exuded sympathy and companionship and coaxed Wolf-Dietrich into exploring his feelings even further. As their conversation progressed, she confided to him how she also felt used by her father. Wolf-Dietrich was intrigued, and together they compared notes and exchanged condolences, then Stefi smiled. "I have an idea. You're a conduit, I'm a conduit. Maybe we could satisfy our fathers' ambitions and still win our freedom."

"How?"

"Your father wants an alliance, my father wants an alliance. If you and I became an 'item,' we might be able to convince them to let us switch from our current assigned partners to each other."

"Well, no offense, but how would that be any better?" Wolf-Dietrich asked. "We'd still have to follow through with some sort of sham partnership."

"We could take our time, have an understanding between you and me, and then, when push comes to shove, we just have a huge blowup and the whole thing becomes impossible!" Stefi gleefully explained.

Wolf-Dietrich looked intrigued. "Who's your father?"

"Traugutt," Stefi announced while discreetly pointing toward him.

"I've never heard of him. Is he important?"

"Not like your dad, not yet, but he will be soon," Stefi answered.

"Ah, it will never work. My father is not interested in promoting other people's careers."

"He won't have to be. Just give my father time. In the meanwhile, you and I can get to know each other a bit. There won't be any harm in that, will there? After all, if it doesn't work out, well, we can still have fun."

Wolf-Dietrich contemplated the chandelier again.

"What harm is there in trying?" Stefi asked.

"We'd have to keep it hush-hush. At least at first. Could you do that?"

Stefi nodded. "No problem. I'm used to secrets."

"Me, too. But won't you get jealous, knowing I'm with another girl sometimes? Knowing that I can't talk about you?"

Stefi shook her head. "We can be friends. You can tell me all about her. Believe me, it won't bother me one bit to keep our friendship quiet, just between us. Not one bit."

═══════════ 45 ═══════════

*T*HE DECEMBER SNOW DRIFTED slowly to the ground, giving the world a silent covering of isolation. Peter watched the flakes through the kitchen window as he chopped onions for Elspeth, his thoughts straying to Allison and times long past. Elspeth sat behind him in a world of her own, a cup of tea untouched in front of her, the radio playing a *Winterfest* speech that she ignored, completely immersed in the romantic novel she was reading, her head bowed forward, her lips moving ever so slightly, her fingers gripping the edges of her book.

The snow was sticky, it clung to everything, gathering in clumps, then falling suddenly to the ground. Not gratitude, he thought as another powdery bomb released itself from a tree limb. It wasn't quite gratitude anymore. The groveling thankfulness had dissipated over the months since his release from working at the factory; still, something in his attitude was alien to the person Allison had known. He finished chopping the onions, dropped them into a bowl, cleaned the board, and started on the green peppers, all without taking his eyes off the snow that drifted so carelessly down to earth.

What would Allison have called it? Submissiveness? Cowardice? Fatigue? Whatever she would have thought of him now, it would have been far kinder than anything he himself would have said. Arrogant and judgmental as he had been, he would have hated the person he was now. Hated, mocked, scorned, pitied. He sighed and glanced down at the fresh green pieces of pepper. Where did they get such things in midwinter? They had been essentially unavailable in London, at least in the stores the English were permitted to use. He eyed the food enviously. Wherever it came from, it was still unavailable to him, at least most of the time. Sometimes he took liberties, or rather, sometimes he gambled, gambled on Elspeth's disposition.

The rules of the game were fairly clear: she wavered, unpredictably, from benign neglect and indulgent good humor all the way to petty vindictiveness; he simply guessed her state of mind and took liberties accordingly. If he won, he could supplement his grimly bland diet or speak his mind or manage in some other trivial way to assert his humanity. If he lost, well, then he paid a price at her discretion. In this way he formalized the disconcerting randomness of being at another's whim and so managed to pass his time and while away his life.

Without obviously moving his head, he glanced at Elspeth and then discreetly shoved a handful of the chopped peppers into his mouth.

"I saw that."

He turned to look at Elspeth, half smiling to beg her indulgence.

Without even bothering to look up from her novel, she commanded, "Spit it out."

He did, throwing the half-chewed handful into the compost bowl with more than a hint of exasperation. As he washed his hands, Elspeth stood and, placing her book upside down on the table so she would not lose her place, walked over to the shelf on which she kept her little book, the one in which she noted his misbehavior.

"I've told you a thousand times not to do that," she admonished, writing something down.

Lost that round, he thought grimly. He was angry that he had so badly miscalculated, but aware that he could do nothing to stop her from recording a punishment, all he said was, "I know, I'm sorry."

"Unforgivable," Elspeth muttered. She shook her head in dismay. "You're behavior is just getting worse and worse. I thought you had finally settled down, but now . . ."

"I'm terribly sorry, *gnä' Frau,*" he said with convincing sincerity.

"You are hopeless!" Elspeth sighed as if exasperated, though she sounded amused.

"I won't do it again."

Nevertheless, two days later he was carrying some sherry into the kitchen to use in a recipe. Thinking Elspeth was still in the kitchen, he mindlessly took a swig from the bottle while still in the hall.

"Peter!" Elspeth nearly screeched.

"Oh, fuck," he blurted.

"Peter!" Elspeth did screech.

He was beside himself. How in God's name could he have behaved so carelessly? Caught out twice in as many days! "*Gnädige . . . ,*" he began lamely.

"You're not going to try and say you didn't just drink straight out of our bottle, are you?"

Abashed, he answered quietly, "No."

Elspeth shook her head in exasperation. "You're beyond belief! What in the world do you think you're doing?" She brushed past him on the way to her book; clearly she did not expect an answer.

His thoughts tumbled over each other as he tried to get past having acted so stupidly and to rectify his situation. As Elspeth picked up her pen, he said on an inspiration, "I wasn't thinking. I'm sorry. I was just feeling happy and at home here. Feeling the spirit of *Winterfest* and . . ."

The way Elspeth glanced up at him encouraged him, and he added, "You know, like part of the family."

Elspeth set her book back down and sighed. "That really is a disgusting habit. You know, you've ruined that entire bottle for us."

"I'm terribly sorry. But look"—he held up the bottle and smiled sheepishly—"there's not much in there anyway."

"All right. You may as well keep the rest for yourself. Go fetch the new bottle."

"Living in an asylum would be less confusing," Marta opined when Peter told her about the incident. She snuggled closer to him under the mess of old blankets and rags he used as a bed. He felt the warmth of her naked body and shivered with anticipation. "Did you get a present this year?"

"No, not this year," he answered with a twinge of regret. "I'm surprised you remembered that I got one last year."

"Oh, you seemed so impressed by it then," she teased.

He felt embarrassed but did not say anything.

"What time is it?"

"I would guess around three," he answered, yawning. "We finished early tonight."

"What time do you have to get up?"

"I could push it back until seven tomorrow. What about you, should I wake you up?"

"Yes, please. Mistress wants me back early to prepare for her party tomorrow night," Marta answered.

"Ugh. Poor baby, you don't get any time off," he commiserated. He draped his arm over her and stroked her back. "You feel good."

"Ah, that feels nice."

"Your skin is so smooth," he commented as his hand gently massaged her back.

"Ha!" Marta laughed. "You're just randy."

"Even so, your skin is buttery smooth," he assured her, leaning over to kiss the small of her back.

"Not my hands," she argued, turning slightly so she could extend one to him.

He caressed it and kissed the veins along the back of her hand. "So delicate!" He traced a pattern along her fingers. "Women's hands are so incredible to me, so delicate yet so strong!" He kissed each finger in turn and then playfully ran his tongue along the length of her index finger.

"I gather you're not sleepy."

"How could I be?"

Afterward she joked, "I guess, what with this being the second year in a row, you could say we have a long-term commitment."

"Maybe we could make it more frequent than once a year. I could find my way over to your place once in a while."

"No!" she gasped. "Don't!"

"I'm sorry. Is there someone else?" he asked, trying not to show how hurt he was by her reaction.

"No, not that. You might get caught and then we'd both be punished."

"I'd never tell them your name."

"They might guess it! Promise me you won't do anything foolish like that! Promise!" she whispered urgently.

"I promise," he said sadly.

"I'll see you next year," she said to console him. "Really. We'll see each other next *Winterfest!*"

He pressed his head against her and murmured, "I look forward to that." And it was the truth.

As he served drinks to the family the following evening, it finally hit him. Next *Winterfest!* Elspeth and Karl sat with their eyes glued to the television, and he carefully placed their *Glühwein* on their respective side tables. Next year, Marta had promised. Next year! He climbed the stairs to deliver Ulrike's cup of cocoa to her in her bedroom. Next year, Marta had said. And he had said he would look forward to it. He *did* look forward to it! God in heaven! He fully expected to still be in this household a year in the future. When, he wondered, had he made that decision?

Ever since he had started working in that factory—when was that? April or so? Ever since then, he had done absolutely nothing with his life. Even when it had ended, he had been too . . . what was the word? Traumatized? No, not that. Fearful? Submissive? Grateful? Yes, grateful. He had been too grateful to have had a single rebellious thought, had not dared to take one independent action. He had not even resurrected his clandestine meetings. He had used excuses: exhaustion, too busy, the holidays. He had congratulated himself on the silly games he played with Elspeth, thinking that somehow that was a sign of his unbroken spirit. Yet he had done nothing, nothing at all. Josef's teasing words, *you'll be saying that twenty years from now,* came back to him. Oh, God, were they right? It had to stop! He had to do something to regain his sanity and reclaim his rights as a human being!

"Peter," Ulrike said almost shyly.

He blinked in confusion at her. "*Fräulein?*"

"Do you know anything about history? I really wish someone could explain this stuff to me!"

The question surprised him. "I know a few things," he finally answered, "but I don't think I could help you very much."

"Why not?" she asked, her eyes straying back to her book.

"We have different histories."

She gave him her full attention. "How so? History is history. Certainly if you know about it, you could tell it to me!"

He smiled and chewed his thumb, wondering at the naïveté of her question and what he should say in reply. Of course, the safest thing to do would be to agree that what she was taught was the truth and then leave as quickly as possible, but, he wondered, what was the point in safety? And he thought of what Konstantin had said to him. Ulrike was one of the ruling class. Maybe he could influence her? Of course, it'd be better if she were a man. As a woman she was essentially powerless, but maybe, one day, she might influence her husband, or even her children. It was a tenuous connection to power, but starting somewhere was better than doing nothing at all.

Her expression had grown puzzled at his silence. Still he hesitated. This would not be like the little games he played with Elspeth where the consequences of a miscalculation were sometimes painfully felt but otherwise irrelevant. Nor would it be like his secret meetings with his friends. This would be crossing that invisible line that separated the life and actions of a lesser being from a member of the ruling class. This would be a violation of the sacred barriers erected within their very house. This would be unforgivable. And if something went wrong, say for instance Ulrike told a teacher what he had intimated to her, then he could easily face deadly consequences. It would be treason, or more precisely, given his status, perfidious treachery. It would be, in any case, a capital offense. He wondered how he could possibly justify risking his life like that, but then he almost laughed as he realized how little was at stake anymore.

"Why not," he said, mostly to himself.

"Why not what?" Ulrike asked, thoroughly confused.

He quickly assessed the situation and deciding it was safe enough asked, "Do you really want to know?"

"Yes!" she answered, impressed by his seriousness, but then added, perplexed, "Know what?"

He walked to the door, glanced down the hallway to be sure no one was listening. He did not want to scare her by beginning with the list of crimes that constituted recent history; in any case, she probably would not believe him, and he had no proof. Rather, he decided to try to gently persuade her to raise her own questions, to overcome a lifetime of brainwashing and propaganda. Satisfied that they would not be overheard, he began by carefully explaining that he had a different version of events: a version that she had never heard before—one that made the world a different place from what she thought it was.

He began by carefully debunking Nazi mythology about their Aryan origins, explaining the origins of people and their movement across the planet. He explained the development of races, tried to convey to her the equality and dignity of all humans and their complex and rich history. He interrupted himself frequently to walk to the door and check the hall, but their illicit conversation remained undetected. He paced back and forth nervously, speaking quietly so that she had to strain to listen. Sometimes she asked questions in a voice that was painfully loud to him. He struggled to answer every question without breaking the flow of his narrative. A sense of urgency drove him, there was so much to tell her.

She looked puzzled by his constant vigilance, but she did not ask about it. She searched his face for an explanation, but he gave none. He continued to speak in an intense, almost rushed whisper until he was interrupted by a summons from the sitting room. He headed for the door but stopped in the middle of the room and stood still, clenching and unclenching his fists. He turned around slowly and scanned her countenance. Was she really so innocent?

"Don't tell anyone about what I've said here," he pleaded.

"Why not?" she asked, suspicion creeping into her voice.

"I don't have time to explain now. Just don't." He paused, then added, "Please. At least, not yet, okay?"

"All right," Ulrike agreed reluctantly.

"Your word?"

"You have my word."

He winked at her and left.

"What took you so long?" Elspeth asked as he entered the sitting room.

"Sorry, *gnädige Frau*. Your wishes?" he replied without answering her question. It sufficed. Tossing the keys to the liquor cabinet in his direction, she commanded him to pour them some brandy and so he did.

Over the weeks his conversations with Ulrike continued, and he covered a range of topics from a perspective she had not even guessed existed. He never got around to explaining why she should keep it all secret, and she did not bother to ask again—it slowly became apparent to her that his worldview could be considered dangerous. Certainly it brought the natural social order into question, and because of that, one evening, she shifted the conversation to a more personal level.

"Why are you here?" she asked.

"What do you mean?"

"I mean, you're supposed to be a criminal—that's what your uniform says. What did you do?"

He smiled. What hadn't he done? In Nazi society, it was so easy to run afoul of the law. But she seriously expected an answer, so he explained, "In England, there is a requirement for all men to serve the Reich."

"Oh, yes, we have that, too. Two years' military service for men, or four years' nonmilitary service. Of course, everyone chooses the military. For women—there is two years' civic service when they're eighteen. That is, if they're not married. Many girls get married then, but I won't! Not for that reason!"

"Well, in England, it's six years, usually abroad, and definitely not military."

"Why not?"

Could she really be so naive? Or was she joking?

"I don't think they trust us with weapons," he responded dryly. This was not exactly true, for there were prisoner battalions scattered across the various fronts. There were also, of course, the collaborators, who saw the military as their best hope of career advancement and redemption from an unfortunate choice of parentage, but such details would complicate the matter unnecessarily, and in general, the choice of two years in the military was not an option.

"So?" she asked.

"So?"

"What about you? You haven't answered my question."

"Ah, yes, well, I was doing my time in a camp and one day we got a new commander, who was a sadist. Do you know what that means?"

She nodded.

He wondered if she really did. "He took a particular dislike to me."

"Did he mistreat you?"

"Yes, you could say that."

"Didn't you tell the authorities?"

"No," he sighed. "He was the authority."

She looked blank.

"Trust me. There was no one I could tell."

She stared at him, unbelieving.

"Poor little sweet Ulrike. There are things in this world about which you have no idea. Haven't you been listening to all I've said? It's not abstract history—it's what is really happening to people. Believe me, I had no one to turn to. The only way to avoid his . . . to avoid his"—he paused, painfully aware that memories were in danger of flooding back—"to avoid him was to leave. So, I escaped. I fled the camp and the country."

Ulrike stared at him, fascinated. "What happened then?"

"Then I was captured and . . ." Again he struggled to suppress images of horrifying darkness; a suffocating tightness threatened to strangle his words. "I was brought back."

"And then?"

The room grew unfocused as he stared into his past. "Then, I was brutally tortured for months." He licked his lips, his eyes remained fixed on a distant point. "And then released so I could work, as I do here."

"But what was your crime?"

He brought his gaze back to Ulrike's face. "That was it. I wanted to be free. I didn't want to be mistreated."

"I think you should have told the authorities. I'm sure they would have handled it."

"Perhaps. It didn't seem possible at the time. Maybe I made a mistake."

"But imagine! An officer of the Reich mistreating people! It's hard to believe. Are you sure you didn't give him cause?"

"I don't think so," he sighed.

On the following evening he was kept busy and did not have time to talk when he brought her evening drink. She wanted to say something, but she did not know what. As he set her drink down, his face betrayed no emotion. He left before she had a chance even to try to express herself.

She stared after him. He had looked tired. How did they manage to keep him so busy? When did he eat? Or sleep? She knew he was up early in the morning; sometimes she heard him moving about as she lay warm and comfortable in her bed, and he stayed up until the last person was in bed, sometimes longer—she had heard him late at night finishing whatever job was still unfinished. Did he have *any* time to himself?

She felt a sudden cold chill. Why had she never asked herself these questions before? *If he were not a lesser being, if he were just like she was . . .* The thought made her uncomfortable. She sipped her cocoa, turned her attention back to her schoolwork, but that night, as she lay in bed, her thoughts returned to him. To the hollowness of his expression sometimes. What did life mean to him? Would he live with them until he died? What would his old age be like? Would they take care of him if he became ill? Would he never have a life of his own? Or a family? What if he had aspirations? Had he really done something so evil that he could never have a life of his own?

Or were some people truly destined at birth to always serve, to never, ever have anything else in their future? If so, couldn't they, shouldn't they, make him part of the family? Acknowledge his feelings? But even Ulrike knew that his feelings were that he wanted to leave, to be anywhere else but in their control. What should be done about that? Was it moral to keep him there? She felt her thoughts were driving her into a trap, and subconsciously she searched for a way out.

She turned over in bed and rearranged her pillow—somehow it had suddenly gotten lumpy. After a few pounds, she found it still did not feel right. She got up and paced the room a bit. She went to the window and listened to the cold rain drumming softly against the pane. She felt chilled and the bed beckoned. She crawled back in and tried to snuggle under the covers, but after a while she felt driven to get up again.

Quietly she pulled on her robe and slipped out into the hallway. Her parents' door was closed—they would be asleep by now. She slid past their door and up the stairs. The door to the attic was open; that surprised her, but then she realized that he would leave it open since it would be warmer that way. Oh, if only her parents knew, they would be furious at the wasted heat! Her intention never to tell them made her feel like a conspirator.

She hesitated, then plunged into the darkness. Even the coolness of the hallway felt warm compared to the chill inside the attic room. She stood for a moment to let her eyes adjust to the dark, and after a moment she spotted him against the wall amid a bundle of old, worn blankets and rags. Really! Couldn't they even afford a mattress?

She went up to him, found his shoulder buried among the rags. She was taken aback to feel bare flesh, wondered why he did not wear clothes to keep warm, but then realized he probably did not want to wear the same clothes day and night if he could avoid it. Somehow, the feel of his warm, bare skin excited her in a way she had not expected. His shoulder felt hard and muscular; she wondered what the rest of his body felt like. She suppressed an urge to find out and instead shook his shoulder lightly.

"Peter," she whispered.

He groaned and murmured, "Allie?"

Ulli. He had called her by a nickname. So gently! And in his sleep! What could it mean? She struggled to restrain her excitement. A little squeak escaped her lips anyway.

"Peter!" A little louder this time.

He tried to turn, mumbled, "Allie," again. Suddenly he awoke, looked at her blearily.

"Ulrike." His voice was completely devoid of emotion. "What are you doing here? What's wrong?"

"I couldn't sleep. I wanted to talk to you."

"Where are your parents?"

"Asleep."

"Oh, Ulrike, go back downstairs. Now."

"But I just want to know some things."

"Please leave. If your parents find you here now, they'll be furious. They'll send me to a concentration camp. Please, Ulrike. Please leave. Quietly."

She felt slighted. Is that all he could think about? She hadn't meant to seduce him, the thought had not even crossed her mind, but she was only wearing a robe and her nightgown, and she was not unattractive! Certainly he should have noticed! He should have hesitated, looked at her longingly, stroked her arm, and then . . . She let the daydream slip away. It was stupid of her to have come into the attic, but then again, he had called out her name in his sleep!

He was staring at her. "Please leave, we can talk tomorrow," he insisted, then added quietly, "It's worth my life."

"Just tell me one thing, and I'll go," she bargained. Maybe he *was* different: surely a German man would never have been so indifferent to her! Or maybe she wasn't attractive. Either way, she felt irritated with him.

"What?"

"Do you have a family? Back in England, I mean?"

"No. None."

"How can that be? Everybody has family!"

"That's just the way it is. Now will you please go back to bed before your parents catch you up here? We can talk tomorrow. I'll find time. I promise."

"Oh, all right." She squeezed his shoulder slightly, she had held it the entire time, then she let go and left the room.

He stared after her, an ache in his heart. He hadn't failed to notice that she was indeed quite pretty, that she was nearly a woman. It had added a measure of desperation to his pleas for her to leave. But that was not why his heart ached. She was too young, too naive, too dangerous to be appealing to him. No, his heart ached because of her question, and because he knew he had hurt her feelings. And because of her touch. When was the last time someone had touched him with such gentleness?

46

NEVER MIND WHEN HE had last been touched gently, when the hell had he last heard a civil word? Elspeth had been snapping at him all day and now this! He stared morosely and shifted his weight uncomfortably from one leg to the other, watching the glasses to see when they were emptied. He thought of the conversation he had promised Ulrike as he saw Frau Schindler's mouth moving rapidly with her yapping complaints. Elspeth finished her drink and he moved quickly to refill her glass, topping up everyone else's as he did so. He returned to his position near the door and waited. The Schindlers had hardly been in the house twenty minutes, but already the visit seemed interminable. He chewed on nothing, his mouth working mindlessly in search of food, but his dinner was in the kitchen, abandoned at the sound of the doorbell, growing cold. Karl motioned for a cigarette. Peter lit one for Karl and for Herr Schindler as well.

Again he returned to his square foot by the door. If only he could talk to someone! Anything to relieve the monotony! He breathed out, trying to calm his growing anger. They were talking about him now, as if he weren't even there, as if he could not understand. To an extent, they were right. He did not care what they had to say, and he listened only enough to recognize a commanding tone.

"Your boy looks uncomfortable, is something wrong with him?" Frau Schindler asked snidely.

"Nothing is *wrong* with him," Elspeth retorted, then pointedly asked, "Do you want something?"

It took a moment for him to realize she was talking to him, but he immediately decided to grab the opportunity her question presented and answered, "Yes, *gnädige Frau*. There's some work upstairs I'd like to finish. I'll still be within earshot."

"You'll do it later," Elspeth snapped in reply.

He had to take a deep breath before he could bring himself to answer, "Yes, *gnädige Frau*."

Later, after he had helped the guests into their coats, Herr Schindler wagged a finger in his face and admonished, "I hope you realize how lenient your master is, boy. If you were in my household, I'd teach you a thing or two."

Though he knew he shouldn't, Peter looked at him, wondering what it was that made some people act so stupidly.

Herr Schindler tilted his head mockingly, "Did you hear me, boy? Are you deaf or stupid?" He turned his attention toward Karl, who was standing beside Peter. "Probably both," Herr Schindler joked. "Give him to me for a few weeks, and I'll beat some sense into him."

Peter decided to stop looking at him, preferring to view the floor rather than his stupid face.

"There's no need for that," Karl returned, distinctly offended. "I can take care of my own."

Laughing his usual loud, boorish laugh, Herr Schindler clapped Karl patronizingly on the shoulder. "Of course! Of course! No offense intended!"

Karl grinned in reply as his guests made their way out, all laughter and smiles. Peter raised his eyes from the floor to stare dismally after them, thinking there had to be a special place in hell for such people.

It was not very late, but there was still a mess to be cleaned. After everything had been cleared up, Peter sat on the kitchen step stool, staring out the window into the night, holding his plate in his hand, chewing his cold dinner. He wondered if he had enough energy to talk to Ulrike, as he had promised, as well as slip out late at night to make a meeting, as he had also promised.

Elspeth surprised him by coming into the kitchen. He leapt to his feet.

"You're not supposed to sit there," she stated.

"My apologies, *gnä' Frau.*"

"And what are you doing eating up here? This is our kitchen—not your dining room!"

She knew he frequently brought his food upstairs, and he was therefore quite taken aback by her question. All he could manage to do was to swallow his food and utter his formulaic "Forgive me, *gnädige Frau.*"

She shook her head angrily. "That won't do this time! You made a fool out of me in front of the Schindlers! Where the hell did you get it into your head to act like that in front of them!"

"My apologies, *gnädige Frau.*" He knew that would not placate her, so he quickly added, "I didn't realize I was behaving inappropriately."

"You didn't realize?" Her voice grew loud and she repeated in disbelief, "You didn't realize!" She shook with anger. "I put up with far too much from you, boy, and now you've made me look foolish in front of my guests! Well, it's going to stop, do you understand?"

"Yes, *gnädige Frau.*" He was not sure what line he had crossed, but it was clear Elspeth was furious. He set down his food in preparation for her next action, yet she made no move to strike him.

She simply stood quaking with rage. Then, as if she had reached some sort of decision, she said much more quietly, "Get out."

"What?"

"I said, get out!"

He shook his head, perplexed. Should he leave the kitchen? Was that what she wanted?

Elspeth quietly clarified, "If you can't follow the rules of my house, then you can just leave." She pointed toward the back door.

He turned to follow her gesture, then he looked back at her in utter disbelief. "*What?*" he stammered again.

"You heard me, get out!"

"Frau Vogel, I *can't* leave." He saw she looked unconvinced, so he added, "It's illegal!"

She grabbed his arm and pulled him toward the door. "Get out."

"Where am I supposed to go?"

"You should have thought of that earlier. Out!"

"It's not permitted!"

"That's not my problem. If you want to enjoy our hospitality, you will abide by the rules of this house, and you will behave respectfully at all times, especially in front of my guests!"

"Yes, *gnädige Frau*. Of course, *gnädige Frau*," he agreed readily. He had let her pull him as far as the door, but he stopped short of opening it. Surely, she had made her point.

"No. That's just not going to do this time. Now get out!" She unbolted the lock and opened the door.

"*Gnädige*, please don't do this." Cold, damp air drifted in.

"I've had enough already. Out!"

"*Gnädigste*, I said I was sorry. Surely—"

"I'm sick of your apologies. Now, out!" She pointed out into the night.

He stared out at the freezing drizzle. The orange security lights reflected off the mists with an eerie glow. Reluctantly, he reached for his jacket and documentation.

"Leave those," she said with cold determination. "They don't belong to you."

His eyes narrowed with a look of disgust, as though she, too, had crossed some line, but he did not take the items and instead stepped outside without further protest. He stood still, staring straight out into the yard, as the door snapped shut behind him and the bolt was thrown.

There was no awning over the door and the eaves were insufficient to shield him from the icy drizzle. He crossed his arms in defense against the cold, but otherwise he stood unmoving, staring sightlessly out into the yard. He felt she was watching him, and he did not want to give her the satisfaction of his reactions.

Eventually though, the cold and the rain grew to be too much, and he began to try to warm himself, breathing on his hands and pacing back and forth. He thought about going back inside, but he could never let Elspeth know how easy it was for him to overcome her locks. No, as long as she knew he was outside, he had to remain outside.

He continued to pace back and forth, swearing quietly under his breath, trying to keep warm. The wind picked up and slammed the tiny crystals of ice into his cheeks with a stinging ferocity. His hair grew heavy, and he shook his head periodically to remove the accumulated ice. The sleet landed on his clothes, formed a thin crust, which then melted with his body's heat and soaked in until he was completely drenched. Cold water dripped down his face like tears. He thought about just walking somewhere, anywhere, but he knew she could reappear at any moment, and if he was gone, then there would be hell to pay.

After several hours—it was well past midnight—Frau Vogel relented and unlocked the door. He stepped inside without either of them saying a word. She was dressed in her robe—clearly she had gone to bed and had only just gotten up to let him in. He was trembling with cold and miserably soaked; he found himself staring at the floor watching the ice crystals drop into little puddles at his feet. He was so furious he was speechless, but he knew that he was no longer afforded the luxury of anger and so he struggled to gain control of his emotions.

She stood waiting and finally he managed to look up at her. "Thank you, *gnädige Frau*. I do appreciate having a place here. I really do. And I know my behavior in front of Frau and Herr Schindler was appalling. I won't do it again."

Frau Vogel nodded her acceptance, told him to finish cleaning up, and then retired for the night. He looked at the plate of food still sitting on the counter. It looked inedible. Ulrike had long ago gone to bed; he had not kept his promise to her. He had missed his meeting, he had not kept his promise to his friends. His eyes burned with fatigue and the muscles of his face felt tired, as if betraying no emotion had exhausted them. He tried to take a few deep breaths, but the effort seemed pointless.

"You never kept your promise," Ulrike gently chided as he set down her cocoa the following evening.

"I'm sorry. I have no right to make promises. My time's not my own," he answered coldly.

"Do you have a few minutes to talk now?" she asked with a pleading smile.

He inspected the hallway, then turned back into the room and nodded disinterestedly. He felt too tired to talk, certainly far too tired to concentrate, so he let her choose the direction of their conversation, only interrupting periodically to walk to the door and listen. She asked a lot of questions about racial theories, and then, out of nowhere, she asked, "Have you ever been in love?"

Her voice was strained, as though she were trying too hard to sound casual, as if the answer were important to her. She seemed ready to cross some frontier, but he could not fathom what it was. He walked to the door, ostensibly to check the hall, but he was furiously thinking about how he should answer her. It was late and he really did not want to enter into a discussion of his past life, but he knew that he would lose any trust she had in him if he lied to her now. He also remembered the look she had given him when he had said he had no family; though it was essentially the truth—a brother who did not even know he was alive hardly counted as family—he knew she thought he was lying then, knew that she was judging his worth as a human being by the answer he gave her now.

Reluctantly he finally answered, "Yes, I have."

"Did she love you?"

"Yes." As he walked back toward Ulrike, an image of Allison's face came to him. He smiled at her memory.

"Did you marry?"

"No, that wasn't possible at the time," he whispered in reply.

"Why not?"

"She was married to someone else."

"Oh." Ulrike paused as if considering the implications of that. "If you could go back now, would you be able to marry her? I mean, would she divorce her husband for you?"

"I don't know what she would have done. You see, she loved him, too, but in any case, it doesn't matter; I have no life other than this one and I will never be allowed to return." He hoped that would sidestep the messy issue of what had happened to her, but he was wrong.

"What happened to her? Is she waiting for you somewhere?"

"No." Again he paused, considering what his answer should be. Just how much should he tell her? "She's dead."

"Dead?"

"Yes. Killed."

"How did she die?"

He sighed. "Ulrike, please don't ask me to explain any more."

"Please tell me, Peter! How can I believe everything else you tell me if I don't know anything about you or where you come from? You're my *only* connection with this other world you describe. You make it real. Just tell me how she died and I promise I won't ask any more."

He looked at her for a moment. Softly he said, "She was killed by the Gestapo, as she was being arrested."

"Arrested! Killed! What for?"

"Shh!" he hissed worriedly, glancing back at the door, then answered, "I don't know." It was close enough to the truth. She may have been arrested for any number of offenses real or imagined. He could hardly tell her that he and Allison were in the English Underground.

"But surely she must have done something!" Ulrike almost pleaded for a reason.

He leaned over her, hissing in her ear. "You haven't been listening to me, have you? What do you think I've been telling you? Fairy stories? Do you think the people I've been talking about weren't real? Do you think the mass murders of the forties and fifties were for a *reason*? That babies and toddlers *did something?*"

She stared at him, stunned. She had never seen him angry; indeed, he rarely showed any emotion at all. She had sort of assumed that he had no emotions or at least nothing profound. "I didn't mean . . . ," she stammered.

He stopped, gained control of himself. It wasn't her fault; she had nothing to do with it. It was his own disbelief that angered him. Why had it taken so long for him to accept the truth, to believe all the evidence he had seen? How could he fault her, she did not even have one photograph—she had nothing but his word. The word of a person who had been branded as traitorous, criminal, beneath contempt, not even really human. Breathing deeply, holding the edge of her desk to steady himself, he continued in a more measured tone, "Ulrike, believe me, people who have done absolutely nothing wrong have been arrested, tortured, and killed. Others, whose only crime is that they want to stop the murder, are dragged from their homes never to be heard from again. Your wonderful founding fathers set up human slaughterhouses—extermination camps—where they carried out the systematic murder of millions of people: men, women, children, old and young."

She shook her head. "It never happened."

"You must have heard rumors or stories, jokes and innuendos," he said quietly, hoping somehow to offer evidence other than his own suspect word. He had himself always had difficulty accepting the worst of the whispered history he had heard as a partisan—he had never questioned it aloud, aware as he was that propaganda was a necessary tool of both sets of combatants, but he had privately wished that the Resistance would use more believable propaganda. After all, what merit was there in using stories about millions upon millions of people killed in extermination camps if no one could believe them? Who could believe whole peoples were slaughtered, entire religions destroyed, nations kept in semi-starved slavery, death camps, medical experiments, gruesome tortures . . . Surely it was too much.

"No." Her head continued to shake as though she could not stop it.

"Yes, it happened! For all we know, it may still be going on."

"Have you seen any of this with your own eyes?"

"No, but I've seen pictures, heard reports . . ." He had seen some photos that had made him shudder, had heard stories which made his guts ache, had experienced enough state terrorism in his own family to know his enemy was ruthless and soulless, but still his mind had resisted acceptance of the reported grotesqueness and scale of the insanity. And despite his determination not to be naive, he had harbored a vague hope that the stories were just that, nothing more than anti-Nazi propaganda manufactured by overzealous partisans or perhaps by the Reich's own propaganda machine for the purposes of instilling terror in the subject peoples.

"They're lies!" Ulrike spoke the words that he had always wanted to believe.

"Ulrike, where do you think all those people went? Look at the numbers before and after. Work it out. Look at old pictures: the names of shops and their owners. Where did they go? Why did so much land open up for colonization?"

She stared at him but did not say a word.

"There's a place in the East called Auschwitz, it's just one of many. They murdered so many people there that they couldn't even bury the bodies. They tried dumping them into the earth, but the swampy ground sent the decaying corpses back to the surface, so, they ended up burning them."

"No! You don't know that!"

"Corpses emerging from the fields! Do you know what burnt flesh smells like? You can't hide that sort of thing!"

"No! It's not true. It's just lies made up by your people. Evil people, jealous people! There was a war—people died, sometimes innocent people. You dropped bombs on our cities! Firebombs! Atomic bombs! But it wasn't like you say, it's all made up and you believe it. You haven't seen it yourself because it's not true!"

"You're right, I haven't seen it. Those who saw it are dead, what can they say? But I have seen other things. You yourself would see it, if only you opened your eyes." He thought of the little bundle of hair he had collected but decided not to pursue that at the moment. If he horrified her too much, she might simply shut him out. There was, he decided, a less terrifying and more direct approach to her disbelief. "What about me? What have I done to deserve this life?"

"You?"

"Yes. Do you truly believe I am so different from you? That I am a lesser being?"

"It's your place to serve," Ulrike whined. "If only you accepted that, you'd be happy with us."

"Says who? Think about it! Listen to your conscience." He tapped her head. "Does any of this feel right? Does it?"

"I . . . It's . . . I don't . . ." Ulrike reached up in confusion to touch her head where he had tapped it.

"If it was so natural to me, why did I have to be tortured into submission? Huh?"

"I don't . . . The Fatherland . . ."

"Do you really think I deserve to be beaten for trivialities? That I deserve no freedom, no family, nothing at all for the rest of my life?"

"You're a criminal. That's why you're here. That's why you—"

"You know I'm not a criminal," he hissed into her ear. "I've told you what happened, and you can even check the documents your father holds on me and see it's the truth; you'll see I've done *nothing!* The criminals are out there"—he gestured broadly—"and the crimes were committed against me! Do you want to know what they did to me and my family? Do you?"

She nodded, her eyes wide with fear. He did not know whether she was afraid of what she would hear or if she was simply afraid of him. He hadn't meant to be so harsh. He tried to calm himself before continuing; he did not want to scare her, it wasn't her fault, it was his for never wanting to believe.

He began, "My mother and father—" but then a sudden horror spread through his limbs. The words died on his lips. He hurled silent imprecations at himself. Idiot! Fool! Slowly, deliberately, he straightened and stood silently with his back to the door. Ulrike looked up at him, waiting for him to continue. For a brief moment he could only hope that his fear was groundless, then he forced himself to turn around.

His ears had not deceived him: someone was standing in the doorway. It was Karl. Peter read his expression in an instant and knew denials would be useless. Involuntarily, he closed his eyes, wishing the clock back five minutes. Just five minutes. He opened his eyes, but Karl was still there.

47

"*I*T'S ALL RIGHT, *it will be all right, everything will be okay, trust me . . .*" She was stroking his hair, talking soothingly in English. The voice was unknown, but eerily familiar, as if he had known it long ago. He turned his head and looked at her. It was a young woman, again strangely familiar. English? Who would be speaking English to him? With a start he recognized her. But she was so young! Mum? What was she doing here? His brain screamed warnings at him. Stop! Don't question! But it was too late, he knew it was a dream and it drifted away from him like sand through his fingers.

Peter remained very still, hoping to recapture some of the lost comfort. He could still feel her fingers stroking his hair, but he also felt pain creeping into every limb as his nerves awoke. He battled to hold it back, to remain numb, but it was impossible. The pain raged through him, like a conquering army, and with a groan, he surrendered to the inevitable.

He raised his hand to his head, where his hair had been stroked. Something scurried away into the darkness, and his fingers came back sticky and damp. He tasted them; it was blood. His movements had caused a shock of pain through his ribs, and he dropped his arm and lay still, fearful of provoking more misery. He tried to open his eyes but they were too swollen. He ran his tongue over his lips and felt the swelling there as well, then he touched each of his teeth in turn and counted two more lost.

Exhausted by his efforts, he rested and waited out the remainder of the night that way, lying there in the dark, taking his breath in short, painful gasps, unable to sleep for the pain. Hours later he was able to open his eyes and was greeted by the gray light of dawn filtering through the window. The light hurt his injured eyes and he closed them again, but not for long. Whatever weakness or pain he felt, he knew he had to get up and begin work if he valued what was left of his life.

Taking it in stages, he climbed carefully to his feet, swaying as the blood pounded in his temples. He held on to a roof strut as his vision faded in and out. When he felt well enough, he selected a rag from his bedding that was long enough to wrap around his chest, then, grabbing his other set of clothing, he went through the house into the cellar. He cleaned himself and washed his hair and wrapped the rag around his chest, binding up the most sensitive area with a sort of bandage. After that he put on the clean clothes and placed his old clothes in water to soak, hoping the bloodstains would come out.

He felt sick while walking to the bakery, but he had already vomited everything up the night before, so he did nothing more than heave convulsively a few times as he walked. Each time he felt sharp, jabbing pains in his chest, and he wondered if his ribs had been broken. When he reached the bakery, he waited silently in the short line at the back door, and though nobody said anything, he was aware that they were staring surreptitiously at him with those same sidelong glances that he had occasionally bestowed on others. When he reached the door, Roman, busy as usual, stopped dead, his mouth dropping open. When he finally found the wherewithal to shut it, he asked, "God in heaven! What happened?"

Peter handed over his ration card, then turned slightly to stare out across the plaza. His vision was obscured by the dizzying sight of steps flying up at him, threatening to break his neck as he tumbled down them. The noises of the plaza were drowned out by the sound of breaking glass as he crashed into the hall table shattering the crystal cigarette lighter and Elspeth's figurines. He could feel Karl's walking stick as it was slammed repeatedly into his back, he smelled the alcohol on Horst's breath as his arms were pinned behind his back so that Karl's fist could crash again and again into his face.

"What happened?" Roman insisted.

Peter continued to stare into the distance. He wet his lips but could not say anything. And through it all, he had not resisted. He had known that to resist was to die, and so he had let it all happen.

Softly Roman said, "I'm sorry," and went into the bakery to fill the order.

Peter returned in time to find Elspeth in the kitchen preparing for breakfast. "You're late. Give me that," she said as she took the bread and shoved the coffeepot at him, adding, "Hurry up, before he notices." She disappeared into the dining room carrying the bread with her.

Setting the pot down, he shrugged off his jacket, then carried the coffee into the dining room. The table had already been set; evidently Elspeth had covered for him. He wondered momentarily if she had tended to Karl as well, or had he managed to tie his own shoes for once? Wrapped in his bitter thoughts, oblivious to everything else in his misery, he did not notice their stares as he served the coffee. He returned to the kitchen and sat down, dead tired. He could not seem to catch his breath, and every time he inhaled, his lungs ached. He also had a raging thirst, and this finally drove him back onto his feet. How in the world was he going to get through this day? It stretched before him, a vast expanse of petty commands and tasks, and at the end of it all, the coveted right to rest, to lay down his head and be alone with his pain, if only for a few hours.

Sticking to his usual schedule, after finishing the breakfast dishes, he went upstairs to clean the bathrooms and toilets. He climbed the steps slowly. Each muscle, every joint, his skin, everything hurt. He entered the bathroom, put on the light, and was confronted by his visage in the mirror. It stung him like a slap in the face. The grim image staring back at him unnerved him, but he was almost as shocked by the realization that he had not even looked at himself since the events of the night before. There it was, staring at him—a testament to the damage inflicted on his life and his acceptance of it.

Though his face was still grotesquely distended, the swelling had decreased enough for his eyes to have reemerged, red-ringed and shadowed. He had cuts around his mouth and on his forehead, but what struck him most was that half his face was bruised and discolored. Blue and purple spread across his jaw and up under his eyes and along his temples like a disease. As he stared disconsolately, he heard a sweet, happy voice in his head. "Hey, Alan, are you going to let me sketch you?"

"Why would you want to do that, Jenny?" he heard his long-ago answer.

"I like looking at you. I'm good at it, really. You've got marvelous lines. Sit for me, please!"

"Oh, I don't think I could sit still that long."

"Aw, come on. You've got a great face. Come on, please?"

"Okay, if you make it worth my while."

"What do I have to do?"

"Give me something to look at while I sit for you. Get naked for me."

"It's a deal!" she had agreed, laughing, and began then and there peeling off her clothes.

What would his little artist think if she could see him now? Without knowing why, he reached out to touch the face in the mirror. The cold surface of the glass offered no comfort, no answers. He brought his hand unsteadily back and probed his face, trying to match sensation with image. Was it his imagination or did the darkened skin feel fragile, like old paper ready to crumble at the slightest disturbance? He looked haunted. Or hunted. Like an animal caught in a leg trap. Stay? Or gnaw the leg off? Either way the result was death.

With a sudden flash of recognition he thought, They're killing me. They're killing me, and I don't even know what to do about it.

"You'll never get anything done like that," Elspeth stated from the doorway.

He looked at her in surprise and studied her face, but he could detect no emotions there, not pity, not regret. Nothing at all. They're killing me, he thought, and I don't even know what to do to stop them.

48

"YOU'RE KILLING ME, you're killing me. Ah, stop, stop!" Adam gasped, rolling on the floor.

Joanna did not give up. With the intensity of a nearly three-year-old she tickled her father mercilessly and giggled uncontrollably at the sight of his abject surrender to her skills.

"You better stop before you pee your pants," Zosia advised.

"Aw, she's all right," Adam laughed, grabbing his little girl and swinging her up and holding her over his head as he lay on his back.

"I was talking about you," Zosia replied.

Joanna stretched out her arms and made airplane noises as her father rocked her back and forth. "I'm a plane. Look, Mama, I'm an airplane."

Zosia nodded. "I see."

"I'm going to drop bombs on you!" Joanna threatened her father. "Boom, boom, boom! You're dead!"

"That's not nice!" Adam lowered her so that she was sitting, straddling his stomach. "How about a kiss instead?"

Joanna leaned forward to kiss him, but just as he puckered up to receive her kiss, she pulled back and giggled. "Fooled you!"

"Yes, you did. Now come on, give me a kiss."

"No, no, no, no, no!" Joanna giggled. "I'm all out of kisses!"

"All out? Oh, no!" Adam moaned. "Well, I guess I'll just have to get one from your mommy instead." He removed Joanna from his stomach and stood to fulfill his threat.

"Ah, always second choice," Zosia grumbled as Adam gave her a peck on the cheek.

Adam got back down on the floor. "Now, at last, to finish my push-ups!" He began, but before he had reached five, Joanna crawled onto his back.

"Sweetie!" Adam chided.

"Go ahead and do it with her as a weight," Zosia suggested.

"One, oof, two, oof," Adam began. "I know—you count, Joanna. I'll go as high as you can count."

Joanna giggled. "Mama taught me up to one hundred! *Jeden, dwa, trzy . . . ,*" she counted as Adam pushed himself up and down.

"Hey, how about *eins, zwei, drei?*" Adam asked.

"I only know up to forty that way," Joanna admitted.

"We'll do German then," he panted.

"Coward," Zosia commented. As Adam worked to Joanna's count, Zosia watched how his arm and back muscles tensed, how a sweat broke on his skin, how handsome he looked.

Joanna had begun smacking her father's arm, yelling, "Gee-up! Gee-up!" as Adam labored under her weight.

Zosia giggled at the sight. "By the way, I sent that paperwork through that you were asking about."

"Good. What about the books?" Adam panted.

"Downloaded. They're in printing now."

"What books?" Marysia asked from the doorway.

"Adam wanted some material for his history class, so I pulled it out of a library and am having it duplicated for him."

"Duplicated? What are you going to do, pass it out to your class?"

"Of course," Adam wheezed. "Or do you think I should keep it all here under my bed?" he teased his mother.

"Well, what I want to know is how you're going to get it to them."

"I'll carry it, on my back!" he teased.

"Adam! If you're caught with illegal printing like that—"

"Oh, Mother, stop sounding like Julia!"

Marysia's face darkened at her daughter's name. "She was right about one thing, Son. You don't take the risks seriously enough."

"And she did and look what happened!" Adam responded breathlessly. "What's the point in worrying? There are people out there who've done absolutely nothing, and they're getting the shit kicked out of them. If I were cautious, I'd be paralyzed, I wouldn't be able to do anything. At least I know if something happens to me, it was for a reason!"

"There's a difference between taking sensible risks and being careless."

"I think it's a sensible risk," Zosia opined. "After all, the printed material will be shown to other people. Adam's effectiveness could be doubled if each student shows these documents to just one other person. Just one!"

"Word of mouth would suffice," Marysia advised.

"Enough!" Adam dropped to the floor as Joanna reached forty. "Let your horsie rest, okay, sweetie?"

"Okay," Joanna nobly agreed, climbing off her father. "I'll go find you some straw to eat."

"Oats," Adam suggested. "Better yet, a steak."

As Joanna rooted around under the sink, apparently looking for oats or a steak, Adam rolled over and looked up at Zosia. Something in her demeanor inspired him. "Hey, Ma. Would you feel safer if I just ran those documents down to the border and had some couriers ferry them into the city for me?"

"And in exchange?" Marysia asked.

"Well, I thought Zosia and I could take a horseback ride with the stuff; I've got to take care of some business down that way anyway, but, you know, what with the snow and all, we won't be back till tomorrow at the earliest."

"All right. I'm sure Joanna would love spending the night at my place, wouldn't you, sweetie?"

Joanna poked her head out from under the sink. "I can stay with you and Olek? Siwa can sleep in bed with me?" she asked excitedly.

"Ugh! How can anyone want to sleep with that stupid cat!" Adam groaned.

Marysia, grinning at her granddaughter's enthusiasm, ignored him. "Yes, we'll all have fun together."

"Yippee!"

"Thanks, Ma." Zosia beamed at Marysia. "You're a gem."

"I expect another grandchild out of it."

"Give us time," Adam remarked. "We need to practice a bit more first!"

"So, have you heard anything from your father?" Adam asked as they bounced up and down, sitting hunched together in the back of the delivery vehicle as it made its way over the rough terrain. Two workmen sat opposite them, one reading a book, the other resting with his head back and his eyes closed. After a particularly bad bump, the one with his eyes closed opened them, surveyed his companions, and closed his eyes again. Adam put his arm around Zosia to steady her.

"On those chemicals?" Zosia asked as she snuggled into Adam's embrace. "He hasn't managed to arrange anything yet, but when he does, he wants you to go along, did you know that?"

"Yeah," Adam replied somewhat dourly. "Did you have anything to do with that?"

"Yes. It was my suggestion."

"My little schemer. Why don't you go? You're much more charming a witness," Adam suggested.

"No, I think you should go. I believe we need to personalize this stuff more. We keep giving them dry facts and figures, and we get nowhere with them. I think you should testify directly about what you saw, give it that flavor of authenticity. Add some color to the facts."

"Hmm. I suppose it's worth a try."

"Yes, and that reminds me," Zosia said. "Remember that worker that Tadek tripped and what happened to him?"

"Of course."

"Include that. Watch the faces when you talk about that. I want to know if they're affected at all."

"But they know that sort of stuff goes on all the time! Hell, we keep telling them!" Adam protested.

"But we don't give it a face. Give this guy a face. Describe him, describe the situation, describe his thoughts."

"His thoughts? Oh, he was so dehumanized I doubt he was capable of thinking anything at all."

"Pretend, then."

"All right. I'll try," Adam agreed. "I still think you should be the one to go."

"I thought you liked visiting America," Zosia said, twisting her head around so she could see his face.

"Oh, I do." He smiled at her and kissed her. "The place fascinates me. It's so odd going from a war zone to a land that is essentially at peace. All their priorities are so different. It's really weird watching the news there. You would think we don't even exist."

"I know. That's a problem." Zosia relaxed and leaned back into his strong embrace.

"I mean, it's not surprising, after all, the geopolitical reality is the status quo. What does surprise me is what they do consider news. Such trivia! They seem absolutely enamored of one subject on one visit, then when I return, they're onto something completely different, and if you ask about the first topic—"

"It's as if they never heard of it," Zosia finished for him.

"Exactly!"

"We have to use that tendency to our advantage."

"How could we do that?"

"We need to put some of our trivia in their limelight. If we could do that, we could get some attention and maybe have a bit more political clout," Zosia suggested.

"Not to mention money." Adam wrapped his arms more securely around her and let his hands stray a bit, trying to find her curves under her winter clothing.

"Indeed, and arms," Zosia replied as Adam undid one of her coat buttons and his hand slipped inside. "The shipments are being hindered. Customs is starting to ask awkward questions. It's really hampering our efforts, and it's not clear why they're doing that."

"Isolationism," Adam guessed. He carefully worked his way deeper through her clothing and finally felt her warm flesh. "I think they're going to pull out of this thing altogether. There's more and more chatter about acknowledging the Reich as the rightful government of Europe and dealing with them as such."

"Oh, God!" Zosia moaned. "Do they have any idea what that would mean?"

"I don't know. They don't care about the murdered millions. What's past is past, they say. Some of these people even say that if the governments sign a peace accord, then the Reich might be pressured into behaving itself."

"Not with the current regime! For heaven's sake it would be a magnificent gift to the hard-liners! It would be like rewarding them for all the recent crackdowns and purges!" Zosia exclaimed. Adam's hand stroked her skin absently. She felt a stirring between her legs.

"I know," Adam sighed. "But they're bored with our fight. They wish we'd get it over with or die already."

Zosia looked out the back of the truck into the deep forest green. They were almost in the borderlands already. There was so little free land, and the thought that they might lose even their tiny enclave of liberty to American realpolitik was more than she could bear to think about.

Adam stroked her fondly, and she huddled in his embrace, enjoying the closeness. With the two workmen riding opposite them, hunched among the boxes, there was little more they could do, and they continued the journey in silence.

They abandoned the delivery truck at a baseline partisan encampment since their intended route diverged from the mainline delivery route at that point. Zosia stopped to discuss some business with the camp's communications officer, and Adam busied himself by doing an ad hoc inspection of the camp and its organization.

"Sloppy," he commented to Zosia as they rode away from the camp afterward. "They all get sloppy after a long enough time without action."

The horse picked its way carefully along the path, and Zosia was enjoying the sensation of warm, strong muscles between her legs and Adam's arms around her waist too much to be seriously concerned about sloppy security.

"We should have brought our skis," Adam commented. "Stretch our legs a bit."

"It's too rough for skis," Zosia murmured, feeling sleepy and relaxed and not at all in the mood for physical exertion. The up-and-down rhythm of the horse's movements were making her feel horny as well, and she wished Adam would concentrate more on the way her back pressed against him rather than think about their mode of transportation. She snuggled in closer to him and murmured provocatively, "Do you know I love you?"

"Yeah, I know. I love you, too."

"I've always loved you," Zosia said as a romantic spirit inhabited her.

"Then why were you so hesitant to marry me, hmm?" Adam asked just to tease her.

"Oh, you know me, I'm not the marrying type!"

"You were afraid that once you tied the knot, I'd tie you down?"

"Well, yes, if you want honesty," Zosia answered. "That doesn't mean you aren't my soul mate. Anyway, I did marry you!"

"After prodding and blackmail and my having to pout! Do you know how many girls would have leapt at the chance to have me?"

"No, how many?" Zosia reached behind herself so she could touch Adam.

"Millions, my dear. Millions."

"Ah, yes. Well, aren't you glad you waited for me?" Zosia asked as a clump of snow descended lightly on their heads.

"Yes, and aren't you glad we did marry? Hasn't it been wonderful?" Adam gently brushed the snow from Zosia's hair.

"Yes, it has. Joanna has been more fun than I ever imagined a child could be, and you're such a loving father."

"Halt!" a voice called out. "Who goes there?"

Adam stopped the horse and called out the day's password. "We're from Central," he added.

The patrol emerged from the woods and checked their passes. Adam and Zosia did not offer identifications and were not asked: the patrols knew that the inhabitants of the Central region guarded their anonymity and only carried a general pass when traversing the borderlands.

Zosia looked from her lofty height at the young kids who surrounded the only slightly older corporal who was their leader. So young! she thought. They were all so young nowadays.

As the corporal handed them their passes, Adam asked, "Is there a shelter nearby where my wife and I might have an hour or so of privacy?"

One of the younger soldiers giggled.

The corporal pointed into the woods. "It's about a mile in that direction, sir. I'll lead you there and then I will personally"—and at that he turned to look at the offending soldier—"personally guarantee your privacy."

"We'd appreciate that," Adam responded with a grin. "Wouldn't we, Colonel?" he added, nuzzling her neck.

Zosia blushed with pride at Adam's use of her title even though it was, technically, a breach of security. It was typical of him. Though he had a reputation of being levelheaded and she had long ago been branded as impetuous, he was the more reckless of the two of them. He just pulled off a better act, first in front of their elders, and later before their political and military bosses. In fact, she had, out of love and because she was already labeled as reckless, taken the blame for some of his more foolhardy actions, just as he had often withstood a great deal of pressure by defending hers. It was one of those bonds of love that was all the stronger because no one knew about it.

"In fact," Adam said, "I think we'll stay the night there. We'll take the afternoon off and finish the trip to the camp tomorrow. Would there be a problem with that?"

"No, sir. I'll inform the relevant authorities, sir," the corporal replied respectfully.

"Would that be all right with you, love?" Adam asked.

"Yes," Zosia murmured.

"Shall we go?"

"Yes, we should," she said as Adam turned the horse to follow the path the corporal was taking. "I feel so incredibly alive," she whispered to the trees. "I wish this day would last forever."

49

*I*F ONLY THE NIGHT would last forever, he thought, as he stared up at the beams of the attic. He could just rest, in darkness, like in death. Peter turned his head languidly to look at the window, and though he lay drenched in sweat, he saw, shimmering enticingly in the cold dawn light, a patina of frost on the panes. He climbed to his feet and stood for a moment, shivering convulsively. A sudden nausea caused him to retch, but he did not vomit. And his head ached. God Almighty, so now, on top of everything else, he was ill! Just great. With the back of his hand he wiped the sweat from his forehead, then he pulled on his clothes and left the attic. After opening the blinds and drapes on the ground floor, he went down into the cellar and washed thoroughly, including his hair. Still shivering, he dried himself, pulled on the rest of his clothes, and looked for something to eat.

By the time he trudged off to the bakery he was already covered again in a slick sheen of sweat. Each bakery was open only one Sunday per month, so the location of the open bakery changed each week. This week's was the farthest away—almost certainly outside the limit of his pass. This had never been a problem before, but he suspected that if there was ever a day it would be a problem, today would be it.

Surprisingly, the walk in the frosty air made him feel somewhat better, and despite his misgivings, nothing untoward happened. In fact, other than feeling somewhat feverish, he felt essentially recovered from the unpleasantness earlier in the week. When he thought about it, from the perspective of a few days, he had gotten off rather lightly. He had known when he had started talking to Ulrike that it was a major gamble, and he had screwed up and allowed himself to be caught. Karl could easily have taken it much further, but, if he remembered correctly, Elspeth had restrained him. Now that it was over with, now that most of his injuries had healed, now perhaps, things could settle back to normal and he could put his life back together.

After breakfast, the family rushed around putting the finishing touches on their Sunday finery. Elspeth wore the new shoes she had bought the day before, and even Ulrike was a bit less subdued. They departed for their rally-cum-religious-service in good spirits. After quickly cleaning up the mess they had left, Peter used the opportunity to pick the lock on the pantry and sort through the food.

After eating, he secreted the remaining items he had stolen in the attic, gathered his extra clothes and bedding, and threw everything into the washing machine. He had never asked Elspeth if this was permitted—he suspected it was not; so, he chose to remain in ignorance and only use the machine when everyone was away. He watched the water as it swirled around and rolled in the large tub. After a few minutes he drained the soapy water while pulling each item out and pushing it through the wringer into the tub of rinse water on the other side. He swished the clothes around a bit then drained the rinse water, enjoying the brief dance of the soap bubbles in the eddies as it swirled down the drain.

Such an extravagant use of water! But it was normal here in their wealthy suburb—the supply never gave out, never gave forth that pathetic spurt of rusty sludge that was so familiar in his youth. Back then, the kids liked to drink the sludge and, on a dare, would down an entire glass. It tasted metallic and they named it tomato juice or orange juice depending on the color. Most of them had never tasted such exotica, but their imaginations allowed them to believe they were drinking the intriguing red or orange liquids they saw served in German establishments.

The sludge was the precursor to no water at all. Sometimes it lasted minutes, sometimes days, but it always happened at the most awkward times. He remembered how his father would howl with dismay and rage whenever the water would quit on the occasions he chose to shower. Better to bathe—then the supply was guaranteed for the duration and the water could be reused, his mother would remind his father each and every time. And each and every time his father would point out that the flat had been supplied with a shower not a tub, and that the tub that they had, stored above the kitchen cupboard, was uncomfortably small for a fully grown man. So his father showered. His brother, Erich, had shown him how to break into the cellar and turn off the water, thus manufacturing a water shortage for the entire building. They did it just to hear their father bellow—like a wounded water buffalo—or so they imagined, water buffalo being fairly uncommon in the streets of London. He or his brother would clamber into the cellar to turn off the supply, and the other would wait outside the door of their flat for the inevitable audio extravaganza. Still giggling, they would turn the water back on within a few minutes so nobody would detect their joke.

On the occasions of genuine shortages, he and Erich, along with all the other children, made the numerous runs, up and down the steps, back and forth along the street, to the firehouse to pick up buckets of water for the evening's activities. They used it for cleaning dishes and bathing. His mother took the unusual step of actually purchasing drinking water—especially in the summer months. Most people did not do that, they would simply boil the water from their buckets. Of course, if the natural gas supply was low or out on those days, there was a problem, and they would drink up whatever preboiled supply they had and then take their chances with the unboiled stuff. Most of the residents also kept water standing in their flats and collected it in vats on the roof, but the main effect of these was that the roof was an excellent breeding ground for mosquitoes and disease since no one bothered to clean their vats out frequently enough. Between the roof vats of standing rainwater and the irregular garbage collection, the English sections of London became deservedly known as foul-smelling, disease-ridden, and thoroughly disorderly. Not unlike the English themselves, his schoolmates had been fond of telling him.

As the rinse water drained away, he put the laundry through the wringer a second time to squeeze out the excess water, then grabbed the resultant sodden mass and took it to the attic to hang it out to dry. It was cold and damp and he doubted the laundry would dry by nightfall, but he had little other option— there was no place by the furnace where he could spread it. In any case, he did not need the extra set of clothes immediately, so they could hang for a day or two. As for the bedding, he would either do without it for the night or sleep with damp covers.

The next thing he did, he knew, was strictly forbidden, and that was to use the family's bathroom to bathe with hot water and good soap. He gingerly washed the remainder of the dried blood from his hair, then thoroughly rinsed away any lingering scent of the soap—not that they would notice with all the perfumes they used. He trimmed his hair using good scissors, then shaved with a sharp razor, carefully cleaning the blade and placing it back into the packet when he was done. After that he washed and dried all the surfaces so no one could tell the room had been used. With that done, he returned to the sitting room, and using one of the couch pillows to cushion his head and a blanket to cover himself, he lay down on the sitting room rug to sleep. That, too, would of course be forbidden if they knew he did it. The thought did not disturb him at all, and within seconds he was sound asleep.

Initially, he had taken his naps on the sofa, avoiding the bedrooms so he could stay near the door and hear them if they came home early, but after he had worked on the armchair, he had taken to napping on the floor rather than have his brief sleep disturbed by the death screams of women—their heads shaven—

as they asphyxiated in poison-gas chambers labeled as showers. He knew it was superstitious nonsense: the inanimate furniture was no more a part of the crimes committed decades ago than the land upon which the blood had been spilled. The criminals themselves had walked freely, lived richly, run an empire with brutal efficiency, promulgated racial laws, and been received as civilized representatives of their regime. They had been and still were beyond his reach, and whatever had happened, he could not undo it. In comparison to the enormity of the suffering the furniture represented to him now, his simple gesture of mournful respect seemed pathetic and pointless, but it was all he could do, so he did it nonetheless.

When he awoke, he checked the time—about twenty minutes yet. No point even thinking about going out. In theory, he could use the time to get a start on the day's work, but he had never actually done that: there really was no point since they always manufactured more. Sometimes he used the brief respite from the family to read, but aside from his lacking the time, there was not much of interest in the house. He considered for a moment perusing the week's newspapers to see if he could sift any news out from between all the self-congratulatory nonsense, but decided he was too tired and his eyes ached. No, better to return to sleeping and get some much needed rest—especially if he wanted to finally put that horrible night behind him.

The thought brought him up short. In a disarming feat of denial he had up to that moment managed to entirely forget Karl's words that night as Elspeth had at long last placed a restraining hand on her husband's arm. "All right," Karl had agreed, "I'll finish with him on Sunday." Sunday, the day when household and family matters were dealt with. Sunday, a day that was infinitely in the future back then. Sunday. Today. The idea dismayed him, but the more he thought about it, the harder it was to dismiss the vague memory. The anger of that night would not be enough to sate Karl's need for revenge or justice or whatever he wanted to call it. There was still a price to be paid.

He debated for a few minutes what he should possibly do. His eyes strayed to the door. The time to leave would be now, before they returned. He could don one of Karl's suits, steal a car, and take his chances on the road. How long would he last? Without papers, maybe an hour or two. Arrested, convicted a third time. He shuddered at the prospect. Perhaps walking. It would be easier to avoid having his papers checked that way. Maybe a day or two. Then what? He realized he was trembling, and he pointedly turned his attention away from the door.

His options seemed rather limited, and he realized that, short of a suicidal escape attempt, there was nothing to be done. Nothing but wait. It made him laugh a bit as he realized that his entire defense system had collapsed to simply hoping for the best, and he rubbed his temples and marveled at the pathetic creature he had become.

When it was nearly time for the family to return, he went and sat on the floor in the hallway by the door waiting to hear their footsteps. When he heard them approaching, he got up to open the door and take their coats and help them settle in. After he had served them their lunch, the family gathered, as usual, in the sitting room to handle the week's affairs. When called, he came in from the kitchen, sleeves still rolled up from cleaning dishes, and took his assigned place. It was clear the children had not yet been dealt with—the week's events had obviously disrupted the routine. They sat in their usual places, their faces taut with anticipation; Ulrike was pale, her jaw clenched. They all looked miserable; even Elspeth, taking her place in the armchair, looked somewhat unhappy and pensive, as if she had disagreed with Karl about something. Only Karl was oblivious to the unpleasant mood; he stood up and moved into the center of the room, relishing his powerful position.

"So, we're all together now," he announced uselessly. "I think you all realize that this week has been somewhat unusual due to, uh, certain circumstances." He threw a scripted look at Ulrike, who, in response, lowered her eyes, as would be expected. "Now, as for you, little ones," he continued, looking at the three youngest, "you've been very good this week. Our beloved Adolf would have been proud of you. You can go outside and play now." He nodded in response to the unspoken question in their surprised faces. He winked at the two youngest as they tumbled with astonished relief out of the room and smiled benevolently after them. Teresa stood up slowly from her seat, gave her parents an odd look, and then left without saying a word. Karl then turned toward Horst and assumed a businesslike manner. "You, too." He nodded toward the door.

"But, Father!" Horst protested.

"No, Horst, it's not your business."

"It is, too! I should know what goes on in this family!"

"Horst," Elspeth interjected softly, "go."

Horst whirled around, wanting to stare her down, but her determination was evident. He glowered at his parents for a moment, then stomped angrily out of the room.

"That boy certainly has a well-developed sense of *Schadenfreude*," Elspeth muttered.

Karl nodded, then shifted his gaze to Ulrike. She sat alone on the sofa, looking for all the world as if she wanted to disappear. Her whole body was pulled in as if she could achieve this goal if only she made herself small enough. She did not look at her father, so he said, "Ulrike," to get her to look up.

She did, frightened.

"Ulrike, child, I don't think you understand yet what dangers you've been playing with." Karl looked at Elspeth, then back to Ulrike. "We feel responsible for that. We haven't been careful enough. When we brought him into this household, we should have made it clear to each and every one of you how important it was to maintain our separateness. We are naturally superior, but even superior folk can be corrupted. Don't you know what his people are guilty of?

Rassenmischung! Decadence! Corruption! Weakness! Betrayal! They are *Volksverräter!* Not to be trusted! They are a sick people!"

That last comment caught Peter's attention, and he stifled a sputter of derision, desperately turning it into a cough. Karl was not deceived and whirled around to confront him, almost shouting at him, "And they are evil!"

If there had been a chance for mercy, Peter knew he had lost it then.

"Evil," Karl repeated, bringing himself under control. "Evil. But they'll be around to do our work for us, and we must learn how to control them and maintain our own high standards. We are superior and stronger in every way, and once you realize that, it'll be easy for you to learn to keep them in their proper place." Karl stopped and let his words sink in. Then he turned toward Peter and hissed, "And as for you, even with your limited abilities, you should have known better. Spreading your poison in my family. Endangering not only yourself, but all of us! Are you so stupid you don't even understand self-preservation?"

"Papa," Ulrike begged to be heard, "it was my fault, I asked him."

"Nonsense!" Karl spat. "There is the weakness," he said, pointing at Peter, "and you must learn to command it! You must learn not to trust them, not to view them as human, not to let slip your position in society! That is your responsibility as an *Übermensch!* Do you understand?"

Ulrike nodded unconvincingly.

"Now I will show you how to be a strong, true Aryan!" Karl said, then he turned away from her and, grabbing Peter's arm, thrust him toward the door, ordering, "Move!"

"Karl," Elspeth finally found her voice, "do you think it's really necessary?"

"She must see."

"That's not what I meant," Elspeth said. "It's just that . . . You already, on Tuesday, you know . . ."

"We've already spoken about this. My anger on Tuesday was just that. This is . . ." Karl eyed Peter. "This is necessary, if we want to prevent such things from ever happening again. There is no place in this household for ingrates and malcontents. *He must learn!*"

Peter's limbs grew heavy with dread. Was survival really worth so much? He eyed the front door again. He could just walk away from it all. Just walk out the door. It wouldn't take long after that. It would be so easy! It would all be over. To give up, after all this time, after all he had endured. To give up any hope of freedom, to give up his life, to just give up.

Karl pushed him. Making his decision, Peter went in the direction he was shoved, down the hall toward the kitchen and away from the door. Ulrike got up and reluctantly followed them out of the room, leaving Elspeth sitting alone in her armchair, stroking her chin thoughtfully. "More work for me," she said to the empty room. "I'll have to do everything myself today. Does he ever think about *that?*"

Karl crossed the kitchen to the cellar door, pushing Peter through it, with an impatient "Go on." Once the three of them were in the cellar, Karl ordered Peter to remove his shirt. As Peter complied, Karl wandered off to the storage cupboard and sorted through the electric cables and wires, eventually selecting one with a grunt of satisfaction.

Ulrike remained close by the stairs as if ready to flee at any instant. When she realized what her father was doing, she looked to Peter, panic in her expression, but he did not see her, he was watching Karl. His expression betrayed no emotion. He looked so calm, Ulrike wondered if he felt things the same way they did.

Peter's dispassion hid a tumult of emotions: fear, outrage, a ridiculous sense of guilt, but most of all he was trying to determine how much danger he was in and weigh his options accordingly. Karl's care in selecting his weapon was reassuring. Both of them were experienced, in their different ways, in torture, and he saw that Karl had selected as his whip a cable which would cause more pain than injury. A moment later, though, a sudden chill ran down his spine as he saw Karl unlock his tool cabinet and remove a pair of handcuffs. Handcuffs? The muscles of his face twitched as he continued to scrutinize Karl's every move.

As Karl stood in front of him, grabbing Peter's left arm to affix the manacles, he came to a decision and forced himself to say, "Please, *mein Herr.*"

Karl closed the metal ring around Peter's wrist and looked up with mild interest.

"*Mein Herr,* I beg you to forgive me. It was a mistake, I understand now," Peter pleaded. Struggling to master his expression, he forced himself to look contrite and continued, "Please believe me. I won't do anything like that again. Please, I am slow and stupid and undeserving of your mercy, but I have learned. Please, this isn't necessary. I *have* learned. Please don't hurt me. Please have mercy on me."

Karl looked him up and down meaningfully, then answered, "I *am* being merciful, and one day you may understand that this is for your own good."

Peter realized that he had made a mistake by not going down on his knees, but it was too late. Karl turned away, pulling him by his bound wrist like a dog on a leash. They came to a stop, and Peter looked up to see a sturdy pipe running along the ceiling and attached to an overhead beam with two closely spaced supports. He stared at the thick pipe and the solid bracing and knew that it would, without a doubt, hold his full weight. He was still marveling at how Karl had walked right to the spot, as if it had been preselected, as his left arm was pulled upward and the loose ring of the handcuffs was threaded through the gap between the pipe and the ceiling. Then he remembered the rumors of a previous *Zwangsarbeiter,* one who had died suddenly. A sick feeling came over him as Karl grabbed his right wrist and shackled that. Had he made a deadly mistake? An uncontrollable instinct caused him to jerk his arms violently downward against the hard metal of the handcuffs, as if trying to free himself. The sharp edges of the rings bit painfully into his skin, and a trickle of blood traced a crooked path down his arm. He heard Karl snicker at his useless effort.

"*Mein Herr,* please. Please don't—"

"Shut up!" Karl snarled. "Not one more word, or I *will* kill you! Understood?"

Peter nodded mutely and stood there trapped with his arms not quite fully extended above his head. Karl walked away from him, but he dared not look to see what was going on. He tried to prepare himself for the inevitable, but there did not seem to be much he could do. He looked up at his bound wrists, then dropped his head to stare grimly at the floor as he waited.

"Papa," Ulrike's soft voice cut through the tense atmosphere; there was a tremor in it. He twisted around to see Ulrike and Karl's reaction to her. "Papa, he said it was a mistake. He said—"

"Don't try my patience. That's exactly the sort of thing I was talking about," Karl snarled in response.

Ulrike appeared to accept the logic of this; she made a simple appeal instead. "Please, don't hurt him. I know what he said was wrong and evil, but he's been punished already." She continued, her words sounding sincere, "It's not really his fault, he can't help what he is. I think he believed what he told me; he doesn't know any better. I know it was wrong, but please don't hurt him any more."

Karl's voice lost its edge. Patiently he explained, "He has to learn his place and so do you. We all make mistakes, but we have a duty to learn from them. It's for his own good, but if it bothers you to see him hurt, just remember that the next time you decide to be foolish. A young German prince had to witness the execution of his best friend because of his own foolish actions. Because he learned from that, he became a great king. So, too, do your actions have consequences for you and for others. Now just sit there quietly and see the results of your folly. It's the least you can do."

"It's all I can do," she answered, turning her eyes, brimming with tears, toward Peter.

Karl resumed his stance and without further warning swung the cord.

Peter heard the whistle of the cable, gasped in surprise as he felt the sharp, cutting pain. Once he was warned by the shock of the first stroke, he steeled himself to accept the following ones in silence. Initially, he was successful, accepting each lash with barely a sound, but as the beating progressed and new blows fell on old ones, his response became less controlled. His face tightened, his mouth stretched into a grimace, and his throat emitted small noises with each stroke.

At one point, seeking some solace from his agony, he turned his head to look at Ulrike, but she had disappeared. She must have slipped away sometime earlier, abandoning him to his fate. Karl followed his glance and, noting Ulrike's absence, muttered something, then struck Peter with furious vigor again and again. His determined silence broke into uncontrolled cries of pain; each wave of agony was followed by another so rapidly he could not even catch his breath. He felt his flesh tearing, boiling, burning. He felt a sudden overwhelming nausea and his vision went black with each pound of his heart. He writhed, wildly trying to avoid the blows, his feet, slipped on the accumulated sweat and blood, and his entire weight fell upon his wrists. He struggled to pull himself back to his feet, but Karl kept flogging him. The blackness of each heartbeat grew longer, the bright flashes of vision grew more and more unfocused, and a dizziness prevented him from being able to work out which way was up. He tried again to stand, then closed his eyes against the pain and let the blackness claim him.

Karl walked over to his victim, placed two fingers on his neck, and found a pulse. Perfect! He could not prevent himself from smiling at his expertise. Firmly holding on to one of Peter's arms, he unlocked the handcuffs, quickly grabbed the other arm as it dropped, and carefully lowered the body to the floor.

He looked at it for a moment, nudged it with his foot, but there was no movement. Then he washed his hands, put away the cable, and picked up the handcuffs. He ran his thumb along the bloody edge; the metal was cheaply cut and surprisingly sharp. Poorly made, like so much else. He thought about getting a better pair as he pulled out a cigarette. He put the cigarette to his lips, then realizing that he did not have a match, he returned to the body lying on the floor, gingerly reached into a trouser pocket, and found a lighter. Lighting his cigarette, he pocketed the lighter and stood over the lifeless body, smoking quietly. His hands were trembling from the adrenaline rush; he could hardly hold his cigarette still. He was exhausted as well—it had been strenuous work, but it left him feeling fulfilled. He missed the old times: nowadays, it was beneath his dignity to interrogate prisoners directly. What a pity!

There was no reason to remain in the cellar, yet he was loath to leave. He wanted to savor the moment: it had been a long time in coming, too long. He should have done this ages ago, the day he had brought the insolent bastard into the house; that would have prevented a lot of nonsense. But now, now it seemed almost too late.

He felt trapped. Despite his threats, he knew he could never recoup the replacement costs if he traded in Peter's contract. Who would take such a useless worker? Only industry, and they never paid enough. And he would never be so lucky a second time in extorting a contract out of someone the way he had out of the Reusches. It hadn't been so bad when he had had a reasonable income stream, but recently he'd been losing his protection rackets to Schindler and others. The bribes had been drying up as well. When he had failed to secure that arms deal, that had been the last straw. His influence was waning, they were all grabbing it away from him; damn, he was nearly destitute, dependent almost entirely on his salary!

Peter groaned and twitched, and Karl thought he might awaken, but there was no further movement. What a disappointment! It wasn't fair! First those stupid fines, then that woman stealing his money, and now this worthless piece of shit. Always scowling and sneaking around and skiving off. Sarcastic, disrespectful, lazy. Always questioning orders, always mouthing off. Half the time he couldn't even open the door on time. The worthless shit! Worse than worthless! Feeding that load of rot to Ulrike. What if she had repeated it? God in heaven, she might have been arrested and then the family would have been ruined! All his work, all his effort down the drain, and all because some stupid, worthless servant couldn't mind his own business! Better if he had tried to sleep with her.

Karl rubbed his head. He had a headache. What was he going to do, what was he going to do? He couldn't get rid of him, he couldn't do without—that would look too impoverished—and he couldn't afford another. He was trapped. He swore and kicked Peter. Damn it! He had to keep him under control, there was no other way. He would have to pay attention to what went on in the house, he'd have to be vigilant and strict. He'd have to bring this one to heel. Zero tolerance. There was no other choice. He'd look like a fool otherwise.

He finished his cigarette and wondered momentarily about where to stub it out. The face? He used to put it in their eyes—the poor buggers never liked that very much. Ah, but he had money invested in this bastard, and besides, he was out cold, he would never even notice. He threw the end on the floor and ground it out with his foot. Then slowly, ponderously, he climbed the steps back to the kitchen.

Elspeth was there. "There wasn't much noise."

"No, I'll give him that much. Get me a cup of coffee."

"Are you finished?"

"For now." Karl lit another cigarette. "For now."

50

"**O**H!" ADAM GROANED AND dismounted, handing the reins over to the young soldier who had walked them into the camp. "Is there any coffee in this place?"

Zosia laughed and lightly slid to the ground. "Tired, darling?" she teased.

The soldier led the horse away without answering, apparently assuming that such questions and conversations were not for his ears. Adam lit a cigarette and turned to Zosia. "Tired?" he repeated. "You wore me out, woman!"

"Put that thing out!" a voice cried out to them. They turned to see Wanda bearing down on them.

"Oh, it's you," Adam greeted her.

She approached and kissed both of them. "Adam!" she chided. "Please, it's hard enough keeping these kids under control without you flouting the rules."

"Sorry." Adam stooped down and ground out the cigarette. "I forgot I was so near the border." He stood and handed Wanda the extinguished cigarette as if he were a naughty schoolboy. "Will teacher forgive me?"

"Here I am training them to blend into the forest, to meld with the night, and you're encouraging them to glow in the dark and send up a smelly stream of smoke!" Wanda laughed. "You're hopeless!"

"So how's things?" Zosia asked. "I didn't realize you'd be down here!"

"Is there any coffee here?" Adam asked.

Wanda threw an arm around each of them and led them off. "Fine and yes," she answered. "Let's get the coffee first, then we can talk."

"So, Adam, what's your excuse for looking so bedraggled?" Wanda asked as she watched him sip his coffee.

Adam held the coffee in his mouth a moment, letting the warmth penetrate his bones, savoring the taste. "Zosia beats me," he answered at last. "She's merciless. Whips me every night. Ah, such agony," he sighed.

Zosia giggled. "Well, you did sound in pain last night. Sort of like an injured elk. Of course, you came back asking for more this morning, didn't you?"

"Ah, I'm a glutton for punishment."

"And again, after breakfast."

"An absolute masochist," Adam confirmed.

Wanda raised her eyebrows. "I'm amazed you two have the energy. When I was your age, with the twins, my God, it was all Jurek and I could do to kiss."

"And how are your boys?" Zosia asked.

"They're here. That's why I came down to the border. They've got leave from their SS unit, and they've managed to sneak in for a visit, but their time is so short that we decided to meet up with them down here to save time."

"So they're not coming up to Central?" Adam asked.

"No, they've got to get back on duty. The Fatherland awaits!" Wanda joked. "We're just glad they could make it here at all."

"Where are they now?" Zosia wondered.

"Out with their dad, taking a walk. He wanted to talk to them, and I had some business to take care of here. There have been more than the usual number of incursions in this region, and I want to work out what the problem is."

"How is their assignment working out?" Adam asked.

"Oh, the usual. They're making good progress, but they're really weary of wearing the uniform, strutting, saluting, shouting '*Sieg Heil.*' It's soul-destroying, as you know. I keep telling them, it will pay off, but they're losing patience."

"At least they have each other," Zosia commented. "Both in the same unit, aren't they?"

"Yes. They say all their friends tell them they look like they could be brothers!" Wanda laughed. As she said that, the two young men came into the tent with their father.

"Colonel Firlej! Colonel Król!" they exclaimed in concert. "How good to see you." First one, then the other bent down to kiss Zosia in greeting.

"Congratulations on your new promotion, Colonel!" Marek said.

"Not so new, anymore," Wanda pointed out.

"Ah, we've been out of touch," Marek explained to his mother.

"And congratulations on your council seat!" Maciej added, kissing Zosia again.

"Thank you!" Zosia beamed.

"And the biggest congratulations on your new baby!" Marek said as both he and his brother kissed Zosia yet again.

"What is she, three?" Maciej asked.

"Not quite," Adam answered.

The boys and their father sat down and poured themselves coffee.

"Do three colonels get us a prize?" Jurek asked.

"No, just a lot of bossing around," Adam quipped. "Especially for you civilians."

"Eh, I never listen to orders anyway," Jurek said.

"All the more so since he's retired," Wanda added.

"If you want to hear orders, then have I got a song to sing!" Maciej interjected. At that point he and Marek launched into long and hilarious tales of their life among the Nazis. Nobody was fooled, they all knew the stress the boys endured, but despite that, Maciej and Marek painted such a picture of idiocy and lunacy that all of them had tears rolling down their cheeks from laughter. As they finished with their anecdotes, Zosia and Adam brought them up-to-date on news, and Wanda added her own version of recent Council events. The conversation turned from one topic to another and the time passed quickly among the friends until Marek glanced at his watch, nudged his brother, and announced sadly, "I'm afraid we have to go."

"Yes, if we don't get back, our carriage will turn into a pumpkin and we'll be dressed in rags!" Maciej agreed.

Zosia and Adam said their farewells as Wanda and Jurek escorted their sons from the tent. "They're growing up so fast!" Zosia commented as she watched the family striding across the camp together. "Wanda and Jurek did a great job with them."

Adam nodded. "Yes, they're moving up fast. They'll be a great asset to us, if they can stick it out."

"They'll do it. They'll do just fine."

The next morning Adam emerged from their tent quite late, stretched, and then looked knowledgeably up at the winter storm clouds gathering. It would be pointless staying another day, and if they hoped to make it back without getting slowed by the weather, they would have to start moving soon. Nevertheless, he decided to wait a few moments. Zosia was nicely tucked up in their tent, snuggled under down comforters, still glowing from their night's activities, the morning air was crisp and invigorating, and he felt so wonderfully alive. He exhaled a cloud of steam and watched it dissipate in the light breeze. God, life was good! So precious, yet so unappreciated in their world. If only everyone in the Reich could stand in the midst of a pine forest on a mountainside blanketed with snow and look up to the winter sky and breathe in the fresh air of freedom. If only.

His thoughts were interrupted by the figure of Wanda coming toward him. Her face looked strained and as she approached, he asked, "What's up? What's wrong?"

She stopped and collected herself as if to speak, but then she threw herself into his arms and hung her head on his shoulder, sobbing uncontrollably.

"Wanda! What's the matter?"

"They're dead," she sobbed. "They're both dead!"

"Dead? Who? What?" Adam asked helplessly.

"Maciej, Marek. My boys," she wailed.

"What happened? What happened!" Adam begged to know. He continued to hold her and stroked her hair as she cried on his shoulder.

Eventually, she brought her sobs under control enough to explain. "Somebody shot them in the street. They were walking to the train station, it was late, dark. They were in their uniforms, of course. Their SS uniforms. Somebody shot them. A terrorist," Wanda groaned.

"Not ours!" Adam asked, horrified. "Not one of ours?"

Wanda looked up at him then, her face red and swollen, her cheeks wet with her tears. "Would it matter who the hell it was?" she asked fiercely.

"Wanda, was it a cock-up? Did we assassinate them?"

She shook her head. "No. It was just terrorism. Some splinter group or disgruntled individual saw the uniforms and took retaliation into their own hands. Just violence," she moaned. "Just random anti-Nazi violence." She blinked hard and looked up at the sky. "My boys are dead and all you care about is whether it was a flaw in our system. Rest assured, Colonel, it wasn't that, it was just a flaw in our whole goddamned world!"

"Oh, Wanda, I'm sorry. I'm so sorry. I didn't mean it like that! It's just so shocking. I'm sorry, it was unforgivable. Please, come into the tent, please, come talk with us. Where's Jurek?"

"He went for a walk in the woods. After all the details filtered in, he asked to spend some time alone. I—I came over here to tell you, and all you cared about was who the murderers were."

"Please, forgive me. Come inside. We should tell Zosia," Adam begged, pulling her gently toward the tent.

Ferociously, Wanda pushed him away. "No, you tell her! Tell her some fool is bragging about his exploit, his courage in killing two SS swine. Tell her how we all encouraged them to go back and wear those stupid uniforms! Tell her how it wasn't the fault of the AK. Tell her it was just someone fed up with the occupation! Tell her what a heroic deed it was! Tell her my boys are dead!"

"Wanda," Adam pleaded.

"You professional killers! You and your wife! You never think about the world you create with your glib murders! With your judicial executions! The world is bathed in hatred and violence, and you go off and kill to make it right again, don't you? The brave assassins of the AK carrying out justice in an unjust world!

Didn't you ever think that you leave behind a host of young wanna-bes? Kids with guns and knives who want to emulate you and get a few of those damn Nazis!"

"Wanda, it's not like that!"

"It *is* like that and my boys are dead because of it! They paid for someone else's crime, don't you understand?"

"Wanda, we try and keep them under control, you know that. You know we can't stop the violence. It's been too many years of murder in our land, we're overwhelmed! Please, don't blame us, don't blame yourself! Lay the blame where it belongs!"

"It belongs at your feet, Colonel," Wanda spat. "Just like Julia's death."

Adam took a deep breath. "Out of respect for your grief, I won't respond to that." His voice had dropped almost to a whisper. "You know it is not our method, has *never* been our method, to kill randomly or to accept the idea of hostages. For decades we have seen our own innocent people killed in retaliation for the actions of others, and we have never, not once, given in to that strategy. That someone else has, is not our fault. You should know better than that, and even in your grief you should be ashamed of yourself."

Wanda opened her mouth to say something, but then she closed it again and tears streamed silently down her cheeks. She came back toward Adam and looked up into his face. "I'm sorry," she whispered. "I don't know what got into me. I'm sorry." She turned and walked away.

Adam did not call her back.

51

"**H**OW'S IT GOING IN THERE?" Graham asked as he peered nervously into the room.

"Would you stop poking your nose in here!" Allison hissed at him. "Just go back to your office and pretend to be busy!"

"Can't you hurry it up?" Graham asked.

"Alan's running the tapes as fast as he can," Allison explained, "and every time we hear someone coming, we've got to drop everything and pick up these mops. Now, would you just leave! We'll come by your office when we're done and let you know, then you can lock up. Now, go!"

Allison pushed the door shut even as Graham was beginning to protest. "He's such a worrier!"

"Ah, he's afraid you and I will get picked up and give him away. I guess it's pretty obvious that if two janitors are caught using the institute's computers, then one of the faculty is responsible."

"It is?" Allison asked.

"No. Graham's just a fussbudget. And maybe he suspects that we're doing more than working here."

"Do you think he'll tell Terry?" Allison furrowed her brow worriedly.

"Why do you care?"

"I don't want Terry to know about us, it would hurt him."

"Then divorce him. We can get married the day after you file the papers."

She shook her head. "You know I don't want to do that."

"Yeah, I know all right. What I don't understand is why not."

"We've been through this," Allison said, a hint of anger in her voice.

"I know, we've been through it: you love me, you love him. Why, I ask myself, do I feel used?"

"It's complicated. I owe him loyalty."

"Why? You're the only person in this country who takes a housing-list marriage seriously! God, what were you, seventeen? He was sixteen? Did you even spend a night together?"

"Not then. But look, he came back from the draft and he joined the Underground just to stay with me. It wasn't his style, but he took the risk just to be my husband."

"Your husband! How in God's name you can be loyal to someone who told you that you did too much, that you were 'too smart'!"

"I told you that in confidence," she hissed.

"You two aren't meant for each other. We are. Just divorce him!"

She shook her head sadly. "It's easy for you to say, you have nothing to lose, Alan."

"And apparently, neither do you. Do you think I can wait forever?" He didn't tell her that he would. The tape drive whirred to a stop, and he turned his attention to the computer. "God, if only we could get our hands on a small version of this thing."

"Do you think they could be smaller?" Allison asked as she stroked the huge metallic beast that filled a wall of the research room.

He nodded. "No reason they couldn't be small. Just technology. In fact, I've heard they have desktop computers in America."

"Wouldn't that make our lives easier!" Allison exclaimed quietly. She walked up to him and threw her arms around his waist. "Once you mount the next tape and program the translation, do you think we could, um . . . ?"

He felt his hostility melt with her touch. "I love you so much," he whispered, too quietly for her to hear. He closed his eyes and imagined what their life together could be like.

When he opened his eyes again, there were no bright fluorescent lights, no smell of cleaning fluids, no laboring computer noises. There was darkness and silence. He was lying down and he was alive, for what it was worth. His arms ached and his extremities were cold, but most of all his back tormented him, causing him to sweat despite the chill. He rolled off his side onto his back, hoping the cold, damp cement would ease the burning sensation. It was a mistake; the agony he felt as he moved nearly caused him to scream aloud. Groaning, he arched his back, rolled back onto his side, and passed out.

Allison. Allie, looking up from her work at him, smiling her tentative, almost somber smile. Allie, waking him up, taking a deep drag off her cigarette, then sticking the end, still moist from her mouth, between his lips and saying, "Here, Alan, this will help you open your eyes." Allie, smiling indulgently at his jokes. Allie, running her fingers over his body. His body, which did not ache incessantly then.

He realized he was awake again, surrounded by darkness, awash with pain. He could see nothing, but he heard himself moan with each gasp he took. He hurt so badly, and he was so cold, but he could not move. He lay very still, doing nothing more than breathing, staring into nothingness with half-closed eyes, wondering idly what it would be like to be dead. Would the pain stop then?

After a while, he turned a bit and managed to work his arms under his chest. He tested his strength and then, ignoring the slick feel of blood beneath his palms, carefully pushed himself up. Sobs of pain escaped as he struggled to a sitting position with his arms still supporting his weight. He paused a moment there, overcoming his dizziness, then continued to his hands and knees. Once he got his balance, he extended one arm outward into the darkness to search for a support. When he could find none, he sat back down to rest.

After a few moments thirst drove him to try again. Panting with the effort of ignoring his pain, he crawled along until he found a wall. He rested his head against it as he gathered his strength. The darkness was so complete around him, he began to wonder if his sight had been damaged. There was a window in the other section of the cellar; if he went to it, he would be able to see some light even at night. With that thought to encourage him, he climbed to his feet, oriented himself by touch, and stumbled off in the direction of the back room.

As he opened the door separating the two rooms, he felt the warmth of the furnace, and shadowy shapes emerged into view. It was still night, but the streetlights cast enough of a glow, even through the shuttered window, to reassure him that he had not been blinded. His eyes adjusted to the gloom, and he had no difficulty finding the sink. He drank until his thirst was slaked, then he rinsed his face and arms. He knew he should wash his back as well, but the prospect of aggravating the almost unbearable pain discouraged him. Besides, he was shivering with cold already; the idea of dousing himself with more freezing-cold water was too much to contemplate.

He dismissed the thought and went to stand by the furnace to warm himself. With half-closed eyes, he stared at the flickering light. *Millions upon millions,* he thought, *millions upon millions.* He closed his eyes so that he would not have to see the image of burning corpses, but the pain he felt ebbing and flowing through his body forced them open again. *This society, these people,* he thought.

Millions upon millions, he thought. *Me.* He stared emptily. When he finally focused his eyes, he looked at the flame and wondered if anyone had tended to the furnace for the night. He stood for a long time, undecided. Eventually, sighing, he gave in to his inclination and banked the ashes and closed the draft.

He stepped back from the furnace and, reaching up among the wood beams, removed his stash of cigarettes. Among the ends were three entire cigarettes. He took two and put the rest back into their hiding place, then using a furnace match to light one, he sat down and smoked. The first cigarette calmed him a bit; the second he enjoyed as a welcome diversion from the pain. As he drew the last puff and sent the smoke in a farewell stream toward the furnace, he ground out the end and decided he had warmed himself enough. He wandered off to find a cloth, and wrapping it around and over his injured back to protect it and absorb the oozing blood, he returned to the other room.

Feeling his way around blindly, he found his shirt where he had left it, pulled it on, and made his way to the steps. He was anxious to get out of the cellar, but when he reached the top step, he discovered the door had been locked. He pressed his hands and head against it, trying to control his frustration, then he slid down into a sitting position on the top step, his head pressed against the wood of the door, and waited for morning.

He woke up when Elspeth opened the door and he nearly fell into the kitchen. Holding on to the doorjamb for support, he climbed to his feet, wincing with pain. The effort of standing left him dizzy, the room whirled around him and he feared he might faint. He gripped the wood, his knuckles white with the effort of preventing himself from tumbling backward down the steps. When he felt sure he had his balance, he moved forward into the relative safety of the kitchen.

Elspeth considered him, a look of faint disgust on her face. "You're going to be useless today—that much is obvious. Damn it! I haven't had a decent day's work out of you all week. And now this."

"I need a doctor. Please."

She continued to study him, stroking her chin, then she shook her head. "No, you don't. Go get some sleep, that'll suffice."

"Mama said to get you up. It's afternoon. She said you've rested enough."

He turned his head and looked into Gisela's wide, innocent eyes. "I'm awake." Nevertheless, she did not leave; she stood shyly observing him until he was driven to ask, "What? What is it?"

"You were bad, weren't you?"

"Maybe," he answered reluctantly.

"Daddy punished you?"

"Yes," he moaned.

"Are you going to be good now?"

He winced as a wave of pain washed over him.

"Are you going to be good now?"

Sobbing with pain, he was unable to answer her.

As she left the room, he grit his teeth and struggled to his feet. Each movement sent tendrils of agony along the damaged muscles and skin of his back. He worked his way down the stairs, panting with the effort. Elspeth greeted him with a nod toward the front door, indicating that it was time for Karl to return from work. He waited, opened the door for his master, and performed the routine he had carried out hundreds of times. Only when it came time to light Karl's cigarette was his routine disrupted. The crystal lighter that usually sat in the hall had not yet been replaced, so he reached in his pocket to find the lighter he usually carried, but nothing was there.

"Here," Karl sneered, and handed him what he was looking for.

He stared at it, embarrassed, but unsure why.

When Karl wandered into the sitting room, Peter followed. Elspeth handed him the keys and he unlocked the liquor cabinet, pulled out the glasses and bottles, and poured their drinks. All the while, the two of them chatted about their day. He set their drinks next to them, and then Elspeth interrupted her diatribe about Horst and his girlfriend long enough to dismiss Peter from the room with an order to go make himself more presentable.

He left the room feeling inexplicably humiliated. Being greeted at the door, having a cigarette lit, having their drinks poured, chattering mindlessly about the children or problems at work—*their* lives were completely unchanged! God in heaven, after what they had done to him, they could at least be smug! But it was as if it were all an irrelevancy. Elspeth had reduced his suffering to an order to clean himself up! Even worse was that it mattered so much to him. His degradation and isolation were so complete that he turned now to his tormentors to care about what had happened!

His eyes strayed to the staircase down which he had been thrown, not even a week before. He turned his head and saw the walking stick, stored in its holder near the door. He let his gaze stray along the hallway where Karl had so brutally beaten him. He stared disconsolately at the walls, at the wallpaper. Afterward, in his dismay he had pressed himself against the wall and carelessly let his blood stain the wallpaper. Even after hours of cleaning, it was still there, his only legacy in the house. Faint traces of blood, his blood, spattered like drops of red rain on the floral pattern. Each drop glinting orange-red from the reflected streetlights. Each drop balanced delicately on the fragile petals as Allison brought the bouquet to her face and breathed the sweet scent. "I can't take them home with me," she whispered.

"I know," he agreed. "I thought you might enjoy them for a few minutes anyway."

"You just wanted an excuse to give that girl a few marks."

"Maybe. Anyone selling flowers in the middle of the night . . ." He did not finish his thought.

"It's almost dawn," Allison said as if disagreeing, but he knew she was just saying good-bye.

"I'll walk you home."

The air was misty and their footsteps were muffled as though they were ghosts treading the desolate streets. He watched her as she slipped into her apartment building, waited long enough to feel sure that she had arrived safely, then turned to head back to his room. En route he stopped and laid Allison's flowers at one of the impromptu memorials to the defenders of the city. A patrolman called out to him but he ignored the summons, slipping down an alley before the policeman could fire off a shot. The narrow escape left him feeling rather apprehensive, and he took extra care for the rest of his long walk home. When he got there, as was his habit, he waited a few moments out of sight to observe his building. It was just a habit and he hardly expected to see anything, so he was rather shaken when he saw three officers exit the building. He could not discern their insignia in the poor light; all he could see was that they conferred in front of the building, in a manner suggesting frustration, and then left on foot.

He stood absolutely still for a moment trying not to believe what the evidence suggested. Had they come looking for him? Why? And how did they know where he lived? The confusion blinded him momentarily to the implications. He knew he should not go inside just yet. There was no guarantee the building was not being watched or that someone was not still inside. No, he should sleep somewhere else tonight, this morning—already the sky was turning gray. It would be dangerous to go to any of his colleagues. . . . He felt a sudden catch in his throat. If they were seeking him, if he had been betrayed, then . . . Oh, God. He turned and began running back toward Allison's flat.

Only years of expertise kept him from being picked up by a patrol during his wild run back to her place; instinct sent him dodging among the shadows at the last minute. He stopped two streets away from his destination to catch his breath. He had to be really careful now. It would hardly do to betray himself in his effort to protect her. Assuming a semblance of calm, he strolled toward the massive concrete tower that she called home. It was late enough that he could join the people stumbling to their jobs as the sun broke through the morning mist. As he walked, he prayed that it was a false alarm. Or that he had arrived in time.

But the small knot of people in front of the main entrance of her building indicated that his hopes were in vain. His heart pounded wildly in his chest. Hardly able to refrain from running, he walked up to the crowd. The entrance of the building was blocked—no admittance to anyone. He thought for a moment about entering through one of the hidden exits they usually used, but a sudden commotion held him fixed in the crowd. With a horrible fascination he watched as the security police emerged from the building.

They dragged a body out with them. It was Terry—unconscious, but apparently alive. Then two more police emerged with another body. He heard his breath catch in his throat as he struggled to breathe through the treacle that suffocated him. That hair, fine and black and beautiful. Those strong, loving arms dangling so lifelessly, twisted at an odd angle as if broken to bits, like his heart. Someone in the crowd shushed him—*Do you want them to take you, too?* He was oblivious. He knew she was not alive, but he stared at the body in a desperate attempt to see some sign of life. Anything.

He wrapped his arms around his chest, clutching his heart. His helpless sobs drew the attention of a bystander—*Do you know them?* He could not answer. How could he say anything to anyone ever again? He still insanely believed it was possible that he was mistaken. He watched, paralyzed by his dread, as they loaded their captives into a van. As they turned to put her in, he saw that the left half of her face was missing. And he saw, from the bloody remains, that it was indeed Allie. A sudden incoherent rage made him want to scream. Why did you fight? Why the hell didn't you let them take you alive! Damn you to hell!

The van drove off and the crowd dispersed. He stood alone on the pavement as workers hurried by, jostling him in their rush to their jobs. Any alert patrol should have noticed him and taken him in for questioning, but he remained undisturbed. The bizarre thought crept into his mind that he led a charmed life. In a daze, he walked away.

He needed to get as far away as possible. Some mindless survival instinct kept him safe as he wandered about. He stopped under a bridge—the same bridge that he had retreated to after his parents' arrest—and stared at the oily swirls of tidal water struggling to flow upstream. The damp air reeked of mysterious chemicals and untreated sewage. It seemed appropriate that he should be here, it seemed a fitting place to think about what had happened. If, as he suspected, they had been betrayed, the betrayal looked complete. He could not return home, nor could he use any of his current aliases, and there was no one to turn to. He assumed anyone he knew was arrested or dead or guilty of the betrayal. Not only were they suspect to him, but he would be suspect to them, and he would be suspect to any other member of the Underground; any other assumption on their part would be suicidally stupid. Given the circumstantial evidence against him, if they knew he was alive, they would almost certainly try to assassinate him. The realization left him stunned: he would be relentlessly hunted by both sides.

He was not sure why he cared to continue to live—stubbornness perhaps, or maybe a desire for revenge—but he began to make plans. There was a set of papers he had, against orders, saved. No one in the group had known about them, not even Allie, and any record of them had long ago been destroyed. They were the ones he had used years ago when he had first joined, long before any of his current comrades had met him. They were old and out-of-date, but they would give him a safe identity, one that had not been betrayed, until he could find better papers. He went to the place he had hidden them and removed them from their protective envelope. He paged through them, looked at the weathered photograph of his younger self, and read the name aloud: Peter Halifax.

It was the identity he had been given by the Underground group that had adopted him not long after his parents were arrested. He had lived scavenging and stealing for about a month, celebrating his thirteenth birthday on the run, when a fellow had simply walked up to him, put his hand on his shoulder and said, "Come with me." The cell had noticed him in the neighborhood, had watched him for a while, and had then decided to adopt him into their ranks. He was given a name, a place to live, and a purpose.

When he reached the age of sixteen, he was supposed to report for the draft, and for the next six years, his life was complicated by this fact. He was given a new identity that changed his name and background and reduced his age by two years. When he reached eighteen, he was given another identity that was excused from service for a year, then his name was changed again and his age was increased by three years so that his records could show that he had completed his service as specified by the law. After that, with each passing year his name was changed and his age reduced until, at the age of twenty-two, his papers and birth year agreed again.

It was a simple albeit disconcerting process that did not end. From then on, for reasons of security and to avoid leaving too long a trail if he were ever taken in, his name and history were changed with some regularity. He got used to it—got used to dropping one persona and adopting another each time he changed assignments or associates. Only the very first time had it bothered him. He was told that the name he had used for three years, a name that he associated with his rescue from the streets and his adoption into the Resistance, was to be discarded. He felt hurt and bothered by their cavalier attitude toward his identity, and he disobeyed orders and hid his papers, feigning their destruction.

And so they had sat, hidden high up in the loose bricks of the foundation of the bridge he had used for refuge and a home. There it was, a name he had not used since he was sixteen, a name that neither his parents nor his boyhood friends would know. A name that anyone who knew him currently would not recognize. Yet, he would have to believe that it was his name and think of himself with that name until . . . until he did not know when.

A desolate feeling of loneliness invaded him; he gasped with the realization of how devastating a loss he had suffered. He reeled with pain as a vision of Allie's destroyed face crossed his mind. Her hair had been damp with blood, the flesh hung in shreds. What the hell had happened?

With an effort, he opened his eyes against the pain. The murky waters of the Temms shifted and swirled into the hallway wallpaper. Stunned, he glanced up and down the hall, wondering how long he had stood there. He could still hear the rise and fall of voices as Elspeth and Karl continued talking in the sitting room. He remembered her order and decided to comply and then get something to eat.

After eating, he went up to clean the kitchen. It was a mess—everything had been left to accumulate, but he did not mind the work. His thoughts wandered back through time as his hands worked mechanically. He stared ahead without seeing; in his mind's eye he was walking the dark streets of east London, breathing his last taste of freedom. It had recently rained, had been raining for some time, and the air smelt of damp bricks. Keeping to back alleys, he made his way out of the old district and into Workers' District #9. It was harder to pass unnoticed here; there were no alleys, just large expanses of muddy open ground between the monstrous concrete housing blocks. A few weeds struggled to survive, but it was a losing battle on this poisoned ground. The air was damp and cold, and the mist glowed ominously under the bright orange lights. He shoved his hand into his pocket, closed his fingers around the day's takings: four hundred *Neue Reichsmark* and a gold watch. Not very good, but better than nothing. The money would pay off the desk clerk for another day. Maybe the watch would help toward the acquisition of good papers. Groceries, acquired at ludicrous black-market prices, would have to wait: he simply had to acquire those papers.

He passed out of the district, reached the slums of East Göbbels. At the bottom of a narrow, dirty alley, he climbed the steps of an anonymous, dilapidated building, a converted warehouse. He had taken a room here because it was the sort of place where, for a price, no questions were asked. The blackmail he had to pay cut into his earnings quite heavily, but he could not get a proper residence, not to mention a food ration card or a job, until he had a proper set of papers.

His thoughts were interrupted by Horst's dropping a pair of muddy army boots on the floor and grunting, "Before tomorrow morning." Horst stomped out, leaving him staring at the boots in confusion. It was unlike the boy to pass on a chance to harass him. He shook his head to clear his thoughts and went back to scouring the pans.

The patterns on the tiling behind the sink dissolved into the dusty shadows of the hallway of his rooming house. A single bulb hung from a cord, accentuating the darkness with its incongruent brightness. Behind one of the doors he heard a radio droning on about the latest Berlin rally. He felt disgusted with himself. Once again he had been obliged to rob his own people. The watch and more than half the money had belonged to a German who had carelessly wandered alone down an unpatrolled alley. Who would have thought that a German wearing a gold watch would only be carrying 250 marks! As the evening wore on without any success, he had become desperate and resorted to burglary. The German residential districts were too difficult to penetrate, and the rest of his night's earnings had come from three separate break-ins in WD8. It was pathetic how poor his fellow countrymen were.

He turned his key in the rusty lock and entered the room. Without turning on the light, he went to the loose floorboard he had prepared long before and secreted the watch with the other valuables that might one day purchase an identity for him. He hid his knife under the same board, but farther out of reach, deep in a crevice. Carefully replacing the board and the furniture, he then turned on the lights. After paying the desk clerk for her lack of interest and paying the night's rent, he had thirty marks left. Enough for a loaf of bread in a government store or about two slices on the open market. Damn! He surveyed his kitchen shelf, located just over his bed, and determined that he had enough for a good meal tonight if he did not worry about tomorrow. There was also half a bottle of gin, and he decided to drink that as well.

When he poured the last shot of gin into the glass, he was feeling well fed and comfortably numb. Tomorrow would be better. He would only rob Germans, and he would get enough to make a difference. He would find another resistance cell, teach them to trust him, get new papers, maybe even find another woman like Allison. . . . He surveyed the clear fluid, savored hope. Maybe he could rebuild his life, he had thought, even as he heard the heavy footsteps in the hallway.

Something told him to panic, but he did not. If they were for him, there was nothing to do but wait—there was no escape from his fourth-floor room. He had noticed and accepted that as an unavoidable risk when he had first taken the room. So he waited, hoping it would be for someone else.

There was a pounding on his door. He finished the last of the gin. The door splintered under an assault of heavy bodies. Three Gestapo burst into the room waving their guns. Strictly speaking, they weren't really from the *Geheime Staatspolizei;* they were, in fact, English. Just local police. Whatever their association, he knew what to do next. He put down his glass and stood to greet them by raising his hands above his head. The game was up: seventeen days and twenty-two hours without an identity, and the game was up.

They made him kneel with his hands clasped together on his head as they searched his room. He mused about who might have betrayed him. Probably someone in the building—maybe even the desk clerk. He felt too numbed by the gin and bereft by his losses to really resent the betrayal. The lure of easy money was hard to beat. Maybe he had been selected at random: it was a good bet that if he lived here, he was guilty of something, and now the guards tore the room apart to determine what that was.

They found only forty-seven marks in total and nothing else. They were rank amateurs: the loose floorboard should never have escaped their notice. Not believing his luck, he stood when ordered. Then they told him to produce his papers. He let his hands down and showed them his identity card. They wanted to know why it was not updated—where were his labor service stamps? He had no answer. They wanted to see his work documents. He shrugged and, knowing he would not be believed, said, "I lost them. Just today." Without even bothering to ask anything else, they threw him against a wall, bound his hands behind him, and led him away.

He spent the time in Green Park prison—it wasn't called that, but that's how everyone referred to it, due to its location—and listened daily to the sound of shots as various prisoners were executed on the grounds outside his cell. He whiled away the time trying to determine what his defense against the as-yet-unstated charges might be, but nothing brilliant suggested itself. Weeks later, when his case finally came to trial, it was determined that the person he claimed to be did indeed exist in the files and matched his description and fingerprints, but there was no record of him ever having fulfilled his national-service labor contract. In fact, it appeared that he had not held a job, accepted ration coupons, or registered his residence since he was sixteen. By a minor bureaucratic miracle his fingerprints were never cross-referenced. That the papers in his possession matched his face and prints was sufficient; nobody bothered to check to see that his prints were also those of a wanted man of a different name. Doubtless his file had crossed some heavily laden desk without even being opened.

It meant that in the end, with the painful lack of evidence, even a Reich court could manage to convict him of nothing more than draft-dodging and lack of proper registration. He was sentenced to fifteen years of labor to compensate for the six he had not done and another five for the insufficient documentation. He remembered looking down at the floor and swallowing in dismay. Twenty years: it was more than twice what he had expected.

"Peter!"

He looked up, shocked back to reality by Elspeth's voice. From the tone, he guessed she must have called more than once.

"Are you asleep?" she snapped. "Hurry up here, there's more to be done. Let me know when you're finished. It's almost time for supper. Hurry up!"

52

"I'M SORRY, the congressman is very busy," the polite young staffer said. "Appointments for his time must be made months in advance!"

"If I knew where I would be 'months in advance,' I would happily oblige the congressman," Alex replied with a forced little smile, "but the nature of my business prevents that. Nevertheless, the information I have is very important to the defense of this country, and I should think it would be the patriotic duty of the chair of the Foreign Relations Committee to make time to hear me."

"We have no proof that your information is important," the staffer replied.

"I'm offering proof!"

"You have no idea how many cranks—"

Alex drew himself up.

"—not to say, sir, that you are one, I'm just explaining that we have such an influx of people with very important information—"

"*Psia krew cholera,*" Alex muttered.

"Sir?"

"Nothing. Never mind. I'll go to the press. I think they'll not only be interested in our evidence, they'll wonder why the congressman wasn't."

"Sir. Please. I wouldn't advise that. If, as you said, this is a very sensitive issue, you could be violating our security laws—and that would land you in prison."

"So what I have to offer is not important enough for the committee to hear, but too important for the press? That in and of itself will make for an interesting headline."

"You'd be risking breaking the law!"

Alex leaned forward and pressed his face close to the staffer's. "Young man, I live in Gestapoland! You can't scare me with your puny threats! Get me a hearing with the committee or I will go to your press!"

The staffer raised his hands. "All right. Look, give me a couple of days to arrange something. It will be behind closed doors, you understand?"

"Fair enough. Two days," Alex harrumphed, and left.

Three days later Alex and Adam were ushered into a small conference room. Along one wall was a table with fourteen chairs, all facing the same way. Opposite the table was a smaller table with three chairs. Adam and Alex were seated at the small table.

"There's no one here," Alex commented to the young woman who had shown them in.

"Oh, the committee will be here soon," she soothed, and left quickly.

"Fuckers," Adam muttered. "They're letting us cool our heels a bit."

"This is ridiculous," Alex concurred, but short of walking out, he could think of nothing to do.

Adam began pacing the room, studying the portraits on the wall. "The setup looks like we're on trial, facing all those judges," Adam commented sourly.

"Oh, that's typical." Alex watched as his son-in-law paced the room, then said, "So what do you think about it?"

"About America? I've seen it before."

"No, about government. You could get elected, move your family to the NAU. Raise Joanna here."

"I'm not averse to it."

"You'd have to give up your, er"—Alex glanced around at the walls—"um, activities."

"I know. I wouldn't mind. I'd miss teaching, but as for the rest of it . . . Well, it's moot."

"Why?"

"Zosia would never agree to it."

"I should have brought her."

"Yes, if your goal was to convince us to leave field work, you should have brought her, not me. Besides, she would have done a better job charming the committee."

"I don't want you to charm them. I just want to give them a sense of authenticity. You were there, you saw it all. Personal testimony is best."

"It's expensive," Adam said. "The money could have been better spent on guns."

"Think of it as educational. There's no point fighting in a vacuum—all of us need experience dealing with the Free World, otherwise we'll lose track of what we're aiming for and how we're going to get there."

"It's still expensive."

"There's a cost to everything we do," Alex conceded.

Within a few minutes two committee members entered the room. Both apologized for being late, made appropriate excuses, then noting that their colleagues had not arrived, one departed, promising to return in a few minutes, and the other opened a file and pored over its contents.

A few more committee members arrived and seated themselves. Adam finally sat down again, tapping his fingers impatiently on the table. When a cameraman entered the room, Adam lowered his head onto a hand and muttered to Alex, "Get that out of here."

Alex was also perturbed and jumped up and, keeping his back to the camera, demanded, "That has to go!"

Two of the committee members looked up. "All proceedings must be recorded," one said in surprise.

Adam, still shielding his face behind his hand, sang quietly, "Get that out of here."

"It's only for the record," the other member explained helpfully.

"A public record!" Alex snapped. "Now get that thing out of here!"

As he made his demands, the chair of the committee walked in. "What's the problem?"

"We can't be filmed," Alex explained patiently. "Our lives depend on anonymity!"

"Anonymity? How can we take a statement from anonymous individuals? This is for the public record!"

Alex squeezed his eyes shut in exasperation. He breathed deeply, opened his eyes, and releasing his words carefully, explained, "You have proof of our credentials from our government in exile. If you peruse the file, you will see that, though you may use our names, it is necessary for us to maintain our security, and therefore we cannot be photographed or filmed."

"What about your voices?" a committee member asked.

Alex glanced at Adam. Adam nodded subtly. "All right," Alex answered for them both.

The camera was ordered into a corner, facing only the committee members, and as the rest of the committee had filed in and taken their places, the proceedings began.

"Great start," Adam muttered to Alex.

"Typical," Alex assured him. "Don't worry, once they hear what we have to say, they'll forget their procedures."

That, of course, was not true. Nevertheless, they managed to work their way through the meeting and inform the committee of their discovery of at least one chemical weapons factory on the outskirts of Berlin. Alex referred them to the maps that had been distributed, he pointed out the documents verifying the chemical analysis of the samples taken, he verified the translations of the smuggled security-service documents that they had acquired.

"Quite an impressive collection of material here," one member of the committee commented. "Almost too impressive."

"What? What do you mean?" Alex asked.

"We're not saying that you're lying, but—"

"Lying?" Adam leapt in. "I was there. I scraped this muck off the ground, risking my life, the life of my colleague, and even the life of a hapless worker! Countless people risked everything to get you this evidence and you say—"

"Calm down, young man, it's not that we don't believe you . . ."

Two hours later it had reached a complete equilibrium and everyone admitted that there was nothing more to be said. Ignoring Alex's weary protests that the "appropriate people" had already seen the evidence he was presenting, the committee assured Alex that his evidence would be forwarded for further study. The committee then reminded their witnesses of the sensitive nature of the material and that it had been classified as secret and warned them not to publicly release any of the information that they had presented. After that, the witnesses were politely dismissed from the room.

"We're doing this all wrong," Alex commented later in their hotel. He paced nervously, smoking a cigarette, as Adam sat on the edge of the bed pulling apart and inspecting a pistol.

"I wonder if this thing is any good," Adam muttered. He ejected the clip and then slammed it back into place.

"I don't know what the right way is, but we're obviously doing something wrong," Alex continued, oblivious to what Adam was doing. "We break our backs getting them valuable information which they could use to justify any action, and they just sit on it."

"Maybe we've got it backward," Adam suggested. He finished inspecting the gun and aimed it questioningly at a vase of flowers. "There, time to test it."

"What do you mean?"

"I'm going out and see if I can't find somewhere to fire this thing."

"No, I mean, what do you mean about backwards?"

"Oh, that. I meant, maybe we should get the American public riled and then the politicians will take action."

"Rile the public?" Alex asked. "How can we? They'd stomp on us in a minute—didn't you hear them? It's all classified. We'd be under arrest the moment we opened our mouths. And given the publicity we'd get, neither of us could ever go home after that—it'd be a virtual death sentence."

"I didn't mean with this information." Adam tucked the gun into a holster. "We need something safer. Completely unclassified. No weapons, no secrets. Something that touches the human spirit. A poster child."

"Oh, they've heard all that. Nothing affects them! If you don't believe me, I'll show you the congressional records from '42 or '43 when word got out about the 'final solution.' If it's not an American . . . I mean, what's going on now is nothing compared to the slaughter of the forties and fifties. And they weren't interested then. Doubted our sources, claimed their hands were tied, blah, blah, blah."

"I think they were overwhelmed by the numbers, and by the gruesomeness of it all. No, what I have in mind is something different."

"What in God's name do you think would work?" Alex asked forlornly.

"Did you notice something odd when I talked to the committee about gathering the evidence—I saw the same thing when we gave a summary to our American friends about what I was doing here."

"What?"

"They asked about that man."

"Which man?"

"The one who was working in the factory. Next time we discuss it with a group of any sort, look at the faces. At least half of them look concerned and interested only then, only when I mention how one person was treated. We would have done better bringing *him* here."

"No." Alex shook his head. "As soon as he opened his mouth and spoke only German, or some other language they don't understand, they'd lose interest."

Adam shrugged. "Eh, I suppose you're right. If he's still alive, I doubt he has much to say in any language." Adam stood and pulled his jacket on. "I guess it doesn't show," he said, inspecting himself in the mirror. "I'll take a subway out toward a park, then see if I can't find somewhere sort of private. Could you loan me a pack?"

"Cigarettes? I thought you had a pack of your own!" Alex exclaimed.

"I did. Now, are you going to loan me a pack?"

Alex handed him a pack and watched as Adam removed one and tucked the rest into his pocket. He frowned as it finally dawned on him what Adam had just said. "You're going to fire a gun in the city?"

Adam grinned at him.

"Where the hell did you get it? Did you smuggle it through customs?" Alex asked in alarm.

"No, don't be stupid. Why would I want to smuggle guns *into* America? No, this one's a free sample from that arms dealer I talked to last night. I just want to find somewhere I can test it."

"How are their prices?" Alex asked.

"Too high if they're giving out samples," Adam replied, lighting his cigarette.

"But that doesn't stop me from accepting their little gifts. I want to try it out and see if it's any good. If I like it, I'll see if I can't get some at a better price from someone else. I've got a couple meetings down by the fish market tonight, so don't wait up!"

"Be careful."

"Me? I'm always careful!" Adam laughed as he opened the door. He gestured a dramatic farewell as he strode down the hall, holding his cigarette in hand, the outline of his holster just barely visible under his jacket.

"Hope he doesn't shoot anyone," Alex muttered in prayer, and shook his head with bemused affection at the retreating image of his son-in-law.

53

"*T*HE FACE AGAIN?" Roman asked plaintively, hoping just this once to evoke a response.

Peter looked up from the pavement and stared at Roman with leaden eyes, then quite deliberately he turned his gaze away and looked across the plaza.

"Everyone misses you. Are you going to come back soon?"

Without taking his eyes off the plaza, Peter shook his head ever so slightly.

"Look, the boys took up a collection. They sent you this," Roman whispered as he reached under the counter and extracted a hip flask. He discreetly shoved it across the counter toward Peter. "We need the flask back, but we thought the contents might help."

Peter looked at the flask, but did not move to take it.

"Take it, already!" Roman hissed. He glanced worriedly behind him. "Quick."

Still Peter did not move, he just returned to gazing across the plaza.

A patrolman paced not far behind Peter, and Roman leaned forward, awkwardly draping his arm over the flask. "Are you nuts?" he asked angrily. "You'll get us in trouble. Come on!"

"I'm not giving him any excuses," Peter explained, still refusing the gift.

"He doesn't seem to need any," Roman commented as he deftly secreted the flask back under the counter. "What was it this time?"

"None of your business."

"Man! He's been going at you nearly every day for months! You've got to do something. If this keeps up, he's going to kill you!" Roman warned.

"Leave me alone."

"What are you going to do?"

Peter turned his gaze back to his friend. "Are you saying it's my fault?"

"No! That's not what I mean."

"Then what are you suggesting? I should file a complaint?" Peter asked bitterly.

Roman scanned the plaza and glanced behind himself as if nervously preparing to impart a secret, then quietly suggested, "Maybe you should leave."

"Looking like this? How far do you think I'd get?"

Roman bit his lower lip worriedly.

"And where should I go?" Peter added angrily. "Do you want to hide me in the bakery? Under a table? Shove a roll in my direction every other day? Huh?"

Roman shook his head.

"In all your years, have you ever heard even one whisper of a place I could go?"

Roman hesitated, then admitted, "No. Never."

"Then you're advocating suicide."

"I didn't mean it that way," Roman whispered helplessly.

"If you don't have anything useful to say, then don't say anything. Give me that much peace."

"Peter!"

"Look, I'm not ready to die. Do you understand that? I've survived worse than this, I'm not going to throw it all away now! I'm not going to risk anything. I know him; he'll grow bored. Until then, I'm going to lie low and wait him out, and sooner or later it will just stop."

"Yes, of course," Roman agreed helplessly. "It will just stop. Maybe even today."

Maybe today, Peter thought as he stopped momentarily to snatch a breath of the bitter, damp air.

"What are you doing? Work!" Karl snapped angrily.

Peter thrust the spade back into the cold sod and turned up another shovelful. Maybe today, he thought over the pounding of his heart, maybe today Karl would finally be sated. Maybe this interminable revenge would finally cease.

"Deeper, put some effort into it!" Karl ordered. "I want this dirt soft, I want it to produce!"

Or maybe tomorrow, Peter amended. He wiped a bit of sweat from his brow and plunged the edge of the spade back into the hard earth. It clanged against rock, sending jarring vibrations up his arms. Not today, tomorrow. It would end tomorrow.

"Is there a rock?" Karl asked, peering down. "Get it out, get it out now! I don't want rocks in my garden!"

"Yes, *mein Herr*," Peter agreed tiredly. He pulled the shovel out and wedged it in at a different angle, trying to find the edge of the rock so he could work it out. Tomorrow? Whenever. He no longer cared.

"What are you doing? What are you doing?" Karl stepped in closer. "Don't do that, use some muscle!"

He could not work out what Karl wanted, but that was not unusual. He acknowledged the order and tried ramming the shovel in at a different angle, twisting it to loosen the rock.

"Work, damn it!" Karl yelled, raising his fist threateningly.

Peter threw his weight onto the handle. Abruptly a piece of the rock chipped off and the shovel flew up, smacking Karl in the shin.

"Oooowww!" Karl howled.

For the briefest moment, Peter felt there was some justice in the universe. "I'm sorry, *mein Herr*. It was an accident." His lips trembled with the urge to laugh as he watched Karl hopping around.

Karl reached down to rub his shin, then straightened. He was livid.

"It was an accident, *mein Herr*. I swear, it was!" Peter repeated, suddenly aware of the danger he was in. "I'm sorry. I'm really sorry. Are you all right? Can I get something for you?"

Karl approached, his face purple with rage. Peter continued to apologize profusely even as Karl snatched the shovel from him. He expected Karl to throw the shovel down and out of the way, and he braced himself for the retribution that would follow.

"Goddamned swine! You did that deliberately," Karl howled, swinging the shovel, not to the ground, but at Peter's legs. "I'll teach you to hit me!"

Only a lightning-fast instinct saved Peter as he leapt backward, out of the way. He tripped, fell, rolled, and scrambled to his feet as Karl swung again. The shovel caught the side of his legs. He fell back to the ground and rolled, all the while trying to apologize over Karl's incoherent shouting. The shovel thumped brutally against the dirt next to him. He tried again to regain his feet; the shovel slammed into the back of his thighs; he fell and rolled again as it came down where his knees had just been. Karl anticipated his next maneuver and smashed the shovel against his right shin. He clawed at the dirt to try to pull himself to his feet. He struggled forward as again the shovel was pounded against his legs. Trapped on the ground, he heard his own cries of pain, his own pleas for mercy, as though they were someone else's.

"Hello there! What's up?" Karl's neighbor called out, distracting him from his hysteria.

Peter rocked back and forth on the ground, holding his legs, moaning in anguish. His legs! Oh, God, his legs! Had even a minute passed?

Still holding the shovel, Karl meandered over to the fence to chat. "The bastard hit me with this!" he explained as he gasped for breath.

"Oh, terrible, terrible. But I'm sure it was an accident," the neighbor soothed.

"That's what they always say."

"Yes, I'm sure they do. In any case, I'm sure it won't happen again."

"Not now it won't!" Karl chuckled, looking at Peter as he lay on the ground. "Get up, you bastard!"

Peter ignored him. His legs! Crippled! Oh, God, senselessly maimed because of a stupid piece of rock!

"I said, get up!" Karl growled.

Peter tried to move, but he was paralyzed by the fear of what he might discover, terrified of a broken bone.

Karl left the fence to come and stand over him. "Lousy, inferior, worthless dog! You're all alike! Now you see what happens when you get ideas. Get up and get back to work, you swine, before I kick some sense into your worthless hide."

Peter struggled to his hands and knees. He paused to find his breath, then forced himself into a crouch with most of his weight thrown onto his left arm. One leg gave way under the strain, and he slid back to the ground. He tried again; his whole body trembled with the effort of pulling himself up. His right arm reached uselessly for a support—Karl was near enough to grab it but stood aloof, watching Peter struggle with a detached curiosity.

Finally he found enough balance and strength to pull his weight off his left arm and stand erect, knees bent with pain, hands hovering uselessly. Karl pushed the shovel into Peter's hands with the clear implication that he should return to work. He used it to steady himself. Pain sliced through him as he straightened to his full height. Like a newborn fawn he stood gasping at his accomplishment on wobbly legs—battered from every angle though they were, they still functioned. He looked down at them: there were no splinters of bone protruding, no unnatural bends. Silently rejoicing at his luck, ignoring the agony he felt, unable to thank the brave neighbor who had saved him, he stumbled back to his work.

Over the weeks that followed, lurid bruises—red, black, purple—discolored his legs; huge, painful lumps as hard as rocks formed beneath the skin. The swollen surface burst here and there to release pus and old blood and ichor. He wrapped his legs and washed them and wrapped them again, praying to no one in particular that they might be whole again.

Elspeth observed him with growing concern during this time, and as she stood by the window watching him wash the car, she came to a decision. She chewed her thumb as she considered her strategy, then glancing back at her husband as he read the Party newspaper, she said suddenly, "How are things at work, dear?"

It took three repetitions, but finally Karl growled, "Ach, all right," from behind the paper.

"This is the third time in two weeks you've come home early."

"Not much has been happening in my section," Karl explained brusquely. He continued to read for a moment, then decided to add, "What makes you ask?"

Elspeth's long silence drew him to his feet. He came to stand by the window next to her. "Have you heard something? Is your mother spreading gossip? Or your brother-in-law?"

Elspeth turned her attention away from the window and smiled with disarming reassurance at her husband. "No, no! Nothing like that. You just seem so tense lately, I thought perhaps something was wrong."

"I haven't been tense! Have you heard something?" Karl asked worriedly. "What makes you say I'm tense?"

Elspeth threw a glance out the window. "You have been rather rough on him of late."

"Him? That's . . . You know what that's about."

"But that was ages ago, darling. Surely it's time to be over that."

"No." Karl shook his head. "No, he'll never learn, he'll never be trustworthy. We just have to keep him on a leash and tug on it now and then to remind him who's boss."

"Yes, of course. But you do realize, it looks bad—I mean, just the other day, when he worked up at the Reichstag Annex, he looked like he was dragged there out of a camp!"

"Pff."

"It does influence people, they think we're out of control. Just look at him." Elspeth turned her attention back to Peter, and Karl followed her gaze. "He really is a good boy. He tries hard to do his job right." They both watched as Peter, on one knee in the driveway, carefully polished the chrome of Karl's car. He hunched over his work, oblivious to anything beyond his task. "He has learned, you know," Elspeth added quietly. "Has he shown even the slightest disrespect recently?"

"Naw! He cringes anytime I even get near!" Karl laughed. "He knows that half the time he's going to get whacked for something!"

"That's my point, dear. He knows his place now, he won't forget it."

"Yes he will. He's stupid."

"But it is his natural place, isn't it?"

"Natural?"

"Yes, isn't that right?" Elspeth turned her eyes back to her husband and surveyed him admiringly. "He's not like us, is he? Not like you. You're strong-willed, forceful, naturally superior. A true Aryan."

Karl nodded his agreement.

"You could never be held down for long, but one such as he, well, his arrogance was forced, unnatural. Now that you've shown him your superiority, he knows and understands his place. He won't want to leave it again because it feels right. Serving you comes naturally to him." Elspeth gestured dramatically out the window. "Just look at the care he lavishes on your possessions! He wants to please you."

"Hmm. Maybe. Still, it doesn't hurt to keep reminding him . . ."

"But it does! Others will wonder why you fret so over such a nothing! They might wonder if you have something to fear!"

Karl looked hard into his wife's eyes. "And do I?" he asked coldly.

"Of course not!" Elspeth breathed. She ran a finger down Karl's broad chest. "Who even glances at cart horses when they have a thoroughbred in the stable?"

"You did."

"My thoroughbred kept leaving his stable!" Elspeth answered, somewhat exasperated. "Besides, all that is long in the past." She managed to focus a loving gaze back on her husband. "Let him go, darling. If you don't, we'll lose another one, and we can't afford that. It was nothing but a conversation with Ulrike. That's all."

"I don't know." Karl rubbed his chin, still watching Peter intensely. "He still worries me."

"He shouldn't. You're the *Übermensch*, he's nothing. You've got to let up—it looks bad if you don't. Besides, he's so beaten up, he's nearly useless! You see the way he is—nearly crippled! We need a healthy, alert worker; there's a lot to do here. Ease up on him. *Please!*"

Karl nodded as he continued to stare at his chattel. "All right. I have better things to do anyway."

Elspeth smiled winningly and wondered how grateful Peter would be to her for her merciful intervention.

The answer was not at all. He did not even notice. Over time, his response to their abuse had become so dulled that, though he knew he should feel outraged, insulted, or something, he had only felt depressed. The sensation had been there for a long time, that much he recognized. The paralysis of emotion had freed itself from the constraints he had unconsciously placed on it and began to take him over. It had started behind his eyes—they had felt tired and weak and unable to focus—then it had spread through his mind like a shadow, and he had had no desire to stop it. It was not a black mood—no, that would imply too much involvement—rather it was the covering blankness of night across his perception, a gray mist enveloping his thoughts. He detached himself from his surroundings, from whatever happened to him, and withdrew behind the shield of unknowing. The leaden cloak of depression settled upon him, and he hunched under its weight, tired and resigned, unwilling to throw off its embrace.

Drugged by his despair, he did little more than carry out his work as best he could and hope his legs would heal completely. He moved through the days of his life cocooned in numbness, carrying out all his duties blindly, wanting nothing more than to be left alone. He did not realize he was fulfilling Karl's ideal, did not know that he was fitting into his natural place in the order of things. If he had known, he would not have cared. It was too much. Somewhere, somehow, it had just grown to be too much.

He walked with his head habitually bowed, the path defined only by the broken slabs of asphalt that lined the road. He kept his eyes downcast, and when he noticed anyone approaching, he stood aside, as obliged, in the wet gutters, letting the spray from the passing cars soak him. He did not look into the face of the uniform that demanded his papers, did not react when smacked jovially on the forehead with his documents as they were handed back to him; he just tucked them away and continued his painful, mechanical pace toward the bakery.

It had rained for the past several days, and now, with the sun and the warmth, the world sprang into life. Shoots of vibrant green grass beckoned from the edge of the park, the leaves of the trees rustled softly in the gentle breeze. He noticed none of it. He did not look up, did not care to notice the emergence of new life around him; nor did he notice the woman sitting on a bench that was located only a few meters away at the entrance to a pedestrian path. As he drew near, she left the bench to approach him. She seemed to be deliberately blocking his path, but he was beyond provocation and blindly stepped out of the way into the gutter to make his way past. She said his name, but he did not hear her.

Only when she nearly shouted "Peter!" did he stop short, turning around to face her.

"Peter. Don't you recognize me?" A car sped by dangerously close to him; she flinched but he seemed utterly oblivious to the danger.

"Frau Reusch." He wanted to say more, but was at a loss for words.

"I need to talk to you." She motioned for him to follow as she went back to the bench and sat down.

At one time, he might have shown his contempt by walking away from her, but now he was so numb that he mindlessly did as he was told and went to stand uneasily by her.

"Sit down, so we can talk," she suggested.

"It is not permitted," he replied.

"Oh, you're with me. It'll be okay," she said.

"It is not permitted," he repeated.

"You didn't used to be like this," she commented, quite confused. After an awkward moment, she added, "You look awful! What's happened to you?"

That penetrated his emotional paralysis—he felt oddly affronted by her question. Now was a hell of a time to feign concern! "Oh, it's not as bad as it looks," he finally managed to answer. "I get by."

"Look, I need to explain what happened," she said plaintively.

He was not sure he could stand to hear an explanation just right now, so he asked, "How did you get here?"

"I have a sister in Berlin, I'm visiting her. I knew Herr Vogel was from Berlin, so while here, I had a friend look up his address in the registry. Then I waited each day in that little park near the house until I saw you. I kept waiting to talk to you when you left the house, but you rarely left and were never alone. Finally, I ascertained your routine and realized that the only time I could see you alone was at this god-awful hour, so I've been waiting for you here."

He nodded absently, distracted by a patrolman who was approaching them.

"*Gnädige Frau,* is this man disturbing you?"

"No, no, we were just conversing."

"Your papers?" The patrolman studied their documents, then looked at Frau Reusch. "He does not belong to you."

"No, as I said, we were just conversing."

"That is not recommended, *gnädige Frau.*"

"Nonsense!" Frau Reusch insisted. "I have . . ."

"Frau Reusch is a friend of Frau Vogel's," Peter quickly interjected. "She was just inquiring as to Frau Vogel's health."

"I see. My apologies, *gnädige Frau.*" The patrolman returned their papers and then leaning toward Peter said softly, "Your insubordination won't be forgotten."

They waited silently, watching him stride away. When he was safely out of earshot, Frau Reusch snorted, "What a man! I have every right to talk to whomever I want!"

"Perhaps. But I have no right to talk to you."

"What did he say to you then?"

He told her.

"What 'insubordination'? You just answered his question."

He shrugged. "I guess he didn't like that I answered a comment directed to you."

"But what did he mean?"

"It means his pride has been hurt, and sooner or later, he'll let me make it up to him."

"How?" Frau Reusch asked, perplexed.

In spite of himself, he smiled. She seemed so incredibly naive. "He and his friends will probably drag me into an alley and beat the shit out of me."

"You're not serious! They can't do that!"

"Oh, they can and they do."

"I won't let them."

"And how long are you going to sit here?" he asked cuttingly.

She thought a moment. "Well, don't you have any recourse?"

"To whom?"

"I don't know. Herr Vogel, perhaps."

"No, he'd probably approve. At least as long as they didn't do any permanent harm." He added under his breath, "He saves that privilege for himself."

"How can you be so calm about it all?"

"I'm not! It makes my gut ache. But what can I do?" And his gut did ache—a visceral pain that warned him that he was losing his protective numbness.

"Oh, Peter, we had no idea. Certainly there must be some way to protect your rights."

"Rights? *Rights?* I have none! It's there, in black and white! No rights! None!" He brought his tone under control. "Didn't you know that?"

"No, I mean yes, it's just that . . ."

"It's just that you never bothered to find out what it all meant. Just like before." He stared at the tree behind her so he didn't have to see the hurt look on her face. "Do I need to quote you the law? Read it someday, find out what's done in your name."

She opened her mouth to say something, but decided better. He stared remorselessly at the tree; the pale green leaves of spring spread in a fine lace against the blue sky. He was beginning to regret his outburst. He felt uncomfortable with the emotions that were threatening to return.

"Peter," she begged, "I want to tell you what happened."

"You sold a slave. No crime in that," he murmured.

"We had no choice." She rushed on before he could interrupt, "Do you remember a stranger coming into the shop after hours a few weeks before . . . before you left? That was Herr Vogel."

He nodded, he remembered it well. It was a Saturday afternoon, well after shop closing, but the store had been busy and Herr Reusch had decided to stay open. Peter was at the cash register waiting for the last customer, a fragile old woman, to disentangle her money and sort out her change. He saw the stranger approaching the shop, but since Peter was in the middle of a transaction, there was little he could do. The man picked up several items, almost randomly it seemed, and approached the register. Peter was at a loss as to what to do. He knew that he should not sell anything to somebody who was not a regular, trusted customer, but the stranger had clearly observed the previous transaction.

As the old lady walked off, the man placed the items on the counter and looked expectant.

Peter hesitated, then said, "I'm sorry, the shop is closed, it's well past two."

"But you just sold that lady some groceries."

"That was a transaction begun earlier, before closing."

"Before closing? It's twenty till three!"

Peter shrugged. "Would you like to talk to the manager?"

"No, I want to talk to you. Why are you handling money? Why are you alone with this cash?"

"I don't know, *mein Herr,* perhaps you'd like to talk to the manager."

"Well, I only stopped in to get directions. How do I get to the Central Hotel, by the train station, from here?"

"I believe the bus out front goes to the center of town."

"I'm in a car, you idiot!"

"My apologies, *mein Herr,* I don't know. I don't leave the estate."

"No, I don't suppose you do. Let me see your papers."

"I'll get them for you," Peter had replied, feeling an overwhelming sense of foreboding.

"You don't have them on you?"

"They're just in the back room. I'll be back in a moment."

He returned with his papers and handed them over. The stranger studied them for a long time, then said, "Will you sell me these items now?"

"I'm sorry, you'll have to ask the manager."

"Then fetch him for me."

After a few minutes, Peter located Herr Reusch. He happily instructed the stranger on the best route into the center of town and then told Peter to sell him the items he had selected. Once the stranger had left, Herr Reusch turned to Peter and said, "What an odd man! And what a fuss over nothing! Why didn't you just sell him the things in the first place?"

"I guess I should have. My apologies."

"Well, let's close up, at last."

The occurrence had stuck in Peter's mind, and he had not failed to recognize Herr Vogel when he returned several weeks later. Yes, he remembered.

Frau Reusch continued, "He knew that we were violating the law. He had proof. And, of course, if interrogated, our customers would corroborate. It would be easy for him to make trouble: he's very high up, you know. Lots of power. Well, he came back and told Ernst he would turn him in if we didn't sell your contract to him. The fines would have done us in! And Ernst might even have had to do prison time. You know, that would have killed him."

"Yes, I'm sure it would have been very difficult."

"And he said we would lose you in any case. He said you would be taken away and could end up anywhere. He told us that you would be considered guilty as well for having worked after hours. It didn't make sense to us—you were just doing as we asked, but he insisted that that was the case and that you would be punished. When he realized that we cared about what would happen to you, he told us all the horrible things that were possible. Then he promised that if we sold him your contract, you would live with them. That you would be safe."

"So why didn't you tell me what was going on? Why did you leave me in ignorance?" Peter demanded. "I felt so betrayed," he added unwillingly.

"We were afraid. After what happened to our son, we couldn't bear to think what you might do. We thought you might try to escape and then you would be caught and tortured or killed. We didn't think you'd understand. We thought it'd be best for you not to know."

"So you made my decision for me."

"Yes."

A heavy silence hung between them. Finally Peter said, "I really must go, I'm already terribly late." He turned to leave.

"Peter."

"What?"

"It took me longer to find you than I expected. I'm leaving today."

He nodded, his back toward her.

"Peter."

He turned and looked at her. She looked so forlorn.

"Will you forgive me?"

His lips trembled. As much as he wanted to, he could not say yes. Instead, he said, "You never told me your name."

"Magda," she responded, surprised.

"Magda," he repeated. "Good-bye, Magda." He started to walk away, then decided to add, "Thank you for telling me all this. It means a lot to me."

He held on to her kind words and the sense of humanity she left with him as he returned to his routine and his life, and even though he struggled to maintain his distance, there were now cracks in his cocoon; the numbness was wearing thin.

======================= **54** =======================

"*L*OOK, DAD! A BUTTERFLY!" Joanna exclaimed excitedly.

The fragile creature fluttered over the stream, wove its way up into the air, and then brought itself down to settle on Joanna's shoulder.

"Hold still," Adam advised. He looked admiringly at the peaceful image of his daughter, bathed in dappled sunlight, the butterfly delicately balanced on her shirt, her little legs hanging over the edge of the rock, swinging back and forth as she tried to contain her excitement and not move her upper body.

Joanna carefully turned her head to look at the creature. "It's beautiful!" she whispered. The butterfly fluttered its wings as if in farewell and flew away.

Adam put his arm around his daughter and held her close. "You're beautiful," he whispered into her silky, golden curls.

"Dad?" Joanna turned her face up to her father with that I'm-going-to-ask-something-important look.

"Yes, sweetheart?"

"Will you and Mommy have another baby? Please? I want a sister!"

"How about a brother?"

"That'd be okay, too!" Joanna exclaimed.

"You do realize that whatever we have, it will be a baby and won't be able to play with you for months, or even years?" Adam warned.

"That's okay. I'd help out with the baby. I really would," Joanna promised.

Adam smiled at his daughter. "Okay," he said, to Joanna's obvious surprise. "Let's go see if we can't convince your mother."

"Aunt Zosia! Congratulations! I've just heard the news!" Stefi enthused as she hugged her aunt in greeting.

"So, you're here." Zosia smiled in response.

"Yes, am I ever glad to take a break from those lunatics! Arghhh. You wouldn't believe . . . Well, I won't go on about it all right now. After all, this is your party, not mine!"

"Yes, Adam insisted on a party to announce the pregnancy. I've never heard of such a thing."

"You know these people—any excuse will do. How far along are you?"

"Nearly two months," Zosia answered. "Maybe it's still a bit early to celebrate."

"Nonsense! Anyway, I'm glad to hear you're knocked up. Still, you have a ways to go to catch up with my mother!"

"Ah, nobody can keep up with her!" Zosia laughed. "At least not any woman who has better things to do with her life than be a brood mare."

"Tch, tch, tch," Stefi chided. "You know she's just doing her duty."

"Is that what it's called?" Katerina interjected as she came into the room.

"Ach, Mother Goose herself," Stefi commented.

"No respect," Katerina muttered, shaking her head. "This lack of respect is intolerable." It was unclear whether she was joking or not.

Zosia hugged her, trying to dispel her bad mood. "Aren't you happy for me and Adam, Auntie Katje?" she cooed.

"No! Adam, yes. He'll continue his work just like before, but for you, no," Katerina growled. "Let others have children, you have too much to do here."

Zosia released Katerina from her hold and waved her hand dismissively. "Ah, the work will get done. And Joanna is such a wonder, we felt it was time to repeat the experiment."

"Yes, Joanna is a darling," Katerina admitted somewhat less sourly, her eyes straying to the corner of the room where Joanna was playing with several other children. "But, Zosia, don't throw your life away. Promise me this will be your last!"

Zosia shook her head. "No, I won't do that. I want children. I want someone to carry on for me."

"It's ideas that are carried on," Katerina argued. "Fight for our ideals. Let that be your legacy."

"Ideals are no good without people to hold them," Adam commented as he joined the little group. He handed out glasses and began pouring shots of vodka in each. "Here's to our future!"

"Your future is with your cause," Katerina objected.

"Ah, you're just pissed off because all your people are dead. Don't wish that on us," Adam retorted.

"Adam!" Zosia breathed.

"Colonel Firlej," Katerina responded, clearly rattled, "maybe one day you will learn the value of . . . Zosia, what is it?"

Zosia was leaning forward slightly, holding her arm across her abdomen, a look of dismay on her face. "No," she murmured, shaking her head as if she had been asked a question. "No."

"Zosia?" Adam and Stefi both asked in alarm.

Zosia turned and fled the room. Adam and Stefi followed her out. Katerina remained behind, staring after them in sorrow. She recognized exactly what had happened, and her heart went out to Zosia even as her thoughts retreated back in time to a young girl whom she no longer recognized as herself. Then it had been malnutrition that had caused her to lose her baby; today, in their ivory bunker, isolated from the misery outside, it was probably nothing more than bad luck.

=================== 55 ===================

"**Y**OU WILL NOT SEE that tramp again!" Elspeth screeched.

"Just try and stop me," Horst yelled in response. He was dressed to impress a girl. That meant that, despite the June warmth, he was clad in his usual tight black leather pants, high black leather boots with decorative metallic clasps along the side, and a matching leather jacket. The jacket had a bit of leather fringe at the shoulders, and this made it not only magnificently stylish, but also one of the pieces of Horst's clothing that Karl loathed the most. He opined frequently that in his day only queers would wear something like that, and they inevitably met with an unhappy and well-deserved fate. Perhaps that explained why, even on a warm night, Horst wore the jacket.

"While you live in my house, you will obey my rules!"

"I'll live at the academy, then." Horst headed toward the door, but Elspeth blocked his way.

"She's unsuitable!"

"She's pure Aryan. They have the documents."

"Those mean nothing! She's a round-faced peasant. She should be out there tilling the soil," Elspeth spat.

"We are all the Führer's children," Horst stated calmly. "And working the land is a noble calling."

Elspeth snorted. "I'm going to get your father to talk to you." She turned to Peter. "Make sure he stays here."

Peter watched numbly as Elspeth disappeared into Karl's study. Horst smirked at Peter, turned on his heel, and left the house.

Elspeth was furious with Peter when they returned to find Horst already gone, but Karl shrugged and said, "What did you expect?" Then, turning to Peter, he said, "Whatever he said, I know he'll be back. Make sure you're up to let him in and see to his needs."

The two of them retired long before Horst returned. Peter sat up and waited. His old habit had been to sit on the floor in the hallway and sleep with his head cradled in his arms, but now he found he could not fall asleep, so he passed the time staring sullenly at the wall opposite, looking for secrets in the pattern of faint bloodstains that were just barely visible.

Horst returned in the predawn hours, drunk as usual. When Peter greeted him, he did not come in, but stood framed in the doorway, grasping the door-jamb with his right hand for support, a nearly full bottle of *Korn* in his left. The orange streetlights cast a surreal glow on the night mist, forming an unearthly halo behind his blond hair. He swayed slightly, then drawled, "You. Again."

Peter stepped back to try to encourage him to enter.

"You. You, you, you . . . ," Horst sang. He screwed up his face in an effort to focus his vision. "Only you ever stay up to greet me. Why's that?"

Peter saw no point in answering.

Horst continued with slurred emphasis, "Do you think it's because no one else cares? Do you? Or do you think it's because they have better things to do? Huh?" His voice suddenly hardened. "Answer me! You"—he paused trying to settle on an appropriate epithet—"subhuman," he concluded rather lamely.

"I don't know."

"I don't know, *mein Herr!*" Horst pronounced with exaggerated precision.

"I don't know, *mein Herr.*"

"Of course you don't. You don't know anything. You're too stupid to live! You're, uh . . . oh, hell, well, at least you're here when, uh . . ." Horst stumbled over his thoughts, hiccuped loudly. Suddenly an idea crystallized and he asked with surprising clarity, "Why do you bother to stay alive?"

Peter had yet to answer that question for himself and had given up trying. Inertia. Perhaps that was the most honest answer. "The alternative is illegal," he finally answered, in jest.

Horst furrowed his brow and stared at him, trying to determine what that meant.

"Destruction of State property," Peter explained. "I'd get the death penalty for suicide."

Horst burped noisily. "Oh, yeah. I guess you would," he said, apparently serious. With that question logically settled, he stumbled inside.

Peter shut the door and started to walk away.

"Come back here, you shit! I'm talking to you." Horst sounded desperately intense. He leaned against the wall, decided that he was more comfortable on the floor, so he slid down into a sitting position. "Come here. I take it back. Come sit down here. You're my friend. Honest. It doesn't matter that you're not an *Untermensch*—I mean, *are* an *Untermensch*, I don't care. Come on, boy." He whistled and motioned as though he were calling a dog. "Come on, sit!"

Peter chose the path of least resistance and sat down by Horst on the floor in the darkness of the hallway. He stared ahead, readjusting his sight to the dim shadows as Horst took another gulp from the bottle. There was a long silence and he wondered if Horst had fallen asleep.

"She left me." The bald statement emanating from the gray silhouette surprised Peter. He turned to look at Horst. "She left me, because she knew they didn't like her. Thought she wasn't good enough. Said she didn't want all the trouble it would involve." Suddenly, Horst turned toward Peter, grabbed him, pulled him close. "She didn't care what I thought! The bitch!" Horst's breath reeked of drink. "I'll be an officer soon. My own man, but she couldn't wait. Shit,

I hate them all." He released his grip, threw his head back, hit the wall. "Ow! Shit."

Peter was hardly listening; he was weary and wanted to leave. There were a few moments of silence; he hoped that Horst had finally collapsed. Suddenly Horst said quite loudly, "How can anyone exist like this? Day in and day out, like a robot. I mean like you, not like me. Like you. Not me, not me."

"Is there an alternative I've overlooked?"

Horst ignored him. "Do you even know what it's like to be drunk? Go on," he goaded, "have a drink—act like a real man!"

Without knowing exactly why, Peter reached over and gently removed the bottle from Horst's grasp. It was a lot of whiskey for someone as debilitated as he, but that did not matter. He raised the bottle to his lips and slowly, deliberately, drank it down.

Horst only slowly grasped what he was doing. When he saw the empty bottle, his mouth dropped open in astonishment and he stammered, "You—you bastard! You drank it all! You drank all my *Schnaps!*"

Already Peter could feel the effects of the alcohol. He stood up, gripped Horst's jacket and dragged him to his feet. "Come on, boy, it's time you were in bed."

Horst's mouth worked up and down, but no sound emerged. Finally he managed to blurt, "How dare you!" but by then he was already being steered toward his bedroom.

After Peter had seen Horst into his room and taken care of the rudiments of undressing him, he climbed up to the attic and collapsed on his bed of rags. The drink made him feel warm and comfortable; thoughts that had eluded him emerged with stunning clarity. His mind was ablaze with emotions and memories and plans. They all jumbled together, competing for attention. It was as if a shade had been lifted and bright sunlight streamed into the gloom of his mind dazzling him with a sudden ability to perceive. It was, he realized, the first time he had felt alive in months.

As the room revolved with ideas around him, he fell into a deep, peaceful sleep. And overslept. He awoke with a start. Elspeth was leaning over him; he had a suspicion she had just kicked him. "What are you doing here? You should be out, it's late!"

"Uh" was all he could manage in reply. He realized his head ached horribly and he felt like vomiting. His mouth was parched, his tongue coated with fur. He grasped at the floor to stop the sickening revolution of the walls: around about halfway, then magically back to the beginning. Right to left and back, right to left and back. He squeezed his eyes shut, wished the effect away, but even the blankness under his lids revolved. He felt like death, wanted to curl up and vanish, wished Elspeth would leave him alone, but most of all, deep inside, he was elated that he felt anything at all.

"Get up." She kicked him again. He rolled over in response and climbed to his feet. He belched and a hot brew of stomach acids burned his throat. He swallowed the foul concoction, struggling to control his urge to throw up. He needed water, and maybe some food in his stomach.

"You reek of booze. What have you been up to?"

He shook his head in response. Nothing, absolutely nothing. If only the damn floor would stop moving! After several deep breaths, he informed her, "Horst came in very late last night. I . . ." He let his voice trail off. He simply could not think fast enough in this condition to come up with the rest of his excuse. He left it to her imagination to fill in the details.

Surprisingly, she had no trouble. "I see. All right, hurry downstairs. You've got a lot to do."

He stood still, concentrating on his balance as he watched her go. What did she see?

As he came down the steps, thoughts tumbled through his head. He noticed that, other than for an appalling and self-inflicted hangover, he was essentially healthy. Karl hadn't laid a finger on him in weeks, since before Frau Reusch had apologized. Frau Reusch had apologized? She had, she had apologized! And the neighbor, the one who had taught him about gardening, the neighbor had saved him! Taking such a risk, coming over to the fence like that to distract his powerful neighbor from his frenzied anger! Elspeth, too, had been almost understanding. She had simply ignored his drunkenness. And Roman told him repeatedly that his friends missed him. He should return to them. He could reorganize his school, he could keep alert and watch for a good opportunity to escape, he had survived his deadly mistake of getting caught talking with Ulrike. He had survived!

Before he reached the kitchen, the doorbell rang. He did up the buttons of his shirt and rolled down his sleeves as he hurried to answer the door. It was a telegram. Elspeth had also rushed out, and when she saw the telegram, she snatched it from the delivery boy's hands, read it several times, and then crumpled it. Disappointed by her reaction, the boy left and Peter shut the door. Elspeth held the crumpled paper in her fist and stared silently at the door for several moments.

Finally he asked, "What's wrong? What's happened?" but she ignored him. She dropped the telegram on the floor and wordlessly went into the sitting room, shutting the door behind her.

It was, no doubt, a capital offense; nevertheless, he picked the telegram up and read it. Uwe, their eldest son, had been injured by a terrorist bomb. There were severe injuries to the lower half of his body. He had lost one leg and might well lose the other. He was recuperating in the hospital and would soon be transferred home. The family should make preparations to receive him and care for him.

Peter snorted: so much for loyalty! The hospitals were overcrowded and caring for an injured man was expensive, so under humanitarian pretenses, he was being released into his family's care far earlier than he should be.

He replaced the telegram on the floor, at a loss for what to do next. Although she had said nothing after reading it, Elspeth was unquestionably distraught. He imagined her holding Uwe as a baby. Imagined her rocking him to sleep, singing a lullaby. He imagined her concern when he was sick, her pride as she presented the baby to her friends and relatives. Had she imagined then the unceasing violence, even in their lives? For reasons he did not fully understand, he felt an urge to speak to her.

With absolutely no pretext, he knocked lightly on the sitting room door and entered unbidden. Elspeth was by the window, her back to him. She stared idly into space, rocking gently back and forth, as though in a trance. He remembered a scene from his distant past—a mother, carrying a young child who had been injured in a shoot-out between some squatters in a cellar and the police. She had hugged the child so tightly, crooned comforting words to it, as tears had streamed down her cheeks. Then as now, he had wondered, where did it all go so wrong?

"What do you want?" she finally acknowledged him, her voice devoid of emotion.

Suddenly his presumptuousness seemed foolish. Nevertheless, he placed his hand lightly on her shoulder and said, "I just wanted to tell you, I'm sorry about your son."

She whirled around to face him; he expected her anger, was not surprised by her indignation. After all, what did he know? How could he understand! It was his sort who were responsible! How dare he touch her! He flinched expecting her to hit him, but instead she stunned him by throwing her arms around his neck and burying her head in his chest, crying, "My boy, my little boy!"

Nervously, he put his arm around her and held her as she sobbed. She continued to press herself against him, and he felt the warmth of her body as he stroked her back and soothed, "I'm sorry," over and over.

Eventually, she pulled herself together and pulled away from him. "Get me a cup of tea," she said softly.

By the time he returned, she had composed herself. "You had no business reading that telegram," she stated coldly.

"I know," he replied just as coldly. He poured the tea and left her alone with her thoughts. They would both act as though it had never happened.

56

"**I** SEE NO REASON you can't join the class. Our next meeting . . ." Adam interrupted himself as he saw a sudden change of expression in the boy's face that sent alarm bells ringing inside his head. Casually, he stood to leave the café, making a quick excuse as he did so, but before he could even turn, he felt someone approach and the muzzle of a gun was pressed into his back.

"Herr Teacher, don't move," the one with the gun said.

"I'm sorry," the boy whispered. "They have my brother."

"I'm not a teacher," Adam said. "You have the wrong man."

"You're under arrest," the voice behind Adam said.

Adam dropped his head slightly so he could see a bit behind him. There were at least three of them. One with the gun in his back and one on either side of him, out of reach. "I said, I'm not a teacher. Look at my papers, you'll see, I work in the textile mill."

The one holding the gun laughed and jammed it into his back. "I'm sure you do, and in the evening you meet with your little group of traitors and spread your lies in your swinish language. Now, come with us."

Adam went with them and was led to a car. He was seated in the back, with a policeman on either side. His fingers picked worriedly at a bit of loose thread in the fabric of the car seat as his mind worked feverishly trying to weigh up his situation. No handcuffs, that was a good sign. They seemed to believe his cover story; that was also probably good. So far it looked like a simple betrayal of a teacher by a student. That meant, of course, that they would not know he could be ransomed and so they might be careless with him; on the other hand, they were unlikely to ask dangerous questions. If they did not realize how much he knew, they could not tear the information out of him. Better safe than sorry, he decided, he would hold with the cover story as long as it lasted and hope that the Szaflary team could locate and rescue him without his tipping them off.

"What's the matter, teacher? You look worried," one of his guards taunted.

"I'm not a teacher."

"It's a capital offense, you know, teaching unauthorized classes."

"I realize that. I'm not a teacher, though."

The guard on the other side of him snickered. "I bet you'll admit it soon enough." He boxed Adam lightly on the face. "They all do."

Adam nodded. He felt sick to his stomach.

In the police station his papers were inspected and he was searched.

"You didn't take this off him right away?" the burly sergeant asked, holding up the workman's knife he had found in Adam's pocket.

One of his guards shrugged and said, "No big deal."

They took his shoes and his belt and led him to a cell that had three cement walls and a fourth wall composed entirely of bars. The old village lockup for drunks. Adam sat on the cot and rested his head on his hands. So far so good. They did not suspect the cover story; he had been appropriately dressed and unarmed; they had treated him with a minimal courtesy. He wondered how long it would take Szaflary to notice his absence. Maybe he could talk his way out of the whole situation before that; after all, they apparently had only the word of one scared boy. Maybe, too, he could get a quick conviction and get his sentence commuted to a concentration camp. There he could hold out for quite a while until an escape was organized.

He rubbed his chin and thought what his textile worker would do. Deny it, deny it all. Besides, a conviction would mean a confession, and that would mean they would want the names of students. It was information that he did not have and could not give them. His students were vetted and registered by people he never met; at the last he gave his final personal approval and admitted each into his class by telling them where and when the next meeting would take place. He had no names, no addresses; all he had were code numbers and the nicknames that he himself assigned to his students. The true names of his students were registered, along with their code numbers, with the government in exile in the free city of Manhattan, thousands of miles away, safely out of the Reich's reach. That's where the information about their scores was sent, that's where their records and degrees were kept. At the end of the course, he left their grades at a dead drop, where he did not even meet the courier; after that, all the students kept was an anonymous certificate, a somewhat innocuous document that they could use as temporary proof of their education. He kept nothing at all.

He stood and went to the small window and looked out at the faint image of the stars against the bright night sky. Joanna would be looking at the same stars. He smiled and thought how he would tell her all about the bad men who had stopped him from coming home on time. Maybe there would be an exciting escape or some clever trickery in the story. She would clap her hands anytime something went right; her face would freeze with fear anytime he mentioned danger. Later, years later, he would repeat the story to her children, embellishing a bit here and there to make it more exciting, drawing out his words as he explained who these people were who had long ago been thrown out of their land and why they were so evil. Then he would take his grandchildren out for a walk into the peaceful night; they would climb a hill together, without passes, without papers, without inspections. There on the hilltop he would point out the stars and explain how he had looked at them through a tiny prison cell window, and how he had known then that everything would come out all right.

"Good morning, Herr Teacher, did you sleep well?"

"I'm not a teacher," Adam responded, rubbing his eyes to wake himself. He had only been resting, and he knew that barely more than an hour had passed. He had heard the shift change at midnight, and the man who spoke to him now was apparently the replacement for the one who had arrested him.

"Come with me, we have some questions for you," the policeman stated as he began to open the lock.

"Oh, can't it wait until morning?"

The policeman opened the cell door and waited in silence. Adam rose and reluctantly followed him as he led the way down the hallway of the prison.

"Ah, Herr Teacher, welcome to our humble prison!" the lieutenant greeted him as he was led into a small, windowless room. He followed Adam's gaze and gestured broadly. "Not as grand as your university, *Herr Professor Doktor,* but we do our best to accommodate our students here. Sit down, sit down!"

"I'm not a teacher," Adam stated mordantly as he sat in the chair the lieutenant had indicated. Besides the chair there was only one other chair and a low table in the room. The lieutenant seated himself on the edge of the table, right in front of Adam.

"No, of course not!" The lieutenant grinned. "Today you're a student, *my* student, and I have some exam questions to set before you."

"Can't this wait until morning?"

The lieutenant shook his head and clucked his tongue. "That's not a very enthusiastic attitude! But, no, I'm afraid I'm on the night shift, and tonight, so are you! By morning, I'll be going home to my good wife and a good breakfast of sausage and eggs and you . . . Well, we'll see." The lieutenant lit himself a cigarette and then offered Adam one. When Adam accepted, the lieutenant lit the cigarette for him. "Now, let's get this over quickly. Tell me everything you know, like a good student."

"I don't know anything, I'm not a teacher."

"The boy said you were."

"He was scared, he'd say anything."

"Why were you talking to him?"

"I thought I could buy some fruit through him. I wanted to impress a girl."

"Fruit? An apple from the teacher?"

"I'm not a teacher."

"Never mind that, we'll get back to your lies later. Just tell me about yourself. As long as you keep talking, my friend there"—the lieutenant pointed toward the corner and a guard holding a rubber truncheon—"won't have to hit you. If you stop, I'm afraid he will."

Adam glanced at the guard; it was an age-old technique and the reason why he had memorized an entire lifetime of details for his cover story. It would, in any case, kill time, but he had to be careful not to let the story come out too pat. "I don't know where to begin," he stuttered, then hearing the guard approach, he said hurriedly, "There's this girl, at the factory. She's real pretty, you wouldn't believe . . ."

Two hours later he was still talking, explaining the details of the equipment he worked with. "Enough of that," his interrogator said suddenly. "Tell me about your family."

Adam paused for breath. He heard the guard with the truncheon approach. Quickly he said, "Could I have a cup of tea?"

The interrogator cocked his head as if thinking about the request, then he nodded toward the guard. "Go get him some."

Adam talked about his family as he sipped the tea. So far so good, he thought, though he was not particularly reassured by their show of civility. It was not unusual for an interrogation to begin gently and decay into sadism.

"Is that when you decided to become a teacher for the Underground?" the interrogator asked suddenly.

"I told you, I'm not a teacher."

The interrogator sprang off the table and slammed the cup of tea out of Adam's hand. "Enough of your lies!"

Adam sputtered, wiping his face with his arm. "It's not a lie."

"I don't like liars!" the interrogator said as he gestured for the guard with the truncheon to come forward. "Show him."

The guard raised the truncheon, but before he could swing it they were interrupted by an orderly at the door. "*Mein Herr!*" he hissed. "A visitor!"

That was quick, Adam thought, wondering at the same time how he came to be missed so quickly. Maybe somebody had spotted his arrest taking place. He glanced behind himself to see the visitor and was surprised that he did not recognize the SS officer who strode into the room.

"You're overstepping your authority by interrogating this prisoner," the officer asserted as he handed a sheaf of documents to the interrogator. "We're taking him into our custody."

"It was our arrest, we have the right to—"

"He's coming with us." The officer gestured to Adam to stand. Adam obeyed and followed him out of the room, leaving his interrogator and the guard behind. In the hall they were joined by two other SS men, and together they marched to the entrance. Once they were outside, they stopped and handcuffed Adam's wrists behind his back.

"Is this really necessary?" Adam asked.

In response one of the guards shoved him down the short flight of steps. Adam stumbled to the bottom, struggling not to fall. Once he had regained his balance, he looked up angrily at his rescuers. What the hell were they playing at? They shoved him into a car and drove a short distance to another building, which he recognized as the local SS divisional office. As they pulled him out of the car and into the building, he swore quietly under his breath.

"So tell me," the young officer asked, "why were you without papers?" He sat on the edge of his desk and surveyed Adam.

"I had papers!" Adam replied angrily. "I told the front desk that!" His hands were still bound behind him, and he shifted uncomfortably in his seat.

"Then where are they?"

"I don't know. Apparently your friends at the police station kept them."

The officer looked over at his subordinate, who then volunteered, "We're having someone check on it. They claimed he came in without papers."

"They have my belt and my shoes as well," Adam pointed out.

The officer walked over to his subordinate. "Do you know what they're up to?" he asked in a low voice.

"I think they're upset we grabbed their prisoner," the subordinate answered quietly.

"The Flying University, and anyone associated with it, is part of the Underground. That's security!" the officer hissed.

"I know, sir. They just think it's a local arrest of a local resident and it should be their feather."

The officer nodded his head toward Adam. "Get him out of here. I don't want those yokels storming in here trying to take him back."

"Where to, sir?"

"Kattowitz. The main lockup will do. Have them handle his interrogation."

The ride to Kattowitz was long and uncomfortable. Adam watched the sunrise through the side window of the car and wondered if he had been missed yet. His first appointment wasn't until nine, and it was unlikely anyone would even know anything had happened to him. It was all moving so fast!

They arrived at the prison and checked him through the front desk. He hoped he would be taken to a cell and left alone for a while, but they marched past the cells and descended the stairs into the unwindowed depths. As he stumbled tiredly down the steps, he began to pray.

He was taken to a room and left to stand. He paced nervously, kicking at the dirt on the floor with his bare feet, scanning the paltry furniture: an old desk shoved up against the wall, two chairs, one in each corner, a broomstick lying abandoned on the floor. About twenty minutes later a weary lieutenant showed up. He held in his hand a single sheet of paper, which he perused with an ill-tempered impatience as he stood in front of Adam. "No papers, huh?"

"No, I had papers. They were kept by the police."

"A teacher, in the Underground, eh?"

"No, I'm not a teacher. It's a mistake."

"Fine, have it your way." The lieutenant shrugged. "Take care of him," he said to the three guards who stood near the door. "I don't care how." He walked toward the door.

"Wait!" Adam called after him.

"What? Are you in the Underground?"

Adam bit his lower lip.

"I want names, I want information."

"I don't have anything. I'm a textile worker. This is all a mistake," Adam pleaded.

"Don't waste my time," the lieutenant said, and left, leaving Adam alone with the three guards.

57

"Zosia, can I have a word with you?" Marysia asked from the doorway of Zosia's flat.

"Sure, come on in!" Zosia replied, intent on spreading the glue for Joanna's cutout doll evenly. Her tongue played along the edges of her lips as she concentrated on the delicate task.

Joanna sat hunched over the pile of colorful paper and scraps on the floor, indicating, with foremanlike accuracy, exactly where her mother should put the glue. "No, not there!" she wailed suddenly. "Her eyes will be funny there!"

Zosia looked up at Marysia to share her exasperation. It was then that she noticed Marysia had not come in nor had she smiled. Zosia shoved the bottle of glue at Joanna. "Put it wherever you want, honey." Zosia stood up. "I want to talk with your grandmother a minute."

Joanna nodded absently, unconcerned.

"What is it?" Zosia whispered once she was in the hallway.

"Adam's missing," Marysia stated dryly. "We think he was arrested."

"Arrested? How? By whom? When?"

Marysia made a calming motion. "He didn't make an appointment this morning. They've checked with his landlady, and she is fairly certain he's been out all night."

"Did he teach his class last night?"

"Yes. After that he was supposed to vet a new student; they were to meet in a café. He had been cleared, but we've learned that yesterday afternoon his brother was picked up on an unrelated charge. We're afraid he may have told his brother about his meeting with an Underground teacher and that his brother may have betrayed that information to the police."

"What about the student?"

"Missing. He may have either accidentally betrayed Adam or was coerced into it to save his brother."

Zosia closed her eyes as she listened, willing herself not to hate blabbermouths who were proud of their University affiliations. "What's being done?"

"We're sending out inquiries from his alleged place of work, asking what's happened to him. We also have someone digging into the files at the local police station today."

"Anyone see him last night?"

"No, none of our people were on that shift in that section of the police building. We used to have five plants but we lost two, so we're temporarily down to three there. We also have someone digging into the files at local security and at security headquarters in Krakau, but so far, they haven't found anything."

"What about the café?"

"We've dug up one witness so far; he said local police took away a worker with blond hair. The young fellow he had been talking to walked off with another policeman shortly afterwards."

"Contingency plans?"

"Tadek, Romek, and Konrad are already in uniform and en route to the city. They'll wait there for information and the appropriate papers to spring him, once we find him. They will also liaise with some local talent in case they need to take more direct action."

"It will take hours for them to get there," Zosia said, pulling worriedly at her thumbnail. "Don't we have anyone on-site who could do the job?"

Marysia looked pensive. "Yes and no. As far as anyone in town knows, they've grabbed a local teacher. Worrisome, but not of overriding concern. We don't want to blow Adam's cover to all and sundry if we don't have to. We're assuming he can hold out a few hours, but if it turns out that the situation merits desperate action, we'll inform our people and they'll do the job from there. Our betting, however, is Tadek and crew will be on-site before it's even feasible to do anything."

Zosia nodded. "What about a ransom?"

"We'd like to avoid that. They don't know who Adam is, and if we tell them, they might release him on exchange; on the other hand, they might decide he has too much information to lose. Currently we're not in a good position with negotiations, we don't have much to offer in the way of hostages, and if they then decide to keep Adam, knowing who he is and what he knows, well. . . ."

Zosia swallowed hard and nodded again. "You said Tadek has already left?"

"Yes."

"Okay. I'll meet up with them there."

"No, you won't."

"Don't be stupid, I have to be there. I might be of use!"

"You are to stay here and take care of Joanna. She can't afford to have both her parents at risk."

"I won't be at risk!"

"I'm sorry, Zosia. Orders."

"Orders? The Council hasn't even met!"

"Colonel, you are ordered to stay put," Marysia stated carefully. "And don't give me that look, because you are not going to get around this. You will not be allowed to leave, and if you try, you will be locked in this room, do you understand?"

Zosia glanced back at Joanna as she sat, humming a little song to herself, on the floor of the flat. "All right. I'm sure—"

"Excuse me," a young soldier interrupted Zosia. "This just came in." The soldier handed Marysia a message and left.

Marysia read the message, then smiled at Zosia. "Good news, one of our people has located his documents in the local police station there; they still think he's just a teacher for the Underground university. We should have no trouble pulling him out with orders from Gestapo headquarters. After all, the Underground is not a matter for local police."

Zosia sighed. "Thank God."

"Go tend to Joanna, honey, it's the best thing for you to do right now."

"Okay." Zosia returned to Joanna's side and, sitting on the floor with her, picked up a pair of scissors and a piece of colorful paper and began cutting out a bird. It would be an eagle, she decided, the emblem of their country, and she and Joanna would draw in the details and paint it in beautiful colors and present it to Adam upon his return. As she worked, she muttered quietly, like a prayer, "Adam, Adam, Adam."

Tadek, Romek, and Konrad marched into the local police station with their impressive array of uniforms and surly looks and slammed the orders down on the front desk. "We were told you are holding one of our prisoners here!" Tadek rumbled.

The clerk gingerly picked up the papers and looked through them. After a few minutes he made his excuses and went to check the files. After about ten minutes he returned with a prisoner list, looking baffled. "I'm sorry, sirs, there's no such prisoner on our list."

"He was arrested last night. Check that list," Tadek ordered.

The clerk shook his head. "This is last night's list. Shall I check this morning's?"

Tadek glanced worriedly at his colleagues, then said, "Yes, check this morning's, check yesterday's. Just find him!"

It took more than an hour of arguing, vague threats, and waiting to find out that Adam truly was not listed as a prisoner in the jail. In exasperation, Tadek finally demanded a personal tour of the prison so that he could see each and every prisoner personally.

That caused a raised eyebrow, and the officer with whom they were now dealing asked politely, "And how will you recognize a man you've never met?"

Tadek hesitated, then answered, "His wanted poster. He's wanted on several other petty counts of acts against the state."

"I'm sorry, *Herr Major,* but I cannot accede to that request. We have—"

"*Mein Herr?*" a young policeman intervened.

"What do you want?"

"I think I know what happened to this prisoner."

"So he was here?" Tadek asked.

"Oh, yes, *mein Herr,* but he was transferred almost immediately."

"Transferred? Why? To whom?" Tadek asked.

"To your people, *Herr Major.* Security was here last night."

The officer smiled. "Ah, it seems you need to do a little housecleaning yourself, *Herr Major.* Your own people are so eager to take our prizes. Maybe if they spent their time tracking down terrorists rather than shadowing our movements, you wouldn't have these problems."

"Shall I call your office for you, *Herr Major?*" the young policeman volunteered.

Tadek shook his head vigorously. "No, no. I'll sort this out personally. My apologies." He motioned to his men and left the building quickly, before any further questions could be raised.

$$58$$

ADAM OPENED HIS EYES as far as he could and looked up at the gray ceiling above him. Every part of his body was screaming with pain. He had often helped edit the reports of human rights abuses that were regularly sent overseas to the American Congress, and he thought with grim humor that now, at last, he could add his own eyewitness account. That thing with the desk drawer . . . He reached impulsively toward his battered groin, but changed his mind and let his arm rest on his stomach. His tongue probed his mouth and discovered four teeth missing, all on the right side. Shit, teeth were a nuisance. Still, they could be repaired, he'd be able to pop them out and terrorize his grandchildren with them. His tongue probed the left side of his mouth and located the one false tooth on that side. It was still intact. Though he had no intention of using it, it was nevertheless reassuring to know a fatal dose of poison was waiting for him if he needed it.

He closed his eyes and worked at memorizing every feature of the faces of the men who had beaten him. The officers would probably not be too difficult, but the three anonymous brutes in that room—they might require some work. Nevertheless, with duty rosters and vigilance, he was sure that someday he would track each of them down and exact an appropriate revenge. They would pay, of that he was sure.

He shuddered a sigh and tried to rest and regain his strength. It would be easiest for their people if he were able to walk out on his own two feet. He should get up and try walking around, he thought, but before he could follow through, the door opened and a grinning young officer appeared.

"Good day, Herr Teacher! Are you ready for another lesson?" Even as he spoke, two guards came into the room and began lifting Adam from his cot.

"What? Wait!" Adam's voice came out strangely and blood trickled from his mouth as he spoke.

"Wait? Why?" the officer asked.

"I haven't . . . Isn't this a bit quick? You haven't let me think at all! I've just woken up! How can . . . It's not usual procedure. Give me some time!"

The officer motioned with his head toward the door, and the two men dutifully began dragging Adam out.

"What's the rush? I've just been . . . They've just . . . Give me time!"

"Herr Teacher, you are not enthusiastic about having another lesson?"

"No, please wait!" Adam pleaded. "Let the pain argue with me for a few hours, please! Oh, God, just a few hours!"

They continued to pull and drag him down the hall. They ended up in an office, and Adam was momentarily reassured. They dropped him unceremoniously into a chair in front of a desk, and a few moments later the same lieutenant he had seen before came into the room and sat behind the desk. He was eating a *Brötchen* with slices of cheese and ham shoved in between. Adam stared at the food, but he did not bother to say anything.

"Hungry, teacher?" the lieutenant asked.

"I'm not a teacher."

The lieutenant continued eating his sandwich while shuffling through some papers on his desk. Finally Adam felt driven to ask, "Could I have some water?"

The lieutenant looked up from his papers. "Are you in the Underground?"

"No," Adam sighed. "No."

The lieutenant sighed and went back to his papers. After he had finished his sandwich and his shuffling, he looked up again. "Are you a teacher in the Underground university?"

Adam shook his head.

The lieutenant looked to the guards, who had seated themselves by the wall. "I'm not in the mood for this nonsense. Take him out of here and beat some sense into him."

The guards approached and began to lift Adam from his chair.

"Wait! Wait!" Adam gasped.

"Are you in the Underground?" the lieutenant asked.

Adam stared at the floor. Quietly he admitted, "Yes, I work in the textile factory during the day and I teach courses in the Underground university at night."

The lieutenant nodded. "Good, then tell me all about it."

Adam did. He told the lieutenant names and some addresses, he mentioned meeting locations and contacts, he described in detail the structure of the university and tried to digress on the content of his courses but was preempted. Nothing he said was true, not a word of it, but it did mean that he managed to kill two hours without being hit.

When they reached the end of his inventiveness, the lieutenant handed him a single sheet of paper. "Sign this."

Adam glanced at the terse admission of guilt to a capital crime and dutifully put a signature at the bottom.

The lieutenant collected the sheet of paper, tossed it onto a stack of papers, and said to the guards, "Get rid of him."

Adam sighed his relief. They would take him back to his cell, and he would wait there either until they discovered that everything he had said was false or until his trial. In either case, it gave his comrades some time to track him down. It would be difficult, he knew, since he had been separated from his papers and had been moved out of town, but there was a good chance his comrades would locate him and he would be freed.

He was taken to a windowless room deep in the bowels of the building. Adam scanned the room and felt a terror grow in him. There was no bed, no sink, nothing to indicate it was a cell. Something like a metal coatrack stood incongruously in the center of the room, and in the corner was a table with various objects—a crowbar, a rubber truncheon, some unidentifiable gadgets.

Panicked, Adam turned to his guards. "I've confessed, I've told you everything!"

The larger of the guards smiled. "We know, so now we have no more use for you."

As they chained his hands and feet to the coatrack, he argued with them, he pleaded to go back and tell the lieutenant more details, he offered bribes, so finally they forced a gag into his mouth.

They used the crowbar and began with the rack upright, but when the force of their blows caused it to tumble, they let him crash to the ground and continued beating him on the floor.

He lost all sense of time, and it was with the distance of a dreamer that he perceived they had suddenly stopped. He concentrated through the screaming agony and recognized the voice of the lieutenant.

"What the hell are you doing?"

"You said get rid of him," a guard replied sheepishly.

"You idiots! I meant put him back in the cell."

"But, sir, policy is we're allowed to practice on condemned convicts."

"Not anymore, you dolts! We recycle them. He'd be a strong worker—we need laborers! We have a quota to meet and you just trashed a candidate!"

The lieutenant walked over to where Adam lay on the floor and looked down at him. "Oh, God in heaven!" he spat in disgust. He stooped down and touched Adam's face. "You've broken his jaw! What if I wanted to get more information out of him?" He then felt the bloody pulp of Adam's legs. "Legs broken, arms smashed. What the hell are we supposed to do with this mess?"

He stood up and returned to berating the guards, promising dire consequences for their foolishness, and then suddenly he said, "Unchain him, put him in his cell. I'll get a doctor to look at him, and then I've got to work out what to do with him."

Adam was released from the coatrack and carried back to his cell. He was laid rather gently on his cot and left alone. As he lay there, he looked up at the window and saw it was still daylight: not even twenty-four hours had passed since they had arrested him. He replayed the lieutenant's words about him and wondered if they were true. Though he was numb now, the pain had been such that he supposed his bones had been crushed. That would take some undoing, he thought angrily. Such a waste, such a goddamned waste. What purpose did all the destructiveness serve? Such a waste! Now he would have to spend months, maybe years, recuperating. They'd have to smuggle him out to America, he'd have to undergo reconstructive surgery on his legs, on his arms, on his face. How would they get him out of the country? he wondered. His mind ran through several scenarios, then he thought about where they might get all the money that would be necessary. If he was going to spend that long in America, Zosia and Joanna should come with him. It would be nice having them there; it would be a good experience for Joanna to see what a normal society was like. Yes, she could gain something from it, and perhaps learn some English as well. That would be good for her future. He imagined her as an adult, giving a report to the American Congress in flawless English. He'd sit next to her, backing her up with facts and perhaps recounting that time, long in the past, when he had fallen into the hands of the Gestapo.

He blinked his eyes to clear the red tears that were filling them. He thought about his little girl and about his mother and about his beautiful wife. They would be so happy to see him, they would help him through that difficult recovery period. He imagined his mother putting a straw in his mouth so he could drink some soup; he felt Zosia steadying him as he learned how to walk again; he saw Joanna encouraging him with her bright smile.

His eyes wanted to close, but he fought the urge. He was afraid of sleep; the little death was more than that to him. As he lay there he heard music, and after a moment he recognized the waltz played at his wedding. The words had seemed innocent then. *Za rok, za dzień, za chwilę, razem nie będzie nas . . .* A year, a day, a moment for you and me, then together we'll no longer be . . .

He tried to speak but his jaw was too shattered to move the way he wanted it to. Nevertheless, he managed to whisper through the blood that filled his mouth, "Zosia . . . Zosia . . . Zosia." He looked back up at the sky, at the blue sky that they would be looking at today as well. The blue turned red as he looked at it, and then the red darkened to black.

59

*T*HE BLACK OF THE night sky slowly brightened into the red of dawn and then the blue of day. Peter watched through half-closed eyes, wishing the short summer night would last just a bit longer. He slept now on the floor of Uwe's bedroom, on a heavy rug with blankets that he rolled up and stored out of sight during the day. His last shred of privacy, his attic bed, had been sacrificed to the unending demands of his irritable and petulant invalid patient.

Every night since his arrival, Uwe had awakened him. Every night. He wondered momentarily if there was anyone in the world, anyone at all, who felt more miserable than he did. He sighed his exasperation and began his day, making his way out of the house and to the bakery as usual. A morning rain had only just stopped, and even though it was July, the air was thick with a cold mist. The usual collection of *Zwangsarbeiter* loitered near the bakery entrance, waiting for their morning ration. He joined the queue, but was too distracted by his thoughts to listen to the whispered gossip around him. He had to ask Roman to yet again convey his apologies to everyone. There was no way he could leave the house with Uwe there. It was impossible.

Eventually he reached the head of the line and looked into the bakery to greet Roman with a smile. A strange face returned his look. The young man was thin, pale, and looked thoroughly harassed by both his bosses behind him and the customers in front of him. Quickly, Peter dug through his papers to find all the appropriate documentation that the man would need. As the order was being filled, he worriedly scanned the interior of the bakery. Roman was nowhere in sight. He turned to the boy in line behind him. He did not recognize him but asked anyway, in a subdued voice, "What happened to Roman?"

The boy ignored him; he wore the uniform of an apprentice, and it would, no doubt, debase him to acknowledge someone of a lower strata. Peter turned back toward the window; the young man presented him with his order and turned his attention toward the next customer.

"Wait," Peter insisted, probably a bit too loudly.

The man glared at him. "What do you want?"

"Where is Roman?"

"Who?"

"The man who used to work here."

"Oh, him. Gone." And with that the young man pointedly turned to the boy. The boy gave Peter a shove as he elbowed his way forward.

Peter scanned the line of waiting people, but none of them returned his look. A lone policeman lounging a few meters away, leaning against a wall and smoking a cigarette, caught his eyes. The policeman seemed to interpret the direct look as a challenge and, throwing down the cigarette, launched himself off the wall and began to walk slowly in Peter's direction. Realizing he had lost any opportunity to find out what was going on, Peter turned and walked away as unobtrusively as possible. The policeman did not bother to follow.

This was an unexpected and unwelcome turn of events! What with his reassignment to sleep in Uwe's room, what with Uwe never leaving the house and demanding attention at any hour of the day or night, he had lost every last chance of contact with all the others. He had become a prisoner of the house and of his patient. His once-a-day visits to the bakery and his chats with Roman had been the sole outlet left to him. And now Roman was gone as well!

Maybe, he thought, as he changed the sheets on Uwe's bed, maybe it was good news. Maybe Roman had found a chance, had learned of someplace to go and taken the opportunity available to him. The thought buoyed him, at least a bit, but whatever had happened, no matter how good the news for Roman, it was a devastating blow for him. He missed his friends terribly, he was excruciatingly lonely, and he was extremely annoyed that Uwe's sleeplessness had so effectively imprisoned him in the house and denied him any chance of meeting with anybody for the foreseeable future.

Uwe slumped in the chair next to the bed as Peter changed the linens and watched his every move with an unnerving intensity. Once the fresh sheets were laid on the bed, he helped Uwe back into a reclining position. His patient was neither light nor cooperative, and as usual, he had a difficult time getting Uwe back into bed safely without straining himself. After he had finally deposited his irritable patient onto the bed and lit another cigarette for him, he finished tucking in the corners.

"Tell me about yourself," Uwe said suddenly.

"Not much to tell. I serve my betters loyally."

Uwe laughed at that. "Well, then, tell me about a woman."

"I don't know any."

"Surely you must have fucked someone! Tell me about the last woman you fucked."

"I've never had sex," Peter replied with a straight face.

"Liar!"

"No, never."

"You're not human!"

"So you all constantly tell me," Peter countered. He moved from one side of the bed to the other.

"Well, it doesn't matter. Tell me about your childhood then."

"Nothing much to say. Pretty average."

"Did you graduate school?" Uwe asked, his eyes closed as if contemplating the great secrets of the universe.

Peter struggled to remember if he had ever answered that question. Yes? No? He supposed the answer must have been that he hadn't. "No."

"Why not?"

"I don't know. I guess education just isn't important to my sort."

There was a moment of silence and Peter wondered if Uwe had fallen asleep. He thought he should pluck the glowing cigarette from Uwe's immobile hand, and he was just about to reach over when Uwe broke the silence.

"What about your parents?"

"What about them?" Peter answered irritably, momentarily forgetting that he was supposed to be a foundling.

"What did they do?"

"Does it matter?"

"You'll show proper respect at all times!" Uwe warned, his eyes snapping open to survey his servant.

"My humblest apologies. Forgive me for my uninteresting life. I seek only to serve," Peter replied with undisguised sarcasm.

"Pff!" Uwe huffed. "All right then, if your life is uninteresting, tell me about your thoughts."

"I have none."

"Come now."

"I don't have time to think. And as you are so fond of pointing out, I'm not really capable of rational thought in any case."

"I asked about your feelings, not your thoughts."

"Feelings? Oh. In that case, absolute loyalty. And gratitude, of course," Peter snapped, more annoyed by Uwe's blatant lie than he should have allowed himself to be.

"Gratitude?"

"Oh, yes, that my life is given a purpose." Peter finished tucking in the sheets. He turned to leave.

"Hey, I'm not done."

"What do you want?"

"Don't take that tone with me!" Uwe growled.

"So sorry, *mein Herr.* How can my most lowly self be of service to my most gracious one?"

"Don't think I haven't noticed your attitude."

Peter raised an eyebrow in response. "Attitude?"

"You think too highly of yourself."

"My humblest apologies, *mein Herr.*"

"You shouldn't be here. It's as simple as that," Uwe stated incongruously.

Peter gave Uwe a long, hard look. Where did Uwe think he belonged? In a work camp? Deciding to deliberately misinterpret, he made another attempt at escape and said, "If that's how you feel, I'll leave. There are other things I'd be better off doing." He started for the door.

"Don't you dare!" Uwe thundered. "I'm not through with you!"

Peter stopped in the doorway. Staring forlornly into the hallway, he agreed, "No one ever is."

"What? What was that?" Uwe asked petulantly. "What did you say?"

"Nothing, *mein Herr,*" Peter replied, half turning to be sure Uwe heard him. "I really must go, though."

"No, come back here!"

Peter could hear Elspeth approaching up the steps. Trapped as he was, he gave up and returned to Uwe's bedside. "Yes, *mein Herr?*"

Uwe wagged a finger at him. "I'm going to catch you out, boy. Just you wait, and when I do . . ." Uwe made a violent snapping motion with his fist. "Your neck, boy! It will be your neck!"

The threat sounded real enough, but Peter was distracted by the fact that Uwe was no longer smoking and the cigarette was not in the ashtray. Peter scanned the bed and finally located the glowing end on the floor. He quickly picked it up and deposited it in the ashtray, stubbing it out with a casualness that masked his annoyance at such childish behavior.

Uwe followed his actions with mild interest, then flicking his fingers in the direction of his pack, indicated to Peter that he should light another one for him. Uwe sighed with pleasure as he inhaled from the cigarette and greeted his mother with a smile as she bustled into the room.

Elspeth returned his smile with a look of syrupy love and undying devotion, then she glanced down at the ashtray and the collection of cigarette ends and scowled at Peter. "You know the doctor said he should not smoke!"

Peter shrugged. "It is not my place—"

Elspeth slapped him before he could say more. "You selfish pig! You don't give a damn about my son's health!" she accused angrily.

That was not really true. He had a real interest in Uwe's recovering enough to finally get fitted with artificial limbs. If he could move about, it would not only circumvent the awful need for bedpans and the like but would also mean Uwe might get enough exercise to be less bored and irritable and would perhaps even sleep through the night and allow Peter to do likewise. No, Elspeth was wrong: Uwe's health was very much his concern, but the boy enjoyed the attention of being bedridden far too much and was malingering in a depression that was more debilitating than his physical injuries.

Of course, Peter said nothing of the sort to Elspeth and simply apologized. He did not bother to specify why he was apologizing: Was it for lighting Uwe's cigarettes? Or for not caring about his health? Or for being a selfish pig? It did not matter, Elspeth had already turned her attention to her son, sweetly reminding him that it was not wise to smoke so much.

"Ah, Ma, but I'm bored!" Uwe whined, and added, nodding at Peter, "And he is always running off leaving me alone. Sometimes I shout myself hoarse and he doesn't come."

Elspeth turned toward Peter, livid with rage. Uwe continued, "He ignores me, Ma! Why, just a moment ago he said he had better things to do."

Elspeth's eyes opened wide with horror. "You piece of filth!" she hissed. "How dare you speak to my son in such a manner!"

"*Gnä' Frau,* I do my best," Peter explained. "I can't come if I don't hear him, and I do have lots of work that must be done."

Behind his mother's back, Uwe grinned at him as if to say: See, I can destroy you in a minute!

"Nothing takes priority over my son's needs! Do you understand?" Elspeth huffed.

"I understand, *gnädige Frau,* but I must do my other work! Certainly you see that?"

"You can do that when he does not need you. And you will make sure that you are always within hearing distance."

"But how can I work outside?" As soon as he said it, he knew it was a mistake.

"You spend far too long outside—there's no need for it. When you do go out, you will always check with me first, and you will check in with Uwe at regular intervals to make sure he does not need you."

Peter grit his teeth at her words and Elspeth slapped him again. "You will not take that attitude with me!" she huffed.

He was not sure what he had done that time—maybe she had read his mind. Resigned, he asked, "And if Herr Vogel has need of me, do I go then?"

"Don't get clever with me! You know that if my husband or I have need of you, then you should come when we call. Don't think, though, that you can use that as an excuse to ignore the needs of my son. He gave his legs to his country, and damn it, you will give him the care and respect that he deserves!" When she mentioned Uwe's legs, Elspeth looked at Peter's with a disturbingly jealous intensity. It was not the first time she had done that, and each time she scrutinized him in that manner, it sent a chill down his spine.

"I'm doing my best," he sighed.

"Well, it's not good enough! Now get out!" she ordered brusquely.

He was more than happy to oblige.

After he finished changing the linens on the other beds in the house, he returned to the kitchen. Miraculously it was still clean and so he had a few minutes to decide what to do next. An endless list of jobs presented itself, but as he glanced around the kitchen, he noticed the sunlight streaming brilliantly through the window, and he was drawn to the back door and the blue sky. He opened it and breathed deeply—the sweet smells of summer scented the air. It was a perfect time to go outside and take care of some yard work, and it would get him away from the oppressive mood of the house, if only for a few minutes.

He hesitated a moment at the door. Usually Elspeth was aware of his every move, and her command that he specifically inform her when he went outside was both redundant and insulting. He smiled at that last thought—was he even capable of being insulted anymore? Elspeth called him a selfish pig and a piece of filth, and he was the one who apologized. What a funny world it was!

The sunshine beckoned; Elspeth was busy upstairs with Uwe. If he went out now, without informing her, he would be in direct and clear violation of her command. She could conceivably get Karl involved, she was certainly already that angry at him, thanks to Uwe, and the punishment could be disproportionately severe, even life-threatening. All he had to do was go upstairs, tell her what he planned to do. There was no rational reason not to. He stood for a moment longer in the doorway. There was no rational reason not to inform her.

He did not inform her. Grabbing the keys to the tool shed, he stepped outside and carefully shut the door behind him. He selected several tools from the shed and busied himself clearing out some ivy that was threatening to strangle the hedges.

As he worked, he thought about Uwe's threats, about Elspeth's strange looks, about Roman's disappearance, and he thought, yet again, about leaving. He had ages ago worked out the logistics—the clothes, the car, the papers he would need. What he had yet to work out was his destination. Always he came to the same dead end. There was nowhere to go, no feasible escape from the Reich, no possibility of a safe haven within it. England was out, he was afraid of his own people there, and everywhere else was an unknown, full of strangers, requiring papers and connections and help that he did not have. What point was there running to another section of the Reich? Life here was tolerable, or at least survivable. What point would there be in taking all that risk just to end up in another suburb of another German city, hiding in alleys, foraging garbage?

He shivered suddenly as an image of a body—hung on a meat hook, arms and legs broken, flesh hanging in shreds—flashed through his mind. Looking up, he was surprised to see that the sunshine was as bright as ever, that no cloud had passed overhead. He wiped the sweat off his hands and forced himself to suppress the image of their retribution.

He thrust his hand into the hedge and grabbed some ivy near its roots. His thoughts always ended in frustration. He felt exhausted, he could hardly find the energy to think, and the whole process seemed so hopeless! With a sudden tug, he loosened the ivy's roots and pulled it out of the earth. He stared at it for a moment, wondering at what had been done to him, thinking of the torture, the drugs, the endless droning propaganda. Had it been more effective than he realized? Uwe was threatening him, Elspeth was eyeing him as though she'd amputate his legs just to even up the score with her son, and Roman had simply disappeared. And here he was, completely paralyzed by indecision and ignorance.

For some reason he started to laugh at himself, at the pathetic shell he had become. The laughter brought tears to his eyes, and as he rubbed them away, his vision blurred irritatingly. He paused, squinting and blinking, trying to restore his focus. When he finally was able to see clearly again, he noticed something among the branches of the hedge. He reached in and cleared away some dirt so he could examine it more closely. Yes, there it was—hidden among the browns and yellows and dark greens—the tiny body of a sparrow. It was fresh with no sign of decay other than the gluey appearance of the closed eyes.

Gently, he scooped the bird into his hand, walked calmly to the back corner of the garden, and there, under a linden tree that he had planted, he dug a small grave with his hands. He carefully laid the tiny body in the earth, arranging it into a comfortable-looking pose, and then silently wishing it well in its new home, he covered it with the earth. It was a useless gesture, but one that he felt compelled to do.

As he walked back across the garden to where he had been working, he heard someone call his name. Surprised by the interruption, he looked up to see Elspeth as she stood framed by the back door like a portrait of suburban calm. Without knowing why, he smiled at the image—not a proper, subservient smile but rather a self-confident, almost happy grin. The sort of greeting one bestows on a friend. He did not know where it came from—perhaps the salubrious effects of the sunshine, perhaps the sheer lunacy of his life. Whatever its source, it surprised Elspeth and before she realized it, she had smiled in response.

She studied him as he approached and the smile dropped from her face. After all this time, after all our efforts, she thought, he still walks too proudly. Even with his limp, he carries himself with grace—his back straight, his head held high. And where in the world did he get the idea he could smile at her like that? Like an equal! Still, she had to admit, he was a lot more amusing than some of the thoroughly cowed workers that her friends had. When she sat with her coffee circle outdoors and he interrupted his garden work to refill their pot or replenish their tray, she would feel a surge of possessive pride as all four of them would look up from their gossip to watch him stride across the lawn. Sometimes they would fill the breaks in their conversation by just staring idly at him as he went about his work.

He stopped in front of her, raising his eyebrows expectantly. Elspeth was standing on the stoop and so they were facing each other eye to eye. She scanned him from head to toe—the uniform, the manacle, the numbers on his arm, calloused hands, scars and cuts and bruises here and there, that malnourished, tired cast to his face—it all clearly pointed to his inferior status, yet he looked her direct in the eyes and smiled. It was not fitting. It was not right or proper! Would he never learn? It seemed they could pummel him into exhausted, mindless subservience, but as soon as they let up, as soon as she took pity, he bounced back to this totally inappropriate behavior.

"*Gnä' Frau?*" he prompted, slightly confused by her silence.

"You did not inform me that you were out here."

"My apologies, *gnä' Frau,* I forgot."

It was clearly a lie, but she chose to ignore it. An hour alone with her son had drained her emotionally. He whined like a child, and she felt much less sympathetic to his complaints than she had when she had issued her commands. In any case, they were probably impractical, and though she would not revoke them, she saw no point in enforcing them either.

"What were you just doing there, by that tree?"

"Burying a bird, *gnä' Frau.*"

"What? With your bare hands!" Her eyes widened in horror. "That's filthy!"

"But so am I," he answered obscurely.

She narrowed her eyes; she was sure some sarcasm was hidden in that comment, but she could not find it and he returned her scrutiny with a look of sincere innocence. Finally she said, "I need you in the kitchen, we need to make something for the ladies this afternoon."

"Yes, *gnä' Frau.* I can finish out here in about five minutes."

"Do it later, I want you now." She wasn't in a hurry, but decided that she had already been lenient enough.

"May I put the tools away?"

"All right. But hurry up."

"Thank you." He turned to go.

"And Peter . . ."

"Yes, *gnä' Frau?*" He turned back toward her.

"Your behavior is totally inappropriate."

"Ah, yes, *gnä' Frau*, but you wouldn't have it any other way." And with that he went to collect the tools before she could even respond.

60

"D ONA EIS REQUIEM, *dona eis requiem . . . ,*" the voices sang mournfully. Zosia had managed to hold up quite well until that point, but upon hearing the words she burst into bitter weeping. She convulsed with sobs, tears streamed down her face, and Joanna's hand fell from her grasp. She could feel her daughter throw her arms around her legs, but she could not reach down to her.

The July sunshine felt cold on Zosia's face, and she shivered uncontrollably. Gnats swarmed under the pines, and she waved at them as if waving away the evil from the world. Her Adam, gone. Gone forever.

Somebody led Joanna away, somebody else put their arms around her shoulders, but all she felt was the enormous void that had opened up in her heart and was threatening to swallow her.

"Is Daddy going to come back?" Joanna asked her grandmother in a whisper as the people around her sang.

Marysia shook her head. "No, honey. That's why we're having this special ceremony. It's our way of saying good-bye."

"I know that. But maybe he'll come back anyway?"

"I don't think so, honey."

"Is he in heaven?"

Marysia nodded, then almost laughed as she thought of some of Adam's antics. "We can hope."

"Maybe he'll come back anyway. Maybe he's just lost and can't find his way home. We should go look for him," Joanna suggested.

Marysia shook her head but could not reply.

"*Babusiu*, why are you crying?" Joanna asked.

Marysia gently stroked her granddaughter's curly blond hair. "First my little girl, and now my little boy. Does it never end?" she whispered.

"Are you okay?" Joanna asked. "Do you miss Daddy?"

"Yes, very much. He was my little boy," Marysia replied. "And they've taken him from me."

"Why?"

"I wish I knew, honey. I wish I knew. When I was a very little girl, they came into our land and they took everything and destroyed anything they could get their hands on. And it hasn't stopped. They just keep taking. I don't know why."

The ceremony ended and the people drifted away. Zosia spent some moments holding on to Tadek and talking with her parents, and then she gathered her composure and came over to join them. "How are you doing, sweetheart?" she asked Joanna.

"Oh, I miss Daddy."

"I do too, sweetie." Zosia reached up and wiped away some tears.

"Do you think he'll come back?"

"No, sweetheart, your daddy's dead. We won't see him again in this world."

"What if I pray? I'll pray every morning and every night and even during the day. Will he come back then?"

"Usually those sorts of prayers aren't answered the way you expect them to be," Zosia replied carefully.

"You go ahead and pray for your daddy and someday . . ." Marysia sighed, unable to decide what to say.

"If you see him wandering in the woods, bring him home. Maybe he forgot where we are," Joanna insisted, tugging at Marysia's shirt.

"Okay. If I see him, I'll bring him back." Marysia looked guiltily at Zosia, who was shaking her head subtly in disapproval.

"And tell the patrols, too!" Joanna added.

"Okay, I'll tell the patrols," Marysia said, grimacing at Zosia in apology.

Zosia shook her head in exasperation. She grabbed Joanna's hand. "Let's go, little one. I need your help greeting all the people at the reception."

As was always the way with these things, the topic of conversation at the reception moved away from expressions of condolences and talk of Adam to more mundane and less emotionally distressing matters. Jokes were told, news was exchanged, and the children began to play among the trees, clambering over rocks, fording streams, shouting, teasing each other, and laughing.

Zosia drank cherry-flavored vodka and discussed with her brother what he had been able to uncover about Adam's death.

"Not much, I'm afraid," Ryszard said. "I've brought a copy of the report for you, but all it says is 'died in custody.' That's not supposed to happen anymore, but controlling the actions of those thugs is nontrivial."

Zosia nodded. "So, they never worked out who he was? It wasn't deliberate?"

"As far as I can tell, no. I can't dig too much without raising eyebrows."

"I understand. Thanks for your efforts on that day. I know you really stuck your neck out there."

"To no effect," Ryszard sighed. "By the time I traced him . . . I still don't know why they moved him around like that. Playing games, I guess."

"Any idea who was responsible?" Zosia asked slyly. "Any names?"

"You know they don't keep records of that sort of stuff. At least not where I can access it. We have the name of the interrogator, but judging from the report, it doesn't look like he was even there at the time."

"What about the body? Any hope of recovering that on a pretense?"

Ryszard shook his head. "Seems they disposed of it almost immediately. There'd be no way to dig it up without making a huge stink. I haven't even been able to locate which site they used and . . ."

"And?"

"It's been over a week, little sister. I don't imagine it was a pretty sight when they dumped it, and they won't have done more than throw it into a hole, probably with a few others. You don't want to see it."

"I suppose not," Zosia said distantly. "It's just that it feels so unreal like this. Joanna's convinced he just got lost. She's so convincing, she has me thinking maybe he's in a hospital with amnesia, or in a camp or something."

"Don't do that to yourself. He's dead. He was murdered. You have to accept it."

Zosia finished her glass and poured herself some more vodka. "I'll try."

Alex came over and kissed Zosia on the forehead. "How are you doing, honey?" he asked as he sat down. "My goodness but Joanna has grown!" he added before Zosia could answer. "She and Genia get along wonderfully!" he said, his eyes following his two granddaughters as they played together.

"Yes, it's too bad they only get to see each other on occasions like this," Ryszard commented. He lit a cigarette and sat back to watch his youngest daughter and his niece.

"Ryszard, you know that's discouraged here!" Alex chided, irritated by his own overwhelming craving for nicotine.

Ryszard shrugged. "Let them fire me."

"So, Dad, tell me," Zosia interrupted, "did you ever manage to wring more out of that chemical weapons stuff? Adam seemed pretty disappointed by the Americans' response."

Alex sighed. "It was a complete waste of time. We're still pushing, using some documents Ryszard acquired, but nothing'll come of it. That's pretty clear."

Ryszard nodded, still watching the two girls chasing each other in circles, flapping their arms like wings.

"So what are the Americans going to do with the information?"

"Keep it on file for leverage in negotiations," Alex replied mordantly.

"What?"

"They're keeping it secret from their own populace for some cack-arsed security reasons, or maybe it was to avoid embarrassing the Reich government or whatever. The upshot is they don't care to use it for publicity."

"I suppose it doesn't matter," Zosia said philosophically. "It's not the sort of thing we'd get a popular response to anyway."

"What do you think would get a popular response?" Alex asked.

"I don't know," Zosia said, looking thoughtful. "I really don't know. Whatever it is, it has to be a human issue, something they can feel in their hearts. No statistics, no technology, just something to make them care."

"Pictures from the camps? We've tried that," Alex said despondently.

"Too distant, anyway," Ryszard interjected.

"You're right. It has to be something they can identify with. And we have to be able to control the story from beginning to end—no meddling with the security agencies, no political quid pro quos. It has to be something we own," Zosia said.

"Sounds like what Adam was advocating," Alex commented.

Zosia nodded. "We discussed it. We both agreed, it should be completely public—no government involvement."

"So any secretly gathered information is out," Alex said.

"Yes, no secrets, no technology, nothing they can veto politically. I just wish I knew what it would be," Zosia sighed.

"If only we could get some defector to talk publicly," Alex suggested.

Ryszard snorted. "Not bloody likely. Any defector knows that would be suicide."

61

*I*T WOULD BE SUICIDE, Peter thought. Trying to leave would be tantamount to suicide. There would be no more second chances, they would kill him, and they would do it very, very painfully.

He put the kettle on and stared into the void of his future as he waited for the water to boil. Months had passed and still he slept on the floor of Uwe's room, still he was awakened at completely unpredictable hours of the night, and still he could not leave the house to meet his students or talk with his friends. And with the arrival of autumn, his last refuge, the garden, was winding down and his last excuse to leave his prison would evaporate with the coming of winter.

It was time to peel the potatoes, but he felt tired, so he decided to make himself a cup of tea before beginning. When the kettle screeched, he poured the water onto some tea leaves he had set aside the night before, stirred it around a bit, and then poured the tea from the pot into one of Elspeth's teacups. Then he gathered the potatoes and bowls and took them over to the table and sat down.

Elspeth came downstairs earlier than he expected and he groaned slightly but did not move. She was humming happily but interrupted herself as she saw him sitting down on her furniture. She glared at him meaningfully but he did not get up nor did he even bother to apologize.

She shrugged, apparently deciding to ignore his insubordination. "What's that?" she asked, walking over to the table and peering into the china teacup he was using.

"Tea," he replied tersely.

"You're out of tea."

"Kind of you to have noticed."

"Where'd you get it?" she asked accusingly.

"It's the leaves from the pot I made for you yesterday evening, *gnä' Frau*," he answered without looking up.

"Our leaves? You didn't throw them away?" Her voice conveyed shock.

"Obviously not, *gnä' Frau*."

"Used tea? That's disgusting!"

"I agree," he answered with irony that was doubtless beyond her.

"And my china as well!"

"What else am I going to use?" He finally looked up at her. "I don't own a teacup. I don't own anything."

"How dare you! You have forgotten your place, boy!"

"I know."

It was insufficient to mollify her, and she went to her little book and picked up her pen.

Without meaning to, he exclaimed, "Oh, for heaven's sakes, what are you doing that for? It's only some worthless, used tea leaves!" As he uttered the last words, he closed his eyes in chagrin, wondering what the outburst would cost him. He attempted to ameliorate the situation and, forcing a smile, added somewhat more diplomatically, "If you provided me with a cup and some tea of my own . . ."

She surprised him by interrupting to say, "All right. You can come out shopping with me and Teresa after our supper—perhaps I'll buy you something then." She placed her book back on its shelf without marking anything in it.

He should have been grovelingly grateful, but he wasn't, and it was all he could do to force a thank-you out of his mouth. He continued to peel the potatoes, setting the unblighted peels into a bowl of cold water so that they would keep and he could cook them later since they were a reasonable source of nutrients.

Elspeth continued to watch and was finally driven to ask, "Why are you putting the peels into water?"

"They'll compost better," he lied.

"Then why aren't you putting all of them in?"

Sighing, he scooped up the separated peels and dumped them in the water as well. "No particular reason," he answered tiredly, wishing her away.

She nodded and continued to watch, smiling at him fondly, and without even thinking, she brought her hand up to stroke his hair, sort of like petting a cat or a dog. She did not notice how he flinched when she touched him, nor did she know the self-control he used to keep from pulling away.

*　　*　　*

After the family's meal, Elspeth and Teresa went to the local shops to pick out some shoes and a few other items and took him along with them to carry the packages. Elspeth had intimated that she would not only buy a teacup and some tea for him but a bit of food as well, saying that perhaps that would improve his grumpy mood. The stores were not far and they walked along the pleasant tree-lined paths, stopped to watch the ducks in the pond, and continued on their little journey enjoying the rare September sunshine. Teresa was her usual impish self, and even Elspeth maintained her good mood, going so far as to direct a few comments about the weather and the flowers to him.

The shops faced inward, away from the street, and formed a sort of pedestrian square, which, at this time of day, was fairly empty. The nearest of the shops was the bakery. Peter cast a glance at it as he went by. He had learned that Roman had simply been transferred to another bakery across town where his experience was needed.

The shoe store was on the other side of the square, and they headed in that direction, veering from their straight-line path only enough to skirt around the war memorial in the center. As they crossed the plaza, they heard a patrolman shout out to a woman who was striding obliviously out of the square. She was dressed in the uniform of a *Zwangsarbeiterin,* and on the shoulders of her blouse could be discerned the patches that identified her as a domestic laborer.

"Halt! Halt or I'll shoot!" the patrolman shouted, waving his pistol around excitedly. He was young and looked thoroughly stunned that the woman seemed to be ignoring him. Her back was already to him and she simply kept on walking without taking any notice of his words. Peter wondered if she was committing suicide.

The three of them stood stock-still watching the drama unfold. The woman walked with a strange almost sideways gait, as if she were half limping. Peter thought he recognized her. He whispered, "No."

"Halt!" the patrolman shouted even more angrily. Then, without a further moment's hesitation he fired.

The woman spun around with a look of surprise and then crumpled to the ground, soaking the pavement in blood. Peter caught a glimpse of her face then.

Both he and Elspeth stared in silent amazement at the patrolman. Teresa retreated a step to stand closer to her mother; she looked repeatedly from the woman to Peter and back again as if making some mental connection. Elspeth put a protective arm around her daughter.

"I wonder why she didn't stop?" Elspeth finally breathed.

"She probably didn't hear him," Peter answered evenly. "She's nearly deaf. Her hearing was destroyed some years ago."

He heard Teresa repeat softly to herself, *destroyed,* as Elspeth turned and looked at him. "You knew her?"

He was watching the patrolman and his colleague as they approached the woman. He did not bother to look at Elspeth as he answered, "Sort of. I've seen her around, but I've never talked to her."

"Why would you?" Elspeth asked. "What could you possibly have to say to each other?"

He turned to look at her then, but she met his glare with innocent superiority. He realized that she had no conception of their lives, and unable to answer her question, he turned back to look at the two patrolmen as they rolled the woman onto her back.

"I wonder who'll compensate her people," Elspeth mused.

Peter felt sick to his stomach. The woman's blood glistened in the sunshine, yet, other than for the patrolman and his partner, everyone else was beginning to return to his or her usual business, afraid that staring too long might be interpreted as criticism of the police action. He wanted to go to the woman to comfort her, yet he lacked the courage. He wished desperately that he had reacted more quickly when he saw her—maybe he could have saved her life.

As if to put an end to the scene, Elspeth sighed to no one in particular, "Rather unfortunate, isn't it?"

Her words washed over his grief, mocking him for his inaction. Before he could stop himself, he was saying, "You put children in uniforms, you arm them with guns, you fill their heads with lies and hatred, then when they murder someone in cold blood, you say, 'How unfortunate.' "

Elspeth drew herself up and said in her most aristocratic voice, "I'll pretend I didn't hear that." With that, she began to walk off, pulling Teresa along, expecting him to follow.

He stood his ground, calling out scornfully, "You never hear anything, do you? You don't see, you don't hear, you don't speak!"

She stopped and turned. Indicating to Teresa to stay put, she walked back to him, then using all her strength, she hit him as hard as she could across the face. There, in the plaza, in public, in front of everyone.

"Keep your hands off me!" he hissed at her.

Elspeth was rubbing her hand, but she stopped when he spoke. Her eyes widened in surprise, then narrowed threateningly. "What did you say?"

"I said . . ."

Teresa was staring at him, shaking her head slightly, pleading silently, *No!*

He became aware of the other people in the square—the two patrolmen, in particular, had looked up from their work and were watching to see what happened next. He shifted uneasily, scanning the familiar plaza as if it were alien to him.

"What did you say?" Elspeth demanded.

Some of the people were staring at him, but nowhere was there the face of an ally. He was alone, as alone as the woman whose corpse now marred the pristine plaza. He met Elspeth's hard look, but it was too late; he had lost this battle years ago.

Defeated, he dropped his gaze miserably to the ground. "I said . . ." But still the words stuck in his throat. He continued to stare at the ground beneath her feet, at the earth that he wished would simply swallow him up. He swallowed and tried again. "I said, please forgive me, *gnädige Frau*," he whispered.

"I didn't hear that."

He took a deep breath and tried to speak louder. "I said, please forgive me, *gnädige Frau.*"

"I thought that's what you said," Elspeth sneered.

He looked up then, his eyes taking in her triumphant look, the woman's blood as it spread on the ground, Teresa's fearful expression.

If it would be suicide, then so be it.

62

PETER TRIED NOT TO watch too closely as Uwe drank the hot, sweet tea he had prepared. Uwe slurped noisily, downed the last drops, apparently not noticing the combination of his own pain pills and Elspeth's sleeping pills that had been dumped into it. When Uwe finished, he yawned and set the cup down on the tray. Peter picked up the tray and asked if there was anything else he could get him. When Uwe said no, Peter left, promising to return in a few minutes to check that everything was all right.

Once he was in the hallway, out of Uwe's sight, he stopped to gather himself. He leaned against the wall, breathed deeply, and wiping the sweat off his palms, returned to his normal routine.

Ulrike was next. As he entered her room, she looked up from her book and studied his face. He thought for a moment that he had somehow betrayed himself, that she could read his intentions in his face, but then she said, "I can't decide which civic service to join once I graduate from high school. It's all so confusing!"

He sighed his relief and silently derided himself for being stupid enough to think that anybody would notice what was on his mind. In nearly three years nobody had ever taken even the slightest notice of his physical state, not to mention anything as ephemeral as his moods or feelings. He acknowledged her unstated question by saying, "Yes, it's a big decision, isn't it?"

"Do you have any suggestions?"

"I don't think it would be appropriate for me to advise you."

She sighed with exasperation. "Nobody wants to help. I wish I had some idea what I want to do!"

"Maybe you could find a service that does acts of kindness for poor, dumb animals," he offered with subdued irony.

She cocked her head at him as if trying to determine if he was serious, then she shrugged and went back to reading her book.

He collected her cup, and as he left the room, he risked saying, "Good-bye, Ulrike."

"Good night," she called back absentmindedly.

As each member of the family retired for the night, he breathed a small sigh of relief. So far so good. Elspeth and Karl were the last to turn in, just after eleven. He returned to Uwe's room and checked on the effect of his ad hoc concoction. He was pleased to see that he had not accidentally killed Uwe and that the boy was sleeping soundly. He went back downstairs and collected Karl's satchel from the hall closet. Then he went to the kitchen and opened the pantry. He selected some supplies and several useful items from around the house and placed them in the satchel; he debated for a second and decided to add several personal items: the handkerchiefs Teresa had given him, the hair he had removed from the chair, and finally, the book from Karl's study that had survived confiscation.

He unlocked a desk drawer and removed the packet of documents that pertained to him. He did not know what purpose they might serve, but since it contained his history, he felt they belonged to him. Satisfied with what he had packed, he placed the satchel by the back door. Grabbing his jacket, papers, and the morning pass, he stuffed them into the bag as well. If his absence was noted early in the morning, it would look as if he had simply gone to fetch the bread. The extra minutes that could afford him might well save his life.

After he had packed his supplies, he stood by the steps and listened for the sound of anyone stirring. All was quiet, so he proceeded to the desk and dug out the masking tape. Carefully, he wrapped the tape around his wristband to prevent the metal from reflecting light and rousing suspicion, and then he shoved the band as far up his forearm as it would go and taped it into place. He decided against trying to cover the numbers on his left arm. If anyone got as far as having him roll up his sleeves, then . . . He decided not to pursue that line of thought.

Once he had finished preparing everything downstairs, he returned to Uwe's room and rested on his rug. It had been a long day, fraught with the fear that he would betray his intentions. Earlier in the day Elspeth had raised her hand to strike him, but he had impulsively reached up and caught her wrist in an iron grip. The look of shock on her face had been priceless. After just a second he had released her, but her fist had remained stuck in midair. He'd taken a step backward, and as she still did not react, he'd turned and walked away before she could reconsider her leniency. It had been, in retrospect, one of the stupidest and riskiest actions of his life: to have waited so long and borne so much just to betray himself at the last minute! Fortunately no ill had come of it. Elspeth had grown tolerant since their confrontation in Uwe's room and chose to ignore his ill-considered action.

After about an hour, he got up and gathered the clothes he had selected from

Uwe's closet and placed them in the kitchen, near the back door so he could change into them just before he left the house. Returning to the first floor, he listened outside of Karl and Elspeth's room. There was no sound. Carefully, grimacing with tension, he bent the door handle downward. Although they rarely locked their door—that would necessitate getting out of bed in the morning to let him in—he had, to be on the safe side, disabled the lock earlier in the day. He had also oiled the hinges, and the door opened smoothly and quietly under his gentle guidance. He slid into the room and waited there in the darkness, listening to the steady rhythm of their breathing.

After a few minutes had passed, he crept across the room and lowered himself to the floor by the bed. Karl snored lightly a few inches away; the bedside stand beckoned. He waited another moment to make sure that they were still deep in sleep. Karl stirred and groaned in his sleep. Elspeth awoke and sat up.

"Karl, Karl, did you hear something?"

Karl mumbled something unintelligible and rolled over. His arm dropped over the side of the bed, dangling a few inches above Peter's nose. Peter lay as still as he could next to the bed, his heart pounding so loudly he felt sure Elspeth would hear it.

Eventually, Elspeth decided nothing was amiss and lay back down. Stuck there on the floor, Peter could do nothing more than stare at the hair on the knuckles of Karl's hand and wait. It took an eternity for Elspeth's breathing to become regular, and then Peter waited another quarter of an hour to be sure she was truly asleep.

Carefully, quietly, he reached up and tugged gently on the drawer of the bedside table. It did not move. He had expected that; he had seen Karl unlock the drawer in the morning once or twice, and he imagined Karl locked the drawer at night and slept with the key in his pajama pockets. Peter pulled out his lock pick and began work. He had opened the lock numerous times, but had never done it with Karl's hand dangling in front of him nor from as awkward a position as he currently was in. He swore silently as sweat dripped down his face. His palms were slick and the pick slipped from his grasp, clanging against the polished wood floor.

"Karl! Did you hear that?"

"No! Now go to sleep and leave me alone," Karl replied groggily, but then decided to get out of bed anyway. Peter only just managed to slide under the bed as Karl's foot landed heavily on the floor. He watched from under the bed as Karl went into the bathroom and returned moments later. The springs pressed perilously close to him as Karl dumped his massive frame back into the bed.

Peter waited again. They both fell back asleep relatively quickly, and this time he decided not to waste any more time waiting. He grabbed the pick off the floor and unlocked the drawer. At this point he was obliged to sit up so that he could see inside. Karl and Elspeth looked deep in sleep so he slid the drawer silently open. Inside were Karl's papers, his gun, and his car keys. Peter removed them,

took a moment to relock the drawer, and crept out of the room with his treasures.

Once he was back downstairs, he took a moment to look at Karl's papers. He
had checked yesterday—while Karl was bathing—that the photograph had not
been updated, but before he bet his life on it, he wanted to be sure that he bore at
least a passing resemblance to Karl's old picture. The cold eyes stared lifelessly at
him. He pulled his face into as arrogant and disdainful an expression as he could
muster, glanced in the mirror, and nodded with satisfaction. Yes, he could do it—
at a glance, at night, they looked the same. In fact, he probably looked more like
Karl's old picture than Karl did. What a charming thought! As for the fingerprints, well, there was nothing he could do about those, except hope that they
would not be checked.

He tucked away the documents and quickly changed into Uwe's clothes. The
boots were the hardest and he cursed and swore quietly as he tried to force them
onto his feet. Although the boots Frau Reusch had given him were old and quite
worn, he packed them in the satchel—they fit much better than Uwe's boots, and
once he was safe somewhere, he might need them. Fully dressed, he took a
moment to inspect the result in the hall mirror; satisfied, he then went to the
back door, ready at last to leave forever. As he placed his hand on the bag, a voice
like a Klaxon cried out his name.

It was Gisela. He cursed his bad luck. His name was called again. It would
wake the whole house! Instantly he made his decision. Stripping off Uwe's jacket
as he went, he bounded up the steps to the second floor. He arrived in Gisela's
room just as she was preparing to call him again.

"Gisela! What do you want? What is it?" he panted. The run up the steps had
aggravated the leg injuries that Karl had inflicted months ago, and he had to struggle to keep his voice from betraying the pain he felt shooting through his bones.

"I want a glass of water."

He restrained an urge to tell her she was quite old enough to get her own
water and said instead, "All right, I'll be right back."

He brought back a glass of water and a pitcher and placed it by her bed.
"Here. I've brought you a whole pitcher so you can get yourself some water
whenever you want. Are you okay now?"

She nodded as she brought the glass to her lips, but there were tears in her eyes.

He sighed and stooped down so he could be near her. "What is it, little one?"

"I had a bad dream."

It was always the same. No one else came when she called them, so she called
him. Water, a blanket, close or open the window, whatever the excuse, the reason
was always the same. "Tell me about it," he said gently as he seated himself next to
her bed.

She told him her dream and he assured her everything was all right. He kissed
her good-night and then held her hand until she fell back asleep. When she was
finally asleep, he released her hand and stood quietly. How much time had he lost?

"Peter?" Teresa's voice called softly from behind him.

"Yes, it's just me. Go back to sleep."

"Those aren't your clothes."

"No, they're not," he replied forlornly. He could not think of any plausible reason for wearing Uwe's clothes, so he did not try to explain. A thousand options crossed his mind, but none seemed particularly hopeful. His plans were like sand running through his fingers. Would it all fall to pieces so easily? He sighed and walked over to her and squatted by the edge of her bed.

"Are you leaving us?" she asked simply.

He stroked the hair back from her forehead. "Yes, I'm going."

"Where will you go?"

"I honestly don't know. There's nowhere safe for me."

"Peter, they'll kill you!" she said, frightened. "I'm scared!"

"I'm scared, too."

"They'll catch you and they'll kill you!" she predicted.

"I know."

"Don't do it then, don't go. Put everything back the way it was. It's not too late!"

"I have to go."

"But we need you!" she pleaded.

"I have to go."

"But they'll kill you, you know that! Suicide is wrong!"

"So is slavery. I used to be a real person, now I do nothing but try to stay alive. I've endured unspeakable torture, I've obeyed ridiculous commands, I've become . . . I hate what I've become. You know what's going on here. You know what's expected of me. I can't be a part of this anymore."

Teresa considered his words for a moment and finally seemed to accept them. "Don't let them kill you," she whispered.

"I'll do my best."

Teresa's eyes strayed from his face to the other bed, to little Gisela now sleeping peacefully. "Don't worry about Gisela. I'll take care of her tonight." She looked solemnly into his eyes, then she added softly, "Good luck."

"Thanks. I'll need it."

"Good-bye, Peter."

"Good-bye, Teresa." He kissed her forehead lightly. "Change the world."

"I will."

63

*H*E SLIPPED OUT INTO the darkness of the night. It was foggy and drizzling, he could not have asked for better weather! The car slid quietly out of the suburban street onto a larger road heading away from the center. Within minutes he had no idea where he was, but he drove steadily, turning each time he reached a larger road. Eventually he saw a sign to the autobahn, and he turned onto the access road without a thought as to where it would lead other than that it would lead him away, toward freedom.

At the bottom of the ramp was a red light and an officer huddled in a tiny booth. The officer emerged as he stopped the car.

"Heil Hitler!"

"Heil."

"Good evening, *mein Herr*. Your papers?"

He handed them over wordlessly. He knew that if the officer accepted him as Karl, then all would be fine; Karl's papers allowed him a rare and enviable freedom of movement. To distract himself, Peter studied the drizzle as it accumulated on the windshield.

The officer perused the papers quickly. Then, as he handed them back, he said, "Very good, *mein Herr,* have a good journey!" He sneezed as he returned to his cubicle.

Peter hesitated a moment. Was the light supposed to turn green? After a few seconds he decided that it was better not to wait, and he drove off and joined the autobahn traffic. He sighed deeply and wiped the sweat off each hand in turn.

The road headed east, and without deciding anything, he followed it. It was nowhere near as empty as he had expected—there were a surprising number of trucks and he decided to casually attach himself to a long convoy of them as they rumbled eastward. When his vision blurred, as it often did, he could follow their taillights, and if there were roadworks or detours or other hindrances, they would be likely to know of them in advance and avoid them.

Time passed quickly, and he drove as if mesmerized by the blurred lights and swishing noise of the wheels rushing through water. He lit one of Karl's cigarettes and began to relax a bit; minutes later, without warning, the traffic slowed and he peered ahead to see why. It was hard to discern anything through the misting rain, but the sudden brightness ahead warned him he was entering a floodlit area. There was nowhere else to go, and inhaling the smoke deeply to calm himself, he slowed the vehicle and pulled into one of the queues. Ahead he could make out some sort of barrier, and it suddenly dawned on him: it was the border for the special administrative region of the capital city. He swore quietly, ground out his cigarette, and nervously lit another; the floodlights were inescapable, and in such light, no one would mistake him for Karl.

The cars inched forward; his heart thundered in his chest. The trail of smoke from his cigarette created a wild pattern in the air as it traced out the trembling of his hand. As each car approached the booth, he saw how the driver's and any passenger's papers were scrutinized, how the guard stared into each face, even making people who wore glasses remove them so his view would not be obscured. He decided then and there that if they wanted to arrest him, he would start shooting, aiming for anybody in a uniform. It would be unfair since nobody but young kids would be on duty at this time of night, but he could not face either alternative of suicide or capture. He would shoot until they killed him.

At last it was his turn. The tired-looking guard leaned out of his booth and asked to see his papers and registration. He asked politely—obviously the car impressed him. Peter brusquely handed over everything that remotely pertained to him or the car as if he were too important to bother to sort out which papers were the needed ones. He then threw his head back with bored disdain and let out a stream of smoke, watching distractedly as it bounced off the roof of the car. The guard fanned through the papers quickly and handed them back wishing him a good journey. The other vehicles had taken minutes, but his inspection had lasted less than thirty seconds!

He drove on, congratulating himself on the impressive vehicle that he drove. Oh, God, if only his luck might hold! He stomped out any flicker of a thought of what might happen if it did not and went blindly into the darkness ahead, not daring to think of where he was going, fearing that if he did, panic would send him fleeing in terror back to the safety of his prison.

A while later, he noticed his petrol gauge was perilously low: he would either have to fill the tank or abandon the car soon. He saw a station shortly afterward, but decided to drive past it, since they would doubtless scrupulously obey the rules, check and note his license number, and cross-reference them to the ration coupons. That would not be a problem now, but it would leave a clear trail. He exited the highway and searched the main roads of a small town for an open station. It was in vain: he only found one station and it had closed at five o'clock.

He decided he would have to head back to the station he had seen on the highway as they were too few and far between for him to try to find the next one. He reentered the highway, again passing through a checkpoint effortlessly, and headed west. The signs advertised Berlin ahead, and he shuddered as the car passed under each. Damn! What a waste of precious time! Over and over he heard the advice: *It's not too late!* He was already heading in the right direction to preempt his suicide, shouldn't he just go home? Back to safety and security and obedience. He grit his teeth and shook his head to dispel the alien voice that pressed him to return to his duty. *The price of disobedience . . .* No! he yelled silently into the darkness. I am free!

The petrol station he had seen slid by on his left, and he swore at himself angrily as he realized that there was no access to it from the westbound side of the road. Luckily, there was another station a few kilometers on, and he stopped there. As the sleepy attendant emerged from the booth, Peter wondered to himself why he had not thought to siphon gasoline from a neighbor's car before he had left. Clearly, any ability at strategy that he had once possessed had been knocked out of him by years of abuse. He wondered idly, as he sized up the attendant, if he had lost his ability to act as well. Well, now would be a wonderful time to find out.

"Good evening, *mein Herr*. How much gasoline would you like?"

"Fill the tank. Here are the coupons."

"And your registration and license, *mein Herr*?"

"Ah, yes, of course." Peter held them in his hand to show the man that he did indeed have the relevant documents, but instead of handing them over, he tapped them lightly against the doorframe. "I'm on official ministry business and it would be better if it were not known that I was in this area at this time. You would be greatly inconveniencing your government, and of course, eventually, yourself, if you were to follow routine procedure. On the other hand, you would be obeying your government's imperative needs if you were to accept this note in lieu of the information you need for your books." He allowed a thousand-mark note to emerge from under the registration. His instinct had argued for simple bribery, but having watched Karl in action on several occasions, he had learned that including a government threat and an implication of following orders was advisable.

The note slipped out of his hand.

"Of course, *mein Herr*." The attendant filled the tank and immediately disappeared into the station without even glancing in the direction of the car's license plate. Better not to know. As the sleek foreign car sped off into the night, the attendant wondered if the lady was really worth so much trouble. Then he set about cooking the books a bit to make sure the gasoline would not be missed. The extra ration coupons would come in handy. And a thousand marks! Oh, what a great night!

The next junction was an intersection with another autobahn, and Peter decided to take this road rather than retrace his steps, thus avoiding exiting and reentering the autobahn system. This one led to the southeast toward Breslau. As he drove on, the blankness of the night shrouded the unfamiliar countryside. He had an impression of woods and flatlands, but it was almost impossible to tell through the drizzle. His lights reflected in a hazy glare off the mist, illuminating the highway just in front of him as a wet ribbon leading to nowhere. The highway grew emptier, and as he glanced in his rearview mirror, he saw behind him a blankness as if his past were being swallowed into the fog.

He crossed the Neisse, and with the realization that it was now too late to return, he began to wonder if he had not made a mistake heading into unfamiliar territory. Surely he would have had a better chance if he had headed west—maybe eventually he could have managed the Channel crossing and found someone in England who would have given him shelter. Maybe Geoff, his old buddy from the labor camp. By now he was, no doubt, well ensconced in that village near Lewes that he had talked of so fondly. On the other hand, the situation always seemed so close to riotous in the East, perhaps he would be able to disappear into the chaos without difficulty? Well, he thought, the point was moot—he had let the first autobahn he had encountered make his choice for him. That and an empty petrol tank. He lit another cigarette and drove on.

As he skirted around Breslau, he had a thought that he should search out Herr and Frau Reusch. He discarded the thought almost as quickly as it came. If they still lived in the development east of Breslau, and if he could find them, he doubted that they could help him, even if they wanted to. And Maria would be utterly horrified to see him—she had made it abundantly clear that he had outlived his usefulness to her. No, better to stay away; he would bring nothing but trouble to their lives. Better to leave them in peace.

Shortly thereafter he crossed the Oder, near Oppeln, and came to another internal border. The drizzle had ceased and the fog had lifted. The officer who took his papers scrutinized them carefully. Peter had secreted the gun next to his seat, and now he pressed his hand nervously against it as he carefully held a bored, detached look on his face.

"You are a long way from home, Herr Vogel?"

Fearing that this was a lead-in to a more detailed inspection of his papers, one he could not afford, he summoned Karl's most peremptory tone and snapped, "That's none of your business!"

"Sorry, *mein Herr*. Have a pleasant journey, *mein Herr*," the officer replied obsequiously. As he watched the car speed away, he added with a sardonic laugh, "And if you don't want any warnings, I don't have to give you any, you arrogant son of a bitch."

As the border post vanished into the distance and his heartbeat calmed, Peter finally managed to pry his hand away from the gun. Each time, Karl's papers had worked like a charm. Ah, the magic of good papers! He felt loath to give them up, and for the first time he had some idea of why Karl fought so viciously to retain his position. And the car, too! Such a fine machine! It would be a shame to dump it in a lake. Maybe he could find some way to keep it. He mused about this for some time as he sped along the nearly empty road. The surface had grown worse and the car jolted now and then—just as well, it helped keep him awake. On the left he saw a glowing region of the sky and he thought it was sunrise, but then he realized it was just the indistinct glow of an industrial region. The air took on a fetid smell, and the trees along the edge of the road, outlined against the industrial fires, looked leafless and dead.

Once he had passed through the worst of the smog, he washed the windshield and marveled at the muddy residue that was swept to the sides and dribbled off the edge of the window. Whatever was in the air had left a foul taste in his mouth, and he reached for the bottle of water he had in his satchel and drank it down. Out of curiosity, he wound down the window and reached out and dabbed his finger in a bit of the accumulated slime. He inspected it and determined it had a burnt orange color, then he brought it under his nose and sniffed, but did not recognize it.

Traffic began to pick up in the predawn darkness, and he considered how he might just merge with the vehicles and go wherever they went. They all had destinations, surely he could just follow one of them and let fate decide what happened next.

Such insane thoughts! He shook his head—it was time to make the decision he had put off since he had chosen this road. Should he head for the anonymity of a city? Or the isolation of the mountains that he knew lay to the south? The mountains were an unknown: he had no idea how to live off the land. It would soon be October, and the nights would be bitterly cold. In fact, that thought had occurred to him before he had left, but he had deliberately ignored the difficulties it had implied because he knew fixating on the details was what had kept him trapped for so long. If he had waited until spring, he would have waited forever.

The other possibility was a city; he was more comfortable with that idea since he had an innate understanding of patrols and papers and life among the crowds. But what about the car? Could he sell it? The money would be enormously useful. Yet the mountains offered a hope of freedom and isolation. He could be alone, truly alone! He could leave the car in the woods and make his way on foot to civilization.

Suddenly he hissed at himself with exasperation. What was he thinking? He could never buy enough papers to cover his numbers! How could he forget that? Society would never be an option—he was marked for life! He sighed at the muddiness of his thoughts—was this the way he had been thinking all along? Or was it just fatigue? His vision had grown blurry, and his head ached with a dull roar. It was getting near dawn, and he was almost falling asleep at the wheel; he pulled out another cigarette and was surprised to see it was his last. An entire pack? No wonder he was so jumpy. He squinted and blinked in a vain attempt to focus his thoughts.

A nebulous panic began to develop as he realized he had reached that point in his plans beyond which he could not see. He had headed out of a fog into a fog with nothing but the path in between illuminated. He had not expected to get this far, and he had left Berlin in the sure knowledge that his destination had to be irrelevant, that as soon as he worried about it, he would be trapped into inaction.

He sighed. The mountains would be good. He would dump the car and start walking. Maybe then something would suggest itself. Live off the land? Try to find the Soviet border? Head for a village and seek help among the natives? Locate some partisans? Whatever. Surviving two or three more days might be the limit of what he could reasonably hope for. Three days of freedom; that was all he would ask for. It would be enough.

═══════ **64** ═══════

*H*E EXITED THE PATHETIC road that the vaunted autobahn had become and headed south deeper into the rolling hills toward the mountains that had emerged with the morning light. He passed through tidy Bavarian-style villages, each oddly accompanied by a miserable shantytown a kilometer or so down the road. The villages looked weirdly out of place, and he noticed on closer inspection that many of the buildings simply had Bavarian mountain-chalet façades stuck onto preexisting structures. The strange architecture, combined with the gray light of dawn, gave the entire region a surreal quality as though he had driven into a gingerbread nightmare.

People were already emerging from the hovels of the shantytowns and trudging along the road toward the fields; they scuttled out of his way as he drove his car along the broken pavement. Peasant workers or slave laborers going to work in the fields: Poles, probably, or maybe Czechs or Slovaks if he had wandered across an old border. Or denizens of a work camp. Or possibly an entirely transplanted population. He wanted to stop and ask them some questions, but he noticed overseers nearby, so he decided not to risk their lives with his interest.

He studied them as he drove along. Despite the cold predawn damp, most were barefoot. The women wore heavy skirts and oversize blouses and had all tied their hair back with scarves; the men had tattered trousers and wore woolen caps. All touched their forehead or lifted their caps in an unthinking salute as he drove slowly past them. He tried not to wince as the gesture was repeated over and over—he had so hated doing that! Most did not look up at him. Some did though—their faces were a mask of oblivious exhaustion. Many limped; most had that malnourished and emaciated look that comes from a lifetime of hunger: the sunken eyes, the absent expression.

They looked weak, diseased, and inferior; their miserable existence condemned them to be exactly what their oppressors claimed they were—incapable of anything more than mindless physical labor. His heart went out to them; he knew what it meant to be robbed of so much, to be so oppressed that he became ashamed of the truth in the insults hurled at him. The times he had shaken with fever while listening to Elspeth berate him for his weakness. Or how she had petulantly ordered him to shut up when he coughed uncontrollably. Or called him stupid when he was too exhausted to think. The humiliation he had felt when his strength failed him as he lifted those countless drums! How he had bowed his head in shame when Karl had called him a cripple because the bones of his legs had been fractured. Or sneered that he stank from his long day's labor. He wanted to stop and tell them: I'm not one of them, I haven't done this to you!

But of course, he drove on in silence, ignoring the salutes, ignoring the occasional sparks of hatred that he ignited with his unwanted presence.

He left the workers behind as the car entered a woods and the last of the villages disappeared from view. He drove for miles with no sign of life anywhere along the road. The trees closed in and the road narrowed as it continued inexorably uphill. After a while he saw a smaller road off to the side, and on an impulse he turned onto that. He was forced to drive slowly as the rough surface of the road twisted and turned, heading deeper into the mountains. Miles passed without a single sign of habitation. Nothing, no one, just the road and the trees. As the car jolted around one particularly nasty turn, a small roadside shrine came into view. The sight shocked him—not that the statue that had sat upon its altar had been hammered into hundreds of pieces and the structure itself was pockmarked with bullet holes, but rather, that fresh flowers were lying at the base of the shrine.

Farther along, on his right, he spotted a small, rutted dirt track. It may once have been a logging road, but now it was clearly unused and almost completely overgrown. He forced the car onto the track and decided to proceed as far as possible. Once the car was stuck, he would cover it as best he could and abandon it. With luck, it would not be discovered until long after he had left the area.

The car continued to inch forward; after the first half kilometer, the track was in much better shape than it looked. It seemed that under all the brush and mud there was a gravel base that prevented the tires from slipping or getting stuck. He began to wonder if he should just abandon the car anyway since by now he was sure his absence had been detected and Karl would have discovered that his papers and car had been stolen as well. He imagined the initial confusion followed by Karl and Elspeth's fury as they berated and blamed each other. He laughed quietly to himself as he saw their anger die down only as they realized they were hungry and there was no bread for breakfast. He could envision them yelling confused orders and struggling to determine who should do what and when to cope with all the morning's routine before they would even think to call the police. He did not know, but would not have been surprised to learn, that Teresa swore to her parents that he had brought water to Gisela just before dawn, and that consequently, she was sure he had been in the house only an hour or two earlier. The authorities were notified accordingly, and Teresa smiled to herself at the farewell gift she had given him.

The vehicle plunged through some low-hanging branches. As the view cleared, a German soldier appeared pointing his automatic rifle directly at him. Shit! Where the hell had he come from? Had some border been crossed? Or had he stumbled into some secret military installation? Was that why it was so devoid of life? Damn! So close and yet . . .

His grip on the wheel tightened and he cursed quietly to himself. The car lurched to a stop and the soldier approached menacingly.

"Get out of the car!" the soldier ordered.

That suited him just fine—there was no way he could hope to escape in the car as the going was too slow. He noted that the soldier's automatic rifle had slipped a bit and was now pointing at the windshield. He emerged and pointed his Luger at the soldier's chest.

"Drop your weapon!" Peter commanded. He knew it was a mistake not to shoot the soldier immediately, but the boy was so young and looked so inexperienced that he decided to try to avoid having to kill him. The youngster stared at him in surprise and let the muzzle of his gun drop a bit farther so that it was nearly pointing at the ground, but he did not release his hold on it.

Although Peter was sure his absence had been detected by now, it seemed unlikely that this soldier in this remote location would be aware that his car was stolen or that he was an escapee. He decided to continue his masquerade as Karl. "How dare you interfere with a government minister on official business!" he barked angrily.

This did not have the desired effect of immediate apologies and docile obedience. Instead the boy's face lit up as though he were privy to a surprise.

"Drop your gun!" It was a female voice and it came from behind. A woman? Something was not right here. Peter calculated quickly: he could duck and shoot the boy, and with some luck he could swing around and aim at the woman before she managed to fire a second shot at him. Chances were that he and the boy would end up dead and the woman would be wounded at the very least. His promise to himself never to be taken prisoner again argued against his urge to avoid a senseless waste of lives. And his intuition insisted, something was not right here.

Peter sighed, dropped his gun, raised his hands, and said, "Don't shoot." He fervently hoped his intuition was right.

"*Babciu!*" the boy exclaimed happily.

"Shut up!" the woman ordered, apparently angry at his breach of discipline.

The boy, looking abashed, obeyed, and taking a precautionary step backward, he raised his rifle and pointed it determinedly at Peter's chest. "If you move, you're dead."

Babciu? Peter's hopes rose. If only he could keep them from killing him long enough to find out what was going on. A woman's hands frisked him, found his papers, and removed them. She stepped around in front of Peter, picked up his gun, and confronted him. She was an older woman at least a head shorter than he—her black hair was threaded with silver, her face was lined, but her brown eyes were alight with a passionate fire. Like the boy, she looked healthy and well fed—not at all like the gaunt remnants of humanity he had encountered on the road. She was wearing dark trousers, a nondescript shirt, and heavy hiking boots. She had a rifle slung over her shoulder, and a small radio and a knife in her belt. Pointing the gun at him, she ordered him to move away from the car.

He did; the boy's rifle rotated to follow him. Still holding the pistol, the woman scanned the inside of the car. She pulled the satchel off the front seat and rooted around inside. She ignored the documents, books, and clothes—apparently they were not what she was looking for. Satisfied that his bag contained no obvious threats, she placed it a careful distance away and dropped to the ground and inspected underneath the car, then reached inside and checked under the seats and in the glove box. After that she removed the keys and opened the hood. Once she had checked under the hood and in the trunk, she shoved the keys in her pocket, tucked the gun into her belt, and began perusing his documents.

"Interesting, interesting," she muttered sardonically. "You're quite a big official, aren't you?" She turned a page. "And quite far from home, eh?" She turned another page, studied the photograph, and then studied his face. "You don't look much like your picture, do you?"

"No. It's not me." With that answer, he destroyed any hope of his being kept alive as a hostage. He hoped instead that immediate honesty would work to his advantage.

"Of course not. And the car is not yours either?"

"No."

"So, you are a thief?"

"I guess you could say that," he agreed nervously. If they decided he was valueless, their most sensible course would be to shoot him then and there.

"What are you doing here?"

"Escaping. I am, was, a slave laborer."

"Oh, really?" She looked dubious. "But you are German."

"No, I'm English—my papers are in that bag," he said, gesturing with his head.

"You idiot! Do you think we don't know the English aren't used that way?"

"Some are. I have criminal convictions."

"For stealing cars?" she asked with a smirk.

"No. Please don't shoot me. Let me explain."

The woman pursed her lips, stared in silence at him for some moments. He knew she was deciding whether to kill him. He knew he was asking her to take an enormous risk, and he was unsure what he himself would have done in her position.

Suddenly she asked, "Why did you not kill the boy immediately upon emerging from the car?"

"I hoped to avoid hurting him."

"Or you thought he would lead you to our encampment?"

"No. I thought he was a real soldier."

She nodded noncommittally.

"Can I put my hands down?"

She nodded again. As he dropped his arms, the boy tightened his grip on his gun, raised the muzzle slightly to correct the aim.

"*Look at me!*" Peter pleaded. "Do I look like a Gestapo agent?" Carefully, so as not to excite the boy into action, he pushed up his left sleeve. "Look at this! Do their agents have numbers indelibly marked on their arms?"

The woman touched the numbers but did not say anything.

"If anyone knows English, I can prove my fluency to them. If you let me remove my jacket, I'll show you the manacle on my right wrist. I can show you scars from beatings I've received. Would any agent go through this effort to convince you?" He knew that, unfortunately, the answer to that question was yes.

She remained silent.

He began to feel desperate. "Oh, God, I haven't come this far to be killed by my own side, have I? Please, you've got to believe me. Give me a chance. I can be useful to you. Please."

"Useful?" The tone of her voice conveyed serious doubt.

"Yes, I know about German life, I can speak without an accent so I can pass for one of them." He had already noticed that neither the boy nor the woman had a discernible accent, and that puzzled him, but he did not have time to worry about that now. "And I can give you this car. I'm educated, I'm healthy, I can work—any sort of work, anything you want! Translations, manual labor, anything! I learn fast! And I know something about codes and strategy and . . ." And it was all wildly out-of-date. "I was in the English Resistance, maybe I can be of help to you," he finished lamely. Why in the world should they risk everything for a stranger? There was no proof he could offer them. Even if he could convince them that he really had been a slave laborer, he had no way to prove that he was not now simply being used as a decoy by the Gestapo. It was hopeless and the woman's face conveyed as much.

"You remind me of my son," she finally said.

He smiled slightly.

"He's dead," she added without emotion.

His smile faded. Had somebody in his cell taken a chance like the one he was asking this woman to take? Was that why they were all dead now? He sighed again. Anything he could think of saying sounded hollow. "If you kill me, you've become what you hate."

She shrugged. "We do what we must to survive."

He lowered his head so he could take a break from staring into the barrel of the automatic rifle. The exhaustion he had felt on the road crept up on him again. If only he could sleep. Finally, without really knowing why, perhaps it was simply to keep them talking to him, he said quietly, "If you do kill me, would you please bury my body? I don't want to be dumped in the woods like some piece of garbage. Maybe you could say a little prayer over the grave? I don't need a headstone or anything since anybody who might care about me is dead anyway." He looked around. "I know the ground is rocky here and it will be a lot of work . . ." If he could divert their attention a bit, then perhaps he could dive into the woods.

It was the woman's turn to smile. "Take off your clothes."

He looked at her in horror. "At least let me die with some dignity! They can't be that valuable to you."

His anger amused her and she laughed lightly. "No, it's not for the clothes. For some idiotic reason, I think I believe you. We won't kill you, at least not right now. All I want to do is check you for bugs or homing devices. You won't object to that will you?"

He didn't. He began by removing his jacket, his fingers fumbling nervously over the military-style buttons. He was not sure whether he should believe her, and his mind kept racing as he tried to think of something he could say to them, something that would convince them that he was genuine and that he was worth the risk of keeping alive. But nothing sounded right. He was tired, perhaps it would be just as well to lie down in the moss and let them blow his brains out—at least his last moments could be spent with the vision of the beautiful forest and the sweet smell of gentle autumnal decay.

He removed his shirt. The woman's eyes lit up with suspicion as the tape on his arm became visible. She stepped forward before he proceeded any further and unwound the tape herself; slowly, the gleaming metal of his manacle emerged. She turned his wrist and held it up to read the inscription and compared the numbers with those on his arm. "Why did you come here, into these woods?" she asked, letting his arm drop and taking a precautionary step back again.

"I chose them at random. I simply fled the city and drove as far as I could before dawn."

"At random?"

"Yes."

"Isn't that a rather idiotic escape plan?" she asked sarcastically.

"Maybe it was my version of Russian roulette—I like to load five chambers instead of one," he answered testily. "You just try and get the information I needed from where I was!"

She laughed. "So you just ended up here. Of all places."

"Clearly I had to end up somewhere. And don't tell me you weren't watching me from a distance. It wasn't so unbelievable that we happened upon each other. After all, *you stopped me*. If only you had watched a bit longer, you would have seen that all I wanted to do was dump the car. I took an exit off the autobahn and headed for the mountains. I thought I might find an old dirt track or even a lake into which I could dump the car."

She did not comment on his assertion; instead she asked, "Why would you want to dump such a nice car?"

"I could be traced to this area if it were found; you see, it belongs to the man whose papers I took." He hesitated, then added with quiet distaste, "The man who owned me."

"Why not head toward England? Why here?"

"The photograph," he said, indicating Karl's papers. "I could never have made the Channel crossing on those papers. And I figured that going to England is exactly what they would expect and that I'd soon be rearrested. It's not like I can ever return to a normal life, not with these numbers burned into my arm."

"They're not burned on," she said as if pointing out a flaw in his story.

"They are to me."

She nodded slightly, then she looked up at the trees and sighed, "What a world we live in!" She made a visible effort to regain her detachment before she ordered, "Finish undressing."

As he shivered in the cold autumn air with his hands on his head, the woman searched him thoroughly. She was gentle and asked his pardon as she invaded his privacy, but he could not help but notice that the muzzle of the automatic rifle never slipped from pointing directly at his heart. The boy's steely gaze held him fixed: he would not be fooled again!

When the woman had finished searching him, she ran her fingers gently over the wounds on his back, satisfying herself that they were real. "When did you get these?" she eventually asked.

"I don't know. I mean," he hastily added, "it depends on which ones you are referring to."

"So you have been beaten more than once?"

"Yes." Beaten, tortured, by more than one person, on more than one occasion. Why did it embarrass him to admit it? Why did he feel as if he had somehow failed?

The woman looked up at him; clearly this revelation, and the physical evidence, made his story more believable. She surprised him by saying, "I am sorry."

Before he could respond, she turned away and went to sit down by the pile of clothing he had left. The boy continued to hold him in his sights as the woman searched each piece. The thoroughness with which she inspected every seam and button implied that not only was she extremely experienced, but that the devices she was searching for were far advanced on the ones he had learned about so long ago in London.

She paused and looked up at him when she reached the waistband of his trousers. Before he could say anything, she slid the slim piece of metal out and inspected it. "A lockpick?"

He nodded. "Yes, I put it so that I could reach it even if my hands were cuffed to the front or the back."

"So you are not completely devoid of talents." She pocketed the lockpick, then continued her inspection. When she had finished, she handed him his clothes, but left the jacket, belt, socks, and boots to one side. She answered his questioning glance by saying, "They're too difficult to search by hand; we'll get to those and your bag later. You can walk barefoot for now. We'll finish questioning you at camp."

After he had dressed, she tied his hands behind his back and took a moment to inspect his gun before she handed it to the boy. He inspected the gun as well, checked the clip, and then slung his rifle over his back and pointed the pistol at Peter. They then set off into the woods with the woman leading the way, Peter in the middle, and the boy following, keeping his prisoner under constant guard.

They dove into the woods, ducking under saplings and trampling over roots and stones until eventually they turned onto a narrow trail. The rocks cut into his skin, the roots twisted around his ankles, loose stones slid out from under his feet, and with his hands bound behind him, each time he stumbled he had no real ability to recover his balance. He fell a number of times, crashing in an ungainly heap, twisting his ankles and bruising his shoulders painfully. Each time they waited patiently, but did not help as he struggled to his feet.

Their path wound up the slope; at points they turned from one path onto another; sometimes they left the trail altogether only to join another a few meters away. Each time they fought their way through the underbrush, Peter was scraped by branches and briers he could not hold out of the way. He tried to keep his head low and lead with his shoulders; nevertheless, his face was soon covered in scratches.

They took their time covering ground; frequently Peter and the boy would rest while the woman disappeared into the woods, presumably to check to see if they were being followed or observed. Nevertheless, Peter felt exhausted: his feet were battered and bruised and covered in mud, his face and arms were covered in scratches and insect bites, and his muscles ached from his numerous falls. He was shivering from the cold, he was hungry and thirsty, and he had an urgent need to urinate. Eventually he had to ask them if he could please stop to piss.

The woman held the gun on him while the boy helped him. Peter was beyond feeling humiliated though—it was such a relief to finally relieve himself! After he was done, the boy used the opportunity as well, and the woman laughed quietly at the odd camaraderie. The boy shrugged, said something to the woman in a language Peter did not understand, they both laughed, and then all three continued their march.

The ground became soft with moss and dead leaves. Birds twittered high above in the branches. The clouds had yielded to a brilliant blue sky, and whenever there was a break in the canopy, sunlight streamed down to the forest floor with a magical dappling of light. Eventually the path they were following dropped down to run along the edge of a small stream. The sunlight created fantastic patterns on the surface—a thousand diamonds dancing to the tune of the water bubbling over the rocks. Peter asked if they would stop for a moment so he could drink.

The woman and the boy waited patiently as he approached the stream and knelt in the shallow water. As he leaned forward, he had a sudden thought, and he straightened and turned to look at them. Why weren't they drinking? "Is this water safe?"

The boy shrugged. The woman pursed her lips, said, "I think so. Your folks— the Germans, I mean—have no access to its source."

He wondered at her slip of the tongue. Were they just taking him deeper into the woods to kill him? The path they had followed had seemed incredibly erratic, as if they were heading nowhere in particular. The water beckoned, his thirst overrode his concerns, and he leaned forward and drank deeply.

They continued along the stream for a long while. The ground was soft and felt good underfoot. Eventually, they came to a large fallen tree that spanned the creek. The woman leapt onto the trunk and began to cross. Peter stopped cold and considered what he should do next. If he slipped off the impromptu bridge with his hands tied behind him, he would probably break his arms falling onto the rocks, but it seemed unlikely that he could convince them to untie him.

The woman was already on the other side and eyeing him suspiciously. "What's the matter? Are you afraid of water?"

"No," he grated, and plunged into the stream. It was less than a meter deep and only about five meters wide, but it was still a challenge not to slip on the mossy stones. He dragged his elbow along the edge of the trunk to help stabilize himself and finally emerged on the other side, dripping wet, but none the worse for wear.

Once he was on the other side, the woman held his arm, guarding him so the boy could cross unhindered. When they were all together, she left the path and scrambled up the bank and up a bracken-laden hillside. Their progress sent up clouds of gnats, which hovered around their faces and seemed to be preferentially drawn to Peter's soaked clothing. He shook his head frantically from side to side to try to disperse them, but they clung to him. He coughed and spit as he realized several had gone into his mouth.

The woman, noticing the commotion, stopped and turned. She took the several steps back toward him and waved her hand wildly at his face. He threw his head back, flinching defensively, his instinctive response a split-second faster than his realization that she was swatting at the bugs. He reopened his eyes and grimaced with embarrassment at his display of fear. She gave him a long look but said nothing, turning instead to resume her climb.

Gathering himself, Peter followed, scanning desperately for any sign of a path. There was none as far as the eye could see. Nor was there any sign that anyone had recently trampled through the bracken. They were clearly breaking a new path. Where the hell were they going? He became increasingly convinced that they were leading him nowhere.

The bracken gave way to a steeper slope of mud and roots and an occasional sapling. The woman climbed up that as well, frequently using her hands to grab on to a root to pull herself up a slippery section. Peter struggled to follow. He wedged his foot into a root and leaned against the slope as he gasped for breath. Behind him he could hear the boy climbing. He looked back and saw the gun still trained on him. "Keep moving," the boy advised.

He continued his ascent. He wedged his foot against a sapling and pushed upward, his next goal a well-buried rock. He reached it, but as he put his weight on the rock, it worked loose and tumbled down the slope. For a few desperate seconds he dug his foot into the remaining dirt, but it did not hold and he went skidding and rolling down the slope.

He came crashing to a stop in the bracken. For a long moment, he lay still in his leafy green bed of ferns, staring up at the sunlight, letting the adrenaline drain from his system. Nothing broken, thank God, just a lot of bruises. Suddenly the sunlight was blocked by the looming shadow of the boy. It took Peter a moment to adjust his eyes, but eventually he could make out the silhouette of the pistol still pointed at him. He struggled to get to his feet, had managed to reach his knees by the time the woman approached. She had pulled her knife out of her belt and was skirting them both to come up behind him.

Peter knew she was fed up and had decided that they had come far enough. He knew she did not want to waste a bullet or risk the noise of a shot. They had brought him all this way with promises to hear him out, just to keep him quiet. They had brought him deep into the woods so they could abandon his body without its drawing attention, without them having to carry it off the road. They had brought him here so his corpse could rot in the sunshine, covered in flies, moldering beneath the bracken. They had brought him where there was no path, where no one walked, so that the stench would not trouble them.

She walked up behind him. He could feel her approach and bent his head forward in expectation of her hand on his hair, the pull that would drag his head backward and expose his throat. He wanted to fight, but he felt paralyzed with grief and frustration. He felt that he should at least climb to his feet—not die on his knees, but he could not move. He knew what would happen next. The knife cutting into his neck, a clean stroke, almost painless. Blood soaking his clothing, staining the leaves, seeping into the rocky soil, draining away without a trace. He would be able to watch as his life disappeared into the dirt, his exhaustion at last giving way to rest. A sudden dizziness made him want to pitch forward . . .

He woke from his daze as he felt the ropes drop off his wrists. The woman gathered the remnants and stuck them in her pocket. "Are you all right? Did you hurt yourself in that fall?"

Some basic instinct gave him the words to answer, "I think I'm okay. Just give me a moment to collect myself."

She pulled out a handkerchief, clambered down to the creek to wet it, and after she had climbed back up, she handed it to him. "Here, use this to wipe the dirt off your face. There's a bit of blood on your left cheek—you'll want to remove that as well."

He obeyed wordlessly, hardly able to comprehend what was happening. He was still alive! And she was showing him genuine kindness.

"Let's go," she said after a few minutes. "I'll have to retie your hands before we reach the camp, otherwise they'll think I've lost my mind taking such risks, but I really think this is the only way to make progress. Besides, I suspect you are thoroughly lost by now and couldn't tell anyone where you've been even if you did escape. Am I right?"

Peter nodded. He was still stunned by the vision he had had.

65

*T*HEY SCRAMBLED ON THROUGH the woods, heading ever upward, until eventually they began a descent into a valley. They crossed a small meadow and Peter breathed deeply the sweet smell of wildflowers and pine. A breeze stirred the upper branches and they swayed slightly, dancing from side to side, but below, the air was still and close. Once they reached the other side of the field and had entered the woods again, the woman stopped and turned to him. "I'm afraid I'll have to tie your hands now."

He nodded his understanding.

"And by the way, don't mention that I ever untied you," she added, taking in the boy with a glance to ensure that he had heard as well. The boy nodded and said something Peter did not understand.

"Don't ever assume that your language is not understood," the woman admonished in German.

Peter took the opportunity to ask, "Is it Polish?"

She gave him a sideways look, snorted with amusement. "So, he goes and disproves me, eh, Olek?"

The boy struggled to remain serious. "Perhaps it's all part of his clever deception."

"Yes, perhaps." Then she answered, "Yes, we're Polish. You are in that part of the Reich which was, for a thousand years, Poland. Is your history that weak?"

"No," he snapped, somewhat irritated, "I just drove without maps and without direction. And there is always the chance that the population of a region is completely transplanted or slaughtered. It has been known to happen, you know."

"Yes, I know. I'm sorry. I didn't mean to offend you." She finished tying his wrists behind his back and then led the way farther on through the woods. After a short time, they were suddenly met by an armed man. He appeared to be in his midfifties, heavily built, with thick brown hair and a bushy mustache.

"Was there a problem?" he asked the woman as he studied their bedraggled captive. He not only spoke in German, but he had a thick Austrian accent as well.

"No, no. But we'll need to have a meeting to decide what to do with him," the woman answered without even pausing in her stride. "Do you want a proxy?" she added over her shoulder, as though it were an afterthought.

"I doubt you'll finish that soon. If you do, I'll trust your decision."

"Fine."

"Is he Austrian?" Peter asked.

"No," the woman answered with a finality that said he could expect no more information for the time being.

They arrived at an encampment and he was led into a tent; it was well camouflaged and inside it was spacious and comfortably furnished. The woman left, leaving Olek to watch over him. Peter paced nervously and waited, wondering what was in store for him. Sometime later a young woman entered; she had a clipboard but seemed otherwise unarmed. She had honey blond hair, blue eyes, and exquisite high cheekbones; her hair was tied back with a ribbon, but untidy curls had freed themselves, framing her face in a golden halo. Untying the ropes on Peter's wrists, she then motioned for him to sit down. She indicated with a nod of her head that Olek should leave. He stepped outside the tent but remained stationed near the entrance.

"My name is Zosia," she said in English as she seated herself across from him. "Please don't try to leave this area; you will be shot if you do. And please don't consider taking me hostage. We don't believe in hostages, I'd just be shot along with you."

Momentarily stunned, he just stared at her. She reminded him of that woman who had winked at him at Elspeth's *Winterfest* party. Was it possible? Whether it was possible or not, he decided it was unwise to mention the incident: if he was wrong, he might offend her, and how could he admit he had used her in his fantasies for months afterward? Finally he stammered, "You, you speak English?"

"Obviously," she answered with a smile, then she explained, "My grandfather was a musician; he ended up in England and married an Englishwoman. My father was born and raised in England and grew up speaking English. He was, by all legal measures, British, but he was the son of a Polish immigrant. That was before the war."

"What happened?" Peter was already enchanted by her, by her soft, deep voice, by her obvious intelligence, and by her ready smile.

"After England was conquered he was 'deported' back to his so-called homeland—a place where he had never been, with a language he did not speak. He married here and raised all of us to speak English as well as German. I've maintained my fluency, since it is a useful skill."

"Just like speaking German without an accent?"

"Yes."

"But you are Polish?"

"Yes. My father named me Sophie—you know, wisdom—and he even spelled it like an English name. All my siblings have English names. I think he wanted us to be English or he was homesick, but we never saw the land, never heard the language except from him or occasional radio broadcasts; so, we are Polish and I am Zosia."

Peter was intrigued, but realized she had misinterpreted his question. "What I meant to ask is, you all here, at this camp, are Polish, right?"

"Mostly."

"But you all speak flawless German, and that boy, he was wearing a German uniform?"

"Yes. We fit in, as necessary. You see, we are very experienced in living an underground culture." She paused, pursed her lips, then added, "Perhaps too experienced."

"And now you are testing one aspect of what I told that woman—what was her name? Babciu?"

Zosia laughed. "Babcia," she explained, "means Granny. She's Olek's grandmother. Her name is Marysia." She smiled at him, then asked politely, "May I see your arms?"

He offered both to her, leaning toward her as he did so. As she leaned in to look closer, her hair brushed against his cheek, and he shuddered with pleasure and a sudden longing. She inspected the numbers on his left arm, then pulling a small bottle of solvent out of her pocket and wetting her thumb with it, she determinedly rubbed at the numbers, but of course they did not smear. Satisfied with her ad hoc inspection, she then looked at the manacle on his right wrist, read the information, and compared the numbers.

"Vogel? Is that what I should call you?"

"No! That's not my name; that was their name!" he answered vehemently.

Zosia raised her eyebrows but did not comment on his reaction. "Of course, their name was used for your identification."

"More for where I belonged. My number was my identity; my name only appeared as part of my history in the full documentation—that's in the satchel that was left with the car."

"I haven't seen that yet. What does it say?"

"Peter Halifax."

She made a note. "Ah, well, what we must do now, Peter . . . Can I call you that?"

Of course she was only asking, with a politeness he had not experienced in years, if she could use his first name. He liked the way it sounded when she said it, and making a quick decision to keep the name, he replied, "Yes, I guess it's my name."

She cocked her head questioningly at his unusual answer, but when he did not explain, she continued, "Marysia argued your case very convincingly. I guess she took a liking to you. Just as well, it's a dangerous idea that we would accept a total stranger from outside our lands into our midst." She got up and went to the entrance and said something to Olek, then reseated herself opposite Peter. "We must remedy that; so, tell me all about yourself. I will represent you to our group, and it is up to me to decide if you are telling the truth. Convince me."

He nodded. Even though it was an interrogation, one with life-or-death consequences, he found he enjoyed talking to Zosia. She had a businesslike manner, but still smiled easily. Somehow, she reminded him of Allison: her determination, her strength, but Zosia was so buoyant that in some ways she seemed to be the antithesis of Allison, almost an antidote. Encouraged by her smile and her relaxed manner, he began his story.

As he was talking, coffee and sandwiches arrived. He interrupted himself to sip the coffee, looked at Zosia in astonishment, and exclaimed, despite himself, "It's real!"

"But of course. We can manage lots of things. Coffee is easy. It's getting those damn invaders out of our country and stopping them from murdering our people which is proving difficult." The smile slid from her face and her look was momentarily distant, but then she collected herself and said, "Please, continue."

He told her everything, or almost everything, shying away, quite naturally, from anything that might be viewed too negatively. He told her about his childhood, about going to the school for German boys, about his parents and his years in the English Underground. For some reason, he did not bother to explain his work, simply describing himself as being in the intelligence branch.

Zosia did not press on any point; it seemed enough for him to simply pour out his heart. She took notes, jotting down names and dates, but sometimes she just listened as he told her all about the people and places and events. He told her about Allison and what happened to her. He poured out his love for her, his passion, his enduring grief. It was the first time since her death that he spoke of his bereavement and mourned her aloud. He told Zosia what had happened to his entire cell and all his comrades. He told her about his weeks trying to live without papers, about his arrest and trial and sentencing to the work camp.

"They threw me in with the normal draftees so conditions weren't too bad, but I was surrounded by a bunch of kids. After I arrived, I met a fellow who had a deferment and had already served three of his years so he wasn't quite as young as the others. His name was Geoff, and we eventually became friends." He watched as Zosia wrote down the name, then continued, "There were a few problems at first, mainly the fact that I didn't fit in. Not only was I older and spoke German far too well, but I even looked, well, as one of the boys put it 'like a German.' By that, I guess he meant I didn't have that pasty, undernourished look that comes from the awful diet most of them had as kids."

"And why not?"

"My father earned good money and my mother was a health nut. She spent a fortune on fresh vegetables and meat and the like. At my school, as well, despite everything else, I was well fed." He could not help himself from looking at Zosia's gorgeous curves, but he decided not to make the obvious comparison with the scarecrowlike beings he had seen earlier on the road.

"This was not altogether a good thing," he continued. "It took ages for me to dispel their resultant distrust, but I think, overall, it was an advantage. When I worked alongside the others, it always amazed me how the boundless energy of youth would give way under the strain of hard labor and poor nourishment. I really felt sorry for those poor boys struggling to fulfill their assignments. The guards harassed them mercilessly for their weakness, and I had to intervene time and again to get them to lay off. I suppose it was that, more than anything, that finally won me their trust and eventually their respect.

"I ended up essentially being the camp leader with Geoff being a sort of second-in-command. We arbitrated disputes, maintained an informal staff, tried to minimize the bullying, carried out negotiations with the *Kommandant*. I really didn't want the part, but it seemed the best way to keep things under control so I accepted the position and they accepted me. They even gave me a history. I didn't do anything to dispel their rumors since I was unable to provide a better story, and besides, wondering about my background seemed to provide the boys with some amusement. Eventually, with repetition, even Geoff became part of the story. I believe we were con artists of some sort, setting up wild schemes to defraud the krauts."

"Not so far from wrong. Why didn't you try to escape during this time?"

"I don't know," he answered with reluctant honesty. "I guess, at first, I was too devastated by all that had happened." He closed his eyes and thought about those years that had slipped by. "I felt sort of numb and uncaring."

Zosia wrote something down when he said this. He could not quite make out the words but he thought he saw "severe depression." He felt affronted, so he quickly added, "Besides, it was difficult and the penalties were high. In my case, as a convict, it was the death penalty."

"So you planned to sit out the full twenty years?"

"No. I was hoping for a reduction in my sentence." Then he added with a small laugh, "For good behavior."

Zosia saw no humor in his words but wrote something else. She looked up and asked in a businesslike tone, "What sort of work did you do at the camp?"

"All sorts of stuff. Usually some industry or farm rented our services from the government and so our treatment and conditions changed considerably from month to month."

"How long did you work?" she asked.

"Oh, the day usually ended around six o'clock. However, during the summer—"

"I meant," Zosia clarified, "how long were you in the camp?"

"Oh. Nearly four years. It was grim, but tolerable."

"You were well treated?"

He laughed. "I guess so, in comparison anyway. I saw some things, awful things. I saw a man, a *Zwangsarbeiter*, shot in cold blood, in a steel mill, because he had broken a bone. I . . . I wanted to help, but I couldn't, I was a prisoner, too."

Zosia tilted her head but remained silent.

"I, there were other things, too, in other factories, in . . . They didn't affect us, we were only draftees, so we weren't usually treated that badly, but the way they . . . It was the *Zwangsarbeiter,* the way they treated the *Zwangsarbeiter.* I thought, at the time . . . It was like they were different people, another species, almost like they couldn't feel pain, or had no lives of their own. I . . . After what happened to me later, after the factory work, I know better, I . . ." He paused, embarrassed by his sudden, confused confession. "I remember, when I was work-ing in a factory, these two officers, one of them tripped me. I swear he did it on purpose. I . . . they . . . I was beaten for that." He closed his eyes against the painful memory. "I don't know why they did that to me."

"What did they look like?"

"I don't know. I don't remember. I don't remember their faces. All I remem-ber is the uniforms and the way they joked with each other and . . ."

"And?"

"And the way they looked at me. It was just the way I used to look at others. Like I wasn't really there, or couldn't possibly understand what was going on. Like I was beyond hope."

"Everything in due course," Zosia said as if to steady him. "Back to the work camp. How was it there for you?"

"There? I felt secure there, even needed."

"Then what?"

He stared at the ground as if he had not heard her.

"Then what?"

"Hmm?"

"Then what?"

"Oh, then?" he asked as he began to pick at some dirt under a fingernail. "Then I attempted an escape."

"Why?"

"What do you mean 'why?' " he asked, moving on to the next nail. "I just did."

"Was it that you had seen too much?"

"Hmm? Oh, yes. That was it. I had seen too much," he answered distantly as he struggled with a particularly recalcitrant bit of dirt.

She shook her head. "There's more to it than that."

"No, really, I just had an opportunity, so I took it," he said, still concentrating on his fingers.

"You're lying."

"Lying?" He shook his head. "No, it's the truth."

"Don't play games with me. Why did you leave the work camp?"

"Does one need a reason?" he asked, forcing himself to look directly at her.

"After nearly four years, yes."

"It took that long to get over what had happened in London. I felt ready—"

"One last chance," she stated coldly.

He threw his hands up angrily. "I don't understand why I need a reason! I changed my mind about waiting it out. Wouldn't you try to escape?"

She stood up and headed toward the entrance.

"Don't go!" he pleaded.

She turned back to look at him.

He sighed, then said, "I found out something." Before she could prod him he continued, "You see, the boys are paid a wage during their conscription: half of their wage is doled out to them while they're working, the other half is saved up until their release. Out of the paid-out wages, they pay for their room and board and buy any of the so-called luxury items such as cigarettes or coffee. Naturally, the prices are set such that nobody saves anything. At the end of their six years, they get the lump-sum payment of the other half of their wages minus taxes, their round-trip fare, and any surcharges they have incurred. As you might well guess, it's a con game and it's not untypical for the boy to return home empty-handed for his six years of work."

Zosia returned to sit down next to him. "So?"

"Well, I was different. As a convict, I didn't merit a wage, nor was I charged for room and board. I figured I was on a different scheme and that was that."

"How did you buy your luxury goods?"

He laughed. "I was camp leader, remember. I assessed fines for misbehavior, and the others chipped in a bit now and then."

"You taxed them?" she asked, amused.

He nodded. "I guess you could call it that. Anyway, I figured prison was prison and after I did my time they'd release me with a hundred marks or something. But then, when I was working in one of the camp offices, I went through the files and found out I was being assessed all along. In other words, the longer I stayed, the greater my debt."

"So after you served your time, you'd be massively in debt to the camp."

He nodded. "Yeah, and the only way I could pay it off would be with my labor. That told me that my sentence was essentially a life sentence and that there was no hope of release other than escaping."

"I see." Zosia noted something down. "So how did you come to be in such a trusted position that you could snoop through their filing cabinets?"

He shrugged. "Somebody had to be assigned to clean those rooms. My turn came up."

"Alone, in rooms with sensitive files?"

"They weren't that important," he answered defensively. "Just prisoner files."

Zosia stood and paced to the entrance of the tent. Speaking softly into the woods, she said, "One clever infiltrator would be the death of all of us. They're not going to take that chance, Peter, they *will* shoot you." She stepped out of the tent.

"Come back!" he yelled desperately. "There's more!"

Zosia stepped back inside and eyed him critically.

He dropped his gaze to his cup of coffee. The black liquid was not as dark as the void he felt he was entering. What was in that corner of his mind? He had not looked there for so long. He stood suddenly and joined Zosia at the entrance of the tent; only Olek stood there, watching them curiously.

"Does the boy speak English?"

"Not really." She grabbed his arm and led him back into the tent to sit down.

Still he could say nothing. He picked up his coffee and sipped it, then stood again. Zosia waited patiently as he studied the fabric of the tent. Eventually he found his voice. "I'd like to tell you everything," he said quietly.

"I want to hear whatever you have to say."

== **66** ==

HE TOOK A DEEP BREATH, then began, "The camp changed *Kommandant*s fairly frequently. They were all alike, all the same sort of bland, ignorable bureaucrat. It was a dead-end job reserved for idiot nephews and brainless pretty boys who could go no further in the hierarchy. The latter group we called blah-blah-blah for 'blathering, blue-eyed blonds.' "

"But *blah-blah-blah* comes from *blond, blauäugig und blöd,* or blond, blue-eyed, and stupid," Zosia corrected.

"I know, we anglicized it. Anyway, they were the sort who advanced through the military with their classic Aryan looks, until inevitably, someone realized that they were simply too brainless to be of any real use. As a group they were generally arrogant, petty, and vindictive, and we avoided them. Well, one day, we got a new fellow, just like all the others. He was driven into the camp one morning, an announcement of the change was made in the evening, and the old *Kommandant* left the following day. At first nothing changed. The announcements were as patriotic and idiotic as usual, the threats just as dire, the routine just as tedious.

"It started slowly; the stories filtered in, hearsay and secondhand, and I did my best to ignore them. Then one of the young lads approached me and described his troubles firsthand. I couldn't ignore it any longer, and after several days wrestling with my options, I decided to confront the *Kommandant* directly."

"What exactly did the boy say?"

"Oh, that he was summoned to the *Kommandant*'s private quarters and given an ultimatum. He must perform sexual favors for the *Kommandant* or face unspecified consequences."

"And he did this?"

"He was afraid."

"And you believed it was not voluntary?"

"Why wouldn't I?"

"I find it difficult to believe he would give in so easily."

Peter turned to look at Zosia. "You've never been a prisoner, have you?"

Zosia shook her head.

"I believed him," Peter reiterated, "and I believed it was involuntary, even though, I guess, the *Kommandant* showered his victims with little favors after the fact. The problem was, I really did not know what I could do about it. I had no real authority."

"You went to see him anyway?"

Peter nodded. "I told him my concerns. I told him to just leave the kids alone. He kept feigning ignorance so I said I'd go over his head, if necessary."

"Was that possible?"

Peter shook his head. "No, not really. I was just grasping at straws."

"Did he get angry that you were threatening him?"

"He didn't seem to, he just told me to come and talk to him later. He seemed like he got a bright idea and said that he was having a party and I should come as a guest, then we could talk afterwards."

"A guest?" Zosia asked, amazed.

"I think he thought I would be entertaining. After the roll call, I returned to the barracks, somewhat undecided about what to do, but within minutes, a guard came to the hut and informed me that the *Kommandant* wanted to see me in his quarters. With an armed escort I was taken back across the compound.

"The *Kommandant* was in a friendly mood. He offered me a brandy and then said, if I was a charming guest that evening, maybe we could work out some arrangement with respect to the problem I had mentioned earlier. So, I worked at being charming. God, it was tedious! I'll spare you the details. Anyway, I did my best. Probably succeeded except for a certain lack of deference. At one point the *Kommandant* hissed in my ear that I had not said even one lousy '*mein Herr*' and it wouldn't hurt for me to say '*Heil Hitler*' once in a while."

Zosia laughed. "What did you say?"

"I told him it wasn't our custom. I didn't tell him that I thought it rather strange to greet other people by invoking a dead psychopath's name."

"Perhaps no odder than having one's wedding day blessed by a visit to a pickled, I mean, *preserved* corpse," Zosia commented.

"Who does that?"

"People in the Soviet Union."

"Wow, that is weird, but then I suppose religious people get married in the presence of a crucifix."

"Yes, some do," Zosia agreed, pursing her lips. "So what happened?"

"Well, when the evening finally ended, I felt utterly drained. Being charming was hard work among those idiots, and I had rewarded my efforts by overindulging in the hors d'oeuvres and *Sekt*. By the time the last guest had stumbled out the door, I felt woozy. I remember just sitting down, wishing I had a cigarette, and wondering how the hell I was going to get a promise of good behavior out of him."

"Did you?"

"Not immediately. The *Kommandant* returned from saying farewell to the last guest and poured me another drink. Brandy. He explained he didn't offer his guests any because it was too expensive. I drank it down in two gulps. He called me a barbarian for that. Said I should savor it. I told him he could fucking savor it, I had to get back and get up early." Peter paused, then said, "He reacted to that word."

"Which word?"

"*Fucking.* I could see it in his face. It was like my 'foul' language had opened a door to him . . ." Peter's voice trailed off.

Zosia waited without saying anything, without voicing her suspicions.

"Anyway, he gave me another, and I know I shouldn't have, but I drank that, too. It just felt so good to break the monotony. He didn't sit down, he stood a few feet from me, pulled out his cigarette case, and removed one for himself. Didn't offer me one. Just smoked a cigarette as I sat there drinking. I began to feel all nice and warm and almost numb. Thought that in a few minutes I'd be asleep. Began to think about Allison, then I noticed he was staring at me.

"Suddenly he said, 'You are very handsome, you know.' That's when I knew I was in real trouble. I said I had to go and I tried to stand up, but he sort of pushed me back into the chair. I was off-balance from . . ." Peter paused, embarrassed.

Zosia remained silent, her face a mask. Outside the tent, the wind picked up and the brittle leaves of the trees rustled noisily in the breeze.

"He said, 'We still have to discuss our deal.' I was worried, but tried to put a brave face on it all. Told him, sure, I'd been to his party, now he would do his part and lay off the boys. He said, no, we weren't done yet. I didn't ask the obvious question, just got up to leave, but he blocked my exit. So finally I asked him what he wanted."

"And he said?"

"Me, of course." He smiled at her, as if he were telling a joke, but the smile was not returned and his dropped from his face. "He offered to leave everyone else alone if I would . . . you know."

"Did you accept his offer?"

He shook his head. "No. I probably should have. Not only would he have left the others alone, but I don't think he was really interested. He wasn't homosexual, he just liked power, and if I had said yes, maybe that would have taken away all the fun and he would have left me alone."

"You had no guarantee that he would have kept his word."

"No, I didn't. And I used that to justify my refusal. That, and the fact that young kids are resilient. I figured that their getting raped was a hell of a lot easier for them to cope with than me getting fucked by him. I guess that was rather cowardly on my part."

"I don't think so. You can't give in to blackmail, it just gets used against you more and more if you do."

"I've done nothing but give in to blackmail for the last four years," he commented bitterly.

"That proves my point."

"It's the only reason I'm still alive."

She straightened a bit, then said, "Please continue."

"Well, in any case, I didn't have the choice. He drew his gun and said I should reconsider. I called his bluff and headed toward the door. He didn't shoot, but his personal guards dragged me back in. They tied my wrists behind my back and left me alone with him."

"But you could still fight."

Peter laughed. "Have you ever fought with your hands tied behind you?"

"Only in training."

"Well, for one thing, fighting implies that there is a chance of winning. If I had managed to overpower him, there was still nowhere to go. All I could do was try and hurt him."

"And did you?"

He nodded. "It was irrational but I wasn't exactly thinking clearly."

"What happened?"

"It didn't stop him. He . . ." Peter closed his eyes as he tried not to remember too clearly all that had happened. He exhaled, then said, "He used the belt of his robe to tie my wrists to my neck, then he started pounding on me, on my head. I spent all my time trying not to break my arms or strangle myself. I think the pounding or the lack of air caused me to black out. All I know is . . ."

Zosia raised her eyebrows and waited. Finally she asked, "What?"

He blinked at the unexpected sight of the tent. "My refusal was moot." His lips twitched but he did not say anything more.

"What happened then?"

"He released me, kicked me out. I pulled on my clothes and left." He gave Zosia a fleeting smile. "That was the really weird part, the way he just stood there and watched me as if nothing exceptional had happened. And me, I didn't know what else to do. I left, pretended it hadn't happened. When I returned to my barracks, everyone was mercifully asleep, and the next day, when they inquired as to the success of my mission, I told them only that I had elicited a promise, nothing more, from the *Kommandant*. About a week later I was told that there were no more complaints, and I was to be congratulated on my diplomacy."

"So you were through with it all."

"So I thought. Two weeks later, I received another summons. It was late evening, most of the boys were asleep, some were playing cards or writing. I was sharing a pot of weak tea with Geoff, talking about nothing in particular, when one of the lads near the door suddenly announced someone was coming. A guard walked in, came straight up to me, and said that *he* wanted to see me in his quarters immediately."

"Did you go?"

"I had no other choice." Peter sighed and continued, "I'll spare you the details of our conversation. The upshot was he wanted to continue our so-called bargain and he wanted a measure of cooperation on my part. I tried to reason with him, appealed to his decency, appealed to his sense of humanity."

"It didn't work?"

"He laughed at me, told me I wasn't an *Übermensch*, so I should just do as he told me and be grateful for his attentions. I pointed out that what he was doing was not approved behavior and it could destroy his career. He said he knew I wouldn't tell anyone because it would cost me my life. He was right, there was nothing I could say that wouldn't make me more guilty than he."

"How so?"

"Corrupting an officer of the Reich, seduction, perverse acts, unnatural proclivities—oh, the list could be endless. Any court would naturally assume I had provoked any illegal or immoral action."

"Yes, it would," Zosia agreed upon reflection. "What happened next?"

"I tried to leave, but he stopped me at the door. I remember how he put his hand on my shoulder." Peter shuddered. "It still makes my flesh crawl. I knew I couldn't physically resist, not with his goons ready to help whenever he called them, so I just kept trying to talk him out of it. All he did was hum the stupid piano music that was playing and go on about how wonderful German composers were." Peter paused as if listening to something. " 'Das Wohltempierte Klavier.' I can still hear it."

He was so obviously distracted by the music that Zosia found herself listening for it as well. When she realized what she was doing, she said, "Please continue."

He looked up at her as if hurt by her words. Distantly he said, "Finally, he stopped humming long enough to tell me I had no choice except one: it could be painful and public or it could be quick and quiet." He turned his head to stare out of the tent into the distance. "I opted for quick and quiet."

Zosia shifted uncomfortably, then asked, incredulous, *"You agreed?"*

Peter nodded. "I knew that nothing I did would make a difference. He had overwhelming force at his beck and call, and he would use it if he had to. It would have been trivial for him to justify my murder . . ." He licked his lips as he stared silently into the distant past.

After a few moments Zosia prompted, "So?"

"I couldn't stand the thought of his goons being there, witnessing it all. I just wanted it over with. I drank a lot of his brandy, to numb my sensibilities, and then . . . Afterwards, I walked back, feeling pretty sick. Geoff waited past curfew to ask what it was all about. I put him off with some lies."

"He believed you?"

"I think so. I don't really know what the others thought. Either they were oblivious or they didn't care. Or maybe they thought it better not to notice, for my sake. After a while though, Geoff confronted me . . ."

"You mean it kept going on?" Zosia asked, her tone betraying distaste.

"Oh, yes, on and on."

"How long did it go on?"

Peter noticed that she had ceased taking notes. "Too long. He did me favors, got me reassigned to easier jobs inside the camp, gave me stuff. It was humiliating." He remembered the humiliation and the strange feelings of filthiness and complicity. Even now his gut ached. "Anyway, Geoff finally asked what the hell was going on, and with some prodding, I told him. It was a wake-up call. He suggested I use my position. Gain his trust, he said, then use it against him. And that's what I did. I got myself assigned to cleaning the offices, made myself appear trustworthy so they'd leave me alone, then I looked for maps, money, anything that might be of help. That's when I found out about my debt.

"Meanwhile, Geoff organized some of the boys into an information network. He wanted to get me the precise information I would need to make it to the border if a chance for escape presented itself. There had always been an underground network—our black market ensured that—so it was not difficult to organize them to a new task. Once they had a well-defined goal, the lads were very efficient at bringing in information. I guess they enjoyed the diversion.

"Finally, I hit pay dirt. It had nearly escaped my notice because it looked so normal, but it was a set of duplicate books. It took a while to compare the Byzantine entries of one set of books with the other, but eventually I was convinced: the *Kommandant* was embezzling.

"Now the Party might indeed be tolerant of 'social errors' on the part of its top officers, but when it comes to money, they're not so forgiving. With the information Geoff had gathered and those books, I knew I could write my ticket out of the country. So, after several days of preparation and planning, it was finally the eve of the ultimatum. Me and Geoff and several trusted lads were celebrating quietly in the barracks with some booze we had got from one of the guards. No one was planning to leave except me, since they all had limited terms and homes to return to.

"Just as we were toasting my departure, I was summoned to see him. That's when I gave him my ultimatum. He essentially agreed to my terms." Peter smiled at that one moment of triumph. He remembered being led into the *Kommandant*'s quarters. The *Kommandant* had been in his robe—dark blue satin with gold cording—sitting in an armchair, his legs crossed, covered by the burgundy satin of his pajama bottoms, his feet shod with black leather slippers each with a gold swastika embroidered at the toe.

"Long time no see," the *Kommandant* had leered, then coughed slightly as he set his cigarette down. Then, his tone changing considerably, he had ordered, "Pour yourself some brandy or whatever you need. Just hurry up, I'm not in a patient mood."

Peter had done as suggested, then slowly, savoring the moment, he had walked over to the *Kommandant* and had thrown the expensive brandy in his face.

The *Kommandant* had sputtered obscenities and threats to which Peter had replied, "*You* are going to arrange my transport out of this country, and I'll tell you exactly how and I'll even tell you why, you goddamned, slime-covered, putrid-brained, shit-faced bastard."

It had taken a long time for the *Kommandant* to calm down enough to stop sputtering, and Peter had not helped matters by continuing to address the *Kommandant* with every insult he could recall or invent, but finally they began to communicate, and slowly it dawned on the *Kommandant* that he had better listen carefully and do exactly as he was told.

"So that's how you got to Switzerland?"

Awakened from his reverie, Peter answered, "Yeah. He was to provide papers and a car and driver to get me across the border. I gave him a week to organize it all and let him know that the compromising evidence was not in my possession, and if anything happened to me, anything at all, no matter how accidental or unfortunate, it would be delivered immediately to his superiors. And to the local newspaper for good measure.

"He wondered how we could manage that, and I remember being quite pleased to inform him that there was no shortage of volunteers to help us out among his own men. Then I explained I would send a postcard from Geneva with an undisclosed code to someone in the camp, and only then would my men accept that I was safe. I've always wondered what happened, since I never managed to send that card."

Zosia made a note, then asked, "What did he do?"

"Fretted that he could be hanged. I told him it would serve him right, but nevertheless, we would help him cover up his actions. The way he looked at me then, pouting and hurt, that's when I realized he was probably truly insane. I didn't want to push him over the edge, so I tried to reassure him." Peter used his thumbnail to scrape some dirt off Uwe's shirt. "That's when he whispered to me that he would miss me."

They sat silently as Zosia jotted down a few more things.

"Now, tell me about what happened in Switzerland."

He explained about the old couple who had taken him in and their kindness, about reporting to the government office, and how somewhere in that bureaucratic maze, someone had betrayed him to the kidnappers. With devastating brevity, he told her of his terrifying return to the Reich and his brutal interrogation.

"Altogether it was about a month or more before I got to trial, and surprise, surprise, I was found guilty." Again he stopped. It was like some weird hallucination: the strange, horrible puppet theater that had been his trial. Zosia waited patiently. Eventually he said, "Actually, I never heard the sentence of death. I was out cold by then."

Zosia brought her hand to her mouth as though to hide the tremble of her lips. He caught the glint of a tear in her eye. She blinked excessively. Without knowing why, he asked her, "Who are you thinking about?"

Too quickly she answered, "No one, please continue."

"At that point, instead of executing me, they reclassified me and dumped me into some sort of reeducation program. I didn't know they did that sort of thing."

"The reeducation?" Zosia asked as she noted something down.

"No, the reclassification. It was completely unnecessary—after all, I was a criminal convict, so they didn't need to do that. It's not consistent with their philosophy. It didn't make any sense."

She smiled indulgently. "Their philosophy is whatever suits their needs. Just read the crap they write about us. We're Aryan in one speech, just in need of some direction, and in the next we're fit only for slavery or extermination."

"Well, when the only thing they have to judge things on is their idea of Aryan looks . . ."

"You mean like Hitler's?"

"Fair point," he laughed.

"You offended them. Your blue eyes and blond hair became irrelevant at that point."

He nodded. "I think worse than irrelevant."

Zosia raised her eyebrows expectantly, but he did not explain further, instead continuing his story. He told her about the Reusches and about his betrayal by them and how he had spent his years in the Vogel household. He spoke of his degradation, his pain and exhaustion, his utter loneliness. He told her about Teresa and Ulrike and Horst. He told her about the scene in Karl's study and his humiliating capitulation to Karl's demands, and about the months he had been leased out like a piece of equipment. He paused to collect himself, then as if he were talking about another person, someone he hardly knew, he told her about the horrendous beating he had received for his conversations with Ulrike and the months of random violence afterward. He told her about Uwe and how he had, by then, lost all track of his life and any semblance of independence. "Two madmen talking at each other," he joked. Then he explained what had happened in the plaza and how perhaps, more than anything, the look in Teresa's eyes had told him he had to risk leaving—that the cost of surviving was simply too high if it meant he had to stay.

When he finished, he felt thoroughly exhausted, but somehow cleansed. They sat silently for a few moments. It was growing dark. Finally Zosia broke the silence. "I need you to fill in a few details here—spellings, full names, and exact dates and places—as far as you can." She handed him her clipboard.

Peter accepted it wearily. He did not know what he had expected, but it wasn't that. She seemed to understand and assured him, "I believe your story. Not only that, but I think we can use it."

"Use?" he asked, almost affronted.

She looked into his face as if trying to read his thoughts, then slowly she explained, "It's my English, I'm sorry. I meant that I think I can convince the committee with it. We just have to check on these details, and if they agree with your story, well, that and my testimony on your behalf should be sufficient."

"Sufficient," he murmured as he scanned the dates and names she had listed. When would it end? Then a thought suddenly penetrated his weariness and he asked, "You can check on these details?"

"Yes. Of course."

"But how long will that take? It could take weeks!"

"No, we'll know enough in a matter of hours."

"*Hours?* How?"

Zosia suddenly looked wary, then she sighed as though admitting defeat. "I'm afraid I've told you more than I should have."

"It doesn't matter, does it? If you decide to trust me, you'll have to trust me completely, anything less would be pointless. And if you decide you don't trust me, well . . . Your secret is safe with me in either case."

"I can't believe I goofed like that. I just assumed you would know."

"Know what?"

"That we tap into their computers. And of course, since they keep such copious files on everyone . . ."

"I had no idea that such a thing was even possible."

"Yes, you have been out of circulation for a long time."

"That, and I think our operations were perhaps somewhat less organized than yours is."

"Well, historically, we do have lots of experience at this Underground society sort of thing—unfortunately. About two hundred years, off and on. And I suppose your people don't need anything quite this elaborate since they are not dependent on their Underground state for their very survival. It has never yet been the stated aim of the Nazis to wipe your culture off the face of the earth."

"No, not yet, though it is clear we have earned their undying hatred."

She contemplated him for a moment, then continued, "In any case, it's hard to compare your organization from then with ours today. In fact, getting information in this manner *wasn't* possible then. All the records went from paper to computer six years ago, during the great modernization drive. Surely you remember that?"

He thought back, shook his head. "I think I was probably harvesting cabbages or something. Somehow, their great leap forward didn't manage to reach us out in the fields." Or in the camp office for that matter, he thought. He still remembered that weaselly secretary stabbing at her ancient typewriter. "Although, come to think of it," he added upon further reflection, "I did do some data entry late in my prison career."

"How in the world did they trust you to do that? Did you introduce spurious data?"

From her tone of voice, he realized he had made a mistake in mentioning that particular job. Sheepishly he explained, "They had a dual-entry system. If I didn't enter exactly what another operator entered, we'd be caught out and severely punished. I didn't know or see the other operator, so we couldn't conspire on our mistakes."

Obviously uncomfortable, Zosia returned to their original topic. "Well, I wouldn't underestimate what your people can do now," she said obscurely.

The thought occurred to him that she might well know more about his erstwhile organization than he did, but of course, she would tell him nothing. "You're probably right," he agreed, still scanning her notes, "I wasn't exactly privy to all their secrets."

"No, I don't suppose you were. You weren't very high up, were you?"

He glanced up at her, rather miffed. "High enough. I was still relatively young."

"But you joined so early—thirteen, wasn't it?—you should have moved quickly to the top. You seem talented."

"Thanks, but I wasn't particularly talented at taking orders." At least not then, he thought morosely as he returned to checking her notes. *Now I'm a god-damned expert.*

"Oh?"

"Yeah, I had some run-ins with the hierarchy early on. I got what I wanted, but I don't think they ever really forgave me. And I had a skill. Somehow people with genuine skills are never moved into political management. Haven't you ever noticed that?"

Zosia smiled at him as if he were telling a joke, but said nothing.

"In any case, I was happy where I was; especially when I was with Allison and that group. A promotion would have pulled me away from her."

Zosia nodded. To Peter she almost looked smug, and he realized, because of her friendly style, he had probably wildly underestimated her authority.

She got up. "Why don't you get some sleep? We'll know enough by morning."

"Now that's a wonderful thought to go to sleep with. Gee, I could be shot at dawn. Or, then again, maybe not."

"Well, you already know if you're telling the truth, so you should sleep easily."

"Unless the bastards have altered the files," he murmured as he corrected the spelling on one of the names she had listed.

"Yes, I guess they could do that. But why would they?"

"Why do they do anything? Why do neutral countries turn out to be collaborators?" That still bugged him. He noted an exact date by the entry Zosia had made for Allison's arrest.

"Everyone knows about Switzerland."

"I didn't."

"Sorry."

"So, is it official policy to return refugees?"

"No. They just tolerate a healthy black market in humans. Money, you know. The Reich pays a bounty for any returned body, a tad more if it's still alive."

"Ah." So it was just bad luck. "Well, with that to comfort me, I think I will sleep. To hell with the dawn, it's still a beautiful evening! And I haven't had a good night's sleep in years."

"Peter?"

"Yes?"

"Does anybody know your real name? Other than me?"

"No. My parents are long gone, my friends from that time would have no idea who I am. I suppose my brother knows about me, but he surely has assumed by now that I'm dead. I doubt if we'd recognize each other if we ever met."

"How old were you the last time you saw him?"

"Eleven," Peter answered, absently drawing a circle around the date of Erich's being drafted. "Eleven," he repeated for no obvious reason. Then, remembering something, he amended, "Actually that's the last time he saw me. I saw him once after that, from a distance. I checked up on him and learned he was graduating in chemistry from some polytechnic institute. I watched from the audience as he was awarded his degree."

"A chemist? Did you think to recruit him?"

"I thought about it, but decided against it. I had no reason to believe he'd be interested in the cause. He had never been before that, and it seemed like an unnecessary danger to reveal myself to him."

"What about Allison? Did she know your name?"

"No, she knew me by the name I used at the time: Yardley." He tapped the place on Zosia's clipboard where she had noted it down. "Alan Yardley. Allison wasn't her name either, I assume."

"So why didn't you ever tell her your name?"

"She never asked."

They fell silent and he stared out the tent door. He could discern a few stars between the branches of the pines.

"I'll see to it that you get some bedding," Zosia said, taking her clipboard back from him. "Do you want anything else?"

"Yes."

"What?"

"Talk to me. Tell me about yourself. I don't really want to sleep this night away."

"I've got to get this stuff to the committee," she said, clearly uncomfortable with him.

"Take it to them. Just promise me you'll come back."

"You're tired. You really should get some sleep."

"Why? This could be my last night! I don't want to spend it alone. I don't want to go to my death alone."

"It's not a foregone conclusion."

Embarrassed by the intensity of his need, he closed his eyes. "Please, Zosia," he pleaded, "please, talk to me. I need company. Please?"

She stared at him for what seemed a long time, then finally she nodded. "All right. It'll take some time, but I'll be back."

=== **67** ===

"**S**O, WHAT DO YOU THINK?" Sitting at Marysia's kitchen table, Zosia spoke quietly since Joanna was already asleep a few feet away on Marysia's couch.

Marysia sipped her tea, then made a face as it was too hot. "I don't know. There's a lot that should be checked out first. If it's all true, maybe he stands a chance."

"Well, I'm pretty sure that bit in Berlin was true—I think I saw him serving at one of those god-awful parties I had to attend, and if I remember correctly, the lady's name was Elspeth."

"Really? Did he recognize you?"

"I don't think so. He didn't say so, anyway. I guess, if what he said is true, he's been through a lot since then."

Marysia nodded understandingly. "Well, if you're right, it sounds like he is telling the truth."

"Not entirely. He's hiding something or things." Zosia tapped the side of her teacup with her fingernails.

"What?"

"I don't know. I just know he was fairly evasive on several points; I let most of it go, but the one time I pressed, it turned out to be something that was humiliating for him, rather than problematic for us."

"That bit with the *Kommandant?*"

Zosia nodded.

"It does prove he's willing to collaborate with them," Marysia pointed out.

"He admitted as much, though he called it giving in to blackmail."

Marysia stirred her tea and tried again. Still too hot. "I suppose, in that light, it's not so bad."

"Still, it's something we should be careful about when we present his case to the Council." Zosia went to Marysia's cabinet, pulled out a bottle of vodka, and poured a bit into her drink. "Too hot," she explained, then added, "You want some?"

Marysia shook her head. "So, you want to advocate his infiltrating our group? You trust him with all our lives?"

Zosia sighed heavily and looked at Joanna sleeping on the couch. "I don't want to see him shot," she said as she sat back down, "and that would be the only other alternative."

"After the run of bad luck we've been having, everyone's edgy about security. They're not going to be very receptive to such a risk. Katerina's already given me hell for bringing him this far. She said I've gone soft." Marysia stared off into the distance. Almost to herself she added, "I don't know, maybe I have."

"Statistically the last three years have been no worse than usual—it just hurts more because they've all been so close to us," Zosia stated dryly. "I'm tired of people close to me getting killed."

"The prisoner is not close to you," Marysia reminded her.

"He is now," Zosia admitted. "You're the one who wanted me to talk to him. I did, and now I care about him. Stupid as that may be."

Marysia pursed her lips. "That's interesting."

"What?"

"What you just said. I mean, you, more than most people, are trained to be analytic about these things, yet you're willing to risk keeping this stranger alive when the stakes are so high. When there's Joanna to think of." Marysia cast a worried glance at her sleeping granddaughter. "She and Olek are all I have left," she whispered.

"I know," Zosia soothed. "But you're the one who insisted I talk to him!"

"Yes, well, I think the physical resemblance to Adam . . . When I saw him, from behind, so self-confident, hurling orders at Olek, I thought, just for a moment, it was Adam come back to haunt us. It was such a dangerous situation, I should have dropped him right then and there, but I didn't! I told him to drop his gun. He could have shot Olek then. I risked Olek's life!" Marysia brought a trembling hand to her face and unsteadily wiped away some tears.

Zosia reached across and stroked her mother-in-law's face. "You followed your instincts, and they were right, weren't they?"

Marysia nodded, unconsoled. "When I mentioned it to him, to the prisoner—"

"Peter."

"—to Peter that he reminded me of my son, he gave me a sheepish smile that looked just like . . ."

"Well, I was forewarned, so it wasn't that, it wasn't the way he looked."

"Then why? Why trust him?" Marysia asked as if seeking answers for her own emotions.

"He's persuasive. And that means, I not only believe him, but I think he has possibilities."

"What do you mean?"

"I mean he'd be the perfect representative to present to the American public. He could speak directly of the suffering inflicted on people here. In English! It couldn't be better!"

"Well, a number of problems immediately comes to mind," Marysia warned.

"Such as?"

"First, we have to keep him from getting shot."

"Indeed."

"Then we'd have to convince the Council—and Wanda in particular—that he could leave Szaflary."

"He could earn trust, if we give him time," Zosia suggested. "We'd make sure he always traveled with someone, then after a while maybe we could arrange a mission or something." She tilted her head in thought. "I think we could do it, it would just take time."

"Everything does. Your father would need time to assess his viability and also work up some presentation format, in any case."

Zosia gnawed on her thumbnail. "Still, letting him loose in America, I doubt they'd go for that."

"We could organize close surveillance," Marysia suggested.

Zosia nodded. "It could get complicated. He'll have to be managed very carefully every step of the way, but we can cross all those bridges if we get to them. First off is saving his life."

"So we need to check out whatever facts we can. Who do you have in mind to do the grunt work?" Marysia asked.

"You, me, and Olek," Zosia replied. "And no one else."

"Us? Why?" Marysia was astounded.

"I want to be sure we dig very carefully. Whatever he's hiding, I don't want anyone else to find out."

"You mean, like the real reason he didn't head toward England?"

"Exactly. I want to have a chance to filter the information before presenting it to the Council."

Marysia sighed. "So what should I do?"

"Olek and I will tap into the archives and check basic facts. You can handle communications with the English. Don't give them much more than the names and just see what they're willing to say."

"You know they're not going to volunteer information without a quid pro quo."

"I know. I also know that whatever he's hiding, it's not that he's a German agent, so whatever it is, it's irrelevant to us right now. Better we remain in ignorance, eh?"

"I guess," Marysia agreed reluctantly. Her eyes drifted upward to the photograph of her son on the wall. Next to it was a photograph of Julia. "I guess," she repeated sadly.

They were interrupted by a light tapping at the door. Zosia opened it and Tadek greeted her with, "Oh, there you are! We were supposed to go out, don't you remember?"

"Oh, I'm sorry," Zosia sighed. "I completely forgot!"

"Well, we can go now." Tadek smiled. "I see you already have Joanna in Marysia's capable care."

"No, there's the Council meeting that's been called. By the way, when is it?"

"That's what I stopped by to tell Marysia. And you. We're meeting at six in the morning." Tadek used the term *we* with special pride since his temporary election to a seat had just been confirmed. "So, we still have plenty of time."

"No, I have to check up on all the facts Peter gave me."

"Peter? Who's that?"

"The prisoner."

"Oh, so he's Peter now," Tadek remarked sourly.

"Even prisoners have names," Marysia commented from her seat.

"I'm told he looks like Adam. Is that true?"

"No, not really," Zosia answered quickly.

"Don't be fooled by him, Zosia. He's the enemy, he knows our exact location now, and if he has a chance to convey that information, he'll be the death of us all."

"He's not the enemy, he's on our side."

Tadek whistled his derision. "Eh, we can discuss it."

"I told you, I can't go out now," Zosia repeated.

"Well, how about afterwards?"

"I promised Peter I'd go back and talk with him."

"He takes priority?"

"He's been through a lot, Tadek," Zosia snapped. "You could have some consideration for others."

Marysia winced and even Zosia regretted her words.

"Consideration? Sure, I'll be damned considerate. I'll give him this night! After all, it is going to be his last," Tadek commented evenly.

"Oh, Tadek!" Zosia moaned. "I'm sorry! Look, could you watch Joanna for a few hours? Marysia needs to go to Communications and check out some details, too. Please? Could you do that for me? Please?"

"Sure, any favor for my little Zosia. And do you know why?" Tadek asked, then without waiting answered, "Because my dear, little Zosienka would never use me unfairly. Not before, not now. Never."

68

*P*ETER HAD FALLEN ASLEEP by the time Zosia returned, and she hesitated to wake him; instead she stood watching him as he slept. She imagined that it was Adam sleeping there, but then he stirred and smiled and the similarity evaporated. "You're back," he whispered in a foreign tongue.

"As promised. So what do you want to hear?"

"Anything. Everything. Tell me about yourself."

She tilted her head to consider him, then agreed, "All right." She sat down and removed a half-liter bottle of vodka and two glasses from her bag. She poured each of them a drink and then set the bottle down, uncapped, between them.

Years of training led Peter to reach for the cap to cover the bottle, but she stopped him: "Old custom." She raised her glass, said, *"Na zdrowie!"* and swallowed the shot in one gulp.

"Naz-dro-vyeh." Peter repeated her version of "cheers," hoping that what he said was at least approximately right, and followed suit; then, pointing to what looked like a blade of grass in the bottle, he asked, "What's that?"

"That's an herb to flavor the vodka. It's grass the bison eat." She refilled their glasses.

He noticed that the bottle had a Polish label and asked, "You make your own vodka?"

"Of course, how else would we get any?"

He wondered at this economy that seemed to function as an entire underground state, but decided not to ask anything that might seem suspicious. He didn't fool himself—he knew she was still judging him. Instead he asked, "That other woman, Marysia?"

She nodded.

"Marysia said I reminded her of her son."

"Adam." She said the name in something other than a neutral tone, but he was not sure what it implied.

"Was that his name?"

"Yes. And, yes, there is some similarity."

"So you knew him."

Zosia laughed. "You could say that."

"What's so funny?" He felt slightly miffed—they seemed to laugh at him a lot.

"He was my husband."

"Oh. I'm sorry."

"Yes, so am I. I mean, I'm not sorry he was my husband. I'm— Oh, bugger!" She looked at Peter as though weighing up the similarities. Then, switching to German, she continued, "I hope you don't mind, but I find speaking in German much easier than English. I've had more practice."

"No, of course not. But why are you so practiced in German? I've hardly heard any Polish at all."

"You must have guessed the answer. You do know that speaking Polish is essentially illegal?"

He shook his head. "I had heard rumors about some languages but . . ." He shrugged, somewhat embarrassed by his ignorance.

"Yes, well, it is and has been for some years now, as a retaliation for, um, certain actions. Anyway, speaking it in the wrong circumstances is quite severely punished. But that's not why we speak German. We, all but a few of us, mix regularly into Reich society, and we must be able to pass ourselves off as *Reichsdeutsch.* We find that the easiest way to have no discernible accent is to speak the language from childhood. So we maintain our fluency this way. We learn our own language as if it were a foreign tongue, and we speak it only with a few select family members—that way we are never tempted to slip into it when we are under stress."

"Stress," Peter repeated the word. Yes, that was a good word for it. Drugs, fatigue, torture—they could all be summed up quite tidily. "But will your strategy work? Aren't you afraid of losing your national identity?"

"As for losing our national identity, well, as long as they want to kill us for it, I doubt we'll forget who we are." She paused, took a deep breath as though remembering long debates, then continued, "Now as for our strategy, well, it has worked before—we sat out partition and an occupation for more than a hundred years and we managed to come back."

" 'A phoenix rising from the ashes,' " he quoted a history text he had read. "But that was different, wasn't it? I mean, the Prussians and Austrians and Russians at least let you assimilate, didn't they?"

"Indeed, to some extent we could move up in society and lose ourselves entirely. That's probably why, this time around, our early leaders took such a dogmatic line about noncooperation."

"They were afraid?"

She nodded. "I think so. I think they thought if we accepted any of the offers of collaboration or a puppet state, then it would be too easy to slip into national nonexistence."

"It has cost you. Was it worth it?"

"You're right, it has cost us dearly," Zosia agreed. "Maybe we should have done things differently. But who could have foreseen how long this Reich would last or this prolonged genocide? Of course, we have so little information, and God only knows what's happening in the bit the Russians grabbed—"

"It's not safe there?"

"Nowadays, that is unclear. Early on, some crossed the Bug River into the Soviet-held territories, but they were either sent back or, we are told, murdered or sent East for slave labor."

Thinking how he had toyed with the idea of crossing that border, Peter raised an eyebrow at that. "Do they still send people back?"

Zosia shrugged. "Sometimes. It depends on politics. Anyway, it's such a fortified border it's almost impossible to cross it now, and for most people, there isn't much point. There are hardly any of our people left over there, so we don't get much information. The Soviets were much more efficient than these Nazis, and even we have trouble remembering it was the same country once." She looked out the tent door and finished quietly, "Between the two of them, we've taken a beating. According to our best estimates, our population now is less than half of what it was in 1939."

"*Less than half?*"

"Yes, within the first five years one in six of us was dead. That's six million people murdered. I'm not talking about soldiers, I'm talking about the entire population: men, women, children, babies. They started with intellectuals, teachers, university students, landowners, political and religious leaders, officers . . . Any potential leaders. Then they went for the Jews. About half that number were Jewish—nearly our entire Jewish population within the German-held regions."

"And the rest?"

"The other half? Those not selectively killed fell to bombings, reprisals, executions, slave labor, starvation—"

"No, I meant the rest since those first five years."

"The famines of '45 and '48 and the epidemic of '46 probably took another sixth or so. Then there was the Warszawa uprising . . ."

What she said sounded like "var-sha-va," and it took him a moment to match it to the German name Warschau and realize she meant Warsaw. "Oh. What happened?"

"As I'm sure you know, it was suppressed. That cost us a few people. Most of our leaders. Since then, it's been mostly just slow attrition: starvation, disease, executions. You know, the usual." She fell silent and Peter did not know what to say.

She looked up at him, her eyes beseeching him to interrupt her thoughts. But what could he say? Suddenly he remembered something. "You said Marysia's son was Adam and that he was your husband, and Olek is Marysia's grandson. So, is Olek your son?" he asked, thinking that she looked rather too young.

"No. He's my nephew, my husband's sister's son. Both his parents are dead, so we're his only family." Zosia paused again, lost in thought. Then she looked up at Peter and said softly, "Maybe when everything has settled, we could find out what happened to your family."

"You could do that?"

"We could try."

"That would mean a lot to me. And there are other people I'd like to trace. And I'd like to know how we were betrayed."

"That's quite an order."

"I think you can understand; as it is right now, I have no history. I need to find some connection with my past."

"Or maybe just build a future."

"Yes, maybe that's enough," he agreed.

"In any case, we'll do what we can. Old records are often erased, many files they did not even bother to transfer, but births and deaths are usually available."

He nodded. He felt a surge of elation just thinking about the possibilities the future held. If only they would let him live.

They talked late into the night. He learned how to spell her name, learned that what sounded, to his untrained ears, like an *sh* sound in her name and in Marysia's was spelt with an *si*, learned some simple spelling rules—that their *j* and *w* were like the German letters, that is, they sounded like an English *y* and *v*, and that the horrendous-looking *dz* that appeared so often was quite easily approximated by an English *j*.

"Our *dz* might look difficult," Zosia pointed out, "but it is not half as bad as what the Germans use for that sound."

He agreed. The *dsch* the Germans used did make a lot of English place names look unpronounceable. There had been enormous confusion after the spelling reform of '59, and finally even the Germans had admitted that some English names were better off spelled with a *j* and officially mispronounced.

Zosia laughed when he explained how renaming and then respelling had failed to take. "Won some, lost some," he remarked, remembering that the Temms had once been spelled *Thames*.

"Here," she explained, "they solved that problem by razing everything and then renaming the new structures. And besides, you can get shot for referring to a city by its Polish name. They are very touchy about that. No sense of humor."

"Oh, I've heard they have a sense of humor—it's just too serious a thing to be laughed at." They both laughed, and as he mocked his erstwhile captors, his mind strayed momentarily to Teresa and her cheerful good humor. He apologized to her mentally but was feeling too buoyantly happy to have any further qualms.

The vodka bottle was emptied, and another, this time flavored with cherries, was brought in, along with more food. They laughed and joked and discussed the state of the world. The stars moved and the night grew cold and they huddled together, a blanket wrapped around them, to keep warm. As the graying of the dawn began to dim the stars and Zosia closed her eyes and rested her head on his shoulder, Peter stroked her hair and realized that he could think of no better way to have passed this, what might be his last, night than by being with her.

Her hair was pressed against his face, and he smelled the freshness of the pine forest in it. He had never before smelled air as clean as that of the forest, never before heard silence as intense as that which surrounded him now. He had never seen a night so dark as this one—never before had he experienced a night without the omnipresent intrusion of security lights. Zosia's quiet breathing, the smell of the pines, and the dim light of the stars were all that he noticed. They filled his being and gave life to his soul, the soul that had lain dormant for so long.

He watched the stars growing dimmer as the blackness of the sky slowly lightened to an intense dark blue, then to a lighter shade that almost obliterated the points of light. He thought of each flicker of starlight as a spirit—some brightly shining but never seen, never understood, others lighting the way for many lost souls. He felt a sudden sadness at his own dismal life. If ever a star was overwhelmed or hidden by clouds, then it was his. He felt as though he had never influenced one person or salvaged one faint hope—all he had managed to do was survive, mindlessly stumbling from one crisis to the next, and he did not even know why.

He felt woozy and considered how he could rearrange himself so that he could sleep without waking Zosia. Before he could move, though, he heard someone approaching the sentry outside the tent. Words were exchanged and then a man ducked under the entrance and faced Peter. He took in the scene in a second, scowled at Zosia's sleeping form, and muttered something. He was tall and lean with dark brown hair and icy gray eyes. He had a look of unquestioned authority, and without the slightest gesture of greeting he nodded toward Zosia and said, "Wake her up."

"Who are you?"

The man did not answer. Avoiding looking at Peter, the man leaned forward and nudged Zosia.

"We need you now."

"Hmm?"

"Zosiu, wake up! We need to discuss matters with you."

Zosia looked up. "Oh, Tadziu, it's you." She looked around, confused. "Good Lord, did I sleep here all night?"

"You've slept about half an hour," Peter replied. "It's dawn."

"Oh my God, I had no idea. Is Joanna okay?" Peter had learned during the night that Joanna was Zosia's three-year-old daughter.

"She's fine, Marysia's watching her now." Tadek sounded less than approving; he said something abruptly to Zosia in Polish, then he turned and left with the clear intention that Zosia should follow.

Zosia looked at Peter, and as she stood, she said gently, "I have to go. I'll see you soon."

"Wait. What did he say to you?" Peter asked, standing up as well.

Zosia looked embarrassed, then said quietly in English, "He said that my husband is hardly cold in his grave and here I am falling asleep in a stranger's arms."

Peter desperately did not want her to leave, so he grabbed at the first question that came to his mind to hold her just a few seconds longer. "What does *kur-vah* mean?"

Zosia looked at him sharply. "*Kurwa?*"

"Yes."

"Did he call me that?"

"Yes. I think. Why, what's it mean?"

She walked to the entrance of the tent, and as she was leaving, she turned and answered cryptically, "It is not complimentary."

The tent seemed empty without her. Peter sat as though stunned on the edge of the cot, then wrapping the blankets around him, he lay down and fell into a deep, dreamless sleep.

69

SOMEBODY SHOOK HIM INTO wakefulness. It was still early morning; the sun, barely visible over the horizon, streamed into the tent, momentarily blinding him. Grunting with incomprehension, he shielded his eyes and struggled to understand what was being said to him.

"Come with me. The Council wants to talk with you."

He got to his feet, stretched, and groaned. The young face of a wide-eyed boy stared at him expectantly. Clearly a response was in order, but Peter could barely remember his own name. Finally he managed to ask in a hoarse whisper, "Why?"

"Just come. They're waiting for you."

"Why? What do they want? Have they made their decision?"

"I was told to bring you." The boy was either adamant or ignorant.

Peter shook his head in vague disgust. What now? He tried to rub the sleep from his eyes. The sunlight seemed excruciatingly bright—why did he feel so ill? Oh, yeah, vodka, no sleep, life and death, all that. Yeah, that would do it.

Zosia appeared at the entrance. She looked tired and almost apologetic. "Sorry to wake you."

"How long have I slept?"

"It's been a little over an hour since I left you."

"Ah." That at least explained the exhaustion.

Zosia clearly had something more to say. She looked at the boy, said, "I want to talk with him," and nodded toward the door. The boy saluted and left quickly, but Zosia remained uneasily silent.

Peter sat on the edge of the cot, trying to rub some life into his face. Eventually, he felt awake enough to hear what he knew must be bad news. "What is it?"

"I'm sorry, I'm really sorry."

"I see."

"The vote was six to four against. Marysia and I, well, I think we convinced everybody that you're okay. Your story basically checks out. The problem is excess caution."

"Uh-huh."

"It's not who you are—I mean, we know that Halifax existed, and we're fairly sure that you are that man, or at least look a lot like him—it's your motives. What was your motive for coming here?"

"But I told you, I had no idea you were here!"

"Then how did you know to turn off the main road, just before our road-block?"

"I didn't." Peter shook his head helplessly. "I didn't. And I was stopped any-way, wasn't I?"

"Yes, but no one expected you to go there. That's why Olek was alone. Except for Marysia, of course."

"I told you what I was doing. I told Marysia," Peter moaned. "It was random chance!"

"And that's unprovable," Zosia sighed. "If there was any reason the govern-ment could convince you to work for them, that's exactly the story you would use. I, personally, don't think that's the case, but . . . It's just that the tiny chance that you are an infiltrator . . . Well, it would be disastrous for all of us. There are so many lives at stake. And you're only one . . ."

"And a stranger."

"Yes."

"And not even the right nationality."

"No. That doesn't help," Zosia agreed. "It all boils down to the fact that we don't know *why* you came here."

Peter closed his eyes. He had to swallow a lump of anger in his throat as he realized that nobody would accept the reality of randomness in the universe. The foundation of all modern science was insufficient to save his life. When he was able to look at Zosia again, he had accepted his fate. "Yeah, I understand. I can't really blame them. But"—and at this he smiled without humor—"do forgive me if I take it personally."

"But . . ."

"Is there any chance of my escaping?"

"No. You'd be dead before you got ten meters."

"Ah, well, at least it would be quick," he said stoically.

"There is still a hope."

"What? Prayer?" he asked sarcastically. They had spoken of religion the previous night, and he meant his remark to sting. He was angry, and even though he did not want to be, he felt annoyed with Zosia for having led him to believe he had a chance.

"That's not what I meant, though it wouldn't hurt for you to have a bit of humility," she shot back angrily. She paused, took a deep breath. "I'm sorry. Look, the Council—"

"Perhaps you could keep me in some sort of quarantine? I don't need to meet that many people."

"For how long? The rest of your life?"

Was one life worth so much trouble? It felt to him as if it was, but how could he convince them of that? "Well, then just escort me out of here. Watch me from a safe distance. You'll see that I'm no threat to you."

"You already know too much. And where would you go?"

He sighed. "I don't know." Without even noticing what he was doing, he ran his right hand up along the numbers printed on his left forearm and then back down again so that the left hand could circle the band on his right wrist. It was a gesture he had done a thousand times before, and every time there was a vague amazement in the back of his mind that the numbers did not rub off, that the band did not unclasp its hold on him.

"You see, we have to make a decision now."

"And you've made it." He looked at Zosia, had a sudden image of troops raiding the mountain camp, dragging her off to a prison to be tortured and killed. He imagined Joanna screaming, torn away from her mother; if she survived, maybe she'd be adopted, like Frau Reusch's son. The image chilled him. They were right, he was asking too much of them.

Zosia bit her lip. "The thing is, the decision is not final yet."

"What do you mean?"

"I don't want to get your hopes too high. I feel I already misled you once, but, Marysia and I convinced them to meet you personally and hear your own arguments, before making the final decision."

"Oh. Great." He had not meant to sound so ungrateful.

"Well, it's better than no chance at all."

"Yeah. I guess I should thank you and Marysia for trying so hard to help."

"You're welcome."

"So that's why the boy came to get me."

"Yeah. We should go now. They're waiting."

"Oh, Zosia, if you couldn't convince them, what hope do I have?"

"Try. Tell them what you told me. You convinced me, I'm sure your story will move them."

He shook his head vigorously. "I can't do that. Those words are gone, I'm never going to speak about that again."

"Never?" she squeaked. "No, no, no! You must! You have to be willing to talk! There's no point, otherwise!"

"I'm sorry. It wouldn't come out right."

"It's for your life!" she argued desperately.

He shook his head. "It won't work. I know it. Those words are gone."

"Peter! You must tell your story to them! You have to say something!"

"I don't know what. I haven't a clue what to say. I've hardly slept in two days. I'm hungry, I'm dirty, I'm hungover. *I wouldn't listen to me!*"

"How about if I get them to wait an hour or so, so that you can prepare?"

"I need to wash and shave." He ran his hand over the two days' growth on his face. "And I need a change of clothes. And some shoes."

"I'll see what I can arrange."

70

*T*HE FACE IN THE mirror stared at him as he shaved. A mirror! And a sharp razor, and shaving foam! Such unheard-of luxuries! It unnerved him slightly that even here in the middle of the forest they lived a more civilized life than he had been permitted. And now he had to think of what to say to convince them to risk their lives just to let him live. A stranger. A friendless stranger. He studied his reflection, saw no answers there; so he turned to the mundane tasks of making himself presentable.

A little over an hour later, he was ready to face his judges and potential executioners. He had washed, shaved, changed clothes, and eaten. He still felt a bit hungover and tired, and he cursed himself for his stupidity the night before, but there was no time to waste on regrets; instead he thought feverishly, trying to plan his strategy. He put aside his anger and disappointment and struggled to design an argument that would convince himself under reversed circumstances. It was difficult: he understood their fears, and eventually, he decided that was the approach he would take. He would not try to convince them that he was safe, he would simply try to convince them that their own ideology required them to take this risk.

The Council consisted of ten members. They were seated casually on large rocks and fallen tree trunks in a sort of semicircle on a slope under the pines. Some of them had mugs of tea or coffee; it looked like a small, cozy gathering of friends. He was led to a spot in front of them, and then his guard withdrew, leaving him alone to face his judges. They had, probably deliberately, positioned themselves uphill with their backs to the sun, which was low in the sky. He squinted against the bright light, struggling to see their faces. He looked around at his surroundings: at least three armed guards within easy distance, probably more out of sight, and a few of the Council members had pistols sitting in front of them at the ready. It was obvious he would not be allowed to escape if they decided against him. He scanned the dirt at his feet: there was no obvious place for him to sit. He decided that in any case he was too nervous to sit still and would be better off standing, pacing now and then to alleviate his tension.

He began by thanking them for hearing him speak. He thanked Zosia for relaying his story and reiterated his thanks that they had checked all the details that they could. At this point he hesitated. He feared that it would be viewed as inappropriate to ask questions of them, but he was afraid of missing what might be his only opportunity. They looked at him expectantly.

"If I'm not mistaken, you did check all the details you could. Am I right?"

There was a general murmur that he was right.

He paused again, bit his lip, then plunged in. "Could you tell me then, what happened to my parents?"

There was a shocked silence. Finally, the man Zosia had called Tadek answered, "Your father died within days of being arrested. Your mother died after about seven months in a concentration camp." Tadek's eyes narrowed and he continued, "At least, that's the story."

Peter did not say anything. He looked up into the sunlight. For a moment he stared unseeing into the inferno, but eventually the excruciating brightness forced him to close his eyes. To his horror he felt tears rolling down his face. Impatiently, almost angrily, he wiped away this betrayal of his privacy. He had long suspected the truth, and it surprised him that hearing it verified hurt so much. So they were indeed dead.

The Council waited silently as he collected himself. He needed to continue with the business at hand, but something else compelled him. In a voice that cracked with tension he asked, "Were . . . were they collaborators?"

Zosia answered quietly, "Apparently most of the files from that time have been wiped or removed from active access; we could find little more than the arrest warrant. Your father was a Party member, about as high up as one could expect a working-class Englishman to reach in the hierarchy at that time. Did you know that?"

Peter stared at her, devastated by the revelation. Finally he managed to stammer, "No." So that's how they got him into that school. Suddenly, lots of little pieces fell into place.

Noting Peter's expression, Zosia hurried to add, "It doesn't really mean anything—I mean, if they were infiltrators, that's what he would have done." She continued, her voice tense with a determination to convey the information as gently as possible, "The records are unclear as to why they were arrested. Our experience has been that they could have been arrested for anything. They may have been collaborating and simply annoyed a political superior. Or they may have been in the Resistance. Or it might mean they were completely innocent of any activity."

Peter nodded. A Party member? Evening meetings, yes, of course. Locked drawers, yes, it all fit. Those trips to the exchange to make telephone calls, comments from the local police, occasional taunts—yes, now it all made sense. But was it all a ploy? Was it some insane, brave, hopeless plot? He stood stunned before the Council, his hand poised over his mouth as if to prevent words from spilling out; yet he said nothing. He had to say something, but still he could not find his voice to defend his own life. An image of his parents together—on a Sunday walk—her hair pulled back into a ponytail, his father's eyes lighting on her face. Both smiling, laughing, swinging their hands as they walked along the street. The image shifted as death claimed them and the flesh dropped from their bones in putrid lumps. Worms and mold and stench replaced their lively presence. Maybe Zosia was right, maybe believing in a God made it all more bearable. It would be so much easier to believe in their spirits soaring to the heavens, freed from the pain of earthly existence, while their corpses became nothing more than cast-off cocoons.

Marysia interrupted his thoughts. "You could not have saved them. Your name was on the arrest warrant as well. If you had been there, you would have been taken."

Peter smiled at her kindness. He swallowed the lump that had formed in his throat. Dead for all these years and now he did not have time to mourn them. With an effort he removed the images of his mother and father from his mind and concentrated on the ten faces waiting for him to speak.

He began by asking if they had any unanswered questions. There were a few, but clearly Zosia had been fairly thorough in relaying his story. He answered their questions and then continued by telling them what he had felt as he had driven away from Berlin. How his spirits had lifted the farther he was from the core of Nazi power. He explained what he had felt when he had driven into the woods and breathed the clean air as a free man. The shock and despair he had felt when he thought he had driven into a secret Nazi military installation, and the surge of hope that had followed when he had realized that he was probably among friends.

"Since then, I have come to realize that this must be much more than a small encampment of partisans—your caution alone has indicated to me that there are much higher stakes involved. But I still can't help but feel that despite that, despite the obvious importance of the work you do, whatever it is, I can't help but feel that we are allies and should be friends. Your fight is my fight, it is the work I carried out for years before I was arrested. And that work is to rid our respective lands of their occupiers, to free our people from slavery and death.

"I know that you fear me, and I understand why. I know well what a lack of caution can do—I've lost everybody who was ever dear to me and I still don't know why or how. But I also know that fear must not be allowed to excuse barbaric acts. I know we sometimes have to make hard choices, sometimes we do things we would not do if we were not at war. But we are fighting, after all this time, not just to defeat the Nazis, but to maintain a way of life, an ideology of justice and human rights. And we cannot apply those rights only when it suits us. I know these are dangerous times, but they have been dangerous times for decades and we dare not assume the methods of our adversaries, for then we will become like them and then our actions will make us nothing more than terrorists.

"Ever since they have conquered our lands, and even before, in their own land, the Nazis have ascribed value to a human according to his nationality, language, culture, or religion. According to his 'race.' They then used fear to justify their actions. They saw the Jews as a force within, out to destroy their society, and they used these fears to persecute their Jewish population—to murder them in cold blood.

"Now, because I am not one of you, because I do not speak your language and you do not know me, you fear what I might do to you. I have offered every proof I can that I am not a threat to you, but your fear is stronger than anything. I tell you, I understand your fear, but you must not act on it. To murder me in cold blood because of your fear—a fear which is virtually unjustified given all the evidence you have that I am who I say I am—such a murder would destroy your own ideology. You will have murdered me because I am alien. For no other reason and you know it."

He paused, hoping he had not offended his listeners by what he had said. He took a deep breath and concluded, "You have to take a risk now. You have to let me live—otherwise you lose your very purpose. Don't use their methods, don't use their justifications, don't kill just because you fear. Don't become what you hate!"

He stopped. There was much more that he could say—he could tell them the same thing many other ways—but he could tell by the look in their eyes that they had heard him and so he had said enough.

At this point Tadek spoke. "All right, we have heard you. Your guard will escort you back to the tent, and we'll let you know our decision shortly."

Peter shook his head. "No."

The Council members stared at him, dumbfounded by his audacity.

"No. If you want to kill me, I want to hear it from your lips," he stated calmly.

He felt very unsure of his chances. He may have swayed one or even two of the six, but he felt they could easily be swayed back against him in his absence. Zosia had indicated to him who had voted against him and which ones were the most likely to change their mind, and now he surveyed the Council and matched her descriptions to the people sitting in front of him.

He turned to one of the ones who he knew had voted in his favor, a woman called Hania, and asked, "Do you think it is necessary for me to die?"

"No, I think it would betray our mission to kill you, or any innocent person."

"What about you?" he asked another who had voted for him. If he had identified him correctly, this was a man called Konrad.

"No. I think it would be unnecessary—and therefore murder." The speaker looked pointedly at Tadek. Clearly he had made this point earlier.

Peter looked to the naysayers. Among them was the man Bogdan, who had spoken with the Austrian accent; according to Zosia, he was the most likely to be swayed. He looked tired, and even as Peter looked in his direction, he was distracted with stifling a yawn. Peter knew he was taking an enormous risk: if the man held his ground, then all was lost. He waited until Bogdan noticed him and looked him in the eye.

"Do *you* vote that I must die?" Peter asked softly.

Bogdan stared at him, then looked helplessly at his colleagues. None of them offered any advice. Finally, reluctantly, he mumbled, "No, I guess not."

Peter noticed Zosia sighing with relief. He did not allow himself the luxury of enjoying his small victory—he knew a five-to-five vote would be debated and overturned. He had to get the other Council members—at least one of them—to vote in his favor.

He turned his attention to an old woman who sat to the side. She looked thin and frail, but he knew that although she had not in any way indicated her rank, she held the Council chair. Zosia had said that her name was Katerina, that she had been an able assassin in her day, and that she was, consequently, extremely practical in her views of life and death. Though she did not fear betrayal for her own sake—she felt she had already lived a full life—she was protective of her younger colleagues.

"Do you think murdering me would further your beliefs?" he asked her.

"It would not be murder if it did," she answered evenly.

He felt slightly exasperated by her pedantry. "Then," he rephrased his question, "must I die?"

Katerina cocked her head to the side, pursed her lips as if weighing up all the possibilities. "I don't believe you should be party to this decision."

"Why not? You want to decide my fate in my absence—then you don't have to see the consequences. What would you do, have me marched off into the woods and cleanly shot by one of your subordinates? You want to make me faceless! If that's what you want, then pick up a gun and shoot me, now, in the face! Take responsibility for your decision." Peter realized his sudden anger had probably destroyed whatever goodwill he had managed to establish. He saw Marysia wince at his words, but it was too late now, he had to stand by them.

The woman surprised him; she laughed and nodded to herself. Then, once her cackling had ceased, she pointed a bony finger at him and addressed her colleagues. "And Alex told me the English were unflappable!" She turned her gaze back to Peter, but still addressed the other Council members. "I was wrong. He'll do fine. Let him live."

Peter felt an incredible weight slip from his shoulders. Relief surged through his body, and he dropped his head so that he could close his eyes and sigh without being too obvious. So the vote was now at least six to four in his favor. Still, his work was not done. That sort of margin was dangerously thin, and if they had changed their minds once . . .

He looked up, caught the look of relief in Zosia's eyes, saw Marysia nod encouragingly at him. He addressed the next Council member: a rotund, balding fellow of about sixty. "How do you vote?"

The man shrugged. "I guess you've made your point."

"And you?" Peter asked the woman next to the man. Her name was Wanda and her vote was extremely important for she was responsible for internal security. Once trusting and outgoing, she was, according to Zosia, now increasingly bitter and withdrawn after having lost two sons to an unauthorized sniper who had mistaken them, while they were in town, for genuine German officers. If anyone understood the bitterness of dying for nothing, she would.

Wanda nodded but looked somewhat disapprovingly at him. "All right, you can live. But I hope you understand what you have asked of us."

"I do," he replied gently.

There were two left. Tadek looked at Peter with something close to loathing. The other man seemed barely more approachable. He was large and his features had a rough look as though he had been carved from a piece of wood but the sculptor had never bothered to refine the work. Zosia had described him well; his name was Wojciech. Peter met the gaze of this man with a questioning look. Would he be accepted?

Wojciech answered before Peter could even phrase the question. "Whatever I say doesn't matter, I'm outvoted."

Peter hesitated for a moment. He desperately wanted to accept the vote was in his favor and stop while he was ahead, but he knew he could not. His vision had grown blurry again, and he found it aggravating not being able to make out the expressions on the Council members' faces. His thoughts were momentarily side-tracked as he wondered if his vision had really been this unstable before he had fled. Probably—it just hadn't mattered much before. He turned away from the group and with his back to them closed his eyes and rested for a moment. The rotting bones that would now be his mother and father leapt into view, and he was forced to open his eyes. The pines looked cool and inviting. Why couldn't he believe in soaring spirits?

He turned back and faced the group. "All right. By my count, it looks like I can live—that is, if it doesn't have to be unanimous. But I also know something about how you must exist in order to survive here. You all have to trust each other, you need to be able to rely on each other. There's no way that I can survive if even two or three of you want me dead, and whatever new decisions are taken later, or accidents happen down the line, it will destroy your esprit de corps, and that will be dangerous for all of you, not just me."

Peter directed his attention to the huge man. His size made him look slow and stupid, and Peter had to fight an urge to speak simply to him. "If you really feel that I cannot be permitted to live—there's the gun." Peter nodded toward the pistol sitting in front of the old woman.

Wojciech followed his gesture, stared at the gun for a moment, and then shook his head. "No, I won't do that. No."

Peter let his breath out quietly. It wasn't an affirmation, but it was enough.

"I will," Tadek spoke at last.

Everyone looked at him in surprise. Zosia leapt up. "You can't! There's been a vote."

"What vote? He asked for opinions and now he asks for unanimity! Since when do we take orders from a stranger?"

"*Tadziu!*"

Tadek picked up a gun and walked calmly to where Peter stood. As Tadek faced Peter wordlessly, he felt his heart pounding in his chest. He raised his hand to stop any of the Council from interrupting and returned Tadek's steely gaze. Finally Peter broke the silence, said as calmly as he could, "I know if you want me dead, I'll inevitably end up dead sooner or later. So do it now, if that's what you really want. If you really want to kill an innocent man in cold blood, then do it now, in front of all your friends."

Tadek raised the gun to point it at his face and grated, "You talk about friends, but where are all your friends?" Still pointing the gun at his face, Tadek turned to address the others. "Don't you find it just a bit too convenient that they are all dead? That there is no one to confirm or deny his story? Huh?" Tadek turned back toward him and added, "Even your accomplice in the prison camp didn't last very long, did he? How *convenient!*"

"What are you saying?"

"Oh, but of course, you don't know about that, do you?" Tadek sneered.

"About what? *Who?*" Peter glanced at Zosia, had a sudden, terrible premonition. "Geoff?" he asked so quietly they could hardly hear the name.

Zosia nodded slightly.

Peter felt suddenly quite ill. Tadek studied him as if interpreting his reactions, but he ignored Tadek, wanted to ignore the gun pointing at him. He had a violent urge to knock it out of Tadek's hand, but he knew that would be pointless. "What happened? I didn't name him," he said to no one in particular. He felt he was losing his balance as the earth kept shifting beneath him.

Katerina answered in a dispassionate voice, "It seems he murdered your *Kommandant*—beat him with a candlestick over the head in his private quarters. Claimed it was an accident and self-defense according to the court report. Of course, they hanged him for that, the very next day."

It was obvious what had happened: with Peter's absence, the insane *Kommandant* had decided to move to his next victim despite the documents they held against him. And poor Geoff had been down to counting the days until he was free!

With a voice like a twisting knife, Tadek added, "So, no friends, no family."

It was completely irrelevant to the argument, but he felt the need to correct Tadek's assertion. "I have a brother," he said distractedly. Though Erich, no doubt, assumed he was dead, he had checked on his brother's progress now and then and knew he was alive and well. But, he realized, the last time he had checked was ten years ago.

No family, Tadek had said.

He looked up past the gun at Tadek and waited for the inevitable. Tadek said nothing, just held the gun steadily pointing at his face.

"I do have a brother, don't I?" Peter finally asked plaintively.

"Oh, yes. The best sort." Tadek fixed him in his sights. "Just your sort."

"What do you mean?"

"He's a Party member. A good Nazi."

Peter felt himself flush. He noticed how intently Tadek watched him, and embarrassed, Peter dropped his gaze as he thought how both his father and his brother had betrayed everything he believed in.

Zosia called out something in Polish, which Tadek answered angrily. Then Marysia said something. Tadek snarled a reply to that as well. As a debate erupted around Peter in words he could not understand, he kept thinking of his father and his brother. Collaborators. Stinking collaborators.

Suddenly Tadek turned back to him and, switching to German so that Peter could understand, said, "Those idiots will believe any ridiculous sob story, but you and I know better, don't we? We both know, you'd be the death of all of us."

Peter felt too dismayed to answer.

"But since you got a majority vote, you know what I'm going to do?" Tadek asked, then without waiting for an answer, said, "I'm going to grant your last request. I'll shoot you in the face, in front of my friends, and I'll even clean up the fucking mess it'll leave."

Peter stared at the cold metal of the barrel. "Fine," he agreed tiredly. After all that he had endured, was this really all there was? He fought back an image of what his face would look like when Tadek pulled the trigger, fought away memories of Allison's face, and wondered suddenly about life after death, about soaring spirits. Would he finally find out?

"Tadziu." It was Zosia. She had quietly joined them and they both looked at her, surprised by her sudden presence. "Put the gun down." Under her breath, so that none but Tadek and Peter could hear it, she added, "That's an order."

Without saying a word, Tadek lowered the gun and turned disgustedly to walk away. The rest of the Council, still in a sort of shock, watched as he walked back up the slope. He climbed to where he had been sitting, walked a few meters farther, then turned again. Waving his gun to indicate the entire group, he snarled, "You're all fools! Don't you see! He'll be the death of all of us! Anyone he's ever had anything to do with is dead!" Anger and frustration nearly choking him, he spat out, "You're fools to trust him! Idiots!" Spinning on his heel, he stormed off, still hurling incomprehensible imprecations as he went.

Peter watched him leave, continued to stare into the sun long after he was gone. Though Tadek had left, his words hung in the air: *Anyone he's ever had anything to do with is dead!* It was no worse than what he himself had thought on many occasions, yet the words stung. He knew the Council was watching him, wondering what he would do, but he did not care to notice them. *Your father died within days of being arrested . . .* Within days. All those years of searching, of wondering. *Within days.* The sun blinded him, turned everything around him into dark, looming shadows. He began to tremble, as if from cold. *Your mother died after about seven months. . . .* How she must have suffered! *Seven months*—and for what? For nothing. All those years he was looking for her, she was dead. *It's all right, it will be all right, everything will be okay, trust me,* she had said. But she was dead. The sunlight caused tears to stream down his face, but he did not care anymore. He did not care what the Council saw or did not see. He could no longer make out even their shadows; they were irrelevant.

He saw nothing, felt nothing, heard no one, only the darkness surrounding and the voices of his past. *Arrested! Killed! What for?* Like a cascade of water, they washed over him. *Do you want them to take you too?* He shook his head, but voices hissed in his ear: *You like games, see how you like this one. . . .* He squeezed his eyes shut. *I'm afraid you've been sold. . . .* He put his hands to his temples to try to still them. *Are you so stupid you don't even understand self-preservation?* He pleaded for silence, but a thunder roared in his head. *The price of disobedience is death.* . . . His heartbeat pounded a rhythm into the cacophony. *Dona eis requiem.* . . . A sickening dizziness caused him to stumble. *Don't let them kill you.* . . . Waves of grief and loneliness and death washed over him, suffocating him—he was drowning. *Were you tortured?* He could not stand them anymore. *Were you tortured?* Slowly, he turned and lowered himself to a sitting position, put his face in his hands, and wept.

PART II

The Darkness Within

"**A**RE YOU ALL RIGHT?" The words emerged from the din with increasing clarity, and by the third time or so, he understood and looked up to see the speaker. Marysia looked down at him. By her side were Zosia and Konrad.

"I guess so." Tears streamed down his face. "I think I just need to get some sleep. Can I do that?" The voices still beset him, but they were quieter, like the sound of a waterfall in the distance. He tried to focus on Zosia's face, but her image was hazy; he squinted, blinked, and tried to get the film off his eyes. Eventually it occurred to him that Marysia had answered him. He looked up at her questioningly.

"Of course," she repeated slowly as though aware that she did not have his full attention. "You're a free man, you can come and go as you please."

Peter nodded. Yes, free. They said so. So go away! he yelled to his voices. He looked at his arm: the markings were still there and the band still clung to his wrist. Free. They said so. Just like that. Like magic. He climbed to his feet and wordlessly stumbled to the tent. Throwing himself down on the cot, he fell into a deep sleep.

It was dark when he awoke. He rolled into a sitting position, sat for a moment trying to recall where he was. A lantern was burning with a low light. Somebody had removed his shoes and set some food on a tray near the bed. He ate the food, climbed under the blankets, and fell back asleep.

He awoke in broad daylight feeling oddly detached from himself and his surroundings. He swung his legs over the edge of the bed to get up, but before he could stand, the realization hit him: he was free! He had done it, he had survived! Ever since the night of his arrest all those years ago . . . How long had it been? God Almighty, eight years! For eight years, he had focused his entire being, all his hopes, everything, on this one moment. And now it was here. He had survived!

He felt an incredible surge of happiness at the realization that all his dreams had come true. Free! And a home! The Council had agreed he could stay! He was safe, he was free, he had left behind all that horror. He could live a normal life, he would return to the living, he would start afresh! What more could any man want from life? What more? He felt tears running down his cheeks, and he wiped at them in confusion. What were they doing here? He was free, he was elated, he was thankful. . . . What more could one want? All the rest of it, all the ugliness and the murders and the years and years and years of wasted life—it was all in the past. He had been purged of all of it! The escape, the trial, defending his life—that was sufficient to cleanse him. He was free, he was free, he was free! What more could one want?

He stood and a momentary dizziness overcame him. He sat back down. His parents. They were indeed dead. That's what that man, Tadek, had said. Peter had known it all along, but somehow it still hurt, and now, after all these years, he could mourn them. But what was there to mourn? People he hardly knew; a life he had never lived. And Geoff. Executed. His friend's ever-present grin, the silly scenarios he would invent, the way the two of them would do a double act that kept the young boys in stitches, laughing at their oppressors, joking their way through years of meaningless labor. Hanged. And Allison. Nothing left but bones by now. The fantasies he had invented, where she survived to greet him upon his return home . . . Home? He couldn't go home. They would kill him.

He shook his head, trying to dispel the thoughts. He was free, he had a chance here at a new life. None of the past would matter. He would start afresh, make a home for himself here. He would be free and that was all that mattered. He would be free of them. Forever!

He stepped out of the tent and looked around—there was no guard in sight. Clearly, they had honored their decision that he was to be trusted, but it left him feeling strangely alone and at a loss for what to do. What did a free man do? Where should he go? He realized with a sudden pang how much of his life had been structured by constraints, and after all this time, without directions, orders, or threats, he was adrift.

His eyes were drawn to the forest around. The pines were tinted with the somber green of autumn, the air was alive with the singing of birds. Insects swarmed here and there, and he saw the movements of a squirrel as it dashed up a trunk. Sunlight glinted through the canopy, warming him as he stood there. It is a beautiful world, he thought. And if he was to begin life anew somewhere, then he could think of no better place.

He cleaned himself up, found a change of clothes and breakfast among the things that had been thoughtfully left for him in the tent, and then went out and tried to find someone. It didn't take long. A camp sentry emerged from the trees after he had wandered a few meters and pointed him in the right direction.

As he walked among the trees, he noted, not for the first time, that there were far fewer tents than the number of people seemed to merit. He took a mental tally: ten Council members, six or seven different guards, Zosia's child . . . Even without assuming that the Council represented a much larger number, that was still more people than the three tents implied. One entire tent for himself, one for the latrine; the third and largest was where he was heading now. Where the hell did everyone else go? Perhaps if he had been less preoccupied earlier he would have noticed, but now, as he looked around, he saw no sign of where they all resided.

The large tent was a sort of kitchen. There was coffee and tea and some food on a long table along one wall, and opposite that were some chairs. Four other people were in the tent, only two of whom looked familiar. One was the old assassin, the other was Wojciech—the man who had grumbled that he had been outvoted. They stared at Peter with undisguised curiosity. He felt daunted that there was no one he considered a friend.

"So you've finally got up?" the old woman asked in a tone that was either sneering or jesting.

He nodded.

"Help yourself to the food. My name is Katerina. Do you want anything?"

He wanted to find Zosia or Marysia, but his newly earned independence made him determined to make his way on his own. "I want this off," he said, indicating the band on his wrist.

Katerina turned to her colleagues and said something in Polish that made them laugh. He bristled but did not say anything. She turned back to him and looked as though she was going to tease him but, upon seeing his face, changed her mind and said in a tone that was kinder than he had expected, "We'll get to that, don't worry. Now sit, have some tea with us, then I'll give you a tour."

"This is amazing," he found himself saying yet again.

Katerina turned a corner and pointed out a chapel. "We have expanded our underground home over the years," she explained. "It is called Szaflary."

"Szaflary," he repeated. "Is absolutely everything kept here?"

"That would be stupid, wouldn't it?" She gestured down a hallway. "Now here are some passages that lead to stuff you shouldn't see for a while. Later maybe. I mean"—here she sidled up next to him as if telling him a secret—"we said we trust you, but you know . . ."

"Frankly, I'm amazed that you have shown me this much. What about security? Why are there so many of you? Why aren't you organized in isolated cells? It's so much safer."

"Yes, it is. We did that early on, but we were dying. I mean, we live here. Some of us were born here. This is where what's left of our freedom, our culture, is carried on. That's more important than safety." She looked around sadly. "This, and other places like it, this is all that is left of us. Out there"—she gestured broadly—"out there, we play roles, but we are not ourselves."

"But if you're discovered here . . ."

"Oh, they know we're here. They're not exactly sure of us, where we are, how many, but they know."

"*What?*"

"The soldiers. They know. We don't let any of them emerge alive from these mountains. They stay away, and they get to stay alive. They lie, they say they patrol these areas, but they know that they better not set one foot inside our borders."

"But if the government finds out, won't they bomb you out of existence?" he asked, confused by the implications.

"They can't," Katerina answered as if unconcerned.

"Why not?"

"Deterrents," she answered, deadpan.

"What do you mean? You have nuclear weapons?" he almost scoffed.

"No thanks to our useless allies. Anyway, our deterrents are strategically based in various German cities. It's another one of those standoff situations. Only thing is, we reached the balance after they had grabbed our country and slaughtered millions of our people. It was too late to set the clock back, but we have at least stopped most of the mayhem."

"You negotiate with them?"

"Nowadays, yes. There was a time . . ." Katerina neglected to continue and he did not ask anything more.

When they had finished the tour, she led him back to the library.

"You said some of your people infiltrate into the general population. What's the point? Aren't they powerless there?" he asked while absently scanning the computer screen visible on a desk. The library was not en route to the room she had said he could use, so apparently Katerina had a reason for bringing him back, but she had not as yet told him.

"Oh, they serve a number of purposes. They keep the morale of the population up, set up schools, disseminate information, teach, organize small partisan groups, help equalize food distribution, recruit into our ranks, and perhaps most importantly, they keep any local or wildcat groups from assassinating our own operatives."

"Are assassinations common?"

"A lot commoner than the Germans would like to have known."

"Isn't there retribution? Murders of hostages and so on?"

"Yes, but we decided early on, we can't be held hostage for what *they* do. Besides, they are so uncontrolled, they defeat their own purposes. For example, in September 1939, just after the invasion, they hanged twenty thousand civilians in Bydgoszcz as a retaliation for military action."

"Twenty thousand? Civilians? Hanged?"

"Yes. You see my point. If they are willing to kill like that, as retaliation for defensive military action during an invasion, then we can hardly take seriously any hope that our so-called 'good behavior' would be rewarded with civility."

"No, I guess they freed your hands. It was never so wildly uncontrolled in England."

"Oh, yes, it was," Katerina corrected. "There was a firestorm of arrests and executions after the invasion. They were rather secretive about it; nevertheless, they wiped out anyone they termed an enemy of the state. Including your entire Jewish population."

She seemed to think he was ignorant of his country's history, and that annoyed him. "Yes, but England didn't have that many Jews in the first place."

"No, you dealt with them early on in your history, didn't you?" she countered condescendingly.

"Didn't you?" he responded, automatically assuming history that he did not know.

"England expelled the Jews in 1290, dear boy, whereas in our kingdom they were granted autonomy and guaranteed their liberties under the Statute of Kalisz in 1264, and in the fourteenth century, during the reign of Casimir the Great, those fleeing persecution in other lands were welcomed here. With the Reformation, tolerance was extended to all religions via the Confederation of Warsaw in 1573. I think you will find that is not only early, but unusual. While the rest of Europe tore itself to pieces with religious wars, here we maintained our diversity and let each keep his own conscience."

She closed her eyes as if recalling something, then said, "We who differ in matters of religion will keep the peace amongst ourselves and neither shed blood on account of differences of faith, or kinds of church, nor punish one another—" She stopped suddenly. "It is a loose translation and I don't remember it all. Anyway, many, many Jews found refuge in the old republic and remained throughout the period of partitions and into the new republic. That is one reason why there were so many of them here for the Nazi invaders to persecute. That is why the Germans based their extermination camps here—this is where most of their victims lived."

"Are you saying, then, there was no anti-Semitism?" he pressed somewhat illogically.

"I said nothing of the sort, child," Katerina chided. "Squabbling between and among neighbors, religions, political parties, and social classes is completely normal in any heterogeneous society. What is not normal is the view we hold of such things nowadays."

"What do you mean?"

"I mean you have swallowed far too much Nazi education. You view disagreements in the past as a prelude to what followed, and you write history backwards. The Jews were a people like any other, they had a rich culture and history, they had strengths and weaknesses and divisions among them. They were no more lambs waiting patiently to be slaughtered than the gentiles here were slaves waiting to be worked to death!"

"I don't understand your point."

"You honor these Nazis," Katerina hissed lightly, "by ascribing such importance to their asinine racial theories that you even look for their roots in normal human disagreements rather than in a madman's rantings. Do you think we laid ourselves open to invasion and the complete destruction of our country just to solve some political disputes? You give credence to Nazi propaganda by never questioning their assumptions. To oppose them is not just to spout opposite nonsense, it is to know the truth and to defend it!"

"You've certainly heard a lot in my few words," he responded unsteadily.

"Are you saying that wasn't your implication?" Katerina asked with tightly controlled anger.

"I don't know what I meant," he answered honestly. "I am tainted by my times, I admit it. I have only one view of the world and it's a very ugly one, but remember, I had no choice in the matter."

Katerina nodded as if accepting an apology, then she sighed. "I grow old, too old for this fight. You are right, we have failed you by handing you this world so devoid of morality. You children, you children must fight battles you cannot even understand. This war we have given you, it is yours to fight, but you do not know what it is about. You have suckled at the breast of war, yet even so, you do not fight, you just survive."

He gave her an uncomprehending look.

"Yes, I mean you. I suspect your story is true, and like so many others you are indeed guilty of nothing. Unjustly condemned, you are innocent of any blood in a time when innocence is in itself guilt. You will know no peace until you accept the guilt of war. You cannot stand idly by."

"I haven't been idle!"

"Your resistance has been ineffectual. You have not killed in an age that requires killing."

"You don't know what I've done!"

"I know what you haven't done. This man, this man who owned you. He was a murderer, a torturer, wasn't he?"

"I would guess so, from what I know," Peter answered with reluctant honesty.

"Yet you left him alive to murder and torture others?"

"I am not judge, jury, and executioner," he replied defensively.

"Over there"—Katerina waved her arms to indicate an area of books—"we have the volumes documenting the specific measures taken against Jews, all of which were legal."

She said it as if the connection to their conversation was obvious, and he realized that it was. "Killing is wrong," he muttered helplessly.

"Blessed is the world in which that is true, but that is not our world, is it?"

He turned away from her and walked over to the books she had indicated. Stroking their backs with his fingers, he asked, "So it is documented?" since he did not know what else to say.

"Oh, yes, we've done some digging. Quite literally. I would suggest, though, that you don't eat anything before you look at the evidence we found. If you think you've suffered . . ." She paused, then in a controlled voice continued, "These are just copies; the original evidence has been smuggled to America for safekeeping. And that's exactly what they're doing with it, keeping it safe. They don't want to upset the political balance."

He said nothing, aware of how close to a flashpoint of anger she was.

She sighed heavily, then added, "You know, they weren't alone. There were others who for political or religious or ethnic reasons were pursued to their deaths, but for the sheer volume of people involved, the variety in their backgrounds—social, cultural, ethnic, age, health, gender—nothing mattered—there is nothing to compare with what was done to them."

"Nothing?" he asked pointedly. "What about the tens of millions in the Soviet Union who disappeared into the earth? Or the eight million or so murdered in the Congo? Or don't they count?"

"Ah, so you are not without some history," Katerina remarked more mildly than he had expected. "Well, perhaps I betray a prejudicial interest." She cast her eyes down and fell silent.

He studied her. Her silence seemed almost prayerful, and so he did not interrupt.

Quietly, so quietly that her words were almost lost to the susurration of the ventilation fans, she said, "My family was Jewish. We were urban, cosmopolitan, assimilated into Warsaw society. When the Germans penned us into that ghetto, with all those transportees, all those villagers and people with their strange customs—"

"You were there?"

"Oh, yes. When the transports started, I left—"

"You could get out?" he asked in astonishment.

"Oh, yes, there were ways. Cellar passages, bribery, the sewers. Individuals could slip in and out. The problem was, where to go? Our enemies held the entire country, controlled most of Europe. But of course, you are aware of that."

He nodded.

"I went into hiding, first one place then another, hidden by people who did not even know me. Brave people, all of whom risked death, not only their own, but those of their family. I was moved out of Warsaw to the countryside and then eventually, through the son of one family, joined a partisan group."

"There were Jewish partisan groups?"

"Yes, after the ghetto uprising, remnants of the ghetto fighters regrouped in the woods and they fought bravely, but that is not what I joined."

"And these partisans—they just accepted you?" he asked almost jealously.

"At first they did not want to bother as I was just another mouth to feed, but then I acquired two *Wehrmacht* rifles and that sufficed as proof of my usefulness."

"What happened to your family?"

"I lost everyone. After the German and then the Russian invasion, some fled to the east, into Soviet territory. I don't know what became of them. Of those that remained, all died. Every single one of them."

"I'm sorry. I had no idea." He replayed his last few comments to see if he had said anything really insensitive. After a reasonable silence he asked gently, "You say 'they' when talking about your people. Are you not Jewish?"

Katerina laughed. "Depends on who you ask. The Nazis would say yes, the religious would say no."

"What do you say? What do you believe?"

"I believe in nothing," Katerina stated coldly.

It was probably an accurate summary of his own religious beliefs, or rather lack of beliefs, but somehow when Katerina said it that way, it seemed much colder and emptier than what he felt. Did he, then, believe in something? The disturbing thought got shoved aside, and he pressed on with another question. "Was there any organized resistance? I mean before the uprising?"

"Yes and no. It's easy to underestimate the terror and confusion of that time. And until 1941, it wasn't even clear that we were targeted for special treatment." She used the Nazi euphemism without irony. "Before then, more were killed because they were part of the intelligentsia rather than specifically for their religion. Later, after the Wannsee conference, things changed, but that wasn't clear at the time, and there were the usual disagreements about what to do. You see, in the ghetto the Nazis created in Warsaw, there was an incredible diversity of peoples and opinions. The consensus opinion, before 1942, was that complete submission was the only way to survive. Guerrilla warfare or coordination with the Polish Underground was ruled out; obedience to the German authorities via the Judenrat was encouraged. The leadership was afraid of giving the Germans an excuse to turn their machine guns on us. So they waited. Such a passive approach had served my people well throughout history, and most of them were convinced that once more they could wait things out. Well, in 1942 the first transports out of the ghetto were begun, and in two months three-quarters of the people had been taken. Then it was clear that obedience and submission would not satisfy the Nazis, that they needed no excuses, but it was just too late."

I'm not giving him any excuses. Peter felt a tremor as he recalled his words to Roman, not even a year before. "What about outside help?"

"Lack of information has always hindered us, that and an unwillingness to believe the unbelievable. Very early on, the Polish Underground, on behalf of the Jewish Resistance, sent emissaries to the unconquered lands begging for help and especially for passports and money to smuggle people out. At least one such emissary was smuggled into the ghetto so that he could return with an eyewitness account—I know, because I saw him. I heard he got through all the way to London, then America, but there was no real response. They didn't want to hear about it. The government also established a Council to Aid the Jews and managed to hide some people and smuggle some people out and a few arms in, but as always, they were hampered by lack of resources—even as they were during the general uprising and even as we are now. As for individual actions, little is known of the anonymous martyrs. Those, like me, who survived can offer our paltry gratitude, but for all those who did not, we have no words nor can we thank those who died trying to save them." Katerina sighed. "In any case, everyone was limited by confusion and terror."

"And antipathy and indifference?" Peter had a sudden memory of how his mother had told him about their good luck in getting their first flat when the previous owners had been deported or arrested or, as she had said, "something like that." Because he had shared her joy, he had never stopped to think what her words must have meant until his grandmother had whispered something to him years later.

"Yes, that, too," Katerina agreed, "but we were also the only land that had the death penalty imposed for helping a Jew in any way whatsoever. I can show you the German directives, if you wish." She pulled down a book and paged through it. "Here's one: 'In view of repeated instances of Jews being hidden by Poles, anyone who shelters Jews and gives or sells them food will be punished by death. This is the final warning.' I myself saw a man shot to death simply for throwing a sack of bread over the ghetto wall."

She handed the book to Peter and he looked at some of the directives therein. Edict after edict—each growing more dire, each more annoyed by the obvious civil disobedience. Each contained commands not to supply Jews with food or shelter or documents, each contained the word *Todesstrafe*, death sentence. He flipped through some pages and stopped in the middle of a list of people convicted under one of the diktats. The entries leapt out at him: October 25, 1942, Zosia Wojcik, along with her two children, aged two and three, executed along with a Jewish man she was harboring. November 1942, Oborki—twenty-two families, the entire population of the village, murdered for giving aid to Jews. He flipped ahead: February 1944, the entire village of Sasow burned alive for aiding Jews hiding in the nearby forests. He turned back a few pages: Maria Rogozinska and her one-year-old son shot for harboring Jews.

A one-year-old? He closed his eyes and shut the book. Numbly he asked, "What about denunciations? Active support of the Nazis' policies?"

"Oh, yes, that happened, too. Some people gloated, and there are always people who want to make money or settle old scores or ingratiate themselves. In every society, there are immoral opportunists, as I am sure you are aware."

He remembered what had been said about his father only the day before, and he felt himself redden.

"And there was not much coordination between allies." Katerina was still answering his question. "You know how it is, what could have been done, what should have been done, what wasn't done . . ."

"Do you think it would have helped?" he asked uncomfortably. For personal reasons he hoped Katerina's opinion would be that it would not have helped. He was painfully aware that in his own family history there was no indication of any heroics. Would his grandparents have risked their lives for casual acquaintances? For strangers? And what about his parents? With them, indifference might have been the best he could have hoped for. He had a dreadful fear that they had collaborated, and a concomitant fear that he was wrong and damning them for things they had not done.

He also had nagging doubts about himself. Would an external observer have said he was indifferent, rather than terrified, when he had watched the woman gunned down in the plaza? Was knowing that he was helpless sufficient excuse for his inaction? Or was it that he had no reason to risk his life for her? Did he then expect of others a courage he had not shown himself?

Katerina was studying him, her lips pursed. "Probably not," she answered at last. "There was very little opportunity for heroics. Now, in retrospect, it's hard to realize how much of a shock the whole thing was. To have predicted the events of 1942 just ten years earlier would have been considered fanatically anti-German." She paused, looking pensive. "Now, it is obvious what their intent was, but then, then we believed better of the world. We were naive." She looked at him with sorrow. "You, you children of this war—you can't ever understand. You're scarred from birth and some part of you will always believe that what we have around us now is normal."

Again that same accusation; he shook his head slightly but did not disagree. He was still too absorbed with wondering about his parents. Whatever they had done, he reassured himself, whatever their choices, they had not initiated the whole thing.

"And let's not forget," Katerina continued, "whatever heroics or indifference or collaboration the local populations showed, they were not the ones perpetrating the crime. Our conquerors were very determined in their efforts, and it is they who carried out the murders and it is they who bear the guilt. And," she added, pausing to make sure she had his attention, "it is difficult to risk your life for a stranger. I guess you can appreciate that."

"Yes, I do." After an awkward silence, he finally said, "I want to thank you all for giving me this chance."

She ignored his expression of gratitude. "There were some, though, who were too willing to capitulate, who volunteered assistance, who blackmailed people. Those bastards . . ." She stopped as though she had finished her thought sufficiently clearly.

"What happened to them?"

"Elsewhere? I don't know. Perhaps in England they lived out their lives in peace. Perhaps they worked in the government and lived in a cozy flat with a wife and three children."

"Perhaps," he agreed with quiet helplessness.

"Here, the Resistance imposed the death penalty for such actions and publicized their executions and . . ."

"And?"

"And those who were not found immediately were tracked down later"—she smiled—"and killed."

Zosia's words about Katerina came back to him. He looked at her lined face, imagining a young girl whose entire family had been murdered. "Were you a part of that?"

"Oh, yes. In my youth, I was quite good with a knife. A secret liaison, get them into an embrace and come in from behind: they never knew what hit them. More's the pity, they should have suffered."

The room felt hot and stuffy and he wished they would leave, but Katerina seemed fixed to her place and her thoughts. To try to change the direction of the conversation, he asked, "Your people in the field—do they live as Germans all the time? Or do they switch roles, German one week, Polish the next?"

"It depends on how well established their position is. Most, if they can, switch; otherwise they'd go mad. But of course, not quite as fast as every week. When our Germans can't stand strutting and saluting anymore, they come back for a break, and when our *Nichtdeutsch* get fed up with hunger and manhunts and risking continual arrest, then they return."

"Manhunts?"

"Yes. I guess you don't have them."

"I don't think so—not if I understand how you are using the term."

"What I mean is, the master race needs slaves and they tend to use up the ones they have fairly quickly, so every now and then—rather frequently, in fact—they simply close a street or raid a building or invade a house or whatever, and they grab everybody there and take them away. It's not really like an arrest since they don't even pretend you've done something wrong; it's just, well, a manhunt. They usually send the adults to factories, farms, mines, and so on. Tadek lost his wife that way."

"Really?" Peter could not imagine that harsh, unyielding man ever having had a wife.

"Yes, newly married, living in Kraków. They closed a street she was on and simply took her and everyone else away. That was ten years ago."

"What did he do?"

"Came here. He heard the mountains were off-limits, so he made his way to the nearest village and then simply walked in. For all we know, he may have been trying to commit suicide. But whatever the case, Zosia—she never follows the rules—Zosia spotted him and escorted him into camp."

"And?"

"Oh, he was interrogated, his story was checked, and he's been here ever since."

"So, he went through the same process that I did."

"More or less."

"And you let him live."

"Obviously."

"But he wanted me to die," Peter stated bitterly.

Katerina shrugged. "Anyway, they still go on."

"What?"

"The manhunts."

"Oh."

"They take children, too."

"Children?"

"Yes. Some get adopted, most get taken for domestic labor, although I've heard that there are such shortages of children that they use adults now for that as well." She looked at him, cocking her head to the side thoughtfully. "I guess you're further proof that that's the case."

Peter met her look, but did not match the small smile she gave him. Somehow all that he had endured did not feel like "further proof" of anything. He was no more a bit of economic data than he was somebody to be bought or sold.

"Of course," she continued, "I have a theory about that."

"Oh?" He wasn't sure what she was referring to and suspected that he would prefer it remain that way, but he could not think of any sensible way of preventing her from proceeding.

"Yes. I think you—and others like you—were simply used to test their retraining programs. They like refining their psychological techniques, and they have come a long way! I think they found an intelligent, well-educated, independent-minded, physically fit adult quite a challenge. Time was, someone like you would simply scare them into chaining you to some machine and working you to death in a few weeks. Don't you think it's interesting that they took so much time and effort to train you and then threw you into the very midst of their society? Hmm?"

"*Interesting* isn't the word I would have used for it at the time," he answered dryly.

"Nevertheless, it's an intriguing commitment of their resources."

"Only four months," he said, aware that this vague defense was quite damning.

"But that's a lot of time to spend on someone who could be put to work in a factory immediately!"

"They've never been known for not wasting time on cruel diversions. Or for efficiency, despite their much vaunted reputation to the contrary. And, in any case," he added, despite that it contradicted what he had just asserted, "I worked every day of those months in some capacity."

"Yes, yes, yes, but that's neither here nor there—the point is, why train an adult to do a job that a child is so much better suited for? Other than shortages, of course."

"They used to use adults all the time."

"But they changed that policy in the sixties!"

"Well, maybe they're changing it back!" He felt more and more irritated without knowing exactly why. He just felt sure that somehow his character was under attack.

"That's exactly my point!"

"I don't know. Maybe I'm just too tired, but I'm just not following you on this."

"What I'm trying to say is, they decided children are the most malleable and therefore the most trustworthy once they've been properly trained. Now for decades they use kids—nearly every adult working among them, in their households, I mean, has never known any other life. But suddenly they use adults again. Maybe it's hard to get enough kids. But then, if there are shortages, why train someone as obviously problematic as you must have been? Someone with your background!"

"I don't know." He worked to keep the anger out of his voice with little success.

"Oh, just think of it! If they could break somebody like you without physically, or even mentally, destroying you, then what a coup that is! What wonderful proof of their superiority! Somebody as confident as you willing to work obediently among them, not threatening their families, not disrupting their society, not indulging in violent acts!"

Peter felt his face grow hot with shame: her words provoked a sharp memory of his humiliation in Karl's study. Why had he given in so easily? But what alternative was there? He looked down at the table, waiting helplessly for her to finish.

Suddenly a thought occurred to her. "You didn't, did you?"

"What?"

"Commit any violent acts?"

For a moment he felt like lying, but he was too tired to construct a careful, consistent story, so he finally answered truthfully, "No."

"No bullet through your friend's brain when you left?" Katerina suggested with unappreciated humor.

"He's not my friend."

"No . . . ?" She drew her finger across her neck and made a noise like a knife slicing through flesh.

"No."

"Whyever not?"

Why not? More time to escape? Less risk? A commitment to nonviolence? The children? He settled on that. "He was a father."

Katerina snorted her disbelief. "That's just an excuse."

Peter looked up at her, but he could not match the intensity of her stare. He looked back down at the table. Could he admit that it had just not occurred to him?

"What about sabotage?"

"No."

"Vandalism?"

A smile flitted across his face as he thought of the useless acts of his youth. In all his years with the Reusches and Vogels he had not even defaced one poster! "No," he admitted quietly, then summoning whatever dignity remained to him, he looked up at Katerina and added, "not unless you count the times I carelessly splattered my blood around."

Katerina took the mild reproof as humorous and nodded her approval of his morbid sense of humor. "But seriously, I bet your progress was tracked, from a distance, and every month you functioned as desired, someone congratulated themselves on their methods."

"Hurrah for them," he responded bitterly. It wasn't enough what he had endured, now Katerina was making him feel as though he had failed to disprove their theories and techniques. But it made some sense. Why hadn't it occurred to him at any point?

"I didn't mean to make you feel bad," Katerina offered.

"No?"

"No, really. I just thought you might be interested."

"I guess I would be, if it weren't all so personal." He remembered his introduction to the Vogel household, remembered Karl assuring Elspeth: *He's quite safe.* How had he been so sure? "Maybe later, when I can put some distance between them and me, maybe then I can analyze it all rationally."

"Yes, we'd be very interested in your responses. If they've become very good at what they do, we need to know. We need to prepare our people."

"Yes, I suppose with the manhunts you are all in danger anytime you enter a town or village," he said, wondering at the courage of the ones who volunteered to return.

"Oh, no. Usually we manage to equip everybody with papers making them essential personnel in their locale—so in general, our people don't get taken. After they're finished with their jobs or need a break, they just come back here."

"Do the ten of you run all this?"

"Oh, essentially. Political parties and a parliamentary representation were maintained for some years after the Germans invaded, but that was unsustainable. We've maintained a political wing with all the trappings of democratic representation so that it will be easier to organize an interim government after liberation, but for the time being, we're run on military principles and under martial law. The Council gets orders from above, but we run the day-to-day stuff."

"Above?"

"Yes, above—and that's all you'll get to know about that."

"Fair enough." He shrugged. He had no interest in probing where he was not wanted. It was one of the hardest things he had had to learn as a young recruit: to dampen his insatiable curiosity. But the lesson had been important and he had learned. In some ways he was astonished that Katerina was so loquacious. He appreciated her answers, but worried slightly that she might be overstepping her authority or the agreed wisdom of the Council. He decided to change the subject to something less dangerous. "Isn't ten an awkward number? What happens if you get a five-to-five split vote?"

Katerina laughed; she almost doubled over with mirth at that question. "We don't get many yes–no type questions," she finally explained. "I know that yours was that sort . . . well, not really—I'll tell you all about that sometime—but anyway, usually when we poll ten people, we get twenty different votes! I swear all we do is squabble. No, the vote never splits in half. It'd be a miracle if we ever got five of us to agree on anything!"

He nodded. Clearly Katerina was prone to exaggeration, and perhaps all that she had told him was colored by an agenda, but he found he liked her, even if, in her abrupt honesty, she was not particularly gentle. He felt tired and his eyes were growing weary, so he decided not to ask any more questions. After they had sat for a moment in silence, Katerina finally told him the point of their return to the library. "Before we finish, I want to show you some documents that we have copies of here. Perhaps you've seen them before, perhaps not."

She led him over to a volume of Reich documents from 1940 and paged through until she found two separate entries. The first was a set of directives signed by Brauchitsch, the commander in chief of the army at the time, entitled "Orders Concerning the Organization and Function of Military Government in England." It contained details of the German occupation of Britain. One plan was that "the able-bodied male population between the ages of seventeen and forty-five will . . . be interned and dispatched to the Continent." That had indeed happened, and many had not returned. During the 1950s the policy had changed, and the internment had metamorphosed into the current six-year labor draft. Other rulings directed how hostages would be taken, how posting placards would be a capital offense, how all but the most mundane household items would be confiscated, and how ownership of a radio would be punishable by death.

Peter was familiar with most of it: he had read pieces of this and other documents, he had learned the history of his people since the war, and he had experienced the day-to-day occupation of his country all his life. There was little in the plans that had not been implemented in one form or another. He looked up from the entry, curious as to what Katerina expected him to say. While he had been reading, she had pulled down several other volumes and had marked entries in each. She indicated that he should read the second entry that she had selected and refer to the other volumes as necessary, then she sat down to wait as he did so.

The second selection was a long chapter of excerpts from diaries, logs, lectures, and directives. It told of the German plans for Poland—to convert the entire population into a slave labor colony, to annihilate the nobility, the clergy, the intelligentsia, the military and political leadership, and to exterminate any and all Jews and other "undesirables." It spoke of how the Poles, bereft of all their leaders, could be forcibly sterilized en masse to prevent procreation and could then be safely worked to a slow collective death as slaves of the Reich. Footnotes, from later dates, sent him to the other volumes for documentation of the occupation and the plan's implementation: gruesome experiments, enslavement, death camps, mass starvation, slaughter. There were handy charts and detailed numbers. All the sources were German officials who were quite proud of their accomplishments, and there were numerous photographs and other proofs that their accounts were valid. The documents were horrific in their cold-bloodedness: there was no expression of dismay, no question about the direction the Reich was taking, only cold, almost gleeful, accounts of human misery.

After a long while he looked up. "Why did you have me read this?"

"I imagine that you are familiar with the realities of the first series of documents."

He nodded.

"So you will have an easier time understanding and believing the second set."

"I do. But that still doesn't explain why."

"No, it doesn't. I won't explain now, because that would be pointless, you are not ready to understand. But someday, remember what you read here. Remember that we, too, have our own sad tales."

"You're being rather patronizing."

She smiled. "Perhaps. But now that you have escaped them, you will look for a fairy-tale ending to your suffering. It won't happen. It never does. And in your frustration, you will look to us to bring your salvation. Do not be surprised when we are unable to deliver."

He shook his head. "But you agreed to let me stay here! I don't need more than that. I won't expect anything. I've never depended on anybody but myself."

Katerina looked at him indulgently as though he were a sweet, naive child, but she did not say anything.

"Is it still going on?" he asked, gesturing toward the words he had read. Anything to stop her from looking at him like that.

"Some of it—"

A spasm of pain shot up from his leg through his body and involuntarily he gasped.

"Are you in pain?" Katerina asked.

"Not really."

"The human body does not bear such abuse well."

"It's nothing. I'm fine."

"I seriously doubt that," she countered coldly. "Although they are less prone to crush bones than they once were . . ."

He heard the catch in her voice. "Who are you thinking about?" he asked gently.

Katerina frowned at him as if embarrassed, but her frown gave way to a sad smile and she said, "All these years and still I don't forget. I was thinking of my sister. She was a courier for the Jewish Underground. She was small and slight and it was easy for her to slip through sewer grates in and out of the ghetto. She was caught by the Gestapo and . . ." Katerina heaved a great sigh. "The last we heard of her, they crushed every bone in her body while interrogating her. Naked, of course. Seems our 'supermen' are not above . . . The note smuggled out of the prison told us her arms were broken and the lower half of her body was in shreds."

"I'm sorry," Peter said, feeling utterly helpless.

"It was a long time ago. As I was saying," Katerina continued brusquely, "unlike my sister, they did not intend to kill you, but they also had no intention of preserving your health, and consequently, you will be weaker and in pain for the rest of your life. You are, how shall we say, damaged goods? That was, after all, their intent: to *make* you inferior, so that you would be a suitable slave."

He ducked his head, unable to deny the truth in her words.

"As a bonus, they were able to demonstrate their complete contempt for your life," Katerina explained into his silence. "From an internal source we have, I know that the attrition rate in those reeducation programs was around fifty percent. Most of those were simply killed when they were deemed unfit for work."

His eyes drifted nervously around the room. One out of every two. He had understood that statistic intuitively at the time, and it was no wonder that he had left their tender mercies and stepped into his new role with the Reusches so full of unnamed and unrecognized fear that he had not ever seriously considered doing anything that might cause him to be sent back.

"You must have survived," Katerina continued relentlessly, "not for any reasons of strength or determination, but because you showed sufficient pliancy."

"It was an act," he muttered defensively.

"Apparently a very good one," she chuckled. "Anyway, they've refined their techniques, thanks to you and your fellows, so that now they claim an eighty percent survival rate. Not bad, eh?"

"If you were already aware of these reeducation programs, why did you doubt my story?" he asked angrily.

"It is not your prerogative to question the decisions of the Council," she answered haughtily. "However, consider this: Was it just coincidence that your owner is highly placed in the Security Ministry? Perhaps he made some sort of deal for your life. You have exhibited an incredible desire to stay alive, and by your own admission you have no loyalties left. No command structure, no loved ones, not even a God that you must answer to."

"It's not like that!" he insisted, but in his mind he heard himself promise: *Whatever it takes.*

"Who knows?" Katerina shrugged. "In any case, we have taken an unnecessary risk in allowing you to live. Show some gratitude."

"Ah, so I should grovel at your mercy?" he snapped, regretting his words even as he spoke. He *was* grateful, but she had managed to make him feel that he had only exchanged one form of servitude for another!

"Your anger is misdirected. It is not our job to rescue you, nor have we ever done you any injury. We owe you nothing. Our rule is, we are not guilty for their actions. And for you, I might add a second rule. You live on sufferance here, and you would do well to remember that."

Peter glared at her but there was nothing he could say. He was grateful. *He was grateful!* But where was that fantasy ending he had always written to his story? Where was the dream that had sustained him? The one where he was welcomed as a hero, embraced and kissed and comforted and thanked? Or even just greeted with a warm smile?

Where were the words that would have made just one hour of torture bearable? Where were the words? Without realizing it, his fingers clawed at his manacle.

"Now," Katerina said, her eyes indicating his wrist, "let's get that thing off you."

2

"**Y**OU HAVE SCAR TISSUE here and here," the physician said, running his fingers along Peter's cheekbones. "It's harmless, just the result of being repeatedly pounded, but it changes the shape of your face slightly."

Peter nodded, unconcerned. Along with organizing the dental work that he had desperately needed, Zosia had insisted on a medical examination. He had reluctantly consented and allowed himself to be poked and prodded by three doctors over several days. They had discovered that he had had broken ribs on more than one occasion, but that most of his injuries had seemed to heal fairly well. They took X rays of his lungs and shook their heads ruefully at the images of scar tissue. They noted old fractures on his arms and legs and skull and told him, uselessly, that he had received a number of severe blows to the head. They also discovered that his recurrent headaches and occasional blurred vision were due to "trauma," which was simply a way of saying he had been hit one too many times in the face. Now he was sitting through the final consultation, and these results were summarized by the staff physician—a balding, gnomelike fellow who wore an oversize lab coat and kept nervously fingering his stethoscope.

The physician pinned an X ray onto a backlit screen. "And see here, you have some damage to some vertebrae. I guess someone really whacked you pretty hard across the back, eh? Kicked you, maybe?"

His eyes drifted off the X ray to the cabinets aligning the wall. "What's the damage?" he finally asked.

"Hard to say. Whenever you're dealing with nerves, you never know when things are going to go wrong."

"Thanks for the cheerful news," he commented morosely, wondering at the wisdom of having a checkup.

"Could affect your back or your legs or your neck around this area." The physician placed a finger at the base of Peter's skull. "That, not surprisingly, can give you pretty awful headaches."

"What can be done about it?"

The physician shrugged. "Painkillers."

"Great," Peter responded sarcastically. "What else?"

"Your legs," the physician continued ruefully. "They healed well enough, I suppose, but I imagine they give you some trouble now and then?"

"Sometimes. Can you do anything for them?"

The physician pursed his lips.

"I know, I know. Painkillers."

"We have these." The physician handed him a small bottle of evil-looking pills. "Very strong, so I advise you don't use them often. And they're addictive."

He nodded.

"Be careful with them, but take one if the pain gets unbearable."

Unbearable. Now there was a concept. He doubted that anything would hurt more now than it did originally, and he had borne that. After having had so many drugs pumped into him involuntarily, he was not sure he wanted to take any more, but he accepted the bottle and dropped it into his shirt pocket, thanking the doctor as he did so.

"Unfortunately, I don't think there's much we can do about your vision. At least not here."

"Where then?"

"In a properly outfitted hospital, they could do some more extensive testing. Maybe they could enact some repairs with lasers or surgery. Usually we get our people into a major hospital with appropriate papers and identifications to make sure they are important enough to get good treatment, then we see to it that our doctors are assigned to work on them. Unfortunately the hospital staff is, naturally, mostly their people"—it was clear from his tone who *they* were—"and getting you in there . . . Well, to put it bluntly, you're a marked man. There's no way we could pass you off as . . . well, you know, not with the scrutiny one undergoes in a hospital."

Peter nodded, unseeing. Would he never escape the bastards? Even here, even now, he could feel their choke hold on his life. He looked up at the physician. "Am I going to lose my sight?"

The doctor hesitated longer than was comfortable; finally he said, "I don't know."

Peter closed his eyes, but he opened them again immediately, irrationally afraid that his sight would disappear if he failed to use it. He looked around the office, savored the view, tried to impress on himself how grateful he was for his vision, as though begging his eyes not to deny him a gift he fully appreciated.

The physician wandered over to a drawer and rooted around a bit. Finally he found what he was looking for and brought it over to Peter. "Here"—he held out a glasses case—"these might help prevent the headaches. Wear them outside and whenever the light is bright."

Peter reached inside the case and pulled out a pair of dark sunglasses in a wire-rim frame. He put them on and leaned back to see his reflection in the mirror that hung over the counter. He smiled indulgently at the unfamiliar image, removed the glasses, and thanked the physician. Maybe it would help. Then he looked down at his arm. "Is there any way to remove this?"

The doctor shook his head. "I'm not an expert, but I don't think so. They really have gotten efficient at that, haven't they? The dyes are—well, it's not my field, but as far as I know, there's nothing that dissolves them that wouldn't take your skin off as well."

"What about burning it off?"

"Ech." The physician frowned, his bald forehead wrinkling with distaste. "I don't think that would work. They inject the dye quite deep—don't you remember the pain?"

"I was out. It did hurt afterward though."

"Well, if you burned the skin off, you'd have to go quite deep; probably you'd get some muscle and nerves. I once heard something about some technique involving lasers, but if there is one, it's not for the likes of you and me—especially you! You'd have to check into a hospital and, well, there's the rub. Anyway, we don't do anything like that here, we're just a clinic really. And an occasional emergency room."

The physician must have read Peter's expression, because he felt inclined to continue, "I think you can understand, we usually have more pressing issues to worry about. I don't think you could find anybody to do it for you, it's just not that important."

Peter ran his fingers along the numbers: one three one four seven oh eight. How many times had he run that through his mind? "It never changes," he muttered.

"What?"

He hadn't realized he had spoken aloud. "It never changes."

The doctor nodded in that absently sympathetic way that doctors do and then, as if to conclude, asked, "Is there anything else?"

Slightly confused by the question, Peter shook his head. Shouldn't he be asking that of the doctor? Then he remembered something unusual that had happened at the Vogel household and decided to ask about it. The doctor was already heading out of the room, so Peter had to call after him. "Wait! Yes."

The doctor turned and raised his eyebrows expectantly.

"Some months ago, in February, actually . . ." In February, when he had been reeling from Karl's revenge, there had been a midday knock on the door. He had gone to answer it and had been horrified to see three officials—one a policeman, the other two in white lab coats, such as doctors wear. As they requested, he fetched Frau Vogel. She came to meet them at the door, equally mystified, and invited them in. They had told her that they had something of importance to discuss and looked pointedly at him. Frau Vogel sent him from the room with a dismissive nod, but within a matter of minutes he was called back into the sitting room. Frau Vogel was by the window, leaning over a table, signing some papers.

She did not even look up as he came into the room; instead one of the white-coated men told him to roll up his sleeve.

A tourniquet was put on him, the white-coated man snapped a finger at a vein in the crook of his arm until it stood out, and then the other white-coated man produced a needle. The needle was injected and emptied and the tourniquet released. Frau Vogel returned the papers, the men thanked her, and they left without a word of explanation.

For the next several days, he had lived in horror of what might have been injected into his bloodstream. He had a fever and felt ill the following day, but with Karl constantly hammering him, it was rare he felt well in any case. The gossip around the town square—all the *Zwangsarbeiter,* and no one else, had been injected—was that it was some sort of inoculation against a communicable disease.

"Nothing came of it, as far as I know. I never got particularly sick or anything. Do you have any idea what they did then?" Peter asked, hoping at last for an answer to the mystery.

"I don't suppose you used to have brown eyes?" the doctor joked.

"No." Peter found the reference to a cruel medical experiment in extremely bad taste.

"Well, clearly they used you as guinea pigs," the physician answered seriously. "They were probably just doing a field test on a new vaccine or something. Certainly, if there was a disease scare and they had something they knew was safe, they wouldn't have skipped their own people. No, it was clearly a test."

"I guessed that much myself," Peter said, somewhat exasperated. Was this fellow good for anything? "Can you tell me what they injected?"

"Your blood doesn't show anything really unusual. You've been sick with some of the normal lousy-living-condition illnesses, and any one of them could have been caused by that shot. Or none of them." The physician looked at Peter sympathetically and added rather uncharacteristically, "Sorry. Don't worry about it, I don't think the shot did any long-term damage."

After the examinations and dentistry were completed, Peter was called before the Council to discuss his skills.

Katerina began, "Clearly, you have much experience that could be of value to us—you know a great deal about the current state of German society—at least a segment of it. In a few days, a psychiatrist and a sociologist will be here to interrogate—"

"Interview," Zosia suggested.

"—question you at length for a few weeks. They'll report back to HQ with the information they've gained. After that we need to know what you can do."

A few weeks? What in God's name could they want to know? Although Zosia had been careful to get Katerina to reword what she had said, he could not help but feel dread at the prospect of being interrogated or interviewed or questioned for such a long time. He remembered his conversation with Katerina in the library—clearly she was pursuing her interests to their logical conclusion. It took a moment for him to realize that everyone was waiting for him to speak. He looked at them blankly.

"Your skills?" Hania prompted.

He began with the basics. He had had reasonable weapons and assault training, but he was no longer a kid, and it was decided that he should not, in general, be used for direct assaults such as sabotage. They were equally unimpressed by his long-ago training as a sniper, though a note was made for future reference.

"We have more than enough people who know how to fire a gun," Wanda commented archly.

"How about propaganda," Peter suggested. "The English Underground put out a so-called German Resistance newspaper; I used to contribute articles now and then. I'm fluent and I'm experienced, so my work is easily passed off as genuine. If you want, I can organize such a newspaper for you."

Tadek, Wojciech, and Wanda started to laugh.

He thought they were questioning his abilities, so he added, "Look, I can make it realistic, I've seen the genuine article. Teresa passed *The Parliamentarian* on to me sometimes, and Geerd had a copy of *The Nationalist.*" Those were both illegal newspapers genuinely originating from the shadowy German Resistance, and they were the only evidence he had ever seen of the German Underground's existence.

Now the entire Council was laughing. Katerina finally motioned for order and stated not unkindly, "Those are ours. I'm sure you can contribute an article now and then, but we have plenty of writers. Is there anything else?"

Angry and embarrassed, he scanned their faces in turn. After a moment's hesitation he mentioned some other minor skills he had picked up along the way: maintenance, repairs, lockpicking, even cooking. It was all greeted with barely disguised contempt.

Zosia cocked her head to the side as if wondering what sort of game he was playing, but she did not question him or his choice of offerings.

Tadek, however, did. "Isn't there anything you can do that we can use?" he asked with ill-humored impatience. Then with a practiced air of frivolity he added, "After all, we don't have any German camp commanders who need servicing."

There were one or two grunts of amusement. Peter stifled his initial reaction of stunned hurt and searched for a quick response. How long had Tadek waited to drop that little gem? With so little warning, all Peter could manage was to maintain a façade of composure and reply quietly, "We all do what we must."

"A real man would have died first."

"Indeed. But all the good men have been killed." Peter paused significantly to let the meaning of his words sink in. Zosia had told him, in strict confidence, about a sabotage mission from which Tadek alone had returned. Years had passed, but no one, especially Tadek, had forgotten. Smiling slightly Peter added unnecessarily, "So, how are you still alive, Tadek?"

Tadek slowly rose to his feet, enraged.

Peter stood to meet him.

"Stop this nonsense!" Zosia interjected angrily, glaring furiously first at Tadek, then at Peter. She turned to Tadek and said something to him in Polish that caused him to sit back down looking somewhat abashed. Then she turned to Peter and hissed in English, "I told you that in confidence! How dare you betray my trust!"

"I'm sorry, Zosia, I wasn't prepared for what he said."

"Well, since you're so keen to betray my confidence, maybe you should know the whole story," Zosia spat, still using English. "He did it to try and save his wife from a military brothel!"

Peter sat back down, feeling extremely foolish. His only consolation was that Tadek looked even more sheepish. Zosia continued in German, "We don't have the resources to fight both the Germans and each other! Now, let's get back to business like civilized people."

Katerina nodded her agreement. "Peter, tell us if there is anything else you might be able to do. Our needs are great, and although another person is always welcome, our resources are very limited. You have to contribute if you are to stay." She gestured around. "As you can see, we have no windows here to clean. Is there any skill, or even interest, that you can offer that we can develop?"

Peter grimaced; he had held his most important and well-developed skill in reserve. He had spent his life being trained for it, yet he hesitated to mention it to the committee, partly out of fear that if they scoffed at it, he would have nothing more to offer, partly because it brought back such strong and painful memories of his time with Allison and his very last years in the Underground. But as he saw the row of faces looking questioningly at him, some hopeful, some full of disdain, he was forced to offer up his last hope.

"I know something about decoding. You know, cryptanalysis."

The sudden look of interest on the faces of the Council was rewarding.

"But my knowledge is old, almost certainly out-of-date," he added, quick to point out the disadvantages before anyone else did.

"But you know the basics?" Katerina pressed.

"Oh, yes, I know the basics," he replied, thinking of some of the idiotic things he had learned. Katerina would surely have opined that his time could have been better spent with a rifle.

"Were you good at it?" Hania asked.

"I suppose. But it was a long time ago."

"Still, you do remember things, don't you?" Konrad insisted.

"Yes. I guess so."

"And you could pick up on new techniques and knowledge quite quickly?"

"I don't see why not. If someone gave me the information, I could study it certainly."

"Good. I think we have a job for him. Don't you agree?" The speaker was the older, balding Council member named Tomasz, whom everybody called Tomek. He was the one who had initially voted against Peter—it was funny how Peter never failed to remember what their votes had been—but had switched rather easily when pressed.

Tadek scowled at Peter and cleared his throat to get the Council's attention. "I hate to interrupt this little festival with something so tedious as a rational thought, but before we rashly take yet another idiotic decision, I think he should prove his skills. Otherwise, we might waste a lot of time and effort on him."

"How would we do that?" Marysia inquired.

"Let him decipher some coded documents. We have some stuff from years ago—certainly we could find something for him to look at. Something out- dated—you know, at his skill level," Tadek sneered.

"What would that prove?" Zosia asked, clearly annoyed.

"It would prove he's not lying to us now. That he's not just buying time to work some mischief. If we set him to learning current skills and decoding stuff, he could be here for years before we'd see a result—or the lack of one."

Zosia began to object, but Peter interjected, "I don't mind. I'd like to see what I can do. It's been a long time and a lot has happened since then."

Tadek smiled with a great deal of self-satisfaction. Zosia glared at Peter for preempting her defense of him.

He explained, "I've been through a lot and I really don't know what I'm capa- ble of anymore. Tadek's right—you would invest a lot of time and effort in me. I'd like to know that I'm up to it."

So it was agreed; he would pass one more test, but this time it would be the sort of test he understood, and for the first time in a long time he felt no real fear.

<hr>

3

"You STILL FEAR ME, don't you?" the voice asked.

He did not know the correct answer, so he said nothing. He lay there, curled on the floor, his eyes closed in defense against the pain.

"I know you're awake," the voice chided, "and you will be punished for not answering."

He opened his eyes to stare at the smooth polished leather of his tormentor's boots. "I'm sorry. I didn't know what to say."

"That's also wrong. As wrong as fearing us. And for that you will also be punished."

"I don't understand what I'm supposed to do," he moaned.

"You're not supposed to understand. You're not supposed to think. Or feel.

Or even fear. You just obey. It's that simple." The uniform came into view as his tormentor stooped down to grab his arm. "You'll like this one. Something really special, just for you." A hand, holding a syringe, came toward him.

"No! No syringes!"

The psychiatrist looked at him in surprise. "But you just said it was okay."

"No. No, it's not."

"It will help you remember," she assured him patiently. "You'll relax."

He shook his head, more to clear it than to disagree. "No needles."

She surveyed him for a long moment, her patience obviously at an end, then sighing, she put the medication away. "Fine. We'll do it your way. But let me warn you, the Council will be informed of your lack of cooperation."

It wouldn't be the first time, he thought.

"Nor the last," Zosia added when he had told her about his interview with Katerina's researcher. "Don't worry, they'll be gone soon enough."

"And when they are, I will never again talk about these things with anyone," he asserted, then he paused and added, "Except maybe you."

Zosia pursed her lips.

Tadek, standing next to her, snorted. "Now, about this decoding test."

"How did you two get assigned to do this?" Peter asked.

Tadek snorted again. Zosia answered, "Apparently we volunteered. Anyway, here's what we came up with." She handed him a single sheet of paper. The entire page was a string of numbers, nothing else. "There are three separate passages."

"Don't tell him that! Let him work it out," Tadek snapped.

"Oh, it's obvious." He grabbed a pencil and drew a line on the page. "One of them ends about here." He drew another line, farther down. "And the other ends around here."

Tadek and Zosia looked at each other in amazement. Finally Tadek stammered, "That's right. How did you know that?"

"You didn't put this together, did you?"

They shook their heads sheepishly. "How could you tell?"

"Who did?"

Zosia and Tadek looked at each other almost guiltily. Finally Zosia answered, "We had HQ send something—they have analysts there. We tried, we looked up some old documents and their translations—but we had no idea what to do. So we explained the situation and asked them to send something."

"Just as well, I suppose they'll have sent something feasible as a test." In fact, he thought as he perused the sheet, they've sent a child's game. He spared a mental thank-you to his counterparts at HQ who had decided to be so gentle with him.

"But how did you know there were three separate codes?"

"Just look at it," he said, enjoying his little triumph. "The patterns are absolutely different."

"What patterns?"

"Look at this first set—the numbers are nearly random and evenly distributed from zero to ninety-nine. So, each number clearly does not represent an individual letter—otherwise the numbers wouldn't be so random. It's some sort of homophonic cipher."

"A what?"

"And that means, since it's so short and I don't have time or computing capabilities, that I almost certainly won't be able to decipher it without more information."

"Oh."

"They did send along some extra information, didn't they?"

"Yes, how'd you—"

"But this next section here—see? They've just strung together numbers that are clearly simply substitutions for letters. And there's a lot of structure—see how often twelve appears? It's probably something fairly simple like a mono-alphabetic cipher."

"And the third passage?" Tadek asked, fascinated.

"Well, it doesn't look random, and again the numbers are limited, so I'd guess they just put in numbers for letters—but the structure looks weaker than the second passage."

"So?"

"So, it's probably some combination. Maybe a Vigenère cipher with a finite keyword—that would be a nice, simple test. I can calculate an index of coincidence and tell you more; it'll just take time."

"How much time?" Tadek pressed.

"I'll tell you"—Peter smiled wickedly—"when I'm done. Now, do I get any background information?"

"Why should you?"

"It's rare that there is absolutely no idea what a document is about. These are rather short passages: to be fair, I at least deserve some sort of realistic scenario of where this originated or some general idea of what it might be about. Even a bit of cleartext—especially for the first passage."

Zosia raised her eyebrows at Tadek.

Peter added, "And besides, I'm sure they told you to give me the extra information, didn't they?"

"Yes," Tadek admitted sheepishly, and handed over another sheet of paper.

Peter knew then, before he had even started, that he had passed their little test. He felt an overwhelming rush of pleasure at the knowledge that it was all still there! All those years of soul-destroying work, numerous beatings, humiliation, sickness, hunger, loneliness—none of it had taken his knowledge away from him. It was all still there! It would take work to recapture the details, to catch up on new developments, to reconstruct a way of thinking, but he no longer doubted his own abilities—they had survived, just as he had. It was all still there!

After he presented the Council with his results, he was quickly put to work analyzing, or at least organizing, stacks of information that had accumulated.

Apparently, for a long time they had not had anybody who could seriously attack intercepted messages. As recently as three years ago, they had had three analysts. Two had been seconded to Warszawa—that is, to the region that had once contained the capital city of Warsaw and was now dominated by the concrete colossus of Göringstadt—to work on a major project. The third had been Marysia's husband. He was supposed to have trained successors, but had suffered a nervous breakdown after the death of his daughter and had wanted to retire to a village with a reasonably safe set of papers. Marysia had steadfastly refused and they had eventually divorced. In deference to his years of loyal service he was provided with a safe retirement, but Marysia's bitterness at his abandonment was still evident, and the subject of her ex-husband was tactfully avoided.

Items of seeming importance had been forwarded to headquarters, but a mountain of presumably trivial information had, in the meanwhile, accumulated. And how it had accumulated! Nobody had bothered to sort the documents, broadcasts, and electronic messages by source or date or possible subject. Peter was simply shown to a storeroom full of papers and tapes and told to do what he could with it.

Over time he managed to sort and prioritize and translate. Week after week he presented to the Council the fruits of his labors. They politely stifled their yawns at the lists of winter coats and orders for fertilizer. He begged for assistance, convinced that if the information, tedious as it was, was correlated, it might provide useful demographic and economic information. They agreed and assigned Olek and a seventeen-year-old, Barbara, as his part-time staff.

During the Christmas holidays, he began to badger the Council to provide him with his own computer. It was simply impossible to do reasonable work constantly begging time on other people's machines. And what were they using them for anyway? He harassed the Council mercilessly, accosting members in the hall, demanding to know when they would finally provide him with adequate equipment. There could be something important among all that dross and they would never know it! Not at the rate he had to proceed!

Eventually they agreed. He appeared at a Council meeting in January with his report in hand, ready to begin his demands again, when he was preempted by Katerina. She raised her hand as he stood to speak and said, "Enough. Enough. Before you say a word, we want you to know that we have pulled every string we have with HQ. We have called in every favor. We have reminded them that they have stolen our two best analysts without replacing them; we brought up the painful subject of our Marysia's ex-husband; we have groveled and implored and cajoled on your behalf. So not a word! You will get your damn machine."

Peter grinned, set his week's work on the table, and without saying a word, promptly left.

It took another month before the machine finally materialized. Peter was summoned from his storeroom office to the Council meeting room. Only

Katerina, Zosia, and Tomek were there. Zosia pointed to the small box on the table and watched with delight as he opened its cover.

"It's so small!"

"But look at what it can do." She almost giggled as she switched it on. "It was delivered this morning and I've been trying it out. It's better than mine!"

He looked at the compact gray box and the screen that had leapt to life. "It's beautiful!" Over the past months, he had learned much from Zosia and others about the current state of computers and software, but he had never seen anything so compact and ostensibly powerful before.

"Isn't it great?" Zosia asked as though she had invented it herself.

"I've never seen anything like it. There's no comparison with the clunky old things that I've seen in the ministry."

"I'm not surprised. We got this from America. Apparently they're sold on the open market there. Available to just about anyone. Can you imagine?"

"No," Peter sighed. What sort of place sold such exquisite technology on the open market? "Why doesn't the Reich just import them then?"

Tomek answered, "Oh, the Americans forbid their export; besides, they're priced in dollars and so are, for us, phenomenally expensive."

"And so you should be grateful," Katerina added.

Peter pressed a few keys, studied the listed files, and shook his head in slight wonder.

"We had some stuff loaded on it for you," Tomek explained. "Latest math programs, that sort of stuff. At least that's what our people in the NAU claimed. Unfortunately, you're on your own in working out what it all does, but they said it would be useful."

"You mean this was specifically sent for me, all the way across the Atlantic?"

"Yeah, the PDA—that's the Polish Defense Association—they organize funds and send shipments of equipment and arms periodically. No doubt your little machine here was part of a fund-raising drive: dinners, speeches, broadsides." Tomek laughed.

Peter laughed, too. What a wonderful thing it must be to live in a free land. Fund-raising dinners! He could barely imagine what a strange world must exist on the far side of the Atlantic.

4

"Y OU'VE BEEN THERE?" Peter asked. "I never have. Tell me about it."

"Of course, I'll bore you senseless!" Marysia laughed. "But perhaps you'd prefer to go there yourself someday?"

"America? Of course, I'd love to see it, but who the hell would pay to send me there?"

"Oh, I don't know. Maybe you could do a speaking tour. You know, talk about what it's like in the Reich."

He shook his head emphatically. "Never."

"Never?"

"One of you could talk—that'd be interesting. But for me to talk about my past? No, I'd never do that. I have trouble enough with it as it is."

"You seem to be doing okay."

"I get a lot of help from you all, from my friends," Peter admitted shyly.

Marysia smiled weakly at him, then raising her glass, suggested, "Here's to friendship."

He raised his in agreement. "To friendship, and to your kind generosity in taking me in."

"How could I ignore a poor, starving stray like you on my doorstep? Sleeping in that lousy dorm room, eating in our, er, 'restaurant,' poor thing . . ."

He laughed at her pathetic description of what was, to him, a wonderful life. It was true that after a short while he had been moved from the one rather comfortable guest room to one of the more spartan dormitory-like rooms that were reserved for the transient staff, but that had only increased his sense of security and belonging. The rooms had no kitchen and he was used to taking his meals in the mess hall, where the much despised menu was, to him, luxurious. Even better, though, was that Marysia apparently had taken him under her wing and frequently offered him meals, often with other guests, or occasionally, such as tonight, alone.

"And speaking of friends," Marysia continued, "I want to tell you about yours."

He lowered his glass. "What do you know?" he forced himself to ask.

"Don't worry." She then told him that, according to the records, every member of his group had indeed been arrested and all of them had perished, but beyond that, the records were removed from access. Too long ago and unimportant or too sensitive and vital? Who knew. Their fates made it clear that if any one of them had betrayed the group, then he or she had been double-crossed or the records had been appropriately adjusted to hide his or her involvement.

"But I always knew it didn't come from within."

"How so? Were they all that trustworthy?" Marysia asked with obvious, but controlled, cynicism.

He shook his head. "No, it's not naïveté on my part." He paused a moment, then came to a decision. "On my first night here, I didn't explain everything as clearly as I could have to Zosia."

Marysia raised an eyebrow. "Then you should clear the air."

"I suppose so," he agreed reluctantly. "All right. The detail I left out was that our research group was large so that we could have a lot of expertise available, but we subdivided it for reasons of safety. There were six separate cells of three or four people each, depending on their discipline. A member of a cell only knew the other

members of their cell, and even then they were only supposed to have the most minimal information on their coworkers. So, unless things had really got corrupted, no
internal member could betray the entire collaboration. With one exception."

"You?"

"Yes. Me. I was the point of contact with the rest of the hierarchy. I not only
belonged to a cell, but I organized the work for all our other researchers."

"Ah, no wonder you were scared!"

Peter nodded. "I was the only one who knew how to contact everyone, and
therefore, I was the only one who could have betrayed them all. After my narrow
escape, I tracked down what had happened to the rest, and when I realized how
widespread the betrayal was . . ."

"You knew they were certain to blame you."

"Especially since I wasn't picked up."

"Ah, but you were working. The higher-ups would have known that, and that
at least would explain why you weren't at home that morning."

He shook his head miserably. "We weren't working," he whispered.

"What?"

"We weren't working," he repeated slightly louder.

"I thought you said—"

"I did. The truth is, we were warned off making that night's contact. Allison's husband wouldn't have known the difference, but anyone higher up, after the fact, would
have known there was nothing going on. I had absolutely no reason to be missing
from my flat that night, none except an affair I had tried very hard to keep secret.
Allison would have been the only one who knew that I had been walking her home,
and she was dead, so I had no alibi. It would have been obvious I was the traitor."

"What about your contact, I mean, your boss? He'd know everyone."

"He worked through me. He was from another cell and leapfrogged me for a
promotion. So, he knew his old comrades and he knew me and the people I
worked with, but that was it."

"They promoted him over you? Did that make you bitter?" Marysia asked
with something like suspicion.

"No. I didn't want his job, I wanted to stay with Allison, but unfortunately
that wasn't the reason for my being overlooked."

"What was?"

"I don't really know. Probably insubordination. In any case, they may well
have thought I felt snubbed, and so my bosses may have thought I was bitter."

"And vengeful?"

"They may have thought so. I didn't tell the Council all this because it only
complicated the picture and I felt the cards were stacked against me sufficiently
as it was."

Marysia tilted her head with curiosity. "Tell me, is there anything else you
kept from us?"

Peter's eyes strayed from Marysia's face to the photographs she had mounted on her wall over a bookshelf. He rubbed his chin as he surveyed them: a picture of Marysia and her husband; another of her daughter, Olek's mother; and another of her son, Adam. A phantom family, just like his, except that he did not even have photographs. He pulled his gaze away to look down at the table. After a long moment he answered her question: "Just some humiliations that I had no desire to relive."

Marysia blinked slowly as if carefully considering her next question, then she seemed to change her mind and said, "Well, if it wasn't you, and it wasn't anybody on the inside, then it must have been a leak from HQ."

"I guess so. I don't know," he replied quietly, glad that she had not probed further in the other direction.

"Or possibly you made a mistake . . . but I am sure you've already considered that possibility."

"I certainly did. I spent weeks examining every detail of what I had done or said. As you know, with hindsight, mistakes are usually quite obvious—but I could find none."

"So, as I thought, you had nothing to fear."

He nodded though he did not agree. Nothing to fear? No, he had lots to fear; all she had done was let him know that they had nothing to tell him. But that *was* a mercy and he appreciated her gentleness. He smiled and said, "Thanks for telling me. I really appreciate it."

"There is one minor disconcerting thing."

He tensed. "What?"

"Yardley is listed as arrested, convicted, and executed."

"Me?"

"Yes."

"That makes it look like I did it! Like they were covering my trail for me!" he exclaimed, horrified.

"To some."

"Why would they do that?"

"The records may have been amended years later; perhaps when they were computerized. Either someone was covering up their mistakes or they had given up on finding you and hoped that that little entry would be discovered by your own people. If it were, you would then be rendered ineffective."

"Or killed."

"That *is* one way of being made ineffective. It's not unusual for them to do something like that."

"Is that why the Council did not weigh it against me?"

Marysia nodded noncommittally, then refilling their glasses, asked, "Do you want to stop by for dinner tomorrow? I'm just making some soup, but there'll be plenty."

"Ah, thanks, that sounds wonderful, but I already have an engagement!"

"You? Who?"

"Zosia's invited me over for dinner."

"Zosia?" Marysia repeated with something like alarm.

"Yes. Why?"

Marysia shook her head and broke into laughter.

"Could you please tell me what is so funny?"

Marysia could not bring her laughter under control. She was giggling so hard her face had turned beet red and she was obviously having trouble gasping for enough breath.

"Marysia! What's so funny about a dinner invitation?"

"How often have you visited her?" she finally managed to ask.

"Oh, you know, I'm always stopping by. She was especially helpful after my talks with that idiotic psychiatrist."

"And did you ever eat anything there?"

He shook his head. "She'd put out bread and cheese sometimes, with our wine or vodka. It was freshly made so I know she can bake."

"You mean like that loaf there?" Marysia pointed to a loaf of bread cooling on her counter.

"Well, yes. Exactly like that," he answered, his face growing slowly warmer.

Marysia burst into laughter again. She spent a moment dabbing at the tears that ran down her cheeks, swallowing her giggles into her throat so that all he heard were strangled little squeaks as he watched her body shaking with mirth.

So, he was not altogether unprepared for the mess he found in Zosia's kitchen the following evening. "It's a nice assortment of ingredients you have here," he said, prodding the rabbit meat with a fork. "What do you plan to do with it?"

Zosia shrugged. "I was hoping maybe you had an idea?"

After they had finished the meal that he had prepared, Zosia carefully wiped her mouth with her napkin, sipped some wine, and then said, "Excellent! Now, I have a proposition for you."

He looked up with alarmed delight.

"I was thinking that maybe you could move in here."

"Move in?" he asked, looking around the apartment in confusion. Though Zosia's two rooms were considered to be quite luxurious, there was only one bedroom.

"Yes, this place is for a family, and with just me and Joanna here, I'm afraid I'll get reassigned unless I move someone in."

"Where would I sleep?" he asked, still glancing around.

"Well, you know, Joanna shares the bed with me, so you could have the fold-out couch. Look, there's even a partition we could put up when you want privacy." Zosia gestured toward a series of panels that lay on the floor under the couch. "Hey, I'll even dig out Adam's clothes—you're about his size and it would do for you to have something more to wear. I should have given all that stuff away long ago, but somehow it didn't seem right."

"And it does now?"

She paused, then slowly nodded. "Yes, it seems right now. You belong here, you're one of us."

"And in return for all this?" he asked, somewhat disappointed but even more embarrassed by where his thoughts had momentarily taken him.

"In return? Nothing! Just your company. I mean, if you want to help out, well, that would be useful."

He nodded his agreement and looked around at his new home. "You have this place nicely decorated, you'd almost think there were windows, what with the curtains and all."

"Oh, that was done years ago!"

"What about Joanna?"

"She already adores you. She said she'd love to have you here. You know, sometimes I'm a bit busy and don't give her the time she deserves."

"Sometimes!" he laughed.

Zosia smiled wanly. "It's hard being a lone parent. And she misses her father so much. I think she believes she's reincarnated him. She prayed every night for him to come back, and then you showed up."

"You know, I'm not Adam," he said worriedly.

"Oh, yes, I know! But you do resemble him a great deal, and not just physically."

Peter felt disconcerted by her words. He knew inevitably that the comparison would break down, and he felt intuitively that at that point he would not be able to compete with a dead man.

Zosia seemed to understand his unease. "Peter, please don't worry. I like you for who you are."

"But what about Joanna? Do you think she's in danger of being terribly disappointed?"

"No. She knows he's dead. She just finds you very lovable—again, just for who you are." Zosia sipped her wine and her eyes took on a distant look. "No, the only one who is being replaced is Adam. It's unfair to his memory, but shortly she won't really know him anymore. It's you who is the reality."

Peter thought of Allison. It had been a long time since he had thought of her—possibly for the same reason: Zosia was the reality. In the end, death was terribly personal, and for all the times over the years he had thought of Allison, he had not died with her. She was dead, long gone, and life went on; the living made their peace with the past and moved on.

5

*M*OVED ON AND settled in. Quite comfortably, in fact. Peter sat out the last of the winter in Zosia's apartment, and now with the spring rains pounding down outside, he felt particularly warm and cozy as he lay on the couch, reading. He had, he realized, made a home for himself. He owed a lot to the people around him, to all the people who had made it possible, and in his own way, he had tried to thank each of them. Sometimes, as with Marysia, words alone sufficed. She instinctively recognized how much her gestures of friendship had meant to him, and she dismissed his attempts at repayment with a wave of her hand and the advice that he should pass kindness down the generations, "where it is needed." For the Council members who had accepted him, he recognized that words would never serve the purpose: they had no use for words, they needed hard work and discipline. And so he worked diligently and obediently, never questioning an order, never turning his back on any job, no matter how unrelated to his own. But the one person he could not thank enough was Zosia. He owed her everything, and though he gave everything he could to her, it never seemed enough.

He set down the technical journal he had been trying to read. It was useless, his thoughts kept turning to Zosia. She was due back today, and any minute now she would be coming through the door.

As if reading his thoughts, the door opened and Zosia came in. "I'm back!"

"I'm so glad to see you! Been back long?"

"Long enough to see Joanna and to chat with Marysia." She tossed her raincoat on a hook and came over to sit on the arm of the couch. "Thanks for taking care of Joanna while I was away."

"Thanks for trusting me with her." He paused, then asked, "By the way, did you tell Marysia to check up on us every five minutes, or was that her own initiative?"

Zosia laughed. "You can't blame her for being nervous. You know, she's used to caring for Joanna during my absences—it was a big step for all of us, having you do the job."

"I appreciate your trust, I really do," he said with heartfelt gratitude.

"I heard from Marysia, you were more than adequate to the job. I believe the word she used was *doting,* comically so."

"Sorry. I just go mad with worry when you're away. I tried to keep it from Joanna."

"Indeed, I heard from her that even she told you not to worry."

"Yes, 'Don't worry, Mommy will be back soon' is what she said as I was tucking her in, trying to find some comforting words," he said with a laugh. Once Zosia returned, he always felt giddy with relief and happiness, and all his worries evaporated into the mist. This time, with Joanna entrusted to his care, his worries had been even greater, as if he would somehow be held responsible if Zosia did not return.

Even worse, though he did not say so, were the times that Zosia took Joanna with her. On those occasions, Tadek would accompany the two of them so that they could form a nice family group. They carried excellent papers and did little more than visit a few shops or a zoo or eat in a restaurant in order to familiarize Joanna with the society around her. Peter understood it was an essential part of Joanna's education, but still whenever they left, his chest tightened with a fear bordering on panic, and the feeling did not ease until they had safely returned in the evening or the next day.

"So how did the job go?" He never asked what the job was and Zosia never said.

"Well enough. Hey, I brought you a little present. A reward for all your efforts with my daughter."

"Eh? What?"

"These." She slid a set of documents out of a folder and placed them on his chest.

He studied the first leaf of the papers. "An SS major, very impressive. So what about them?"

Zosia waited patiently until he had paged a bit further.

He came to the photograph and studied it momentarily. "Adam, I presume."

"Yes."

"Is that his real date of birth?"

"No, but close to it."

"He was younger than me."

"A bit. But that doesn't matter. We don't need to change anything except the photograph and then they can be yours."

"I don't want them." He handed the papers back to her.

Zosia studied the photograph. "Actually, the photos on these things are such bad quality, we don't really even need to change it."

"I don't want them."

"But I suppose we should, it's safer that way."

"I said, I don't want them."

"Nonsense," she finally replied. "You have to have a set for emergencies. These will do fine."

"Can't I have something a little less"—he considered which word was appropriate, finally settling on—"obnoxious?"

"Nope. You need a very good, safe identity when you come to town with me and Joanna."

"Town?"

"Yes, the place with all the big concrete buildings."

"Zosia," he moaned at her idea of humor, "I don't want to go into town."

"You need to, Peter. You can't stay cooped up here. It has been months since you arrived. Winter's past, spring's well under way, it's time."

"No, it's not," he answered grimly. "It'll never be time. I'm not going back out there."

"You have to! We need you to!"

"How so? I do good work here. Why do you need me to go out there?"

"It's . . . Well, it's for your sake. You need to confront them. It's unnatural staying here, cloistered."

"Pray tell, which part of my life out there was natural? Prison? Torture? Slavery?" He raised his eyebrows as if expecting an answer, then added, "I'm happy here. I have everything I want. Can't I just stay put?"

Zosia sighed. "It's not good for you to withdraw like this. I know you have nightmares, I see the way you hit the bottle. Everything's not all right. You've got to confront that fact."

"I said, everything is fine."

"Peter," she pleaded with him to understand, "you don't act fine."

"What do you mean?"

"Well, for instance, when we argue, you flinch if I wave my arms around, as if you think I'm going to hit you."

That seemed a thoroughly unfair comment to him: *they* did not argue—he was far too satisfied to have many complaints, and the ones he did have did not seem worth emotional turmoil; any and all yelling was done by Zosia as she would explode whenever she was upset. Her fury passed quickly and her boisterous and happy side more than compensated for these outbursts, but during them, he hardly thought it unnatural that he should avoid her wildly flailing arms. He decided not to raise these points, though, and said instead, "I don't do that. And anyway, our interactions here are hardly relevant to my walking normally down a street in town."

"But there are other things as well."

"Like what?" He felt faintly disgusted that she had been observing him so clinically.

"You don't defend yourself. You always take the blame for everything, whether it's your fault or not. You always give way. Have you noticed how in the narrow hallways, you always give way?"

He stiffened. "That's just politeness."

"Every time?"

"It's just courtesy." His voice had grown cold.

"*Every time*," she repeated, emphasizing the syllables.

"You're acting like I'm not quite human, Zosia. Like I've been programmed."

"No, it's you—you act like you're not quite equal."

"I freely choose how I behave."

"You seem to be strongly influenced—"

"I am not an *Untermensch*—my personality has not been molded to fit their ideal! And I resent you—"

"Peter! You must be able to see—"

"I don't see anything!"

"—how much you've been changed," she hurried on, determined to finish her thought. "And I know why that is: I know that you've been conditioned for years—"

"Cut the psychoanalytic crap. You have no idea—"

"—but you can overcome that. You just need to practice a bit—"

"I'm not like that!"

"—and you'll be your old self."

"What do you know of that?" he finished bitterly. They had been talking at such cross-purposes that they had hardly heard each other.

Zosia sighed. "Please come into town with me and Joanna. She'd like you to come to celebrate her birthday. She'll be four—"

"I know that."

"She wants to show you the zoo and eat in a restaurant with you and act grown-up."

He looked down at the floor, so she could not see his expression. She reached out to touch his hair and felt the slight movement of his head as he flinched at her touch.

He was silent for a long moment, as if considering her request, then he said quietly, "Zosia, I'm afraid."

She noticed he was trembling. "I know. You have every right to be."

"They hurt me," he said simply.

"I know." She stroked his hair. "I know," she repeated quietly.

The next day Zosia convinced him to have Adam's uniform tailored to fit him. It did not take many adjustments, and even the tailor noted the similarities between the two of them. Peter stifled a scathing remark: he was sick of hearing the comparison, sick of Adam, sick of his heroism, sick of his renowned level-headed, cold-blooded confidence. Lot of bloody good it did him when it came to the crunch, Peter thought uncharitably, then immediately regretted the sentiment. Still, he felt rather melancholic that no one knew him when he was younger—before all the unpleasantness. Then, he, too, had been brilliant and strong and unflinching and confident; now, he was a wreck, and despite his denials, he knew it.

The papers were reprocessed to carry the new photo—dutifully out of focus and weathered—and he began the tedious learning of yet another life history with all its interminable details. A week later the little family group was ready for its outing. The night before, Peter spent restlessly; whenever he managed to fall asleep, he was beset by nightmares that centered around horrific fantasies of his getting them all arrested through some stupid indiscretion. He gasped out Zosia's and Joanna's names as they were dragged off to some terrible fate, and then he awoke panting and drenched in sweat.

Finally the clock told him it was morning and he could walk away from his dreams. He dressed in the uniform he was to wear that day. He put a lighter and a new pack of cigarettes in the jacket pocket and then, after a moment's debate, decided to carry one of Teresa's handkerchiefs. Of the three, two had become rather bloodstained, but he had kept one in reserve, and so it had remained pristine, the little swastikas still dancing along the edge in the purest Aryan white. It would go well with the uniform, and Teresa would probably approve the subtle irony.

That done, he left the bunker. Near the entrance, he asked one of the sentries if the uniform would be a problem—he was assured that they would not mistake him for an enemy and he could wander freely.

The chill dawn air was filled with mists, and the trees were shrouded in gray shadows. As he wandered, he felt he had entered a world that was truly apart from all else. His footsteps were muffled, his thoughts blanketed by the fog. As the sun began to lift some of the fog, he realized he had been gone quite a long time and he should probably head back to the encampment. As he turned and strode purposefully in that direction, suddenly, out of nowhere a bullet sped past his head and he heard the report of a rifle. Instinctively, he threw himself to the ground.

"Don't shoot!" he yelled in the first language that came into his head—and that was German. He immediately followed it with Polish and, for good measure, English. He collected himself enough to repeat his yell in Polish and followed it with, "I'm one of you!"

A moment later he heard footsteps, and he rolled over to see a young kid pointing a rifle at him. The boy did not wear any uniform—just an armband with the letter *P* that terminated in a *w* as an anchored cross. The letters stood for *Polska walczy*, "Poland fights," and was the official symbol of the Armia Krajowa, the Home Army.

Peter remained on the ground, among the leaves, careful to keep his hands up and away from the pistol he was wearing. "I'm one of you!" he repeated, trying to recall if he could say anything else. One of Joanna's nursery rhymes came to mind, but that did not seem as if it would be useful.

"No, you aren't," the boy said.

"Yes! Yes, I am! I'm from the encampment. Really. I'm the Englishman—you must about me hear!" He knew he had really screwed up the grammar on that sentence, but he was pretty sure the point had been made.

The boy stared at Peter with a look of confusion. That Peter did not recognize the boy at all warned him that perhaps, despite the armband, he should not say much more. As he was deciding this point, someone else approached. This was a somewhat older lad whom Peter recognized. He nodded at Peter and smacked the young boy on the head in a less than jovial manner.

"You idiot! You're not even supposed to be patrolling here!"

The boy looked dismayed. He pointed at Peter and said, "But, but he isn't one of us."

The older lad smacked the boy again, said, "That's not for you to decide! You nearly shot one of our own! The least you could do is apologize."

Peter climbed to his feet and brushed the leaves off his uniform as the boy stammered a timid apology. Peter nodded his acceptance and watched as the two headed off back into the woods, the elder lad still randomly smacking the younger and hurling insults and orders at him. Peter's heart was still pounding, but as he calmed down and began to walk back, he thought he should probably work more assiduously at his language lessons.

As he approached the entry to the bunker, he spotted the sentry he had spoken to earlier. Though disturbed by her previous false assurances, he did not mention the shooting incident to her and instead returned to Zosia's rooms. By the time he got there, Joanna and Zosia were ready to depart. He told Zosia about the incident and she seemed quite concerned, asking him details of where he had been and what the lad had looked like.

He answered, then asked, "Why didn't I recognize him? I thought I knew everyone here—at least by sight."

"Oh, he almost certainly doesn't live here." In answer to his questioning look, she continued, "We patrol a huge area and we could never afford to have all the kids who patrol for us live here; many are volunteers from local villages and farms. Lots live in camps in the woods. Genuine partisans. They get orders from us, and supplies, but they really have no idea exactly what we have here, or who we are. And for that reason, they can be quite dangerous."

"That explains his blank look."

"Yes, and it's just as well you didn't mention more than you did. They're supposed to be posted to the outer sections, farther than you should have naturally walked. Either you really went a long way, or he was way out of his area."

"I think the latter—that's what the other boy said. Now, him I recognized, though his name escapes me."

"If you recognized him, then he's from the encampment—so he'd either be the boy's superior officer and had tracked him down, or he'd be assigned to patrol one of the inner sections, presumably the one you were in. Anyone from the encampment should recognize you on sight since that's part of their job, and of course, they should also be aware that we're going out today and so should be on the lookout for that uniform."

"Ah, so the sentry was right, there should not have been a problem."

"No." Zosia shook her head emphatically and wondered to herself why this little cock-up bothered her so much.

"What about when I drove in? Why didn't one of the outer patrols shoot at me then?"

"The car," she answered tersely. "They radioed your presence and we told them to let you through: we wanted to find out what you were up to. And besides, we wanted the car—it's a nice one."

He nodded. So, that stupid car had saved his life. He smiled at the thought of how many times he had cursed it as he had polished the chrome.

"Well, I'll check it all out later," Zosia assured him. "It should be in the daily report. For now, though, let's just thank God that you're okay and get this show on the road."

They rode the delivery vehicle down the mountain and into a nearby farmstead. There they picked up a car that had been prepared for them and drove the rest of the way. It was a long trip—they avoided the local village and smaller towns; instead opting to travel a bit farther for the greater anonymity afforded by the district capital, Neu Sandez.

The journey passed pleasantly, with Joanna playing quietly with some toys in the backseat as Peter and Zosia chatted about trivialities in the front. Only when

Joanna began humming a tune to herself was the mood broken. She had barely sung a half dozen notes when Zosia recognized it, turned angrily to her, and yelled at her to shut up. Peter replayed the offending notes in his head and realized that it had been a Polish folk song, but still he wondered at the vehemence of Zosia's action. When he turned to look at her, it became clear: she was as pale as a ghost and shaking like a leaf. He had never seen her afraid before and realized, for the first time, that her studiously casual behavior up to that point had been for his and Joanna's benefit.

Zosia gained control of herself, turned to her daughter, and apologized. "But you know, Johanna," she continued, using her daughter's German name, "not even tunes."

"I know, Mama. I'm sorry, I forgot."

"Please don't ever forget."

"I won't," Joanna solemnly assured her.

Once they reached the town, Zosia directed him to a place where he could search for parking. "Where in the world did you ever learn to drive?" she asked as he turned a corner.

Distracted by pedestrians, he answered, "I watched the bus drivers when I was fifteen. I got a working license that year so I could get a job with a delivery firm. I was still using the Halifax name, so it was in those papers." He paused to glance down a side street, but there was no parking there. As he drove on, he added, "I remember how mad Karl got at me when he noticed it in my documents."

"Why was he mad?"

"Because I hadn't volunteered the information. He had me get the chauffeuring license the next day. Threatened me with all sorts of dire consequences if I didn't pass the test. That sure made for a relaxed test," Peter said with a sarcastic laugh.

"And London bus drivers turn corners in that awkward manner? How come?" she asked as he turned onto another narrow residential street.

"Oh, they don't do that. It's a bad habit," he answered, suddenly embarrassed. "I'll stop doing it."

"But why do you do it?"

He rounded a corner and selected an alley before explaining, "When I drove for the Vogels, I had to handcuff my left wrist to the steering wheel. It made for rather awkward turns, especially since my right hand was busy shifting. I could let the wheel slide through my grasp, but I never knew when it would suddenly catch on the ring. I compensated by holding fast to one place and moving my arm with the wheel."

"But why? I mean, why the handcuffs?"

"It was the law." Peter scanned along the street. "At least that's what I was told."

"But what was the point?" Zosia asked, mystified. She pointed to the right. "Try down there."

"Of the law? I haven't a clue. There weren't any inane posters explaining that one. Maybe so I couldn't hijack the car. Who knows. Just one of a million idiotic laws on the books."

"I've never seen anyone else have to do that," she commented. "Look, there's a place!"

He aligned the car with the space. "I guess Herr Vogel was one of the few people who actually obeyed that law—far be it for him to miss a chance to humiliate me. But that one *was* particularly stupid. Even his mother-in-law chided him about it once when I drove them all back from the train station."

As he backed the car into the small space, he remembered how Karl had repeatedly explained to Frau von dem Bach that it was the law, and how Elspeth, as if translating, had repeated the words to her mother. Only minutes earlier, in the train station, Karl had lashed out at him in public, leaving him profoundly humiliated, and as a result, Frau von dem Bach's concerns had been the least of his worries, but he didn't mention that to Zosia. "If I think about it, I don't do it. It's only when I'm concentrating on something else that the old habit takes over." He threw a smile in her direction. "Don't worry—I'll soon unlearn it."

She shook her head a bit sadly. "Sometimes, it all seems a bit too much," she sighed.

"At least I don't try to drive on the left," he said to lighten her mood.

"Do they still do that in Britain?"

"No, they got rid of that fairly quickly, but for a time, it was sort of a protest—driving on the left when the law said the right was the correct side. You can imagine what a mess that made of things. By the time I learned to drive that was long in the past—although some irresponsible types would still do it occasionally." He smiled at the memory and Zosia laughed at the implication.

"You didn't, did you?"

He turned the engine off and pulled the key out of the ignition. "Not often. I had a job driving a delivery van, and I only got to drive on the job, of course. My superior officers in the Underground made it very clear that they would not tolerate such nonsense. They didn't want me to lose my job, and they didn't want to have to get me out of prison for something idiotic like that. But I was just a kid and a rather bloody-minded one at that."

"You? Bloody-minded?" Zosia asked disingenuously.

"Unimaginable, eh?"

It was already early afternoon, and so their first order of business was to get some lunch. The meal in the restaurant went smoothly and was followed by a visit to the zoo and then a quick look in some of the shops. Peter noticed, here and there, attached to park benches or over shop doors, the at one time ubiquitous *Nur für Deutsche* signs, but they were all old and fairly rare. Clearly the rules were known to all, and nobody even needed to remind the *Nichtdeutsch* who scurried nervously about that they were not wanted, that they were only just barely tolerated. Despite the signs, despite the uniforms, despite the seething resentment of the *Nichtdeutsch* and the downcast eyes of the *Zwangsarbeiter,* he began to relax and even to some extent enjoy the visit.

They decided to splurge and have their evening meal in a restaurant as well. Again, everything went as planned, and as they left the restaurant, he basked in a well-fed glow as he strolled down the street to promenade along the river with "his" family.

Zosia's sudden viselike grip on his arm destroyed his reverie. Without realizing it, he had nearly stepped aside into the gutter to let another couple pass. He shuddered a sigh as the couple skirted around them, naturally deferring to his imposing black uniform. Joanna, walking on the other side of her mother, had not even noticed, but only Zosia's warning had saved him from an action that would have been both out of character and inexplicable.

It was the only incident of the entire visit, and though it shook him to the core of his being, Zosia shrugged off his apology when he mentioned it the next morning. The couple, she assured him, would have assumed it was an eccentricity on his part, and in any case his uniform would have kept anyone from noticing anything he did. Thereafter, however, he made it a point to accompany Zosia into town whenever possible: he was not going to be wrong-footed again.

6

WITH THE SUMMER the weather settled and the nights warmed and Peter began sleeping outside with some regularity. Many times, on clear nights, Zosia and Joanna joined him, and they cuddled together under the stars. Many others from the encampment had the same habit—clearly the fresh air and starry nights were preferable to the safety and claustrophobia of the bunker. On those clear nights, the woods around the entrances took on a strange quality as sleeping bodies were scattered under the trees amid desultory conversations and restless, pacing sentries.

Peter found his greatest peace out there in the forest. If Zosia and Joanna were with him, he enjoyed the warmth of their company, the feeling of belonging, the quiet buzz of conversations drifting around him. Even when the nights were chill or damp, he often slept outside; then he had the woods nearly to himself. On those nights, he was equally happy. He would retreat far from the entrances to a small escarpment and sleep undisturbed, breathing in the pungent odors of moss and wet leaves, protected from the misting rains by the rocks. After a time, the sentries learned his habits and were careful to avoid pacing too near so that he had a sense of aloneness and privacy such as he had never enjoyed in his life.

Whatever the weather and however many other people were outside with him, he rarely slept through the night. He would awaken from uneasy dreams, listen to the breathing of those nearby or the soft rustle of the leaves, and he would invariably be drawn to his feet to walk among the pines in the embrace of the blessed darkness. At first he made a point of quietly announcing his presence to any unseen guards, but eventually they came to know his peripatetic ways, learned to recognize his slightly arrhythmic gait, and he could walk in silence, undisturbed and with the illusion of total isolation.

Sleeping outside also solved a recurring problem that he had in Zosia's flat. Tadek had the irksome habit of visiting Zosia, spending hours talking to her in a rapid, complex, and incomprehensible Polish and staying far, far too long. Peter had initially tried to join in the conversation, but his halting attempts were sneeringly rebuffed. Then he tried simply listening, so that he could learn the language, but Tadek glared at him as though he were eavesdropping. Eventually, he simply tried to sit out the visits, reading a book or doing some work at the kitchen table, but even that felt awkward. He finally gave up and learned to abandon the flat anytime Tadek visited. Now, at least, he could leave for the entire night, and by morning he managed to suppress his irritation enough so that Zosia was unable to detect it.

He knew that Zosia's hospitality in inviting him to live with her and Joanna had not been an invitation to run her life. He knew that with Joanna asleep in the bedroom, Zosia had no place to sit in her flat with guests other than on his bed. He tried to adhere to the necessary courtesies of close living, and so he did not groan when Tadek came to visit, and he hid his dismay when Zosia invited Tadek to dinner. He grit his teeth at the snide remarks about his "limited language abilities" and ignored Tadek's satisfied smirk whenever the two of them returned from long walks together. He knew that whatever Zosia did with Tadek was none of his business, that it was presumptuous of him even to notice their actions, but whenever he saw them together, his eyes followed them. He could not stop himself from wondering, but he did not dare ask Zosia anything directly, and since she did not volunteer any information, he was left unenlightened.

Nevertheless, he was not averse to picking up clues about their relationship from other sources. It inspired him to work on his new language so he could better follow the encampment gossip, and for that he found a great source in his two trainees, Olek and Barbara. They were hard workers and fast learners, and though their youthful chatter sometimes irritated him, he quite liked working with them, and in between the happy laughter in the office and their dispensing gems of local gossip, they helped him clear away the backlog that had accumulated. Their routine was fairly straightforward: Peter perused all messages, and if they fell into the category of familiar, he delegated them to either Barbara or Olek to interpret. The unfamiliar ones he attacked himself. Once the gist of these became clear, Olek would help him, keeping track of the information that emerged and reporting to Wanda accordingly. If the nature of the message was too sensitive or revealed details unknown to Peter, he was obliged to hand it over to Olek to finish the translation, using lists and code names to which Peter had no access. It was frustrating work, for Olek did not have the requisite expertise, but Peter could only offer his help by working blind—and that was inefficient. Nevertheless, despite such hindrances, the three of them worked well together and managed to do a good job.

Only one series of communications, picked up by one of their listeners in a Breslau military installation, stymied them. It was a series of intermittent and aggravatingly short messages that did not fit any of the patterns of codes they were aware of, but it was low priority, so though it remained unbroken, they did not forward it to HQ, nor did Wanda forbid Peter from working on it. So, whenever he had some free time, he puzzled over the code, musing on possible structures during walks in the woods, attacking it from different angles during the day. There was no reason to suspect the information it contained was important, so he quietly gnawed at the problem as a sort of amusement, simply curious to find its solution. It was as he was working through a paper sent from the NAU on new cryptanalysis techniques that he realized that his code did not fit the usual mode, not because of its sophistication, but because it was old-fashioned. It was the sort of code that might have been devised by someone, trained as he had been, years before, in a backward land, long before computers dominated their trade with their tedious ability to do phenomenal calculations.

This code, he thought, needed something more substantial behind it, and he began perusing the usual suspects: *Mein Kampf,* biographies of Hitler, and other patriotic texts. Then he got a break, a bit of cleartext that stated angrily: "Note!!!" followed by a number. It was the sort of frustrated mistake that a bright junior partner would make when dealing with stodgy, stupid, and uncooperative seniors. It was, he presumed, the publication number of the correct edition of the book that they were using as the base for their code, and the reason for the message was that complaints had filtered back about garbled messages, obviously due to another edition of the book. He went to the library and with the help of the librarian located the text with that publication number. It did not take long after that to break the code and to translate the texts.

The messages that he uncovered were no less perplexing than the strange code itself. They carried irrelevant information to and from scattered and apparently unrelated sources; nevertheless, he did not stop to ponder their significance but quickly relayed the information to the Council for political and military analysis.

Not long afterward, he began receiving similar coded strings from HQ. Apparently, they, too, had been picking up odd messages, and they began sending what they thought might be similarly encrypted information to the encampment for him to work on. He translated it without comment, refusing to explain the solution to his unseen counterparts. They began probing his knowledge, planting their own text within the genuine messages, so in retaliation, he only returned bulk results, refusing to identify which bits of text came from which encrypted messages and translating as loosely as possible without compromising message integrity. It was a game both sides played with neither side admitting the game even existed. He knew that eventually he would have to lose, but for the moment he enjoyed his advantage and the obvious frustration of his Warszawa counterparts.

Without its ever being specified exactly why, two analysts were eventually sent in person to speak with him directly, "in order to exchange ideas and share information." He was less than enthusiastic in his reception, speaking in vague terms about his work and explaining that most of what he did was by intuition. He freely volunteered to work on anything they sent him but confided that he really wasn't able to be of any more help than that.

Zosia sat in on one of the interchanges and watched him with growing perplexity. In the evening they took a walk together, and as Joanna skipped ahead to explore a hollow log, they stood together, watching her play, in silence. It was that time of day when the sun hovered on the horizon—bright enough to irritate his eyes, yet casting too little light for him to wear his sunglasses. He took the glasses off and turned to smile at Zosia, but she did not look at him; instead she stared intently after Joanna. The silence grew heavy between them, and he waited uneasily for Zosia to say what was on her mind.

Finally, still without looking at him, she spoke. "You were lying to them today."

"Yes, I was."

"I think they knew it, too."

"It doesn't matter. They got the message."

"And what was that?" she asked, apparently distracted by something in the distance.

"I'm not telling them anything," he answered, following her gaze though he knew nothing was there.

"Why not?"

"Isn't it enough that I decode the documents for them?"

"But what if something should happen to you?" she asked.

"Indeed."

"Oh."

Joanna had spotted another, more fascinating goal and had run on ahead. They walked after her in silence for a few minutes. Then Zosia finally asked, "Do you really think you need to do that? Don't you think you can trust them?"

"Why should I? Why should I give away my only advantage?"

"So you think as long as you're unique, you'll be safer," she guessed, kicking at a bit of sandy soil with her toe.

"I think they'll be a little less careless with me. It won't last all that long though. They'll work it all out sooner or later on their own."

"Maybe not. We're always short of trained people, and those we have are always short of time."

"Well, then, you'd think they'd be a little less cold toward me, wouldn't you?"

"The world doesn't revolve around you; maybe they have other concerns."

"Yeah, but then I've got to look out for myself, don't I?"

"Yes, I suppose you do." Zosia's voice had taken on a resigned and somewhat cold edge.

He felt that she was misjudging his motives. He didn't care what any of the others thought, but he didn't want her to think of him as selfish. He took her hand, stopped her in her stride, and turned her toward him so that she could see the sincerity in his eyes. "Zosia, it's not like that. I mean, it is a bit, but you've got to understand I've had so many people tell me my life was worthless, that it was hanging by a thread. Even your friends were willing to just blow me away." He sighed heavily. "Don't you understand? I need some sense of security, some feeling that I am indispensable or . . . or at least not so easily trashed."

It was growing dark, and in the dim light, he could not discern her expression. He added somewhat ruefully, "In any case, I'm not denying them much. It's just a bunch of dross sent out by some conspiring officials, it's not important. They know that, that's why they weren't all that upset."

"It's all right, you don't have to explain."

"Is it really all right?"

"Yes. I think I understand. And I trust you to do what's right."

He sighed again. What the hell did that mean?

They both stood in silence watching Joanna skip stones off a tree trunk. She went to pick up the stone she had thrown, then as if she had suddenly seen something, she broke into a run and disappeared down a slope. Zosia stared as if entranced, then gasped and ran in the direction Joanna had taken. Peter ran after her, calling to Zosia, "What's wrong?"

At the bottom of the slope Joanna was standing stock-still. Zosia skidded to a stop just behind her. Both of them stared at a small white stone planted discreetly under a large pine.

Peter had stopped with Zosia, and he gasped quietly at the pain the sudden exertion had caused him. *"Co to jest?"* he asked softly.

"It's Adam's gravestone," Zosia replied in English. Obviously she did not want to include Joanna in the conversation. She stroked her daughter's hair as she spoke.

"Is he buried there?" Following Zosia's lead, Peter had switched to English as well.

"No, of course not. I have no idea where his body is."

"I'm sorry."

Joanna stood quietly looking at the stone. Zosia continued to stroke the child's hair. "We always have a service and a memorial stone for our lost ones. I had not noticed that we were so near to it—not until Joanna ran down the hill."

"You are *sure* that Adam is dead?" he asked, perturbed by the twisting he felt in his gut. What if the answer was no?

Zosia threw him a glance that made him wish he had not been so crass. What in the world had led him to ask something so incredibly insensitive? "Yes," she answered finally. "His death was registered in their files. They don't usually bother to send us formal notification," she added sarcastically.

He had not meant his question to sound the way it had come out. Wasn't it possible that he had wished there was hope for Adam? "What did he die of?" he asked, hoping to sound conciliatory, but realizing immediately that this question was even stupider than the last.

"A heart attack," Zosia answered as if repeating an oft-told lie.

Joanna turned to her mother, wrapped her arms around her leg. "Can we go home?"

"Of course, dear."

Peter picked up Joanna and they began walking slowly back to the camp. Joanna wrapped her arms around him and rested her head against his shoulder; within minutes her steady breathing told them that she was dozing. They continued walking in silence, each immersed in his or her own thoughts. Peter felt comforted by the trusting child in his arms and pressed his head against hers affectionately. He struggled to find the right words to apologize to Zosia without putting his foot in his mouth again, but Zosia interrupted his thoughts before he had decided what to say.

"What does it feel like?"

"What do you mean?"

"To be questioned. To be tortured. What did Adam feel?"

"I don't know."

"But you were tortured, weren't you?"

"You know I was." Nightmarish images flashed before his eyes. "I imagine it wasn't the same for him though."

"Then what do you think it was like? I mean, to be interrogated like that? Did he feel hopelessness? Despair? Did he feel abandoned?"

"I can't say, Zosia. I'm sure it's different for each person. For me, I'd say there was always a strong feeling of being betrayed by humanity."

"All of humanity?"

"In a way. I think people in pain want the rest of the world to offer help, or at least sympathize, but for me the only people I saw were ones who enjoyed seeing me suffer. My pain was not only preventable, it was deliberately caused by other people. I think anyone who is used to normal human interactions finds that a bit of a shock."

She did not say anything, so after a moment's reflection he added, "Until one gets used to it, and comes to expect it even." He did not add, *And comes to believe it is justified.*

"Do you think that's what Adam felt?"

Peter shrugged. "His situation was quite different from mine; in his place, I might have been more concerned about not betraying anyone. Most of the time, I wasn't even asked anything. Nothing relevant, anyway. That relieved any fear of betraying anything, so in some ways I was less afraid than I might have been. And I didn't have a family to lose, so maybe that made it easier for me to accept the thought of dying."

Zosia walked on beside him, her face set in stony silence.

He paused, trying to recover some of what he had felt in those horrible prison cells when left alone with his pain. When he realized that she had not said anything, he turned to look at her questioningly. Suddenly it occurred to him that he was being stupid again—she wasn't asking about his experiences at all! What must she have felt when she learned of Adam's capture? When she knew he was almost certain to die a horrible death? He thought about what Adam must have felt and wondered what his own feelings would have been if he had known that Zosia and Joanna were praying for him. Would it have changed anything?

Carefully, so as not to aggravate the pain he knew she must be feeling, he said, "Zosia, when I said I had nothing to betray, it also meant I had nothing to hold on to. When I said that I had no family to lose, it also meant that there was no one worth dying for. I only know that my greatest fear was dying alone, unknown and unmourned. Adam had you, and even if you weren't there, he knew he had your love. And he knew that Joanna would carry something of him into the future. Don't worry, Zosia, you were there for him."

She stopped walking for a moment and looked up at him. Gently he wiped the tears from her eyes.

7

*T*HE FOLLOWING MORNING he told the visiting analysts how to decipher the nonstandard code. They were grateful and genuinely surprised.

"It would never have occurred to us!" Teodor asserted. He was the elder of the two—short and nearly bald, looking like a somewhat belligerent gnome.

His young companion, a woman named Halina, nodded her head in agreement. She was also short, with dark hair and a tired-looking, thin face. "We've been working at this too long! To miss such a schoolboy's trick!"

"Yes, yes, yes!" Teodor agreed. "We're overbooked, that's the problem. And one would hardly expect such a sophisticated system to be used to carry someone's private code. Still that's no excuse . . ." He shook his head in consternation.

"Do we know yet what their little conspiracy is about?" Peter asked.

Teodor laughed. "World domination!"

"Either that or a woman." Halina giggled. "It's always one or the other with these types."

"Just as well we didn't prod the American Security Agency into helping us," Teodor commented. "We tried, but they ignored us."

"They always ignore us," Halina observed.

"They're so incredibly jealous of their information there!" Teodor grumbled. He looked to Peter. "I don't suppose your lot ever got any useful information out of them?"

"Yes and no."

"Ah, now that is cryptic," Halina said with a laugh.

"Well, 'no' because we rarely got any real-time information out of them," Peter explained. "Everything seemed to be jealously guarded, and as far as I could determine, the whole Underground structure was viewed as so much cannon fodder, even the HQ staff. But 'yes' because we'd get some help with the training. I, for one, was tutored by an American. Not really an American—an American-born Brit, actually. Anyway, they'd come over for a year or two and try to make themselves useful, so they could get to know what it was all about. Then they'd go back claiming to represent us. In fact, I think it was a requirement to run for a position in the government in exile, spending time in England, that is. At least it seemed to be the custom."

Peter reflected on the number of Americanized Brits he had seen. Each had come "back" to the "homeland" eager and enthusiastic and full of energy and ideas. By the end of their stay most were tired and disillusioned and desperate to get out. Their romantic dreams were shattered as they discovered that the heroically brave freedom fighters were nothing but a pack of ill-tempered, often drunk, chain-smoking humans who had no patience with and no respect for idealistic children playing at war. They learned the awful truth that there was no nobility in suffering through the usual government punishments, that rotting in prison for a few years was often sufficient to break a person's resistance, that petty bureaucratic harassment and the inability to find work would silence most protesters, that those who continued the fight were often considered, quite rightly, fanatics. They were particularly horrified to discover that a good portion of the Underground's revenues came from illegal activities such as bank robberies and drug and alcohol sales, and they were dismayed to learn that the "unified front" that was presented with such success in the NAU was a complete sham, that hatred of the Nazis was not enough to cause Monarchists, Republicans, Socialists, Communists, and others to genuinely love each other.

". . . same thing here," Teodor was saying, "except it is a requirement, written into our emergency constitution, that all our representatives are born and raised in the Reich. The exiles are always trying to change that, but so far, we've managed to at least hold on to that much control of our government. Of course, once one of our people—usually from HQ—is called to serve, they immediately forget where they came from and start catering to their American constituency. And since we don't get a vote, there's not much we can do."

"Our one great advantage—the Empire—has been turned against us," Peter commiserated. "Now they rule everything from Toronto instead of London and we're just another damn colony. We don't even get a vote. They said it was just too impractical and would be too dangerous for us."

"I heard," Halina added, "that there is pressure from the NAU government to keep so-called foreign influence to a minimum. They're afraid of the Communists. They don't want to recognize governments on their territory voted in by people who are not under their jurisdiction."

"What a crock of shit," Teodor commented. "The Communists have virtually no support here—which should come as no great surprise with their big brothers next door being so helpful murdering our people."

"Oh, Comrade Teodor!" Halina mocked the singsong Russian accent. "Do you not know, they were not murdered! They went happily to their deaths in the Siberian mines to help the Soviet war effort against . . . er, who was it again? Oh, yes, that belligerent little group of nations that stood between us and the Reich!"

"Psychopaths to the left of us, murderers to the right," Teodor sang.

"And the Reds and the Nazis always kiss and never fight!" Halina joined in the chorus.

Peter joined them as they laughed uproariously. Rubbing the tears from his eyes, he opined, "Clearly you two have worked together far too long."

"Yeah. With no help. To get back to our original track," Teodor agreed.

"Single though it may be, it is well beloved," Halina chimed in.

Peter nodded. They had already told him about the perilous state of their human resources. During the first several years of their occupation, before America even entered the war, the Nazis and the Soviets had murdered nearly everyone with any higher education whatsoever, and though, over the years the Home Army had pieced together an education network and had tried to recoup their losses, the attrition rate was still appalling, and experts in any field were few and far between. However, because the regime was so brutal and murderous, there was no shortage of volunteers to carry out less specialized tasks, and it was this great army of volunteers, most of whom lived tragically short lives, that provided the backbone of their cryptanalysis: most of what they knew about the enemy's security systems they simply stole, often at a terrible cost in young, idealistic lives.

"But to get back to what you were saying," Peter said, "for all their political pressures, it still doesn't explain why they can't offer more technical assistance. Especially with espionage and analysis. We risk our fucking lives and they sit on their arses and fret about trivialities."

"Well, you know, they never know when we'll be infiltrated or simply crack under torture and give up all their precious secrets," Halina offered as a diplomatic defense.

"Humph! They just can't be bothered—they don't give a shit if we rot here, just as long as their balance holds. They threw us all away"—Teodor included Britain and most of Europe in this statement by waving his arm in an expansive way to include Peter in his definition of *us*—"for what they call peace. Just as long as their bloody trade deals aren't jeopardized. I've seen some direct quotes from some of their politicians—essentially they say, hey, we don't care who the Nazis or Reds murder, as long as they do it inside their own borders."

"And quietly," Peter added.

"Yes, and quietly." Teodor nodded vigorously. "Some even say if it's quiet enough, then it isn't even happening."

"I know," Peter agreed, wrapped in his own thoughts. "Just a few prisoners here, a bit of judicial torture there, nothing much, nothing that can't be dealt with. Just a few unfortunates on the wrong side of the law."

"Yes, some minor lack of civil rights, a couple of unnecessary executions, occasional famines—all accidental, all due to mismanagement," Teodor continued the list.

"Oh, the Americans have applied sanctions." Halina seemed to know she had been assigned the role of devil's advocate.

"Sanctions!" Teodor snorted. What more needed to be said!

Peter had heard variants of the same conversation numerous times before, in English, in London years ago. There, it had been a particular complaint that the British government and exiles had had the rest of the Empire and, in particular, all of Canada to fall back on. After a decade or so, the suspicion grew among those left behind that the island was being consigned to the category "expendable." The subsequent union of Canada, Quebec, and the United States into the NAU confirmed these fears in the minds of many. The British leadership was drawn into the huge and powerful political structure of an entire continent, their children grew up there and assumed the roles of power, their grandchildren were born there and knew no other home.

The world was thus neatly divided into spheres of influence: the Latin gangster regimes, the North American democracies, the Asian patrimonies, the Russian Communists, and the German National Socialists. Only Africa seemed up for grabs—the scene of continuous skirmishes between the great powers. It was, to all intents and purposes, a stable geopolitical division of the world, and that one small island on the edge of the German hegemony should be grabbed back, at an unconscionable cost in American lives, was, in the eyes of more and more Americans, a rather unsettling and unattractive idea.

Peter had not subscribed to this view; it wasn't clear to him that the ancestral home of the British Empire was being abandoned to its fate, but he was convinced that the political paralysis that emanated from the far side of the Atlantic was only hurting their cause. He wondered then, as he did now, at the sort of social structure and the complex international economic and political policies that were involved. There were so many contradictions between the public statements and the actions of the NAU that none of it seemed to make any sense. And information was so hard to come by: having spent his life, like the rest of them, sorting through the propaganda of a totalitarian regime, how could he ever believe anything he read or was told?

"Now they want to organize some trade deals and so they're putting pressure on our organizations there to lay low and offer us less help," Halina explained to no one in particular.

"They buy goods made by slave labor on one day and talk of freeing the world on another," Teodor countered.

"I don't think they buy anything from the Reich. I think it's illegal. They are still, after all, technically at war," Peter suggested.

"Oh, they buy—I know all about that—just not directly. And as for being at war, they only seem to remember that when we need something. Then their Ministry of State refuses to let information or equipment into our territory because they're at war with the occupiers! Talk about logic!"

Peter thought about his computer: obviously there had been no exaggeration in Katerina's assertion that they had truly exerted themselves on his behalf. He should have shown more gratitude; perhaps later he could express his thanks.

"Well," Halina said in a conclusive tone, "whatever we say here won't make a damn bit of difference."

"No, it won't. But I know what will!" Teodor agreed, looking meaningfully at Peter.

"What?" Peter asked suspiciously.

"You!" Teodor announced triumphantly. "Why don't you come up to Warszawa? We could use you there."

"I can't," Peter explained as he rolled up his sleeve and showed them his numbers. "Out there, these are a death warrant; here they don't matter."

"Ech. Can't they do something about those?" Halina asked as she leaned forward to have a closer look.

"They say not."

"Don't believe the quacks here, get another opinion!" Teodor snorted.

"But if they're right . . ."

"Well, then you're right, those would be a problem," Teodor conceded.

Peter rolled his sleeve back down, pleading, "Please, don't get me transferred. I don't want to leave here, it's my home."

They looked at each other as if communicating telepathically, then they both nodded. "It'd be a pity not to have you up there with us, but we'll honor your wishes. We'll tell HQ that it's best you remain here," Halina offered.

"Thank you. And do visit often, okay?"

Teodor nodded his head. "I can see why you want to stay. It's a cozy arrangement here."

"What's your rank?" Halina asked as if agreeing.

"Rank? I'm a civilian."

"Oh, heavens! Don't do that! Get commissioned!" Teodor insisted.

"I'm averse to taking orders."

"Doesn't matter," Halina insisted. "If you're here, you take orders, and if there's fighting, they'll draft you in an instant. Get a commission—you'll get better pay and at least then you can give orders, too!"

"Pay?"

"They aren't paying you?" Teodor asked, astonished.

"Room and board." Peter replied, then added somewhat humorously, "And all Colonel Firlej's old clothes."

"Those bastards," Halina murmured. "Demand a salary."

"It's that Katerina, she's a skinflint! That tightfisted old . . ." Teodor stopped himself and grinned sheepishly. "Ah, mustn't say that. We're all brothers in the bond, now aren't we?"

"And a commission!" Halina urged, ignoring her comrade. "Zosia is a big shot, she should arrange something decent for you."

Peter considered their words and wondered why he had not thought to ask earlier for some compensation. Had he assumed they all worked for free, or was he just simply grateful not to be shot? "A salary. Money for my work!" he scoffed, mostly at his own timidity. "Sure, why not, I'll ask." Then with mock severity he added, "No, I'll demand!"

"Good for you!" They smiled, sat back, and relaxed. Peter thought that though their age difference was enough for them to be father and daughter, they looked more like two peas in a pod. One plump pea and one skinny one. Peter laughed to himself as he wondered how long it would have taken Maria to pluck these two peas out. Halina consulted her watch, showed it to Teodor, and said, "What do you think?"

"Yep, I've had enough."

They looked at him. "Shall we join the others now and have some vodka?" They were not strangers to the Szaflary encampment and knew about the regular parties. On Saturdays a group of the "regulars" got together along with some of the visiting or temporary staff and indulged in vodka and conversation and debates; sometimes there was singing and even dancing.

Early on, Peter had attempted to join in; nevertheless, he felt rather uncomfortable despite the general merriment and relaxed atmosphere. Notwithstanding their protocol to the contrary, the language invariably switched to Polish as the evening progressed, and anyone who then bothered to converse with him was clearly doing so only to be polite. And if there was dancing, then Zosia made an impression on the floor as she whirled around gracefully with her partner. Not only did he not know how to dance, but the lingering pain in his legs had made him awkward and self-conscious when he had tried to learn, and eventually he had given up. He simply sat back and watched, usually drinking far too much vodka, envious of the man dancing with Zosia, aware that all too often it was Tadek and that the two of them looked painfully natural together.

He shook his head at Teodor's and Halina's questioning look. "You go ahead, I have some work to do."

======================================= **8** =======================================

"**N**OW WHAT THE HELL did I do with it?" her victim muttered. She stood there carelessly with her back to the open door, shuffling papers and mumbling to herself in confusion.

Stealthily Stefi crept up on her, her arms poised for action. When the moment was right, she sprung like a cat, leaping forward to throw her arms around her aunt and shouting, "Boo!"

"Good God!" Zosia exclaimed, jumping with fright and dropping her files. She turned around even as Stefi released her hug. "You scared the hell out of me!"

"You should be better prepared!" Stefi teased. "Ever on the alert."

"That's a good way to have a nervous breakdown," Zosia chided, patting her chest to try to settle her heart. "I'm at home, dear. I relax here."

Stefi giggled. "You're just getting soft." She stooped down and gathered the dropped papers together.

"And you, I see, have come a long way in these four and a half years," Zosia commented, remembering back to that traumatic day when she had helped Stefi with her first kill.

"Yes, I have," Stefi agreed, suddenly serious. She stopped her paper gathering and looked up earnestly at her aunt. "Did you know, I had to take out Til?"

"No! That was you? Oh, I am sorry. What did he do?"

"He was a bad boy. Tried to blackmail Father," Stefi explained.

"You liked him, didn't you?"

"Yeah, he was nice." Stefi stood and handed Zosia her files.

"You should know better than to get emotionally involved with anyone who might one day be a target."

"Pff! Look who's talking!" Stefi laughed. "Olek told me you slept with a prisoner the very night he arrived."

"I interrogated him," Zosia answered defensively.

"Is that what it's called?" Stefi asked slyly.

"I was tired! I fell asleep! Anyway, I have my reasons for what I do, and it is not your prerogative to question them!" Zosia scolded, then added quickly, "I didn't realize you were coming so soon. Why are you here?"

Stefi tapped her teeth. "Time for some dental work, if you know what I mean."

"You're rather old for that, aren't you? What are you, twenty now?" Zosia asked, turning away long enough to stash the files in a drawer.

"Yes, I'm twenty, and no, this isn't a first implant. The dentist says that my mouth is still growing and I have to come back for frequent maintenance if I don't want the capsule to crack. I'm also due for some weapons training, and the best ranges, as you know, are here."

"Not to mention Olek."

"Not to mention that," Stefi agreed with a wink.

"Are you hungry?"

"Ravenous! Where's Joanna?" Stefi asked, glancing around the flat.

"Out playing." Zosia wandered over to the kitchen to see if Peter had left any prepared food around. She found some leftovers and brought those out. "Do you want this?"

Stefi sniffed the casserole. "Smells good. Is Marysia still cooking for you?"

"No, I've acquired a housemate. The English fellow."

Stefi giggled. "Still interrogating him?"

Zosia glowered.

"I've heard he's the spitting image of Uncle Adam. Is that true?"

Zosia shook her head. "Not at all. I don't know why everybody says that."

"Probably to annoy you. What's he like?"

"He's nice. Good company. Very useful, too," Zosia summarized. "Takes care of everything here and Joanna loves him. He's out with her right now."

"Is he any good in bed?" Stefi asked impishly.

Zosia raised her eyebrows at her niece. "You should know better. It has only been a year."

"I'm sorry. I wasn't thinking. What's he do here?"

"He's our cryptanalyst. And speaking of which, it's good you're here. I need to talk to you."

"Me? What about?"

"I'll tell you while you warm this up." Zosia began rooting around in the cupboards, muttering, "Where the hell are the frying pans?"

Stefi held one up in the air. "You mean this thing sitting on the stovetop?"

"Yeah, that. Do you know how to warm food?" Zosia asked, dumping the casserole into the pan.

Stefi shook her head. "Naw, that's servant's work. Or Ma's." She watched as Zosia put the pan on the stovetop. "Maybe you should put some oil in first?"

Between the two of them, they finally managed to heat up the dinner without burning it, and as Stefi sat eating, Zosia explained what was on her mind. "It's something Peter found—this unusual code sent out from an unlikely source. We sent the results on to HQ and determined that they have also stumbled across part of this network. It seems there is a conspiracy within the security services, and the code is used more to exchange information between members of the conspiracy and to hide it from their own colleagues than to exclude us."

"Fascinating," Stefi mumbled as she sipped the wine Zosia had poured for her. "How do I fit into this?"

"I talked with the analysts from Warszawa, after they had talked to Peter, and they're as baffled by the information being sent out as we are. Place names in the middle of nowhere, code names for people that we can't match up to anything, no obvious rhyme or reason for any of it. Then it dawned on me that maybe it's somehow linked to that thing you've been pursuing—that project that Schindler had. Have you found out any more on that?"

"I've more or less let that drop. I got some place-names out of Wolf-Dietrich, but then he had to go back to work and I have no way to get at him there."

"Hmm. I was hoping you could pump him for a bit more information. I'd like to see if these things are linked."

"Well, we do keep in touch. He said he'd be in Göringstadt sometime in the near future. I could try and arrange a meeting."

"Do it," Zosia ordered. "I have a suspicion this is important."

9

"**I**S THIS IMPORTANT? Can I help?" Joanna asked as she stood wide-eyed in the kitchen watching her mother pull bowls and pans and ingredients out and place them on the counter.

"Yes, I'm making dinner." Zosia ducked her head into a cupboard and began ruthlessly rooting around, muttering imprecations to herself.

"Why don't you get Daddy to help you?"

Zosia brought her head out and looked at her daughter with something like disapproval on her face. "Daddy?"

"Yes, he's good at making things! I help him out all the time," Joanna explained, oblivious to her mother's look.

"Well, the reason I'm not asking Peter for help is, I meant it to be a surprise party for him."

"A birthday party?" Joanna asked excitedly.

"No," Zosia answered irritably. "It's been a year since he came here, and I thought we should celebrate that. Especially since he made such a fuss for both our birthdays, and then I missed his altogether."

"A party! Great!" Joanna jumped up and down and clapped her hands. "I'll decorate!"

"Fine, sweetie. Maybe first you could tell me where the potatoes are?"

Joanna took her mother's hand and led her two steps to the storage bin. She opened it and pointed inside. "Those are them."

"I know that much!" Zosia growled. She picked up one and inspected it. She poked at the small eye growing out of a dimple.

After a moment of watching her mother, Joanna said, "I still think you better get help."

"I think you're right."

A short while later, Zosia munched on a piece of chopped onion as she watched Peter put a pan on the stove. "I can help out now, I'm all dressed," she offered.

"Good, chop this up." He shoved some boned pieces of chicken toward her.

"How did you ever learn to cook so well?" She picked up a paring knife.

He handed her a cutting knife, then threw some butter into the pan. "What I want to know is, how did you ever get to this stage in your life without learning how to do even the simplest things in the kitchen?"

"It was never really necessary. And I was busy with other things," she said, busily hacking at the chicken.

"All your life?" He raised an eyebrow disbelievingly as he twisted the pan to melt the butter evenly.

"Well, I depended on my mother until my parents moved out. After that, Marysia did a lot of the cooking for us," she answered as he dumped the onions into the butter. As they changed from white to almost clear, he shifted them to the side of the pan, reached for the chicken, and added that to the center. The meat sizzled as it hit the hot surface.

"So, now, you've delayed answering long enough; where did you learn to cook so well?"

"No big secret, I've watched others." He stooped down to inspect the flame and adjusted the gas accordingly. "When I was home from school, my mother taught me some basics." He remembered how normal life had been then. She had advised him that a man should always be able to fend for himself, and that it would help him find a good wife if he wasn't helpless in the kitchen. He turned the meat, pushed it around a bit, pensively. If they had lived, what would life have been like for him? A respectable government job, a wife, a child, a one-bedroom flat, maybe eventually even a car. Could it ever have been like that?

Zosia was looking at him questioningly. He gave her a fleeting smile and continued, "My grandmother taught me as well; I used to stay there sometimes." Again he stopped speaking as he remembered the frail old woman who had given him so much love. "I paid her back by cooking for her when she got feeble. I was in school then, so I didn't have much chance, but when I was home on break, I'd go over and try to help out, at least until she died."

"So, this is all from when you were a child?" Zosia asked as if to prove she was far too old to learn.

"No, not at all. Most of what I know is from when I worked in a restaurant kitchen. Later, in the labor camp, I was occasionally assigned as kitchen staff in restaurants or industrial cafeterias. Then Frau Reusch taught me some things, and even Frau Vogel wasn't that bad at cooking. She said her mother had never taught her anything since they always had servants, but she learned a bit from a Polish woman who worked for them."

"A Polish woman?"

"Yeah, she was temporary. Came in a few years after Gisela was born and left a month or so before I came. I guess before that they had some man."

Zosia made a face and Peter thought it was in response to the implication of what that woman must have had to endure, but she dispelled that thought by saying, "She should have never cooperated! The traitor!"

"Zosia! All she did was cook! Don't be so judgmental!"

"My goodness, aren't we touchy!"

"That's because I cooperated," he muttered.

"No, you didn't."

"By your definition, I did. And," he added, thinking of Maria, "I didn't even have the excuse that I was raised from childhood as a slave."

"That was different. What you did was different."

"No, it wasn't. We do what we must to survive."

"Offering recipes is more than surviving; it's collaboration!"

"Well, as long as there is no other option, we need to live as well." His own uneasy guilt mixed in with thoughts of how Frau Vogel had sobbed on his shoulder after the telegram about Uwe, about how sometimes they would discuss the best way to work the garden, or how he had felt when Teresa had given him the *Winterfest* present. It was clear that if he had been more cooperative, or had cooperated earlier, his life could have been a lot better. He thought of Maria, too: she had been determined to live as happily as possible, to have needs that could be fulfilled, and to ignore those that could not. Was it so evil? Could anyone so helpless and alone really be a traitor?

Zosia was shaking her head. "Cooperation of any sort just enables the Reich to continue. It legitimizes it!"

"I'm not so sure. We failed to defend our liberty adequately during the war, and revolution seems unlikely now. Perhaps we can change the system from within. Perhaps evolution is the way out."

"Failed to defend? Failed to defend! We fought like hell! We kept our side of the bargain—rejected Hitler's unholy alliance, took the brunt of the first attack, but you, you French and English sat on your hands! Don't arm, you said, don't provoke the psychopaths! Just hold out two weeks, you said, two weeks! Ha!"

Peter rubbed the back of his neck. "I wasn't even born then, Zosia."

"But you talk about us not defending liberty! What was it called then? The 'phony war'? While they were murdering us here, you laughed about this so-called *Sitzkrieg!* Hitler's troops from the west, Stalin's from the east! We were being slaughtered and you did nothing! Nothing when it would have made a difference to do something! When they were weak and vulnerable, you sat there!"

"I wasn't even born then," he repeated quietly. He had heard the excuses and explanations of those who were alive then, but he did not repeat them for her.

"So now you think we can sit it out. That the way out is evolution! They're trying to *exterminate* us! *You* can wait for the system to evolve, you *English*"—she somehow imbued the word with as much tone of betrayal as any German had ever managed—"but if *we* wait, we'll all be dead! No, no, that's not the way—she should never have aided the enemy in any way!"

He did not appreciate the way his simple suggestion had been exploited to attack his entire nation, but decided not to argue it further. It had been, after all, a rather insensitive remark given all that had happened and was still happening around them. Still, he felt a kinship with Frau Vogel's previous servant. He understood that she had only wanted to live her life for whatever it was worth. He felt a need to justify both the woman and himself to Zosia and said somewhat deadpan, "I really don't think handing out a recipe is aiding the enemy."

Zosia looked at him as though reevaluating him in light of that comment. He felt discomfited by her stare and so he added, "It's easy to be unforgiving about things one has never encountered personally. Perhaps if you people offered us an out, then you could judge us."

"Who do you mean by *us?*"

"Us. Me and that woman."

"I'm not judging you."

"Yes, you are." Or was he simply judging himself and blaming her?

"Well, what are we supposed to do? We're fighting for our lives! Do you mean we don't do enough?"

"I mean for all your activities, I never once heard of something like an underground railroad to free forced labor. You didn't even free Tadek's wife, did you?"

"You know I didn't agree with that decision." She did, though, understand the logic: if they had not only let Tadek live, but had taken the risk of trying to free his wife as well, they would have opened themselves up to a deluge of refugees and requests.

"So, once they take someone, that's it, isn't it?"

"What are we supposed to do?" she asked, clearly angered. "We can't feed and house everyone!"

"How about smuggling them out to America? Or somewhere else?"

"Do you have any idea what that would involve? And do you realize how few countries are willing to accept refugees? Just try and get into America! For all their big words about freedom, they'll throw you right back out if you show up destitute at their border!"

"I'm not judging you; I know what you're up against. I know you can't go saving every poor fool like me who ends up in their hands; though I do think you could be a bit more willing to accept those of us who do make it out on our own." He said this without bitterness, but he had not forgotten the humiliating experience of having to defend his life to the Council. Though they were ignoring it, it was the anniversary of that as well.

Zosia frowned slightly but said nothing.

He continued, "But still, I'm not judging you, and I don't expect you to judge me either. I'm not proud of everything I did, but I know it kept me alive and sane. If you aren't there to offer help, then don't offer condemnation."

"I wasn't even talking about you!" she moaned plaintively. She watched him cook for a few minutes in determined silence, then finally ventured, "It's nice that you learned so much. Is this a recipe from the restaurant?"

Joanna put down her book to come and stand by them; though she could not understand most of their English, her curiosity had been piqued by the varying tones of their conversation. Peter plucked a piece of tomato off the counter and handed it to her to eat, then answered Zosia in German so that Joanna would understand. "I'm just making this one up as I go along, based on the ingredients at hand. Since I've come here, I've learned to improvise—out of necessity—to keep from starving." He gave Zosia a fleeting, hopeful smile.

"Are you complaining?" she asked lightly.

"Not in the least. I couldn't be happier." He leaned toward her and kissed her, then picked up Joanna and kissed her as well. He spun Joanna in his arms so that she could do a handstand, held her there as she giggled, and then let her gently down to the floor. "You have no idea what a joy it is to eat the food I've prepared rather than watch hungrily as someone else wolfs it down."

"Didn't you at least get to taste the leftovers?"

"Pff. You must be kidding! I wasn't even supposed to touch what they threw away."

"But you did?" Zosia asked, trying unsuccessfully to hide her revulsion. Joanna, back up on her feet, wrinkled her nose but remained quiet.

"Of course I did!" He tasted a piece of chicken; it was done, but he needed to correct the spices. When he was satisfied at the balance, he scooped up the chopped peppers and tomatoes and tossed them into the pan. "No, my rations were, as Frau Vogel would say, completely separate. That is, when I got a chance to eat them; there were really no concessions to the possibility that I had human needs." He fell silent, then added softly, as if to himself, "None at all."

Zosia studied him as a distant look came into his eyes, but she said nothing to interrupt his reverie.

He caught her look and explained, "Sometimes I'd only manage to find time to eat early in the morning and very late in the evening. Near the end of the month, it was often half-rotten, as well. Still, I suppose that was nothing compared to . . ."

"To what?" Joanna asked.

He looked at her, aware for the first time that she had been listening to him. The words he had been about to say died on his lips. The memory had come upon him so suddenly, so casually, he had almost spoken about it in front of Joanna! How could he speak such obscenity in her presence? He grit his teeth to force himself into silence as it played through his mind. He shut his eyes, wishing it away. He felt himself shaking uncontrollably.

"Daddy? Are you all right? Daddy?" Joanna's sweet voice penetrated the horror.

He opened his eyes and saw her wide eyes, the soft curves of her tiny, delicate face. Daddy. She had called him Daddy. He shook his head. "Don't worry, honey. It's nothing."

"Are you sure?" Zosia asked gently. "You've gone as white as a ghost."

He nodded. "It's okay. Really."

"How have your headaches been? You haven't mentioned any recently," Zosia asked, carefully changing the subject.

"They're much less frequent. I still get them and the blurred vision, but not as often."

Zosia grabbed a bit of meat out of the pan; she was about to pop it into her mouth when Joanna tapped her and pointed to her own mouth. Like a mother bird offering up a juicy worm, Zosia dropped the meat into Joanna's mouth and they both giggled. Then Zosia said to him, "You have one now, don't you."

"Yes, how did you know?" He was annoyed that he had not been able to hide the pain more effectively, and annoyed that his head ached in the first place: it was like someone screaming at him continuously. He lowered the heat under the pan and in a separate bowl mixed some flour into sour cream.

"Oh, I just guessed. You know, your tone of voice, the way . . ." Zosia waved her hand vaguely.

He ran through a mental inventory wondering if there was any red wine to be had. White perhaps. Were the spices too heavy for that? If he had thought of it earlier, he could have compensated for that. If only he didn't have this god-damned throbbing in his head. It took him a moment to notice that Zosia had not finished her sentence. "The way what?" he prompted.

"It's just that they seem to be quite coincident with certain topics of conversation."

"I'm not making them up!"

"I didn't mean it that way! Really, you've got to stop being so sensitive!"

"I'm sorry."

"And I wish you wouldn't apologize so much."

He had to force himself not to apologize for that.

She continued, "You're allowed to disagree with me. I won't be offended!"

"Really? You seem to get so worked up."

"That's just your interpretation. I like discussing things with you, I like that you have different opinions from me, but I don't like the way you take everything so personally."

"I'm sorry," he said without thinking. "Oops, I wasn't supposed to say that, was I? Sorry!"

Zosia giggled and he laughed as well. The laughter felt good and he said, "At least you've managed to clear up my headache."

"So, I'm good for something?"

He beheld her for a long, silent moment biting his lip as if to contain a torrent. Finally he nodded and agreed, "Yeah, for something."

=========================== **10** ===========================

*T*HE LITTLE PARTY was a great success. Marysia even brought along her cat, Siwa, since the feline had taken such an obvious liking to Peter. Siwa's affection was not lightly given, he had been assured, and this had delighted him—all the more so when he had learned that she had not been fond of Adam. Now she sat curled on his lap purring as he scratched the fur between her ears.

All the guests had enjoyed the dinner and, winking at Peter, complimented Zosia on her culinary efforts. They then clustered around the sofa, sipping vodka and waiting for him to open his presents. He was amazed that everybody had managed to bring one, even though, as Marysia noted, it was no great accomplishment finding something for the man who had nothing. He received some tools from Konrad, who laughingly pointed out that now Peter would no longer have to borrow his when he fixed something for Zosia, and Tadek gave him a Polish-German dictionary dating from the 1920s—one of the few that had escaped being burned after their language was declared illegal, Tadek noted. He almost said more, but Zosia fixed him with a look that kept him judiciously silent.

Finally, it was time to unwrap Marysia's present—she had insisted on saving it until last, obviously convinced he would be pleased. From the shape, he knew it was a book, and that alone pleased him. When he finally removed the cloth in which she had wrapped it, though, he was speechless. It was a volume of poems that Zosia's father had given Marysia upon the engagement of her son to his daughter: not only were the poems in English, but the beautifully bound volume was William Blake's *Songs of Innocence and of Experience.*

Marysia saw his expression and explained, "Zosia told me."

He read the inscription that Zosia's father had written, and below that another that Marysia had written to him. Finally he stammered, "I can't accept this, it's too much."

"Yes, you can. Nothing can be brought out of the ashes, but some things, at least, can be replaced."

He nodded. "Thanks, Marysia." He couldn't say more, but he did not need to—she could see the gratitude in his eyes.

She hugged him, said quietly, "Welcome home."

At that point, it was decided by consensus that they had been somber for quite long enough and the party lightened up considerably. Vodka flowed, languages spilled out in a babble as each conversational group chose whichever seemed the appropriate tongue, and eventually they all got drunk enough to convince each other to sing bawdy folk tunes. As the last guest stumbled out the door, and Peter crawled into his bed, he was still giggling from the last joke, feeling well-fed, happy, and at home.

He awoke with a start from a completely different world. The small light that Zosia left burning cast comforting shadows; still he could feel his heart pounding furiously. It had been the usual dream—the one where Karl had just knocked him down the steps. He tumbled endlessly feeling his neck snap, his back break, his teeth smashed by granitelike protrusions. He observed his destruction with an odd detachment, felt no surprise when at the bottom of the steps, he could climb to his feet. Overwhelmed by pain he was unable to escape: his feet dragged as though his legs were of lead; he could not catch enough breath to move; his hands grasped uselessly at objects too far away to reach. By sheer force of will he tried to get his body to move; in response, his legs inched forward. To the right was a door—escape, he knew—but inexplicably he always turned to the left. Karl was somehow in front of him now, armed with a club. Karl swung at him, beat at him mercilessly. And Horst. And Elspeth. And others: faceless tormentors, dead friends, his parents . . . He felt his flesh pulverized beneath the blows, every bone of his body snapped like dry twigs, the sharp fragments jutting grotesquely through his skin. On and on it went, he could not move, could not scream. He turned toward the door, toward escape, and always, always it was Allison who stood there, blocking his path. She stared at him unseeing, expressionless. He reached for her, but she drew back. Her eyes were white—no, no, they were on fire. She held a club as well—he screamed at her to recognize him, to stop, but his voice caught in his throat. Unrelenting, she swung the club at him and his body shattered to bits; he collapsed into a heap of blood and pain—nothing left, unable to move. And then, always, he awoke.

He swung his feet to the floor, sat for a moment in the dark with his right hand pressed against his mouth, taking comfort in the solidity of his jaw, the unbroken line of his chin. He always woke racked by pain, and he wondered aimlessly if the pain caused the dream or vice versa. His hand moved up to touch the skin over his cheekbones where the doctor had indicated there was subcutaneous scarring of the muscle tissue. What had he said? It changes the shape of your face slightly. Not shattered to bits. No, not that simple. They had left their mark in other ways: *it changes the shape of your face slightly*. Gently, he touched where so many others had felt free to brutally slam. His hand trembled as his fingers traced a line along the ridge of bone under his eyes.

Quietly, so as not to awaken Zosia and Joanna sleeping in the next room, he went to the cupboard and pulled out the Scotch. It was a present from Zosia. An officer supply train had been raided, and some single-malt Scotch whiskey had been among the luxury goods on board. He smiled at the thought of how much Zosia must have wrangled to get him a bottle; she had presented it to him shyly, said maybe it would make him feel at home.

He poured himself a glass and sat in the underground gloom, contemplating what he should do with his life. What could he do to stop being afraid of his dreams? Would time heal all wounds? He felt that he needed more than time, he needed a direction. Never before in his life had he had the opportunity to make choices for himself, to have a direction to his life. But where to? He began by examining his desires, replaying boyhood dreams, imagining anything he fancied irrespective of the logistics or likelihood of fulfillment. His mind wandered. Should he return to England? No, there was no particular attraction in that idea. Seek revenge? There were prospects there. But a life goal? No. He could not devote his life to or find his purpose in vendettas. Politics? He smiled at the image of himself, a world leader, rousing the NAU to action, ridding his land of the Nazi scourge, bringing peace to the world. He shook his head, rejecting the image. Maybe he could do something, but even in his wildest dreams, the image of himself as a charismatic leader was ludicrous. If he had ever possessed the sort of fire that such a person needed, then it was long ago extinguished.

He continued to sip the Scotch, relaxed, and daydreamed. He closed his eyes and wondered what he would like to hear, what he would want to see when he opened them, if he were an old man. What could possibly surround him that would make his life feel worthwhile? He kept his eyes closed and listened into his future. Laughter. Giggles. The mischievous sounds of little children teasing a sleeping old man. Slowly he opened his eyes. Instead of the gloom of the little room, he saw a warm, well-lit room full of children. He saw Zosia smiling contentedly at him. He saw Joanna, and their other grown children, chatting amiably. He saw himself a husband to Zosia, a father to Joanna, a man with a family. It did not matter where; it did not matter what else he did.

He took another sip of the whiskey, sighed with satisfaction. Quietly he stood and crept to the door that separated his room from the bedroom. It was open a few inches and he peered in and looked at Zosia's and Joanna's sleeping forms. His dream was possible! It was all he needed. Calmed, his heartbeat quiet, he returned to the chair to finish his drink.

Zosia emerged from the bedroom. "Are you all right?" she asked in a sleepy whisper.

She was so beautiful, he wanted her so much! And he wanted to stay with her, to raise Joanna, to make a home for himself. If only this time he didn't lose it all. "Yeah, I'm fine."

"What's the matter?" she asked, responding more to his tone than his words. She sat on the edge of his bed, curling her legs beneath her, and pulling at the blanket to cover herself.

He told her about his dream. Then, before she could say anything, he asked inexplicably, "Zosia, have you ever killed anyone?"

"You tell me first." She did not seem surprised by the question; rather it seemed as though she had been expecting it for a long while.

"What? If you've killed anyone?"

"No, silly, if you have."

"No." He considered her for a moment as Katerina's condemnation rang through his mind. "It was never in the Underground's plans for me."

"And what was?"

"Infiltrating as *Reichsdeutsch* into a weapons lab outside London. I was trained to that end."

"But you didn't want that?"

"No, I wanted to be English."

"What happened?"

"I was told to shut up and follow orders." He remembered how they had said "grow up" with such disdain that all he could do was study his hands, his head bowed in utter shame.

"And?" Zosia prompted quietly.

"I more or less refused. I think they were ready to shoot me for insubordination by then."

She nodded and he continued, "It went on for years. I kept studying all the background I needed in order to infiltrate but kept arguing that I didn't want to. Finally we compromised: they would scrap the idea of me working in the lab, and in exchange, I would use my analytic skills for them. Us, I mean. I was to analyze from the outside what I refused to find out from the inside."

"You mean the research lab?"

"Yeah, they added cryptanalysis to my training so that I could decipher stolen documents and interpret them."

Zosia tilted her head in confusion. "With so much background, why did you hesitate to tell the Council what you knew?"

"I don't know. I guess because it was all dated, and I didn't know what was still in my head."

She looked dubious.

"It's the truth. I really don't know, Zosia! Maybe it's because I spent so many years lying about my skills—pretending I knew nothing, sometimes pretending I couldn't even read. Maybe I had come to believe my own lies."

"Apparently that wouldn't be the first time."

"You've talked to Marysia." He sighed. "Look, I'm sorry I misled you. She told you why, I'm sure."

Zosia ignored his apology. "So this time, tell me the truth, how was your group organized?"

"Small cells of scientific specialists, at least one of whom had some knowledge of cryptanalysis. Most of them had jobs at the university or in institutes and lived relatively normal lives. Someone, usually me, picked up or bought information from our sources, then I took a preliminary look at it and farmed it out to the appropriate cell for further study. They consulted with each other and reported back to me. I collected and organized the various reports and presented it all to our liaison."

"So you only oversaw the work that others did?"

"No, I had a cell as well, so frequently I'd assign something to our cell to be analyzed."

"Was Allison in your cell?"

"Yes, she was a chemist. She and I were so-called 'full-time'; we had both joined young, had been specifically trained to the job, and our external lives were meaningless: we weren't pursuing careers and we didn't have family commitments to hold us back."

Zosia nodded, apparently satisfied. "What was Allison's husband?"

"He wasn't a specialist, just security. He had come back from conscription to discover his wife was in the Underground, so he joined to stay with her. He was only assigned to our group because of her."

"Oh, so that's how you two spent so much time alone together," Zosia guessed.

"Yes," Peter admitted dryly.

"No doubt she was attracted to your ability to understand her work. Unlike her husband," Zosia continued in her investigative voice.

"No doubt," Peter replied bitterly. Before he could stop himself he said, "He was thick. God knows what she saw in him. God knows why she wanted to keep us both." He should never have kept the affair a secret! He should have done what everyone else did and blithely announced their attachment to the world. Terry would have left her in a minute. Then she would have seen how much her loyalty to him was worth!

Zosia shrugged. "Did it work?"

"Did what work?" Peter asked, still thinking of Terry and Allison.

"Did you find out what they were doing?"

"Oh, yes. I think we had a pretty good view of the entire establishment. We had people inside who stole documents, and we sat on the outside and analyzed it all and passed it on to the Americans. And that's it, that's all I did, I gathered intelligence and I never killed anyone."

"Maybe you should have," Zosia suggested. "Perhaps it would have purged you of your dreams."

"What an odd idea. But the dreams came later."

"I suppose they did," she conceded. "Well, maybe you should talk to someone about what happened to you. Maybe that would help."

Even though it was dark, she could see the sharpness of the look he gave her. "I did. I told *you*," he replied evenly. "That was quite enough."

"I meant someone else. Anyone. Maybe—"

"I'm not ever repeating what I told you, not to anyone," he insisted somewhat brusquely.

"But if you told your story to other people, maybe it would not only make you feel better, maybe it would even help our cause, you know, show what's going on—"

"Enough!" He did not raise his voice, but it was clear he was furious. "I'm not going to speak with anyone else! No one! Is that clear or are you stupid?"

Zosia pressed her hand to her lips to keep from saying anything. They remained silent for a moment, and she could hear him breathing deeply as he tried to gain control of his anger. Finally she said softly, "I was only trying to help."

"I know, I'm sorry. I'm really sorry." Quickly he added, "Now, enough about me, what about you, have *you* ever killed anyone?"

"I was hoping you'd say you had." She turned her attention to covering her toes.

"Why?"

"Because then you wouldn't think less of me," she whispered.

"So, you have?"

"Oh, yes."

He waited, hoping she would expand on her answer. When she didn't, he finally asked, "Why?"

She smiled at him. "What a silly question! I'm a soldier! Don't I look the part?" She shimmied comically from side to side so her breasts jiggled provocatively under her nightshirt.

He smiled at her teasing. "Well, then, when? How many?"

"Oh, I'm afraid I've lost count." At the look of surprise on his face, she added, "All the kids who are raised here work guard duty patrolling the mountains, and then later, of course, we become group leaders to the partisan encampments: keep them pointing their guns at the right people, as you know. Our policy is simply, nobody uninvited ever reemerges. Of course, we don't have prisons, so . . ." She gestured helplessly.

"Haven't they ever done an all-out assault?"

"Against whom? We're not officially here. These mountains are officially conquered, and you know the Germans, they are a very literal folk. They haven't seriously tried since 1970. Anyway, it's not all that easy to capture and control every inch of ground, especially territory like this. You should know that."

"Yes, I guess I do," he answered, distracted by her proximity. The dim light made her look all the more ephemeral, like the vision of an angel who had come to visit him. The thought of her patrolling against invading soldiers just didn't seem to fit. "How old were you?"

"I started at fourteen. I stayed at it for twelve years, on and off. Of course, I did other things as well, training and such. Just like your Barbara and Olek, too."

"Yes, of course." Peter had a sudden image of sweet little Barbara blasting away some hapless foot soldier, then wandering back to the office to help with some data entry. And if he had not personally had Olek point a gun at him, he would have had just as difficult a time imagining that fresh-faced kid shooting at anyone. He suddenly felt very ignorant of the people and events around him. He rubbed his eyes and face to try to soothe a growing sharp pain in his temple.

"It's not as bad as that," Zosia responded perceptively to his frown. "The soldiers know our boundary and they know better than to cross it. Only the fools or would-be heroes who insist on following orders rather than, er, prevaricating get caught out." She paused to rearrange the covers more securely over her feet. "I must admit, though, it was rather unsatisfying: all I ever shot were poor dumb privates. I never really aimed at a genuine target—you know, someone truly evil."

"I can't imagine you aiming at anyone," he said somewhat despondently.

Zosia looked at the shadows that hid his expression. She felt dismayed by his tone. Clearly, it was time to shatter some illusions; indeed, she had obviously waited far too long. Perhaps, she thought, she had enjoyed being the woman he had created in his mind. She had tried subtly throughout the year to enlighten him, but his illusions had been sturdy. She was the woman who had saved his life, defended him to the Council, fallen asleep in his arms on his first night of freedom. The doting mother, the caring friend. He had not wanted to know more, but now it was unsustainable. He could not remain in ignorance forever, no matter how much he wanted to.

She forced herself to sound cheerful, tried to recall the callousness of youth, tried to impress on him that she was not the kind and gentle creature he had invented in his mind. She plunged in: "I started patrolling at fourteen. I did my first lone patrol at fifteen and killed my first victim a month later. It was a difficult kill; I screwed up and wounded him. There was no time to go get help so I had to track him down to kill him before he got out. He was shot in the leg. He ran, I followed. After what seemed an eternity, he collapsed. I came up close—didn't want to mess up again—and looked him in the eyes. He begged me to spare him. He pleaded with me. He was crying. Then I shot him in cold blood."

"What else could you do?" he responded to her story mechanically, without sympathy. He hoped she had finished, but she had only paused.

"I got much better at it after that; I realized that wavering was worse than doing nothing. There were times when we didn't see anyone for months, then there were other times when somebody got zealous, and we had to drop them like flies. Patrols would be sent in and the idiots would actually come in! Five, six at a time. We'd have to pick them off, one by one. Shoot and disappear. They'd respond with a barrage of fire, but we'd be gone. Then, the next kid, a kilometer away, would pick off another until there was one desperate fellow running to get out of the woods. We'd make sure he never made it."

He nodded. What he felt and what he wanted to say conflicted so badly that he was left speechless. Zosia continued, driving her point home, dispelling his last stubborn doubts.

"That's how Adam and I got to really know each other. We'd keep score and try to outdo each other. Later, when we got older, we'd make love anytime we made a kill, right then and there, as close to the body as was safe. It was fantastic. The adrenaline rush was so incredible, you can't imagine what it felt like."

"Please stop."

"It was, though, after a time, unsatisfying. Not personal enough. So Adam and I moved to assassinations. We worked as a team. We'd get sent out to remove somebody, do the job, and if we could, we'd fuck right there in the room with the corpse."

"Please stop."

"I still do it, Peter. What do you think I do on all those missions? Do you think they need someone to lug along a computer every time? Why don't you ever ask anything about me?"

"Zosia, please stop!"

She did, abruptly. There was an awkward silence as he tried to think of something to say. She glared at him. "You want to know me?"

"Yes, I do."

"But not the real me!"

"No, it's not that."

"You think I'm horrid, don't you."

"No, no, I don't. It's not that." He struggled to find the right words, to clarify nebulous concepts. It was too much though: to process the information, filter it through his thoughts, and then explain what he felt in a few seconds. How could he hope to tell her what he felt when he himself didn't even know?

"What then?"

"Why are you trying to provoke me like this?"

"You're an idiot," she hissed in reply.

"*Mommy!*" Joanna's plaintive cry drew them both up. She stood in the doorway holding her ragged stuffed bear.

Zosia stood up, threw a last, unreadable look at him, and then went to her daughter. "Let's go back to bed, honey. Sorry we woke you." She herded Joanna back into the bedroom and shut the door tightly behind them. As she climbed back into bed with Joanna, she pulled the covers up close around them and tried to sound reassuring as she said good-night, but when she put her head back against the pillow, tears rolled silently down the sides of her face, puddling uncomfortably in her ears.

Peter remained in the armchair, stunned into paralysis. It was just as well Joanna had interrupted them, he would almost surely have answered Zosia's brutal comment with anger. Why in the world had he asked such a stupid question? What had he expected her answer to be? No—of course. She had been right; the moment she had said yes, he had not wanted to hear any more. Or he had wanted to hear an apologia. Her life didn't fit his script, and so he had wanted her to rewrite it.

His head ached with a brutal fury. He buried it in his hands, tried to claw the pain out with his fingers. It hurt as it had when Elspeth used to hit him and hit him and hit him all day long. It was probably her unabated pummeling, her continuous, insatiable displeasure that caused him such pain now, that threatened his sight. Yet, he had never believed she was cruel; though she was the one who had pounded at his face every day of those first weeks, he had always blamed Karl. Why had he done that? Why had he rewritten Zosia's life for her? He should have known, should at least have asked. Why had he been so determinedly blind to the real woman?

He thought about Zosia—the real woman this time—and realized that he had failed her miserably. She had wanted to tell someone her story, had wanted someone to understand the actions of her youth, the necessary compromises of her life, maybe even give her a context in which to forgive herself. All the times she had listened to him, all the times she had soothed his memories! And the one time she had opened up to him, he had asked her to stop! Maybe she had told her story so brutally because she was bothered by it. Maybe she had been afraid of his reaction and so she had presented herself as cold and hard and unhurtable. And he had wanted to know why she was provoking him! God, she was right, he was an idiot.

11

*T*HE NEXT MORNING, when Zosia emerged into the room, she found Peter still in the armchair, sound asleep. She nudged him and he woke up and smiled uncertainly at her.

"I'm sorry about last night," she said flatly, then turned away and busied herself in the kitchen section before he could even respond. It was, he realized, the first time he had ever heard her apologize for anything, and unusually, since Joanna was not around, she had spoken German. Her choice of language was an unambiguous insult and the words held little conviction—it was as though she had decided to say them only in the interests of keeping things running smoothly in the tiny flat. With her back to him, she asked a bit too cheerfully, "Do you want some tea, or should we have coffee?"

"Zosia . . ."

"What?" She almost snapped the word—almost but not quite. Clearly she was trying hard not to be angry. She still had her back to him, so he could not read her expression.

"Zosia, I don't know how to say this."

"Then maybe you shouldn't." Again her voice carried a tension—as though she hoped he might take her response as a joke, though it clearly was not.

"Zosia—"

"Would you stop repeating my name?" she grated, thoroughly exasperated.

"Sorry." It was one of those useless, meaningless apologies. His thoughts digressed for a moment on how harmful they were—worse than not apologizing at all, perhaps.

"Anyway, I'm sick of German. Why the hell can't you speak Polish yet?"

"That's not fair. You know I'm trying. It's not like I get much help here . . ."

"You always blame someone else."

Tadek's perpetually snide rebukes of his attempts came to mind, but rather than dispute her assertion, he chose to ignore it. "I'm sorry. I really am trying, it just takes time. We can speak English."

She responded in Polish. "No. If you can't say it in Polish, I don't want to hear it right now." She managed to slam the knife down on the counter as she was chopping at something. He wondered what it was she was pretending to make for breakfast. Chopped onions?

He paused. Now, she really was provoking him, but he decided not to be waylaid. He ran through his vocabulary, struggled to construct a sentence that would convey at least the gist of his rather complex thoughts, but it was hopeless. Every time he started a sentence, he ran into a word or a phrase he couldn't translate. And even if he knew all the words, he never knew what order to put them in, what endings the nouns should have—dative? Locative? Should he use a perfect or imperfect verb, and what was the masculine first-person past tense? All he had available to him were phrases that he had memorized syllable by syllable—and none of those would do. If he wanted to express an original thought, he would have to construct the sentence from scratch and risk sounding extremely stupid. Exasperated, he tried to simplify what he wanted to say even further. At this rate, he thought grimly, we'll both die of old age before I say anything.

Zosia clearly had the same idea. If he could have seen her face, he would have seen that she was smiling. Gently she said, "I can hear the cogs grinding from over here."

He didn't understand half the words, but he guessed the phrase from context. That's it, he thought, I don't care how simply or stupidly I have to say it, I'm going to speak! So, without groping for any further subtlety, he simply announced, "*Kocham cie, bardzo, bardzo mocno,*" which he hoped meant, "I love you, very, very much."

She spun around to look at him, her mouth slightly open with surprise. "*Kochasz . . . du liebst . . .* you love . . . ," she gasped in a confusion of languages.

He plunged in, mindless now of the grammatical niceties of her complex language. "You don't have to say anything. I know you don't love me, not yet. So, please don't worry." At this point he was stuck. Even butchering the language wasn't sufficient to convey his thoughts, so he switched to English to continue, "I don't expect a response. I don't expect anything. I know that I haven't given you any reason to love me—I've been too self-involved. But I promise, if you give me a chance, I promise there will be something to love. Just give me a chance to prove myself to you."

She smiled slightly. Then wetting her lips, she lowered her head. When she looked up again, she seemed to have come to some decision, but she did not say anything. She walked over to where he sat and set herself down on the arm of the chair and stroked his hair.

He pressed his head against her shoulder and wrapped his arm around her waist. Embarrassed by his admission, he said, "Do you know you're my best friend?"

She laughed lightly. "The competition for that position doesn't seem to be all that fierce."

"No. But you still manage to come through for me—even without having to compete."

"Well," she said, swinging her legs like a little girl, "you're my best friend, too."

They sat together quietly. He was enjoying the moment, but when he looked up at Zosia, he saw she was staring at the framed wedding photo of her and Adam on the wall. His face fell, but then he remembered how he had failed her the night before, and gathering his courage, he asked, "You grew up together?"

"Yes."

"He was always there for you." It was not quite a question, he knew the answer.

"Yes," she whispered, still staring at the picture.

Peter stood and went to the picture, looking at it closely. She seemed to be wearing a gown made entirely of lace. "Where did you get the dress? You got married here, didn't you?"

"Oh, that!" She giggled. "Yes, we had a little ceremony here in the woods. I wore a white dress that Marysia loaned me—it's held on with a belt. And then I wrapped my granny's lace curtain around it and over my head. Pretty campy effect, isn't it?"

"You look beautiful."

"White was hardly an appropriate color."

"It's always appropriate when you're in love."

"And that we were. Sometimes I think he was the only one who—" She stopped abruptly.

"The only one who really understood you?"

"Yes," she admitted quietly.

He turned to look at her, saw tears running silently down her face. He turned back to the photograph and contemplated the happy couple for a moment, then in a low voice said, "Zosia, if I could, I'd take his place. I mean—my life has been an utter waste. If I could have died in his place and he could have come back to you, I'd have made that trade—just to know you and Joanna were happy."

"Peter . . ."

"I mean it, Zosia. It's not a bunch of empty words. I know it sounds hopelessly romantic, but I don't say things like that. I've never said or felt anything like that. I just know that it would have given more meaning to my life than I ever had."

She fell silent. He walked over and stood next to her, putting his arm around her. "I'm sorry, I didn't mean to make you feel uncomfortable. And whatever I wish, I can't trade places with him, so I guess it was stupid of me to even say that.

I just wanted you to know you can feel free to talk about Adam. I won't be jealous, I won't be hurt. I promise."

She slid off the arm of the chair into his arms and buried her head in his shoulder. He felt her crying and held her as she sobbed quietly, "Oh, Peter, I miss him so!"

"I know," he said, holding her and stroking her hair. And I love you so much, he thought.

He could not think of anything else to say, so he just held her closer. They stayed that way a long time, then Zosia shook herself free and walked over to the photographs and pictures on the wall. She stood in silence contemplating a watercolor of Warsaw's *Stare Miasto*—the old town. Peter came up behind her and gently placed his hands on her shoulders. He could feel the warmth of her skin through the fabric of her nightshirt. He had an intense desire to feel the softness of her skin, to move his hands forward under the fabric, but he knew it was not the right moment. He distracted himself by looking at the picture.

"It's quite beautiful. Was it really like that?"

"I guess so," Zosia replied as if from another world. "At least that's what everyone says."

"Funny, isn't it?"

She thought that the way he held her felt nice; he did not lean on her like some men did, bearing their weight carelessly down on her small frame. Indeed, in all his gestures, he seemed to have that rare talent of understanding their relative size difference. His touch was always light, his presence, even in the tiny apartment, never overwhelming, never obtrusive. Of all the men she had known, none had ever achieved that level of comfort with her, not even Adam. She realized she had not responded, so she asked, "What's funny?"

"You and me, and those like us. We live in a world of illusions, a world of other people's memories, it's like we don't really exist. Photographs from other people's worlds, watercolors of cities that are no more. Yearning for, fighting for, things that have long disappeared, things we never knew: freedom, tolerance, peace. Peoples have disappeared, cities lie in ruins, and we have never known anything else. Your world and mine is concrete and ruins, guns and uniforms. Our lives are lies."

"Or maybe our lives are hopes." Zosia leaned back into him. "It's happened before. Dreams can resurrect realities."

"Were those realities really so good?"

"They were better than what we have now," she sighed. "I wonder if the people then appreciated what they had."

"I don't know." Did *they* appreciate not being in an even worse world? Did he fully appreciate not having been thrown into a concentration camp? Surviving that industrial job? Being allowed to live more than the three days he had asked for? "I guess it depends on whether or not they believed things could be different."

"I believe it *can* be different. I believe there does not have to be perpetual war. I believe—" She stopped abruptly.

"What?" Tenderly he massaged the tension from her shoulders.

"I believe there could be a world where it would seem unnatural and wrong for me to kill another human being."

"A world where death is not the penalty for every infraction against the state . . ."

"Or the penalty for being born on the wrong side of a border . . ."

"Or with the wrong name . . ."

"Or . . ." She stopped their mantra, asked instead, "What does London look like? Was it spared?"

"Oh, the initial destruction was not too bad, but over the years, section after section was taken hostage for various reasons and deliberately destroyed. What was left has fallen into ruin. All but the German residential and office areas." He sighed as he thought of some photos he had seen. "The parks are gone: the trees were either removed through official vandalism or died from age and neglect. Nothing new was planted. The Gestapo built a huge prison in Green Park—I was held there for a time. Outside the prison they had an execution ground. Very grand."

"What about the theaters? My father used to mention them all the time."

Though she couldn't see him, he just shook his head. The theater district was an utter shambles. Still, that did not prevent the regime from putting on productions for the benefit of the people: comedies, dramas, musicals. All with the same theme: National Socialism triumphs over evil. How many different ways they could present the same awful idea! He had seen—been forced to attend—dozens of productions at school. Always the same shit.

Only once had he seen something truly different. When he was eleven, after his brother had been drafted, his parents treated him to a Shakespeare play. It was a rare production, held in a warehouse in a seedy district south of the river. He had been overjoyed at the prospect, had studied the play for so long in advance he could quote whole passages verbatim. *King Lear.* How could he ever forget? The magical night arrived, they filed into the theater and took their seats, and finally the curtain was raised.

He remembered his chagrin as he heard the first lines of the play—in German. Furious with his parents, with the actors, with everyone in the audience, he had begun humming an obscene anti-German ditty he had learned from his friends. His mother shushed him, she jabbed him, she tried to cover his mouth, but all to no avail. He hummed it throughout the entire first act. At the end of the act, his father had grabbed him and literally dragged him out of the theater. Outside, in an alley, his father had begged him to shut up and sit through the play quietly. In response, he had begun humming the song again. His father, who rarely hit him, swung at him and cuffed him on the side of the head. The blow sent him tumbling into the mud.

He did not get up, just stared furiously as he sat there. "Why the hell did you bring me to this bloody awful play?" he had asked in English, using a thick accent he had only recently perfected. Unusually, his father had answered him in English. He had apologized then. Apologized for hitting him, apologized for the play. They had not known it would be in German, they had assumed it would be in English and would please him. His father extended his hand, pulled him out of the mud and cleaned him off, and together they went back in and sat through the rest of the play in silence.

Puzzled by his silence, Zosia turned to look at him. She was so close, he could feel the warmth of her body. His eyes held hers, then he leaned in and they kissed. He gasped with the urgency of his desire for her, and he wrapped his arms closer around her, but she pulled gently back. Kissing him lightly, she whispered, "I've got to go," and delicately extricated herself from his embrace.

She disappeared into the bedroom, and he stood for a long, long time staring at the cheerful watercolor on the wall, at the world he had never known.

12

"*E*XQUISITE! OUT OF this world! Unlike anything I have ever known!" Richard whispered into her ear. He closed his eyes and groaned inaudibly as his fingers traced a pattern down her body to find a new wonder. What was her name again? Oh, yes. "You are magnificent, Helga."

"You don't think I'm fat?" she asked nervously.

He pulled his head back so that he could look sincerely into her eyes. "No! What in the world would make you ask that!"

"I just thought—"

"You have a woman's luxurious curves," Richard assured her as he stroked her flab, "soft, enticing . . ." He moaned expressively.

"Some of the other women . . ."

"Who wants to touch a boy? That's what I want to know," Richard asked as he leaned over to kiss her. "I like women. This current fad for stick figures . . ." He shook his head in dismay. "I'm so lucky to have found you! Ach, but it can't last long. Alas, I must leave Berlin soon."

"Maybe you'll get transferred here," Helga suggested as he planted little kisses on her chest, just above the frill of her rather demure nightgown.

He looked up. "Oh, to be with you!" he sighed, then said sadly, "Still, I don't think there's much chance of it, or have you heard something?"

"Well, I know my boss really wants you here. He thinks you'd be marvelous to fill Schacht's position."

"Oh, is he leaving?"

Helga sighed. "No, unfortunately not. Even worse, he's dead set against having you in Berlin."

"Really? Why's that?"

"I don't really know. I think he's afraid of you and doesn't want the competition. That's sort of what his secretary said to me, but you should ask her directly."

Tried that, Richard thought, but she was unreachable. So, here he was making love to an insignificant and insecure lump of womanhood, trying to wring every last bit of gossip out of her. It was stretching his talents to the limits, but he could at least console himself that every word he said seemed to make her feel happier about herself.

He reviewed all the information he had gathered and decided that his source had served her purpose. Now, it was time for one grandiose, final act of lovemaking, then tomorrow he could have one of his men discover her, woo her, and shortly thereafter, given the choice of a married man in a distant city and a young, handsome, unmarried man in Berlin, she would be able to let Richard down gently. If that didn't work, a sudden, guilt-induced impotency always did the trick. In any case, there'd always be a special place in her heart for him, and he would always give her a longing, albeit resigned, sidelong glance. Sometimes, when he entered a crowded room, he had to let one such look serve for four or five women at a time. It was getting ridiculous. Ah, but enough digression, it was time to get to work.

"It is well past time to take a break from work!" Richard enthused as he trotted down the Ministry steps into the early November night. "Don't you agree?"

"I have a thousand other things I should be doing right now," Schacht grumbled as he followed Richard. "I see no reason why I should be wasting my time going to the club with you now."

"Ach, my dear colleague, I know you are a very busy man. After all, you've turned down three of my invitations so far! If the Führer himself hadn't insisted I seek your advice, then I would let you go home to your dear wife and eight children." Richard walked rapidly, pulling his comrade along in a friendly manner.

"I have nine children."

"Yes, of course, nine children. But he did insist and he himself suggested we do it this evening over a beer." They turned the corner together and approached the construction site that was adjacent to the club.

"I'll have to ask him about that," Schacht muttered.

"Yes, do that. Tomorrow." Richard slowed his pace as they walked past the placards posted on the wooden wall surrounding the construction site.

"I really don't understand why this can't wait," Schacht groused.

"Just one evening, dear colleague! You won't deny our Führer that, will you? Well, look at this!" Richard stopped dead and pointed in amazement at a handwritten notice on the wall. "It's pure smut!"

Schacht bent forward to have a closer look.

"Herr Traugutt!"

Richard swung around to see who was calling him. At the corner, his assistant, Stefan, stood panting, holding one hand against his chest as he gasped for breath and holding out a piece of paper in the other hand. "It's a message for you!" he gasped.

"I'll be right back," Richard said, but Schacht was too intrigued by the letter on the wall to take note of him.

Richard sprinted over to Stefan, grabbed the note from his hand, and began to peruse it. Stefan scanned the street, reached discreetly into his pocket, and pressed the button on a small device. Not two seconds later they were both thrown backward by a blast emanating from the construction site, from behind the point where the letter had been posted. Both men looked in alarm to where Schacht had been standing.

"Bloody hell," Richard swore. "Terrorists." He motioned to Stefan. "You go get help, I'll see if Schacht is okay."

Stefan took off at a run back toward the Ministry. Richard ran toward Schacht's body. A few pedestrians were reasonably near, but they stood unmoving, paralyzed by fear.

Richard gently rolled the body over. The bloody, charred mask that was Schacht's face greeted him. Richard reached down to the neck and frantically searched for a pulse. He was startled to find one, strong and steady. Convulsively, his fingers dug into Schacht's throat with a sudden, violent force. Schacht's eyes popped open; he stared unseeing into the night sky.

A policeman approached. "*Mein Herr,* it's not safe here. There's usually a second blast. Please come away quickly."

Distraught, Richard looked up at him. "I can't find a pulse! I think he's dead."

Gently the policeman tugged on Richard's arm to pull him away. "Come, *mein Herr.* Your bravery won't do your friend any good now. Please, come away."

As they crossed behind the police cordon, Richard was greeted by others from the Ministry. A flurry of negotiations took place around him as the various branches of the police tried to determine who would take responsibility for the investigation. It was finally determined that Richard and Stefan would give their statements the following day to RSHA investigators. The local police were left to clean up the mess and clear the area of any unexploded bombs.

As they walked Richard back to the offices, Herr Schindler placed an arm around his shoulders. "Close call there, Traugutt; we're lucky that thing didn't get both of you."

Still obviously shaken, Richard only nodded.

"Maybe you should go to the hospital and get checked out," someone else opined.

That opinion was seconded by a number of voices.

Richard stopped and rubbed his face. "No, I'm okay."

"Hell of a Berlin welcome, eh?" a third voice asked.

Richard nodded. "It's okay. We have blasts in Göringstadt as well."

"I've heard they're a lot less frequent since you took over that division. Maybe you should come to Berlin," Helga's boss suggested.

"Yes, maybe." Richard gestured back in the direction of the blast. "Do you have any idea who was responsible?"

"Oh, lots of ideas!" Schindler assured him. "Too many!" He laughed and some of those around him ventured to laugh as well.

"You don't think it was random terrorism?" Richard asked, somewhat concerned.

"Could be, I suppose," Schindler explained. "Still, Schacht had so many enemies!" At Richard's surprised look, Schindler laughed again. "Don't worry, there won't be a shortage of suspects. You want to get in on the investigation? There'll be a lot of people who'll have to be questioned. It could be fun."

Richard shook his head. "No, sorry. I can't stay more than a few days. I'm due back. After I make my statement, I'll have to catch a train to Göringstadt."

13

*R*ICHARD SAT GLOOMILY staring out the window of his first-class compartment, his feet resting casually on the seat opposite, as Stefan handed over their papers to the conductor. The train was crowded and the conductor scowled meaningfully at Richard's feet but after perusing his identity papers decided not to comment.

Click-click, click-click. Thump-thump, thump-thump. The rhythm of the train's wheels kept reminding Richard of Schacht's pulse. It had been so unexpected! He had almost not bothered to check! He felt unusually rattled by the whole affair. It had taken so much to lure Schacht out that, if he had survived the blast long enough to speak, he would definitely have pointed a finger at Richard. Not only that, but the gruesome interrogations that had followed: some of the suspects had been genuine lowlifes—apparently Schacht had been deeply involved in some criminal conspiracies—but still there were the others, the various Danish nationalists who had been brought in. Richard closed his eyes and sighed. It shouldn't have to be like this, he thought.

He opened his eyes and stared out the window as the countryside sped by. The old Reich lands had long ago given way to the new Reich, and now as they crossed yet another internal border, the colonial lands emerged. Vast estates with their worker townships dotted the terrain. Gated German villages stood out in isolation on the plains or were surrounded by miserable dilapidated housing. Military installations with mile upon mile of barracks and airfields, warehouses and firing ranges, loomed large on the landscape. Huge tracts of forest lay in ruins—clear-cut, the logs left to uselessly rot—either in retaliation for resistance or out of fear of what, or who, might lurk within. Huge industrial complexes rose up out of the horizon, defiling the land for mile upon mile with their concrete and their pollution, then vanished back into the earth as the train moved on. Miles of electrified, barbed wire lined the track at various points as the train passed by concentration camps.

The towns the train stopped in were sometimes reconstructed, or even newly constructed, with a heavy emphasis on fortifications, walls, gates, and barriers. Other towns, older cities, where the train did not stop, were bombed out and consisted of nothing but ruins and weeds. They sped through wrecked stations—ghostly shells of metal and broken glass. Bridges arched over the railway line and then fell away to nothing. Burned-out farmsteads, their chimneys rising above the charred roof struts, hinted at a life gone by. Animal corpses, bones whitewashed by the sun, littered fields here and there as if no one dared collect them. A landscape of wanton destruction, of resistance and waste, of oppression and fear.

Richard decided to stretch his legs and left the compartment. He took up a position against the compartment window so that he could look out across the landscape. He was the only one who did so. The other passengers in the aisle—mostly Germans—seemed determined not to look out the windows. It was supposed to be their triumph, it should have been their proof of superiority! Yet, judging from their faces, their animated conversations carried on with everybody casually leaning with their backs to the outside windows, it was an embarrassment to them. An undeniable sign that they had put their fates, their country, and their hearts into the hands of madmen.

He wondered at what had brought each of his fellow passengers to the region—the incentives were high: money, land, prestige, and slave labor being just a few. But still, for every three immigrants to the colonizable lands, one returned within five years. And that despite the social stigma and low-level government harassment that they had to face upon returning. It was not a well-known fact, yet it spoke volumes. How many people were shocked when they learned the reality about the "New Lands"? How many came expecting green fields and friendly, compliant peasants offering baskets of fruit and bouquets of flowers to their new masters? The image of the ubiquitous poster appeared before him, contrasting sharply with the desolate landscape, the result of decades of pillage and hatred and destruction, that rolled past.

As the train headed north to cross the river, the landscape began to change. He returned to his seat to watch as entire suburbs of ugly, squat, but serviceable concrete-block houses began to appear. The houses grew more substantial, and occasionally a wealthy suburb of proper pitched-roof houses passed by. The beginnings of Göringstadt and their final destination.

"Write out the chit when he drops you off," Richard ordered Stefan, as he climbed out of the taxi. Richard stretched, rubbing the small of his back to relieve a pain there, and surveyed the Party-assigned house that he called home.

For as far as the eye could see, cheaply built, ugly, squat houses surrounded his manor, like concrete mushrooms springing up in its confiscated fields. Only a generous yard and the house itself remained of the old estate.

Stefan collected the luggage, told the driver to wait, and followed his boss as they proceeded to the front door. Kasia herself answered the door, and as Stefan deposited the luggage in the hall and took his leave, Richard embraced her.

"How was your trip?" she asked. "Successful?"

"Yes, I'm going to be transferred to Berlin soon," he answered, accepting the cigarette that she offered him. Then, glancing around, he asked, "Have the guests arrived?"

"Not yet, the servants are upstairs making the last-minute preparations. I've doubled up the children so we have two bedrooms free. We'll put your sister and her mother-in-law in one room. We'll put her nephew in the other, and her daughter can . . ."

Richard nodded disinterestedly as Kasia continued to explain how she would arrange everyone. "What about the servants?" he interrupted suddenly.

"I've given them weekends and the evenings off. I can't do better than that. They'll need you to write them special transport passes—it'll be too early in the evening to use their usual ones. And you should give them a little extra to cover the higher fares."

"All right, all right," Richard groaned. He wandered into his study and began picking through the small pile of accumulated post.

Kasia watched for a moment from the doorway, then she ventured, "Your father called this morning. He said he had important business and would meet up with us here, this evening."

"Then who's . . . ?"

Kasia raised her eyebrows.

"All right. Which train?"

The train arrived on time and she was one of the first to descend to the platform. Richard greeted his sister with a peremptory hug. "Welcome to Göringstadt, dear . . ." He stopped dead and stared at the SS major who had stepped off the train and stood expectantly behind her. Richard took a step back to better survey his guests, then drawing in his breath slowly, he stated, "I didn't realize your husband would honor us with his presence."

"Yes, I thought I'd surprise you," his sister answered breezily.

Richard continued to stare at the stranger, who at first met his gaze with a fleeting smile, then after a moment, nervously averted his eyes to watch an incoming train. "I guess we should go," Richard announced without even bothering to greet the others.

As they drove back, Richard searched feverishly through his memories trying to answer the jumble of questions in his head. An Englishman. That's what he had heard. But where else? An Englishman who looked a bit like Adam. But not just Adam, somebody else. Who? Where? Those mannerisms. So familiar! Someone from the RSHA? An agent? Richard glanced nervously at his unexpected guest and then at his sister. Damn her anyway! He lit a cigarette to calm himself and decided to wait until he could speak to her in private.

Kasia was no less surprised by the unexpected guest, but with the servants present, she put on a brave face and kissed her supposed brother-in-law warmly, then carefully explained to the servants where to place the luggage. The family all retreated to the sitting room and conversed stiffly as drinks and hors d'oeuvres were served. Richard's parents arrived and the conversation continued in its oddly stilted manner until finally Richard announced to Kasia, "I think we don't need the servants anymore."

Kasia readily agreed and leapt to her feet to help hustle them out the door.

"Polish?" Zosia asked as Kasia shut the door on them.

Richard stood and paced to the window, watching silently as the servants left the property.

"Ryszard?" Zosia pressed.

"Yes, they're Polish," Kasia answered testily. "We prefer the risk of a knife in the back to being spied on by German employees."

"No luck with getting some of our own?" Marysia asked.

"Not yet. We've been making do ever since the last pair were reassigned."

Ryszard turned away from the window to face his sister, ready to lambaste her, but was distracted by the way the stranger shifted nervously in his seat, rose suddenly, and walked aimlessly around his chair. When he realized that everyone was staring at him, he smiled nervously and sat back down.

Ryszard noticed how the man met his eyes only briefly, then turned his gaze away, off to the side again. Why was that expression so familiar? Unbidden, grimy images crowded his mind: a bare bulb, concrete walls, an officer's incomprehensible curses, the sound of a truncheon striking flesh. He winced at the familiar, unwelcome imagery and glanced again at the man's face. It was the eyes. That look of an impenetrable distance, of an isolation defined by pain. The look of a prisoner. Ryszard felt relieved: it wasn't the man he recognized, it was that look. If their paths had ever crossed, it had probably been during one of his numerous prison tours, and that made the man unimportant and forgettable. And fragile. Ryszard let out his breath slowly, deciding to hold his tongue for the moment.

"So, how about introducing us to your husband?" Alex suggested jovially to his daughter.

Zosia gladly obliged, the ice was broken, and everybody relaxed and exploded into conversation. Joanna disappeared upstairs with her younger cousins to play. Olek shyly excused himself to go talk with Ryszard's eldest—their daughter Stefi. Marysia and Anna retreated to the kitchen to sip vodka and exchange Council gossip. Kasia busied herself as hostess, not taking part in any conversation except in passing. Alex sat himself on the edge of the couch near Peter's chair and insisted, in English, that they get to know each other, and Ryszard rubbed his face tiredly and sat down to talk with Zosia.

She, however, was not interested in answering questions. Instead she started talking about Adam and how nothing was the same without him. Ryszard nodded his head wearily and let his mind wander.

"Make Zosia speak it to you—and make her listen to you in it!" Alex was advising Peter. "And don't worry if she laughs. Hell, they all still laugh at my accent!"

Ryszard listened to his father's nasal whine, and though he could tell Peter's accent was quite different, he did not know what significance that held, if any. He furrowed his brow as he listened in, trying to follow the rapid, fluent English. He could not catch everything, but they seemed to be discussing the corruption of English by German neologisms and comparing it with American English. "I would suppose that the Americans have always considered their language 'proper' English," Peter was saying.

"Yes, but we know better, don't we?" Alex laughed.

"So what do you think?" Zosia was insisting.

Ryszard drew his attention back to her. "Hmm? I don't know yet. Tell me more."

Zosia launched into the details.

"*Ananas?* That's pineapple!" Alex was saying, sounding surprised. "Didn't you know that?"

"But we'll need to get him out and about, to prove he can be trusted . . ." Zosia was saying.

". . . the English word for those, dear boy, is *venetian blinds,*" Alex was explaining. "Just what sort of language are they speaking back home nowadays?"

Anna and Marysia wandered back into the room. Their voices rose and fell in the happy exchanges of old comrades-in-arms. Kasia kept refilling everyone's glass with cherry-flavored vodka, and Olek and Stefi ventured downstairs, giggling and blushing as they exchanged their last-minute private observations before joining the adults.

"Sunny-day showers, eh? Never heard that one," Alex was admitting. "There is some silly American joke about April showers, but I doubt there's any connection. God only knows what obscure rhymes kids will be singing in five hundred years about the invasion and good ol' Uncle Adolf."

"Hopefully, irrelevant ones," Zosia chimed in, apparently giving up on her one-sided conversation with Ryszard. She had switched to English as well, and Ryszard noticed that she now spoke it with a confidence that was greater than his own.

"By then, the question will be, are they *them* or *us?*" Ryszard suggested, switching the conversation back to Polish so that the others could join in.

They did, and the discussion ebbed and flowed around the room, eventually settling on the question of whether the Warsaw uprising should ever have been allowed to take place. Some said that if they had only thrown open the city from the first to the German invaders, perhaps it would have been spared the way Paris was. Others said nonsense, Hitler had always been intent on destruction—and besides Paris was a backwater sleaze joint for Party officials now. It was pointed out that whatever the French had saved by giving away Paris, they had lost in pride. Someone responded that pride was a bit pointless when you were dead. Olek opined that an uprising would have occurred sooner or later whether or not it was sanctioned, and at least a sanctioned uprising was organized. That was answered with a derisive "Organized suicide! Big deal!" Nearly the entire leadership had been wiped out and it took decades to rebuild, Marysia reminded everyone. Zosia noted that it had at least brought the world's attention to what was going on, but then countered her own opinion with the observation that it had not changed anything as far as she could tell. And why should it have? her father asked. They then veered off into international politics and why any country should risk its own security to protect another. General human rights, national integrity, the trickiness of presenting an aggressive foreign policy to a voting public—all went into the soup.

Only Peter remained silent, with that intense look of one trying desperately to understand what was being said. He rose suddenly and went over to Zosia and said something into her ear.

"No problem. Just don't get lost," Zosia answered cheerfully.

"I won't," he laughed and headed toward the hall. There was a sudden silence, which caused him to turn around at the door and look questioningly back at them all.

Ryszard was wondering what exactly to say when Kasia interrupted the awkward moment by putting down the cheese tray she had brought into the room, saying, "Wait for me, I'll go with you. I can use a break."

Ryszard stood and accompanied them into the hall. As Kasia changed her shoes, Peter opened the box of cigarettes that sat on a little table in the hallway. "Do you count them?"

"Heavens! Why would I do that?" Kasia looked up to reply.

"Just wondered."

"Help yourself," Ryszard suggested.

"Thanks." Peter gingerly selected one. He lit it, then held it out and spent a long time contemplating it.

"Is there something wrong with it?" Ryszard was finally driven to ask.

"Funny how life changes. If I had done this just over a year ago . . . Well, never mind."

As Ryszard closed the door behind them and returned to the sitting room, Olek and Stefi, sensing that they were better off elsewhere, made a quick excuse and hurried upstairs. Alex took a deep breath, fixed Zosia with a stony look, and said in a low, angry voice, "What the hell was that all about?"

Zosia shrugged. "We said we trusted him."

"Not with all our lives!" Ryszard replied.

"What other sort of trust is there?"

"Why do you insist on taking reckless chances? Why did you bring him here?" Anna asked.

"Because I trust him," Zosia hissed angrily.

"Then risk your own damn life—not my wife and kids! My God, now he knows all of us and where we live and everything!" Ryszard yelled. "Twenty years of my life I spend building up this position, and you mindlessly go and bring any random stranger in here to destroy me!"

"And letting him go out alone. Are you mad?" Alex added.

"Apparently," Zosia agreed, undaunted. "You all didn't trust Tadek either, and now he's one of our best."

"Tadek was different. We could check on him and learn his history. We knew there was no indication of any collaboration or connection whatsoever between him and the Nazis," Anna explained patiently to her daughter. "But this fellow, even he admits no one in Britain would vouch for him, and the only living name he could dredge up, that of his brother, is a goddamned Nazi!"

"A what!" Ryszard exclaimed.

"I see you've done your research," Zosia accused bitterly.

"I told her," Marysia said.

"You!" Zosia charged. "I thought you agreed with me about him! You helped me defend him!"

"Yes, I think he's genuine," Marysia admitted. "Not only that, but I like him as well. The trouble is, Zosia, we still must be careful; we don't know who he is. We can't be blind to the risks. And doing this without clearance! You *lied* to me!"

"I've never been wrong in my instincts yet," Zosia reminded them.

"Yes, Zosia, your instincts are good. But you only have to be wrong once, and with such carelessness, we'd all be dead," Alex pointed out.

"Joanna certainly loves him," Anna said, apparently relenting a bit. "She came in the kitchen and told me all about him."

"So now we're basing our security on a four-year-old?" Ryszard asked angrily. "You should never have brought him here. He had no need to know!"

Zosia shook her head sadly, pushed her hair back. "Well, he's here now, there's no getting around that. I can finish my business tomorrow, and we can leave the day after. That'll solve your problem."

"Zosiu, child, the damage is done. He knows us now. There's no point your leaving early," Anna pleaded.

Zosia went to stand by the window, pulling the drapes back so that she could see out into the street and watch for Peter and Kasia's return. In a low voice she said, "All right, maybe it was a mistake. Maybe I shouldn't have brought him here. But it wasn't his fault—he didn't ask to come, I asked him. And I told him he would be welcome."

The others listened but did not comment.

Zosia continued, not looking at her family, rather keeping her eyes on the street and the front door, "He's not stepping out to make contacts or to betray us, he just needs to get out and about, especially in the evenings. I think you might understand why if you get to know him better. Anyway, you can keep an eye on him if you want. For God's sake, just don't let him know."

Ryszard ran through his available options. The damage was done, there was no point in anger. And he seemed to recall from what he had heard of Zosia's conversation that she had some use in mind for the Englishman. "All right," he agreed for them all. "We'll take it in turns and try to be subtle."

"And I want you to be hospitable. Your suspicions are only that and they are unwarranted. It's important he feel accepted. Very important." She sounded so intense, they wondered what she could mean, but none dared ask.

So it was agreed, they would allay their fears by never letting him out of their sight—whatever that took—but they would also assume the best under all other circumstances and treat him accordingly. Alex had only two conditions—the first was that Peter not meet Zosia's other siblings; the second was that Alex wanted to talk to Zosia, alone, later in the week.

They seemed settled when Ryszard suddenly smacked his hand against the table in exasperation. "Shit!"

"What?" Anna asked for them all.

"The telephone." Ryszard got up and went to his study where the phone was kept. Telephones were not only unusual, they were rarely kept anywhere but in a small, separate, and well-insulated room. Thus, even though the lines were invariably tapped—especially for Party officials—at least the telephone itself was not an easily accessible microphone for listening into the rest of the house. He unscrewed the bottom of the receiver and removed the microphone. He thought he might just detach one of the lead wires, but then realized any moron would be able to fix that, so instead he just put the bottom back on without replacing the microphone diaphragm.

He returned to the sitting room holding the microphone in his hand. "I removed this so you'll be able to hear anybody who calls, but you'll have to put this back in if you want to speak. I'll leave it with Kasia since she's here during the day."

"I thought your study had a lock," Zosia noted bitterly.

"It does, but it's not very good and he can pick locks, can't he?"

Zosia admitted tiredly that he could.

Peter and Kasia returned, and shortly thereafter Zosia said that she was ready to retire. Kasia looked uneasily at Alex and Anna before explaining to Zosia and Peter, "I only have two spare rooms, and with the servants, well, it would look odd if you two didn't share . . ."

"I could sleep on the floor, if you wish," Peter offered halfheartedly.

Zosia laughed. "Nonsense! We'll be cozy. Don't worry about it, Kasiu!" Zosia kissed her sister-in-law and waved good-night to the rest of the room. "Are you coming up now?" she asked Peter, motioning with her finger.

Ryszard saw the look on Peter's face and knew immediately: he was hopelessly in love with her!

====== **14** ======

"**J**UST AS WELL we never removed the major from their files. You pass easily as my husband!" Zosia said, pulling her dress off over her head. Peter was sitting on the edge of the bed, digging into the satchel that he had packed, the one he had stolen from Karl. She noticed how he stopped looking at what he was doing and fumbled mindlessly in the bag, his eyes unable to leave her. His hand reached absently into a side pocket of the satchel, and she was surprised to see it emerge holding a tiny bundle of hair.

"What's that?" she asked, coming over to look.

He stared at it, obviously as surprised as she was. "Hair," he answered at last. "I accidentally pulled it out of one of the Vogels' chairs."

She bent to examine it and took it into her hand. "Is it human hair?"

"I think so."

"I suppose you don't have to kill someone to steal their hair."

"No, you don't. But they did, didn't they?"

"Yes. I would guess the owners were murdered." She handed it back to him, treating it with careful respect.

"I thought as much."

"Why did you keep it?" she asked as she placed her suitcase on the bed and opened it.

"I don't know. Maybe it was the way Elspeth reacted to it."

"How was that?"

"She demanded that I put it back, then she walked away and ignored it. Seeing her so able to shut it out of her mind, I guess made me determined not to do likewise. So I kept it."

"Are you ready to throw it away now?"

"No. I'll never be ready to do that"—he ran his fingers over the soft hairs—"but maybe someday I'll be able to bury it. Until then, I think I'll just tuck it back into this pocket."

She nodded. She did not know what to advise, and it seemed as good a solution as any. Too much had happened in the twentieth century to ignore it all, and too much had happened to remember it all. Perhaps a small memorial like Peter's made sense. She reached into her suitcase and pulled out a small, locked case. From that she removed her gun and, sitting on the edge of the bed as well, began inspecting and cleaning it.

"An assassination?" Peter had stopped unpacking and was watching her with undisguised curiosity.

"Yes," she answered tersely.

"Who?"

"Nobody special," she responded cautiously. She became aware of a prolonged silence and looked up from her work to study his expression. He gave her one of his fleeting smiles in response. There was no accusation in his eyes, just a realization that his curiosity had strayed too far.

"Can I ask what he's done?"

It was a genuine question. She reminded herself that Peter was unaware of yesterday's conversation, and there was no reason he should view her professional discretion as insulting. "Yeah." She smiled. "A blackmailer. Turned in some of our own to the Gestapo. He's unimportant, it will be trivial."

"How are you going to do it?"

Again she studied him. His curiosity was genuine and only that. She was sure of it, yet the warnings of her parents and her brother echoed in her head. Oh, to hell with them, she thought, and said, "A stiletto should do the trick. It should be a clean job."

She pulled out a piece of jewelry and showed it to him. The oblong, silver pendant flared slightly at one end and had filigree running along its length. She pressed against a bit of the pattern and a thin, sharp blade leapt out of the end—straight out.

He started. "I never realized that was a weapon!"

"Usually I carry it in my purse, but, as you know, sometimes I wear it around my neck. Of course, the blade is a bit shorter than usual so that the handle is not recognizable as such."

"Is the short blade a problem?" he asked, touching it.

"No, I just put it here." She reached around his neck and placed her fingers at the base of his skull. "If one gets the right angle, it makes it so quick that they rarely even bleed much."

"Will you have to sleep with him?"

She laughed: that was certainly not the typical concern of a spy!

He ducked his head, embarrassed by his presumptuousness, so she reached over and gave him a hug and a kiss. She could feel him quiver as the soft material of her slip brushed against his skin.

"Be careful," he murmured.

"Don't worry. I always am. Everybody agrees I'm overcautious," she said as she laughed inexplicably.

Zosia returned unharmed and successful from her endeavors, and the following day, when Ryszard went into work, she and Peter hitched a ride into the center of town. She gave Peter a tour of the city, and they laughed in their sleeves at the Nazi monuments, each more grotesque and tasteless than the last. In the afternoon it began to rain, so they decided to visit the museums. They started with art and walked through the wretched exhibits with good humor. After viewing enough heroic sculptures of work and war heroes to last a lifetime, they wandered into the wing with painted art. There the workers were even brawnier, the invariably blond women had children nearly dripping off their hips, and the sun never stopped shining.

They tried an archaeology museum next, sure that that would be more immune from the effects of propaganda, but the main display was pottery shards and jewelry, circa 200 B.C., dug up in the region of Göringstadt. Of course, all the shards and all the jewelry could clearly be labeled as Aryan and specifically Germanic in nature. Neither of them knew enough archaeology to determine if the artifacts were real or to offer up alternative explanations, but both were well enough trained in logic to spot the inconsistencies, and they amused each other by pointing out paradoxes in the little historical paragraphs that accompanied the displays.

After that they wandered into the natural history museum. There they discovered an entire floor devoted to the development of races and an explanation of why the Aryan race, as exhibited in the modern German nation, was the pinnacle of this development. They moved on to the exhibits of dinosaur bones and ancient fossils, but these displays were poorly labeled and badly presented, as if the curators could not decide—or had not been authoritatively told—whether the idea of dinosaurs walking the earth without Nazi guidance was sacrilegious.

Since the natural history museum was so disappointing, they had about an hour before closing to peruse the science museum to see if they wanted to return to it later in the week. "Now what," Peter asked, "can they do to science?" He need not have asked. The biology wing explained all about blood and racial mixing through bloodlines and how tainted blood produced inferior beings—a two-headed calf and a deformed lamb carcass being the main evidence offered. Chemistry was somewhat better: it stuck to noncontroversial topics, although there was a penchant for crediting German scientists with every discovery from the periodic table onward, as well as a good bit of alchemy before that.

Physics was disappointing—the only genuine amusement provided was when Zosia read the subtitle under the great "German" astronomer Copernicus. She snorted so loudly that a number of the patrons gave them a curious glance. They wandered into the section on modern physics, curious to see how that was presented. The German-speaking Jews who had worked on modern physics in the beginning of the twentieth century were nowhere mentioned. Indeed, modern physics, with all its technological wonders and horrors, got rather short shrift. Clearly the regime was still of two minds about this wild, uncontrollable, and yet powerful tool. It had been derided as Jewish voodoo science in the beginning of the twentieth century, but the nuclear weapons it had produced were all too enthusiastically used in the middle. The love-hate relationship was clearly more than the curators could handle, and they offered only a few of the acceptable figures of modern physics as paragons of German logic and intelligence. Mathematics was similarly muddled, and since the museum was closing, Peter and Zosia left, deciding that there was little point in returning later.

The rain had stopped with the coming of dark, and they walked in the park. Now and then a snowflake drifted down from the clouds, but otherwise they were alone. They walked to the river Vistula—a river that, like so many other places, had more than one name. The water flowed lazily past the city; here and there cinders floated on the surface. Zosia said that on bad days, when the wind was high in the southeast, where the ruins of Warsaw lay, then the river would run black with ash. She told Peter the myth of Syrenka, the mermaid of Warsaw, and he laughed and asked how an inland city had a mermaid as its symbol.

She explained, as a marine biologist might, about freshwater and seawater mermaids and their various habits, concluding, "Clearly, from the evidence at hand, some mermaids swim in rivers." They both laughed lightly. He hugged her and they held each other against the chill breeze and looked out over the almost tranquil river.

Zosia took care to go slowly as they climbed the steps back up the embankment to the paved path that ran along the river. At the top she stood still to rest, waiting patiently, trying not to notice how Peter winced with pain. A small group of SS Jugend came jogging by, their hair cut bristly short, their faces covered in sweat despite the evening chill. Courteously, they gave Zosia and Peter a wide berth, sprinting agilely onto the grass in an overzealous show of deference. Peter watched them as they passed, turning his head to stare bitterly after them as they ran off into the distance. Zosia looked at his expression—it was a study in pure hatred. She felt slightly disconcerted and tugged on his arm to distract him, leading him over to a bench to sit down.

They sat in silence for a moment, then without preamble she asked, "Do you ever dream about the *Kommandant?*"

"No," he answered almost too quickly.

"I wonder why not."

"Maybe because it never happened," he said without inflection.

She snapped her head around to look at him. He was staring down the path, his head turned away from her. "Never happened?"

"No, never," he replied, still not looking at her. From some distance away, a young couple walked along the path toward them, and he seemed to be intent on them. "I made it up to gain your sympathy. I didn't expect you would tell everyone. Now you can tell them all it never happened. Okay?"

"I'm sorry." Zosia remembered Tadek's cruel remark. "I had to tell them in order to . . ."

"Well, it never happened, so we don't ever need to discuss it. Right?" His voice came out of a distance.

"What about your reeducation?"

"What about it?"

"Do you ever dream about that?"

"No." He was watching the approaching young couple as if mesmerized. The woman was pretty; she leaned her head in toward the young man as he said something. They were obviously enamored of each other.

"You know, you've told me about the first month, but you never told me what happened after the officer visited you," Zosia prompted.

"I don't remember."

"Three months of your life? None of it?"

"None of it."

They fell silent as the couple came within hearing distance. Zosia looked at the woman Peter was watching so intently—she had a provocative sway to her walk. He turned his head to watch the couple as they passed by the bench, and eventually his eyes fell upon Zosia's face. He smiled wanly at her. "You don't want to go down that path," he said, then his eyes strayed back to the retreating couple.

Zosia thought for a moment whether she should continue, then she decided to try a more direct approach. "Why is it that of all your experiences, you seem to think about the Vogels the most?"

He pulled his attention away from the couple and looked at her for a moment as though he would disdain to answer, but then he seemed to reconsider. "I've thought about that and I think it's because of everything that I saw or experienced, they were the most disconcerting. In prison or in a prison camp one expects a level of insanity. One believes that if there are sadists or nuts, then they will naturally gravitate to positions of authority, so nothing comes as a shock. Torture and death, it's all part of the natural order of things. But you sustain yourself by believing that out there, out among normal people, it is different. You like to think, if only they knew, if only they could see it with their own eyes! But when it's all transplanted to a nice home in the suburbs with a happy, healthy family of children, a back garden with flower beds and trees and birds . . ." He shook his head. "You learn, firsthand, how violence can permeate a whole society, and even in a room of pretty floral wallpaper and delicate glass figurines, it's easy to feel terrified."

He sighed, looked back at the water down below. Zosia followed his gaze. It had grown quite dark, but still she could see that the ashes were a bit thicker now—the wind had picked up with the early evening. She slid closer to him, leaned into him, and he put his arm around her. He held her in silence and then quietly, almost under his breath, he added, "I know you don't want me to say it, Zosia, but I love you."

She did not say anything in response.

=15=

H E OPENED HIS eyes to utter darkness. He had known it was there all along, it was never far away. Curled, bound, gagged, and dying in his coffinlike crate, he had managed, in his mind, to find his freedom. The realization that it had all been nothing more than a protracted hallucination caused him to moan with despair. The desperate sound of his gasping echoed noisily in his ears as he struggled to fill his lungs with the useless air. He was so dizzy he could not tell which way was up. Each exhaled breath came back at him hot and fetid. He tried to move his fingers, to once again scrape at the ropes, but they were bloody and numb. Though he was racked by thirst, sweat streamed down his face. He brought his hand to his face and wiped some of it away. The gesture surprised him and he opened his eyes to the dim light of a bedroom and the soft whisper of Zosia's peaceful breathing.

Peter lay there in the bed, his eyes open, staring at the patterns of shadows on the ceiling of the bedroom. If he closed his eyes again, it would return, he knew that. He calmed his breathing and tried to relax, but he was afraid of falling asleep, afraid of disrupting his dream of freedom. He slipped out of bed, pulled on his clothes, and quietly descended the steps to the main floor. In the hallway he pulled on his boots and jacket, checked that his papers were in order, and then turned the doorknob gently, so as not to awaken the household. The door was locked. As his eyes adjusted to the light, he was able to see that it was a deadbolt lock that required a key for indoors as well as out. That was not unusual. Nor was it particularly unusual that the key was missing, although he was terribly disappointed. He sighed with exasperation. Not wanting to wake his hosts, he decided to use the back door. It let out into the yard, but presumably there was an easy way to get outside the fence.

At the back door there was a simple bolt lock. It was thrown shut and he pulled it back to open it. The door did not give way. He looked up and noticed a second lock—a rather jury-rigged affair of two pieces of metal bolted to either side of the door and held together with a keyed padlock. Was crime really so awful in this region? What if there was a fire? He shrugged and supposed that the windows were always available in that case. What was it somebody had once said? Oh, yes, it was in a factory where he had, as group leader of the prisoner contingent, questioned the safety arrangements—in particular, padlocked emergency escape doors. The foreman had answered with flawless German logic that the emergency doors were locked because they were not used very often.

Putting aside his frustration, he considered his options. The padlock meant that he was effectively locked in along with the rest of them. He might be able to open it, but he decided that even trying might appear rather rude. As would using a window. So he was stuck. The somewhat absurd thought occurred to him that the servants must either use the front door, or Kasia must get up early in the morning to let them in. Both situations would be unusual, but then, he reminded himself, they would want to always be aware of when the servants were in the house to avoid any possibility of speaking the wrong language at the wrong time. What a horribly complicated existence they must lead! He felt a surge of pity for the family and went back into the hallway to remove his boots and jacket.

He thought he heard a rustle by the stairs as he moved from one room to the other, but when he called out softly, no one answered. Probably one of the kids, he thought, and dismissed it from his mind. He went into the sitting room and sat in the darkness, looking out the window by holding the heavy draperies back. He was seized by an inchoate fear that left him trembling, and he nearly jumped when he turned and noticed Kasia watching him in the doorway.

"Oh, it's you," he said rather lamely.

"Are you all right?" she asked tiredly.

"Yes, I'm okay. Did I wake you? I'm sorry, I tried to be quiet." He said it in German; Kasia did not know English and he did not feel up to trying to converse in Polish.

"Oh, I'm a light sleeper—you know, the ever-vigilant mother."

"Yes, I used to be a sound sleeper myself. But not anymore." He turned back toward the window, gave a last glance out into the night, and let the drape drop back into place. Softly he added, "I would give a lot to have undisturbed sleep again."

Kasia nodded. "It's stressful times for many of us."

Realizing that he had been rather selfish, he said, "Yes, I admire what you and your husband are doing. And I admire your bravery and endurance. I don't think I could handle it."

"No?"

"No."

They were silent for several moments. Kasia made no move to sit down or to leave. She seemed to be undecided about what she wanted to do. Finally Peter broke the silence. "You lock the front door with a key?"

"Yes. That's the sort of lock the house came with."

"Why don't you leave the key in the door?"

There was a silence, then she said rather hesitantly, "It's not our custom. Is there a problem?"

"It's just that I like to go out at night. I have good papers, a curfew pass and everything, so it should be no problem. Maybe you could leave the key accessible?"

Again there was a long hesitation. Finally Kasia said, "I don't think it's wise. It might raise questions. The curfew pass is probably not valid in this region. And it's not safe out there—especially in a uniform like yours."

Wondering at the plethora of reasons for his remaining indoors, he simply nodded his agreement. "How about if I just go into the back garden?"

"Please don't," Kasia said almost desperately.

She offered no reason why it was unwise, but he decided that her request was sufficient. "Okay. I'll stay in. I don't want to trouble you or your family. God knows, you have enough to worry about."

"Yes, that we do."

"Especially with your pregnancy now," he added perhaps unwisely.

"How did you know?" she asked, stunned. "I haven't told anyone but Ryszard!"

"Just guessed. You look tired and distracted, and, well, pregnant."

She gave him a critical look. "Well, you guessed right. Please don't mention it to anyone else. Especially not the children."

"Won't they be happy to have another sibling?"

"Oh, I think they think five kids is quite enough. But the real problem is that a toddler in the house again will mean everybody has to be extra careful— they don't understand enough not to repeat anything they hear. So we'll have to speak only German in the child's presence, especially when we move to Berlin."

"Berlin?"

Kasia sighed at her error. "Zosia didn't mention it."

"No. Is Ryszard going to be promoted?"

She hesitated, then decided it was pointless trying to deny it. "Yes, it looks like he will. It's more of a sideways move, but that's always the case when one is relocated to Berlin. Just being called to the city is considered a step up."

"He's at about Vogel's level I guess."

"Who's he?"

"My onetime owner." Peter had long ago grown tired of circumlocution and had settled on this phrase as the shortest explicit explanation of who Karl was.

"No bitterness?" Kasia asked, referring to Peter's unemotional tone.

He shrugged. "What would be the point?"

"None, but that doesn't stop most of us." She contemplated him a moment, then seemed to make some sort of decision, for she came into the sitting room and sat on the sofa near him. "Would you like a drink?"

"Yes, I'll get it. What would you like?"

She smiled with delight. "Just your offer of help was enough! I shouldn't drink, you know."

"How about tea? I'll make you some."

"I'd like that." She settled into her seat, ostentatiously enjoying the unusual break from her duties as hostess.

Peter put the kettle on and poured himself a generous whiskey, then rejoined Kasia on the couch. They chatted for a while longer with Kasia asking a lot of questions about his experiences, but he managed time and again to turn the subject away from that. Then, quite timidly, she touched his wrist. "What are those scars from?"

"I don't know. Handcuffs, probably."

"And your hands—do you know what caused that?" She held his hand in hers as she said that. Her touch felt gentle and he felt a strange thrill along his arm.

"You can tell?"

"Not in this light, but I noticed in daylight, the skin looked"—she paused trying to find the word for it—"different."

"Chemicals, I think. I don't know what sort. I think they're what messed my lungs up as well. I had so many illnesses and beatings, though, it's hard to know when my breathing became difficult. I only really noticed most of these things after I left."

"Do they hurt?" she asked, stroking the skin of his hand gently.

"Not usually." He looked down at his hands, added softly, "I guess they made a tidy little profit for Vogel." He had, though, never learned how much the Vogels had received for his labor, nor had he ever found out how much he had cost Karl in the first place. The complete lack of knowledge always annoyed him, and he had scoured the house for information, but Karl must have kept the receipts—if there were any—at the Ministry. It was quite irrational, but not knowing how much money had changed hands either for his life or his labor made him feel even more dehumanized.

She lifted his hand to her lips and kissed it. "There, maybe that will make it feel better."

"Yes, it does." He had a sudden memory from long ago of a desperate need for one word of kindness, and he smiled at her gesture. She had not released his hand, and he felt he should remove it from hers, but something prevented him.

"I notice you wear sunglasses, even on cloudy days. Why's that?"

"You must know that veterans of Africa wear them all the time."

"Yes, of course, I guess it's their way of bragging. But I didn't think Adam's papers—I mean, your papers—said anything about Africa."

"They do now," he laughed. "I had them amended so that I have an excuse for such an affectation."

"But why?"

"The light hurts my eyes. I don't know why. Sometimes my vision gets so bad, I think I'm going blind."

"And are you?"

"I don't know."

The kettle shrieked and he started as if hit. She looked at him, but he did not explain, he just removed his hand from hers and went to make her a cup of tea. She rewarded him with a tired smile and a "Thank you" when he brought it back.

"I can't help noticing, you don't get much help around here."

"Well, there are the servants. But frankly I spend more time avoiding letting them know what's going on than the work that they save me is worth. I'm always shuffling someone or something out of the way."

"I meant from your family."

"Oh, that's just Ryszard's way. He has a lot on his mind—it's not easy for him. And the kids—well, they have so much to keep track of—friend and foe, languages, school subjects, illegal knowledge. They do double studies—learning what they have to in order to pass the exams, and then learning what we want them to know." She shook her head. "It's a lot to ask of kids. More even than Ryszard went through—after all, he had the safety of the bunker."

"I guess your children at least have each other."

"Yes, that's one reason I keep getting pregnant—it gives them comrades-in-arms. Of course, as a German hausfrau and Party wife, it's politically advisable to have a lot of kids in any case. But I think this will be the last. I'm just too old to keep up with them."

"I hope you don't mind me asking," he said, emboldened by her candor, "but you seem to speak German with an accent. Weren't you raised using it?"

Kasia laughed. "No. I wasn't raised like Ryszard or Zosia. I was raised among the general populace—as a Pole. I joined the Home Army and worked my way into an office as a secretary. I didn't know it, but they were prepping me to work as Ryszard's secretary. So, naturally, we spent time together and got to know each other quite well. When he asked me out, I assumed it was my duty to go, and despite the fact I thought he was one of them, I liked him. I guess he liked me, too, because rather than have my bosses tell me who he was, he did so himself. He asked me to what he called 'a conference,' and my AK bosses said I should go—I guess they had gotten word from above—so I went and that's when Ryszard showed me his home and who he was."

"That must have been quite a surprise."

"You can't imagine, I was flabbergasted! I mean, I had heard about the place, everyone has, but to be taken inside like that! Of course, we only met his parents, and I had no idea where we were, but still, I felt so honored. Anyway, we fell in love and wanted to marry. Since he had a government position, it was decided I should become *Volksdeutsch* and we could marry officially and my job would be to support him in his career." She paused, then added quietly, "My parents never forgave me for turning traitor."

"Your parents don't know then, what you're doing?"

"No, unfortunately none of my family does. Some of them are in the Home Army, but none are in the Intelligence Section, nor are they at the level where they could be told." She looked to the side so he could not see her expression as she said, "It's not really even safe for me to visit them, I am so loathed. So you see, I am totally alone." Her voice took on a note of sadness as she added, "An outsider."

He felt guilty at the thought of what his own virulent reaction would have been to Kasia's apparent betrayal. Had he unjustly condemned his own brother in the same manner? "You have Ryszard's family," he consoled.

"They have each other," she said with some bitterness. "They have that strange background that makes them unfathomable to us petty mortals. Even my children are ciphers to me. No, like you, I am an outsider and always will be."

She finished her tea, then said, "I've got to get up early, so I had better go to bed. But it's been pleasant chatting with you."

"Yes, thanks for keeping me company."

"Sleep peacefully."

He got up, poured himself a full glass of whiskey, and then sat back down in the darkness to stay awake.

16

"ARE YOU SURE you want me to do this now?" Stefi asked, glancing nervously around the café. "I can postpone our meeting."

"Don't do that! You said his being in Göringstadt was a great opportunity. I don't want you to miss it because of me," Olek urged. "I'll just wait here."

"You won't try to follow us, will you?" Stefi asked worriedly.

Olek shook his head. "I would never interfere with your work. I promise."

"Okay then. Time to go." She stood and Olek stood with her to help her into her coat. She smiled at him. "It will only be a couple of hours. Three at the most."

"I know." He kissed her lightly. "Don't worry, I understand."

Stefi left the café and strolled across the street to the hotel, entering through the door that led into the restaurant. She paused at the entrance to look out the window back in the direction of the café; she could just make out the form of a man standing by the window, looking out into the street, but she could not discern if it was Olek. She smiled at the shadow and then turned to the maître d'.

When she gave him the name of her dinner partner, he led her through the restaurant and into a hallway of the hotel. "Your husband ordered room service, *gnädige Frau*," he informed her with a half smile. "He's in room one-twenty-five. Do you need someone to show you the way?"

"That won't be necessary." Then Stefi suavely pulled out a note and handed it to him and, using her most confident, married-woman sort of voice, thanked him for his assistance.

Wolf-Dietrich laughed when she told him this. "What a waste of money!" he grumbled cheerfully. "Now he'll know we aren't married!"

"I know. It's just that his know-it-all assumptions annoyed me."

"You would have been better off saying, 'Room service!' That cheap little miser!" Wolf-Dietrich laughed.

"So where is the food?" Stefi asked, glancing around.

"Didn't order any. Are you hungry?"

"How about some wine." Stefi slipped her shoes off and sat on the bed.

"Good idea. Can't really afford anything great though." Wolf-Dietrich picked up the telephone and tapped the button. "I've blown all my cash on this room!"

"Is it that expensive?" Stefi arranged some pillows and then lay back on them languorously.

"It is when you're as badly paid as I am." The operator answered and Wolf-Dietrich placed his order for the wine.

Once he had finished, Stefi asked, "Ah, so how is work?"

"You know I'm not supposed to talk about that."

"That's like saying you're not supposed to talk about your life," Stefi groused. She reached up under her skirt and began to undo the fasteners of her stockings. "I mean, who's silly rule is that anyway?"

"Rattenhuber's," Wolf-Dietrich answered, his eyes intent on her legs.

"Who's he?"

"Oh, he's handling the petty details for the project. Overall organization, security, and so on." He stared as Stefi began to roll the stockings down.

"You don't mind, do you?" Stefi asked innocently. "They're rather itchy."

"No, not at all."

She finished removing the second stocking and relaxed back onto the pillows. "Is he any good at it?" She dangled one of her stockings playfully in the air.

"He thinks so. I don't get to do anything. He does everything himself." Wolf-Dietrich sat timidly on the edge of the bed. "Takes the information in, 'encodes' it in some magical way, and distributes it to the staff when he's good and ready. I'm told he even set up the network for sending coded documents from one place to the other, but my father is too old-fashioned to trust that."

"Wise man. Those things are full of holes. 'Every official has some way of getting his hands on codes,' " Stefi quoted in an appropriately gruff fatherly voice.

Wolf-Dietrich laughed, then corrected, "Oh, no, I mean he set up a completely separate network with its own codes and everything, but my father still won't trust it."

"What's he do instead?"

"He lets trivial stuff go out via the network, but anything he thinks is important has to be hand-carried. That's why I'm here, in fact. I'm a courier. It's the one job ol' Ratti trusts me to do."

"If he's such a big shot, why does he have to do everything himself?" Stefi tossed the stocking at Wolf-Dietrich and giggled as it landed on his head.

He blushed, removed the stocking, and gingerly laid it back on the bed. "I don't know, maybe he doesn't trust me. He must know that I have to report everything he does back to my father."

"Well, since you're not allowed to do anything, you must have plenty of time for visitors?" Stefi asked winningly, leaning forward and stretching toward Wolf-Dietrich.

"Maybe I shouldn't be talking about this," Wolf-Dietrich suggested nervously.

"Good idea," Stefi huffed, pulling back suddenly. "Instead, you can tell me why you got us a room with a bed. I thought we were having a nice dinner."

"You said you wanted privacy!" Wolf-Dietrich protested. "Said you just wanted to talk!"

"With a bed in the room?" Stefi asked, lightly offended. "What are you suggesting?"

"Nothing! Really! It's just hard to get privacy without a bed!" Wolf-Dietrich explained sheepishly. "Nobody offers rooms without beds. I didn't mean to offend you . . ."

"Didn't mean?" Stefi repeated as she angrily grabbed for her stockings. "Didn't mean? First you get us a bedroom, then you say you can't talk about anything!"

"I misunderstood, I'm sorry. I thought, I mean, it seemed to be what you asked for."

Stefi began pulling her stockings on, struggling as she was too angry to do it right. "What I asked for was a chance to get to know you better! So you do all this 'can't talk' stuff, like I was some sort of blabbermouth farmer's daughter. Look here, my father's important, too! You can just go and keep your secrets to yourself, if they're so damn valuable!"

"They're not valuable," Wolf-Dietrich pleaded. "It's just that . . ."

Stefi stopped her befuddled attempts at putting on her stockings. "Just that what?"

"Oh . . ." Wolf-Dietrich stared at her. She had raised one leg to pull on her stocking, and from where he sat he could see the smooth curves of her upper thigh. "Oh, it's just that they're so hush-hush about it all, I feel, I don't know. It's so stupid."

"What are you talking about?" Stefi asked, suddenly quite sympathetic. She let her stocking drop to the floor and slid over to sit next to him.

"It's this stupid project of my father's, the one I mentioned before."

"I thought it was the Führer's idea." Stefi grabbed Wolf-Dietrich's hand in hers and then let their clasped hands settle on her lap.

"Not really. I mean, he knows about it, but it's really my father's project. I think the Führer is interested in it only if it works, if you know what I mean."

"Covering himself from political fallout, eh?" Stefi absently stroked his hand, turning it over so his palm rested on her bare thigh.

"Yeah, so everything has to be carried out by just a few people, in a sort of deniable way."

"What do you mean?" She leaned in toward him so that he could speak more confidentially. Her hair brushed against his cheek and she heard him sigh.

"I mean"—Wolf-Dietrich's fingers traced a light pattern on her skin—"I mean, like none of the work actually takes place at the military installation—everything is in the main house, the place where ol' Ratti himself lives. Big mansion, beautiful."

"Really? That sounds sort of creepy." She shuddered and pressed herself against him, her hand reaching out to the solidity and comfort of his chest.

"He's converted half the cellar into his office for the files, and then there's an annex of offices and things. It's really weird because it's not supposed to be there—all the soldiers just think it's just the normal sort of junk about running the place. You know, orders for food, fuel, that sort of stuff. That's one of the reasons I'm there—to keep an eye on things. I mean, he has the house patrolled, but it's sort of casual—you know, so that no one gets wind of the project."

"But how can they do something this big with just a couple of offices?" Stefi asked as she playfully began undoing the buttons of his shirt.

"Oh, they don't do any of the testing there. The field tests are conducted elsewhere, usually under the guise of something else. My father has overseen some in and around Berlin, he's got a colleague in Breslau doing some stuff, and there's one or two other places."

"What do they do?" Stefi's hand slid inside his shirt and she felt how he shivered at her touch.

"I don't know. Test farm animals, I think. They got some tame chemists in labs at the university. I don't know," Wolf-Dietrich answered absently. He continued to trace patterns with his fingers on her thigh, but now his hand slid along, edging its way upward. "Your skin is very soft," he whispered.

"I know some people in Breslau, who's the guy working there?"

Wolf-Dietrich turned to look directly at her. "I don't know," he said with a hint of suspicion.

Stefi shrugged. "Doesn't matter. I don't suppose my father is in on all this, do you think?"

Wolf-Dietrich shrugged; his hand had stopped moving.

"But you still haven't told me what you do." Stefi pouted, turning toward him so that his hand slid down between her legs. "Enough of all these cloak-and-dagger types, what's been happening in your life?"

"You know," Wolf-Dietrich said, cocking his head to the side, "I don't know a thing about you."

"Well, I'll tell you," Stefi answered with a smile. "Maybe I'll even show you," she added, reaching up to her blouse and undoing a button.

17

"**T**HE PRICE OF disobedience is death!" the voice ranted, echoing through his brain. He shook his head in irritation and tried to concentrate on the twitter of the birds and the rustle of the dry leaves underfoot. "You are parasites, a burden to society, and you shall work until you die to repay your debt!" it warned. Peter reached into his pocket and unfolded his sunglasses, hoping to diminish his dizziness more than the sunshine. "Corrupt blood! Tainting our pure society with your foul stench! You deserve nothing better than death!"

Shut up, he thought.

"Now those squirrels are a bit different than the ones we have down south," Alex was saying.

Peter blinked back the hissing denunciations. Shut up already!

"It's getting cloudy, maybe we should stop for a cup of tea," Marysia suggested.

The family discussed what to do at this point in their Sunday walk. They had been strolling for about an hour along the scrupulously maintained gravel paths that rambled through the woods adjacent to the convention center. Each path was edged by a neatly trimmed lawn that then gave way to trees, and under the trees there were dry leaves and needles, but not a single fallen twig remained in sight.

Peter walked with them, chewing absently on a knuckle, not taking part in the discussion. The chants from that morning's political rally had provoked a flood of memories, and though he heard members of the family greet passersby and had nodded his head at their inconsequential comments about the birds and the squirrels, nothing, not even the fresh air and the chill sunshine, could shake the uneasy images from that morning. It was the local equivalent of what the Vogels had attended every Sunday in Berlin, and it had also been eerily reminiscent of the ranting propaganda sessions he had been forced to attend during his reeducation.

Zosia tugged on his arm and he found himself going with the group that was heading toward the café, while Ryszard and Kasia remained with the younger folk, taking a different path, deeper into the woods. Peter gave Zosia a quick smile, then his eyes were caught by the uniform of a *Zwangsarbeiter*. He stared, mesmerized, as the man worked on his hands and knees, painstakingly picking tiny bits of gravel from the lawn and carefully placing the little stones back onto the path. It reminded him of that first day of his reeducation when he had scrubbed the latrine on his hands and knees. Years later, with the Vogels, he had still been forced down to scrub floors or pick litter from the lawn. Years later.

He barely perceived how the worker rose and backed away as they approached, deferentially moving out of their way so as not to hinder their passage; Peter only saw images of Frau Vogel's carpet as he picked lint and dirt off the delicate fabric. Years of such shit! Years of his life! He did not notice what provoked the anger of a passing policeman, but he suddenly became aware of shouting and the policeman striking the *Zwangsarbeiter*.

Without thinking about the consequences, he turned back and approached the two, grabbing the officer by the shoulder and swinging him around. Then, using full force, he slammed his fist into the policeman's face. The police officer landed heavily on the ground, blood running from a cut on his mouth. He looked up at his attacker in utter amazement; the *Zwangsarbeiter* also stared, stunned and unmoving. Peter ordered the officer to stand. The man did so trembling.

"Your papers!" he demanded angrily.

The policeman handed them to him.

Peter looked at them quickly and said, "I have noted your name, don't think you'll get away with this!"

"But, *Herr Major . . .*"

"Shut up. If you ever abuse your authority again, I will see that you are arrested! Do you understand?"

"Yes, *Herr Major*," the man answered, shaking with uncomprehending terror.

Peter threw his papers back at him and went to rejoin his group. They all looked at him in utter shock; even Zosia looked stunned. He ignored them and began walking along the way they had been heading, and they quickly joined him.

"*Idiotisch!*" Anna declared before they had even shut the door of the house.

She did not stop there, but Marysia was yelling in Polish and Alex's voice drowned her out with "Childish insanity!"

Peter was not naive, he had expected to be called on the carpet, but even so, he was surprised by the vehemence of their reaction.

"What the fuck is going on?" Ryszard was trying to ask over the cacophony.

Peter listened to the tornado of words, trying to pick out sentences here and there—how could he endanger them all so cavalierly? Didn't he think about the children? What if someone else had come along? How could he hit a German officer in public! What had he thought he was doing? What did he think he would accomplish? How dare he take unilateral action. Was he nuts? He could have destroyed everything with his childish outburst!

It had been stupid, he knew that; he could tell just by looking at Zosia's face that she also thought he had been reckless, though she had said nothing so far. The children looked on; he felt particularly foolish being upbraided in front of them—especially Olek, who was his subordinate.

Mercifully, Kasia interrupted Ryszard's increasingly heated and loud queries by grabbing his arm and virtually pulling him from the room. As she did so, she turned back and ordered the children—all of them—upstairs. Immediately! Unused to their mother ever being so assertive—she was dragging Dad out of the room!—they hastily obeyed. In some ways, the scene of her manhandling their father was far more entertaining than that of the three old folks yelling at the guest in an incomprehensible babble. Olek was the only one who had an understanding of what might actually be occurring, and he tried to give Peter a look of camaraderie and support as he left.

Peter did not see Olek's gesture of solidarity; all he could see were the people he most wanted to accept him screaming multilingual denunciations at him. He

felt a complex defense structure begin to crumble in his mind, felt that some barrier was collapsing in the face of such an onslaught of anger and rebuke, and he
felt helpless to stop it.

His eyes strayed from their faces and he caught sight of Zosia behind the
three. She theatrically placed a finger to her lips indicating that he should not
give her away. Then, positioning her hands on either side of her head she wagged
her head and simultaneously flapped both hands and her mouth rapidly to imi-
tate the three elder statesmen expressing their all too vociferous opinions.

Peter watched the little puppet show and had a hard time suppressing a
laugh. Of course, it was so simple! The pieces fell back into place, the dam held,
and he realized he was not that fragile after all. Zosia continued to mimic them
and Peter burst out into laughter.

"What is so damn funny?" Alex demanded. Anna and Marysia said something
similar in their respective tongues.

Peter took the opportunity their momentary silence presented him to say in
English, "Look, I'm sorry. It was stupid, all right? I realize that." Gratuitously he
repeated it in German to Anna and in Polish to Marysia.

Faced with such an admission, the three looked at each other and realized
they had perhaps gotten carried away. They all began to reply, and then realizing
that they were using three separate languages simultaneously on him, they all
began to laugh. Peter and Zosia laughed as well, and though Peter was direly
warned never to do anything so stupid again, the seriousness of his infraction
was lost in their mirth.

18

DURING THE WEEK, Zosia chose to visit her other siblings and some friends.
She seemed surprisingly coy about where she was going, and though she never
made it explicit, she made it clear that Peter should not plan to join her on these
visits. Most of the time she took Joanna with her, and the other members of the
house disappeared to work or school. Marysia and Olek disappeared on most
days to visit relatives, and only Kasia, the two servant girls, and sometimes Alex
and Anna were around. During the day, they all had to maintain their façades,
and Peter grew rapidly bored with reading books and pacing the garden. Even
walking the neighborhood lost all appeal as he realized somebody always felt
obliged to accompany him. Maybe they thought he needed the company, maybe
they wanted to make sure he did not run into trouble. Whatever the reason, he
noticed that he was always preempted whenever he headed for the door by a
friendly offer of company.

On Wednesday evening, as he finished his novel, ignoring the conversation around him, he decided he would go into town the following day. He had noticed a jewelry store during his visit there with Zosia, and he thought he might be able to find something nice to give her for *Wilia,* as the special celebration of Christmas Eve was called. Zosia planned to visit her brother, and so it would be a perfect opportunity for him to buy something without her knowing about it.

Early Thursday morning, after Zosia and Joanna had left with Ryszard, he approached Kasia and asked her quietly if there was some public transport into town.

"Why?" She seemed appalled at the thought.

"Well, I would have gone with your husband by car—but I didn't want my wife to know about my trip, so I could buy her a surprise present."

Kasia shook her head. "No, I'm afraid it's just too convoluted a route—I could never adequately describe it to you."

"But there is some sort of route? I can just ask the driver."

"No, that just won't work."

"Well, how far is it to town—ten kilometers?"

"Walking, yes. But that's just too far."

"I have all day. Look, I even noted the shop's number so I can call and check their hours."

"No!"

Peter looked at her, stung by her response.

"I mean," Kasia amended, "the phone's not working. And you shouldn't walk all the way into town. After all, what about your legs?"

"Walking is no problem. In fact, it relieves the pain."

"Still, I don't think it's a good idea."

"So there's no way for me to get there."

"I could . . . well, I'm really busy. No, it's just not practical."

He nodded, a slow burning sensation spreading through him. "I don't suppose," he tried without much hope, "that there's a jewelry store nearby I could walk to on my own."

Kasia shook her head.

"And I don't suppose that I could call a taxi."

She looked at him with exasperation.

"I didn't think so," he said and walked into the library. He stood by the window and looked out into the street. He felt a complete fool. How could he not have noticed? The locked doors, the telephone, the ever-present company. It was obvious. In fact, he realized, he had never been unobserved since his arrival. His lonely walks through the woods were an illusion. If he had ever tried to leave the mountains alone, he was sure he would have been stopped. Politely, perhaps, but forcibly.

He knew he should not feel insulted; in fact, it was rather kind the way they had tried to hide it from him, but that did not stop him from feeling hurt and betrayed. Zosia knew all along, knew and never said a word! That awkward silence the first evening when he had said he was going out—everybody in the room knew and he was left looking like an idiot. An oblivious idiot. She should have told him! He had trusted them completely and believed them when they said they trusted him. He had accepted their hospitality in good faith, and they had been nothing but a bunch of hypocrites. He felt a sudden urge to simply walk out the door—let Kasia try to stop him! What would she do, physically hold him back?

He knew, though, that he could never return if he did that, that he would probably be shot—he knew too much to be allowed to wander freely. He laughed bitterly at himself. His life was as much in their control as it had been in Karl and Elspeth's. They were kind to him, but they owned him every bit as much as the Vogels had. He even agreed with their logic. He knew what danger he could put them in, knew that they could not risk everything for the sensibilities of one man, but agreeing with their rationale made it no easier to accept. He did not hate them for what they had to do, he did not even disagree with their decisions, nor with his being kept in the dark about it all—that was, after all, an act of kindness. No, what he disagreed with was the entire world. He hated everything about the world and the society around him. Did it have to be this way? he wondered. The bare branches of the trees outside swayed in the wind but offered no answers.

19

"*T*EA?" ZOSIA ASKED, AMAZED. "I thought you wanted to talk seriously."

"Yes," her father answered, "seriously enough that we should both remain sober."

"Oh, that bad, eh?" Zosia just could not bring herself to act serious; after all, she was no longer a little girl and she found her father's summons to a tête-à-tête a bit too rich for words. Nevertheless, she had come as requested, alone, to her parents' town house where they could discuss the details of her life in private.

"Sophie, please!" Her father switched to English for some unfathomable reason.

Zosia was no longer daunted by the language, and she quite happily switched as well. "Where's Mother? Doesn't she want to put in her two pfennigs' worth?"

"Tuppence," her father said with irritation.

"Two cents," Zosia continued the linguistic game.

"Enough!" Alex smacked his hand on the table. Then he sipped his tea and wondered if vodka would not have been a better idea. "Your mother says she trusts you and that she doesn't want to take part in this . . ."

"Charade? Cross-examination? Nonsense?" Zosia suggested in rapid succession.

Alex decided not to be drawn in. He relaxed a bit, began to reminisce. "You know, Zosia, we were among the first to try this—raising you children the way we did, underground, completely untainted by their society, ready to play roles. From the first we worried a great deal about what it would do to you all. We were very careful and took pains to try and make your lives as normal as possible. We watched Ryszard's development and it all seemed to work out fine. He didn't seem too traumatized by the dual personalities, by all the"—he looked for an appropriate word, decided on Zosia's earlier suggestion—"nonsense."

"But?"

"Well, with each successive child, we got more relaxed. I'm afraid by the time you came along, we were completely casual about it all. Even the guard duty—a necessary evil—no longer seemed so unusual. And I think you've latched onto that casualness. I think you have yet to learn how to be careful. And in our business, caution is all that stands between us and death."

Zosia had heard some variant of the speech many times before and had learned that the quickest way to get it over was to appear to listen. Nevertheless she said, "It's a *war,* Father. It is not a business—it's a war. A bloody long war. And no matter how much you tried to make our lives normal, they can't be, because it's a war." She did not bother to add, as she had on previous occasions, that she was happy with her life and with herself, and that she was a thoroughly competent and professional soldier and that her decisions, though apparently impulsive, were sound. That she had survived as long as she had was proof of that. She was not going to change, no matter what they said.

"Well, be that as it may." Alex used the phrase as most people did, to politely ignore what had just been said, and continued, "I want to discuss several things with you. First off, Ryszard has informed me that all three of the men who were in some manner responsible for Adam's death—"

"Murder," Zosia corrected.

"—have managed to meet with unfortunate fates over the past year and a half."

"*Really?*" Zosia asked, intrigued.

"Yes, really. One murdered, one committed suicide, one seemed to step in front of a train. What do you know about this?"

"Nothing, of course," Zosia answered, looking her father directly in the eyes.

Alex considered his daughter, weighing her answer in his mind. "Fine," he said at last. "There's no reason why you should, of course."

"Of course. Judicial executions were ruled out, so naturally I obeyed the constraints of our treaties and let nature take its course. If they died, it was their fate. Now what else did you what to know?"

"Tell me," Alex said, ignoring her tone, "what about this man, this English fellow?"

"What about him?" Zosia sipped her tea, made a face, then added a spoonful of sugar.

"What makes you think he's genuine?"

"Ah, he's genuine all right!" she assured him as she stirred the tea. "Physically he's a mess: fractures, burns, scars, eyesight . . ." She shook her head. "Nobody would set themselves up quite so thoroughly to support an alibi."

Alex disagreed but did not say so; instead he said, "It doesn't matter, the point is, we don't know anything about him. Nobody does. Despite his injuries, he might still be an infiltrator."

"A plant! Why would anyone who has had all that done to them spy for the Nazis?"

"Perhaps to save his own life or maybe for a greater goal, say, to ransom a child." Alex looked at his daughter and wondered what he could have been black-mailed into if Zosia had been at stake.

"Subtlety has never been their strong point, Dad. If they knew enough about us to put him in with us, then they would have destroyed us by now." She sipped her tea again and made an even more disgusted face.

"Maybe. Maybe not."

"Anyway, none of the facts supports that thesis. But more to the point"— she preempted his interruption—"I've talked with him, spent a year getting to know him. I trust him because I know him." She stood and went to the cabinet. "Where the hell do you keep the booze?" She found the bottle before Alex could answer and, turning back to the table, added, "If you demand more of someone than that, then you've become a robot and we're fighting for nothing at all."

Alex looked somewhat taken aback by that vehement statement. He stroked his chin and uncharacteristically gave in. "All right. We'll work on the assumption he's genuine."

Zosia looked disbelievingly at her father, then she smiled as she recognized that he had been ready to be convinced all along. She walked over to her cup and poured in some vodka. "Do you want some?" When her father nodded, she added some to his tea. "So what do you think?" she asked as she seated herself.

"Think?" Alex was stymied. He had not expected Zosia to want his advice, but he had been prepared to offer it in any case and most of his thought had gone into how he could get her to listen—not into what he would say! Deciding he would alienate her if he leapt in with negative comments, he started with, "Well, he's intelligent. And well-spoken. And your mother thinks he's charming."

"Yes, he's very sweet."

Alex paused, but Zosia did not interrupt. "You know he loves you," he added.

"Yes. He's told me."

"Joanna thinks the world of him."

"Yes. She's said so repeatedly," Zosia agreed.

"I watched him playing football with her the other day in Ryszard's back garden."

"Yeah, he taught her the basics this summer." Zosia smiled at the image her father had conjured up.

"He's really good with her." Alex sipped the strange alcoholic concoction in front of him.

Zosia tilted her head to look at her father. "I brought him here so that I could get your opinions. I didn't expect all this shit in between, but if you *have* looked at him as something other than a threat, I'd like to know what you think."

"Well, I'd be careful, child. He's moody," Alex offered tentatively.

"He's been through a lot."

"So have we all, in our own way."

"Most of the time, back home, he's quite happy. Really. You just haven't seen him at his best. I think being out here makes him nervous—Ryszard's house is too much like the Vogels'."

"Hmm."

"Really, I don't think that will be a problem."

"Are you in love with him?"

"Of course not," Zosia snapped.

Alex nodded that noncommittal, I-don't-believe-you nod.

"Why are we talking about love?" Zosia demanded. "I wanted to know what you think about using him for propaganda purposes! Like I told you about months ago!"

"You mean, you don't love him?"

"Why would I? I just want to bring him to the point where he will speak on our behalf! What do you think? Do you think we could use him?"

"Use him," her father echoed, disconcerted. "Zosia, it's one thing to see possibilities in him for our publicly stated goals, but it would be very unwise if you are personally manipulating him toward that end. Are you?"

"Why would it be unwise?"

Alex furrowed his brow as he struggled to quickly organize his thoughts. "You're playing with fire, sweetheart. I see what you're doing, but I think you're too close to this thing to play this game. He loves you and I see something in your response to him that's not as controlled as you'd like to believe. I don't want to see you hurt."

"How could I get hurt?"

Alex didn't answer; instead he said, "Marysia says he cooks for you and takes care of all the other chores as well."

"You know I've never been good at all that stuff. I depended on Ma too much."

"You know, he's very fragile, he'll do anything to be liked right now," Alex warned.

"Why does it matter why he does things?"

Alex regarded Zosia fondly, wondering how his daughter could be so mature in some ways and so adolescent in others. "Because if he comes to believe you're using him, things could turn very unpleasant. You know nothing about this man—nothing at all."

Zosia sipped her tea. "He likes taking care of us, he's said it makes him feel at home. Hell, he's always doing stuff for everybody around the encampment—he must enjoy it."

"And you genuinely like him? It's not just a convenient excuse for using him?"

"Of course not! I mean, of course I like him, and, no, I'm not using him." Zosia paused, then asked in retaliation, "Are you using Ma? Is Ryszard using . . . Well, forget that!"

"Touché." Alex sipped his tea. It was true—he rarely helped out around the house, and all his children seemed to have taken after him. Perhaps Anna had done too much for them all their lives, but that was not the point of this discussion. It seemed they were only capable of touching on the most tangential issues. How could he explain his gut feeling to her?

Eventually he said, "I think he might work out for us, Zosia. I'll talk to him a bit more and get a better feel for how effective he'd be and whether or not he'd like to do this sort of thing, then I'll have to spend time organizing something. In the meanwhile I want you to stay out of it. Move him out of your flat, stop seeing him so much. Put some distance between him and you."

"Why?"

Alex bent his head forward and rubbed the back of his neck. He knew he could not hold Zosia's attention for long, and in any case he wasn't quite sure what it was his intuition was telling him. When he put together what he had read in the psychiatrist's report, his own experience and difficulties in adjusting as a foreigner in a foreign land, and his knowledge of Zosia's character, all he could see was emotional disaster ahead for his little girl. Both her and the Englishman. Peter was floundering, in danger of being swept away by forces none of them properly understood, but of all people, Zosia was not the one to extend a hand into those dangerous waters. She was, herself, far too delicately balanced.

"Why, Dad?" Zosia repeated, rather exasperated.

Alex sighed. "Torture is not really designed to break bodies—that's easy enough—it's designed to ruin a person and anyone associated with him or her. Your friend has a darkness within that will shade everything he experiences from now on. I don't want you to go into the shadows with him."

"If what you said is true, someone should be there for him."

"Maybe someone should," Alex agreed. "But it shouldn't be you. I know you, you're no more patient than me or Katerina. The point when he'll most need help will be exactly the point when he will most try your patience. He'll resent you. And all the things you view as helpful or strengthening, he'll view as threatening. You won't be able to handle it, sweetheart. You're a wonderful soldier, honey, but sometimes you're a bit . . ."

"Heartless?" Zosia asked bitterly.

"Oh, honey, I didn't mean it that way!" Alex saw how Zosia's lower lip trembled, as if she were a little girl ready to burst into tears. He came around the table to hug his daughter. "That's not what I meant at all!"

Zosia pushed his hands away. "Don't try that on me now, Dad! You always left that 'emotional crap' to Mother. I've known all my life how to please you, and that was to get results, so don't go changing the rules of the game on me now!"

"Zosia, maybe I've made some mistakes. . . . It was hard for me, adjusting to being here. I didn't belong. It's hard living among foreigners. The English, we're . . ."

Zosia gave him a sharp look. "It was your choice. You molded me and Ryszard and the others into little war machines, now accept the job you've done and listen to my plans!"

Alex grimaced. Though it broke his heart to have hurt Zosia's feelings, hugging her like that had felt unnatural and a bit silly. He shrugged and went back to his seat. "What do you have in mind?"

"I'm not going to distance myself from him. He's a good friend and he's getting along just fine. I'm going to help him, and I think that the best way to do that will be to get him more involved, to build up his confidence slowly. It will not only serve our purposes, but I'm sure it will help him out as well." She paused to sip her tea. "And you needn't worry, Dad. I won't get hurt, because I don't love him, and I'm not going to fall in love with him. I loved Adam, and that has cost me enough to last a lifetime."

"Of course, honey," Alex agreed helplessly. "Of course."

20

PETER REMAINED AT HOME the day Zosia went to her parents'. It was raining and cold, and he did not even suggest leaving the house. It was the third day in a row he had spent entirely indoors while Zosia went out visiting. He had spent his days reading and staring morosely out the windows. Once or twice he played a few notes on the piano—letting his fingers slide up and down the keys, a chord or two, a phrase from a long-forgotten piece of music. But he did that standing; he could not bring himself to sit down and play in earnest. He knew that that part of himself, his mother's gift to him, was lost forever.

As he watched the rain pounding down, he could hear Joanna with the other children upstairs playing happily. They shrieked and giggled and shook the house as they ran from one room to another playing tag or hide-and-seek or whatever. It was Saturday and the servants had been given this weekend off as well. Ryszard would be home from work in an hour or so; Kasia, Marysia, and Anna were busy in the kitchen. Anna had arrived by taxi a short while ago and after greeting him had immediately retreated into the kitchen. Stefi and Olek had gone on a shopping trip to the local shops; they had invited Peter along, but he had decided not to accompany them—they obviously wanted to be alone and he had lost all interest in doing anything other than staring out the window. They should be back soon, the shops were closed already. It was early afternoon, the rain had been pounding down for hours, and he had been drinking even longer.

A taxi had picked Zosia up in the morning. There were no taxi stands nearby so it must have been requested. Clearly the telephone worked—at least for some people. The taxi, idling on the street, waiting for its passenger, was the last straw. Once Zosia had left, he had grabbed the bottle of whiskey and a glass from the cabinet and had taken up his position by the window in the library. He poured himself a shot, sipped it, then started smoking the pack of cigarettes that he usually carried. They were stale; he had placed them in the pocket of the uniform without even thinking about it when he had prepared to go to Neu Sandez back in the spring. They had remained there unsmoked all these months. Now, methodically, pausing only to sip his whiskey, he worked his way through the pack. When he finished, he wandered over to the cigarette box in the hallway, grabbed a handful, gave an angry glance at the door through which he alone could not pass, then took up his position by the window again.

He smoked and drank, watching as the black branches of the trees faded into the mist that rose from the sodden earth. The whole world merged into a uniform haze of November rain: no color, no blacks, no whites, just layer upon layer of gray. The smoke from his cigarette misted on the window, and unthinking, he wiped away a bit to be able to see more clearly, but there was nothing but gray as far as the eye could see. The unaccustomed surge of nicotine caused tremors throughout his body; the whiskey soothed his nerves, made his trembling hands feel as if they belonged to someone else. Someone who was nervous. Someone who felt angry and unwelcome. Someone who was unsure of himself, scared, and alone. Someone else—not him. He was almost numb.

Ryszard returned from work, saw Peter standing in a cloud of smoke with the bottle of whiskey, and grabbing a whiskey glass from the cabinet, came over to join him by the window. Peter spared Ryszard a bleary glance, then pointedly turned his attention back out the window.

"Long day?" Peter asked for no particular reason.

"Yeah." Ryszard grabbed one of the cigarettes from the little pile and lit it. The two of them smoked and drank in silence.

"How much do I owe you for the booze and cigarettes?" Peter asked.

"Nothing, of course. You're our guest!"

"No, I insist. I've consumed more than my fair share. I'd buy you replacements myself, but . . ." He paused, then finished bitterly, "But I haven't had a chance to get out. I don't know the prices, how much does it all cost?"

"Forget it," Ryszard said, obviously affronted. When he finished his cigarette,

Ryszard tipped the rest of the whiskey down his throat and went into the kitchen to say hello to everyone.

Kasia came into the library with a cup of coffee and a pastry. Peter did not look away from the window, and Kasia did not say anything—she just put the plate and cup near him. He muttered his thanks as she left. Stefi and Olek returned shortly thereafter, and several hours later Zosia and her father arrived in his car. They both saw Peter in the library, and Zosia went up to him while her father stood near the entrance as if undecided about whether to stay.

"Are you okay?" Zosia asked, waving some of the smoke away.

"Leave me alone, I have a headache," he answered in a shaky, hoarse voice.

"I'm not surprised," she said, looking at the accumulation of cigarette ends and the nearly empty bottle of whiskey.

He turned his attention away from the window to look at her, but she kept moving, in fact the whole damn room was moving. Shit, I'm drunk, he thought. How had that happened?

"You're plastered!" Zosia said as if reading his thoughts. "Good Lord! Joanna's here—do you want her to see you like this!"

"You're one to talk," he replied fiercely, and before he could stop himself, he added, "screwing Tadek on my bed while she sleeps in the next room!" He noticed out of the corner of his eye that Zosia's father chose to leave at that point. He wondered if he had spoken loudly enough for him to hear.

"Shut up! You don't know what you're saying!"

He struggled to focus on her. His head pounded horribly. Trying to speak clearly, he said, "Why didn't you tell me!" His voice broke with the effort, and he turned back to look out the window and light another cigarette.

"Stop that already!" She angrily snatched the lighter away from him.

He grabbed it back with some force. He tried to light the cigarette, but he couldn't get the lighter to work properly. He threw it down angrily. God, he thought, I'm making a complete fool of myself. He wished something would stop him, and as if on cue, Kasia called out that dinner was served.

Zosia grabbed his arm and gently tugged. "Come on."

"No, you go. I'll just stay here."

Zosia contemplated him for a moment, then went into the dining room. She returned with some meat and cheese on a piece of bread. "Here," she said, offering it to him, "eat this, it will make you feel better."

He ignored the sandwich, continued to stare out the window. "Why did you bring me here?" he asked forlornly. "I didn't ask for this. Why did you do this to me?"

She shook her head. "I'm not debating with a drunk." She turned to leave, adding, "We're leaving early tomorrow, you'll want to pack tonight."

In the evening, after the younger children had gone to bed, the rest of the family congregated in the sitting room to have a quiet drink together. Peter did not join them, and nobody asked why not as they had all noticed his sudden moodiness. No one was sure what had prompted it, but Zosia hinted that he became withdrawn if he was in pain, and that seemed a sufficient excuse for his melancholia. They were, therefore, quite surprised when he staggered into the doorway late in the evening. He stood swaying slightly, squinting at them as though he could not quite focus.

"Would you like to join us for a drink?" Kasia suggested.

"I'm going out," he stately bluntly. Then, scanning each of their faces in turn, he asked bitterly, "So, who has the leash this time, eh?"

Finally Olek stood and walked over to him. Gently grasping his arm to steady him, Olek said kindly, "I think a bit of air will do you the world of good. Come on, we'll go out."

Peter threw off his hand, hissing angrily, "Get your fucking hands off me!" He gathered himself, glared at them, and repeated, shaking his head for emphasis, "All of you! Keep your hands off me!"

The next day, on the train back to Neu Sandez, Peter had to leave the compartment several times to be sick. Each time Olek accompanied him to the end of the carriage and stood waiting in the aisle as he retched and heaved in the minuscule toilet compartment. The lurching of the train and the confined space did nothing to help him overcome his hangover. He emerged each time looking like death warmed over, and Olek helped him open the window near the door so he could breath some fresh air.

"God, I feel such a fool," he finally managed to stammer to his companion. His voice rattled in his throat; in between being sick, he had spent a good part of the morning coughing.

"Ah, you're human," Olek consoled him. "And that family is not the easiest group of people to deal with."

He looked at Olek—there was no irony intended; clearly, though Olek had taken part in keeping a watch on him, Olek had dissociated himself from the decision to do so. Peter realized with a sudden insight that he would never understand military discipline.

Zosia joined them in the aisle. "You look like hell," she said cheerfully.

"Oh, God," Peter moaned. He felt particularly embarrassed about what he had said to her in the library; so embarrassed he did not even want to refer to it to apologize. He made a sudden lurch for the toilet again.

When he reemerged, Zosia laughed behind her hand. "We call that giving it back," she teased gently.

Peter slid down so that he could hold himself up by letting his feet rest against the wall opposite. The corridor was narrow so he was only down to Zosia's height when he did that. He looked her in the eye. "I don't suppose there's any point in my saying I'm sorry?"

"There's no need." She leaned toward him and kissed him on the cheek. "We're sorry, too."

====== **21** ======

"*T*RAUGUTT! IN MY office, now!"

Richard stopped dead in the corridor and pursed his lips. He blinked slowly, weighing up his response, then sucking a deep breath in through his teeth, he turned, smiled graciously, and entered Schindler's office.

"Ach, Herr Schindler, always a pleasure." Richard bowed slightly in greeting.

"What the hell do you think you're doing?" Schindler snapped, not even bothering to stand.

"Oh, just investigating housing and other details in preparation for my move to Berlin," Richard replied suavely.

"I'm not talking about that!" Schindler fumed, waving his hand in annoyance. "It's this!" He raised a piece of paper high in the air. "What the hell do you think you're doing, requesting permission to nose around my facilities!"

"You're responsible for southeast England, aren't you?" Richard asked innocently. "I have no plans to go there."

"Hamburg! I'm talking about my laboratory south of Hamburg!"

"I'm sorry," Richard soothed, "I didn't realize that was yours."

"I told you about it at dinner!" Schindler grated.

"Oh, it's that one!" Richard smiled. "You were so clever then as to not pinpoint its location. Now I know! But don't worry, the Führer's project, as I believed you termed it at that time, is safe with me. I wouldn't bellow out the information, even in a secure building such as this."

Schindler reddened. "Well, if it wasn't that, why did you request a visit?" he asked rather more calmly.

"As it says in my request, I'm in the middle of studying social management techniques and ways of calming a roused populace."

"Our society has no need of such rot."

"Not now, of course, thanks to the wonderful social management carried out by the Party to date. Techniques and methods of enduring quality such as you yourself have displayed! Nevertheless, we must be ever vigilant. There are occasional rumbles, which we would ignore at our peril. I wish to get a sampling of the command and control structure of various social institutions, including military bases, and use that overall view to put together a report on the state of our society."

"It's still all rot. You manage with this!" Schindler snorted, slamming a fist onto a copy of *Mein Kampf*. "And with this!" He raised his fist demonstratively in the air.

"It's at the Führer's behest."

Schindler glowered but did not respond to that. He glanced around the room as if contemplating the possibility of unseen listeners, then in a softer tone said, "It's not possible for me to sanction your visit to that institution. I'm sure, given the nature of your research, that you could choose another, more convenient installation."

Richard rubbed his chin as he contemplated the suggestion. "It would be difficult . . ."

"But not impossible."

"There are so many factors that must be considered. Size, location, style of governance . . ."

"Nevertheless."

"There would be little sense in changing plans now . . ."

"I'm not giving you clearance," Schindler said politely, though his lips twitched.

"I wouldn't have to see everything."

"I'm not giving you clearance," Schindler repeated courteously.

"Perhaps my aide would suit you better?"

"Your aide. Yes, my son told me he applied for that position. Imagine that! And he didn't get the post."

"No, he didn't. Now, would my aide be a better choice?"

"He won't get clearance either," Schindler replied with a tight smile. "I'm not giving you or any of your lackeys clearance."

"Really," Richard emphasized, "this is unnecessarily obtrusive to my project . . ."

"I'm not giving you clearance, and the decision is mine to make, so, dear Herr Traugutt, change your plans!" Schindler stood suddenly and gestured toward the door. "Good day!"

Richard grit his teeth, then after a moment's consideration, he gave Herr Schindler a slight bow and left the office.

22

"**Y**OU'RE WORKING TOO HARD," Zosia said as she pulled a glass out from a basket, filled it with wine, and set it in front of Peter. "Look, I've brought a picnic." She gestured toward the freshly baked bread, cheese, and ham that filled her basket.

Removing the reading glasses he had recently acquired and rubbing his face tiredly, Peter agreed. There was, however, no way around it—a large volume of coded material had been seized and had to be interpreted as quickly as possible. He was in the middle of a preliminary sort, and the stacks of files towered in unstable heaps around the office.

"Is there any way that I can help?" Zosia asked. "I'm not doing much right now that the New Year festivities are over."

"Maybe, but first let's enjoy this lunch you packed. One of your better cooking efforts," he teased.

"Oh, Marysia made the bread."

Peter laughed. "I would have never guessed!"

They ate there in the office. He leaned back in his chair and, being careful not to topple any of the stacks, put his feet up on the desk. "So, any news?" he asked.

"The paperwork on your commission has gone through."

"Ah, what'd I get?"

"Captain. Just like I requested. And the salary has been approved. Back pay and all."

"Great."

"I also talked with my parents today," Zosia said between bites.

"Ah, how's everything there?" he asked with feigned casualness. His behavior on the last day of his visit had tactfully been ignored ever since they had returned, although he suspected everybody at the encampment had heard about it anyway. Nevertheless, Zosia had warmed to him considerably since that visit, so he felt that it had not been a dead loss.

"Well, Mom's worried about the move to America. She doesn't want to give up her work here, but she doesn't want Dad to have to go it alone there. And she's worried about leaving Ryszard and Kasia alone—especially with their upcoming move to Berlin. But Olek should be happy."

"Olek? Why?"

"Oh, with Ryszard and Kasia moving to Berlin and Mom and Dad going to America, Stefi's decided to move here."

"America," Peter repeated. What a strange place it must be. Alex and Anna would now simply emigrate there and become part of the government in exile. Alex had won a seat in the cabinet and now had to leave the land he had lived in since his youth, but his children and grandchildren would stay behind, carrying on the fight. Zosia might never see her parents again once they moved, and Joanna would grow up without her grandparents. It made Peter think of his own family, and he was tempted to ask a question that had bothered him for some time now. The problem was, did he really want to know the answer?

"Zosia," he began in a tone that let her know he was heading into dangerous territory, "why was Tadek so sure at my trial that my brother was a Nazi?"

"Oh, you don't want to rehash that, do you? It was so long ago!"

Peter ignored her protest. "Given that he knew about your brother, why was he, why were you all, so sure he was not doing what your brother is doing?"

Zosia picked a bit of bread out of her teeth. "Oh, we didn't know anything for sure. Tadek just used that to goad you into a reaction."

"Ah." What a charming man he is, Peter thought.

"He wanted to know if you were genuine."

"Okay then, why was my name on the arrest warrant, but not Erich's? Presumably he has a clean slate as far as the government is concerned—after all, he was able to get Party membership."

"Yes, it does look like he wasn't tainted by whatever affected your parents and you. Perhaps because he wasn't at home at the time."

"That's what I thought at first, but it really doesn't make sense."

"Doesn't it?"

Without knowing exactly why, Peter knew then, she was lying to him. He had suspected it for a long time. If his parents had been arrested and he had been picked up as a matter of course, then that would not be unusual. But if his name had been on the warrant as well as theirs, then the whole family was suspect, and Erich had not been gone long enough to be disassociated from whatever they were suspected of. So why had Erich been left off the warrant? "Why are you lying to me?"

Zosia sighed. "Do you really want to know this?" She waited while he decided; then, when he nodded his head, she said, "Are you sure?"

"I can't believe it could be worse than what I might imagine."

Her silence was not reassuring.

"Oh, for God's sake, Zosia, tell me!"

"You don't believe in God."

"Don't try to change the subject. What haven't you told me?"

She sipped her wine, then looking into the glass rather than at him, she said, "You were the only one on the warrant."

"Me?"

"Yes, you."

"What did I do?" he asked, rather stunned.

"Was there some sort of street gang?"

"Oh, that. Yes, but I had been kicked out by then."

"Well, that might have been the ostensible reason. It's not clear."

"But none of the other gang members were arrested."

"Perhaps the informant didn't know their names."

"But why were my parents taken?"

"Presumably, they did not tell the arresting officers where you were—so for noncooperation if nothing else."

"But they didn't know! I just went out for a walk." He had a vivid memory of how his mother had tried to console him, how he had rejected her explanation and stormed out of the flat. He could still hear the door slam behind him. And then when he had returned home, his life had been changed forever.

"That wouldn't matter."

"But how did the informant know my name? Why would they want me?" He felt a growing sense of panic as he relived the terror and abandonment of that time of his life.

"If you knew the other gang members, you could be made to give their names, so from their point of view, you had reasonably useful information."

"But they were just kids!" he argued plaintively.

Zosia looked at him somewhat sorrowfully.

Peter realized what a stupid assertion that had been and said, "I know. When have kids been spared?" So, that stupid gang he had joined had cost his parents their lives. They had saved him. Deliberately or not, they had saved him and died in his place. Zosia was right, he probably did not want to know that. He looked at her, saw there was something more. "Who was the informant, Zosia?"

"Peter . . ."

So she knew. They had known all along. He had assumed that the informant was anonymous, but they had known all along. "Who?" he insisted.

"Peter," she repeated helplessly. "You don't want to know. It's gone and in the past. Forget it, there's nothing you can do."

"*Who?*" The neighbors? One of the kids? A schoolmate? A teacher? Had he confided in somebody? He could not remember. Had he condemned himself with a thoughtless story or joke?

"It was your brother," Zosia whispered.

"My brother? But that's nuts! He loved Mom and Dad! And he— It would have looked bad for him!" But Erich had hated him and everything he did. It *was* conceivable—especially if Erich was naive enough not to realize that such a denunciation would put their parents at risk as well.

"He probably didn't realize what the fallout would be. He probably thought all you'd get was a good scare. And he could curry favor by turning you in."

"There's no doubt? This isn't conjecture?"

Zosia shook her head. "No, his name was listed as the informant. I can think of no reason why the files would have been falsified." She waited a moment as the reality of her news sunk in, then asked, "Are you all right?"

He nodded but could think of nothing to say. His brother. The bitterness of it left a foul taste in his mouth. "Anna was the lucky one," he finally said.

"Anna?" Zosia was momentarily confused, thinking of her mother.

"My little sister. She died before we could tear each other apart. We would have destroyed her, too. She's the lucky one."

"It wasn't your fault, Peter."

"No, but I didn't help. I provoked Erich. I joined that stupid gang. I never took any of it seriously. It was all a big joke. I didn't think I was risking their lives . . ."

"You were a kid, how were you supposed to know?"

"I was old enough to cause their deaths."

"Peter, it wasn't your fault!"

"No, it wasn't. Could you go now, Zosia? I have loads of work to do."

"Peter . . ."

"Really, I've got so much to do, I'm simply swamped. I'll see you this evening."

She realized that she wasn't going to change his mind, so she gently kissed him and left. His back was to her as he lowered his head over his work. She watched for a few minutes from the doorway, but he did not look up and his pen scanned across the lines without interruption. Zosia walked away, leaving him to his thoughts. She stopped by a bit later and watched him from the doorway, but he was immersed in his work. An hour later she checked again, but he was still completely absorbed. She shrugged and decided that he would have to deal with it in his own time.

Olek came in shortly thereafter. Peter greeted him with a muted hello, but did not look up from what he was doing. When Barbara showed up for work a short time later, Olek gave a subtle shake of his head to Barbara's buoyant greeting. Recognizing the cue, she quietly began work, entering the data that had been set aside for further analysis. So the three of them worked; occasionally Olek and Barbara exchanged a comment or two, but essentially they worked in silence.

Thus, Olek and Barbara both nearly jumped out of their skins when Peter stood and in one swift motion knocked stacks of files off his desk onto the floor. The carefully sorted stacks landed in a heap, which Peter then kicked across the room. His own brother! As the mess of papers floated back to earth, Olek and Barbara stared in stunned silence.

"Shit," Peter swore quietly as he realized he had just undone hours of work. His own brother. He sighed and went over to the mess to put the papers back into their file folders and try to reconstruct the priority assignments. It reminded him of his life. Anytime he thought he had put everything back together, some ill wind from the past stirred it all into a mess again.

Without even asking what had provoked his outburst, Olek and Barbara came over to help him, and together they reconstructed the stacks.

"I can't tell from where it was lying—was this low or high?" Barbara asked, holding out a file.

Peter took it from her and scanned the cryptic notes he had written in the columns. "Low," he replied, handing it back to her. Olek handed him another, and he scanned it and remembered that it had been rated low as well. Both files had been one of a number that had puzzled him. Statistics about animals. Now why was farm data encrypted in the first place? And whose farms? He had not taken the time to translate them properly. There was so much else to do, so many other documents that had not even been perused, that he felt uneasy at the thought that while he puzzled out the farm data documents, important information could be moldering on a stack.

Nevertheless, the documents nagged at him; there was something there, a coincidence of some sort. He jogged his memory but could not quite find the connection; then as Olek questioningly placed another file under his nose, it suddenly hit him. He jumped up and consulted his atlas. It was the place-names!

Many of them were near to ones he had encountered in that strange code he had translated a half year before, the code that still trickled in now and then. Irrelevant meetings between nonentities on the one hand, and stacks of meaningless information on the other. Could they somehow be connected? It was, at this point, nothing more than intuition, but he decided to play his hunch.

"Olek, Barbara, once we've cleaned this up, I want you to both stop what you're doing. Olek, go through the low-priority stacks I've already sorted and look for notes like these on the first page, or for this structure." He opened a file and indicated some of his markings. "If you find that, set the files aside in a separate stack. I want to see how many we have. Barbara, I want you to help me with the unviewed stacks. I'll show you what to look for."

They worked late into the night. Neither Barbara nor Olek pointed out it was well past their usual quitting time—they had realized without Peter's saying a word that something important might be involved. Olek stepped out to get their morning guard-duty shifts reassigned and returned with some dinner for the three of them.

They continued their work the next day and the next and the next, unable to explain exactly what it was they were looking for, aware only that the farm data stack grew to an uncomfortable height. Olek finished sorting the low-priority stacks and joined Barbara in scanning the unsorted information. As they became more competent and practiced at their job, Peter left them to it and turned his attention to the higher-level codes that had been set aside.

It was a problem. He could usually recognize on sight when something had been given a higher security code, but it was still tedious and time-consuming interpreting each document—and he felt sure, irrationally so, that there was no time. He decided not to try to translate them; he just wanted to look for certain words: in particular, anything that would relate to the stacks of low-priority farm data. He went to the list of keywords they had for the various security levels for the past month. Out of thirty days, they had twenty-five third-class keywords, twenty-two second-class keywords, and twelve of the first-class keys. He used each to write a program that would translate entered data and search for the unusual words that had repeatedly appeared in the low-priority data: *fertility, reproduction rate,* and *mammalian.* He did a quick mental calculation—the limiting step would still be data entry. He would just have the first ten lines of code entered. Or maybe twelve? If the words did not occur within that range, they would have to assume the document was irrelevant—at least on the first round.

Once he had the program set up, he reassigned Olek to entering the codes, telling him to start with the first-class stack that Peter would give him and explaining how to handle the data entry. Peter then sent Barbara out to locate another computer—preferably Zosia's if she wasn't currently using it. If that was unavailable, she should steal one, he said, smiling at the crisp salute she gave him in response. Once he had Olek established at his job and Barbara was off on her acquisition mission, he set about sorting the high-priority stack into first-, second-, and third-class codes. It was a nuisance—they all required different handling, and trial and error was too time-consuming. The quickest method was for him to look at each and decide by sight which category it was. It was not something he could quickly train either of his assistants to do; in fact, he was no longer sure he was very good at such instantaneous visual pattern recognition. He took a deep breath, reminded himself that he used to be quite skilled at this game, and plunged in.

With twelve out of thirty keywords known, and assuming the data was accurately entered, nearly half of the first-class stack should have been readable. Their hit rate was less than a quarter. Peter sighed—either he was screwing up or it was just bad luck. He scanned the stacks of information around him and cursed quietly. An office move: from a dilapidated building to a new concrete structure in Breslau. One of the moving vans had been hijacked for the loot inside, and as a bonus there were several crates of encrypted files. Just their luck it was all paper files. It all had to be done by hand. And what if there really was nothing there? He swore again.

"I might not know much English," Olek interrupted his thoughts, "but I sure can swear fluently in it now—thanks to you."

Peter laughed, and Olek continued, "I shocked my grandmother the other day. She said I had picked up your accent!"

"Yeah, I really should stop doing it—it'll ruin the purity of your German if you slip in English vulgarities. That could be dangerous."

"Oh, no problem—I only let it integrate into my Polish. I run German through a separate part of my mind."

Peter wondered if Olek really was that good at keeping it all separate. They spoke German in the office, invariably worked on German-language documents, so if Peter constantly swore in English, the natural place for it to fall into Olek's head was in his German vocabulary. But Olek was like Zosia—raised from birth here— and Zosia was phenomenal at keeping it all separate. Was Olek equally adept? Well, in any case, Peter would have to stop using English in the office: Olek or Barbara's life, or perhaps even his own, might one day depend on such a subtlety.

Eventually Barbara returned with Zosia's computer, and Peter took some time to copy his program onto that and get Barbara started entering the data from second-class documents. They had a much better hit rate on those and he felt reassured. Several hours later with stacks of what he hoped were well-sorted files, he took a break. Even with his reading glasses, even with the lights dimmed and focused, he could barely see a thing. He cursed what they had done to him as he rubbed his eyes and thought that the Council would be holding its usual weekly meeting soon—this would be a good time to inform them of his suspicions. He told Barbara and Olek to take the rest of the evening off, then went on his own to see the Council.

He was a few minutes early, and he waited impatiently in the room they used as their chambers. In fine weather they would meet out of doors, but with the coming of winter, they remained indoors and used a storage room to meet. Tadek was the first to arrive.

"What are you doing here?" he asked accusingly. "We haven't summoned you."

Peter ignored the gibe and offered a serious answer: "I have information that I think you should know." He felt the beginnings of one of those piercing headaches and hoped grimly that the pain would hold off long enough for him to make a coherent presentation to the Council. As he saw Tadek pull out a bottle of vodka and uncap it, Peter added undiplomatically, "And it would help if you would remain sober for once."

"Since when do I take orders from Zosia's houseboy?" Tadek asked pointedly, then drank straight from the bottle. "Ah, good!"

The others filtered in and took their seats. Katerina was ready to call the meeting to order, but Tadek raised the point that they must at least start as a closed meeting. Zosia scowled but did not object as Peter was politely ejected from the room and told he would be called back as soon as possible.

He stood in the hall, waiting impatiently. He paced a bit, angrily aware that the headache was beginning to dominate his thoughts. A few more minutes and I'll be incoherent, he thought, cursing yet again the anonymous multitude that formed the "them" of his past. A nameless sergeant—he must have weighed at least 130 kilos—had swung that rubber truncheon with such enthusiasm. Peter could remember the sergeant vividly but had no idea which interrogation it had been, could not even remember his nationality. How he had hated that behemoth with every fiber of his being!

He had stopped pacing, was leaning against the wall, clawing at his temples. God, it hurt like hell! Worse than usual. He slid down the wall into a sitting position, his hands tearing at his hair. He heard the chamber door open, heard Konrad tell him they were ready to hear whatever he had to say. He shook his head, climbed to his feet, and mumbling "I can't," he stumbled off back toward his office.

Olek and Barbara were still there, still working. When they looked up, both of them abandoned their work to help him sit down. Barbara lowered the lights while Olek went to get a cold compress. Zosia stormed in only moments later.

"What the hell was that all about!" she yelled, furious at the embarrassment he had caused her. Everybody had turned to her for an explanation and she had none.

"Leave him alone!" Barbara snapped defensively. Colonel Król only outranked her by a zillion ranks, but Barbara did not care.

Zosia turned to look at the slip of a girl who had just yelled at her, stunned by her audacity. Then Zosia looked at Peter and asked in a much more concerned tone, "Are you all right?"

"I'm sorry, Zosia," Peter muttered through his pain. It was worse than ever!

He thought they had been getting better, and he was not only furious at himself and embarrassed, he was dismayed at the realization that nothing had improved.

Olek returned, took in the scene with a glance, and ignoring Zosia's rank, asked his aunt bluntly, "What are you doing here?"

"Your loyal troops," Zosia said to Peter, nodding toward Barbara and Olek.

He smiled slightly in return, but the smile faded rapidly as he winced with the uncontrolled pain. Barbara clambered over some stacks to stand behind his chair so she could gently massage his head. Olek went to fetch some water. Zosia realized with a sudden unexpected jealousy that she was superfluous and said softly, "I'll go back to the meeting and explain. Come later if you can—if not, you can tell me later and I'll relay the information." She leaned forward and, ignoring Barbara's possessive and defensive scowl, kissed Peter on the forehead. He had his eyes closed and did not seem to notice.

An hour later the worst of it had passed. He thanked Olek and Barbara for their care, then asked them to please quit work for the night, pointing out that errors caused by tiredness were extremely counterproductive. When he said that he was going to speak with the Council, Barbara agreed that they would stop work if and only if he allowed them to accompany him to the Council chambers. "You need some moral support against that arrogant bunch," she asserted.

"Sure, why not," he agreed, truly touched by her offer. Three against ten—it seemed fair odds. Barbara could take on five, Olek would take on five, and he could fight the devils in his head. It seemed reasonable.

Together they set off, carrying a few documents to back up their assertions. Careful not to make the same mistake twice, he knocked on the Council door and waited for someone to answer. He and his staff were invited in almost immediately. The fluorescent lights buzzed aggravatingly overhead—he appraised them and guessed that he had about five minutes before they would provoke another wild headache. Perhaps ten if he could shield his eyes somehow.

"What is the problem?" Tomek asked, interrupting his ruminations.

Forcing himself to organize his scattered thoughts, he launched into a brief description of what he had found so far among the captured files. "I think they're related to those other messages we pick up now and then. They're up to something, I just can't tell exactly what. I just thought it would be wise for you to have a progress report, and maybe you can cross-reference my information with HQ. Maybe then it will be more obvious what this is all about. If you can give us a direction to look, that will help enormously. We could also use some extra help."

A series of glances back and forth among the Council immediately informed him that they already knew something. At the very least, they suspected something and he had just confirmed their suspicions.

"Thank you, Captain." Katerina spoke formally for the entire Council, using his newly acquired title somewhat snidely. "It is imperative you keep looking through the material and see if you can find anything else. This information has been very useful to us."

It was a dismissal.

Peter debated with himself, glanced at Olek's and Barbara's exhausted faces. They were disappointed as well. Katerina was seated behind a table, and he went up to it and placed his hands down on its surface so he could lean in toward her. "Comrade Katerina," he said with heavy sarcasm, "do tell us what it is we are looking for!"

"That information is classified," Katerina answered.

He slammed his hand on the table so hard even cold-blooded Katerina jumped a bit. "Damn it!" he yelled. "Do you have any idea how long this work takes!" He gestured broadly back toward Olek and Barbara. "We haven't got the time to play your games of hide-and-seek!"

Katerina gave him a murderous look.

"Peter . . . ," Marysia said quietly, to try to interject some calm.

"Look," he interrupted her, pacing back and forth, "I know you have your security to worry about, but you don't have much choice. As long as I am the only qualified analyst around, you're going to have to trust me, otherwise you're just wasting our time."

Still they greeted his plea with silence. Zosia would not look up at him, she seemed to be doodling something on a notepad; Marysia was looking at Olek as though concerned for his safety. Peter leaned against the table, opposite Katerina, and looked at each of them in turn, though most did not return his look. Then he said softly, intensely, "If we know what we're looking for, we have a much better chance of finding it. This material is dated, we don't have much time, I'm sure of that."

There was no reaction. He took a deep breath and tried again, offering up the only assurance he could: "If you're afraid of telling me something that will compromise your people in the field, then just keep me prisoner here for the rest of my life." He stepped back from the table, and turning away from them, he added bitterly, "It's what you're going to do anyway."

Nothing had changed since his visit to Zosia's parents. He never left the encampment alone, he had no access to Communications. He was essentially a prisoner. He knew it and he had decided perhaps it was time that he let them know that. It was time to end the charade.

The buzzing of the lights intensified. Barbara approached him; in a whisper she asked, "Prisoner?"

He nodded in a somewhat noncommittal way, indicating that he would explain later. The Council was still silent; perhaps all he had managed to do was arrange his court-martial. Sighing with exasperation, he motioned for Olek to join him and Barbara and said, "Come on, we'll work with what we have."

They were at the door already when he heard Zosia call his name. The three of them turned to look at her. In fact, the entire Council was looking at her, some members clearly menacingly. Zosia ignored them all. "We know that certain members of the Führer's inner circle have resurrected the idea of secret, mass

sterilization for inferior populations. There'd be"—she waved her hands to indicate that she was guessing—"something like contamination in the water. I don't
know, maybe they'd have an antidote for themselves and so they could wipe out
populations at will, and without needing to bother with the messy business of
mass murder. We clearly need to find out more about what they are up to and
find a way to prevent it. We need to get the information to our biologists; we
need chemical formulas, effectiveness, methods of counteraction."

"Zosiu!" Katerina nearly screeched. "Enough! We haven't got clearance for
this!"

"We don't have time for that. And he's right. We need them! We need to let
them know what's going on and what to look for."

"Let her speak," Tadek said. Marysia and several others nodded.

Peter raised his eyebrows slightly, but otherwise made no response. Tadek?

Zosia continued, "We believe the Führer himself supports the program, but he's
maintaining deniability by running it through the greater London section of the
Sicherheitsdienst, through an official named Schindler—he's a crony of Vogel's."

Peter made a face as he remembered all too well that obnoxious man.

Zosia continued, "The experimental operation has been farmed out to several
provincial sites, including the Breslau office from which we got the files you've
been working on. They're trying to keep things quiet, so after they amass the
data, we think they're forwarding it to Berlin for review, but then moving it out
to somewhere more politically quiet for analysis."

"Where?" Peter asked.

"The outskirts of Hamburg. There's a military installation in a cleared area
near the village of Undeloh, and they're using the headquarters and the fellow
who runs the place to accumulate their findings. They have a small staff working
right in the director's residential mansion. Everything seems to fall under a special section and outside the normal chain of command there. Schindler runs the
Berlin end of things; the director at the lab is named Rattenhuber. Most of the
information is transmitted via couriers since they don't trust the codes—that's
why there are all these paper and tape files. One of our agents has tried to get
inside, but that has fallen through."

Zosia stopped, somewhat stunned by the enormity of her decision to speak.
She stood and turned toward the Council. "There, it's said. The damage is done. I
take full responsibility for this decision." She looked back at Barbara, who was
observing her with renewed respect, and smiled, thinking: I'll probably be
pulling guard duty under your command next week.

There was a rancorous debate after the three left. Tadek insisted they present
their breach of discipline to HQ as a majority vote of the Council. Katerina was
adamant that Zosia had acted alone, and Zosia insisted that the record reflect
that. The message was sent the following day and passed on to a Warszawa
Council member—Zosia's mother, as it happened. She shook her head at her
daughter's decisive impetuousness, presented the request of the Szaflary moun-

tain encampment to inform their analyst of the top-secret information, argued their case, received the clearance, and wired it back to the mountains the following day. So, Anna Król thought, the minutes of the various Councils won't match exactly. Nobody would ever be the wiser.

By the time the Szaflary Council received the surprise clearance and Zosia realized there would be no sanctions against her—even Katerina could not stay angry at her for very long—Peter and his staff had filtered through two-thirds of the documents. And they had something.

The crucial names had helped them home in on a copy of a communiqué sent from Breslau to Berlin and Hamburg. Upon translation, they learned that an adjutant from Berlin was being sent out to pick up data from experiments conducted in the neighborhood of Breslau for review in Berlin and would then transport the files to the laboratory in Hamburg. They had missed the adjutant's visit to Breslau, but learned that he would be leaving Berlin for Hamburg in five days. A brief physical description of the adjutant was included—apparently nobody in Hamburg knew him personally—as well as a description of his travel arrangements.

Barbara's hands shook as she showed Peter her version of the translation. He scanned her work and complimented the job she had done. She beamed with shy pride.

"Let's stop," he said, and went over to the bottle of Scotch that had relocated itself from Zosia's flat to the office. He poured each of them a shot and they toasted their efforts. Once they had finished their impromptu celebration, Olek and Barbara took the document and went to round up the Council. Peter insisted they should have the fun of presenting the information, and besides, the less he saw of that group, the better.

23

THE SECOND DAY after the Council had been presented with the communiqué, Zosia took the unusual step of having Peter summoned from his office back to their apartment. As he walked down the narrow hallways to their rooms, he thought that now everything else had settled down, she might have decided it was a good time to return to the unresolved conversation about his brother. Since their lunchtime discussion, they had hardly even seen each other. He had been totally absorbed in his work, slipping into the flat long after Zosia and Joanna had gone to bed and leaving early in the morning before they were up. Joanna had come to say hello and help with simple tasks now and then, and Zosia had found time to stop by, but they had never found an opportunity to talk in private.

His brother, and the information Zosia had given to Peter, had occasionally come into his head as he had worked, but he had not really spent much time thinking about what it meant to him. His dreams and nightmares had not changed, nothing seemed different, and he had essentially put the issue to rest—there was nothing to be done about it and it was long in the past. Besides, the chain of events his brother's action had set into motion had brought him here and he was happy with his life. Even as a virtual prisoner. It was, after all, exactly what he wanted: to remain safe and secure. And who in this world, he asked himself philosophically, wasn't severely constrained?

He ascended the ladder to the level of their flat with a technique he had perfected using mainly his arms and thus avoiding stress on his legs. As he carefully stepped off the ladder and gently set his weight back onto his feet, he realized that the boy who had summoned him had used his military title. Clearly Zosia was not calling him to talk about his past—it must be business, and that it could not wait until evening implied it was bad news. The January winds howled outside the encampment, the snows had piled up deeply, and Peter, on the several walks he had taken, had come to feel that they were living in an entirely isolated and independent part of the world. Zosia's summons and the serious look on her face as she asked him to sit down warned him that his illusion was only that. The world was intruding again.

She offered him a drink and then began without preamble, "We've organized and gotten clearance on what we need to do with respect to that communiqué you unearthed for us. We'll remove the adjutant and insert our own man in his place."

"Who?"

"Tadek fits the physical description the best, and he's a good man to have in there. Unfortunately, since he's supposed to bring information and pick up a general report on how things are going, he's not supposed to receive much in the way of specifics. So, we still need to get at their files, and that means into their computer."

"But he doesn't know anything about computers, does he?"

"Not much, so I'll be accompanying him as his wife."

"What'll happen to the real adjutant?"

"If possible, he'll be held hostage and exchanged for someone we want. If not . . ." Zosia shrugged ruefully.

"And where do I fit into all this?"

"Well, you'll be coming, too."

Peter took a deep breath, then let it out slowly, but he did not say anything.

"We've learned that . . ." Zosia continued. "Well, we've ascertained—from other sources—that nearly everything is on the computer there."

"So, you'll hack into it. Remotely?"

"No, they've been careful, it's not on a network. So, the problem is, we not only have to hack into it, we have to do it on-site, and at the same time we have to overcome any security arrangements protecting the data. We don't know what we're going to come up against, so we want you along. With your expertise we'll have a better chance of actually retrieving something from their system."

Peter furrowed his brow. "Just like that?"

"Well, I'll be along to help. We're hoping you'll be able to overcome whatever file-protection mechanisms they have in place."

He shook his head. "You should know that's impossible! You don't sit down at a foreign computer and break into protected data just like that—don't they know that?"

Zosia shrugged. "We were hoping that the file protection . . . We know they're trying to keep this secret and so it's all run by one officer. Apparently he doesn't have much training in this stuff."

Peter shook his head forlornly. "That might well make it more difficult. I wouldn't even know where to begin . . ."

"We were hoping that it might be simple enough to break in one night."

"You'd be better off praying."

She ignored his comment. "The security officer is the director of the laboratory—this Major Rattenhuber. He's the one who devised their network code. You've already defeated him once, maybe you can do it again. Maybe he's been careless."

"Well, that at least is a good bet, especially with the military, but I still don't think it's a realistic plan."

"Nobody will blame you if you don't succeed."

Peter snorted in disbelief. "How long will we have?"

"We'll be there three days, we'll probably manage access for one night. We'll have a three-pronged attack: Tadek will try to get information from the major directly, I'll talk to the wife, and you'll . . . While we're there, Tadek will do everything in his power to get the major to show him things on the computer. He'll pass on whatever information he can get to us, and we can try to formulate a plan of attack. I'll help you hack into the files as far as possible, and then you can make a stab at accessing them."

Peter nodded absently. One night! What were they thinking? "If Tadek is the liaison, how am I going to be integrated in? As some junior officer?"

"No, they know only one officer is coming."

"As a guard?"

"Again, they know only one military person is coming. We can only manage to come along as the personal retinue of the adjutant."

"How then?" Peter asked, afraid that he already knew the answer.

She glanced at his left arm apologetically.

Peter followed her eyes down to the numerals on his arm. "No," he breathed softly, shaking his head. "No, Zosia, you can't ask me to do that. There must be another way!"

She raised her shoulders in a gesture of helplessness.

"I could go as a brother-in-law or a friend or something."

"Do you really think they'd believe that the adjutant would be bringing along rogue members of his family?"

"Why not?"

"Be serious. This is the best strategy."

"There must be some other possibility."

"Think about it. This is the safest. If anyone sees your arm, well, there's no problem this way. And what about Vogel's trips? You told me sometimes he would take his wife and you to tend to her. It's not unheard of. But any other grouping, well, it would raise suspicions immediately."

"Then get somebody else. I can't do it."

"You must," Zosia insisted coldly.

"What do you mean 'must'?"

"It's not a request."

"Oh, I see." Did she think he was stupid? Since such missions were completely dependent on the acting ability and the conviction of the agents, everyone knew that ordering someone into a situation with which they were uncomfortable was not only ineffectual but dangerous. It was, therefore, also against policy.

"We *are* a military organization," she explained. "Your rank means something, you know."

"Yes, of course." He looked away from her. She clearly assumed he was unaware of the policy, and so, to save herself the trouble of convincing him or having him participate in the planning, she was issuing orders. Worse still, he knew he would obey them—not because they were orders, but because they came from her. Couldn't she have just said please?

"Peter! Don't be like this. We wouldn't ask you if we didn't think this was the best way to do it."

"Oh, don't worry. I'll do it. I'll do my best for you. All of you."

"It's for your people, too."

"I have no people. Don't you know that? Don't you remember what Tadek said?"

"Oh, forget that already! He was angry. Look, it's your chance to prove yourself!"

"Prove myself? It's almost impossible, it's dangerous, and, I swear to you, Zosia, there *will* be trouble. You don't take it seriously, you don't understand—if you put me in that uniform, if you put that band around my wrist, I won't be able to move freely, I'll get harassed for trivialities, and if anything happens, anything at all, I'll be the first person they suspect! That will put all of us and our mission in jeopardy!"

She rubbed her head, pushed her hair back in exasperation. "Look, we're not naive. We know the dangers involved. But have you got any better ideas?"

"Take someone young, then they could be your son or daughter."

"The adjutant's too young: a glance at his pass will tell anyone that. We're already pushing the age thing a bit."

"Well, then, let me go as the adjutant. Nobody there knows him, do they?"

"No, we don't think so. But you don't fit his description."

"So what? Dye my hair. If nobody knows him . . ."

"He's taller than you, and lean, like Tadek, and there might even be a photograph . . ."

"Then make me military, some junior officer."

"I told you, they know only one officer is coming."

"So, the information is wrong. People change plans all the time."

Zosia shook her head slowly as she thought over the idea. "No," she whispered as if, upon consideration, the idea was impossible.

"Why the hell not?"

Zosia bit her lower lip, thought a long moment, then said hesitantly, "You're not ready for that."

"Not ready?"

"I know from your experiences you've never done this sort of infiltration, isn't that right?"

Peter glared at her, wishing he had never told her anything about himself.

"You've never masqueraded for any length of time or acted out a role, have you?"

Still he did not answer.

"You're not trained for this, and we don't have time to go through the necessary training."

"I lived with them," he reminded her angrily. "I know better than anyone how they act. Damn it, I acted for four years!"

Zosia looked away, drummed her fingers a bit, then suddenly she reached toward him.

He flinched visibly and cursed silently at his all too obvious response. "That proves nothing!" he asserted angrily.

"What if someone in uniform jovially slaps your back and you cower in response? Who knows what that sort of proximity to those uniforms and people will provoke. You wanted to step into the gutter in Neu Sandez. Remember your outburst in Göringstadt? And look what happened the other day, in front of the Council. We can't take the chance!"

Humiliated, he kept silent. She had proved her point; nevertheless, he was sure there was more to it than she was saying. Making it an order! What was she hiding?

Apologetically she added, "We just don't think it's practical. You know, in view of . . ."

"In view of these?" he asked, holding up his arm. "Or is it in view of the fact that the Council still doesn't really trust me?"

"Both, I guess."

"They want to make sure I'm in a position to be closely watched!"

"Perhaps."

"Admit it!"

"Yes, there were some words to that effect; after all, you never have been completely vetted. You know we can't reorganize everything around your being a special case. It would be irresponsible," she defended herself tiredly.

"Then why not send someone else altogether? Why put me in there at all?"

She sighed. "There is no one else we could get. Politically, it's important that the Szaflary group manages to handle this on its own; we've been losing too much authority to Warszawa. We predate them, yet now we have to ask them for permission to do anything! But that's not the point, it's more than that: you're good at what you do, creative, intuitive. Brilliant. We need that." Her voice had dropped as she spoke, and she ended by staring at her feet and mumbling something.

"What?"

She looked up at him, repeated softly, "And I need you. I specifically asked for you."

He stood up and paced the room. He stopped at the lace curtain hanging on the wall and ran his fingers along it. It was long and wide and intricately made with a fine pattern of flowers and leaves running the length of it. Zosia's grandmother had hung it on a balcony window of her town house, which overlooked the market square. Zosia had worn it at her wedding. Now it hung, a forlorn reminder of better days, against a damp, underground, concrete wall.

He spoke so quietly she had trouble hearing him. "All right, I'll do it. We'll need to change my numbers—they'll be checked when we travel. And we should change my nationality. Polish is good, I know enough words now, and besides, I shouldn't have to speak it."

She nodded even though he couldn't see her; he was still staring at the lace, his back to her.

"When do we leave?" he asked, his fingers still tracing along the leaves of lace.

"We take the overnight train tomorrow from Neu Sandez to Berlin. We'll leave Berlin on Thursday morning."

"So we'll be staying a day there?"

"We have a safe place," she assured him.

"That doesn't give us much time."

"I know."

"What about Schindler? You said he heads up this laboratory. He'll recognize me, if he sees me."

"Don't worry, he's in London now. There is no reason to believe he'll make a surprise inspection tour. And if he does," she added before Peter could debate that point, "we'll keep you out of sight. It'll be easy—he'll have no interest in meeting my servant."

"No, I don't imagine he would," Peter agreed. He suddenly laughed.

"What?"

"Oh, I just realized, I was being an idiot! Schindler's such a racist, I'm sure the only thing that he ever saw was what was on my shoulder. If we change that, he won't have a clue who I am. I could spit in his face and he wouldn't recognize me!"

"The son might be there—do you think he'll recognize you?"

Peter really didn't know the answer to that question. If he told Zosia that Schindler's son would recognize him, then he would have an excellent excuse for not taking part in the mission. And he would disappoint her as well. With a conviction he did not feel, he answered, "No, I probably saw him once, years ago. I can't remember what he looks like, I see no reason why he'd remember me. Still, it might be safer, if he's around, to keep me in the room, or whatever."

"We'll do that," Zosia assured him. "Any other concerns?"

"I'll need to practice an appropriate accent—I'll need your help with that."

"Don't worry, we'll prepare everything."

Peter turned and gave her a look that conveyed his doubts. "And will you prepare Tadek enough that I could turn my back on him?"

"You shouldn't be so hard on Tadek."

"Hard? The man wanted to *kill* me!"

"He didn't know you—he is trustworthy. Believe me."

"Of course." Not for the first time, the question of Tadek's place in Zosia's heart worried him.

Zosia's eyes were drawn from Peter's strained face to the lace curtain he had been fingering. Unlike it, she had never known another home other than the heavy, damp concrete walls around her. What would her grandmother have thought? What would it be like to live unafraid in a town, windows open to the daily passage of life? "I wonder what the world would have been like if we had won. Or if the war had never happened," she said dreamily.

"I can't imagine. It's funny, isn't it? Whatever the reality is—it seems so set in stone, as if all of history led to this point. Yet, there must have been a point, in the thirties or forties maybe, when a few different decisions could have changed everything."

"Do you think so?"

"Logically, yes. What if Hitler had never been born? Were the forces at work in Germany at the time strong enough to have produced another leader just like him? Or what if Hitler had attacked the Soviet Union? They say he really wanted to—only his astrologer stopped him. Or what if the German nuclear program had been less successful? What if the Nazis hadn't believed in it wholeheartedly? Maybe . . . But you know, in my heart, it's hard to believe things could have happened differently. The world is what it is."

"So you believe in fate?"

"No." He paused, shook his head for emphasis. "No. I think the future holds any number of possibilities. And I really do think history could have been different—it's just hard for me to truly believe it here," he finished, tapping his chest. "What do you think?"

"I think believing in other possible pasts opens up a terrifying door for most humans—for if all of history wasn't working to this point, this particular present, then who can guarantee that they would themselves have existed? It's scarier than death, because with death you can believe in immortality, but how do you counter the possibility of nonexistence? Better to believe things had to be the way they are—then you know, deep down, that you had to exist and you had to be the person you are. It still leaves room for any possible future—until, of course, the future becomes the past."

Peter nodded. When he was younger, he could never have imagined his current situation and all the experiences he had had in between, but now, he felt that this point in his life had been inevitable. As the infinite possibilities of his future had been narrowed to one past, he had set it in stone. He wondered how Zosia's belief in God tied in with her perception of the past and future. Did having an immortal spirit mean that you were sure to have the same personality no matter what circumstances you were born into?

Before he could phrase the question, Joanna interrupted them by running into the room. She had been playing in the woods with some of the other children, and she came in flushed and excited. Peter smiled at her and took Zosia in with the same glance. How could he believe that he might never have met them? It seemed impossible to imagine life without them now.

Joanna tugged at his sleeve. "You're home!" she exclaimed in Polish. "Are you staying?"

He felt slightly guilty at his abandonment of her over the past week. "I've been here, little one," he said in careful Polish, "you've just been asleep!"

She made a face, then asked, "What are you making for dinner?"

"Perhaps your mother is cooking tonight," he teased.

"Yech! You cook better! It's been awful without you!"

Zosia laughed. "Well, I guess that's decided! Anyway, I've got work I have to do."

"All right," he conceded; the rest of the files would wait until his return—if he returned. He stood and grasped Joanna's outstretched hand. "Let's go see what we've got."

24

THEIR TRAIN APPROACHED the outskirts of Berlin at dawn. Peter had been unable to sleep for the last several hours of their journey, and he had finally abandoned the *couchette* compartment he shared with Tadek and Zosia and gone to stand in the aisle. The conductor spoke to him deferentially, the occasional *Zwangsarbeiter* skirted nervously around him. Funny what the color of a uniform can do, he thought, looking down at the ridiculous insignia and medals on the neat black cloth. The clothes he would wear tomorrow, that other uniform, waited safely tucked away in the safe house along with the papers and wristband and other paraphernalia they would need for the job ahead. He pushed his hair back and leaned against the cold glass of the window. The train slowed as it approached the city, and he watched with a fascinated dread as suburb after suburb passed by. He had checked the railway maps and ascertained that they would pass nowhere near where the Vogels had lived, but still the tidy houses and trim lawns of the infrequent well-to-do suburbs evoked a visceral reaction in him.

Zosia stepped out of the compartment, yawning sleepily. Her dress was rumpled and she had not even straightened her hair. "Are we almost there?" she asked between yawns.

He nodded.

She came up to him, put her arm around his waist. "Don't worry. It'll be okay. We won't be here long."

They arrived at the pension without difficulty, having changed taxis several times en route to make sure they were not followed. After they registered and had their papers stamped, the elderly gentleman led them into a back room. There they were joined by an old woman, and Zosia greeted her warmly and asked them if they had swept recently. When they assured her everything was secure, she hugged and kissed them both. They greeted Tadek by name—they clearly knew him, albeit less intimately than Zosia—then they turned to Peter and greeted him without saying a word.

The three of them were led into a private dining room, and there they settled down to a hearty breakfast and exchanged news and gossip in whispered Polish. Peter studied the old couple who ran the pension—they looked thoroughly exhausted and they confirmed this with their own words.

"Oh, it is so difficult, Zosia—we don't know how much longer we can put up with it," the woman whispered in a singsong accent as she poured another cup of tea for Peter.

The old man nodded his agreement. "We are so lonely. It is so hard to live like this. We've got to go back."

Zosia consoled them, assured them that they were essential, needed, appreciated. She begged them to be patient, to wait until there was an adequate replacement. They sighed and looked at each other wearily. "Ah, but what are we doing, complaining like this to you?" the woman sang. "We should be welcoming you. And you have suffered so much—we have heard about Adam! We are so terribly, terribly sorry."

Zosia bit her lip and nodded mutely.

Then the woman turned toward Peter and asked the question that had clearly been bothering her since she first set eyes on him. "But who is this? And why are you so silent?"

Peter had been able to follow almost all the conversation, but had not felt comfortable interjecting any comments. He noticed Tadek had been silent as well and was surprised by the woman's almost accusatory question.

Zosia, however, understood. "He's not a ghost, Auntie. Your memory of Adam is flawed; he does not look that much like him. Say something, Peter—that will dispel her doubts."

"Say something" was exactly the sort of command that guaranteed an almost moronic inability to say anything in a foreign tongue, and Peter found himself momentarily stymied.

"He's not Adam," Tadek filled the silence, "he's just a cheap, imported replacement model." The joke carried a note of bitterness that even the old couple could not fail to notice. They looked at Peter all the more curiously.

Compelled to say something, he finally managed to say, "This is a very fine breakfast."

Noting his accent, the old man turned to Zosia and asked, "He is German?"

"No. I'm English." Peter could think of nothing else to say, so he turned his attention back to his plate and continued eating.

The old couple looked at Zosia and she replied to their unspoken question by saying, "We've vetted him completely—he's quite safe."

"Yes," Tadek added, "we all agreed, didn't we?"

Zosia shut him up with a look.

Peter chewed his food, thinking, And tomorrow I'll be in a position where he can easily get me killed. Oh, God, what have I let myself into?

25

*I*N THE EARLY AFTERNOON, once they had all settled into their rooms and relaxed a bit, Peter ventured out to find Zosia. She was not in her room, but he quickly located her with the elderly couple in the little sitting room they kept at the back of the pension for their private use. Peter interrupted apologetically, then called Zosia aside to ask her if the car was already arranged.

"Yes. It's on the street."

"Give me the keys. I want to check it out."

"Check it out?"

"Yes, it's a long trip—we should make sure everything is running smoothly."

Zosia furrowed her brow as though she thought she was being deceived. "Don't you think it would be a little inappropriate for you—in that uniform—to go poking around a car?"

"No, not at all. Give me the keys and show me which one it is."

She excused herself from her godparents—for that's who they were—and walked to the front of the pension with Peter to show him the car. They paused there, on the stoop, and he looked into her eyes, willing her to trust him. He needed to go alone—unobserved—and he needed her to let him go.

"Wait here," she said. "I'll get the keys." It took her some minutes to return. When she did, she handed him the keys and said, "Whatever you do, don't take too long. Otherwise, we might worry."

Peter kissed her on the cheek and said, "I've just got to check it out. I'm sure you understand."

She nodded and left.

Normally, he would have confided in Zosia, but he knew that while they were on a mission, they were bound by their military procedures and ranks. Tadek outranked him, and Zosia outranked them both, and though it was not usually relevant, in this context, when he was going to do something that was so fool-hardy, he could hardly ask her permission. She would have had to refuse him. Better Zosia could plead ignorance, even if, as she so clearly indicated, that was not the case.

As any high-level official would do, he quickly scanned the underside of the car. Satisfied that he was not a terrorist target, he then slid into the driver's seat. Despite the cold it was a bright day, and he put on his sunglasses. He had memo-rized the map in his room, and without further hesitation he started the car and drove away confidently. Forty minutes later, he turned onto the familiar subur-ban street and parked the car two houses down from the Vogels' house. Although he would raise suspicions by his presence, nobody would harass him. The uni-form, the quality of the car, the military license plate—it would all keep him out of danger. The neighbors and the Vogels alike would assume that he was observ-ing somebody on the street, but they would not dare to wonder more than that.

He lit a cigarette and began to smoke, but the reflection of the smoke off the windshield reminded him of all the times Karl had blown smoke in his face, and within a few seconds he extinguished the cigarette. He tapped his fingers on the edge of the ashtray pensively, wondering what it was he had come here for. What did he hope to achieve? What demons could he dispel just by looking at the house? As he watched, the front door opened and Frau Vogel and a woman emerged. The woman was obviously his replacement, and he felt a surge of pity and guilt. Doubtless her life would be a lot more miserable because of what he had done—they would feel that they had been too lenient with him and would take out their vengeance and frustrations on her. He almost felt like going over to her and apologizing, and perhaps if she had been alone, he might have done so—though, wearing the uniform that he was, he would probably have provoked only uncomprehending terror in her.

He shook his head to dispel the thought and imagined a different scenario: he could walk up to Frau Vogel and demand to see her papers and harass her merci-lessly about their being out of order. Even if she thought she recognized him—and how could she not?—she would not dare to disobey him, not while he was wearing this uniform. He imagined her stunned face, imagined her thinking,

How can this be? He smiled at the ludicrous image, suppressing a childish urge to actually do it, since it would be pointless and dangerous, but he allowed himself to enjoy the brief fantasy.

He sat for a bit longer, watching the house. Frau Vogel and her servant returned. The children came home from their various activities. It was a Wednesday, so that would mean that Rudi and Gisela were returning from school, Teresa would be returning from attending her Bund Deutsche Mädel meeting—or more likely, from not attending her BDM meeting—Ulrike would by now be enrolled in the N.S. Frauenschaften and would doubtless be busy with a training program and a schedule that he would be unfamiliar with. He wondered if she had passed her school exams, wondered if her modern history results were as poor as his had always been. Probably not, she had apparently learned her lessons and would fit well into her place in society. And Horst would not come home until late—if at all. Perhaps he had moved out permanently. Uwe, Geerd, then Horst. They all seemed to run away, but there was nowhere for them to run—they were, in some ways, more trapped than he had ever been.

He realized that whatever he was looking for—the cure for his dreams, the peace of mind that still eluded him—it was not here. He could take no revenge, could not even gloat that he had managed to survive. He had to remain silently missing from their lives, and though Karl and Elspeth had scarred him terribly, probably permanently, he had to live with the fact that he would never influence them in the same way that they had warped his life. He had been a tangential concern of theirs, a thorn in their side occasionally, a commodity to be used; whereas they had been the very definition of his life for three long years. They had held life or death over him; pain, sustenance, even sleep, had been at their will. The balance was unfair and could never be redressed.

He started the car and drove back to the center of Berlin, deciding en route that there was one small thing he could do. He parked the car near the pension and walked about until he found a shop that sold note cards and stamps. He purchased the local postage and wrote a brief note to Teresa, making it so obscure that even she might not guess what it meant. He did not sign his name, and no one in the house had ever seen his handwriting, so he figured it was safe letting Teresa know he was alive and well in this manner. He wrote: *Enjoying my new location, but miss seeing you at school. Hope all is well with you. All is well here. Change the world! F.*

He chose to sign an initial on the assumption it would make the note look less suspicious, say from some rather shy boy, and he used the letter *F* for "Freedom." The last line would probably cause Elspeth to interrogate Teresa, but he was sure she could handle it. He smiled as he dropped the card in the postbox and hoped that there was no unforeseen danger associated with such a whimsical gesture.

As he walked back, he noticed a jeweler's and on an impulse decided to go in. It was already shop-closing time, but when he rapped on the window, the owner came and opened the door for him. He looked into his wallet to see how much he had with him. It was a reasonable amount, and since this would be the last evening he could carry money, he decided it would not be unreasonable to spend it all. He perused the display cases. Most of the jewelry was gaudy and unappealing, but a fine silver chain with a solitary diamond centered in a setting of filigree shaped like a delicate and distant star caught his eye. It cost rather less than he had planned to spend, but it was the only piece of jewelry that he liked, and he imagined it would look beautiful on Zosia.

He gave the clerk the six thousand marks and asked if he would wrap it. The clerk asked to see his papers so he could note the transaction in his books. Peter frowned with annoyance—he had forgotten that expensive purchases were recorded for tax purposes. He handed over the papers and the clerk perused them; noting that he was married, the clerk asked, "Shall I send the invoice to your home or, uh, your office?"

Neither, of course, would do. Glancing nervously back at the other customer the clerk had let into the shop, Peter placed five hundred marks on the counter and said, "Just store it here for me."

The note disappeared and the clerk agreed, "Of course, *mein Herr.*"

Just as well, Peter thought, that so many Party officials have mistresses. Once outside the shop, he placed the small packet in his pocket. He would send it back with the uniform and pick it up later to give Zosia the gift at a more appropriate time. Then, realizing that he might not return, he decided to scribble a note on the wrapping paper to make sure Zosia knew it was for her, and if neither of them returned, that Marysia would save it to give to Joanna. There wasn't much room on the small package to write what was in essence a last will and testament, but he found space enough to tell them he loved them both.

When he returned to the pension, Zosia, her godparents, and Tadek were in the sitting room. Zosia greeted him warmly. She asked in German, "So does it run well?"

"No better than one might expect."

"Ah, I'm sorry you didn't discover anything useful."

"So am I. But what can one expect from a car? Certainly not miracles."

Tadek scowled. "Cut the crap. You were AWOL."

Peter shrugged. "When's dinner?" he asked in Polish, picking up a biscuit and chewing it thoughtfully.

"Now," Zosia's godmother said. "We were waiting for you."

"Sorry. I did not intend to take so long."

She smiled at him and shook her head at the suggestion that he had caused any problem at all. Clearly she and her husband had decided that he was Adam reincarnated, and they were quite willing to forgive the dead-returned-to-life almost any discourtesy. Peter wondered how Adam managed to be so well loved by so many people. Was it just a side effect of being dead? His question, at least in the case of Zosia's godparents, was answered later in the evening when the old woman drew him aside and said, "Zosia thinks highly of you and that's all that matters to us. I just thought you might want to know, she said many kind things about you. Take care of her—she trusts you, and she is very precious to us."

Peter, stunned, took a moment before he could construct an appropriate reply. Finally he managed to stammer, "I'll do my best."

26

*I*T WAS A WINDY and bitterly cold morning in Berlin. They had finished their preparations and now it was time to go. It was getting late, he should have been dressed long ago, but still Peter had trouble pulling the uniform on. Once he put it on, he was stuck—there would be no alternative for at least three days. His military uniform and the papers that went with it would be sent back separately to Neu Sandez, and until then he would be obliged to wear the uniform and carry the papers of a slave. And in a society that defined a person by their documents, that is what he would be. Again.

It was only an act, he told himself; just a role. It should be simple; all the difficult things had been done already. He had the metal band on his wrist, designed to look as solid as the real thing but more easily removed, and his numbers had been changed, but only with ink.

The familiar blue uniform lay on the bed waiting for him. He stared at it as though it were alive and he expected it to attack at any moment. The uniform was certainly in better shape than what he used to wear, but no more appealing. He remembered how much fuss it had taken to get Elspeth to replace his worn clothes. His old uniform had grown stained—mostly with his own blood—and torn and thin. He had tried to soak out the stains, had repaired the seams and patched the tears, but when the threadbare material of his shirt had worn so thin that nearly every move caused another rip, he had finally been forced to approach Elspeth with a request for new clothes. Of course she had grumbled that he had not taken enough care with his uniform, of course she moaned about the expense, and of course she told him to wait. So wait he did. Only when Frau Schindler made a rather snide comment about his unkempt appearance did Elspeth finally relent. So, even Frau Schindler had her uses.

The new uniforms were purchased from a supplier in the city—and, oh, how that had triggered yet another torrent of complaints about how much trouble and expense he caused! Then Peter had to carefully remove the shoulder patches from his original uniform and sew them securely onto his new. He remembered how Elspeth had inspected his work, carefully pulling at the edges to make sure they would not easily come off. Once that was done, the old clothes were returned to the supplier for recycling.

He shrugged off his thoughts, pulled on the uniform, and surveyed himself in the mirror. He no longer had that malnourished, terminally tired appearance, but otherwise he looked fairly convincing. Well, if anyone knew how to play this part, he did. He put on the jacket, stuck his papers in his pocket, and left the room. As he descended the steps of the pension, a young man and his girlfriend began to ascend. Without giving it even a thought, he backed out of their way. Once they were past, giggling at some private joke, he made his way to join the others waiting in the private dining room. They looked him up and down, Zosia's godparents with curiosity, Zosia with a smile of commiseration in her eyes, Tadek with a satisfied smirk.

Zosia took affectionate leave of her godparents, Tadek said his brief good-byes, but Peter found himself completely at a loss for words. Somehow, the old woman understood. She came up to him, took his hands in hers, and said, "You are one of us and our prayers will be with you. Go with God." She made the sign of the cross before him, then standing on tiptoe, she kissed him on the cheek.

The three of them made their way outside, Zosia and Tadek leading, Peter following, carrying the luggage. As they stepped onto the street, the January wind cut through the thin fabric of his jacket, and he looked with envy at the thick wool coats that the other two wore. Wordlessly, he opened the doors for them, loaded the luggage, and then lowered himself to inspect the undercarriage as he had done numerous times for Karl. Satisfied that there was no obvious danger, he climbed into the driver's seat to chauffeur them to their destination. Tadek, only half-jokingly, suggested he follow regulations and chain himself to the steering wheel. At that Peter allowed himself to step out of character, and military discipline, long enough to tell Tadek, in three different languages, to fuck himself, then he started the car and drove off.

As he drove, he glanced in the rearview mirror at Zosia and Tadek. Zosia had lightened her hair to the appropriate platinum blond and had pinned it back into a bun with two braids running along the side. She had also done something to make her hair smoother and the usual halo of frizz and disorganized curls were missing, making her look very tidy, very organized, very proper. They sat in stony silence, each staring out his or her respective window. Tadek's briefcase sat on the seat between them with Peter's computer safely tucked inside: Tadek would use it for transferring the data that Herr Müller was bringing and for other simple uses. To acquaint him with the basics of its use, Peter had tutored him for hours. Zosia had assured him that Tadek would never let personal animosity jeopardize any mission, but still Peter had been surprised by Tadek's attentiveness and cooperation.

The drive was slow. The roads were slippery, and a number of accidents brought traffic to a standstill. Once they were clear of Berlin's endless sprawl, they drove into a turnout, and Tadek and Zosia walked a few meters into the woods as if to get a breath of fresh air. As soon as they were out of sight of the road and the parked traffic, they were met by the group that had intercepted Herr Müller and were given the data that he had been carrying. They returned to the car, and sitting in the back, Tadek and Zosia spent some time looking it over while Peter waited outside, keeping a watch for any police or suspicious civilians. It was another bright day, and he sorely missed his sunglasses, but it was impossible for him to wear them at his present social rank. He breathed on his hands to try to warm them, then rubbed his eyes wearily, hoping to coax them into maintaining their focus for the rest of the drive, while wishing profoundly that his head would stop aching.

Zosia had already cooked up false data on Peter's computer in case there had been any complications with Herr Müller, but once she had a chance to peruse the real data, she decided they should dump theirs. "It's just too different," she stated despondently.

"Let's alter what you put on the computer to look more like this stuff," Tadek suggested.

"That'll take too long."

"But we shouldn't miss this chance to ruin their experiment."

"I don't think one set of cooked data is going to ruin their experiment, and it's just too risky to throw any old crap at them. Let's give them the real stuff—it'll make it easier for us to pass as legit."

"Why can't you alter your faked data?" Tadek asked.

"We just don't have that sort of time!"

"Then why don't you introduce spurious results into the real data?"

"I don't want to risk that—I can't tell if they've built in any checks. If they know we've tampered with this stuff, then we'll be screwed," Zosia explained.

"Surely you can do something?" Tadek insisted.

"Hey, if you want to be the expert, then you do it! Otherwise, keep your fucking computer illiterate mouth shut and let me make the decisions!"

Peter had listened to the debate from outside the car, and Zosia's voice had risen considerably during the interchange. He decided it was time to stop the argument, and besides, he was freezing. He went around to the driver's side, got in, and lied matter-of-factly, "We've got to push on. I've spotted trouble." The debate ended; Zosia deleted the false data as they headed west while Tadek sulked.

27

T HEIR ARRIVAL AT THE laboratory headquarters could not have gone better. Major Rattenhuber was a jovial host, well pleased to meet both the adjutant and his charming wife. He showed them to a well-appointed room in what had clearly once been a private mansion and indicated its various comforts to them: the lovely view, the fireplace, the comfortable furniture. As Peter set down the luggage, the major furrowed his brow in thought and then offered, "I could find separate, er, accommodations for your boy here. We didn't really expect . . ."

"Oh, heavens no!" Zosia crooned. "We wouldn't want to put you out, and anyway I want him here to be of help. Could you just locate a cot perhaps?"

"My pleasure!" The major rushed to the door, then stopped to consider something, drumming his fingers on his lips as he did so. He sighed, said, "Forgive me. It just occurred to me. There's no, er, facilities anywhere on this floor for him. Of course, you wouldn't want him using your bathroom—which is right through that door, by the way—and I'm afraid the nearest appropriate toilet is in the cellar. Unfortunately, the building isn't really secure, and he'll have to get a guard to accompany him on such, er, you know, occasions."

Zosia smiled her most perfect smile. "I'm sure it won't be a problem, Major."

"Well, then, if you don't mind . . ."

"We'll manage just fine."

"Good. Well, I'll be off then." Pausing only long enough to remind them when dinner was, the major then took his leave. Even as the three of them were sighing their relief, he popped his head back in to say, "I'll be sending an escort to bring you to dinner—you could get lost in this place without help! Isn't it just gorgeous!" And he disappeared again before they could answer.

Peter unpacked their cases, glad for something to do, while Zosia sat on the sofa and nervously tapped her foot against the coffee table. Tadek paced the room, suspiciously scanning the furniture, pictures, and drapes. When he had finished unpacking, Peter politely inquired if they wanted a drink. They both nodded, so he went to the bar and poured a portion of brandy into a glass. He drank it down in one quick gulp, then filled it and another for Zosia and Tadek.

The cot arrived and was set up, then they were left alone to relax. When Peter had traveled with Karl, he had always been at a loss for what to do at such times. Clearly, he could not relax, not with Karl in the room, yet there was little in the way of work that needed to be done in a hotel room. With Zosia and Tadek, it seemed even worse. He could, of course, sit in one of the chairs and read quietly since that would never be noticed by a possible undetected listener, but he did not want to step that far out of character; so instead, he went and stood by the window, pulling back the curtain to stare out at the countryside, thinking of what lay ahead, thinking of what lay behind.

There had been a particularly unpleasant trip with Karl once. Elspeth had not come along; Karl had made it clear she was not invited. For three days, Peter had spent his time a virtual prisoner of the hotel room. Each day had been tedious, but the nights were much worse. Karl spent each successive night out drinking. The first evening, he had come back sick-drunk and in dire need of help. Peter had greeted him at the door, helped him wriggle out of his clothes, washed Karl's face after he had puked, and washed himself and his clothes after Karl had vomited on him. He had cleaned the bathroom so it did not smell, and since Karl had insisted on vomiting into the sink, he had removed handfuls of undigested food from the clogged sink drain and flung them down the toilet in nauseated disgust. He had helped Karl into his pajamas, guided him into his bed, and helped his master in and out of that bed with each succeeding wave of *Korn*-inspired nausea. In the moments of peace in between, Peter had lain on the floor, at the foot of the bed, and had wrapped himself in a bit of sheet that hung over the edge.

On the second night, Karl had returned drunk again, but this time in the company of his conference buddies, who stayed and played cards late into the night. As he stared out the window of the château, Peter shied away from remembering exactly how long that night had lasted, exactly how much petty abuse had been meted out to him in the interests of humor and fun.

The third night had been the last. Karl had come back late and drunk again, this time grasping at a prostitute, who was, to judge by appearances, equally drunk. They had stumbled into the room giggling, then the prostitute had caught sight of him. She gasped her surprise and looked him up and down with undisguised curiosity. He took their coats and Karl maneuvered her to the bed and they began undressing. There was nowhere for Peter to retreat to, and he had stood uneasily staring out the window into the night, trying to ignore the sounds of their frenzied, drunken, grotesque attempts at sex.

When the woman got up to leave and was pulling on her clothes, Karl had called him over to the bedside. "Hey, you, *Fräulein*. Do it with him," Karl ordered, pointing at him.

The woman ceased struggling with her stockings and looked up in alarm. "Him?" she asked, trying to determine if she had misunderstood.

"Yeah. I want to see you two at it. Do it. Don't worry, I'll pay his costs." Then, turning to Peter, Karl had added, laughing, "There, now don't say I never give you anything! I mean, surely you want it, don't you?"

Peter felt his cheeks growing hot. Karl knew what would happen, knew he could then gloat at his obvious superiority and masculinity. Peter surveyed his options: blatant refusal and the attendant violent punishment, or a humiliating inability born of shame and the resultant denunciations of impotence and inferiority, which Karl would continually broadcast thereafter, or compliance and success and the knowledge that he had performed sex on command for his master's amusement.

The quandary had been nicely solved by the prostitute's appalled response. "I cannot do that! I am a good German, *mein Herr!*" she had declared, "and I will not violate the race laws in this manner!"

Karl had hesitated a moment, as if deciding whether to pursue his little theater, but then he had given in and said, "Good girl. That's what I wanted to hear. I respect and salute your purity."

Zosia said something to Tadek, which broke Peter's reverie, and he let the curtain drop back into place. He thought of the prostitute's kindness. She had given up good money and risked Karl's wrath to rescue him. Or, he wondered, had she meant what she had said? Had she viewed sex with him as akin to being asked to copulate with a dog? He would never know, he thought. And maybe it was better that way.

The seconds ticked by, the minutes slowly accumulated. Eventually, it was time for dinner; there was a light tap at the door, and a gangly young private indicated that he would escort them to the dining room. He seemed almost obsequious in his manners, but nevertheless balked at the idea of Peter being left behind in the room.

"I'm terribly sorry, ma'am, but this area is not secure. We can't just leave him here. If he doesn't accompany you to dinner, then he'll have to be locked up elsewhere."

Zosia and Tadek exchanged a look. "He'll come with us then," she said while Tadek glanced back at Peter and rolled his eyes. Peter did not know if Tadek was expressing exasperation at him or the rules, nor did he care.

The dinner was held in an ornate dining room with the major and his wife, and the mayor of the local village and his wife. A crystal chandelier sent splinters of light dancing around the room. The table was intricately carved and richly set with candles and china and silver. Heavy draperies muffled the noise of the howling wind and the pounding rain; the thick carpeting gave the room a warm, isolated atmosphere. Peter stood uneasily near a wall listening to the soft strains of music that came from the cleverly hidden speakers. Everything—from the drapes to the warmth to the music—reminded him of the *Kommandant,* and he shuddered with revulsion. He knew Zosia had thought she was defending his interests when she had insisted that he accompany them, but he would really have preferred to be elsewhere, anywhere else. As personal property, he was sure he would have been well treated, and he might have been able to engage his guard or some kitchen help in conversation. Now, he was stuck here, bored beyond belief, tortured by the smells of the food, watching everybody else eat as his own hunger gnawed at him.

The conversation covered the usual range of topics, and Peter forced himself to listen to everything the major had to say in order to learn as much as he could about the man's knowledge base. Several times during the evening, Zosia or Tadek subtly tried to turn the conversation to security or computers or codes, but the major was determinedly intent on his anecdotes and jokes and did not seem to notice their attempts. He talked at length about his experiences in England and about his musical interests, his family, and his dog. He seemed to have a wonderful time with his attentive guests, and he suggested that they have dinner together the following evening.

"That would be absolutely wonderful," Zosia replied, then looking at Tadek, asked, "Do you think we'll be back in time, dear?"

Tadek nodded. "I don't think my family expects that I'll be able to visit for very long. They understand that duty comes first. And I would certainly view it as a duty to enjoy another of your wonderful meals, Major!"

"Good, good! We'll be eating a bit later tomorrow, and there will be more guests as well—I'm sure you'll enjoy meeting them! Oh, it really is a bit hard having such a difficult job!" the major joked, and downed the last of his wine. "And speaking of work—we'll need to look at that data you brought tomorrow. I'll send someone around for you in the morning so that we can transfer it to my system."

"Yes, of course." Tadek smiled and nodded.

They relocated to the drawing room for after-dinner drinks, but Zosia, mercifully, pleaded fatigue and had Peter accompany her back to the room. Once they got there and had the door shut behind them, she groaned and kicked off her shoes and threw herself down on the couch in a display of exasperation. Peter waited until she looked up and then mimicked eating.

"Oh, yes, of course!" Zosia leapt up and went to the door, but no one was there. She went to the phone and tentatively picked up the receiver.

"Yes?" the operator inquired.

"Yes, this is Frau Müller. Could you send up some food for"—she squinted at Peter's frantic shaking of his head, nodded her comprehension, and finished, "me. I've grown hungry."

Once she had set the receiver down, she inquired with a look why she should not order food directly for him. Was he supposed to not eat? Peter mimicked his answer: "Yes, but it would be appalling food!" Zosia shrugged almost as if she didn't believe him, but let the subject drop. In any case, a hearty snack for her arrived a few minutes later, and he ate it gratefully in silence.

The following morning Tadek was called away to work with the major. Zosia was entertained by the major's wife, who planned to give, at her guest's request, an impromptu tour of the mansion. Peter and Zosia arrived in the main hallway at the appointed time and were greeted by Frau Rattenhuber. At the dinner the major's wife had eyed Peter up and down, and now she repeated this maneuver. Suddenly, without preamble, she spoke directly to him. "You speak German, don't you?"

"Of course, *gnädige Frau.*"

She scowled at his rudeness but did not comment. "I know that some of you don't understand very well—stupid I guess."

He did not respond.

"Do you understand me?"

"I understand, *gnädige Frau.*"

"My brother went out East, to where your people still are." She emphasized *still* as though this were an indication of some sort of failure. "He settled a farmstead out there."

Again Peter did not respond.

"Are you listening?"

"Yes, *gnädige Frau.*"

"Do you know what happened to him?"

"No, *gnädige Frau.*"

"He was murdered! By your people!"

"I'm sorry, *gnädige Frau.*"

"Don't give me that! You're all alike, you're all filthy swine. Murderers! He had three children! We should have destroyed each and every one of you when we had the chance."

Zosia shifted uneasily. "Are you sure it was the, er, natives?"

"Of course. It was a robbery attempt, as he was coming home. Who else could it have been? German resettlers would never do such a thing!" Frau Rattenhuber looked as though she were ready to spit on Peter.

"Of course not." Zosia smiled tightly.

Frau Rattenhuber turned to her, said, "I would never trust him in my house!"

Coolly, Zosia replied, "Oh, he's very well trained. Been with my family since he was a young child—completely trustworthy, loyal, and well behaved. We're very lucky to have him." Then, with a superior little toss of her head she added, "And besides, we're the master race. Certainly, *we* can handle *them.*"

"I suppose." Frau Rattenhuber shrugged and decided to change the subject. She indicated the pendant Zosia was fingering and commented, "That's an unusual piece of jewelry. I noticed you wore it last night as well."

"Yes, it was my poor, dear departed mother's. It reminds me of her and I'm never without it," Zosia confided with a rueful smile.

"Ah," Frau Rattenhuber agreed, then decided to add, "It's lovely. I see it matches your ring."

Zosia held up her hand so her heavy silver ring with its black stone was more visible. "Yes, it's a set."

"Charming. But come now, I'll show you the house. It came into government hands in 1936. Before that it belonged to a merchant, I've forgotten his name . . ." she droned on as she led them through the vast halls past the portraits of political figures and into the dining room.

"Phew, I can't believe I didn't belt her one!" Zosia exclaimed. They had driven away from the mansion on their planned visit to see relatives. En route they had stopped in a village to eat, and then they had decided to take a stroll in the local cemetery.

They maintained a sensible order: Zosia and Tadek hand in hand walking in front, Peter walking deferentially behind, but there was no one within earshot and Zosia had angrily relayed the story of Frau Rattenhuber to Tadek.

"But if she lost her brother, you can understand why she is so upset," Tadek suggested diplomatically.

"Understand? *Understand?* What the hell was he doing there in the first place! He knew that he was settling land that belonged to someone else, someone who had almost surely been murdered to make way for him."

"Perhaps he didn't know. Perhaps she doesn't know."

"Well, she should! And she's so sure that it wasn't his own compatriots! How could she know that!"

"You must admit, the chances are if he was deaded, it was by one of ours."

"And damn right, too!" Zosia exclaimed.

"But what if it really was only robbery, would you approve of murder then?"

"If it gets the job done."

"You know, if he wasn't specifically targeted, then his murder accomplishes nothing except to promote hatred," Tadek argued coolly.

"She didn't care about specifically targeting anyone—murder them all, she said!"

"But she does not define us," Tadek reminded her.

"No, but she defines them! We ought to murder all of them!" Zosia retorted.

"Zosiu," Tadek soothed. He said something to her in Polish that Peter could not understand. She nodded, replied quietly, and then sobbed slightly. Peter watched with growing jealousy as Tadek put his arm around her and held her as she cried. He had realized long ago that Tadek carried a torch for Zosia and that only his sense of decency had kept him from revealing his feelings immediately after Adam's death. And then it had been too late—Peter had stumbled into Zosia's life and destroyed everything. No wonder Tadek hated him. That was understandable, even forgivable, but what truly hurt was watching how close Zosia was to Tadek, how she held on to him, how she took comfort in his words, in his ability to speak her language fluently, in their shared history. And in their common belief in a God.

As they skirted around a small chapel, Peter fell back a few steps so they could have a bit of privacy. His eyes danced from gravestone to gravestone, each with its flowers and weeds, each with a name that was important to someone but meant nothing to him. The barren, rain-soaked limbs of willows and chestnuts arched gloomily overhead. He so much wanted to hold Zosia and comfort her that his arms ached with the effort of restraint. He replayed the words in his head that Tadek had said to her. He had not heard it clearly, and the wording had been too complex for him to understand, but he thought he recognized at least one word—the word for God. Had it been a prayer? Or had Tadek simply comforted her with some trite religious reassurance?

The sodden ground sucked at Peter's feet as if trying to put even more distance between him and Zosia. He felt ashamed of himself. If what Tadek had said had comforted Zosia, wasn't that enough? Didn't that, in itself, prove that it wasn't trite? Was it only jealousy of Tadek that had led him to think that, or was it his own inability to understand what it was they both believed? On the rare occasions he felt that there was a God, it was only because he thought he had heard a mocking laughter from the heavens.

Zosia would have rejected that outright. She was no stranger to misfortune, she was not blind to the troubles that beset the world, and she was not naive. No, she did not believe that God would magically intervene and remove all pain, but she also did not believe in a God that enjoyed the suffering of creation. He had once suggested to her that God must enjoy suffering, since the world had been set up in such a way that it seemed to lead to nothing but misery, but she had shaken her head vigorously at that and had gone on to expound upon the gift of free will and the constraints that it would place on even a deity. He had then asked about the constraints her Catholicism placed on her. She had laughed and given him a little speech about just wars and Saint Augustine, then added that since she wasn't in any case particularly dogmatic, it was irrelevant to her what the "old farts" in the Vatican said. They had, she said, quite clearly abrogated all rights to spiritual leadership of her church when they had been so accommodating in the face of Nazism and had so completely abandoned her people, all of them—gentile and Jew alike, she emphasized—to their cruel fate. The conversation had been marvelously freewheeling, influenced, not a little, by a blackberry-flavored vodka, and now he regretted that he had never seriously pursued her line of thought.

Zosia stopped and, detaching herself from Tadek, wiped away her tears. She noticed that Peter had fallen back out of earshot, and she waited for him to catch up, then, speaking German so that she could be sure he understood, she said, "I'm sorry about that. Sometimes, I just get . . ." She shook her head slightly. "I just get, you know, upset." She glanced up at the sky, at the lowering clouds, then down at the drizzle that had accumulated on her shoulder. She brushed the drops off her coat and sighed. "I guess it's about time we get down to business."

28

THAT EVENING THEY all attended the major's little dinner party. Of course, they were there in different roles, and Peter stood unobtrusively near a wall while Zosia and Tadek ate and drank and laughed and joked. The obnoxious little mayor and his wife were there again, and some local Party officials and their wives as well. Having seen Peter the night before, the mayor had managed to bring a member of his personal staff to stand in wait as well. The young woman stood near Peter, perplexed as to exactly what her function at the gathering was. They did not talk to each other or even look in each other's direction; they stood bored and hungry, keeping their silence and their thoughts to themselves.

Eventually all the innumerable courses had been served, the multitude of wines tasted and the after-dinner brandy consumed. The hostess suggested they all retire to the drawing room for further drinks and chocolates and the guests gladly complied. All but Zosia. She confessed to having drunk more than she was used to and asked the forgiveness of her hosts as she made her way, woozy and flustered, out of the room.

Initially Tadek made to accompany her, but she assured him with expansive words and gestures that her boy would be sufficient to see her back to the room, and that Tadek should stay and enjoy himself as long as he wished. He, protesting ever so slightly, eventually consented, and she staggered genteelly out of the room, rejecting the idea of hanging on to the arm that her servant offered, but clinging instead to the cloth of his shirt for support, apparently convinced, as were the other guests, that this was proper etiquette.

Only when they were back in the room did she lose her stagger. Quickly and without exchanging a word, they assembled their equipment into her generous handbag. Zosia opened the door and peered out—all was quiet. She motioned to Peter, and together they slipped down the hall to the stairs. They descended quietly down one flight, past the merrymakers starting yet another round of drinks and beginning to sing good German *Lieder*, down another flight and into a hallway. They passed the kitchen with its overworked staff struggling to prepare the next set of snacks and drinks while cleaning the dishes from dinner, slid down a corridor, and then pressed themselves into a doorway to wait for the guard to do his rounds.

The door they were aiming for was in a short hallway, just around the corner: the hallway formed a part of a long complex that a single private patrolled. He paced his round methodically: down the short corridor, turn a corner, down a long corridor that was out of sight of the door they needed to get through, turn again, down another longish corridor, turn around and walk back. Tadek had observed and reported on the routine, and they had debated the merits of knocking the guard out, but decided that since the guard was changed every two hours, an unobserved intrusion would give them the greatest amount of time to do their work. No bodies, no missing guards, no questions. So now Peter and Zosia pulled out a stopwatch and timed his rounds.

Peter nodded at her. From the description of the lock that Tadek had given them, Peter felt he could easily open the door before they were detected. Zosia nodded in return. Together they listened to the private's steps. As he left the near corridor and turned the corner, they sprinted into action. Silently, they entered the little hallway and Peter dropped down in front of the lock. Zosia stationed herself nearby, handing him his tools and watching the stopwatch.

Peter worked feverishly. As he heard the private's precise footsteps enter the distant corridor, the lock gave way. He dropped the duplicate keys and tools into Zosia's bag and was ready to turn the handle when they heard footsteps approaching from the way they had originally come—they were trapped between the approaching footsteps and the pacing guard! Peter stepped back from the door and looked up in time to see a young private rounding the corner. He glanced quickly behind himself and realized that Zosia, with all the damning equipment and the computer, had disappeared. She must have ducked into the long corridor, but there were only seconds before the guard on duty would be turning into that very same hallway and he could not fail to see her.

Knowing he only had seconds to clear the way for her, Peter strolled brazenly past the young man and around the corner leading back to the kitchen. The surprised private watched him as he walked by, his mouth gaping in surprise. After all these months of boring guard duty, finally, something had happened when he wasn't even patrolling! Peter had smiled so casually at him that it took him a moment to remember to pursue him down the hall. He raised his gun, pointing it at Peter's back, and demanded, "Stop! Hands up!"

Peter complied, turned to face the boy, and volunteered cheerfully, "I'm sorry! I seem to have stumbled down the wrong corridor. Could you tell me where the drawing room is?"

"What are you doing here?"

"I guess I'm lost. I was looking for the major's party." Peter noticed the gun was shaking in the boy's hand.

The boy stepped backward so he could glance back down the hall Peter had been in. Nothing there, nothing at all. He heard the guard's precise steps approaching, and he waited until his comrade was in sight before he asked him, "Have you seen this fellow here before?"

"Who?" The guard was nonplussed. "What's up?"

"I found this boy skulking around here."

"I was lost," Peter amended patiently as the guard broke his precise routine to peer around the corner into the section of the house that was not on his route.

"Nope, never seen him."

"I said, I was looking for the major's party. I was sent with a message," Peter repeated helpfully.

"Hmm." The guard seemed somewhat less excited than his young colleague—perhaps because he had not spotted the intruder himself. "Take him upstairs and check his story. They're all in the dining room, or the drawing room," he suggested, then realizing he had left his route unguarded for seconds longer than usual, he turned precisely on his heel and strode back along his well-worn path.

The two of them climbed the stairs together: Peter leading the way, his hands held somewhat lazily in the air at shoulder height, and the young private, his hands slippery with sweat, holding his pistol pointed at his prisoner's back. He was less afraid of what his prisoner might do than what his superiors might do to him if they objected to this intrusion. He swore quietly to himself with frustration. What was a guy supposed to do? If you ignore something, they might court-martial you; if you see it, they yell at you for interrupting their party and being stupid and obtrusive.

Once they reached the ground floor, the sounds of the party were unmistakable. The noise strained the credibility of Peter's alibi, but the soldier seemed too nervous to notice. Peter also assumed an air of trepidation appropriate to the situation. It was only in part faked—at this point he was completely dependent on Tadek's playing his role flawlessly, and that thought caused him some consternation.

They followed the sound of the revelers past the dining room and to the drawing room. The private had Peter stop at the large, open French doors and stood anxiously waiting for someone to notice him. Eventually, one of the ladies tapped Major Rattenhuber on the shoulder, and raising his eyebrows in query, he wandered over to see what the problem was.

Most of the party had, by this time, taken notice of the pair and fallen into a curious silence. Tadek looked up from the woman he was chatting with—the mayor's wife—and for one unguarded moment a look of panic flashed across his face as he saw Peter but not Zosia. But then he took control, excused himself from the mayor's wife, and went to join the little group by the door.

As he approached, the major turned from the private, who had obviously just explained the circumstances, to ask Peter, "What were you doing down there?"

"I was looking for Herr Müller. Frau Müller sent me."

"Downstairs?"

"Yes, *mein Herr.* I lost my way."

The major seemed poised to pursue this line of questioning, but Tadek interrupted with alcohol-inspired rage, "Lost? Lost!" He raised his hand and theatrically slapped Peter hard across the face, fuming loudly, "You simpleton! Can't you do anything right!"

Then regaining control of his temper, he turned to the major and explained apologetically, "You know, he's always screwing up. Doesn't listen. Doesn't pay attention. Too stupid to get anything right." Tadek threw an angry, frustrated glance at Peter and continued in his conciliatory manner, "If I had my way, I'd . . . But my wife, you know, he's been with her family for years . . ." Tadek sighed, exasperated.

The major smiled indulgently. "Say no more—I know exactly what you mean. The simplest instructions . . ." He finished the sentence by shaking his head and hands simultaneously.

"Sorry for the disturbance," Tadek added. "I hope he hasn't perturbed your guests." He threw a glance back at the interested onlookers.

The major caught his meaning and nodded. "Please don't apologize. No problem, no problem at all, but I should get back to my hosting duties. You seem to have the situation well under control—I'll leave you to sort it out." With that, the major returned, smiling, to his guests, and soon a polite buzz of conversation indicated that Tadek and Peter were no longer the center of attention.

With a terse "Well done" and a nod of his head Tadek dismissed the now somewhat disappointed private. The lad holstered his pistol, clicked his heels, and gave a slight bow before he marched off. They had not even bothered to note his name. Well done, indeed—the self-centered, drunk bastards!

Tadek watched him for a moment, then with his back still toward the room, he mouthed, *Zosia?*

Safe, Peter indicated more with his eyes than his lips. He was not sure that it was true, but he could not afford to explain: he was still facing the party and he could see that many of the guests were carrying on the sort of one-ear, one-eye conversations that indicated they had not entirely lost interest in what was happening by the door.

Tadek then surprised Peter by asking, very quietly, "Did I hurt you?"

Peter shook his head slightly.

Without missing a beat, Tadek began to speak loudly, slowly, and simply, as if to a moron. "Now what did Frau Müller want?"

Peter, fidgeting nervously, explained in his heavily accented German that Frau Müller had wanted to know if she should remain awake or if she should retire for the night.

"Oh, I'll probably be late—tell her to go to sleep."

"Yes, *mein Herr.*" Peter hesitated slightly, then added timidly, "And should I wait up?"

"Of course, you idiot!" Tadek held his hand to his head and shook his head in annoyed disbelief. "What do you think you're here for?"

"Forgive me, *mein Herr.*"

"Idiot," Tadek snorted. He was ready to send Peter away when the major approached them. Tadek looked mildly surprised. "Major?"

"I'm sorry to bother you, it's just that he shouldn't be out unescorted—this place is a little understaffed and we don't patrol the main house. Let me call someone—"

"Oh, no. Don't do that. That won't be necessary. I want to have a word with my wife directly anyway—before she goes to sleep. I'll take him upstairs and then I can remind her not to send him on errands without an escort. I'm sure it'd be better coming from me."

"If you don't mind."

"Of course not. All this fuss is my fault in any case."

"Nonsense, it's been a pleasant little diversion!" The major dropped his voice conspiratorially and added, "It gave me an excuse to get away from that obnoxious little mayor! God what a bore!" The major made a dismissive gesture with his hands and added, "I really should get hazard pay for the sort of conversations I have to put up with—I'm in danger of death by boredom!"

"Ah, but your hospitality has been most wonderful!"

"Well, yes, but you have no idea of the incompetents I have to deal with. Why, just the other day . . ." The major rolled his eyes in contemplation and took a deep breath in preparation of a long story.

Tadek interjected quickly, "Well, if you'll excuse me." And grabbing Peter by the arm, he steered him toward the steps.

Back in the room, they stepped into the bathroom, ran the water, and Peter quietly explained what had happened. "I think," he concluded, "Zosia is inside the office. I think she slipped in while I was walking away from the private and before the guard rounded the corner."

"Thank God!" Tadek closed his eyes. The sudden torrent of fear and now relief had left him thoroughly drained. "What do you think I should do?"

Again, Peter was surprised by the question. He considered for a moment, then answered, "Escort me to the cellar. If we're noticed, say we're heading to that toilet the major described. Then, once I'm inside the office, I think it's best for you to return to the party. You can keep an eye on things from there and perhaps preempt any further difficulties."

Tadek nodded. He had tried to limit his alcohol intake during the evening, but it was difficult to get visibly drunk without drinking—especially at dinner where everybody could watch if one's wineglasses and cordial glasses were emptied. Now with all the tension and fear of the past few minutes, the alcohol that he had consumed—little as it was—made him feel woozy and a bit ill. He wished Peter luck and told him to wish Zosia luck as well, then they left the room together in silence.

They reached the hall near the office without incident. As the guard's steps faded down the long corridor, Peter indicated that Tadek should wait to see if he got in, then head back upstairs. Peter slipped around the corner, turned the handle, and slid into the soft glow of the dimly lit data room. He glanced behind him: as he expected, Zosia was waiting, her little lead cudgel in one hand, her gun in the other. She looked like a very huggable thug. He grinned at her and they giggled silently for a moment.

He gestured to the room around them questioningly.

"Yeah, I swept it," she whispered. She removed a small case from her bag and showed him the three separate devices tucked inside the soundproof cocoon. Two of the devices looked similar; one looked fairly ancient—it even had wire leads.

"Have you got into any files yet?" Peter asked as he slipped on the thin, skintight gloves that Zosia handed him.

"First tell me, what happened to you?"

Peter smiled at her unprofessional curiosity. He began explaining, but she interrupted, "He hit you!" Her whisper had turned into an angry hiss.

"Yes. I thought it was a good call."

"There was no need for that!"

"Really, it's okay—it seemed to work. It diverted the major's attention from questioning me or seeking you out."

"Well, if you think so."

He finished his story quickly, then asked again, "Have you made any progress?"

"Yeah. Good news and bad."

"What?"

"Well, he didn't do much to protect local access. It took me only a few minutes to use that terminal there." She indicated the source of the dim glow. "The major's ID is his name—how very original—and his password is, get this, Pikkadilly—his dog's name. It's spelled with two *k*'s by the way."

"How did you work that out so quickly?"

"Well, usually I try something patriotic first, but the major didn't seem the type. Dogs are a favorite next guess. He fouled me up with the spelling, but then I remembered seeing the name of his horse on its portrait—that was Kovent Garten—also spelled with a *k*."

"You're a bloody genius!"

"I know." She smiled. "Of course, he was very kind to be so predictable. But at least he didn't write it all on a little note taped to the back of the computer."

Peter gave a short laugh at the image.

"Don't laugh—I've actually seen that more than once."

Peter nodded in silent agreement. It was true: one could usually count on a certain level of incompetence or overconfidence, and in a society where so much was considered secret, there was always carelessness caused by the security overload. If nearly everything was classified, then it was hard to treat genuinely sensitive information seriously.

"Now," Zosia said, "for the bad news."

"You can't find the files?"

"Oh, they're there all right. They seem to be encrypted."

"So? We can sort them out later. You don't need me! Just copy them and we'll get out of here." His relief was palpable.

"Me and whose truck?"

"What do you mean?"

She motioned him to a small door and opened it. Inside was a room filled by a full-size, old-fashioned computer. "That terminal accesses this monster. It may be slow and stupid—but it's big. I've estimated the size of the files, and we couldn't get even twenty percent of the data onto ours."

"But we don't need all the data! Just the theory and conclusions. You know, chemical formulas, effectiveness . . .'"

"And how are we going to tell where that is?" she responded with exaggerated patience.

"I guess you're telling me he hasn't neatly labeled a file 'Formulas and Effectiveness,' subtitled, 'This is the one you want to steal.'"

"Well, if he has—I can't read it."

"So we've got to break the code just to know which files to copy."

"You've got it in one. It's worse than that, though. The files are copy-protected so we can't even steal them at random—we'd have to pack up that entire machine! Anyway, we can read the files on the screen, but it's all coded, so it's just gibberish. I think this operating system is so old it doesn't have its own built-in security, so the major just jury-rigged something. Or maybe this is Schindler's way of avoiding too many people at the RSHA from finding out about what his little laboratory is up to."

Peter swore quietly. He chewed his thumb for a moment. "Maybe it's not so bad. If he's left them in a readable state, it's probably because that's necessary to decode them, which would mean the decoding program should be on this machine as well. Once that is run, it probably removes the copy protection so that the major could pass the information on to authorized parties."

He wandered into the little room, looked at a few manuals lying around, read any labels he could find. Nothing, nothing but numbers. Not even suggestive numbers. Meanwhile Zosia was scanning around as well. She circled the beast, inspected various bits in the hope that there would be something tangible they could use, but there was nothing. Peter looked at her. She shrugged in reply, and they left the room and went to the terminal on the major's desk.

"I guess getting into his file is the best we can hope for," she said as she sat down at the desk.

"Do you know much about the sort of computer that is?"

She shook her head. "Not much. It's old. I wouldn't have been surprised to see a card-reader."

"I'm surprised a lab this important doesn't merit better equipment," Peter said, leaning over her shoulder and looking at the incomprehensible strings of numbers, letters, and symbols that were appearing on the screen as Zosia tried various commands.

"Oh, it's not at all unusual. The government pours money into various technological pet projects, and they achieve occasional peaks of performance. That, and industrial espionage, carry them a long way, but the economy just can't produce the goods. As soon as you take a step away from these monumental triumphs, everything else seems to be in a state of near collapse. But then what do you expect? Slave labor may well be cheap, but it's hardly reliable or loyal." She interrupted herself to lean forward and peer at something on the screen. Deciding it was useless, she continued her typing and her monologue. "One can hardly expect cooperation from the labor force, nor innovation. Corruption is rampant and industrial sabotage . . ." She paused again to look at something, leaned back, and continued hacking. "You worked in industry for a while, didn't you?"

"Yes." He did not want to hear the question he knew she was going to ask.

"Did you sabotage anything?"

"No," he sighed. "I would have, I just didn't see any opportunities. At least none that would have left me alive at the end of it."

Zosia fell silent. She looked intent on what she was doing, but he felt sure she was simply trying not to indicate how disappointed she was in him. He paced away from the screen, looked contemplatively at the books on the major's shelves. He did not even know what they were looking for or what Zosia was attempting to do, but he wasn't surprised to hear her say somewhat indignantly, "Can't you at least watch the screen?"

He returned to his position behind her chair and leaned forward, resting his arms on the back of the chair so his head was just above hers and he could clearly see the screen. But he did not watch it; instead his eyes strayed around the room. Then, suddenly, something he saw out of the corner of his eye on the screen caught his attention.

"Wait!"

"What?"

"What was that?"

"Which?"

"What have you been doing?" he asked.

"I've been opening files and listing the first hundred lines, hoping we'd see something recognizable."

"Oh."

"Well, you didn't seem to have any better ideas," Zosia explained.

"No, I mean, yes. But I thought I saw something. About three or four screens back."

"I'll repeat the last several files."

She typed a few commands and Peter watched closely. "There! Stop!" She hit a key and the screen froze. Peter peered at it silently for several moments. Zosia turned from the screen to look at him, raising her eyebrows in query.

"I think," he said, releasing his words slowly as if speaking quickly might destroy a spell, "this might be the algorithm for encrypting the documents."

"So we can run it backwards?"

"More likely, it decodes them as well, or there's a similar program that does the job. After all, we can hardly expect the major to decipher each file by hand every time he wants to read something. Run it forward a bit—just a few lines."

Together they studied the program; it was written in an outmoded language that had been specifically designed for military purposes by the German government. Though he was unfamiliar with the programming language, it was similar enough in structure to ones he knew that he could guess most of it, and Zosia explained the rest.

"I think that's it—see those lines there? I think all we have to do is call this program and it will decipher the files for us," he concluded. He and Zosia had exchanged places—now he was sitting at the terminal and she was leaning over reading from above.

"Great!" Zosia exclaimed in a whisper.

"Not really."

"Why?"

"It'll ask us for a password," he replied despondently.

"I can start guessing at the password, while you try other, more rational approaches," she offered hopefully.

"I think it's worse than that. The password is cross-referenced to the file that has been called."

"But there are hundreds!"

"I know," he responded.

"Well, how can the major remember hundreds of passwords?"

"Presumably there is some method to them. I suppose they could all be the same, but I think it's more likely they can be generated somehow using information contained in the file names. Some sort of mnemonic." He sighed heavily, bent his head forward, and rubbed his neck. Already his eyes were bothering him, and he had not eaten since lunch.

Zosia gently pushed his hand aside and gave him a massage. "Are you hungry?" she asked as she soothed the pain in his muscles.

"Yeah. I wish I had eaten something. Idiotic planning on my part."

"Ah, but you didn't contend with my superb organizational abilities." With that, she continued the massage with one hand while reaching with the other into her bag. After rooting around a bit, the hand reemerged holding a wrapped sandwich.

"You are a genius!" he declared, reaching for it.

She pulled it away. "Uh-uh-uh. Not until you say I'm a superb cook as well!"

He laughed. "Have I ever said otherwise?"

"Say it!"

"Ah, but it is so obvious. The chefs of the world sing your praises! You are a culinary genius beyond compare!" He lunged for the sandwich and managed to snatch it from her grasp.

She giggled quietly.

"Look at that," he said between bites, pointing to a line on the screen.

"What about it?"

"Well, I don't understand the formatting. Is it a number or more general?"

"Could be anything. Is that where the program accepts the password?"

"Yeah."

"Should we run an iterative routine?"

Peter shut his eyes and did a quick mental calculation. He shook his head. "We don't have time."

They fell into silence. Zosia studied the screen along with Peter, but she saw nothing of interest. She turned her attention to him as he sat mesmerized by the lines of program displayed before him. He held the last of his sandwich in his hand, near his mouth, as if preparing to take a bite, but he did not move. After a long moment she asked, "What is it?"

"I think I know what he's doing," he said, almost as if speaking to himself.

"Really? Can I help? What should I do?"

He did not seem to hear her. She looked back at the screen, wondering what it was he saw there.

"I need my computer," he said suddenly. "And the data that we gave the major this morning."

She pulled his computer out of her capacious bag and helped him set it up, next to the major's terminal.

"Now what?" she asked. A tingle of excitement crept through her, she felt so alive!

"Give me time," he answered, shoving the last bite of his sandwich into his mouth. "Just give me some time."

Zosia took up a position in the armchair and waited. Her relaxed attitude quite effectively hid that she was guarding the door—her ears keenly tuned to any approaching sound, her gun and cudgel resting at the ready in her hands, on her lap. She watched Peter as she waited. She noticed how he was thoroughly engrossed in his work, how his eyes scanned back and forth between the two screens with an intensity that excluded the rest of the world. She realized as she waited, guarding the door, that she was the only one who would notice an intrusion quickly enough to prevent disaster. And she acknowledged, for the first time, that she would be devastated if something happened to him.

The strangely mixed dark and blond of his hair, the graceful way he carried himself, his wicked sense of humor, his intelligence, strength, and gentleness—these reminded her of Adam. Yet, there was so much else, so much that was different. Like Adam, yet not like him. Maybe like a ghost of Adam returned from the dead, traumatized and changed by a vision of hell. The moods, the sudden frowns of pain, the distant looks followed by his brief, elusive smile as he noticed her looking at him, the trapped look in his eyes after one of his nightmares. She wondered what he had been like before the camp, before the *Kommandant*, before the torture and beatings and slavery. Was his smile less fleeting then?

As if from a dream Peter looked up at her. "I have a password," he said quietly. He sounded exhausted. She leapt up and came to look. On a sheet of paper he had scribbled a number. "When you type this in at the prompt, the program decodes our data file and removes the copy protection."

"Wonderful! How's it work?"

"This number initiates the generation of pseudorandom numbers that are used as a one-time pad for encoding and decoding the relevant document. Put in the wrong password, and you get a different number so the decoding becomes meaningless."

"Did you try the same number for the other files?"

"No, not yet. It's worth a try but I don't expect it will work." He ran the program, entered the name of a different file and the same password. As expected the resultant output was useless.

"It didn't work," he said, stating the obvious.

She looked at her watch, suggested that he rest a few minutes, and sat down to try various permutations of the password on a test file. Peter sat for a moment, listened as Zosia swore quietly every time the screen filled with gibberish. Then he began pacing the room again. One matched set. They had one matched set. A file name, written as a number, and a password—also a number. He mentally toyed with the pair, trying to match letters to the numbers to see if he could invent appropriate words. None of his naive attempts worked. He continued roaming the room. One matched set. How could one generalize anything from that? He returned to the desk and started unlocking the drawers and rummaging through them.

"What are you doing?" Zosia asked as he shuffled through papers.

"Looking for a list. If there's no mnemonic, then there must be a list."

"Fair enough. But the major might not keep it here."

"Well, if he doesn't, then we're screwed. Any luck?"

"You would have heard." Zosia turned her attention back to the screen and tried to ignore Peter poking around underfoot as he struggled to open the lock that held the bottom drawer shut. Suddenly he managed to pull it open with a loud clang. She winced and glanced at the door. Was the guard near enough to hear that? They both froze, waiting, but there was no sound outside.

Peter sighed miserably. Other than for a broken pencil, the drawer was empty.

"Maybe he didn't use it because the lock was broken," Zosia suggested humorously.

"Probably. Well, we can always charge him for fixing his desk." Peter rose to his feet, paced the room some more, and stopped in front of the bookshelf. "Zosia, remind me. What did the major talk about at dinner?"

"Himself," Zosia answered sarcastically. She stopped her futile attempts at the keyboard and, pursing her lips, added, somewhat more helpfully, "Dogs, horses, politics, music . . ."

"Not music," Peter corrected, "musical instruments."

"Ah, yes, the domineering father who pushed him into the military and cut short his brilliant career in . . . What are you doing?" Zosia asked as Peter suddenly moved forward and scaled the bookshelf. He stood with his head above the top shelf and peered downward.

"Looking for dust. Or rather, the lack of it." He climbed back down and pulled out two books.

"What's up?"

He turned to her, holding a book in each hand. His smile was so triumphant, she grinned in response, not even knowing why she was so happy.

"What do you have?" she asked.

"An acoustics book and math tables," he said with a laugh. "Our poor major couldn't bear not leaving his signature on his masterpiece."

"I don't understand."

"The solutions to the equations in this book"—he shook the acoustics book—"are tabulated in a book like this." He waved the math tables. "Get it? Something the major is keenly interested in, translated into a nice series of random-looking, but well-matched numbers."

"His list of passwords," Zosia sighed. She eyed the large tome Peter was holding and said, "I don't want to sound discouraging, but even if you are right, will we have time to work through all the possibilities in that book? How many pages are there?"

"Twelve hundred," Peter answered as he flipped to the back of the book.

"Even with a computer, that's a lot of trial and error. We have a shitload of files to check out, and we really don't have much time left."

"I'll do it faster than trial and error," he assured her, as he sat down in the armchair. "The sorts of equations you use for dealing with musical instruments will narrow down which tables to look at—and when I find a pair that matches our password and its file, then we'll have the list. I guarantee it."

Zosia bit her lip, worried by his confidence, but within fifteen minutes, he proudly presented her with a page of the book. "Try it," he said. "Match the fourth, fifth, and sixth digit of the file name to this column, and the password is here, backwards, in this column."

Zosia grimaced, selected one of the file names off the computer, matched the name to the appropriate password, entered both into the decoding program, and waited.

Results spilled out on the screen. Fertility data for sheep in Denmark before and after treatment.

Zosia stared at the screen, utterly stunned. "You did it!" she whispered. "You did it!"

"Is there a file zero zero zero?"

"No, unfortunately the numbers don't seem to be sequential. Files older than ours have higher numbers. And lots of numbers are missing."

"Damn. That means we've got to examine each one by hand until we find the most useful information."

"I'm afraid so. I'll start by looking at size and date, and maybe we can pick out the most relevant stuff that way. Why don't you guard the door," she said, pushing her gun and cudgel in his direction.

It took Zosia ages to work her way through the files, and still she found nothing of significance. He tried to relieve her from the tedious work, but his eyes were failing him, and they quickly gave up on that idea. So instead he sat guarding the door, listening to the sound of the sentry's footsteps—more a thud than a click from this one—as they came and went back and forth, again and again.

Zosia continued her scanning and copied several relevant files. He glanced at the clock; they did not have much more time. To have come this far and leave essentially empty-handed! He sighed.

"Don't sigh, boychick, I've found what we need."

"You have?"

"Yes, I've been quietly copying it for the last five minutes."

"Oh, thank God!"

"Or whomever," she teased, reminding him of his own favorite reply to her constant use of that phrase.

A short while later she stood up and groaned. She pressed the lid of his computer shut and shut down the major's terminal. "Done," she announced, her voice hoarse with fatigue. "I suppose if the major is really observant, he'll note that somebody was using his computer, but somehow, he doesn't strike me as the observant type. Anyway, they'll work it out soon enough when the adjutant turns up missing."

They reorganized the desk, checked that the furniture and the books and everything else was exactly as they had found it, then slipped out of the office and back upstairs. Entering their room quietly, they greeted Tadek silently as he emerged from the shadows, nodding to him to let him know that all had gone well. He sat down on the sofa and let out a loud sigh of relief.

29

ZOSIA WAS UTTERLY exhausted from the long hours she had spent inspecting the files and the constant fear of discovery; without saying anything at all, she used the toilet, then returned to the room to slip out of all her evening clothes. Both Tadek and Peter found themselves turning away uneasily so that each would not see the other looking at her. She seemed oblivious to both of them; after a lifetime of enforced closeness in the encampment, it had not even occurred to her to seek privacy.

Tadek gave Peter an unreadable look, removed his clothes—he also had not changed out of the uniform he had worn the previous evening—and slid into the luxurious double bed next to Zosia. Though Zosia's soft breathing told them both she was already asleep, Tadek rolled next to her and wrapped his arm around her to keep her warm and safe.

Peter grimaced. Leave it to the major to have rooms furnished, somewhat unusually, with double beds. And of course, since Tadek and Zosia were playing the role of husband and wife, what would be more natural than the two of them snuggling together in the same bed? Without bothering to undress—what was the point, he'd be wearing the same thing in an hour—Peter lay across his cot and stared at the ceiling. They had placed his cot near the door, out of sight of the bed, but he could still hear the two of them breathing deeply. He was tired, but sleep eluded him. Finally, he got up and went and sat on the sofa. From there, he could watch Tadek and Zosia sleeping and could torment himself with his jealousy more effectively.

After about an hour or so, he got up from the couch and went to splash some water on his face and shave; then he went over to the bed to wake them both up. He knew they would want to be dressed and ready to leave as soon as possible after breakfast, but somehow, as he watched the covers rise and fall with their breathing, he found himself unable to disturb them. As he stood there watching, Tadek opened his eyes and looked accusingly up at him.

"What are you doing?"

"I was just coming to wake you up, *mein Herr.* Breakfast will be here soon."

"Oh, all right." Tadek nudged Zosia. "Time to get up, darling."

She rolled over and mumbled something incoherent. Finally her eyes fluttered open and she looked at Tadek. "What is it?" she asked sleepily.

"Time to get up, *gnädige Frau*," Peter said flatly, and walked away to get her robe. He dropped it on the bed wordlessly and went to stand with his back to them by the window. He felt embarrassed by his churlishness and wondered at the intensity of his feelings. He remembered the first night he had spent with Zosia—how she had fallen asleep on his shoulder, and he remembered Tadek's bitter words of reproof. Now he felt like saying something similar, but recognized immediately not only that his words would have no effect, but that they would be unfair as well. Zosia was Zosia, raised in a strange mixture of secrecy and intensely close community, she had no qualms about such things and would never understand either his or Tadek's jealousy. He would at least not make Tadek's mistake of possessiveness. If he loved her, it was his problem to deal with her openness and lack of inhibition, not hers.

As Zosia and Tadek dressed, he packed the bags in silence, carefully placing his computer and their equipment in Tadek's briefcase and locking it. The late winter dawn finally approached. The sky turned a soft gray, the birds began to sing, and then slowly, the edge of pink marched upward from the east and lit the room with a rosy glow. Zosia and Tadek finished dressing and sat on the sofa, talking in a desultory manner. Peter, of course, did not join in; he was more nervous than the other two, and he paced uneasily from one window to the other as if looking for something or someone to arrive. He watched as the clouds gathered on the horizon, obliterating the feeble sunrise with their threat of yet more rain. The thought kept running through his mind: just a few more hours, just a few more hours. There was breakfast, a short meeting between Tadek and the major, the drive to Neu Sandez, and then he could be rid of his uniform and manacle and . . . He had almost added his numbers to the mental list, but those, he reflected sadly, would remain.

A soft knock announced the arrival of their breakfast. As with the previous mornings, it would consist of two hearty trays of food: sausages, ham, cheese, and liver paste; fresh rolls and butter and jams, fruit and yogurt—more than many families would eat in a day. There would be a pitcher of juice with two glasses and a pot of steaming coffee, cream, sugar, and two cups with saucers.

The first morning the breakfast had arrived, Tadek and Zosia looked momentarily perplexed by the service. There was clearly enough food for three, so why only two of everything? Peter had smiled to himself as he reached under the trolley and, with a flourish, produced the small tin of food from the second shelf: stale bread and some hard cheese, moldy around the edges. He had made a point of emptying the tin—to leave the food might raise difficult questions—before he joined the other two in indulging in the bounteous breakfast.

He opened the door, expecting the same sullen orderly who had brought the food on the previous mornings. Instead, he was greeted by three officers: one was the major, the other two he did not recognize, but they were wearing police uniforms—one a captain, the other a lieutenant. Peter stepped back as the major pointed in his direction and said, "That's him."

"What's going on here?" Tadek demanded.

The lieutenant grabbed Peter and pulled his arms behind him, fixing them there with handcuffs even as the major explained, "There's been a theft. I'm afraid your boy here is under arrest." He sounded somewhat apologetic.

"A theft? What's missing?" Zosia asked, and wondered at the same time why a captain and a lieutenant were investigating. It seemed like overkill.

"Some silverware, *gnädige Frau*," the major answered before his companion could shush him. The captain mumbled something to the major and then he added, "I'm afraid I can't give more details without compromising the investigation. I'm afraid your boy is the prime suspect."

"Nonsense!" Zosia snapped. "He hasn't stolen anything!"

"We can't be sure of that until we have finished our investigations, *gnädige Frau*," the captain assured her, leering in such a manner that Zosia instinctively glanced down at her blouse to make sure that all the buttons were fastened. "We have to take him in for questioning."

"You can't do that!" Tadek blurted. In answer to the questioning looks, he added, "He's our driver, we need him to get home today. We must leave immediately—I have work that must be done."

"We'll provide you with another driver."

"Then he won't be able to get home," Tadek insisted.

"If he is found innocent, we'll transport him to your address. If not . . ." The captain shrugged. "If not, I suppose the authorities will provide you with a replacement."

Zosia eyed Peter. He hadn't in any way resisted having his hands bound, and now, keeping his head lowered, he glanced from one speaker to the other as if casually watching a play in which he himself was not involved. There was something in his expression, but what was it? She remembered his manic pacing and the way he had kept checking the windows and wondered if he had expected this. Had they been set up? Had he managed to contact someone in Berlin after all? She bit her thumbnail nervously and turned her focus back to the argument as Tadek was saying, ". . . there was no time for that, he's been with us!"

"But he was seen out of your presence at least once! Remember, he was discovered wandering around lost," the major pointed out.

Tadek hesitated before continuing, "Well, yes, but that was a very short time."

"And there are so many other people in this building! How do you know none of them did it, knowing that our boy would automatically be blamed?" Zosia added.

"They are all officers in the *Wehrmacht* or guests of the major, *gnädige Frau*. Surely you are not suggesting that they would indulge in such behavior?" the captain asked.

"All things are possible. We are, after all, only superhuman," Zosia retorted slyly.

"With all due respect, *gnädige Frau,* we really have only one suspect, and it is your servant. I know it will be a hardship to do without him, but I'm sure he will be replaced eventually. You don't want to make the job of the police difficult now, do you?" the captain said snidely.

With a sudden shock, Zosia guessed it might well be a setup, but not the one she had initially suspected. The captain was eyeing Peter not as a suspect nor as a comrade who needed to be freed and debriefed, but as an acquisition. *They wanted him!* He had to be worth a small fortune in bribes and deals. The Müller's well-trained and trusted servant would simply disappear into the criminal justice system only to reemerge the property of some other wealthy and connected individual. With a palpable horror, Zosia realized that it may have been her zealous comments to Frau Rattenhuber that had initiated their current situation.

Her thoughts followed several tracks simultaneously. If Peter was their agent, letting them take him would mean the death of everyone she loved and the destruction of all they had fought for, and he could not be allowed to leave the room alive. Similarly, if there had been a theft, he would be trapped in a prison, vulnerable to interrogation and might possibly betray them all, and again, the risk was too great to accept. But if the entire charade was nothing more than a hastily constructed abduction, then there was hope, for what the policemen were doing was illegal, and a sufficiently obstinate Frau Müller could well fend them off. Zosia weighed the evidence and her intuition and made her decision.

She turned to Tadek. "Darling, you really do have a lot to do. Why don't you *get away* now. Take the car; I'll stay here and make sure that things are sorted out. We'll take the train later, I'm sure that won't be too inconvenient."

Tadek stared at her helplessly. He looked at Peter, at the briefcase, at Zosia again. Carefully he said, "Are you sure that's wise?"

"Yes," Zosia replied with delicate precision, her tone conveying that it was not only her choice, it was an order.

Reluctantly he agreed to her plan. "All right." He turned to the major. "I'm afraid, Major, we should finish our business and I'll have to leave."

"But of course."

Tadek turned to the captain, said without preamble, "We are not without our own connections, Captain. I'm sure the boy is innocent, and I'm sure it'd be in your best interests to ascertain that *immediately.*" He turned away before the captain could reply and approached Peter to say, "Don't worry, lad, I'm sure these men will soon realize their mistake. I'll see you soon." He turned to Zosia and paused. She could see the tears glistening in the corners of his eyes as he struggled to control his fear for her. His mouth moved but no words emerged.

"I'll see you back at home," she assured him, but her words were empty.

"*Auf Wiedersehen,*" Tadek said, his voice quavering on that simple phrase. He kissed Zosia and, then casually picking up his briefcase, left the room with the major.

As the door shut behind them, Zosia, knowing that everything incriminating had left the room with Tadek, said, "Now, gentlemen, I know it is somewhat unconventional for me to suggest this, but perhaps we should look for some evidence of guilt or innocence? I propose that you search my servant and see if you can find this missing silverware. If not, then I think we have proof that you have the wrong man."

The two men looked at each other, somewhat taken aback by her boldness. Eventually the captain nodded, and the lieutenant went over to Peter and frisked him carefully. After that they searched the baggage. When they still found nothing, they painstakingly searched the entire room, suggesting to Zosia that she retreat to the dining room for breakfast and return later since the search would be tedious. She, however, declined the invitation.

As they searched, the lieutenant suddenly asked, "What about the briefcase?"

"It was locked," Zosia answered authoritatively. "It could not have been in there."

They accepted this without comment and continued their search. After another half hour had passed, the captain suggested, yet again, that Zosia might want to relax for the duration, but she politely refused, staying irritatingly alert. Finally the captain came up to her and said, "It's not here, he must have already passed it on to an accomplice."

"Really, Captain! Don't you think that inventing accomplices stretches the imagination a bit? After all, there's no one here but *Wehrmacht* officers and guests of the major, and they would never indulge in such behavior!"

Stung by the repetition of his words, the captain stated coldly, "We will have to interrogate him."

Zosia realized she had overplayed her hand. With a conciliatory smile she suggested, "Perhaps I could simply pay you the price of the silverware and that way you could make reparations."

"We will have to interrogate him. That is the only way we'll get the truth out of him."

"Look, you've searched everything, you've wasted our time, you've caused me enormous stress. It is time to admit your mistake and release him. We need to get home," Zosia fumed.

"We will not do that, *gnädige Frau*," the captain responded. "We need to question him. It is standard procedure."

Zosia grit her teeth as she considered her options. Finally she conceded. "Fine, you can ask him yourself about the silverware. Go ahead." She gestured helpfully toward Peter.

"We will do it at headquarters."

"You will do it here and in my presence!" Zosia demanded.

The captain glared at her, then he walked over to his lieutenant. "Do you know who she is? Is she someone's daughter?" he asked desperately. Though he had spoken in an undertone, Zosia had no trouble guessing his words.

The lieutenant shrugged helplessly. "I don't think she's anybody, but if we get him to admit to something in her presence, then it won't matter, will it."

The captain nodded thoughtfully, then paced back to Zosia. "All right, *gnädige Frau,* we'll do it here, but it's not something for a lady to watch—this isn't a tea party. We're investigating a crime and we're used to dealing with criminals using methods which they understand."

"I understand. And I'm sure you understand that you are dealing with an innocent man. You have no evidence against him and you have two stout character witnesses for him, so be careful how you treat him!"

"He's an *Untermensch!*" The captain slammed the table with his hand, his exasperation finally showing.

"But he's mine and I've—I treat all my subordinates with civility. Do you understand?" Zosia had nearly said "and I've grown fond of him," but decided that that might be interpreted as being too close to violating some race law.

"Frau Müller, you are getting dangerously close to hampering my investigations. There are standard procedures for questioning this category of suspect. They have no incentive for telling the truth, so we must give them one. You may not like that, but that is the way it is done. In point of fact, your very presence here is a hindrance, as we know from long experience that your boy will say whatever he thinks pleases you. So, if you wish to stay in the room, I will graciously allow that, but I must insist that you keep quiet or I will have you expelled!"

Reluctantly Zosia nodded. This compromise seemed the best she could hope for. "I'll be quiet, Captain, but don't forget that I am watching you!"

She sat on the sofa, across the room from the three of them. They began gently enough, seating Peter in one of the upright chairs, facing Zosia, and draping his bound arms over the back. For a moment they were stymied as they searched for a bit of rope; they finally settled on the heavy cord used to hold back the drapes and used that to tie his wrists to the spindles on the back of the chair, thus keeping him securely in place. As the lieutenant tightened the knots, the captain asked Peter, almost seriously, if he was comfortable. At this Peter raised his head—he had been staring downward—and looked the captain full in the face for the first time. He nodded slightly as if to acknowledge that he understood the question was meaningless, then he turned away, letting his eyes meet Zosia's before they turned downward again.

As if this were his cue, the captain slammed his fist up under Peter's chin. As Peter's head snapped backward, the captain leaned forward and shouted from only inches away, "You will answer all questions appropriately! Do you understand?"

Zosia had jumped to her feet, but she forced herself to sit back down.

Peter lowered his head back to a normal position, his eyes closed as he struggled to control his anger. Quietly he answered, "Yes, *Herr Hauptmann.*"

The captain glanced back at Zosia, then proceeded. "Good, good. Now, tell me, do you understand the charge against you?"

"Yes, *Herr Hauptmann.*"

"Good, very good. Now, tell me, why did you steal the silverware?"

"I did not steal the silverware. I have stolen nothing."

The captain bit his lip at this as if in serious thought. He paced away from Peter, then dramatically, he turned on his heel and surveyed the suspect. The lieutenant stood next to and a bit behind Peter, silently intimidating by his proximity.

"You're lying," the captain stated. The lieutenant smacked his fist threateningly in his hand, but the captain shook his head slightly. "I want you to tell me the truth. Just tell me what I want to hear," the captain continued not unkindly.

"I did not steal any silverware," Peter answered almost mechanically.

"Maybe it was to buy cigarettes?" the captain suggested helpfully. "We know you do these sorts of things. It's all right, you know. You can admit it."

"I did not steal any silverware."

"Then how do you know it was stolen?" the captain cleverly asked.

"You've told me about it. Maybe you're lying," Peter replied unwisely.

The captain's eyes widened at that, and the lieutenant stepped forward and backhanded Peter. Zosia winced and shifted uncomfortably, but remained seated.

"What if I were to tell you we have a witness?" the captain asked.

"I know you don't," Peter asserted, not in the least bit deferential, "because I did not steal the silverware."

The lieutenant glanced back at his boss, saw him nod, and slugged Peter in response.

Zosia cringed, half turning away. *It's not a request,* she heard herself say. How could she have been so stupid?

The captain walked forward, and the lieutenant fell back to make room for him. The captain lifted Peter's chin. "That hurt, didn't it?" When he received nothing more than a glare in response, he added softly, "Just say you did it."

Peter continued to glare at the captain. Zosia saw how he had to swallow something, saw a trickle of blood dribble from his mouth. She also saw how furious he was and understood why he had so senselessly provoked the captain. This angry, useless bravado was, she realized, one of her first glimpses into his real personality. It made her sick at heart to watch. Her own impotence, his reckless bravery, shades of Adam.

"I said, just tell me you did it," the captain repeated.

She hadn't been there for him, Adam had faced his fate alone.

"If I had stolen anything, don't you think you would have found it?" Peter asked provocatively.

The lieutenant swung his fist into Peter's ear for that.

And now she was useless for Peter. He was suffering before her eyes and she could do nothing at all.

"You're being very clever, but that's not good enough," the captain snapped angrily. He grabbed a chair and swung it into position next to Peter's, and then straddling the back in a casual, almost friendly manner, he sat down so that he could lean forward, his face only inches from Peter's ear. "You don't need to tell us where it is. Just admit you stole it. That's easy, isn't it?"

How could she have got him into this? Oh, God, why was she so helpless now!

"I didn't steal it," Peter whispered.

Zosia felt a pain in her hands. Looking down, she realized she had been twisting her fingers around each other until they hurt. Carefully, as if they belonged to someone else, she unwrapped them.

"Come, come. Admit your crime, you'll feel better." The captain's voice dropped and he added in a confidential whisper, "You know exactly what I want to hear, you know exactly what to say. It'll go much easier for you if you just do as you're told. It's always that way, you know. It's always much easier. Just tell us that you stole the silverware. All we need is for your mistress to hear your confession. Then she can go home and we can take you in. It will be easy after that. We'll type up our report, and before you know it, you'll be back home. It will all be over with."

"I didn't steal anything," Peter stubbornly insisted. The lieutenant slammed a fist into his face. The captain pulled back in alarm. Zosia closed her eyes in pain.

With a warning glance at his lieutenant, the captain leaned forward again, close to Peter's ear. "A simple yes!" he pleaded quietly. "Just one word. Say it. Just say it."

Peter remained silent.

"Captain—" Zosia began.

"Frau Müller," the captain interrupted, glowering at Zosia, "any interruption is an interference in police work. I can arrest you for that." Zosia fell silent and the captain turned back to the prisoner. "*Wahrheit macht frei*," the captain hissed at him. The truth will set you free—it was a cruel pun on the concentration camp motto: *Arbeit macht frei*.

"Then you'll be interested in knowing," Peter said, meeting the captain's look, "I didn't steal anything." It was an obvious challenge.

The lieutenant raised his fist, but the captain shook his head. He leaned back, confused. He had expected denials, but certainly nothing of this sort. He stood up and stepped back as if trying to regain control of the situation. "We don't like hurting you. Just tell us the truth and we can stop. Please." The captain paused, raising his eyebrows expectantly, but Peter remained silent.

"Don't be stupid, just admit it. Now!" the captain exclaimed.

The lieutenant tensed, awaiting the captain's signal, but the captain turned to Zosia instead. "Tell him it's all right to confess. Tell him!"

"I can't do that. But, Captain, don't—"

"Fine!" the captain snapped angrily, and gestured to the lieutenant.

Zosia bowed her head rather than look. She hadn't been there for Adam, and now, again, she was useless! Over and over she heard Peter's objections in her head, heard her flippant dismissals of his concerns. She thought of how they had talked afterward, of all the wonderful, intelligent conversations they had had, of how he had confessed his love to her in a confusion of languages. She remembered falling asleep in his arms that first night, the desperate need in his voice as he told her his story. She remembered how he had worked the evening before, the intense look of concentration on his face as he had struggled to rapidly untangle the code. The way he put seed out for the birds in the depths of winter, how he allowed himself to be "ripped off" when bargaining with the local villagers. The cheerful chatter of his office, the way his face lit up whenever he saw her.

A soft moan from Peter penetrated her thoughts: the lieutenant was resting his hand, rubbing it to relieve the pain; the captain was collecting his thoughts for his next question. Peter looked up and their eyes met. His face was covered in blood, his hair was damp with sweat, he was trembling violently, yet there was an intensity in his gaze, something there she could not read. He looked as though he were going to say something, but then, without prompting, the lieutenant hit him again.

The captain looked at the lieutenant, somewhat surprised, a little disdainful, but he did not say anything. Peter did not move from where the lieutenant's fist had left him; he had to be pulled back into a straight sitting position. He was rasping, his breaths coming in short gasps. His eyes were half-closed, and though Zosia longed for him to look at her again, he did not.

Zosia turned her attention to the captain. Should she feign telephoning someone? It would be an easy bluff for them to call. When dare she make her move? Too soon, and she could be forced to make a decision she did not want to face, but if she waited much longer . . . Again her eyes were drawn to Peter and her heart ached.

The captain studied his prisoner. He glanced at Zosia and scowled a rejection of her eager, questioning smile. He wandered over to the drinks cabinet, pulled out a bottle of whiskey, and poured two drinks. He walked over to the prisoner, ignoring the lieutenant as he reached expectantly for the second drink. The captain put the drink to Peter's mouth. Peter took a sip; some of it dribbled down the sides of his mouth as the captain miscalculated how far to tilt the glass. The captain offered more and Peter drank it. The captain continued to hold the glass for him, and he drank the rest of its contents.

The captain stepped back and drank his whiskey pensively. He stood tapping his fingers and his eyes darted from Peter to Zosia and back again. The captain bit his lips, then sighing his frustration, he moved toward Peter again.

Zosia stood and walked toward the captain. Smiling courteously, almost seductively, she gently touched his arm. The captain jumped nervously at her touch. "Captain, if I may have a word in private with you?" She nodded toward the corridor.

The captain stared at her, obviously confused, somewhat worried. He then nodded and led the way out. He sent the guard by the door to stand farther down the hall and then impatiently asked, "Frau Müller?"

Zosia fingered her pendant. *"Herr Hauptmann,* I think that the investigation has run into a cul-de-sac. You are clearly an excellent interrogator and no real criminal could have withstood your efforts; therefore, I think we should assume that the boy really is innocent. Certainly he would not dare to deceive an investigator of your caliber for this length of time. So, perhaps the best option at this point would be to release the prisoner into my custody. I will personally guarantee that he will be kept under close guard. Then, he can be picked up whenever there is new evidence or whenever the investigation is to be continued. I'm sure *mein Herr* has our home address. We will be there, at your convenience."

The captain stared at her silently for a moment. His lips twitched, he glanced nervously back toward the room and his prize.

"And I will be sure to mention your wonderful professionalism to my uncle when I am back in Berlin," Zosia added winningly.

The captain sighed heavily. "Fine. I'll release him into your custody."

"Thank you, Captain," Zosia crooned in reply. "I am in your debt."

Later that day the captain would nearly choke upon learning that Herr Müller's wife was a nobody. He decided the best course of action to cover his humiliation was to never mention the incident and never pursue the matter further.

30

AFTER THE POLICE had left, Zosia got Peter some water to drink, and then tenderly she washed his face. They said little, still aware of their surroundings. When the major returned, he suggested that they be provided with a car and driver to take them back to their home, but Zosia insisted that that would be far too much trouble. No, a ride to the train station and a military pass to get them intercity tickets without the usual delays would suffice.

A car and driver were provided for their trip into Hamburg. Zosia sat in the back of the car, Peter in front, with the driver. He rode unconstrained—even the military did not follow the rules about transit with the same zealousness as Karl. They rode in complete silence through a cold, driving rain. Peter's thoughts returned to the interrogation. He had not allowed himself to analyze his feelings at the time, but now, he found himself wondering at his reactions.

Always before when he had been in a dangerous situation, his entire being had been intent on survival. This time, though, his thoughts about what might happen to himself had been almost marginal. Instead he had found himself thinking about Zosia. He had wanted her to leave with Tadek, or instead of Tadek. He had been desperate to get her out of danger—enough so that he had wanted to provoke them, had even considered confessing to the alleged crime, just so they would take him away and leave her alone. It wasn't that he didn't want to be with her, for he did. And it wasn't that he no longer cared about his own life; it just suddenly was not as important as knowing that Zosia was safe. He had never felt so strongly about anyone—not even Allie. How could that be? The intensity of his feelings terrified him.

The car pulled up to the station, and he jumped out to open the door for Zosia. As she wrapped her coat more tightly around herself, he removed the bags from the back. They headed into the station without exchanging a word. The pass provided by the major allowed Zosia to requisition a one-way ticket to Berlin for travel that day. Peter waited with the luggage near the door as Zosia went into the ticket office with their documentation. When she returned, they passed through the gates and out onto the platform. It was cold out under the great roof of the station, and the next train to Berlin was not leaving for nearly an hour, so aside from a few patrols pacing back and forth, they were nearly alone. They stood a discreet distance apart, Zosia staring off into space so that he was only in her peripheral vision, Peter standing with an attitude of attentive deference, staring downward at the luggage as though guarding it.

He spoke softly, without looking up. "I want to thank you for what you did back there. You risked your life to save mine. I won't forget that."

"I'm sorry about all that," Zosia replied equally quietly. "I'm really, really sorry."

"All's well that ends well," he replied without conviction.

"How do you feel?"

"A bit stunned still; it's sure to hurt more later." After a moment he added, "I must look like hell." He was suddenly aware he did not want her to be embarrassed to be seen with him. "Do I look all right?" he asked rather sadly.

She looked around to make sure nobody was near, then smiled at his battered face. "You look . . . you look fine." She blinked back some tears, then repeated unconvincingly, "You look just fine." She looked back out across the tracks into space, took a deep, unsteady breath of the cold air, then without turning to face him said, "They didn't give me a ticket for you—just this pass with my name and travel information on it. It looks more like a baggage claim than a ticket."

"You could say that."

"But where do you sit?"

He found he could keep his eyes off her no longer. He looked around to be sure that they were essentially unobserved, then he looked directly at her beautiful form. She still faced the track, and all he could see of her face was the curve of her cheeks and the edges of her eyelashes. "If I'm lucky, they'll have a boxcar with wood benches where I can go; the apprentices and indentured servants have first priority and we get the leftover seats. Everybody calls it the cattle car. If there isn't one, I just get to stand around in the aisles and try to stay out of everyone else's way. If the train is crowded, the best place to be, in that case, is between the carriages—it's cold and uncomfortable, so nobody wants to be there and they usually leave us alone."

"Us?"

"Yeah, there's always a few other *Zwangi* on the train. It's a great place to pick up jokes and gossip." He noticed she was shivering slightly. She was wearing a wool coat with a fur-trimmed collar and had a silk scarf underneath, but still the damp air carried a bitter chill. He wanted to put his arm around her to warm her, even though, with his thin jacket, he himself was cold.

After a few minutes passed in silence, he asked, "Your ticket only goes to Berlin—what do we do then?"

"I don't know. We didn't plan on this, you know." She paused and pulled out a silver cigarette case. He came over to light the cigarette and had a chance then to look into her eyes. She smiled warmly at him. "We could, of course, return to the pension. Or maybe Frau Müller will be able to bully the ticketing office there into issuing a priority ticket on to Neu Sandez. We'll figure out something."

"Which station are we arriving at?"

"Friedrichstrasse."

"Ah, that's near Karl's office."

"Were you ever there? The Ministry, I mean."

"Yes. A couple of times." He decided he did not want to think about that other life anymore. He changed the subject. "I didn't know you smoked." Naturally, smoking was forbidden inside the bunker—the ventilation system would not have been able to cope. Outside, in the forest, it was the custom not to smoke because the guards were forbidden to do so for security reasons—they could be detected miles away by the smell, and conversely they could use the smell of approaching Reich soldiers to detect them well in advance of any sight or sound of them. This simple and efficient detection system was slowly being superseded by more advanced technologies, but the custom was still observed.

"Yeah, well, as you know, none of us really have the option back at camp." Irritatingly, Zosia had turned back away from him, so he could not read her expression. "I only smoke when it's appropriate to my character, and I think Frau Müller has had a difficult enough morning that right now she would light a cigarette." She blew some smoke into the air, stared at it absently.

He looked down the platform. People were beginning to gather: they should probably not talk anymore.

Zosia seemed to come to the same conclusion. Without looking at him she said, "Check the board and see where we should be standing for my carriage. It's"—she consulted her ticket—"sixty-one oh two." Her voice had assumed an imperative tone, and although he understood she was reassuming her role, he nevertheless felt a chill. He responded appropriately and then walked over to the large board that displayed the carriage numbers and how they would line up on the platform.

*　　*　　*

The train arrived at the station fifteen minutes late, and the anxious passengers boarded hastily. Peter helped Zosia on board and then returned to wait with the luggage until the last of the Germans had boarded; after them the few *Nichtdeutsch* boarded, followed by the apprentices and indentured servants with their baggage. Then, and only then, did he and the several other *Zwangsarbeiter* climb the steps with their loads of luggage. As was usual, the conductors chided them for taking too long and blew the whistle to shut the doors before the last of them had stepped completely inside.

He carried the luggage to Zosia's compartment and loaded it on the overhead racks. He casually reorganized the bags of the other passengers to make room for Zosia's. He knew they would not object—given his presence, she was obviously their social superior. The other passengers in the compartment stared at him with a long-practiced mixture of contempt and envy but indeed did not object as he carelessly shoved their bags together. They had been obliged to carry and store their own luggage and resented that. They were also annoyed that arriving in the compartment first had not sufficed to reserve them extra luggage space. Their only revenge was to let him see how superior they felt to him—even if they were somewhat in awe of his mistress. She, obviously, had to be someone rather important.

Peter smiled to himself—he had seen exactly the same reaction hundreds of times before when he had gone shopping or traveled with Frau or Herr Vogel. They had always reveled in other people's reactions, whereas Zosia seemed somewhat embarrassed by the vignette and stared determinedly out the window.

When he had finished, he had to draw her attention. "Frau Müller?"

She looked up at him, perplexed.

"Is there anything I can get for you?"

"Uh, no. No."

"In that case, *gnädige Frau*, I'll find a space. I'll be back in a bit to see if you need anything."

It turned out there was no place on the train for him to sit. He was in no mood to talk to anyone, so he meandered the aisles, looking for a comfortable, unoccupied spot. Between the last passenger carriage and the baggage car, he found it. Wind whistled through the gaping holes and the metal ramp swayed wildly to and fro with each bump and curve on the poorly maintained tracks. The frigid isolation suited his mood, and he huddled against the flexible sides and peered through a crack in the fabric at the passing countryside, carefully trying to ignore how much his face hurt, trying hard not to reach up and touch the damage.

He checked on Zosia several times throughout the journey. Her carriage companions changed—the seats were now unoccupied except for two old ladies who sat demurely opposite her. He suppressed a sigh as he looked at the comfortable empty seat next to Zosia. He was tired and he ached from all his injuries. He would have loved to sit next to her, place his head on her shoulder, and fall into a deep, peaceful sleep, but that was impossible. They had only one train ticket, and even if he could discreetly change into different clothes, he had no identification papers and no ticket to match. Zosia caught his glance at the empty seat and gave him a commiserating look.

He returned to his isolated post. He had had a bad feeling about this mission, about his role in it, from the beginning. He was not superstitious, nor did he believe that he had unusual intuition, but it was hard to shake the feeling that he had known things were going to go badly. Not only that, but they still were not home safe, and the nagging fear that had plagued him throughout the mission had not left him. He wondered idly what else could possibly go wrong as he stared at the beginnings of the Berlin suburbs. They were still far from the center, but the housing estates already stretched endlessly as the city of 12 million sprawled like a concrete cancer into the surrounding countryside.

As he checked one last time on Zosia, the train made a final stop in the suburbs before heading into the city center. It was a popular stop—the last in a residential region and also a connecting station for journeys continuing east. Consequently, there were fewer people now, and he could relax in the warmth without being in anybody's way. He paced the aisle of Zosia's carriage and finally settled on a position near the door, leaning against the window opposite an empty compartment not far from hers. The anonymous gray housing estates of huge concrete towers had given way to smaller buildings of brick and plaster and then to small houses on little plots. Eventually apartment buildings reappeared, and then the landscape gave way to the commercial and urban center of Berlin. The train slowed so as not to make too much noise or jar the foundations of the buildings as it began to rumble past vast government ministries of marble and sculpted concrete. Their immense façades dwarfed the pedestrians outside their walls, reducing them to tiny cogs of the state. He rested his face against the cool glass to try to relieve the pounding headache he had endured since his interrogation. He wondered about the lives of the people he saw through the glass. What did God see in their lives? In their fates? Was there such a thing? And if so, was he fated to always return to subjugation? The thought struck him as irrational, inspired by pain and fatigue, yet he could not drive it from his mind.

"Hey, boy!"

The interruption caused him to jump. It was a male voice and his blood ran cold at its sound. He knew the voice, he knew what he would see when he turned to face the speaker.

"So, you've changed nationality, eh? That's an interesting development—maybe we'll investigate that. But still I see you know your place in the world." Karl grinned at him, inhaled from his cigarette, and blew a stream of smoke into his face. Peter noted the gun pointed at his stomach, raised his eyes to look into Karl's. He kept his face a questioning blank even though he knew there was no hope that Karl would think he had made a mistake. Not enough time had passed and they knew each other far too well.

Karl poked him with the gun. "What are you doing here?"

Peter wondered if he could grab it away from him, but then what? The carriage was not empty, and they had already caught the attention of some of the people loitering at the far end of the aisle near the other door. They looked on, mildly interested, apparently unable to hear the words being said, almost certainly unaware of the low-held gun.

Using his left hand—the cigarette perched between his fingers—Karl reached over and grabbed Peter's arm. He twisted it around and read the numbers to himself. "What's going on here?" he snarled, confused and suspicious. "Answer me, you bastard!"

The cigarette was beginning to burn Peter's skin, and he pulled his arm away as he said, "I'm sorry, *mein Herr,* I don't understand what the problem is."

"Drop the phony accent, that ploy is useless! I know who you are, just like you know me."

Peter returned Karl's accusing stare with one of complete confusion. He could not believe that of all trains, Karl would have to be on this one. Such coincidences don't happen, he kept thinking uselessly. He struggled to organize a plan, but his disbelief interfered with his ability to reason, and a soul-destroying fear nearly paralyzed him. Was there such a thing as fate? Was this his fate?

"You belong to *me!* Did you think you could steal my property? Did you think you could take what was rightfully mine? Did you think you could get away with it? Did you?" Karl poked him with the gun again. "Answer me!" he grated, forcefully swinging the gun up and into Peter's chin.

Peter fell backward, landing heavily in a sitting position. He sat on the floor staring up at Karl, stunned. The passengers at the far end of the aisle were giving their full attention to the interchange now, although they clearly could not hear the dialogue.

"Now I've got you, you swine. And you know what I'm going to do to you, don't you?"

Peter knew. He also knew that he would not be taken alive. Not this time. Never again.

Karl could barely contain his elation at having cornered his errant slave. I found him! he gloated. The whole damn security service can't locate him, and I stumble across him on a train! He dropped his cigarette on the floor, ground it out with his foot, and contemplated his prisoner for a moment, savoring his victory. Then he collected a mouthful of saliva and spat at him.

Peter carefully wiped the spit from his face. Karl could restrain himself no longer and launched into a tirade concerning how he had been wronged and how, in revenge, he was going to destroy Peter piece by piece. Peter remained on the floor, out of reach, as Karl hissed that he would break every bone in his miserable body, that he would burn every bit of flesh inch by inch from his bones, that he would use starvation and beatings and electric shocks to elicit information from him. "That's right, boy, I'm going to interrogate you. Personally! I'm going to enjoy every minute of tearing you to pieces. You'll drink my piss, you'll eat my shit, and then I'm going to listen to you beg to die. It's the least you deserve after what you've done, and it will be music to my ears."

"*Mein Herr!* I'm not who you think I am!"

"I know what I'll do . . ." Karl seemed to change his mind about killing his prisoner. His exhilaration was such that his mind was awash with conflicting scenarios for revenge. "You'll come back with me, but this time we'll make sure you stay put." He licked his lips, his eyes widening as he envisioned how he would make Peter pay for the humiliation that had been inflicted on him: his car, his gun, his papers, his slave—all gone, all in one night! Oh, he'd show all those who had implied his household lacked discipline! "First, we'll see to your legs: you won't run away again, you won't even walk," he planned out loud, oblivious to Peter's slowly climbing to his feet. "You'll hobble, and every painful step will remind you of your crime! Then castration—that will bring you down a notch, won't it?" Karl grunted in appreciation at his own imaginary pun. "And your rations, yes, yes, I'll make sure you learn discipline. I'll show those—"

"*Get fucked.*"

Karl's reaction was exactly what Peter had expected. He had been so involved in his tirade, he had not noticed that Peter was standing, had not noticed how close Peter's hand had moved toward the gun. The shock of hearing such words directed at him threw him off guard long enough for Peter to twist the gun out of Karl's grip and discreetly point it back at him.

Peter did not know if the passengers at the end of the aisle could see what was going on, he could only hope that they didn't—he certainly could not afford to look at them. How much time did he have? Minutes? Seconds? Had somebody noticed the sudden exchange of the gun and gone to get help? Or had he hidden his action well enough?

A voice inside him told him to shoot Karl while there was still a chance. *Now!* it yelled. He wondered what he could do then; once he had shot Karl, there would be no escape, he would have to kill himself if he did not want to be taken alive. He argued with himself: there was Zosia to protect, and Joanna; he could not get them involved! Karl had recognized him, he could never get away now, not unless he killed him, and then he would have to die as well.

Nervously he licked his lips. He had to act quickly, before it was too late, but he did not want to die. His thoughts turned to Zosia again, his beloved Zosia. It was worth his life to save her, to know that she had walked away unscathed in the confusion of a murder-suicide in the narrow aisle of the carriage. She would disappear long before his papers were checked, long before the questions about his strange double numbers would arise. She would be safe, and she and Joanna might remember him with fondness and carry him into the future in their hearts.

His eyes strayed momentarily to her compartment. He wanted to protect her by keeping her away from the situation, but did she *need* protecting? What had she said? *If one gets the right angle, it makes it so quick that they rarely even bleed much.*

She didn't need protecting! Not only that, she could offer him a chance for life.

He made his decision in an instant and whispered intensely to a stunned Karl, "Now, you listen to me you shit-faced motherfucker. You'll keep your mouth shut. Do you understand? You know I have nothing to lose, so I'll happily use this if you make one wrong move. Got that?"

Karl nodded. He was shaking and visibly sweating, his dreams vanished.

"Turn around slowly, look casual."

Karl obeyed. Peter poked the gun into his back, tried to hide the metal in the folds of Karl's jacket. If only the passengers lose interest. If only they haven't seen enough to know what's going on. If only the conductor doesn't come through. "Okay, now walk slowly down the aisle. Be calm. Just two compartments. That's good."

Peter glanced at the loitering passengers at the far end of the carriage as he proceeded awkwardly down the aisle. Nobody seemed to be paying much attention. Clearly a *Zwangsarbeiter* being smacked around was nothing particularly noteworthy. And a bewildered, drunken oaf who would do such a thing, in his confusion perhaps attacking the wrong man or his own man for no reason—it was embarrassing, nothing more. Something to watch with mild interest or, at most, a slight unease, then when it was over, something to ignore and forget; it was none of their business. They had gone back to their conversations and observations; the train was approaching the station, and they needed to get to their seats and get their luggage. They had lost interest.

Karl's terrified silence gave Peter the chance to finally speak his mind. Calmly, quietly he hissed into Karl's ear, "We met as strangers: I had never done any harm to you or your family—keep moving, that's right—yet, you worked me to exhaustion, denied me food, insulted and beat me endlessly and without mercy. And I never did you any harm. I did not raise one finger against you or your family in violence. Consider that, *mein Herr,* consider how lucky you are that all I did was leave."

He doubted the words would even penetrate Karl's prejudices enough to be examined, but Peter had needed to say them anyway, and though he recognized it was ill-advised to divert his attention from the dangerous job at hand, he was glad he had spoken.

They stopped outside Zosia's compartment. She looked up, immediately assessed the situation, and rose to her feet. Peter was surprised to see that instead of reaching for her necklace, she adjusted the silver ring she wore. A matched set, Zosia had said to Frau Rattenhuber. A matched set! Of course, it was a weapon as well. She stepped out and hugged Karl, who stood confused by the door.

"Darling! There you are!"

"Who the hell are you?" Karl bellowed, his surprise overcoming his fear of the gun.

Peter mouthed *Karl* to Zosia; she nodded and tightened her hug and pressed her hand forcefully into the base of his neck. Loudly she continued, "You know you shouldn't drink when you take your medication! The doctor said so! You really must be more careful, dear. You know how it makes you dizzy and confused!"

Karl's quiet "Ow" and surprised grimace went undetected through Zosia's little speech. He gave her a glassy, cross-eyed stare, then he slumped in her arms. Peter caught his weight, and with Zosia's help, pulled him into the compartment. They set him in the seat next to her—a drunken, peaceful soul. It wasn't the first time that a passenger had collapsed from too much drink on a long train ride, and it wouldn't be the last, but the two old ladies shuddered with delicate revulsion nonetheless.

31

*T*HE SNOW CAME DOWN in large, lazy flakes, melting even before they hit the ground. It was a wet, cold, uncomfortable day, but the heavy gray clouds and the messy splatters on the windowpane looked beautiful to Peter. He rolled over and stretched, soaking in the unaccustomed luxury of a feather pillow, crisp white sheets, and a down comforter.

They had gone to the pension. Since they were unexpected, there was no room for them, but Zosia's godparents had insisted they stay in their own private room. There had been a minor debate about that, but in the end, the old woman had had her way. She and her husband would take turns sleeping on the sofa, and besides, they did not need much rest. They told Peter and Zosia not to worry, they would arrange everything—clothes, papers, travel passes, transport. The identity band was removed, the numbers covered. The old woman ran her fingers knowledgeably along Peter's jaw, where Karl had hit him with the gun, then applying a cold compress, she had assured him that it would be okay. She and her husband did everything they could to make Peter and Zosia feel comfortable, and then they withdrew to give them the privacy they seemed to need.

"Do you think he was still alive?" Peter asked as he lay in the bed, watching one snowflake after another hit the window and annihilate itself.

Zosia rolled toward him, hugged him. "I don't know. The dose was supposed to be sufficient to kill, but it wasn't well placed and he was a real tub of lard; he may have survived." She had buried her face in his neck, so that he had trouble understanding her answer. She pulled her head back, looked at him, and asked gently, "Did you want him dead?"

"As a matter of practicality, yes. But if I had planned that encounter—well, I don't think I would have made it so painless."

"So you wouldn't have shown him your moral superiority by showing him mercy?" she asked, raising herself up on one elbow.

"I doubt it. Oh, who knows what I would have done," he sighed. He would have liked to believe better of himself, or at least have Zosia believe better of him, but the fantasy of inflicting on Karl what he had inflicted on so many others was too appealing. "Anyway, you didn't hear what he said he'd do to me. And I know he meant it."

"Oh, I don't blame you. I myself . . ." She scowled, then let her expression relax. Her head slid down her arm, and she snuggled back under the covers. "Well, let's not think about that now. He's either dead or alive, but we're safe for the time being."

"But there is one thing that does bother me."

"What's that?"

"Well, you had your poison; presumably if you got captured, you could make a convenient exit?" he asked.

"Yes, that's the intent."

"Why in a ring? That's the sort of thing they take from you."

"The ring is extra, because of my profession. For things like, well, like with Karl. I carry some in a tooth as well—that's the way most people carry it."

"Most people," he repeated gloomily. "Why wasn't I provided with anything similar?"

"It wasn't thought to be necessary."

He did not fail to notice the passive voice of her answer. "Why not?" he asked almost too gently.

She looked away from him, clearly embarrassed. She got out of the bed and walked to the window, watching the snow for a few moments. The light from the window silhouetted her form. Finally she spoke, keeping her back to him so he could not see her face. "It's a trust thing: the poison is very convenient for us, but it is only useful as long as they don't suspect that we have it. If they knew we had it, they would remove it upon our arrest, so we could only use it at the moment of arrest. Most of us prefer to wait a bit and see if there's any hope of wriggling out of a tricky situation."

"So they . . . you were afraid I'd betray your secret."

"We didn't want to take the chance," Zosia admitted.

"What exactly is it that you use?"

"I don't know."

"Is that the truth?"

"Yes, I really don't know," Zosia sighed. "I asked once, but was told that I had no need to know. All I know is that if you don't specifically look for it in an autopsy, it's pretty much undetectable. That's why it's important that as few people as possible know about it."

"I understand why I wasn't told about this by the Council, but I thought you trusted me. Why didn't you tell me about it?"

"Orders. I was very specifically warned not to mention anything that I didn't have to."

"So, you tell me all about Ryszard—which was useless to me and clearly annoyed the hell out of him—but nothing about this poison—which would have given me a great deal of comfort! You know, it wouldn't hurt if there was just a bit of consistency in what you guys are willing to tell me," he replied witheringly.

"We obviously need some Germanic organization," Zosia said, deadpan.

Peter sputtered and they both broke out in laughter. After a moment the laughter died away and they fell into a comfortable silence. Zosia seemed intent on watching something out in the street. "So what would you have done?" he asked suddenly.

"What do you mean?"

"I mean," he said carefully, "given that I had no poison to protect myself, what were you planning to do if those two had taken me out of your sight?"

"Oh, one of our operatives would have kept tabs on you."

"Your network doesn't extend to Hamburg," he said, feeling rather nauseated. "Please tell me the truth, Zosia. Just this once. What would you have done?"

"I don't know, Peter," she answered distantly. "It didn't come to that."

"You would have killed me, wouldn't you?"

"I don't know. Maybe," she said as if the question did not really interest her.

"And if you had done that, then you would have been as good as dead yourself," he guessed.

"I don't explore hypotheticals, it just destroys one's ability to act."

"I almost gave myself up to them," he admitted, "so that you could leave. God! It would have got us both killed!"

"What stopped you?" she asked, still staring out the window.

"The lieutenant hit me, for no apparent reason. Remember? That stopped me long enough to make me reconsider the idea."

Softly she said, "You know, I think perhaps hope springs eternal. If they had taken you, if I was unable to prevent them, then I would probably have let you go." She traced a pattern in the mist on the window. "It goes against everything I know, everything I've been trained to do. They might have tortured every bit of information out of you that you had, or you might have been working for them all along. Either way, it could have been a death sentence for everyone I know. Rationally, letting you go would have been the most indefensible action of my life."

His heart stopped, he did not dare say a word as he waited for what she would say next.

"There's only one explanation for such a lack of discipline," she whispered.

He tried to quiet his breathing so he would not miss a word.

"It's that I love you." She said it so softly he wondered if he had simply wished the words into being.

She turned and smiled shyly at him. It took a moment for him to catch his breath, then he smiled broadly. He beckoned and she returned to the bed. As she crawled in, he moved toward her and embraced her gently. As he held her to him, he whispered in her ear, "I love you so much, Zosia. I love you so much."

They hugged each other for a long time in silence; he savored the warmth of her body against his. Her eyes were closed and she sighed quietly, and he wondered if she had fallen asleep, but then she stretched and yawned luxuriously like a cat after a nap. He smiled to himself, and then assuming the traditional British stance for a proposal, he raised himself up on one elbow and said, "You know, love, you've saved my life three times now."

"Have I?" she asked, arching her back and throwing her head back as she lay on her side.

"Yes, and do you know, it's an old English custom, when a woman saves a man's life for the third time, she has to marry him?"

"Oh, really?" she replied, opening her eyes to give him a dubious look.

"Yes. No exceptions. So, will you?"

Zosia rolled onto her back, stretched again, and grinned. "Sure. Why not?" She giggled, turned toward him, and added, "But I'm not going to let you get away that lightly—you coldhearted Brit. You're going to have to work harder to get a proper yes out of me." She snapped her fingers. "One order of romance! Heavy on the charm! I want a symphony!"

He smiled broadly. He felt so giddy with happiness that it did not matter what had happened to Karl. It did not matter that he had narrowly escaped death or that the Council's treatment of him was inscrutable. Nothing in the world could intrude on their happiness!

He put his arm around her, began to kiss her neck, moved downward slowly, teasingly. As she began to respond, breathing deeply, sighing slightly, he looked up, could not resist asking, "Is this what you had in mind? Or would you like me to add words to my music?"

"Only in Polish." She traced a pattern with her finger along his neck, down his chest.

"*Kochana Zosiu.*"

"That's a good start," she teased. "How about some more?"

He shook his head helplessly.

She giggled. "Then you'll have to work your magic in silence."

32

"**W**ELL, COLONEL?" he asked mischievously.

"Yes, Captain?" she responded with a luxuriant stretch and a satisfied smile.

"Was that a reasonable salute?"

"Um-hmm." She stretched, moaned, and turned over in the bed so her face was away from him.

He raised himself up enough to lean over and kiss her cheek. "You're marvelous," he whispered softly into her ear.

"Umm," she responded, already half-asleep. He continued to lean over her and watched as she drifted off. With her eyes closed, her long eyelashes looked even more seductive. And whatever she had done to her hair to smooth it down was wearing off—obstreperously frizzy curls were beginning to emerge here and there. He looked at the curve of her face, ran a finger gently over her cheekbone and down along to her chin. She continued to smile even as her breathing became regular.

Peter settled back down among the covers, resting his hands behind his head. He had not slept the night before, he had endured a miserable day, the adrenaline surges from two life-and-death situations had left him exhausted, and Zosia had agreed to marry him. Despite his fatigue, he did not feel like sleeping.

It had been so long since he had slept with a woman. A year and a half? No, better not to think about that; *that* was not sex—it was something else: a quid pro quo, a bargain, a way of staying alive. Besides, he had never told Zosia about it. It had embarrassed him too much: that selling of the very last bit of his soul in exchange for a little peace in his life. And until Elspeth had hit him in the plaza, in public, he had thought it had worked. He thought that he had bought some human dignity from her. But when she had hit him like that, for voicing his opinion, then he had known he would never be human in their eyes. That was when he had known there was no price he could pay that would satisfy them. That was when he had known he had to leave, whatever the cost.

He smiled to himself. Just as well: look at what he finally had now! Zosia would be his wife, Joanna his daughter. He had a home, friends, and a purpose, and given his outing alone in Berlin, the doubters in the encampment could not fail to trust him now. He had proven himself. Even the disastrous encounters of the past day had served their purpose—he had shown what he was made of, had proven his loyalty. They would have to accept him.

He got out of bed and went over to the window. It had still been daylight when they had begun making love and they had not drawn the drapes. He wondered if anyone had seen them. Now, the night sky was lit a brilliant orange as the omnipresent security lights reflected off the dusting of snow on the sidewalks. The overcast sky merged into the mist of orange making the city look somewhat like a dimly lit backdrop in a theater. It was still reasonably early, but the streets were nearly deserted. A patrol paced along the pavement under the window; a few soldiers emerged from a bar across the street and debated the direction they should take. A taxi turned a corner and disappeared from view. The usual workings of a city. A city gone discreetly mad.

Peter lowered the shutters and returned to the bed. He should sleep; they were not yet home safe, and the last thing Zosia needed was an exhausted partner if anything should happen during their stay in the pension. She had already saved his life three times, he did not want there to be a fourth. And he hoped he would never have an opportunity to try to repay the debt. What he wanted was a chance to live something akin to a normal life. A chance to be human.

That thought brought Elspeth to mind. He grimaced in annoyance, she did not belong here in his happiness! Was it only three days ago he had watched her leave the house with her servant? Had daydreamed about harassing her? Now all he wanted was to be rid of her, her and her stupid husband—may he rest in peace! But how would she cope if Karl was dead? Did she have a pension? Would she have to move out of the house, sell the slave? Would she miss Karl? Or would she secretly be pleased? Funny, he had never learned what was inside her head; sometimes he suspected that she herself could not have answered the questions. She was such a paradox.

What had he said that day that had finally caused her to take action? She had told him his behavior was totally inappropriate, and he had answered something like, she wouldn't have him any other way. *Ah, yes,* gnä' Frau, *but you wouldn't have it any other way.* He remembered saying it with a flippant air of complete disregard. He had just buried that sparrow and had found himself, once again, thinking about his own death. The realization that he had accepted it as a given, that he would die in the near future, there, as an unfree man, had left him feeling somewhat freed from all the constraints of his life. So he had smiled at her when he had seen her; he had found within himself the broad and happy grin of a man who had accepted his fate and had ceased to care. And she had chided him for it in that strange way she had of seeming both pleased and displeased simultaneously. Sometimes, sometimes when she forgot who she was and the seriousness and probity of her position in society, sometimes she even looked attractive.

He had come inside, scraped the dirt off his boots, washed his face and hands, and presented himself in the kitchen ready to make whatever she would later take credit for. There was, however, no cooking or baking that day; she had changed her mind. "We'll just buy something from the bakery later," she had said while scanning him from head to toe. He had been used to the way she looked at him, so he had not really taken much note of her action. Not until she had said, in that strange tone of voice, "Come with me."

She had led him to her bedroom and shut the door. Uwe was in his room napping, the children were at school, Karl was at work. "You look tired," she had said. "Take off your shoes and lie down."

"*Gnädige Frau,*" he had protested, shaking his head, "it is forbidden."

"No, it isn't. I have commanded, so you are permitted."

"I cannot."

"Yes, you can; are you telling me that you will not?" she had said with only the slightest hint of malice.

It should have taken more than that; it should have required threats or something, but he knew the game, he knew the score, and he knew there was no way he could win. So he had immediately conceded defeat and tried to snatch whatever advantage he could from the situation. If they were caught, it was the death penalty for him; but he was dying anyway and the particular impetus for his death was irrelevant.

He could have failed to satisfy her since that would easily have been explained and easily excused: the fear, the poor living conditions, the coercion. But he was frighteningly lonely as well. So, he had opted for treating her as a lover, for telling her sweet lies, for responding to her touch, for closing his eyes and thinking of Maria. He had initially tried to think of Allison, but it was too much of a stretch, so he had thought of Maria and smiled at the irony. He remembered Elspeth telling him then that he looked happy, and he remembered agreeing. "I've always wanted you," he had lied with disturbing ease.

Zosia stirred and moaned in her sleep. He raised himself up on an elbow and looked at her as she slept. The covers could not hide the deep arch of her waist, the way her hips curved up and then her body gently tapered along her thighs. The sweet smell of her sweat perfumed her skin and encouraged even more curls to emerge from beneath her temporarily tamed hair as it lay scattered in a mass about her head. She was so beautiful! He loved her so much.

He remembered his first night of freedom—the night they had spent talking and watching the stars move. At the time he was uncertain whether it would be his last night on earth, but he had enjoyed it all the more for that. He remembered how they had huddled together against the cold of the night, how she had fallen asleep in his arms with the coming of the dawn. They had shared so much, learned so much about each other on that night. More than most couples learn in a lifetime. And now, finally, the love that had been planted then would come to fruition. Was it possible to be happier? He sighed contentedly and lay back in the bed ready at last to sleep. At long last he could wash away Elspeth's memory.

"Can I wash?" he had asked, indicating the bathroom suite in her room.

Elspeth lay in the bed, smiling dreamily. "What's the hurry?"

"Work," he answered tersely. "A shower would be nice." A shower with hot water and enough soap to scrub away the feeling of complicity. A shower, because Karl always bathed.

"No"—she sounded annoyed—"use the cellar. I don't want you to mess everything up in there."

Now there was a concept, he thought. I clean the bloody bathroom every day but I can't be trusted to use it. But of course he knew the real reason. She might stoop to having sex with an *Untermensch*, but she sure as hell wasn't going to let him use her bathroom—it was just too personal!

He pulled on his clothes and shoes, finished tying the laces while sitting on the edge of the bed, and thought of Elspeth's refusal to let him shower. He turned to contemplate her as she lay on the bed with the covers pulled demurely up to her chin. "Is there anything else, *gnädige Frau*?" he had asked with more than a little sarcasm.

"No," she had answered quite seriously, assuming her usual distance, "you may go. Oh, yes, go see if Uwe needs anything."

"Of course, *Gnädigste,*" he had said, and left to check on Uwe.

As he lay next to Zosia, he remembered how that first afternoon, as he served the coffee to Elspeth's friends, she had smirked at him. She clearly wanted to reveal her triumph to her friends but did not dare, at least not with Frau Schindler present. Elspeth kept eyeing him, and he remembered feeling disgusted, embarrassed, and used as he realized she was not looking at him as a man, but rather as an object that she owned. Owned completely.

Zosia turned toward him. "Aren't you asleep?"

"No, just thinking."

"What are you thinking about?" She yawned.

"Nothing important." He rolled toward her. "You are so incredibly beautiful."

She yawned again, managed to reply, "You're not half-bad yourself."

"Do you want to do it again?"

"Are you up to it already?" She sounded tired.

"I think so. Anyway, there's lots to do in the meantime." He grinned at her and reached tentatively toward her to stroke her skin. "You're so beautiful, I just want to touch you. All the way from your hair down to your toes—starting here."

She rolled onto her back but did not pull away from his touch. "Umm."

"Go back to sleep, if you want. If you don't mind, I just want to feel the contours of your body." He ran his fingers along her face, enjoyed the rise of her cheekbone, the down of her cheek, the curve of her jaw.

"No, I don't mind," she replied sleepily.

He let his fingers stray across her lips. Such sensuous lips! "You are so heartbreakingly lovely," he whispered.

She sighed, wet her lips with her tongue.

He traced around her ears, felt the folds and the curves, the soft skin of her earlobe. Slowly, savoring the sensation, he let the back of his hand slide along her neck, felt the delicate pulse of her life's blood beneath his hand, the wisps of hair that strayed into his path.

"That feels good," she murmured dreamily.

"Your skin is so incredibly soft here." He lingered at the base of her neck just above the swell of her breasts, traced little circles just to feel the softness of her skin. But then his hand was drawn farther down.

"Yeah, I think I'm ready for some more," she sighed as his fingers caressed the soft skin of her breast, teased her nipples to harden. "Umm. Definitely ready."

"So am I," he whispered in reply, bending down to kiss her, letting his lips follow the progress of his hand.

=====**33**=====

"**W**ELL, I NEVER THOUGHT I'd see you alive again," Tadek joked with just a bit less than his usual degree of spite.

Peter grinned at him. "Great party, isn't it?" he said, glancing around at the revelers who were celebrating their successful mission and safe return.

"All the better as our engagement party," Zosia contributed as she joined them. She hugged Peter and added, "It's all right if I tell everyone, isn't it?"

His grin broadened.

"You're getting married!" Tadek shouted. The crowd fell silent and stared at them in amazement. "Zosia, can we talk? Now? Please?" Tadek pleaded.

"Mommy?" Joanna called out from across the room. She abandoned her friends and began plowing through the people.

"Please, Zosia!" Tadek begged.

"Later," Zosia replied coldly. As Tadek tugged at her arm, she repeated, "Later!"

Tadek downed the rest of his vodka in one gulp, then muttered, "Congratulations," and wandered off to refill his glass.

"Don't worry about him," Zosia said, watching him walk away. "He'll be fine."

"Mommy!" Joanna squealed as she threw her arms around her mother's legs.

"Funny," Peter responded, "worrying about him hadn't really occurred to me."

Joanna released her hold on her mother and threw her arms around Peter's legs. "Daddy!" He lifted her into his arms and hugged her. "Married! Married! Will you be my father? Will you adopt me?" she asked excitedly.

"If there's an official way of doing it, I certainly will. But you know, I already have." He gave her a big kiss. "Now, why don't you come with me, little one. I'm going to get your mommy a present."

He returned to the party with the necklace he had bought in Berlin. He had not taken time to rewrap it, and despite his protestations that she should not, she read the melancholy farewell he had scribbled onto the wrapping paper. Her voice caught in her throat as she realized how close she had been to losing him, and they looked at each other with a shared knowledge of devastating loss. Then Zosia smiled and opened the gift. She declared it was absolutely wonderful and quickly fastened it around her neck and traipsed around the room for all to admire it.

As Peter remained holding Joanna, Barbara came over to him. "I'm glad you made it back," she said shyly.

"Yeah, so am I." He smiled at her.

"I'm sorry about . . ." She gestured toward the injuries still visible on his face.

"They'll be gone soon enough."

"May I?" she asked as she gently kissed his cheek. Their eyes met as she pulled back, then she quickly looked away, scanning the room as if searching for someone. Without looking at him she said, "Congratulations on your engagement."

"Thank you."

She finally decided she could not find whomever she was looking for in the room and brought her gaze back to his face and said softly, "It's quite a surprise. No one expected it."

"It's what we both want."

Barbara nodded noncommittally. "I guess. But please, be careful."

Zosia returned before he could decide what to say to that. She and Barbara exchanged a glance: Barbara's look was inscrutable, Zosia's amused. Barbara made her excuses and walked off. Zosia watched her walk away, said, "I think you have a fan."

"She's a nice kid."

"She wouldn't appreciate you thinking of her as a kid."

He shrugged. She was indeed a young woman, bright, pretty, experienced. She had probably already killed a dozen enemy soldiers. Still she had that youthful enthusiasm, that sure knowledge of the world that he had long ago lost. There was a lifetime of compromises and bad decisions that separated the two of them. She was a kid.

That night, as they lay in bed with Joanna sleeping between them, Zosia turned on her side, reached over her sleeping daughter, and gently stroked his face to see if he was awake.

"Hello," he said as he felt her fingers. He hoped she did not notice that he had recoiled—it was just that her touch was so unexpected and he had nearly been asleep.

"Joanna?" Zosia whispered quietly, but there was no response from the child.

"I think she's asleep," he whispered. "She's a lovely child, isn't she?"

"Yes, she is." Zosia sounded sad.

"What's the matter?" he asked, worried by her tone.

"You can't adopt her," she replied forlornly.

"What? Why not?" He raised himself up to look at Zosia, but she had turned her face away. He felt vaguely desperate, whispered intensely, "I promised her I would!"

"You should have asked me first," Zosia said stiffly.

He fell silent, utterly furious with her. He decided, however, not to show his anger; there was too much at stake. He gritted his teeth and said, "Look, I'm really sorry I didn't ask you first. You saw, though, she just asked me—how could I say no?" Zosia didn't say anything to that, so he added, "I'm sorry, I'm really sorry I didn't get your consent before announcing it to everyone, but please Zosiu, please let me adopt her."

"No, Peter. It's just not possible."

"Why not? I *said* I was sorry!" It was hard to whisper and be so angry and desperate at the same time.

"I promised Adam."

"You what?"

"He said if anything happened to him, he didn't mind if I remarried; in fact, he even encouraged it. But he made me promise that no one would adopt Joanna. He wanted to be sure he was not forgotten, that he remained her father."

Damn the man's ego! "I'm sure he didn't mean it that way, Zosia."

"You know the life we lead, Peter. If Adam or I talked about death, it was entirely serious; we liked to keep our affairs in order. He meant what he said."

"I'm sure if he knew how much Joanna wanted it, he would change his mind."

"No, that's exactly what he was afraid of. That he would be replaced."

"So he'd deny his daughter a chance to have a father?"

"You can still be a father to her. You just can't make it legal. I made a solemn vow."

"Damn! What am I going to say to Joanna?"

"You should have thought of that before you made your promise."

Damn them both, he thought, and slumped back down into the bed. Damn their stupid egos and their genetic connection. He was Joanna's father now, he should be allowed to say so to the world. He sighed noisily.

"I'll tell Joanna, if you want," Zosia's voice came softly out of the night.

"No," he responded, resigned, "I'll tell her." That her mother is a wicked old witch and her dead father a selfish egomaniac. Well, maybe not. Maybe Adam deserved this last vestige of a part of Zosia's and Joanna's lives. It was, after all, just a legal nicety. It wouldn't change anything—he would still be a father to her. Being there—that was what mattered.

He lay quietly thinking of what he would say to Joanna. Perhaps if he invoked her father's memory a bit; perhaps they really were forgetting him already. What had it been? Not even two years. "Zosia?" he asked quietly to see if she was still awake.

"Yes?" she answered with tears in her voice.

"How did Adam get taken?" He had never bothered to ask. He had, he realized, done everything he could to hurry the process of forgetting the man.

"He was teaching a class—in town. A university course. He was betrayed by a new student."

"Teaching?"

"Yes, that was one of his passions. He taught history. We try to keep an education system going so that our population can be ready to resume control of their lives at some point in the future." She paused. "Of course, teaching is a capital offense."

"What happened to him?"

"Died in custody is all the records say."

"I'm sorry, Zosiu," he said quietly. He decided suddenly to learn more about Adam, to try to help Zosia preserve his memory. It was the least he could do. "He was on the Council, wasn't he?"

"Oh, yes, more senior than me. Once he was gone, we elected Tadek to the Council."

"Ah, Tadek." The one who had given him such trouble at his trial. After all he had endured—to face that cold judgment, those unfeeling eyes. "So, I might have had an easier time at my trial if Adam had lived?"

"I doubt it."

"What? Do you think Adam would have been keener to shoot me than Tadek?"

"I don't know. What I do know is I got a lot of sympathy votes for your cause. Without that, it's doubtful we would have gotten a majority in the first place, and Adam's opinion would have been irrelevant."

Peter did not say anything. He wished he had not asked the question.

"Or more likely," she continued, unaware of his discomfort, or perhaps unconcerned about it, "Marysia would not have been feeling quite so sentimental and would have had Olek shoot you the minute she realized you were unimportant."

"Unimportant," he repeated.

"Yes, unimportant," she agreed.

He did not fail to detect her implication. How dare he think of himself and his own pain, when Adam, marvelous Adam, had made the ultimate sacrifice. "Ah, yes," he responded bitterly. "How stupid of me to have forgotten my place." Worthless and unimportant and in a lifelong debt for being allowed to live. Why did it sound so damn familiar?

A long silence ensued, then softly she said, "I'm sorry, Peter. I didn't mean it that way."

"Yes, you did," he replied quietly, and turned over to fall asleep.

There was a classroom. A few scattered chairs, a table, a place where he could stand and talk. Three or four students sat looking at him, waiting for him to speak. He talked about literature, about Shakespeare. The class grew noisy—he looked up and saw twenty or so students—all in neat rows of tables and chairs. He quoted from *King Lear*. He tried to use English, but German kept coming out. Someone asked if there was a line about serpent's teeth and mad governments. No, he said, it was a hound's tooth and Mozart. He heard a key scrape in a lock, began to tremble in terror. He looked up at his students. There were hundreds of them packed into a huge lecture hall. How could they have been so careless! Hundreds!

They were all waiting for him to say something. The rusty key scraped like a razor across his raw nerves. His limbs grew heavy with dread. He began to speak again, but his voice caught in his throat. He looked up but no one was there. He was alone. No, not alone, for someone hit him. He sputtered as blood filled his mouth. Someone hit him again. *You self-satisfied, arrogant little worm! You think you're so damn intelligent, don't you!* He spit blood, choked, and coughed on his teeth as they swam loose in the blood in his mouth.

"Are you all right?" Zosia was kneeling on the floor by his side of the bed, looking at him in the dim light.

"Oh," he moaned, then realized where he was. "Did I wake you?"

"What were you dreaming?"

He shook his head in answer, then got up out of bed. "I'm going for a walk."

Zosia stood, put her hand on his arm. "I'm . . . I didn't mean . . ."

He kissed her. "It's all right about Joanna. She and I will work something out."

Zosia nodded.

"And," he continued, unsure of himself, "I'll do what I can to help her remember"—he swallowed, forced himself to say the words—"her father."

"Thanks," Zosia said quietly, and turned to crawl back under the covers.

He pulled on his clothes, a pair of tall boots, and a long, wool coat and wandered to the exit. It was a cold, almost cloudless night. A sentry's voice came out of the darkness. "Captain Halifax?"

"Yeah, it's me." Peter peered in the direction of the voice, but could not recognize who it was.

"I wasn't able to come to your party, sir, but I wanted to offer my congratulations."

"Thank you." Peter paused, then added, "I hope you can make it to the wedding."

"Sir?"

"The wedding."

"Which wedding, sir?"

"Mine and Colonel Król's. Wasn't that what you congratulated me about?"

"No, sir. I didn't know about that, sir. No, I was referring to your success on the mission. I heard how brave you were—and resourceful."

"Oh?"

"We're proud of your work, sir. Olek and Barbara came out earlier and relayed your story."

"They did?"

"Yes, sir."

"Oh." They had relayed his story, but they had not mentioned the engagement. He smiled to himself. "I'll just be walking about a bit."

"No problem, sir." Then pointing into the woods, the sentry said, "It's easier going in that direction, there are some paths through the snow."

"Thanks." Peter went in the direction the soldier had indicated. He walked a bit into the darkness, then brushed some snow off a rock and sat down to watch the wisps of passing clouds through a clearing in the trees. His head ached as though someone had been pounding it, so he picked up a handful of snow and held it against his eyes. The melting snow ran like tears down his face.

34

"TIME TO GET UP, Daddy. Shh! Don't wake Mom!" Joanna said, nudging Peter gently. "It's today!"

Together they dressed warmly, gathered their candles and written vows, and slid out into the predawn darkness. It was Joanna's simple solution to her mother's diktat: if she could not officially be adopted, then it would be unofficially and secretly witnessed only by her friends.

They arrived at the tree that marked Adam's grave as the first light of dawn touched the horizon. As they dusted the snow away to find the marker, they were joined by Joanna's classmates and even her teacher—a young woman, a teenager actually, called Basia. Peter gave Joanna a questioning glance, and she shrugged and said under her breath that it was hard to invite her classmates without the teacher noticing, so she had invited the teacher as well. "And besides," she whispered, "she's a good sort."

Joanna's friends sat in the snow in a semicircle around the two and waited expectantly, clearly accustomed to such odd rituals. Joanna had involved her entire class in the writing of the ceremony, and it was she who led the proceedings. They lit the candles, they sang some songs, they explained to her father what they were doing and that he would not be forgotten—ever. This last promise sounded as though it had been used before on many other occasions—all the children knew the words by heart. Peter listened to their chant with a growing sense of wonder at the strange world he found himself in. Their words, their voices, were beautiful, enchanting, yet also quite terrifying—that such young children had such a certain knowledge of death, of killing, of dying as a people.

They reached a point where he was asked to make his promises to Joanna and her family, and he did so, vowing to take care of her as best he could, vowing to love her, vowing to help her keep the memory of her father alive. So that he could say it all in Polish, he had written the words down and had Barbara help him with the grammar to be sure he had it all correct. He held the paper in front of him, but his vision had become so unfocused he could not see the words, so he said it all from memory, hoping that they would not laugh too much at his mistakes.

Joanna made her promises as well and then the children sang again—a church hymn to their blessed Virgin, then their national anthem, and finally another song, which could only be described as pagan in its words of ancestor worship and memory. They extinguished the candles, and Joanna came over to sit on his lap and to hug and kiss him as the other children and their teacher turned to head back to their classroom.

The two sat there awhile surrounded by the silence of the snow-shrouded woods. Joanna leaned against his shoulder, and he stroked her curly blond locks. A shaft of sunlight made its way through the trees, illuminating her hair. It glinted a coppery gold, and he marveled at the subtleties of its color. Gently he lifted a curl and studied the complex twists and turns of the individual strands. As he held the hair, he recalled the matted stuffing he had pulled from the Vogels' armchair. Had there been the hair of a child among those strands?

After a long while sitting in silence, they stood, brushed the snow off their clothes, and returned to the camp. Joanna went to her class, but Peter returned to the flat. Zosia had already left for work, and he decided to take the rest of the day off and spend some time putting up some shelves. He gathered his tools, determined what else he might need, and went about scrounging materials and equipment. Eventually he had everything he thought he might need and began trying to mount something onto the rather unyielding concrete of their flat.

"Why don't you just put in a work order for that?" Zosia inquired; she stood in the doorway munching an apple, looking up at him on a ladder.

"We did—about a year ago. I'd like to have these shelves this decade." He spoke around the bracket he was holding in his teeth. "In fact, I'd like to have them up before our guests arrive—this place looks . . ." He sighed.

"Disorganized?" Zosia suggested as she tried to extract a bit of apple skin from between her teeth.

He gave her a wry look.

"Non-German?" she asked.

He smirked.

"Polish?"

"I'm afraid where I came from the standard synonym for unkempt was *English*." What was it the kids at school said? *Foul-smelling, disease-ridden, and thoroughly disorderly. Not unlike the English themselves.* It had hurt then; at least he could smile at it now. "But is it really so awful of me to want my books up off the floor?"

"No, I know you have this inexplicable *Drang nach Ordnung*," she teased.

He laughed and glanced down at the books that he had acquired over the past year and some—they were getting moldy sitting in their stacks on the floor, his office was full, and Zosia's stuff already filled every other available space. Technically, the work order should have solved the problem, but somehow, and not surprisingly, the overworked maintenance crew had given the new bookshelf a rather low priority—in spite of, or perhaps because of, Zosia's rank. So, he had decided to try his hand at installing the shelves himself. The bunker's concrete was notoriously difficult to work with, and he did not have enough experience to feel comfortable with Zosia watching him. He thought he had solved that problem by waiting until he knew she'd be out before attempting the job, and therefore, he had been rather taken aback to see her in the doorway. She wouldn't help, but she would offer lots of advice, even though she herself had never once done anything of the sort.

He climbed down from the ladder and set down the tools. "How about a cup of tea?"

"No, I don't have much time. I just thought I'd stop by on my way back to my office."

"Oh, where were you?"

"Research. I wanted to check on Karl."

"Did you find anything out?"

"Yep."

"And I suppose you're going to tell me at some point?" He smiled at her. "Or do I have to bribe you with a dinner invitation?"

"Hmm. Yeah, I think a dinner invitation will do."

"Fine. I'll cook tonight."

"Not tonight. I have to make a quick trip up north. How about when I get back?" she suggested.

"Okay. Now, tell me what you found out."

"Well . . . we were right, he survived."

"Too bad." Peter turned to put the kettle on for himself. "Do you think there'll be any fallout?"

"I don't know. The train staff found him and took him to the hospital. Diagnosis: heart attack. I doubt he's told them more than that—it would look rather embarrassing to have had you and lost you like that. If he did tell them, I doubt they believed him. They'd probably assume it was delirium. But even if he did tell them, and even if they did believe him, there's no harm in it. He has no idea where you've gone."

"He's seen you now."

"Oh, that was so brief, he'll never remember me." Zosia breezily dismissed Peter's concerns. "I'm sure he was disoriented by it all. Anyway, I don't imagine there's any problem there."

"He worries me, Zosiu. He's vindictive and now he'll have an ax to grind."

"Oh, don't fret it, he knew you were alive before this. After all, he would have been told if your body had turned up somewhere."

"I suppose, but now I've rubbed his nose in it. And he knows there's something weird going on. He noticed I had changed nationality and numbers. It'd be worth his tracking me down just to sort that out."

"Not really—he would probably figure you had gotten kidnapped after your escape. Someone would just slam a nationality on your sleeve and a new number on your arm and sell you off. After all, what would you do then, complain?"

"Does that commonly happen to escapees?"

Zosia shrugged. "Who knows? What does happen is slaves who haven't escaped are sometimes kidnapped—sort of like what almost happened to you."

"You mean those two officers at the laboratory who tried to arrest me?"

"Yes. My bet is if those two cops had taken you, you would have never made it to the prison. En route, they'd have bundled you into another car and claimed you escaped. Then you'd have found yourself dumped into a factory with locked gates and guards with guns. Or you'd be beaten into admitting a crime and your 'punishment' would be to be reassigned. They'd give you a new number, and you'd answer to whatever name they told you. You'd have no reason to disbelieve them, but even if you did, who would you turn to?"

"Well, I would have come right back here."

"I know that. I meant, who would a typical *Zwangsarbeiter* turn to?"

"What if someone like that does escape and informs their previous owner?"

"I suspect that they pick politically weak owners who wouldn't believe the story, and even if they did, they'd be too terrified to pursue any legal action. They'd be wise to just slam the door in the face of their returning chattel."

"Hmm. Well, maybe then Karl won't concern himself with the details, but he still worries me. He has a long memory. As soon as he gets a chance, he'll try and do something."

"But he can't, so don't worry about it."

Easier said than done, Peter thought as Zosia kissed him and turned to leave.

"Hold on, there!" Marysia warned as she came into the apartment, her arms laden. "You're not going anywhere, young lady, until you help me sort through all these invitations!"

"What about Peter?" Zosia asked.

"He's already given me his. Handwritten as well."

"One of the advantages of not being so very popular as you, my little princess of the Underground," Peter joked.

"Anyway, he has another task," Marysia consoled Zosia. "Here, learn this, so you know what you're doing," Marysia ordered, handing him a well-worn pamphlet. She seated herself at the table and began organizing stacks of paper. Zosia dutifully followed suit.

Peter looked at what Marysia had handed him. It was a Roman Catholic missal. On the right-hand side of each page was the mass in Latin, on the left a translation into Polish. Zosia giggled when she saw the expression on his face.

"Latin?" he asked.

"Just the mass," Marysia answered, all business.

"And the vows?"

"They'll be in Polish," Marysia stated with an irrefutable finality.

He had never actually considered the practicalities of marrying Zosia within her own community. He had imagined a quick exchange of vows in front of a few friends, a big party, and that would be it. Certainly marriages in Britain were usually much less formal. The first marriage—the one that typically happened about a week before the boy turned sixteen—that was a quick affair in the registry office and then an excuse for a going-away party and a teenage brawl. The bride and groom usually left at the end of the party, sick drunk, to return to their respective parents' flats.

Six years later, when the boy returned from conscription, they had the advantage of having been on the housing list all those years. A jump on everybody else, except of course, everybody else did the same thing. So, there were a lot of young couples who knew nothing about each other and had nothing in common other than a place on a housing list. They usually stayed together—it was worth it to keep that coveted priority placement, though they often lived almost completely separate lives. Upon finally being assigned a flat, they would share it and continue to live their separate lives. Inevitably they would meet other people, and divorces and remarriages would be arranged almost simultaneously. It meant that, in the end, a first marriage was a rather casual affair. It was a slip of paper, a place on a list, a sometime partner for nights out at the pub, and little more.

"Is there anywhere I have to say I believe in God?" he asked as he scanned through the pamphlet.

Zosia screwed up her face in thought. "I don't think so. Not if you don't say the creed. If you just stick to the vows, you should be okay. But God is invoked a lot."

"You should be comfortable doing that," Marysia remarked sardonically without looking up from what she was writing. "According to Olek, you invoke God all the time."

Ah, yes. He really should clean up his English. "Sorry, it's part of my local dialect. I'll try and be more—um—circumspect, in the future."

"Yes, do try."

Zosia looked up at him, gave him a conspiratorial shrug.

The kettle whistled and he turned to make his tea. "Do either of you want a cup?" he asked, but they both shook their heads. As he cautiously sipped the brew, he asked, "I don't need to, er, eat anything, do I?"

Marysia looked up at him, a look of utter disapproval on her face. "If you mean receive the host, no—it's an honor. One you haven't earned."

"Ah. Again, my apologies. I'm a bit untutored in this religion thing." He had almost said *crap* but had caught himself in time. "But it is permitted for Zosia to marry me and still use your ceremony?"

"Yes, yes, yes. We can accommodate heathens and atheists," Marysia replied impatiently.

"Good." He grinned at her. "And where exactly do I get to work in my blood sacrifice to the tree gods?"

Marysia glanced up at him sharply. "You— Oh, you're joking."

Zosia laughed, said, "What I want to know is, when do we get to sacrifice a virgin? I haven't had one in ages!"

"No respect," Marysia muttered shaking her head, "no respect." She looked up at Peter again, tried to maintain a serious expression. "You know, young man, we take these things seriously, not like you British."

"Oh, so you've heard about English marriages."

"Yes, everyone has. The Germans point to it as proof that you're all corrupt. Marrying to be on a housing list!" Marysia tried to sound disgusted.

"Well, don't the locals do that here?"

"No," Zosia replied, suddenly quite serious. "Marriage is essentially forbidden for *Nichtdeutsch*."

"What? You're kidding!"

"No, unfortunately not," Marysia agreed with Zosia. "The law was enacted in 1942 that the only way to be legally married is to prove that it will 'raise the racial standard of the Polish people.' "

"And that," Zosia continued, "as you may guess, is not easily proved. I mean," she added impishly, "how can you improve on perfection?"

Peter shook his head in amazement. "So marriage is basically illegal?"

Marysia shrugged. "You are surprised? After all, it was for you, wasn't it?"

"Yes, for me, everything was illegal."

"In any case," Marysia explained, "it serves a useful technical purpose for them. As long as marriage is forbidden, it is impossible to have children legally, so whenever they want, they have the legal right to seize the children and throw the parents in prison."

"Ah, so any *Nichtdeutsch* who marries or has children is a criminal."

"Yes, it's very easy to be a criminal here."

"I never understood why they bothered with all the technicalities, you know, why they feel the need to have laws to back up their immoral acts."

Zosia shrugged. Marysia said, "Maybe if they make it legal, they think it is moral as well. Many people confuse legality and morality, then they never have to examine their own conscience about what they do."

"I really don't have time for this right now!" Zosia said abruptly, and got up and left. Both Peter and Marysia stared after her, taken aback by her sudden departure.

"What was that all about?" he asked helplessly.

"Oh"—Marysia dismissed his concern with a wave of her hand—"she must be nervous. Maybe she feels she's rushing things."

"We're not rushing, we've known each other more than a year now."

Marysia sputtered, "I tell you, this isn't like her at all. She's not one to marry. Even with Adam, she hesitated!"

"Even?"

"You know what I mean. They knew each other for years, they were a natural couple, not like you two."

"Not like . . ." He paused, looked at her a moment. "You don't think we should marry, do you?"

Marysia looked down at the piece of paper on which she had been writing as though it contained a script she should read, but she did not say anything.

"Why not?"

She sighed. "You are from wildly different backgrounds. I don't think either of you have thought this thing through."

He bristled slightly.

"Oh, don't bother taking offense, it's the truth. I mean, never mind about all you've been through, or Zosia's unusual upbringing. What about culture? What about religion? What do you two really have in common?" Marysia asked, almost as if pleading. "All I'm saying is, I think you both should think long and hard about this marriage idea."

"I've already thought about it quite long enough, thank you," he stated coldly.

"Well, then, nothing I say will matter, will it?" she concluded somewhat forlornly.

"No, it won't. I'm not going to let your jealousy over your son ruin my only chance at happiness."

"That's not my motivation," she said stiffly.

"I think it is. You've finally worked out that I'm not going to step into his shoes, I'm going to displace him altogether, and you don't like that."

"Oh, what do I know about marriage." Marysia sounded resigned. "I'm just an old woman whose husband ran away . . ."

"Oh, don't trot out that old song, we're not talking about how your marriage was fucked up here."

"I'll thank you to watch your tongue in my presence."

He sighed. "I'm sorry. Zosia's not the only one on edge."

"Don't worry, son, it's normal."

He smiled at her calling him son. "Thanks, Ma. I don't suppose you'd like to have some vodka with me?"

"You drink too much," she said as he went to the cabinet to get a bottle.

"I know."

35

"SO WHAT'S GOING ON?" Zosia asked as Anna poured out some vodka for her and Ryszard. From where Zosia was sitting, she could just manage to see out the window of her parents' town house to the windswept street below. The gusts whipped up whirlwinds of snow and hurled them along the desolate canyon formed by the huge blocks of public housing. The windows clattered in their frames, and though the flat was warm, Zosia shuddered.

Alex made a face. "Bad news again, I'm afraid."

"What now?"

"The information we've sent them on that sterility program. It's been classified."

"Peter and his team haven't even finished decoding it all!" Zosia exclaimed.

"I know, I know. Nevertheless, we've already sent the headline news, and they've thanked us for the information and put a gag on it."

"What would happen if you ignored the gag order?"

Alex shook his head. "The Cabinet feels we have too much to lose. Nevertheless, don't tell Peter—have his office keep up the translations. Maybe we can find something we can use—maybe we can leak the information to the American press via another route."

"I think we should just ignore their gag order. They don't have the right to issue us commands. Especially now!" Ryszard grumbled. "Have you told HQ yet about the secret talks?"

Alex nodded. "They're worried, but they agree with the Cabinet that it's not sufficient reason to take such a drastic step. Besides, if we violate the gag order on this, that could scupper our chances at those talks."

Ryszard sputtered. "We have no chances. We have no representation there!"

"What are you talking about?" Zosia asked.

Alex pushed a folder of papers across to his daughter. "This is one of the reasons I wanted to talk to you personally. I want you to officially convey this information to the Szaflary Council. I've already presented it to HQ, and they know we'll be sending the relevant copies back with you."

Zosia opened the folder and began scanning the papers as Alex continued, "It seems there has been an official invitation from within the NAU Foreign Ministry to begin some sort of talks with the Reich. They've suggested Helsinki for the venue. As you can see, there are several items on the tentative agenda which are . . ." Alex hesitated as he searched for the appropriate diplomatic phrase.

"They are an outright betrayal of us," Anna filled in the silence. "They want to negotiate formalizing the status quo and accepting our land as being official Reich territory in exchange for some vague human-rights statements."

"A peace accord?" Zosia asked.

"A sellout," Ryszard said.

"Yes," Alex agreed. "They feel that there's no longer any point feigning our independence. There are elements within their Foreign Ministry who feel we would be better served if we were given an official status within the Reich. Then they could agitate for our rights from that platform, rather than refuse all dealings with the Reich government. Perhaps they have a point."

"No!" Zosia scolded. "You know what happens! They turn a blind eye to anything that happens once it's within the sovereign borders of a state!"

"They're not seeing much now anyway, and anytime we show them something, we get stomped on." Alex sighed. "That's the other thing I wanted to talk about, and that's why I called you up here in person and without Peter. I've looked a bit further into using him as you suggested, and I've already made some tentative arrangements. The problem is, we're going to be able to pull a stunt like this only once. If we use Peter, we'll be throwing all our eggs into one basket."

"One very unstable basket," Ryszard added. "I think we'd be better off using an actor. Or anyone else."

Somewhat annoyed, Alex shook his head. "We've already discussed your concerns." He turned his attention back to Zosia. "Now Ryszard said that Kasia talked to Peter at length while he visited and she was of the opinion that he was not very keen on talking about his experiences. She said his story was compelling but she had to drag the details out of him. We'd need more than that. He'd have to wholeheartedly prostitute his history if we're going to have any hope of getting people there to listen."

Zosia nodded. "When he wants to be, he's convincing."

"What about the psychiatrist's report?" Anna asked. "You know, she said this sort of thing could push him over the edge."

Zosia shook her head. "It won't."

"Anyway, he only has to make it through the month," Ryszard observed, "then it doesn't matter. In fact, a suicide, halfway through—now *that* would be effective!"

Zosia gave Ryszard a sharp look, but then her expression changed to one of cold agreement. "Yes, that's all we need."

Anna raised her eyebrows in surprise, but did not comment.

"What about his loyalty to us?" Alex asked. "We have every reason to believe he's genuine, but no real reason to believe he's loyal to anything or anybody other than himself. Everything he endured, he did for himself, for survival. There was no element of heroism in it."

"All the better for proving our point," Zosia observed.

"Yes," Alex agreed, "but we need to know that he'll do a good job, and even more important, we need to know that he's devoted to us so that he's not inclined to deliberately cause problems."

"Why in heavens name would he deliberately cause trouble?" Zosia asked.

Alex cast a glance at Ryszard and Anna before answering. "We've found out a bit more about his history. Seems that betrayal that cost everyone their lives and cost Peter his freedom, well, it was a messy business. It came from over the pond."

"Won't that actually make Peter feel better to have that question answered in his mind?" Zosia asked, somewhat confused.

Alex shook his head. "I doubt it. The hierarchy knew his group was in danger long before they sent a warning. Once they learned about the danger, they decided to wait and use his group as bait to catch the traitor. Clearly, they cut it too close."

"Oh, God!" Zosia moaned.

"It gets worse. There was a trial for the traitor, a reasonably quiet affair, resulting in a short-term prison sentence. He had royal connections, you see. The problem was, the group used as bait—Peter's group—were from the 'allied faction,' that is, the antiroyalist Republicans who were only working with the government as part of a united front. Citing the government's obvious carelessness with its allies, the Republicans in Toronto tried to use that betrayal as leverage for more power, but it all backfired—they were actually temporarily excluded from the government instead, and the whole incident was hushed up."

"So how did you find out about it?"

"A friend of a friend remembered it personally. She was able to dig up some microfilm of Republican newsletters from that time, and putting those together with her reminiscences and with what Peter said, it all becomes clear."

"So that's why we had such a hard time finding anything," Zosia mused.

"Yes. Just as well, too. If you had had access to the official archives in Toronto, you would have found that they ascribe the whole fiasco to unknown causes with the strong implication that it was a betrayal by Yardley."

"What!"

"Well, that neatly covered up any carelessness on their part, and since they thought Yardley was dead, I guess they figured it wouldn't do him any harm."

"Those bastards!" Zosia spat. She squinted in thought, then muttered, "He was right. If he had run back to England and told them who he was, someone from the organization would have killed him."

Alex shrugged. "You see, if the Germans knew about that and told him—they could have turned him—he might be out seeking vengeance, just using us as a way to get to the English, especially the higher-ups in America."

Zosia shook her head. "No, he honestly doesn't know."

"Well, it has to remain that way!" Anna warned. "He certainly showed no tendency toward self-control during his visit to Ryszard's!"

"And whatever your feelings may be, little sister," Ryszard added, "he still hasn't been left out on his own. We have no proof that he wouldn't run right to his handler and spill his guts the minute he gets a chance."

"Oh, I've already tested that," Zosia said. "I let him loose in Berlin and had an agent tail him. He did exactly what I predicted. He went to look at the Vogels' house and did nothing else."

"You took that sort of chance! Who the hell gave you permission!" Ryszard nearly screamed.

"I gave myself clearance!" Zosia retorted. "I explained it all to Wanda and the others afterwards as proof of his trustworthiness."

"Yes," Anna sighed. "But as they noted in their report to us, he may have known he was being tailed."

"Anything is possible!" Zosia sneered.

"And he stopped in a shop," Anna added.

"He bought a necklace," Zosia asserted wearily. "This one, in fact." She fingered the diamond.

"And he wrote a postcard," Anna continued.

"The agent saw the Vogel girl's name on it," Zosia sighed, exasperated. "There comes a point where questioning his story is just paranoia, and I think they've passed that point."

Ryszard glowered but did not disagree. "Nothing we say to her is going to make a difference. Our little Zosienka is in love."

"I am not!" Zosia exclaimed.

"Yes, you are, little sister," Ryszard insisted.

"I am not in love!" Zosia hissed.

"You're not?" Anna asked. "Are you . . . are you pregnant?"

"No," Zosia answered brusquely.

"Then why are you marrying him?" Anna asked.

Zosia stared out the window. She did not look at any of them as she answered in a muted voice, "Because I told him I would."

"Oh, Zosiu! Didn't I ever tell you there's a time to stop playing games! Why did you do such a thing?" Anna asked.

"Well, we had just finished working together at that lab, you know. We worked the whole night together, we really made a great team. And then there was that fiasco at the end. They hurt him so badly . . ."

"Always the cold-blooded professional, eh?" Ryszard scoffed.

"He had warned me and I hadn't listened to him. And I felt so . . . Then on the train, with that Vogel man—I almost lost him then! God . . . I don't know, I guess I felt guilty about how badly he was hurt, about putting him in such danger."

"Guilty? You're marrying him out of guilt!" Anna almost shrieked.

"No, no, no!" Zosia waved her hand in frustration.

Anna sighed and looked out the window to see what Zosia was staring at so intensely, but there was nothing unusual there. She turned back to her daughter. "If you don't love him, then why?"

"Well, I thought I did. I mean, when I thought I might lose him, then afterwards . . . I just felt so happy he was okay. And in that pension, while he was recuperating, I felt so close to him, I just wanted to be with him forever."

"And how long did that last?" Ryszard asked perceptively.

"Oh, about a week," Zosia moaned. "Then I realized, it just couldn't work."

"So why not back out?" Anna asked gently. "There's still time."

"I've already announced it to everyone—I don't want to look like an impetuous fool. And it made him so happy, I couldn't bear to hurt him, and I thought it would be good for Joanna, she was really happy with the idea."

Alex and Anna exchanged a significant glance but did not interrupt.

"After Adam, I know I won't ever fall in love again," Zosia sighed. As she watched the snow swirling around, she said to herself, "God, I miss him so." She blinked back some tears and brought her gaze to rest upon her mother's face. "But I know life has to go on—so I have to see to more practical needs."

"Practical needs," Ryszard repeated disdainfully.

"Yes. Some of us can't leave everything to our wife to handle!" Zosia returned angrily. She rubbed her neck, then her eyes. "He wants it so much, and it really doesn't seem like such a bad idea. I don't want to hurt him, not after I said yes. I mean, if I back out now, he'll see it as a betrayal. He'll think I've deliberately tried to humiliate him, and . . ."

"And what?" Alex asked.

"And, and, and . . . ," Zosia stammered, wondering if she really wanted to confide so much.

"And what?" Anna pressed.

"And if he thinks that, then he'll never speak out on our behalf!"

"Oh, Zosiu! Marriage is a holy sacrament! How could you use it as a propaganda tool?" Anna groaned.

Zosia's eyes strayed from her parents to Ryszard and back again. "It will not be the first time in history that a marriage is contracted for reasons other than pure love," she stated dryly, "nor will it be the last."

Anna shook her head, disconcerted once again by the children she had raised.

Alex smiled. "No one could say you're not devoted to the cause, little one."

"Zosiu, it's your life," Anna pleaded. "I don't know about him, but you take marriage seriously. You can't afford to marry someone you don't love—even if it seems practical. Even if it means he'll refuse to help us."

"But all my hard work will be wasted!" Zosia wailed. "I can't back out now!"

Before Alex or Anna could reply, Ryszard said, "She won't cancel it, Mom, no matter what you say. No matter what she says. Our little Zosienka is in love!"

"I am not," Zosia whispered, but her voice was unsteady.

36

"**R**YSZARD! So GOOD to see you! Are Kasia and the children here?" Marysia asked as she welcomed him into her flat.

They embraced and he kissed her three times. "They'll be along later, closer to the big day," he answered, then turned his attention to the other two guests as he lit himself a cigarette.

"Hey, that's not allowed here," Katerina chided.

Ryszard walked over to her, embraced her, and kissed her cheek. "And is my auntie Katje going to plunge her little dagger in my neck for bad behavior?" he whispered.

As Katerina fended off his arms with ill-tempered impatience, Wanda chimed in, "Ryszard, it's hard enough to keep discipline here, why do you insist on being so difficult? You know the ventilation can't cope if we all smoke."

"Then don't," he snapped.

"And it would help if you stuck to speaking German with the staff," Wanda added. "You haven't spoken a word of it since your arrival!"

Ryszard raised his eyebrows at her. "I speak enough of it out there. Now, are we going to get down to business or are you ladies too intent on your bitching?"

"Please, let's sit down," Marysia suggested, gesturing toward her dining table and the four glasses of vodka she had poured out. As they seated themselves, she began, "We think we've found a couple who could work in your household when you're in Berlin." She handed Ryszard two files. "She says her mother is ill and they shouldn't go, but it's your call. Look at their files, interview them, and let us know."

"Anyone would be fine," Ryszard remarked, as he leafed through the pages. He looked up at his listeners and grinned malevolently. "Though, what we should do is save Zosia before it's too late and use her husband-to-be. After all, he's experienced!"

"No!" Wanda snapped angrily.

"No," Katerina agreed.

"It was a joke," Marysia explained, somewhat perplexed. Then she turned to Ryszard. "Wasn't it?"

He shrugged. "I thought so. I thought you wouldn't want to lose him. I've heard he's turned out to be reasonably useful."

"Who said that?" Wanda asked, her eyes narrowing.

"Tadek, of all people. Said you got a highly trained, highly intelligent analyst quite cheap—free in fact! If only he weren't . . ." Ryszard declined to elaborate.

"Useful or not, he mustn't leave this place," Wanda explained. "He's one of the few people here who knows your undercover identity, and we still haven't been able to vet him properly. He's a security risk!"

"Pff. I must admit I was stunned when I saw him in Göringstadt. It just didn't seem like you to clear something like that."

"I didn't," Wanda replied acerbically. "It was that sister of yours acting on her own again."

"So I heard. I also heard you reprimanded her so severely that she followed orders for what? Two whole months afterwards?"

"I was hoping maybe you could get through to her. You're the only one with any sense in that crazy family of yours."

"Ah, it's that impetuous English blood in our veins," Ryszard suggested humorously.

Katerina laughed, but Wanda did not. "Zosia's got some harebrained scheme and now your father is behind her as well . . ." Ryszard's gaze wandered around the room as Wanda fulminated. His eyes lit upon Julia's picture mounted on the wall, and he discreetly stared at it for some time. That long, dark hair, those passionate eyes. He sighed silently and brought his attention back to Wanda as she was saying, "I want to finally put a stop to this nonsense. I'm not going to give the clearance for him to leave here. No more trips out. None!"

"That's *your* prerogative, isn't it?" Ryszard asked Katerina.

Katerina sipped her vodka, eyeing the three of them. "In the final analysis, yes.

I've heard Wanda's arguments, and I'm convinced she's right. I just wanted to hear what you had to say before I made my decision. I assume you agree with her."

"What about the rest of the Council, don't they get a say?" Marysia huffed. "People here won't like it that you're trying to stop Zosia from doing something which could be very, very useful for us."

"They don't need to even know about it," Wanda retorted.

"What do you think, Ryszard?" Katerina asked. "After all, you're the one at greatest risk."

"Ach, the closer I get to Führer, the less I'm able to care." Ryszard laughed. He leaned back in his seat and sent a stream of smoke toward the ceiling.

"Do you really think that's a possibility?" Marysia asked.

"Yes." Ryszard laughed hoarsely and ended up coughing. "After all, I have a phenomenal political machine backing me up, don't I? All unquestioningly loyal, too. Much better than the measly mafias my competitors can muster." He laughed again at the concept of the entire Home Army as his personal entourage.

Wanda rolled her eyes impatiently, and Katerina prodded, "Well, what about this stupid idea of Zosia's. You've met this man, what do you think about him?"

"About him? He's a wreck, he drinks too much, he's moody, unpleasant, and rude. And I think Zosia's making a big mistake. But if you want to know what I think about the idea of using him, that's quite different."

"Then what do you think about it?" Marysia asked.

What did he think? Ryszard reflected on the long debate he had had with Zosia after their discussion in Göringstadt. She had convinced him of nothing, but then, upon returning home, Kasia had spoken quietly for no more than ten minutes and had completely changed his mind. His eyes strayed up to Julia's picture again. If only Julia had had Kasia's sense. He brought his attention back to Katerina and said, "He poses no particular danger to me."

Katerina raised her eyebrows in surprise. Wanda looked ready to object, but Ryszard raised a hand to silence her. "He may or may not be loyal to us, but the one thing I know for sure is, he's in love with Zosia, and for as long as that lasts, he'll do whatever she tells him."

"How can you be so sure?" Marysia asked.

"You don't understand what they did to him. He doesn't either. But I do. They made him afraid of freedom. So afraid that he would never leave. The fact that he left anyway shows a remarkable strength of will, but it also left him . . ." Ryszard paused, trying to find the easiest way to express the concept. "It left him seeking another prison, one to satisfy that fear they burned into his brain. His love for Zosia is that prison. He's bound to her by more than affection, he needs her, and he'll do anything to satisfy that need. So, if you want to use him, all I can say is, the sooner the better."

"But what if he loses control of himself? Like he did in Göringstadt?" Katerina asked.

"That wasn't losing control. He knew there was no real danger." Ryszard leaned forward, looked at each of them in turn. "I'll tell you this: he survived eight years slaving away for them. Eight years of abuse, months of torture, and he never once hit back! Now, that's control."

"Controlled or not, he's not going," Wanda insisted. "I don't trust him. I don't know what it is, but he's hiding something."

"Maybe," Ryszard agreed.

"None of us have perfect lives," Marysia noted, then turning to Katerina, said, "So you see, Ryszard is not against it. I think you ought to throw the idea out to the encampment. See what they say. I think you'll see that Zosia's idea is generally supported."

Katerina pursed her lips. "I'm not going to take any votes, Marysia, but you, Wanda, should remember that the final decision is mine."

"I don't like the way the rest of the Council isn't being consulted," Marysia commented.

Katerina waved her hand in annoyance. "Wanda's security, you're vice chair, that's sufficient consultation! Now, Ryszard, since you aren't adamantly opposed to Zosia's plan, maybe you could do some research for me. I was wondering if you could check Halifax out a bit further." She pushed a thick file toward him. "Study his record and talk with him. Your impressions will be useful."

Ryszard accepted the folder wearily. He opened it and scanned the one-page summary at the front. "Hah! So, that's why he's familiar!" Ryszard laughed.

"Why?" Marysia asked.

Ryszard tapped the paper. "This place in Breslau he was at—he must have been one of Lederman's pets." He stroked his chin thoughtfully. "You know, I vaguely remember him showing me some English prisoner . . ."

"Did he look like Peter?" Wanda asked.

Ryszard shrugged. "He was covered in filth, starved, and half-dead the time I saw him up close—he could have been anyone." He looked back down at the paper. "I suppose I must have seen him at the Vogels' the time I was there."

"Zosia said she thought she saw him there," Marysia commented.

"Did that man look like Peter?" Wanda asked Ryszard.

Again Ryszard shrugged. "Exhausted, pale, coughing up his lungs. Same sort of hair though, face . . ." He screwed up his eyes as he thought. "Sorry, I didn't bother to memorize it. He hardly merited attention."

"But you think he is genuine?" Marysia pressed.

"Oh, I've never doubted that he's genuine. He's far too fucked-up to be acting!" Ryszard laughed. "Though what that says about his motives for coming here or his loyalty to us, I can't say. All I can do is repeat: whatever his motives might have been, he's now bound to Zosia by love, and as long as that lasts, we own him."

"I don't trust him," Wanda repeated. "He's hiding something."

"You don't trust him because he's English," Ryszard snapped. "Just like the hard time everyone gave my father."

Katerina patted the air with her hands, as if calming children. "Maybe when you talk with him, Ryszard, you'll learn more."

"I'll do what I can."

It took several days before Ryszard managed to stumble across Peter as he was heading out on one of his walks. He invited himself along and Peter reluctantly agreed. The two men walked in uncomfortable silence as Ryszard led the way along one of his favorite boyhood routes up snow-covered inclines and down steep, icy slopes with the intention of eventually reaching a small waterfall.

Ryszard enjoyed the climb and the brisk air. It had been a long time since he had been home, and he missed the mountains in winter. He stopped and stretched and turned to say something, but saw that Peter had fallen some distance behind. Ryszard crossed his arms and waited, tapping his fingers impatiently against the wool of his coat. He listened to Peter's labored gasps and studied the frozen sweat on his cheeks as Peter climbed the last few icy steps up the slope. "Do you need to stop?" Ryszard asked brusquely.

Peter took a deep breath, said, "I'm all right, we can . . ." There was a long pause as he stared into the distance, breathing heavily, then he pointed toward some rocks nearby. "If you don't mind," he muttered.

They sat in silence, or almost silence. Ryszard scanned the dark branches of the pines and wondered how he was going to initiate a conversation, all the while trying to ignore the way Peter was sitting there, his eyes squeezed shut, gasping with pain. "What is it?" Ryszard was finally driven to ask.

Peter dropped his head so that Ryszard could no longer see his face. "My legs," he finally stammered. "I don't usually climb when it's so icy."

"Ach, sorry. I didn't realize that you were that weak."

Peter looked up at that. "It's not weakness," he whispered angrily.

Ryszard shrugged. "If you say so."

"I'm ready to move on."

"Never mind. It's a good enough view here." Ryszard pulled out a pack of cigarettes and offered Peter one.

"I thought that's against policy."

"Fuck policy."

Peter shrugged, took one. Ryszard lit it for him and Peter gave a short laugh of approval.

"What?" Ryszard asked.

"Oh, I think the last person to light a cigarette for me was an insane psychiatrist who had just had me tortured. He tried to get my reaction to his methods. They were always interviewing me."

"Hmm. Fascinating," Ryszard replied without interest. What in God's name did Zosia see in this man? he wondered. Was a passing similarity to Adam so damn important? They smoked in silence for a moment, then he said, "I need your help. You see, my background placed me in London when I was young, and now that I'm going to Berlin, I'll need more information about the place."

"London?" Peter asked rather incredulous. "Why in the world did you choose somewhere so unfamiliar? Certainly it would have made sense to use somewhere you were familiar with."

"Perhaps," Ryszard agreed testily, "but the reasons were straightforward. First of all, there are not many Germans who could claim the Tatra mountains as their home, so wherever I claimed to come from, it would have been unfamiliar to me. I assumed the London background because around here it was almost guaranteed that no one would be able to call me on it. Now, as I move to Berlin, that is no longer true."

"I see."

"The name is a bit unfortunate as well," Ryszard confided.

"Really, why? Richard Traugutt sounds like a perfect German name!"

"Oh, I chose it for the irony. Keeping my first name wasn't risky, but Traugutt was a Polish nobleman who took over the leadership of the January Rising in 1863. He was hanged by the Russians in 1864."

"So you think it's a bad omen?"

"No, I just don't think giving them hints like that is a good idea. At the time, I didn't expect this identity to last so long. Now it's too late to undo it." Ryszard stopped and stared at the trees, then mentally preparing himself to feign a great deal of ignorance, said, "Now, tell me about London."

"Well, I'll tell you all I know, but I'm afraid that I have very little information about how the Germans of London lived since most people maintained strict racial separation back then."

"Do you know anything about the Horst Wesel Academy, near Slau? My legend has me attending there."

"Eton," Peter said.

"Eton?"

"If you went there, you should know that was what the students called it. It's the historical name. Well, at least for a part of the school. Even my Herr Vogel referred to it by that name."

"Not to me he didn't," Ryszard objected.

"It's sort of an insider's thing," Peter explained.

"Then how do you know?"

"I went there."

"*You?*" Ryszard responded, carefully imbuing the word with amazement.

"Yes, me," Peter answered as though quite fed up. "Do you carry poison?" he casually asked.

Ryszard gave him a sharp look.

"Don't worry, I already know all about it."

"Of course I do."

"Good," Peter responded cheerfully.

"Me, my wife, and my elder children," Ryszard continued darkly. "As for Jan and Genia, we just have to hope they'll die quickly and without being questioned. Does that satisfy you?"

"I'm sorry. That was uncalled for." Peter rubbed his forehead. "Now let me construct a life for you at Horst Wesel and in London."

They talked for hours, moving now and then from one location to another to keep warm. Peter offered up a wealth of experiences, retelling anecdotes with the emotions and hesitancy of one who had actually experienced the events long in the past. Ryszard listened intently, using all his skill and experience as an interrogator, but he could hear nothing that implied a memorized legend. What he did hear was the voice of a lonely, ignored, and frequently harassed schoolboy, retelling the jokes and stories that had rebounded around him in locker rooms and the dining hall as he lived his life alone in a crowd, unwanted and invisible.

"Now, let's see, you'll probably want to know some of the standard insults they used," Peter said, furrowing his brow in thought. "Those I know!"

Ryszard listened, laughing at some of the more amusing puns the boys used. Despite himself, he became interested in what Peter was saying and asked, "Why didn't the English boys join forces together?"

"I believe most were genuinely trying to fit in. The last thing they wanted to do was mix with their own underclass. In fact, more often than not, it was some English kid trying to prove his loyalty that I had to fight. But even if they had wanted to gang together, I doubt if they, we, would have dared—we were too few in number and the retribution would have been horrific if it was perceived that we were forming our own gang."

"It must have been pretty brutal," Ryszard sympathized.

"Yeah, I don't know why we feel the need to torment our children with schools like that. Maybe we think it makes them strong," Peter responded. After a moment, he added, "Or self-reliant." He pulled a bottle out of his coat and offered it up. Before Ryszard could drink, Peter cautioned, "It's pure."

Having been properly warned, Ryszard poured a few drops of the pure spirits onto his tongue and let the alcohol evaporate. The liquid left his tongue numb, and the vapors had a quick, dizzying effect. "Most people dilute this stuff," he commented, handing the bottle back to Peter.

"It's more efficient this way." Peter drank some down.

They sat there for some moments. Ryszard smoked distractedly and watched as a few flurries floated to earth. The silence was crystalline and he was surprised when Peter broke it by saying, "I'm sorry about the way I acted at your house. It's just that, it was only then that I realized that I was still a prisoner."

Ryszard turned to look at Peter, but Peter did not meet his gaze. "Don't worry," Ryszard found himself saying, "you'll get used to it." He wondered at his own words as he added, "I did."

====================== **37** ======================

ALEX AND ANNA ARRIVED in February, a week before the wedding, saying they wanted to spend some time with their daughter and granddaughter and old friends before absconding across the pond. Everyone knew that contrary to their plans and promises, they would probably never return. No one ever did. Of course, the first plan—the one that was trotted out as the most likely—was that the Third Reich and the Soviet Union would be overthrown, a new Poland would be established, and the government in exile would be able to return home in triumph. Just a couple of years. A decade, maybe two at the most.

After everyone dutifully agreed that they would, of course, see each other again on that triumphant day, the conversation always turned to the next line of defense: even if things progressed more slowly than they all hoped, the departing couple would return in the line of duty or on business or even perhaps just to visit. There was no way they were going to be separated for the rest of their lives. No way. The exorbitant cost of travel for a government that had to beg every penny of free currency, the danger, the impracticality—none of this was mentioned. And the cultural changes that émigrés underwent—the way they began to view the war and their homeland as a political playground, as a distant and unseen fantasy world—these things were not mentioned either.

Peter observed the little theater, the glib reassurances and the unspoken misgivings, and mused about the likelihood of Alex and Anna ever returning from the land of milk and honey, the land of peace and prosperity, to their homeland—a shattered corpse that lay decaying under the Nazis' heel. The wedding, he realized more and more, was just an excuse for a great gathering of the clan—the marriage ceremony itself seemed rather tangential to the family gathering, to the farewells being said to Alex and Anna, to the fond wishes for Ryszard and his family as they headed to Berlin. This did not annoy Peter—indeed the changes in their lives were far more disruptive than what he and Zosia planned, and he did not begrudge them their family reunion. However, he was slightly perturbed by the interactions of the group at large. It was so obvious to an outsider—one such as he—that they had been surviving for too long in isolation, that the Underground society might well collapse under the accumulated weight of preserving itself against the Nazi regime that surrounded it and threatened it with death at every turn. They had learned to cope with the most extreme of circumstances, but they were losing every other aspect of themselves as a result. The children's chants at his adoption of Joanna returned to haunt him. How long could a people survive surrounded by murder and mayhem and still hope to maintain a semblance of normalcy? Could it continue even ten more years?

"In any case, my dear friends," Alex was saying quite loudly, "I know I'll get to see my youngest daughter here and my granddaughter quite soon since I'm sure they'll be accompanying Peter on his visit!"

"What?" Peter responded in alarm, unable to reconstruct whatever had gone before.

"Ah, yes, the dear boy, he's going to speak on our behalf! It will be a great coup!" Alex did not address Peter directly, but aimed his comments at the crowd of well-wishers.

"What are you talking about?" Peter yelled over the heads of the crowd between himself and Alex. He was being set up, it was clear, but he saw no way out except to walk into the trap and try to get out the other side. The room fell quiet, and everyone turned to Alex to hear his answer.

"*Alex!*" Katerina warned.

"You!" Alex enthused, pointing at Peter. Alex winked at Katerina, then continued, "You're the perfect piece of propaganda. A living, breathing example of the tyranny visited upon our two lands! Your experiences, your fluency in English—it will all go down wonderfully there. And because you'll be serving the purposes of the Brits as well, they'll foot the bill for getting you there!" Alex smiled broadly. "We're thinking of August. Good time—just before the Canadian elections. And the USA will be into election fever as well! Hot though. Hot as hell then."

Alex had spoken German to be sure Peter would understand every word. He did not miss the implication: he was being offered the chance to help the cause in front of everyone so he would have no opportunity to refuse.

"Father! You promised to be subtle," Zosia chided.

So she knew. And she had not warned him! He bit his lip as he considered his reaction. He noticed Wanda's scowl, saw how Ryszard spoke into Katerina's ear as they both studied him. It was unclear to him all the subtleties of what was going on, but one thing was clear: it was too late to ask for privacy—whatever debate took place would have to take place in front of everyone, and they were all *Alex's* friends and *Alex's* comrades and *Alex's* relations.

"Ah, subtle." Alex waved away the objection. "We have a dire need—I'm sure your future husband has no objection to doing his bit!"

"He might have less objection," Peter said evenly, "if he were granted the courtesy of being told exactly what 'his bit' is."

"Captain"—Alex used Peter's military title quite deliberately—"all you have to do is come to the NAU, talk a bit about your experiences to various groups, and help us in the election campaign."

"That's all," Peter responded sarcastically.

"Yes, it's not asking much." Alex chose not to notice the sarcasm.

"Is it an order?" Peter asked carefully.

"I can't imagine why it should have to be. Surely you want to help. You must have heard how bad things are getting there."

Peter shook his head; he had heard, but he wanted to hear Alex's version of events. It would give him time to think.

"Well, in the last local elections in the USA, the Republicans swept the polls. You must know they've been running on a platform of isolationism. They rant that there are too many problems at home, that they can't afford to be the world's policeman, blah, blah, blah. And they want to pull out of the NAU or at least trim back their role in it. They want to cut all funding for so-called overseas adventures—that's us, you realize—so they can balance the federal budget and give tax breaks to everyone. As if we were genuinely a big-ticket item!" Alex waved his hand in annoyance. "But that's neither here nor there. The amount they spend is irrelevant—it's their outlook. They want to abandon any role in our future. They want to begin talks; they're working their way toward a treaty with the Germans, and they would just give us all away as a lost cause.

"The situation in Canada is just as bad—the Nationalists want to pull out entirely—and they're leading in the polls. Any party that bothers to speak up for us is taking a hammering. They say all our claims are just hype—that the regime here is just not that bad. Statistics are meaningless to them, they can't understand numbers. They're dealing with emotions and that's the way we have to fight them. With emotions. With you! You've experienced everything we say happens . . . well, short of being shot"—Alex laughed—"of course, but, anyway, there you are—winning smile, blue eyes, blond hair—the perfect American image of his European brother. They'll identify with you, with your youth, your ability to speak English. They'll adopt you as their own, then you'll tell them what happened to you, and they'll feel that it has happened to one of their own. Their son, their husband, themselves. You have to do it—you are in a unique position and we need every bit of help we can get."

"And do you think this will influence an entire election?" Peter asked to gain more time. He glanced at Zosia to try to gauge her feelings, but she was looking raptly at her father. Peter was on his own, that was clear.

"Not really, but that's not our goal," Alex answered. "We're just one tiny issue on an entire election platform; all we have to do is remove this issue from the agenda. Make isolationism a vote-loser!"

"Or at least not a vote-winner," Anna inserted.

"Yes, yes," Alex agreed. "It doesn't matter who wins the elections in either place—they're all the same—we've just got to change the attitude of the voters on this one issue, make the pollsters find out that abandoning us is politically unacceptable. Make the whole concept seem immoral. If we can do that, then there's a chance this item will get dropped from the agenda, and we can work with these clowns the way we usually do."

"How could they do a turnaround like that and save face?" Basia, Joanna's teacher, asked.

"Yeah, if I understand you, Alex, they've already put a lot of effort into promoting this idea," Konrad added.

Alex, Anna, and several of the other, older members laughed. "Don't worry,"

Anna answered once she had contained her laughter, "if they find out that something is unpopular, they'll forget it overnight. As if it never happened."

"Don't the people press them about such lack of conviction?" another voice inquired.

"No," Marysia answered. "No, they forget as fast as the politicians—if they even bothered to know about the issue in the first place. Generally, the pollsters tell them, by asking the right questions, what they're worried about, and they tell the pollsters which way the wind should blow that day. The politicians happily oblige. When a new issue comes along, it displaces the old one and everyone forgets about it. Even if voters were concerned about a particular but unstylish issue, they often have trouble determining where the politicians stand. So in general, they just pick and choose according to whatever issues are spotlighted."

"And our goal," Alex picked up the thread, "is to spotlight this issue, but differently from the attention it has been getting. We have to humanize it. Make sure that those sums of money which seem all-important now suddenly seem trivial when faced with the human cost. Once we've done that, we can let them quietly forget that they ever wanted to dump us, and they can fight the election about other things—like whether or not the vice president really did have an affair with his male secretary."

"So you see," Anna chimed in, looking directly at Peter, "we really need you to come over. And it will be a great experience for you. You've never been there, have you?"

"No."

"Then it's settled!" Alex stated.

"No, it isn't," Peter replied with deceptive calm. He was so furious at the way he had been ambushed that he could not possibly think clearly about the implications of agreeing to this venture, nor could he rationally judge the likelihood of its success. All he knew was that he felt an uncomprehending terror growing within him. That and an overwhelming sense of being utterly alone.

"What? But of course you'll go!" Anna said. She was followed by other voices.

"Peter, how could you not?"

"Yes, it's so important!"

"We need to convince them—"

"Stop it! Just stop it!" Peter snapped angrily at all of them.

"What? What's the matter?"

"I'm not a show animal! I'm not for sale!" he replied to no one in particular. Where was Zosia, why did she not come to his defense?

"He shouldn't go," Wanda stated without emotion.

Peter was surprised by her defense of his position, but before he could say anything, several other voices interjected, "Yes, he should!"

"It's a great opportunity to serve *your* country and *ours!*" Tomek said with a definite emphasis on the distinction.

"If you had had your way, Major, I wouldn't be alive to carry out this great service," Peter retorted. "I do remember you voted to have me shot!" Peter saw, out of the corner of his eye, Barbara's sudden, angry look in Tomek's direction.

"Hey, hey, hey," Katerina roused herself, "this is all classified! Enough!"

"And my life isn't? How dare you all just sit here like vultures making decisions for me!" he said, gesturing around the room. Then, turning to Alex, he said, "And how dare you try and blackmail me like this! Why couldn't you just ask?"

Alex glanced at Katerina, smiled sheepishly, then turned his attention to Peter. "Well, since the issue has been raised here, now, with everyone obviously in agreement that it's a good idea—"

"I'm not," Wanda interjected.

"Almost everyone," Alex corrected. "What about it? Huh?"

All eyes turned to Peter, awaiting his answer.

Just like that, he thought, without even five minutes alone to consider the ramifications. Just like that, without any warning. Like the way they'd come and get him in his cell—he never knew when, he never knew for what. All those faces staring at him as he stood helpless and alone. All those uniforms standing around, waiting for the entertainment to begin. Using him as if he were not really human, just some sideshow set on the earth to amuse them all. He felt his heart pounding in his chest, and though he tried hard to hide his fear, he realized he was trembling.

He looked again to Zosia. She was busy rubbing the back of her neck, her head down. When she finally looked up, she had an absent expression on her face; her tongue probed along the edge of her upper lip as though she were deep in thought. She did not look at him. "I'll think about it," he finally said aloud.

"Oh, come on, what's there to think about?" Alex pressed jovially.

Peter considered a moment, then said in a conversational tone, "Tell me, Alex, have you ever been tortured?"

Alex glanced at the others, realized that the tables had been turned on him and that it was too late to do anything but answer the question. "Er, no," he replied with reluctant honesty.

"Beaten?" Peter suggested as a precisely pronounced alternative.

"No."

"Forcibly sodomized maybe?" he asked, drawing out the syllables.

"No, of course not!"

Peter snorted at Alex's horrified response; he noticed a number of raised eyebrows among the guests—clearly gossip about him had been less widespread than he had guessed. "Interrogated?" he asked with feigned gentleness while he still had the initiative.

"Um, no."

"Arrested even?" His tone had degenerated into the patient pitch used when asking a backward child a difficult question.

"No, well, er, yes," Alex answered, relieved he could answer something other than no.

"When?" Konrad asked with surprise. "Certainly you're not talking about your deportation from England?"

"Well"—Alex cleared his throat—"yes, that was the time I was thinking of. It was traumatic, quite traumatic."

There were a few grunts of derision from their audience.

"I see." Peter smiled grimly.

"But it's not my experience we're talking about," Alex said, clearly embarrassed.

"No, it's mine. And therefore any decision is mine to make—in private and after careful consideration."

"It's for the good of us all! You really must do it." Alex regained his wind, prepared to launch into a long and persuasive speech.

"*I said,*" Peter interrupted in a tone that caused even Alex to fall silent, "I'd think about it."

There was, Alex realized, no point in pushing further, and not a few of his audience looked at each other in surprise when he neglected to continue his assault. They were even more surprised when Ryszard did.

"For reasons which, for some of you, must remain unclear," Ryszard drawled over the whispers that had followed Peter's comment, "I know something about the methods of the security services." The few mutters that had begun immediately dropped to an attentive silence. Peter glared at Ryszard, but did not interrupt.

"There is a method to their madness," Ryszard asserted. "Most victims are released alive—there is a reason for that. They are meant to convey a message to the community at large, and that is, obviously, don't do what this person has done, or else this is what will happen to you or someone you love. This is why ordinary objects are often used to inflict pain—so that terror will be provoked by the most innocent situations *after* the victim is returned home."

"I wasn't sent back home," Peter asserted, angered but unsure why. "I wasn't a 'message' for my compatriots!"

"Oh, yes, you were," Ryszard disagreed. "You were placed among a population of fellow forced laborers, most of whom, I would guess, had not been tortured, and most of whom, I would further guess, ascertained that you had been. Maybe it was a coat hanger or a bottle or some other innocuous item which made you tremble. Maybe it was just certain words. Whatever it was, they would have noticed, and they would have understood the connection, even if you did not."

Peter felt that somehow Ryszard was implying he was stupid, but before he could respond, Ryszard continued, "As useful and widespread as it is, though, torture has rather negative political implications, and no modern government indulges in it openly. They hide their complicity behind periodic assertions that a few 'rogue elements' have gotten out of control, or by labeling their victims as terrorists, criminals, or insane. All these devices help to distance governments from the procedure, and further to put some distance between the victims and the public's perception of itself and its own innocence or sanity."

Peter thought of his own constant irritation at the green triangle he was obliged to wear. He wet his lips as if he were going to say something, but no words emerged.

"Nevertheless," Ryszard emphasized, "nothing is so successful at suppressing public outcry as the silence of the victims and the perpetrators themselves. This is efficiently achieved in two ways: first by planting in the victim's mind an absolute distrust of humanity, thus destroying his ability to relate well to anyone or to trust anyone with the sensitive details of his life, making him see enemies and phantoms even among—"

"I am not insane!" Peter hissed.

"*I* didn't say you were," Ryszard responded coolly. "Second, they make the proceedings utterly humiliating. In general, that is the reason for the sexual violations, for denying the prisoner clothing or simple toilet facilities, for placing bags or buckets on their heads, or attacking their genitalia. There are more efficient methods of inflicting pain and lasting damage, but that is not the goal. The goal is to make the victim a silent witness, to make that person terrifying to all who know him, but at the same time to make him unable to carry any message of what has happened to him to the world at large. To make it all too humiliating to speak about."

Peter found himself staring at the floor as Ryszard spoke. Could he ever tell anyone about having his stomach grotesquely distended with contaminated water, of being drenched in his own excrement? He looked up to see Ryszard's eyes boring into his. "As long as you remain silent, you remain their tool," Ryszard warned, "and if you think that speaking out will damage you, just think of the damage you do to others by remaining silent!"

Peter felt like a coward and at the same time resented Ryszard and the others for making him feel that way. They thought they were asking him to sit on a stage, fully dressed, and talk calmly. But if his words were effective, he would be inviting hundreds, maybe thousands, of strangers to strip him and see him as he had been then: naked, beaten, filthy, and violated. Drooling, scabrous, swollen, and discolored. Obscene and repulsive.

And what if he let them look into his mind? That part of himself that was damaged the most? What if he let them see the "phantoms" that stalked him, the self-doubts that beset him, his inexplicable feelings of guilt? What if he let them know of the overwhelming fear that even now made his heart thunder in his chest? He shuddered at the thought. Even worse, though, what if his words *failed* to convey those humiliating images about himself? Then his efforts would be pointless, and he would be seen as whiny, self-pitying, and weak!

He walked toward Ryszard, the crowd parting before him as he crossed the room. When he was face-to-face with Ryszard, he stopped. "You left out one small detail," he said so quietly that only the complete silence of the onlookers allowed his words to be heard.

"And what is that?" Ryszard asked.

"The third component of the silence: no one wants to hear about it! It embarrasses the audience, makes them uncomfortable, so they tune it out. 'It can't be that bad!' they'll say. 'You're exaggerating!' they'll say. 'Jeez, can't you make it a bit less, you know, unpleasant!' they'll say," Peter said with a sneer. He glanced around the room to make sure everyone was listening. "They won't want to believe such things happen—not to good people, anyway. So, they'll either decide I am evil or foolish or hopelessly foreign, and deserving of my fate, or they'll point out I'm still alive, relatively healthy, and I should stop whining and thank God that I've been granted my life!"

He took a deep breath. "The only way out of that trap is for them to dehumanize me—make me the perfect sacrificial lamb, suffering in noble silence! Heroic and redeemed! But then I can't be bitter, can I? I can't be fallible or human or scared. In fact, I should view the whole thing as an inspiring adventure! I should find Jesus! I should write a *fucking book* about it!"

Ryszard raised his eyebrows at the sudden vehemence of Peter's reaction, but his expression said that he had expected no less. Peter turned away from Ryszard and his all-knowing attitude. He was one of them. One of those faceless uniforms who watched impassively as others suffered, screaming, weeping, begging God for mercy.

Peter turned to the others in the room, almost pleading with them to understand. "That country is filled with asylum seekers, many of whom have stories worse than my own. The victims of torture walk around like ghosts, no rational person wanting to believe they exist. And if they do speak up, the truth of their words is doubted, their motives are questioned. If the Americans haven't heard anything yet, it's because they don't want to. Would you? Would you listen? Would you do anything?" He scanned the faces. Nobody said anything. "The sad truth is, even if I were to speak, you wouldn't be able to find anyone who would listen."

Peter turned and walked out the door, ignoring Alex's "I'll handle that part of it!" He strode down the hall to the entrance and left the bunker for the anonymous peace of the cold, snowy night. As he walked slowly through the trees toward the escarpment where he usually sat and looked at the stars, he heard someone running up from behind, panting loudly from the effort of plowing through the snow. It was Zosia. She smiled at him and joined him, and they continued to walk in silence for a few moments.

When the warm feeling of her hand in his had calmed his heart, he asked, "Why didn't you help me in there?"

"Well, mainly because I think you ought to do it, so since I couldn't say anything useful to your cause, I said nothing at all. But also because I thought you should be seen to fight your own battles. I knew you could handle it."

"Why didn't you at least warn me?" He couldn't tell her of the terror Alex had provoked, of how it was like another show trial: all those faces waiting to condemn him, waiting for him to condemn himself. But certainly she must have had some idea!

"Oh, I'm sorry. If I had known Dad was going to pull that stunt, I certainly would have. He just mentioned it in passing, and I said I thought it would be a good idea, but I told him he should talk to you directly—that it was completely up to you. I assumed it would be in private, so I just advised him to be subtle so he wouldn't jar old memories, and he said he would be. God, I'd hate to see what he thought unsubtle was!"

"I can't believe he ambushed me like that."

"Me neither. But I'm sure he had his reasons." Zosia wrapped her arm around his waist, and he put his around her shoulders. They felt comfortable together like that, as if they belonged together for all time. They stopped at the escarpment, and clearing away some snow, they sat and looked at the stars, holding each other and enjoying the biting cold of the cloudless night. Eventually Zosia shivered and suggested they should head back. They walked along the trail they had made, the snow muffling all sound save the whisper of their breath. They continued in their warm togetherness, but just before they reached the entrance, Zosia pulled him to a stop. "You know, I was just thinking about my father's idea and about what Ryszard said. Maybe you should do it."

Peter took a breath and then exhaled carefully.

"Maybe talking about it would help you heal. Maybe it would help stop your dreams."

He shook his head. "You know better than that."

Zosia contemplated the stars. Peter followed her gaze upward and they stood in silence together. "It's important to us," she said quietly.

"I know. I wouldn't even consider the idea otherwise."

"So you'll do it?"

"I need some time to think about it."

"What's to think about? Didn't you hear what Ryszard said? Don't those people matter to you?"

"And didn't you hear what I said? I'm not so sure he's right. I'm not so sure that it will do any good at all," Peter replied. A shooting star drew a fiery line across the sky and then disappeared forever. "What I do know is that it may well destroy me." He waited for Zosia to respond to that, to say that she now understood what a difficult decision she was asking him to make. He waited for her to echo the words of her question, to say that not only all those anonymous people mattered to her, but he did as well. When she said nothing at all, he added, "I don't know what motivates Ryszard, but I know what makes your father tick. What he wants out of this is political advantage, money, and weapons. He doesn't want to help people like me, he's just using our misery to buy guns. I'm not sure I want to be used like that."

"You owe it to us," Zosia whispered to the firmament.

"I know. I owe you my life, I owe you everything. I owe you all a debt of gratitude that I will carry to my grave. I've tried hard to repay you, but I know it will never be enough. Still, I will beg one more favor of you."

"What's that?"

"Allow me the dignity of making this decision for myself. Release me from my debt, just this once."

Zosia brought her gaze down from the heavens to study his face. She looked at him a long time, her mouth working its way back and forth between a smile and a frown. She bit her lower lip and seemed to come to some decision.

"What is it?" he asked.

She wrapped herself around him, burying her face in his coat, then suddenly she pulled back and looked up at him again. "Do you love me?" she asked tenderly.

"With all my heart." Stroking her hair back from her face, he kissed her.

"Would you do it for me?" she asked breathlessly. "As a wedding gift?"

He narrowed his eyes as he studied her, but he could not quite grasp the significance of his nebulous suspicions. She looked up at him, her face suffused with love, and his heart melted. "All right, as a wedding gift."

38

THE LARGEST ROOM available was too small, so the ceremony took place outside under the pine trees in knee-deep snow. Everybody was bundled up against the bitter cold, and the wind carried their words away before they had even finished speaking each sentence, but it was, nonetheless, a beautiful exchange of vows. Peter had chosen Olek as his best man, and in a fit of matchmaking, Zosia chose her niece Stefi. Zosia and Peter removed their warm leather gloves long enough to put the rings on each other's finger. The ring Zosia had worn for Adam was an heirloom, so Peter agreed to use it again and placed it on her finger in the certain knowledge that it represented far more to her than simply their wedding vows: it was for her a symbol of her current marriage, her previous marriage, and her ties to family and cause. In contrast, he had no heirlooms, no previous marriages, and if, by some chance, he had ever owned a gold ring, it would have been taken from him by force long ago. So, she presented him with a new ring that she had bought, and as she placed it on his finger, it represented only his marriage to her, and that, he felt, was enough.

The priest, who had traveled to the encampment for the ceremony, was convinced by the biting cold to limit his advice to the happy couple to just a few brief words. An altar boy held a small crucifix mounted on a staff to one side so that the couple could be married in the presence of Christ. The lonesome, agonized figure on the cross looked incongruous in the snow under the pines, and Peter eyed it wryly, remembering his comment to Zosia on his first day at the encampment. He listened as the congregation repeated the Latin phrases of the mass in a jumble of meaningless syllables, watched as most of them took a bit of bread and a sip of wine, and sighed his relief when the incomprehensible ceremony finally came to an end.

The reception was held inside the bunker, spread out among rooms and hallways with food in one area, dancing in others, and people milling happily about the hallways drinking and conversing. Initially Peter and Zosia stayed in the largest room, but Zosia eventually felt obliged as a hostess to mingle and greet each guest. She tried to convince him to do likewise, but since she declared it "silly" to march around as a couple, he steadfastly refused, opting instead to sit with Joanna on his lap or idly drinking and watching the festivities as though through a window. He chose a chair in a corner of a room where there was dancing, placed a full liter of vodka on the floor nearby so it was available as necessary, and let his thoughts drift through the haze of conversation and music and dimly lit faces.

Zosia returned to him several times during the evening to try to convince him to take his duties as host seriously, and by the third attempt she seemed somewhat annoyed by his unwillingness to actively socialize. "Could you not be so rude!" she pleaded angrily.

"I'm not rude, I'm talking to everyone who cares to chat with me!"

"You should go out and greet them! It's your duty to make the guests feel at home here," she insisted, leaning over his chair so she could speak quietly.

"They're *your* friends and family, Zosia, and they feel more at home here than I do. I don't feel comfortable talking to people I don't even know—it's not something I've ever done."

"Can't you do it anyway? You're embarrassing me!"

"And can't you just get off my back!" he snapped. "I said it makes me uncomfortable!"

Zosia opened her mouth to say something to that, but decided better of it. She stood looking at him for a long moment. He gave her a hopeful smile, but she did not respond. He tried to find the words to soften what he had said, but she turned and walked away before he could say a word.

He watched her leave, unable to decide what to do. He thought maybe he should make the effort of circulating and chatting to people he did not know, painful as that would be, to show Zosia that he did care, but by the time he had decided to move, Barbara came over to chat with him for a bit, then Olek and Stefi did likewise. Halina and eventually Teodor spent some time with him nattering about business and the troubles they were having with their computing needs. Eventually the priest who had conducted their ceremony sat down, uninvited, in the chair nearest to him and began a one-sided conversation.

There were two priests who visited the encampment with some regularity. Although Peter could not fathom the hierarchy, one seemed to outrank the other, and it was the lower-ranked of the two who had performed their ceremony. Peter had met the senior priest on a previous occasion and had decided he was a venal and uninspired man. He expected nothing better from this junior colleague.

". . . have remained outside the church despite your marriage to Zofia," the priest was saying when Peter finally decided to listen.

"Do you have a problem with that?" he asked the priest without any interest in the reply.

"Not on my account, no," the rather young man replied. "I just thought you looked like someone who needed something in his life."

"Not what you have to offer."

"No? I've talked with others like you, people who have endured much. Always, it is the believers who are able to best sustain themselves, to find themselves afterwards."

Peter turned his head with exaggerated care to look at the priest. "I would think that the essential characteristic of a believer is believing. Now, how exactly does one get around that? I can't force myself to believe in something that I don't believe in, now can I?"

"You can open your heart to the possibility."

"I'd prefer opening a bottle," Peter retorted, reaching for his vodka and filling his glass.

"Maybe someday you should come and talk. I think you'd be surprised."

"Sure. And when you feel like discussing the wrongs of religions throughout the centuries, you can come and talk to me, eh?" Peter replied, perhaps rudely.

"I'd like that," the priest surprised him by responding. "You have no idea how much I enjoy a good discussion!" Then, suddenly growing quite serious, the young man asked, "Do you believe governments have been without evil?"

"No. Of course not."

"But you are not an anarchist, are you?"

Peter sighed, seeing the obvious connection. "No. It seems a necessary evil to have some structure in our lives."

"So, the manipulations of men which have fouled religion in the past are not necessarily proof that God cannot be found in those same religions!" the priest trumpeted, jumping ahead a few steps in the desultory debate.

Peter paused long enough to down a bit of his drink before replying. "It's entirely possible that your views contain the truth of the universe," he said to his annoying guest, "but I, for one, shall never know." He then turned his attention back to the room and refused to be drawn further into debate.

Later in the evening Katerina joined him and sipped some of the vodka he offered her. Despite both their best attempts, they began to talk business as he tried to convince her that he needed a higher security clearance—it was nonsense his working with such a low priority! Katerina agreed that it did not make his job any easier and that it was somewhat confusing, but was adamant that without a better vetting, he had no hope of getting a proper clearance.

"How can we show you sensitive material," she asked in her usual matter-of-fact tone, "when we still don't know who you are?"

"But you must see that I can be trusted. For Christ's sake, I know all your names and faces and the location of this place and so much more—it's stupid denying me access to files that I need to do my job!"

Katerina shrugged. "We'll be the judge of that."

"But didn't everything that happened at the laboratory prove I'm not one of theirs?"

"Prove?" Katerina looked at him skeptically. "No. The evidence is in your favor, but it could have all been set up to secure your position here."

"Isn't that just a little bit paranoid?" he asked, exasperated.

"Before 1942," she said solemnly, "I believed in paranoia." She looked away, waited a moment as he digested that thought, then, still without looking at him, stated, "They'd give away laboratory information, they'd risk your life a million times over to get at us. If you were truly devoted to the Fatherland, you would have suffered your injuries gladly to prove your case."

"I think," he responded quietly, "that it is quite clear I don't suffer them gladly."

"Even if that were clear, it doesn't prove anything."

"It doesn't?"

"No. I can come up with many reasons you might obey their commands, whatever they've done to you. You have yourself admitted a tendency toward collaboration. What haven't you admitted?"

"Nothing!"

"I don't know that." Katerina finally turned back to look at him. "But let me suggest a scenario—just one of a multitude. Let's imagine that everything you said was true and that you lived your life as a lonely *Zwangsarbeiter* in Berlin. You meet a woman, a *Zwangsarbeiterin,* and you fall in love. She becomes pregnant, there is a child, and you love the child as well."

Peter sighed heavily since it was obvious where she was going with the story, but he did not interrupt.

"Of course, such an event cannot remain hidden, and the woman is arrested and eventually implicates you."

"No, I go to the police voluntarily, out of love for her."

"Fine. In any case, they help you escape, pointing you in our direction. They know it is a difficult, dangerous task, but they have nothing to lose—just your life, which is worthless to them. They give you plenty of time, say three years—"

"Make it five."

"Yes, five years. If you haven't returned by then—"

"Enough already! If that's how you feel, why are you letting me go to America? Why not forbid it?" He didn't mention that he would be rather relieved if she did.

"Because Alex managed to get the entire encampment behind the idea." She breathed deeply and added almost reluctantly, "And because I basically do trust you."

Peter looked at her in surprise. "Then why can't I get the sort of clearance I need to do my job properly? Why do I have to hand everything over to Olek as soon as I stumble across sensitive information? Don't you know how inefficient that is? Why hamper my work?"

"Because if I am wrong, as it stands now, you will cost us dearly. You might help them pinpoint the location of Szaflary, you would cost Ryszard his life, and you would prevent many people here from ever infiltrating again—but the one thing you would not be able to do is destroy us entirely! You know nothing of Warszawa, you know nothing of our deterrents or the agents who maintain them. As it stands now, you could harm us, but you could not exterminate us." She looked away from him to scan the room and her expression softened. Without looking back at him she repeated softly, "As it stands now, you could not exterminate us."

He followed Katerina's gaze to watch Joanna skidding across the floor between the dancing couples. She was in a competition with some other children to see who could slide the farthest. It hurt to see her like that: so adorable, so vulnerable. He felt cheated by fate. Katerina was right and there was no argument he could use to prove he was genuine: it was not enough that he knew he was. He had spent years in *their* hands, months of it under torture and reeducation; he was tainted and it could never be undone. He had survived, but in some ways they had killed him.

After Katerina wandered off, Alex joined him. "So, you've agreed to come and speak for us after all!" he enthused, seating himself in the chair Katerina had just vacated. "That's great, that's just fine. And Katerina has approved your absence—so everything's all set. I'll get you more information about what your schedule will be and the arrangements . . ."

Peter ignored him, watching instead as the dancers whirled around with complete abandon. Zosia was among them—going from partner to partner, but eventually ending up in Tadek's arms. She looked incredibly happy and flushed as they finished executing a series of complicated maneuvers—the result of years of practice and natural grace. Peter reached for the bottle he had placed near himself, unintentionally interrupted Alex to offer him a shot, then poured himself a generous serving and turned his attention back to the dancers as they held each other so closely, so intimately.

After Alex gave up talking at him, Peter spent a good amount of time alone. He preferred it that way. He watched from his comfortable distance as the in-laws and friends fussed over Kasia, now that her pregnancy was obvious. He remembered her bitter words about being an outsider, and as he looked at her glowing smile, the way she leaned into the kisses and blushed at the comments, he wondered if the only time she felt included was when she served as a brood mare, providing yet another little soldier to add to the Underground aristocracy.

He turned his eyes away from her, away from all of them. He felt awash with homesickness, with a longing for people and places that he had not seen for an eternity. He missed belonging, he missed being trusted. When he had allowed himself to imagine his escape years ago, he had always imagined that he would be greeted with open arms, welcomed as a hero, congratulated for his bravery and endurance; instead he felt as if he had contracted some sort of incurable disease.

Picking up the bottle of vodka he had been using, he looked at its contents. It was surprisingly low—had he given Alex and Katerina that much? He poured the rest of the bottle into his glass and settled back to watch the roomful of people. The alcohol slipped down easily—the lights, the music, the sounds of conversation, all blurred into one meaningless babble. He tried to amuse himself by imagining he was home among friends and family. That he had met Zosia in England and . . . well, some complicated scenario that left him free to marry and left his friends alive. He tried to imagine his parents attending his wedding, standing together, congratulating him. How old would they be now? Always the same age, they had never grown older. He had such fleeting memories of what they looked like. His mother had dark brown hair, long and straight. His father? Light brown hair? Tall?

"Can I join you?"

He looked up to see Zosia's mother. He nodded and offered her the chair next to him. She was carrying a drink so he did not offer her one. They sat in silence for a few moments, then she said, "You looked deep in thought. What were you thinking about?"

"About my parents," he answered as he stared off into the distance.

"Do you miss them?"

"Yes. I mean, I miss having had the chance to get to know them." Encouraged by her sympathetic tone, he added, "I've lost so many people in my life, I miss them all."

"Like that Allison of yours?" Anna asked.

"Yes, I miss her," he admitted forlornly. "I loved her."

"More than Zosia?"

Aware that he had spoken foolishly, he turned a contemptuous eye toward Anna. "That's a stupid question."

"No, it isn't. It's my daughter's future we're talking about. All I asked is, do you love Zosia more than you loved that married woman?"

He did not miss the opprobrium in her tone. "For Christ's sake, let it rest. Allison's dead!"

"But what if she weren't? Which would you choose?"

"They are two different woman, in two different times, and I love them, or loved . . . This is stupid. It's like asking Zosia whether she loved Adam more than me."

"But that's easy—she'd choose Adam. Everyone knows that."

He stopped dead, hurt more by her confidence in her prediction than by its brutality. He found himself staring at her, trying to think of some sort of reply, but he couldn't think for the noise of her words echoing through his head.

Anna's expression softened as she realized what her words meant. "I didn't mean to offend you."

"No, of course not," he sneered. "You just didn't care. My past isn't quite up to your standards, so my feelings are irrelevant. That's always the case, isn't it? Pious people are given carte blanche to hurt anybody, aren't they?"

"I'm not pious. I'm just interested in Zosia's welfare. After all, we won't be here to look after her."

"You weren't anyway. Besides, she's a full-grown woman."

"But she's still my daughter. Maybe someday you'll understand—"

"Maybe." He thought of Joanna. Yes, he would probably be protective of her for the rest of her life.

"—when you have a child of your own."

Pointedly he said, "I do now."

"Joanna?" Anna asked with poorly concealed alarm. "You're not adopting her, are you?"

Peter looked at her directly to try to read her intent, but her face was a mask. She would learn the truth from Zosia in any case, so he answered, "No, Zosia won't let me."

"Oh, too bad," Anna said before making her excuses and departing.

He was still gnawing on the all too obvious tone of Anna's words when Zosia's godparents came over and sat down with him. They congratulated him and told him that Zosia was a wonderful girl and not to worry if he felt nervous—they must have read his expression—because it was normal for grooms to feel nervous at their wedding. "Don't be overwhelmed," Zosia's godmother advised. "A new family always takes getting used to. It's the way of almost all marriages." He smiled at their kindness and thanked them for their advice. A waltz began as he finished speaking, and he noticed the room had grown relatively quiet and that Zosia was approaching him. With a growing panic, he looked at Zosia's godmother questioningly.

"She's suppressed a lot of our traditions because she knew it would make you uncomfortable," she explained as Zosia came nearer, "but you owe her at least this."

"What am I supposed to do?" he asked hurriedly.

"At least one dance, son. She needs at least that."

At least one dance! How in the world could he, with no practice, with no preparation, in front of so many people? But he knew the steps, he had learned them long ago to please Zosia, and though he had given up on the practicality of ever enjoying the movement when it caused him so much discomfort, he did still remember what to do.

He stood and smiled at his wife, stepped forward to greet her. She took his hand and led him to a seat in the middle of a ring of onlookers. He sat down as indicated and she sat on his lap. The audience held hands and began singing a folk song as Stefi came forward and began removing the veil that Zosia wore. Because it was a lace curtain and not a real veil, Stefi was only able to remove it from Zosia's head and wrap it around her shoulders; then she took a scarf and used that to tie up Zosia's hair in the traditional fashion of a married woman of long ago.

Everybody applauded and Peter smiled at the transition from blushing bride to old married woman; Zosia grinned impishly in return. Then she stood, pulled him to his feet, and they began to dance. Their movements were gentle, the twists and turns kept to a minimum, and the vodka he had drunk kept the pain in his legs at bay. They did in fact appear graceful and natural together, and as they looked into each other's eyes, the rest of the room faded from view. As they danced, the curls began creeping out from under Zosia's scarf, and with a shake of her head she let her hair emerge and the scarf dropped onto her shoulders. The dim light glinted off her golden tresses and reflected in her eyes. He felt the voluptuous curve of her waist, the sensuous muscles of her back. She was so incredibly beautiful!

All around them held hands and sang their folk song about love and marriage and a life together, then as the song finished, the other couples quickly joined in dancing so that soon the two of them were lost in a sea of dancers. In the middle of the floor, in a privacy almost as complete as being alone, they beheld each other and slowly drifted around each other. And the two of them became as one.

39

"*T*RAUGUTT! I NEVER thought you'd be invited to this sort of soiree!" Herr Schindler said with too perfect a smile.

"Ah, Herr Schindler, always a pleasure," Richard answered suavely, nodding his head slightly. "And Frau Schindler, you are a perfect picture of pure Aryan beauty. Such loveliness I had no hope of seeing!"

"Richard! Why so formal? Please, call me Greta!" Frau Schindler replied, offering her cheek to be kissed. Once Richard had greeted her appropriately, she turned to his companion and exclaimed, "So, we finally get to meet the mysterious Frau Traugutt!"

"Ach, I'm afraid not," Richard confessed. "My poor wife was taken ill early this evening, and my daughter Stefi volunteered to step in for her."

"Your daughter!" Frau Schindler trilled, her eyes running along Stefi's body as if valuing a racehorse. "Young lady, I hope your father warned you about the sort of men you will meet at one of the Führer's parties. They can be absolute snakes! And with one so young and beautiful as you!" She clucked her tongue in warning. "We'll have to make sure you stay out of trouble tonight. If I had known you were going to be here, I would have insisted that Günter bring his son along. He'd be better suited to your age!" She cast a glance up at her husband, who had not yet stopped leering at Stefi, and asked, "Isn't that right, dear? Or do you think your son is too old for such a young child?"

"I'm twenty-two," Stefi volunteered, moving ever so slightly out of Frau Schindler's grasp. She saw how her father's eyes narrowed in warning, and she changed her position and warmed to Frau Schindler's embrace. "So I do feel quite vulnerable here. Maybe you'd be kind enough to introduce me around?"

"My pleasure, darling," Frau Schindler soothed as she guided Stefi away from the men. "Come with me, I know everybody! Who would you like to meet?"

"The Führer," Stefi answered without hesitation. Before Frau Schindler could object, Stefi added, "I've only met him once before, but since you are so highly regarded, I'm sure he's a great friend of yours!"

"You've met him?" Frau Schindler wondered aloud. "That must explain why you've been invited here. It really is unusual, someone so new to Berlin as your father . . ."

Stefi did not volunteer the answer to the puzzle. She did, however, smile to herself as she thought of how her father had somehow convinced one of the secretaries to simply add his name to an invitation list.

". . . but perhaps you've already met," Frau Schindler was saying as she stopped near a lone and rather unimportant-looking man. "This is Herr Karl Vogel. He's also a resident of Schönwalde and works in the same office as my husband and your father."

Stefi looked with intense interest at the man as Frau Schindler concluded the introduction. He noticed her avid look and smiled pompously in reply.

"I've heard about you," Stefi volunteered. "My heavens, but I never thought I'd meet you!"

"About me? What?" Herr Vogel asked somewhat worriedly.

"Oh, that you are especially talented at keeping the lower orders in their place." Stefi could barely control her expression as she saw Herr Vogel blush with pride. He drew himself up, ready to launch into a self-congratulatory discussion of his talents, so Stefi quickly added, "Frau Schindler here has promised to introduce me to the Führer! I've only met him once, I wonder if he'll remember me?"

"The Führer?" Herr Vogel asked, half-turning to glance in his direction. "He looks fairly busy now. You might not get a chance—"

"Oh, but Frau Schindler is his dear friend!" Stefi insisted. "But maybe I'm being foolish, maybe you know him as well?"

"Not as well as me, my dear," Frau Schindler huffed, and pulled Stefi in the direction of the Führer, leaving Herr Vogel behind, full of steam with nowhere to blow it.

The two ladies reached that critical distance where the hangers-on buzzed intensely around the great man, and Frau Schindler slowed her pace to a circuitous stroll as she looked for an opening in the crowd. She seemed to be losing her determination, and Stefi quickly ran through a few strategies in her mind, trying to decide which was the most likely to make Frau Schindler a stout ally. "Be quick and direct," her father had advised, "you won't have much time, and she's already advertised her willingness to make a deal. There's no need to waste time on subtlety." And so, she decided not to.

"My father has spoken of you often," Stefi confided. "He's right, you know, you are stunningly beautiful."

Frau Schindler raised her eyebrows in surprise. "He's said this to you?"

"Oh, no, I've heard him talk to other men." Stefi paused just long enough to seem pensive, then added, "I think he's lonely. Mother is very busy with the children, you see. And she's due to have another in June."

"How many does she have?"

"This will be the sixth. It's quite a strain on her. And I don't think Father wanted that many—one or two, at most. But she insisted, she's very devoted to children." Stefi looked meaningfully into Frau Schindler's eyes. "I think she's holding him back, you know. I think he needs a stronger woman, one with more political sense. One who isn't tied to so many children."

Frau Schindler glanced at her husband as he chatted to an attractive young woman and then over to Traugutt as he spoke with a group of officers. Her eyes darted back and forth between her paunchy, aging spouse with his drunken stance and lecherous stares to the tall, handsome, and much younger Traugutt with his earnest demeanor and charming manner. Stefi counted the seconds silently as she saw Frau Schindler not only weighing up each one's prospects of advancement, but the likelihood that she would be present to share in the rewards of her efforts.

Frau Schindler turned back toward Stefi and smiled. "You're right, you know. Having the Führer as a personal friend is very useful to one's career, and, I'm told, he is not particularly fond of matronly women. Nor," she added somewhat sadly, "even women of my age. But a girl like you, yes, that will keep his interest!"

Stefi smiled shyly.

"Don't worry, darling, I'll see that we get through that scrum, and once I've introduced you, I'm sure the Führer will be interested in talking to us. But, maybe you've heard, the Führer has some odd tastes. Perhaps, before you talk to him, I could offer you a few insights, so that your conversation will be fruitful. Would you care to stroll outside for a bit? It's not too cold for spring."

Stefi nodded.

"Good," Frau Schindler purred as she wrapped a protective arm around Stefi's shoulder. "Now, dear, what do you know about discipline?"

"Discipline? You mean like in school?" Stefi asked with confused innocence.

Frau Schindler smiled. "Yes, like in school. Just imagine there's a naughty schoolboy and you're the headmistress . . ."

40

"**O**H, BUGGER!" Olek swore, throwing his pen across the room.

"What's the problem?" Peter asked without even bothering to look up. He already knew the answer. It was the data. They had no trouble translating it all using Rattenhuber's program, but there was still the messy business of interpreting it. And it was a mess!

"I thought I had this perfect, line after line made sense," Olek moaned, "but now it's all crap. A two-hundred-fifty-year-old man, a one-hundred-seventy-three-year-old woman. Shit! Shit, shit, shit!"

Barbara looked up at him and smiled bemusedly. "Don't worry, I've got some good stuff here. I'm not done yet, but I think we've finally found some human subjects!" She held up an annotated file. "Look. I'm not sure how they're numbered, but . . ." Her voice trailed off.

It took Peter a moment to notice that Barbara and Olek had started whispering. He turned and leaned out of his chair so that he could see the papers Barbara had been holding under Olek's gaze.

She snapped them back out of his reach. "It's all right, Olek and I sorted it out already."

"Let me see them anyway," he said, extending his hand in her direction.

She casually pitched the papers onto her laden desk. "Really, there's no need to waste your time!"

"Barbara?" he asked, confused. "Come on." He motioned for her to hand him the papers. She did, but it was a different set.

"The other set, those there." He pointed.

Still she hesitated, then finally handed him the papers. It was a printout of one of the innumerable decrypted data files, and as usual, it consisted of a few words and a tedious series of numbers. Barbara had attached a page of notes with a heading and had organized the numbers into a matrix with various assumed category headings.

"My interpretation could be entirely wrong, you know," she said worriedly. "After all, they're just numbers."

He perused the conjectures she had scribbled along the sides. If she was correct in her assumptions, then it was a good find: the experimental subjects, though numbered, were almost certainly human—the ages and location would not really match anything else. "It looks good to me. I think we're talking about real people here, the poor sods. If you're right, then this will be excellent proof of our claims." He smiled as he started to hand the papers back to her, but then he stopped and took another look.

Berlin, about two years ago. Numbered subjects injected two years ago in and around Berlin. His hands shook as he scanned the list. Barbara and Olek exchanged a surreptitious glance. Peter's eyes found what they were looking for: 1314708. There it was, just a number, a seemingly meaningless number. In the column next to it, according to Barbara's translation, was an indication that the subject had been tested. Then his age and gender, and next to that an address zone; he recognized the postcode for the Vogels' suburb. The next column was an assessment of the subject's general health on a scale of one to five. After that was a column that indicated follow-up diagnosis, but there was none for that particular subject.

Not a test vaccine. It was not a test vaccine after all. He looked up from the list of anonymous, involuntary test subjects; from a list of subjects of a medical experiment on inducing infertility; from a list that he was on. Barbara and Olek were staring at him. He did not see them, did not see the walls of the office surrounding them. He saw the white-coated technicians, the quick conversation with Elspeth, the way he had been dismissed from the room. He saw her signing papers he could not read, he felt the tourniquet, the quick injection, and then they were gone. Not a word of explanation, nothing. He was not a human, he had no rights, no feelings, no opinions, no future. The law said so; how could it be otherwise?

"Are you all right?" Barbara asked, concerned.

His mouth moved, but no words came out. He was shaking so hard she must have been able to see. Not a vaccine at all. It was April already and Zosia still wasn't pregnant.

"Is that you?" Olek asked much less subtly.

"Are you all right?" Barbara repeated.

He shook his head, stood, and headed toward the door. In the corridor, before he managed to walk two meters, he retched and was sick. Barbara and Olek rushed over to him as he slid down the wall into a kneeling position, and they stood helplessly nearby as he curled over himself, vomiting. He remained that way for a long time, long after he had finished being sick.

Olek made a move to help him up, but then changed his mind. Barbara stooped down next to Peter, asking softly, "Captain Halifax, are you all right? Can I get you anything?"

He shook his head, still not raising himself from his fetal position. If only they would go away and leave him in peace. All of them! Why couldn't they just leave him alone? What had he done that they could toy with his life, destroy every hope and murder every dream he had ever had? Why would they never leave him alone? What had *he* done?

The words he had hissed at Ulrike came back to him: *Do you think the people I've been talking about weren't real? Do you think the mass murders of the forties and fifties were for a reason? That babies and toddlers did something?* He had really been talking to himself then, he had actually believed that somehow he was not one of them, that they were a group apart: the victims, the innocents who had known intuitively from birth what their fate was. He was not one of them. He was immune.

"Captain?"

He looked up to see Barbara stooping down next to him. He saw the pity in her eyes. Pity and her own immunity. Had it been that way for all of them? Had each and every one of the millions thought that they were special, that they would be exempt, that it was someone else's fate to die? As the poison gas had filtered into the showers, had even one person thought, yes, this was my fate from birth? As the babies died in their mothers' arms, had even one mother thought, Yes, this is why I gave birth to this child, so it could die meaninglessly?

He answered the question in Barbara's eyes with a brief smile, said in a shaky voice, "Would you please get me something to clean this mess up with?"

She nodded, glad for something useful to do, and went to fetch some cleaning supplies. He watched her disappear down the hall, looked around, and noticed Olek standing a short distance away, as if guarding him. During the time he had been kneeling there, he had been aware that one or two people had wandered down the hall but had been shooed away. He closed his eyes and felt the sweat trickle down his face. He felt incredibly ill, sick to his bones. What, he wondered, had they done to him to leave him so vulnerable? What poison had they injected into his soul?

Barbara returned with the bucket and some rags and began to clean up the mess he had made. He insisted that he do it, and they debated briefly until they compromised and both cleaned the floor. As Barbara wrung out her rag and did a last swipe over the concrete, she asked without looking at him, "Do you remember them doing it?"

"Yeah. I had no idea what it was about. We all got injected—all the *Zwangsarbeiter* that is. None of us knew what it was."

"Do you think they . . . it had any effect?"

"I hope not. Now that I think about it, both men and women were injected, so I'm not sure what they were looking for. Maybe just testing to see if it would kill us or cause long-term damage of an unexpected sort. Maybe it was just a base compound and not actually a test."

Or maybe they didn't care what happened and they had injected women as part of their camouflage for causing chemical castration in men. Was his ability to have sex proof that nothing had been done? Or had they hoped to achieve infertility such that it would be essentially unnoticed except for an inability to make babies? And how, he wondered, were they planning to do a follow-up study? They did not test him beforehand, so how could they know what changes had been wrought? What sort of science was it that tested arbitrary, unknown subjects?

Lousy science, careless science, inhuman science that wasted lives as if driven to do so. Nazi science.

"I'm sorry," Barbara said, finally looking directly at him.

"Yeah, so am I. My life wasn't supposed to be like this," he said, more to himself than to her.

She looked confused but did not question his statement. Then shyly she asked, "Do you want children?"

"Very much so."

"I'm sorry. Maybe nothing will come of it."

They were still on their knees in the hall. Several more people had been sent away by Olek, and Peter decided they really should move back into the office. "Maybe," he agreed as he offered his arm to Barbara and they stood together. "In any case," he continued as he picked up the bucket to carry it to the nearest toilet, "what's done is done."

But what, exactly, had been done?

When he returned, Barbara made him a cup of tea and the three of them settled back into the office. Peter did not feel like discussing anything, but he also did not feel well enough to leave the office. Luckily, Olek and Barbara seemed to sense his mood, and they conversed between themselves about trivialities while he stared absently at the stacks of papers and books and ran his fingers along the hot surface of his cup. When should he tell Zosia? What should he tell her? That she had received damaged goods? Would she want to annul the marriage? Was it considered acceptable grounds for an annulment? Would she do that to him? She really wanted to have another child, and that had clearly been one of her reasons for marrying him. Had it been the only one?

"What a fucked-up mess," he sighed, unaware that he had spoken aloud until both Barbara and Olek turned toward him. Seeing their surprised looks, he pointed at the piece of paper that contained his number and added rather sardonically, "There's the real obscenity."

"We weren't offended, sir," Barbara said rather more formally than usual. "It's just that we want to help, but we don't know how. I wish I knew what to say."

Olek nodded his agreement. "Do you want us to leave?"

Peter shook his head. "Not unless you want to. I guess I'll take the rest of the day off though. I don't think I'll be much good here." He did not move, however; he didn't know what to do—he did not want to be alone with his thoughts.

Barbara seemed to understand his hesitation and said tentatively, "If you like, I'll go with you. We can go for a walk. We don't have to talk about anything. You know, just walk."

They grabbed their coats and headed outside into the gloomy day. A tent was set up but they ignored that and walked off into the woods. It had been raining for days, and piles of melting snow and wet leaves made the paths slippery.

Eventually they abandoned the well-traveled routes and crossed over unmelted snows heading ever upward away from everyone. The steep climb hurt his legs, but the pain felt reassuringly familiar. He slipped and fell several times. Each time Barbara helped him to his feet and held on to him for a few steps. She made it seem as though she were seeking his protection rather than guiding his steps and in this way assuaged his already battered ego.

After a while she noticed he was panting with the pain, so they took shelter in a copse and sat on a fallen log. The leaden skies promised more rain, and as they sat there, a few drops soaked through the wool of their coats. They were silent for a few moments, surrounded by the hushed sounds of woods. Despite the thaw, the dampness made everything seem colder. He noticed she had leaned against him and seemed to be trembling, so he asked, "Are you cold?"

She nodded and he put his arm around her to warm them both. He thought about Emma, or Jacqueline, or whatever she was called nowadays. She would be just a bit younger than Barbara now; a young woman grown to maturity in slavery. He wondered if she had been taken by anybody yet, wondered if she had slept voluntarily with a man, wondered if perhaps she was pregnant. He pushed the thought of children away. If that route had been denied him, he was going to have to accept it, he could not let this last straw destroy everything that had been reconstructed over the past year and a half. There was too much to lose.

He thought of the dreams he had dared to set up for himself. They had been simple dreams—a wife and a family and a chance to live something like a normal life. He had not asked for vengeance, had not asked for fame or riches or even an answer to all the suffering. Just a home and a family. Was it too much? Or was simply daring to dream more than he was permitted? Was there some jealous god that ruled his life, who had determined that he could never rejoin humanity once he had been torn away? Was his god a Nazi?

"What are you thinking?" Barbara asked.

"I was wondering, why me?"

She looked up at him questioningly.

He smiled at her look, said, "I don't think anybody plans to be the victim of oppression. When I was your age, I was invincible, just like you, and I knew I always would be. They had not gotten their hands on me yet, and therefore I felt sure they never would. These horrors that surround us, they were for someone else. Not for me."

"Captain—"

"Call me Peter. You used to."

"I, well . . . before you were, it's just that, since you're the colonel's husband . . ."

"Ah."

Barbara was silent with embarrassment, then she said, "I've heard that that is not your real name anyway—is that true?"

"It depends on what you mean by real. I think of it as my name, but my parents named me something else."

"What?"

"Niklaus. Niklaus Adolf Chase," he laughed. "My father and brother called me Klaus. I hated it. My mother stuck to Niklaus most of the time, but my friends—my real friends—called me Nick."

"Why wouldn't your brother use Nick?"

"Probably to annoy me. We didn't get along all that well."

"Is he still alive?"

"Yeah, the last I heard he was. I haven't looked up anything on him personally—they don't like me snooping around, so I stay obediently uninformed about everything. And everyone."

"Where is he?"

"In England. Apparently, he's a Nazi." Peter looked into the distance as he said, "He *frenched* me to the police as a kid, so I think he takes it all seriously." He had translated the English slang for betraying someone into its literal equivalent in German, but Barbara seemed to recognize the verb anyway.

"He turned you in? What for?"

"Trivial stuff. A street gang. Though I doubt it was his intent, that little betrayal ruined our lives. Got my parents killed. Funny, I bet Erich didn't even know that I had been kicked out of the gang by then."

"Why were you kicked out?"

"They didn't trust me anymore—not since my parents sent me to a school for German kids. And I guess they must have known or suspected that my father was a Party member."

"That must have been awful! Why did your parents send you away to school?"

"I guess they thought I could make a place for myself as a collaborator. They at least wanted me to fit in with the Germans."

"Did you?"

"I tried. For a time, I really tried." He had tried, too. It had been made clear to him during his first year that he could be accepted, but it would be on their terms. Not for him just the slavish obedience to some older students; no, as an English boy, he had to pay an extra price: to take the absolute bottom rung of the pecking order, to deny his own heritage and ethnicity, to heap scorn on his own people, to prove superloyalty and admiration for all things German. They had wanted him to participate fully and joyously in his own denigration, to carry out his own humiliations to prove that he was appropriately grateful for being allowed into their ranks. It was more than he could accept and he had spent the rest of his years alternately harried and shunned.

"What did your school friends call you? Klaus or Nick?"

"The other students," he answered carefully, "referred to me by some variant of my last name. The usual mispronunciation was 'sha-zeh' or sometimes 'shah-seh'—you know, as in *schassen,* to kick out." He remembered how they would warn him, using his name to get his attention before they attacked. They lost nothing by giving away the element of surprise—he was always outnumbered. He had learned to fight on the streets, but he could not have prepared for the physical advantage of his tormentors. During the first months, when he had only just turned nine, he had been beaten so badly the school officials had intervened to put him in the clinic. When, even then, his parents had not visited, he had realized that he was completely on his own.

After that, he had learned to handle himself better. When there was a gang, he usually provoked a one-on-one conflict by insulting just one member's courage. That evened up the odds a bit, though he was never given a fair fight—if his opponent was not bigger and stronger, if he showed any signs of winning, then the boy's friends intervened to bring him down. So, he opted for a strategy not of winning, but simply of inflicting harm, careless of his own well-being. Over time, even the bigger kids learned that they would end up injured if they beat up on him, and the attacks became less frequent.

Once he had established himself as a loner willing to defend his small space, he had turned inward. He continued as a member of some sports teams, always careful to attend only official practices where he was relatively safe with an adult in attendance. Friendless, he had spent his time studying, excelling in virtually every subject for want of anything better to do. He was especially proficient in math and the sciences because it was much more difficult for the instructor to judge his answers to be inadequate or wrong. Even in his more subjective classes, he often impressed his teachers, and he was, on occasion, shown some kindness by them. But by then it was too late. He was distrustful and hurt and closed to any but the most rudimentary human interactions. If anyone had wanted to befriend him after his first year, it would have been impossible.

"Have you forgiven him?"

"Hmm?"

"Your brother, have you forgiven him?"

Peter shook his head. "I doubt he even wants my forgiveness."

"I'm sure he does," she said with the conviction of youth.

The raindrops began to fall more frequently, and Barbara suggested that they start walking back. They made their way out of the copse and down a steep, snow-covered slope. His right leg buckled under the stress and he began to fall. Barbara grabbed for him, lost her balance, and they ended up rolling down the slope together. They landed at the bottom, tangled in each other's arms, unhurt and laughing, covered from head to toe in snow.

"Are you all right?" he asked, trying to control his laughter.

"I'm fine," she giggled in reply, and unexpectedly kissed him. It lasted longer than a friendly kiss, and suddenly they both pulled apart. Barbara looked away, back up the hill.

"I'm sorry," Peter breathed. "I didn't mean to . . ."

"It's all right," she said without looking at him, "it was my fault." She paused, then still looking up the hill as if trying to determine where they had stumbled, she said, "If your news . . . if Colonel Król . . ." She stopped and they sat in silence for a moment.

He studied her profile; she was a very pretty girl.

As if exasperated, she suddenly blurted, "If you need me, I'm here." She paused, obviously embarrassed, then sighed and added, "Colonel Król is a very lucky woman."

Tenderly he brushed a bit of snow from her hair. "Yes, and I'm a very lucky man to have her. And to have a friend like you. Whatever's been done to me, given what I have now, I consider myself a very lucky man."

Barbara nodded, turned to him, and asked matter-of-factly, "Shall we go?"

He nodded and they stood and brushed each other off. He put his arm around her, happily using her shoulders to steady himself as they continued their descent. When they approached the entrance, he requested that she and Olek please keep the information they had discovered a secret until he had told Zosia. "I mean a real secret, not even gossip. And tell Olek not to tell Stefi either."

"No problem. I'm sure Olek will keep his mouth shut. Especially around Stefi."

"Why especially?"

"Haven't you noticed?"

"No, are they on the outs?"

"No! He's just mortified of her seeing him with his face all pimply! He's been avoiding her like the plague." Barbara giggled.

He laughed, "Ah, the unsolvable problems of the world."

41

*H*E RETURNED TO their flat and poured himself a drink. It was still quite early, Zosia would not be back for hours from her interminable meetings, and Joanna would not be back from her classes for another hour or two. He drank the whiskey and poured himself another. What if Zosia decided she could not bear this latest revelation? What if she decided that she wanted someone who could father a child, someone who had not been defiled by medical experiments? Could he blame her? He finished the glass of whiskey and went to see Marysia.

She was not home yet, but as he was writing a note asking her if she would watch Joanna for the evening, she returned. She greeted him with a kiss, then exclaimed, "Good Lord! Have you been drinking again?"

"Don't worry, I'm not a drunk."

"One would be hard-pressed to tell the difference."

"There's a reason."

"There always seems to be."

"If you feel that way, why not have the Social Welfare Committee sanction me?" he suggested caustically. "Cut off my supplies." They had indeed already issued an unofficial warning, or as they called it, a "friendly suggestion." He had efficiently dealt with their concerns by supplementing his ration with expensive, bootleg vodka made in some of the villages to the south.

"I don't want that. Come on, I'm just trying to help. You know alcoholism is a problem in all the Undergrounds. Didn't the British have antialcohol campaigns?"

"All the time," he sighed, exasperated. "Preached at us continually. Sort of ironic since drug-running was one of their major sources of money. But you know, it's not alcohol or drugs that's the problem, they're just the effect. The problem is stress, you know that."

"I know," Marysia agreed. "And I know how devastating its effects are, especially on you young people. You children of the war are stress junkies. Addicted to killing, drugs, alcohol . . ."

"You forgot sex."

"How in the world you'll ever establish a stable society . . ."

"I seem to remember when we first met, *you* held me at gunpoint, forced me to strip, searched me, marched me bound and barefoot through the woods, and threatened to kill me."

"Those were all necessary precautions!" Marysia objected.

"So is preserving our sanity any way we can. Now, if you don't mind, can we drop the bogus philosophy, I'm not in the mood for this right now. I just wanted to know if you could watch Joanna for me this evening. I need to talk to Zosia alone."

"Fighting again?"

"Not yet."

Marysia gave him a critical look. "What is it now?"

"I think Zosia needs to know this first, before anyone else."

"That bad?"

"Could be." He turned away so she could not see his face. How could they have done that to him? How could he have not even suspected? "Could be."

"Oh, Peter. What is it?" Marysia asked, suddenly very worried.

He shook his head. "I really have to talk to Zosia."

"All right. Bring Joanna over whenever you want, she can stay the night here."

"Thanks."

"And, son . . ."

"Yes?"

"Lay off the whiskey. If you've got something serious to discuss, you should stay sober."

He nodded and almost laughed. "All right, Ma."

He returned to their rooms and decided to follow her advice, capped the whiskey, and put it back into the cupboard. He paced a bit, tried to read, looked around to see if anything needed doing. All to no avail. Barely an hour had passed. Continuously the thought pounded his mind: What if she did not want him anymore? Finally he gave in and went back to the cupboard to pour himself a drink. Before he began to pour, though, Joanna returned from her classes. She bounced into the room full of her usual stories and smiles, and he hugged her in greeting. His dear, wonderful daughter—Adam and Zosia's child.

"Are you all right?" Joanna asked perceptively, squirming uncomfortably.

He released her. "I'm sorry! I didn't mean to squeeze you, sweetie."

"Is Mommy yelling at you again?" Joanna asked, pulling back so she could see his face.

He shook his head no, wondering why everyone seemed to think they fought all the time.

Joanna was looking at him questioningly. "Do you want me to go to *Busia*'s tonight?" she asked with a calm maturity that both he and her mother seemed to lack.

He nodded. "If you don't mind, honey. I have something important I need to discuss with your mother."

"Shall I go now?"

"No, let's wait until your mother gets home. She'll want to see you first."

Zosia seemed annoyed that he had arranged a tête-á-tête for that evening, especially without warning her first; nevertheless, she sat at the table as he requested and waited as he set out two glasses and began to pour drinks.

She waved hers away. "What's so important that it couldn't wait until Joanna was asleep?" she asked impatiently.

"I found out something today. Olek and Barbara already know, so it's only a matter of time before the entire place knows about it. I just wanted to make sure you heard it from me and not from whispers."

"What already?"

"You know the lists that we acquired from the lab—the medical experiments to induce sterility?" he said carefully.

"Yes."

"We've been translating them in the office, and Barbara found some with human subjects listed."

"Human subjects?"

He nodded.

"If we could find one of these people, they could talk about their experiences, and they wouldn't be connected to us," she said, thinking aloud. "We'd be off the hook! That'd be . . ." Her eyes lit up. "Great!"

He nodded noncommittally, looking down into his glass. "I guess so."

She looked more closely at him, tilted her head in anticipation, but he did not break the silence. "So what's the problem?"

"I'm on the list," he answered without looking up.

"Oh!" she exclaimed, and then repeated much more softly, "Oh."

"What do you want to do?" he asked after a moment had passed.

"What do you mean?"

"I might not be able to father a child, Zosiu. We haven't managed it yet."

"Oh, that—we haven't even tried!"

"It's been months without success," he argued forlornly.

"Not really—we've been busy all this time with the wedding and Joanna. Hell, we've certainly not gone at it every day. We probably just missed the crucial days."

"Probably?" he asked, astonished that she wouldn't know.

"Well, definitely."

"Definitely? Zosiu, I thought you wanted a baby. Have you been deliberately avoiding getting pregnant?"

She glanced around the room as if looking for something.

"Zosia?"

"Well . . ."

"Well what?"

"Well, I've been waiting for a reasonable period of sobriety on your part to coincide with fertility on my part."

"Sobriety? I don't get drunk!"

"No, your tolerance is phenomenal, but you do drink a lot."

"You know why."

"Yes, I do, and that's why I haven't said anything. But don't worry, if you abstain and we really try, I'm sure I'll get knocked up."

"What if you don't? What if they succeeded with their little test?"

"Was there any indication what was tested?"

"Not that I know of. Maybe Olek or Barbara found something out since this morning."

"Well, then, we'll cross that bridge when we get to it."

"Zosia!"

"Oh, for Christ's sake, Peter. Why should we panic now?"

"I was experimented on!"

"I know, darling, and I'm sorry, I'm terribly sorry."

"But what do you want to do? I mean, if they have succeeded? If I'm . . ."

"I don't understand what it is you're asking me. What *can* we do?" she asked in confusion. "Do you want me to track them down and assassinate the bastards?"

"No! I want to know! Will you want a divorce?"

"A divorce?" She stopped and shook her head slightly. "A divorce?" She stood, pulling him to his feet. When he continued to look down, she gently placed her hand beneath his chin and lifted his face until he looked into her eyes.

"I thought I would lose you."

She embraced him, held him close, stroking his hair affectionately. "No, you're not going to get rid of me that easily," she whispered soothingly. Then she maneuvered him to the sofa and they sat down together. She stroked his face, ran her fingers through his hair, kissed him gently. When he seemed calm enough, she asked, "Do you have any idea what was done?"

"No. I remember being injected. I don't remember if I bothered to tell you about it. I told the physician, and he said they had not detected anything unusual in my blood."

"Yeah, you told me about it. It's one reason I set up the appointments for you with the doctors in the first place."

"Oh."

"Well, you were an unknown quantity then," she explained, her hand trailing gently along his chest. "I didn't want you introducing some deadly diseases into our community."

"Oh, I thought those exams were for my benefit."

"That, too," she comforted, her fingers tracing an indiscernible pattern as she spoke. "Anyway, as far as we know, they could have been testing just about anything. There's no reason to suspect they were successful."

He gave a short laugh. "Perhaps not, but with my experiences, I'm not exactly an optimist."

"I've noticed," she agreed somewhat sadly. "Anyway, one thing we can do is get you tested by the physician . . ."

He did not respond.

"Or," she added suggestively as she began undoing his buttons, "we can do our own tests . . ."

He smiled at her with a glimmer of lust.

". . . and let nature take its course." She paused as he reached up to touch her face. She brought his hand to her lips and kissed it. "However, there is one thing we should do in any case."

"What's that? Assassinate someone?" He had been touched by her earlier offer. She was thoroughly professional, and the fact that she had offered to kill his tormentors, illegally and against all her military training, had moved him—though even in the depths of his despair he had recognized the extremely black humor of such a valentine.

"Well, if you want. But what I was thinking was that we should make your adoption of Joanna legal."

"What? You'd go against Adam's wishes?"

"Adam's dead," she replied rather coldly. "It was unfair of him to ask such a thing and stupid for me to agree. After all, I had no right to determine Joanna's fate like that. It should be her choice, and she has already made her opinion abundantly clear."

"Oh, Zosiu, that would mean so much to me!" He hesitated. "But are you sure you want to defy Adam's wishes? After all, Joanna and I sorted it all out for ourselves."

"Yeah, I heard. But it's important we make it legal whatever you and Joanna think. During the wedding, when I was talking to my parents, I realized that they would be very likely to take Joanna to the NAU if something happened to me. They assumed it would be the best thing for her, you know, a normal life, a family, et cetera. I mentioned that she should stay here with you and Marysia, and they were rather dismissive of that idea. I think they think raising their kids here was a mistake—maybe I'm to blame for that—and they would want to remove Joanna from this environment."

"Oh, God, I hadn't thought of that. I just assumed she would stay here with me. Or at the least with Marysia."

"Yeah, I sort of assumed the same. But what with my father in government there—well, he'd be sure to get his way. The only way to make sure they don't get custody is for you to adopt Joanna legally. Then if I get wasted on a mission, she can stay with you. And that, I'm sure, would be Adam's preference as well—he would have never guessed that she might be taken away to another continent because of his stupid request."

"It wasn't stupid. I understand what he must have felt."

"Stupid or not, it's currently impractical. So, unless you have a problem with it, I think we ought to make the adoption legal."

"No problem. No problem at all," he responded happily.

Zosia reached out and touched his cheek. "You know, we have a whole evening and a night to ourselves, and I haven't noticed any empty bottles recently."

"I haven't needed any recently."

"And I'm probably fertile, ready to be plowed, so to speak."

He smiled in response, but the smile faded as a last bitter thought disturbed him. "You're not afraid to be with me? I mean, I feel pretty polluted, Zosiu. I'd understand if you were a bit put off."

In answer to his question she crawled on top of him and began unbuttoning his shirt as she kissed him, starting at his forehead and working her way down.

Two weeks later, Barbara and Olek were beginning to comment openly about Peter's frequent absences from work. They had not found out anything more about the test done on him, but he seemed reasonably unconcerned—certainly he did not work late trying to unearth more information. Indeed, he barely found time to work at all. He would leave midmorning and sometimes return before lunch, then he would leave again in the middle of the afternoon and sometimes he came back to finish the day, sometimes not. Whatever he was doing, it seemed to leave him in a thoroughly jovial mood. He joked and laughed and folded the coded documents into paper airplanes, which he sent skimming over their heads, then he would get up, stretch, mutter something about having something to do, and would disappear again.

Zosia was suffering from similar illnesses or appointments and was unable to attend meetings, turned down two assassinations that would have taken her out of the encampment, and never did quite get around to hacking out some data that she was supposed to unearth. Her dereliction of duty seemed to leave her in similar high spirits, and the two of them were often seen strolling arm in arm through the woods, calf deep in mud and slush, grinning giddily like two lovesick teenagers.

Several days before the expected onset of Zosia's menses, Peter began asking as soon as she awoke, "Anything yet?" The answer was no, not yet.

Half a week later when he asked, Zosia said, "Apparently not," with something bordering on hope.

Three days later both of them were walking around with an air of expectation: Peter would simply raise his eyebrows in query and Zosia would simply shake her head. With each passing day, she shook her head more emphatically and smiled a broader smile.

By the time she was a week overdue, neither of them could contain their hopes any longer, and Zosia went to see the physician. It was the gnomelike fellow with the nervous habits. He reported the news to them without any apparent idea of its significance: Zosia was pregnant. They accepted his brief congratulations with a dignified thank-you and left his office to go celebrate properly and in private.

They spent the weeks following their good news in a state of ostentatious happiness. They had dinner parties and invited their guests over to hear their news in person—gossip was such that it was unreasonable to expect anybody not to have already heard, but they had fun making a presentation of it in any case. Even Tadek had a wonderful meal cooked for him—and it wasn't that Zosia had suddenly learned how to cook. Peter was feeling that great about the world.

42

EAT IT, the voice intoned. This time he did not hesitate, he knew better than that. He immediately grabbed the capsules and threw them into his mouth, forcing himself to swallow before he could lose his nerve. Rough hands grabbed his face, forced his jaw open, and probed expectantly. He retched involuntarily and someone hit him for that. *Don't you dare!* the voice warned. The fingers found nothing, he had indeed swallowed the pills, whatever they were, and now he waited in dismay for the inevitable effects, whatever they would be.

Peter opened his eyes to the soft darkness of their bedroom. He cast a longing glance at Zosia and Joanna as they slept undisturbed, then with a sigh of resignation, he rose from the bed and went into the kitchen to pull out a bottle of whiskey. His abstinence over the past weeks had cost him dearly in terms of sleep, and he did not hesitate now to pour himself a tumblerful and end the charade. However happy his state of mind during the day, there was still only one way he could face the nights, and as he drank the fluid, he felt the nightmare dissolve back into the past where it belonged.

"Good morning." Zosia yawned from the doorway. "Rough night?" she asked, glancing at the bottle and his glass.

"It's all right now." Peter studied her as she leaned sleepily against the jamb. It had been only three weeks since the doctor had confirmed her pregnancy, yet already he could not help but look at her and see their child within. Their little miracle. It would be nearly six weeks old—a minuscule lump with tiny arm and leg buds. Visible fingers probably, the brain just beginning to develop. He glanced up at the clock. "You're up early."

"I have a lot to do today."

"So do I," Joanna said as she slipped past her mother into the kitchen. She greeted her father with a quick kiss, grabbed some bread and a slice of cheese, and headed for the door. "My class is going out on a morning excursion!" she explained as she waved good-bye.

Both Zosia and Peter laughed. "My God, but she's growing up fast," he commented.

"So busy!" Zosia agreed.

"Well, that makes two of you," he said, wishing she would take more time off. She really needed her rest. He had done everything he could; it was up to her to work the miracles from now on, and she just worked too much, ate irregularly, and there was too much stress in her life. "Anything happening today?"

"Not really. I did talk to Ryszard yesterday."

"Any news?" Peter got up to put the kettle on for some tea.

"Just a bit of gossip. I found out something about your friend Karl."

"What?" he asked, wondering momentarily what Karl would think of being referred to as his friend. He would probably be horrified.

"He's had another kid since you left. Or, I suppose, his wife has."

Peter spun around in surprise. "What! That's impossible! Are you sure it's not an adoption?"

"No—clearly a birth. At least from what Ryszard heard. But why's it so impossible? She's young enough."

"I didn't think so," he responded with a little more control.

"Well, I was curious so I checked. She's only forty. She had Uwe quite young, just after her marriage, in fact."

"But she had her menopause years ago. She told me Gisela was definitely her last," he replied casually.

Zosia looked at him as if wondering something, but said, "Well, how old was Gisela?"

"Eight when I left."

"Hmm. Maybe she simply meant that she intended Gisela to be her last."

"No. She said she couldn't have any more. She lied," he said as though it surprised him.

Zosia tilted her head. "So?"

"She lied. Outright lied," he repeated despite himself.

"Why were you even discussing it?"

He hesitated, turned to put the tea into the teapot. "No reason," he said, his back to her.

Zosia disappeared into the bedroom to get dressed, but called out, "Well, I can't imagine you wouldn't know anyway. I mean, you did all their laundry and cleaned all the garbage, didn't you?"

"You know I did," he answered, trying not to sound bitter. He hated when she mentioned things like that—her words always had a patina of disgust.

"Then you could not have missed when she had her periods."

"I did. I guess she was discreet," he replied, as he painstakingly wrapped the tea back up. "At times she was a very private person. Anyway, they have these little disposable things—tampons I guess they're called. I gather Teresa and Ulrike used them and just flushed them away; maybe Elspeth did the same."

"Really?" Zosia said, amazed. "I never saw anything like that in Göringstadt."

"Maybe you should ask Kasia about it. They're imported and I guess they're at least available in Berlin."

"That would make life a bit easier, wouldn't it?"

"Yes, especially for whoever does the laundry around here."

"Oh, I do my share!" Zosia protested as she reemerged from the bedroom.

He turned to look at her, not even bothering to show disbelief.

"Well, I'm busy! Damn it, I hold down three jobs!"

"Yes, I know you are. And you know I wish you would cut back on what you do, at least now," he said gently. At least they had managed to change the subject.

"I'll think about it. But I really must dash. See you later!"

With that she left, but he noticed that she turned to the right, toward Communications, rather than toward the meeting room.

Once she was gone, he poured himself another drink and sat at the table staring miserably at the amber fluid. Elspeth had lied. Outright lied. Clearly it had been for a reason. The only question was, how old was the child?

He sipped the whiskey, letting his mind wander back to those days. Did he even recognize that man? Could he really have been like that?

"I got you something," Elspeth had said as she dropped her packages onto the table in the hall. She selected one of the parcels and handed it to him.

He opened it and looked at the contents. Leather work gloves.

"Your hands are rough."

He nodded, studying the gloves as though they were incomprehensible. Work gloves.

"What's the matter?"

"Am I permitted to wear these?" He fingered the leather absently.

"Of course!"

Of course. His hands were too rough for her, so he could wear gloves when he worked. It was permitted. There was no law against his wearing gloves. *There was no law!* Yet they had let him burn his hands on those chemicals for months.

"What's wrong with you?" Elspeth asked, quite angry. "You should say thank you!"

"Of course, *gnädige Frau,*" he responded from habit. "Thank you, *gnädige Frau.*"

"No, come upstairs and thank me properly."

He carefully set the gloves back on the table. "It will be my pleasure, *Gnädigste.*"

His pleasure. Such lies! He brought his hand to his mouth, nearly sick with the thought of what he had said and done. How long had they done it? More than three months. More than three months. Nearly every day until he left. Without protection. They did not need it, she had said, she was past her child-bearing years. Well past.

There had been a pattern to it all, he could see that now. They had had sex, or rather she had had sex nearly every day, sometimes twice in a day. She paid him enough attention, was sufficiently patient for him to grow excited and erect so that he could serve her needs, but he rarely came. His exhaustion and incessant pain and fear made it physically difficult, the remnants of his pride and dignity argued against participating in such sham pleasure, and she rarely bothered to give him the time to overcome these obstacles. Her efforts were diverted to directing him how best to please her, and as soon as she was satisfied, she pushed him away, leaving him stranded to cope, on his own, with whatever emotions and physical desires had been ignited.

Then, overnight, it had all changed. She had grown solicitous, friendly even. She had treated him with some dignity and respect, even when they were not in bed together. She showered him with little gifts, food, and kind words. His workload eased; pointless jobs that he had done for years suddenly became unnecessary. He had thought that perhaps she had finally learned to view him as a fellow human being and to like him for who he was, not for what he could do for her. She had given him time and encouragement and tenderness in bed, and he had responded to his newfound humanity by coming time and again, day after day. The frustrations of the prior weeks only served to ignite his passion, and he had responded like a well-trained dog to her commands.

Just as it had begun, it had all stopped. If he had not been drugged by despair, it would have been obvious that he had clearly served his purpose, and that he had simply been demoted back to his natural, inferior status. For that week and some, he had been completely and blatantly used, and he had been utterly blind to that fact. The next month the pattern had repeated itself, and yet, he had blamed it on her moods without giving it any further thought. And now there was a child.

He groaned and buried his head in his hands.

Zosia returned while he was still sitting at the table. "Peter," she called out rather brusquely.

He looked up at her, saw that she was only barely managing to contain her fury.

"Is there something you'd like to tell me? You know, your wife, your close comrade, the mother of your child?"

He turned away to rub his face with his hands so she could not see his expression and shook his head slightly.

"I went back and checked," she said coldly, "after that little discussion about Elspeth's fertility. Do you know what I learned?"

He shook his head again.

"The babe is a year old next month. That means Elspeth was pregnant when you left. Two or three weeks gone, I'd guess. Did you know that?"

He shook his head.

"Is that why you left?"

He shook his head. "No. I didn't know."

"How could you?"

"I didn't know!" He had never meant to abandon his child!

That was not Zosia's meaning. "How could you *sleep* with her?"

Oh, there was that, too. He should have told her long ago; now it was too late to explain. All he could say was, "You weren't there, Zosiu, you can't know what it was like."

"But I do know what collaboration is like!" she said coldly.

The accusation did not surprise him. It was exactly what he had expected and exactly the reason why he had not told her earlier. Quietly he asserted, "I wasn't collaborating."

She was unconvinced. "You slept with the woman!" she yelled. "You can't claim she raped you, not like . . . Or was that voluntary, too?"

"Zosiu!"

"Do you just throw yourself at any of the master race who deigns to want you?"

"Please, enough!"

"Did she enjoy you? Did you like pleasing her?"

"I don't need to hear this." He went toward the door, but she did not move out of his way.

"Do you enjoy pleasing your masters?" she taunted, blocking his path.

"Get out of my way," he said, his voice low and threatening.

"Does it give you a thrill to be with these superhumans?"

"Move!" he ordered furiously. Still, he hesitated to push her; he felt far too violent to trust himself.

She raised her hand. For some reason he was sure she was going to slap him, and without thinking he grabbed her wrist and wrenched her hand back down. "No!" he shouted. "Don't you ever do that!"

"Oh, so only your masters can hit you," she hissed angrily, pulling her hand out of his grasp and rubbing her wrist. "You needn't have worried, I wasn't going to touch you. I'm not like your precious Elspeth. Or your superhuman *Kommandant*."

"Get out of my way."

"No." She glared at him.

For a brief moment he contemplated simply lifting her out of the way, but she would fight him and he might hurt her accidentally, and there was no telling what she might do to him in her fury. He turned back into the room and returned to the table to stare at the unfinished whiskey.

"Did you enjoy being slapped around by them?" Zosia sneered.

"Please . . ."

"How did you do it? Did they punch and kick you to get you excited? Or did they do that afterwards as a reward?"

"Stop it," he whispered, trying to remain calm.

"How *could you* have sex with one of them!"

"I had to."

"Had to?" she nearly screamed. "Had to? You—" She choked on her words, then spat out angrily, *"Collaborator!"*

"It wasn't like that," he said bitterly. But how could he explain?

"What was it like?"

He looked up at her deciding whether he should answer. How could he justify himself? Why should he have to? He looked into those angry eyes, searched for even a hint of jealousy. There was none. "You could at least pretend to be jealous."

"Jealous? Of what?" she asked, truly confused.

"Never mind."

"Why did you do it? What, in God's name, did you get out of it?"

The question sounded genuine. What did he get out of it? "A bit of peace," he stated dryly.

"But you didn't have to do it!"

"I really had no choice." He tried to recall his state of mind at the time, but it was too hard to remember, much less explain.

"Men always have a choice! No one can force a man to get an erection! Certainly you didn't have to come with her!"

"No, but she would have made my life miserable if I hadn't shown that I wanted her."

"I thought your life was already miserable!"

"Even more so."

"But it was—is—completely illegal. She could hardly have turned you in or complained to Karl if you refused."

"She had other powers, Zosiu. She had the power to make my life a living hell. As it was, I gained a few things instead."

"Like what?" Zosia scoffed.

"Some better food. An occasional hot shower. Less punishment." A pair of work gloves.

"Oh, so after your performance, what did she do, pop a bit of sausage in your mouth and say, 'Good boy'?"

"Something like that," he answered caustically.

"Ooh—you do sell yourself cheap!"

"It was the only price I could get," he hissed angrily.

"That's it? That's your entire reason for sleeping with the enemy?"

"And I had a bit of human contact."

"You call that human contact?"

"I did then. I was so lonely . . ." he began, but Zosia's look of contemptuous disbelief stopped him. He was infuriated and a torrent of words exploded from him. "It's so damn easy for you, isn't it! Judging everyone from your ivory bunker here! You've never experienced any of the things you so thoroughly loathe. You have no idea what you ask of others! You just throw that word *collaborator* around as a catchall condemnation with absolutely no idea what you're saying! You're despicable."

"And you're a collaborator!"

"And you're a murderer—better to fuck than to kill!"

"Those are judicial executions!"

"What about the hostages? You cause them to die!"

"If we give in to blackmail, we're doomed. You know that!"

"But it's always someone else who suffers, isn't it? When have any of your precious family or friends been put on a hostage list?"

"We protect our own," she replied evenly.

"And I protected myself!" he yelled in reply.

"By collaborating! You didn't have to do it—you know the difference!" She sounded exasperated by his inane comparisons.

"All I know is I didn't cause anyone's death by sleeping with Elspeth."

"Yeah, that's you all right, just lie there and take it." Zosia's voice had dropped to a low hiss. "Let others do the dirty work so you can maintain your pristine martyr complex! Pick up a gun and fight, damn it! There's a war on! But, no, you prefer to be beaten and fucked by your master race! You enjoyed it!"

"And you murder people and sit in judgment of me!"

"At least I don't—" She stopped abruptly.

"What don't you?" he asked, sufficiently furious that he did not care what she said.

"Nothing."

"What!"

"I said—nothing!" Zosia clamped her mouth shut as if physically fighting back her words. She stepped into the room and closed the door behind her. The whole corridor must have heard them—just as well they had argued in English. She came over to the table, stood on the opposite side from him. In a measured voice she asked, "What about the child?"

"What about it?" he said wearily.

"Is it yours?"

"I suppose so. I can't imagine any other reason for her behavior." He remembered how Elspeth had always stared at him as if determining his suitability for breeding purposes.

"Would you have stayed if you had known?" Zosia interrupted his thoughts.

He nodded. "I would have had to; I couldn't abandon my child into that world."

"You would have been its slave."

"I know." He picked up the glass of whiskey, swirled the liquid around. "But I couldn't have abandoned my child into their hands. Not after what I had seen. Maybe when it was old enough, I would have taken it with me."

"You wouldn't have done that. You knew it was almost certain death."

"I know."

"And you would not have been able to tell it who you were. That would have been too dangerous for the child."

"I know."

"But you would have stayed anyway?"

"Yes."

"Why?"

"So I could be there. Try to have some influence. Try to . . . Oh, I don't know."

"I don't understand. Why would you sacrifice everything for Elspeth's kid?"

"It would have been my child, too." He set the glass back down without drinking anything.

"Why do men think that one sperm makes a kid theirs? If you couldn't raise it as a father, how could you think of it as yours?"

"I just would have."

"This baby isn't yours, Peter. You contributed one minute of your time to its creation. You were duped. You shouldn't feel any loyalty to it."

"Obviously many men would agree with you. They'll happily walk away from their 'one minute's contribution.' I can't do that, Zosia. I'm not like that."

"So you would have stayed and served the family loyally just so you could be there for the child, just so that one day the kid could spit in your face."

"I would have stayed. I don't know what else would have happened."

"You would never have left," Zosia said rather sadly.

"Probably not." He pushed his glass around the table absentmindedly. "You're right, I was fairly sure I was committing suicide, and Elspeth's pregnancy would have tipped the balance the other way. It would probably have been enough to chain me there until I died."

They paused, both exhausted by the argument, by the emotions they had released like nuclear weapons on each other.

"Would you like some whiskey?" he finally asked.

"Yeah. I'll get it." Zosia went to the cupboard, poured herself a small amount, and added a bit to his glass. She stood next to him, lifted her glass. "Here's to your fatherhood."

They gently tapped their glasses together, miserably silent, miserably aware of how much damage they had inflicted. How much irreparable damage.

After he had taken a sip, Peter asked, "Is it a healthy child?"

"I suppose; there's no indication otherwise."

"Is it a boy or a girl?"

"I don't know. I'll check for you." She paused a moment, chewing on her thumb, then asked, "Do you think Karl will ever suspect it's not his own?"

"Not if Elspeth has been clever about it. And I assume it was planned, so I assume she was." What had Elspeth said? There had been a man before the Polish woman. A man whom Karl, in an unexplained rage, had apparently murdered. Were Rudi and Gisela that man's children? Had Karl stopped producing the goods before Elspeth had reached her own self-set quota? Wasn't eight the bare minimum for a respectable Party wife?

"I have to go. I'm already late." Zosia sounded exhausted. She turned slowly toward the door, walked reluctantly into the hall.

She was already gone before he said softly, "I'm sorry about what I said."

43

HE STARED UP at the ceiling. Elspeth was sated; he was tired, wouldn't mind sleeping, but there really wasn't time. There never was.

"Why don't you play the piano for me sometime?" she asked coquettishly, still nestled under the covers.

He turned his head to look at her, responded dryly, "I do believe someone said they would have my fingers broken if I did that."

"Oh," she sighed exasperated, "I was just annoyed that you lied about that Chopin number you played. Calling it Schubert. Did you think I was an idiot?"

"Your husband wouldn't have known the difference," he responded, returning his gaze to the ceiling.

She did not deign to reply to that. "Anyway, I'd like you to play something now and then."

"I can't remember anything."

"You can practice."

"I don't have time to practice."

"You'll make time."

"Uwe will hear."

"I'll tell him it's me. Stop making excuses!" she said with finality.

"I can't play the piano," he replied nevertheless.

"I know you can, do you mean you won't?" Her tone had grown threatening.

"No, I mean I can't." He leaned toward her so he could hold his hands above her face. "See? *Meine Gnädigste* didn't need to have my fingers broken after all; my lady managed to destroy my hands anyway." Funny, despite what they did together now, it still seemed appropriate to refer to her with excruciating formality.

"What?" she asked, confused and annoyed.

"Can't my lady see?"

"See what?"

"The scars."

"Scars? Oh, those. Where did you get those?"

He snorted, slumped back to stare at the ceiling. "Kind of *meine Gnädigste* to have noticed."

"What?"

"It was that stupid factory I worked in."

"Oh, that. Why didn't you wear gloves or something?"

He glanced at her, muttered, "And they say Germans don't have a sense of humor."

"What are you talking about?"

He did not respond. The ceiling actually looked rather dirty—smoke-stained. He should have cleaned it ages ago. Or maybe it should be painted.

"Anyway," Elspeth insisted, "that shouldn't stop you; I'm sure you can play anyway."

That was probably true. The tighter skin, the stiffness—he could probably work around it. But he did not want to play the piano for her and was determined that she would not get everything she wanted. "No, it's simply impossible. You've destroyed my hands."

"Me? What did I have to do with it?"

"Oh, absolutely nothing at all." His voice dripped with sarcasm.

Elspeth narrowed her eyes as if trying to work out what he was talking about. Finally she gave up and said instead, "I think you're forgetting your place, boy."

"Where's that?" he asked flippantly. "On top of you?"

She flung her arm over and hit him in the face. It did not really hurt, but her intention was clear enough.

"You really know how to inspire a man," he said, sitting up and getting out of bed. "I'm taking a shower."

"No! Use the cellar."

"No, I'm showering here." He did not wait for her response, simply walked into the bathroom and turned on the water so he could drown out whatever she might say. As the hot water washed over him, he wondered idly what sort of price she would make him pay for this insubordination. And how would she disguise her anger? Since they had begun their liaison, she had been much less enthusiastic about enforcing a strict discipline, but she did not desist entirely. Perhaps she knew her husband would be suspicious if there were any precipitous changes. Or perhaps she did not associate his being punished with his moods and ability to please her during the week. After all, it was his natural place in life—why should he mind? No doubt he should be delighted to have the privilege of fucking an *Übermensch* no matter how he was treated before and afterward.

He stepped out of the shower and pulled on Karl's bathrobe. She was still in bed, and as he emerged from the bathroom, he leaned against the doorjamb and contemplated her. His eyes strayed to the left, to the framed portrait of the Führer on the wall, and then to the right, to the portrait of Hitler in white armor, riding a charger. Over Elspeth's head was a brass-relief eagle, its talons clinging to a swastika. He regularly cleaned the wood of the frames, polished the brass of the eagle. Elspeth's unnatural platinum-blond hair lay in a halo around her head; it had been so overbleached for so long, it felt like steel wool to his touch. He sighed and closed his eyes against the grotesque image of what his life had become.

He opened his eyes to see the glass of whiskey in front of him. He drank it down and stared at the empty glass. With that woman he had produced a child. Oh, God, what had he done? Would a son be driven into madness by Karl? Would a daughter follow in her mother's careless, vicious footsteps? Could he have in any way influenced the child if he had stayed? Or would it, after a lifetime of seeing him ordered about and hit, have spit in his face?

Oh, God, what had he done?

"Do you really think I'm a murderer?" Zosia's low voice made him jump. She was standing in the doorway, tears in her eyes. She must have left the meeting early, or perhaps she had not gone at all.

He shook his head, speechless. "No, no," he replied quietly.

"I know hostages die. I've known it all my life," she said as though he had not answered.

"I'm sorry, Zosia, I didn't mean it. I was just angry."

"They come to me in my dreams. I hear them in my sleep," she said, staring down at the floor.

"I didn't know that." He had never thought to ask; she seemed so sure of herself, so confident, he had never thought to ask! "I'm sorry. I didn't mean what I said, I was just hurt."

"When I read the lists—do you know they put children on the lists? When I read the lists, I think to myself, And how many of these people are going to die because of me?"

"Zosiu, it's not your fault. It's not you."

"You said it was." She did not look up at him.

"I was hurt. I didn't mean it!"

"But you thought it, so it must have been in your mind all along," she replied to the floor.

"No. It's not your fault. They've made it a dirty war, but we've got to fight. I know that. We can't stop fighting just because they've made it brutal. That would justify their methods."

"But you think I'm a murderer. You think I don't feel anything."

"No, I don't," he breathed. Why in God's name had he said such awful things! "I know they'll kill people no matter what we do. I know the mass murders that happened, I know those weren't hostages. They kill because they kill, not because of you. Please forgive me, I didn't mean it!" He wished she would look up at him. He had an urge to walk over to her and lift her face so that he could look into her eyes, but he knew from experience that would be a mistake.

"You think I'm a murderer." She still did not look at him, just continued to stare grimly at the floor.

"No! I just said whatever I thought would hurt you! I wanted you to stop what you were saying—you were hurting me so much! Of course I don't think you're a murderer! I mean, do you *really* think I'm a collaborator?"

There was a silence that stung him worse than anything she could have said. He waited a moment to see if she was just trying to form her words carefully, but the silence lingered. He gave her a few more moments, desperate to hear something, anything. Even an accusation. But there was just silence.

Finally, when the silence had lasted too long to deny, he said in a measured tone, "I'll have the housing staff find me a room somewhere. Until then, I'll stay with a friend." He turned to go into the bedroom to gather a few things, then added, "I'd like to see Joanna every day. You won't stop her from seeing me, will you? You won't take her away from me, will you?"

"Peter."

He stopped in the doorway, unable to turn around and face her contempt.

"You don't have to go."

"You can't live with a collaborator," he responded bitterly. He went into the bedroom and shut the door. He grabbed the satchel he had stolen from Karl and began to stuff his clothes into it. One word. One word stood between them. Ah, but such a word! A word he had battled all his life. Everything he had suffered could have been avoided if only he had not feared that word.

What had he said to Emma? *Remember to love yourself. Don't blame yourself. If they commit indignities, it reflects on them, not you.* Yet the woman he loved with all his heart did not love him. She felt the indignities committed upon him reflected back on him. Not just Elspeth, all of it. He was tainted by what they had done to him: he had let them do it. He had lost everything in his life so many times, had had it all torn away from him because he would not collaborate, because he could not play by the rules they had set. And now he was losing it all again.

He stopped packing and looked at the jumble of clothes he had shoved into the bag. He was losing it all again. Unbidden, his hand reached into the narrow side pocket and extracted the matted hair he kept there. They had lost everything as well, and they had not even been given the choice, nor had they been given the chance to start again. *Where there is life there is hope.* What a ridiculously trite sentiment! But he had lived by it for all those awful years; he had believed that if only he could stay alive, he could recover the things that made life worth living. And he had done it! A home, a woman he loved, a daughter, and another child en route. And he was losing it all.

But why?

This time no one was tearing him away. He could not blame the nameless, faceless *them* who had destroyed so much of his life. It was by his own choice: his pride could not stand what Zosia had said to him.

Could he give up everything for pride?

Zosia had said he did not need to go. What would it look like to Joanna if he just walked out of her life now? If he gave her up, gave up everything because of something her mother had said. Because of a word.

Had he collaborated? Or had he simply responded to human need?

A different image of Elspeth came to mind: the look on her face as she had read the telegram about Uwe, the way she had sobbed in his arms, the way she had sometimes interceded with Karl on his behalf. He remembered one time they were together—they had already been doing it for about three weeks. He had done what he could to satisfy her, but his fantasies had not been up to erasing the experience of that morning—Karl had responded violently to a trivial provocation, and as a result, he was still in some considerable pain. He had thrown himself off her and sighed with exasperation; he had managed to do just enough to leave her resentful and himself frustrated. And now she would be able to throw impotence in his face. He had known he should act quickly to rectify the situation and try to satisfy her in other ways, but he had felt so frustrated that he could only lie there stupidly with his eyes shut.

He remembered feeling her lips brush against his: she had kissed him! She never kissed him! He had opened his eyes in surprise and saw her looking down at him sympathetically. "Did he hurt you?" she had gently asked.

He had nodded, reddening with irrational shame as he did so.

"Sleep here a bit," she had said as she climbed out of bed. "You look like you could use some rest. I'll get you up in plenty of time." And with that she had left him alone to sleep.

Was it collaboration?

Did it matter what name it was given? Was it enough to cost him everything he had now?

He realized he was shaking his head. He could not do it; he would not lose it all again—not by his own actions. He unpacked the clothes while thinking about what he should say. By the time he had finished, nothing had come to mind, but he decided to step out of the bedroom anyway. Zosia was still there, sitting on the sofa. She looked directly at him but did not say anything.

"I'm not going," he said.

She nodded, then her eyes strayed to their wedding photo on the wall, the one they had placed next to the picture of her and Adam. He wondered briefly which photo she was looking at as he sat down next to her and reached for her hand. She put her hand in his, and they sat next to each other in silence for a long, long time.

Eventually Zosia broke the silence. "Why?"

"I was scared," he answered simply. "I knew how badly I could be hurt, and I didn't want it to happen again."

"So she threatened you?" Zosia had lowered her head to look at her belly, continued to stare downward as she rubbed her hand over where she knew their child was developing.

Peter watched her actions as he answered, "Not really. She didn't need to."

"No threats? What, just a suggestion? Sort of a 'Hey, sailor'?" Zosia imitated a leering prostitute's voice.

"Please don't mock me." He explained the circumstances of Elspeth's first approach, explained what they had both known at the time: that she did not need to say anything at all about the consequences if he did not accept her proposal. Her anger and resentment would have been sufficient to make his life miserable, whether it was her intention or not.

"Realistically," Zosia argued, "what's the worst she could have done?"

"Oh, she might have told Karl I had propositioned her. I know that whatever else he might have done at that point, he would have been certain to beat me to a pulp."

"But you could have told him the truth! That she propositioned you!"

He grunted his derision at that suggestion. "Then he would have beaten me for propositioning her and again for lying about it and again for impugning his wife's honor. No, my word was meaningless and what she said was, by definition, the truth."

"But couldn't you have—"

"Face it, Zosiu, she owned me," he interrupted bitterly. "That's what it means to be owned: you do as you're told if you want to survive. You don't get to pick and choose which commands you'll obey. Millions of people have learned that lesson over the centuries, and I learned it, too."

Zosia kept her head down and did not say anything. She was avoiding looking at him again, as if she could not bear the sight of him.

His heart ached at this sign of her rejection. "Zosiu, I told you what I was! You knew how I spent those years. Did you think it was just a party game? Something I did so I could go on American TV and talk about the Nasties?"

She shook her head slightly but still neither looked up nor said anything.

"This society condones slavery! That's one of the reasons we fight them, one of the reasons we claim they are immoral. It's not an abstract concept either—it's done to real people. Real people with real feelings and"—his voice grew increasingly unsteady—"your husband was one of those people and he did everything they required of him. Everything. From slopping out Uwe's bedpans to polishing the car to servicing the wife. It was *all* degrading, it was *all* humiliating, and it was *all* unavoidable as long as I wanted to live."

He paused to steady himself. "That was the only real choice I had: to live or to die. I chose to live and perhaps that was wrong, perhaps that was collaboration, but it was a choice that you knew about long before this. A choice that you accepted as reasonable that first night that we met. This thing with Elspeth changes nothing."

"Yes, it does! It is different."

"It's no different than"—he bit his lip, turning his head away to finish—"than the *Kommandant*. You knew about that, and you accepted it."

"But it *is* different from that! When you made that baby, you proved that you had gone from victimization to active participation. To collaboration!"

Peter shook his head violently but could say nothing.

"That was the one thing she could not force from you, Peter! That's the one thing I don't understand. How could you do that? How could you be her *lover!*" Zosia pounded her fist against her thigh to emphasize her last sentence.

He sighed. "It's complicated. Human beings are complicated. No matter how many rules and regulations there are for how *Übermensch* and *Untermensch* are supposed to interact, when you put two people that close together for that long, there are going to be complications. She couldn't live by her strict philosophy, and I certainly had no desire to reenforce her prejudices!"

Zosia did not react, so he decided to emphasize his point. "I lived day in and day out with her for two and a half years. We interacted every single day, and sometimes she treated me decently, sometimes like dirt. But however she acted toward me, she was virtually the only person I saw; if I ceased to react to her as a human, then I ceased to be human. I simply couldn't spend every moment hating her or being bitter about her treatment of me—that would have destroyed me faster than anything!"

Zosia made a dismissive noise.

"In any case, there was nothing else in my life. With Uwe there, I couldn't leave the house, I was trapped and alone. When I was obliged to lie with her, there was just one choice left to me: I could hate her and fail miserably or I could try and enjoy it and get some physical pleasure. I chose the latter. I'd summon up some of her better moods, I'd think about Maria or just fantasize like crazy . . ." He hesitated, then added, somewhat embarrassed, "Mostly about you."

"Me? You didn't even . . ."

"You were in Berlin that winter, weren't you?"

"Yes."

"I saw you. You were kind to me. I spent maybe two minutes in your presence, and I'm sure you don't remember it at all, but it was two minutes I savored for months afterwards. You see, that's what my life had been reduced to. A stranger winks at me and . . ." With an effort he regained the thread of his explanation. "Anyway, as time went on, she started talking to me, we'd actually converse a bit—never freely, but we exchanged some ideas. It was like during that time I was human to her. I sort of hoped that I could extend that time beyond the bedroom and that maybe I could get her to see me as human all the time." He stopped, aware he was making no real impression. He sighed. "The whole thing was bizarre, it was grotesque, but it was my life—it was all that I had."

Zosia continued to stare at the floor; he could see she was chewing her lip. "I really do have to get to work," she said in a low voice. "We should probably talk about this later."

Though she would not look up to see him, he nodded his agreement.

=== 44 ===

NATURALLY, THEY DID not discuss it later. It was too sensitive for either of them to dare bring up. It was, nevertheless, clearly on both their minds, and as Zosia yet again tossed and turned in her sleep, Peter felt a strange combination of guilt and pity that he had caused such distress. He got out of bed and came around to kneel by her side so he could reach her without disturbing Joanna. Zosia was mumbling something in her sleep, and he wanted to hear what she had to say in the hopes of gauging how she felt about him and his actions. He listened as she repeated a word over and over, and slowly he realized that she was saying, "Adam, Adam, Adam."

He ground his teeth and decided to return to bed, but Zosia stirred and looked up at him. "Adam?" she asked in a confused whisper.

"No, it's only me," he replied, his heart aching.

"Peter," she said as if clearing away cobwebs of confusion.

He reached out and touched her hand and held it in silence. He wanted to ask her a question, but he hesitated. If only he didn't love her so much, then she wouldn't be able to hurt him so badly! He felt a sick apprehension in his gut, a worried fear of what she would answer when he finally asked. He clung to the silence, to the hope that it offered, then at last he asked quietly, almost hoping she was asleep, "Do you still think I'm a collaborator for what I did?"

She moved slightly, so he knew she was awake, but she said nothing and his heart sank. He waited an eternity, feeling hope slip away, before she finally said, "You know, without having lived it, I just don't have the experience to say."

"You were willing to say before."

"That was an argument. It was foolish of me to . . . I was angry."

"And now you're not, so tell me what you think."

"All right," she sighed. "I'm sorry, Peter, I still don't understand what you did. I don't condemn you for it, but I . . ."

He rubbed his forehead, patiently prompted, "Yes?"

"I don't think I would have done it."

He shut his eyes for a moment. There, on his knees, beside her, it looked as if he were praying.

She tried to explain. "It's the voluntary nature of it all . . ."

"Okay, enough," he said, dismayed.

She did not say anything, just spent a long moment looking at him. He wondered if she was comparing his actions to what Adam would have done. "I guess we should cancel my trip to America," he said tiredly.

"What? Why?"

"I think it's obvious," he stated without rancor. "If even my wife considers me a traitor, I can hardly hope to gain a sympathetic hearing there."

"You don't have to talk about this stuff! You must go!"

"I don't see how I can. The whole point of my going was that my story would be genuine. If I have to lie, it'll all fall apart."

"No, it won't! You convinced me on that first night. You can do it again."

"This whole messy business was one of the reasons I was so reluctant in the first place; now that it's out in the open, I just don't see how I can pretend it didn't happen."

"You can do it if you try. We're depending on you! A few changes here and there to your story won't take anything away from it. You *must* go! You *promised* you'd go!"

Something in her tone made him look at her for a long time, but the intensity of the love he felt for her left him unable to voice his misgivings. Instead he said, "We can discuss it tomorrow. I'm sure it will all be clearer then." His voice assumed a hypnotic tone, and he gently passed his hand over her eyes so she would close them. "Just go back to sleep now. You need it, the baby needs it. Forget everything else, think about your beautiful daughter, and your wonderful child-to-be and a husband who loves you dearly. Sleep and dream about how good life can be. How sweet life is."

He continued to kneel by her side and stroked her forehead as she drifted off. When he knew she was asleep, he kissed her tenderly and then returned to his side of the bed. He lay in the dark and listened to Zosia's and Joanna's peaceful breathing. He lay very still, stifling a sob of quiet fear at the demons that awaited him behind the veil of sleep.

The child was a girl: she was about three and looked remarkably like Joanna had at that age. They walked along hand in hand to the park. A patrolman scowled at them but decided their familiarity was for the child's safety and so did not harass them. He felt grateful he could hold his daughter's hand—soon she would be old enough that there would be no need and therefore no excuse to do so. She chattered amiably and he responded cautiously. He wanted to teach her

English, but he did not dare. He wanted to hug her, but the opportunities were rare. Still, the walk to the park was enjoyable, and since Elspeth frequently grew bored with the child, he often was able to care for her.

At the park she was surrounded by her friends; they whirled around him singing some song he could not recognize. She was among them, whirling around him as well.

"Who is that?" someone asked in English, pointing at him.

"My father," she replied happily.

He spun around to see her, stunned by her response; so they repeated it for his benefit.

"Whose is that?" someone asked, pointing at him.

"My father's," she replied happily.

"No," he whispered, and wanted to say, "I belong to me," but he could not find his voice and he could not find her among the children. They all wore uniforms and she was completely indistinguishable from the others.

But now she was grown. He was waiting for her by the car—to chauffeur her. A beautiful young woman with bleached-blond hair. She hung on the arm of a young man in a military uniform. "Whose is that?" the young man asked, pointing at either him or the car.

"My father's!" she answered gaily.

And this time, he did not object.

He awoke and lay quietly for a moment thinking of the dream, of the image of himself walking with his child to the park, holding her little hand. He could still feel how her delicate fingers clutched at his, could still see the bright sparkle in her eyes as she pointed out a squirrel. He felt a terrible longing for her, for that part of himself he had unknowingly left behind.

Again he drifted off to sleep and to dreams. Again the child. A boy this time, grown to a handsome and strong young man, wearing a crisp black uniform with high black boots. Yawning and stretching, the young man threw himself into a chair and, pointing at his boots, said, "These are dirty."

"Do you wish to take them off, *mein Herr?*" he asked the young man.

"No, I'm going right back out."

So, the father knelt at his son's feet and cleaned his boots. As he wiped away the dried mud, then used a brush to clean the crevices, he contemplated telling his son of his true parentage. The boy, however, preempted him. "I have a story to tell you. A fairy tale."

He spread the polish on the smooth leather. "*Mein Herr?*"

The boy smiled. "The story is from India. You know where that is, don't you?"

"Yes, *mein Herr.*"

"Good. Anyway, you see there was this Brahman woman—you know what that means, don't you?"

"Yes, *mein Herr.* She was of the priestly caste."

"Exactly. Noble blood. Well, she married a wealthy and wise man and spent her days strolling through the gardens of his estates, but then one day she grew restless and secretly wandered into the village. There she saw a man who fascinated her. She had never seen one like him—almost half-devil, you might say. He smiled an evil, enticing smile and seduced her then and there. Are you listening?"

"Yes, *mein Herr.*"

"The poor woman became pregnant and was beside herself with shame. She gave birth to a healthy child, but because of the miscegenation, she had to keep the parentage of the child a secret, and she raised him as if he were her husband's son."

He ran the cloth back and forth over the leather.

"The child was happy and successful and had a promise of a good life. The pure blood of his mother won out over the polluted blood of his father, and it was clear no one would ever need know the shame of his parentage. However, the outcaste father contrived to visit his child and tell him the truth of his birth. The boy turned the beggar away at the door, but still the evil man was insistent: he would do anything to reveal himself. He thought in this way he might gain some advantage for himself. He did not care if it destroyed the boy's life; he did not understand that truth is not such a simple thing. He did not realize that the boy's true father was the man he had looked up to and admired all his life, the man who had provided for him and who offered him a world of opportunities."

He changed cloths and worked on the final shine to the luxurious black boots.

"Do you know what the boy finally had to do to let the poor worm know that he and his miserable stories were not wanted? Do you?"

"No, *mein Herr,*" he answered quietly. He looked up from his work to confront his son's cold, cold stare.

"He spit on him, like this." The boy collected a mouthful of saliva and spit at him.

Peter started. He stared at the ceiling; his heart felt like a stone in his chest. He ran his hand over his face, convinced that it would come away covered in spittle, but it was dry. Would it have been like that?

Afraid of what his next dream might invent, he decided to go for a walk instead of sleep. A few minutes later, he emerged from the bunker into the cool night air. Heavy clouds made the darkness complete. He stood a moment to get his bearings and then headed into the woods. He thought not of his dreams, nor of Elspeth's child, rather he thought of his father. In a fit of helpless anger, he had spit at his father once. Now, it was far too late to apologize.

A few hundred meters into the trees a familiar voice asked softly, "Captain Halifax?"

"Good evening, Barbara. Why are you out now?"

"I'm just heading back from duty near the perimeter. You know I run a group of partisans."

"Oh, yeah. Everything go well tonight?"

"Yes. All quiet on the western front."

He smiled at her literary allusion. On an impulse he asked, "Are you tired? I'd like to talk if you have some time."

"I'd love to, Peter." She swung into step beside him.

They walked to the escarpment that he usually retreated to, and he pulled out the bottle of grain spirits he had brought from the apartment. After they had exchanged a few pleasantries and shared a few swigs, he told her what was on his mind. He told her about Elspeth and what he had done with her. Then he asked, "Was that collaboration?"

"Why would it be?" She seemed stunned by his question. "You weren't exactly helping their war effort!"

"Oh, I don't know. I just wondered what you thought." He accepted the bottle as she handed it back to him. He took a swig. "It seems there's a child now; I have every reason to believe it's mine."

"Oh! Good for you!" Barbara took the bottle from him to toast his fatherhood. "*Na zdrowie!* That's one less kid with her husband's genes! And one more for us." She drank another large gulp and then handed him the bottle.

He smiled at her uncomplicated response, returned her salutation, and drank to her toast. "But," he replied after he had swallowed, "it's not one for us. The kid is in their camp."

"Well, steal it back!" she suggested with the casualness born of a happy alcoholic glow. "Why not? They take our kids all the time. And this one is one of ours anyway."

"Why not," he repeated somewhat more seriously. Save the child from a life as a Nazi. Why not?

They talked in great detail for several hours about the Vogels and his life with them. Once Barbara realized he wanted to talk, she quite openly asked for details and listened with rapt attention to everything he had to say. And she talked freely about her own life—her weird life under the ground, as she put it. "My parents don't understand us, they think their children are strange, part of the elite," she said, using the word as though it had gained a special significance among the denizens of the encampment.

She reminded him of Zosia when he first knew her, when she did not judge him so harshly. He smiled at Barbara's openness, hugged her to keep her upright as she slipped into drunkenness. She clung to him, moaning or singing softly to herself as she put her hands into his coat to warm them. Finally, after swearing her to secrecy, he decided it was time to see her back to her room before she fell asleep in the woods, so he walked her home and delivered her safely into her parents' arms. They looked at him rather curiously but did not ask any questions. They were both low-ranking—her father did maintenance work, her mother cooked in the mess—and neither felt comfortable questioning Colonel Król's husband about why he was delivering their daughter home, hours later than her shift ended, and in such a state of drunkenness.

He muttered an incoherent explanation and then returned to his bed to sleep for a few hours in peaceful forgetfulness.

======================================= **45** =======================================

"Y ES, I AGREE, Peter shouldn't stay in our flat. It'll be crowded enough with you and Joanna here." Alex's voice emerged from a small box set on the table on which Zosia was sitting.

"I was thinking more that we don't want him associated with us," she explained.

"Oh, that won't be a problem. He'll be surrounded by hundreds of Americans—why should two more make a difference?"

"So, I'm going to be an American?"

"If anything. I don't see why you'll be discussed at all. Anyway, as my relatives, you're safe from retribution for any action taken under my auspices."

"I realize that. I also don't think they'll imagine anybody who has made it safely to America would ever want to go back. I was thinking more along the lines of my undercover work. Say somebody in Berlin is assigned to go through the publicity photos where I happen to be present, and there I am in Berlin pretending to be somebody's wife or something!"

"We'll make sure you're not present. And you two shouldn't see that much of each other anyway. You're going to be in D.C. a good part of the time, aren't you?"

"Yes, it's a great opportunity to do business—what with the British picking up the tab and all. But what about surveillance photos?"

"Their network here is pretty pathetic—mostly some amateurs from the brethren associations. They're more likely to heckle Peter—that's the level they work best at. Anyway, I have confidence in your masquerading abilities, my dear."

Zosia wrinkled her nose in amusement at the term. She swung her legs back and forth as she sat on the table, pressing the little buttons that let her converse with her father. Alex continued, "But, honey, why are you fretting so much? You know how to take care of yourself."

"Oh, I think it's Peter. He's so jittery about this, he's got even me seeing ghosts."

"What isn't that boy jittery about?"

"Once burned, twice shy."

"Don't worry, sweetie. Nobody'll link you to him. We'll put him in a hotel, on his own. I managed to get the Brits to promise to pay for that as well."

"How about some spending money? He'll need to look around and buy things—you know, in order to better present himself."

"I'll do my best to wring more hard currency out of them," Alex replied after some hesitation. "But I don't hold out much hope for their cooperation."

"Why not?" She waited as the answer wended its way through the ether.

"Well, apparently, there's a strong movement for them to dissociate themselves from us. Seems they think we don't have a snowball's chance in hell—and they don't want to be dragged down with us. As they put it, twenty years of independence in the past two hundred is not much to pin one's hopes on. They assume our culture is on the verge of annihilation and our people will soon be extinct or totally assimilated."

"What about the eight hundred years of statehood prior to that?" Zosia asked huffily.

There was silence and Zosia guessed her father had resorted to shrugging, then realizing his listener would not hear that response, he said, "Well, if you'll excuse the phrase, I think they are indulging in realpolitik. They're not the majority, but I can understand where they are coming from. They view their own position as weak but salvageable—hoping to gain some concessions from Berlin, maybe autonomy. Cultural rights, education in English, the usual—sort of on the Flemish model. They know there is no hope of our ever being given any of that—not with the current bunch of ideologues in power. Besides, half our country is in Soviet hands and the NAU is currently trying to cozy up to them. Anyway, they figure they're in better shape negotiating alone, and to prove some measure of loyalty to Berlin, they want to dissociate themselves from us. We're considered to be extremists and all that has occurred in our land is—they say— our own fault for not cooperating. I've even heard some of the more extreme of them refer to our Carpathian exclusion zone as a 'terrorist-controlled zone.' "

Zosia winced. "But you say they're not a majority."

"No, I'd guess not, but nobody is, really. Ever since the hard-liners gained the upper hand after Braun's death, there's been utter chaos among the strategists here. These so-called Conciliators are the only ones who have a consistent and convincing line right now. The other English factions are in complete disarray— united only in their belief that the Conciliators are would-be traitors. The Polish contingent has been spared that to some extent since the Nazis so kindly ruled out the possibilities of collaboration or conciliation for us. Since we turned down that anticommunist alliance with them at the beginning, they've made our decisions easy—fight or die."

"And we're dying," Zosia could not refrain from saying.

"Yes, I'm afraid so—soon we'll just be another historical footnote. We need action—whereas the Western powers, and especially the Brits, they have time to come to some better solution. And the NAU, well, it's hard to convince people to die or even pay money for someone else's pipe dreams of nationhood and survival. I'm afraid that as long as we keep insisting on not disappearing quietly, we're a bit of an embarrassment to them all. A lot of politicians just wish we'd go away so they can ignore Nazism's meaner aspects and deal with the Germans as just another political force. Every time we make a noise about mass murder, starvation, deprivation, et cetera—well, we're just spoilers.

"That's where Peter's so important. We've got to make them see that the various groups targeted so far are not all special cases. First the Jews, Gypsies, political inconvenients, religious types, and invalids, then they move on to groups that had possessed statehood prior to the war—us and our neighbors and then . . . It's obvious, there's no particular reason for them to stop."

"But they've never professed a desire to annihilate the British. At least not consistently," Zosia countered.

"Ah, yes, and their word has been worth so much in the past!" Alex's voice took on a bitter edge.

"I'm just playing devil's advocate."

"I know, and I know that everyone else thinks they won't be next. It's our job to make them think that they will—our survival depends on it; it's irrelevant whether we're right or wrong at this juncture. If they're not clever enough to find some relevance in the fact that the Reich is murdering us, then we'll make it relevant to them in other ways. Again—that's where your husband comes in. We're getting his travel money from the anti-Conciliation factions—they're hoping he'll prove that it can happen to anyone and that the Reich has no intention of treating anyone equitably."

"Just as I've always said!" Zosia could not stop herself from saying. "But it's the *anybody* part I'm worried about. The Americans will assume he was a criminal, everyone does. How do you think we should redo his history?"

"Well, he's going to have to mention the Underground, otherwise you're right, disappearing like he did will make him look like he joined the criminal underground, and as honorable as that may be, we don't want to confuse our audience. Besides, it will make him more heroic. Freedom fighter, et cetera. He should just stick to the Halifax name and story—abandoned as a babe, raised in an orphanage. Then say he was adopted at eight or so and his adoptive parents were arrested when he was twelve, at which point he was on his own. That'll work, won't it?"

"Yes, I suppose." Zosia tried out the story in her mind, began to fill in details for later use.

"At that point, he should stick with the German-documented history. He can join the Underground at sixteen—that'll explain his sudden disappearance. From then on, he can pretty much tell the truth, just the names are changed to protect the innocent."

"Why even have his parents arrested? Why not stick with his documents all the way through to sixteen?"

"Pathos. We need that lone-kid-standing-on-the-street-corner imagery. Very, very powerful image. Beats the hell out of his arrest as an adult."

"I see. But the Germans might spot the inconsistency."

"So? What are they going to do, complain? Ask for equal time? If they grumble about that, it will only serve to verify everything else. Oh, yeah, that reminds me; have him change that Allison thing. Make her his wife, dump her husband from the picture."

"Why not leave her out altogether?"

"Same reason, love interest—makes him more human. But make her his wife or at least fiancée. We don't want him to be too human!"

"All right. That only leaves one thing he's worried about: he still assumes that the English might assassinate him as a presumed traitor. What should we tell him about that?"

There was a longish pause and Zosia wondered if they had lost the connection, but then Alex spoke. "Well, tell him I gave them the Halifax name and they didn't recognize it as one of their own. Their only information on that name is the information that the Germans hold in their files—presumably when he was supposed to destroy those papers, they wiped all information about that identity from their records."

"So I'll tell him he can use that name without them linking it to Yardley or Chase or anyone else."

"Exactly."

"But once they hear his story, he thinks someone is sure to make the connection."

"Tell him the history of that incident is sure to be safely buried in diplomatic files and long ago forgotten."

"But there are people who would recognize him on sight as Yardley. He wants to know how to stop them from denouncing him as a traitor," Zosia explained.

"Tell him his story will speak for itself, and besides, it would be politically disastrous for them to attack him. Tell him to stop fretting, he'll be safe."

"Maybe we should just tell him the truth?"

"No! For God's sake, Zosia, it's taken this much to bring him this far! That could blow everything."

"I may have blown it anyway."

"How so? What's happened?"

Zosia paused. "Nothing really. Look, don't worry, I'll sort it out. Don't worry."

"Please do that. I'm really banking on him now. And it was your idea in the first place!"

"I knew you'd remind me of that if things didn't work out." She laughed. "I'm going to work on sorting everything out today, don't worry."

"What did happen? Why the big upset? Did you lose your temper?"

"It was nothing, really nothing. Just newlywed stuff, that's all."

"Good. Well, get to work on him, girl. You've got what you asked for, now deliver the goods."

"Yes, sir! Daddy sir!" Zosia laughed and signed off.

================================== **46** ==================================

WHEN PETER FINALLY dragged himself out of bed and into the kitchen, Zosia was not only already awake and dressed but she greeted him with a cheerful good-morning, a boisterous kiss, and an attempt at fried eggs.

He poked at the overdone eggs with his fork and wondered at her change in mood. Call him a collaborator, invoke saintly Adam, then let it all slip away! When she went into the bedroom for something, he discreetly poured a generous serving of vodka into his coffee and then sat down to begin eating the eggs she had cooked for him.

"How are they?" she asked cheerfully as she sat down opposite him.

"Awful. Why did you cook them so long?" he replied with unnecessary honesty, and sipped his coffee with surreptitious pleasure.

"Oh, I was reading this article and I just forgot about them." She shoved a story about life in the NAU at him. It was written by an American, so it was, he thought, of doubtful value to an outsider. He paged through to look for photos, but there were none—the article had been downloaded from an illegal satellite link and reprinted as a samizdat publication, and any photos had been sacrificed in the process.

"Does it have any useful insights?" he asked somewhat dubiously.

"Who knows? I didn't get very far when I realized that I was burning the eggs!" She laughed. "You should read it though. It's important we present your story well. There are a number of things we'll have to refine. I'll go over the list with you later. And about that other stuff—you know, well, we'll just forget all that, okay?" Then leaping up, she blew a kiss at him and announced, "I've got to run—there's a problem with some of the partisans in the northern sector we've got to sort out. Ta!" She was out the door before he could say anything.

So much for a discussion, he thought. He forced the eggs down, resupplied his coffee with more vodka, and then sat down to look at the article. He scanned it, looking for insights, but it was full of nothing but trite and self-congratulatory generalizations. It talked glowingly of the American spirit of independence, their drive and self-reliance—as if, he thought, no one else has a spirit of independence or drive or self-reliance. The article continued with folksy stories of the typical American's willingness to help his or her neighbor in times of need. It rapidly became clear that *neighbor* meant "American neighbor" and that the author was an isolationist.

And this was the culture he would try to impress into action! What a hopeless, thankless, and unpleasant task! He tossed the article into a corner. A few seconds later, he got up, picked it up, and carefully filed it among Zosia's stack of current readings, then he went to the cabinet and poured more vodka into his mug. He scanned the supplies, realized that he needed to restock the kitchen, especially the vodka supply, and decided to do that before he went in to work.

Later in the day, Zosia stopped by his office. She looked for a moment at Barbara and Olek as if deciding what to say, then spoke to him instead. "I need to talk to you alone," she said, indicating the other two with her eyes.

Without even being asked, they both rose, made excuses, and left. He felt a slow burning sensation at her usurping his authority in the office but did nothing more than raise his eyebrows expectantly. Zosia watched as the two disappeared down the hall, then she shut the door and said, "There's a minor problem with Barbara."

"What? What's wrong?"

"Her parents want her reassigned. It seems rather abrupt, I don't even think Barbara knows."

"Oh, shit," he groaned. "She's of age, isn't she? Do they have the right to do that?"

"Who knows? Whatever right they have or don't have, they can make trouble for her—she lives there after all."

"Yes, but she could move out."

"There's hardly room for independent young people. Besides, I'm interested in sorting the problem out, not destroying Barbara's family. Now, do you know what this is about?"

He admitted that he probably did, and he relayed the incident of the previous night.

"Oh, for Christ's sake, what the hell were you thinking about?" Zosia scolded.

"Nothing!"

"Clearly!" she agreed sarcastically. "Didn't it ever occur to you that a married man twice their daughter's age bringing her home, drunk, in the middle of the night might worry them?"

"I just wanted to make sure she got home okay. I didn't expect her to get drunk; we didn't have that much."

"Not by your standards."

"What do you mean by that?"

"I mean, my dear, even vodka has a smell. You're not exactly discreet." She nodded her head meaningfully toward his coffee cup.

"Oh, leave me alone!"

"Look, I don't care how much you drink as long as you can handle it—and usually you can. But don't go getting young girls drunk out in the woods! We have to maintain some sort of society here, and these people have sensibilities about these sorts of things! Do what you want, screw the girl if that's what you want, but for God's sake, be discreet!"

"Zosiu! All we did was talk, all I wanted to do was talk . . ."

"I know, you wanted a sympathetic ear. But don't you realize she has a crush on you? She'll be sympathetic no matter what you say. And you're leading her along. Don't you have any consideration for her feelings? You're using her."

"No, I'm not, she's a friend, I like talking to her. You talk with Tadek—how's this so different?"

Zosia apparently felt the differences were sufficiently obvious that she could ignore his question. Instead she said, "She's very vulnerable. Be careful. You're not the only person in the world who can be hurt."

He decided it was not worth another fight and surrendered. "Okay, I'm sorry. Is there anything I can do to calm her parents? An apology?"

She shook her head slightly. "I don't think an apology makes sense; after all, you didn't really do anything. And it was kind of you to see her home. No, I think an apology would just send the wrong message."

"Then what can we do? She's good at her job, I don't want to lose her."

"What you have to do is behave yourself from now on. Otherwise, I think I've already handled the problem."

"How?"

"I suggested that if she leaves your office, she be assigned to do assassinations with me as her mentor. Somehow that cooled their enthusiasm for her being transferred."

"I wonder why," he mused humorously.

"Apparently my reputation is even worse than yours. I am reputedly quite a difficult woman," she answered with obvious amusement.

"So I've heard, and it's true."

Zosia feigned a pout.

"But I wouldn't have it any other way." He rose to lock the door. "I've missed you terribly during this disagreement. Maybe we can just put it all behind us?" He approached from behind to kiss her neck.

"So you won't cancel your tour?"

"No, I promised you I'd go, and if you think it'll be all right, then it'll be all right." He moved his hands forward and began undoing her buttons.

"Oh, it'll be all right," she agreed happily. His hands moved under the material of her blouse, and she moaned slightly. "I don't think this is the right time," she protested gently. "This is hardly the way good, decent folk behave!"

He ignored her scruples, began telling her how incredibly beautiful she was, how he longed to hold her, touch her, stroke her. He ran his fingers through her hair, kissed her silken curls. He cajoled, flattered, complimented, stroked, and eventually overcame her not particularly forceful objections.

As they lay on the floor, among the stacks of documents and books and desk chairs, Zosia snuggled closer to him and thought about the last woman he had made love to. She had never been jealous in her life as it had not suited either her disposition or her purposes; still, she could not help but wonder at the comparisons Peter might make in his mind. Was Elspeth's power an aphrodisiac? How had he managed to drum up enough enthusiasm to actually do it with her? If he had no desire at all for Elspeth and still managed to have sex with her, was there any possibility that he was doing the same now?

He was such a great lover, so wonderfully satisfying of her needs. Indeed, though she hated to admit it, he was much better than Adam, for the two of them had grown too casual and Adam had never bothered to exert himself to find out what she might want beyond what pleased him. Peter was completely different: he made her feel as though she were the most extraordinary woman in the world, that simply being able to lie next to her, to enjoy her body, was more than he had ever hoped for. In the middle of the day, he might do no more than run his finger along her face—yet the smile of pleasure, the obvious enjoyment he received from such a simple gesture, left her feeling sexually charged. Or the way he sometimes just brushed his lips against her hand—not a prelude to sex, not a come-on; he did it just for the joy of kissing her. It all made her feel so special. And he seemed to read her mind, to hold back when she needed time, to push forward despite protestations when she wanted that as well. How did he do it? His whole being seemed intent on pleasing her, or rather, seemed pleased by her—she had never experienced anything so sexually stimulating. And it seemed that he gained the most pleasure from her happiness. It was wonderful, electrifying, but was it all part of a service? Did he feel any real desire for her?

The questions plagued her, not because the philosophical or theoretical elements appealed to her—she would never do anything so foolish as to analyze a sexual relationship that worked so well—but because, for the first time in her experience with him, she had faked her response. She had been unable to enjoy his attentions because she had kept wondering if he had behaved the same way with Elspeth. What sweet, meaningless words had he whispered to her? What tone of voice did he use with her? Did he betray his cynicism or did Elspeth believe that he really wanted her? Had he really wanted her? Had he voluntarily made love to a woman who had treated him so inhumanely? Had he been so warped by his experiences that he might even have enjoyed it? Had Elspeth been attractive to him? Zosia grimaced at the thought, realized that she was as intrigued by the idea of seeing that woman as he was with seeing his child.

She stretched and accidentally knocked over a stack of files with her arm. She rose up on an elbow and looked at Peter as he lay with his eyes closed and with a satisfied smile. "Peter?"

"What?" he asked dreamily.

"Would you like to see your child?"

He opened his eyes to look at her. "Yes, you know I would. But how can I?"

"Well, I've been thinking. There's some difficulty with Ryszard's household help—he has a man and a woman, they're a husband and wife team. They need to handle some personal problems. I guess the wife's mother is dying, and they want about a month out of Berlin. We could go in as a temporary exchange, you and me. Then we'd be in Berlin and maybe somehow we could arrange for you to see your kid."

"I'd love that." Peter's voice brimmed with gratitude. He sat up and kissed her, hugged her, then contemplated her for a moment. "Zosiu, would you even consider doing this if it weren't for the kid?"

"Heavens no! My brother can be a pain at the best of times. The last thing I'd want to do is spend a month under his thumb, but I know it's important to you to see your daughter."

"A daughter? It's a girl?"

"Yes, I finally got a chance to look it up today. You have a little girl. Her name is Magdalena."

"A little girl. A little girl." He wrapped his arms around Zosia, kissed her warmly. "Thank you! Of course I want to go. Thank you! A little girl!"

47

*H*EADQUARTERS HAD NO difficulty with Zosia's idea, but it took a lot of convincing to get the Szaflary Council to agree to it. Why, Katerina wanted to know, were they going to risk their most highly trained analyst and their best assassin and a member of the Council on such a ridiculous assignment?

Zosia argued that she needed the experience, that she wanted to be based in Berlin, that Joanna needed the education. And finally, at Peter's suggestion, she argued that Kasia needed her as she approached her due date. Zosia argued, cajoled, called in favors, and finally managed to get Katerina's objections overridden.

They transported themselves to Berlin as the major and his wife and daughter, but upon their arrival at Ryszard's house, they took up their new identities as a young cousin from the East and her two servants brought in on a temporary trade. Joanna was placed in Genia's room, and her parents were given two cots in the attic for their use whenever necessary, but Kasia had given them the guest room as well so they could spend most of their visit in comfort. There in the guest room they put on the finishing touches.

They laughed at each other while they put on their costumes, poking fun at the presumed sudden change in their blood as they dived down through the ranks of humanity to the very bottom. Zosia had dyed her hair a dark brown and donned a shapeless and ill-fitting blue shift. She spun around in front of Peter and asked, "What do you think?"

"You look gorgeous."

She smirked. "That's not supposed to be the effect."

"Sorry. I can't help you're beautiful."

She smiled at his compliment, went into the bathroom, and putting some grease on her hands, rubbed it into her hair. "This should help a bit." She pulled the oily brown mass back into a sloppy ponytail. Then, using an eyebrow pencil, she darkened her eyebrows and just under the inside of her eyelids. The action was obviously painful, and her eyes turned red and teary from the abuse. She turned toward him, scowled slightly, and asked, "Better?"

He nodded. "But you're still gorgeous."

"Oh, you're no help!" she exclaimed, exasperated.

"What about me?" he asked, presenting himself for inspection.

She studied him for a moment: the transition was heartbreaking. They had colored his hair using an easily dissolved brown dye, and he had done nothing beyond that other than don the uniform, yet he looked completely different! He raised his eyebrows as he awaited her evaluation. She smiled at him, came forward, and gently grasped his hand, brought it to her lips, and kissed it.

He laughed slightly at her silence. "I know, I look like hell."

"No, you look afraid." She saw how his tongue moved back to touch the false tooth that now carried poison for him. It was an involuntary probing that they all did at first. Death whenever one wanted it. Funny, but no one felt reassured. "I am, too," she confessed.

He looked at her in surprise. "You?"

She nodded. "Scared shitless." Her hand moved unbidden to her abdomen, and her eyes dropped to contemplate their unborn child. "More afraid than I've ever been."

They presented themselves downstairs to the general merriment of the family. With Stefi at the encampment, the eldest child at home was Pawel, a witty and bright sixteen-year-old boy. He teased his aunt mercilessly but had either been forewarned or was sufficiently intuitive that he did not harass Peter at all. His younger brothers, Andrzej, who was thirteen, and Jan, who was ten, joined in. When Zosia scolded Jan for teasing her too much, he stated quite impishly that he had nothing to fear as long as she wasn't wearing her necklace. Andrzej joined in, asking, "Auntie Zosia, what are you going to do without your necklace to keep us in line?"

"Ah, just you wait and see." Zosia's eyes glinted with feigned menace. "The next time you visit us, I'll show you where your father used to be locked up by your grandfather! It's the darkest, dankest part of the bunker and there's no way out!"

The boys drew back slightly, unsure of the reality of the threat. Joanna gave both her parents a hug and told her mother that she looked awful with her hair all messed up. Zosia thanked her for that information and then set about practicing her character by making tea for everybody.

Zosia settled into her role surprisingly well. She was not only supportive of Kasia as she struggled through the last awkward days of her pregnancy, but she let Peter teach her the basics of how to handle a household and carried out her self-assigned duties with a cheerful gusto. Only in the early morning when she would moan about killing herself rather than getting up yet again to go and fetch breakfast rolls was she less than enthusiastic in her job. Peter tried various ways of waking her up, but nothing really worked. Eventually he would ask if she wanted him to go, and she would groan that it was too dangerous and finally manage to roll out of bed.

She found the whole process extraordinarily disconcerting. The first morning Kasia accompanied her, and as the two women walked slowly to the bakery, Kasia stopped to explain Zosia's temporary presence to the patrols. They were deferential toward Kasia, and though Zosia kept her head and eyes down, they seemed to treat her courteously enough—one of them even stooping down somewhat comically so he could peer into her face. The next day, however, when she went on her own, they treated her with an ill-tempered brusqueness that promised violence at any second.

"I hadn't done anything!" she moaned to Peter. "I'm sure of it! I was walking like you taught me, careful not to look at anyone, doing everything you said, and still they came over barking at me like . . ." She looked up at him plaintively. "Did I screw up? I thought I was doing it right."

He embraced her, stroked her messy, greasy hair. "I'm sure you were perfect. They just harass people, especially new people. There's no way around it. It sounds like everything went just as it should have done."

She pulled back to look at him. "Really?"

He nodded, pulled her back into his arms. "I'm sorry, darling, that's just the way it is. They'll probably lay off in a day or two. Just be especially careful for the next couple of days."

"What more can I do to be careful?" she asked quite seriously.

"I don't know, it was useless advice."

It was also useless worrying, his sitting by the back window each morning waiting for her to reappear, but he did it nonetheless. From the moment she went out the door until the moment he saw her opening the back gate, he sat and uselessly fretted. Sometimes he ventured out into the yard to the back gate to watch for her approach down the alley, but he felt that this might be viewed as suspicious behavior by the neighbors, so he did not often indulge himself.

Eventually he came upon the idea that Joanna and Kasia's five-year-old daughter, Genia, could walk each morning with Zosia to the bakery. The children were under strict instructions never to try to interfere, just to run home and report any serious trouble. They were happy to take on the responsibility, and Zosia enjoyed the company. Knowing how the patrols tended to behave themselves in the presence of Rudi and Gisela, Peter felt sure that the girls would act as a reasonable deterrent to any unpleasantness.

Once the morning routine had been sorted out, the days were quite pleasant. Zosia and Peter managed to keep the house in a reasonable state; Kasia helped out when she felt up to it and sprawled awkwardly in an armchair to rest when she did not. The children were self-sufficient, and there was plenty of time for visiting and conversation. The only annoyance, and that was fairly minor, was that it was considered too dangerous for Peter to leave the property given that the Traugutts lived in the same Party-favored area as the Vogels. He accepted the inconvenience and used the time wisely, studying material that he had brought with him about America and its culture.

Ryszard came home in the evenings invariably exhausted by the stress of his day. He did nothing to help around the house; he rarely even interacted with his family. He just sat and smoked, sometimes reading the Party newspaper, often just staring off into space, sipping a whiskey. Sometimes Kasia would sit and join him and try to converse, but usually he was so unresponsive that she gave up and left him to his thoughts. Occasionally he argued with his son Pawel. He wanted Pawel to move out of the house as soon as possible, to move into Szaflary with his sister Stefi under the pretense that he had left home for a military academy. But Pawel, having only just turned sixteen, was not yet ready to leave home. He wanted to remain with his family and especially wanted to be there for his mother. He was aware of his father's stress-induced depression and felt the need to shoulder the burden of taking care of the family as his father struggled with his own internal demons.

Pawel confided his difficulties to Peter, and the two of them discussed the best approach to use with Ryszard. Pawel, and Andrzej as well, both leapt at the opportunity to talk to Peter and learn whatever he could teach them. They seemed completely starved of fatherly attention and complained bitterly of their father's increasing withdrawal from the world around him. He had always been somewhat preoccupied with his work, they said, but since their move to Berlin, his preoccupation had deepened into something much more destructive.

Peter tried to explain their father's behavior to them, tried to ease them into communicating with him, but all that seemed to happen was that the boys latched onto Peter as a substitute father, and as Ryszard finally took notice that he was being usurped, he fell ever deeper into his self-absorption.

Within a week, Peter decided there was nothing to do for it but talk directly to Ryszard. It was not hard to find him alone; he actively encouraged the children to avoid him, and with the birth overdue, Kasia was ever more tired and napped frequently. Peter asked Zosia if she would like to help, but she shook her head in mock terror and exclaimed, "Not my brother! No thank you!"

So, Peter entered the living room alone to try to talk to his brother-in-law. Ryszard was sitting in the armchair, sipping some whiskey, immersed in his newspaper. Peter poured himself a drink and sat on the couch.

"Ryszard, we need to discuss your sons," Peter began abruptly.

Slowly Ryszard lowered the paper, gave Peter a well-practiced look of disdain, then raised the paper again.

"This is serious."

Ryszard lowered the paper again. "Let me guess: you know better than me how to raise my boys."

"It's not that." Peter tried to be gentle. "It's your withdrawal from them. They need you."

"What would you know about families?" Ryszard asked contemptuously. "You couldn't even *act* the part of gracious host at your own wedding!"

Peter had never thought about his encounter with Zosia's family in those terms, and it made him realize for the first time that he had been quite insulting in his behavior. His own family, when it had existed, had interacted so little with each other and with anyone else that in some areas he was completely ignorant of standard social behavior.

"Even your friend Karl would have had enough class to greet guests at his own wedding!" Ryszard goaded.

The cruelty of the remark did not make it any less true, and Peter felt thoroughly embarrassed. He did not want to be sidetracked, but nevertheless said, "I'm sorry about that. I was feeling rather, er, worried at the time." On the spur of the moment he decided that it was a perfect segue and continued, "I was insecure in my position, and so I withdrew into myself and as a result hurt the ones nearest and dearest to me. Like you're doing now."

"Give it a rest." Ryszard ruffled the paper noisily.

"They're your sons—not mine!" Peter retorted angrily. "Look at them! If I do anything around your house, they're there asking me questions, trying to help, interested in learning!"

"Oh, so they can be plumbers!" Ryszard responded scornfully. "What the hell are you doing fixing faucets anyway?" He had seen plenty, but that had really bothered him—all three of his sons in the bathroom, Pawel half under the sink, Andrzej holding on to the tap from above, Jan handing tools to his brothers, as Peter sat on the edge of the bathtub and directed their efforts.

"It was leaking!"

"Kasia should have called a plumber."

"Kasia should have! Do you have any idea what state your wife is in? Do you have any idea what it is like inviting complete strangers into the house? The security precautions? Do you even have any idea how difficult it is to get hired help under normal circumstances? You should know better than that!"

"Well, then go ahead and show them your trades," Ryszard agreed haughtily. "Fix broken panes of glass and unstick windows and whatever the hell else it is you're always doing!"

"If you're not competent at the simple jobs associated with living in a house," Peter responded with equal vitriol, "then perhaps you could find some other way to talk to them. Try taking a walk with one of them! Or is using your two hind legs beyond your technical competence as well?"

"Fucking *Untermensch!* You haven't a clue what my life is like."

"Yes, I do," Peter replied calmly, reminding himself that he was trying to help

Ryszard's sons, not win an argument. "I know what it is like to become a completely different person and live that lie day in and day out. I did it for survival, you're doing it for a cause. Otherwise, it is the same."

"It is not," Ryszard replied weakly.

"So you don't feel like a prisoner?" Peter asked, remembering Ryszard's one unguarded moment months before.

"I don't . . ." Ryszard fell silent.

"You have three wonderful boys and a marvelous little girl here who need a father. Don't abandon them," Peter pleaded. "Maybe you want to feel distant from them in case something happens, but don't do that. They need you and they need you now, not later when you reach some distant goal."

"I just don't have time to fool around with all this . . ." Ryszard waved his hand to indicate the house and his children.

"Ryszard! You need to have a life! It is the only thing that will save your soul. For God's sake, each and every day you don the most unfeeling persona, you deal with the most heartless people in one of the cruelest ministries of an evil government. It's a poison! You can't do that to yourself and not have an antidote."

"I'm afraid," Ryszard said quietly.

"Of what?" Peter asked. There was so much to be afraid of!

"I'm afraid that if I relax a bit here, I'll slip up out there. And then we'll all be dead."

"There are other deaths to avoid."

Ryszard fell silent, perhaps thinking about what his brother-in-law had said. After a moment, he picked up the newspaper again, saying, "All right, you've said your bit."

Peter sighed. Was that it? He sat and watched as Ryszard read, then making a decision to interfere just once more, he went to the cabinet and pulled out a deck of cards.

"Here," he said, shoving them at Ryszard. "Go play poker with your kids. I've taught them the game."

"You *what?*" Ryszard asked, confused, as he stared at the deck of cards under his nose.

"Joanna regularly takes me to the cleaners. Watch out in particular for Jan—he has an excellent poker face."

"What?"

"And I think Joanna has passed on some of her tricks to Genia—so don't be surprised if you're out of pocket by the end of the evening."

"What?" Ryszard could not stop saying.

"Just do it. Whoever is home. Call them downstairs, suggest a game," Peter ordered, pushing the cards into Ryszard's hand.

Ryszard stared at the deck for a good long time, then, closing his hand around the cards, he stood up and went into the hallway to call his children down.

=================================== **48** ===================================

"**H**ERE, I THOUGHT THIS might interest you." Ryszard tossed the heavy, spiral-bound notebook onto the coffee table.

Peter was sitting, in uniform, with his feet up on the coffee table reading the Party newspaper. He had been ready for duty in the event that Ryszard arrived home with someone, but as he had seen him walking up the path alone, Peter had not bothered to get up or interrupt his reading. Still, he welcomed the diversion from the endless printed garbage and pulled his feet off the table to lean forward and look at the book. "What is it?"

"Oh, the rules and regulations governing domestic workers. There's a huge section devoted to you and your ilk," Ryszard answered absently as he lit a cigarette. "Want one?"

"Yeah, sure." Peter accepted the cigarette, began paging through the heavy book. "Do they provide this to every owner?"

"Naw. It's property of the Morality Ministry. I just borrowed it. I guess the average owner is just supposed to know intuitively what all the laws and regulations are."

So, as he had so long ago suspected, there was a book! He read the paragraphs. Even obsessive Elspeth had been unable to comply with most of the regulations. They appeared to be listed chronologically, and though there was an index, it was not particularly useful. Within minutes Peter found several regulations that were inconsistent with each other and several more that were not indexed. It all depended on which page one looked at! He laughed scornfully.

"What's so funny?" Ryszard asked as he poured himself a whiskey. "Do you want one?"

"I should be getting that. Yeah, I'd like one."

Ryszard handed him the drink, and Peter explained the source of his amusement. He continued paging through the book, and his eyes landed on some fee list for several years prior. "What about these? Is this what I cost?"

Ryszard scanned the page. "More or less."

"One hundred thousand NRM," Peter read the appropriate category with something like dismay. There it was, his price, published in a book. "What do you make?"

"Annually, I have a base salary of about a million."

"Base? What, do you earn overtime?"

Ryszard laughed. "You could call it that."

"So my lifetime labor cost one-tenth of a year's base salary?"

"Well, yes, but I am well paid. A very well-paid laborer only makes about a hundred grand."

"So even a worker could afford to buy me on one year's salary?" Peter felt a sudden shock of . . . what was it? Bitterness that his price was so low? Wasn't that a ridiculous thing to feel outraged about?

"No, a worker could never afford you," Ryszard answered. "Those are the official fees involved in transferring the contract from the state to a private individual. They could even be waived altogether. Where the money comes into the picture is getting that contract transferred in the first place. You have to have some political muscle, or an overriding social need or a really good bribe."

"What sort of bribe?"

"Varies with availability. Could be up to a million, usually much lower. In your case, I'd guess Karl didn't pay a pfennig—just hounded the Reusches into signing you over." Ryszard paused, then added with unnecessary callousness, "I would guess your birthrights were sold for less than a pack of cigarettes."

Peter ignored the comparison. "And the Reusches?"

"I would guess they were being bought off to keep quiet about their son's death. They probably paid a minimal amount and maybe even had the fees waived."

Peter vaguely remembered something about "in lieu of the usual fees . . ." Why, he wondered stupidly, did he feel so insulted?

"You almost certainly went cheap," Ryszard said.

"What makes you say that?"

"You were a test case, so to speak. That reeducation bit had only just been introduced, and placing you with a family was risky. I had you pegged for a powerful family—"

"You?"

Ryszard laughed. "Took me a while to recall the event, but after I perused your file—"

"*You?*"

"Yes, I arranged your release. I thought you'd make trouble so I suggested a politically powerful family as your placement."

"*You* were responsible for what I went through?"

"No, not me. I was just on an inspection tour."

"Who was, then? What's his name?"

Ryszard shook his head.

"*What's his name!*"

"No need to thank me for saving your life; it was, after all, just a joke," Ryszard said pointedly. "In any case, they obviously did not feel comfortable about letting you out to someone important. The Reusches were nobodies. Maybe they deliberately chose someone they didn't care about, so if you slit their throats in the middle of the night, it'd be no great loss."

Peter breathed deeply trying to control his fury. There was no point in asking Ryszard again, so instead he asked, "So how did I end up with the Vogels? Wasn't he valuable?"

"Depends on who you ask. But I think he just wanted someone on the cheap, and there you were, owned by politically weak people who had committed a minor crime. Plus, by then, I guess you had proven yourself, if he even bothered to take such things into account. He is, about certain things, rather thick."

So am I, Peter thought. He took a moment to swallow all the information Ryszard had so casually passed along. Ryszard knew who had tortured him, Ryszard had organized his release, Ryszard had saved his life. As a joke. A joke. Peter blinked away the bitterness he felt and to distract himself scanned through a few more pages. On one was a list of regulations for subletting workers to industry, and it prompted him to ask, "How much do you think I earned for Karl in that factory job?"

"Did they feed you?"

"No."

"Full day?"

"No, just eight hours."

"Seven days a week?"

"Yes." Day in and day out without a break. Work at home all day, work in that god-awful factory all night. Breathe those foul fumes, walk home barely able to put one foot in front of the other. Two hours of sleep, naps whenever Frau Vogel wasn't looking. God, it had nearly killed him.

"It has gone up, but I'd guess at the time you probably pulled in about three thousand a month."

"Three thousand?" Peter could not believe his ears. "One hundred per day?"

"Yeah, that'd be my guess. I suppose I could ask him, but"—Ryszard grinned—"for some reason he doesn't enjoy talking about you—except of course to grumble."

"A pack of cigarettes per day," Peter translated, using Ryszard's scale. "They nearly killed me for a fucking pack of cigarettes a day."

"Which he no doubt smoked without thought."

"How much are rations?"

"For you, they'd have been . . ." Ryszard looked pensive. "What class of rations did you have?"

"I didn't realize there were classes."

"Oh, yeah, there are. What color was your card?"

"Blue."

Ryszard laughed. "The cheapest! I could have guessed. Those run about two hundred a month. So you bought your food with two days' work. Add another day for clothing and the rest was pure profit."

"It nearly killed me," Peter said rather sadly. He did not expect Ryszard to understand and he had not meant to say it out loud.

"How so? Was it the chemicals?"

"Partly. But mostly it was that I was expected to continue to do everything at home as well. I was getting two hours of regular sleep then."

"Well, in any case, it couldn't have lasted more than a week or two. Still, I suppose two weeks with such a schedule would be devastating."

"Two weeks! Try"—Peter counted silently—"nearly five months!"

"What? Five months!" Ryszard laughed. "I'm amazed he got away with it for that long!"

"Why not? I wasn't dead; that seemed to be the only criterion," Peter answered bitterly.

"No, no! It's against the rules, look for yourself." Ryszard pointed at the book. "If anyone had caught him pulling that sort of stunt, Karl could have lost you back to the state. You weren't supposed to be used for personal profit; after all, if it's factory work they wanted you to do, it's the state that should have made the profit."

Peter felt a sudden chill.

"But, of course, you didn't know that," Ryszard said, interpreting Peter's expression.

Peter shook his head.

"He didn't either. Not until I told him," Ryszard guessed. "I think, if I remember correctly, he had you quit that very night."

"*You* told him?"

Ryszard grinned. "Yes. Seems I saved your life a second time."

Peter nodded numbly.

"Though almost too late, judging from how you looked then. You seemed pretty shattered." Ryszard paused as if remembering, then asked, "You don't even remember my visit there, do you?"

Peter shook his head, mouthing the word *no*.

"And it was all unnecessary. Illegal even," Ryszard added.

That was true, and the fact he had suffered so unnecessarily was indeed a bitter pill, but even more so was the knowledge that he had been grovelingly grateful to Karl for having finally ordered him to quit. He felt sick at the memory of how he had reacted to Karl's alleged mercy. It had not been mercy at all!

"Not that I expect gratitude, or anything," Ryszard said jokingly.

Peter could not even respond; he had an urge to vomit.

"Are you all right?"

Peter shook his head as he stared at the smooth, pale, damaged skin of his hands. "No," he breathed.

Ryszard did not know what to do with that answer, so he left his brother-in-law alone with his thoughts while he went to unpack his briefcase and change out of his suit.

"Why the gloomy look?" Zosia asked as she walked into the room several minutes later.

Peter jerked his head in the direction of the regulations. As Zosia began to peruse it, Joanna burst into the room. "Hi, Ma! Hi, Dad!" She bounced across the room, giggling the entire way, and at the last bounce threw herself up and onto

Peter's lap and wrapped her arms around him to hug him while still giggling. He joined in her laughter and stood up while holding her so that he could spin her around before dropping her back down to continue her bouncing. She bounced around the room one more time, then stopped and announced breathlessly, "Genia wants to show me the park. Can I go with her?"

"Sure, if you promise not to fool around, not even a tiny bit," Zosia answered, trying to maintain a stern air.

"I will, Ma."

"This is serious!" Zosia emphasized. "Not one wrong word. Remember everything I've told you and do everything I've taught you. Do you promise?"

"Of course!" Joanna sounded offended at the repetition.

"And only if Genia's mother thinks it's okay," Zosia added as an afterthought.

"She's napping," Peter interjected worriedly.

"Oh, I guess we shouldn't wake her. What do you think about them going out alone? You know the turf better than me."

"It's not usually done that way. Besides I'd feel a lot better if one of us went along."

"That means me," Zosia sighed.

"Why can't Dad come?" Joanna whined.

Zosia grimaced slightly. "Nice to know I'm so welcome!"

Joanna threw her arms around her mother's thighs and said, "I meant both of you!"

"I might be recognized by someone in the neighborhood, sweetie," Peter answered, "so, I'm afraid I'm housebound."

"What would they do?" Joanna asked, suddenly serious.

"They'd kill me," Peter responded just as seriously.

Joanna's face dropped, but then she remembered her original request and said, "So we can go?"

"Yes, you and Genia get ready while I get my papers together," Zosia answered.

Feeling lonely and abandoned, Peter watched out the window as Zosia walked with the two girls in the direction of the park. As he stood there, he absently swept his fingers across the windowsill. They came away covered in dust, and he shuddered with the knowledge of what would have happened if Elspeth had ever discovered such an accumulation.

49

"**S**O YOU THINK Uwe is depressed and that's what's prolonging his illness? Is such a thing possible?"

"Yes, *gnädige Frau*. The mind is very powerful," Peter answered, wondering if a cigarette was possible.

Elspeth nodded to herself. "Interesting. I hadn't really thought of things that way." She looked at him and smiled kindly. "It was rather nice today, wasn't it?"

"Yes, it was," he agreed without having to lie. He glanced at the time and decided not to try for the cigarette today. Maybe next time. He climbed out of the bed and pulled on his clothing. "I guess I should get back to work."

Elspeth glanced at the little clock on the bedside table and smiled provocatively. "There's plenty of time, come back to bed."

He hesitated to answer as he contemplated how he could say no without offending her.

"Oh, don't give me that miserable look!" she snapped, exasperated.

It was too late, he would never be able to summon up enough enthusiasm to make up for his faux pas. "Forgive me, *gnädige Frau,* but I have so much work that must be done . . ."

"Oh, I don't know why I expect any response from you. You have no appreciation of what I do for you . . ." He recognized the beginning of a tirade and there was nothing to do but wait it out. Though it was no worse than usual, he felt inexplicably hurt by her words, but he did nothing, said nothing, until she was finished, at which point he apologized and asked permission to leave to return to his work.

". . . you must have so many wonderful stories to tell about her!" Kasia's voice floated into his perception.

He peered through the gap between the curtain and the window frame into the garden below and watched the two women as they sat there sipping their tea and eating their tiny sandwiches.

Elspeth picked a bit of lettuce out of her teeth, then motioned for Zosia to refill her teacup before saying, "We've just changed caretakers, so I'm afraid I haven't heard anything amusing recently."

Bad enough that Elspeth had not brought Magdalena with her, despite an explicit invitation to do so, but now Kasia couldn't even wring a story out of her! He turned away to look into the darkened bedroom and sighed his exasperation.

"Oh, did you have trouble with the last one?" Kasia asked.

"No, she was just a schoolgirl on a month's course. Like the others. I'm afraid Magdalena hasn't really taken to any of them much."

"Maybe she'd like more interaction with her mother, or her father," Kasia risked saying.

Elspeth's face darkened for a moment. Her thoughts seemed to be elsewhere. Then she smiled, sipped her tea, and shrugged. "Frankly, my husband never took much interest in the girls. And as for me, well, just between us, I'm a bit fed up with children."

"I understand," Kasia murmured, and nodded her head. "I understand."

The obvious truth came out in bits and pieces in the conversation. The child was an irrelevancy. She had served her purpose by being born; she was a number—number eight, a quota fulfilled. Peter stared down at Elspeth's dark roots with growing dismay. His poor little Magdalena, whom he did not even know. She was fated to be an extra mouth to feed, a burden on the family, a nonson. He closed his eyes and sighed heavily. How could Elspeth feel so cold toward her own child? Was she mad? And if so, how had he ever managed to maintain his sanity in her household?

Maybe he hadn't. Could a sane man have accepted the verbal and physical abuse she meted out one minute and make love to her the next?

". . . so you were able to get another servant besides the nannies?" Kasia was saying.

"Oh, yes, I wasn't going to try and manage all on my own! That house, oh, there's just so much to do!"

"I know." Kasia nodded agreeably. "It's so hard to get the help to do anything right. I thought, though, you would have had trouble given, er, that little incident?"

Elspeth blushed. "No, no problem. We, well, it was obvious that it was not our fault and that his training was defective. We had problems—mind you, nothing serious, but still—we had problems with him from the first."

"Oh, really?" Kasia exuded sympathy.

"Yes, terrible. He was an asocial. Never fit in, never showed proper respect." Elspeth shook her head. Her words sounded almost memorized and did not match either her tone or expression. To Peter her tone sounded as though she felt betrayed; her expression was one of poignant, perhaps even fond, memories. It sickened him, and he placed his head on his arms on the windowsill and listened to the rest of the conversation without looking at her again.

Elspeth finally left, and Zosia came to the bedroom door, pushed it open, and slipped inside. She stood silently contemplating him in the dim light, then she asked, "Are you all right?"

"Yeah, I'm okay," he answered, resigned to hearing a diatribe about his cowardice. With her? How could he? She was even worse than expected. Such a Nazi-ette! Not even pretty. And so on.

"You look . . . are you sure you're okay?" Zosia asked as she came to stand by him.

He nodded. "I guess I forgot how much I hated her. Or maybe I never really realized it at the time."

"I'm sorry she didn't bring the baby," Zosia soothed as she stroked his hair.

Without meaning to, he pulled his head away, then realizing what he had done, he turned his attention to her. She was so loving, how could he possibly shy away from her? He stood and reached toward her and they kissed passionately. He would make it up to her, make amends for that moment of defensiveness, and besides, it would feel good to purge the emotions of the afternoon. They continued to kiss and embrace and stroke each other, moving slowly toward the bed.

They undressed each other, rolled onto the bed together, and continued their passionate kissing. He began kissing her body, moving down the smooth skin to nibble at her breasts, to run his tongue over her hardened nipples. He moved downward kissing her stomach, stroking between her legs with his hands, caressing the curves of her waist with his lips, exciting her to groans of expectation.

When she seemed thoroughly excited, he began to raise himself, but she stopped him. "Go down on me," she pleaded as her hands convulsively stroked his face. "You've never done that." Ever so gently she guided his face farther down.

He let her hands guide him so she would not recognize his hesitation. He bent his head toward her, but stopped. "I'd rather not," he said simply, and moved upward in the bed.

"Oh, why not?" she groaned with disappointment. "Really, we've never . . . I just wanted to try it with you."

"Please. No." He kissed her on the lips.

Something in his tone woke her out of her dreamlike state. She opened her eyes and stared at him. "*That woman!*" she accused. His silence was the only acknowledgment she needed. She rolled onto her side putting her back toward him. He raised himself up and reached for her, but she pushed his hand away.

"Zosiu . . ."

"Is she all you think about?"

"No, no! It's not like that."

Zosia's eyes narrowed with frustrated anger. "What is it like, huh? Tell me about it. Tell me all about it."

"You don't want to know."

"Yes, I do; you couldn't be bothered to tell me before."

"It's humiliating!" His voice was strained.

"And it's humiliating for me, never knowing when I'm going to cross some unseen boundary!" she retorted angrily. "If you cared about my feelings, you would at least let me know where I stand!"

"Can't you just respect my privacy?"

"I do. But when your memories interfere with our lives—then I have a right to know about them."

"It's not the memories that are interfering. My response to your request was not out of line. *Was it?* Or do you expect unquestioning obedience to your every whim?"

"That's exactly the sort of thing I'm talking about—everything gets blown way out of proportion by you!" she accused.

"It isn't *me!* You're the one who can't let go. Ever since you found out about Elspeth, you've jumped on every mistake I've made, the slightest wrong move, the smallest gesture. You can't get over her and you're blaming me! Ever since you've found out about her, you've been faking with me—we haven't had any real sex since then. You've completely shut me out of your life."

"Well, then, include me back in," she suggested coldly. "Tell me all about it."

He did not reply. He was emotionally exhausted, and there seemed no easy way to refuse without escalating the hostility, but still he could not tell her. He could not let her wallow in his humiliation, and especially he could not bear to think she might tell her friends. He had already provided them with far too many laughs. Simply and with finality he said, "No."

Zosia did not respond. She remained silent with her back toward him.

He lay back in the bed, closed his eyes, and tried not to think about it, about Elspeth, but of course he was unsuccessful. He would lie next to her, trying not to think, trying not to understand. He would lie there until a decent interval had passed, keeping his eyes closed because he did not want to see. It had been useless though; she did not let him go so easily. She made him see, made him understand. At some point she made it clear she wanted oral sex from him. She began with subtle hints, which grew increasingly unsubtle as time progressed. He knew what she wanted and shuddered with revulsion at the idea. It was one thing to climb on top of a woman he did not love and pretend she was someone else, but to do that . . . He determinedly ignored the hints, and eventually Elspeth was forced to instruct him directly.

When she told him what she wanted, he turned his head to look at the wall and muttered, "I'd really rather not."

There was a long silence as she seemed to be deciding what to do with his refusal. He turned toward her, reached for her face, stroked it gently. "You're a beautiful woman," he said not altogether untruthfully, "and I like to see your face when we make love."

Elspeth smiled slightly, and he thought perhaps he had salvaged the situation, but then she said, "So why do you always look away?"

"I'm overwhelmed by your beauty," he lied egregiously.

"Do as you've been told," she responded, unmoved.

Somewhat hopelessly he tried, "Please, Elspeth, let me take the initiative. Allow me that much self-respect."

"Self-respect?" she snorted derisively. "You?" She sat up and twisted around to lean over him. "You've always had an inflated sense of your worth, haven't you? You're a worm! And now, just because I let you crawl into my bed, you think you're my equal! Do you have any idea what my husband would do to you if I let him know about us? Do you?"

"And what would he do to you?" he asked, afraid that she might impetuously carry out her threat.

"Not much. He knows how it would reflect on him," she answered as though speaking from experience. "But you—your life wouldn't be worth living!"

"It isn't now," he muttered to himself.

"What? What did you say?"

"I said . . . I said it wouldn't be worth living without you," he replied desperately. "Please, let's not fight. You are my beautiful, merciful lady," he said, returning to addressing her with stiff formality, "and it breaks my heart when my lady is unhappy with me. Please let me make it up to my lady."

Elspeth smiled. It was unclear whether she believed him or simply enjoyed his groveling. Whichever, it seemed to work as an aphrodisiac, and she lay back down in the bed and indicated that she would allow him to show the sincerity of his words.

From another world Zosia's voice interrupted his thoughts. "I'm sorry I pushed you. I didn't mean to."

He glanced over at her. She was still facing away from him. Had she really said something or had he dreamed it? "I'm sorry, too."

"About what?" she asked dreamily.

"All of it. I love you." He got up on an elbow to look at her and perhaps start again, but she had closed her eyes and seemed to be falling asleep.

He lay back in the bed and thought again of Elspeth. He remembered how in the throes of passion she would push him away the moment she no longer wanted his attention, careless of any emotional or physical involvement he may have had at the time. She was sated; what else was there? As he yielded to her demand for oral sex, she had been driven into paroxysms of pleasure, and then suddenly, her back still arched, her eyes still tightly shut, she had rudely shoved her hand into his face to indicate he should stop.

He had sat on his heels and watched her from his odd perspective as she settled into a breathless afterglow. It was like watching someone else's life—a documentary on television, perhaps—he was so detached from her and what he was doing. Then, as the force of her passion was spent, she reached out toward him, pulled his body on top of hers. As he lay on her, she noticed he was not excited, not ready for the next obvious step, and she was surprised. Her surprise was more telling than the immediate anger that followed. Of course she was angry— a desire was not going to be instantaneously fulfilled—but surprised? Yes, surprised because she had no real concept of his independence, of the fact that what pleased her did not automatically excite him. At the time it had not seemed at all strange to him. In fact, at the time, he remembered thinking that he had been stupid for not foreseeing her desire and preparing himself accordingly. At the time, she had owned him.

He turned his head to look at his wife. Zosia was wrong: it was not collaboration, it was just sick. Not only what had been done to his life, but what had been done to Elspeth's and Karl's as well. They all suffered from a sickness.

Gently he tugged at Zosia's shoulder. She resisted him, moaning slightly, but eventually she rolled onto her back, her eyes still closed, apparently asleep. He kissed her and began whispering in her ear how much he loved her. He stroked back the unruly locks that struggled to break free from her grease-bound hair, he let his lips brush across her cheeks as he reminded her of how she had saved not only his life but his soul. "Please, Zosiu, come to me again. I need you, I love you," he pleaded quietly.

Her eyes fluttered open and she opened her arms to him and he fell into her embrace.

*　　*　　*

He awoke to music. Somewhere, someone was playing a piano. He held his eyes shut for a moment and half-dreamed that his mother was alive and demonstrating how to play a piece. She had been surprisingly good at the piano; perhaps in a different world she would have had a career as a musician. The music continued, and he awoke completely, aware that he was at Ryszard's, aware that Zosia slept next to him and that it was the middle of the afternoon. He smiled at his sleeping wife and replayed the last few minutes of their passion. Her reactions had been genuine, he was fairly sure of that, and he was enormously relieved. She had, at last, forgiven him, or at least she had managed to put his affair with Elspeth out of her mind long enough to enjoy his attentions.

Quietly, so as not to awaken her, he climbed out of the bed and dressed, then went down the stairs to see who was playing. At the entrance to the music room he paused and watched as Kasia's hands swept swiftly across the keys. If he had even for a moment contemplated trying to play their piano, the thought was completely swept from his mind by this demonstration of her expertise. As he stood there, Joanna and Genia joined him in the doorway, one child on each side of him. They listened in silence and then, when Kasia had finished the piece, they all applauded.

"Mommy's teaching me how to play," Genia informed him proudly.

"I wish I could learn," Joanna sighed.

"I can teach you a bit, while you're here," Kasia offered, still glowing from the applause, "but I'm afraid you'll have to find someone else to help you once you've gone home."

Not surprisingly Joanna turned to her father. She looked up expectantly. "Can you teach me, Dad?"

He looked away from her toward the piano, then shifted his gaze uneasily out the window. "I don't know how, honey."

The lie was obvious to Kasia. She smiled gently and asked, "Who taught you?"

He bit his lip, deciding whether to admit his lie, then answered, "My mother. I didn't get a chance to learn much before she was arrested. After that, I didn't see a piano until I was at the Vogels."

Understandingly Kasia offered, "You don't need to know much to help Joanna begin."

He studied his hands, flexing his fingers. "My hands hurt," he said, hoping Kasia would excuse him from trying.

But it wasn't Kasia, it was Joanna who tugged on his sleeve. "Please, Dad! Please play something. Then you can teach me when we're back home!"

He glanced nervously from Kasia to Genia and back. Kasia was so talented, he would feel humiliated if he tried to reconstruct what he knew in front of her. She understood his hesitation, and saying, "Come along, Genia, there's something we must do outside," she led her daughter away and left him alone with Joanna.

Joanna looked up at him expectantly. "Please!" she begged.

"I'll try, honey." He walked over to the piano and studied the keys. "It's been a long time, just give me a moment," he explained to her as she stood eagerly at his side. He closed his eyes and tried to remember what to do, but all he heard was Elspeth's voice: *If you ever touch my piano again . . . I will have my husband break your fingers.* He breathed deeply trying to purge her from his mind and began playing the Chopin polonaise. He didn't get far before he got so confused he had to stop, but Joanna was nonetheless impressed.

She jumped up and down and clapped her hands. "Oh, you can play! That was marvelous!" she enthused, apparently unaware that he had managed no more than a few bars. "Do you know anything else?"

He smiled at her enthusiasm, and then, out of the depths of his memory, he recalled something. His left hand played a series of triplets while his right moved through a simple melody of two-note chords that switched gently from one key into another, repeating the theme almost hypnotically. It was simple, far too simple to be considered real music, but it was nevertheless charming and relaxing in its poignant lack of sophistication.

Joanna stood with her mouth open, stunned by the tune. "That's so pretty! Where did it come from?"

"I made it up, sweetheart. When I was a boy," he explained, blushing at her approval.

"What's it called?"

He shrugged.

"Call it 'Nick's Song,'" Zosia's voice suggested from the doorway.

He jumped up, knocking over the piano bench as he did so. He looked at it with a feeling of distaste. Just like with Elspeth. Would he never escape her baleful influence?

"I wish you wouldn't react to my presence like that."

"You just surprised me." He righted the bench.

"Can you play something else?" Zosia asked.

He stared at her in shock.

With a mixture of sarcasm and sadness, Zosia guessed, "Your dear Frau Vogel again?"

There was no point in denying it; he could construct no other plausible explanation. "Sorry," he muttered.

"Just go ahead and play for Joanna," Zosia replied, shaking her head slightly. "I have things to do."

She left and Joanna turned back toward her father. "What did Mom mean?"

"Huh?"

"Why did she call it 'Nick's Song'?"

"That was my name, when I was a boy."

"Can you play more?" Joanna pressed, oblivious to the way he stared at the empty doorway.

Why had he hurt Zosia like that? Why couldn't he forgive her Elspeth's sins? There was no easy answer, and he put the question away to turn back to his daughter and answer her question. "How about you sit here and I show you how to play a melody?"

Joanna grinned from ear to ear and immediately clambered up onto the piano bench.

<hr>

50

"*I* THINK I HAVE an idea for getting Magdalena over here," Kasia said over her cup of coffee. Ryszard had just left for work, and the three remaining adults had settled into their morning ritual of relaxing and chatting before beginning the day's work. Kasia had deliberately waited until Ryszard was gone since she had not told her husband about Peter and Elspeth. She was sure he would use the information badly, so she had opted for silence. Her husband's attitude toward Peter puzzled her. Initially, when he was an unknown quantity, Ryszard's caution was understandable and she had shared it, but once Peter had proved himself in Hamburg, she had warmed to Zosia's husband. Nevertheless, Ryszard had been almost fanatical in his denunciation of "that man" during their entire visit to the encampment. He had grumbled ceaselessly to everyone: his wife, his parents, his friends, and even Zosia. Kasia had once questioned Ryszard why he was so determinedly negative about Peter, but she had not received a coherent answer.

She noticed Zosia and Peter were looking at her expectantly. "Oh!" She stirred herself. With each pregnancy it seemed to get worse—this absentmindedness. She could barely remember what it had been like with Stefi—that was so long ago—but even then, she was fairly sure that there had been weeks, or was it months, when she had had trouble keeping track of what she was doing. With Pawel and Andrzej, she had been so busy with her other children that she had blamed that for her inability to concentrate, but with Jan and Genia, there had been others around to help, and then it had been clear that her thoughts were anything but clear. As if her brain were leaking out of her ears, she remembered thinking. And now it was happening again.

"What's your idea?" Peter prompted.

"Oh!" Kasia repeated, surprised that she had once again drifted. What was her idea? With an effort, she collected her thoughts. "The girl who watches Magdalena is from a local household. She comes in early in the morning and leaves in the evening to go home. She's only fifteen and doing it as part of some training scheme for her youth league. Anyway, she spends as much time as possible in the park—I think she hates being inside with Elspeth and Uwe."

"No surprise there," Peter commented.

"Indeed. I think Elspeth tries to get her to nurse Uwe, so she just takes the baby for walks to get away. Anyway, I thought maybe I could get Pawel to flirt with her and strike up a relationship. He could then suggest that she leave the baby here at our house so they could spend time together. Since we're known to that family and quite respectable, there should be no problem. If they establish a routine, you could conceivably see her every day until you leave."

"Would Pawel do such a thing?" Peter asked.

"Of course, if he's ordered," Zosia answered. "He's a professional."

Peter looked to Kasia for an answer.

She nodded. "I can ask. He'll view it as a useful opportunity to refine his skills."

"*Ask?*" Zosia repeated, incredulous.

"Yes, Colonel," Kasia answered patiently. "I'm not as well trained at giving orders as you are. I'm afraid I have to ask my children for favors."

Zosia snorted but did not comment further.

They set their plan into action that very afternoon. Pawel accompanied Kasia on her walk through the park with Zosia in servile tow. Kasia spotted the young lady and, on the pretense of saying hello to the baby, introduced herself and her son Paul to the nanny, whose name was Liesel. Kasia chatted quite amiably about the Vogels to reassure the girl that they were indeed friends while Pawel made a point of engaging her with his eyes and smiling most approvingly. Liesel carefully noted Kasia's expensive clothing, the presence of a servant, Paul's fine build and handsome features, and smiled shyly in return.

Pawel managed to stumble across the young lady an hour or so later; this time he was alone and he invited her to have an ice cream. Liesel was quite amenable to any company; she was bored to tears with her job and the child, and she found this charming young man quite intriguing. She had carefully noted his last name and had determined to learn later that evening all she could about his family.

The next day, having discovered that her new friend was not only from a respectable family but a highly placed and wealthy one, she scanned the park in forlorn hope. He would never reappear, never be interested in a nobody like her. She should have smiled more, should have laughed less loudly! Oh, darn, why had she talked so much! She should have listened with rapt attention! Magdalena cried and Liesel shoved a bottle into her hands and hissed at her to shut up. Where was Paul? Would he come to the park today?

To her utter amazement, she saw him strolling. Not only that, he was smiling and walking toward her. It was as if a dream had come true! She had herself married with eight children and two or three servants before he even said hello. Frau Traugutt, the beautiful wife of a government minister! A grand house, servants to order about, and not one, but two cars! When Paul suggested that perhaps they could leave the baby at his house—Frau Vogel would never be the wiser—Liesel happily agreed and they walked in that direction together. She handed Magdalena over to the slovenly servant she had seen the day before, passed on a few instructions, and without looking back, tripped off happily with Paul.

Zosia held the little girl in her arms, somewhat stunned by it all. Kasia stood nearby, and they both waited for Magdalena to wail at being left completely alone with strangers, but instead the child wrapped her arms around Zosia's neck and hugged her.

"She doesn't seem afraid," Zosia ventured.

"Maybe she doesn't see enough of anyone to feel at home anywhere," Kasia suggested. Zosia handed Kasia the child and she hugged Kasia as well.

"Peter," Zosia called, "I think you can come in now."

"Already?" he asked quietly from the doorway. He had remained out of sight so that the nanny would not see him and report his presence to anyone, but also the three of them had guessed that Magdalena might be wild with fright and was more likely to calm down with women rather than a strange man. Pitching his voice as softly as he could, he asked tentatively, "Madzia?"

The little girl looked at him, curious and unafraid. When Kasia moved to hand her to him, Magdalena put out her arms and went naturally into his. Peter held her and hugged her and stroked her hair, saying her name over and over again. Her willingness to grab on to anyone, her determination to find a protector, tore at his heart. He had abandoned her without even knowing what he was doing, and now she was as alone in the world as he had ever been. "Oh, my little girl," he almost sobbed, "my lonely little girl. How can I undo my mistakes?"

Kasia excused herself, and Zosia and Peter spent the afternoon getting to know the little girl. They tried all the standard games and rhymes and songs to see if she recognized anything, but she greeted each offering as if it were completely new. She was quick though, and during the afternoon Zosia taught her how to clap her hands, and with their enthusiastic encouragement, her ability to walk improved markedly. Peter watched with a growing sense of guilt and frustration as he realized that no one had taught the child anything, that she probably spent her time alone in a playpen or strapped into a carriage, making her way alone in the world with only the necessities shoved at her at the appropriate times.

Without thinking, he lit a cigarette. Zosia looked up from the finger game she had been playing with Madzia and snapped, "Put that thing out. It's hard on the baby—both of them."

"Sorry," he muttered, and went to the ashtray to stub the cigarette out.

"It's bad enough in here already without you adding to it," Zosia continued peevishly. "No matter how many times I tell you, you always forget!"

"I said I was sorry," he emphasized as he ground the end into the tray.

As if on cue the baby began coughing, one of those baby coughs that rack the entire body. Zosia picked her up and cuddled her while she coughed, then suggested, "We should feed her something. Let's go to the kitchen."

Genia and Joanna came in for their meal as well, and as they sat down at the table, Joanna pointed at the baby and asked, "Who is that?"

"Her name's Magdalena. She's . . ." Peter was going to say something innocuous, such as a neighbor's child or just visiting, but the words stuck in his throat. Could he deny his daughter?

He looked up at Zosia, and they carried out a silent discussion, then Zosia said, "Go ahead."

"Come with me, sweetie," he said as he picked up Joanna. "I need to talk alone with you for a few minutes."

Genia watched, glancing at her aunt for an explanation, but none was forthcoming. She shrugged; used to secrets as she was, she knew it was not her place to ask, and besides, she'd get Joanna to tell her later!

Peter retreated into the sitting room with Joanna and sat down with her on his lap. "Do you remember what I told you about my life before I came to Szaflary?"

Joanna nodded.

"You know, I lived and worked in a house near here. The people who were my . . ." He sighed, started again. "The lady who gave me orders was named Elspeth. She visited here a few days ago. Do you remember?"

Joanna nodded again.

"For nearly three years, she told me what to do, and I did it, because I had to, because I was . . . because I had to."

"I understand," Joanna said helpfully.

"Well, one day, she told me to behave as if I were her husband."

"Did you?"

He nodded. "Yes, and I did with her what husbands do with their wives. We had to be very careful, because such games are illegal, and if anyone had found out, I would have been arrested and killed."

"Did you want to play this game?" Joanna was used to dangerous games and to people giving and taking orders. None of it was really surprising.

"No, but I did. And as a result Elspeth had a baby. That's the baby in the kitchen. She's my daughter." He paused but Joanna did not interrupt. "We have to keep it very secret though; you can't tell anyone else. Not even Genia. Do you understand?"

Joanna nodded solemnly. "I swear, Dad, I'll keep it secret."

"Good. You understand what I did? Do you have any questions?" He felt that if she was going to chide him for his behavior, he'd prefer to get it over with.

"Does this mean she's my sister?" Joanna asked gleefully.

"I guess so, honey," he responded, relieved. "She's your secret sister."

Joanna grinned. "I have a sister! A secret sister!" she giggled. Genia had all those brothers and Stefi, but she had a *secret* sister!

They returned to the kitchen, and Joanna grinned at Genia, bursting with her news. But she had solemnly sworn to keep the secret, and she would do so because, as her mother put it, she was a professional.

Pawel continued seeing Liesel, indicating to his uncle, "You owe me for this, big time!" as he headed out the door yet again. Within a week, they had arranged that Liesel would come straight to their house to drop off the baby so that Pawel did not have to locate her in the park each day. Magdalena quickly established herself as a member of the household, and eventually even Ryszard became aware that the Vogels' child was visiting with inexplicable regularity. He was finally driven to ask Kasia what was going on, and she explained the situation to him as they lay next to each other in bed.

The next morning, Ryszard snickered when he saw Peter and commented, "I should have guessed." Ryszard surprised Kasia by not saying anything more, though one evening when Pawel groaned in the presence of the four adults about how tedious Liesel was, his father snapped, "Get used to it. Lie and smile and smile and lie. You'll never be able to be yourself out there. Not until we're free."

Feeling somewhat sorry for Pawel, who looked stunned by the rebuke, Peter changed the subject by asking, "And when do you think that will be?"

Blowing a stream of smoke toward the ceiling, Ryszard answered, "Not in my lifetime."

"You don't think there's any hope?" Peter asked.

"Not for us," Ryszard replied. "Your people—the English—they have a chance. You have the Commonwealth, and besides, nobody's trying to annihilate you. You might one day get autonomy, some cultural rights, then perhaps independence and then you can rebuild. But for us, shit, there's nothing but ruin and extinction in our future. I'm surprised we've lasted this long, if you call the mess we have left in our land 'lasting.' A half-starved, illiterate population of ten or fifteen million standing on top of twenty million corpses, waiting their turn. No industry, no economy. Our language spoken in whispers, our heritage looted or destroyed. Our entire land has been turned into a strip mine—pull out all the resources and leave nothing but a wasteland."

"We'll survive. We did it before," Kasia argued.

"They only tried to annihilate our culture then," Ryszard replied. "Genocide wasn't part of the *Kulturkampf* or Russification, as far as I know."

"Well, we have managed to stop that, haven't we?" Kasia responded.

"Just barely. Given half a chance, they'll start again, and this time they won't quit until the job is done," Ryszard answered morosely.

"Do you really think that's the case?" Peter was trying to determine if Ryszard's gloomy predictions were based on rational observation of his colleagues or if it was simply an expression of his obvious depression.

"Perhaps it's not that hopeless," Zosia interjected.

"Maybe it's like 1850," Kasia suggested, referring to roughly halfway through the 125 years her country had endured occupation and nonexistence. At the questioning glances, she explained, "You know, too long in the past to remember independence and decades away from liberation."

Ryszard snorted. "Great. Just like us, they lived to see neither end!"

"Nevertheless," Kasia persisted, "it was necessary to keep the dream alive. What would have happened if our people had lost faith then? Hmm?"

"Dream on, if it keeps you sane," Ryszard responded sarcastically. "But just look how efficiently the Soviets have destroyed the other half of the country. They shot or exiled or deported into the Reich anyone who claimed to be Polish, awarded some cultural rights to the Ukrainians and Lithuanians and Byelorussians, and that's it"—he snapped his fingers—"we're gone! Like we never even existed! Even we accept it as a fait accompli! Look at how our demands have changed!"

"What exactly are your demands?" Peter asked.

"They are irrelevant, is what they are," Ryszard snapped.

"Nevertheless, what are they?" Peter insisted.

"In the most extreme form," Kasia replied, "we demand the status quo when the first international crime against us was committed: our prepartition boundaries of the old republic. Nobody takes that seriously though, centuries of violence and occupation having left their mark. The criminals have gained legitimacy through the passage of time. A fact, which I am sure, many other criminal governments have noted."

Pawel continued, "More hopefully, we demand our independence and the territory that was ours prior to the 1939 invasion. That's the publicly stated goal."

"But now," Zosia picked up the thread, "we're working toward accepting just the territory under German occupation back. It's just a tiny bit of what we once had, but thanks to murder and deportations, it's the only area that still has a reasonable number of ethnic Poles."

Kasia added, "And it's a concession to the NAU's attempts to normalize relations with the Soviet Union. They can stand us having aspirations contrary to the wishes of the Reich, along with all the other captive nations, but to have a quarrel with two empires . . ."

Ryszard interrupted angrily. "We don't ask for reparations or even apologies, we don't ask for our lands or for the resurrection of the millions of our war dead. No damages for pain and suffering, no recompense for our anguish, for the children who saw their parents murdered, for the people who lost their eyes and their limbs, for the people worked to death, for the women raped to death. We don't ask for our loot back or for the reconstruction of our hospitals and schools, the rebuilding of our capital, the restoration of our ancient heritage—nothing, none of that! We touch our forelocks and beg the international community to acknowledge our right to breathe! And for that we are scolded for being troublesome and uppity!"

The four of them studied Ryszard, surprised by his vehemence.

"There are some in the West who denounce us as terrorists," Ryszard fumed. "They say we deserve our fate, that we should have lain down and died quietly, that by fighting back we only cause trouble. They would call me a wrecker, Kasia is a saboteur, Zosia here is a murderer!"

Zosia glanced at Peter but he looked guiltily away. Why had he ever said something so stupid?

"They grumble that we make things difficult for them to normalize relations!" Ryszard continued. "They whine that they are tired of war, that there's nothing to fight about, that what's done is done! To them we are dead already, and they can't bury our heaving corpses fast enough!"

"There are those who recognize your bravery and your courage, who defend basic human rights," Peter offered.

"Well, they don't do it loudly enough," Ryszard retorted. "The mass of the NAU population is uninformed and therefore unwilling to support us. And without them, we have no hope. They'll stand idly by and watch us be murdered, strangled to death for our criminal proximity to psychopaths. They tell us our screams disturb the peace and couldn't we please shut up! Then they'll feign surprise and whine that they were not warned when the psychopaths turn on them!"

Like Neville Chamberlain and the Sudetenland, like the Fourth Partition of Poland, like the phony war that existed before France was invaded. History lessons that had remained unlearned. Were they doomed to be repeated? Peter did not need to say any of these things, he knew the others were all too aware of what had gone before. Nevertheless, the Reich had been halted, there was no invasion of America, there was a balance of terror to be maintained. Were the lessons of the past insufficient to dictate the actions of the future? Was there some other way out of the mess other than direct confrontation?

He really wanted to know what Ryszard had dispassionately observed from his politically powerful position. Trying to work around the grim responses that sprang from Ryszard's mood, Peter pressed, "Don't you think things have settled down inside the Reich? Do you really think they're going to try and reimplement their original plan, after all these years? Don't you think the moderate element has a chance of holding power?"

"Other than a few people here and there, like Katerina, the entire Jewish and half-Jewish population of Europe was murdered. Where was this moderate element then?" Ryszard asked.

"But certainly there's been some evolution within the Reich government. After Hitler died and there was that shake-up . . ." Peter suggested.

Ryszard shrugged, suddenly tired. "I don't know where they're going. They don't know either. That's the problem with absolute power—it's so dependent on the whims of one or two personalities."

"But then, what is your genuine goal?" Peter pleaded to know.

Ryszard responded, "There are many divergent opinions about what we can hope for and what is achievable, but our unstated and genuine goal is simply survival. We hope to maintain a sufficient population base and enough of our culture to one day reconstruct our nation. Maybe if we get a few concessions from a future government, we can parlay that into a bit of autonomy and some cultural rights."

"So you are willing to deal with them and set yourselves up as a client state?"

"Personally, yes," Ryszard answered.

"Client state!" Zosia snorted. "That would be an extreme demand from our Ryszard!"

"She's right," Ryszard agreed. "I'm working toward something more basic."

"What?"

"A guarantee of, shall we say, second-class human rights. The right not to be arbitrarily murdered, the right not to be taken hostage for other people's actions, the right to a fair trial, the right to marry and to keep our children. Maybe, in an optimistic scenario, the right to speak our language and to schooling for a year or two."

"How about land ownership?" Peter asked.

"No hope. I doubt we could even get them to outlaw arbitrary expulsions. If I were being really optimistic, I might demand wages for services rendered. That would help your people."

"The English?"

"No, the *Zwangsarbeiter*."

"So you hope there'd be an end to slavery?"

"Just wages at first. If we could outlaw land expulsions, abductions, and forced *unpaid* labor, then those would be the first steps toward ending slavery. Make it uneconomic. Of course, one could argue that it would be better to extend the unpaid labor system."

"Why?"

"It causes a great deal of social tension. Every job done by a *Zwangsarbeiter* is a wage-paying job taken away from a German. The working classes hate you. You force them into military service as the only alternative because they simply can't compete with slavery. As the union movement grows stronger—"

"There's a union movement?" Peter asked, remembering those Germans who had long ago shared a prison cell with him after he had been recaptured. Were they part of a larger phenomenon?

"A weak one," Ryszard answered. "If they were to grow stronger, they might be pushed toward revolution if they see no alternative. But I think that's unlikely. I think a minimum wage would be more likely to cause the changes we want to see."

"You're not asking for much," Peter commented somewhat sarcastically. The idea of forced paid labor was not particularly attractive to him. What could he have done with the money? Still, it might have been a disincentive to waste his labor, and that might have made the conditions of his existence a bit more palatable. Perhaps, too, he could have bought his freedom at some point.

"No, it's not asking much, but it's more than we have, and it could mean the difference between survival and extinction. With the prevailing morality of categorizing the vast majority of people as not quite human, the only hope we have for keeping them from being killed is to make them economically valuable. They don't even need to receive the wage—it could be paid to the state, like a tax. Then the state would have an interest in preserving their lives and the industrialists would have a vested interest in not wasting their labor. As it is, workers are too cheap and are treated like so much garbage—and you can see what it's doing to our economy."

"*Our* economy?" Peter asked pointedly.

"The economy, if you wish. But I won't apologize for referring to the economy that dominates all our lives as 'our' economy. We must acknowledge that it is no longer a war between us and them—we're conquered and we're trapped within this society and whatever affects it, affects us. We must work with the system that we have—it's idiocy to pretend that there is any alternative."

Zosia made a face but did not comment.

"My sister thinks I'm a fool. Or brainwashed by being out here too long. But I don't believe a few rabid partisans lurking in the mountains makes for a convincing foreign enemy. Whatever happens is going to happen from within. We are past the point of winning a war, we must look toward either evolution or revolution. And since I see no indication that revolution is imminent, I look toward evolution. I think it's our only hope: *collaboration*." He emphasized the word, looking pointedly at Zosia. "There are others who think that any acknowledgment of their power is a betrayal of our cause, that we must maintain our long-standing 'stiff attitude toward the occupant,' but I'm a realist and won't argue for their point of view."

"Whatever our personal differences on that score," Kasia interposed as if to preempt an argument, "it doesn't matter as long as they are unwilling to treat with us. Whether we would accept second- or third-class status or demand equal rights is irrelevant to the government. They have not forgiven our previous rejections of their overtures, and as long as that is the case, our varying strategies are irrelevant."

"Yes, and because of the survival issue," Zosia added, "whatever our differences on strategy and goals, we present a completely united front to the world. We keep our differences to ourselves, all the more so since they are, at this point, only theoretical."

"Not always," Pawel interjected.

"What do you mean?" Peter asked.

"Oh, because of the varying strategies and the leadership's unwillingness to ever criticize any action, there are independent actions that don't exactly coincide with our stated goals or strategies. Dad takes advantage of that." Pawel indicated his father with a nod, and then plunging on as if doing something extremely brave, he added, "We all know that he's pursuing his own agenda for recognition of basic human rights for our people. The Warszawa Council is aware that they can hardly control his actions, that he only takes orders when he feels like it, and yet they don't do anything to sanction him." As if to soften whatever punishment he was going to suffer for his exposé, Pawel looked at his father and added, "Isn't that right, Dad?"

Ryszard brought his cigarette to his lips and sucked on it pensively as he contemplated his son. A brave, bright boy growing into manhood. Perceptive, well-spoken, and from all accounts quite convincing in the roles he played. He could be proud of his son. "You're right, I haven't been sanctioned yet, son. Not yet."

=====**51**=====

"**P**ETER!" KASIA APPEARED in the doorway of the sitting room, panting. "I'm in labor!"

Peter jumped up from the floor where he had been trying to build a tower with Magdalena. Zosia stood as well. "Shall we call Ryszard?"

"He won't be home in time; these things happen fast for me. You're going to have to drive me to the hospital," Kasia answered as she groaned and reeled into Peter's waiting arms.

"You can't go!" Zosia fretted at Peter. "I'll have to drive. Is Pawel nearby?"

"No, he's out with Liesel, of course," Kasia hissed through her pain. Berlin and the lack of Ryszard's parents had led her to plan to rely on Pawel to take her to the hospital, and she wondered momentarily at their group absentmindedness in that none of them had accounted for his being away once he started seeing Liesel.

"I won't be recognized," Peter assured Zosia as he steadied Kasia. "It's better if I go, the laws at least allow me to chauffeur—you might get stopped. You watch the kids and call Ryszard; we'll take Andrzej along as the figure of authority."

Both Kasia and Zosia laughed at Peter's choice of wording. As he gathered all the appropriate papers together, Zosia went to the back door to call Andrzej in from the yard. "Well, Master Andreas, it seems you're in charge," she advised her thirteen-year-old nephew, then smacked him on the shoulder to send him in the direction of the front door where Peter and Kasia were waiting. Andrzej drew himself up to his full height, took his mother's arm from Peter, and with Peter grabbing her overnight bag, they made their way out the door and to Ryszard's car.

The hospital was in an older section of the suburb, and there was no parking nearby. "I should have taken a taxi!" Kasia fretted through gritted teeth, then suggested that Peter just drop them off and drive home, but he pointed out that he did not have any papers allowing him to do that and it was worth his life not to lose sight of them at this point. He should have changed identities, he admitted, but it was too late now and they were stuck with him for the duration—he needed their protection. Kasia agreed as he pulled the car up and over a curb and left it parked illegally, in the style of anyone with any authority. The vehicle would not be towed—it would be worth the patrolman's life if he did that.

At the reception desk, the attendant stated that their servant would not be allowed to accompany them any further, but Andrzej replied with surprising force and authority, "He's coming with us." And since the attendant had already scanned their documents and noted Ryszard's job title, that was the end of any argument.

Together they made it as far as the maternity floor, but at that point Kasia was whisked away to be handled by the medical professionals in an antiseptic and impersonal assembly-line procedure. She had a look of near panic as she gave herself up to their tender mercies and left the only people she trusted behind in the waiting room.

With each previous child except Genia, she had managed to return to Szaflary, where she could give birth in safety, free to express herself in her native language, able to depend on those she knew and trusted. With Genia, the Council had arranged for a midwife, and though it was unusual for Germans of her class, she had given birth in the comfort and safety of home. With their move to Berlin, however, they had been unable to arrange anything, and Ryszard had decided that another home birth would raise suspicions; so, Kasia had arranged everything with the hospital and with a local doctor, and now she had to face the entire process among strangers, remembering throughout not to say one word in the wrong language. It was her sixth birth and yet it was the first time that she was genuinely terrified.

She thought of Ryszard and the grim look on his face every morning as he went into the office and decided if he could do it every day of his life, she could maintain her composure through the birth of her child. The nurses were amazed by her behavior: that such a highly placed woman did not scream and bark orders and tear at her sheets. Party wives usually used the opportunity of giving birth to one of their multitudinous children to vent their years of frustration, and to some extent the exclusion of their husbands from the wing was a fulfillment of those same husbands' desires. They shrugged and blamed the hospital rules and let paid professionals put up with the tantrums that such wives felt free to throw at this time of their life.

Andrzej and Peter felt no such desire to be away from Kasia. Andrzej paced nervously in the waiting room, while Peter stood discreetly in a corner near a window, trying to be as inconspicuous as possible. Every now and then he scanned the crowd to make sure there was no one he knew among them, but otherwise he stared at the floor so as not to offend any of the waiting men by accidentally catching his eye.

Hours later they were still waiting. Andrzej had grown weary of pacing and had seated himself in one of the lounge chairs, glancing repeatedly at the entrance to look for his father. Peter had grown weary of standing, but he remained by the window, glancing now more often at the forbidden seats than at the faces of the men sitting in them. Now and then a name was called and a worried husband jumped to his feet to be escorted away.

"Traugutt!" an orderly barked into the room of expectant men.

Andrzej jumped to his feet and approached. "That's my mother."

"Sorry, son, only husbands allowed back here," the orderly informed him gleefully, obviously relishing his position of power.

"My father has not arrived yet," Andrzej stated, motioning to Peter to join him. "I am going to see my mother now."

The orderly smirked, but then his eyes strayed to the boy's servant and he paused to reconsider. "All right," he finally agreed, "you can see your mother, but he stays here."

"Out of my way," Andrzej ordered, and as the orderly instinctively stepped aside, Andrzej brushed past him, motioning for Peter to follow. The orderly's mouth opened, but no words emerged. He then hurried after the pair so that he could show them the way to the physician.

The physician greeted Andrzej politely and asked, "Your father is not here yet?"

"No, unfortunately. How is my mother?"

"She's fine. You have a little brother. Both mother and son are doing well. Would you like to see her?" the physician asked even as he pushed open the door to Kasia's room.

The physician took his leave of them as Peter and Andrzej stepped into the large room. A number of women were on beds in the corridor, but despite such obvious overcrowding, Kasia was alone in the room, having been given the privacy that her good papers called for. In her arms she held a tiny bundle.

She acknowledged them wearily and asked her son, "Where's your father?"

Andrzej shrugged. "I guess he had trouble getting away."

Peter smiled a discreet welcome at the baby, not daring to say anything even in the privacy of Kasia's room. Kasia understood his caution and smiled in return, saying, "They wanted to take the baby to the nursery, but I insisted he stay with me." She grinned. "And for some reason, they listened to me."

"Do you have a name for him?" Andrzej asked, touching his brother's tiny little nose.

"Piotr," Kasia said so quietly they had to read her lips. She winked at Peter and said aloud, "We'll call him Peter."

Peter blushed and wondered if Ryszard had agreed to the name, or if Kasia had chosen it then and there as retribution for her husband's absence.

As if reading his thoughts, Ryszard burst into the room at that moment. "Oh, I'm sorry, love!" he groaned. "I was in a meeting! Contrary to my orders, someone had left instructions that there should be no interruptions, so I only just got the message."

"What an unfortunate mistake!" Kasia replied sarcastically. "But, just as well. You would only have wasted your time waiting in the lobby. And I had no need for you, after all; our son and our loyal servant were here for me." She looked down at the baby and stroked his face. "And now you have another son. I've named him Peter."

Ryszard took the baby into his arms. Not reacting to the name, he asked instead, "How are you feeling?"

"Fine."

"They want to keep you here for two weeks, to recover."

Kasia shook her head. "No, get me out of here. Today."

Ryszard nodded, recognizing that he had no option but to obey. He handed the baby to his son and said, "Stay with your mother, I've got to go and yell at some people."

Andrzej sat on the edge of the bed and chatted to his mother until Ryszard returned and informed his wife, "I've got them to agree to tomorrow morning. Will that do?"

Kasia shook her head. "I said today," she reiterated in a cold voice. "I will not spend a night here alone!"

Ryszard leaned against the wall and lit a cigarette. He glared at his wife while he smoked, but when he finished, said, "All right, today it is." He pushed himself away from the wall and left again.

He returned twenty minutes later looking rather frazzled. "We're stuck at tomorrow—they've got some laws on their side." He looked at Andrzej and asked, "Apparently you signed something when you came in?"

Kasia answered for him. "Of course he signed whatever he had to. After all, *you* weren't here."

"Well, I can't get them to budge. But you don't have to spend the night alone. They don't want me here—afraid I'll want sex or something—but your female servant can spend the night with you. Will that do?"

Kasia scowled, then agreed, "All right."

"I'll take him home now." Ryszard indicated Peter. "Then I'll come back with your girl and spend the evening here. She can stay the night, and I'll pick you both up in the morning. Andreas can stay with you until I get back. Will that satisfy you?"

"Yes. But make sure the baby gets to stay the night with me. I don't want him to ever leave my sight."

"I understand," Ryszard assured her.

"And make sure we get a cot in here for my girl." Kasia could imagine her sister-in-law's fury if she was forced to spend the night on the floor!

"I'll do that," Ryszard agreed, "but I doubt she'll spend much time sleeping."

Indeed, Zosia spent most of the night pacing. Time and again nurses bullied their way into the room and she had to deferentially remind them they could not abscond with the infant just because the mother was sleeping. Each time Kasia awoke and reiterated what Zosia had said, and only then did the nurses withdraw from the room.

"But the babe needs to be in the nursery! The mother will roll on him and smother him," one nurse argued.

"They are both sleeping just fine," Zosia replied. "My lady wants her son to remain here with her."

"How dare you be so insolent!" the nurse huffed, and tried to push past her.

Zosia did not move. It was a delicate balance—not giving in, but not appearing to resist. Luckily before the disagreement went any further, Kasia awoke and said wearily, "Please leave the room."

"But you'll smother the baby!"

"I'm here to prevent that," Zosia replied smoothly to the idiotic assertion. "Now do as *meine gnädige Frau* requests."

The nurse scowled and left. Zosia sighed heavily and turned to Kasia to give her an apologetic smile. "I had hoped *meine gnädige Frau* would get to sleep undisturbed."

"So had I." Kasia tried not to laugh at poor Zosia. Cold-blooded assassin, government minister! The self-confident colonel was struggling hard to maintain her composure and to play her lowly role.

Zosia glanced around, then bent down to kiss her sister-in-law's forehead. "You'll be home soon," she whispered, then moving away from the bed, she began her vigilant pacing again. Back and forth, back and forth, back and forth throughout the long night.

Both men had equally disturbed nights as they worried about their wives. Ryszard dreamt that the SS Lebensborn inspected Kasia's documents and decided that although she had been declared *Volksdeutsch,* her blood was sufficiently tainted that she did not deserve to keep her child. He saw them tearing the babe away from her as she screamed and fought them. Groaning, he rose from his bed and made his way down the stairs to the liquor cabinet.

"Ah, so you're up as well," Peter greeted him.

"Dreams. You, too?"

"Yeah. Keep dreaming Zosia kills the nurses to stop them from stealing Piotr, and then she gets dragged off and executed. Decided I'd rather remain awake than see that one more time."

"What time is it?"

"Nearly three. Want to play some poker?"

"Sure. That'll kill a few hours. Besides, I could use the cash."

"In your dreams." Peter laughed. "But two's no fun, let's see if Pawel and Andrzej want to play."

"Good idea." Ryszard laughed as well. "If we get them when they're sleepy, maybe we'll manage to win for once."

52

DESPITE THE FEARS and nervous agitation suffered all round, the night passed without incident. Ryszard managed to rescue Kasia, Piotr, and Zosia from the hospital the following morning, and over the next few days life in the household returned to normal. Piotr was adored by all, Pawel continued seeing Liesel, and Peter and Zosia continued to see Magdalena nearly every day. Several times, perhaps out of sheer boredom, Teresa accompanied Liesel to the Traugutt household and stayed there with her sister while the nanny went off on her husband-catching venture. On those days, Peter was trapped upstairs, out of sight while Zosia and Teresa tended to Madzia and Piotr. Pawel made a point of having an appointment and returning earlier than usual on those days, so Peter's exile was not interminable. More than once though, when Liesel and Pawel returned to the house, the two girls from the Vogel household stayed on and visited. Teresa seemed to enjoy talking to Pawel, and he seemed in no great hurry to leave when she was around. Liesel sat with her arms possessively around her man but was usually unable to interrupt the conversation as it strayed into topics with which she was totally unfamiliar. Eventually Pawel would have mercy on both Liesel and Peter and would disappear to go to his appointment; then the two girls stayed only long enough to appear polite before taking their leave.

"She's a bright girl," Zosia opined as Peter emerged into the sitting room soon after the girls and the baby had left one evening.

He nodded sadly.

"Tomorrow's the last day," she reminded him needlessly.

"I know."

"While we watched Madzia together, I've managed to talk to Teresa a bit. I guess she likes slumming."

"No, she's just a sweet kid, and I would guess, a bit lonely." He stared down the path that Magdalena had taken.

"She told me about you, about when you tried to teach Ulrike, and what happened to you then. She said that you taught her about courage."

"Courage," he repeated, somewhat disconcerted. He had only just come to terms with his cowardice during those years of abject submissiveness. Courage?

"I had her promise to take care of Magdalena, to make sure she wasn't ignored. I told her that Madzia deserves love, that she's a special little girl. She seemed to know what I meant." Zosia winked at him.

He nodded, embarrassed. "How did you manage to convey such privileged information?"

"Oh, I used my mysterious Gypsy-style voice. It's very useful when one wants to convey information while maintaining a façade of ignorance and inferiority."

"Yes, I should have resorted to it," he murmured. Courage?

"And Kasia told her to come by with the child at any time. She likes Pawel, so you can bet she'll be here. Magdalena will be well cared for."

He smiled his thanks, but still his eyes strayed unbidden to the path his daughter had taken.

The following evening he watched the path even more hopelessly as Liesel and Pawel approached the house. He gave his daughter one last kiss, and Madzia gave him a hug and wiped at the tears that ran down his face. She giggled at the wet warmth and sucked her fingers to determine its taste. Making a face at the salty water, she squirmed in his arms and he set her down. She toddled over to Zosia, who went into the hall to deliver her into Liesel's care. As was now her habit, she howled at the disruption in her playtime and clung to Zosia's neck. Zosia carefully extracted her and, ignoring Liesel's presence, kissed the child. Liesel gasped in horror and looked meaningfully to Pawel to upbraid his uppity servant, but he just shrugged. As Liesel said her good-bye to Pawel, Zosia withdrew into the sitting room to see how her husband was coping. Peter watched from a window as Liesel retreated back down the path with her charge. He brushed the tears from his face with an impatience that betrayed his embarrassment.

"I'll miss her," Zosia ventured. "She has a lot of personality."

Peter nodded. "I'm glad you talked with Teresa. I feel a lot better about her care."

"Don't worry, love, something will work out."

He shook his head slowly. What could they possibly do? There was nothing short of stealing the child, and unlike their adversaries, they did not indulge in kidnapping. There were far too many pressing problems to waste resources and political advantage on sorting out the details of one person's life; Tadek's wife was certain proof of that. No, he would never get permission to abduct his own child, and without permission and therefore without a place for her to live, he could offer her no life at all.

They returned to Szaflary and spent the remaining time before their departure preparing for their trip to America. In order to arm himself with both the relevant facts and the emotional fire to convince the American public of the justice of their struggle, Peter went to the library and delved into the archives that Katerina had pointed out to him. He was not unfamiliar with the history therein; nevertheless, the documented brutality and mass murder still horrified him. His head swam with images of humans packed into quicklime-laden freight cars and agonizingly burned to death, of gas spraying from shower heads asphyxiating helpless, naked, shaved people, of mass graves with broken and distorted bodies, of starved children with staring eyes, of walkways paved with the ashes of the dead, of shattered bones and bombed cities, of massacred villages and hanged hostages and millions upon millions of murdered innocents. The words appalled him, they haunted him, and they also raised a question in his mind: What was the point in telling his story? How was his paltry, miserable tale possibly going to impress a people who had remained unmoved by all that had gone before?

Alex listened to Peter's question patiently and explained that history was insignificant to most people: "Hell, on a world scale, most of this stuff pales into insignificance! What we need is someone these people can see and hear and touch. Your story alone will be sufficient. Your hurt will become their hurt, your anger will become their anger. Don't look at any history—we've had too much of that and to no good effect. Work on presenting yourself, just yourself. Do whatever it takes to make yourself acceptable and sympathetic to the Americans. That's an order!"

So, Peter read magazines and newspapers and watched a series of videos that Zosia scrounged up for him. Using the reviews and political fallout from each documentary or press conference or personal interview, and discussing details with Alex and Anna, they homed in on what they believed would be an acceptable television persona for him to present to the world.

First and foremost, they decided that absolute honesty was out. Genuineness would have to be sacrificed to avoid aggravating vocal segments of the American population. They decided Alex was right: though love was something that he could talk about freely, and sex he could mention indirectly, it was essential that Allison be his wife rather than another man's wife. The pain of their separation, the depth of his feeling, the grief at her death, would not be believed otherwise. He would be labeled an adulterer, and all else that followed in his story might be interpreted as divine retribution, as unlikely as God was to use the National Socialist regime to carry out heavenly justice.

His affair with Elspeth was clearly off-limits, not only because it would offend a segment of right-thinking Americans, but also because it could endanger Elspeth and by extension Magdalena. And they would have to avoid the fact that he had technically committed a criminal offense by draft-dodging. In a society as fanatical about crime and punishment as America seemed to be, the label *criminal* was all too likely to provoke a response that he only got what he deserved.

They decided he would have to work on his accent. Too strong an accent would be viewed as too foreign and therefore not only incomprehensible, but also not worthy of attention or sympathy. Also, it was clear from the entertainment media that his accent was appropriate to the lower classes and would be ascribed to a criminal milieu, and again, it would then be likely that the rest of his story would be considered irrelevant. Gangsters and street thugs could expect to live a life of random violence and arrest, what did they have to do with social justice on a worldwide scale?

It wasn't difficult for him to change his accent; for although he spoke as everyone around him in London had spoken, he had earlier in his life learned a more old-fashioned accent from his parents. Only when they had given up speaking English to him and had switched to German had he adopted the rough tones and vocabulary of his boyhood friends and later his Underground comrades. With a bit of effort he recovered his parents' accent; that, combined with his usual speech patterns and some deliberate Americanisms added for clarity, left him with an understandable and reasonably pleasing voice. "Mid-Atlantic" Zosia called it, though to himself, he sounded like a foreigner in his own tongue.

Upon Alex's insistence they decided he would have to give up smoking and drinking for the duration of the visit. He could indulge in a social drink on rare occasions in public, but he should not, even once, light up a cigarette. "You can do it in private," Alex confided. "Everyone does, just don't do it in public—not unless you want to get dragged into a debate on alcohol and tobacco."

"Maybe a debate would be amusing," Peter suggested.

"No!" Alex almost screamed. "You have no idea! For God's sake don't comment on any American issue. All you'll do is divert attention from our cause, make enemies, and get screamed at by fanatics. No discussions of cigarettes, alcohol, drugs, crime, racism—except as it applied to you—abortion, religion . . . Well, you get the point. It will become obvious which topics to avoid when you're here. Oh, yeah, make sure you leave the *Kommandant* out of your story. If you aren't condemned for being a queer, you'll be accused of being homophobic. And some women's group would no doubt claim you are degrading women."

"How so?"

"Oh, let's say, you'd be trivializing the trauma of rape by implying it can happen to a man . . ."

Peter listened somewhat aghast as Alex constructed possible scenarios for which Peter could be denounced by various interest groups. Would it really be like that? Like stepping into a snake pit? Each word placing him near to some poisonous jaws waiting to inject their venom? He had no conception of the pitfalls of free debate in a free society and had naively thought that his story would be accepted for what it was: his story.

". . . In fact, no sex at all, if you can avoid it. They're squeamish about that," Alex concluded.

"Sex? What about violence and murder?"

"No problem there. Their kids have it served up on TV with their breakfast cereal. And that reminds me: learn what a typical diet is and don't admit to preferring anything else. They think it's odd if you don't have cereal and milk for breakfast. And watch your sense of humor—they might think you're weird, and you're going to have to be careful about your childhood—their assumptions are going to be completely different from yours. No gangs, make sure your parents are warm and caring, and your school—try to make it sound like a positive experience—"

"Nobody had a childhood like that," Peter protested. "I'll sound like a freak!"

"No, you'll sound like a kid with an ideal American childhood rather than a Nazi-English one. Look, we want them to give money to help us overthrow the government, not support the various social programs they might think we need there. And that reminds me, make sure everything now is just perfect with your life, okay?"

"Why?"

"They like happy endings. Your escaping is like Cinderella putting on that glass slipper. That's it, no adjustment difficulties, no reality afterwards, just smiles and warm, understanding revolutionaries welcoming you into their arms and praising you for your noble sacrifices. Your experiences are going to be an analogy for our entire land, and we want to make sure when they give us money, they can walk away smiling, knowing that everything's going to be all right now."

"How about if I just keep quiet about the afterwards part?" Peter asked. Zosia sputtered quietly.

"Yeah, that will work, too. They'll assume the best. Just be careful that we don't turn their sympathies away from our struggle and towards some soft-hearted victims' groups. In any case, try to be a bit more buoyant. They often misinterpret the Brits here, think they're too cold and unfeeling. If you're not a bit more bouncy—"

"Bouncy?" Peter asked in amazement.

"Yes, bouncy. Otherwise, they'll think you're miserable even when you aren't. And don't forget, for heaven's sakes, clean up your vocabulary . . ."

Alex continued with his advice, and Peter nodded his head, forgetting for the moment that Alex could not see him. As Zosia noted her father's suggestions, Peter wondered why they didn't just hire an actor. By the end of their refinements, he would be unrecognizable. "What's the point of my going?" he finally asked.

Alex seemed to understand his frustration. "You'll do fine. Don't worry. And despite these limits, the essential truth of your story will be very moving. When you tell everyone what's happening there, they'll believe you, because they can see the reflection of our people's pain in your face. An actor would never be able to convey the poignancy of our suffering the way you will."

Zosia raised her eyebrows at her father's almost poetic efforts. Maybe studying public relations tactics had influenced him. He dispelled that idea by concluding, "And besides, actors are expensive and you're free! Beyond that, truth is stronger than fiction."

"Stranger," Peter corrected.

"Huh?"

"Stranger. Truth is *stranger* than fiction."

"Stronger, too. Your story will never be disproved because it's true, and that is a very strong point in our favor. The point is, we want to make Americans feel that they would be as vulnerable as you were. So we must avoid anything that the average American is sure he or she is not and that includes adulterer, alcoholic, drug addict, criminal, homosexual, dirty, smelly, or low class. And, oh, yeah, atheist."

Zosia smiled at her father's idea of tact.

"You forgot polluted by medical experiments," Peter added wryly.

"Oh, that's not your fault," Alex assured him. "Anyway, they're used to being poked at by obnoxious physicians here."

"Thank God for small mercies. Anyway, that's one I've decided to leave out."

"What? Leave out? What do you mean?"

"There's enough there without me talking about the medical experiments. Besides, from my point of view, it was nothing more than a needle jabbed into my arm. I don't think it's very impressive. We can let the data I translated speak for itself. Has it been released over there yet?"

"Released?" Alex repeated nervously. "Er, yes. Making quite a splash. Still, I think you should talk about your experience with that. It is important to have the personal touch."

"No. Not on that. I don't want to. Make sure it stays out of any previsit publicity. I really want to avoid discussions of my sex life. It could get complicated. It's important, Alex, I mean this. No discussion of that sterility program!"

"You're free to talk about whatever you want. If you want to leave that out, fine. Leave it out."

"And, Alex?" Peter asked somewhat hesitantly. "Katerina said I can't do any engagements for anyone else—you know, like one of the international prisoner-rights organizations. Do you think you could talk to her about that?"

"No. She and I are agreed on that. You speak for us alone. We don't want to dilute our message."

"But maybe I could help by—"

"The answer is no. You are speaking for us, for the Reich-wide resistance movements. Nothing else."

"But, Alex—"

"You owe us loyalty, Peter!"

"I know that. I know I owe you my life, and I am grateful to you all. And you *have* my loyalty. I just thought that maybe I could do some good—"

"No. We need to keep this thing under our control. The answer is no."

53

"**I** THOUGHT WE HAD this damn thing under control!" the Führer fumed, so furious that his nails dug into the fine leather of his armchair. "You told me your source said everything had been taken care of! What is this, Günter? A betrayal? Are you trying to make me look bad?"

Schindler shook his head, genuinely perplexed. "No, no! I don't know what's going on—"

"Why not!"

"I haven't been able to make contact recently. It's very complicated, everything has to be run through various levels of government. Maybe my source got it wrong—"

"Wrong? Wrong? You're the one who promised me your stupid sterility program would be carried out in the greatest confidence! You . . ." The Führer paused, at a loss for how to express his anger. His face had turned a dangerous purple.

"*Mein Führer,*" Schindler pleaded, "whatever leaks we have had with regards to the Hamburg lab, it does not help to bring even more people in on it." He nodded toward the third person in the room, standing quietly off to the side, smoking pensively. "Why is *he* here?"

"Herr Traugutt was good enough to personally warn me of your lax security," the Führer answered with suppressed rage. "He has gained my trust from his astute observations."

Schindler glared at Richard remembering the inebriated dinner conversation that had led him to reveal state secrets.

"With only the most minimal digging, he managed to come up with details about your arrangements that no one should have been able to find out!" the Führer continued. "He worried, quite rightly, that if he could learn our secrets so easily, then so could the Americans! He warned me even before that incident in January."

"You mean the attaché being kidnapped? That was nothing! He had no real information!"

"Well, as we both know, there was a breach somewhere. Now I'm being humiliated in America. It's common knowledge there! Information has been officially released by their government about our secret sterility program—and you promised me that your people would keep a lid on it! If only I had listened to Traugutt back then, rather than you!"

Schindler's look turned from one of fury to one of confusion. "How did you find out so much?" he accused Richard. "Is that why you wanted to snoop around there? I knew you were up to no good!"

"No, the request to visit was legitimate," Richard explained. "Don't you remember, it was you who told me that the laboratory was special to you."

"You son of a—"

"Not only that, Günter," the Führer continued darkly, "but my dear friend Richard also warned me that your source in America was misinformed. He warned me that the project would be made public despite your agents' efforts, and it's only thanks to him that I was able to take abortive action!"

"Abortive?" Schindler asked worriedly. He glanced involuntarily over his shoulder, looking instinctively for an arresting officer.

"Don't worry, I don't have to sacrifice you," the Führer sneered. "Not this time, anyway. It seems neither you nor I knew anything about this secret laboratory. It was that underling of yours, Rattenhuber, who cooked the whole damn thing up. You can thank Traugutt for that. With his timely warnings, I was able to have my own people discover the sterility program and close it down before the Americans publicized their information. Rattenhuber is being appropriately handled, and you, ignorant as you were of the whole thing, are being let off with a warning to keep your people on a tighter leash! Understood?"

"A tighter leash, yes, of course," Schindler muttered contritely. "What about my son?"

"Amazingly," the Führer explained, "he knew nothing about it at all."

"Excuse me, *mein Führer,*" Richard interrupted, "but I believe he was the one who tipped off your people in the first place. It was a clever move on Herr Schindler's part to put his son into that laboratory."

Schindler nodded his gratitude. "Yes, yes. My son, quite the hero. Saved the day . . ."

"That's right. This time. All I can say is, there had better not be a next time!" the Führer warned.

"A next time?" Schindler asked. "You're not really going to kill the project, are you?"

The Führer sighed. "I have no choice. This was too close a call. They have an entire overview of the program: experimental data, human subjects, supply sources. Where the hell they got such information . . . As it is, my ability to deny any high-level involvement has been severely strained, and the idea that one underling was responsible for the entire conspiracy hardly holds water. Only the fact that I closed it down *before* they released the information has saved me. Or rather, you."

"This is certainly going to be an unpopular decision amongst our own people!" Schindler argued. "My God, it's a complete capitulation to the capitalists!"

The Führer pulled out a cigarette, and Richard lit it for him before Schindler could even react. "I know. I'm not happy about that, but I can't afford to be linked to anything like this—it violates several treaties we've signed on biological warfare."

"Damn the idiotic treaties."

The Führer shook his head. "I wish we could. It's these trade deals: oil, plutonium . . . The bastards are killing us, they keep putting pressure on all these neutral countries, them and their damn money."

Schindler snorted his disdain. "We don't need them, any of them!"

"Yes, we do. I don't really understand all the details, but the Economics Ministry never stops yammering at me. And Defense. And Labor, too. It's a mess. You don't see the reports, you have no idea what a mess it is."

"We've managed to keep going this long!" Schindler retorted.

"We've managed to keep going this long," Richard explained, "by using up every resource of our erstwhile neighbors, but that's not sustainable, we're going to be in trouble soon."

"If we show weakness, that's when we'll be in trouble!" Schindler snorted.

"Maybe you're right," the Führer sighed. "But we're not showing weakness here. By preempting the Americans on this, it doesn't look so bad for us."

"Our own people will know," Schindler pointed out. "They'll know you rolled over for the capitalist dogs."

"It'd do well for you, Günter, to remember to whom you are speaking."

"My apologies, *mein Führer*. It is only my absolute loyalty to you that makes me worry so much."

"Ach, well, anyway, we don't have to worry about what our own people think—most of them weren't supposed to know about the project. As for those who did, well, the program wasn't working anyway, and as far as they are concerned, that's why it was abandoned."

"It just needed time!"

"Perhaps, but we don't have the time. According to the rest of the world, we've stopped a small-time conspiracy cooked up by some overzealous fanatics, and thanks to Traugutt, you're in the clear this time." The Führer waved toward the door. "Now go see if you can't put your house in order for me, so that I can maintain my trust in you as a senior adviser." As Schindler hesitated, the Führer waggled his fingers impatiently in the direction of the door. "*Go!*"

Richard sighed his relief once Schindler had left. He had taken the calculated risk of alienating Schindler to ingratiate himself to the Führer and set himself in obvious and direct competition for the title of heir apparent. He still was unsure of the wisdom of his move. The Führer was notoriously unreliable, his own position was still extremely tenuous, his power base weak, and Schindler would be a powerful enemy. It was possible he had made his move too soon, but the opportunity had arisen and he had not been able to pass it by.

"Do you think he's going to cause trouble?" the Führer asked.

"I think our real problems are going to come from elsewhere," Richard guessed. "There has to be a reason our people lost control of this issue, and I'm afraid we're going to find out what it is, all too soon."

"Will you advise me, Richard?" the Führer asked almost plaintively.

"It would be an honor, *mein Führer.*"

"Maybe you could bring your daughter along to the consultations? Whenever she's in Berlin. We'll need someone to take notes, and she seems like a clever girl."

"Yes, she's clever," Richard agreed worriedly.

"A very pretty girl."

"That she is." Richard paced to the window and stared out for a moment. He brought his cigarette to his lips and could not help but notice that his hand was trembling. "I'm sure she'd be very pleased to be of service," he said without turning around. "It would be a great honor for her."

54

"AND WHAT DID you do then?" The reporter's soft voice conveyed genuine concern.

Peter was impressed. He knew she was only showing concern as part of her job, part of the caring persona she projected on television, but she did it well. No wonder she was so highly paid despite her incredible shallowness. He answered, "What could a twelve-year-old boy do? I ran and hid."

"Why? Certainly you were not guilty of anything."

"Of course not, but the idea of 'innocent until proven guilty' is"—he wanted to say "is unknown," but realized that would convey the wrong impression, and so he said, "is not honored by our oppressors. Of course, our people always remember their ancient human rights—the rights which our two cultures have in common and which inspired your wonderful Constitution—but what can one do in the face of such evil?"

"But you were just a *child.*"

"Oh, yes, but children are not immune. Think of your own child," he said, turning imperceptibly toward the camera, "see how innocently he or she plays and think of how you would feel knowing that they could be arbitrarily arrested or kidnapped. Stolen, enslaved, killed—you would not know which—you simply would never see your son or daughter again."

"He's good," Alex muttered to Zosia as they sat off-camera watching Peter. "He never misses a trick."

"I told you he'd do well." Zosia nodded. "We watched hours of American shit to learn how to present his story, and he made a point of getting that reporter to like him—she'll see that it's well edited. We had several meetings beforehand where he turned on so much charm with her I was ready to puke."

"Yes, she has a reputation for being tough, and here she is eating out of his hand." Alex laughed quietly. "I didn't know he had it in him."

Zosia nodded. "I guess it's just one of those suppressed talents that none of *us* ever get to see."

Alex covered his mouth to contain his laughter. Anna shushed them and Zosia whispered more quietly, "Just as well you told him not to smoke though. We had no idea Americans had such a visceral reaction to it."

"Apparently they view it as a drug addiction," Alex whispered. "That and drinking. Is he staying off the booze?"

"As much as possible," Zosia replied. "He's got some sleeping pills for the bad nights, but he swears the vodka is better."

"Tell him to stick to the pills."

"I will. But why is it better to pop narcotics than to drink a bit of alcohol?"

"Beats the hell out of me." Alex turned his attention back to the interview.

"I'm going to take a break," Zosia whispered, and she discreetly slipped out of the studio.

By the time she returned, the reporter had covered considerable territory and was saying, "I assume you've heard the Reich's response to these recent accusations of medical experiments?"

Peter dropped his gaze briefly to the floor as he considered what his answer should be. He looked back up with sincere concern at the reporter and said, "I had heard some rumors there, but our news services cannot be trusted. Which experiments are you talking about?"

"A sterilization program! Our security service received detailed information from Underground agents about it, and the Führer himself was moved to comment on the allegations."

"And what did he say?" Peter asked warily.

"Oh, he said his own investigators had already uncovered a minor conspiracy among some low-level officials. A single laboratory was immediately shut down and the officials were dismissed. Apparently they cooked the program up among themselves."

"You know that's not true. Such a program would be approved at the highest level."

"How do you feel about it? Your involvement, I mean."

Peter shook his head slightly. "My involvement?"

The reporter had a momentary look of confusion, but then hid it expertly. "Yes, we have information that you are listed among the human subjects tested. You didn't know this?"

"Wow, look at that!" Alex whispered. "He looks genuinely shaken. My God, he fakes astonishment well."

"That's not astonishment," Zosia hissed in reply, "that's fury!"

Into Peter's stunned silence the reporter added gently, "I'm sorry you had to find out in this manner. We assumed you had already been informed."

"I didn't . . . I didn't . . ." He wet his lips and fell silent.

"You didn't know, of course."

"No, I never expected to hear such a thing. I . . ." He took a deep breath, his eyes briefly wandering toward the dark corner in which Zosia and her family sat.

Zosia muttered angrily to her father, "We had agreed that we wouldn't use this angle!"

"No," Alex explained, "we had agreed that *he* would not use this angle, but the threat that he would reveal an entire secret program, using his *own* experience, was enough to force the security service to do a preemptive announcement before he even arrived. It was a reasonable exchange, and don't worry, he's coping just fine."

Zosia had to admit that he was. She turned her attention to Peter as he was saying, ". . . just shows you the utterly inhumane way in which a portion of the population is treated, and the fact that it was uncovered by Underground agents and that the program was, as a result, closed down, shows how important it is to support these people in their efforts. Some Americans have an image of the Underground as a bunch of people with rifles creating mayhem in an otherwise peaceful society, but these revelations show how wrong such images are. These are brave people who risk their lives to uncover the truth in a society of lies. Their efforts save lives and prevent untold misery!"

He continued for some time in that vein, and slowly the color returned to his face.

Altogether the interview lasted over six hours, far longer than anyone had expected. Afterward the reporter thanked Peter for his cooperation. "You understand that this will all be edited down to a twenty-minute segment." She sounded as though she wanted to avoid his being disappointed.

Peter smiled graciously. "I'm just pleased that I have had this opportunity to tell my story. I'm sure that your expertise will ensure that the twenty minutes will convey the essence of my message."

The reporter blushed, assured him she would do her best, and took her leave of them all. Peter kissed her hand in farewell. Out of sight of the reporter, Zosia rolled her eyes. Once the production crew was safely out of earshot, Zosia asked, "The Brits don't kiss hands, do they?"

Peter did not answer her question, just said quietly, "See if you can't get me a bottle of whiskey from somewhere."

The taped, edited interview was to be shown on a popular current-affairs program in two days' time. The day before the airing, Alex received a call from one of his comrades. As Alex cradled the phone, he turned to Zosia and Peter, who were relaxing in the living room, and said, "It looks either really good or really bad."

"How's that?" Zosia asked.

"The network is advertising the interview as an hour-long special. They're canning the other segments to highlight his story"—Alex nodded toward Peter—"for the entire hour."

"Good Lord! That must be good news," Anna inserted.

"Unless they've discovered something awful and they're going to spend the hour destroying his and our reputation."

"We'll just have to wait and see," Peter said with a calmness that surprised the others. He could not find it in himself to get particularly worried. He had done his best and there was nothing more that he could do. He had made the complicated journey out of the Reich and into the NAU, had been given a few days to adjust and absorb the cultural atmosphere, and then he had given what was probably the most important interview of his visit. It was done and he felt nothing but an overwhelming relief. It was up to the editors and propagandists to make something of his words.

He checked his watch, indicated that it was time they should get going, and the four of them left for that evening's appointment: a brief lecture at a university followed by a question-and-answer session. Peter traveled with Alex and Anna; as usual, Zosia traveled separately and remained well out of sight of cameras and curious reporters, and Joanna remained at the apartment with a trusted friend.

They need not have bothered; the lecture was well attended but drew no obvious media interest. Still, it was successful as a fund-raiser. Numerous checks were signed then and there, and even more names were added to the list of prospective sponsors of the freedom fighters in Europe.

"You're good at this," Zosia commented to Peter as they casually met during the cocktail hour afterward. Or rather, the diet-soda and decaffeinated-coffee hour.

"Pleased to meet you. Um, what was the name again?" He grinned at her.

"Oh, call me *Interested*." She leered at him, running her tongue over her top lip in mock seductiveness. "From what I can see, I wouldn't be the only one called that here. You're obviously a handsome, exciting man."

"Kind of you to say so, miss. Interesting, isn't it, how years of violence and misery can be summarized as 'exciting,' don't you think?"

"Oh, it's not their fault. Too much TV, I think. All that violence where nobody ends up hurt—unless of course they end up cleanly dead, but then, that only happens to the bad guys."

"Yeah, just like real life." He sighed, looking at the watery brown beverage they called coffee. Decaffeinated. What was the point? "God, I could use a real drink!"

"How about if we accidentally meet in the bar across from my parents' apartment? Ten o'clock okay?"

"It'd be great, but where are we going to get the money to buy anything?"

"I'll cajole my dad."

"Aren't you a bit old for an allowance?"

Zosia shrugged. "What can I say, it's either that or go without."

"Good point. Right, meet you then. I'll be the one with a rose in my lapel."

"Okay, we ought to separate before anyone notices us." Zosia looked around nervously.

"Yeah, love you. Miss you."

"See you later." Zosia motioned a discreet kiss in his direction and then melted back into the crowd. Peter pasted the smile back on his face and went to do his duty as a guest speaker and fund-raiser.

55

*T*HE NEXT DAY nothing was scheduled, and Peter and Zosia took the opportunity to look around the city together. In what seemed an excess of caution, she wore a wig, makeup, sunglasses, and borrowed clothing that was completely different from anything she might wear on the job back in the Reich. Even though it was the fourth month of her pregnancy and there was an unmistakable swell to her abdomen, when they met at the corner of Fifth and Sixtieth, Peter did not even recognize her until she stepped up to him and said hello. He looked her up and down, smiled at her American-girl-style outfit, and greeted her with a kiss. Though she was admirably unrecognizable, their precautions seemed unnecessary; he had generated no particular interest, and there were no paparazzi willing to snap his photograph on the street either with or without a mystery woman by his side.

They had a great time. So many things that they had heard or read about were so different in reality. Peter was amazed by the pedestrians, who blithely ignored traffic signals. Zosia stared almost stupidly at lasers used simply to read prices. "This is military technology!" she whispered. He replied by pointing out the discreetly placed detectors near the door—clearly the merchandise or something was being monitored. They both had fun finding out that real coffee was available, as was a full selection of wines, beers, spirits, and cigarettes, although the fact that customers had to register their purchase of such was a bit disconcerting. Summoning up his best foreign accent, Peter asked the clerk about it.

"Oh, for cigarettes, we can only sell those to registered addicts. As for the other stuff—it's rationed so that nobody buys too much. We type your registration into the computer, and that references your previous purchases—if you reach your limit in a month, then you're out of luck."

"But we bought stuff in a bar the other night without registering it," Peter risked admitting.

The clerk shrugged. "Yeah, that's not controlled. I guess they figure the bar prices will slow you down. Anything for those with money," he added somewhat bitterly. Clearly, despite the fact that his income and quality of life would be considered extravagant by working-class Reich standards, he did not consider himself well-off.

"Oh, so can we buy some whiskey?" Zosia asked.

"I'll need to see your ID."

Zosia pulled out the passport she had used to enter the Union. The clerk shook his head. "Sorry, you're not a registered resident."

"I didn't say I was."

"You need to be a resident to buy booze," the clerk explained patiently.

"Then what am I supposed to do if I want some?" Zosia asked with growing impatience.

"I don't know. The legislation doesn't cover illegals and foreigners."

Zosia seemed prepared to argue, but Peter gently pulled her away. "It's all right," he assured her, "I'll manage without." They left the shop wondering at the ubiquitousness of idiotic legislation in the name of concerned government and headed down the Avenue. "Just as well I brought cigarettes with me," Peter commented as he lit one. "I thought they'd be expensive, not unavailable!"

"In any case, make sure you don't smoke when you're in the spotlight," Zosia reminded him as she waved the smoke away.

"Yeah, yeah, I know. Wasn't I a good boy all day yesterday?" he muttered while scanning the shop windows.

"Yes, very good. And I'd appreciate it if you wouldn't do it when I'm around. You know it's not good for the baby."

"Not even outside?" he asked, incredulous.

"If you don't mind."

"All right, all right," he groaned as he stopped to extinguish the cigarette on a stone wall. Seeing a trashbin nearby, he ceremoniously went over to it and threw away the end. "There! Satisfied?" he asked sarcastically.

"Yes, you're a dear," Zosia answered seriously. "Thank you." She grabbed his hand and placed it on her abdomen to soothe him, and he smiled sheepishly in response.

A short distance along they found a computer superstore, and the two of them wasted several hours drooling over the computing power readily available to the hoi polloi. "Kids write their school reports on these!" Peter whispered to Zosia, repeating the information he had learned from a salesclerk who had assumed he was shopping for his child.

"Well, I heard that I'm supposed to want to put recipes on them!" she giggled in reply.

"Shit. What a fucking waste. We could use this stuff!" he moaned while fingering one of the fantasy-world price tags. Twelve thousand Union dollars. It might as well be a trillion.

They left to get lunch. There was such a profusion of restaurants and cooking styles to choose from that they took some time before they settled on Chinese. Afterward they had dessert in another establishment, and Zosia declared that she was in love—with hot fudge sundaes.

"Decadent," she muttered between mouthfuls. "Sinfully decadent and depraved."

Peter laughed and used his napkin to wipe off some of the fudge sauce that dripped down her face. "Yeah," he agreed, "I could get fat and happy here."

"Don't do that! I like your lean and hungry look."

The bar that served the desserts had alcoholic drinks designed along some pseudo-European patriotic lines, and when they saw the fanciful names, neither could resist the temptation to try one. Peter nearly retched on the sickly sweet mixture that they called a Union Jack, while Zosia was absolutely enamored of the vodka, cream, and coffee combination that was called a White Eagle.

They emerged from the bar and counted their money. The five hundred Alex had given them was disappearing rapidly. Back home, it would buy several years off an automobile waiting list; here it was a good day's outing.

Their next stop was a clothing store. There was nowhere outside the NAU that they could wear anything they bought—imported clothes would immediately be noticed within the Reich, and the style in the bunker was, to say the least, rather casual, so they simply browsed with the intention of learning about the fashions of the country.

Nevertheless Zosia held up a pair of blue jeans and suggested Peter try them on.

"No fucking way," he replied rather more rudely than she had expected.

"Oh, come on, contrary to rumor, they're nothing like what you wore. The color's much nicer, and there are all these double seams and extra pockets and these quaint little rivets here."

"I know, and I'm pleased by that."

"Then why not?"

"The material—it's too similar for comfort."

She was however insistent, and after a bit of back and forth he conceded, "I'll try on a pair of black ones if you like, but not those."

"You're obsessive," she replied, but did not press further.

Once he had dutifully tried on several styles and they had discovered the right size, Zosia insisted that they spend their dwindling supply of cash to buy the jeans. "They look smashing!" she exclaimed.

"They're hot," he protested as sweat streamed down his face.

"Oh, come on. You don't own anything, and Adam's clothes are getting worn. Buy them, you look great!"

He decided not to pursue her referring to his wardrobe as Adam's clothes and instead argued, "It's stupid to spend this much on something I can buy back home for marks."

"You can't buy these. Oh, treat yourself. Treat me! I like you in them. And besides, you can wear them for your next interview. It'll be an investment. We'll charge the Brits."

"They're too hot to wear here, at least in August."

"They'll have air-conditioning," Zosia answered, and that was the final word.

Once they were outside the store with the package under her arm, he leaned over to kiss her. "Thanks. I'm glad you think I looked nice in them." It was a deliberate effort on his part to accept the purchase gracefully and was completely contrary to what he actually felt. He had indeed found her attention quite flattering, but it had also been disconcerting to him, since the last person who had fussed over him in any way had been Elspeth. Little presents and worrying about how he looked had taken on an ominous significance in his life, and it was not easy to forget the price that he had always paid for her attentions.

Next they visited a music store. Peter stood, entranced, for more than an hour in the shop listening to one recording after another at the little machine that played selections. The depth of feeling expressed in the music did not seem to match the cheerful materialism of American society, the lives without trauma. Perhaps, he thought, there was distress and pain even in a free society; even without tormentors, there seemed to be torment. Indeed, the very stability and generally peaceful nature of the society around them seemed to give voice to music and musical poetry that cut to the quick of his soul. They were the missing themes of his life—somebody else sang of his alienation, of his loneliness, of the desperation of his soul.

Zosia tugged on his sleeve a number of times, bored once she had examined all the technology, and he finally detached himself from the earphones. She promised solemnly that if he came up with a list of recordings, they would find the money and the wherewithal to smuggle them back, and with that promise she was able to entice him away and farther down the Avenue.

Their next stop was a huge bookstore with a coffee shop and comfortable chairs and couches scattered about. After scanning the popular fiction and political sections, they both naturally gravitated toward the science, mathematics, and technology section. Zosia found an incredible selection of documentation on computers—too much in fact. After spending a moment gathering her courage, she selected an apt title and seemed intent on reading and digesting the book then and there. Peter left her to her research and began inspecting the titles farther along. He found a sealed three-volume series on cryptanalysis that left him cold. It was humiliating. According to the table of contents listed on the back cover, the first volume summarized everything he had spent years risking his life to learn. In the second and third volumes was information with which he was only partially familiar. He had scrambled desperately to get his hands on the latest research, had risked the lives of smugglers to get research papers and books into the bunker, and there it all was for 450 Union dollars. Algorithms, protocols, codes—everything publicly available to anyone with the money and the time to read it.

Freely published in a free society. His complete admiration and respect for America's First Amendment took a momentary backseat to his utter rage at the damage that would be done. Of course, Nazi agents in the NAU would get their hands on these books, and of course they would use the information to their advantage—even their bloated and corrupt regime would eventually see its value. Meanwhile, when Alex had, upon his request, tried to set up some sort of liaison with the American Security Agency, they had completely refused any contact. "Not if he's going back," they had said. Alex had pointed out that someone who was bravely willing to risk his life to take the best analysis techniques back to where they would be the most useful should be rewarded with equipment and information that would make his job easier, but they were adamant. Even assurances that Peter would not survive long enough to betray any information at all if he was ever taken into custody had not impressed them. What did they care about suicidal courage? They would not compromise their security and that was that.

Peter turned pointedly away from the books. He did not have enough money to buy them now, and in any case, it would take some effort to smuggle them back. He looked around and spotted a book on computer-generated musical compositions. He paged through and smiled. What a thing to do—use mathematics to derive music; what a marvelous way to waste one's life. He replaced the book and walked down the aisle to the next section, labeled *sociology,* presumably located there because it was alphabetically after *science and technology.*

A treatise on child abuse caught his eye, and he picked it up and perused it. It was a depressing little work, detailing the lifelong implications of a violent upbringing. Peter felt a wave of sorrow for its unnamed victims and a twinge of guilt at his preoccupation with his own troubles. He looked at the forward to learn why the author had written the book, and there the author explained that the effects of violence on children were so profound that they would affect not only the child but also society for the rest of the victim's life. "How can we expect anything else when they have no basis upon which to reconstruct a normal life?" the author asked. "The silent killer of personality" she called it and added that "even adults, who come armed with other experiences and strongly held beliefs, often cannot cope with systematic violence directed against them." At this point, she quoted a survivor of Nazi terror to support her supposition: "Anyone who has been tortured remains tortured. . . . Anyone who has suffered torture never again will be able to be at ease in the world. . . . Faith in humanity, already cracked by the first slap in the face, then demolished by torture, is never acquired again."

Peter shook his head as he read the words, rejecting outright the prophecy. Nevertheless, he also felt a strange comfort in knowing that maybe someone out there truly understood what he felt. Perhaps since those words were printed, the writer had found hope? Maybe he could trace the man or his writings and see if there was some solace to be had in his story. He turned to the footnotes at the back of the book and there read the man's name and a brief biography. An Austrian who had fled to Belgium because he was Jewish, he had been tortured for his role in the Belgian resistance and deported to Auschwitz. He had escaped during the uprising there in 1946 and fled to America. After writing several treatises on his experiences and being largely ignored, the writer, apparently unable to escape the demons that continued to pursue him, committed suicide in 1978.

Peter gasped. He did a mental subtraction: thirty-two years. Thirty-two years and the man had still not escaped! Carefully he set the book back on the shelf. He went back to where Zosia was studying her book and convinced her to take a coffee break. They went into the little coffee bar, Zosia still clutching her book as though it would run away, and settled down with some fancifully flavored coffees. Peter told her about the cryptology volumes he had found.

"Yeah, my father told me about them when they were published," she responded.

"Oh, why didn't you tell me?"

"He wanted to buy them for you and give them as a gift when you arrived, so it was a secret. But when he went to buy them, he found out they're restricted to citizens only—not even a residency document is good enough. So he couldn't get them."

"That's stupid. That'll never stop the Germans from laying their hands on them."

"I know. Us neither. It'll just take a bit longer. After that we have to get them out of the country, but sooner or later you'll see them."

"Thank your father for his effort in any case," Peter replied, still distracted by the quote he had read. Was it a prophecy? Was he doomed to never truly be free again?

"I think it'd sound better coming from you."

"Yes, of course. I'll do that." He sipped his coffee, then to change the subject he told Zosia about the curious music book he had seen.

"How odd! To think someone would do research on something so useless!" She sighed and shook her head, then switching to quiet German in the interests of privacy, she added, "They really do have shallow lives, don't they."

"Oh, what makes you say that?" he asked, also in German.

"Well, they don't seem to have any purpose. They just go to school and work, buy a house and a car, and then they die. It's so meaningless."

"And you think we have meaning?" he asked somewhat sharply.

"But of course! Don't you?" she responded with surprise.

"No. Or rather, less than they do."

"How can you say that? We have a cause. We have a purpose to our lives."

"In your terms, it's a pointless cause," he countered mordantly. "Think about it. Our cause, our entire purpose for living, is to overthrow the government and establish national independence. In the best of all possible worlds, if we succeed, and if all turns out well with no civil wars and everybody working together"— his voice took on a sarcastic note at that thought—"the most we can hope for is to be their poor cousins. With smashed economies, uneducated populations, and a devastated environment, our greatest achievement would be to be like them. If we started today, it would take us at least a generation or two. At least! They're already there. Doesn't that make us the ones with pointless lives?"

"No, no, no, no, no," Zosia disagreed, shaking her head for emphasis. Still she could not quickly formulate a reply; she just knew intuitively that he was wrong.

"We're struggling to be like them. If you think they're shallow, maybe you should rethink what you're doing for a living."

"No, no." Zosia continued to shake her head. Something in what he said really bothered her, but she could not put her finger on it. She didn't think it was the idea; rather it was something like the hopelessness in his tone, the way he so blithely devalued everything they did. "No," she said as she finally formulated a reply, "I'm sure it will be different. It would be madness to give in just because we're not sure of where the future will take us."

"But once again, you're blithely able to condemn that which you do not understand. You think that because that woman over there doesn't have to kill to survive, her life is meaningless?" He discreetly indicated the young woman at a table near them.

"No, that's not what I said!" Zosia replied, annoyed.

"Well, what would you have them do? What would give meaning to their so-called shallow lives? Do they need a revolution just to keep themselves ideologically sound? Would their lives be more meaningful if they had to fear arrest at every turn?"

"No!" Zosia grew slightly angry. "You're taking it all out of context!"

"Well, if it's not the outcome that makes our struggle meaningful, are you saying then it's the stress and weariness and fear? Does spending our lives looking over our shoulders or sleeping badly give us purpose? I, for one, am sick to death of it!"

"Why are you badgering me? I just said it to make you feel better about the books!"

"But you quite willingly trash other people's lives because they don't conform to exactly your standards!"

"Oh, *that!* Come off it. Look, I apologized, but you *wanted* my opinion. You *asked* me, remember!"

"And you were so certain you knew what it was all about."

And so it went, neither giving ground, both offended that their enjoyable little break had been spoiled by the other's obstinacy and ill will. They argued for nearly an hour, slowly dragging in one thing after another. The topic strayed, the passions were directed here and there, but the rancor was a constant. Neither had the sense or the ability to realize they were hot and tired and stressed. Finally they both managed to fall silent simultaneously and for long enough to realize that they had argued over nothing. Yet again.

"I think we should go," Zosia said quietly and in English. Their strategy of speaking German had probably protected the topic of their conversation, but it had naturally drawn much more attention than they had anticipated. It was clear as bits of their language were overheard that the patrons had wondered, what were two Germans doing in the Free City?

Peter nodded his agreement and they both stood. The number of people who watched them as they rose and left was embarrassingly large. At the barrier that separated the coffee shop from the bookstore, he turned to face the curious stares and said, "Yes, we're from the goddamned fucking Reich, and no, we're not goddamned fucking Nazis so you can stop your fucking staring at us!"

Zosia slipped away and waited at the first bookshelf as he spoke, beside herself with embarrassment. When he turned away from his audience and joined her, she grabbed his arm, dropped her book on a convenient shelf, and rushed them out of the store. Outside, they avoided looking at each other. She was angry at the scene he had inflicted on her; he was furious at her lack of loyalty and the way she had rushed him out of the store. They walked in silence trying to cool down, each painfully aware from previous experience that although the argument was about nothing, it would return and would take ages to dissipate.

Finally, several blocks away, Zosia ventured, "We've got to do something about this."

"Oh, everybody argues. It's no big deal," he said, trying to reassure himself more than her.

"It *is* a big deal. We do it all the time and about nothing! Things are going well and we still can't handle it. What if there were genuine trouble in our lives?"

"You think our lives are going well?"

"Yes, don't you?"

He sputtered his derision. "Yeah, sure, everybody spends the best years of their lives hiding from the authorities in an underground bunker."

Zosia chose to ignore his sarcasm. "Maybe you should see a psychiatrist while you're here. Maybe they'll help you with your dreams and stuff. After all, they're not Reich-trained. I'm sure they can help."

"So, it's all my fault. I'm nuts and that's why we argue," he responded bitterly.

"No, that's not what I'm saying. It's just that maybe—"

"I get it. It's me. If I weren't so fucked-up, we'd get along fine. Just like you and Adam did. The perfect couple, the perfect husband," he grated, walking along even more rapidly, as if he could outpace his anger.

"Peter, maybe they can help!"

"No!" He stopped walking, grabbing her arm to stop her as well. Several people collided with them, and it was a moment before he could continue, "No fucking way!"

"But—"

"Was this all your idea? Bring me here for these interviews just so you could get some head doctor to look at me? Was it?" He tightened his grip on her arm.

With deliberate, calm strength, she removed his hand from her arm. "Don't do that again," she warned quietly. She waited a few seconds so her warning could sink in; a sea of people flowed around them as they stood in silent confrontation. "It was not a plot. I just thought it might help." She raised her hand to silence his nascent objection. "Let me finish! I know our bringing you here hasn't helped, but you're getting almost paranoid. It has got to stop. Isn't it about time you got over it already?"

The words he had only just read played through his mind. *Anyone who has suffered torture never again will be able to be at ease in the world. . . .* Is that what some-one had said to the author, thirty-two years later? Get over it already? He lowered his head. His shoulders rose and fell with each deep breath. "I wish I could," he said at last. "But the one thing I know is that I need to do this on my own."

"I know you've always been self-reliant, but maybe this is the one time you really need help. I've tried to give it but I don't know how and I'm afraid all I've done is make things worse. Maybe it's time to accept outside help?"

Faith in humanity . . . is never acquired again. He shook his head. "They won't be able to help if I don't trust them," he whispered.

"All right. I'm sorry. Let's just go."

56

OTHER THAN FOR his appearance on the current-affairs program, Peter's visit had not attracted as much media interest as Alex had hoped. The network show was, nevertheless, a genuine accomplishment and would in itself have been worth the visit. It was the result of Alex calling in a few favors and the producer's own background: his family had fled Austria in 1938 and had lost everything they owned. The reputedly irascible old man would do anything to embarrass the Nazi regime, including airing a risky and possibly audience-losing interview with a strange and eloquent Englishman.

Once the old man saw samples of the footage, he decided to take an even greater risk and asked the reporter to put together an hour-long show. Marcia Long was more than happy to oblige. She knew that not only the man's story but the man himself was intriguing. And who could blame her if she gloated at the prospect of an hour-long show to herself! Her reputation was well established, her interviewing techniques superb, her background work impeccable, and now—now the payoff! The show would win an award, she was sure of it. She and her staff worked feverishly and together came up with an hour-long segment with all the appropriate background footage.

The network advertised the program, and it drew a reasonably large audience, which, surprisingly, grew as the hour progressed. Peter could not watch the show for embarrassment, but the rest of America did. It struck a chord. All the protectionist, isolationist whining had raised the hackles of a silent majority of Americans, and they had felt a growing sense of shame at their inability to act on the world stage. What was this withdrawal into rural utopia? Were they not a world power? Were they not the most advanced country—or countries—in the world? Was their word, given long ago to their defeated allies, worthless? Calls flooded into the station, and telegrams, faxes, and electronic mail. The word came from across the continent: the people were interested! And the media sat up and noticed that there was news to be had here. Good, easy news: no dangerous travel, no difficult background to understand, no complex issues to uncover, just a man and his story. They lapped it up as the free information-entertainment that it was.

Overnight Peter became a celebrity. Overnight the great American publicity machine kicked into gear and looked for a way to make a profit. Overnight, his calendar for the rest of the month became booked solid and he lost his privacy to a host of sympathetic, concerned journalists, television reporters, handlers, and interested onlookers.

Within a week the media ceased to report explicitly on him; rather they filled their pages and shows by reporting on the media attention given to him. Then there was the analysis of what it all meant, what the American people wanted, and what the politicians should do. It worked like a charm. The agenda was set, and the debate was heavily weighted against the isolationists. Luckily for them, the isolationists rapidly evaporated from the political scene. The Nationalists took a nosedive in the polls, the Republicans restated their policies, more carefully explaining that they had never meant to abandon America's brave allies, and the Democrats rallied to the obscure plank of their platform that had always supported international involvement. Politicians rushed to be seen with the appropriate freedom-fighting support organizations, and the debate ended in a draw: everybody agreed that withdrawing support had never really been an issue and that the foreign governments in exile were not only welcome but had the full sympathy and support of the various American governments. At least for the time being.

Peter bore the attention with stoic calm. It was a flash in the pan and he would be forgotten not long after he left, but the damage to the isolationists would be done, and with that he could feel some satisfaction. He did not fool himself into thinking he was important; it was not his story that had fueled the political firestorm—the tinder had been there waiting for ignition, and Alex had been right, his story was the perfect match but indeed nothing more than that. He would, at the end of it all, go back home and sink into obscurity.

An obscurity that was looking ever more blessed, he thought, as he walked onto the set of a very popular and extremely crass live talk show. This one would be tough, but it was going to reach the widest audience, and as Alex put it, low IQ or not, they still had a vote, they still had money.

Peter waited in the comfortable little room provided while the first guest chatted to the host. He had a TV set in the room and could follow the dialogue onstage if he so desired, but he preferred sipping the coffee and daydreaming as he looked at the tasteless art on the wall.

". . . And finally, what do you think of all the fuss being made about our next guest?" the host asked his guest.

Fuss sounded rather pejorative, and Peter listened with interest to see if the guest took the bait.

"Just another diversion from the true issues which are dividing this country," the woman asserted. "Why should Americans be concerned about what happens over there when every day there are thousands of crimes against people of color in this country? We're facing genocide—we cannot and must not divert precious resources from solving our problems at home to policing the world!"

She continued for some time in her diatribe, repeating in various ways the same theme and misquoting history and statistics. Peter looked more carefully at the screen and noted for the first time that she was what Americans referred to as black or African. Judging from her words, she seemed to be a professional at it. Since his first encounters with Africans had been at diplomatic functions where he had served canapés, he had come to associate the term *African* with the extremely dark skin of the people he had served; it was something of a shock to him to discover that so many African-Americans were incredibly light-skinned and looked not at all like the stereotype promulgated in Reich propaganda. He reached over and picked up the photocopy of the guest list and read her credentials. An academic trained in sociology and an author of some note. Well, she had not been required reading at the Horst Wesel Academy.

There was a light tap on the door, and a well-dressed young woman came to escort him to the stage. He groaned inwardly and smiled in response. She brought him to the edge of the stage, indicated when he should step out, and then left him to proceed alone. The host announced him, and Peter stepped out, aware of the awkward distance he had to walk under the scrutiny of so many unseen viewers. His legs hurt worse than usual, and in spite of his best attempts, or perhaps because of them, he could not hide his limp. The host grinned at him with big, white, shiny teeth. He shook Peter's hand, introduced him to their first guest, and indicated his seat.

"So what do you think of Miss Whitmer's assertions?" the host asked.

"I'm afraid I didn't hear them," Peter responded, determined to stay outside any messy all-America issues.

Dr. Whitmer, infuriated not least because of the host's mistitling of her, broke in with, "Certainly you realize it is inappropriate for a white man to lecture us on slavery!"

"I'm just recounting my experiences," Peter replied evenly.

"What could any *white man* understand about slavery!" She imbued the words *white* and *man* with such derision that she had no need of further adjectives to give her opinion.

Peter, seeing a minefield of possible answers, decided on, "And what could you?"

"You ignorant man! Don't you know what the black experience has been? Don't you know what my people have suffered? And are still suffering at the hands of the white power structure?"

"What have you personally experienced?" he asked calmly.

"I have seen my share of pain!" she boomed.

"I'm sorry to hear that," he responded quietly. "So have I. Perhaps we can learn from each other."

"We have learned enough from the white man throughout history—to our cost! You could never understand the black experience!"

"Because I am white?"

"Yes!" she answered, infuriated.

"And you can?"

"Of course!"

"Even things you have not personally seen or experienced? Even things in the distant past?"

"Don't act stupid!"

"My apologies. I'm just curious. You see, I'm afraid I don't ascribe to racial theories of guilt or hypotheses of tainted blood, but I do know some people who do. Maybe you'd enjoy talking to them?" he asked disingenuously. The audience tittered.

"You!" Dr. Whitmer responded. "You with your blond hair and blue eyes! You weren't oppressed, you weren't targeted for your skin color or your religion! You brought your troubles down on yourself! You have no understanding of racism, you—"

"You're right," Peter interrupted forcefully. "I could have fit in and I chose not to! That's exactly the point, isn't it? Don't be fooled by the nonsensical ideas of Nazi mythology, they'll happily change their tune whenever it serves their purposes. If it suits their needs, they'll flatter and wine and dine representatives of peoples they claim are inferior—I know, I served the damn drinks! They'll imprison and torture and enslave anybody who disagrees with them—no matter how pristine a pedigree they might have! That's the way of these gangsters, they oppress anyone who stands in their path, anyone who disagrees with them. And if you could, for just a few seconds, detach yourself from your precious group-think politics—"

"You're a fool! My people are oppressed as a group, they must react as a group!"

"And that makes you their ally!" he spat in reply, suddenly understanding Katerina's anger during their first discussion. "The Nazis and their ilk would like nothing better than to have you think of yourselves as different! If you can't see that we are more than just a member of a group, that we aren't defined by hair or eyes or—"

"Get real! You're a member of the ruling class! Even the way you are treated here shows that! Do you think you would be listened to if—"

"You don't get it, do you? Why do you think I am speaking out? You have a substantial movement in this country to tolerate these criminals, to treat them as acceptable. You have people here who believe they would be immune from oppression because they belong to the right group or because they are Americans. They don't know that their actions, their beliefs, the things they take for granted here, would be enough to mark them out as enemies there! Like me. I did nothing but disagree with them, nothing at all! No one is safe when intolerance, *any sort* of intolerance, is accepted! That's what makes us alike, more alike than any of our superficial differences that you're so intent on pointing out!"

"*We're not alike!*" she almost howled. "One pathetic man's experiences do not compensate for the oppression of centuries!"

"Who's talking about compensation?" Peter began, but then he stopped. He was getting into exactly the sort of argument he had promised himself he would avoid. He frowned as his head throbbed with pain. What, he wondered, could he say to back out of the situation?

Dr. Whitmer used the pause to good effect, launching into a tirade against his uneducated, insensitive bigotry. Peter rubbed his chin thoughtfully and answered tersely on occasion, never saying more than that he had nothing but his own story to tell, refusing to again take the bait. After ten minutes had passed in this manner, with Dr. Whitmer showing no signs of letting up, the host finally restrained her.

"Let's let Mr. Halifax here speak a bit. I think the audience would like to ask a few questions. I know I certainly am curious as to what he thinks about us and American society."

At the prompt Peter launched into a pat speech about the wonders of the Land of Opportunity, and with a brief nod to his fellow guest he acknowledged that there were problems to be solved but that America was a great continent, and with such a brave and dedicated people there was no reason why they could not offer help to their brethren overseas even while addressing the inequities that might exist at home.

He was then prodded by the host to briefly recount his life history for the "one or two hermits" who had not yet heard about him. He dutifully did that, concluding with, "But I managed to survive by holding on to the hope that one day we might be free, that we might one day be like America, and that one day the Americans would rise up as a people to help us in our hour of need."

Dr. Whitmer rolled her eyes and made a slight snorting noise, but did not dare to interrupt. She had bargained for her position as the opening act on a highly publicized show only on the understanding that Halifax would be allowed to speak when it came to his turn. She had made the pact in order to have a huge public forum, and now she had to stick to her part of the bargain in the interests of future speaking engagements.

Peter found himself silently agreeing with Dr. Whitmer's snorted opinion: it was crap, but he had learned that such sentiments went down well with audiences, and indeed, the audience was soaking it up.

As his guest spoke, Jerry Mann worried a bit. He was rightfully famous for the controversial nature of his shows, and this little festival of warmth would kill his reputation and eventually the ratings. Yet, to turn on a debate between his two guests seemed unwise; for one thing, the Englishman seemed uninterested and nearly unprovocable on the race issue—he honestly felt no white man's guilt and would not even pretend to feel it. Nor would it help to let that Whitmer woman rant at him—she was just plain boring without opposition. He should have got a member of a Nazi sympathy group to go on opposite, but after last year's onstage melee and murder, the government had vetoed the idea. Damn censorship. So, the job was left to him to provoke something. The question was, what would get a response? As Peter finished speaking and the audience applauded warmly, Mann came to a decision.

"Very interesting, very interesting. But certainly you could have avoided such unpleasantness?" Mann asked.

"Which part in particular?" Peter asked, unwilling to rehash every detail.

"I mean, someone as bright as you. You are hardly typical or average, now are you?"

"I'm not sure who is typical," Peter responded, confused by the direction of the questioning.

"Certainly not someone as educationally elite as you! We all heard about your doctorate from EUM. And in mathematics!" Mann gasped his astonishment.

"The English University of Manhattan doctorate was honorary," Peter explained. "Just part of my visit."

"Ah, yes, but I heard it was truly earned. You have an extensive education in some very arcane subjects, isn't that true?"

Peter wanted to ask if there was supposed to be something wrong with that, but then he saw the direction that Mann was heading. Add elite and overeducated to Dr. Whitmer's denunciation of him as a white European male and the next logical step was pampered, whining aristocrat who pined for lost privilege and did not merit the support of the honest, simple, and hard-pressed American working class.

"Perhaps," Peter answered carefully, "I had no opportunity to compare my experience with others since higher education is essentially forbidden to my class." He let slide that his class was essentially self-defined by an unwillingness to collaborate. In any case, it was sufficiently true in that higher education, and in many cases any education, was denied to numerous people. "You see," he continued, turning toward the audience, "that is one of your freedoms that we value so highly. The right to learn. We know how hardworking Americans educate their children and work to put them into university so that they might better themselves and make this a strong and just country."

Dr. Whitmer opened her mouth to say something, but Peter, acknowledging her with a nod, continued, "And we recognize, as you do, that equal access to education is crucial. We recognize your struggle to make your educational system fair and available to all your citizens, just as you recognize the hardship our children must endure as they read illegal books in dark cellars, as they study forbidden texts, fearing arrest at any minute, fearing that their parents will be taken because of their commitment to learning . . ." Peter continued, weaving a tale of two noble peoples separated by an ocean: the one society struggling to regain basic rights, the other striving relentlessly for a better, fairer society.

Mann tried other questions, tried different accusations. He laid them subtly, never daring an outright attack, and Peter answered them just as subtly, never taking offense, never noticing the way the host tried to twist Peter's words or reinterpret his message. With each answer, Peter tightened the web around Mann, and the audience loved it—their love-hate relationship with the host having swung toward hate for the moment.

From their living room, Anna and Alex together with Zosia and Joanna watched the live program. Alex smoked nervously; Anna kept leaping up to refill someone's glass with tea or to offer snacks; Zosia, sprawled on the floor, chewed her thumb. Only Joanna, sitting on the floor next to her mother's prone form, remained calm; she knew her father would do well.

"I wonder why Mann decided to go after him?" Anna asked as she once again shoved a plate of cheese and crackers in front of Joanna.

"I don't know," Alex admitted. "I never watch this show. But Peter's handling him well."

"I would have snapped that woman's head off," Anna admitted. "She has no clue how lucky she is."

"Yes, but Peter's right, there is no point in debating her. It would only make him look unsympathetic. Better to go the route he's taken and suck up to the Americans."

"I wonder how he manages to say all those obsequious things with such a straight face," Anna commented to no one in particular.

"Just part of the service," Zosia answered bitterly, thinking of how he must have spoken to Elspeth. And herself as well? "Seems he has a whole slew of personalities he can use when he's in the mood."

"So which one is the real thing?" Anna asked.

Zosia shrugged. "I'd be surprised if even he knows."

Anna looked at her daughter, wondering at the source of her remarks, but did not say anything because Alex shushed them both. "I want to hear him!" he hissed, leaning closer to the television.

Out of the corner of his eye, Mann watched the reaction of his audience and felt elated. He did not care that he was the object of their hate at the moment—he'd rectify that situation soon enough—all he cared was that they were involved. They were beginning to make noises, small cheers, occasional boos. It was great. It was perhaps the most intellectual discussion he had managed to maintain for any length of time without losing them utterly. With a glance he looked toward his guest. The man was tiring of the harassment; a few more good swipes, and he should change the pace lest he look too mean and petty.

Despite all his intentions to the contrary, Peter found himself rubbing his forehead. The pain was excruciating. It was those damn lights—they were in his eyes and had bothered him from the moment he had stepped onto the stage. He felt certain in a few more minutes the pain in his head would overwhelm everything else, and he was afraid of the consequences.

As the host asked yet another aggressive question, Peter decided to take a small risk. He indicated with his hand and a brief smile that he had heard the question, then said, "Excuse me, just a second here," and reached into his shirt pocket for his sunglasses. He bowed his head to put them on, mostly to rest his eyes and stretch his neck, but it looked quite humble to the audience, and on the close-up monitors most of them could discern that he was shaking. Still quivering, he looked up, smiled sheepishly, and explained, "I'm terribly sorry, but my eyes were damaged over the years, and these lights are causing me excruciating pain. I do hope you don't mind."

"Damn it! What's he doing?" Alex growled.

"Have you noticed, his accent has changed?" Zosia pointed out, ignoring her father.

"Yes, now that you mention it . . ." Anna looked intrigued. "Why did he do that?"

"It's unintentional," Zosia explained. "He slips into that tone anytime he's angry or stressed. I don't think he's even aware he does it." She was though. The distance, the distinct courtesy—as if he were talking to a stranger. It was offensive when he used it with her, and he used it all too often, pronouncing her name with a disapproving precision that irritated the hell out of her.

"However he speaks, I want to know what the hell he thinks he's doing!" Alex grated.

"Don't worry, this will work," Anna assured him. Whether it was deliberate or not, the tone of voice, the courteous wording, the apology, even that sheepish, pained expression: it was all there. It worked for her—she wanted to hug him and apologize for anything she had ever said, so she knew it would win over the audience, or at least the women. She glanced at the scowl on her daughter's face and amended to herself, at least those women who did not love him dearly and apparently, painfully.

It did work. Peter had not intended to look pathetic, he was just in pain and quite embarrassed by that fact; nevertheless, he looked heroic as he suffered in brave silence. The audience felt suddenly protective of him, and as one they turned toward Mann daring him to try one more aggressive question.

But, no, Mann realized it was time to save his own image, and this thing with the eyes gave him a great idea for a publicity stunt. His audience, his beloved audience, ready to rend him limb from limb at the moment, would in a minute do a complete turnabout and be the heroes of the day. The American public, they were wonderful, generous to a fault, and they loved themselves and that image of themselves quite dearly. They would happily pay to keep that image, and Mann knew exactly how to get them to do that.

He made a discreet hand gesture to his offstage staff and then went into the audience to have them ask the questions. The tone changed markedly—no more innuendo, no more vague accusations. Suddenly Mann was the epitome of concern, nodding his head sympathetically as someone asked, "What exactly is wrong with your eyes?"

"I wish I knew," Peter answered tiredly. "My vision comes and goes, and bright lights provoke phenomenal pain."

"Will it lead to blindness?" an older woman asked.

"I don't know. We don't really have the facilities to diagnose something like this."

"What caused it?"

"I don't know. Chemicals maybe. I was exposed to a lot of"—he shrugged—"junk. There are no safety requirements for us, just use us until we drop dead." His voice had taken on a bitter edge. The pain was making it impossible for him to keep up the façade he had so carefully constructed. He could hardly construct a coherent sentence, let alone try to sway an audience toward supporting armed insurrection in distant lands.

It was the perfect opportunity for Dr. Whitmer to jump in, to point out that any money spent abroad was a criminal waste of resources when there were so many unsolved problems at home. He would never be able to stay calm in the face of another attack, she was sure of that, but she knew instinctively that even if she managed to pummel him verbally, he would win any debate in terms of audience sympathy. She weighed her pride and urge to argue against that insurmountable truth and kept silent, consoling herself that at least she had managed to reach a much wider audience than usual and that she had already said her piece.

"Or maybe it was simply physical abuse," Peter continued. "I was hit in the face a lot." He paused as if remembering something or someone, then repeated distantly, "A lot."

"What about treatment?" someone asked.

Peter shook his head. "That's not available to my class of people. We work—in whatever conditions—until we drop dead. Now, of course, after speaking to you all, if I made myself known to the authorities, I'd simply be shot out of hand." He thought for a moment, then added with a winsome smile, "If I were lucky."

"So you *are* planning to return?" Mann jumped at the implication.

"As I have said, I cannot comment on my plans."

"But what about here? In America?" Dr. Whitmer felt inclined to inquire. "Surely you could find something out?"

Peter nodded. "Yes, I've thought about that. I've thought about lots of things. Having my legs broken and reset, having this tattoo removed, tracking down these headaches, sorting out my vision problems, talking to psychiatrists to soothe my nights. Lots of things. I don't know what's possible; probably there's nothing much that can be done about most of it. Not at this late date."

"Oh, don't underestimate our medical community!" Mann admonished. "With such a wish list, what would be your most pressing desire?"

"I guess my eyes. I don't want to lose my sight," Peter responded without much hesitation. "But there's no point having a priority list since I can't afford any of it anyway."

Alex frowned as he watched the proceedings. It was going well by most measures, the audience certainly loved Peter, but it was not going the way Alex had expected. The topic was digressing terribly, getting more and more personal and less focused on their cause. "Why does he keep talking about himself?" Alex grumbled to himself.

"That *is* what he's supposed to do," Anna reminded him. "Remember, he's supposed to personalize it all."

"Oh, he's personalizing it all right. It's a goddamned one-man freak show!" Alex fumed. "Where are the appeals for arms or political support?"

"I think he's tired," Anna defended him, "or sick."

"Both," Zosia opined from her position on the floor. "I'd guess he's concentrating on not vomiting onstage."

"He gets that ill?" Anna asked.

"Frequently." Zosia grabbed a piece of cheese from the tray Anna had set on the coffee table, broke it in half, popped one bit into her mouth, and offered the other piece to Joanna.

"Has he seen a doctor?" Anna asked, concerned.

"Yes. The guy back at Szaflary thought it was linked to the headaches which come from all his head injuries. He said there's nothing to be done about it."

"What do you think?"

"I think that might be true. Or it might be psychosomatic. Peter just gets terrified now and then; I think his fears provoke a lot of his physical symptoms, but he says that's not the case."

"What about the booze, that can't help much," Alex suggested caustically.

"Naw, the symptoms predate the drinking, and the alcohol actually seems to help, which is why I think it's stress-related."

Alex harrumphed his disbelief.

"Has he seen anyone here? They have some wonderful advances in medicine," Anna pressed.

"He asked the physician who gave him his physical about it. That fellow suggested some pills; some sort of stomach wonder drug."

"And?"

"I don't know. Peter wouldn't fill the prescription, said he was sick of drugs."

"He should at least try," Anna insisted.

"Maybe," Zosia agreed. "But the physician just sort of scribbled this prescription, he didn't really seem interested in diagnosing the problem. Anyway, unknown drugs scare Peter, so there's no point forcing him to take them even if they do work. The stress alone would make him sick."

"What *did* they do to him?" Anna asked almost to herself.

Zosia glanced at Joanna, then decided to answer anyway. "I gather one little game was making him swallow something which would make him violently ill."

"Why did they do that?"

Alex sputtered at the stupidity of Anna's question, but Zosia interpreted it correctly. "They were teaching him to obey any command, no matter how painful, immediately and without thought. Since he knew what was going to happen, he might well hesitate, but if he hesitated, they just upped the stakes, thus punishing him for self-defense mechanisms and, in that way, attempting to destroy any reaction on his part other than absolute, mindless obedience."

"It still affects him, doesn't it?" Anna asked, though it was clearly not a question.

"Oh, yes," Zosia agreed. "In ways not even he is sure of."

"I guess that's why he—" Anna began, but before she could say more, Alex hushed them both and they returned their attention to the screen.

They were still talking about Peter's assertion that he had no money.

"How could you afford to come here?" someone asked.

"My expenses were covered by the generosity of some local residents," Peter answered obscurely. His visit had never gained official status with any of the governments in exile, and the anti-Conciliation coalition had asked to remain anonymous for fear of indicating to the public at large the raging internal divisions of the exile community. "Understandably, given the Reich's vindictiveness, they have asked to remain anonymous."

"And they won't help you?"

"They can ill afford the expense of medical treatment for the millions of victims of the Reich's human rights abuses. I am relatively lucky—there is much, much worse. But in any case, our need is not to treat the victims; it is to prevent the abuses in the first place. We must fight them and we need your support to do that," he answered, rallying slightly.

They were not shaken that easily. He was the one they could see, he was there. If they could solve his problems, then in their consciences, they would have solved the world's problems. It was a touching approach—the one little candle into the darkness philosophy—and Mann played it for what it was worth.

"I know!" he intoned at the appropriate moment. "We have the resources! We have the ability! We can do it! Let's get a toll-free number up on the screen." He gestured theatrically toward his crew. "Can we do that? Can we get a toll-free number? Let's do it! Let's see what we can do about restoring this man's vision!" Mann thought for a moment about linking eyesight-vision with the social-vision thing, but decided it was too difficult on the spur of the moment. "Come on, America! We have a need! Let's see some response. Let's get together enough to get this fellow into medical treatment! We can do it, we're the greatest country on earth—the most generous people! Let's see what we can do!"

"Oh, God Almighty!" Alex howled, echoing Peter's thoughts fairly accurately. "What the hell is that maniac doing! We're not looking for doctors. Speak up, boy! For Christ's sake say something!"

"I thought he made a good stab at a turnaround," Anna opined.

"If it didn't work, it wasn't any good!" Alex almost shouted.

Zosia motioned to him sharply to tone it down. Not only was Joanna in the room, but as she had explained to her father on numerous occasions, yelling loudly at the television did not cause the people on the screen to hear him—it only annoyed his fellow viewers.

Peter did not speak up. He answered the questions that were put to him, conversed in general about various things, and let Mann take the show along the agenda he had set. Now and then someone announced the running total of the impromptu collection to rousing cheers from the audience.

Dr. Whitmer finally asked why they were collecting money for this man's medical treatment and not for a poor, black child of the notorious Docklands area. "Europe is always a mess! You Europeans are always killing each other! Why should we get entangled in another one of your stupid and interminable wars?

Why all this money for a white foreigner when our own black children go without!" she accused, looking to Peter for an answer.

Peter had lowered his head during the debate, and he kept it down as he considered her use of the word *foreigner* as if that meant he were a lesser being. Why an *American* child? Why imply that helping him excluded helping another? There were many answers to her question. Many and none. In any case, he felt too sick to argue, so he simply turned toward her, removed his glasses so she could see his eyes, the blue eyes that she so reviled, and answered distinctly, "I don't know."

Alex groaned as if in pain as he watched the proceedings. The audience had completely taken over the debate with Dr. Whitmer and Jerry Mann screeching their opinions into the general melee of noise. Peter sat quietly, apparently breathing deeply to contain his nausea, probably with his eyes closed. Meanwhile the total for the collection climbed. Suddenly Alex sat up. There was a way to salvage the situation after all. Certainly they could convince the station to sign over whatever was collected not to a medical fund but to Peter personally. It would only make sense given the danger that they could claim he was in. "He has to go into hiding," Alex muttered, practicing.

"What are you talking about?" Anna turned to see if he was talking to the television again.

"We've got to convince the station to make sure Peter gets the money personally—tell them his life is in danger or some such nonsense. We'll tell them he'll use the money as soon as it's safe, or better yet, under an assumed name."

"Why?" Anna asked.

"So that Dad can get his hands on it," Zosia explained.

"Do you think you can get your husband to sign it over to an armaments fund?" Alex asked Zosia.

"Oh, I think he'd be willing to divert most of it to something useful. He might want to reserve a bit to himself for a few things like upgrading his computer."

"Wouldn't that be unfair to him?" Anna interjected. The cold-blooded calculations of her husband and children sometimes worried her. Was she the only one who thought that maybe saving his eyesight was useful? That it would be unfair to ask him to throw away this chance he had been given just to buy more guns?

"He's already looked into it a bit, Ma," Zosia soothed her mother's ruffled sensibilities. "The physician said that there was only a forty percent chance that they could even determine what was wrong. And then he said there wasn't much guarantee they could do anything about it even then. He said it could take months of incredibly expensive tests and procedures, and that the risk of complicating whatever damage had been done might preclude treatment. All in all, he said, we'd end up a lot poorer and not very likely much better off."

Anna sighed. It was possible the physician had known they were impoverished and had proffered his advice accordingly, in which case a second opinion would be worthwhile, but she did not say that. When her husband and daughter had their sights set on a goal, there was little point in arguing. If the station released the funds to him directly, Peter would sign over the money to the cause. He would have no choice.

"I've got to get down there before he does something stupid with that money. You stay here," Alex said to Zosia as he rummaged for his documentation and credentials, "there might be cameras around. I'll see what I can do." As he headed toward the door, he turned toward Anna and asked, "Do you want to come along?"

Anna shook her head emphatically.

57

As the show wrapped up, Peter walked off the set. He was not interested in the numerous people who approached him; he just made a polite apology and forced his way through to the backstage area. There, a security guard kept the crowd at bay as the same young woman who had escorted him before came to greet him. "We need to go to the back office so you can see about this collection Jerry organized. What a marvelous humanitarian he is!"

"Yes, he's something all right," Peter responded mordantly. He still felt like puking.

As they entered the office in the back, Alex looked up from harassing the man behind the desk and beamed guiltily at Peter. "Ah, my boy, there you are!"

"Isn't it customary," Peter asked in Polish, "to wait until the corpse is cold before stealing the coins from its eyes?"

The office staff looked at him blankly, Alex's smile wavered just the briefest second, then he replied in English, "Good to see you, too! What a wonderful man that Jerry is, isn't he?"

"A marvelous humanitarian," Peter responded, borrowing his guide's words.

"How do you feel?" Alex had not noticed on the television how pale Peter was.

"Ill," Peter responded tersely.

"Sophie sent you some lemonade," Alex said, picking up a sealed cup he had set on the desk and handing it to Peter. "Homemade."

"Oh, we have drinks here!" Peter's guide responded with alacrity. "I should have offered you something. I'm sorry! Would you like a soda?"

"No, this will do. Thanks," Peter murmured as he tasted the vodka and lime. Thank God for Zosia's sense of humor.

As Peter began to relax, Alex explained helpfully, "I was just discussing this collection—"

"What's the total?" Peter interrupted to ask the man behind the desk.

The clerk tapped a few commands into the computer on his desk, waited a moment, then announced, "Four hundred fifty thousand has been promised so far."

"Is it genuine?" Peter asked as he studied the high technology scattered about like so much cheap office equipment.

"We've collected a lot by credit card—that you'll get. The rest are pledges—expect about fifty percent of those to materialize." Clearly they had this operation well established.

"Um," Peter agreed noncommittally as he finished the last of Zosia's drink. "How's it disbursed?"

"Once we've collected it all, we'll deposit it into a special account to pay your medical bills." The clerk hesitated, then added, "Of course, we'll need to take a minor administrative fee. Fifteen percent."

"That won't work," Peter replied, feeling a bit better, or at least a little more numb. "I'll probably have to go into hiding and change my name. I won't be able to use the funds if they are in a medical account."

"We could deposit them directly into your personal account," the clerk offered. "Of course, the administrative fees will be higher. Twenty percent."

The woman who had escorted Peter shifted uneasily.

"Five percent," Peter replied, "and I won't feel obliged to mention these fees to my next audience."

There was a slight hesitation, then the clerk pressed a button and picked up the phone. He explained the situation, nodded his head, and cradled the phone, smiling. "Ten percent and we won't mention the redirection."

"Three," Peter countered. Alex smiled—he could have saved himself a trip.

"Three? That wouldn't even cover our expenses!"

"Charge it to advertising costs," Peter suggested.

The clerk excused himself and left the room. When he returned, he suggested timidly, "Five?"

"Done," Peter agreed.

"We'll need your bank details."

"I live under a pseudonym and have no accounts or legal standing in this country. Sign it all over to my agent here. Mr. Przewalewski will see that it is used as intended." Peter indicated Alex with a brusque wave of the hand.

Alex could not believe his luck—no cajoling, no bargaining, no sharing with the Brits! A list formed in his head: rifles, bullets, detonators . . . How much could they get? He suppressed an urge to hug his son-in-law.

"All of it?" the clerk asked.

"Every fucking penny," Peter answered bitterly. He picked up a pen and a loose sheet of paper off the desk, and at the bottom of the blank page he signed his name. "Fill in the details," he ordered curtly as he handed the page to Alex. As Alex stared nonplussed at the signature, Peter, without another word, walked out of the office.

The woman who had been assigned to help Peter stared after him. She thought perhaps she should follow, but he had seemed so determinedly rude that she decided he could find his own way out. He had been so charming upon his arrival and now he was so sullen! "Moody fellow," she muttered to herself. Alex and the clerk nodded their agreement.

As he walked down the hall toward an exit, Peter was unable to shake the feeling that it had been an utter disaster. Not financially—that part had at least been salvaged, but in every other way it was a pointless and humiliating experience. He had been there to talk about their fight for freedom and had ended up in a debate about medical expenses. Had anybody been convinced of anything? The media circus was beginning to wear on him. And these headaches, the nausea— they were so overwhelming and so unpredictable! God, to show such weakness in front of so many people! He had been obliged to retreat into morose silence throughout the last portion of the show. What would people think?

He walked out the back door into the sultry late afternoon. The heat hit him in the face like a blast from a furnace. Even with his protective shades, he winced at the bright sunshine, and it took a moment to realize a small knot of people were gathered there, ostensibly waiting for him. One or two had cameras mounted like second heads on their shoulders, a few others had the intense look of local reporters, but the rest seemed to have no news affiliation whatsoever. The heavy metal door clanged shut behind him, and he realized it was too late to retreat back into the building.

As he descended the few steps into the crowd, he noticed that a number of the people were in a group. They were all young men with shaved heads, each wearing, despite the oppressive heat, heavy black boots. They sported sleeveless T-shirts and an array of tattoos on their arms including the crossed-ax symbol that was the ubiquitous replacement for the illegal swastika.

"Hey! Nigger lover!" one called out to him.

Huh? That would not have been Dr. Whitmer's opinion, he thought in a sudden confusion. The heat pummeled him, and the sun had reignited the pain in his head.

"Fucking Jew!" another shouted.

"Faggot!"

"Motherfucker!"

Then somebody yelled, "Traitor!"

He turned toward the one who had said that. "To whom?" he asked, genuinely curious.

"To the white race!" the youth shouted in reply. "You're a weakling!"

"Inferior!"

"They're defending our race and you betray them!"

"They should have shot you!"

"Bet he's not even white! Bet if we scrape a bit, we'll find he's a nigger!" a lad asserted, pulling out a knife and brandishing it threateningly.

Peter sighed. They were blocking his exit. Then another of them pulled out a small gun; his comrades pulled back slightly to form a loose circle around Peter. The several reporters and cameramen jumped back in alarm, or perhaps excitement. They had been sent out to get a "local-color segment" lasting a few seconds and more likely to be canned than screened, and here they were witnesses to a confrontation, maybe even a murder! It would make the headlines!

Peter glanced at the media people, thoroughly disgusted. It was clear he could expect no help from that quarter. As they whispered excitedly into their microphones, he turned his gaze back to the boys and surveyed them contemptuously.

"Call that a gun?" he asked, pointing at the ridiculous weapon. Diplomacy, explanations, even a debate, might have been more effective than ridicule, but he was in no mood for chatter. His head hurt.

"Want to try it?" the boy answered.

"Sure," Peter responded, and indicating the spot in front of him, said, "Stand here—the cameras will get a better view of your ugly face."

The boy hesitated, realizing suddenly the possible consequences of his brazen action. His mouth jerked convulsively as he tried to think of a way out, but it was too late. His options were to commit a felonious assault with a weapon on-camera or to back down in front of his comrades. Actually, he had no choice. On the one hand, the justice system would imprison him, he'd be a hero in the jail, and he'd be a hero when he got out. On the other hand, his buddies would humiliate him, beat him up, and possibly kill him. Unaware that he was taking orders from his intended victim, he went and stood where Peter had indicated.

The fellow with the knife was looking quite surly at being upstaged. Peter glanced at him, fixing his height, weight, and location in his head, then he turned back toward the boy with the gun and waited. At the moment the boy raised the gun, Peter executed a sweeping kick that knocked it out of the boy's hand and continued up and into the knife wielder's face. Peter landed slightly off-balance, hammering a knee into the ground, but he quickly recovered into a crouch and spun around, prepared to take on all comers.

There was no reaction—they stood with their mouths stupidly open. The boy who had held the gun stared disconsolately at his hand; the one with the knife was on the ground moaning and holding his face. Seeing their condition, Peter straightened and walked over to the gun. It lay outside the circle of bullies, and as he went through them, they found the wherewithal to move aside. All but the knife wielder turned to look at him.

Peter picked up the gun, sputtering derisively as he looked at it. "Little boys shouldn't play with grown-up things," he muttered to himself, and removed the clip. He tossed the gun onto the ground near the reporters and pocketed the clip.

Contemptuously, he scanned the boys, who were only just beginning to recover themselves, and said, "You really are too stupid for words." Then he turned and walked off.

One of the men whom Peter had thought was a reporter jogged after him.

"Mr. Halifax!" he called out as he caught up with Peter. Peter did not stop walking, but the irritating fellow jogged jovially around in front of him and kept pace with him by trotting backward. "You don't believe, sir, do you?"

"What?"

"Jesus. You don't believe in Jesus, do you?" He shoved a pamphlet toward Peter.

"I'm sorry"—Peter shook his head in vague disbelief—"I don't understand." When would they leave him alone?

"Jesus loves you. Jesus will solve your every problem. It's all in here! Read it!" The man pushed the pamphlet into Peter's hands.

Peter nodded as he grasped the literature. Was the *entire country* insane?

"You should love your enemies. Turn the other cheek! Remember, Jesus loves you."

Peter formulated a scathing response, but then, remembering the presence of the microphones, he decided against saying anything. There were a lot of religious people among their financial backers; it was better to remain silent. He smiled and responded to the man's assertion by saying, "I'm sure he does." Peter pocketed the pamphlet, putting it next to the bullets and, waving farewell, quickened his pace so that he could lose his new backward-trotting friend.

The phone rang and rang. It took forever for Peter to drag himself out of the deep sleep into which he had retreated. Elspeth would be furious, he had to wake himself up before she noticed he was sleeping, before she started kicking him. Oh, God, those new shoes of hers. They hurt. His whole side hurt from yesterday morning. And he had not cleaned them yet, even though she had told him to. But how could he, she was always wearing them! He had to wait until night, and last night he had forgotten. He would have to do them tonight, he dare not forget again. Was it night? Had he forgotten again? Was that why he was having trouble waking up? Damn, the telephone!

He rolled over in his bed and stared at it. A bed. A telephone. America. It was still daylight; he must not have slept long since returning from the studio. Certainly not long enough to lose his headache. He sighed and picked up the receiver.

"What the hell happened?" Alex's voice leapt out at him.

"Huh?"

"Why didn't you call us?"

"What?"

"You're on the news. That little encounter with those boys. Did you know it was filmed?"

"Hah! How could I not know? They were five meters away—those cowards!" Peter rubbed his eyes.

"Why didn't you call us?"

"Why?" Peter squinted and blinked, trying to bring his vision into focus.

"So we could prepare!"

"Prepare what?"

"A statement." Alex stopped short of saying, "*You idiot!*"

"I think the incident was self-explanatory," Peter responded angrily. For this his blessed sleep had been disturbed?

"But it was a great opportunity!"

"What are you talking about?"

"Well, you blew your chance to say something profound there, but we could still have issued a statement after the fact."

"Oh, fuck off."

"Peter! I don't expect to hear that sort of language."

"Then I'll spare you." Peter hung up the phone. He turned over to fall back asleep, but the phone rang again almost immediately. He stared at it a moment, then swearing quietly to himself, he reached over and picked it up.

"What?" he grated into the receiver.

"It's me," Zosia's voice greeted him.

"Oh. Hi, darling. Sorry, I thought it was your father."

"I'm sorry about all that."

"Not your fault."

"But it was a great opportunity, and now it's gone," Zosia chided without meaning to, having redirected her anger to something other than that she was still trembling with fear.

"Oh, for Christ's sake! Look, I'm sick, I'm tired, and I really need to rest. I'm sorry I missed a great chance to turn on the propaganda machine, but for heaven's sake, Zosia, I'm only human. Couldn't you at least congratulate me on handling the situation?"

"You took an unnecessary risk there." The local news program had opened by announcing, "International violence on our streets, foreign visitor greeted by mob as he leaves local studio," and had shown a teaser of the newsclip. Only after interminable commercials and introductions had she finally seen the outcome even as her father was getting no answer from Peter's room. When Zosia saw the gun pointed at her husband, she did not know whether he had survived the encounter, did not know as she sat there appalled, her daughter hugging her in fear, if she was witnessing his execution: he had not bothered to call when he got back to the hotel.

"I called it the way I saw it," Peter argued wearily.

"You could have talked them out of it. You should have at least tried diplomacy."

"I decided action was best."

"But you should never have tried to get both at once; that was unnecessary. The guy with the knife was no threat," she lectured like the training coach she had once been.

"It worked, didn't it?"

"What if it hadn't? They might have all jumped you if you landed on the ground."

"But I didn't!" he responded angrily. Thanks for your support and advice, he thought sarcastically.

"You hurt yourself on that landing, didn't you?"

"My knees always hurt," he replied defensively. It was not lack of skill on his part that had thrown him off-balance; rather, both assailants had offered less resistance than one would have expected—as a consequence he had overcompensated on the force of his kick and had to absorb the unused power on his landing.

"You may have done permanent damage."

"Zosiu, I called it as I saw it! Damn it, I've worked hard to overcome my physical limitations and get back into fighting form, the least you could do is congratulate me on my obvious success!"

"Congratulations." Her voice sounded cold.

"Where's Joanna?" he asked suddenly.

"I'll put her on," Zosia replied in a subdued voice.

"Hi, Daddy!" Joanna's cheerful voice greeted him a few seconds later. Funny to think she was only a few blocks away. "I saw you on TV! You looked great! But I was scared when that man pointed the gun at you." She spoke German to him—it was ironically the easiest language for the two of them.

"Yeah, I was scared, too, sweetie," he responded in German while wondering if they should not switch to a dual-language communication—she could speak Polish and he would reply in English.

"Why didn't you call us afterward?" Joanna asked. Somehow, the question was different coming from her.

What had he been thinking? "Oh, I'm sorry! I didn't think you would see it. I felt so ill, I just climbed into bed and fell asleep. I'm sorry, baby, I didn't mean to scare you. I just wasn't thinking."

"I was really proud when you knocked them both over."

"Thanks, sweetheart, I needed to hear that." He imagined the look of pride on her face and smiled at the image. "I love you, little one."

"I love you, too. I miss seeing you."

"I miss you, too."

"Will you visit us this evening?"

"I'm afraid I can't. I have another talk show to do. I'll try and sneak over there tomorrow. Okay?"

"Okay. Love you, Daddy."

"Love you, too. And tell your mommy, I love her."

"I will."

"And tell her I'm sorry I didn't call. I just wasn't thinking."

"I will."

58

*T*HE LATE-NIGHT TALK show was live, and so it was dark when Peter left the hotel to walk to the studio. A few reporters from tabloids and one magazine reporter greeted him at the entrance of the hotel. Ever since they had discovered where he was staying, it had been that way—a small coterie of journalists plying their trade.

Peter had woken up feeling much better, had eaten a good meal in his room, and had left for the studio a half hour early so that he could stop and answer questions en route. He laughed and joked with the reporters and explained about the earlier encounter with the Nazi sympathizers. He extolled the virtues of the reporters' free society where political opinions could freely be expressed without fear, then pointed out that the boys had shown exactly the tendencies that on a large scale were used to rule a continent.

"Don't be fooled by the diplomatic efforts and conciliatory rhetoric of the Nazi government. They are simply lies used by people whose base philosophy is just like that of those young men: hatred, intolerance, and violence," he lectured into the tape recorders.

"Of all the insults they hurled at you, you responded to only one," a reporter asked, "and that was being called a traitor. Why was that? Did it strike a chord? Do you feel you are betraying your government?"

"I don't accept those gangsters as a government, and I certainly feel no loyalty to the murderers who have claimed power over my people. The reason I was intrigued by that insult in particular was that my entire nation has been labeled 'traitors of the folk' because of our lack of support for and active opposition to Nazi doctrine. I was curious to see if the young man was aware of that and was referring to my being English, or if he was just hurling a random insult."

They continued chatting with him even as he decided it was time to start walking to the studio. They walked along with him, holding out their recorders or jotting down notes. Peter felt relaxed and friendly and did not bother to insert much in the way of propaganda or appeals into his answers. He just responded as truthfully as he could, feeling that in some ways the truth was the most eloquent appeal that he could make.

His mood remained good as he stepped into the studio and was introduced to the crew.

"We'll provide coffee for you during the show," a young man explained. "Since it's a late-night show and we want everyone to be relaxed and cheerful, we offer the option of spiked coffee. Which would you prefer?"

"Spiked?" Peter queried.

"With whiskey. It's called a Manhattan coffee by the people in the USA proper. Most of our guests prefer it."

"I guess I'll have to go with the spiked. I wouldn't want to break any traditions."

"Right-o." The young man made a note on his clipboard.

There were three guests, and Peter was the last to be brought on. He could not discern if that was a place of honor—save the best to last, tease the audience with promises—or whether it was simply a filler for the late-night gap. Whatever the situation, he received an enthusiastic welcome and a cheerful greeting from the host and his other two guests.

The host's name was Winston—a name that no one who knew him dared to contract to any nickname. Good-natured and humorous, he made his place on late-night television by never covering a serious topic on his program, and he had no intention of doing so that evening either.

"Well, Mr. Halifax, or rather, is it Dr. Halifax?" he began jovially after shaking Peter's hand.

"Call me Peter, please."

"Ah, good. First off, I wanted to explain that you have quite a serious message to convey to the American audience, isn't that right?"

"I think they are aware of the seriousness of the situation overseas."

"I mean, we're talking a pretty messy business here, and I don't want to give the audience any misimpressions. Among other things, you were, I believe, interrogated by the Gestapo?"

"Among other things."

"I've heard that's worse even than an IRS audit. Am I right?"

Peter wrinkled his nose. "Well, I must say, I've never been audited by your tax service, so it'd be hard to compare." He thought of a phrase he had heard only the day before. "In fact, I've never filed taxes, so I don't know what it's like to be a wage slave, just an unwaged one." The audience laughed, pleased at the humble, humorous response.

"Ah, yes," Winston continued, "but they are also aware that you're only human, and for once you might like to just relax and chat to us a bit and show us the less serious side of life in the Reich."

"Yeah, the place is an absolute barrel of laughs," Peter joked, and sipped the coffee provided.

"Maybe we should start with something easier—like your impressions of America. Certainly something about this country must have surprised you."

Peter laughed as he thought about his afternoon experiences. Then he quite judiciously launched into a series of anecdotes concerning his adventures in the NAU. In order not to mention Zosia or anyone else, he happily incorporated all the humorous stories he had ever heard about first impressions of America as his own.

He talked about being stranded at the crossing as the other pedestrians streamed across the street against the light, wondering where the toilet was when all the signs indicated some sort of employee lounge or "rest room," watching an insanely brave tourist actually *voluntarily* approach a patrolman to ask directions, getting service from a store employee—who might even apologize for not having been more prompt! The list went on. There were the ubiquitous telephones with their direct connections to anywhere, the inexplicable gadgets, the laser scanners and exotic fruit. And there was the incredible wealth of choices. Peter retold a story he had heard about buying a razor.

"It really is quite remarkable. I brought nearly everything with me since I don't have any real money, but somehow I forgot my razor. So, I went into a store and asked if they had a razor. Now, the answer one would get back home is yes or no. If the answer was yes, you would purchase said razor; if it was no, you might try again in a week or so. Of course, if you hear no three times in a row, you might check to see if razors had become illegal or needed a permit or ration card, but in general, the procedure is fairly straightforward. Anyway, I asked at this store here and this fellow behind the counter points to a display and there it was—a wall of razors! It took me half an hour to sort through the selection. I bought a disposable, and I must admit, I was quite proud when I got back to my room and discovered I really did have a razor. And not only that, the next time I went into the store, I was able to purchase a razor in less than three minutes!" The audience laughed. "Of course, I had studied beforehand and had notes in my pocket just in case I panicked." They roared their approval.

Peter continued his stories, often taking in humorous comments and observations from his fellow guests or the host. They added their own stories and impressions—one of the guests was an émigré—and the evening flowed smoothly aided by the Manhattan coffees they all drank.

"When this thing started wrapping itself around me in the car, like some sort of snake, I nearly panicked." Peter was laughing at the memory of a friend of Alex's story. "It struck me as a particularly odd way of arresting someone. Or was it an abduction? Just as well I didn't attack the driver! Thought I had gotten nabbed by the Gestapo or something. You understand"—he turned to address the audience—"nearly anything that happens to us, that is our first assumption: you know, girlfriend dumps you, must be the Gestapo! Et cetera. So there I was—"

"So you don't have seat belts there?" the host interrupted.

"No, and I never even suspected they existed! For me, a restraining device in a car meant being handcuffed to the steering wheel."

"What?" Winston looked stunned.

Peter explained the rules about his chauffeuring the family, then added, "I think I was the only one in the Reich who had to follow that rule."

"What purpose did it serve?" the host asked. One of the guests, an artist named Itto, was making odd motions as if trying to work out exactly how he would steer around a turn with such a restriction on his movements.

"I haven't a clue," Peter responded bemusedly as he watched Itto's attempts. Peter did know though: it was humiliation, pure and simple.

"Isn't it dangerous without seat belts?" Winston asked with practiced naïveté.

Peter laughed again. "I suppose it would be if the cars ran, but since they spend most of their time on the sides of the roads, it's not really a problem." The audience laughed and Peter decided to repeat the old joke. "In fact, do you know why they put rear-window defrosters on Volkswagens?"

"Why?" Itto asked, giving up on his pretend driving.

"So that you can keep your hands warm when you're pushing the car."

That got a good laugh, and Peter continued repeating all the VW jokes he could remember. It was the "people's car," Hitler's pet project.

They took a break finally, and when the cameras were back on, the host asked, "Jokes aside, what about *your* life in the Reich? Is there anything you could tell us about that?"

"You're looking for humor?" Peter had expected that but was still undecided about exactly how to handle this turn of events.

"Well, something other than doom and gloom."

"I suppose if you find stupidity funny, you'll love hearing about my previous owner." Peter had made his decision. He needed to remain human in the audience's eyes, he needed them to think of the victims of the oppression as human as well. If it took humor to do that, then he would find humor for them.

"Now, you say *owner*—what do you mean by that?" Winston asked.

"I mean the guy who owned me," Peter replied impishly.

"You mean like bought and paid for you?"

"Precisely."

"Doesn't that bother you? I mean, you just said *owner* the way I might say *boss*. Like it was a completely neutral concept."

"Oh, at first it bothered me. I guess it still does, deep down, but there is only so long that you can play pretend. After that, you have to face facts, and eventually, I realized that he was the one who should have been ashamed. Not me." Peter's words were bolder than his true feelings—he did feel ashamed and he knew that Karl never would.

"So, like, what were you called; I mean, was there a job description?"

"Yes, quite funny, but they seemed rather reluctant to call me what I was. That's one reason I'm here; I feel the populace there is uncomfortable with the system they have and might well overthrow the wretched edifice if given half a chance."

Peter expected them to follow that line of thought into social upheaval and resistance, but instead Winston asked again, "So what did they call you, then?"

"Hmm, that's difficult." Peter closed his eyes and tried to think of a suitable translation for the cumbersome phrases in his documents without mentioning the word *criminal.* "Something like 'subhuman, life-sentenced, privately maintained, domestic forced laborer on trial term available through the largesse of the department of internal affairs and in the end responsible and returnable to that department.'"

"What!"

"It's a clumsy translation, but you get the gist."

"Wow! You sort of lose track of the fact that you're talking about a person."

"Indeed. In fact, my name appears only incidentally in their files. Everything about me is registered either according to my number here"—Peter tapped his sleeve—"or under my owner's name. You know, like you'd register a dog or a steer."

"So, what was this owner guy like?"

"What was he like? I'll tell you." Peter then regaled them all with story after story of Karl's idiocy. An occasional rearrangement of events, speaking words out loud that were only thought, providing a voice-over type of narrative, forgetting the pain—a portrait of Karl emerged: venal, petty, vain, stupid, lazy. The list of Karl's flaws and foibles made for good anecdotes.

"So what did you do then?" the other guest, a model named Arieka, asked. She had been laughing so hard tears were streaming down her face as Peter recounted some of his discoveries during his first days on the job.

He took a swig from his fourth cup of coffee and answered, "What could I do? I tied his shoes. I mean, you make the simple assumption that a grown man knows how to tie his own shoes and . . ." Peter made a face and threw his hands up. "But I should have known better," he continued in between the laughter. "After all, he *was* in the government."

"Now that sounds familiar!" the host chimed in. The audience roared.

Arieka lit a cigarette and offered the pack around. Itto accepted and on an impulse Peter did as well.

"Oh, now that's interesting," Winston observed, "I was under the impression you didn't smoke."

"Oh, I don't usually," Peter replied with deceptive honesty. "For most of my life it's been illegal or unavailable."

"Illegal?" Arieka asked. "Do they have the same registration of smokers?"

"No, not at all. When I said illegal, I meant illegal for me. You see, I had no rights—not even the right to smoke myself into an early grave." The audience laughed at the absurdity. "I would guess I was the only person in the Reich who wasn't legally permitted to kill me."

"So it wasn't concern for your health?" Arieka asked disingenuously.

"I don't think so." Peter winked at her. He quite liked her—she had helped him out on a number of his stories, offering the obvious straight lines or leading questions like an unrehearsed double act. "In any case, I certainly inhaled a lot. You see, *mein Herr* had me light his cigarettes—apparently his mother told him not to play with matches either"—Peter paused to let the laughter quiet down—"and every time I'd light a cigarette for him, he blew smoke at me. I just thought I'd find out what it was like to smoke a cigarette from the filtered end."

Something in Peter's whimsical tone of voice and studiously overcasual attitude made the audience roar with laughter. He himself marveled that he could be so humorous about things that had hurt so very much.

"I blow smoke at a man to turn off unwanted sexual advances," Arieka admitted.

"Now there's something I bet you hadn't considered," the host offered.

"No, I hadn't." Peter drew deeply from the cigarette—not at all like a curious novice.

"What about the women? Did you get it on with any of them?" Itto asked.

"You'd have to see his wife to believe her." Peter shook his head in mock horror.

"Probably not unlike mine," the host joked. The audience gasped appropriately. "Oops, did I say that?" the host responded, then turning toward the camera, made a mad plea to be forgiven by his spouse. When he had finished, he turned toward Peter. "But certainly that's a long time to go without! Maybe a daughter?"

"There is a difference between dying to have sex and being willing to die for it," Peter answered somewhat seriously. "Besides, a well-raised German girl would never have considered tainting herself by mixing with an inferior such as myself. I was, to them, a lesser being," he added, a note of bitterness creeping into his voice. He caught his error as he noticed the look on his host's face, so he quickly added, "As you would be as well."

"Me?" Winston asked with what sounded like genuine astonishment. "But you don't know anything about me!"

"Your decadent behavior betrays your low origins," Peter stated dryly.

Expertly following Peter's cue, Winston asked, "Decadent? What do I do that's decadent?"

"Ah, what don't you Americans do?" Peter answered casually, pleased that he could make it clear to his audience that he was not, by their standards, an exception. Of course, it wasn't quite true, but it was close enough, and he began, without hesitation, to list off typically American behavior—actions of which they would normally be quite proud—and explained how each could be interpreted as decadent, disruptive, or insufficiently deferential. "Your First Amendment alone is proof to them of an incorrigible lack of discipline in this society," Peter stated as part of his list. "You're so disorganized, you let people name their children anything they want to—no book of names for you! And your marriage laws—or lack thereof—show a complete disregard for racial purity!" he concluded, nicely bringing the topic back to where it had started.

"Phew! Do you think they actually bought into that?" Itto asked.

"Clearly."

"But the sex thing. It sounds confusing, how do they keep track?"

"For the average citizen, believe it or not, there are actually posters explaining what is and is not allowed. In particular, sex with a non-Aryan would not only have been immoral, it would have been akin to treason."

"We have something similar where I came from," Arieka said. "I lived in the city before the civil war, before I fled to America, but back in the village, if you mixed with the neighboring people, you would be shunned—even killed."

"Were they white?" the host asked.

Arieka raised an eyebrow in obvious disbelief. "In the middle of Africa? No, they were black, like me."

"How could you tell the difference?" Itto asked naively. He had been hammering the coffee as well.

Peter snickered into his hand. Arieka laughed outright. "How do Europeans tell each other apart? Tribal hatreds always find a way."

Winston veered the conversation away from such serious topics, and it continued for some time in a lively and generally lighthearted manner. After his third cigarette, Peter decided he had pushed the curiosity idea far enough and he refused more. At a break in the topic, the host pointed at Peter's left hand and said, "I notice you're not wearing a wedding ring. Does that mean the young ladies in the audience have a chance? Or is there a Mrs. Halifax out there?"

Peter thought it would be amusing to say there was no "Mrs. Halifax," only a deadly colonel, but he had trained himself to respond differently and he dutifully replied, "I cannot comment on my personal life. Too many other lives would be put at stake."

"Oh, just a hint," Arieka begged.

Peter shook his head.

"Well, what about your handler? Information is that a member of the Polish government in exile is handling most of your trip. How in the world are you mixed up with them?" the host asked.

"A coalition of interested parties representing a wide variety of European nationalities sponsored my trip here," Peter lied, "and they elected one member as their representative. It was quite arbitrary."

"Are you going back?" Itto pressed.

"I can't comment."

"Will you be staying in America?" Itto cleverly rephrased the question.

"I can't comment."

"The man has survived Gestapo interrogations, Itto," Arieka chided. "Do you think you're going to trick him now?"

"Why in the world would anyone go back to such an awful place?" Winston asked, breaking his own rule.

"Perhaps to fight for his homeland," Arieka said, saving Peter from answering. She looked directly into Peter's eyes and predicted somewhat sadly, "You will go back."

"I can't comment," Peter replied with a rueful smile.

"You will go back, and you will fight," Arieka insisted. "We all saw you on the news this evening—you will fight. And even if you won't say it, I will." She turned toward the audience and admonished, "You should support him. He fights for freedom and justice in this world! There is too little of that, and we should support these people wherever they are. He will give his life; at least you can write a check!" She turned toward Peter and said, "Whom do you recommend?"

Peter considered for a moment, then allowed himself the rare pleasure of answering truthfully. "My personal favorite is the Home Army. Their American fund is registered at 666 Fifth Avenue, Manhattan F.C. Send your checks there." He was mindful of the furious English response he could expect from that, and it might also give the Nazis a hint as to his current location. Oh, well, he thought, somewhat drunkenly, to hell with them. None of the English contingent had bothered to say so much as a word to him yet. The Armia Krajowa, the Home Army, *was* his favorite; after all, they paid his salary, such as it was.

<hr>

59

*T*HE NEXT MORNING Peter went to his in-laws for a late breakfast. For the first time since his arrival, he noticed that he was being tailed. He wondered if he had been followed all along and had only just noticed now or if it had just started. Either way, he felt disgusted by the Underground's lack of trust in him. As he jumped off and back onto a subway, finally losing the fellow, he thought that perhaps the Underground had been concerned for his safety after his encounter with the Nazi sympathizers and he was frustrating them by losing his bodyguard. Serves them right for leaving him in the dark, he thought as the train sped out of the station.

Joanna jumped on him at the door and would not let go, wrapping herself tenaciously around him. He held and hugged her and kissed her repeatedly as he watched Anna mix up the pancakes. It was an American recipe she had picked up, and he thought he might add it to his repertoire. Anna assured him, though, that the essential ingredient was the maple syrup that would be poured on afterward, and since that was completely unavailable back home, there was little point in learning how to make them. Nevertheless he watched; it gave him an excuse to stay away from the table and not converse with either Alex or Zosia. He suspected both were somewhat miffed by his performance on the late-night show, and that no one had mentioned it yet added to this suspicion.

"So what did you think of last night?" he finally prompted.

"Great job," Alex enthused.

"Great," Anna agreed.

"Yet another personality, eh?" Zosia muttered somewhat incongruously.

He frowned at her, but before he could ask what she meant, Joanna chimed in with, "I thought you were wonderful, Dad!"

"You stayed up?"

"Of course!" she giggled.

Alex ground out his cigarette and urged, "Why don't you sit down, boy, you look tired."

"You've registered as an addict?" Peter asked.

Alex studied the smoldering butt and replied, "Yeah, we both did. They have special waiver forms for émigrés to make registration easier. We get to skip all the 'smoking will kill you' classes. They figure we're all a lost cause."

"You registered, too?" Peter asked Anna.

She nodded as she added some more flour to the batter. "Yes, but I've quit. Alex uses up my allotment."

"Two packs a day, eh, Alex?"

"Yeah, yeah, yeah, don't tell me about it. Anyway, I give some of Anna's away. Makes me look generous."

"You shouldn't smoke in here," Zosia said between yawns as she stared sleepily into her coffee cup.

"No," Anna agreed, "I've asked you not to, at least not while Zosia's here. And Joanna."

"Okay, all right," Alex groaned, getting up. "I'll be back in a couple of minutes. Peter, why don't you come out with me?"

Peter considered Alex's invitation. He did not want to talk to Alex, but on the other hand a cigarette would be really nice. After smoking almost a pack the previous night, he had been craving them all morning. "All right," he agreed, setting Joanna down. "I'll just be a minute," he assured her.

They leaned against the wall of the hallway near the door. It was not legal to smoke in the hallways, but to go down and out to the street would take too long what with the pancakes already on the griddle. Alex offered Peter a cigarette and lit it for him, then lit one for himself.

"Well, what do you want?" Peter asked abruptly.

"Hey, maybe I was just being friendly. Don't get much chance to talk to you, old boy."

"Tell me, do the other Brits here speak with your accent?" That awful, whiny, stilted accent.

"Yeah, the old ones do. The young ones—their kids—have a sort of American twang to it all. Sounds really odd."

"I can imagine."

"Course, some of the new arrivals sound like you. Is your accent common in England now?" Alex asked without mentioning how low class it sounded. It grated on him terribly.

"Can't say. It seems to be ubiquitous in London," Peter answered, then added just to annoy Alex, "We're all the same now, same lack of rights, same low *Nichtdeutsch* classification, same accent. Those clever Germans have managed to solve a thousand-year-old class problem in just a couple of decades."

"Replaced, rather than solved. It's the Normans all over again."

"Let's hope not. Can you imagine grammarians, a thousand years from now, chiding schoolchildren for the vulgar habit of *not* putting prepositions at the end of their sentences? Anyway, what did you want to ask me?"

Alex sighed. Was he that obvious? "All right. I wanted to know exactly how truthful you've been about that messy business with your arrest and your friends' deaths."

"Why?"

"I've been keeping in touch with our English friends here—the ones who paid for your trip—and, well, either no one recognizes you or they're keeping quiet about it. Even after you laid out the details on that show."

"So?"

"So after your performance last night—by the way, good job on that plug at the end. Did you set it up with that woman?"

"No. It was spontaneous."

"It was great. We sent somebody posthaste to the office in the middle of the night to take calls after that, and it was just as well. The phones have been ringing off the hook ever since."

"Thanks. So, you were saying?"

"Oh, yeah. Well, our friends were a bit upset at being excluded."

Peter shrugged. "She asked for one name."

"Oh, I don't blame you." Alex ground out his cigarette on the wall, flicked the end onto the floor, and lit another cigarette. "In fact, I was very pleased. No, it's not that. They just seemed to realize that they've been snubbing you. They were afraid of the negative consequences of being associated with your visit, you know, divisiveness, et cetera. Now, as the money is rolling into our office, they've realized that might be a mistake. So, they've invited us all to a reception at England House. I wanted to check with you before I said yes or no. I wanted to give you a chance to back out without Zosia knowing just in case there's something you're not telling her."

Peter stooped down and picked up the end that Alex had dropped.

"Oh, there's a cleaning person here."

"So that requires you to act like a pig?" Peter asked rather quietly as he shoved the end into his pocket. As he straightened, he answered Alex's question, "I've told you everything I know about what happened then. If they know more, I'd be glad to hear it."

"So you really have no idea what happened?"

Peter shook his head.

"Okay then. Do you want to go?"

"Yeah. Yeah, I don't care if they know me. I have nothing to hide. It should be obvious by now that I wasn't the one who ratted us out. There's just one thing."

"What?"

"No cameras, no press, no publicity. I'm tired. Just an evening out. Okay?" Peter pleaded.

"I'll make that a condition of your acceptance."

"Thanks. Let's get some food."

"Sure."

Over breakfast they talked about how Alex and Anna were adjusting to their new home.

"Your third homeland, huh, Alex?" Peter asked between mouthfuls of Anna's delicious pancakes. She was right, he thought, the syrup was essential.

Alex nodded pensively. "I'm getting used to it." He added philosophically, "I guess you get used to anything."

Zosia glanced at Peter as if expecting him to react badly to that comment, but he did not. Instead he said, "Life here certainly seems to be agreeing with you."

Alex patted his stomach and laughed. "Yeah, it took me a while to get used to so much food, but I'm learning to control myself now."

"I was more commenting on your other changes. You look quite different."

"Quite deliberately. I got rid of some of the gray and acquired these." He pulled off his glasses and contemplated them. "Spectacles. Didn't realize I was missing so much before!"

"Ah. Why the hair dye? Do you think it makes you more American?"

"No. You remember, we were Ryszard's parents in Göringstadt, don't you?"

"Oh, yes."

"Well, he was sure to have been observed throughout that time. We think we've purged all the photographs of him and Kasia with us, and with you and Zosia, by the way, but we can never be sure. So, now that I'm a public figure, it's best if I don't look like that fellow that may turn up in a photograph in some security file on Ryszard. You can imagine how disastrous it would be if at some future date someone stumbles across a photograph of Ryszard in the company of a current member of a government in exile."

"Yes, I can."

"So, I do what I can to minimize that danger, however remote."

"Makes sense. How are you fitting in otherwise?" Peter asked. Zosia looked at him, as if surprised by his question.

"Well enough. Better than the last time I changed homelands." Alex laughed.

"How old were you when you were deported?"

"By the time I actually landed in the General Gouvernement—eighteen. Prior to that we spent a number of years in an internment camp."

"Who's we?"

"My family, my mother included, though by no stretch of the imagination could she be considered foreign. But she had married an immigrant, so . . ." Alex's voice fell off as he reminisced.

"What happened to them?" Peter asked.

Alex shrugged. "I got pulled out at eighteen. That's the last I saw them. Never was able to trace them."

"I'm sorry," Peter responded softly.

Joanna looked up from her food. "You lost your mommy and daddy?" she asked her grandfather.

Alex nodded. To try to lighten the mood for her sake, he said, "I don't know what happened to them. Maybe they lived happily somewhere."

Joanna nodded in agreement, determined to accept the unbelievable in order to cheer up her grandfather.

"What happened when you arrived on the Continent?" Peter asked, trying to gently veer the subject away from Alex's missing family.

"I suppose I was being sent to work somewhere. There was a huge transport of us and it was terribly disorganized. We were marched all over the place. At some point, I realized I was near to where my father said he had come from, so I just walked away from the march. Walked into the woods and disappeared. Stumbled across some partisans."

"And?" The ending was not obvious to Peter.

"Oh, I guess I looked bedraggled enough that they took pity on me, and I knew a few words of Polish. They knew there was a transport of English deportees, so they had no trouble believing my story, and they let me stay with them. They thought my language abilities would be useful. I fought a bit with their group, then moved on and into the city."

"Kraków?"

"Yes. Moved up in the Home Army, and, well, you know the rest."

"Vaguely. But how did you manage to learn German without an English accent? You were quite old."

"Oh, I learned it when I was a kid."

"In the internment camp?"

"No, I just refined it there. You see, my father was from a village near Kraków, or Krakau, as it was called, so he fell into the Austrian partition of Poland and had been schooled in German. He was a musician and worked in Kraków, but then after the first war, he moved to Vienna to work there. When anti-Semitism became a problem for him there—"

"He was Jewish?" Peter and Zosia asked simultaneously.

"Seems so. Anyway, he got a job in London. I guess he told the immigration authorities he was Catholic because there was no record of his being Jewish in their files when they got captured by the Nazis. Or maybe they didn't record that sort of information. I think in the internment camp, he told the doctor his mother had been American, so that he could explain being circumcised. Or some such nonsense. They bought his story—at least while I was there. He and Mom always fretted about that, though."

"What was she?" Zosia asked suspiciously.

"Anglican. Didn't you know?"

Zosia reddened. "No."

"Ah, it wasn't important, neither practiced anything."

"Your father converted to marry me," Anna explained, glancing at Peter meaningfully.

"As I was saying," Alex continued, "despite marrying an Englishwoman, my father's dream was to return to Vienna, once things there settled down. He kept preparing for the big move and insisted the whole family learn German, so I did, from childhood."

"That explains the Austrian accent," Peter commented.

"Yes, and the fact that I never really learned Polish. A few words here and there, but he thought it was too much to ask us to be trilingual."

"So, you were a rather reluctant Polish patriot," Peter remarked.

Alex shrugged. "I was British, what can I say? I never expected to be anything else, except maybe Austrian. Circumstances and the Germans changed my mind and here I am. Or rather, there I was. Now I'm here."

"And you've changed allegiances yet again," Peter teased.

"How so?"

"You used to say *we* when talking about the British, now you say *we* and mean the Poles."

"Ah, well, dealing with the ex-pat community here has made me a bit less British than I used to be. I imagine someday you'll have trouble thinking of yourself as British."

"English," Peter corrected. "I've never felt any connection to those others."

"Divide and conquer," Anna interjected.

"I suppose," Peter agreed. "In any case, I never had any affinity for the ex-pats, either. Nobody at home does."

"Well, my guess is, you'll have trouble feeling at home among the English pretty soon," Alex reiterated.

"Probably. My connections with home have already grown pretty tenuous."

Anna shrugged. "I guess we all learn to adapt."

"Does that mean you'll become an American?" Peter asked.

"Never!" Zosia snorted.

"Maybe," Alex corrected her, "but I'm old and it's a bit late to change. Besides, I'm only here as a foreign representative. But"—and here Alex switched to English to try to exclude Joanna from the conversation—"if something happened to Zosia, I would raise her daughter here as an American."

Anna began conversing with Joanna to make the rude language transition and their sudden exclusion from the conversation less noticeable to her. They chatted about Joanna's plans for the day in Polish, and their words filled the awkward silence that followed Alex's words.

"If something happens to me," Zosia said deliberately and too calmly, "then she will be raised by Peter in Szaflary. He is, after all, her father."

"I don't think that's all gone through yet," Alex replied, but then showing his palms in a defensive gesture, he added quickly, "But I misspoke. I meant if something happened to both of you."

"And Marysia and Stefi and Tadek," Zosia stated coldly.

"Oh, Zosiu! You had us as the guardians before! You trusted us then!"

"That was when you lived there. I don't want my daughter raised here."

"Why not? It's a good life. If both you and Peter are dead, don't you think she'll be sufficiently traumatized? Don't you think she'd deserve a better life than what can be offered there?"

"No!" Zosia slapped the table. "The last thing she'd want is to lose her home as well as us! She'll stay there!"

Alex made a face as if he disagreed, but realized that arguing with Zosia was useless. "Well, let's hope it never comes to that," he said finally, then switching to Polish he joined Anna and Joanna in their conversation.

60

ONLY ONE APPEARANCE WAS scheduled for that day. It had been arranged well before all the publicity, and so the tiny church hall on Lexington was completely inadequate to accommodate the audience. Folding tables laden with pamphlets, magazines, books, and membership forms were set up at the back, each one staffed by several representatives from an exile organization. Peter and the host sat on folding chairs at the front on a small, raised stage and waited for the program to begin. As he waited, Peter scanned the tables: arms-running fronts for well-established Underground groups, political action fronts, religious affiliations, the Prisoners-of-Conscience International Foundation, friendship organizations, aid organizations, nationalists, internationalists . . . Some names he did not even recognize. Of those he did, some he wholeheartedly supported, others he had his doubts about, and a few worried him with their alarming agendas and uncontrolled memberships prone to acts of wanton and useless violence.

He studied the contents of one table loaded with various devices: long rods with handles, short rods that looked like torches or flashlights, a heavy belt with something attached, a curved metal object, odd-looking knives . . . He squinted to read the table's banner: an aid organization for political prisoners. Putting the name together with comments he had heard, he guessed the devices were instruments of torture manufactured in the NAU that somehow found their way into the hands of the secret police of repressive regimes.

Feeling vaguely ill, he turned his gaze to the walls. Maybe it was those coffees he had drunk the night before, or possibly it was the American cigarettes—they were different from what he was used to. Filtered, for one thing, but they also had a funny taste. They must have something in them, he thought.

There seemed to be a minor commotion at the back of the room. The people who had bought tickets in advance were the sort who had been interested in European affairs even before the media circus. They were trying to get in past the crowd clamoring for the few unsold tickets. Those were the ones who would be fascinated this week and forget his existence by next. Oh, well, as long as their money was good, he didn't really care.

Eventually one of the organizers decided to move the folding tables to another room and use the extra space for more chairs, thus increasing the at-the-door admissions. The grand rearrangement would delay the start of the modest program, that was clear. Resigned to the inevitable, Peter lowered his head, closed his eyes, and let his mind wander.

Zosia, Joanna, impressions of America. Home, the smell of pine, the claustrophobic damp cement. Young faces, children—all staring at him. He checked; no, it was not the Vogel children. Row upon row of faces. All scrubbed clean, all boys in uniform. He looked down on them from an adult height. Not something from his school days. Where in the world . . . ? Their expressions were a mixture of curiosity, contempt, boredom. He was supposed to say something, he knew that, but what?

His hands were shaking, he looked down at the small length of chain connecting his wrists. Another chain led down from his wrists to one that bound his ankles together. Shackled such that he could hardly walk. Now he remembered, he had hobbled into the schoolroom under guard, had been presented to the students as an object lesson. It was part of his reeducation, something from long ago that he had chosen to forget, a day from those three months of special treatment. Under torture he had been taught what to say, had memorized pompous words of self-denunciation. But they were lost to him. The boys waited expectantly but he was speechless. They had used so much pain to teach him the words, all he could remember was the pain. He was shaking with fear, with the knowledge of what they would do to him if he failed, but he could not remember what he was supposed to say!

Someone prodded him roughly. Speak! But he couldn't; he could not even remember the first word. He knew the gist of it, that he was evil and recognized his evil and begged the Fatherland to accept his service as expiation, but that was useless—he had forgotten the words and he had none of his own. He stood helplessly shaking; the boys grew restless. Somebody prodded him again, then he was hit several times. That only terrified him more, pushed the words even further from his mind. Finally, fed up, somebody had grabbed him and dragged him stumbling over his chains out of the room.

Their retribution for his failure had been horrible and, even now, completely forgotten.

Why that memory? Why now? he wondered as he opened his eyes and looked at the audience. Not the rows of faces, not the people looking up at him; it wasn't that. Another table, now empty, was turned sideways; its legs were unlocked and folded down with a distinctive creak. The metal legs snapped into position against the wooden surface with a resounding thunk, and he flinched in response.

That was it—the tables! *Their retribution.* Suddenly it all came back to him.

In their rush to punish him for his insubordination, for his eloquent, unintended silence, they had not even bothered to take him back across the vast installation to the prison; instead they had hustled him along the hall, hurled him down the stairs into the basement of the school. He remembered how he had tripped over his chains, tumbled to the bottom of the steps, and lain in a miserable, helpless heap. The words had come to him then, as if by magic, and he had desperately recited them, begging them to return him to the classroom. But they were far too furious with him; screaming obscenities and threats at him the entire way, they had dragged him to his feet and into the boiler room, and there, shutting the massive steel doors behind them, they had unfolded a stored table. He could still hear how the legs groaned, how the metal catches snapped noisily into place. They had thrown him onto the table on his back, not even bothering to remove his chains, letting his head hang partly over the edge. The edge of the table pressed against his skull, and he remembered the view as he had looked up and backward: asbestos-covered pipes and a concrete wall. They had tied a length of rope from one elbow, down under the table, to the other; he remembered the cutting pain as they jerked the rope tight, how it pulled the chain between his wrists taut. They had used another rope and the chain between his ankles to tie his feet down and had then beaten him mercilessly with a length of electrical cord, the old-fashioned way. No drugs, no equipment, just pure, unmitigated anger, for he had humiliated his trainer.

His hands had been trapped by the way they had tied him, and he remembered how he had struggled vainly to spread them over his lower abdomen and groin to protect himself. The cable had cut across the tendons on the back of his hands, leaving welts that had taken ages to heal. "A folding table," he muttered, inspecting his hands for identifiable scars.

"Hmm?" the host, next to him, asked.

"Oh, nothing. Are you from this area?" Peter's voice shook slightly.

"No." The host smiled. "I moved to the Free City ten years ago. I'm trying to raise my family here. It's a bit rough, you know, overcrowded, the prices are so high, the extra taxes . . ."

Peter listened to the reassuring litany of complaints, nodding his head in solemn agreement.

The program went well and the questions were knowledgeable, coming mostly from the front of the room—the location where the advance-ticket holders were seated. There were a lot of questions about England from people who had left decades ago. What was it like, how were the people faring? Was his experience in some way typical? They were thirsty for any uncensored news, and Peter felt sorry that he had nothing new to offer; he had not been home in over ten years.

Then the questions turned back to him and one woman rose and asked, "Mr. Halifax, you've been through a lot. You were imprisoned or enslaved for a long time. Are you free now?" She tapped her chest. "Free here?"

He held her gaze for a long moment. He did not know what to say. The audience was expectantly silent, not even a cough or a shuffle of feet. The woman gave him a weak but encouraging smile, and he realized he was talking to someone who also had experiences of some sort. He felt he owed her something, but he did not know whether it was the truth, or a comforting lie.

He scanned the faces in the room, looking for the answer. Did he dare tell them what he felt? The pain, the isolation, the unending fear? The irrational anger, the sudden surges of overpowering hatred? The horrible feeling that his own mind had been turned against him? The weariness at being perpetually grateful to everyone? The pathetic and selfish desire that someone, somewhere, might recognize his self-sacrifice and maybe, just once, say thank-you? Did he dare speak the truth for the sake of the one or two in the audience who might feel comforted to know that they were not alone in their perpetual torment? Or must he betray them and tell comforting lies to serve the greater good? His eyes fell upon Alex, and he recognized the growing anger in his handler's expression. There were only seconds left before his silence would say more than any words. Spit it out! Alex was telling him. *Give them what they need!*

"Yes," he said at last, his voice more unsteady than he would have liked. "Yes, I'm free. Completely free."

There was a silence after that, as if they all expected something more to be said. He lowered his head as he waited for the host to select the next question, but nobody wanted to intrude.

Peter raised his head and spoke into the silence. "I've escaped. And that's what I want for others—the freedom that I have, the peace that I have found. If you can support us in our fight, I want you to know that it would make all that I suffered worthwhile." His voice dropped to a whisper as he forced himself to emphasize, "All of it." He took a deep breath, saw that Alex's expression had softened to approval.

"I want to thank all of you," Peter continued. "I want to express my deepest gratitude for what you who support us have done, and I want to encourage those of you who have remained aloof to please join us. We need you, we need your help, and we are truly grateful. Your money will do wonders for us—my own story bears witness to that." He paused and swallowed, then allowed himself to add, "I would also like to take this opportunity to publicly express my undying gratitude to those who have personally helped me and for the infinite patience they have shown me." He did not turn his head toward her, but he let his eyes stray to where Zosia was discreetly sitting. She caught his look and returned a cautious smile of recognition.

Afterward he wandered down into the audience and continued to chat with the various people who approached him. Nobody came up and spat out the word *traitor,* and Peter imagined if he had disappointed anyone with his words, then they had already left, perhaps to pick up the bottle or the knife or whatever gave them solace. How many suicides? he wondered. How many suicides would now be on his conscience? A few people who spoke with him did use the word *inspiring* and he blanched but accepted the praise without comment.

The host eventually came over and asked if Peter would casually move into the room with the tables so that the crowd might follow. "We've done them a bit of a disservice, hiding them away like that, and it would be nice if we could get these people to that room to look at what they have to offer," the host explained sheepishly.

Peter followed him to the other room, and as predicted, many of the audience wandered along with them. The crowd milled around talking to the representatives at each table, or to each other, and a small group continued talking with him. He wandered mindlessly with them, chatting, listening to their stories, relaxing as the mob became more diffuse and he became less the center of attention and more just another body in the crowd. As he talked with an enthusiastic young woman, he casually leaned against one of the tables and his hand brushed against something strangely familiar. Without interrupting himself, he glanced backward and stopped in midsentence.

His hand was resting on a small black device the size of a flashlight. One end had a handle with a trigger, some sort of dial, and a switch; the other end was narrower and had some exposed metal prongs. He tried to move his hand, but it felt like lead; his mouth went dry and his breathing became heavy. The bright lights overhead washed out the images of the people around him, and the noise of the room blurred into an indistinct roar as his heartbeat thundered in his ears.

Unfair, that had been the word that had ridiculously come into his mind at the time. It had been unfair and undeserved. His torturer had arbitrarily chosen him, pulling him out of a work gang, to demonstrate a new device imported, he had said, from America. He had called it a stun gun and had casually prodded Peter with the end to show its effect to a group of officers touring the prison. The result had been staggeringly painful. His legs had buckled and he had collapsed to the ground under the agonizing effect of the jolt of electricity it had delivered. They had pulled him to his feet, and as he saw his torturer approach him with the device again, he had pulled loose from the hands that held him and protested his innocence, almost yelling, "I haven't done anything wrong!"

"Now you have," the man taunted. His torturer had punished him for that insubordination by having two of the entourage hold him and, with the help of other hands pulling brutally at his face, ramming the device down his throat. When the trigger was pressed, an excruciating current raced through his body. He remembered hearing his own muffled screams, remembered his convulsive struggling, remembered how timeless moments later they had surveyed him, commenting on the device's effectiveness as he lay crumpled in agony on the ground, drooling blood and drenched in excrement.

A voice or voices emerged through the roaring waterfall of his pain. "Are you all right?" he heard. Marysia, Konrad, Zosia . . . No, someone else, and English words, not German. He was looking across at a face so he had to be standing. He shook his head to clear his vision and looked again. "Are you all right?" an intense-looking, thin, bearded man behind a table asked again.

Peter turned half around and saw the woman he had been talking to. "Are you all right?" she echoed.

"Did they use these on you?" the man asked, his concern suddenly turning to avid interest. He interpreted Peter's stunned silence as an affirmation. "Could you speak on behalf of our group? We really need to raise consciousness. Could you speak for us?"

Peter shook his head and said softly, "No."

"Please! We really need to raise funds, to get legislation passed. You must!"

"No," Peter repeated softly.

"You must speak out!" the man pressed almost angrily. "It's not fair! You must help us!"

"No," Peter mouthed. He kept shaking his head and saying "No" over and over even as he backed away, even as he thought of Teresa's word for him. Courage? "No," he said, crossing the room to the exit. "No," he was still whispering as he left the hall.

The following day there were two magazine interviews. Both were mass circulation, nonintellectual newsmagazines; both had not been interested in his story when offered exclusive interviews before his arrival. Peter had scanned both magazines to determine their styles before the interviews, and other than for the typeset and paragraph layout, he was unable to discern a difference between them. They were identical competitors for the same soft-news, gee-whiz market, and he responded to each reporter's identical questions with identical answers.

"Should have just shown the second one a videotape of the first interview," he told Zosia over the phone.

She grunted as she pulled on her stockings while holding the phone against her shoulder with her head. "Did they take photos?"

"Yeah, maybe I'll make the cover." He laughed. "We went into the park for the one magazine. Settled for the lobby with the other."

"Did you at least get lunch or dinner out of them?" Zosia struggled with her other stocking.

"Lunch from the first one. But Alex said there'd be food at England House tonight, so I turned down dinner."

"Are you ready yet?"

"Yeah. You?"

"No, not yet. And I've got to help Joanna. I should get going."

"Okay, uh, Zosia, one more thing."

"What?"

"Do I have a bodyguard now?"

There was an embarrassed silence, then a quiet, "Um, yeah."

"Since when?"

"Since that incident with the Nazis," she answered reluctantly.

"Was that your idea?"

Again a silence.

"Was it?"

"Yes. Why? Do you mind?"

"Yes, call him off."

There was another silence.

"Did you hear me?"

"Yes. All right," she agreed, resigned. "I'll see you there," she added and hung up.

61

*T*HERE WAS DINNER, a very nice dinner. The reception had been organized in honor of a substantial donation from the estate of Lillian Rose Devon, and therefore, though Peter drew curious glances, he was not the center of attention.

"Next year," the woman next to him at the head table confided, "we're going to establish a Devon award for notable contributions to the Underground cause. I'm sure you'll be a shoo-in for that!"

"That would be a singular honor," Peter said agreeably, thinking that next year, they would be hard-pressed to remember his name. He did not bother to ask how they hoped to honor people who by the nature of their work needed to remain anonymous. Instead, he made polite conversation about the award and the Devon family while scanning the tables to see if he could locate Zosia. Finally he spotted her. He continued to look in her direction, hoping to catch her eye, but she was deep in conversation with someone and at length he gave up.

He was not asked to make a speech, was not even mentioned by any of the speakers. Apparently the invitation had been solely to win him over rather than to have him win over the audience. Indeed the audience—volunteers, government officials, Underground liaisons—was already completely committed to the cause and had no need to hear from him. It was a relief, and in a rush of gratitude he felt slightly guilty that he had not mentioned an English organization on the late-night show. They had rescued him from the streets, had provided him with a raison d'être, were fighting for his homeland; didn't he owe them some loyalty?

After the dinner they mingled over cocktails, made with real alcohol, thank God! Alex was in his element. Some of the government officials had not seen their homeland since the fifties, and therefore their memories were no different from Alex's. They talked together like old buddies and reminisced about the place as if they had been there only yesterday. They spoke of a land that no longer existed, discussing policy for a people they did not even know.

Zosia fit in naturally as well. She spoke animatedly to a small group of second-generation exiles using a nearly neutral accent that was neither her father's nor her husband's. As Peter stood next to her, listening to her speak, he marveled at how she had nicely canceled both their influences.

He looked around and noticed Anna and Joanna sitting off to the side. Anna was becoming more familiar with English with each passing month, but she was still obviously uncomfortable in sustained conversation. He whispered his excuse into Zosia's ear without interrupting her continuous stream of conversation and went over to join Anna and his daughter.

He lit a cigarette, one of the ones he had brought from home, and offered Anna one. She shook her head.

"Oh, that's right. You've quit," he said in German.

"Did the police get hold of you?"

"The police?" he repeated, alarmed.

"They wanted to interview you about that incident with the neo-Nazis. They called Alex today to try and track you down. We told them where you were."

"No, they haven't called yet," he muttered.

"They said it shouldn't take long, they have everything they need on the videotape."

"Good. For some odd reason, I have an aversion to police."

Anna nodded her understanding. "What do you think of them?" She indicated the surrounding British exiles.

"It's nice being able to just relax at a gathering. I appreciate that."

"Do you feel at home?"

He shook his head. "Naw, I don't know these people. Maybe I read their names on a directive in the distant past, but I don't *know* them. And they," he added quite pointedly, thinking of the growing distance between the government and the governed, "don't know me."

"I wonder," Anna mused, misinterpreting, "I wonder how it is that no one recognizes you or your story."

"I'm glad they don't. The idea scares me a bit."

"You're assuming they don't know what really happened."

"Yes, I suppose I am." He scanned the crowd yet again. Did he want to be discovered? Might they be able to tell him what had happened all those years ago?

Anna studied his face for a moment. "You really loved her, didn't you?" Her tone carried none of the accusation of their previous conversation.

He nodded without looking at her.

"It may be your only chance, son. Go see what you can find out. Somebody here must know."

"Yeah, I guess I'll walk around the room a bit." He kissed Joanna, then kissed Anna on the cheek. "Wish me luck."

"Good luck."

He wandered the large room, mingling with the crowd, sipping the champagne provided, and conversing with the occasional person who came up to him. There did not seem to be anyone who could offer him further information or explanations on his past, and he was about to give up and rejoin Anna and Joanna, when behind him he heard a familiar voice.

He turned carefully and studied the speaker: a man, not much older than he, talking knowledgeably, or at least pompously, to a small knot of English-Americans, that is, second- or third-generation exiles. The voice and the face belonged to a man he had known as Graham. Peter had given the Council what little he knew about Graham, but nothing had turned up in the files: he was not an acknowledged German agent nor had he been arrested nor was his name linked to their arrests. That was not surprising—Graham had been his immediate superior and their link to the rest of the organization; most of the group did not even know him, and nobody but Peter had known how to contact him.

Peter waited until Graham had finished his current exposition and had not yet launched into the next to walk up to the group and say, "Excuse me."

Graham turned toward him, as did all the others. There was a pause as Graham studied him, then he smiled and said, "Yardley."

Peter was stunned and it took him a moment to say, "So you *do* know me?"

"Yes. It was hard to tell from the TV since not everything in your story matched up. You know, you changed a few dates, added a wife . . ." Graham paused significantly, then suggested, "That was Allison, wasn't it?"

"Yes," Peter responded somewhat embarrassed.

"So, you finally got your chance to marry her. At least in your imagination, eh?" Graham added snidely.

"I amended my life under advice," Peter replied calmly.

"Naturally, of course, of course," Graham rushed to assure him. "Well, other than the details, I still had trouble feeling certain it was you. Your accent's changed. Milder, i'n'it? And you look a bit different. Older, of course. Or is it something else? Not sure . . ."

As Graham mused, Peter studied his old comrade for clues. Why wasn't Graham, or whatever his name was now, accusing him, or at least questioning him? Why no curiosity?

"But in person," Graham continued, "there's no mistaking you!"

"Kind of you to remember me," Peter said with subdued irony. His suspicions were growing stronger with each overenthusiastic word Graham spoke.

"Let me introduce you to my friends here." Graham was all smiles. "This is my dear old friend Alan Yardley, also known as Peter Halifax, also known as, er, any others?"

"Some."

"And this is . . . oh, the group." Graham gave up in good-natured confusion.

There were several pleased-to-meet-ya's, which Peter essentially ignored. "You seem to be doing well for yourself," he said to Graham.

Graham's grin broadened. "Oh, yes. I'm here permanently now as an adviser to the Home Office."

"Working *in* the government? Congratulations." Peter could hardly keep the sarcasm out of his tone.

"And you?"

"Surviving," Peter replied tersely.

"Staying here?"

"Can't say."

"Oh, you should. You don't want to go back there. It's so . . ."

"Filthy?" Peter asked, using one of the typical complaints of the Americanized English. "Miserably damp?" he suggested into Graham's embarrassed silence. "Or is it the appalling food?"

Graham glanced at his young friends and shrugged a chagrined apology.

"Oh, I'm sure they've said it all themselves. Horrid place full of ill-tempered, violent, chain-smoking—"

"Alan!" Graham looked abashed; his friends glanced at each other with guilty recognition.

"—alcoholics who insult them all the time and don't appreciate the sacrifices they've made to come and learn about us and our vile culture." Then, indicating Graham's friends, Peter added, "Isn't that right? Isn't that what you think?"

None dared to answer, though several shifted uneasily.

"So you're alive," Graham said to say something.

"Obviously. And you're not surprised?"

"A bit. But you always were slippery. If anyone was going to survive that fiasco, it would have been you." Graham smiled at his young friends.

"Doesn't that raise any questions in your mind?"

"What? Questions? Um, well, I guess I'm curious how you pulled it off. Bad luck about the arrest afterwards. Hey, where'd you get the lousy papers? Street purchase?"

"No, they belonged to me when I first joined."

"Oh, that was clever." Graham sucked on his cigarette. The little audience was fascinated, and he obviously loved being the center of attention. "But you know, you aren't supposed to keep things like that."

"Well, it's not too late to issue a sanction," Peter sneered.

"Oh, we'd never do that! No, my boy, we're just glad you pulled through. Messy business, what?"

Peter rubbed his chin, then risked saying, "Yes, you don't come out of it all that well, do you?"

"Oh, so you heard." Graham's voice conveyed disappointment.

"Yes, but I'd like to hear your version. It only seems fair."

"It wasn't anything like what you heard! I told them to warn you all immediately. I really insisted waiting was too dangerous. I argued so vociferously, I was nearly cited for insubordination!"

"Obviously. You know, I appreciate your concern. We all do, every last fucking corpse!" Peter stopped, then resumed in a more conversational tone, "But despite your best efforts, you couldn't convince them."

"No! But you know, they were in a bit of a bind. They could hardly go arresting someone that high up without a reasonable suspicion."

"Of course."

"And I couldn't disobey orders and tell you that he had your names. You might have let on that we were on to him!"

"Couldn't have that, could we?" Peter replied coolly. He had noted Graham's change from *they* to *we*.

"No, you might have blown the operation. You know, gone into hiding or something."

"And there was no reason for us to do that, was there?"

"Well . . ." Graham snorted with anger. "Blasted security! They just don't take it seriously enough here! Why they ever let him get hold of so much information! They should have been more suspicious earlier on. Of course, that is what tipped us off in the first place."

"So you had our names on a list in a file drawer, eh?" Peter asked sardonically.

"Oh, not that bad!"

"A *locked* file drawer," Peter amended bitingly.

Graham's eyes widened with sudden suspicion, then he asked, "How did you know all this? Who told you?"

"You just did."

Graham seemed to swallow a few curses, then filled in the awkward silence by saying, "Well, if it's any consolation, old boy, the moment he gave you all away, we had him then."

"Ah, that is consoling. Hanged him, no doubt."

"Er, no. The Americans won't let us hang traitors. They'll happily fry drug dealers, but I'm afraid we have to put our baddies in prison."

"For ever and ever?" Peter asked, sure of the answer.

"Well, he was released three years ago."

"You can give me his name," Peter spoke gently, "or I can look it up in the news files. Which?"

"Oh, Yardley. Alan! He was really *quite* senior! And with the royal connection . . ."

"I thought we both belonged to the English *Republican* Army," Peter hissed. "Since when have we started covering *them* for their stupid loyalties!"

"Alan, come now, you know the political realities!" Graham let his eyes stray meaningfully toward his groupies. "We had to be careful! Strength in unity, my boy."

"Don't 'my boy' me!"

"Come on," Graham pleaded, "you don't want to pursue any vendettas. It'll look bad for us if you go digging up old dirt!"

"Oh, you needn't worry," Peter assured him in a cold tone. "If I'm going to take revenge on anyone, it will be you. You're the one who didn't warn us. You're the one who sacrificed all of us to please your royalist masters. You're the one they're calling for."

"Alan! It wasn't my fault!"

"I hear them calling you, don't you?" Peter raised a hand to his ear, listening to ghostly voices.

"Alan! Aren't you listening? It wasn't me! It wasn't my fault!" Graham insisted desperately.

"*Come join us, Graham, we miss you!* That's what they're saying," Peter interpreted for his audience. "I think it's only fair I help you join them, don't you?"

"Don't joke like this, Alan. It's too weird. Stop it. Please, stop it! They told me to hold off warning you! They just mistimed it, that's all. The flight, I was going to leave more time, but . . . It would have been such a scandal if they had got it wrong—they couldn't just arrest him without firm proof! I was just following orders! Honestly . . ."

Peter shook his head, dropping the psychic act. "No, Graham, or whoever you are, I'm not buying that. Our lives were always cheap to our American-born masters. We all knew that and we had nothing but contempt for those buffoons! *But you were there! You knew us* and you let us swing! I always knew you were a pompous arse, but I never took you for a murderer!"

The little audience of American-born future masters backed off slightly in preparation for the violence that was sure to follow, but Peter disappointed them; showing a self-control they had not expected, he turned and walked away.

Graham stared after him, watching as his old comrade left the room, then he recovered his composure and, smiling weakly at his little audience, raised his glass. "Excitable sort!" he toasted with a forced little laugh.

Peter went out the massive front doors and into the hallway. There he hesitated a moment, wondering what to do. He was furious, but he was equally helpless. Retribution was impossible unless he wanted to spark a diplomatic incident and destroy everything they had worked for. Squabbling among and within the allies was one of their greatest problems; it weakened their position in the NAU and left them vulnerable to attacks from the Nazi sympathizers in America.

He sighed heavily, lit a cigarette, and stepped cautiously outside. The traffic on Fifth Avenue had abated a bit, but it was still impressive. He glanced around—no reporters anywhere, the embassy had kept their word. He sat on the steps in the evening heat and smoked, enjoying the momentary solitude, thinking of his lost friends.

He ran through Graham's words in his mind and heard again his half-swallowed excuse: *The flight—I was going to leave more time* . . . Therein probably lay the entire truth: they had held Graham in America until they were sure of what orders to give; Graham had been sent back with a warning but had arrived too late. The ministry had cut it too fine, waiting for their irrefutable proof, Graham had screwed up getting the message to them fast enough, and probably, somewhere, something inevitable like a late train or a flight delayed by a thunderstorm had cost all his friends their lives.

He cleaned some nonexistent dirt out from under his fingernails and wondered: Had a message been sent to his flat that very night, the night he was out with Allison? Was there an unanswered knock on his door, a sheet of paper shoved under it? He was the only one who knew how to contact everyone else quickly. How close had Graham come to warning him? That very night would have cut it perilously close, but there would have been time, time enough. He should ask Graham if he had made it as far as London, if a messenger had knocked on an unanswered door. He should ask, he thought, but he would not; he did not want to know. On that score it was better to remain in blessed ignorance.

"Dad?"

He turned around to see Joanna standing at the top of the steps and motioned for her to join him. She sat next to him and he gave her a hug.

She waved her hands around her face and grunted.

"What's the matter?"

"Those things stink." She pointed at his cigarette.

He looked at his cigarette as if seeing it for the first time and thought of all the times Karl had blown smoke in his face. It had been a ritual every time he had lit Karl's cigarette, and it had stunk then. "Yeah, they do, don't they?"

"They're awful."

"I'm sorry, sweetie, I didn't know they bothered you." Of course, Joanna had not grown up surrounded by constant smoke. "You'd make a good American," he added to tease her.

She grimaced. "Uncle Ryszard's place smelled awful—I could hardly breathe!"

"Oh, I'm sorry! Why didn't you say something? Maybe we could have done something about it."

She shrugged. "Genia said not to. She said her father would yell at me."

"You should have told me; I would have talked to him."

"But he would have yelled at you."

"I'd have just yelled back, honey."

"Doesn't Uncle Ryszard outrank you?"

"Not on things like that, sweetie. Next time something bothers you, you tell me and I'll see what I can do. Okay?"

"Okay."

He inhaled from the cigarette, suddenly feeling a guilt he had never felt before. He made a point of blowing the smoke away from her, of holding the cigarette off to the side, but still he felt guilty. How odd!

"And I've heard they're not good for you," Joanna said suddenly.

He smiled at her concern. "Yeah, I've heard that, too."

"So why do you do it?"

"I don't know," he replied truthfully. "Habit, I suppose." At the time he had heard of the dangers, it had not seemed particularly relevant since the risks he was taking were such that his future health was hardly a concern, but maybe now they were important; maybe it would determine whether he would see Joanna's children grow up. He didn't want to miss that. Nor did he want to spend years hacking and coughing and spitting like so many of his elder colleagues had, the way Alex did. "Your mother doesn't let me smoke near her now that she's pregnant. And I can't smoke at home. Seems a bit pointless, doesn't it?"

Joanna nodded, clearly surprised that an adult could see sense so easily.

"Would you like me to quit?"

She nodded enthusiastically.

Never before had it mattered. Never before was a future so possible. Maybe the past would not matter if the future was full of hope. "Okay. I'll stop." He ground the cigarette out on the stone steps. "There! All done."

Her look of happiness was more reward than anything he could have asked for. He looked around for a place to put the end, but there was nothing obvious, so he shoved it into his pocket. "So, how do you like America?"

"I think it's great!" Joanna placed such an odd emphasis on *great* that he had to laugh. "Can we stay?"

"I'd like that. But I don't think it's possible."

"Why not?"

"Your mother doesn't want to."

"But if we stay here, she'll have to stay!"

He had discussed this with Zosia extensively, but she had been adamant. He was welcome to stay wherever he wanted, she had said, quite magnanimously, but she was going back. And that meant, of course, that Joanna was going back as well.

"I'm afraid it doesn't work that way, honey," he explained. "You have to go where your mother goes, and she's going back. Anyway, wouldn't you miss the mountains and the forest? Wouldn't you miss your grandmother and Olek and all your friends?"

Joanna nodded. "Yes, I suppose I would."

"I would, too. Look, we have a few more weeks here. I've got to do a bit of traveling and some more interviews, and then I'll be done. We'll go home and I'll get to spend lots of time with you. Not like here. Would you like that? We can go into town, visit the zoo. Wouldn't that be nice?"

"Yeah!"

"Do you want to go for a walk?" He indicated the park across the street.

"Sure!"

"Okay, go tell your mother where we're going." He watched as she ran happily back up the steps and inside the building. She emerged a moment later, and they set off across the Avenue and into Central Park. At the first rubbish bin they located, he not only threw away the cigarette end but discarded the rest of the pack.

Joanna skittered around happily. "You're really going to do it?"

"Of course, I said I would." He realized he had at that point absolutely no option of backing out. A little girl, a five-year-old little girl, had broken the habit of a lifetime. What power her smile had!

PART III

Coming Home

1

*E*VERYONE NOTICED how the Führer's frown deepened as he listened to the whispered message, and the conversation in the room quickly died away to an expectant silence. The propaganda minister continued his worried, intense whispering as he handed the Führer an American magazine, already opened to an article.

"Another one?" the Führer exploded. "Who the hell is this man!"

There was a whispered answer.

"I know that! But who is he? Is he a fake? Why don't we have a file on him?"

"Presumably, during his alleged reeducation and forced labor, everything on him was refiled by number. Perhaps Security can explain to you why their files are not cross-referenced by name," the minister explained, looking pointedly at a number of the guests in the room.

The Führer sat up and put his drink down on a side table. "Enough of this, already! We're going to sort this out now!" He stood and scanned the room. "Everyone in Security, into the library. Now! You, too," he added, indicating the propaganda minister. "Everyone else, continue with the party!" The Führer walked toward the door followed by an obedient group of men, their heads hanging like dogs who had just had their noses smacked. The Führer stopped at the door and looked around. "Traugutt, bring your daughter along, we'll need a secretary."

That last comment caused a number of the guests to throw surprised glances at the various secretaries in attendance, and there was intense interest in the young, dark-haired woman who walked confidently through the parting crowd to the door. Once they were in the library, Stefi sat demurely at the Führer's side at the head of the conference table.

"You can take notes?" he asked quietly as he handed her a notepad and pen.

She nodded shyly, then, once the Führer's attention was elsewhere, she threw an inscrutable glance at her father.

"Gentlemen," the Führer began, "I think all of you are, to some extent, aware that there has been an intensive American propaganda effort directed against us this past month. Most of you, however, have not been apprised of the extent of the damage done to us." He paused and looked at the article in front of him, then sighing, added, "I don't understand where this is coming from. We were right on track for talks, I had the personal guarantee of some of their most senior politicians that things would be kept quiet—"

"You had the word of Jews and gangsters," Schindler interjected, "and it was worth exactly what I told you it would be!"

There were a few murmurs of agreement, and someone began, "These Americans—"

"These Americans," Richard interrupted, "have a different system. One which few, if any, of us truly understand. They are not able to control their own people. It leads to chaos, crime, and corruption, but it is clear that the politicians who gave their word to our Führer have not violated it. This is not a political initiative, it comes from below."

The Führer nodded gratefully. "It comes from this man. Can anyone tell me who he is?" He pushed the magazine toward the nearest seat. The occupant shook his head and passed it on. As the magazine was passed from one to the other, the Führer motioned toward the propaganda minister. "Tell them what's been going on."

The minister shifted uneasily in his seat. "It seems to have started about a month ago with an interview on American television. This man did nothing more than describe what he called his life story . . ."

As the magazine reached Richard, he looked at the photograph in the article. It was small but clearly focused, and the features of his sister's husband were unmistakable. It had been a difficult decision, but they had opted for not cloaking Peter in anonymity, as they feared it would lessen the impact of his story. Alex had hoped Peter and Zosia would remain in the NAU, but Zosia had been adamant that she would return, and Peter had wanted to stay with her, whatever the cost. So, he had returned, trusting to the seclusion of the mountains and the anonymity afforded by the Reich's multitudes, bound by the chains of love more securely than he had ever been by any other chains. Richard shook his head at the picture and passed it on.

". . . backlash against isolationism and against our interests, which we have not adequately addressed," the propaganda minister was saying.

"What do we care what they think?" Schindler asked sharply as he picked up the magazine.

"It has already had real consequences," a representative from the border police explained. "We've had a significant increase in the number of arms we've detected being smuggled into the country. We can only assume that there has been a concomitant increase in the supply."

"There has been a Reich-wide increase in terrorism."

"And there have been riots!"

"And an upsurge in union activity."

Schindler ignored the comments. He looked up and smiled at the Führer. "I know this man."

"You do? Who is he? Is his story real?"

"I don't know how real it is, I don't know what he's been saying, but look in Vogel's file. Karl Vogel."

"Vogel? What does he have to do with it?"

"Vogel owned him," Schindler laughed. "And I warned him, from day one, that boy was trouble. He should have beat the shit out of him when he had the chance."

"We'll make amends for lost time when we get our hands on him," the Führer promised. "He's going to wish he had never seen the light of day."

"There's no guarantee he's within our reach, is there?" someone asked.

"Our agents lost him in Mexico City. They ended up following someone to California, but they think it was the wrong man. They lost the double in Los Angeles, so they can't be sure."

"Morons!"

There was a generally noisy and rancorous discussion of the ineffectiveness of various subdivisions of Security until the Führer was driven to slam the table with his hand. "Enough! Enough."

There was a moment's silence, and then the propaganda minister ventured to ask, "What sort of security measures have been taken so far?"

"So far, nothing organized," Schindler answered, throwing an accusatory glance at the Führer. "While we've been awaiting our orders, we have managed to crack down on illegal publications, border patrols have been enhanced, smuggling rings broken up. I think it's time for a retaliatory strike. This man is English, isn't he? We should have started executing hostages in England ages ago."

"He claims to be sponsored by a coalition, and his handler is from the Polish government," someone pointed out.

"Then hang a couple of thousand of them as well!" Schindler demanded. "Burn a hundred villages and their inhabitants. We must teach them that they can't play these sorts of games with us!"

The Führer leaned back in his chair and smirked at his challenger. "Perhaps it will interest you, Günter, to know that an executive order was signed today for massive retaliations to begin on the morrow. And this, this traitor, he claimed to work in London, so we're going to sweep London clean of every terrorist suspect. Within the week, they'll have their trials and will be fertilizing Green Park shortly afterwards."

"Ah," Schindler stammered. "Good, that's good. We don't want to look weak."

"We aren't weak," the Führer reminded him. "Nevertheless, retaliations aside, there is still much to deal with from this mess." He stroked his chin thoughtfully. "It's late, and none of us are thinking clearly. I'll be assigning task forces to deal with the various problems raised tonight: riots, increased arms, terrorism . . . uh, what else?"

"Unions."

"Yes, unions, and of course our official protests to their government about all this, and whatever. Anyway, I'll expect you all to work in close concert with each other since all the problems stem from the same root. My office will be handling overall coordination, and you are all to report to it and cooperate with each other. Is that understood?"

They all agreed it was.

"Good, go out and rejoin the party. We'll pick up on this tomorrow." As the men rose and turned to leave, the Führer called out, "Traugutt, stay behind." He turned and smiled at Stefi. "You too, *Schatz*."

Richard waited patiently until the last of the others had left and the door was shut, then he turned to the Führer expectantly.

The Führer waved his hand toward the chair next to him. "Come sit here, I want your advice on some things. You always seem to have a good eye for what's going to happen. Maybe you can give me some ideas about how to handle our answer to the Americans."

"Of course, *mein Führer*," Richard answered obsequiously. "But first, I think it's important that we consider this retaliation order you have signed."

"Why?"

"I worked out East, remember? I know who you're dealing with there, and I believe there's a good reason that the coalition that supported this Englishman chose the handler they did. If he's a representative of the Polish government in exile, then he has ties to the Home Army."

"So?"

"They have the most efficient assassination unit of all the terrorist organizations. We have only been able to keep them in check through a complicated series of protocols established over decades of negotiations. If we strike at anyone within the Reich for an action of one of their government spokesmen in the NAU, then we have violated the protocols."

"So what?"

"If we violate the protocols, they will strike back in proportion to the violation—that's part of the deal. None of your officials in the East will be safe. Even the majority of us in Berlin will have to fear for our lives. Though you personally have sufficient protection, the rest of the officials don't, and as they are knocked off, one by one, they may believe that it was a deliberate action on your part to remove them. Especially Schindler. It could provoke a coup."

"Oh! But wouldn't it be clear that it was not my doing?"

"By violating the protocols, it would be your doing," Richard explained.

"Oh! What should I do?"

"Cancel the retaliations. All of them," Richard advised.

"Oh." The Führer rubbed his chin. "What about the arrests in London? We can still do the sweep, can't we? Those will be genuine terrorist suspects, after all."

Richard shook his head. "Not worth it. They'll know why there was a crackdown. They'll know it was retaliation, and when your own people start dropping dead, Schindler won't hesitate to point a finger at you."

The Führer groaned slightly. "But then the populace will think they can get away with this sort of thing."

"Since we have absolute control of the media, the populace is completely unaware of what has been happening in America. All they know is that there is some level of disruption within the Reich. That is all we must deal with."

"What about Schindler, and the others? They'll think I'm being weak."

"You only show weakness by worrying about them. You are, after all, the Führer. You are our leader, and we have all pledged undying loyalty to you. All of us!"

The Führer nodded his head wearily. "So is there no way to punish this criminal for his actions?"

Richard took a deep breath, then explained reluctantly, "Halifax himself is not a member of the government in exile, so he is still bound by our laws and you could charge him with crimes against the state if he were ever to return."

"We'll do that! We'll scour London, we'll scour England! We'll find that bastard!"

"You can do that, but you know, he'll never come back."

"We'll kidnap him!" the Führer suggested excitedly. "As soon as he shows his face again."

"That would set a dangerous international precedent."

"Oh, yes. You're right," the Führer sighed. "Well, I'll tell you this, my friend. If he is ever foolish enough to come back, he'll regret it! How long did he talk about us, stabbing us in the back, twisting the knife? A month? It was a month, wasn't it?"

"Yes, I believe so."

"One month. That's how long I'll make sure he stays alive. A month before we'll let him die. Thirty-one days! And for each and every one of those days, he'll beg us to kill him!" The Führer was sitting bolt upright, his eyes gleaming with excitement, but then he threw himself wearily back into his chair. "It still won't be enough though. He's hurt us. Like a thankless child he has spurned his own Fatherland. It will take ages to undo the damage he's done to us." The Führer sighed heavily. "You're a father, Richard. You understand what it would feel like to have a child who behaves so cruelly, so unfairly . . ."

Richard and Stefi remained respectfully silent as the Führer struggled to cope with his grief. Gathering his courage, the Führer collected himself and appealed to Richard, "I need to know how to handle these Americans. You seem to know a lot about them, what do you think?"

Richard considered for a moment. The Reich had responded to the Halifax affair by protesting directly to the American government. Not only had the protests been ineffective, but the lack of a public-oriented response had been interpreted as guilt and had only enhanced Peter's story. Now, though, with Peter's tour finished, the best thing to do would be to stir things up a bit, so Richard advised, "The Propaganda Ministry needs to strengthen its response. I think it has been a mistake to remain quiet for so long. It is interpreted as guilt."

"Hmm. Maybe you're right. Why don't you handle that end of things? You seem to understand these Americans."

Richard shook his head. "No, no, not me. I wouldn't know what to say at all. Americans confuse me, they are corrupt and immoral and chaotic. I would never know what to say."

"Who then?"

"Give Propaganda their head. They're trained in this stuff. See what they come up with. And if, after a time, they aren't handling it right, I'm sure by then a candidate will suggest himself."

The Führer nodded wearily. "All right, I'll try that. Now, why don't you go back to the party."

"Yes, *mein Führer.*" Richard stood, gave a slight bow, and motioned to Stefi to join him.

"No, no, you stay here for a few minutes, *Schatz.*" The Führer motioned to Stefi to remain seated. "I need to go over these notes with you."

Richard studied the Führer, quickly weighing up his very limited options. Then Richard looked at Stefi and realized that his intervention would, in any case, be unwelcome. They had both been angling for this sort of access for months—what business did he have fouling up her plans at this stage? She was thoroughly professional and completely dedicated, and at that moment he recognized that he not only trusted her with his life, he trusted her with her own.

"We won't be more than a few minutes," the Führer assured him, as he waggled his fingers in the direction of the door.

Richard grit his teeth, bowed slightly again, then quickly turned and left before he could change his mind.

As the door shut behind her father, Stefi set the notebook down and, moving to stand behind the Führer, began massaging his back and neck.

"Oh, that does feel good," he moaned in response.

"I'll type up these notes and submit them to your office tomorrow."

"Naw, just burn them." He slid into a more comfortable position. "Ah, yes, right there, that's good!"

"You feel so tense! You've made so many command decisions," she soothed. "I'm very glad you're not going to carry out those retaliations."

"I don't know, maybe I will. I could use a few additions to my tape library." He gestured to a bookshelf laden with videotapes. "Some of those are getting quite old. I'd like a few new ones. We could view them together. Just you and me."

Stefi walked over to the shelf and picked up one of the tapes. There was a single-word label on it. It was either a person's name or perhaps the name of a village. "What are they?" she asked.

"Torture, retaliations, confessions. Some are really quite gruesome," he warned. "My favorites are the subtle ones—some of my cinematographers are quite good at nuance. No blood at all, yet you can feel the pain. It sends shivers up and down my spine. Makes me feel quite randy, you know."

Stefi shuddered and set the tape back on the shelf. "But you would be taking such a risk. I don't think it's worth it for a bit of film. Do you?"

"Risk?"

"Yes, like my father explained." She came back over to him and continued her massage.

"Oh, yes, forgot about that. Oh, oh, oh, that feels so good! Remind me about that tomorrow morning. Oh, yes, that's great, oh, oh, yes. I don't want to forget. What did he say, provisions?"

"Protocols. I'll tell your personal assistant tonight and he can make sure it's stopped before tomorrow. That way we won't have to worry about forgetting and I won't have to worry about your safety. And my father's."

"Good idea," he sighed. "Exquisite! You have exquisite fingers! Why don't you come to my office every day and give me a massage?"

"I'm not in town much."

"I know!" he pouted. "But where are you?"

"I take care of my great-aunt. She lives out East, in a colonial region, and has fallen ill. She needs someone to help her out. Someone she can trust."

"You're wasting your talents."

"It's family." Stefi let her thoughts stray only momentarily to the old woman who had been established in a farmhouse just to provide her the cover she needed to return to Szaflary. The neighbors knew of the brown-haired young woman who visited her regularly and, if asked, would make their reports accordingly. "She needs me."

"What about your mother, she's just had a baby. Doesn't she need you here in Berlin?"

"Not as much as my aunt. My mother has the other children to help her."

"Well, you tell your aunt to take good care of you. If she doesn't, she'll have me to answer to."

Stefi leaned forward and kissed his cheek. "I'll tell her. Now, shall we return to the party before my father starts to worry?"

The Führer laughed heartily. "Yes, of course! We wouldn't want him to think we're up to anything!"

=============================== **2** ===============================

BY THE TIME Peter came home, the effusive welcome and celebratory atmosphere that had greeted Zosia and Joanna had abated somewhat, but he was still greeted warmly and congratulated and thanked for his efforts from all around. He learned that his words had been more effective than anyone could have predicted and that the increased flow of money and equipment into Europe had begun even while he was still in America.

"They aren't being very discriminatory," Tadek informed him during a game of poker. "A lot of stuff is falling into the hands of loonies."

"I think," Peter replied as he ordered his cards, "they think we're *all* loonies here." He shrugged and thought of what they all took for granted as normal. "Maybe they're right."

"Well, this helter-skelter approach is causing some unfortunate strains in our resistance efforts. The number of random bombings and snipings is up considerably. Not only here, but in the rest of the Reich as well. Security has been tightened everywhere."

"They've called up reserves," Romek interjected, contemplating the mess in his hand.

"Unfortunate," Peter replied, "but I think it was unavoidable."

"Perhaps," Tadek agreed as he laid down an initial bid. "You could have been clearer about whom you supported and more willing to denounce the crazy fringe element while you were on television."

"What crap," Peter muttered, looking at his cards.

"It's all pressure on a system that must sooner or later collapse," Romek suggested as he threw in his cards.

"Yes, the fringe element serves the purpose of making the regime more willing to deal with us, since we are at least reasonable," Peter said, growing annoyed at Tadek's undertone of condemnation. "It wasn't my job to direct the flow of funds; I did what I was supposed to do, and that was to raise American awareness of the situation in Europe and to gain sympathy for the cause of the Resistance."

"Random murder is random murder," Tadek pronounced solemnly.

Peter glared at him, thinking of how close Tadek had come to randomly murdering him upon his arrival. He decided not to mention that though, and as he met Tadek's bid and raised him, Peter replied instead, "And wanton violence has been a way of life here for decades, my *dear* colleague. Maybe it's about time that the Germans feel some pain."

"We're not looking for revenge," Tadek reminded him, meeting Peter's bid and indicating that he wanted only one card.

"No, that would be impossible." Peter motioned for two cards. "But if a little bit of hurt gives them an idea of what they are doing to the rest of us, maybe it's not such a bad thing to have terrorist bombs and random murders."

"The Jewish leaders in Warsaw formally requested that of the Allies back in '42, I think," Romek remarked. "Tit-for-tat executions of Germans living abroad. They hoped that the request, at least, would draw attention to their desperation."

"We should have listened to them," Peter said. "We still can."

Romek nodded noncommittally. Tadek shook his head. "I don't think it will work." He tossed in two more chits.

"You have no idea how many of them are cowards," Peter retorted, matching Tadek's two and adding another six. "I *do* know! And, I'll tell you this—if *mein Herr* had suspected that he might one day have *his* bones fractured with a shovel in retaliation for his actions, he might just have decided to restrain himself."

Tadek glanced at Peter's face but got no indication of his thoughts. Tadek scowled at his cards and then threw in his hand.

"If you feel that way, why didn't *you* take revenge?" Romek asked.

"I should have," Peter said as he drew in the pot.

Tadek was right. The sudden American interest in the various resistance causes had led to an upsurge not only in random terrorist acts, but contributed to a growing sense of political chaos within the Reich. There were more well-planned sabotage, heightened resistance in mountain retreats, greater efforts at intra-Reich diplomacy, nascent strikes, and new underground newspapers. The Reich authorities debated the appropriate reaction to these changes, one side arguing for greater repression and heightened vigilance, the other for a loosening of controls to release steam without letting the pot boil over. The political infighting between the two factions only added to the growing sense of instability.

For Peter, the changes were almost moot. He ventured out to the local village on several occasions, but otherwise had little to do with the outside world. He retreated into his mountain fastness and picked up the threads of his life where he had left off. He continued with his physical retraining, sharpened his already impressive shooting skills, and began trying to play the piano so he could teach Joanna. He played poker with his friends, attended parties, went for long, pleasant walks with Zosia, and took Joanna out to harvest mushrooms and berries, or to picnic and swim, or just to observe the wildlife. He returned to tending the garden he had planted, thanking his friend Kamil profusely for keeping it during his absence, and even decided to expand the plot now that he knew what he could and could not plant in the harsh mountain climate. When he stopped to rest and leaned on the shovel, breathing in the fresh autumn air, sometimes he thought of the garden he had tended at the Vogels'. An image of those horrific few moments when Karl had attacked him with the shovel would occasionally flash through his mind, but he did not react to the memory; he just stared off into the distance and let the vision of the meadow wildflowers and the distant rustle of the wind in the trees soothe him.

Sometimes, too, he thought of Elspeth and the weird experiences he had had with her. He thought often of Madzia, wondering what he could do for her, but he never came to any firm conclusions. At other times, especially on dark or rainy days, he thought about the times he had spent in prison. He tried to approach the memories with a detached air of wakefulness, and to some extent it worked. He could view his past self with something like pity and was relieved that it was no longer he. Once in a while he tried to send messages of comfort back to that miserable wretch, whispers of hope from the future, but he could not remember if he had ever heard these time-traveling thoughts. For good measure, he sent a few words of comfort into the future as well so that they would be there when he needed them. It was a habit he had acquired in childhood, at a time when his only friend was his future self, and it was a folly that he still occasionally indulged.

Other than for these visits into his past, he lived a contented life. The two months' absence, first at Ryszard's and then abroad, had sharpened his appreciation of the encampment. It was not that he had not recognized the freedoms that Americans enjoyed, it was more that he had been obliged to be diplomatic for so long, it was a welcome relief to voice his opinion openly among people he knew and trusted and who understood the basic issues about which he was talking. That was probably what had annoyed him the most in America: not his missionary role, but that so many people had no clue what he was referring to and that he often found himself reduced to simple diagrammatic discussions of a deeply complex situation.

Not unlike the conversation he and Zosia had had with Katerina, he mused, as he leaned on his shovel and stared into the sunset. The encampment had many accreted flaws, which he more keenly recognized since his tour of America, and to remedy them he and Zosia had had Katerina over to dinner to try to persuade her to reorganize and reprioritize a number of things, in particular his work. But all she had left them with was the comment at the end of the evening that if she did not know better, she would think they were saboteurs trying to destroy whatever unity and organization had been established. Zosia had turned crimson at the remark, but in deference to Katerina's age and standing had said nothing. Peter had not been so controlled and had blasted the old woman for having turned into a calcified and useless old fossil, and as he had closed the door behind her, he had said, still within her hearing, "She's obviously gone senile."

Katerina's attitude only compounded a problem that was already growing in his mind. It was necessary to reorganize the office and catch up on missed work, but he knew once that was accomplished, there would be little point to what he did. To keep up with the fast-paced developments in his field, they needed a massive commitment of resources and people, a commitment that they could not afford and that was not realistically available given the constraints of their existence. Logically, if he was to make a genuine contribution, he should be seconded to Warszawa or to the NAU, but the first was impossible and the second he did not desire as long as Zosia wanted to remain in the Reich.

Worried by the developments in his work, he often sat and pondered what else he could offer the encampment, never sure of what it was he was looking for. Since completing his visit to America and the conception of their child, he somehow felt as though he had reached the end of his shelf life, as if his only purpose had been served and the only point to his current existence was caring for Joanna and tending to Zosia. He felt it was all well and good enjoying a life of leisure earned by his hard work in America, but he wanted to contribute more. He needed a new career, and for that, he thought, he needed to improve his knowledge of the language he now spoke so unsteadily. His goal was to be able to understand every nuance of Tadek's speech, no matter how rapid or complex, and he hoped to be able to speak fluently enough to switch languages with Joanna so that they no longer used German as their common language of communication.

"I'm not sure switching is a good idea," Zosia said when he confided his goal to her. They were sorting through some baby clothes that Zosia's friend Franciszka had given her, and Zosia's attention was momentarily diverted as she sought the match to a sock. Finding it at last, she continued, "You know, she needs to be utterly fluent in German, and your speaking it to her is good practice, you have such a lovely accent."

"I don't want to practice German with Joanna. I want a language that we love as our common tongue. English or Polish. But not German," Peter responded as he held up a tiny white gown. How was it possible that a human could wear something so small? Babies were wonders of miniaturization!

"Oh, it's so close to English, why don't you want to speak it?"

"It's not close to English!" he sneered. "Anyway, it gives me the creeps. I've had it shoved down my throat so many years of my life. You can speak German with her. I'd rather use something else."

Zosia held up a pair of tiny socks. "Marvelous, aren't they?"

"The socks?"

"No, babies! Marvels of miniaturization!"

Sometimes they really did seem to think as one. "You scare me, woman," he joked.

"Rightly so. Now, what shall we name the sprog?"

"Ah, how about Geoff, if it's a boy."

Zosia made a face. "After your friend?"

"Yeah. Do you have a problem with that?"

"Only that I wanted a Polish name. That doesn't translate well."

"What's wrong with an English name?"

"It's my culture that's under attack and it's me that is doing the hard work here. I want a Polish name."

"The baby will be more English than Polish, my dear. Let's see . . . ," Peter mused, should he count Alex as entirely English or half-English? "For argument's sake, let's say your father is only half English. That makes you one-quarter, and the baby is . . . five-eighths English."

"Oh, rot. He or she is pure Polish."

"I thought your mother had some Ruthenian as well."

"Utter rot!"

"Or was it Cossack?"

"Nonsense. She's purebred Polish!"

"Not even a hint of that wild Eastern blood in her?"

"None at all!"

"Now with Alex's mother being English, his being born there, and assimilation," Peter continued teasing Zosia, "I'd say your father is completely English, which would make the baby, hmm, three-quarters English."

"Luckily, our family tradition is the woman names the baby since she does all the work. So, whatever your clever calculations, I get the final say."

"You are joking, of course?" he asked humorously.

"No, I'm not," she replied without any humor at all.

There were, he realized, the seeds for a huge argument there. His pride insisted that he have a say in the naming of his child, and now that she had made a point of rejecting it, he also felt like insisting on an English name. For a moment he felt that his personality, his independence, his culture, his pride, everything was on the line. Everything except his love for Zosia: that he took for granted, and he expected her to take it for granted as well. Hmm, now there was a thought.

Carefully he asked, "Joking aside, is this important to you?"

Zosia looked up at him from the pile of clothes. Something like surprise was in her eyes. She nodded slowly. "Yes, it is," she said in a quiet voice as if the words were a revelation to her.

He examined his own feelings and realized that, except to spite her, the origin of the name was not really important to him. There were lots of beautiful names in both languages. It was important to her, it was not important to him, and he said he loved her. Was that enough to convince him to give up a stranglehold on this decision? Was that enough to convince him not to fight her about it just because he wanted to make sure that she did not get her way easily? Or to teach her a lesson for not having asked him in the appropriate manner? Put that way, it seemed silly to argue, yet still, something inside him said he had to fight for his rights. If he gave up this piece of territory, it would never be regained.

What an odd way to think. They were not adversaries in a war fighting over a border, they were supposed to be partners in life. He claimed to love her, believed he would give his life for her, had seen her risk her life for him, yet this simple thing was so hard. He gave her so much that she did not appreciate, yet something that she wanted, he found difficult to concede. Indeed, that he had mentally termed it a *concession* revealed a lot.

"You've gone all quiet," Zosia commented on his sudden silence.

"Oh, just thinking of the baby," he lied. "What would you like to name it?"

"If it's a girl, I'd like to call her Irena."

He hesitated, then slowly, as if the words were so foreign to him that he was not sure what they would sound like, he said, "I'd like that."

"You would?" Zosia did not hide her surprise.

"Yes. I think it's a pretty name."

"You mean there is nothing else that you would rather have?" she asked suspiciously.

"I don't think it would be first on my list, but I like it, and if you want it, why should we search further?"

"No reason," she conceded.

"What about a boy?"

Zosia bit her lips. "I always liked, before that is . . ."

"What?"

"I always wanted to call a son Karol."

Peter took a deep breath; though Zosia had emphasized the slight difference, it was pronounced nearly identically to *Karl.* "I don't suppose there are any other names you would like?" he asked painfully.

"You could think of it as your father's name—Charles."

"That wouldn't help much."

"Well, how about Adam?"

Peter breathed deeply. Beloved Adam. What better name to give his son? "Firstborn," he whispered, thinking of his brother. He had always known his brother's firstborn status had been special to his parents.

"Not my firstborn, and since I'm the one giving birth . . . ," Zosia interrupted his thoughts.

"Of course," he replied, snapping himself back to the present. "Yes, I suppose we could name our child Adam," he offered quietly.

"Good! Then Adam it is!"

3

"**D**O YOU THINK MOM WILL FEEL BETTER by the time we get home?" Joanna asked. The day had grown cloudy, and as they walked along the path to the cemetery and the river, a wind kicked up and Joanna had to clutch at the package of sheet music that they had bought.

"I think so, honey," Peter answered as he scanned the tombstones, reading their inscriptions as they walked down the path. It was a German cemetery, yet some of the names leapt out at him with their obvious Polish roots. *Passing* they had called it in the American South; here the corpses were "passing" even in death. It would be quite a hilarious farce if it had not cost so many lives and so much suffering.

They stopped at the edge of the cemetery and looked out across the river. "She has some terrible headaches with this pregnancy," he explained, "and it was best for her to stay home and relax in the quiet."

Zosia had woken up with the headache early in the morning and informed him that they would not be able to go into town that day. It created yet another argument. It seemed that no matter how hard they tried, they fought about everything. The planning that had gone into their trip would be wasted, it would take ages to organize another outing, and he and Joanna were both desperate to get out and about. He had promised to get her the sheet music for her piano lessons, and they had already delayed once because of weather. With these considerations in mind, he had launched into a tirade about trust. He was sick of being watched, he was sick of being treated like a second-class member of the establishment. If Zosia was too sick to go, he and Joanna would go alone.

Zosia had looked worried, but she was clearly in pain and not prone to prolong the argument, and she quickly conceded defeat. "Fine, go," she had said wearily, "I'll inform them of the change of plans."

Joanna grabbed on to her father's hand and looked up into his worried face. "Why do you and Mama fight so much?"

Peter closed his eyes with embarrassment, then he opened them to look down at his daughter. "I'm sorry, baby, we don't mean to. It's just that we both have strong and different opinions. We don't do it that much, and we're getting better, aren't we?"

Joanna nodded noncommittally. "At Uncle Ryszard's house, they never fought."

"Uncle Ryszard and Aunt Kasia handle things differently than your mum and I do. And besides, maybe you never heard them fight."

"Genia said they don't."

"Ah. And what did you tell Genia about us?"

"I lied," Joanna admitted sadly. "But she knew anyway, because you and Mama fought even there."

"Oh, I'm so sorry, little one!" he moaned. "Do we embarrass you?"

Joanna remained silent, staring out at the murky waters.

He stooped down and swept her up into his arms. He held her and stroked her hair as she buried her face in his uniform jacket. "Look, sweetie, I think I've worked out a few things over the past month in America, and, well, I realize that a lot of the time I'm not fighting your mother, I'm fighting things from my past. I've told you a bit about the time before I came here, didn't I?"

"Uh-huh," Joanna murmured through the cloth.

"And do you remember how I said a lot of it was very difficult for me?"

"Uh-huh."

"Well, it's like when you trip and fall and hurt yourself. Sometimes everything still hurts long after you've gotten up and walked away. And if you've hurt your-self really badly, sometimes you're afraid to even go back anywhere near where you fell. That's sort of what happened to me, I think. And I think that sometimes I get afraid that your mother is taking me back to that place where I was hurt, so I get scared and I fight with her."

"You get scared?" Joanna pulled her head back to ask in amazement.

He nodded. "Yes, and sometimes I do things like yell at your mother for things other people did to me."

"That's silly, though."

"I know it is, and I'll try to change. Will that make you feel better?" he asked. He wished it were that simple, he wished that he didn't often feel as though Zosia were viciously goading him.

Joanna nodded.

"Why don't we walk back into the center and buy your mother some of those chocolates that she loves. We can surprise her with them when we get back."

"Oh, that would be nice," Joanna agreed readily, not mentioning how much she loved those chocolates as well.

"And we can go to the bookstore, too. Maybe I'll buy your mother a cook-book."

Joanna giggled in reply.

So it was they strolled back into town, doing a last bit of window-shopping as they turned into the street with the chocolatier. They stood and looked into a large shop window, admiring the display of dolls, and he wondered if one would be appropriate for Joanna at Christmas. It was unusual to give bought gifts, but he thought that this year he might break the tradition and buy each of his family members something nice.

They turned away from the window, and Peter was unable to decide if Joanna's interest had been genuine or just a passing attraction. The street was fairly crowded with rush-hour pedestrians and traffic, and as they passed the dis-play windows of a large department store, Joanna strolled in front of him as there was not room to walk side by side. The flash of the first explosion—per-haps only a detonation—was visible out of the corner of his eye. He lunged at Joanna even as the other pedestrians, less trained and more complacent, walked unperturbed. He was down on the ground on top of Joanna before they even heard the noise or felt the percussion of the second, larger blast. A wall of glass and debris erupted outward, toppling the standing people like so many rag dolls. He felt the fierce wind of shrapnel buffet him, and then it was over. He rolled off Joanna, realized that he was bleeding and in pain. He glanced at himself, saw pieces of glass covered in blood embedded everywhere along his exposed back and sides. He looked at Joanna as she climbed to her feet. She looked uninjured, albeit winded.

"Are you okay?" she asked, looking down at him.

He nodded. "I think so. What about you?"

"I'm fine. You're bleeding." She reached toward his head.

He felt his hair; his hand came away covered in blood and splinters of glass. "I'll be all right." He pulled himself into a sitting position. He sat still, afraid that further movement would drive the shards that covered him deeper into his clothes and skin. He was nauseatingly dizzy and shaking violently. He tried to take in their situation, and he realized with a slow horror that the body next to them was not moving. A few yards away he saw a little girl, about Joanna's age. Her dark curls lay in a mass about her still head, blood dripped from her ears, her mouth hung open filled with something dark and wet, her eyes stared at nothing. There was mayhem around them. Glass and bodies and people running about trying to help.

They had to get out of there. He tried to stand, but a long shard of glass lodged behind his knee prevented him from moving. He pulled it out, wincing at the pain. Joanna extended her hand and helped him to his feet. He stood there as the world whirled around him, fading in and out. They had to get out of there, he had to move. Joanna looked up at him worriedly. Her lips moved, the word "Dad?" echoed through his head. He wanted to say something to her, but he couldn't find the word. Something important. The world spun around him, he saw someone coming to help, he wanted to say something to Joanna, but the ground was hurtling upward to meet him even as the world went black.

───────────────── **4** ─────────────────

"*T*HEY GOT HIM!" Karl gloated, walking uninvited into Richard's office.

"What? Who?" Richard managed to feign interest. Another poor dumb shit who had got caught. He hoped he was not expected to be present at the interrogation. He had grown somewhat inured over time, but it was still not easy watching torture. Joking about it afterward was particularly taxing. Maybe he could have an important prior engagement . . .

"That bastard—that ingrate. The one who stole my car and gun and papers!"

"What? Where?"

"Out East of all places. In Neu Sandez. I know one of the junior officers there. He phoned just to let me know! Goes to show you—they never really looked for him. I told them he was trouble, but they had to wait until he went and showed his face on American TV—then they took me seriously!"

"Hah. Poor bastard. What are you going to do with him?" Richard tried to sound calm. Was Zosia okay? Did they get her as well?

"Oh, nothing. He's out of my hands now. Seems he's offended someone much higher up than me." Karl winked and pointed upward.

What, the elevator shaft? Richard wanted to say, but he nodded knowledge-ably instead.

"They'll take good care of him, I'm sure. I just hope I get a chance to witness some of it."

"Is that likely?" Richard wondered.

"Well, I hear there's going to be a film."

"Really? How did they get him?"

"Oh, he was waltzing around town—in an officer's uniform, can you imag-ine!—and he got caught by one of those terrorist bombs. Probably set it himself. Anyway, at the hospital, I guess they identified him."

"Ah, was he, uh, alone?" Please, God, say yes.

"No. Seems there was some kid with him. Couldn't be his though, she's about five, and, well, he wasn't having kids five years ago." Karl scowled suddenly as if his thoughts were heading in a direction he did not like.

"I assume they'll just release the kid," Richard said, not believing that he had actually voiced such a naive opinion.

"Yeah, right!" Karl laughed. "That's good. I'll keep you posted! Maybe we'll get to see the film. Would you be interested?"

"Very. I'd really like to see you get what you deserve, Karl," Richard replied with a winning smile. Then, reaching for the phone, he added, "Now, if you'll excuse me, I have to make a call."

5

"**H**E's WAKING UP," the voice emerged from the darkness. His eyes fluttered but closed against the bright fluorescent lights. Finally he managed to open them, saw an unknown male face looking down at him. Behind that he could discern banks of lights, rows of beds. A hospital.

"So, Halifax, you've decided to come home."

Peter grimaced in confusion.

"Oh, yes, your numbers gave us all the information we needed."

Peter glanced down at his arm, at the numbers that had betrayed him, but he could not see them, they were bandaged—as were his other injuries. He was in a hospital bed; the back had been raised so he could see the room easily, and he realized as he tried to move that his wrists and ankles had been bound to the frame. He shuddered with fear. Joanna was nowhere in sight. Had she escaped?

"Or should we say Herr Doktor Halifax, hmm?" the voice prodded. "Seems you've made a little name for yourself, eh? A mathematician. Goodness, we never appreciated your talents, now did we? Maybe we'll have you do some sums for us, eh? Calculate how long your life is going to last, eh?"

Peter closed his eyes against the moronic prattle, took a mental tally of his physical state. He felt hot and rather dizzy, and every part of his body hurt as if stabbed repeatedly. Yes, of course, the glass.

The bland voice continued as if tutoring him. "Did you enjoy your sojourn in America? Hmm? You said some terrible things about us there, didn't you? About your homeland. See? We know!"

Peter opened his eyes to see a facsimile of a magazine page held in front of his face. It was in English—a page from a magazine article written about his American tour. The page was pulled away, and the head shook and a tongue clucked in disapproval. "You're going to have to pay for that, you know. You belittled our land and our Führer. Such disloyalty! We can't have that."

Peter looked at the speaker, but he could think of nothing to say, so he remained silent. Where was Joanna? Was she safe?

"And then there is this fine uniform of yours and these papers! Now there we do have some questions. A five-year-old daughter—"

Peter closed his eyes in an attempt not to show any emotion. His tongue reached to the tooth that had been loaded with poison. Still intact.

"—when we know you were otherwise engaged five years ago. Confusing, eh?"

The man waited as if for a response. When Peter said nothing, he finally said, "Clearly you have friends we'd like to know about. But what were you doing getting involved in such an unprofessional bombing?"

"I had nothing to do with the bomb."

"Probably not. Oh, well, just bad luck, eh?" His inquisitor smiled. He motioned to the guard nearby. "Untie him."

They released him from the bed and helped him to his feet, then handed him his clothes and helped him to put them on. His arms were grabbed before he could do up the buttons of the uniform jacket, and his wrists were locked behind his back, then he was pushed in the direction of the door. As they half-walked, half-carried him out of the ward, he realized that he was surrounded by victims of the bombing. A visitor looked at him and his entourage and hissed aloud, "That's one of the terrorists!"

"Kill him," someone said.

"Slowly," someone else muttered.

A woman who was walking between the rows of beds overheard and turned to look at him. "Murderer!" she hissed, and spat at him.

He shook his head but did not otherwise respond as his guards hustled him from the room. They led him out of the hospital and into a car. A short journey later they arrived at a nondescript town house. There was no sign over the door, no indication of what lay within. Inside, they passed two sentries and walked along a hallway and down a staircase into what was presumably the cellar. Peter's inquisitor rapped on a door and it was opened to reveal a small, dark room with a window looking into another room. The guards remained outside as he and the inquisitor stepped into the room.

Peter's heart sank as he looked through the one-way mirror. It revealed a similarly small room with only a table and a chair and one lonely occupant. Joanna sat calmly at the table. In front of her was a bowl of oatmeal or something, which she ate dutifully as though she had been ordered to do so. Peter's companion smiled at his reaction. "So you know her."

"No," he replied steadily, "she's just a kid."

"I don't think so. Her papers say you're her father."

"You know I'm not. She's just some kid."

"Then you won't mind if we harm her." The inquisitor pressed a button recessed in the wall. A woman entered Joanna's room. She had a piano wire in her hands.

"No. Don't," Peter breathed.

"So, she means something to you?" the man asked as the woman stretched the wire between her hands. Joanna sat stiffly, staring determinedly straight ahead; she did not even turn to look at the woman.

"No, I just don't want to see a kid hurt. Let her go! She's just a kid," Peter pleaded.

The man pressed the button again and the woman left the room. "Thank you," he said sardonically. "You've told us all we need to know."

Peter was led out of the room and back into the corridor. The turn of events surprised him—what were they playing at? He was led to another door and into a slightly larger room. There were few furnishings: a table off to the side, a high-backed metal chair with sturdy crosspieces near a wall, both bolted to the floor, and a camera on a tripod pointed so that it focused on the chair. It looked all too familiar.

He sighed. He had hoped they would wait a bit—give the encampment time to organize something. What could he tell them that would buy time? What useless information could he offer in exchange for a few hours? How much should he tolerate before he started talking? He was afraid they might resort to drugs immediately—if they did that, he would have to decide quickly, while he still had a free will, whether suicide was the only option. Would they release Joanna if he was dead? He suspected not; he suspected that she would remain alive only as long as they thought she could be used as a way of getting him to talk. So, he would have to stay alive even if they started using drugs. And he would have to keep his mouth shut about so much! He trembled as he realized how desperate his situation was—could he buy enough time? Could he get them to use violence instead of drugs? Perhaps he could provoke them into knocking him out: that would buy a few hours . . .

He glanced around. There were two guards as well as the interrogator, but no one was holding him at the moment. He bolted for the door. It was slammed shut before he could reach it, and his arms were grabbed by the guards. The interrogator hit him in the face, but only once. He struggled against them with all his might, tried to kick them, but all they did was drag him into the chair and tie him to it. He fought them the entire time, making their job as difficult as possible, but they remained unprovoked. His arms were draped over the back and bound into place, and his ankles were tied to the legs. The base of his skull was pressed back against the top crosspiece, and a length of insulated electrical wire was wrapped around his neck, twisted once, and then wrapped around the crosspiece and the two ends carefully twisted together. The wire was not particularly tight, and given that his arms were already wrenched behind the chair, it did not affect his mobility greatly. Nor did it affect his breathing, and if he did not move, it did not even hurt him, but it did prevent him from lowering his head, and he guessed its intent was to keep him from bowing his head out of sight of the camera. Once he was safely immobilized, one of the guards punched him viciously in the stomach in retribution for his resistance; he jerked forward violently, discovered the exact painful limits of the wire, but did not, unfortunately, lose consciousness.

He closed his eyes for a moment to collect himself and waited for the inevitable. His tongue probed his tooth again. He had to stay alive for Joanna; he had to die if they came at him with a syringe. Which? Would they just release her if he died? Could he stay alive and say nothing to betray the encampment? Perhaps he could lead them on a wild-goose chase—start with useless information and drag them through an entire false confession. Then if they resorted to drugs, they would probe in the wrong direction, and he might say nothing useful. He took one second more to gather his courage and then opened his eyes.

The interrogator seemed to be waiting for something; he glanced nervously at the door and drummed his fingers on the table. After a moment, an SS officer entered the room, placed a file on the table, and went to stand, somewhat disinterestedly, by the door. As if this were his cue, the interrogator motioned toward the camera, and one of the guards went over to it and pressed a button. A red light indicated it was filming. The interrogator straightened, indicating his awareness of his important role as narrator, and approached his prisoner.

Peter surveyed the man calmly. Working around the pain in his jaw and stomach, he asked conversationally, "What do you want from me?"

"Many things. Many, many things. But that can wait," the interrogator replied ominously. "You'll talk to us by and by. I'm sure you'll tell us everything you know. You'll beg to talk to us, then you'll beg to die. But we have other business to tend to first."

"What other business?" Peter asked, hoping to initiate some sort of dialogue. He ignored the interrogator and directed his question toward the officer with the assumption that he was in charge; he hoped his action would distract the interrogator by irritating him. Anything to waste time.

The interrogator slugged him, snarling, "I ask the questions here!" Then, calming himself, he reached inside his jacket and removed a pair of dark sunglasses. He held them up and dangled them in front of Peter. "Do you recognize these?" he asked rhetorically.

Peter shook his head. They were not the pair he had worn in America, but they looked a great deal like them.

"Seems you are fond of talking about your eyes. Worried that we have damaged them, isn't that so?" The interrogator did not wait for an answer, but instead clumsily shoved the glasses at Peter's face to put them on him.

Peter winced, held his eyes shut as an earpiece jabbed into his eye. Finally, the interrogator managed to seat them correctly on Peter's face. Cautiously, he opened his eyes; the interrogator had stooped down to look directly into his face and said sardonically, "There he is: darling of the American media. Doesn't look so self-confident now, does he?" The interrogator glanced at the SS officer and was rewarded with a grunt of approval.

Peter felt himself trembling, but there was nothing he could do to calm himself; he knew all too well the odds against him.

The interrogator stroked Peter's cheek. "Look at how the coward shakes!" he mocked, then smacked him lightly across the face. "Such a fine face—it would be a shame to cut it up. Hmm?" The interrogator's hand stroked gently along Peter's skin, plucked a piece of glass from his hair that had been missed. Then the interrogator smirked a bit, shook his head at the sunglasses. "But no, no—they just don't work for you. We'll have to do better." In one abrupt motion, the interrogator backhanded Peter at the temple, sending the glasses flying across the room. They landed near a guard, who then stooped to pick them up.

"Crush them," the interrogator ordered, and the guard mindlessly obeyed and destroyed the glasses.

It seemed an odd thing to do, and Peter did not bother to search for the veiled threat—it would be made clear soon enough. Indeed, the interrogator did explain the action: "You won't be needing those! You won't be needing anything! You so bitterly complained about what was done to your eyes—well, we'll show you what you missed! After all your grievous accusations against us, we feel obliged to help. We will solve your problem for you and make sure you have no reason to complain about your vision ever again."

With that the interrogator pulled out a switchblade, and holding it near Peter's face, let the blade leap out. In response, Peter's head jumped back the few centimeters that he had between his skull and the back of the chair. The interrogator menacingly brought the blade forward, and once Peter could move his head no farther back, the interrogator brought the blade in to touch his eye. Peter had squeezed his eyes shut in fear, but dared not move farther as he felt the razor-sharp edge against his eyelid. The interrogator drew the knife slowly over the eyelid and along the skin above and below his eye as if tracing a surgical pattern. Involuntarily, Peter squeezed his eyes ever more tightly shut, but he could do nothing to protect himself and he knew it.

The cold knife edge danced over his skin. With a brief prayer to no one in particular, Peter resigned himself to losing his vision. He summoned up the last bright image that he had—Joanna looking down at him, asking if he was all right—and ceased trembling. He would probably not survive long in any case; it seemed unlikely, given the Führer's interest in him, that the encampment would be able to effect a rescue, and even if they chose to try to bargain for him, he doubted that he was ransomable. He had offended the powers-that-be, and no price save his life would satisfy them.

Then suddenly, the teasing stopped, the knife was pulled away and plunged into his thigh. Peter screamed and opened his eyes to see the knife embedded deep in his flesh. Blood seeped warmly into the fabric of his trousers. The interrogator smiled sheepishly, then turned to look, almost apologetically, at the officer. The SS officer, looking somewhat bored, shrugged his indifference.

"Not yet," the interrogator said with an air of disappointment, reaching forward to remove the knife. He primly wiped the blade, closed it, and put it back into his pocket. He looked pensively at the blood as it continued to seep into the material—the flow indicated a muscle wound, no major blood vessels cut. He shook his head in genuine annoyance at having exceeded his orders, but the flow was slow enough that the wound did not need to be bound, and he decided to ignore it and continue his monologue.

"Not yet, boy. You still need them—there's something we want you to see. In Berlin, in person, there you can provide some amusement. Live entertainment! Isn't that what those idiot Americans say? Live! Heh, heh—at least for a time. No, it will have to wait a bit, then we can remove your eyes properly, perhaps with a sharpened trowel, hmm?"

The interrogator paused as if expecting a response. As there was none, he continued, "And then let you eat them for us—how will that be? Eh? Will that solve your problem?"

Aware of the camera, Peter was torn between trying to reason with them and wanting to spit in their faces. He could think of nothing sensible to say in the face of such madness, and in the sure knowledge that he was going to die, he wondered if they couldn't perhaps just get on with it. They were going to drag it out, that was clear, but maybe once he was dead, the Council could ransom Joanna. Once they had their revenge, maybe then she would be safe. By that reasoning, he could not kill himself: they would feel cheated and might turn to Joanna as a substitute. No, he would have to bear whatever they did to him—at least until he knew she was safe or until he was dead. The prospect of what the next few days or even weeks might hold for him terrified him.

The interrogator beamed. "Well, now, as promised we have a special treat—something we want to be sure that you see!" His voice assumed an air of authority, as though reading a judgment, and indeed he was reading something. "Let it be known, that you have been judged to have offended against the dignity and pride of the Fatherland. You have insulted the person of the Führer himself. Your disloyalty has caused untold distress, and now we shall return the favor." He paused, took a deep breath, and continued, "The Führer himself is interested in seeing that this crime does not go unpunished. He wishes you to understand the distress you have caused for all our peoples with your disloyalty. He wishes you to understand how, after all the mercy that has been bestowed on you by the

Fatherland, you have behaved like a thankless child. It has been determined that the best way to teach you this lesson is to take your own child from you."

Could they possibly mean . . . ? Peter prayed that he had misinterpreted the threat. His mind worked feverishly for some sort of response, something to stop the madness, some way to buy time. Fervently he begged, "What if I were to apologize? Publicly. I can make an appearance—denounce everything I said, swear it was all lies. Why don't you go find out what your superiors think about that?"

The interrogator ignored him, motioning toward one of the guards to go out and bring Joanna in.

"No, wait!" Peter pleaded. "Before you do anything—contact your superiors, I'm sure they'd want to hear what I have to say. Go call them, I'll wait, I promise! It'd be a mistake to do otherwise!"

The interrogator did not respond; the guard continued as if programmed. He had Joanna stand in the middle of the room, only a few feet from Peter and facing him but out of sight of the camera, then he withdrew to stand by the wall. Joanna looked at Peter and bit her lip but did not betray any other emotion. She waited silently to learn what role she should adopt.

"She's not my child!" Peter asserted in a voice shaking with terror, his glib line of defense vanished.

"But close enough." The interrogator smiled.

"No. I hardly know her. She's just a kid. Let her go!" he begged. He was aware of the camera recording his emotion, knew how much pleasure his agony would give someone, but he was oblivious to all but the need to save his daughter. He struggled to hide his fear, to sound unconcerned: at any moment, someone would come bursting through the door, machine guns blasting, and they would all be saved. At any moment. He searched for the bravado to continue to make offers, to play for time.

But there was no time. The interrogator nodded toward one of the guards—a large man with a blank expression. "Strangle her," he said bluntly.

The guard approached Joanna.

"I am a German!" Joanna's confidant voice rang out. "And if you touch one hair on my head, you will be made to pay the price." She spoke flawless German, played her role perfectly. Her years of training had not been wasted.

Peter felt a surge of pride in her; she was so convincing, so utterly confident!

The large man stepped back, somewhat worriedly.

"I said strangle her!" the interrogator demanded.

"But . . . ," the guard stammered. If there was some sort of cock-up, he knew exactly who would be the scapegoat.

"She's a Pole!" the interrogator asserted angrily.

"I am a German!" Joanna retorted haughtily.

"Then," the interrogator asked her directly, "why were you with this terrorist?"

Joanna hesitated.

"She's a hostage. Her father is rather high up," Peter answered for her, "and we were using her as a shield. I hardly know her, there's no point in harming her—she's meaningless to me."

Joanna straightened and looked at the interrogator with brave determination.

"Kill her," the interrogator demanded.

The guard looked confused.

"They're lying, you idiot!"

"No, she really is a hostage! If you harm her, you will be in deep trouble," Peter reiterated. Joanna's acting was so good, he almost felt confident of their success.

The interrogator raised an eyebrow in disbelief.

"She's one of yours. She doesn't mean anything to me," Peter assured him. "If you touch her, you'll just be harming an innocent kid for no reason at all. One of yours!"

"Then why," the interrogator asked as he pulled a piece of paper from the file that had been placed on the table, "was she with you in America?" He shoved a facsimile under Peter's nose.

Peter gasped involuntarily. Along with some printed details was a reproduction of a photograph of him with Joanna sitting on the steps of England House. Somebody had scribbled "Halifax" under his picture. Beneath Joanna's picture was a question mark, which had been scratched out and "Przewalewski" written below it. It was a good shot of the two of them—he held a cigarette in one hand, his other arm was draped around her shoulders, both of them were smiling. The photograph was obviously taken from a distance with a telephoto lens, probably from somewhere within Central Park. He knew the precise moment: he had just promised her he would quit smoking.

He fought back his shock and dismay to assert, "That's not her—you have the wrong child."

The interrogator shook his head, unconvinced.

Glancing at the photo again, Peter decided to change tack. "You have me," he offered desperately, his voice strained with emotion. "I'm the one who spoke out. *You have me!* Take it out on me, I'll do what you want, whatever you want. I'll say what you want. I'll make killing me enjoyable for you. You can drag it out for weeks and I'll do whatever you say. *Whatever* you want. Anything, really!" He indicated the camera with his head. "Look, does he have any tapes where the victim cooperates? It will be unique! Don't give up that chance. I'll help you out, I'll do what you want! I'll do it to myself, with a knife or whatever! It will be a unique tape. Just don't hurt the little girl. I don't even know her!"

The interrogator hesitated, he glanced at the SS officer, who shook his head in response.

"Go ask someone, you'll see, it's what the Führer will want. Please!"

Growing suddenly angry at the delays, the interrogator motioned to one of the guards standing behind Peter. "Shut him up!" The wire was jerked taut and as Peter choked in response, a cloth was shoved into his mouth and held in place by a hand. Joanna stiffened but said nothing. She knew that she was not supposed to care about what happened to her captor. That done, the interrogator turned toward the reluctant guard. "She's that terrorist Przewalewski's grandchild! Now strangle her! That's an order."

Still uncertain, the guard glanced questioningly at the SS officer. The officer nodded in response.

Reassured, the large guard with his spadelike hands approached the little girl and placed them around her neck. The last view Peter had of Joanna was with tears appearing in her eyes as the massive hands closed around her throat. As her body was lifted from the floor by her delicate neck, the interrogator snapped his fingers in Peter's direction and the gag was removed from his mouth. He roared in agony, trying to say something, anything that would stop them. He struggled with every fiber of his being against his bonds to try to stop them physically, he pleaded, he begged, he threatened, he offered bribes and deals, he screamed "No!" as the massive hands tightened their hold. He fought like a wild animal, to no avail.

It took an eternity to wring the life out of her little body. With her tiny fingers, Joanna tore at the hands that strangled her, dug little fingernails into callused skin; she kicked wildly but in vain. Her struggles ceased; a bit of blood appeared at the corner of her mouth, urine trickled down her leg, then her executioner dropped her like a rag doll onto the concrete floor.

As he saw her body drop, Peter stopped struggling abruptly. All his words stopped. He stared forlornly at the lifeless form, hoping against hope that she was still alive, that it was all part of some insanely cruel game. Apparently the interrogator had the same thought for he ordered brusquely, "Finish the job."

The executioner seemed to know exactly what that meant, for without hesitation he stooped and grasped Joanna's ankles. Standing a few feet from the wall, he swung her body with vicious force. Peter screamed silently as he heard her skull crack against the concrete, as brain matter spattered messily against the pristine surface. For good measure the executioner swung her body again as Peter continued to scream his voiceless dismay.

The guard dropped her battered body to the floor and backed away. Peter's entire body shook, his muscles seemed frozen, and he was unable even to gasp for breath. His ankles and wrists were slick with blood, but the ropes and handcuffs still held him bound. Blood or saliva dripped from his mouth, and the wire that had held his head up hung loose about his neck. He stared wide-eyed, almost uncomprehending, at the body in front of him. They all ignored him; the SS officer left, motioning for the guards to follow him. The interrogator, taking only enough time to reattach the wire to the chair—more securely this time, left as well, quietly closing the door behind him.

They left him there with Joanna's body and the camera rolling. Left him to contemplate the evil of his ways and the words he had spoken so boldly in public. Left him to suffer before the camera so that his audience could have their revenge. He heard himself ask Ulrike: *Do you think that babies and toddlers did something? Did a bright and happy five-year-old girl?*

6

WHEN THEY CAME TO UNTIE HIM, they realized he was burning with fever. Cursing angrily at the prospect of losing him to infection before they had a chance to ship him to Berlin and interrogate and execute him in an appropriately gruesome manner, they rushed him back to the hospital for treatment. His muscles torn by his exertions, his mind in a fevered haze, Peter stumbled in their grasp and fell into a delirium.

He was dimly aware of being bound to his hospital bed, of an injection or two, but little else penetrated his consciousness. All he could see was Joanna's look of horror as her face grew bruised from bursting capillaries, as her mouth opened in a desperate bid for air. He saw her look pleadingly at him as she realized he was helpless to prevent her murder. Had she tried to say something? *Father?*

His daughter. His little girl. He saw her grinning at him, her bright eyes, her happy expression, her messy blond curls glinting in the sunlight. The fire of his fever consumed her image, and he screamed over and over again for them to stop as her life slipped away before his eyes. People told him to shut up, he was given more injections, liquid was forced down his throat—but none of it was reality. The only reality was the impersonal red light of the camera and her little body lying at his feet growing cold out of his reach.

His bed was moved and he was loaded into an ambulance of some sort. He realized they were probably moving him to a more secure location. Though they had placed him in a private room with a guard, the hospital was not in a prison and was probably deemed inadequate to their needs. He stirred and a face peered down at him. It looked like Tadek.

"What happened?" he heard the Tadek look-alike say.

I'm delirious, he thought. Can I keep my mouth shut, or should I kill myself now? There was still something to live for: Zosia and their unborn child. Revenge. But if he was delirious, could he risk staying alive? His tongue moved to the tooth. Still intact.

"I think he's in shock—and he's feverish," the Tadek look-alike said to somebody else. "Better unload that tooth."

Peter felt someone gently pry open his mouth with a strange little instrument. "Where is it?" he heard an almost panicked voice ask.

"Oh, yeah, Zosia said it's not in the usual place—I guess he already had some false teeth. I think she said that one." The Tadek look-alike poked a finger into his mouth.

Don't touch me, he thought and tried to turn his head away.

"Hold still!" the other voice commanded angrily as they proceeded to do something he could not quite understand. "Got it. That should stop him from doing anything stupid. I swear that stuff causes more trouble than it's worth."

"What happened?" yet another voice asked. It emanated from a third face he did not recognize at all.

"Peter! Wake up! It's me, Tadek! Where is Joanna?" A hand smacked his face gently.

Peter looked at the Tadek look-alike. What a stupid question for an interrogator to ask! Well, if he did not know what had happened, there was no harm in telling him that. "She's dead," he croaked. "Strangled."

"Oh, God!" Tadek moaned. He turned to his companions. "I'll stay with him, you two go and find out if there's any truth to what he said. Maybe he's mistaken. It should be easy enough to find out, somebody will be talking about it, I'm sure." Tadek was ready to have the ambulance pull over to let his companions out, but then decided to see if Peter could assist them further.

"Where did this happen?"

Peter blinked and looked at him. It was beginning to feel like reality. Was it really Tadek? How did the impostor know Tadek's name? Had he already betrayed them all? Again though, there seemed no reason not to answer his question. "In a cellar. In a town house about a kilometer from the hospital—toward the train station, I think."

"I think I know where that is," one of the other two said. "They have that whole block near the market square converted to cells."

Tadek nodded grimly. "Okay, see what you can learn." He turned to Peter and, stroking the sweat from his forehead, said softly, "Don't worry, you'll be okay. You're safe now."

Peter remained in their farmhouse for a day and then they moved him to the encampment. He was recovered enough to be aware of what was happening, but he did not react to the events around him, preferring instead to withdraw into his illness. At Szaflary, he was placed in the infirmary for observation; people came and went, discussions were carried out over him as though he were insentient, and effectively, he was.

He heard a male voice, one he did not immediately recognize, asking, "Will he make it?"

"We think so," Marysia's voice answered out of the haze.

"And it has been confirmed about Joanna?"

"Yes. There's confirmation," Marysia replied sadly.

Peter felt his own overwhelming sadness blur the words into undifferentiated tears. He turned to listen closer, but when he moved his head, the burning heat of the flames seared him and he had to duck back into the pool of tears and view the world through their murky waters.

"Dad?"

He shook off the last of his sleep haze.

As he opened his eyes, Joanna peered at him with a look of concern. "Are you okay?"

"What are you doing here, sweetie?" he asked, aware that his words sounded muffled. Maybe it was the noise of the flames. He should bank the ashes for the night. Had anyone done that?

"They said you were sick. Are you okay?"

"I have a fever, I guess." Why did her face keep shifting like that? "I thought I lost you."

"No, it was just one of your nightmares." Joanna absently plucked some ashes off her sleeves.

"Oh, just a nightmare. Of course, I have lots of them," he responded, relieved. He thought he had lost her! He had thought she was dead! Killed! What a relief. He decided not to tell her just how awful the nightmare had been, she might take fright. The flames roared in his ears. He could hardly hear what Joanna was saying. She looked happy, bouncing up and down across the room. Then she decided to fly and swooped low over him, up to the ceiling and back down again. "Where are your wings?" he asked, surprised she could fly without them.

"Oh, they got dirty, so I took them off." Joanna swooped past him again, then settled on the chandelier overhead. The flames from the candles leapt around her. He shook his head in confusion. Something was wrong—she didn't know how to fly without her wings! He struggled to ignore his confusion; deep down he knew what would happen if he pursued his doubts.

Instead, he turned away to tend the fire. They were running low on fuel. Somebody threw a log in, but the log was moving. He looked at it and realized it was his mother. Then his father fell in as well. He reached for them but the flames beat him back. "More fuel!" somebody shouted, and he saw Allison and Terry and Geoff and his other friends dumped in. Then Adam.

"That looks fun!" Joanna declared, and leapt into the flames.

"*No!*" he screamed, and leapt in after her. "Come back!" he howled as the fire burned his flesh and his skin turned molten and slid off his bones. "Come back," he moaned.

Marysia mopped his forehead. "It's all right," she whispered. "It's all right."

After a while it was decided that he could rest in his own rooms more easily. Zosia tended to him, and Marysia, and Joanna's teacher, Basia, and others. They placed cold cloths on his forehead, washed him, treated his injuries. As he showed signs of recuperation, they read to him and kept his mind occupied with trivialities. No one discussed what had happened, no one asked, not even Zosia.

She chose to read Thackeray's *Vanity Fair* to him and spent long hours narrating the amusing and irrelevant story. Once she was done with that, she tried Mickiewicz's *Pan Tadeusz*, but he shook his head in incomprehension too often, and she finally decided it was too difficult. As she put the book down by the bedside, she looked into his eyes and decided he was well enough to talk.

"They've learned Joanna is dead," she said, her voice distant and detached. "Did you know that?"

He nodded.

"They said you witnessed it," she stated calmly.

He nodded again.

"Do you know why they killed her?" she asked gently.

He closed his eyes and nodded.

"What happened, Peter?"

He took a deep breath, and keeping his eyes closed so that he would not be distracted by her reaction, he said, "They strangled her in front of me, to punish me for my interviews in America."

He kept his eyes shut waiting for her next question, but there was silence. Finally he opened his eyes, but she had left the room. He cried out, "Zosia?" but there was no answer. Calling out her name repeatedly, he climbed to his feet and staggered into the living room, but she was not there either. He was too exhausted to continue farther, and he sat on the couch and buried his face in his hands and sobbed uncontrollably. Marysia found him there and walked him back to his bed.

"Where's Zosia?" he asked as the room spun around him.

"She went into the forest to mourn her daughter. She stopped on her way out to ask me to come and see to you."

"Why did she leave me like that?"

"Maybe she needed the privacy, or maybe she went to find someone who could console her."

7

*T*HE MEMORIAL SERVICE was held the following day, when Peter was well enough to walk. Olek and Tadek supported him as they progressed slowly through the woods to the sight of Adam's gravestone. The day was beautiful— crisp and clear—the sort of day Joanna loved.

Peter did not join in as they said the requiem mass—he had never bothered to learn the words. Usually he stood aloof and remained respectfully silent or, some might say, cynically observant, as they carried out their rituals. This time he stood beneath the branches of the pine with Zosia at his side, with Olek ready to offer an arm if he needed it. He stood and listened to the alien words, to the mournful chants, and wished that he could believe in soaring spirits. *Dona eis requiem*, they pleaded. Grant them rest.

The wind rustled the needles of the pine, a few drifted down to the ground. The simple white stone, devoid of any inscription, was placed next to Adam's. Peter heard Zosia sob next to him. He wanted to reach for her, but he was afraid she would reject him, would push him away as the one who had failed to save Joanna.

The accusations he had hurled at himself ever since the explosion played through his mind. Why had he insisted on going into town alone? Why had he let them see he recognized Joanna? Why couldn't he come up with a better explanation for her presence? Why did they have to go down that street then? Why didn't they leave town earlier? Why hadn't he told her to run the moment he had realized what had happened? Why did he ever walk out of that party? How could he have been so careless as to be photographed with her? Why didn't he send her back inside the moment she had appeared on the steps? How could he have spoken so freely in the NAU? He knew what they were like, did he really expect they would ignore his words, let him live in peace after what he had said? Why did he come back?

He should never have come to Szaflary in the first place, he should have stayed where he belonged—at Elspeth's side, serving her needs. He should have killed himself immediately upon realizing he had been captured. Or during those few seconds between their telling him what they were going to do and their doing it. If he had committed suicide, maybe, just maybe, they would have spared Joanna. They might have used her as a hostage; she could have been ransomed. He could not get around the thought that it was his life that had cost her hers. If he had never met her, she would still be alive, still reading her books and singing her songs. It had been his responsibility to see Joanna safely in and out of the town, and he had failed. It had been his bold words on camera that had provoked their revenge. It had been his . . .

He stopped. Such thoughts were useless and with them one could go insane. There was always risk, there was always a possibility of doing something wrong. There was also the possibility that he had unknowingly saved her life a year ago and gained a year of happiness that they might not otherwise have had. Who knew what the future might have held if he had done things differently. There was, he knew, no point in berating himself. They had murdered her to punish him, and the more he fixated on his own actions, the more successful they were. They had murdered her because that was their way—they were the killers, it was not his fault, even if he had made a mistake or been careless. He could not have been expected to have foreseen the sequence of events that led to her death.

Yet, the rational argument carried little weight in his mind, and even as he mentally looked around for other possible culprits, he knew that the others, Zosia in particular, would be thinking the same thing about him. How could he reach out to her when she might think it was all his fault? She must certainly blame him! It was not fair, they were at fault, too! Why had Alex insisted he come to the NAU? Why didn't Alex realize what it would mean? Why hadn't Anna insisted that Joanna stay safely indoors at that party? Or better yet, not even go? Why did Zosia let him go into town alone? Why couldn't the Szaflary Council control the terrorists who had exploded the bomb? Why didn't they warn him that the situation was so unstable? Why wasn't Tadek there earlier, before they had a chance to kill her? What had taken them so long? It was their fault—they were the ones who had raised her to be an enemy of the state, who hadn't supplied her with a safe identity. It was Zosia who was the assassin, who continued to fight the government when she could retire to the countryside and live a life of relative security. Why did she even have a child if she wasn't prepared to give up the fight to take care of her? Why had she ever let Joanna out of her sight?

Kyrie eleison. Lord have mercy, they begged repeatedly. Yes, someone have mercy. Someone.

When they all went down on their knees, he knelt as well and prayed to whoever might hear him to take care of his little girl. His beautiful Joanna. He begged Adam's forgiveness for his failure to protect her, he asked Allison to watch over her for him, he looked to his parents to sing her to sleep. Long after the others had returned to their feet, he remained kneeling, his fists pressed to his mouth to stifle his sobs. Oh, little girl! Oh, sweet, precious, lively, intelligent, happy little girl! What have we done?

The children, her school friends, gathered into a group and sang a special song they had composed for her. Peter could not move, he could not raise himself to his feet. The tears blurred their faces, and their words were drowned out by the throbbing in his ears. He heard the melody through the ocean of sorrow that washed over him. Salt water and waves of sadness.

"Captain?" He looked up to see Olek squatting down next to him. "It's over, sir. Shall we go?"

Peter was still on his knees, the crowd was drifting away. Barbara stood next to Olek. Marysia stood behind them looking at him rather strangely. "Where's Zosia?" he asked.

"I don't know, sir."

"She's with Tadek," Marysia answered. There were tears in her voice, and her face was red as though she had been crying. "Go to her, she needs you," she added softly.

With Tadek?

Marysia extended her hand, encouraging him to stand. Once he was on his feet, she said, "I know they've done something terrible to you; I know you will need time to heal. But you don't have that time right now. Go to Zosia, you two should be together."

"Why would she want to talk to me?" he asked forlornly. "She must think it's my fault, she must blame me." His own vicious thoughts trying to lay the guilt on Zosia's shoulders ran confusingly through his mind. How could he have thought such things! He felt ashamed.

"She's smarter than that. She needs you, Peter! She's lost her daughter—you should be with her. Go to her," Marysia insisted.

"It's *her daughter*, sir," Barbara said.

Her daughter? Even Barbara could see what he had blindly missed!

Zosia's daughter! Nine months in her womb—a heartbeat, kicks, hiccups under the ribs. Nine months, day and night—there inside of her, a part of her. Then birth: the contractions, the pain, the struggle; a tiny wrinkled newborn, eyes squeezed shut, sleepy and afraid—a newcomer into a cold, bitter world. A baby, playing with her toes, batting at toys, sucking milk. A year at Zosia's breast, sleepless nights, a tiny bundle to hold. Crawling, exploring, the first step, the first word. Sentences and giggling and running in circles around trees.

Zosia's daughter. The death of a father, holding Joanna close at night so that she would not be afraid, hiding her own tears to keep from breaking Joanna's heart. None of these things had he seen or been there for. Joanna had sprung into his life three years old—full of happiness and confidence and love. Things she had received from her mother; things that he had never fully credited Zosia with giving Joanna simply because Zosia had never trumpeted her own role in her daughter's happiness.

Joanna had adopted him and made him feel at home, she had loved him and trusted him because she understood love and trust. She was confident and independent because her mother had taught her confidence and independence. She shared what her mother had already given her, and all he had done was congratulate himself on how well he had behaved as a father. He had loved her as his own daughter, but that was only possible because Zosia had made room for him. She had not been jealous, she had not competed for her daughter's attention, she had even let herself be excluded a bit in order to cement his own position in the family. She had shared her most precious treasure with him: Joanna's love.

That wonderful little girl! And now they had lost her, and all he had thought about was his own pain. He was so used to being tormented in his own private hell, so used to the idea that those around him inflicted or enjoyed his pain, that he had never once thought of all the people who were this time suffering with him. Joanna: Zosia's daughter, Marysia's granddaughter, Olek's cousin, Tadek's goddaughter, Basia's pupil, Adam's only heir.

Stung by Barbara's gentle rebuke, he looked around the dispersing crowd. In the distance, under some trees, he saw Tadek with his arms around Zosia; her head was buried in his shoulder. Peter walked unsteadily in her direction.

Tadek saw him approach, gave him a long look as if deciding what to do. When Peter came close, he bent his head and whispered to Zosia, "Your husband's here," and tried to gently detach her from his chest.

She tightened her grip and between sobs, stammered, "I can't . . . Not now. Please . . ."

Unbeknownst to Zosia, Peter was already close enough to hear her response and he felt ashamed. He wanted to retreat, but a desperate, almost angry gesture from Tadek told him to stay put. Tadek whispered something to Zosia that Peter could not hear. She released her grip and pulled back enough to nod at Tadek, then she turned toward Peter. Tadek's hands dropped from her shoulders, and he walked away while the two contemplated each other in silence.

"Hi," Peter said softly.

"Hi," Zosia replied unsteadily.

He offered his hand to her and she reached out to him and clasped it. Both of them were shaking. He wanted to apologize, beg her forgiveness, explain what had happened, but he realized that she did not need to hear about his feelings or fears at that moment. She did not need an apology for that would only provoke an analysis of his sense of guilt. It was not about him; it was about Joanna. "She was a marvelous little girl," he said.

Zosia nodded.

"She brought a lot of happiness into our lives."

Zosia smiled shakily in reply.

"Can I hold you?"

She nodded and they embraced and held each other and wept.

<hr>

8

*T*HE NEXT DAY Peter appeared before the assembled Council. The weather was fine so they sat outside. Zosia was not present, and despite the casualness of the gathering, he noticed that the secretary kept the minutes and a tape recorder was present as well, though it was not on.

Katerina began. In a voice that was about as gentle as she had ever managed, she welcomed him back and then said, "We have gathered bits and pieces of what occurred, but we need your version of events formally declared to us for the record. We realize you are still recuperating, and we are sorry to ask you to recount something so painful, but time is of the essence—we need details before your memory of the events fades, and we need to trace these people and administer justice if necessary."

"If necessary?" Peter asked.

"If they have violated a law, then they have committed a crime for which we can punish them."

"Violated a law? How can they possibly not have violated a law?"

Katerina motioned to the secretary to stop writing. "Please understand," Katerina replied patiently, "here in the mountains you have been shielded, and for our own purposes we have kept you deliberately ignorant of many things, but in this land we are surrounded by murder every day. Many crimes have been committed on our territory and against our people. The murder of an innocent child is not something in and of itself which we can either prevent or avenge—this is the tragedy of our existence. That does not mean we either forgive or forget; it just means that within the confines of our current existence, we cannot pursue personal vendettas."

Peter looked ready to argue with that, but Katerina raised her hand to silence him. "Joanna is not the first child to die, Peter, and she will not be the last. Thousands have starved, thousands were gassed, thousands . . . well, the list is endless. We have only managed to bring the mayhem under some control by virtue of certain protocols with our conquerors. We are in a very weak position—we cannot demand much of these murderers, and this is the price we pay for bargaining with them. An unlawful revenge against your child's murderers will provoke massive slaughter, and it will not bring her back."

Katerina paused and it looked as though she were swallowing back her emotions. Even Katerina? She took a deep breath and emphasized, "If we were to avenge Joanna's death when they have not violated the protocols, then all we will do is cause another child to die, and you do not want that, I am sure. However, if they have violated the protocols in the slightest possible way—believe me, we will seek revenge. Therefore, we need every detail, as painful as that may be."

He nodded his understanding, and she motioned to the secretary to proceed with the minutes and to activate the tape recorder. Quite formally Katerina then said, "Do you swear, by all that you hold sacred, that what you are about to tell us is the truth, and that you will tell us this truth completely, to the best of your ability?"

"I swear."

"Please proceed."

He told them his story. He summarized briefly their visit into town, and then with the explosion he told them every detail that he could remember. When he mentioned the camera, there was a stir.

"Excuse me," Konrad interrupted, "but for whom was this film made?"

"They never said explicitly, but there was a strong implication that it was intended for the Führer. They said that the Führer himself was interested in my being punished."

"Was Joanna ever visible on the film?" Tomek asked.

Peter shook his head, then when Katerina pointed at the recorder, he said, "No, I'm pretty sure no one was visible except me and maybe the interrogator's back. Maybe at the end his face may have appeared—when he tightened a knot . . ."

"Ah, please continue," Katerina prompted.

"But her voice would have been heard," Peter added to his previous answer. "She spoke so bravely . . ."

Several of the members nodded their sympathy as they remembered the courageous little girl. They waited patiently while Peter collected himself. He continued with the details, trying as best he could to quote the interrogator, but it was terribly difficult. However, when he described the photograph and the interrogator's last sharp command to the executioner, there was an audible hiss of breath as the assembled members gasped their surprise.

"Did he actually use the name Przewalewski?" Katerina asked.

"Oh, yes, he wanted to reassure the guard that they knew exactly who she was—that she wasn't a German hostage. 'She's Przewalewski's grandchild!' he said," Peter answered, then added softly, "I won't ever forget that."

"Was the camera rolling when he said it?"

"Yes. It should have recorded his voice. I assume it was recording sound . . ."

"And the photo?"

"Her name—or rather his—was on it as well. They had 'Halifax' under my picture and a question mark under Joanna. The question mark had been scribbled out, and beneath that—in a different handwriting—someone else had written 'Przewalewski.' "

"Not Przewalewska?" Marysia asked.

"No," Peter replied, wondering at the pedantry.

"So they were clearly identifying her with her grandfather," Marysia commented.

"Was it spelled correctly?" Hania asked.

"I think so."

"I think it's clear," Tadek said softly. "We have a witness, a voice record, and print record. We have the bastards."

"What?" Peter asked. "How?"

"A deliberate assassination of an envoy's near relative," Katerina said, then added, "But we must not get distracted from your deposition. We'll present this evidence to the court and due process will be followed. Please withhold your comments," she said to the Council, then to Peter, "Please continue."

He finished his story. He did not describe his thoughts during the hours they had left him alone with Joanna's body—they were clearly irrelevant. When he was done, a few words were said to bring the proceedings formally to a close, and then the Council dispersed. Peter remained sitting on the grass, absently plucking at a few blades. Tadek approached and stood uneasily near him. He noticed several others nearby as well, but he ignored them all.

He knew exactly the sort of thing Tadek would say. He had heard it often enough, and he could not bear to hear it again. Not now. Without looking up, he said to Tadek, "I don't need anybody to twist the knife, thank you."

"Peter, I . . . ," Tadek said uncertainly.

"I know she'd be alive if she had been with you or with Zosia or with anybody else. No one else walks around branded as a criminal; she would have been safe with *anyone else*. No one else advertises to millions what *they* have done and then just stupidly walks about with his daughter like he had a right to live like a human!" Peter's voice shook with bitterness and sorrow.

"That's not what—"

"Everyone I've ever had anything to do with is dead; you don't need to say it this time," Peter spat his anger. "So no sly comments, please. There's nothing you can say that I haven't already thought a thousand times."

"Peter, please . . ." Tadek stooped down to be able to talk directly to him.

"And the funny thing is"—Peter laughed between his sobs—"my getting her killed, that would not have been good enough, would it? They could strangle a little girl to punish her father and that would have been okay with you all. But let the bastard mention some official's name and . . ."

"There is no action that we can take without their retaliating, but the retaliations vary." Tadek leapt at the opportunity to explain. "A 'terrorist' act is one that is not covered by the protocols: our retaliating for murders within concentration camps, for deportations, enslavements, or starvation falls into this category. If one of our acts is deemed to be terrorist, then it results in the wholesale slaughter of entire villages or sections of a city."

Peter looked up at Tadek and shook his head in horrified disbelief. It was all so legalistic!

"However, an action on our part which is justified by the protocols is called 'partisan' and results in varying actions: sometimes nothing, sometimes the murder of a set number of listed hostages. A judicial assassination falls into this category. It was thought that it would be impossible to maintain a government in exile if we did not have some manner of guarantee for the envoys, so the murder of an envoy's relative merits a judicial assassination. Don't you understand?"

"And the murder of a little girl?" Peter asked, climbing to his feet. Tadek stood as well.

"Is not covered in the protocols. As they intend to eventually annihilate us in any case, we have very little in the way of staying their hand—we fought to achieve whatever we could and we have managed a few compromises—a slowing down of the slaughter, if you will. In a case like Joanna's, we're clearly pushing the point, but if he had not mentioned her grandfather, we would have no case for a judicial assassination; in which case, any action we would have taken would have provoked a bloodbath."

"So her murder would have remained unpunished?"

"Illegal actions taken by individual members on their own initiative are not unheard of. We can hardly control the behavior of every private citizen," Tadek answered obscurely.

"I see," Peter replied, disconcerted by the cold-blooded calculations involved. "It's all very tidy, isn't it?"

"We do our best," Tadek answered, growing impatient. "If the reality of our existence is not to your liking, then let me be the first to apologize to you for it. But let me also say this, Halifax: you've done precious little to change it. You were well enough able to stand the murder that was happening all around you when it didn't affect you personally! If you can't stand finding out exactly what our existence here means, then perhaps you should just pick up your sorry excuse for a personality and get the hell out of here!"

Peter was so stunned by the sudden attack he said nothing.

Tadek warmed to his task. "We took you in, gave you a home, gave you a rank and a purpose! Our most wonderful Zosia gave herself to you, tried to include you in her life and her family. And how do you repay her? All you can do is blame us when something goes wrong! Why don't you just once remember who the hell is doing the murdering around here in the first place! *It's not us!* We didn't kill Joanna, not even you did! God damn it, if you can't see that, then you're an idiot!"

Tadek took a deep breath. "We didn't ask for this!" He gestured furiously toward the area of occupation. "And if after all these decades we are a bit weary and jaded, then let me apologize to your incredible sensibilities, once again! But if we don't live up to your grand expectations, then why don't you just go back to England and fight your puny battles from inside a cozy office there! Get the hell out of our country, we have enough problems without your continuous accusations against us!"

Peter glanced at the others who had remained. They stood a short distance away watching the two of them. Obviously they had heard every word of Tadek's vehement denunciation of him. They said nothing, their faces betrayed no emotion, yet he knew from their stances that they agreed with Tadek and were relieved that someone had finally expressed what they all felt.

He swallowed. Tadek was right; because miracles were what were needed, he had expected miracles from them. As an antithesis to evil, he had expected perfection, and so he had condemned them for their human frailties. How many impossible decisions had they been forced to make over the decades? How many times had they wept with the bitter knowledge of failure? These thoughts prevented him from mentioning the painful fact that if only they had deigned to let him know about the details of the protocols, he might have been able to bargain for Joanna's life. It was too late to say that though, it would serve no purpose except to exacerbate their pain.

Tadek shook his head in disgust at Peter's silence and had already turned to walk away by the time Peter found his voice. "Tadek . . ."

Tadek stopped, sighed heavily. With his back to Peter he snapped, "What?"

"Tadek, do you remember the day I arrived here? When you pointed the gun at my face?"

Tadek turned to look at him, his eyebrows raised in expectation. "What about it?"

"If you had killed me then, Joanna would still be alive today."

Tadek opened his mouth to speak, but then thought better of it.

"You should have pulled the trigger, Tadek. You should have done it."

Tadek said nothing for a moment, then he slowly shook his head, turned, and walked away.

9

RICHARD STOPPED BREATHING at points. If he just stopped, did not actually hold his breath, it seemed to take only thirty seconds to begin to feel uncomfortable— so much so that all else became irrelevant. That was good—it was the only way to show absolutely no emotion. If he was diverted to wondering at the involuntary resolve of his lungs to grab for air, then he would not have to think about Joanna's brave little voice speaking off camera. Nor was Peter's suffering easy to bear. He had no particular fondness for the man, but his agony was obvious, and knowing what he must be witnessing, Richard could empathize. Could, but did not dare, not here, not now.

Karl had already filled him in on the details of Peter's escape from the hospital in Neu Sandez. The idiots apparently thought he had managed it alone or something. God, they were stupid! How in the world had they managed to conquer so much land? Was mindless brutality enough? Or had they grown stupider with success? Was their repressive system finally reaching the point where only idiots were promoted? Idiots promoting ignoramuses?

Clearly that was the case with Karl. He had gloated about the escape; even though it had robbed him of the opportunity to know that Peter had been suitably punished, he had gloated. The reason was simple—it vindicated him wonderfully. If the goddamned security service in Neu Sandez couldn't hold Peter when he had offended the Führer personally, who in their right mind could blame Karl for letting Peter slip away when he was nothing more than another forced laborer? Who could blame Karl now?

Richard had heard Karl go on and on about it. Richard, his friend whom he trusted, had heard it all. That English traitor! *Volksverräter,* Karl had said, all of them! Why had we ever thought they would be of any use? he had wondered. I don't know, Richard had truthfully replied. That cripple, Karl called Peter. Knowing the answer, Richard had once asked what had crippled him—was it some accident? Karl had shrugged as if he truly did not remember, then answered that he supposed it was simply genetic inferiority. Yes, of course, Richard had replied.

Now Richard had the wonderful opportunity of personally viewing the tape that Karl had acquired at great cost. Richard sat, grunting occasionally with amusement, snickering at Karl's comments, suppressing an overwhelming urge to strangle the oaf as he sat there giggling next to him. Richard did not think of his sister, he did not dare. He did not think of his parents—they had to be pushed out of his mind forcefully. And he did not think about Joanna—his dear little niece who had romped so happily through his house such a short time ago. As the fatal few seconds played, he did not even, despite a strong urge to do so, mentally list the mistakes that they must have made to allow Joanna to get into such a terrible position. Mistakes were inevitable—the only hope was that they were not fatal. No, he knew better than to look for fault anywhere but exactly where it lay: in the hands of their Nazi government.

What he did do, to distract himself, was plot. His own efforts to stop the murder had come too late. After a painful series of phone calls just to determine who had any authority in Peter's case, after the delays in the long-distance exchanges, after he had cobbled together a convoluted excuse for wanting to see Halifax alive and unharmed, he had cheerfully been informed that the prisoner would indeed be transferred shortly to Berlin, and, oh, by the way, the girl was dead.

Richard swallowed the gall that the memory produced; it was time to move past that. How exactly could he get this tape from Karl? How could he get it copied? How could he get it distributed? How could it best be used against them? Karl would never believe he owned a videocassette player: they were like computers and facsimile machines—not the sort of thing one would find in a person's home. So, what excuse could he use to borrow the tape? Stealing it seemed impractical, borrowing would have to do, but under what pretext?

Karl stood up and hit the stop button on the machine. It only took him three tries to find the right one.

"Why'd you stop?" Richard asked.

"Oh, well, I saw it before and, well, not much happens now."

"No?"

"No, he just sits there, looking stunned and sick. Doesn't say anything, doesn't do anything. Well, I'm wrong there, he sheds some tears. Doesn't make a sound, they just roll down his face—proves his weakness, if you ask me. But otherwise, boring."

Richard wondered momentarily what they had thought Peter might say or do. A soliloquy to the camera? A mea culpa? They're idiots, he thought once again.

"I heard the Führer was furious when he viewed the tape," Karl said.

"Oh, why?"

"Well, you heard it: if they hadn't killed the brat, they could have got him to do all sorts of stuff. It would have been unique. I mean, you heard him, cut himself with a knife, maybe he would have gouged his own eyes out!" Karl laughed. "But they blew it. Following orders, I guess, but I mean, you have to show some initiative now and then. They should have consulted with someone about his suggestion."

"Yes, that was definitely a mistake."

"They blew the whole thing. Hell, he was much more amusing when I had him out cold on the cellar floor," Karl gloated, reminding Richard of his previous triumph over Peter.

"Ah, yes, when you brought him to heel." Richard wondered if Karl noticed the logical inconsistency of complaining about Peter's escape after he had supposedly been brought to heel. Probably not.

"Yes"—Karl smiled proudly, pleased that Richard remembered—"that god-damned cripple learned who was boss."

"Clearly," Richard answered obscurely. "Anyway, the tape . . ."

"Oh, that. Well, as I said, not much more on it."

"Ah, but I'd be interested in seeing the rest anyway."

"You would? Whatever for? There aren't any more laughs in it." Karl motioned in the air with the cassette.

"Yes, but there is so much you can tell about the *Untermensch* mentality if you study their facial expressions. It is a hobby of mine. I'd really like to view this at some length."

"Oh, I see. I just thought they looked stupid," Karl joked.

Richard laughed. "Yes, but still there is something under all that stupidity—as you know, they can be quite treacherous. It really is an understudied field. I'm thinking of initiating some research projects in that direction with funds from . . ." He nodded his head upward in the usual manner. "Very hush-hush right now. But with your experience—especially with this fellow—well, I'm sure we'll find your insights very, very valuable. And it would put paid to all those nasty, nagging questions . . . you know."

Karl nodded enthusiastically. "I'd love to help, but I'm afraid I just don't have the time to sit and watch this now. I have a meeting I've got to get to! Maybe we can arrange a later time?"

"Oh, you don't need to stay, just give me the tape and I'll get it back to you as soon as I'm done."

Karl made a face. "I'm not supposed to let it out of my sight," he moaned, "and I've got to get it back to my source by tomorrow."

Richard shrugged expressively. "Oh, well, if you don't want to help . . ."

"It's not that! It's just that . . ."

"If you don't trust me . . ."

"No, of course I do, it's just that . . ." Karl grimaced. Handing Richard the tape, he whined, "Just don't tell anyone! And make sure you keep it very safe!"

Richard smiled. "You can trust me, Karl."

"Oh, I do, Richard, I do!"

"Oh, and Karl?" Richard asked as Karl headed toward the door.

"Yes?"

"How long did you book this room for?"

"Oh, I just booked this hour, I didn't know you'd want to stay . . ." Karl grinned, unsure what to say at that point.

"No problem, I'll just stay until someone comes in. Have a good meeting." Richard dismissed Karl in his best management voice—the voice and manner that had given him so much illusory power. With people like Karl, it always worked.

Once Karl had left the room, Richard contemplated the videocassette player. There was no way to make a tape from another tape—he would need two machines. Tucking the tape into his jacket, he left the room and went to another well-equipped conference room. Nobody was inside and the hallway was quiet. Praying for a bit of luck, he pulled out his lockpick and opened the door. Using a handkerchief so that he did not touch the machine directly, he quickly unplugged it from the television and other equipment attached to it, and with a brazenness that was his only answer to having no real plan, he picked it up and carried it out of the room. He used the handkerchief on the underside, taking most of the weight on one arm, and only used the fingernails of his other hand to steady the machine as he carried it. It was unfathomably heavy. What did they put in these things? Lead?

A secretary passed him in the hall and deferentially stepped aside. Then he met up with a junior officer. "Can I help you, sir?" the younger man asked.

Richard swore to himself. Damn, a witness. "No, thank you," he replied, willing the man to move on and forget Richard's presence there. Finally he reached the second conference room, and kicking the door shut behind himself, he dropped the stupid machine down next to the first and hurriedly attached the wires. As his hands fumbled with the connections, he feverishly thought of any excuse he could use if someone walked in while he was making the tape copy. Once the machines were connected, he realized, with a sudden dismay, that he did not have a blank tape. Swearing at himself for his stupidity, he left the two machines connected and walked to the nearest secretarial office.

The woman looked up as he leaned in. *"Mein Herr?"*

"Pen's just gone out," he said, mixing boylike helplessness with a charming smile.

"I'll get you another, *mein Herr.*" She made a mark with her pencil on the document she was typing.

"Oh, no, no—just point me toward the cupboard," Richard said, already en route to the supply cabinet.

"In there, *mein Herr.*"

He disappeared into the cupboard, found the locked cabinet, and hurriedly unlocked it. The secretary called out, "Is there a problem, *mein Herr?*"

"No, just found them now," Richard replied happily as he quietly opened the cabinet and removed one of the empty tapes with his handkerchief. He stuffed it into his jacket, closed and locked the cabinet, and grabbing a pen from the shelf, stepped out into the outer office. "Had trouble finding a blue one," he explained with a sheepish smile, "one as blue as those eyes of yours."

The secretary blushed.

"Put it down on Vogel's account," Richard said, indicating the pen. "It's his fault," he added with a wink.

Richard left the office, and the secretary dutifully accounted for the pen under Vogel's name, smiling at a brief fantasy of marrying that kind, good-looking, high-ranking official, whatever his name was.

10

*O*UR *FATHER, WHO ART IN HEAVEN* . . . In between refining his story if anybody walked in, Richard repeated the prayers he had learned as a boy. There was nothing else to do as the one machine reproduced the tape playing on the other. He had located a "high-speed-dubbing" button and used that. After twenty seconds or so, he had stopped the machines and checked that he was doing it right. Convinced that it all worked, he started at the beginning again—that way there would be no mysterious breaks in the footage—and now all he could do was pace nervously around the room. How long should he leave it? The entire tape? Or would the first half hour be sufficient? The tapes whirred. Would the speed compromise the quality? And what did they mean "high-speed"? It took an eternity!

He lit a cigarette to steady himself, stopped pacing, and studied the smoke rings that he blew into the air. Yes, the story was gaining plausibility; he could carry it off. Besides, no one could tell what was being copied just by walking into the room; it would only be after the fact that the evidence gathered might be used against him. As usual, he thought. As usual, if he fell under serious suspicion, there was no hope: there was too much accumulated odd behavior, too many little pieces would fall into place if anyone asked any serious questions. It was little consolation that the same was true of all his coworkers: just working in the system left one incredibly vulnerable to denunciations.

He smiled at that thought and let the plan expand in his head. Surveillance, yes. Accumulated evidence, yes. The security services did more surveillance of their own than anyone else. There would be photos somewhere. A master and his slave. Maybe in a hotel, maybe at the house. Peter had mentioned to Richard that he was fairly certain that there had been no surveillance inside the house, but still, there was sure to be something from outside, or from one of Karl's business trips. If not, the identification that Peter had brought with him to the encampment would suffice. It would work. Richard leaned his head back and blew a stream of smoke into the air and laughed as it rose to the ceiling.

His sudden surge of confidence convinced him to copy the entire tape. Once the machines clicked to a stop, he removed the two offending tapes and tucking them into his jacket returned to his office and locked them in a filing cabinet. He then returned to the conference room and without difficulty disconnected the two machines and returned the one he had borrowed to the other conference room. The door was still unlocked and apparently no one had noticed the recorder's absence. He placed it back on its shelf, rewired it, and with a flourish left the room, locking the door behind him. Success! Two witnesses had seen him with the machine, but neither had really taken notice; one secretary might report that he had signed out a pen, but she did not know his name and would probably not connect his visit with the tape that would turn up missing at the end of the accounting cycle. Of course, she would have to pay for the missing tape—consumer prices, not office-supply prices, and she might even lose her job, but nobody would assume the tape went missing for anything other than the usual black-market reasons.

Richard returned to his office. He opened a desk drawer, removed some solvent, and putting a bit on his handkerchief—a nice white one with swastikas woven around the edge in white thread—carefully wiped both tapes. The one he copied should have been clean but he did it anyway; the other, however, he had been obliged to touch when Karl had handed it to him, and he paid careful attention to removing his prints from that. He put the copy in a safe place, picked up the original with his cloth, and inspecting it one last time, headed for Karl's office. He was not sure how he would hand it to Karl without touching it, but need not have worried: Karl was not back yet. Richard smiled winningly at Karl's secretary, explained he had borrowed something and was returning it, and marched into Karl's office just long enough to place the tape in an unlocked drawer.

Richard returned to his office and rubbed his face wearily. The conference room might have been bugged; it would be routine and the signal would simply have been recorded on tape and eventually discarded. How long until they dumped such tapes? Three months? His voice would be unmistakable as would Karl's and the sound track of the tape. There was no camera in there—of that he was fairly certain, but that tape, if it existed, could be his death warrant. Was it worth waiting before he did anything with the videotape copy? He lit another cigarette and thought about it. Patience was one of the most difficult requirements of his job; he was not a patient man. Patience could save his life. Yet, the American elections were coming up, and if he acted fast enough, there was the faint hope that the publicity from Peter's visit had not yet entirely died down. The timing was crucial—he could not afford to wait. He would get the videotape released and take his chances that the government would look for the leak elsewhere. There would be no a priori reason why they should look in his direction or Karl's or at that conference room; there was no real reason to expect that conference room was currently bugged. Patience, he sighed to himself, was a virtue he did not possess, and that would one day get him killed.

He stubbed out the unfinished cigarette and made a mental note to request a special mission by one of their operatives to find out about the conference room and erase any evidence as soon as possible. Then he lit another cigarette and contemplated what he should do next.

The phone rang and an uninterrupted stream of calls and visitors kept him from thinking further about the problem until it was nearly time to leave. How to get the damn videotape out of the building. There was, in theory, no hurry, yet the longer he delayed the greater the danger of its being discovered in his office. He rubbed his eyes and thought: there was the perfunctory search of his briefcase when he left the secure wing—it would probably not escape detection there and would raise questions. On the other hand, there was usually no frisking, but sometimes there was—even of high-ranking officials. If he carried the videotape on his person and it was discovered, there would be no suitable explanation—he and his wife and his children would be as good as dead. The thought scared him momentarily, and he had a sudden urge to fling the videotape out his window and be rid of it—and that thought solved his problem.

He wrapped the videotape securely in crushed paper, put it in a large envelope, and sealing the envelope, went up two flights to the top floor and into the men's toilet. No one was there. He opened the window, looked across the shaft to the unsecured wing of the building that was used for documentation of new residents, and listened for sounds from the men's toilet that was opposite and one floor down. The window was open, not surprisingly—the room was small and unventilated—and no one seemed to be inside. He quickly checked that no one was around or looking out and casually flung the envelope across the chasm. It landed with a thud on the linoleum and Richard smiled: not bad for never having practiced!

With deceptive calm, Richard left the secured wing and crossed the great marble hall of the entrance where Peter had stood in terror so many years before. The hall was nearly empty now—the orderly queues of applicants had been sent home long ago to come and wait in line another day. Richard laughed to himself at what passed for organization nowadays. People who had managed to complete three-quarters of the process were told to throw away their documents and come again to start fresh on the morrow. Why should they expect service or courtesy—it was a government office!

He showed his identification to the solitary guard posted at the entrance of the unsecured wing and passed into the building without difficulty. Although it was not late—only six-thirty—the wing was essentially empty. Richard had expected that—the offices were open to the public for limited hours so that the late afternoon could be used to finish all the paperwork; however, the officials were not so easily coerced into being helpful. They slowed the process by doing the paperwork as the public waited and waited. The morning crowd was then dispersed as the offices closed for two or so hours for lunch and then reopened for the afternoon, starting the process over again. At the end of the public hours at four, the officials had little to do and could head for their homes at an early time—usually by five or six.

Richard climbed the steps to the appropriate floor, walked casually down the hall and into the men's toilet. He found the package lying on the floor of a cubicle and picked it up as if he had just noticed it and thought to turn it in to the front desk. Carrying both the briefcase and package seemed cumbersome, so he conveniently stored the found package in the briefcase and just as conveniently forgot about it. He used the facilities, then strolled into the hall, poked his head into an empty office, and shrugging at the absence of his friend or acquaintance, headed toward the door.

Outside he hesitated a moment to light a cigarette and contemplate his options. Should he take a taxi or the train? Should he get rid of the tape immediately or head home? It was a long enough pause for him to notice that he was being followed, and he cursed to himself. Often being tailed was a good sign, it meant a promotion was under way, but today, it meant he could not rid himself of the videotape. So, he could not go to the bookstore; he would have to go home. He sighed and hailed a taxi.

His tail followed him but abandoned him near his house. Clearly the house was under separate surveillance. It was a bit soon for a promotion, and the more he thought about it, the more the surveillance worried him. He was cursing as he walked into the house, and Leszek, as he took Richard's coat and briefcase, frowned at his superior officer's infinite capacity for bad moods.

"Anybody here?" Ryszard asked in German.

"No."

"What about . . . ?" Ryszard gestured around the room.

"Nobody's been here since the last sweep."

Ryszard glared at him.

"Nevertheless, I checked this morning, as scheduled. What's up?"

"I'm being followed. Make sure you and your wife are on good behavior when you're near the windows. No smoking, and so on."

"We know the drill."

Ryszard scowled, then motioned for Leszek to light him a cigarette.

"I suppose next you'll want me to smoke it for you?" Leszek suggested humorously.

"Just do your job," Ryszard snapped. "And tell the kids no Polish outside— not even a whisper in the yard. Oh, just tell them to speak German all the time, inside as well as out."

"They won't like that."

"Neither do I. Just tell them."

"It would be better coming from you," Leszek ventured. "They need to talk to their father now and then."

Ryszard had a sudden urge to hit Leszek. Of course, he didn't; but he understood now why Karl had so regularly pummeled Peter. It was just too easy! Any mood, any irritation, any unappreciated comment, and with one quick gesture all the tension could be released. Why practice self-control, why respond with reasoned argument when it was so easy to just blow off steam?

Leszek waited expectantly.

"Yeah, okay," Ryszard mumbled. "I'll tell them. Would you fetch Andrzej for me? I have a job for him."

Ryszard explained to his son that he wanted him to take the videotape to the bookstore, adding, "If you're caught with this one, Son, we're all dead. Do you understand?"

Andrzej wondered at his father's serious tone but did not question it. He nodded solemnly. "I won't get caught."

"You know the routine? You know how to make sure you're not followed?"

"You know I do, Dad."

"Turn around if you have even the slightest doubt."

"I will. You can depend on me," Andrzej answered bravely. Why was his father looking at him like that?

"I don't have any choice," Ryszard sighed. "Make sure they know I want it to get all the way to the NAU, into my father's hands. I don't want this held up for clearance in Warszawa. They can send a copy there if they want; in fact they can distribute it to everyone if they want, but I want a copy to go directly to your grandfather. He'll know what to do with it. Do you understand?"

"I said I did."

"Fine. And when you come home, I want you and Pawel to begin packing. You're going by the end of this week."

"What! You can't! I won't!" Andrzej protested.

"You will and that's my final word. I want both of you out of my house by the end of the week. Aunt Zosia and Stefi will see to you in Szaflary."

"Dad! Ma needs us! You can't make us go."

Ryszard lit another cigarette and contemplated his son. Joanna's voice as she spoke her last words played through his mind, and though he shook his head, he could not shake the image of her murder that he had seen reflected in Peter's eyes. "You're going," he said, and walked out of the room.

11

*I*T MAY ONLY HAVE BEEN COINCIDENCE, but a few days later Peter was called again before the assembled Council. Zosia was there this time—they looked at each other across the short distance and he gave her a brief smile. She smiled back and then hurriedly looked down to rifle through some papers sitting in front of her. They had not talked much since the funeral—she had immersed herself in her work, and on the rare occasions they had spent together, he had been unable to find the right words to say. He for his part had lost himself in learning yet another branch of obscure and quite probably useless mathematics. It was maddening—the progress in the world of cryptanalysis was such that he had no real hope of keeping pace from his isolated location. The published information seemed deliberately obfuscatory—often published more in the interest of tenure than of promoting knowledge—while genuine progress was well guarded and inaccessible.

His position was becoming increasingly untenable: he could offer little more than routine translations of well-known codes and keywords, something that both Barbara and Olek could do with equal facility. He did not have the computing power, the human resources, or the knowledge to attack the genuinely secret information that now and then found its way into his office. More and more often, he was forced to forward their findings to the team in Warszawa, and he suspected, more and more often, they sent the codes on to the NAU. Politically it was disastrous, for if, after the risk of numerous lives, a code ended up in the NAU and was broken there, the powers-that-be were all too likely to decide that the information was too sensitive to share with their allies back in Reich territory. Thus, critical, perhaps lifesaving, information moldered in secret diplomatic files or in the hands of an inept and risk-averse American secret service, and the great price paid for its discovery was completely wasted.

"Captain Halifax," Katerina began, "thank you for attending our meeting. Before we begin, let me express the gratitude of the entire Council for the work you and your staff have done on decoding and correlating the data for our propaganda efforts in the various NAU elections."

Peter nodded, waiting for her to get to the point of his being there.

"As you know, prior to the bombing in town which has so disrupted our lives, we were intending to address the issue of your position here. We understand the problems you have encountered and your complaints since your return from the NAU. As your translations of the Hamburg data are completed, it has become increasingly apparent that the current system is unworkable.

"Therefore, we have decided to scale back our operations here and to coordinate more closely with the Warszawa Council on the interpretation of seized data. Whatever cannot be routinely and immediately translated will be immediately forwarded to them—they will in turn attempt to establish a larger center using analysts who will be seconded from the NAU."

Peter nodded. Clearly there was little place for Olek and Barbara in the office anymore. He would become a glorified clerk and they would be reassigned. Or worse yet, he thought with a sudden horror, they would want him to go to Göringstadt and work in the newly coordinated operation.

Katerina continued, "Olek will be handling the routine work here. Do you think he can manage without your help?"

"Yes, he'll do fine."

"Good. Now as for you." Katerina paused, glancing at the Council members, her eyes settling on Zosia as if to check on whether she should proceed. Zosia continued to study the papers in front of her, biting her thumbnail. Katerina sighed slightly. "We would like you to go to London to work as our liaison there."

"London?" Peter asked, stunned.

"Yes, of course you'll be perfect since you know the city and the language, and you'll be trusted by their, or I guess, *your* people there. We've asked the British to send out an explicit clearance of Yardley, so there won't be any problem if any of your old comrades recognize you." Katerina pursed her lips. "Though I don't think they plan to tell anyone you're alive, so you might get one or two shocked looks. Anyway, there's no longer any reason to avoid the place."

"No," he replied, distracted by Zosia's complete lack of response, "no, none at all."

"Congratulations, Peter, you get to go home," Marysia said.

His eyes darted from Zosia to Marysia. Was it sarcasm? A position that would use none of his talents or skills—as rare as they were, as hard as they had been to acquire! A job usually reserved for eager young recruits with no experience! Congratulations?

"It is a position of great trust," Konrad said. "We know that was what you wanted."

Konrad, too. Peter glanced at each of their faces in turn. They were laughing at him—they were throwing him out and they were laughing at him about it! He dropped his head, preferring to stare at the ground rather than to look at them.

"You will be given a new identity with a young wife," Katerina informed him.

He glanced up sharply. What?

"She will serve as an aide and bodyguard."

What?

"Barbara has requested the position and we have acceded to her request."

What?

"It will be excellent experience for her to leave Szaflary. She has learned a great deal of English since your arrival and she is very skilled with weapons. You'll be well protected," Katerina assured him.

"Zosia?" he finally managed to ask.

"Colonel Król has too many commitments here. She has no authority to act in that arena and would be wasted if she were to accompany you," Katerina answered coldly.

"Zosia?" he stammered, hoping to get her to look up.

She finally did. "It will be good for you to get away from here, Peter. You have personally offended the Führer, they know you are here: this region is too dangerous for you now—they'll never be looking for you back in London."

"London?" he repeated helplessly.

"Your presence here endangers us," Katerina explained. "You are a challenge to them, one which we cannot afford to make at this time. They have recognized that you must have met Alex's daughter in America and that she is, in some manner, connected with this region, but they have not firmly linked *you* with *us,* so it is better that you go before they do."

"You're not coming with me?" he asked Zosia, ignoring Katerina.

"You get to go home, Peter," Zosia replied evenly.

"*Home?*" He could not say more in front of the entire Council. Certainly she understood what they were doing!

"It will be a great experience for you, and we've recognized you're unhappy here," she added as if in explanation.

We. She had declared her loyalty and it was with them. His wife, the woman who had said she loved him. He dropped his head again, tried not to let them see how deeply they had cut him. "What about our child?" he finally asked.

"Our Zosia will be well looked after," Marysia answered.

"Better than she is now," Tadek muttered. There was a quiet titter from those around him.

Peter realized he was shaking with suppressed anger. In the back of his mind he heard a young voice from the distant past: *Sorry, kid, bloody unfair. Now off with you.* He looked for support among the faces, but even those who had befriended him upon his arrival showed no particular concern. "How long am I to be assigned there?" he asked, resigned.

"That's indefinite."

"And if I refuse to go?"

There was a momentary silence. Finally Katerina asked, "Why would you do that?"

"If I refuse?"

"It's an order. You have no option of refusal," Katerina replied brusquely. Then her tone changed and she asked gently, "Why be difficult with us? You do want to contribute to our effort, don't you?"

"Oh, yes," he replied bitterly, "I just wanted to know where I stood."

They spent some time discussing the details and asking his opinion on certain things. He answered their questions, commented when asked, but he did not really listen. His eyes kept straying to the woods, expecting to see Joanna jump out from behind a rock and say "Boo!" His ears kept expecting to hear her giggle as she ran around and around a tree. The movement of a sentry, the twitter of a bird, all of it caught his attention and made him scan instinctively for his little girl, but she wasn't there and would never be there again. His heart ached, and he turned his attention to Zosia to see if she would look at him, but she kept herself busy as a member of the Council, picking through the papers in front of her, offering suggestions now and then. Finally he gave up and disengaged himself from his feelings, from any emotion whatsoever. The important thing was not to let them see how he felt, and the easiest way to do that was to feel nothing.

"Would you at least answer the question?" he said with exaggerated patience as he poured himself a cup of coffee. It was the second and last cup of the day—the supply had gotten noticeably more erratic recently and the rationing had intensified accordingly.

"What question?" Zosia asked.

He controlled his anger, did not say, The question I've asked you ever since you finally decided to come home last night. He had waited up, had greeted her as she stumbled in, and had tried to discuss the Council meeting with her, but she was too tired. Carefully enunciating each word, he asked for the fourth time that morning, "Do you *want* me to go?"

"We need a replacement for our liaison there."

He decided not to be distracted this time. "But do you want *me* to go?"

"The Council thinks you'll be perfect for the job."

"But do *you* want me to go?"

"And it's a great opportunity."

"But do you want me *to go?*" he almost yelled.

"You have your orders," she answered without emotion. "There is no question to answer."

"Then let me try another one," he said, barely containing his ire. "Do you want me to come back?"

There was a pause that was almost sufficient to answer this last query, but then Zosia said, "Of course I do—you are the father of my child."

"Is that all?" he asked, while another part of his mind wondered, Am I?

"No." She drew the word out slowly. He waited but she did not embellish her answer.

"I'll miss you. Will you miss me?"

"Of course I will. Now can we stop with this interrogation?" she answered impatiently. "There are a million details to sort out." She bustled about and handed him a set of papers. "Here's your life, learn it. We've dropped six years from your age and added five to Barbara's so you're not so mismatched. You'll both be German—sorry about that, but there's less hassle that way, better rations, and since Barbara's English isn't that good, well . . . Anyway, you won't have to be military—a veteran though, Africa, wounded in a bomb blast, that will explain everything nicely. We'll have a special light cast to wrap your arm—part of an old injury, of course. It's removable, just use it out of doors." Her voice dropped off as she said to herself, "I guess we should have done that ages ago."

He remained in stunned silence.

She resumed her businesslike attitude. "We'll dye your hair"—she picked up one of the dark strands that ran through his blond hair—"this color. Bits of your hair are quite dark—it will look natural. And we'll give you brown eyes . . ."

He pulled back, freeing his hair from her touch. "Don't change the eyes."

"Why not? We'll fit you with contacts."

He shook his head. "I'll never be able to wear them for any length of time. You know my eyes hurt so much as it is."

She nodded. "Oh, yeah, right. Okay, we'll amend that—blue eyes, dark brown hair," She paused and cocked her head to look at him, "Yeah, I guess that will work. Barbara will be platinum blond—naturally . . ."

"Doesn't that bother you?"

"What? Platinum?"

"No—Barbara. You know she has a crush on me. Doesn't it bother you—sending me away for an indefinite period of time with her?"

"Oh, she'll do her job. She's very competent."

"That's not what I mean."

"What then? Oh!" Zosia laughed suddenly. "Oh, yes, that. Well, I suppose if you're so inclined . . . Hmm. I wouldn't advise it. Half your age, and so vulnerable."

"It's pretty damn convenient, isn't it?"

"What do you mean?" Zosia paged through some papers, trying to find something.

"Send me off with some substitute wife; you stay here with Tadek."

"Nonsense."

"I noticed your private so-called conversations with him haven't decreased since our marriage."

"This jealousy of yours . . ." She shook her head, still sorting through the documents. "I noticed it from the first. I didn't think you'd make trouble with it though."

"I've been very patient!"

"Patient?" she asked angrily, finally looking up from her papers. "Patient? As if I'm a child? As if I'm disobeying my lord and master? Patient? As if you have a right to tell me who to spend my time with? Why do you men think that just because a woman marries you—"

"Don't twist my meaning! You know damn well that I've never tried to control you!"

"And for that I am supposed to be grateful? That you don't *forbid* my visits?" she spat at him.

"My God, the time you spend with him!" His voice wavered with a terrible confusion of anger at her and fear at what he was losing. Somehow she made it sound as if he demanded unreasonable things—but all he wanted from her was what he offered her freely and lovingly.

"Where, in the marriage ceremony, did it say I had lost all rights to have friends?"

"Turning to him at the funeral!"

"Well, I could hardly turn to you!"

"You didn't even try!"

"Would you just back off this crap? We really don't have time for this," Zosia snapped.

"Why don't *you* cut the crap. You're fed up with me, so I conveniently get posted out of here!"

Sighing heavily, she said carefully, "Look, it's not a divorce: it's an assignment. Pure and simple—got that? Everybody here has a job to do, everybody is open to being posted somewhere, even places they don't want to go. You're not being sent away, I'm not getting rid of you. If, however, after your time there, you were to choose to stay, there is nothing we could or would do to force you back, but it would be your decision. It's not some plot on our part, so you can just stop weaving your paranoid fantasies."

"Paranoid fantasies? Fantasies? Who the hell sat there without looking up throughout the entire meeting? You knew they were going to do this, but did you warn me? Did you bring the idea to me first? No! You let them spring it on me in front of everybody so I could sit there and look like a complete fool!"

"That's all you ever care about—how you look!"

"You must have known about this for ages. Barbara knew about it! Why the hell didn't you tell me first?"

"Because of this! I knew exactly how you'd react and I just didn't want to have to deal with it!"

"Deal with it? *Deal with it?* My God, Zosia, you're having me sent away for months—or years—or whatever, and you don't want to deal with my reaction? What? Am I supposed to not care?"

"No," she replied patiently. "Look, I think you should feel a lot; it's just that with Joanna's death . . ."

"I think you're using her death as an excuse," he said bluntly.

"What?"

"You're excluding me from your life and you're using her death as an excuse!" he asserted brutally.

"That is exactly the sort of helpful analysis I have chosen to do without!" she replied angrily.

He shook his head in sad confusion. "I'm sorry. I don't know what it is, maybe you've finally realized I'll never be Adam, maybe it's that thing with Elspeth. I'm sorry about those things. I'm sorry I wasn't able to comfort you at the funeral. I'm really sorry. Whatever it is, I apologize, I'll make amends—but I need to know *what* I've done!"

"Please," she sighed, pushing her hair back. "Enough already."

"Enough?" He took a breath, was ready to launch into a tirade, but Zosia held him with a look. What was he doing? Trying to convince her to let him stay by yelling at her? Whatever truth there might be in what he was saying, it was not the right approach. He took a deep breath and tried again. "Zosiu, I need you."

She looked at him sadly, then glanced away, biting her lips. She collected herself, breathed deeply, then said, "Peter, right now, you're just too hard to live with. Joanna's death has left me so . . . I have so many . . . I just don't have the strength to deal with your needs right now. Please give me this bit of space; after a time, once I've healed a bit, then I'm sure—"

"Please let me stay, Zosiu. I can be there for you."

"You're *never* there for me!" she said bitterly.

He looked at her, his heart breaking with a sense of inexplicable and complete failure. He turned away, walked over to the curtain that hung on the wall, and studied the lace for a moment. "I have tried," he said softly.

She didn't say anything to that. As he stood there, fingering the material, he could feel the knife pressing against his eyes, could feel the way the blade had traced a pattern on his skin. He shuddered. "I can put aside my needs. I can help you. Please let me try again."

"Okay, you can help me. Go on this assignment, do that for me."

He closed his eyes against the unanswerable logic of her request. Finally he nodded slightly, then asked plaintively, "Am I really so useless to you?"

Zosia sat down, ran her hands through her hair, then gave herself a little neck rub. After a moment, she looked up at him; she seemed near to tears. Finally she said, "No, you're not. But through no fault of your own, you are in no position to help me now, and if you stay here, I will feel compelled to help you. Not only do I not feel up to that task, I know I will eventually resent it. Do you understand?"

He shook his head. "No, I don't understand."

"Please, just take the assignment. Please?"

"All right," he said, resigned. "I know I don't really have any choice, not if you don't want me here."

He hoped she would rebut the blunt assertion, but she did not. He let his head drop, there was nothing more to say. He remembered, early on in his days in the Vogel household, once or twice trying to reason with Karl, almost arguing with him. In view of his reeducation, where anything but immediate and completely docile obedience provoked the most vicious retaliation, it was amazing he had ever tried anything so foolhardy. He must have felt insanely brave. If so, it was a bravery he no longer owned. He could not bear to argue anymore—Zosia had succeeded where they had failed. Such were the powers of the heart.

They were silent for a time. Zosia noted the change of eye color back to blue wherever appropriate; he stood and watched her. When she had finished, he waited for her to look up, but instead she gathered everything together and made as if to leave. As she dropped her files into her case, he finally found his voice. "Can I just ask one favor?"

"What do you want?" she asked cautiously.

"Can I come back to help out when you're due to give birth? Just temporarily?" he pleaded.

She closed her eyes as if the request pained her. Finally she said, "Okay, I'll see if it can be arranged."

12

ALEX RECEIVED THE VIDEOTAPE and knew exactly what to do with it: publicize it to all and sundry. The job was more difficult than he had expected. The interest in Peter's visit had faded, the networks claimed the video was too violent and of remote interest. He went to the current-affairs show that had originally aired Peter's story. The executive producer was interested, but was also afraid of government pressure and claimed the strange and graphic nature of the video was problematic. "Either way you look at it," he said, "it's a problem. It's too graphic in that it portrays a child's murder and therefore will be condemned as sensationalistic, and yet because you don't actually get to see the murder—it won't attract audience interest. We'd be stomped on for showing it, without any benefit from the publicity."

"You are kidding, right?" Alex replied.

"No. And it really doesn't help that it's in German. The audiences don't want to read subtitles."

"Next time they murder a child, I'll remind them to do it in English for you. And make sure they get a goddamned close-up of the blood!" Alex snarled bitterly.

"I'll show a still from it and report that Halifax was arrested. It'll be a follow-up to the original story."

"All right," Alex sighed. "Here's a picture of the girl when she was alive. Maybe you could show that as well." He handed over a picture of Joanna. He had not told the man it was his granddaughter on the videotape, and Alex thought momentarily of volunteering that information to elicit more interest; perhaps they could even interview him. But he did not have the heart for that. Any moron who paid close attention would hear the name, but then again, most Americans so egregiously mispronounced his name that they probably wouldn't hear it in the stream of German.

He tried the news agencies next, and they dutifully reported in brief paragraphs the attack against a member of a government in exile's family. The murder raised interest in the exile community—not least because most of them had relatives or friends back home—but it never managed to make it beyond the special-interest pages.

Not until a lone financial newspaper decided to splash the story on its front page. The *Wall Street Times*—a merger of the *Financial Times* and the *Wall Street Journal*—decided that it was sheer cowardice on the part of the networks not to air the story in prime time. They highlighted government pressure that had been brought to bear after the Halifax visit and concerns raised about destroying efforts at normalizing relations. The front-page story with all its accusations was supplemented by a two-page story on the inside pages. That story contained the translated text of the entire videotape as well as still photos taken from it.

The news reported the exposé, and the following week one of the newsmagazines that had interviewed Peter used the picture of him with the knife pressed against his eyes as its cover photo. "Are we blind to what is going on?" it solemnly asked America, and it touched off the expected furor. Soon each network was finding time and reason to air segments of the videotape with subtitles and explanatory notes.

$$=13=$$

*J*AN, GENIA, PIOTR, KASIA, Leszek, and Lodzia. And himself, of course. That was quite enough victims for them. Nevertheless Ryszard was sad to see his sons go, and he did not know if he would ever see them again. They would leave today while he was at work; he had said his good-byes that morning. Both boys had been determinedly unemotional. Ryszard as well. He did not dare show how much he wanted them to stay. If he did, they might convince him to change his mind, and he had already delayed their departure by far too long. Well past the week he had promised himself. No more delays! They were off to the military academy where they would be safe; it was time to get over it.

The school was a subterfuge that he himself, as a youth, had never had to undergo, but which the Home Army handled marvelously well. They had established their very own military academies, high standards and all, and this was one of the best! His boys would be present for any scheduled inspections by state officials, and the school administration would conveniently cover their absences otherwise. Just another couple of spoiled brats with a well-placed father who bribed their continuous progress through the curricula even if they were almost continuously AWOL, off somewhere boozing and whoring, as would only be expected of them. He laughed to himself as he thought of how his colleagues occasionally mentioned the academy as a shining example of their superior educational system. The school itself was rather a challenge to the educators of the Underground as they dealt with a motley mix of young boys being prepped to infiltrate and genuine Nazi youngsters who were impressionable enough to perhaps have the brainwashing of their culture subtly impaired by conveniently available Resistance propaganda, overzealous teaching of idiotic Nazi ideology, and the occasional ineptly censored textbook.

Ryszard shoved thoughts of the school and his children out of his mind as he approached the office. Time to assume his persona, time to become the mindless, soulless cog in the great Nazi security apparatus. Anyway, he had a lot to do, he had to get to work on Karl.

Slowly the videotape was gaining publicity in America, slowly it was having an impact. A lot of people—average Americans—were angry. Quite angry. They had taken Peter into their homes, had adopted him as one of their own, and had written a fairy-tale ending for the conclusion of his visit. His injuries would heal, his eyes would be repaired, he would meet a nice American girl and buy a house in the suburbs, and if he disappeared from their view and from their minds, it was only to settle into an idyllic American life. They had solved the problem and they did not need to think about it any longer. Not until they saw the videotape.

That he had gone back surprised no one in retrospect. It had always been clear that he would. That his government had taken such offense was also not surprising. How had he ever thought he would get away with it? All that was common sense, it was expected. But the gibes at America, the murder of a child in cold blood, the destruction of their dreamworld ending to his visit—that was just too much!

The foreign offices of the three ruling American governments came under sudden irresistible pressure: we must not deal with these monsters! Third-party trade deals were scuttled as the pressure increased; arms shipments to rebels were allowed past without the usual delaying tactics; money was funneled into the coffers of the Undergrounds and their competitors and imitators. It even became the fashion for individual Americans to head toward Africa and to join militias with the idea of eventually infiltrating into the Reich to help with the imminent revolution.

The isolationist plank of the U.S. election campaign was not only a dead issue; an interventionist plank began to gain a following. The message was carried by a small but vocal minority: We have been patient long enough! We must do something!

The response from the Reich was predictable. As it became apparent that they could not simply ignore the issue, that it was having genuine repercussions and was fouling the air in all sorts of arenas, they felt the need to act. Of course, that meant find the leak and destroy its source, but also, they needed to do some damage control. They needed to respond appropriately. Somehow the bland denials of gray-suited officials to other government officials were not making an impression, and there was a minor panic as various Party hacks tried to work out how to handle these emotional and reactionary Americans.

It was once again the topic of discussion during the morning coffee break. The deferential old woman who served the coffee withdrew from the lounge leaving the powerful men alone with their coffee and pastries and great thoughts, and Karl was the first to make a suggestion.

"The trouble with those boys over in Propaganda is they haven't had to earn their living in decades. They've been spoiled by all the good work of their predecessors and the excellence of our educational system. They have no idea what it's like to deal with an undisciplined populace like the American public."

Good, good, Richard thought, he's got it almost perfect. Richard had carefully put the words into Karl's head by voicing that opinion several times in advance in his office.

There were grunts of agreement. Everybody knew that Propaganda were a bunch of lazy, overpaid slobs. Not a one had the genius of a Göbbels, and they usually made Security's job a nightmare with their idiotic initiatives.

"What they need is someone who understands how to talk directly to the Americans," Karl continued, pleased by his newly reinvented prestige.

"Someone like you, Karl," Richard suggested. Karl beamed with pleasure.

The others fell over each other rushing to agree with this simple suggestion. "We ought to put your name forward to those boys, Karl," someone agreed.

"Yes, as a spokesman you'd be able to bring this thing under control," another chimed in.

"Here, here." There was a general murmur of agreement. If Traugutt was suggesting it, it probably came from higher up. Everybody knew he had special connections with the Führer's personal office and that he always seemed to be in the know. They even liked him as well. For all his power and prestige, he never took credit even for his own ideas. He seemed happy to let others take the credit for initiatives.

So it was agreed. Karl would be suggested as the spokesman and damage-control expert to help those buffoons dig themselves out of their difficulties. He had the winning presence of prestige and knowledge, the style and flair for public speaking, the blond hair and blue eyes that would give his words weight and authority. And he knew the bastard who was causing all the trouble in the first place—Karl knew Peter's weak points and could destroy his reputation as necessary.

Karl offered his services to the Führer's personal office, which had taken over responsibility for dealing with the implications of the fiasco. His offer was accepted, and he was given a small staff and time to prepare appropriate statements and presentations to the American public. They certainly didn't understand why the NAU government was in thrall to its own subjects, and they felt helpless to put the right spin on the events. Maybe Vogel could get through to them—after all, he was the one who even understood that the Americans had a concept of "spin." Before he had mentioned it, the propagandists in the office had been clueless.

Karl returned to his office flushed with success, realized what he had done, and ran immediately to Richard's door.

Richard laughed to himself when he saw Karl's breathless body blocking the light. "What can I do for you?" he asked politely.

Karl panted a bit, then smiled. "Er, nothing really. Just stopped by to say hello."

"Hi, then."

"I got the job."

"Congratulations."

"You always, er, have lots of ideas, Richard. Perhaps you'd like to have some input on this? You know, er, throw some more ideas around."

"Oh, I wouldn't want to steal your thunder, Karl! If it got around that I was involved, some people, well, you know how they talk, they might say you weren't up to it."

"But I am!"

"I realize that, but others might not," Richard replied coolly.

"Ah, yes. Of course. I just . . ."

"However. If you're careful not to let anyone know I'm, say, offering my opinion for you to consider in the grander scheme of things, well, I'd be pleased to submit my humble ideas."

"You would?" Karl sounded as if he might faint from relief.

"Yes, you know I make a casual study of the wiles of *Untermenschen* and inferior races. I'm convinced a large proportion of white Americans are genuinely subhuman. It's all that interbreeding. The Germanic blood in that country . . ." Richard shook his head sadly. "Anyway, I have studied them a bit and I might be able to help you. But keep it just between us. You don't want anyone to think you needed my help, do you?"

"No, of course not. But I would like to hear your opinion. Just so I can compare it with my own ideas. Refine them, perhaps."

"Yes, as a refinement." Richard smiled his most endearing smile.

14

T HEY SAID THEIR FINAL GOOD-BYES outside in the woods near the entrance to the bunker. The luggage—such as it was—had been sent ahead; all Barbara and Peter had to do was walk to the pickup point to be transported to the farm and from there into town. They would travel by train and ferry since it was easier to arrange than a flight.

Peter gave a final kiss and hug to Marysia, thanked her for all she had done for him, then turned to face his wife. He looked at the bulge in her stomach where their child grew. He wanted to reach out and touch it, but he did not dare. Zosia put her hands out and he grasped them; they stood that way together in hopeless silence for a few moments. There was so much between them that both were speechless. Too much had been said, too much had been left unsaid.

"May I kiss you?" he asked finally. He had been so humbled by the events of the past weeks, he felt unsure about even the simplest assumptions.

"Of course," Zosia replied with an air of frivolity. As if nothing had happened.

He leaned down and kissed her gently on the cheek. She looked slightly affronted but did not say anything. He said quietly, "Good-bye, Colonel," and turned to join Barbara.

Before he had gone even two steps, Zosia called out, "Peter."

He turned back to look at her but did not come closer. She stepped forward so she could speak quietly. Pressing herself against him, she reached up to stroke his face. "I love you."

He shook his head slightly and backed away. "I don't think so." He turned and walked off to join Barbara. He put his arm around her shoulders to help steady himself, and together they headed down the slope without looking back.

Zosia went back to her rooms—to the luxurious two rooms that were now hers alone—and poured herself a small glass of vodka. She downed it in a gulp as a toast to her husband's departure, then she went into her bedroom and opened the carved wooden box that held her small collection of jewelry. Solemnly she twisted the wedding ring from her finger and placed it inside next to the necklace Peter had given her. She looked at it lying there for a moment, and as she stared, she noticed that tears were staining the wood of the box.

She looked away, and her eyes lit upon a classified report lying open on the bedside table. Peter had been reading it for her, so he could offer her a summary of its contents and in that way save her time. He always did that sort of thing, took over any bit of her workload that he could. She turned her back on it, but then her eyes caught sight of Joanna's cupboard. The doors worked properly now—he had fixed them—and there were the happy little folk designs he and Joanna had painted on them. Zosia thought of how Peter would always get up for Joanna, early in the morning, or anytime she had a bad dream or was sick. No matter how tired he was, he always took care of the child so that Zosia could sleep undisturbed.

Zosia grunted with annoyance. It was best this way, she told herself. She did not need him, he was nothing but a drain on her. Who needed the gestures of love, the tenderness, the lively conversation, the humor? She didn't! Who needed the songs sung just to please her, or the way he held and comforted her when she wept about Adam? None of it mattered, she would miss none of it!

Olek would miss him, surely, for Peter had provided the father figure that Olek had so desperately needed. Peter seemed to intuitively understand how important such things could be. Not like Adam. Adam had never felt comfortable with the role of mentor, perhaps being too immature himself. But Olek would do fine on his own. And Marysia, too. She wouldn't miss Peter—the way he always helped out, the way he always found time for her. Damn it! Why was it even a question in her mind? She didn't need him! He was a drain on her! He would ruin her professionalism. Katerina was right. It was better this way. It was better!

There was a light knock on the door, and she closed the lid of the jewelry box and returned to the living room. Marysia stepped into the room unbidden. Zosia quickly wiped at the tears in her eyes and smiled at Marysia.

Marysia did not smile back. She stared down at Zosia's hand. "You didn't lose much time removing your ring, did you?" she noted.

Zosia glanced down at her hand and then back at Marysia. Shrugging, she replied, "It was bothering me."

"What was that all about?"

"What do you mean?"

"Haven't you had enough, Zosia?"

"What are you talking about?"

"That 'I love you.' What was that for? You've never loved him—why not let him leave in peace?"

"I thought he'd like to hear it."

"You thought you'd like to keep a hook in him so that you can draw him back whenever it suits your fancy!" Marysia accused. "For Christ's sake, Zosia, haven't you bled him dry? You got what you wanted out of him! Why couldn't you let him go? He'd have had a chance in England, with Barbara, she'd have been there for him! Now, he'll never take it—he'll keep remembering that you said you loved him!"

"Oh, he'd have come back no matter what I said. He wouldn't abandon the child."

Marysia sighed. "I suppose you're right." She walked over to the couch and sat down heavily. "But what are you doing, Zosia? What have you become? Where is the sweet little girl who loved Adam?"

"Still in love with him." Zosia sat down as well.

"Does that give you the right to abuse others?"

"I've been kind to Peter. Look, he freely admits that most of the problems we have are his fault."

"And you freely accept that. How very fair of you."

"He's too needy to ever be there for me. I treat him fairly, considering how little I get out of the relationship."

"Oh, Zosia! You're beginning to believe your own propaganda! Just think what he's done for you! If only you would open yourself to accepting—"

"Oh, get real. He couldn't even comfort me at the funeral!"

"Comfort *you?* He was the one injured in the bomb blast, he was the one who was arrested and stabbed and forced to watch Joanna's murder!"

"My daughter!"

"His daughter, too! For Christ's sake—they did it to hurt him! Are you in collusion with them?"

"*Marysia!*"

"He's barely recovered from his wounds and a deadly infection, we pull him out of a sickbed and drag him to the funeral, and where are you? Holding on to Tadek!" Marysia spat. "Your husband was nearly murdered and you publicly cling to your lover!"

"He's not my lover."

"And I bet," Marysia added bitterly, "*he* apologized for not being there for *you*."

"Marysia," Zosia begged, "have some mercy. I've lost Joanna—"

"And I bet," Marysia continued, "that you let him take the blame for that as well."

"He was the one who had to insist on going into town with her."

"Who insisted that it was important for him to go into town regularly? Who dragged him out of the encampment when he didn't want to go?"

"That was ages ago! He didn't have to go into town once he got back from America!"

"He didn't know you were done with him!" Marysia hissed. "How was he to know he had served his purpose?"

"He got Joanna killed!"

"And why was she killed?"

"To punish him for speaking out in America," Zosia answered, exasperated.

"And who insisted that he speak? Who gave him no choice about the matter?"

Zosia shook her head, refusing to be drawn in.

"And how did they identify him once he fell victim to the bomb blast?"

Zosia didn't answer.

"His numbers, wasn't it? Who insisted that he not spend a penny of the money he raised on himself? Who said it was too expensive and pointless looking into having those numbers removed?"

"He didn't have to go into town!"

"And who insisted that she just had to return here?"

"He could have stayed in America, if he had wanted."

"You knew that he couldn't stay, not if you returned. Oh, Zosia, you never once thought of what your brilliant strategy was doing to him."

Zosia rolled her eyes. "I happen to remember that you were a party to all these decisions, a long time ago. You thought it was a good idea then, now you're suddenly shocked by what it involved?"

"No, I'm shocked by what you've become. You're trying to be as cold-blooded as Ryszard, but that's not you, honey. And in compensation, you're being cruel."

"I've not been cruel!" Zosia protested. "I saved a man's life, I gave him a home, and I provided him with a family and some sense of stability."

"You told him you loved him, and then you ruthlessly rejected every opportunity he gave you to make that true. You let him think he was unlovable, that he had somehow failed you, and you let him take the blame for everything that went wrong after that point. You complained that he was never there for you, but you never let him close. You manipulated his actions, using his gratitude like some sort of cattle prod, and his love for you as a chain around his neck."

"He didn't need to fall in love. That was his choice."

"You took advantage of someone who was vulnerable, and you haven't stopped. Jesus Christ! At least Elspeth Vogel would have called it by its real name!"

"Marysia, you've said quite enough!" Zosia stood. She was trembling with anger and her hand shook as she pointed at the door. "Get out!"

Marysia stood as well. "And what have you done it for? Cold-blooded professionalism? The cause? Honoring Adam's memory?" She shook her head. "I don't want my son honored in this fashion. And I wonder at a cause that would turn the kind woman that I knew into this monstrous being."

"I said, *get out!*"

Marysia did not leave. "Zosia, we have all given away a part of our humanity in order to continue this fight—that's the price we must pay. But don't give away the ability to love." Marysia reached up to try to stroke Zosia's cheek, but Zosia angrily pushed her hand away.

"I am not going to fall in love again," Zosia hissed. "I will not be hurt again! Damn it, if I choose to organize a propaganda campaign and have to convince the speaker to take part, then I hardly think I should be condemned as monstrous! And if I make a mistake and marry someone I shouldn't have, I refuse to be vilified for the rest of my life because of that!"

"If you feel that way, then why not let him go? With your three little words, you've destroyed his chance for freedom."

Zosia swallowed, unable to answer the question. Why had she said those words?

"It's not wrong to love someone, Zosia. Not even your husband. Why not give him a chance?"

Zosia shook her head. "It would never work."

"Have you ever tried?"

"Please leave, Marysia." Zosia gently grabbed Marysia's arm and led her to the door. "I need to be alone."

She saw Marysia out the door and closed it tightly behind her. Then Zosia turned back and surveyed her living room, seeking the comfort of the familiar as Marysia's wild accusations reverberated through her mind. Only then did she notice the small vase of wildflowers. They were freshly picked; Peter must have collected them early in the morning and left them for her. There was no note, no promises, no pleas—just the flowers that he knew she so loved. She knelt then, knelt to pray as she had not done since Adam had died, but no words came to mind: the years of inattention had left her barren of comfort. She began to cry in earnest then.

15

"**I** WONDER WHY JÄGER?" Barbara asked as they stood alone on the deck of the ferry. "I mean, Niklaus is obvious, but I wonder why they chose Jäger for our last name."

"I think it's their idea of a joke. A play on my last name," Peter replied, staring off across the water. He could not help but think how much Joanna would have enjoyed the ferry crossing. The wind carrying the taste of salt, the untrammeled view to the horizon . . . She had so loved taking that cruise around the island of Manhattan with Zosia. They had been careful then, he had not gone along in case there was any media attention, but Joanna had filled him in on all the details.

"Halifax?" Barbara repeated a bit more loudly, thinking that the wind must have swallowed her words.

"Chase," Peter responded. "The English verb *chase* can be translated to the German *jagen.* Get it?"

"Oh. *Jäger,* hunter; chaser, Chase. I see." Barbara wrinkled her nose in annoyance at her tenuous command of English. "Don't you think it's dangerous using such a name?"

"No . . . or maybe, or I don't know." It was hard to care. Mistakes were so inevitable that it seemed that only luck kept them alive in any case. Would it have hurt less if Joanna had been killed by the bomb blast? Or by a car accident? Or by disease, like Anna? She would still be dead, the only difference is he would have been unaware of that surveillance photo. They could have pulled it off; she had been so convincing! But for that photo, she might still be alive.

Barbara huddled closer to him and he put his arm around her. It was cold out in the bitter sea breeze, and even the bright sunshine could not warm them, but the air felt fresh and they both preferred shivering in the wind to the crowded and unprivate atmosphere below.

As they stood and gazed in silence, the nebulous shadows on the horizon became recognizable as the white chalk cliffs of Dover. He pointed them out to Barbara.

"I know," she said without thinking. "I've been watching them for ages."

"Oh." He suddenly felt foolish. He fumbled in his coat and located his new sunglasses. He held them a moment trying to convince himself that they were not ominous, but as he brought them toward his face, he could feel the knife tracing a pattern over his eyes, and he decided to put them back in his pocket and settle for squinting. As he let his eyes relax again, the cliffs slipped back into unfocused possibilities, and his thoughts turned to his last words to Zosia. He should have said something more profound or more conciliatory. The problem was, each time he thought about it, he thought of something different he should have said. Her declaration of love had surprised him—perhaps he should have told her he loved her as well. It would have been a lot better than what he had said. If he was killed, would she raise their child knowing that the last thing he had said to her was so stupid?

"You don't have to wear that just because we're posing as married," Barbara said, pointing to the ring that he was twisting round and round his finger. "German men often don't."

He stopped fidgeting with it. "I know," he responded absently. After a moment he added, "I want to."

Several hours later their train was speeding through the Kentish countryside and they both watched the view in fascination. Barbara had never been to England, but he was equally unfamiliar with most of his country. He had in his life only ever been outside the Greater London Administrative District—GLAD, in its ludicrous English acronym—on six occasions, only three of which had been legal, and none of those journeys had taken him southward except the one-way trip he had made in a closed and windowless carriage en route to his imprisonment.

The tunnels of the coast and rolling hills inland eventually gave way to the sprawling housing of the suburban villages: the English slums, the German estates, the petit-bourgeois apartments of mixed German low-class or English Conciliators. Here and there were the "unreconstructed" zones—areas that had never been rebuilt after the invasion—and then there were the "illegal" zones—areas where the local administration had withdrawn housing permission and had then exacted a destructive revenge on the resultant squatters. The burned row houses looked abandoned, but Peter knew the streets of rubble hid thousands of homeless sheltering illegally among the crumbling brick walls. By virtue of their undocumented residences they were subject to immediate arrest or deportation for resettlement; nobody really knew what happened to them after that. Not surprisingly, "terrorist" acts were almost invariably followed by a city zone being declared illegal, or as the administration put it "unsafe," and the resultant homeless population was driven to bribery and acts of desperation to find other legal residences.

They stepped out of the carriage into Victoria train station. He scanned around, confused by the changes wrought during his absence. "Ten years," he muttered.

"What?" Barbara asked.

"Nearly ten years to the day since my arrest. A lot has changed, there's so few English signs anymore!"

"It's not illegal," she stated as a sort of question.

"No, just discouraged. You know, if you wanted to advance in a career, or stay in a good school, it was better not to speak it. Still, there used to be a lot of information posted in English." He looked around a bit more. "That seems to have changed."

The taxi took them to a busy road near Eva Braun Station, just west of what had been Regent's Park. It was a relatively undestroyed region of town and at the beginning of the gated German residential community to the north. Their area was not inside the gated community, but was easily accessible to the Germans who lived there and therefore attracted German specialty shops and their attendant low-ranking German residents.

They looked at the row of buildings pressed one against the other and located their address. Downstairs was the bookstore they would manage—above that was their tiny flat. There were two more floors above theirs—both were apartments reached by a stairway located in the next-door building and therefore completely separate from their residence.

They entered the store. A woman looked up questioningly from the book she was repairing.

"The owner of the shop has sent me to take over the management of his store," Peter said, handing her a thick packet of papers. "Here's my letter of appointment and references."

"Ah, yes." She smiled. "I've been expecting you."

That night they stayed in a bed-and-breakfast. As Barbara slept, he pulled back the curtain and stared out the window at the desultory nightlife, listened to the yapping of a dog, watched the mist settle on the ground. He tried to remember what life in London had been like, what he had been like back then, but instead, all he remembered was another strange little room and another sleeping city.

It had all been because Karl had taken a business trip. Mercifully, Peter had not been required to go along, but less fortuitously, Elspeth had been forbidden from accompanying her husband. She fumed over her exclusion, mulled over it, and then, on Karl's first night of absence, she had tiptoed into Uwe's bedroom, tapped Peter on the shoulder, and indicated that he should follow her. She ignored his desperate, silent objections, and he had eventually followed her into her bedroom. As she shut the door behind him, he had pleaded quietly to be allowed to leave. With the children at home, with Uwe perpetually waking up, how could they possibly spend the night together?

It was one of the most unsettling nights of his life. He had spent the entire time listening for movements outside the door, listening for Uwe to call him. He was completely unable to give Elspeth the attention she expected, and eventually, tired of cajoling him, she had fallen asleep next to him. He got up to leave then, but she awoke and commanded him to stay. So he did, nervously napping next to her the entire night. It was not even flattering—she did not want to spend the night with him, did not want to hold him as she slept, she was just using him to express her anger at Karl's absence, and if they were discovered, he was the one who would die.

The next day, at breakfast, Elspeth abruptly announced to the children that she would be visiting her sister Constanze near Dresden. Ulrike would be in charge, Teresa would help out, and Horst was warned not to bully his sisters during her absence. And, by the way, Peter would be coming with her.

They left that evening, arriving late and checking into a hotel with the plan of visiting Elspeth's sister the following morning. Once they were alone in the room, Elspeth ran her finger seductively down his face and along his shirt. "There! Now you not only don't have to worry about the children, you also have plenty of time. But first"—she turned away to pick up the room-service menu—"what shall we have to eat?"

It was the nicest meal he had eaten in a long, long time, and in the carefree atmosphere of their private room, Elspeth was almost charming. His worries eased as he refilled their wineglasses and he began to relax. He even toasted his "beautiful, merciful lady" with something approaching neutrality, if not actual sincerity. It was odd; upon their return everything would be back to the usual highly polarized hierarchy, Elspeth included, but for that night, she treated him as though he were an equal—give or take a few bad habits on her part and a few typical concessions on his. Long after she had fallen asleep, he stood and stared out the window looking at the nightlife of a city he knew not at all, but one that had, for a brief time, given him a measure of humanity.

The next morning Elspeth made the trip to her sister's house. She took him along like some sort of trophy to be sniffed at and inspected. The sisters hugged enthusiastically, then Elspeth plucked at his sleeve and pulled him to stand in front of Constanze, announcing proudly, "And this is my manservant."

"Not at all what I expected," her sister exclaimed as she walked around him. "Mother described him quite differently."

"She would, wouldn't she."

"Yes. Never quite satisfied with anything, is she?"

"No," Elspeth agreed tersely. "What did she say?"

"Oh, that he looked nearly dead on his feet," Constanze answered as though he were incapable of understanding her. "But he looks quite lively! I guess, though, that was when you had him working in a factory job?"

"Oh, that was my husband's harebrained scheme. Anyway, that's long in the past."

"Yes, just as well, judging from what Mother said. You certainly don't want to tire this one out." Constanze smiled at him as though, unable to comprehend her words, he might still be made to understand that she was complimenting him. "You've had him, what, three years?"

"Not quite."

"I'm really surprised you haven't visited earlier."

"Ah, well, you know, after last time . . ."

Constanze nodded knowledgeably.

He felt his face grow hot with embarrassment as he continued to stare at the patterns on Constanze's fine wool carpet. From behind him Elspeth reached up and petted his hair. He visibly shuddered and Constanze frowned slightly, then asked knowingly, "Touchy, though?"

Elspeth nodded. "High-strung."

Constanze reached up slowly toward his face as if trying not to frighten a wild animal. She touched him gently, seductively, then let her fingers trace down his face, along his chest, and onto his thigh, which she then smacked approvingly. "Well done, Elspeth!" She nodded happily. "Well done."

He was sent off to the kitchen to get something to eat while the two women visited. Elspeth's sister seemed to run a much more relaxed household, and the plate of food that was set before him by a smiling old woman was reasonably generous if simple.

"So, you're the new one?" she asked.

"I guess so," he answered between bites of fresh bread and cheese. God Almighty, why couldn't Elspeth be this relaxed! Fresh bread!

"How long have you been lying with her?"

He glanced sharply at the old woman, then returned his attention to his food. "I'm afraid," he answered dryly, "that would be illegal and therefore completely out of the question. Besides"—he smiled wickedly at her—"it would be immoral and immorality does not exist among our *Übermensch*."

She nodded. "Good boy, very wise. But be careful."

"I do my best."

"Well," she said as if changing the subject, "I suppose we'll be seeing you around here sooner or later. The mistress isn't a bad sort, but don't make her husband angry."

"What are you talking about?"

"Oh, your lady will get tired of you, and my lady is not averse to castoffs. I imagine you'll make an extended visit at some point."

Traded from one to the other! No wonder Constanze had looked at him with such interest.

Observing his reaction, the old woman breathed, "Dear boy! It's not by choice, is it?"

Utterly ashamed, he turned away from the woman's probing eyes, shook his head slightly, and answered softly, "No."

"Oh, I am sorry. I just assumed . . ." She did not bother to finish her assumption. Instead she whispered, "I think it's worse for you men."

He looked up at her quite perplexed. "Worse? How so?"

"Yes, worse. When the men expect, er, favors from us, that's all they expect. The women, the women though, they always believe you're going to fall in love with them. It's not enough to submit, is it?"

Keeping his eye on the entryway, he shook his head. "No, whatever I do, it's never enough."

"Not just your body, but your soul as well."

He nodded, then asked, also in a whisper, "You seem to speak from experience."

"Yes, in my day, I was quite pretty." Her eyes took on a distant look and she added melancholically, "They robbed me of my youth." She fell silent a moment, wrapped in bitter memories, but then she revived. "But I was smart and I played along and I'm still alive now and in not too bad a position. And one day"—she winked—"one day the revolution will come."

She smiled and continued without prompting, "It wasn't with her husband." She indicated with her head in the direction of Constanze's voice. "It was her husband's father. The wife didn't seem to mind, maybe she was relieved not to be bothered herself. Who knows. Anyway, once I was no longer interesting to him, I was allowed to stay, and then I was given to the son when he married."

He rested his head in his hands and thought about the Vogel children. Would he be given to one of them when Elspeth grew bored with him? Which one? Horst? Horst would be the worst, and Elspeth knew that, too. It would be Horst then; it would be her retribution for his failing to fall convincingly in love with her.

The curtain dropped back over the window and the dimly lit street disappeared from view. Peter shook his head at the thought of what his life might have been like, but then again, if he had stayed, Joanna would still be alive, he'd be caring for Magdalena, and maybe, just maybe he would have settled into his role in life.

══════ 16 ══════

*R*ICHARD DECIDED HE WOULD ACQUIRE the surveillance files himself rather than request an outside operation. As an insider, they would be reasonably accessible to him, and since there was nothing particularly secret in their contents, they were not well guarded. Anything truly sensitive would be removed long before they were archived. Of course, he would have to be careful not to be seen with Karl's file, but otherwise the acquisition should be fairly easy given his high rank.

As he headed down to the archives, he worried that the files might have been purged. He had already checked the computer, using passwords that should have been unknown to him, and there had been precious little of use there. He said a little prayer as he descended the metal steps to the bowels of the building and hoped that the last several years of information were still intact and that Karl had elicited enough interest in his career to have merited at least occasional surveillance.

He reached the bottom of the stairs and glanced along the hallway's length. To the right were cells for the prisoners and interrogation rooms. Someday, he would probably be dragged in that direction never to emerge. The thought was not reassuring, nor were the occasional noises that filtered down the long hallway. He finished his cigarette and lit another one. Thank God Pawel and Andrzej had left. At least they were out of harm's way, he thought simultaneously with yet another prayer, and thank God the surveillance had apparently ceased. Just another false alarm.

He turned to the left, leaving behind his morbid thoughts, and called up one of his most charming smiles.

"Good afternoon, Herr Traugutt. I haven't seen you in a while." Beate smiled at him.

"Ah, my good Fräulein, it has been far too long!" Richard grinned at her. "But they have you buried here so deep in the bowels of the building, it's hard to find you! Maybe, they want to keep your beauty from dazzling everyone and stopping them from working!"

"Oh, Herr Traugutt! The things you say!" Beate tittered in response, reddening and grinning and ducking her head in a charming-shy manner.

He chatted with her for a while, complimented her, leaned across her desk to sniff her perfume: "Marvelous! Heavenly!" Then he explained the reason for his visit. A newspaper was under investigation. Seemed there were hidden unpatriotic messages in the text. He'd need the files on all the contributing writers, editors, and anyone else involved. Quite a list actually—that's why he had come personally—too much for his secretary to carry. Could she track down this list of names while he ferreted out some others? Oh, of course, he would help, it was a lot to ask and together the work would go much faster!

As she smilingly agreed and went to track down the names from the top of the alphabet, he headed toward the other end. He grabbed one of the folders on his list then went to Karl's file. Grabbing the material from the relevant years—it wasn't empty!—he stuffed it into the folder and then finished gathering the other folders. He would actually peruse them at some point. The newspaper was loyal beyond reproach, and it would serve them right if one or two of them were denounced. It always helped to stir the pot a bit: good, loyal Party members being arrested for disloyalty not only advanced his career—he was the first to spot them, the clever bastards—but also sowed disaffection among the populace.

Beate returned with an armload of files and checked them off along with the stack that Richard presented her. When they were done, he made a point of chatting to her some more, then returned to his office to read through the data. He could probably manage to pluck out a few interesting items and return the rest before the end of the workday.

Karl's file contained several envelopes of photographic negatives. Apparently Karl had been surveilled at least four separate times for a period of several weeks, each time during the years he had owned Peter. There were also isolated photographic negatives from the trips Karl had taken and from the various functions that he had attended. Richard quickly sorted through them. He was only interested in photos that had Peter in them as well. Once he managed to get Karl to deny the entire Halifax story, the release of such pictures would prove singularly embarrassing.

A number of suitable candidates were among them. Most were in the garden surrounding the Vogel house. In fact it seemed Karl was rarely outside without his servant—either ordering him around or harassing him at his work. In several shots both their faces could clearly be seen, and Richard sorted those into a pile. He specifically looked for the incident with the shovel, but unfortunately there was nothing from that time; however, he found a sequence of three photos that would serve as an adequate substitute. The first shot was of Peter lying on the ground near the car, obviously working on something like removing rust or mud from the lowest part of the frame. The next shot had Karl saying something to him; Peter was still on the ground, but had rolled over to look up at his master. The third shot had Karl aiming a kick at Peter's face.

Richard snorted with pleasure at his good luck: nothing could be clearer—a vicious, unprovoked attack on an unarmed man in a defenseless position. Both faces were clear, especially in the second shot, especially if magnified. Perhaps these would be even better than the incident with the shovel since, as far as he knew, Peter had not even bothered to mention its occurrence to his American audience. Such was the brutality of the regime that the incident had passed for normal in his life.

The second picture in the series drew Richard's eye again and his glee subsided. As good propaganda as it was, it was disturbing as well, especially the look on Peter's face. He clearly knew what was going to happen next, yet he was helpless to prevent it. Richard focused his magnifying glass on those eyes, thinking of his own momentary terror as he had looked down the right branch of that long corridor, and he felt suddenly ashamed of himself for his quick and harsh judgment of the man.

Why, he wondered, had he and Tadek been so determined to poison the waters of Peter's marriage to Zosia? Why the brutal humor at Peter's expense? Well, the answer was obvious in Tadek's case. With himself though, it was less apparent, but he suspected it might have been fear. Fear and recognition. Peter was a living reminder of all the things he tried not to think about, of all the right turns down that terrible corridor. Peter was the silent witness that Ryszard himself had spoken about, and his own reaction to Peter had been disturbingly predictable and exactly as desired. It would seem, he mused, that the wall of distrust between the tortured and the rest of the world had builders on both sides.

There was a knock at his door, and as Richard closed the folder over the evidence, Karl entered grinning. "I just wrote up a memorandum to send to the NAU government—I thought you might like to peruse it."

"No," Richard responded almost angrily. Karl looked devastated so Richard quickly explained, "You don't want to talk to their government. They're impotent. What you want to do is prepare a statement to read directly to the American people. I'm busy right now, but why don't you keep tomorrow afternoon free and we can work on it then."

Karl looked stunned by the idea, and Richard realized that in his haste to rid his office of the man, he had not been sufficiently subtle. He summoned up his last shred of charm. "You can trust me on this, Karl—I know what to do."

After Karl had left, Richard reopened the folder and continued sorting through the negatives. He found a poignant one where Peter looked near to death. Karl was berating him for something, and Peter hung his head with a look of resigned dismay. With the transposed colors, it was hard to tell exactly, but Peter had clearly been terribly beaten, and though only the injuries to his face were visible, his expression of hollow misery spoke volumes. Richard set that aside for later use. It would work well in a before-and-after sequence once he had driven Karl into admitting Peter's existence as his slave but had convinced him to deny any brutality. Poor Karl, Richard thought, he was in for a singular run of bad luck on the timing and tone of the statements he would make to the American public.

Once he had finished sorting through the photographs, Richard selected several useful documents and made photocopies of those. Again it was unusual that he did these things himself, but his poor secretary was momentarily over-worked, and being the wonderful boss that he was, he did not mind taking a few minutes from his busy day to queue-jump at the photocopier and make a few quick copies of documents that he needed. He was even sufficiently cour-teous that he would have waited for his turn if the secretaries in the queue had not absolutely insisted that he go in front of them. As he walked away, he bestowed on them that special private smile that each knew was intended specifically for her.

"He's the only one who knows how to work that machine among the men," one commented. The old system, where each and every copy had been funneled through an office for approval and copying had been scrapped, but since then, only the secretaries had learned how to work the one cumbersome machine allotted to their wing.

"He's married," another observed incongruously.

"Doesn't mean he isn't nice," yet another noted.

"And marriages don't last forever," the first opined, giggling.

"Hands off, he's mine."

"We'll see at the *Winterfest* party!"

"Maybe we should roll a die."

They all laughed and continued their musings. Perhaps they were all like that in Göringstadt? It would sure be a welcome change from the pompous and self-important buffoons who paraded around their Berlin office. Transfers anyone?

Back in his office, Richard put the collected negatives and photocopied docu-ments together in an envelope and locked them in his briefcase. He had decided to copy the documents since they formed a complete normal set and any gaps might easily be noted. The negatives, however, were not indexed, and the absence of several would not be obvious even if Karl's file was closely inspected.

He returned to the archives, not pausing this time at the junction at the bot-tom of the steps. He had with him four files. He handed the top three—all from the beginning of the alphabet—to the archivist and indicated that he was fin-ished with them. The fourth, he volunteered to put away himself since it belonged on the other side of the room among the *V*'s. She smiled, noted the returns, and accepted the three folders. Richard went to Vogel's file, dropped the documents back in his folder, and filed the folder he had carried in. He breathed a sigh at his apparent success, said yet another small prayer, and after investing some time in keeping Beate happy with him, returned to his office satisfied with his day's work.

He lit a cigarette, poured himself a small glass of whiskey, and contemplated going home early. After such a day of expended charm, poor Kasia would be in for a grumpy husband. He shook his head in wonder at what she put up with. Ah, how he loved her!

17

OVER TWO DAYS, the bookstore manager showed Peter and Barbara what they needed to know about the management of the store, the codes and contacts, and the equipment they would use. After that, with a satisfied grin that she was finally going home, she vacated the attached flat and the two of them moved in.

Barbara immediately set about making the place into their home—unpacking her clothes, dividing up closet space, sorting out the kitchen. Although she was supposed to help Peter manage the store and handle the contacts and communications, she had also obviously decided to assign herself the role of a proper housewife, and before he had even managed to finish the cup of tea she had made him, she had unpacked his suitcase and begun preparing a dinner for the two of them.

He sat unmoving on the couch, listening to the sound of something frying in the little alcove kitchen just around the partition, and thought about the codes and equipment and contacts. The job did not require his special skills, and his thoughts bifurcated between a growing resentment at this waste of his talents and wondering how soon he could send a personal message. Their communications were relatively secure—they depended on equipment that was smuggled in from the NAU and was allegedly years ahead of what the security services could handle—but there was always the possibility of detection and arrest. Their messages might be secure, but the senders definitely were not. It was a stressful and lonely job with a great deal of risk and little tangible reward. There was no sudden joy of breaking a code, no surge of accomplishment as a train line was dynamited, no congratulations on a job well done. In fact, nothing was ever completed; they were nothing more than a cog in a huge machine passing dangerous information back and forth between directors and operatives or from one political ally to another.

Katerina had indicated to him that on account of his rank and experience and being a native Englishman, he would probably be asked to do more than simply file messages back and forth, but he was sure that she was only softening the blow. Neither side had any reason to trust him politically: the British had lost contact with him too many years ago, and he had never established himself among the Poles. The diplomatic fiasco of his interactions with the British government in exile would not soon be forgotten, and in any case he had spent too much of his life in the hands of the enemy. Collaborating, as Zosia would say.

No, he would not be put to use as a diplomat between Underground groups, he was far too tainted for that.

"Look, Dad!" Joanna's sweet voice broke into his thoughts. He glanced around, but of course, she was not there. He missed her so! Such a happy child, so full of life. In her brief time, she had given so much to him, so much hope, so much confidence. Never before had he felt so unconditionally loved, wanted, and at home. He thought then of his other daughter—little Magdalena, whom he could not see. What lay in store for her? Would she harry her servants mercilessly, held back by no social convention; permitted, encouraged even, by society to be infinitely impatient and demanding? Would she be like her mother? The thought of Elspeth left him feeling cold, and he jumped to his feet as he felt her hand stroke his hair.

"Sorry," Barbara's voice came from behind him, "I didn't mean to scare you."

"Oh." He turned around, thoroughly abashed. "It's just that I thought for a second you were Elspeth."

"Who? Oh, yes, Frau Vogel! Did she come up from behind and stroke your hair when you were sitting?" Barbara teased.

"I wasn't permitted to sit," he replied obscurely.

She looked at him questioningly, but then decided that sizzling noises from the kitchen took priority. "I just wanted to ask you to set the table—the dinner will be ready soon."

"Of course," he responded absently.

After the nice little dinner that Barbara had prepared, they cleaned the kitchen, relaxed a bit, and then retired for the night. Tomorrow would be their first day on the job, and they were both intrigued and a bit nervous. As he undressed, Peter reviewed, once again, all that he had learned. He was sufficiently distracted that it took a few minutes for him to notice that Barbara, sitting on the bed in her nightgown, was staring at him. Once he noticed the vague look of horror on her face, he stopped to consider its possible source. Only a double bed was provided in the apartment; perhaps his assumption that they would share it was the problem?

He looked at her quizzically. "Do you want me to sleep on the couch?" It would not be particularly practical since the couch was not large or comfortable, but there was nowhere else readily available.

"No, no," she said as if in a daze, still staring.

"You don't mind sharing?"

"No, of course not. If anyone should sleep out there, it should be me. After all, you're the senior officer."

Peter smiled at her gentle euphemism. "Then?" he asked, hoping she might explain.

She shook her head at him, chagrined by her obvious gaffe. "I had no idea . . ."

He glanced down at his scarred body. "Oh, yes, of course." Fucking sons of bitches, how he hated each and every one of them who had trampled on him so happily.

"Do they hurt?" she asked, motioning toward the injuries.

He shook his head. "Only when pretty young girls point them out to me," he teased.

She reddened. "I'm sorry! I didn't think . . . I, it's just that . . . Oh!" She threw herself facedown onto the bed in a fit of girlish embarrassment.

"Barbara. It's okay, I was joking!" He laughed. "Here, I'll turn out the lights."

In the dim shadows he saw her emerge from her self-imposed exile; he could just barely discern her face. "Would you put the lights back on?" she asked timidly.

"Why?" he asked as he reached for the switch.

"If we're supposed to be married, I think I should know what you look like. I'm sorry about . . . It was unprofessional."

He nodded and, turning on the lights again, let her look at him as he stood there.

"Would you come sit by me so I can look more closely?"

Was she trying to prove her cool by being so clinical? He nodded and went to sit by her. Without even asking, she ran her hand over his back and along his arms. He turned his head away slightly so she would not see how much her presumptuousness annoyed him. She may have thought she was being sympathetic and open, or perhaps even seductive, but all it felt like to him was the prodding and poking of so many others who had given themselves the rights to his body.

As she caressed him further, he grabbed her hand, forced a smile onto his face, and holding her hand in both of his, assured her as gently as he could, "That's probably enough for now."

She nodded, suddenly aware that she had offended him and grimaced as she turned over to hide her face in the pillow once again. He turned out the light and crawled under the covers without bothering to console her.

"Niklaus, wake up! Are you all right?"

He opened his eyes to see Barbara's anxious face peering down at him.

"What's the matter?" he asked sleepily. The dream was there—or rather the nightmare. Damn, if only he could have slept through it. The vision was still painful.

"You were shaking!"

"So?" he snapped angrily, stunned by the unnecessary cruelty of her waking him. He might have slept through it, would have forgotten it by morning, but now it was there in his memory. Damn it, sleep was so precious, and now it was lost!

"I thought . . ." Barbara fell silent, then tried again. "I just . . . I'm sorry. I thought that I might . . ."

He felt a sudden pity for her confusion. How was she to know? Masking his anger as best he could, he said, "It's okay, don't worry. Thanks for, uh, the concern. But next time, if possible, please don't wake me. I get little enough sleep as it is. Okay?"

"Okay," she agreed sheepishly.

"Do you think I'll bother you?" he asked, trying to soothe her feelings.

"No, no, I'll be all right. Now that I know." She turned over as she said that and buried her head under her arm.

He reached over and stroked her arm. "I'm sorry, I didn't mean to snap at you."

"It's okay. I'm just an idiot," she said forlornly.

They lay silently for a long time, each thinking the other was asleep. Barbara occupied herself with her thoughts, Peter tried not to occupy himself with his. Finally after several hours he fell back asleep.

The bomb exploded silently this time. It all happened in silence. The blast, the way he threw himself down on Joanna, the terrible wind of shrapnel impaling him with thousands of daggers as he lay there. He rolled off the child, felt again the stabs of pain as each piece of glass dug its way deeper under his skin. There was mayhem; he looked down, saw the piece of glass in his leg. He was standing, swaying dizzily, and then he screamed at Joanna to run, to run as far away from him as she could, to run and hide. Sound bombarded the scene as he yelled his warning. He could hear her footsteps as she took flight, could hear the glass still tinkling to the ground, could hear the people running about, trying to help. He felt himself pitch forward, saw the ground coming up to meet him, but Joanna was gone, she was safe, she had run away.

He awoke panting. Why hadn't he told her to run? Surely there must have been time! The scene had played itself out in his mind so many times—both asleep and awake—that he knew each terrible microsecond. *Run!* How long does it take to say that? Why hadn't he told her to run?

The word repeated itself over and over in his mind as if trying to tutor him. This is how you say it, this is how to do it next time. Run. Run away and hide. How many times did he have to hear himself say it? Over and over he heard himself speak, saw her take flight in his imagination. He greeted her again back at the encampment sometimes; congratulated her on her escape. "You said run," she told him, "so I did."

He sat up in bed and rubbed his face. It was going to be one of those nights. Though he was exhausted, he rose and went to the desk, gathered a few sheets of paper and a pen, and decided to write a long letter to Zosia. It would be ages before it reached her; perhaps there would be no opportunity to send it at all. It was futile, there would be no comfort to be had from her reply if there even was one, but still he wrote. Without preamble, he told her about his dream, that was uppermost on his mind; then he wrote about his memories of Joanna and the good times the three of them had had together. He mentioned over and over how much he missed Zosia, how much he loved her.

"I wish I could write poetry," he wrote, "so that I could let you know just how much I miss you. It's like a physical pain, hell, it is a physical pain. Oh, Zosiu, I love you so much, why do we have to be apart? What have I done?"

He looked at the words and realized he had written something almost identical only a few paragraphs before. Such repetition looked foolish; better to write something else. He let his thoughts wander, and he began telling her about his impressions on his return to England:

"Both Chase and Halifax are far in the past (other than those few weeks just before my arrest), and nearly all my memories of this place come from Yardley. He was such a different fellow—not the lonely boy, not the determined and rebellious youth. He went to pubs and slept around (before A.) and violated curfew to watch the stars at night (there are some dark corners near the river—and yes, we do have an occasional cloudless night!) and generally he had a pretty good time of it all. Confident, happy—if a bit lonely—he would have gone mad for you and your adorable daughter. I don't know if you would have liked him though. Maybe better than you like me (I've gathered that's not saying much anymore), maybe not at all. I wonder how much of him was me, I wonder how much I can become him again. And do I want to?"

Peter scowled at the page. It was stupid referring to himself in the third person, but it seemed apt. He wasn't Yardley anymore, and he hardly remembered how he could ever have been so unfettered. Worse though, was that last parenthetical remark. He wanted to remove it, but it was in ink and he'd have to rewrite the entire page. Maybe he could scratch it out? Knowing Zosia, that would only convince her to find out what lay underneath and she would then give it even more significance for the difficulty of discovery.

He decided to let it stand as it was. Zosia would probably never even see the letter, and even if she did, she would probably skim its contents in her always rushed way. Deciding to explore his thoughts without worrying about Zosia's reaction, he continued, "Would you want me to be more like him? I think he might have reminded you of Adam. I don't know whether that would have been good or not. I'm sure that he'd never have matched up to"

He hesitated, realizing he had written himself into a corner. The first words that came to mind were "your super husband," but that sounded far too bitter, albeit an accurate reflection of his feelings. He constructed Zosia's thoughts on the subject: Adam would never have let Joanna get taken, Adam would never have copulated with a Nazi-ette, Adam would never have . . . Peter snorted his derision. He would probably have liked the guy if he had known him, would probably have respected him as well, but this competing with his ghost—that was pure folly. He had known it would happen, had warned both Zosia and himself, but still it was worse than he had expected. It seemed unwinnable. Turning his attention back to the paragraph he had been writing, he tried to construct a tactful exit. He decided on "some of your expectations though," and left it at that.

He then turned to a description of their first several days in London, the weather, the people, the changes that he had noted. He wrote about how he had taken Barbara to one of his favorite pubs on their first night in town to get a meal, but realized just as they approached the door that as Germans they would probably be made to feel extremely uncomfortable inside. He had led her away, and they had found a quiet German-friendly establishment close to their new home.

"It's strange," he wrote, "but I never experienced it from that angle and it made me feel irrationally angry at them all. I just wanted to have a nice meal yet I knew that we'd probably get beer spilled on us or someone would vomit in our direction or do something else unpleasant. There could have even been a stupid fight if anyone was feeling brave enough to risk police intervention. I wonder if there are any places where Brits and Krauts mix freely. I didn't know of any before, but after all these years, perhaps things have changed. I'd like to mix in with them but I'm afraid it's just not going to happen."

The words looked strange. He had said *them* in reference to the English and he had clearly written it as if he were a German living in London. How odd! Still, the way they were treated defined to a great extent who they were, and they were treated as Germans—there would be no way around that fact. With all the privileges, with all the jealousies, with all the suffused hatred that would involve. It was ironic and unfair, and it pushed him toward sympathies that would otherwise have been abhorrent. It was, he realized, exactly what he had hoped to avoid when he had argued with the Underground leadership so long ago.

He wrote for several hours more, digressing into whatever topic crossed his mind—the way the mountain wildflowers bloomed in a profusion of color, the sound of the pine needles underfoot, the glistening of diamond-scattered sunlight on the fast-flowing streams. He told Zosia how beautiful she was, how he missed her, and asked how everyone was doing—each by name. He realized he missed more than Zosia, he missed the entire place and the people there.

He also realized, quite suddenly, that he had spent the time free of nightmares or visions. He felt tired and relaxed and somewhat sure that he would fall into a restful sleep. And he had not drunk a drop! Pleased with his discovery, he got up, stretched, and returned to the bed. Barbara had confiscated his side of the bed. Gently lifting her up and back onto her side, he lay down and fell into a peaceful sleep that lasted the rest of the night.

18

"So, KARL, LET'S SEE WHAT YOU'RE GOING TO SAY to the American public," Richard offered in his most friendly voice, atoning for the previous day's snub in his office.

"I'm not so sure I should address the public directly. It's so low class."

"No, you must! The American government has no control over its people. They're a bunch of impotent fools—that's what comes of democracy. The entire place is run by opinion polls of the voters' preferences, and those opinions are manufactured by their Jewish-controlled media. It's pointless defending our interests to their government—they're toothless. We must win over the American populace!"

"But if the media are controlled by Jews, how can we possibly get a fair hearing?" Karl moaned.

Richard smiled knowingly. "We have some friends there. I'm sure I can arrange something for you if you want."

"You could?" Karl sounded stunned by his friend's reach and power.

"Yes. And I'll make sure you get credit for everything you do! My role will simply be to facilitate whatever you choose to present," Richard offered magnanimously.

"But what should I present?" Karl wailed. "The boys in Propaganda had no luck, and the Führer's office couldn't get a good response either. What can I possibly do?"

"Their mistake was they protested to the government to suppress the whole affair. That won't work. We've got to fight fire with fire. We've got to give our side of the story directly to the American people, and we've got to make it attractive so that they listen to it. That's why we need you—you've got the presence we need!" Richard tutored Karl yet again. How many times did he have to explain to the moron!

Karl's hand went impulsively to smoothing his naturally blond hair. "So what should I say?"

"What I would do is deny the whole thing. It's all a plot. They—that is, the American Jewish media—hired some actor and had him fake the whole damn thing. Every word of it. Then, they faked the video as well. It's all a fake and there is no way they can prove otherwise."

"No way," Karl repeated, entranced. He had not thought of that, but, yes, they had no way to prove any of it. All a fake. Every last word! What a brilliant idea.

"But I'm sure that's what you had in mind already." Richard blew a stream of smoke into the air and watched it dissipate. "Wasn't it?"

"Oh. Yes, yes," Karl hastily answered. "I was just thinking along those lines. How very disconcerting that you should have so accurately reflected my thoughts!"

"I was just building on something you mentioned the other day. It must have come to you in a flash, but of course, it took me several days to understand what you were saying."

Karl grinned. It was clever of him, wasn't it! If only he could remember what he had said and if anyone else had heard it. He wouldn't want someone else taking credit for his idea, after all!

"Tell you what," Richard continued. "I'll lay out a script for you and you find a translator." Best for Karl to organize the translation—there was a good chance he'd screw it up and that would only make their reply to the Halifax video all the more ridiculous.

"A translator?"

Richard dug a fingernail into the back of his skull to distract himself for a moment. When he had located his patience again, he explained, "Yes, as you noted, they don't speak German there and we could hardly hope to get a sympathetic translation from those gangsters who run their media."

"Oh, yes, I, um . . ."

"Organize the filming for next week—that will be plenty of time. Don't you think?"

Richard spent the rest of the workday creating a script for Karl, and then to say that he had officially accomplished something, he randomly picked four files from the stack of folders on his desk and handed them to an underling, saying, "I've studied these and found their behavior extremely suspicious. I want them put under round-the-clock surveillance, and I want you to determine why they are acting suspiciously." Laughing to himself at the grand idiocy of it all, he then went home.

In the taxi on the way home, he mused about the possibility of having some evidence planted against two or three of the four. It would look good if he had once again managed to spot wreckers or saboteurs or infiltrators among the most loyal and patriotic segment of the population. Of course, he would have to get clearance, and that was always a nuisance; the other organizations were terrible about sharing information as they naturally wanted to protect their operatives' identities. He would have to put in a request to HQ this week, but once the suspects were cleared, he could have some fun with them. He laughed hoarsely, his laughter dissolving into a coughing fit before it ceased altogether. Then he lit another cigarette.

His thoughts turned to his genuine work. He would have to get those documents and negatives and an outline of the plan off to his father quickly. Maybe he and Kasia could stop by the bookstore on Saturday morning. A family outing. Should he show Kasia the negatives first? There was no particular reason to do so, but he knew she would be interested, and she might have some good ideas about how to time everything. She had a real knack for that sort of thing. Yeah, he'd show her. Of course, that would mean he'd have to explain the contents of the videotape. He did not like the thought of doing that, but he could not really leave her in the dark about it. He should have told her long before, when he was forcing his sons out of the house. She was not ignorant of the danger they were all in, and he was stupid to think he was shielding her by not telling her about the videotape. He started coughing again, but this time it dissolved not into laughter but into sobs. Poor little girl. Poor sweet, happy, lively little girl.

As Ryszard walked up the path, he pulled out his packet of cigarettes, but it was empty. Somehow that infuriated him, and as Leszek opened the door for him, he walked in fuming. He reached for the cigarette box, but Leszek preempted him, picking up the box, opening it, and offering it to him.

"Enough of this shit, already," Ryszard snapped. "The surveillance is off for now, so would you just stop with all this crap?"

"Look," Leszek said, lapsing into familiar speech, "mine and my wife's life are just as dependent on this little charade never being detected as your family's. If you can't handle it, why don't you just pull out?" And get us out of this hellhole assignment as well, he did not need to add.

"Who the hell do you think you are!" Ryszard yelled in reply, raising his fist threateningly. Kasia stepped into the entryway; she motioned with her head toward the sitting room, and Ryszard sheepishly went in.

Kasia asked Leszek to bring them drinks, then joined her husband in the sitting room. She didn't say anything for a long moment, then tenderly she advised, "Ryszard, my love, you must relax a bit."

Ryszard looked ready to reply but Leszek came in with their drinks. After he had set them down and left the room, Ryszard said quietly, "I despise that man."

"But why, dear?"

"He thinks he knows this job better than me."

"He's a good man."

"My sweet wife, you think that about everyone."

"He wants to expand his contacts here. He thinks he can organize something among the workers."

"*What?* No! I don't like that you let the two of them out and about as much as you do."

"Ryszard, you have no idea what it's like here for us! We wait, day in and day out, with virtually nothing to do. It's both dangerous and boring. You've got to let them have some diversion. Something to make them feel useful."

"They're useful here, doing their job. That's enough."

"Darling, please. They might be able to—"

"I said no," Ryszard growled. "It's dangerous and we can't afford that sort of risk. I won't have it."

"But—"

"I said no!"

Kasia sighed. "So how was your day at work?"

Ryszard pulled out the envelope of negatives and documents, explained about the contents of the videotape, and outlined his plan to Kasia.

"Yes, I think it will work. It looks well laid out." Kasia sounded reassuring. She squinted at the negatives. "I can't really make much out. Do you have a magnifying glass?"

"Yeah, here."

Kasia accepted the glass and looked at the pictures. "Oh, that's a nasty one. He looks awful here, too." She looked up at Ryszard and smiled. "Yes, I think it will all work well."

He was surprised that she did not show more emotion. "I thought you liked your brother-in-law. Don't those pictures bother you?"

Kasia tilted her head in surprise. "Not really," she finally answered. "It's all so long in the past."

"Yeah, I guess it's all over and done with," Ryszard said without conviction. It bothered him that Kasia was less perturbed by the photographs than he had been. Was he losing his cool? Perhaps, he consoled himself, it was actually seeing that videotape. Simply describing it did not do it justice. Or perhaps it was fear. He identified with Peter in the videotape. It was the sort of revenge they would take on him. They would use his family's deaths to torment him. They might even let him live a good long time as they murdered each member of his family one by one in front of him. They would rape Kasia, repeatedly and brutally, just so he could see it. His tongue probed back to his tooth. Could he expect his family to kill themselves? Would his children do that? Could he kill himself immediately and abandon them to their fates, hoping that his death would preempt any action against them? Or would he, like Peter, suspect that only his long and tortured death would satisfy them? It was clear Peter had guessed that if he stayed alive they might leave Joanna alone. It was clear he had guessed wrong, but who was to have known? Would he know when the time came?

"You need an eyewitness," Kasia said, interrupting his morbid thoughts.

"What?"

"Well, they can claim the pictures and document copies are fake as well."

"They're negatives," Ryszard pointed out.

"Even so," Kasia replied.

"I won't write that into Karl's scripts."

"Still, he might take the initiative. Or someone else might suggest it. You need a living witness."

"To what?"

"To anything. Any indication that Peter was genuine." Kasia paused. "Didn't he say there was a daughter who was rebellious? Maybe she could be suborned."

"Too young. Besides it's not really feasible. We'd have to convert her and spirit her out of the country and . . . I just don't think that would work. And they could say she's an actress as well."

"Yeah. It needs to be somebody already known."

"I just don't see that as being possible."

"What about a diplomat?"

"Hmm?"

"Well," Kasia explained, "didn't Peter say he served at diplomatic functions sometimes? And they're always kept under surveillance. Maybe there would be a diplomat who was at one of those and would remember him."

Ryszard shook his head. "Even if we could somehow trace the parties he worked . . ."

"I'm sure you could get that information directly from Karl."

"How would he remember?"

"His accounts. He must have them from that far back. He'll have been paid for Peter's labor."

"If it wasn't done as a favor."

"You can be sure he kept track of those as well."

"Yeah, I might be able to get the information from him. Okay, say I can locate a list of functions—so what? Nobody remembers servants. Who'd remember him? And what good would it do?"

"You only need one person of standing from a nonallied country to say he saw Peter at one of those functions. Just one. Then his existence and story are undeniable."

"Hmm. It would be a nice extra touch." Ryszard wondered if it would be worth the extra work. Tracking the receptions—reasonably easy; getting the surveillance photos—probably not a problem, he could invent a plausible reason. Identifying the people in the negatives would be tedious but not particularly taxing. But finding someone who remembered Peter, a nameless, faceless servant in a foreign country?

"If you get a reception during the period when this photo was taken"—Kasia held the one where Peter was an obvious wreck—"then he might have been more memorable."

"Yeah. But Karl might not have loaned him out at that time."

"Leased," Kasia corrected.

"So?"

"Money, dear. Do you think he'd be ashamed of his handiwork?"

"No. He's quite proud of it."

"And with money involved?"

"You're right. I doubt he bothered to keep Peter under wraps just because he looked battered."

"Also, Peter is rather distinctive, at least for that class, and with the criminal stripes on his arm, he may have aroused curiosity."

"Yeah, that criminal link is a problem." Ryszard was distracted by that thought.

"But it's just arbitrary! He wasn't any more criminal than . . ." Kasia was going to say "you or me" and realized just how stupid that would be.

"The Americans have a real problem with criminality. They take the label seriously whether it's deserved or not. In news articles they use the word *prisoner* as if they were not humans, as if they're a different species."

"Or subhuman?"

Ryszard laughed. "They do that with prostitutes as well. Rarely do they refer to them as women. 'A prostitute was murdered,' they'll report, as if her job defined her existence. Part of their piety and drug-war siege mentality, I'd say."

"How was his criminality handled on his original visit?"

"He tiptoed around it. Didn't actually mention he was classified as 'criminal.' Just kept mentioning the facts of his case, rather than the labeling. But if Karl mentions that label—well, the American public is likely to think Peter deserved whatever he got."

"They're not that naive, are they?"

"Some are. They seem to think that once you're found guilty in any legal system, then whatever happens to you is your own fault."

"Obviously the result of never having lived with a mad government."

"Obviously," Ryszard agreed. And what assumptions did *they* make having *always* lived with insanity as the norm?

"Well, if Karl wants to mention it, maybe you should point out how bad it would look that he harbored a criminal in his house. Would that work?"

"It just might." Ryszard grinned. "Anyway, Karl is such an arse, he won't even think to mention it if I don't tell him to."

"Good, now back to my eyewitness idea."

"I think it's great. I'll see what I can dig up." Ryszard got up and went over to his wife and kissed her. "*Moja kochana Kasiu*, do you know how empty my life would be without you?"

"I can only guess."

19

*I*T WAS THE FOURTH NIGHT IN A ROW that it had happened. Awake and disturbed, he lay there. No nightmares, nothing horrible; yet it was so disconcerting and uncomfortable. He lay perfectly still on his side, turned away from Barbara. She was asleep but pressed up against him so that he could feel every curve of her body against his back. He was hard, erect, on fire with desire. He had been dreaming about sex, but couldn't even remember with whom. Just sex with some woman, any woman it would seem. The warmth of Barbara's body, the softness of her hand as it lay casually draped over him, all of it was driving him wild with need.

Carefully, so as not to wake her, he reached downward. Maybe he could at least relieve some of the physical tension. If he didn't, the resultant lower-abdominal pain would add insult to the injury of his frustration. Damn Zosia! Did she want him to sleep with Barbara? How long did Zosia think he could tolerate having a beautiful young woman who was madly in love with him in the same bed with him night after night? What in God's name had Zosia been thinking when she had imposed this exile on him? Or did she just not care?

His hand moved slowly, up and down. His breath came in more labored gasps as he felt the unbearable tension building. He began to stroke a bit faster, struggling to minimize his movements without unduly distracting himself from the pleasure.

"Are you awake? What are you doing?" Barbara mumbled.

That slowed him down a bit. What he would give for just an iota of privacy in his life! "Nothing," he answered through gritted teeth, hoping she'd get the hint to leave him alone to get on with it before he lost the threads of his fantasy.

Her hand slipped forward across his stomach, under the waistband, and down to join his hand. She stroked the veins on the back of his hand, twined her fingers in his.

"Barbara . . ."

"Let me do it."

"I don't—"

"As a friend. Just massaging you, massaging away your tension. Don't do anything, just relax." Delicately she began to caress him. He started to pull her hand away, but then he stopped. What harm would it do? It felt so good to be so gently touched.

"Turn a bit."

He did, rolling onto his back so she could reach him more easily. She rested her head on his chest and positioned herself so she could use both hands. Her fingertips danced over his skin, located scars from electrical burns, from cutting cords, from any number of brutal tortures; she memorized their locations and thereafter deftly avoided touching the fragile skin with its painful memories. He began to relax as he recognized her caution, and he took her at her word and closed his eyes, not even thinking of reciprocating or of kissing her or of doing anything except accepting her attentions. He wasn't doing anything, he assured himself, wasn't being unfaithful, and it felt so nice. It felt really, really nice. So relaxing, so . . . Again the tension built, more intense this time on account of the delay and on account of her alien touch. He wanted her, wanted to pull her on top of him, kiss her passionately, thrust himself deep inside of her, ah . . .

When his brain started functioning again, he wondered momentarily who "she" had been. Was it Zosia he had wanted or Barbara? Or maybe nobody in particular? He lay on the bed, covered in sweat, trying to keep the sticky puddle on his stomach and chest from dripping down his sides. He felt too happy and relieved to even think of being embarrassed but did laugh to himself at the thought of what he must look like.

Barbara slipped out of the bed and returned with a washcloth and washed him, making a special effort to avoid hurting him. His scars weren't all that sensitive, but it was sweet that she was so careful, and he grinned at her idiotically. When she was done, she left to wring out the cloth, then she returned to the bed, kissed him on the forehead, and curled up next to him, throwing her arm across his chest.

"Where in the world did you learn to do that?"

"Oh, girl talk. Intuition," she answered obscurely.

He pulled the covers up over the two of them, relaxed as she held him, did not even mind as her hand slipped downward and rested, holding him gently, almost possessively. He wondered if she had expected him to reciprocate, but her soft breathing indicated that she was only interested at the moment in sleeping, and he fell into a dreamless and peaceful sleep in her arms.

20

ALEX SCANNED THE OUTLINE of what Ryszard planned for his next release. It was all going wonderfully. That pompous Vogel arse droning away at the American public, telling them they had been duped, implying they were stupid and naive, explaining that the entire Halifax story was a hoax generated by inferior exile-types. Heh! Just as things had begun to settle down, the Vogel presentation had hit the air. Alex could hear his son's dripping cynicism behind each and every one of Karl's words. It was marvelous and it all sounded so incredibly patriotic. Karl would think he was doing wonderfully. Even his bosses would praise him. Until . . .

Alex listened carefully to the recording he had made of Karl's presentation on American television. It had been difficult to find a full airing of it, and even then they had so carefully jacked up the translator's voice that Karl was almost inaudible behind him. Alex wanted to hear the German so he could work out what Karl was really saying. The translation was appalling: ungrammatical, uncolloquial, stiff, and even occasionally wrong. It was a nice touch. Alex wondered who had arranged it.

"What's this request to get in touch with this diplomat?" Anna interrupted him.

"Shh!"

"Oh, shush yourself. Put that thing on hold and answer me!" Anna snapped.

"It's 'pause,' " Alex corrected as he pushed the appropriate button. He had noticed that Anna was becoming more and more—what was the word for it?—aggressive? Pushy? Emancipated? It was annoying.

"Pause-shmause. What's this about?"

"Ryszard has tracked down a real person who met Peter at a diplomatic function in Berlin. He's from some African country or kingdom or whatever. Anyway, he's currently here in the NAU, and there's actually a photograph of him conversing with Peter."

"Conversing?"

"Well, he seems to have stopped at his drinks tray for longer than it takes to say 'another one of these'—through three consecutive photos, in fact. So we're hoping he remembers Peter and can verify his story or at least his existence."

"What was Peter doing attending a diplomatic function?"

"Weren't you listening! He was serving!" Alex laughed.

"Serving? Who'd remember a servant?"

"Well, here's a copy of one of the photos. What do you think?"

Anna studied the photograph. "Oh, God, he looks like hell. Maybe the other fellow will remember him. I guess the picture will help jog his memory."

"No doubt. Unfortunately, he's more likely to find forgetting convenient. They get money from the Reich."

"Are they allies?"

"No, but he's unlikely to want to upset them. We need a way to convince him it's in his best interest."

"Does he get money from us?" Anna suggested.

"From the NAU—yes. From us, no."

"You know what I meant."

"Yes, but the point is, the NAU authorities have no interest in putting pressure on him."

"Wouldn't they want the truth to come out?"

Alex snorted his derision. "Yeah, sure. Anyway, I have a much better lead. Remember that woman on the late-night show? She's from the same country and is famous."

"I never heard of her."

"Others have. Anyway, I'm sure she gets invited to their embassy parties. She almost certainly knows this guy, so I'm going to ask her to talk with him. She's coming over later this week." Alex turned his attention back to viewing the tape.

"Oh." Anna raised her eyebrows. She stood silently for a moment, then said coldly, "I guess I should prepare some hors d'oeuvres or something. Shrunken heads perhaps."

Alex glanced up from the videotape machine, confused by Anna's unusual archness, but she had already left the room.

"So, you want to speak with me," Arieka stated between draws off her cigarette. She leaned back in the chair and surveyed her hosts coolly. They had all sat down at the dining table rather than on the sofa as if they were expecting to conduct business. Arieka noticed how the man held on to a file as if anxious to show it to her. "And why do I want to talk to you?"

Anna sniffed as Alex explained, "As I said to you on the phone, it's about Peter Halifax. I believe you were friends?"

"I met him. I'm here. What about him?" Arieka's eyes scanned the tiny flat. A few photographs on the wall near the sofa, some small carved wooden boxes scattered about, a black shawl with a pattern of bright roses woven into the cloth, currently used as a small tablecloth; otherwise everything looked as though it had been acquired in Manhattan. Naturally, they would have come nearly empty-handed.

"You saw the videotape?" Alex asked. Call me Alex, he had said when she had greeted him at the door with a questioning stutter.

"Yes, a bit of it. And some stills in a magazine." Arieka felt suddenly sad. "I knew he'd go back. I told him not to."

"After the show."

"Yes, we went to my apartment." Arieka noticed how the woman stiffened. She had hardly said a word since her heavily accented greeting, just offered Arieka a drink and some cheese and crackers.

Anna got up from the table. "I have an appointment." Grabbing her purse, she left the apartment.

"She thinks I slept with him?" Arieka asked after the door had snapped shut.

"Perhaps."

"And she disapproves."

"Quite probably."

"She does not approve of a white man with a black woman?"

"More likely"—Alex decided to drop all pretense of coyness—"she does not approve of her son-in-law with any woman other than her daughter."

"Her son-in-law?" Arieka repeated. Then as she began to piece together the facts, a look of realization came over her face. "So that was your grandchild on the tape?"

"Yes. It gets lost in the translation, but it's my name the interrogator invokes."

"Sheval . . . ?"

"Yeah, Przewalewski. My daughter's child and Peter's adopted daughter."

"Adopted! Oh, that explains the age. I am so sorry!" Arieka moaned. It was to Alex's ears one of the few reactions he had heard about Joanna's death that sounded genuinely sympathetic.

"So am I," he said simply.

"So he wasn't lying . . ." Arieka sounded distant.

"When?"

"How did you know he went to my apartment afterwards?"

"We called the hotel after the show. They told us he said he'd be out."

"Oh, yeah, he wanted to call you—his handler, he said—directly but then he guessed you'd all be asleep, so he left a message at the front desk. Then we went over to my place and had drinks."

"And?"

"Does it matter?"

"Not to me," Alex replied truthfully.

"We talked a lot. Played my guitar. He had me teach him some songs from my childhood. God, I could hardly remember the words, and my voice is not the best, but he wrote down what I sang and then sang it back to me. I guess he liked the alien words and rhythms. And we drank, smoked cigarettes—I gather he was not a nonsmoker, despite appearances to the contrary."

"He is now."

"Really?"

"Yeah, Joanna—that's the girl on the videotape—she asked him to quit."

"Oh. And he did?" Arieka remembered how much he had enjoyed smoking, how he had savored each cigarette.

"I think he'd have done anything for that little girl," Alex answered ruefully. "He really wanted to be a father to her." He frowned at a memory, then said, "So that was it? Nothing else?"

Arieka smiled. "I wouldn't tell *you* if we did. But, you can tell his wife he didn't. He said he would like to, but he couldn't. I thought he was just putting me off; that maybe he was embarrassed."

"Embarrassed?" Alex asked despite himself.

"You know, from the scars."

"Oh, and how did you know about those?"

"He told me," Arieka answered with a bit of surprise. "He said his clothes hid a lot of unpleasant history. Anyway, I guess that wasn't the reason after all. Well, I digress."

Alex nodded his agreement. He pulled out the photocopy of the photograph, pointed to the relevant section of the photo, and then produced a magnified copy of that section. Only two people were in the magnification—Peter holding a tray and an African diplomat in a long robe and wearing a hat with multicolored bands. "Do you know him?" Alex pointed at the diplomat.

Arieka held the photocopy and stared at it a long time. She knew the diplomat quite well, in fact, but that was not what she was looking at. It was Peter, he was unmistakable; yet he looked so different! She looked at the black eyes, the bruised and beaten face, and heard his voice in her mind as he joked about his years as a slave. They had all laughed, had not wanted to hear anything but humor, had turned away from the possibility that there had been genuine pain. She heard the gunfire in her village, remembered her father dragging her by the hand as they ran for cover, remembered how in the city she had disowned it all and in America it was the stuff of anecdotes and colorful stories. "Yeah, I know him," she said finally. "What can I do for you?"

Alex explained what they needed, and Arieka nodded her head. "He's hot for me, so I'll have no problem getting him to do my bidding, foreign aid or no foreign aid."

Alex thanked her, and when they parted, he kissed her warmly on each cheek, figuring that since she was not an American, he did not have to stick with the cold American custom of shaking hands.

Arieka was on the street before she recalled that Alex had used the present tense: *he is now.* So he was alive! Her heart leapt with happiness for her friend. Somehow, miraculously, he was alive.

21

SHE DIDN'T EVEN BOTHER TO ASK the next time; in fact, he was not even quite awake. Still, his need was obvious, and Barbara reached over to be helpful—as a friend. Peter woke with her hands working their magic and his body on fire with desire.

"Stop it," he muttered while trying to hold on to the dream she had inspired. Allison, of all people. She used to do that, wake him up like that. After all these years, he had been dreaming of Allison. What would Zosia think? What would Barbara think?

In response to his feeble command, Barbara draped one of her legs over him. He could feel the damp heat between her thighs. She continued to tease him and he moaned with agonized pleasure.

"Please, Barbara, stop it," he said, trying to put some conviction in his words, pushing her hand away. It didn't work. She held him closer, grasped him more intimately, and kissed him passionately on the shoulders and neck. He tried to wake himself, to call up all the arguments against letting her continue, but it was too late, and still half-asleep he gave in and without in any way reciprocating he closed his eyes and enjoyed her kisses and caresses.

He jerked convulsively and the movement woke him up. He opened his eyes and stared at the ceiling. His hand compulsively wiped his face, but there was no blood there, nothing at all. Barbara was sound asleep and he guessed hours had passed. He felt the familiar dread, that awful fear of sleeping, and sighing his resignation, he got up. He made himself a cup of tea and spent some time writing a letter to Zosia. Then when his eyes had grown tired, he closed them and began thinking about where his life was going and wondering what to do about Barbara. It seemed stupid that two people could have such desire and suppress it. Whom would it hurt? Zosia didn't care what he did; he could even tell her and she would just shrug her shoulders, if she even bothered to listen. She didn't even love him, had just sent him away into this impossible situation. Why in God's name was he showing her a loyalty that was not only meaningless to her but probably undeserved? Doubtless, she was finding comfort in Tadek's arms whenever she needed it.

He wondered momentarily why he had never asked her outright what her relationship with Tadek was. She would probably tell him the truth—that is, if she deigned to answer. More likely, she would grow angry at the implied constraints on her independence. So, she guarded her independence and privacy jealously, while he pushed Barbara away just for the sake of some idiotic and unappreciated loyalty. Where was the sense in it all? Whom would it hurt?

Zosia didn't care, he would satisfy his physical needs, and Barbara would finally have a chance to express her love for him. She had tried in so many ways. She made their little flat as comfortable as one could want, she cooked lovely meals and did most of the shopping and cleaned everything before it was even dirty. They went for walks together and she listened with rapt attention to anything he had to say, she took an interest in anything he was interested in, she studied English and tried to learn about English culture. She did everything to make herself attractive, not only physically but as a companion. A lifelong companion.

And there was the rub. If he began a liaison with Barbara, she would be sure to misinterpret it. No matter how clearly he laid out the ground rules, she would think that he either loved her or would soon love her. The simple fact was that he didn't. He found her pleasant and pleasing, physically attractive and a comfortable companion, but he did not love her. There was too little feedback. She was like a mirror, working to reflect his ideas and desires; it was fun and flattering, but it was terribly insubstantial. He needed someone with experience, with independent and vociferous opinions. He needed a partner, not an appendix. He needed Zosia.

With years and experience, Barbara was sure to grow into a wonderful maturity, but it would take time, and if she were to spend that time as his companion or wife, he suspected they would never escape the almost father-daughter relationship that their friendship resembled. He would teach her and she would learn, but her experiences would be those of a student. She would have nothing to offer him except what he himself had helped develop. It could work, but it was more likely not to. And more to the point, they would be working toward the possibility that he might one day love her. Everything would hinge on his emotions developing according to a plan while she would have to maintain an almost infinite patience. It would be pointless and insulting. He would be trying to turn her into some gentler version of Zosia, and if Barbara ever understood that, she would learn to hate him forever.

So, anything they began was doomed to be temporary. Even so, it might be a pleasant diversion if only Barbara weren't so in love with him. Even worse, he would, as far as he could guess, be her first sexual partner. What a history to establish! Her very first man would be doing nothing more than using her to make up for missing the woman he loved. All her hopes of cajoling him into loving her would be used against her. When it all ended, as it surely would, she would have nothing more than the knowledge that the man she had dearly loved had treated her so shabbily. She might well come to loathe herself or the feelings that had led her into such a trap, and she would surely have nothing but contempt for him. Two years from now, could he stand the look of disdain that she would give him? He could hear her thoughts of the future: there he is, that loser, that louse who used me just because I was momentarily in love with him. How could I have been so stupid, how could I have not seen how contemptible he is?

He did not want to hear that about himself.

So, Barbara was out of the question. Not so much for the sake of his loyalty to Zosia, but for his own self-esteem and for the sake of his friendship with Barbara. As a friend, he would advise her against getting involved, and as a friend, he would do what he could to prevent her from making a mistake. Someday, perhaps after she had gone through some relationships, after she had more experiences and had formed her own opinions; someday after Zosia had kicked him out for good; someday when they could approach each other as equals—then perhaps she would be available to him. But by then he was sure she would not want him anymore.

The next day he was determined to bring up the subject with her. It had to be a daylight conversation, one where he would not be influenced by irrational desires. Breakfast was too early and a bit too rushed as he got up late. During the workday, in the shop was inappropriate—there were too many interruptions. Lunch was impossible because one of them had to keep an eye on the shop while the other ate. So, it had to be at dinnertime.

Barbara shopped and cooked again although Peter offered to take a turn at it. She claimed to enjoy it, and besides, he looked tired, was it a bad night? He had to admit that his sleep had been pretty brief and unsatisfactory. Too bad, she commiserated, perhaps tonight would go better. And with that she disappeared to do the shopping as he relaxed through the afternoon, keeping an eye on the customers and helping them to find the books they needed.

The meal was lovely, and they finished it off by splitting an orange that she had splurged to buy from one of the German-only shops. He told her how the children in his neighborhood had used to refer to the rusty, sludgy water as orange juice, and they both laughed at his humorous description of drinking the muck.

After cleaning up the dishes together, they relocated to the couch and had another glass of wine while chatting about various things. She asked for more stories of his childhood, pointing out that it was useful research for her, and he willingly obliged, glad to have a reason to put off the difficult discussion he had in mind.

He told her about how his brother, Erich, and he used to turn off the water to their father's showers and how they would roar with laughter at his discomfiture. "It was quite unusual to have a shower to ourselves, and I think he was proud of it—so it was all the more painful for him when the water inevitably and inexplicably gave out each time he was all lathered up. We worked out a really convoluted signaling system from our hallway down into the cellar, and one of us would get to sit upstairs and watch the fireworks."

Barbara shook her head in amused disapproval as he continued relating some of the things he and his brother had done. It had been nice then, when he and his brother still got along, when they weren't competing for what seemed like a limited supply of love and attention.

"You should go see him," Barbara suggested.

"Erich?" Peter was astonished at the suggestion.

"Yes. See what he has to say for himself."

"I don't think so." The security implications alone were horrendous. Besides, what in the world would they have to say to each other? "No," he reiterated as if Barbara had argued with him, "no, that wouldn't be a good idea." He paused, then added, "Anyway, I don't know where he is."

"Oh, I think you can assume he didn't move from London."

"No, perhaps not," he replied distantly. Funny, they could stumble across each other on the street and not recognize each other.

Barbara picked up the bottle and poured the rest of the contents into their glasses. Then she slid over on the couch and, curling her feet up under herself, leaned against him and said, "Here's to families," and tapped her glass against his.

He draped his arm around her and agreed, "To families." It felt nice with her curled up against him. Peaceful and friendly and not worth disrupting with complicated discussions about their strange relationship. Besides, he was getting tired and it was nearly time to retire for the evening. Better to leave it to another day.

22

"**W**E'VE GOT TO DISCUSS THIS!" Karl exclaimed. He had managed to remain calm as he had walked down the hallway and snapped at Richard's secretary in a normal fashion, but once he had entered Richard's office and closed the door behind him, he could maintain calm no longer. They were sunk! "What are we going to do?" he wailed.

Richard glanced down at the calendar. Four weeks until the U.S. elections, just about right. "We?" he asked innocently.

"You're the one who told me to deny everything!" Karl fumed. "Now they've gone and proved the videotape was made here. Some technical details I don't understand."

"They have a different video system there. I never told you to claim the videotape was made in America. I just said to say it was not authentic!"

"But they've got his identity documents. They've released them to the press!"

"Who are they?" Richard asked out of curiosity.

"I don't know! Someone just gave the documents to the American press. They clearly state his history, and most of it matches his story! We're sunk!"

Richard smiled at Karl's naive addiction to pieces of paper. He made a common assumption—that once something was on a document, it was the truth. Karl stared at Richard, desperate for a response, but Richard let him stew a few seconds longer as Richard ground out one cigarette and calmly lit another. Satisfied at the delay, Richard said, "Now, tell me exactly what *they* have done."

Karl explained that his presentation had, to his surprise, been shown on American television exactly as Richard had predicted. Karl was sure it had had a good effect, but unfortunately, not long afterward, the documentation that Peter had taken with him when he'd left was released to the American media. Also the original videotape had been analyzed, and it had been ascertained that it was unlikely that it was produced in the NAU.

"So," Richard summarized, "they know the videotape was made here and they have some documents. Is that it?"

"Yes." Karl seemed stunned by the simplicity of it all.

"Okay. The technicalities of video systems are beyond me. Let's concede that point. Maybe it was made here. But," Richard continued before Karl could interrupt, "the production of fake documents is hardly a fine art. I suggest you claim the documentation is fake and that all they've done is film the videotape using our type of equipment. Clearly they have such—otherwise they would never have been able to play the tape."

"Oh," Karl replied, at a loss for words.

"You were thinking along those lines, right?"

"Yes, of course. I just wanted to see what you thought," Karl replied quickly.

"Now, tell me," Richard added coolly, "did those documents specify you as the owner?"

"Yes," Karl admitted, clearly worried by the implications.

"And did your name appear on the original presentation, the one you put together?" Richard asked, knowing the answer.

"Yes," Karl answered even more worriedly.

"Wonderful!" Richard applauded, to Karl's surprise.

"Wonderful?" Karl could not help asking.

"Yes! What better person to deny the whole thing! You never met the man! Obviously, when they faked the documents, they chose your name because it was the only one they knew, because of your presentation!"

"But that isn't what happened," Karl moaned. "I *did* own him!"

"Karl," Richard sighed, wondering yet again what had happened to the incredible German war and propaganda machines of decades ago, "the Americans don't know that. Tell them you never even saw the man before he appeared on television. Tell them it's all made up. Every word. So they made the videotape here instead of there. Big deal. And they faked a few documents. So what? Child's play."

Karl nodded, trying to memorize every word.

"Oh, and throw in the kid's age."

"Huh?"

"The child—she was five. That's inconsistent with his own version of events. He was, by his own words, otherwise engaged at the crucial point in time."

"Oh, yeah. How did he have a daughter that age?"

"Don't know. But the inconsistency is there. Let them chew on that!" Richard grinned.

Karl left with a script and complete instructions. All his own idea, of course. All of it had nothing to do with Richard. Karl's friend had simply helped him clarify his own brilliant thoughts. They both agreed emphatically on that point. In parting, Richard subtly insisted that Karl make sure he had a good translator. Somewhere, somehow, Richard had heard the translation was a bit rough, and this time he wanted to be sure the message was clearly heard by the American people.

As Karl left the office, Richard lit another cigarette. He started coughing uncontrollably, and it was a moment before he could inhale the sweet perfume. As his cough subsided, he chuckled. He really looked forward to Karl's next ridiculous propaganda tape and to the release of Joanna's adoption papers and the photograph—an innocent one—of Karl speaking to Peter.

23

"WHERE SHALL WE WALK TODAY?" Barbara asked. It was Sunday, time for a long, leisurely stroll.

"Down by the river?" Peter suggested.

"Again?"

"I like the river. I never got to walk along the embankment as a kid since it was closed to *Nichtdeutsch*. You know, too close to Westminsterschloss."

"But we've gone there the last several weeks. And it's cold by the water. Isn't there somewhere else?" Barbara moaned.

"How about the ruins of St. Paul's then? I used to like going there. They're quite spooky, but you get a good feel for just how grand it must have been."

Barbara shook her head sadly. "Haven't you looked at any maps?"

"No, why?"

"They redeveloped that area ages ago. It's all offices now."

"Oh. I didn't know that." He paused, remembering the ghostly remains of the great cathedral with a fond sadness. "Hmm. Okay, then, how would you like to see my gravestone?"

"Your what?" she responded, appropriately confused.

"I'll show you. Come on, it's a nice long walk and the orphanage grounds are nicely gardened. Though I suppose nothing looks good this time of year."

So they bundled up against the cold, damp wind and set off. They took a taxi for the first part of the journey through East Göbbels and the Worker Districts, both of which were neither pleasant nor safe to walk through, and alit at Bekton, near a long dock just off the Temms. The area was not particularly pleasant either, but it was safe enough for Germans, or at least it was the last time he had been there.

As they walked along the dockside, Barbara commented, "So, you still get to walk by your beloved water."

"I always dreamed of following it out to the sea. But just like the freshwater, I got trapped by the tides always shoving me back upstream."

"That's quite poetic," Barbara commented. It was not clear if she was teasing.

They strolled along the dock to the river and along the river for a short while until they were driven away from the banks by industry.

"This isn't the direct route, is it?" Barbara asked as she peered at the rows of houses along the tiny lanes.

"No. I just thought you'd like a stroll."

"And you get to dream of sailing away?"

"Yeah."

As they turned a corner, a blank brick wall came into view; they walked along the wall and then through a gate in it. Nobody challenged them, it was not that sort of place. They strolled along the grounds, skirting the concrete-block buildings that formed a square of barracks around an enclosed playground. It was not yet afternoon and nobody was outside—presumably the residents were inside attending a rally or some other appropriately patriotic function.

Peter and Barbara continued past the barracks and around several other buildings that might serve as a school or administrative center, or perhaps the mess hall. Behind those, the well-kept gardens suddenly grew unkempt and wild. Here and there white stones had been placed like paving stones, but they were not conveniently laid out, and as Peter led Barbara over the weeds, he avoided stepping on any. The ground grew increasingly swampy, and eventually they came to a tiny stream. They walked along it for about twenty meters so that they were directly behind the cluster of buildings. There, a few meters from the water, was a large block of concrete. They went around it and looked at the face. On this side, the weeds had been cut a bit and a path led directly back to the administrative buildings.

Peter pointed to the buildings, to a group of windows on the lower right. "I believe that's the orphanage's hospital," he said as if that were relevant.

Barbara glanced at where he had indicated, but her attention was drawn back to the large stone. Names were chiseled into it. Row upon row of names. Along the top of the stone was the inscription "To our foundlings." That's all it said.

"What's it mean?" she asked.

"I think it's the gravestone for all these children."

"But why so obscure? And there's only one date by each name—like that one, two-sixty, February 1960."

"I don't think it's February, I think it's two," he explained. "I think the child was born in 1960 and was two when he died."

"Is that a typically English format?"

"No, I think they were deliberately obscure because they never admitted that any of these children died. My guess is, they buried the bodies under those paving stones but kept them alive in the record books so they could get the extra rations of food and medicine."

"Oh, so they wouldn't want any evidence like gravestones around—just in case a nosy official wandered back here." Barbara glanced uneasily at the grave-yard she had just walked over. Swampy ground—what a mess! And there was mud all over her shoes now. Was it somebody's remains?

"Yeah. I'd guess though that someone felt uncomfortable not commemorat-ing the poor little ones, so they put this up. If you add the ages to the years, you'll see that a lot would have died during the various epidemics. That would make sense."

"What brought you back here?" Barbara asked, glancing at the semiwild appearance of the little plot of ground in the middle of the city's eastern edge.

"Oh, I came out here to see where Peter Halifax was supposed to have grown up. Authenticating research. I stumbled across this, and his name there." He pointed to the inscription. "Born same year as me, but the poor little tyke didn't make it past two."

"Do you think they murdered these kids?" Barbara motioned toward the white paving stones.

"I don't think so. They'd be unlikely to advertise it like this if they did. Look, see all the Coventrys and Halifaxes and other nuked-city names? My guess is those babes were pretty sick when they were brought here. Besides, I toured the place once, on the pretext of looking for my brother, and it seemed okay inside."

Barbara nodded as though reassured. Funny that it would matter after all these years. "What did they do when the kids were supposed to be released into society?"

"That happens at twelve. My guess is they sold or gave the names to the Underground. Good, clean, genuine backgrounds—their papers would be valu-able." Unlike the children themselves, he thought sadly.

"My shoes are soaked and my feet are getting cold."

"Yeah, we should go before someone notices us." Peter threw one last glance at all the names. Row upon row of names. If he was right and they eventually ended up as Underground identities, the monument could one day serve as a death warrant for hundreds of people. The dates on the monument stopped abruptly and no other stones were around. Maybe that was why. Or maybe as the staff had continued to secretly bury the endless stream of little corpses in their backyard, maybe they had, from sheer heartache, ceased to care.

24

*T*HE SS OFFICER WHO HAD BEEN PRESENT at Peter's interrogation was reassigned to Scotland within days of the action. Nevertheless, his body was found in a Glaswegian alley only weeks later. He had been stripped of his clothes and bludgeoned, apparently with a cricket bat. Citing the protocols, the Home Army claimed responsibility, though they had not actually carried out the execution. Judging from Peter's testimony, they had determined that he was the senior officer present and therefore responsible for all that had happened, and as a result they had condemned him to death. They had only just been arranging the fellow's demise when their procedures had been preempted either by an informed friend or by an assailant with a different and unknown agenda. In any case, the court shrugged its shoulders, declared justice as having been done, and left well enough alone. They decided to take no action against the guards involved since they were clearly only following orders. The responsibility to be apportioned to the interrogator, it was decided, was sufficiently unclear that he, too, was not condemned.

Zosia accepted the decision of the tribunal without question—a clear sign to those who knew her that she had not accepted it at all. She struck first against the guard who had actually strangled Joanna. He was not particularly bright and it was easy to entice him alone into an alley with a promise of a special deal on some smuggled fruit. Tadek came up from behind him as he sniffed at the oranges and placed a gun in the small of his back. They quickly bound his hands, then Zosia informed him that she was the mother of the little girl he had strangled. She smiled sweetly as she placed the piano wire around his neck. Realization slowly took root and a look of terror spread across his face. Zosia waited only that long, not long enough for him to beg, then she garroted him.

He was too large to swing into a wall, so Tadek obliged Zosia by breaking his head open with a concrete block. Although the man was already dead, Tadek was clearly perturbed by such a retribution on the corpse, and he threw the block down in disgust afterward. "It's to leave a message, Tadziu, for the protection of the living ones," Zosia reminded him as she stared at the grotesquely damaged corpse at her feet.

The second guard was no greater a challenge. He was removed on the same day, before news of his comrade's fate reached him. He was intercepted by Tadek and Jacek, another friend of Zosia's, as he left a bar. They pulled him into a bombed-out store and bound him to a chair. He stared drunkenly at his attackers, trying to explain that they could have his money if they wanted it and did not seem to understand the coldly worded explanation of his situation. Not until

Zosia appeared before him, her blond hair haloed by the diffuse light from the street.

"Ah, an angel!" he guessed. "An angel."

"You murdered my daughter. And tortured my husband."

"No, that must be someone else. I don't do that sort of thing!" The man shook his head, slurring his words in his sudden attempt at sense.

"So unimportant that you don't even remember," she said sadly, then refreshed his memory.

As he recognized the incident and realized that there was no denying his involvement, he began to plead. "But I didn't do anything! I was just there! I was just following orders!"

"Too bad," Zosia replied coldly.

"Oh, that poor little girl! I've dreamt about her, oh, it was terrible. I had no idea. Please, please, please don't hurt me! Oh, how you must ache, I know, it's terrible. I've protested, did you know? I've made a complaint, it was so terrible . . ."

"No, you didn't."

"Other children died. Did you know that? Your bomb killed innocent children, civilians—"

"It wasn't ours," Zosia cut his defense short as she saw Tadek make a motion about time. With her delicate hands she grasped the man's neck, and with one firm motion she drove her thumbs into his throat and crushed his windpipe. Nervous about the possibility of a patrol detecting them, Jacek and Tadek did not wait to see if he was dead; they unbound the body, grabbed one leg each, and on the count of three swung the body clumsily into a wall. They dropped the body, panting with their exertion and nervous fear.

"It's not like doing it to a five-year-old, is it?" Zosia asked no one in particular. Though battered, the guard's head was not broken, and he looked up at her with wildly unseeing eyes. Sighing heavily, Zosia picked up the stone she had prepared and raised it high over those staring eyes.

"Let me do that!" Tadek insisted quietly.

Zosia hammered the stone down onto the man's head. She winced at the spray of blood, raised the stone, and brought it down again with greater force. The third time she raised the stone, Tadek intercepted her and removed it from her trembling hands. "Let's go home," he soothed as Jacek hurriedly wiped her face and arms, then threw a cloak over her shoulders.

Zosia stared unmoving at the corpse as Tadek repeated, "Let's go home, Zosiu, it's over."

The interrogator proved to be more troublesome. His natural caution had been heightened by the fate of the two guards who had happened to work a shift with him one evening some time ago. He went to his superiors and explained his suspicions about a vendetta being carried out, but he was assured with wide smiles and generous pats on the back that no such thing was possible. When he pressed, he was asked if he had ever before exhibited such a lack of patriotic trust. No, he insisted, it was just that circumstances . . . What circumstances? So, he explained how both guards had been left in a state similar to that of the little girl who had been . . . and here he hesitated. Had been what? he was asked. There was a girl who had died in custody from wounds from the bomb blast, he was forced to concede. So? they asked. Nothing, he replied.

He applied for a transfer and waited nervously for the answer. He learned of the SS officer's death in Scotland on the same day that he received the rejection for his transfer. He sighed his resignation. Perhaps it was just coincidence. There was a lot of crime in the city, much of it kept under wraps for fear of scaring away colonists. Perhaps it was just two coincidental acts of wanton violence so typical of the Slavs. Perhaps there was nothing to fear.

Nevertheless, he carefully locked his doors and windows, he only went out with well-trusted friends, he never went out alone if he could help it, he stayed away from all but the most well-guarded parts of the town, and he looked behind himself constantly. His life became a misery of fear.

He applied for a transfer again, this time to Berlin, citing family difficulties at home. He received his transfer and left as soon as possible for the safety of his hometown. There, for the first time in weeks, he breathed easily as he walked the pleasant tree-lined streets. If only everywhere in the Reich could be as marvelously organized and purely Aryan as Berlin! The peace and prosperity, the calm domestic bliss, he thought, as he skirted around some *Zwangsarbeiter* collecting litter. Away from all that violence, he mused as he walked past the blank walls of the local prison. Safe, among good people who know what's right, he ruminated as he perused the windows of a shop that had changed names decades ago and whose owners had disappeared forever. So tranquil, he pronounced as he strolled past the posted newspapers declaring the complete destruction of some resistance somewhere and the hanging of hundreds of terrorists. Ah, if only the rest of the world could be so virtuous and organized!

Sometimes the interrogator's mind strayed to the little girl whose death had led to his transfer. She had been quite charming; pity that the parents had been so careless with her life. Even if she was a natural inferior, it was not pleasant seeing the results of their folly. He did not know exactly what the father had done, but it was clearly something quite horrendous; even he seemed to be aware of that. And there had been numbers on his arm! Clearly a renegade. What business had he destroying the social order, running around loose like some wild man, breeding his filth and corruption into their society, disrupting the purity of the populace? And he had denied his own daughter! What a piece of filth! What a traitor! Better to end that poor girl's life than let her carry that criminal's blood in her veins.

So, the proceedings had been right and just, yet still he suffered. It was so unfair! His transfer had removed him from the fast track that he had worked so hard to place himself on, and in his file, no doubt, was a line about his "fears" and possible disloyalty. Doubtless his determination to do whatever the Reich required would now be questioned, and his precipitous move away from interrogations would be a black mark on his record that would take years to wash away. That one day of work had utterly ruined his career! Always, his thoughts progressed along the same line, and he always found himself quite furious at the perfidy of Peter's unknown crime and the disgusting fact of his continued existence. Troublemakers, all of them!

Upon hearing of the transfer, Zosia pounded her fists and wept with frustration. Tadek advised her to let it go—whatever message they had wanted to send had been sent. Enough of the local soldiers knew about the other two that they would soon all know. Still Zosia was not satisfied. Each time she walked into her empty little apartment, each time she did not hear Joanna's voice singing in the corridor, each time she thought of her innocent child's brains being crushed against that concrete wall, she pounded her fists and wept. Gone, gone forever, and the man responsible walked free and happy in Berlin. It was intolerable!

25

"*T*HIS IS INTOLERABLE!" the Führer fumed. "The Americans! This videotape fiasco! Close that door!"

Richard pulled the door to the Führer's office shut behind him. It closed with a muffled click that made the security of the room seem even more oppressive. Richard took a moment to smooth his clothing. The frisking always annoyed him, but this time they had been exceptionally thorough. Clearly the Führer was feeling edgy. "*Mein Führer?*"

"Oh, Richard, I'm so glad you could come here on such short notice. You're the only one who talks sense to me. I can't trust any of them. Günter, I swear, deliberately tries to mislead me, forcing me into situations where he can embarrass me. I swear it!"

"So it was his idea to murder the little girl?"

The Führer pursed his lips. "No," he answered sourly, "that was my idea. I wanted to keep that Halifax bastard alive so that I could roast him slowly, and when they said there was some brat involved, I thought it would be a nice opener to a long series of tapes. I didn't think it would have such an effect!"

"You should have consulted me first," Richard chided. "I warned you about the protocols."

"I have a whole damn Reich here to run, how the hell am I supposed to keep track of every region's petty compromises?"

"Always check with me first," Richard suggested.

"Besides, I never expected someone to go and steal the videotape," the Führer griped. "We're going to have to track that bastard down and hang him by his balls!"

"And is the investigation proceeding at all well?"

"No! We can't locate any leak at all. Maybe I'll just remove everyone who had anything to do with the tape!"

"That would be unwise," Richard cautioned. "Given the speed with which the tape made it to America, I think it's clear the leak occurred very early. That probably means a copy was made right in Neu Sandez, before it even got to Berlin. It was probably done by one of the men present at the interrogation. Perhaps they thought they could sell it on the black market."

"Can they do that? Copy a tape like that, I mean."

"I don't know, but if you haven't already questioned the men present, I would do so now."

"Oh, that's another problem. Three of the four of them are already dead!"

Richard raised his eyebrows. "Three?" he asked.

"Yes, the fourth is hiding out in Berlin. Obviously, they were murdered. We must retaliate, massively!"

Richard shook his head. "That would be disastrous. Given the evidence on the tape, we clearly violated the protocols; we're lucky we've gotten off so lightly."

"Lightly? Since when do we take orders from some hooded bandits? We cannot be seen to be weak!"

"Their judgment on those men was, no doubt, based upon the protocols and publicized to the local administration accordingly. Everyone there will know that what happened were judicial executions. The local officers probably haven't been told, but I'm sure they suspect that the original violation of the protocols was at your order. They will already be pretty upset about that. If you violate the treaty again and retaliate, no officer in that region will be safe, and they will know it was you who put them in that sort of danger. You'd have a mutiny on your hands."

"Oh, really?"

"Yes. It's what I've told you about before," Richard explained as patiently as he could. He offered the Führer a cigarette and then lit one for himself. "It's all very delicately balanced there. We try hard to keep things quiet so that we don't scare the colonists, and things like this ruin everything, besides creating bad publicity abroad."

"Well," the Führer huffed, "I wasn't trying to kill an envoy's grandchild! That was only mentioned incidentally to prove she was not a hostage! I should shoot the interrogator myself for blathering that on tape. My intent was to punish that renegade, and you told me that I was in my rights to do that!"

"Punish him, by all means, but next time, do be careful about collateral damage," Richard suggested rather snidely.

"Well, what the hell do you think I should do?" the Führer moaned. "I can't be seen to be weak. Now, not only is this English criminal loose and, I'm told, back in America, but I'm taking orders from Polish partisans and worrying about officer mutinies! We can't look weak like this. We must act! I'm going to order an invasion of that mountain area near where he was discovered."

"Not a good idea."

"Günter's pushing me to do it."

"Proves my point."

"Are you telling me it's not within our rights to suppress terrorist enclaves on our own territory?" the Führer asked angrily.

"Not at all. But it might look like a retaliation against the envoy's involvement in the Halifax affair, rather than what you really want, which is a direct punishment of the traitor himself."

"Bah! It's high time we reclaim that land! It's ours, damn it!"

Richard shook his head. "Face it, our troops are not at all prepared for that type of warfare, nor will they be very motivated; whereas they will face a very prepared, very motivated resistance. It will be an embarrassing failure."

"They've never lost a battle!" the Führer trumpeted.

Richard coughed. "They haven't fought a real battle in decades! They go into some village with overwhelming manpower and technological superiority and a willingness to kill anything that moves, and we call that a military victory! We're deluding ourselves—which is fine, as long as we don't start to believe our own propaganda!"

The Führer sucked in his breath. "Herr Traugutt, you are out of line, questioning the military prowess of our forces. I suggest you reconsider your words."

Richard sucked on his cigarette and then slowly let out a stream of smoke as he surveyed the Führer. "*Mein Führer,* whatever the strengths of our troops, I don't think it's a good idea. If it succeeds, you will have achieved nothing that you can publicize since we do not publicly admit to the existence of this partisan enclave in the first place, and if it fails, you will be humiliated. Schindler is pushing you to do it for that very reason."

The Führer dropped himself heavily into his padded leather desk chair. "Richard, you're not there at these meetings! They all advise me to act tough! I don't know what to do."

"Be tough by sticking to your decision. No retaliations, no invasions. You understand diplomacy, they don't, that's all there is to it."

"I'll think about it," the Führer sighed. "I'm not really sure I understand diplomacy. I'm having no luck at all with the Americans. I thought I had them all nicely lined up to work with us, and now this fiasco." He shook his head. "Nobody knows what to do with them."

"How is your new spokesman turning out?"

"Oh, I thought he was doing really well, but he's had one piece of bad luck after another. I don't know if I should keep him on or what. He's a friend of yours, isn't he?"

"Vogel? I think his wife is friends with my wife," Richard answered obscurely. "I believe they sometimes take the babies for walks together."

"Ach, that's right, you have a baby. How is he doing? What is he now?"

"Five months."

"And your eldest? How is she?"

"She's away at the moment," Richard answered, trying not to show his irritation.

The Führer smiled wistfully. "She's a fine young woman. Make sure she visits me the next time she's in town. I'd like to see her."

"I'll do that."

"They grow up so fast, don't they?" The Führer did not wait for an answer as he waved Richard from his office and buzzed his secretary to send in his next appointment.

26

THE FOLLOWING SUNDAY, Barbara asked to see where Peter had really grown up. It wasn't that long a walk, and Peter wondered why he hadn't bothered to look at the old place sooner. But then again, why should he? It was just an apartment near the top of a prewar block of flats. They had not been too awful. Round and about a lot of the prewar terraced housing had been destroyed to make way for concrete high-rises, but his building had been tall enough to escape deliberate destruction.

Where the brick or masonry had crumbled or been damaged during the war, the repairs had been done in concrete slopped on like some sort of bandage paste, and the cracks that had appeared in the walls after a terrorist bombing had never been repaired. The chimneys for their small coal fires were unreliable, the water arrived in rusty spurts, and all the flats had been subdivided and divided again. Their flat had originally been one large room with three windows facing the street. A wall had been built dividing off one window and that part of the room for his parents' bedroom, and a kitchen had been shoved in a corner near another window. The bathroom had been torn apart and the bath replaced by a shower. The saved space was used to make a closet, whose wall cut right across the old bathroom window.

The flat had high ceilings, a leftover from better days, and even though the plaster dropped from them in little powdery bombs whenever a lorry rumbled down the street, they gave the pathetic room a wonderful sense of space. The windows were marvelous as well. Huge old windows that pushed up to open in a way that modern windows would never allow. The glass leaked cold air and it was impossible to find replacements for the cracked panes, but the bitter winter draft and the patches of taped cardboard were a small price to pay for such a luxurious view of the world.

The route to the apartment had changed considerably from what Peter remembered. A highway cut a swath through what had once been residences and one of his favorite hangouts. They clambered over the railings and strolled across the vast, empty, pitted lanes. On the other side they climbed over the guardrail and dropped about a meter down to ground level next to a terraced house that had inexplicably survived as an isolated outpost of the past. An outline of an old stairway climbed up one of its outer walls, and some plaster clung in a decorative diagonal stripe up the length of the ghostly stairs. There was no door on the brick house and the windows were boarded up, but the smell of burning wood and trash emanating from within told them that it was certainly occupied nonetheless.

They walked along. Again the layout had changed, and they had to walk some distance out of their way to skirt around a huge administrative center. As they rounded the front of the building, Peter read the small sign over the main doors: CRIMINAL COURTS AND DETENTION CENTER. There was always money and space for more prisons. Local residents, those who would not lose their homes, usually liked having new prisons and competed for the influx of money and the promise of well-paid jobs.

" 'And they sold their birthrights for a mess of pottage,' " he quoted quietly to himself, unaware of the religious allusion.

His family's old apartment building was right up against the wall of the new courts and not surprisingly had a sign in front indicating that it was slated for eventual destruction to make room for an expansion of the detention center. The date of completion of the new wing was set for a month prior, but there was no sign that any action had been taken other than to dispossess the previous residents of their homes. The old building loomed in front of them, officially empty, clearly occupied by hundreds of squatters.

"Have you been inside since that day?" Barbara asked in a subdued voice as if she expected ghosts to leap out at them.

"I went in to listen at the door of our flat after my parents were arrested. There was somebody living there. After that, I never came back," he answered distantly. He had been afraid of being recognized, of somebody turning him in for a reward. Even now, he felt a chill of terror as he remembered the van parked on the rubble-strewn street out front. The neighbors had looked out from behind closed curtains, had peered around the corner to watch. A small group of passersby had stood respectfully distant and waited until they were given permission to continue on their way.

As they stood there, some children emerged from the shadows and scrambled past them. Even from a distance they stank. Their grime-covered faces indicated that there was no water in the building and had not been for months. Peter wondered what he and Barbara must look like to them. What were two clean and well-dressed Germans doing here in the center of all this garbage? Inspectors? Social workers?

Peter began walking toward the building, but Barbara hung back. "Do you think it's safe?" She looked worriedly toward the dark, glassless windows.

"I think so." Linking his arm in hers, he strode purposefully down the path. There had once been small patches of grass on either side of the entrance—a luxury that bespoke the building's prestige. Now the lawns were nothing but hard-packed mud covered with piles of discarded building material from the works next door.

They stepped out of the unusually bright November sunshine and over the threshold of the lobby. Though the sudden contrast left them nearly blind, Peter did not hesitate even a second since he knew that pausing would be taken as a sign of weakness. He walked confidently across the lobby, holding on to Barbara to reassure her. Somebody grimaced at them from across the room but did not make a move toward the strangers. As they approached the base of the stairwell, a group of four youths moved to intercept them, standing with crossed arms in front of the steps.

Without even breaking his stride Peter tossed three fifty-mark coins to the side of the steps and said in English, "Bugger off." The boys overcame their surprise to scramble in the direction of the coins, leaving them free to climb the steps unmolested.

At the sixth floor they turned down the hallway and came to the door of the flat. It hung crookedly on one hinge, the other having been torn loose when it was kicked in at some earlier date. Inside there were clear signs that the rooms were occupied, but nobody was currently in the main room. Peter glanced around. The furniture was gone, everything, even the sink and the light fixtures. The last legitimate resident had apparently stripped the place bare upon receiving orders to move out. Or the squatters had sold off anything they could carry. He was glad to see that the piano was gone; he had hoped he would not have to see its ruined hulk sitting in a corner of the doomed building.

He went into the bedroom and found a family of four gathered around a pot of food having their lunch. The wife looked deranged, the husband simply tired. The two children stared up at him with weary expressions. Peter guessed the second child had been unofficial and had eventually cost them their housing and their jobs. Or maybe they were original residents who had been obliged to leave when the apartment block had been slated for destruction, and now they had to squat in their own home, ever fearful of a police roundup, beset by crime, cold, and unable to find enough food.

He opened his wallet and pulled out two five-hundred-mark notes. The woman licked her lips sloppily, then carefully wiped the saliva onto her sleeve. He handed the notes to the man and said in English, "Don't come back until evening."

The family rose as one and left the flat. One thousand marks? What sort of weird sexual perversion drove a man to bring his girlfriend to a place like this and pay them off with a thousand marks? The woman argued that they should turn the couple in to the police since they were obviously up to something and clearly they would get a reward for *frenching* them. The man hit her and she shut up.

"A thousand marks?" Barbara asked.

"It will feed those kids for at least a month. That is, if the parents don't spend it on some miracle cure or drink it all away," he replied, somewhat ashamed of his spontaneous and useless generosity.

"Why until evening?"

"I don't know. I can't really see spending more than fifteen minutes looking around." Nevertheless, he had felt an intuitive need for time. There was something he had meant to look for, something that he had put out of his mind years ago because it had been so impossible. Now was his chance, he just had to remember what it was.

To jog his memory, he gave Barbara a tour of the place. He gestured with mock grandeur and said, "This room contained the artfully combined foyer, sitting room, kitchen, library, boys' bedroom, formal dining room, and music room!" He explained where everything had been: the fold-down couch, the armchair, the television and its table, Erich's closet and Anna's cupboard.

"Where did you keep your things?" Barbara interrupted to ask.

"Hmm? Oh, behind the couch, on the floor." He gestured toward a corner.

She raised her eyebrows. "On the floor?"

"Yeah, I called it my 'cave.' I would vault over the couch and duck back there to sort through my things in my own private little world."

"Didn't you resent the fact your sister and brother had closets?" she asked.

He looked at her, surprised by the question. "Resent?" He lowered his head as he tried to think back. "I guess I never really thought about it. Anyway, I did get Anna's cupboard eventually, after she died." Again he thought back, then added, "It took about two years before my mum could remove her clothes and I could use it. I felt guilty using her space like that, but, no, I don't think I resented it."

"I would have," Barbara asserted, but he was already explaining how his mother had also squeezed in a piano as well as a table with six—imagine six!—chairs: no fold-up coffee table for their dinner, they had a proper dining table. Against the wall the hanging wires and pipe ends testified to where the cooker and sink had been. Later, they had even acquired a refrigerator—an unheard-of and completely unnecessary indulgence.

Looking around like that, with the place empty of furniture or people, he realized for the first time how large the two rooms were, much larger than the flat he and Barbara shared. A young couple living on their own in two large rooms with a private bath, a kitchen that they did not have to share, three children, private-school fees, good clothes, fresh fruit and vegetables, meat—often beef—at least three times a week. What had once been obscure was now obvious: his father had to be in the Party, how else could they have afforded such luxury? Other couples, where, of course, both husband and wife worked, could barely scrape by, lived with in-laws, limited themselves to one child, whereas his family had bathed in luxury on his father's salary alone. His mother's job, which she had kept throughout his youth, had been needed only for the extras: the bottled water, the chocolate, the books, the piano.

"What're you thinking?" Barbara asked.

Surprised out of his reverie, he answered, "Oh, I was just wondering if it was worth it."

"If what was worth what?"

"My mother working. She had a really lousy job, and with three children, it must have been absolutely exhausting, especially when we were young, but despite the fact that my father obviously made good money, she never gave it up."

"Maybe it wasn't enough money for her. Some people never have enough."

"That's true, or maybe she enjoyed her friends at work."

"Or her independence."

They walked into the bedroom. Though smaller than the living room it was still quite spacious; there had been room enough for a double bed, a writing desk, and while she was still alive, Anna's little bed. Now there was nothing except some wires dangling where the overhead light had been and the meager possessions of the squatters.

The only remaining room was the bathroom. Due to the overwhelming stench of urine in there, Peter and Barbara did nothing more than poke their heads through the doorway so he could point out the now-famous shower. The toilet and sink were gone, but the shower was still there, though of course the water was permanently shut off.

"Shower!" he said suddenly, clicking his fingers with recognition.

"What?"

"Oh, it's a word in a rhyme my mother used to recite. As a kid, I always thought it was just a standard English nursery rhyme—you know, one of those poems that are almost nonsensical because they are so historical or garbled. Well, later, after they were arrested, I never heard it again, and much later when I just happened to quote it to a girlfriend, she claimed to have never heard of it. That didn't surprise me, but then I started to ask, just casually curious, and I learned that nobody else had ever heard of it. It might have just been old-fashioned or regional or just something my mother made up. Then it dawned on me that it might be some sort of code that my mother was passing on to me. It seemed a bit too much to hope for, and besides, there was nothing I could do with it since I had no idea what it meant and it was all so far in the past."

"So you think it's a code?" Barbara asked, intrigued.

"Yeah. I think it was. I think she was afraid of what might happen and wanted to leave a message for me."

"How's it go?"

"It's really odd: 'Sunny-day showers, grow exotic flowers, in places you'd never suspect; twist to the right, reach for the light, and suddenly all will connect.' "

"Sounds like a set of instructions."

"Yeah. What threw me was I thought of showers as rainfall. But what about this?" Peter stepped into the smelly little room.

Barbara took a deep breath of fresh air and followed him in. "Well, the sun is shining and you're at the shower. Now how do we grow exotic flowers?"

"Perhaps the exotic flower is my reward," Peter guessed. "Which means I have to twist to the right and reach for the light." He did that, reaching up toward the location where the wires of the old overhead light dangled. He stood still for a moment wondering what should connect. The wires? Seemed dangerous and not particularly useful.

After a few seconds without inspiration, he turned back toward Barbara and shrugged. "Any ideas?"

"Under the ceiling? There by the light?"

There was no furniture in the flat and the ceiling was rather high, so he lifted her up on his shoulders and she peered inside the hole left where the light had been. She reached an arm inside and felt around. "Nothing," she informed him, disappointed.

Nothing. It had been stupid to expect otherwise, he thought.

Barbara repeated the poem to herself, going over each word. "What did you call this room?"

"The toilet. Or sometimes the bathroom."

"There's no bath in here."

"I think there had been in the prewar apartment before it was all torn apart and subdivided, but, you're right, that was a misnomer."

"You never called it the shower?"

"No. That's the shower." He pointed at the tiny cubicle. "Ah, I get your point." He stepped inside the cubicle, twisted to the right, and scanned the wall. There was no light to reach for and there did not seem to be anything to connect. Nor was there any sunshine. What could she have meant? Did he have the wrong idea entirely?

The showerhead was gone but the pipe was still there. He reached inside with his little finger and ran it around inside the pipe. Crusty mold. He tried turning the pipe, but it did not move. What had he expected, a secret wall to open up? He mentally chided himself for being silly, but still kept looking. He stepped out and inspected the sewer. Twisting it to the right only tightened it, but maybe she had got it backwards or used poetic license. He opened the sewer grate and reached down. There was no light, no connections, nothing but really foul dried muck. He retched as he pulled his hand back out. Barbara handed him a handkerchief and he wiped his hand on that. Next he inspected the faucets and the tiling. Still nothing.

He stepped around the outside of the cubicle, to the board that covered the pipes. It was low to the floor and he got down on his knees to look at it. Nicely fitted into the wall, surrounded by a fancy molding that was a remnant of a more extravagant age: it ought to be removable, easily so since it would give access to the plumbing. He tapped on it with his knuckles. Hollow naturally, there had to be space for the pipes. And exotic flowers? He ran his hands down the molding along the edge. It had to be easy if his mother was hiding something; it had to be something she did not have to tear apart, something that would remain undetected. He found the handholds that were used to put the cover-board in place. Funny he had never noticed those when he was a kid, but then he had determinedly spent as little time in the flat as possible—*his* hiding places had been down by the river. He pulled forward, twisting the board to the right, and it slipped naturally out of its mooring.

There was nothing in the space other than the pipes and the valves to turn the water on and off. Palpably disappointed, he sat back on his heels and sighed.

"Reach for the light," Barbara reminded him.

He lowered himself even further, but he could see nothing. Barbara went to the window and pulled down the shade, then she shut the door to the bathroom. In the semidarkness, he could just discern a crack of sunlight coming through the outside wall. Had that been there all those years ago? He reached up toward it, but his arm would not fit. He twisted his arm around the pipes, tried to force his bones to comply, but he could not reach the light. He swore and pulled his arm back out.

"Can you try?" he asked Barbara.

He moved out of her way, and she got down on the floor and reached up for the tiny shaft of light. "Got it." She slowly pulled her arm back out. In her hand was a book, covered in dust. She handed it to him and, saying, "I'll see if there's anything else," reached back up among the pipes.

Peter looked at the book's cover. It was cloth, and the printed pattern was one of exotic flowers. What a sense of humor his mother had had.

Barbara's arm reemerged and she held another book. "There's another," she said, and returning her arm to the cavity, she extracted that as well. She handed them to Peter and struggled to reach around inside the wall cavity. After a few minutes she declared, "I think that's everything." She stood, dusted herself off, and looked at the treasure she had recovered.

"What are they?" she asked as he blew the dust off and opened the cover of one.

The pages were filled with his mother's handwriting. It was her diaries. He looked up at Barbara, an expression of wonder and disbelief on his face. "It's my past."

===========================27===========================

*B*ARBARA PACED NERVOUSLY, checking the hall and windows repeatedly as Peter
sat against a wall inspecting his treasure. He opened the first of the diaries, read
the simple inscription: *Catherine Sinclair Chase*. She must have written that later
because the first entry was before she had married. The handwriting of an inexperienced girl filled the page:

> Oh, I am so tired of war! We can only hope that the government—now
> that they've completely fled the island—will make peace and let there be a
> peaceful laying down of arms. There are so many who say they will refuse
> and that they will fight at any cost, but it is such nonsense! Why are we
> defending that corrupt social order? Why do miners fight for royalty and
> privilege? The workers die to defend the castles and estates of the rich
> while the factory owners flee to Canada! The National Socialist German
> Workers Party may be German, but they are for the workers. They are not
> fighting for their aristocracy. Maybe if we work with them, we will find
> out that we have so much more in common than we were led to believe.
> Maybe we can make this a green and pleasant land of peace and prosper-
> ity for all—not like the class-ridden system they have overthrown but one
> of equality and justice. I don't believe all the propaganda against them!
> I'm sure that it is just the American Capitalists trying to prolong the fight-
> ing. What do they care if we die? They sell arms to both sides!

The entries were fairly irregular, and years passed within pages. Each time
Catherine mentioned the invasion or their new government, she talked of peace,
of getting along, of starting again. There were quotes from propaganda posters
and the "reactionary" opinions of the people she knew. About a quarter of the
way into the book her future husband gained an entry:

> Edmund White and Charles Chase have returned from internment.
> They're sending back the youngest ones first, which is odd, since they
> don't have wives or children. But maybe it makes sense—after all, they
> had the least to do with all the resistance. They were both only fifteen at
> the time. I can't believe so many years have passed—they look so different.
> Anyway, it's good to see some of the boys come back. Or, I guess, they're
> men now.
> Ed had some news about Tom—says he's been writing to another girl.
> I guess that explains why I've heard so little from him. He could have been
> a bit more honest! I know we didn't have anything special when he joined
> up, but still.

Charles has grown so much I hardly recognized him. I didn't really know him all that well before. He seems really nice, though he looks so terribly pale. He says he wasn't mistreated. He says he saw some other blokes who had it much worse, but that those who cooperated were usually treated fairly. He said that the terrorists (he actually used that word!) back home made it rough for them all over there and that they should just give up fighting and accept defeat gracefully.

After several pages the entries became more frequent albeit still irregular. Sometimes Catherine wrote daily, sometimes there were gaps of months, many were undated and Peter only guessed they were made at different times because the ink was different. Apparently she only wrote when the mood struck.

Charles says that he has had enough—that he is tired of this perpetual fighting. He says that the Underground violates international law—that they are nothing but terrorists who don't want to give up the power that they have finally, rightfully lost to their military superiors. Sometimes he seems a bit harsh in his judgment of them, but I respect his opinion. I just wish he would be a bit more careful what he says to others—lots of people think he is a traitor. He isn't—he's just a realist. And he is so handsome! I'm sure he's going to ask me to marry him soon.

Peter skimmed the pages: his father's charms were detailed, his mother's hopes were laid out. Her handwriting tightened a bit as though conserving paper, but it still carried the excess of loops and curves that made it difficult to read.

Mum expressed concern about my political opinions. I should just avoid the topic with her altogether. Ever since Dad was killed, she hasn't been herself—she blames the Germans for his death, but it was the war and now that is over. She's part of the old order—she'll never understand that it is time for good, decent, honest folk to stand up for themselves and take what is rightfully theirs. We really must clear out the scum—they've driven this country to ruin. We need to return to the old ways—the young people see that. You can tell that there is a lot of support among the young for the new ways (I mean, of course, returning to the old ways!) because there was a rally in Trafalgar Square (they pushed the debris out of the way) and it was attended by lots of young people. They're sick of war, they want peace, they want justice, they want a home for their future. Speaking of futures, guess who asked me out for tomorrow night!!! Very solemn—do you think???

The next entry was made the day after that and bore out his mother's suspicions:

Well, I'm going to be Mrs. Charles Chase! I'm so excited and happy. Charles says that he is going to work with the system—that we'll be able to be well-off and get housing and even a car. I hope he's right. There's a lot of resentment in the population—I'm afraid if we're seen to be conciliatory, there might be trouble. On the other hand, the Germans are rather slow to accept us—I think they are afraid of terrorists. There are so many jobs and positions not open to us right now, but that will change, they say. I'm sure with time they will see that there are those of us who are willing to try and work things out. It was so horrible all that happened here, but I'm sure it was horrible there, too. War is like that. I'm sure there were atrocities committed against them as well—we really shouldn't fixate on the massacres here and there—they are just isolated incidents and the perpetrators will be punished. Anyway, it's all in the past. The people who keep talking about the horrors of occupations in other countries are just troublemakers. I mean, all those strange places have always been rather barbaric—I'm sure once order is established there it will all settle down. It won't be anything like that here.

Peter felt a sudden surge of nausea. He slammed the diary shut, and Barbara turned around from her lookout in surprise. "Are you okay?" she asked, concerned by the look on his face.

He nodded. "Do you think we can spare five more minutes?"

"Sure, no problem." She turned worriedly back toward the broken window and the view of the rubble-strewn street.

He opened the book a number of pages beyond that last entry.

They've enacted new racial laws. It's all very confusing. They used to say it was just a matter of clearing out all the troublemakers and inferior sorts and then we would be united with the Deutsche Volk. Now it is much more complicated. I've heard that they've had so much unexpected trouble that they figure the population must be corrupt. I think maybe they're mishandling people and getting their backs up. The new scheme is going to divide everyone up. We all have to go in for an interview and answer questions about our parentage and our views. I guess they already have some information on file, so if one lies, they'll know it and the punishments are severe.

Charles told me we have nothing to worry about. There will be the highest classification, which no one here will get because that will be pure German. Then there will be the immigrant Germans, those with partial German blood, and finally those with Germanic attitudes. I guess the latter means that you have to prove you are pure English and loyal to the regime. I'm really scared of the interview, I don't know all the details about my great-grandparents! Charles said I shouldn't worry—that they're mostly checking one's attitude, and we should be fine.

I think we shouldn't have all these classifications! I mean, after all, what is the point of overthrowing the old order if we have another class system thrust upon us? Charles says we can use these classification schemes to our own benefit. He wants me to find out from Mum if I have any German relatives, but I don't think she'll take well to my asking.

Heard about more executions today. I wonder if they're true. I hope not. I'm sure things aren't as bad as people say. The laws will be made fairer soon—it's just leftover effects from the war. The conscription is worrisome—no one seems to know what is going on. They won't say when the deportees will be allowed back.

Maybe I should start hiding this diary.

Several pages further she wrote:

Three days ago Charles and I were married. Finally! Different offices kept demanding different bits of paper from us. We had to prove that none of our great-grandparents, grandparents, or parents were Jewish (or Gypsy or some other things, like West Indian)! Luckily we managed to find baptismal or marriage records for everybody, but what about when the records are lost or were destroyed? The ceremony was odd, too. It was in English, but all the paperwork was in German. All that funny Gothic script. I have no idea what I signed—I'm not sure the clerk even knew. Well, it only took this long to get married because they had such a backlog handling all the new regulations. I guess we could have gone to the church to have a religious ceremony, but neither of us saw the point. My mother was disappointed, but I told her we were lucky to get the official clearance when we did and that we had better not complicate matters by trying to get a church service.

We've moved in with Charles's mother—her flat is a bit larger and in better shape than Mum's. Charles's brother still lives here so it is a bit crowded, but he got orders yesterday to report for conscription on the Continent, so we'll have a bit more space soon. There's no indication of how long he'll be gone, but I hope we have a place of our own before he comes back. God, we need space! Had to climb over a family sleeping in our doorway today—gave me the creeps! I wish the government would take care of these people and put them in a camp or something. I heard they put the Gypsies in special camps so that they're not annoying people anymore. They ought to do that with all the homeless. It feels so unsafe having so many people just hanging around—they look jealous and angry. They scare me, I wish they'd go away.

Promised myself I'd learn German—there are so many signs and papers and things that are in that language, it seems the only sensible thing to do. There are classes being held at the school a few blocks away. They're free and I heard that if you test well at the end, you get extra food ration coupons! I'd use mine to get some chocolate—I'm absolutely dying for some.

Peter smiled at that last line. His mother always had a passion for chocolate. He remembered his dad once surprising her with an entire box of chocolates for their anniversary. She was ecstatic and inundated them all with kisses.

Charles got a job at a government office! It's really low level but there are possibilities! His knowledge of German really helped and he has been studying and taking courses, so he's even better at it now. Oh this is great news—he'll have priority for housing and we'll get a better ration book. If things go well, we might even get permission to have a child soon. Lots of people are going ahead and having kids without permission, but I think that's a mistake. They're realizing it as they get dumped off the housing lists and find their rations cut. Sometimes the kids are even taken into custody if the parents are deemed to be so irresponsible that they are unfit parents. That seems a bit harsh. I know it's irresponsible to flout the regulations, but still. Anyway, there are so many orphans that it hardly makes sense to make more. They've pretty much given up on trying to track the relatives of the foundlings—especially in the neighborhood of the nuclear zones. I guess they've just started giving the kids the names of cities. More and more keep turning up—you'd think with the cessation of hostilities that things would have settled down! Someone at work (did I mention I found a job in a packing plant!) mentioned that parents are abducted if they are suspected of political crimes and that's where the orphans keep coming from, but I don't believe that. I bet that their parents were just irresponsible and can't afford to feed them so they just dump the baby near an orphanage. The cold-blooded monsters!

Or maybe their parents get arrested and they go foraging for garbage, Peter thought angrily. How could she have been so naive? Or was it simply that she was full of endless hope, always waiting for the brave new world that would never materialize? Just a kid weary of war and desperate to believe that the end of fighting was the same as peace. A page later she wrote:

Maggie said she was held up at knifepoint yesterday. There really should be something done about all the criminals. All they took was her groceries. She went to the police, but they said they could not issue her new ration coupons—so she and the kids will just have to do without! It's so unfair. That horrible criminal! Absolutely hateful! He should be hanged!!!

The words grew unfocused. Peter blinked hard to try to bring them back, but instead all he could see were a series of faces, angry, afraid, contemptuous: the expressions of his victims as he held them up at knifepoint. He had never hurt anyone, but in his desperation he had earned their hatred. Groceries were part of what he took during those dangerous days immediately after Allison's murder. Money and jewelry, too. Anything that might buy him an identity. What would you have thought? he wondered to his mother's ghost. After spending seven months scrabbling for crusts of sawdust-laden bread, would she have forgiven him his crimes against his own people?

His vision finally cleared and he read further:

Alice didn't show up for work. I checked at her home after work and her mother said she went out last night and didn't come back. She's the one who told me about the political abductions. Nacht und Nebel, she said. Night and fog, I guess. (I really must study more.) Isn't that odd? She must have said it all to make her disappearance more dramatic. She's probably run off to Scotland to get married and didn't have the right paperwork or something. Still, I feel worried. I wish things would settle down. It has been so many years, yet still there are all the wartime regulations and so many soldiers and military police in the street. I know it's difficult bringing order here when so many people are resisting, but it seems that nearly everything is illegal.

There were some arrests down the block. I don't know what for, but I peeked through the curtains and it looked like they were just kids. This martial law is wearing on my nerves. I wonder when things will change for the better. I wonder when the rest of the POWs will be released. You can tell it worries Charles's mother, she doesn't say anything, but she's always rereading his father's old letters. They started requiring all the letters to be in German, I guess it's easier for the censors that way, but it's really hard on everyone. People are always running around looking for someone to translate the letter they've gotten from their husband or son or whomever. I've been told that if the censors don't like the quality of the German used, they just throw away the letter. I guess they don't know how important these letters are to the people back home. Charles has asked me again about asking my mother if I have any German blood. Maybe I should look into it.

Several pages later the mood changed:

Great news! We have a flat of our own. Charles said he knew his hard work and loyalty would pay off. We went to look at it this evening; it's a mess and the building next to it has crumbled so there will be squatters everywhere, but it's legal and it's ours! A neighbor there said a young couple used to live in the flat but they were arrested for something. Poor sods, but their bad luck is our good fortune! Oh, a place to ourselves, this will make it easier to get a birth permit. I want a son—a boy who will grow up just like his dad.

Well, you got one, Peter thought grimly; that would be Erich, the bringer of your destruction. Peter felt thoroughly depressed; all the hopes he had held about his parents' intentions were evaporating before his eyes. He closed the book and rested his eyes for a moment. They should leave, it was dangerous staying there so long. He picked up the third book and skipped to the middle. The entries were now in German and his heart sank, but then he read:

> I don't know what to do about Niklaus. I'm worried he won't know what to do if something happens. I wish I could tell him, but Charles insists I don't—at least not yet. Says he's still too young. What am I to do?

Peter sat up and stared at the pages as if not believing the words written there. Tell him what?

"We should go," Barbara said. "There are patrols in the streets and it's getting late."

"Yes, of course," he replied quickly, scanning the rest of the page for further clues. There was nothing else though. It was pure folly, but he decided to take the books with him. He couldn't let his past go now that he finally had it in his hands.

Barbara watched nervously as he tucked the diaries into his coat. "Do you think that's wise?"

"No. But I can't just leave them here. Do you mind?"

"No, of course not." She smiled. "My father told me that at some points in our history all my people have had is our past. I wouldn't want to deny you yours."

They left then, the books carefully tucked into his clothes. They walked the route home in silence, Peter scanning for trouble, Barbara praying that they would not be searched. Their papers were checked twice, but the officers were polite in both cases and they had no trouble.

"Are you going to spend the night reading those?" Barbara asked, though it wasn't really a question. She knew the answer well enough.

He smiled and nodded.

"You'll be wanting these." She went over to the shelf and retrieved his reading glasses. She brought them over and handed them to him.

"Thanks," he replied sheepishly. They really did help, but he often forgot to use them. Barbara seemed to think it was a forgetfulness fueled by vanity.

"Would you like some tea?" she asked.

"I'd love some." He settled onto the couch and opened the first book. He decided that he would start at the beginning and read through without skipping ahead. That way he would get a clear picture of what was going on as his mother wrote each entry, and if there were disappointments ahead, it would delay them. He didn't want to jump ahead and find out that what his father believed he was too young to know was that he was embezzling or going to be promoted or had found some German relative so they could all be *Volksdeutsch.*

His fear was tangible. With her words his mother could destroy a lifetime of hopes. It was stupid of course; nothing would change what had happened and who he was, but still, stupid or not, he so wanted to have something in his past to be proud of—something other than greedy, collaborating parents. Something other than disappointment, betrayal, and abandonment.

The words swam in front of him. He could just throw the books away, burn them before it was too late. Then he would never know and he could maintain his hope. But he knew he would not do that: worse than any knowledge was the uncertainty. If they had believed everything they had foisted on him, well, he'd have to live with it. It would be only a minor perturbation on all the horrors that he had to live with. It was not like Joanna's murder or Allison's, or what had been done to him. It was just a point of view two people long ago had had—a point of view that had become irrelevant with their deaths.

He laughed aloud. No matter how rationally he debated with himself, he knew the truth deep down. *It was important.* They were his parents and it was his childhood. He could live with what he found out, he could hate or love them, forgive them or not, but he could not deny that it was important—as stupid as that might be. Odd, he thought, how things so long ago seem so much more significant. For all the terror of his later experiences, he had faced them as a man, a man with well-formed opinions of himself and the world. They could scar him, but they did not form him, not the way his experiences as a child had.

He heard the kettle whistle, and with renewed courage he began reading.

28

*T*HE HOURS PASSED. Barbara refilled his cup, supplied him with a sandwich, turned on the lights as the room grew unbearably dim, but otherwise she stayed out of the way. He read as if possessed, and she watched as the shadows passed across his face. Eventually, she told him good-night, kissed him on the forehead, and went to bed. She awoke several times and realized he was still reading, but then she settled down and slept well.

Entry by entry Peter uncovered the thoughts of a girl and then a woman as she grew into maturity in a strange, new world. Satisfied with the birth of one son, she detailed the boy's developments, the first words and phrases, his first attempts at drawings. There were notes on his size and weight as he grew, and she had scraps of paper inserted in the pages—crayon drawings Erich had made, little notes he had written. Despite the expense, there were photographs as well. Charles and Catherine proudly holding their young son, Erich. They looked happy and complete. A perfect little family coping with the brave new world around them.

Catherine seemed truly happy in her role as wife and mother, working her job, taking care of her husband and son. Great long happy passages were written, devoid of all comment on what was happening in the world around her, and great long equally happy silences occurred between the entries. They moved to a better flat, the one Peter would call home; Charles's career progressed and he moved forward in the Party. Charles eventually found a job for his wife in a government office as a file clerk, and she wrote happily of the chance at last to get off her feet and work in a clean building, but eventually the peace was shattered as Catherine wrote:

> Pregnant again. Haven't done the paperwork in advance. All a bit of a surprise. Charles is furious with me, but as I pointed out, I didn't manage it alone. He yelled about space and cost and his career. We've been screaming at each other for days. He told me I should get an abortion, and he arranged an appointment for me in a good clinic. I'm not so sure I want to do that, though. I'll have to do some thinking in the next couple of days.

Peter looked at the date. For a moment he could not move, then he stood, went over to the bottle of gin, and poured himself a glass. He held the glass up and looked at the light through the clear fluid. Well, he thought, what would he have advised? Given the crowding, the poverty, and the government, his father's actions were perfectly rational. Peter thought of his boyhood friends. Nearly every one had been an only child. Those that weren't had seen their families dragged down into poverty by the extra, often-illegal burden, and the parents of those children had seemed particularly ill-tempered toward them. And there were all his friends later in life: the women with their countless abortions, the itinerant husbands and boyfriends who made it clear another child was not on the agenda. How many times had he accompanied a female friend to the clinic because the man responsible couldn't be bothered or hadn't even been informed?

No, there was nothing unusual in his father's demands. What was unusual was that Peter was there to read the words years later. What, he wondered, had provoked his mother to keep the baby? He drank the gin down, poured himself another glass, and went back to the diary. The issue was not raised again until several weeks later when Catherine wrote:

> I didn't go to the appointment. I really want a little girl, and this is my chance to have one. Charles was furious, but after a while, he calmed down and said he'd see what he could arrange to expedite the paperwork so we won't be blacklisted or lose our housing or Erich's placement in school. He got the permit yesterday, and everything is sorted out now. It will be great having another baby. I'm going to name her Anna, after my grandmother. I think it's a beautiful name. Charles says I should think

about picking out a boy's name, just in case, but I'm sure it will be a girl. I so want a daughter and I want Erich to have a sister. He's such a wonderful boy! Yesterday, I was feeling ill and he went and got me a glass of water all on his own! He's so thoughtful. I'm so proud of him.

This was followed by an unending stream of anticipatory entries:

> Got some baby clothes from my cousin Sandra. Pretty little dresses and some ribbons and even a lovely little hat! It's going to be so wonderful when my daughter is born. I can already imagine her with her blue eyes and blond hair and delicate features. She'll have a big brother to look out for her and we'll be the perfect family, just like in the posters!

Peter sputtered his disdain at the reference to those grotesque posters of hardworking, brawny men, voluptuous but demure mothers, and their two happy children, always an elder boy and a younger girl. Nobody ever achieved the ideal: the Germans had as many children as the mother could tolerate, doubtless inspired by different posters, and the English rarely bothered to produce more than one offspring, inspired, for their part, by overcrowding and despair. The background was always incongruous as well: bountiful farmland with German-style farmhouses and villages as inspiration for the city dwellers living in their concrete wastelands. Maybe only in the villages were the posters full of gleaming cities and the wonders of modern technology.

He read on through the pages as Catherine chose a middle name for her daughter and even started eyeing toddlers who might one day be suitable husband material. The words were unrecognizable as the thoughts of the woman he had known. It was as though she were living in some dreamworld, brainwashed by propaganda and her own desire for peace and normalcy. Every now and then she expressed a worry that the child in her womb "felt like a boy," but she dismissed these notions as superstitious nonsense just as readily as she embraced any omens that the baby was a girl.

Eventually, a note of trouble entered their lives as Catherine's pregnancy became obvious.

> Last week the big boss came through our office. He stopped to talk to one of the managers, and during that time I got up to file some papers. He stopped dead in his conversation and just stared at me. Then he asked the manager if I was pregnant. The manager sort of shrugged and said that he guessed so. Then the big boss asked if I was married. The manager said again that he thought so. "Fire her," the big boss said. And just like that I was fired. He didn't say one word to me, like I was too dumb to understand or like it was beneath his dignity to address me directly. It was so humiliating! I had to clean out my desk then and there. I guess they had a

policy against married women that I didn't know about and which everyone else ignored.

After looking around, I realized no one will hire me with this big belly. Charles said with another baby on the way, we can't afford for me not to work. It's unfair but his pay is lower than his colleagues' because of the race laws (we don't have the extra expenses of maintaining a proper Aryan lifestyle since we're used to the filth—that's not what they say, but that's what it comes down to). Nor does he get the extra compensation for working abroad that all the Germans get. We have to pay more in rent as well since we don't have the right papers to live in the subsidized districts. There are extra taxes, too—the reconstruction taxes (for rebuilding our cities) and the restitution taxes (to pay for all the damage we did to their cities). Obviously the German employees don't have to pay any of those.

Anyway, the packing plant agreed to take me back, but I've lost all my seniority. Still it was nice to see all my friends again and I'll get a little time off from work for the birth. This pregnancy sure has been hard on me now financially as well as physically, but I'm sure when I get to see my little girl's face, it will all be worth it.

The date of the birth passed without comment, naturally enough, but three weeks later Catherine made her last entry in the first book:

Had a son. Healthy. Charles named him Niklaus Adolf.

Charles named him . . . Peter took off his reading glasses and cleaned them while staring at the unfocused words. He cleaned them slowly, carefully removing every trace of dirt from the lenses, then for good measure he polished the metal of the frame. He pulled out his knife and used it to tighten the screws, then took a moment to bend the frames back into a more comfortable shape; then he checked the lenses and cleaned them again where he had accidentally touched them. He replaced the glasses and finished the gin that he had poured for himself. Sighing slightly, he picked up the second book, but without opening it he set it back down and rested a bit, laying his head back against the couch and closing his eyes.

A piece of paper: high-quality bond, clean on both sides, white as freshly fallen snow. A real find, his little treasure. It was early in his school career, he was five, maybe six? He remembered finding the sheet of paper in the schoolroom and hiding it in his notebook. At home, he climbed up the makeshift ladder of a chair on a table and took his father's fountain pen out of its hiding place, then he clambered onto the window ledge, and looking out onto the street for inspiration, he drew a picture. It was a beautiful drawing: the street as it should have been with trees and happy people and nice houses and buildings. Horses pulled carriages, dogs chased children, the sky was littered with birds. He turned the

paper over and continued the scene with the street leading off into the countryside and a forest of animals peering out from the trees.

His mother was the first one home after him, and as he heard her heavy sigh
in the hallway, he signed his name to his masterwork and jumped off the ledge in
time to greet her at the door. He held out the picture for her to see as she entered,
exclaiming that he had drawn it for her. A tired smile appeared on her face as she
set down the bags of groceries and took the sheet into her hands. "It's lovely," she
praised, but as she felt its quality, a look of confusion came over her face. Where
had he got the paper? He explained. She turned it over and saw that both sides
were covered. "Oh, Niklaus," she chided gently as she handed it back to him, "you
shouldn't waste such good paper." He held the paper outstretched for minutes
after she had picked the bags back up and turned into the kitchen, but she did
not notice: there were groceries to unpack and cooking to do, the baby had to be
picked up, and the laundry needed to be collected from the roof.

The light seemed bright and he got up and turned it off, opting for a small
lamp instead. Wandering into the kitchen, he put on the kettle for another cup of
tea. He started with cold water, dumping the tepid water into the sink in a display
of wastefulness that would have gotten him smacked as a child. Though the kettle had a whistle, he stood by it anyway, waiting for the water to boil. Once it was
ready, he poured it into the teapot and waited for the tea to steep. He knew what
he was doing: delaying. He was afraid of what might come next. After that brief,
heartless entry that greeted his arrival into the world, he was so afraid of what he
might find out. Perhaps, he reflected sadly, perhaps it was because he already
knew.

He returned to the couch and picked up the second book. Carefully he dusted
off its cover, held it unopened in his hands. Would the explanations lie within its
pages? He opened it; there was no inscription, not even her name. The first entry
was dated two days after the last. It was in German and from then on she used
only that language.

> I forgot how tiring babies are! I gave all the pretty dresses and clothes
> away, Amanda was glad to get them. I have some boy's clothes left over
> from Erich, but not much, most of it I gave away after he was a baby. I
> guess what we have will do, and maybe I can scrounge up a few more
> things. Oh, God! What are we going to do with two children? It's so
> crowded and I just don't have the energy for this anymore. I feel exhausted
> every time I feed him, I have to run out on break and meet Mum at the
> plant entrance. I'm still bleeding, and standing all day hurts. Work all day
> and take care of the baby all the rest of the time—thank God Mum is on
> the evening shift. Soon he'll be old enough to leave at the workplace care
> center, until then I hope Mum remains available.

It was a month later before she made another brief entry:

> Shopping and cleaning and endless nappies! It is so crowded, the baby
> is always crying, Erich won't behave, and Charles expects so much! God,
> there is just no room and I don't get a minute's peace. I wish Charles
> would help more, but he's busy, busy, busy with his career.

Peter closed the book and walked over to the window. As he stared out, rubbish bins and water tanks and the usual courtyard detritus stared back up at him.
It wasn't he, he reminded himself: it was a demanding, anonymous baby. She was
tired, overworked, without help or comfort. Growing increasingly disenchanted
with what life had to offer her, an intelligent woman condemned by society to
play the fool. An ambitious woman whose only hope of advancement was for her
husband, a man not quite as bright as she. A woman who took on all the burdens
of household and childcare while working an exhausting job, because that's what
everyone expected of her. Still bleeding after three weeks. Was that normal or was
it a sign of how much her body was stressed? And the smudged ink; was it tears?

There was a sudden clatter and two cats yowled at each other angrily. He left
the window and returned to the book. There was more of the same for about a
page or so, the words becoming ever more despairing, his mother's thoughts
bordering on suicidal. Her husband seemed useless, often coming home from
work long after the children were asleep, or traveling to various Party functions
as part of his drive to succeed within the system. Peter could hear the weariness
in his mother's voice, the dismay at how her life was slipping away into empty
tasks and meaningless work.

Into the darkness of the past he whispered words of comfort to his mother,
assuring her that her time had not been wasted and that he had remembered her
and had taken comfort in her long after she was gone. He understood what it was
to be ambitious, understood what it felt like to see every chance at making a
name for oneself evaporate. He knew that no history books acknowledged the
sacrifices of those who spent their time caring for a child, yet he also knew that
after his long years of imprisonment, the loving trust of a child had saved his
soul.

He turned the page. A series of doodles, squiggly lines, circles, and letters
were run together as if only for artistic effect. It was almost as if she were trying
to write but could not bring herself to say anything. The next entry was dated
several months later, by which time she seemed to have come to terms with her
situation as her words carried virtually no emotional overtones whatsoever.

> Charles and I have decided to bring the boys up speaking German, that
> way they won't have problems dealing with the bureaucracy and they'll fit
> into the better part of society. We made a mistake not starting sooner with
> Erich and he's having trouble in school now; so we're going to start off
> immediately with Niklaus. We plan to use English as well—can't help but
> do that since their granny refuses to speak anything else, but we want to

make sure they're comfortable in German, so they don't sound like street thugs whenever they're dealing with the bureaucracy or in school. We'll have to work up a schedule or something. It will be good for me to practice more—my friends think I'm nuts when I try speaking it to them. They always ask me if I've "gondoich."

He had almost forgotten that phrase, it had been so long since anyone had used it, but seeing his mother use it brought a smile to his face, for the phrase, derived from *gone Deutsch,* meant "gone insane."

Three years passed. Catherine's entries were infrequent and often commented only on how busy or tired she was. She noted changes in Charles's job, Erich's progress in school, the death of a few relatives and friends during an epidemic. There were more changes in the law, more deportations and shifting of populations from one place to another; there was the codification of some established practices and the abolition of others. Another spelling reform was introduced; the names and spellings of places were changed and changed back and changed yet again. The currency was rationalized and all residuals of the imperial system were finally done away with.

About her second son, she wrote very little. There were no saved scraps of paper, no record of his early words, no celebration of his first steps. His first and second birthdays passed unremarked; she wrote about Erich's progress and about her husband, but of Niklaus, there was next to nothing: neither good nor bad—almost as if he didn't exist.

Tucked into the pages were half a dozen photographs from those years: Charles and Catherine, Charles receiving an award, Erich receiving some minor school award, a portrait of Erich with his proud parents, Erich and his father at an official function, Erich in some sort of uniform. Erich's younger brother was nowhere in sight. Peter swallowed the implicit insult; presumably his mother's lack of attention in words was reflected in her deeds, but he did not remember. Presumably it had affected him, but he did not want to think about how.

On Niklaus's third birthday, Catherine commented:

I talked to Charles last night about having another child. He said that the two seemed to tire me out so much I shouldn't even consider a third. He argued that nobody has three, but I told him that nobody's husband is as highly placed as he is. His German coworkers regularly have buckets of kids and he should think of himself as one of them—not one of the common herd that surrounds us. He's bound to get promoted soon and then I can quit work, and I'm sure soon we'll move out of this dump into a better neighborhood, and when we do, three children will be just right! He finally agreed to apply for another permit.

Less than two months later, Catherine got her wish:

Great news! Charles got the permit! I'm going to get pregnant as soon as possible. I've been reading all sorts of articles about how to make sure the baby is a girl. This time I'm sure it will work.

Peter chuckled to himself. His mother always did have a weakness for pseudo-science; indeed, in that, she was no different from the mass of the population. Though there was no direct or obvious government encouragement of the practices, he felt sure that there was a great deal of subtle support. The official tolerance of all the occult bookshops and inner-strength seminars, and mystical half-religions, was sufficient testimony that they must have served a marvelous pacification and propaganda purpose. Dissatisfied? Turn to a psychic healer. Unhappy? Your astrologer will tell you it is simply fate. Discriminated against? The biotherapist will explain it's all in your genes. Take these vitamins, use this oil, rub on this balm—your kids will be more Aryan. Life will be good.

For the more practical-minded, there were Party memberships, sports associations, genealogy societies, and scholarships to good schools. There was that tantalizing possibility of belonging, of being one of the new Aryan aristocracy. All the old guard had been swept away—the top was open to any, well, almost any, who wanted to belong. Blond hair and blue eyes were optional! Just salute the flag, swear allegiance, speak the language of command, obey all orders without question, and you, too, could be one of the leaders of society!

For the remorseless cynics, there was an endless supply of gin and cigarettes. Weedy from alcoholic malnutrition, trembling with nicotine overdoses, they worked their dead-end jobs and cursed their conquerors, they bemoaned their impotence and remembered the glory days of empire until they dropped dead of cirrhosis or lung cancer.

It did not take long for Catherine to get herself "knocked-up," and she wrote how some friends expressed amazement at this turn of events and how others advised her on effective birth control, the most direct being her boss, who told her that it was all right to say no to a man, even a husband. Catherine, however, was pleased by her pregnancy, and as her condition grew obvious, she walked proudly with husband, two children, and the third on the way, and only three days after Anna's birth, she wrote:

A little girl! I have a daughter! Oh, and she is so beautiful! Her name is Anna and she is the sweetest little thing! I feel fairly exhausted, but oh so happy! Now our family is complete. I sent the boys over to my mother's for the past couple of days. Erich will come home tomorrow so that he can go to school. I'm going to let Niklaus stay with his grandmother for a while longer. He seems happy there and my mother thinks he's marvelous. She says he's not difficult at all, just intelligent, and that intelligent children are always a challenge. Well, whatever the reason, they seem to get on together.

The diary detailed little Anna's progress. Again the pages were filled with details of the baby's every move, of the noises she made, of her progress toward crawling, then walking. There was a record of her growth and there were snippets of paper with scribbles and dabs of paint. There was a photograph of Catherine and her daughter, dressed primly and posed solemnly, another of Anna alone, and yet another of Anna with her parents. Peter scanned them quickly, unsurprised, but the last photograph caused him pause.

It was a picture of his parents with Anna and Erich. He looked at the four of them, his father's dignified, calm demeanor, Anna cuddled in his arms, Erich standing proudly mature in front of his father, his mother's indulgent smile as she gazed down at her two children. The perfect little family. Where was he, he wondered, *where the hell was he?*

It was a Sunday, he could tell that from the clothing. He was probably at his grandmother's; they must have gone for a walk, stopped on a whim by a photography studio. It was just a whim, that was all. A sudden impulse to take a photograph, and he, quite by chance, had not been around. In fact, it had almost certainly been his decision not to be there. He had always preferred visiting his grandmother to those tedious Sunday walks. That was all there was to it. Carefully placing the photograph back in the pages, he read on.

With Anna's birth, Catherine's mood improved considerably, and she even began to accept her second son's presence as something other than a burden. She wrote glowingly of how he cared for his little sister, of how Erich and Niklaus played so nicely together, of their progress in school and in the local youth groups. She even reported how perceptive and caring her second son was on at least one occasion:

I guess I must have looked tired the other day or maybe I had been complaining out loud. Niklaus came up to me when I plopped down in a chair and asked if he should go live with Grandma permanently. He spends a lot of time there—I admit it's convenient dumping him on her and she seems to enjoy the company, but still I was surprised. I know a lot of people do that, and I thought about it but decided that I don't want her raising him—she has such ideas! So, I said no, he should stay at home and we'd find room for everybody. But it was so genuinely considerate of him to ask, I just had to hug him. And do you know what? When I went to put my arms around him, he just froze, as if he didn't know what I was doing. Have I never hugged him? Funny, but I can't remember.

He really is quite lovable despite being so rebellious and independent; he's such a happy kid, always laughing and telling jokes and trying to make us laugh. He's especially good with Anna; he takes her outside to play on that little patch of grass and they go for walks to the river and he teaches her all sorts of stuff. He seems to think she's his special responsibility. Funny, I would have never guessed he'd be so caring. She absolutely adores him, too. He's just turned seven, yet he's so bright, he's already explaining things to me and reading books I haven't got around to reading yet! It looks like his hair might stay blond or at least light brown, and he has nice blue eyes as well. I think he might do really well—we'll just have to give him a push in the right direction.

One thing I'm going to do is try and teach him how to play the piano. He has a good ear and I think he'll be able to do well. Now all I need to do is find the patience and the time to teach him! And a piano, of course. Charles says there isn't room for one, but we'll make room! I wonder if it will require a permit?

Peter laughed out loud as he read that last question. Permits had ruled their lives. Queues at government offices, arguments with bureaucrats, forms that had to be filled out time and again, journeys from one office to another, surly replies and shrugs of the shoulder. Snapped commands, silent peremptory points of the finger, the ubiquitous experience of having waited, hours usually, in the wrong line. Don't point out the sign over the window—it's no longer valid or you've misread it. You're in the wrong line. The counter has closed. Come back later. Those forms aren't valid anymore. Are you trying to make trouble?

Handfuls of money dropped accidentally behind counters, filing cabinets that magically came unstuck, tears and shouting and vicious arguments over nothing. A rubber stamp with the word DENIED written entirely in capital letters. Red ink that could spill over from the application form onto your identity documents if you weren't careful. Do you want to make trouble? Do you want us to look at your job performance? Is your ration book too high a priority? Do you want your child to lose his place in school? Go to the end of the queue. Don't make trouble.

Peter got up and put on the kettle for another cup of tea. Barbara had gone to bed already, and only when he washed up the plate his sandwich had been on did he realize she had made it for him. He walked over to the bedroom door and peered inside. She was curled up on her side of the bed, the blankets off her shoulders. She looked chilled, so he went over and touched her shoulder. It felt cold and he pulled the blankets up and tucked them around her. He spent a moment watching her sleep and then, as the kettle whistled, returned to the kitchen to pour the tea.

With the pot refreshed, he sat down to continue reading his mother's history. The little family continued its journey through the bureaucratic maze and the political confusion. Catherine reported on the progress of her children, now apparently proud of all three of them. Charles's career continued to prosper. Their ration booklets were upgraded once again, and there was even some chocolate available to slake Catherine's addiction. There was also a nice photograph of the three children tucked into the pages: Erich standing and Niklaus sitting with little Anna on his lap. All three smiling broadly. Peter looked at the date; not much time left for the three of them, soon Anna would be dead.

29

CATHERINE DID NOT NOTE the epidemic at its beginning. It was just another wave of disease through the poorer sections of town, weeding out the homeless and the weak. This one, however, was worse—the winter was colder and wetter, the harvest had been bad, and following the five-year plan, the export of crops had been increased. The population was hungry and weary and weak, and the influenza spread from the poorer sections into the middle class and even into some of the German districts. When it hit the German population, there was a rush to the hospitals, and suddenly, with a shortage of beds and food and coal, a rationing system was instituted that gave overwhelming priority to the ruling class. The *Nur für Deutsche* signs that had been falling into disuse were dusted off and placed over door after door. Segregation was again strictly enforced, and the *gemischt* population was effectively excluded from government services and well-stocked shops as long as the pure Aryan population was in need.

The Underground, which had struggled to survive in the face of apathy and exhaustion on the part of the populace, had a sudden change in fortunes; recruitment went up, activities were reorganized, and a new long-term plan of attack was established. It was clear that there would be no quick changes, no revolution and overthrow of the conquerors in the near term. It was also equally clear that the minor concessions and rights that the native population had won through compromise and collaboration would be withdrawn as soon as they proved even a minor inconvenience to the government. The occupiers had shown their hand: the English would never be granted full equality. The leaders of the Underground smiled and began to lay their plans. They were in for the long haul, but now at least a part of the population understood the reason why the fight was necessary.

For the Chase family, the epidemic brought personal tragedy. Catherine wrote how Niklaus succumbed first, probably having contracted it from one of the lower-class English children that he was always hanging around with. She berated herself for not having forced him to stay indoors, but it was too late, the enemy was in the door. Anna and Catherine were simultaneously next. Catherine made a quick entry in her diary at that point, but wrote no more until well after Anna's death. Between her family's and her own illness, there was no time to write, no strength in her arms. After Anna's death and everyone else's recovery, she wrote about the events, concluding with:

> As I saw her little body taken away, wrapped in its shroud and placed tenderly in the truck that would take her and all the others to be buried

outside the city, I thought to myself how I've lost my beloved daughter. I'm too old and tired to have another child—she's gone and I can't replace her. Erich and Charles were too sick to come out, and I was only barely back on my feet. Niklaus was recovered, and he held my arm and walked me down to the street so I could wave good-bye to my little girl. He was the only one who was well and he had been absolutely wonderful taking care of everything. Fetching supplies and preparing food and everything. He was particularly good with Anna and I think it really hurt him that his efforts were all in vain. I guess it's the first time that he realized that sometimes sheer effort is not enough to get what you want. If it were, he would have saved her.

When we were climbing back up the steps—I took a long time— Niklaus asked me if I thought it was his fault for bringing it into the house. I felt so bad when he said that, I just hugged him and then of course I assured him that it wasn't his fault, that it was everywhere and sooner or later it would have hit us. I hope I sounded convincing.

Catherine did not write again for a long time after that. It was a time of conflict for the family. Niklaus had grown convinced that his parents were wrong in working with the system, and the epidemic and its aftereffects only confirmed his beliefs. Meanwhile Catherine and Charles seemed even more determined to work their way out of the mire of English London and into the rarefied atmosphere of the ruling elite. They turned their attention toward Erich and Niklaus, determined to make them into proper little mock Germans. Erich seemed happy enough with their plans, but Peter remembered how he had grown more and more angry and ever more determined to maintain his separate English identity. His grandmother had abetted him in that, passing on history and language and culture to him. He had also turned increasingly toward the street gangs, and his casual association became a full-fledged membership. Catherine noticed the change and remarked accordingly.

Worried about Niklaus. He is such a bright lad with such promise, yet the way he speaks! I can't believe some of the words that come out of his mouth! Such language. And such a low-class accent! Where in the world did he learn to speak like that?

Ever since Anna's death, he just rebels against everything. I think he's in one of those gangs. They're awful—some stupid patriotic (i.e., English) name, lots of slang and jargon. I don't know what else they do. Vandalism, dealing drugs, theft? I heard anytime they get a German boy on his own, they beat him. God only knows what would happen to a girl! Luckily the patrols usually stop it, but I'm afraid someone could get really hurt. What if Niklaus is caught doing something like that? They could put him in juvenile detention or worse. How are we ever going to get him back under control? He's just a little boy!

His mother was right, the gang did all those things and more. It was rare, but when they found some German kid who had dared stray into their neighborhood without protection, they would jump him. He remembered how, as a new member, he had protested, feeling that somehow things weren't quite right. Later though, after some of his buddies had been badly beaten by either German gangs or by the police, after some arrests, after a few executions, after the epidemic with the signs *Nur für Deutsche* over most of the hospital doors—after all that, he simply stood aloof, unable to participate but also unwilling to offer any aid or defense to the victims. Anyone who was stupid enough to be caught out alone deserved his fate. It was, he realized, an easy, childish rationalization that haunted him as a self-condemnation throughout most of his life: he had been caught out alone and he had paid the price for youthful arrogance.

He read further and came across another entry where his mother bemoaned his behavior.

> Niklaus is driving me nuts! Why can't he be more like Erich? He moans continuously—like some little English propaganda machine. Where does he get all this stuff? Sometimes I just want to throttle him for making so much trouble. It's "bloody this" and "fuck that" all the time. He pretends that he doesn't understand us when we speak German. I know discipline and punishment are all the rage now, but Charles and I just believe there has to be a better way than beating a kid into submission. Still, I wonder if we aren't spoiling him by being so tolerant. I think he gets some of his worst ideas from my mother. She really is a bitter old cow. Maybe we should keep him away from her. If only we could make him see sense somehow. In any case, Charles and I have decided—no more English at home. Not a word, not until he admits he's fluent in German. And no dinner either.

Peter remembered that time well: it was a battle of wills that he was fated to lose. His mother only purchased enough food each day for that evening's meal, his brother happily wolfed down the extra portion of rations that went begging at each mealtime, and his friends rapidly grew tired of him asking them for food. They all knew his father's ration card was far superior to their parents', and they resented the imposition. Finally, a friend, well, actually a gang leader, gave him a way out. "Know thine enemy," he had said philosophically between draws on his cigarette, thus giving implicit permission and a justification for caving in. After that, it did not take long to admit defeat.

> At last! A breakthrough. Guess who today finally asked if he could join us for dinner! He not only asked in German, but he agreed to converse throughout dinner. Thank God, the kid has some sense! I've saved some coupons, I'll buy some of his favorites and make a really nice meal for him

tomorrow to celebrate. We can tell him our news then. I hope he takes it well.

The news was that they had obtained a place for him in the Boys' Academy. Needless to say, he did not take it well. It took several minutes before his shocked horror had subsided enough for him to realize they were not only serious, but thought he should be pleased. He begged, he pleaded, he tried to bargain, but all to no avail. He was going to be dumped in a good private school, one intended for the sons of German bureaucrats and officers. Three days after breaking the news to him, his mother made her next entry.

Niklaus is still furious with us. Calls us traitors, swears at us using English phrases he certainly never heard at home! At other times he argues with us, trying to change our minds and cajole us—he even uses German then. I just don't understand it, a good education will make sure he has a fighting chance in this world, but instead he acts like we've betrayed him. I'm so desperate to get him out of this neighborhood and away from the influence of these gangs, I wouldn't even care if it were a bad school, but it isn't, it's the best in London!

Charles really had to work to get him a place, and the fees will bankrupt us! He didn't even manage to get Erich in, only Niklaus's scores on that aptitude test and a lot of favors pulled it off. He really exerted himself to get Niklaus this opportunity and he has gotten no thanks at all for it. In fact, Niklaus actually spat at him yesterday. Charles was so surprised he swung at him and knocked him right off his feet. Luckily, he was controlled enough to leave it at that. Niklaus just sat there on the floor utterly silent. What did he think? That he could spit at his father and get no reaction? Where in the world does he get his ideas? I never imagined an eight-year-old could be so difficult. Erich was never like this. He must be getting his ideas from somewhere. It must be those kids on the street.

Niklaus claimed they'd kill him at the school. I told him he'd fit in just fine, but he swore it wouldn't matter. Then Charles assured him that the school authorities would make sure he was okay. I don't think he believes us. It wasn't like him at all, he seemed genuinely scared, not one of his usual stunts. He begged not to have to go—promised that he'd do better in all his subjects and promised solemnly to speak German all the time. I almost changed my mind then, but then I asked if he'd quit his gang and he said there was no gang!! Erich laughed then. I wonder if he's in one, too? He's mad at us as well. Says we spend all our effort on "that little ingrate." What did we do to get such children?

There followed a lot of entries that dealt with the trivialities of life. One mentioned that Charles had been inducted into a proper level of the Party—no longer an associate member. After that there was a mention of taking their son to his new school and the tears Catherine had shed on the way back home at the realization that her little boy was growing up.

Over the following weeks, Catherine seemed to make a determined effort to pay more attention to Erich and to detail his accomplishments, but then there was a disturbing little entry:

> School authorities said Niklaus fell down a flight of steps. They said no reason to visit and that everything's being handled. I had Charles call from the office and they assured him that a visit from us would only embarrass the boy.

A flight of steps! Peter felt chilled and read on quickly, determined not to remember those first horrible months as he had tried to establish himself. His mother wrote about how he was getting along: joining sports teams, doing well in classes. Her entries had a note of forced cheerfulness, as though she herself was unsure of them. Just before the end of the first year, she wrote:

> Curfew has been changed again. It's later now but you still need a special pass to go out and the old ones are no longer valid. Such a nuisance. Well, there's not much reason to go out anyway. The crime seems to be only getting worse. You would think with so many soldiers and patrolmen on the street . . . What am I saying, I'm sure they're doing their best. The bombs don't help—they can hardly do their proper job when they have to spend all their time cordoning off areas and tracking down the terrorists.
>
> Niklaus has been injured during a football practice. They say he'll be okay but he'll look a little beaten up when he comes home in a couple of days. Poor boy, I should make something special for his homecoming dinner.

Peter almost laughed aloud at that. Yes, it had been football practice, but it was in the locker room, not on the pitch. One of the times that the verbal harassment had turned nasty. Six on one: he hadn't stood a chance. They had finally scattered when the coach had entered the room, predictably that bit too late. Peter remembered sitting on the floor, blood dripping from his nose and mouth, unable to say a word when asked what was going on. *Answer me! Are you deaf, what's wrong with you, boy?* Still he had remained in stubborn silence. They knew and they chose to do nothing, so why should he endanger himself by seeking their worthless protection? The coach had shaken his head in nameless disgust, pulled him to his feet, and walked him to the clinic. Football practice, indeed!

Catherine's next entry was after the end of the school year.

> I am absolutely furious with Niklaus. He hardly ate any of the special foods I prepared. He's never home, but when he is, he just stares sullenly. He hardly speaks, in any language! I asked him about his sports injuries

and he just stared at me like I was nuts. Didn't say a word. What a brat! I could throttle him.

Yesterday, he and Erich skulked off together, I heard them laughing in the hall. It's good to see the boys getting along, but I wonder what they're getting up to. I do worry about them. There are so many bad influences out there. Some of the stories I've heard at work . . .

Oh, some good news—more detainees released. I guess these were the problem cases. I can't imagine any other reason why they should have been detained so long. Maybe Charles's father will get to come home soon. His mother still reads those ratty old letters he wrote from years ago. I guess they cheer her up after she's read one of the recent ones. I've read some and I must admit they are quite odd, completely devoid of feeling. Just little reports on his life there. He's working in some canning factory. I don't know what he'll do when he comes back. Of course, there are no jobs or housing for any of them, maybe that's why they were kept away so long. It will be tough on them coming back to nothing. It's hard to imagine so much time has passed. So little has changed. The streets are still filled with rubble. I'm still working in the packing plant. The shortages never seem to stop, and instead of building new housing, they're always knocking something down.

Peter remembered when his grandfather had finally been allowed to come home. It was after the beginning of his second year, and Catherine made a short note in her diary but did not otherwise comment. Peter had received special permission for a Sunday trip home just so that Charles could take his family to meet his father. There, in his grandmother's apartment, they stood in a row, he, his mother, and brother, as if on military inspection. Charles's father, prompted by his wife, walked across the room with a funny, stooped gait; he stood in front of them and confronted them with a look that seemed like disapproval. Charles had smiled at his father and introduced each member of his family, explaining that there had been a daughter as well. The old man had stared grumpily at the wife and two boys, grunted his greeting, and then had returned to sit down in an armchair. He asked if Charles had a cigarette for him and he smoked it in silence, listening to the radio, nursing a single beer, and not saying anything for the rest of the visit.

On their way home, Catherine had wondered aloud, perhaps hoping to make an excuse for their sakes, if the old man wasn't perhaps sick or still recuperating from the shock of his transition back to civilian life.

"Naw," Charles had replied, "he was always like that, at least in front of us kids. He must have been a bit better before we were born, or maybe when he was alone with Mum, 'cause she seemed to have fond memories, but as far as we were concerned, well, he hasn't changed!"

Erich had ventured to ask, "Did you like him, Dad?"

"Of course!" his father had answered. "He had a job, he didn't hit us or Mum, and he didn't drink too much. What more could a kid ask for?" Charles laughed as if he realized that perhaps he had hoped for more; that he wanted to provide the guidance to his sons that he had lacked as a child.

Peter remembered feeling a faint guilt then that he had not only expected much more from his father but had been so willing to judge his every move and so unwilling to accept his help. Perhaps he should try to do better at school, Peter had thought, perhaps he could make a go of it. He returned that very evening to the school, determined to do his best. He worked at his classes and studied assiduously, but the constant harassment did not cease, and he soon felt as abandoned and betrayed as on the first day he had been sent away.

At the end of term, Catherine wrote:

> I wish Niklaus would tell me about school. Before you could never shut that kid up, now he's so silent! At least when he is home. I saw him out on the street the other day with his friends, he was joking and laughing and seemed his old loudmouthed self. I was glad to see it, even though it hurt to know that the silent treatment is reserved just for me and Charles. It's particularly bad with Charles. He gets so little chance to see the boy, what with work and all, and when he finally finds time, Niklaus acts like he's not even there. Charles tried to show him some models he built when he was a kid. I swear Niklaus looked ready to spit on him again, but I guess he remembered last time, because he didn't. He just stared at his dad like he was speaking some incomprehensible language. I could see how much Charles was hurt, but luckily he didn't get mad. He just wished him good-night and left him alone.
>
> His behavior makes even good news taste sour. I asked him if he had any special news or maybe had won any awards and he said no. Only when I showed him the letter the school had sent about his math award did he admit he had won anything. He said he had forgotten about it. I asked what he did with the prize money and he said, "Spent it," and refused to say more. Such a lot of money to waste! I am so disappointed!

The math award had come as the result of an exam given in one of his classes. The math teacher was a weird old fellow who never showed any of his pupils the slightest sign of favor. When he gave the exam, he had each student write only a number in his exam book and then write that number on a slip of paper with his name. They had made a great show of dropping the slips into a locked box, and the teacher had promised that the box would be opened only after the exams had all been graded. Naturally, no one had believed him, at least not until an assembly several weeks later when various awards were announced. The math award was announced; Peter remembered how his name was mangled as it was called out, how he had been obliged to rise up and walk down the aisle followed by the jealous stares of his classmates. He was handed the prize money and plaque in front of all the others, and the master congratulated him but somehow forgot to shake his hand.

He knew he was bound to lose the money, and when he had looked at the plaque and seen that nowhere did his name appear on it, he knew it would be fair game as well. With that thought, he descended the steps of the stage and walked along the front row of seats where most of the gang leaders had managed to acquire places, each sitting with arms crossed, head thrown back in haughty disdain, and surrounded by loyal lieutenants. He chose one of the most powerful and simply handed the money to him, then walked a few meters along and handed his plaque to another before returning empty-handed to his seat.

The next day he was called into the main office and disciplined for his very public display of disrespect for the school awards, but it had been well worth it. Everyone knew he had nothing to steal so he avoided numerous confrontations and as a bonus managed to foment a nasty battle between the two gangs whose leaders he had singled out. After that he made a point of never excelling on any paper and so won no more awards.

That was the last entry in which he significantly figured for the entire remainder of the second book; clearly, out of sight meant out of mind. His mother noted his coming home for the summer holiday and his return to school for his third year, but otherwise seemed to assume from that point on that his silence was usual boyish reticence and that no news was good news.

She talked of Erich's efforts in school and the government-sponsored groups that he joined. She wrote endlessly of the problems she had talking with him, how he mindlessly parroted propaganda and didn't seem to think for himself. Peter laughed as he read that. So Erich hadn't escaped the baleful judgments of her manic depression either! Well, Peter supposed, there was a lot for an intelligent person to be depressed about. He closed his eyes and thought about his boyhood friends. Not one, he remembered, had trusted his parents. Not one. In many ways, he and Erich had been rather fortunate in that his mother's stress had manifested itself in such nonviolent ways, in bitter thoughts that she mostly managed to confine to a diary that no one else read. He had known some kids who had suffered a lot worse. And that included some of the elite children who had attended his school. Not unlike Geerd and Uwe and Horst, he thought. And where had Karl and Elspeth learned to behave like that? Was the entire culture, the entire Reich, creaking its way to a nervous breakdown? Was that how the sins of the fathers were to be visited down on the next generation?

He shrugged away his urge to indulge in profound distractions and picked up where he had left off. Catherine took to walking in the early morning before her job began and simply observing the state of the city around her. She alluded to some political discussions at work but disdained to explain further, perhaps out of fear. Peter could not discern what had created the crack, but it seemed that her general dissatisfaction with all those around her, and her overwhelming dismay at the lack of hope in her life, finally found a focus. Her eyes were slowly opened to the reality around her, to the relevance of what had happened to others. It was not a smooth transition; for long periods she flew into a rage at the thought of "those terrorists" and chided the people who would still not work to make a peaceful society. Then at other times she would mention how odd it was that she should feel obliged to hide her diaries, how she felt she had the right to question the status quo, how it was unfair that women automatically got shunted below men in all jobs and in education.

Why am I still in that packing plant? Why haven't I moved up one notch? I'm just as smart as Charles, yet his career moves forward and here I am stuck on the shop floor. I've tried to become assistant manager, but they wouldn't even accept my application. I've looked for other jobs, but nobody wants to hire a woman, especially a married woman—we should be at home taking care of the family, we shouldn't be taking good jobs away from the men! Of course that's easy for the German women, their husbands get enough pay! It isn't fair that Charles can't get any further in his job just because he was born here. He should get equal pay, after all, he does as much work (if not more). The extra taxes for us aren't fair either. Where does all the money from the Reconstruction tax go? Nothing ever seems to get done. Why are we still paying Restitution taxes? Aren't we all one country now? They bombed us, too! I've even heard they started the war, that they staged that Polish provocation. We didn't ask for their bloody invasion, why are we still paying for it? It isn't fair. It isn't right.

There are things I've heard that worry me. I always thought it was just anti-Nazi propaganda, but there is so much talk, it's hard to believe it is all made up. They (the government, I mean) don't help by making so many damn rules. They keep tearing down buildings! God in heaven, they move people around like they were cattle. Whole areas get uprooted and relocated. They've invented some new factory towns and they simply notify people that their job and their residence has moved! It is unnerving.

There's that horrible prison they put in Green Park. God, all the trees have been left to die. The city is an absolute mess. Why do we have segregation? Charles keeps trying to get us a better flat, but we always hit some roadblock. Do you know what one official said? He said, stop making so much noise if you want to stay out of trouble! All we were doing was asking for the new forms to apply for new housing! He called that "making trouble"!

The third year of school passed, Catherine's son grew another year older and another year more distant from everyone and everything. Erich was drafted in the spring, and when Niklaus returned home for the spring break, with both Anna and Erich gone, he found himself the center of attention for the first time in his life.

Niklaus came home again for break. I really don't look forward to seeing him anymore. It's a terrible thing to say about one's own child, but he
is so sullen when he is here, he spoils everybody's mood. If he's not out
and about with his friends, he just sulks at home. Charles keeps trying to
talk sense to him, but he just acts like he doesn't hear. Or even worse,
sometimes he "toes the line" acting like he agrees and mouthing all the
right words to Charles. He does it without a hint of sarcasm, and more
than once Charles has been fooled into thinking Niklaus is agreeing with
him. It breaks his heart when all of a sudden Niklaus just laughs at him
and walks away.

Who knows what that kid is thinking? I don't think anybody will ever
get inside his head. Were we this hard on our parents? He's just a little boy!
I wonder if a daughter would have been different. It's really quite odd, but
I can't look at him anymore without thinking of my poor little girl.
Sometimes, God forgive me, I wonder what life would be like if we had
lost Niklaus, rather than Anna.

Peter read those words several times, refusing to allow any feeling to disrupt
his thoughts. Eventually, a small smile crept across his face. So what else is new,
he thought, and turned the page to continue reading. Several pages later his
mother wrote:

With Erich gone, I've been trying to talk more to Charles about my
feelings, but he doesn't want to hear it. I'm not sure what to do. I think
we'll have to do something to cheer Niklaus up. I'll see if I can't find something he would like.

And a few days after that his mother made a short note:

Really strange several days. Two days ago Niklaus came back early, well
before dinner, and he did not go back out again. He just sat in a chair all
evening and read the German dictionary like it was a book. I guess he was
teaching himself new words. Then yesterday, he spent the day at home. I
stopped home during the lunch break to drop off some groceries (Margot
took the morning off and stood in the queue and let me join her at my
break) and there he was just sitting in that same chair reading the English
dictionary this time. I tried to chase him out to go get some fresh air, but I
don't know how long he stayed out. He was home when I returned from
work and did not go out in the evening. Today it's the same—I'm writing
this in our bedroom because I can't get him out of the house. I swear if it's
not one extreme, it's the other with that boy.

Peter remembered the source of that behavior, remembered it all too well. It
was the day he had gotten "the word." He had been walking along the street and

had spotted one of his mates, who apparently did not see him. The next time he called out to a friend and was ignored, he knew something was up, and he took off at a run and caught the fellow by his shirt. "Can't talk to you," his erstwhile friend had screamed in terror. Peter had let him go and had searched out some older member of the gang. He found one—a boy named Dennis, who promptly grabbed his arm and immediately marched him to one of their cellar hideouts. There was a meeting of the leaders—all boys of about fifteen. Most of them were engaged to be married, most only months away from conscription. The little coterie of pseudo-adults looked up from the business they were conducting with something like alarm.

"He needs to hear it from us directly," Dennis announced. "We owe him that much."

So they told him. He was exiled, shunned, out. He had asked why and they had said he could not be trusted, that he was being corrupted by the school he was at, that it was a violation of their security to allow such collaboration. He had protested his innocence, had explained how much he needed their support, had literally begged, but the decision was final. If he mixed with any of the members or was seen at any of the gang locations, he would be treated as any rival gang member or German would.

He had continued to beg—they were his only lifeline. Didn't they know what it was like for him all alone in that horrid school? At that point one of them rose threateningly from his seat, ground out his cigarette, and looked ready to personally enforce the banishment. At that point Peter had switched pleas. He no longer begged to belong or to mix freely with them or to be associated with any of their actions, he just pleaded that one or two members who were his close friends might be allowed to speak to him occasionally on the street. Nothing much, but they had been close friends, were unavoidable neighbors—just a few words now and then?

The leaders put their heads together and agreed. They allowed the exile to name two of his closest friends who could talk to him occasionally without being sanctioned. The rest would shun him completely, and he was advised on pain of severe punishment not to try to initiate any contact with any other member. He had nodded his agreement, shaking with fury at the unfairness of it all.

Dennis had walked him out of the meeting, draping his arm over his shoulder. Once they were on the street, the elder boy had said, "Sorry, kid, bloody unfair. Now off with you," and had given his young companion a shove in the direction of his home.

It had, in a way, been a relief. The growing distrust of his friends had been undeniable, and now the situation was clear: he knew there was nobody in the world he could turn to. The ache of his parents' betrayal, the sorrow of his grandmother's ever-increasing confusion, the pain of the growing distance between himself and his friends, the utter loneliness of his existence at school— they could all be turned off. If he did not care, then he could not be hurt. If he did not show his pain, then they could not enjoy his suffering. He thought of himself as a human machine, an organism that had to live in a hostile environment and would play whatever game was necessary to do that. He was precious to no one in the world, and so he could ignore everyone and concentrate on simple survival. All the emotional land mines, all the efforts at pleasing, all his determination to belong—all of it was irrelevant.

He became more studious after that, branching out into subjects that were neither required nor encouraged by his school, his grandmother often supplying him with old books. He read and studied; he practiced the piano as if driven; he took long, lonely walks; he observed and analyzed and thought. At school he had to continue to fight to maintain his position, but as he withdrew from everything and everyone around him, as he often did not even hear the provocations that at one time would have led to a fistfight, he was more often than not simply left alone. He lay in his bed at school as the morning light warned him that another day was beginning and would murmur to himself: *Alone, alone, alone.* It was both a plea and a statement of fact.

His mother detected his change in behavior and made occasional notes in her diary accordingly. She was not overly concerned; after all, he was by all standards, at last, behaving himself, but she did puzzle over it a bit. Finally, at the end of his third year, she saw fit to ask him directly if there was anything wrong. She recounted the conversation in her journal.

> Today before Charles came home from work, I asked Niklaus about things at school. He's been home for a week and nothing has changed from the last time he was home. Still studious, quiet, well-behaved. Practices on the piano a lot and he's getting really quite good. He treats his father with respect now and even, sometimes, asks his opinion or advice. It really pleases Charles, it's so good to see the two of them acting like father and son. No fighting about language. When we speak German, he is well-spoken, uses proper grammar and a very good vocabulary (much better than mine). As a reward to him, we sometimes speak English now. His accent is remarkably improved (none of that street slang) and he doesn't swear anymore.
>
> After he went back to school last time, he even started sending letters home. They were filled with the usual stuff: good news about grades, gossip about school. If I didn't know him better, I'd say everything was simply wonderful. But it is so unlike him, and such an abrupt change, and when he's not actively engaged in conversation, he looks so distant, like he's on another planet.
>
> I really didn't know what to ask him, I mean, how can a mother say, "My boy, you've been behaving, giving us no trouble, your reports from school are good—what's the problem?" yet I felt I had to find out if something was going on. So I talked with him. I really tried hard to find out what's going on in his life, what things are like for him, how he's getting

on with his friends. He just kept assuring me everything was wonderful. He fretted about why I was quizzing him. Wasn't I pleased with him? Had he upset me in some way? I don't know. I just don't know. Either everything really is fine or he's a consummate and shameless liar.

Peter laughed quietly to himself as he read that. "It was the latter, Mum," he said softly into the darkness. He closed his eyes to rest them a bit and thought of the mistakes he had made in his life. She had reached out to him then, he should have grabbed the hand that offered to pull him out of the flood, but it was too late, he no longer believed in her or anyone else.

He reached behind himself and turned off the small light he had been using to read the diaries. His eyes ached, and he knew that if he did not rest, a headache and the attendant nausea would preempt his efforts. The darkness surrounded him. From the next room he could hear Barbara's regular breathing, the ticking of the clock. The sounds of a sleeping city drifted through the window; the regular steps of a patrol punctuated the desultory noise of the infrequent traffic. A dog barked; it sounded like one of the shepherds that the patrols used—perhaps they had spotted some kid violating the curfew or an unsavory character stealing food. In the distance he heard the ominous thumping rhythm of one of the ubiquitous police helicopters. His city. The place of his birth. His homeland. The place where he had spent his youth, had joined the Underground, had found the woman he thought would be his forever. Never once had he walked its streets without fear of challenge by a patrol; never once had he cast a vote for the government that regulated the city's life; never once had he felt free or at home.

His thoughts returned to his mother's words. What had they had then? It had been the summer break, just before his fourth year at the school. There was still fall, winter, and spring term, summer break, and then she would be gone. In fifteen short months—just two weeks before his thirteenth birthday. Their time together was running short; his mother's time on earth would not last two years from when she wrote those words.

If only he had known.

Their lives were so brief and so unsure. How could he have spent the time he had been allotted with them so badly? It was a mistake, he realized, that he was doomed to repeat: the constant arguing with Allison about her dual affections. Wasted time. Words wasted on a future they did not have. Was it happening again? Was that the road he and Zosia were traveling?

He got up from the couch and went to the table and penned his thoughts in a letter to her. He could not read the words he wrote, nor did he even try; he just used their blurry outlines to keep them straight on the page. He did not expect the letter would be read, he just hoped that by putting his thoughts in print, he might be able to clarify what was happening.

30

"*H*EY, SLEEPY, WAKE UP." Barbara jostled his shoulder.

Peter awoke and stretched. His whole body ached and he realized that he had spent the remainder of the night sleeping in the chair, his head on the table. He stretched and yawned and moaned. "What time is it?"

"Nearly time to open the shop. Did you finish the books?" Barbara set down a cup of coffee in front of him.

"No," he sighed. Now he'd have to wait until the evening. Oh, well, he had waited this long in his life.

She seated herself opposite him at the table and began munching on her *Brötchen*. It was a day-old roll, anathema to a true German, but neither of them could be bothered to run out to the bakery early in the morning. "And what have you discovered so far?" she asked in between bites.

"More than I should ever have learned. I learned a lot about my mother. Made me feel rather sorry for her. She had so much promise and then to see it all just wasted like that."

"Did you learn anything about yourself?"

"I'll tell you about it while we're working." He smiled at her as he sipped the coffee. It was nice having someone to talk to, someone so understanding and unjudgmental. Such a sweet kid.

He blinked away the last of the morning muck from his eyes and glanced down at the letter he had been writing. He could not be sure, but it looked as if it had been moved. Barbara looked away, twisting around in her seat so she could look out the window.

"Did you read this?" he asked.

There was a long silence.

"Did you read what I wrote?"

"I'm sorry."

"Barbara. I need my privacy."

"We're supposed to be married," she replied defensively.

"We're supposed to *act* married in front of others. We're not married!" he snapped.

Finally Barbara twisted back around so that she was facing him. "I said I was sorry."

He rubbed his forehead; he felt tired and had a headache. "I'm sorry, too," he said at last. "It's no big deal. Nothing you didn't already guess, I'm sure."

"She doesn't deserve you," Barbara stated baldly. "She doesn't treat you right."

"Be that as it may, it's not your business."

"It is if it affects my work, and it does. She doesn't want you. Not really. You should get a divorce, get your freedom."

"I made a commitment that is meant to be a little stronger than that," he replied unsteadily.

"She treats you like . . ." Barbara could not summon up an appropriate analogy.

A lot of words came into his mind. Barbara was only saying what he had thought a thousand times, yet he responded, "I'm not easy on her either." He wondered at how he suddenly felt obliged to defend Zosia's honor. Maybe there was more there than he realized. He saw her smiling face, heard her easy laughter, remembered the way she had held him and listened to him on so many difficult nights. He saw her popping a strawberry into Joanna's mouth, the two of them giggling as they chased each other down a hallway, Zosia's face white with fear as she heard Joanna hum a dangerous tune. He thought of the beautiful golden curls that never stayed where she put them, the womanly curve of her hips, the lines of knowledge and maturity that made her face warm and beautiful to him. He closed his eyes and imagined what she looked like now growing heavier as their child grew within her. She had looked tired when they had said their good-byes, weary of the constant load, the burden that could never be put down even for a second. He should have said something else when she had said she loved him. God, how he missed her!

"You're not even listening to me!" Barbara huffed.

He looked up at her, stunned. "What?" he asked, confused. He tried to replay what she had just said, but it was lost.

"Never mind!" she replied scornfully.

That evening Peter let Barbara close up the shop and made his way back to the flat so that he could finish the diaries. He had not marked his place and it took him a while to determine exactly where he had been. Finally, he found the appropriate page. Catherine seemed to accept her son's word that all was well at school and did not comment further on that, though she did continue to wonder at his strange behavior at home.

Niklaus still not going out much. He plays the piano a lot and is getting really good at it. I've found some old sheet music that my mother had and I've passed it on to him. Mum looked at me sort of funny and asked if I really wanted the music, but then, she's always acting queer now. Niklaus seems to really like it, he spends hours and hours each day working on the songs. Just a few, over and over. He seems to be trying to pound them directly into his brain. Really irritating, especially when he first starts learning a new piece, but I don't say anything.

That was a bit rich! Peter thought. It was the technique, if one could call it that, that his mother had taught him. No scales, no practice songs, just dive into a difficult piece and learn it bar by bar. Like the sheet music she had given him: it was far too difficult for him to read and play simultaneously, so he had memorized it bit by bit, and after months he could play one piece. It was also why, after years of absence, he could sit down at Elspeth's piano and draw up physical memories in his fingers without knowing which note would come out next.

The entry continued:

> Had to chase Niklaus out of the house again today. I guess he really has no friends left in the neighborhood. I know that is what I wanted, and it's the best thing for him, to keep him out of trouble, but still he seems lonely when he's here. I guess he misses his schoolmates. He doesn't talk about them much, but when I ask, he assures me he has loads of friends there. He tells me all about them and their families, he just doesn't visit them over breaks because they live in gated neighborhoods, and as Niklaus so delicately put it, it would be awkward to try and reciprocate with an invitation here. We really should see about moving in or at least closer to those areas. I hear there are satellite neighborhoods that are mixed and don't require the bloodline proof for residency. They are so much nicer and the crime is so much lower!

Catherine wrote how she had learned of a production of *King Lear,* which she hoped Charles and she could take their son to. She was astonished by her son's reaction to the news, writing how his eyes lit up with anticipation and he spent hours studying the copy of the play that she had acquired for him. In late June they went to see the play, which he remembered so well and which had cost him such humiliation at Karl's hands. Even as he read his mother's words, he could hear that single word *"Later"* hissed at him with such venom. The whistle of Frau von dem Bach's departing train, the malevolent smile, the subdued threat of *"It's later,"* played through his mind so vividly that he nearly missed the impact of his mother's words:

> . . . told Charles I was really upset. He asked why and I couldn't really explain. Of course I should have known that if it didn't explicitly say "in English" that it would be in German, but as much as I should have known, it still bothered me. Why not in English? That's what the play was written in, that's what we all speak! Damn it, I've been trying for all these years to accept their presence on our island, and now it seems like all that's been achieved is that it is we who have to be accepted. We've become aliens in our own land. I just can't hide that fact anymore. Charles, for all his efforts, is getting nowhere, and that is the least of the injustices we have seen.
>
> I look at what we have done over the years and I realize that it is worse than nothing. We have been so ineffectual, our lives have been a waste. I think of my relatives and friends and I can think of not one person who has made a difference. Even worse, we've taken out our frustrations on

our kids. How could we have accepted this government? This idiotic ideology? It's corrupt, unjust, unfair, cruel. Nothing but a pack of thugs and murderers and we let them carry on with it all. God Almighty! Niklaus is right, he's been right all along, it's no wonder he hates us. I thought we had peace, but all we've done is refuse to fight, and what a mess we've left for our sons and daughters. We called it peace but there is no peace without justice. There is just this never-ending war that has poisoned us all, and now we've passed it on to our children and left them to fight it, alone and without any support or help or understanding from us.

Peter read and reread those words, finding a comfort in them that was beyond measure. Her words had made it clear that the school was to them what they had said it was: a chance for his advancement, not the secret plot he had always hoped. His disappointment at that discovery could now at least be tempered by her admission: even though they had imposed such a hell on him, his parents, or at least his mother, had come to realize that collaborating with such an enemy was hopeless. He read on eagerly as she described her feelings in more detail. Over a period of days, she apparently had long conversations, or rather arguments, with her husband, the result of which she summarized:

I've agreed to have Niklaus return to school. I'm sure it's awful for him there, but since Niklaus refuses to say anything, I can't convince Charles of that. Besides, he says, Niklaus will be entering the Upper School this year, and that is sure to make things better for him. I told Charles that I'll agree to send him there, but now my intent is for him to learn the ways of the enemy so that he can fight them more effectively! Charles told me not to be so melodramatic. He also said I'd better not say anything to draw suspicion to us, because there are always sorts within the bureaucracy who are looking for ways to get rid of so-called foreigners (meaning us!). He said that some people get arrested on simple suspicion of this or that, and then they just disappear. God in Heaven! I was furious that he hadn't mentioned anything about this earlier. He said he didn't want to worry me!! The only reason I didn't say more was I could see he was truly worried. He doesn't know what to do—he doesn't want to lose all he's worked for, yet if he keeps moving up, he's afraid that these jealous sorts will target him. He feels completely trapped. We're going to have to work out what to do.

I told Charles I was scared and he assured me it's not as bad as all that. Just some whispers over the years. Still, I'm scared and I'm really and truly angry as well. After all our efforts to fit in, to receive such a welcome! What a waste of our lives.

As time went on, Catherine's opinions against their occupiers only hardened. She actively sought out information and began attending clandestine meetings held by the Underground to educate the populace. Once such meeting impressed her sufficiently to merit a special entry.

> They had a guest speaker tonight. We've been warned about this meet-ing for ages and I took extra precautions. The speaker was a man who had been in the military some thirty years ago. SS, I think. He described some of the things he saw and the reasons why he had joined the Resistance. I was nearly sick just listening and I think everyone else felt the same. I don't think he was lying or that it was exaggerated—at least in part because he broke down in tears. We asked if all this is still going on, and he said he didn't know, but he did know that they never brought the guilty to justice and that the actions of those years have been accepted as "neces-sary" and "for the benefit of the Reich." As he said, if that's the sort of thing that benefits the Reich, then I must fight it with all my being.
>
> There was a handout as well. It was an eyewitness account presented to the American Congress in 1950. I'll tuck it into these pages as a sample of what I heard that night.

Peter pulled out the badly printed piece of paper. The ink had faded and smudged, but the words were still readable. It was not unlike some of what he had read in the archives at Szaflary:

> They brought an aged woman with her daughter to this building. The latter was in the last stage of pregnancy. They put her on a grass plot and several Germans came to watch the delivery. This spectacle lasted two hours. When the child was born, Menz asked the grandmother whom she preferred to see killed first. The grandmother begged to be killed. But, of course, they did the opposite. The newborn baby was killed first, then the child's mother, and finally the grandmother.

Peter shuddered a sigh and stood up to pace around the darkened room. It was no different from what he had read or heard hundreds of times, yet there were some things to which he could not become inured and this tale in particu-lar stung. If only it weren't the truth! If only it were some madman's fantasy that remained nothing but words on a page!

It was so long in the past that it should not have mattered, but it did. It did. Once he had realized that these words and words like them were the truth, once they had broken through his defensive barrier of denial, then they became a part of him, burning their way into his soul. Now he had his own sad words to add to the tale, and he could inform his mother that, yes, it was still going on, and, yes, it was worth fighting with all of her being.

He glanced at the clock—three in the morning. He felt fine and would proba-bly be able to finish the diaries tonight. The thought perturbed him in a way he had not expected. It was as if he were running out of time with his parents all over again. He had only just found them and now there were so few pages left in their lives! He poured himself a drink and tried to slow the pace of his reading.

Catherine described how the words of that evening stayed with her, how she felt guilty at her own lack of action and virtual collaboration over the past years. When her son came home for break, she began to discuss her ideas with him, and slowly, ever so slowly, he responded.

Been trying to talk to Niklaus. Even though Charles is coming around to my point of view, I find Niklaus is most open when his father is not around. I can tell he's beginning to let me know a bit of what he thinks—just a little, as if he thinks I might be leading him into a trap and he has to be careful. We talked in generalities about what sort of government should replace this one if a revolution were to happen (neither of us daring to say that we actually thought one should happen) and he had a lot of ideas on that topic. I asked where he had learned about democratic politics and he just cocked his head at me and smiled in that knowing way of his—as if to say, I've not yet earned enough trust to have that question answered, but maybe in the future. He's such a smart boy, yet he is just a boy and I'm afraid he won't be cautious enough if I tell him all of my thoughts.

Decided I have to hide my diaries in a more secure place. If Charles might be the target of anti-English sentiment at work, then it is possible this place might be searched on a silly pretext and the words I've been writing would be damning. I found a really good place in the shower and I've put the first two books that I started before we even got married way up inside the wall. I put them in a crevice that's so narrow, I don't think a grown man's arm could get into it (mine just barely fits). Since all the police are men, I figure they'll be safe there like that, since even if they find the hiding place, they're not likely to reach that far into it. I store this diary in there as well, and since it is a nuisance to get it out, I don't make as many entries anymore, but better safe than sorry. I sometimes wonder why I write anything at all. When I started writing, it was because my aunt had given me the diary; now it has become a habit. I suppose I thought Anna would be interested in my words when she became a mother, but that is long past. I don't think Erich would have any interest in what I've written, but maybe someday Niklaus will—long after I'm gone.

Speaking of old age, I've been stopping by to see Mum every day recently. She's not doing very well at all. Seems like her mind is always in the past. All of a sudden she seems so old and frail. Niklaus is very helpful whenever he's home, running errands for her and even visiting when I'm at work to cook her meals and clean for her. In one of her clearer moments she thanked him and he told her it was the least he could do since she had always been there for him. (So that's the thanks I get for my years of effort!)

Niklaus and I talked some more as we walked home from Mum's together. He even told me a bit about school. Not much, but it was different from the usual rubbish, so I guess it was the truth. I hinted that maybe it was all for a purpose but didn't say more, mostly because I had no idea what I was talking about, just the inkling of an inspiration.

Peter found himself grinning. So it hadn't been his imagination or just wishful thinking! No wonder he was so confused about his parents' motives: they had been confused! He read on as Catherine described how her husband began more and more to agree with her point of view. He did not attend any of the meetings for fear of discovery and denunciation, but he listened eagerly to her reports of what the Underground had to say and what they were doing.

With each page, Catherine reported more of her mother's deterioration. As Peter read the words, he shared again his mother's sadness. It had been a painful time for him as he saw the one person who had supported him throughout his childhood slowly and irreversibly failing. It was equally painful for Catherine as she could not communicate to her mother the turnaround in her own beliefs. One day, Catherine's mother walked out into traffic and was killed by a car. It was a mercifully quick death, but one that left the family stunned by their loss.

Erich could not come home for the funeral, but Niklaus was there. He only made it in time to meet us at the graveyard, and it was one of the rare times I've seen him in his school uniform. Usually he changes out of it before he even reaches home—God only knows where—but this time, there he was all properly dressed with his neat suit and tie and the school's insignia and swastikas. I used to think that uniform looked quite handsome on him.

Niklaus didn't say much but I could tell he was really heartbroken. She was always so good to him and I think she taught him a lot. My sister Emily and her children were there, but as usual we didn't have much to say to each other; just the usual courtesies that strangers exchange on such occasions. She had a man with her and she introduced me, but I didn't bother to remember his name, though who knows, maybe this one will stick around for a while.

I tried to talk a bit more to Niklaus afterward as we started the long walk home, but when he saw a bus heading west, he said he had to hurry and catch it because he had not, after all, gotten permission to leave, so he had just skipped out, and the sooner he got back, the less severe his punishment would be. He was gone before we could ask him what he meant by that. He seemed to think we would know. What, in God's name, do they do there? Why hadn't he got permission to come home for his grandmother's funeral? Charles even called from his office about it yesterday.

It was simple spite, Peter thought to himself. The master had called him to the office and coldly told him of his grandmother's death, then added that he would not be allowed to attend the funeral because he had not been sufficiently deferential over the past several weeks, so how could he possibly pay his respects to the dead when he did not even show a proper attitude to his betters? There had been no argument, he had simply waited until early morning, had climbed the wall, and had hitched a ride to the cemetery, arriving only just in time. On the way back, he had hopped a series of buses and run several miles, managing to scramble over the wall even as his name was being called over the loudspeaker with the command that he report to the main office. It was not the first time he had been called that day, and he did not even bother to pretend that he had been on campus; he simply accepted the caning as the price for saying good-bye to his grandmother.

"Hey, you still up?" Barbara's sleepy voice broke into his reverie.

He gave her a gentle smile and nodded, asking, "What's wrong, can't you sleep?"

She yawned, came to sit down next to him, and curled up so that her head was on his shoulder. Peter was eager to read more of his mother's words, but Barbara seemed to need his company, so he patiently closed the book and set it down. "What's up?" he asked, stroking her hair away from her eyes.

She sighed and pressed herself closer to him. After a long while, she said softly, "I wanted to apologize for reading your letter."

"Oh, don't worry about that."

"I don't want you to think you can't trust me. I respect your privacy."

"It's all right, little one," he soothed, still stroking her hair. Like Joanna after a bad dream. "Why don't you go back to sleep, you sound tired."

"I'm not like that, you know."

"I know, don't worry. It really is all right. I'd already forgotten about it."

She looked up at him suddenly, as if insulted by his last phrase. She didn't say anything but her expression asked, Am I so forgettable?

He sighed and continued to stroke her hair. Then he leaned over and kissed the top of her head. "I take a lot of comfort in your being here, Barbara, I really do."

She leaned back against him and closed her eyes, obviously unwilling to leave him, obviously afraid of saying more. He held her until she fell asleep, then he picked her up and carried her back into the bedroom. It was unlikely that she slept through being moved, but she did not open her eyes, perhaps enjoying the sensation of being a child in his arms. He laid her on the bed and covered her, and indulging her in her feigned sleep, he stroked her hair back from her face again and kissed her cheek, whispering, "Sleep well, child."

He sat for a few moments by her side, watching as genuine sleep reclaimed her, then he sighed heavily. He was tired and every page he read was one less page in his mother's life. With deliberate patience, he decided to prolong her life for at least one more day. He returned to the sitting room to place the last diary safely on a shelf and turn off the lamp, then he went to join Barbara in their bed.

$$31$$

*F*EELING THAT HE WAS REALLY PUSHING his luck by not finishing the diaries when he had a chance, Peter went into work with Barbara the next morning as usual. Despite his premonitions, nothing untoward happened; they worked their usual shift in the bookstore, then after they had eaten their meal and Barbara had retired for the night, he began reading again. With Catherine's prodding, Charles decided to turn his disillusionment to good use and, through his wife, offered his services to the Underground.

> The local leadership has a hard time believing we don't want money for this stuff—that just makes us seem more suspicious to them. I guess they've never heard of people having a change of heart or being disillusioned before. Anyway, they're beginning to trust us, but now they're expressing disappointment at the low-quality information that Charles can get his hands on. I've tried to explain that it is not caution on his part so much as the fact that nothing else is really available to him. I hope that is the truth. I feel thoroughly fed up with this regime and am ready for a revolution of any sort, but I think Charles is still maybe acting more out of bitterness and revenge against those who have made his progress so difficult.
>
> The Pure German faction has gotten more brazen recently and there have been minor incidences against "foreign" Party members and even Charles has been harassed a bit. He knows who is behind it, but there is no proof against them and it's not clear that, even if he had proof, any of it would be taken seriously by the higher-ups.

Peter read his mother's words again, trying to determine which of their two dangerous games would eventually cause their deaths. It seemed obvious now that their arrests had not been as accidental as had seemed. Clearly, if it was known that Charles was feeding information to the Underground, then he could be arrested outright, without the need for a charade, but perhaps there was only a suspicion, or perhaps there was some political reason to keep his indictment secret, such as the fear of providing ammunition to the Pure German movement. Under those circumstances, being arrested for allegedly hiding his wanted son might be enough to set him on the path of a long and deliberately deadly interrogation. It would not be unusual for the Party to dispose of a troublesome member in such a fashion.

Still, if Charles had been suspected of treason, it seemed unlikely that the Party would have had the patience to wait for such a coincidence as his son's being denounced. How could they have known that the son would not be at home and that both his parents would be at the moment they decided to arrest him? They would not have waited for such accidental luck when they could easily have manufactured something more straightforward. Only if the timing had just happened to coincide with their suspicions, or maybe if Charles or Catherine had said something unexpected while under investigation, would it make sense.

That last thought was rather scary. He reread his mother's words. *Ready for a revolution of any sort.* Had she said something like that to her interrogators? Had it all been just bad luck and Erich's denunciation up to that point? Though the end result was the same and long in the past, he somehow hoped it wasn't true, for then the root cause of their deaths would be his old gang membership and the conversations he had had with his mother.

Ready for a revolution of any sort. It was a direct quote from him. He had used it in his younger days, quoting the more radical elements of the freedom movements. The implication was that a reasonable approach had failed to produce results and that change, any change achieved in any manner, was preferable to the current state of affairs. It was naive, of course; a bloodbath was not really preferable, and the Gestapoland imposed out East was easy proof that life for the native Britons could have been much worse. Nevertheless, it was a common sentiment, usually not reflecting a genuine philosophy, but rather frustration.

Peter turned his thoughts to the Pure German faction and their possible complicity in his parents' deaths. The movement clearly did not wield enough power to act openly, but they might jump at any opportunity to purge "foreign" elements from the Party and the bureaucracy. A chance arrest of the parents of a wanted boy would provide them with the perfect opportunity. Charles's death might then have been either deliberate or the accidental consequence of an intention to scare him out of government. In either case, his wife would have had to be silenced to keep her from pursuing a vendetta or exposing their crime to the authorities.

The latter scenario fit in slightly better with what little he knew. Due to its apparent lack of political power, the Pure German faction would be dependent on dumb luck to put one of their enemies into their hands, and the secretiveness that followed Catherine's and Charles's arrests seemed more in keeping with what their methods would have to be. Everyone would know what had happened, and all the English could read the writing on the wall, but nobody could be held accountable as it had been an accidental death under interrogation.

Peter read on. There were more hints that the Pure German movement was making trouble, and as his parents' involvement in the Underground deepened, Catherine worried about her son's future:

Our initial plans for Niklaus were that if we got him into a good university, he could get a deferment or even carry out German-style service. Now, of course, I doubt we could talk him into the military for two years, especially since I get the impression he would not be welcomed among his comrades (I've heard there are a lot of deaths from hazing). Recently, I've been thinking of withdrawing him from that horrid school and letting him finish his schooling locally and then eventually he could work with the Underground, but then he'd have to go through those six years in the labor draft.

Now, there is another possibility. One of the locals suggested they could use him when he's finished schooling. Their plan would be for our son to disappear and for Niklaus to reemerge with a new identity which would allow him to infiltrate directly into the security services or some other branch of government. It seems amazingly long-term thinking, for they could not possibly hope for him to achieve anything for at least a decade, but I guess after all these years, we're in for the long haul.

Charles and I have debated the pros and cons endlessly. On the positive side, Niklaus could do something useful for his country and I think he would like that, also he would not have to be drafted (they said they could handle that though they didn't say how). The negatives are fairly obvious: we would almost certainly lose all contact with him, he might not want to pretend to be a German or Volksdeutsch, and it would be dangerous.

There's one more thing I really didn't like: we've talked about him a lot to the Underground, discussing his fluency and his suitability and his talents, but they never asked what he would want. They seem to assume he's sort of our commodity to do with as we please! I know that we have pushed him into certain things, like his school, but we've always had his best interests at heart. This is different, they only seem to view him as someone to be used. I've mentioned that he's a very independent-minded boy, but they brush that aside. They seem so hungry to have him that I'd worry about how they might treat him.

Peter thought back to that moment when that unknown man had put his hand on his shoulder and said, *Come with me.* Clearly they had heard Catherine's words and heeded her warnings, for they had waited a full month, letting him know hunger and terror, before they had offered him their assistance. He had been led to believe that they had only happened to observe him wandering the streets and their assistance had been completely altruistic. They had expressed surprise at his background and schooling, marveled at his fluent, unaccented German, and presented their plan for his future as if it had materialized out of thin air. They had also maintained a stony silence about his parents, insisting that they had no information whatsoever. Doubtless, as far as they were concerned, the unfortunate demise of his parents was a boon for they no longer had to negotiate to get their hands on him.

A burning sensation spread through his body as he remembered how he had been overwhelmed with gratitude and a desire to please them once they had so mercifully rescued him from the streets. His gratitude had carried him through excruciating interrogations, preventing him from betraying anything—not one name, not one location, not one code word, ever left his lips. Even after Graham and his superiors had let him and his friends serve as bait for a trap, he had maintained loyalty to them! Even now, he used the name they had given him then in preference to the one his parents had given him.

It had all been a farce. They had used him from the start, like a well-trained chimpanzee. Like a commodity. It was true, he consoled himself, whatever their motives, they had saved his life. Still, they could have treated him as a human being, they could have told him what they knew, they didn't have to treat him like that. Or had they been so poisoned by the society around them that they, too, no longer knew how to trust anyone?

He reread his mother's words, feeling the love and concern in them that she had so often denied him in his youth. It made up for a lot, it made up for much of what she had written earlier, and as he continued reading, he felt comforted. She had not been the perfect mother, nor had she been an idealist all her life, but neither was she heartless or relentlessly collaborating. And, she had loved him after all. That was worth something.

Catherine's words continued to outline her worries about harassment at Charles's workplace, about anonymous poison-pen letters, and she continued to debate with herself the merits of the Underground's plans for her son. Around *Winterfest,* she seemed to take a break from it all and wrote about other things— about the price of sugar and the renaming of streets, about how her in-laws were faring and news from Erich; still her mind was never far from her problems, and buried in the middle of a description of that year's *Winterfestmarkt* was the line Peter had found before:

> I don't know what to do about Niklaus. I'm worried he won't know what to do if something happens. I wish I could tell him, but Charles insists I don't—at least not yet. Says he's still too young. What am I to do?

The thought had slipped out of her pen as if of its own accord, and she determinedly changed tack again and wrote more about the weather and what they had had for dinner that evening, detailing things as if to preserve forever a memory of normalcy. On the following page, she allowed herself to return to her troubles and came up with a tentative solution:

> I thought my diary might be of help to Niklaus if something accidental should happen to us. Trouble is, I don't think he'd find it and I can't tell him where I hide it, at least not yet. I've decided to sing a little song to him that maybe someday will make sense. It's all so wild an idea, I feel a bit

silly, but if Charles and I are taken in for something or if we just disappear or whatever, well, maybe he'll be inspired to look for a reason and maybe my words will lead him to this book. If so, Son, I want to tell you I'm sorry about the mistakes we've made in your life, and I want you to know that we both love you dearly. I can't give you any names or useful information, but maybe with the background that I've written, you'll be prepared to accept help if it's offered, and you might have a better idea of why things happened the way they did.

God, it's scary to think my entire legacy to my children might be nothing more than a few obscure words scribbled into a book. I get so scared. Maybe it's all for nothing, maybe the Pure German movement doesn't want to do anything but scare us. I guess, though, that I'm not the first person in this world to feel afraid.

That was the last entry that mentioned anything about her fears or in any way presaged the future. She took up her pen for twenty or so more pages to describe her life and those around her, but her fears were buried, and if any more incidents of harassment occurred or if any conclusions were reached in her discussions with the Underground, they were not mentioned. With a growing sadness, Peter read her last entry, dated eight days before she disappeared from his life:

Niklaus will be home in about a week, I look forward to seeing him. I wonder if the feeling is mutual. The flowers in Mrs. Stone's window box are blooming. They always bring a smile to my face when I see them. Someday, I'm going to get around to putting window boxes outside this place. I don't think we'll ever get another flat, but the neighborhood isn't that bad, after all.

There's a concert being held in the new hall they built in Covent Garden. It's martial music, which I don't like, but I'd like to get tickets just to see the inside of the new building. It's supposed to be as ugly on the inside as on the outside.

Price of bread went up again. I heard there were some riots in Lincoln about that, but who knows what the truth is. All seems quiet here. Maybe if the fine weather holds, Charles and I will go to the park on Sunday. It's always crowded and the grass is completely worn-out, but still it will be nice to get out and about. We can take some wine with us. Maybe that and some bread. Buy a loaf before the price goes up again, ha, ha. Didn't someone write "a loaf of bread, a jug of wine, and thou beside me in the wilderness"? Well, a scruffy park is going to have to do!

Peter paged through the rest of the book, but there was nothing else, just empty pages testifying to yet another life cut short. He set the book down and wiped the dampness from his cheeks, then turned off the light and stared into the darkness for a long time.

32

"**H**AVE YOU SEEN WHAT THEY'VE DONE!" Karl flapped his arms, utterly panicked.

Richard guided him down the hall, shushing him as he led him into his office. Once the door was shut behind them, Richard asked, "Now what?"

"They have a photograph!"

"Get control, man! What are you talking about?" Richard snapped.

"A photograph!" When Karl saw Richard's angry look, he made a determined effort to control his panic. "They released a photograph of me and that ingrate to the American press! There I am clear as day talking to him in front of my own house!"

"Who's they?" Richard teased.

"I don't know!" Karl moaned. "But now the Americans have proof I'm lying. They have a photograph of me and my *Zwangsarbeiter* together, well before this all happened!"

Richard stopped to consider. Logically, there were a lot of escapes from this situation. The photograph proved nothing, but if Karl did not realize that, there was no reason to head in that direction. There were only two weeks until the election—things were going well, but time was running short.

"Do you have any ideas for a response?" Richard asked, just to be sure that Karl had not considered any of the denials that had just run through his own mind.

"Would I be here? Oh, yeah," Karl added now that he was on a roll, "that thing with the kid—dead end. She was adopted. That envoy went on record saying it was his granddaughter and that Halifax had married his daughter and adopted her daughter."

"Oh, too bad." That must have been good for some sympathy points: distraught grandfather being interviewed about his beloved granddaughter. Richard felt a momentary surge of anger and sadness as he recalled Joanna's smiling face, as what they had done to her flashed through his mind. It was, unfortunately, not a propaganda stunt.

"Married!" Karl harrumphed.

"Huh?" Richard asked, momentarily confused.

"Married! What's he doing getting married? He's a criminal. Criminal blood. All we need is that sort breeding their filth into society. Married! What a pervert!"

"Yes, yes," Richard agreed tiredly. "So what are you going to do about the photograph?"

"It's all your fault! You told me to say it was all faked!"

"Ah, yes. Well, I thought we were just working off your inspiration, but if I've led you astray, let me see if there is anything I can suggest." He paused and bowed his head, deep in thought. Karl waited impatiently.

Karl really did not have any ideas, that was clear. He apparently had not even noticed that Peter's papers, though genuine, had been touched up to include adoptive parents so that it would all be consistent with what he had said on television. So, Karl was clueless; with that knowledge, Richard felt safe jumping a few steps and suggesting, "All right, admit that you knew him. So we have a different system from theirs. That does not make it wrong. They must learn to appreciate our culture; our culture is different, but that does not make it wrong. Diversity, they used to call it; or cross-culturalism." Richard waved his hand in genuine annoyance at his lack of memory. "Or was it anti-cultural-imperialism? Oh, something like that. Anyway, they're wrong to judge us so harshly. Yes, you, er, 'owned' this Peter Halifax, but it was only part of an employment system which they do not fully understand. Workfare—I think that's what they call it."

"Workfare?" Karl fumbled in his pocket for a notebook and pen.

"Yes." Richard handed Karl what he needed, spelled the word, and gave him a translation. "Tell them he was an asocial, homeless. He needed a place in society, a job, a skill. You provided all these things and a home as well. He might have called it slavery, but it was nothing more than providing useful employment to someone who would otherwise have been a drain on the system. Emphasize that it was for his own good. That there was no brutality, that it was an education for him. No violence." Richard's voice took on a patronizing air. "None of these negatives that he emphasized in his presentation. Just good, healthy work. Yes, yes, it had a bit of coercion, but they have chain gangs in some of the American states. They understand that sometimes a bit of coercion, a bit of discipline, is necessary. Still, it was all an education. Not brutal, not violent, just organized, disciplined. Not slavery at all. An apprenticeship. A work-release program. That's all."

Karl was delighted with the suggestion. Together he and Richard put together a presentation that would, in Karl's mind, emphasize the advantages of their system. Richard was careful to include everything and anything that an American might find repugnant. He inserted the word *independent* as an insult wherever possible, he threw in racism, sexism, anti-Semitism, and every negative prejudice he could invent. He even managed to insult the Nazi sympathizers in America by referring to them as "little brethren" and implying they needed guidance from their superiors overseas. He emphasized time and again that there was no brutality, that Karl was essentially a philanthropist, a nice guy who had provided a poor, antisocial outcast with a place in society. Richard gave the whole tone of the presentation an obnoxious, arrogant, and patronizing air. He insisted Karl make a personal appearance, that he arrange a press conference in some neutral third country. That would give the entire affair far more import than it would otherwise gain. He timed it all for one week before the election. Two days to percolate and then the countermeasures and the release of that most damning series of photographs. There would be no time for a response. It would work wonderfully!

Both finished their complicated work ecstatic with the result. Both had their reasons for being happy, and Richard could smile at Karl with genuine pleasure as he sent him on his way to carry out his task as spokesman for the Reich and the National Socialist agenda. Let the Americans hear it the way it really was! Let Karl speak the truth!

Karl's press conference went as might be expected. It gained a reasonable amount of coverage simply because of the novelty value. Richard had made a point of choosing a suitably warm and sunny resort island not far from America; cheap to get there, a nice little break from the beginning of November with all its miserable wet and cold. The reporters were falling over themselves to cover it.

At first Karl had difficulty getting the Propaganda Ministry to agree to the trip and the press conference, but Richard armed him with persuasive arguments and had him point out that several ministry officials would probably need to accompany him on the jaunt, and suddenly all was possible.

Karl returned tanned and gloating. "Idiot Americans never knew how to reserve a place for themselves by the pool!" He laughed. "I mean, once you got used to the fact that there were no reserved places, all you had to do was have the maid drop your towel on a lounge chair first thing in the morning, and it was there waiting for you after breakfast!"

"Ah, how clever of you to do that," Richard commented agreeably.

"Yes, but it was inconvenient getting the hotel staff to do my bidding. I don't know why you insisted I not take my own servant along."

"Maybe you should have." Richard and Kasia had debated the merits of that. Should he let Karl blow everything all at once, or were they better off letting out the information slowly? To influence the elections, probably the former, but the elections were pretty much guaranteed already. The Republicans had completely backed away from isolationism, and both parties now emphasized the importance of keeping their age-old commitments to their defeated allies.

What Richard was pursuing now, more than election results, was funding. The newly elected Congress would be voting on appropriations; the American public would be asked yet again to donate personally. A steady stream of uncomfortable revelations would better suit these purposes, and in that case it had been decided that Karl should not take his servant with him to the press conference.

So he went alone and was forced to deal with the services provided by the hotel staff. Even so, the American reporters were not unaware of the arrogant and demanding nature of the speaker. Was it typical? No one could be sure, and it did not really matter; it was enough that he annoyed the hell out of them. They took their quiet media revenge with their unbiased reports carried in certain tones of voice, using well-chosen words, emphasizing particular events and illustrated from bad camera angles. It was, of course, all unbiased; they were reporters just reporting the facts.

Karl rubbed his hands with glee at his performance. His bosses were well-satisfied with his defense of the Reich, and the American public shuddered at being tutored like ignorant schoolchildren by a pompous and unattractive bureaucrat. Still, some with open minds considered his words and wondered, if it is just a training scheme, if it is just a cultural difference, have we been too judgmental?

Alex waited the several days until this opinion emerged in the news and discussion groups, and then he released the three-photograph sequence. The press didn't hesitate this time: the negatives were accepted from their mysterious source immediately, and the photographs appeared everywhere. There was an explosion of anger as those who had disliked Karl and had trusted Peter's story suddenly had proof positive of their intuition. The man was not only pompous and arrogant, he was brutal and a proven liar. Nothing he said could be trusted, nothing in the Halifax story had been disproved. In fact, the poor fellow had been rather soft-spoken about all he had endured. And now he was almost certainly dead, brutally tortured to death after witnessing the vicious murder of his beloved daughter. All because he had dared speak the truth.

In the last days before the election the politicians fell over themselves trying to get to the nearest microphone to denounce the Reich and its policies toward its subject peoples. They vowed funding, they vowed support. The resounding silence from across the sea that greeted their denunciations only further convinced the Americans of the justice of their words. For once, as rarely happened, the truth had gained the upper hand in the propaganda stakes.

33

RICHARD CAME INTO THE OFFICE on Monday morning and waited for Karl's inevitable arrival. Richard had taken Saturday off as a sick day just to prolong his response and to see what Karl might do on his own. The answer was nothing—Karl waited for his adviser. The U.S. elections were to be held on the morrow, and Karl dutifully panicked when Richard casually mentioned this.

"You mean, they have an election tomorrow?" Karl yammered unhappily.

"Yes, remember I told you about them before." Richard removed his cigarette and coughed.

"But are they important? I mean, the outcome is fixed, isn't it?"

"I don't know," Richard responded truthfully. He had never ceased to be amazed at the reports that the American elections were free and fair. Certainly money and other influences played their roles, but apparently news reports and photographs could also affect the results. The past months had proven that, and it had gone some way toward removing his own doubts about democracy. "Everyone claims it isn't fixed, but maybe they're just very clever about it. In any case, they seem sufficiently clever that they are forced to bend to public opinion."

"Well, with this current disaster, that means . . ." Karl paused, unsure what it meant.

"What current disaster?"

"Haven't you heard?" Karl was stunned.

"No, I've been sick. What's happened?"

"Oh, it's terrible. After that little speech I gave emphasizing no brutality and all, well, there's been another leak. A set of photos of me and him."

"So, you've admitted he worked for you. Big deal."

"But I'm kicking him."

"Kicking?" Richard asked as if he must have misheard.

"Yes. He was on the ground and I kicked him in the face. Somebody caught it on film."

"You kicked him in the face?" Richard did not hide his contempt.

"Yes," Karl responded timidly.

"While he was on the ground?"

"Yes." Karl's voice was even quieter.

"What did you do that for?" Richard asked with sarcastic patience.

"I don't know. Discipline?" Karl ventured. He gained steam and asserted, "It's reasonable, you know, we are their superiors, after all. I had the right!"

"You kicked a man in the face when he was lying on the ground?"

"Yes, I guess I must have. I'm sure he turned his head—he was good at dodging. Anyway, I'm sure it wasn't very hard, just, you know, letting him know who was boss," Karl whined.

"You kicked him in the face," Richard repeated yet again. "What had he done?"

"I don't remember. I'm sure it wasn't as bad as it looks. It looks worse in the photographs. I'm sure it wasn't that bad. Anything can look unreasonable if you splash it on hundreds of newspapers."

"Is he threatening you or disobeying you, at least?"

"Not obviously," Karl admitted ruefully. "He probably said something disrespectful or gave me one of his goddamned stupid looks."

"Go get me a copy of what the Americans have seen," Richard ordered. Karl was so distraught that he obeyed immediately, not even upset by the command in Richard's voice.

Once he was out of Richard's office though, his confidence returned. He even felt slightly angry. He did have the right! Everyone had said so. Halifax had not complained, had not even reacted really. Just rolled and ducked, as Karl knew he would. His foot had hardly grazed his face. Besides, what if it had? He had the right to mete out punishment, he had the responsibility to maintain order. Nobody thought about him, about the great responsibility he carried with respect to his family and his chattel. If things fell apart, he was held responsible! He was expected to keep order, it was his job, and without discipline, where would they be? Let an inappropriate comment or a sly look pass unpunished, and next would be chaos! What was this? Were they getting soft? Were they becoming American? Why in God's name should he have to defend an action that was legal and moral?

When he got to his office, he found another press release on his desk. It had been left there without comment by someone from Censorship. They must have picked it up off the American wire and decided he should see it. It was yet another photograph of him and Peter. Damn that man! Karl looked at the picture. Outside again, Peter was listening to him with that vacuous expression he so often used. It had irritated the hell out of Karl. He could tell that Peter was hardly listening! His face was terribly beaten, and Karl guessed it must have been shortly after he had discovered Peter talking to Ulrike. Now the American public should know about that! What would they think if they knew why Peter had been hit? Didn't they worry about their daughters? Didn't they care if their children heard lies from their servants? How did they keep their inferiors under control? Certainly they would understand.

He picked up the photo and took it along with the three-photograph sequence to Richard's office. This time Karl would be the one with the ideas. Richard had got it all wrong. This time Karl would tell them exactly what was going on and they would understand!

Richard looked at the photographs that Karl had brought him. "I don't know," he muttered, "I just don't know."

"You're the one who got me into this mess!" Karl fumed.

"I had no idea you had, er, meted out discipline quite so, er, efficiently. Why didn't you tell me when we were working on your response last time?"

"I thought you knew. Besides, there's nothing wrong with what I did."

"Of course not," Richard responded sarcastically. "And I suppose you pluck the wings off flies and strangle puppies in your spare time?"

"What does that mean?" Karl grated.

"It means, even if they are inferior, we have a responsibility to exhibit, shall I say, civilized behavior toward them. That means, as their superiors, we should never allow ourselves to get angry or irrational, especially not in their presence. Certainly you realize that."

"I was never irrational!" Karl sounded nearly hysterical.

"Of course not. There is, however, an unfortunate angle to these photographs that makes it look as if you were."

"So what shall we do?" Karl brought his anger under control. He was desperate, he needed Richard's help.

"We?" Richard asked archly.

"Please, Richard, I don't know what to do," Karl begged.

"Let me think about it. Come back in a couple of days."

"But isn't that after the elections?" Karl asked, panicked.

"What do we care about their stupid voting? This will take time to sort out. I'll have to think about it. Come back in a couple of days." Richard grabbed Karl's arm and steered him toward the door. "I've been ill and I have to catch up on my own work right now."

Richard chuckled silently as Karl left. Once the elections were over, they could respond, but for now, let the Americans hear only a guilty silence, an arrogant lack of response from the Reich. Let the politicians make their last-minute promises and let the voters go to the polls with the image of those photographs etched into their minds.

Like clockwork, Karl appeared on Wednesday morning in Richard's office. Richard came in to find Karl already seated in one of the chairs. That infuriated him and he felt like haranguing his secretary, but decided it would be pointless. She would have been unable to stop Karl in any case, and besides, he had decided to string Karl along for just a little longer, so he needed to be nice to the idiot.

"Richard!" Karl greeted him without standing.

"Ah, what a pleasant surprise," Richard responded with toneless sarcasm as he set his briefcase and files on the desk. "Would you like a cup of coffee?"

"Yes."

Richard buzzed his secretary and requested two cups of coffee. Then he turned to Karl. "And what can I do for you?" he asked sweetly.

"The photographs! Don't you remember?"

"Oh, yes, almost forgot."

"Well?"

"Well, you could explain that what they see is part of normal discipline and that Peter was never really hurt, say that the photographs are misleading. Or you could deny their reality, say they were staged with actors."

"Are those my only options?" Karl whined.

"No, as I see it, you have two choices: denial or admission. Under denial you can deny the severity of the photos, or even their reality. If you deny the photos, you could even deny Halifax's reality, say you were mistaken, say he isn't the man that was under your, uh, shall I say 'care'?"

Karl looked unhappy.

"Or you could opt for admission. You could admit the photos are genuine but explain their circumstances, the provocation for your disciplinary actions, or you could admit that there was no real provocation and tell them it's none of their fucking business and that it's our country and we'll do what we damn well please with our people." Richard said the last not as a genuine offering; he wanted to put the thought into Karl's head for later use, so that it would slip out at some inappropriate moment when he was under pressure.

"I like that last option," Karl said, much more happy all of a sudden.

"I thought you might, but I'd advise against it."

Karl was crestfallen. "Why?"

"I just don't think it's wise. But of course, it's your decision." Richard smiled. He knew Karl would follow his advice, but now that thought, that opinion, was there, waiting like a bomb to explode. Richard had no idea how long Karl's fuse would be, but it did not matter. The trap was complete, the duration until he hanged himself was irrelevant.

Karl studied his cigarette. He had to make a decision, be forceful, take command. "All right," he said decisively, "which way do you think I should go?"

Richard thought. They had that diplomat waiting in the wings, but there seemed no point in driving Karl into denying Peter even existed. Richard decided to go with something fairly simple. "If I were you, I'd claim the photographs were faked. Claim you never hit him like that."

"You think that will work?"

"Yeah. I mean, what can they possibly do? If they release more photographs, then they could be fakes as well. It's the simplest solution, don't you think?" Richard smiled winningly.

"Yes, the photographs are fakes. In fact, it's all fake!"

"All fake? You could say that, but then you'd have to go back on what you said earlier."

"Oh, yeah, I guess that wouldn't be wise."

"Probably not."

34

"**M**EDICAL RECORDS!" Karl yelled as he threw down the clippings on Richard's desk. "Medical records from a respected and disinterested source!"

Richard picked up the news items. It looked bad. Who would have guessed that Halifax had gone to a physician while he was in the NAU? Eye damage, bone fractures, scar tissue, it was all there. A history of repeated violence. "Perhaps," Richard suggested to amuse himself, "you could suggest he was a masochist?"

"Do you think?" Karl asked, intrigued.

"It was a joke," Richard replied sardonically. He scanned the summaries. "You know," he said almost to himself, "we treat cattle better than this."

"Oh, it's blown all out of proportion!" Karl snapped in reply, eyeing his friend suspiciously.

"Yes, clearly." Richard was still studying the clippings. "I suppose you could claim this all happened later, or earlier. Perhaps the fellow was in an accident?"

"Yes, yes." Karl nodded enthusiastically, his worries about Richard's loyalty apparently having evaporated. "You're a genius!" he exclaimed, so happy with the quick solution that he did not even bother to claim credit for it this time.

"Ah, I was just inspired by your lead," Richard reminded him with an engaging smile.

As Karl left and the door shut behind him, Richard sighed heavily and rubbed his forehead. God, he was getting careless! What had he been thinking?

It took more than four weeks for the response to the latest Reich press release to emerge. Alex had decided to take his time because the reply had been so pathetic it had almost served their purposes directly. An accident! Good Lord, how had Ryszard managed to convince that idiot to say something so transparently stupid? No question of the integrity of the records, no clever dodges, just claim it was an accident like some child caught acting naughty! The pundits were quick to pick up on that one. Starvation? They forgot to eat! Burned to death? Must have been playing with matches! Beaten to death? Uh, they tripped!

It seemed almost a pity to disrupt the fun, but now with the elections over and well won, the goal was to keep the European problems in the news, to keep the funds flowing to the cause. After three weeks the noise died down, and after giving it all a week's break, Alex decided it was time to stir things up again. He asked Arieka to have her diplomat come forward and make himself and his recollections public.

He did. He approached the news agencies with the photographs in hand, explaining that they had been mysteriously posted to him. Once he had seen them, he remembered the incident clearly, and he thought it was his duty to come forward with the truth. He knew personally and could stake his reputation on the fact that not only was Peter Halifax in Berlin at the time that he had been there, but he had seen the man shortly after he had been brutally beaten. Out of curiosity and a sense of outrage, he had tried to engage the man in conversation at a diplomatic function, but the look in his eyes had told the diplomat that Peter knew he would be severely punished if he dared say so much as a word.

That last bit was an invention concocted by Arieka since the diplomat's genuine recollection, that the man had seemed moronically obtuse, was not sufficiently sympathetic nor did it tally with the obviously intelligent man who had spoken up on television.

"The reason I spent so long with him," the diplomat explained to Arieka, leaning close to speak confidentially, although they were alone, "was that I wanted to know if any of the drinks on his tray were nonalcoholic. I thought maybe my German was too accented because I couldn't get an answer, he just stared downward like some moron. Finally, he looked up and I saw what he looked like. That's when I asked what had happened."

"What did he say?"

"Absolutely nothing. Just stared at me stupidly, like a subhuman." The diplomat laughed at his command of Nazi mythology. He stopped laughing when he saw Arieka's expression. "Anyway, at the time I thought he was just subnormal and had gotten himself into a fight. You know, the way retards often get themselves into trouble."

"Clearly your thesis was wrong."

"Ah, yes. Obviously. You know, I caught a glimpse of that other guy on TV and I would have never put the two of them together. Never! At least not until you showed me this picture. He was so different!"

"I see. I guess to avoid your looking foolishly duped, you should maybe change your memories ever so slightly."

They settled on an accurate recollection of the facts, a slight change in the diplomat's remembered perceptions, and a few extra words of advice. Consequently, the diplomat stated publicly that not only was the photograph that was sent to him authentic, but he felt sure that every picture and every word of Peter's story had been genuine, and he was equally sure, given what he himself had witnessed, that the videotape was sadly true as well. The Americans should face facts; they owed at least that much to the courageous man who had risked and lost everything to tell them the truth.

The diplomat was excellent. He was sober and concerned, and he even took the heat from his own government with stoic calm. "It was my moral duty," he said, dabbing a bit of sweat from his forehead.

"Oh, that Arieka must be great in bed!" Alex commented as he watched another interview of the calm, dignified, and very believable diplomat. He wondered if Peter had any idea what he had missed.

"You don't know she did that!" Anna responded, having decided to defend Arieka's honor now that she knew how Peter and Arieka had spent their night together.

"No, but I'm going to send her flowers anyway!" Alex laughed. He was in a great humor. Their funding was way up, donations were rolling in. Congress was making appropriate noises, parliament was fuming, and even the Quebecois had taken time out of their feuding over Indian lands to comment. The onetime accepted status quo in Europe had suddenly become the European Question, to be debated at cocktail parties and on documentaries. They had not made one misstep in the entire plan.

Next, he thought, we'll move it away from Peter. Keep up the heat with photographs of the camps, of the factories, sweatshops with child labor . . . Release statistics and life stories and perhaps even a book. Maybe a documentary. A movie—yes! A made-for-TV movie "based on a true story." There would be interest now. It would be easy to get the backing they would need. He should send Peter some flowers as well. What had Zosia said, he was in London?

35

T HE WOMAN HAD BEEN PERUSING the glass-encased shelves for a long time, leaning over the long counter to peer at the titles. Peter was busy serving the customers and only noticed her subconsciously. He always kept a mental tally of what each customer did, and something in her behavior or her stance caught his attention. Nevertheless, he could do nothing about it for the moment; Barbara was out doing the shopping and he was busy with a steady stream of people.

Finally the miniature rush ended and the woman was left alone in the shop with him. She casually wandered over to his counter and smiled. Clearly she was a contact. He awaited the usual coded sentences so that they could carry out the ritual of her passing information on to him, but she said nothing. Instead her smile changed to a perplexed frown.

"Alan?" she asked so softly he hardly heard her.

He looked closer at her. "Can I help you?"

She looked confused.

After a moment he repeated, "Can I help you with something?" but this time he used English.

"Alan!" she said, her face breaking into a smile.

Peter surveyed her. Ungainly, slouching in that way that Englishwomen often used to launch themselves into middle age. A sort of clumsy, chummy maturity that announced: indifferent wife, tired mother, dead-end job, but a good friend to chat to over a lovely cup of tea. He regauged her age as younger than he had initially guessed, mentally subtracted two or three stone from her body, and studied the unchanging eyes and mouth and voice.

"Jenny," he replied. "Jenny." She was a member of the English Underground, an ex-lover, a woman with whom he had had an affair while her husband was away at the labor camp. She was three years younger than he and had at the time been quite attractive. A friendly face, a slender albeit unmuscled body that would naturally, once she had stopped actively dieting, tend to slackness. It was almost a philosophy of living among that type, a statement of settling in, a confession that all efforts at remaining pretty had been for external reasons, that there was no particular pride in appearance once life was comfortable, or at least tolerable. Retirement at thirty. He supposed that it may have been offered as a comfort to their husbands or partners, a deliberate abnegation of any attempt at attractiveness. Even their clothes advertised that they were uninterested and unavailable. He could have predicted the transition, he had seen it often enough.

The two of them had grown quite serious, or rather, she had. He had enjoyed her company, she was friendly, chatty, artistic. They had maintained a long relationship, but when it was clear that she planned to divorce her husband as soon as he returned, Peter had ended the affair. After that, since they were not in the same group, they had seen each other infrequently and had not had much chance to interact. He had learned that she had picked up another lover not long after him, divorced her husband, and married the new man. She gave every indication of having no bitterness at all toward Peter. "A mutual misunderstanding of intent" was how she had referred to their affair. For his part, he had simply realized he did not want to spend his life with her.

"I heard you were dead," she said softly, glancing around to see that no one had entered the shop. "But obviously not," she added, indicating that explanations were not required.

Barbara returned at that point and they fell silent as she walked through the shop into the back room. Jenny studied her carefully as she passed by.

"I heard there was a team here and I could deal with either of you. So, she's the other one?"

"Yes."

"Your wife?"

"Yes."

"She's not English, is she?" Jenny asked perceptively.

"No, she's not." There was obviously no point in denying Barbara's complicity in their network, but there was also no point in explaining any more than necessary.

"She's not German either."

"What makes you say that?" he asked, somewhat astonished.

"Her face. She has those high cheekbones. Some Germans have them, but it looks more Nordic or Slavic to me."

"My little artist. You always were quite perceptive."

"I would have killed for those in my younger days." Jenny sighed, then she cocked her round face at Peter. "But you look different. You've dyed your hair."

"So have you." She had become a platinum blonde.

"Ah, it's getting fashionable among Englishwomen. But I can't believe you've colored your hair! It was so nice before."

"It was unavoidable."

She looked quizzical, but he did not explain further. She continued to study him. "There's something else. You really look different somehow."

"I'm older." He smiled, not commenting on how very different she looked.

"No, no, no. It's more than that." She tilted her head the other way. "Your face!"

"My face?"

"Yeah, remember, I drew portraits of you; I know the lines of your face intimately, and they've changed." She reached tentatively toward his cheeks; he leaned forward obligingly so she could stroke her hand along his cheekbones. "Here and here. How . . . ?" She could not find the right phrasing for her question.

"I was in prison. That's where they would hit me all the time."

"Oh, I am sorry! I didn't think! That was rude of me, wasn't it?" Jenny was overwhelmed by embarrassment. She obviously wanted to know more, but did not dare to presume to ask.

"It's all right," he responded with a shrug. "It is what it is."

Barbara emerged from the back room. Obviously she had seen Jenny stroking Peter's face, and she came directly over to the two of them. Skirting around Jenny to go behind the counter, she went up to Peter and kissed him. "Hello, darling."

"Hi, love," he responded dutifully, then waited in silence for Barbara to give him the privacy he obviously wanted. She made a pretense of sorting some things under the counter, straightened a shelf, then finally gave up and walked a short distance away.

"How did your new marriage turn out?" Peter asked once Barbara was out of earshot.

"Oh, him." Jenny laughed. "Long gone. I'm on number three now."

"Sorry."

"Don't be. With you it would have lasted." Jenny smiled winningly, then too embarrassed to hear his response, she continued, "So, you're still in the game."

"Yes, and you, too."

"Not really. I just run messages now and then. I can't really afford the time with two kids."

"Two?"

"One from number two and one from number three. What about you?"

"Ah, one en route, another—my adopted daughter—was killed." For some reason he felt compelled to tell her the truth. Maybe for old times.

"Oh, I'm terribly sorry. How did it happen?" Jenny asked while scanning Barbara, looking for hints of the pregnancy.

"It's complicated," he demurred.

Something in his tone caused Jenny to look back at him. She studied his face as if remembering something, or comparing a mental picture with what was in front of her. Then she nodded and said quietly, "You're him, aren't you?"

"Who?"

"That Halifax fellow. I read an article about him. Was that you?"

"Yeah, that was me."

"Was what you said the truth?" she asked, suddenly aware of the meaning behind his obscure answers.

"Essentially. I'm surprised you heard about it."

"How could we not? Well, I suppose the general populace here didn't hear much, if anything, but those of us with connections—well, let's say, you made quite an impression."

A customer entered, and Barbara went over to assist and keep the man away from the two of them. Jenny lowered her voice still further. "What you did there was really brave, and you should know, it really helped. Not just funding, but it helped our morale here. To know somebody was speaking out about what is going on, telling them that things aren't settling down or getting normal."

"Thanks. You know, it cost me my daughter."

Jenny's face conveyed a look of unspeakable shared sorrow. She shook her head and let her eyes drop to the floor, probably in some mistaken and typically English belief that she had put her foot in it by expressing her gratitude for what he had done. Eventually she found the courage to glance up at Barbara again and ask, "Is that the mother?"

"No. She's not really my wife, that's just our cover. The child was the daughter of the woman I'm currently married to. She's"—he sighed—"back home."

"Good Lord!" Jenny exclaimed quietly. "You're in love, aren't you! With your wife! You of all people!"

"Why of all people?"

"Oh! I'm sorry, I didn't mean it like that. Is that why you're here? I should think you were too valuable to be in this position normally. Is it like a sabbatical?"

"You could call it that." He was rather embarrassed that the appropriate word was more like *exile*. "I'm supposed to be making better contacts with the British Underground eventually. We need more coordination between our two groups."

"I'll say! Whoever you're with now, we could use more help. That's the problem, they've got us so divided that we're conquered. Who, by the way, are you with now? The French? The Scots?"

He shook his head.

"Oh, come on, you can tell me! After all, whoever is sending the message I'm carrying already knows!" Jenny then glanced at Barbara again. "Norwegians? Poles?"

He smiled at the correct answer and Jenny laughed quietly. "The Home Army, of course. How in the world did you ever get hooked up with them?"

"I stumbled into their midst and asked them nicely not to shoot," he replied nearly truthfully.

"We could use some closer ties with them. They have a lot of resources for infiltration—fluent German speakers and whatnot. Proximity to Berlin. Absolute dedication," Jenny said excitedly. Something of the youthful woman was reemerging, and she sounded as though she had not renounced her role in the Underground as willingly as she had initially implied. "What are your orders? Have any meetings been arranged?"

"None yet."

"Well, why don't we circumvent all the bureaucratic nonsense? I'm in contact with some people and I'm sure we can arrange for you to meet with them and discuss things of mutual interest."

Another customer entered the store, then another.

"Look, I better pass this on and get out of here before it's too late." She handed over a book that she had been holding in her hands. "Standard. One twenty-seven, third para."

Peter nodded, memorizing the numbers.

"I'll be back in a couple of days, see what I can arrange by then. All right?"

"Yes, I'll have the book repaired by then. Thank you for coming, ma'am." He watched as she clomped through the shop and out the door.

Barbara and he tended to the customers and were kept busy and separated for a time, but as soon as there was a break, Barbara headed directly toward him and wasting no time at all asked, "Who the hell was that?"

"An old lover."

"What? Her?" Barbara sputtered her astonishment.

"Yes, her," Peter confirmed unapologetically, smiling with fond memories.

"So she was good enough and I'm not!" Barbara hissed angrily.

"We need to talk. Tonight," he asserted quietly, then pointedly he turned away to continue their workday in silence.

They closed up the shop and returned to the flat. He cooked up the dinner since Barbara seemed to be in a huff. She had not spoken one word to him since the afternoon, and when they had entered their home, she had poured herself a drink without offering him one and had set herself down on the couch to stare at the television in stony silence.

A parade was on: row upon row of soldiers marched past, then rockets and missiles and tanks. *Your tax dollars at work*—Peter remembered the phrase he had seen at an American roadworks. Maybe the phrase for the Reich should be *Your wrecked economies and slave laborers paid for this!* All for the Fatherland, the omnipresent Fatherland. He felt suddenly sick with Reich fatigue and wished that he and Zosia and the baby and whoever of their friends wanted to go along could just relocate to some quiet village in the Canadian wilderness, as far from rockets and missiles and tanks and marching soldiers as they could get. They could have a little bonfire— well, a big bonfire—and burn the masses of documents and ration cards and travel permits and every worthless scrap of paper they had to carry. They could burn the uniforms and the regulation books and the endless propaganda pamphlets. The mess would keep them warm for a winter. Then they could build nice log cabins and plant crops and speak whatever language they wanted to and forget everything they had ever learned about living with institutionalized violence. They would become vegetarians so that none of them would have to kill again.

He walked over to the television and switched it off, announcing that dinner was served. They ate without speaking, the clinking of the forks on the plates incongruously loud in the moody silence. Once they had finished dinner and cleaned the dishes, he poured drinks for both of them and invited Barbara to join him on the couch.

She stood unmoving for a moment, making a face, but she relented and sat down next to him.

He sipped his whiskey while he found his courage, then he began, "Barbara, we need to straighten out what we're doing here. We've got to put this relationship back on a professional level."

Barbara did not respond. She stared at the wall, her head turned slightly away from him so he could not read her expression.

"Our marriage here is just a pretense. I not only did not marry you or ever promise anything of the sort, but I am already married and I love my wife."

Barbara turned to look at him then. "Why?" she asked coldly.

"That's not relevant to this discussion."

"Why?" she insisted angrily. "She doesn't love you! She doesn't even pretend to! She cheats on you."

"Do you know that?" he was drawn into asking despite his best intentions to avoid such a digression.

"Everybody knows!"

"Do you *know* that?" he repeated angrily.

Barbara hesitated, then frowning, she admitted, "No. I don't know for sure." She paused. "But the fact that you're not sure shows how she treats your feelings with contempt! If she cared, she would not raise such a question in your mind. She'd . . ."

"What? What do you think she should do? Enter purdah?"

"What's that?"

"It's . . . Never mind. My point is, she has to work and continue to live whether I'm around or not. I don't want to own her or control her behavior or choose her friends. I trust her—it's part of what I want in a marriage." He managed not to add that, at least that was the case in theory. In practice, well, things were more complicated.

"You'll be able to trust me."

"I know." He sighed and stroked her hair. "I find you very attractive and a joy to live with, but I already love Zosia, and you're too young for me."

"I don't believe you love her—not after what she's done to you. That's just a lie you tell to protect yourself and excuse your behavior. Everything you've done with me, the way we've spent our time together—that's the truth. And the truth is you love me! You're just too stubborn to admit it."

"You're too young," he argued weakly. He did not want to debate whether he loved Zosia nor did he feel that dissecting his marriage was relevant to getting Barbara to realize he did not love her.

"I'm not. I'm more experienced than any number of older women."

"There's something to be said for the passage of time, little one. You still have so much to learn and so much growing to do. I don't want to hamper that. I don't want to spend my life always saying something stupid like, 'In my day . . .' I need a woman with independent life experiences, someone who has as much background and excess baggage as I do—so there's some balance."

Barbara was shaking her head. "No, you don't! If you wanted that, you wouldn't resent Colonel Król's involvements and past as much as you do."

Peter felt stricken by her remark. Was it that obvious? He had completely forgotten that Barbara had read at least one of his letters to Zosia and was simply mirroring his own words back to him.

Barbara continued, "You don't want what you say. What you want is a tabula rasa so that you don't have to compete with anything! And the stupid thing is, I can give that to you! I'd make you happy because you'd never have to guess where my love or my attention or my memories were! No saintly dead husbands, no great family ties. You would be the center of my life. And that's what you need! Now that Joanna is dead, there is nothing to hold you back! I could be there for you in a way she never could."

"Oh, Barbara," he moaned, unable to answer her any other way.

"It's embarrassing to admit it," she sobbed, "but I not only love you, I admire and adore you. I would fill those gaps in your heart that the colonel leaves blank. I would never outrank you, I'd never one-up your experiences or knowledge, I'd never arrange your assignments behind your back. I'd simply love you. Deep down, that's what you want. An old-fashioned wife. Not an experienced woman, just someone to look after you and care for you and love you without question and without expectation. I could do that."

He closed his eyes tight against the temptation. God, what a blessed relief it would be. He could win every fight—or there would be no fight! He wouldn't be known as Barbara's husband, rather she would be known as his wife. Cooked dinners and a clean home and thoughtful little presents! No sudden surprise reassignments, no competition on knowledge. The announced winner of every future contest. Or no contests at all. She would not drag out a rusty Russian to counter his smattering of French, she would not explain about the Great Northern War when he talked of the War of the Roses. She would not claim the analyses he had carried out for her as her own, using *I* when *we*, or better yet *he*, would be more appropriate. In fact, she would probably use her valuable time to help him in his work! She would be his student and he would be her teacher, with all the wonderful confidence and restoration of his damaged ego that would imply.

He shook his head slowly. Maybe for a year, at most. "Even if you could keep up that sort of devotion—and my experience is that nobody can, not really—but even if you could, and even if I admit that it would please me now, I'm sure that it would grow wearisome for me. And I'm equally sure, you would learn to first resent me and then hate me as you realized you had given up everything to become my shadow. That's what I mean by experience, Barbara. If you had experience, you would know that what you feel now will not last forever. It can't."

"So you think I'm a naive fool!" she responded furiously.

"That's not what I said," he argued helplessly.

"You goddamned bastard! You use me, you string me along, you let me make a complete fool of myself, and then you calmly throw away everything I have to offer!" she yelled at him between sobs. Tears streamed down her face and her voice was strained with emotion.

He remained calm. Since he did not have any strong emotions about her, it was easy to treat the entire thing rationally, and rationally he knew that she would explode. She had invested far too much of herself in him and her dreams for their future to let go easily. She upbraided him, swore at him, tore apart everything he had ever done or said. She leapt up from the couch and paced angrily around the room, throwing off his arms as he tried to console her, slamming the door to the bedroom as she said her final word, only to reemerge a moment later to continue her scathing denunciation.

Knowing that complete silence would be interpreted as disinterest, and knowing how much more that would hurt her, he responded softly to her accusations and tried to explain how she had misinterpreted or overinterpreted. It gave her more to yell at, more fuel for her fire, but he felt it was best to let her purge herself completely. Whatever remained unsaid tonight would probably be resurrected even more painfully later. Better to let it all come out now.

Only when she tried to hit him did he stop her. He grabbed her slender wrists in each of his hands and held her arms until she ceased to struggle. Then he released her and immediately she swung at him. Again he caught her arms in an iron grip and held her fast. He would concede a lot to her pain, but not that! This time though, she did not try to trick him by ceasing to fight, instead she tried to kick him. As he realized what she was doing, he threw her away from him and she landed against the wall with a heavy thud.

"Don't!" he ordered angrily as he saw her begin to launch herself at him. She stopped and stared at him like a leashed, raging dog. Despite her youth, she was a lot weaker than Zosia and apparently less trained, or at least less rational in her anger. Zosia would never have attacked him like that, and if she had, she would have done a much better job of it. He found himself admiring his wife's self-control even as he warily held a hand out to warn Barbara to keep her distance.

"You should know better than that," he could not help himself from chiding. "You of all people!"

"You betrayed me!" Barbara wailed as if that excused her behavior.

"I will *not* let you hurt me! Only spoiled brats behave like that!"

Infuriated by the insult, she ran at him again, intending to scratch him. He caught her arms and twisted her around so her back was against him and her arms crossed in front of her. It effectively kept her both from hitting or kicking him.

"Stop this!" he snarled, but she was struggling so hard he was sure she didn't hear him. He took a moment to regain his equilibrium. Her behavior was so unexpected, so unlike that of Zosia or Allison or anyone else he had ever cared about, that it had taken him completely by surprise. After a moment she began to tire and finally she stopped struggling. He did not release his hold; instead he held her and hissed into her ear, "Where's that love now? Listen to what you called me, look at how you've tried to injure me. Is that love? What kind of love is it that can't even survive one conversation? You want to build a life based on this?"

He let her go and she spun around. He flinched, but all she did was throw her arms around him. She buried her head in his shoulder and wept as he wrapped his arms around her and held her. "It'll be all right, it'll be all right, little one," he assured her over and over.

It wasn't all right though. The next morning and for days thereafter she completely ignored him and only spoke to him when absolutely driven to do so by the necessities of their job. He bore it stoically, attempting conversation now and then, carrying out most of the daily chores, smiling encouragingly at her whenever he caught her eye. He marveled at his ability to be unperturbed; he was sure if Zosia had pulled such a stunt, it would have driven him mad with irritation, but then, he did not want to make a life with Barbara and so it was easy to set aside her weapons of rejection. Her behavior did nothing more than convince him that he had been right all along—she would never be the woman for him.

During that time Jenny got in contact with him and arranged several meetings. That kept him out of the apartment for a few evenings, and Barbara obligingly disappeared on others. After about two weeks, Barbara relented; she was tired of keeping her opinions to herself. She did not converse though, rather she limited herself to one-sentence observations, sniping at him continuously. The snide, insulting, endless comments got on his nerves, but he determinedly ignored them, refusing to take the bait and restart an argument. There was nothing to argue about—she knew his opinion and it would not change. Everything else was irrelevant. He had not tried to mislead her, but he accepted her hurt anger and would do nothing but wait until she forgave him. If, after that, she had legitimate complaints about their various duties and actions, then he would willingly discuss whatever troubled her in order to make their work easier.

Remarks about his appearance, his habits, his marriage, his past, his abilities, his motives—all went in one ear and out the other. Their fleeting presence in his mind left painful dents, but still he was able to brush them off with relative ease. As the days went on though, he grew more and more weary and less and less tolerant, and it was with gritted teeth that he ignored another insulting tirade as he pulled his clothes on in the morning. He glanced at the pair of socks on the bed and wondered if they would not be more usefully employed shoved into Barbara's mouth, and only that thought prevented him from otherwise reacting.

All of a sudden Barbara sighed and sat heavily on the bed, ceasing her grumbles. She picked at some lint on the blanket, the slope of her shoulders indicating that she felt excruciatingly sad. "Did you dream about the *Kommandant* last night?" she asked softly, the tone of her voice completely different from the strident, angry tone she had just been using.

"I don't know, why?" he asked warily.

"It sounded like you were enjoying yourself," she replied with feigned innocence.

It was the last straw. Hurt or not, there was no excuse for her behavior. With a voice that just barely contained his fury, he said quietly, "Enough. It stops today."

She tilted her head to look at him, then she got up and boldly walked up to him. She was a small woman, and even standing, she had to tilt her head back to look into his face. He winced as she raised her hands and placed them on his shoulders, but he did not pull away or say anything. He looked at her, resigned to hear yet more shit. Short of gagging her, there was no way he could realistically hope to stop her.

"I'm sorry. I didn't mean to hurt you."

"Yes, you did," he replied, unconvinced. "You wanted to hurt me because I'm not what you think I should be and I don't act the way you want me to. You can join a long line of people who've felt that way; I'm not sure it's a group of people you want to be part of, but you've become one of them. Congratulations. You wanted to hurt me and you've succeeded. Now can it please stop?"

"It's only because you hurt me so much."

"I'm sorry. Now, can we call it quits?"

"I wanted to learn to hate you," she confessed, "but I'm afraid all I've managed to do is make you hate me."

"I don't hate you." He wondered how many days it would take until that statement was true. Sweet little Barbara existed no longer in his mind and he was weary of the woman who had replaced her.

"I know you don't want to leave your wife and child. I understand that now," she said, assuming a woman-of-the-world stance. Slipping off her blouse, she added in an almost husky voice, "But that doesn't mean we can't enjoy each other's company." She pressed provocatively against him, but he pushed her away.

"Have you listened to yourself these past days?" he asked, incredulous. With her vindictive and injurious words, she had made herself utterly unattractive to him.

The come-hither look melted from her face and she spun angrily away. "Fine! Have it your way, you self-righteous bastard! You're so old-fashioned and conventional and tied down, you'll never know what you're missing!"

Oh, he had some idea, which was exactly why he had chosen to give it a miss! He watched in silence as she stood with her back to him, furiously combing her hair. He knew exactly the words to destroy her, to take revenge for the verbal abuse she had meted out to him, and he was momentarily tempted, but as she stood only in her slip, he could see the tension in the muscles of her back, and he took pity on her. He decided he would have to do something to rebuild her confidence, even if it meant lying. After all, he could do it for Elspeth, the least he could do was lie as effectively for a friend. It would work well: the words he had spoken to Elspeth, called up from the depths of his spirit by her power to ruin his life, he could use with Barbara. He could let her believe she had the same power, the power of an attractive, desirable, and unattainable woman, the power of denying him what he desperately wanted but could not have.

He took a deep breath and began by telling her how beautiful she was and how much he desired her, how her youth and energy were like sirens to him, calling him to his doom. He told her how each time he had denied himself the chance to hold her, his body had burned and he had gone nearly mad with frustration. He told her that he knew he wasn't good enough for her, that he was too old, too damaged by all he had experienced. He knew that she would be extraordinary if only she could fly freely, unhindered by a man like himself. He explained how she would loathe him for his lack of loyalty to his wife, how she would weary of him if he gave in to temptation, and how her rejection would utterly destroy him. He told her how he would have to spend his life watching jealously as other men would notice her and desire her.

"I don't doubt you'd remain loyal to me," he explained, "but look at what I would become: an old man whose wife stays with him out of pity, a man who had abandoned his own loyalties, his first wife and child, just to be with a woman because she was so incredibly beautiful and intelligent, but who would then discover that he was the very thing that stopped her from becoming all she could be and doing all that she could do. You would learn to hate me, and with good reason.

"You don't know how much your presence has helped me over the years. You have no idea how often just realizing that you're my friend has pulled me out of a depression or seen me through a terrible night. Please, can't I just enjoy your presence in the world? Can't I take pleasure in seeing you smiling at me from across the room? Can't we be friends again and I can be your secret, silent admirer?" he finished on a note of truth. He *had* taken comfort in her, and he would dearly love to do so again.

Barbara looked at him with liquid eyes, then bowing her head, she murmured, "Okay."

36

"**H**EY, THIS IS ABSOLUTELY MARVELOUS!" Jenny pronounced yet again as she shoveled in the last mouthful.

"Thanks," Peter accepted the compliment. Barbara and her guest, a fellow named Mark, concurred with enthusiastic nods.

"You always did serve up great meals," Jenny continued, then wiped her mouth on her napkin and took a sip of wine. "That's at least one reason I wanted to capture you for my own." She laughed.

Barbara turned toward Mark. "Can I get you anything else?" she asked solicitously.

Mark eagerly gestured toward the kitchen. "I could do with another serving."

Barbara smiled charmingly and, picking up his plate, went into the kitchen alcove to refill it.

Jenny winked at Peter. She had not failed to notice Barbara's snub and she guessed reasonably accurately its source. Asking "Do you mind?" she lit a cigarette without waiting for a reply. She offered the pack toward both men, but they both declined. Mark was clearly waiting for his next plate of food, but Peter's refusal surprised her. It was the second time he had turned one down that evening, and such self-denial was totally unlike the man she had known.

It raised a question in her mind, but to ask it she had to regain his attention—he was staring out toward the kitchen. She was momentarily stymied as she wondered which name she should use. He had been Peter Halifax in the NAU and, according to him, that was what he called himself now, but he was Niklaus Jäger here in London, so that would be more consistent, but she could only think of him as Alan Yardley, and though that name was long gone, it was the one that sat on the tip of her tongue. She compromised with "Um . . ."

Peter turned his attention back toward her.

"Have you given up smoking?"

"My daughter asked me to."

He did not seem to want to dwell on the subject further and Jenny nodded without replying. Everything he said indicated that he had loved the little girl dearly and that her absence still weighed heavily on him. In the face of such sad devotion, Jenny almost felt guilty for having left her two children home alone with her husband. "Business," she had said to explain her absence, not deigning to tell them that they would be missing an excellent dinner.

She had taken on the role of ferrying information and arranging meetings for Peter and his English contacts, and during one of her trips to the bookstore, he had invited her and her family to dinner and indicated that his colleague would be invited as well. Jenny had accepted the invitation on behalf of herself, but declined for the rest of her family. Although the other woman—he had called her Barbara—would be present, Jenny had hoped to gain some time alone. She had come early, and he had explained that Barbara had in the meanwhile invited a friend as well. "I've seen them together in the shop a few times and I know she's gone out to the pub with him once or twice, but I haven't met him yet," he had explained.

Jenny looked at her old lover with a fond smile, but he was too busy studying his other guest to notice. She looked across the table at Mark as he accepted the plate from Barbara, and the three of them sat and sipped their wine while he launched himself into the food.

Hungry, Jenny thought, all our boys seem perpetually hungry at that age. Mark ate as though he had never seen such quantity or quality of food, and indeed he might never have. He was tall and weedy with black hair and extremely pale skin. He said he was English, though Jenny guessed some Irish blood was there. They had learned he was a courier for the Underground, and indeed that is how he and Barbara had met. He had joined at the age of fourteen, following in his father's footsteps, and had in that way avoided the draft. Now he was nineteen, never married, and still boyish in his appearance. A few years of decent food, Jenny thought, and all of a sudden he'll be a man. Two or three more years after that, she mused as she noticed a few wisps of gray in his jet-black hair, and he'll look old, older than Alan, or Peter or whatever his name was.

She turned her attention back toward Peter. He looked good, really good. If she had not gone back and reread the interviews he had given in the NAU, she would have said that however he had spent his time over the years had agreed with him. Luckily, she knew better than to say something so insensitive, and upon closer inspection she could see hints of an abiding depression. Was it lingering pain or something else that gave him such a resigned and unhappy smile?

Mark finished his second helping and they had their dessert and after-dinner drinks, and then Barbara rose from the table and announced, "Mark and I are going out. See you later." Mark looked up somewhat surprised.

"Where are you going?" Peter asked. Barbara said something Jenny could not understand, and Peter switched languages to answer her. The tone grew heated, and Jenny and Mark watched in confusion at the incomprehensible argument that passed over their heads.

Barbara crossed her arms, said something with finality, then, switching to German and softening her tone of voice considerably, she said, "Let's go, Mark. The old folks want to be alone." Mark stood, smiled sheepishly and said his thanks, then helping Barbara with her coat and grabbing his own off the hook, he obediently followed Barbara out the door.

As the door snapped shut, Jenny burst into quiet giggling. "Poor boy!" She laughed. "He's already whipped!" She drank some more wine, refilled their glasses, and added between swallows, "I know you would never put up with such a dominant woman."

Inexplicably, Peter burst out laughing then.

Jenny stayed a long time and they talked about all sorts of things. After sufficient glasses of wine, she even managed to cajole Peter into talking about his marriage and what had happened since his return from America. "The more I try to hold on to her," Peter confessed about his wife, "the more she seems to slip away from me."

Jenny gave him a sympathetic smile, encouraging him to continue, far too wise a woman to offer useless insights.

"I don't know why I feel so tied to her," he continued, the words spilling out almost uncontrolled. "I think she's made it pretty clear I'm not wanted anymore. I think it must have been pity all along, and now that's worn off. I don't know why I don't just accept it and get out of her life—you know, make a home for myself here. They've given me carte blanche to leave." He sniffed his derision. Finally freed from his prison, he did not want to go.

"It's because you love her."

He nodded, disconsolately. "The problem is, I don't think she loves me, so everything she does in our marriage seems more like a kindness than genuine emotion. Does that make sense? It's like it's all an effort for her. My heart leaps when I catch sight of her and she gives me a courteous smile in return."

"Maybe that's just her way of expressing her emotions."

He nodded, unconsoled. "Maybe." He sipped a bit more wine, then without meaning to he asked, "Do you know what it's like to love someone who doesn't truly love you?" He was so embarrassed by his admission that it took a moment before he noticed that Jenny had not answered.

Their eyes met, but still she did not answer the question. A wan smile played across her lips, then faded again into a memory. "I thought I did once," she answered at last, "but I was wrong; it was just a childish infatuation."

"Lucky you."

"Yeah, lucky me."

As he closed the door behind her, he had a sinking feeling. The wine was beginning to wear off and with it his urge to reveal himself and all his problems, but it was too late. Though she had offered helpful words of advice and seemed sympathetic, he nevertheless felt that he had somehow embarrassed himself and Zosia by being so open to someone who was virtually a stranger to him. It was really quite stupid, he realized that, but there was no way to shake the feeling that he had exposed himself to the whole world and would, as a result, be the butt of jokes and the source of amusement at her next meeting with the Underground.

He rubbed his forehead and wondered if he would have a better chance of sleeping it all off if he had another glass or two to ease his mind. As he stood wondering, he heard Barbara and Mark returning, and he opened the door for them.

"The old bag gone?" Barbara asked in Polish; she was quite drunk.

"Do either of you want a cup of tea?" Peter asked in German. "I'm going to put the kettle on."

They giggled as if he had said something quite funny, so he turned into the kitchen without waiting for further reply. By the time he had put the kettle on the coil, they had disappeared into the bedroom and shut the door.

He stood seething for a minute, wondering what the hell he should do. He decided to drink his tea and see if they might finish quickly. They were not quiet, and as he sat in silence in the living room, he could not help but hear their noisy lovemaking. It reminded him of all the times Karl would bring prostitutes to the hotel room and he could do no more than stand idly by waiting for them to conduct their business.

Now, of course, he was not so powerless, and he could in theory march into the bedroom and order the lad out so that he could retire for the night, but the common law of cramped living was that such invasions were not acceptable. Mark lived with his parents, Barbara needed her private life, there was nowhere else for them to go. Nevertheless, he was furious. The common law of cramped living also included unwritten clauses about the uninvolved partner: he needed to sleep, it was his bedroom, and there was nowhere for him to go either! They should at least have asked his indulgence or arranged something in advance. Clearly Barbara was deliberately trying to annoy him and clearly she was succeeding. When, in God's name, would her petty revenge end?

After a long while the noise died down. After an even longer while, when they had still not emerged, he got up and went to the door. No sound at all. He opened it and saw they were both sound asleep. Without further ado, he shook Mark's shoulder. The boy looked up at him in confusion.

"Time to go," Peter announced unceremoniously.

"Whhh . . . ?"

"Get out," he clarified, and to help matters along he pulled Mark from the bed and sent him stumbling in the direction of the pile of clothes on the floor. Mark dutifully pulled on his clothes and let himself be escorted to the door. Peter snapped it shut just a little too quickly behind the boy and then returned to the bedroom to fall asleep.

When he crawled into the space Mark had vacated, Barbara stirred but did not waken. In her sleep she threw her arm around him and curled her naked, sweaty body next to his. He did not bother to push her away.

37

*T*HANK GOD! Richard thought as the phone rang. Karl stopped midsentence and looked at the device on Richard's desk as if it had betrayed him.

"Haven't you stopped your calls?" Karl fumed as it rang a second time.

"No, I'm expecting someone important." Richard winked and nodded his head upward in the long-accepted gesture meaning "from the Führer's office." "We'll have to continue this strategy discussion later."

Karl scowled, apparently upset at being out of the loop, yet again.

Richard waved Karl out of his office and picked up the receiver. His secretary announced a long-distance call and completed the connection upon Richard's approval. A woman's voice that Richard recognized as one of the Warszawa HQ staff said softly, "Nephew! It's your aunt Sybille—do you recognize me?"

"Ah, yes, of course. What's the occasion?"

"Oh, it's your uncle, dear boy. He's traveling through Berlin, making a connection at the station there near you, and I'm afraid he left without his wallet. He has his tickets and papers, but no money. Would you be a dear and go to the station and see if you can find him and loan him some cash?"

"But of course." Richard wondered what was so important that it required this charade. "Give me the details so I can locate him."

An hour later he was at the station and the courier had spotted him. The man hugged him in greeting and Ryszard felt something drop into his pocket.

"What's up?" he asked as he plucked off a few hundred marks and handed them to the courier.

"You have a photograph and some names in your pocket. The names are coded, entry-level twenty-four."

Ryszard nodded. It was a straightforward substitution using the telephone directory available to officials. "And?"

"The photograph is of a prisoner currently in your Ministry. An American, traveling under the name of Wim van Wije."

"Dutch?"

"Guess so."

"What's his real name?"

"Don't know. Anyway, the French desperately want him."

"So?" Ryszard asked, unconcerned. If the French wanted him, let them get him.

"They don't have anyone in position. They want him alive if at all possible. Dead if not."

"What does this have to do with us?" Ryszard pressed.

"We've agreed to do them a favor."

"I hope we've set a reasonable price."

"Not my business. Anyway, see what you can do."

"Me alone? Or is there some backup?"

"Don't pull in any of ours; we don't want to get that deeply into it. The names are four of their agents who will offer you assistance as necessary. They are in lower positions at other ministries and so can't do anything on their own. Naturally, we did not keep a copy of such sensitive information and you should destroy it as well."

"Naturally." Ryszard almost laughed. "I'd have to reveal myself to them?"

"Yes."

"I'll do it alone," Ryszard mumbled. Certainly Warszawa should have guessed that, but it was a nice touch that they had gotten the names for him in any case. The French had to be truly desperate to give up the names of four agents. "Who is this fellow?"

"An American. He's running arms for them, purely for profit. There are four consignments expected that he controls. They don't want to lose the arms, they don't want the Germans to get them, and they would like to get him out because he is so useful."

"But if not, they think he's better off dead?"

"He knows some faces and locations."

"French only?"

"Yes, he's no danger to us. We've never dealt with him."

"Ah. I'll do what I can," Ryszard promised, uninterested. Arms! To the French of all people! They would bury them in haystacks and let them rust before doing anything useful. "How long do I have?"

"We told them we wouldn't even be able to contact our people for two or three days."

"Good, good."

"We implied that we would organize a forcible breakout. So, they probably won't suspect you have anything to do with us."

"Good." The last thing Ryszard wanted was for the French to have him in their files: given the French sense of honor, he could figure on being betrayed within a month. "How was he picked up?"

"Somebody prepared him well. Army papers, he even had the appropriate clothes for a young, off-duty officer. He got picked up in a café, awaiting his contact. There seems to have been some minor fracas and he ended up betraying himself with his accent."

Ryszard snorted his amusement. "I can work with that." He took his leave of the courier and headed directly back to the office, planning as he went. If the man was already in custody, they probably did not have much time.

By the time he stepped into his office he had decided on a tentative course of action. He looked up the coded names and memorized them, then destroyed the scrap of paper in his ashtray. As for the photograph, he decided to keep it; it might be useful in supporting his plan. He scribbled *Van Wije* across the back, then dried the ink on a bit of paper so it looked slightly washed out. He stapled the photo to a piece of paper, and then carefully removed it, so that only the two staple holes were left to mar the photograph. He dropped the photograph into his pocket and headed down into the cells.

"Where's the American?" he asked the officer on duty.

"*Mein Herr?*" the officer stuttered in confusion.

Richard snapped open his badge and repeated his question.

"Cell nine," the officer answered promptly, motioning to a guard to accompany Richard. "No, wait," the officer called as they stepped through the first set of heavy doors. "He's probably in interrogation three—Hauptsturmführer Schmidt just came through a few minutes ago."

"Fine," Richard acknowledged. Interrogation three: that would give it the right level of drama.

The guard led him to the appropriate room, tapped on the door, and entered. Three men were in the room, two in uniform, both standing. The third man was in civilian clothing, seated with his hands folded together, resting on the table in front of him, the wrists bound by handcuffs. Blood was spattered around the room, clearly not from the American since he looked unharmed. Nevertheless, the spattered blood and the grim room had had the desired effect: he looked terrified.

The senior officer, Schmidt, looked up with curiosity at the intrusion.

"Traugutt," Richard announced. "Release this man into my custody."

"I can't do that, *mein Herr*," Schmidt replied as politely as possible. "He's Herr Spengler's fish."

"No, he's mine. Get Spengler down here. Now!" Richard ordered. Spengler was technically superior to him, but that was not important. Politically, the man was a nobody.

Schmidt certainly reacted as though he was aware of the hidden hierarchy. He immediately ordered the junior officer to contact Spengler and request his presence.

Richard lit a cigarette to pass the few minutes until there was a response. He did not waste his breath on Schmidt or the prisoner; it was Spengler he needed to convince. He studied the prisoner and decided that someone had indeed had some inkling of what they were doing, but probably not this man himself. He was appropriately dressed in the black leather that the younger generation so favored. His jacket had a smattering of stylish fringe, his trousers were cut tight, and he wore tall boots with the almost obligatory metals clasps and buckles running up the sides. Pawel had acquired a similar set of clothing not long before leaving, and Richard had groaned in dismay.

Richard picked up the American's papers from the table and paged through them. They looked completely in order. If the man had managed to keep his mouth shut or stick to the phrases he had been taught, he would certainly have passed without a hitch. Ah, well, there was no accounting for traffic accidents or bar fights. He tossed the papers back onto the table.

The American looked up at Richard, confused, unsure if he was being saved or damned. With a sudden, insane courage he spoke up, asserting in loud, slow American English, "I am an American and not subject to your jurisdiction! I demand to speak to a representative of my government!"

Richard walked over to the American, skirting around the table so he could confront him directly. The man looked up at him expectantly, and Richard replied with vicious force, swinging his fist into the man's face.

"Shut up!" Richard ordered in English. "I'm your handler, you worm, and if you've tried to double-cross me, I will personally see to your execution!"

Shocked by the outburst, the American fell silent. He brought his bound hands up to his face, wiped a bit of blood away from his mouth, and looked at it with a vague horror.

Richard surveyed him indifferently. He could imagine the man's thoughts. The reality of everything he had heard, all the warnings he had been given, were slowly penetrating. He had felt smugly safe, he was an American, but now it seemed that was irrelevant. Richard, seeing how he swallowed hard several times, controlled an urge to laugh.

The junior officer returned and indicated that Spengler would be along shortly. Spengler arrived ready for an argument, but Richard smiled winningly when he entered the room and preempted the debate. "Ah, Herr Spengler! Thank you for coming down. I gather some of your boys nabbed my agent here."

"Is that who he is?"

"Yes, yes." Richard nodded, pulling the photograph out of his pocket. "Here's his file photo."

Spengler looked at the photograph, compared it with the prisoner. He turned the picture over and read the name on the back.

"Where did you pick him up?" Richard asked, eyeing the prisoner as if trying to decide if he was trustworthy anymore.

"Near Calais. He's supposed to be arranging the drop-off point for a consignment of arms."

"Ah, he's not supposed to be anywhere near there!" Richard fumed, mentally noting the singular used. A consignment. "Sorry about him trespassing on your turf."

"What are you doing involved in arms shipments?" Spengler asked, accepting the apology with nothing more than a gracious nod.

"Bait. That load is supposed to be heading toward my territory. I'll be interested in seeing what game he was playing at, working with the French. But first we have to get it routed on its original course, otherwise a perfect trap will have been wasted. Months of effort!"

"That would be a shame," Spengler commented without sympathy.

"Yes," Richard agreed distractedly. "I really want to thank you for your diligence here."

"My pleasure." Spengler's tone betrayed surprise at the compliment. "Well, look, if he's yours, you can have him. I'll send the paperwork over to your secretary for your signature."

"Great. Thanks!" Richard beamed. He turned toward the prisoner and said in English, "You're coming with me."

"Your agent doesn't speak German?" Spengler asked.

"No. He really is an American," Richard ad-libbed. He had decided there would be no point pretending that the American was faking his ignorance of German. "Killing two birds with one stone: infiltrating their network while using their system to bait the terrorists here."

"Impressive!" Spengler conceded. "And you know English?"

"I went to school in London." Richard smiled. "Same school as Vogel."

"Ach." Spengler nodded and kept the rest of his thoughts to himself.

Richard grabbed van Wije's papers and led his prisoner out of the interrogation room and down the corridor to the entrance. He signed him out, explaining that the paperwork would follow eventually, and took him up the stairs. He was not interested in offering the man any comfort or calming his fears, quite the contrary, but he found the atmosphere in the cells intolerable. It just seemed all too close for comfort; so, they went to his office.

Richard gestured toward a chair, and his prisoner sat down. Richard offered him a cigarette, but the prisoner, in a fit of newfound confidence, not only refused but asserted that he did not smoke.

"Ah, so you really are an American," Richard said with a laugh.

"How do you know English?" Van Wije's voice was muffled a bit by the swelling around his mouth.

"I'm asking the questions," Richard reminded him as he sat on the edge of his desk and lit his own cigarette. It was a bit of a delicate situation; he did not know whether his office was currently bugged. Probably not, but one could never be sure, so everything he said had to fit into a consistent story. He smoked for a moment and contemplated the man in front of him, trying to size him up. Reasonably cool for one so young, but inexperienced in this sort of thing and rather naive. Profit, the courier had said, that was good. Richard would not have to fight against any ideologies.

"Why did you deviate from your assigned course?" he asked suddenly.

"I didn't," the American replied, somewhat surprised.

"The French were paying you?"

"Yes, of course," he responded with refreshing candor.

"Yet you accepted our money to deliver those goods elsewhere."

"No! I don't know anything about that!"

"Don't lie to me," Richard growled. "You want to stay alive, don't you?"

"Yes," the man answered timidly. "Honestly, I did exactly as I was told by . . . by the people I work for in America."

"And who are they?"

"I don't know their names," the man answered wretchedly.

"I don't suppose you do," Richard agreed, to the obvious relief of his prisoner. "They've set you up, betrayed you, and tried to betray me."

"I . . . I'm sorry, if . . ."

"Never mind. All's well that ends well. All you have to do is carry out the original deal. I'll forgive this little diversion, except of course, you'll accept your life in lieu of payment."

The man looked miserably confused. He hesitated, afraid of speaking, but finally he ventured, "I don't understand what I should do."

Richard smiled at him benevolently. "Don't worry, all will be made clear. When you've done exactly what you're supposed to, you'll be able to go home and kiss your wife and children, walk your dog, and watch your baseball games on television."

The man nodded. He was divorced, had no children, loathed dogs, and did not follow baseball, but he said none of these things.

Richard scribbled something on a bit of paper and handed it to van Wije, removing his handcuffs as he did so. "Go to this hotel, it's just across the street and down to the right about a hundred meters. Register using these papers you were carrying. I'll have the secretary clear you, so you won't have any trouble. Do you know enough words to register for a room?"

The man looked dubious.

"Never mind. They'll be expecting you. Just put your papers on the desk and sign where they indicate. We'll send your luggage after you. I imagine you're tired of wearing that . . ." Richard paused and thought of Pawel again. Pawel liked his leather uniform. "I imagine you could use a change of clothes. And a bath.

Anyway, wait there until someone contacts you. We'll get you back on course and wrap up this assignment without anyone even noticing their little flirtation with double-dipping."

"But what will I say to them when I return?"

"Say? I imagine, since you're an American, you can sue them for getting you into this mess in the first place!" Richard laughed and gestured for his prisoner to stand.

The man stood; he looked as though he were beginning to comprehend that whatever the game was, all he had to do was play along and he would be safe. He hesitated as if he wanted to say something, but then he changed his mind and simply nodded his agreement.

"But remember," Richard added in a quiet, threatening tone, "I'll forgive you only once. I'll be watching your every step until you complete this mission. Every single step. Do exactly as you're told if you want to redeem yourself. Exactly! And if you even dream of listening to a French agent . . ." He made a discreet slashing motion across his throat.

Richard had Stefan escort the American out of the building and to the hotel. He sat at his desk for a few minutes and wondered exactly what to do next. Three shipments of arms for free. He'd get them dropped somewhere where his people could pick them up safely—in fact, he'd just have Warszawa decide where, contact them tonight, have them handle further contacts with the American. Or should he handle this himself? Avoid a diplomatic incident and take personal responsibility for ripping the French off. He laughed to himself as he thought of how angry the French would be. "But we had to do it to save your man," he mentally explained with a guilty Gallic shrug to his French allies. "You did say any effort to save the man, didn't you?" Yeah, he could pull off some bullshit excuse—the shipments were seized by the Germans, some such nonsense. The French network was terribly disorganized, rife with corruption, understaffed, constantly battling betrayals. They'd never find out, and if they did, they would do nothing about it. Nothing—just as they did in 1939. Letting us twist in the wind like that, when there was still a chance to defeat the Germans militarily!

Richard shook his head and let his mind turn to that fourth shipment, the one Spengler knew about. What should Richard do with that? The most consistent picture would be to have them delivered and be picked up by somebody who could then be nabbed by the security forces. Sacrifice a few lambs for another feather in his cap and to secure the other three shipments. But who? The Communists came to mind. They were pathetic, hanging on to some ludicrous loyalty to Moscow. Toadies! The same Moscow that had ordered the deportation and murder of their comrades across the border. The same Moscow that had murdered thousands of Polish officers in cold blood in the Katyn forest. The same Moscow that had signed a secret pact with the Nazis. The same Moscow that had happily swallowed half their homeland, wiping out every last vestige of the Polish culture that had flourished there for six hundred years. Their opposi-

950 .ß **The Children's War**

tion to the Germans was nothing but blind loyalty to the Russian Communists. They were no less dangerous than the Nazis they so loathed. The Communist Resistance then. He could set them up to find out about the shipment, line up some troops, and voilà, wipe out a few of them, maintain the consistency of his story, and achieve a political coup.

Richard rubbed away a nagging pain in his forehead. It was the end of the day, and as he packed his briefcase, he wondered whether he should go talk to the American now, perhaps with an evening walk in the park, or head for home. He decided to let the man stew a bit, and besides, he wanted to run a few things by Kasia first. Something didn't quite sit right, and he was loath to play out his hand without thinking things through with her.

On the way out, he told his secretary to make sure there was some relief for the guard he had assigned to the American's hotel, then he left the building, stopping at a sidewalk stand to buy some flowers for his wife. They looked cheerful, in contrast to the grim and blustery day, and he had been rather ignoring Kasia of late.

In the reflection of the small vanity mirror that the vendor had pinned up on the back wall of his booth, Richard caught sight of somebody following him. He was sufficiently surprised that he spun around and had to recover from the gesture by slapping at his coat as if something had annoyed him. What the fuck? Again! So soon? What the hell were they playing at? He paid for the flowers and headed toward the taxi stand.

This did not make sense. Whatever had sparked the last surveillance had finished, and now here he was being tailed yet again. It was infuriating! No wonder this goddamned country is on the road to ruin! he thought angrily, nothing better to do than harass their best and brightest! It flashed through his mind as a serious thought, and only upon reflection did he recognize the irony. Maybe Peter was right, maybe he was ingesting poison.

He shook that thought away and turned his attention to the taxi that followed his through the boulevard traffic. Did this have something to do with the American? Was there more to it all than just supplying arms? Or was it the videotape? Were they onto him? His mind raced through various possibilities as the taxi sat at a traffic light. Giving in to his impatient anger, Richard tapped the driver's window.

"Yes, *mein Herr?*"

"When the light changes, I want you to drive to the middle of the next block and stop without pulling over."

"In traffic, *mein Herr?*"

"Yes. Just stop dead and let me out. I'll leave my briefcase in the car. What I want you to do then is to drive on as soon as I step out and go to the address I gave you. Do you remember it?"

"Yes, *mein Herr.*"

"Good. Wait there. I'll pay you and there'll be an extra hundred in it for you as well. Got that?"

The driver nodded solemnly.

"Good."

The light changed and the driver did as instructed. The car behind them almost hit them as it slammed on its brakes and skidded to a halt. Richard stepped out and noticed that the taxi that had been tailing him also stopped in the ensuing traffic confusion. His taxi drove on and Richard walked calmly over to his tail. The passenger sat in nervous confusion, not knowing what to do. If he drove on, then he would lose his prey, but if he stayed put, stopped in the middle of the road, it was obvious what he was up to.

Richard opened the passenger door and slid in beside his colleague. His gun was out and he pointed it at the terrified man and asked, "Who are you working for?"

"Herr Traugutt! Please don't shoot! I'm only following orders!"

"Whose?" Richard asked again with ice-cold anger.

The man looked at the gun and then at Richard's angry visage. He could conceivably shoot, he looked that angry, and they both knew that more likely than not Richard would not be held accountable for shooting a pesky subordinate. Maybe a fine, maybe a few bribes to clear his record. "Schindler," the young man admitted. Better to face his boss's anger than this man's unpredictable temper.

Schindler! If it was that weasel, then it wasn't a promotion! "Let me see your papers," Richard ordered.

The man reluctantly handed them over. Richard put them in his jacket, saying, "If you're lying to me, I'll have you shot. Now, tell me again, who are you working for?"

"Schindler. I swear!"

"Okay. Get out." Richard gestured with his gun toward the door.

"My papers?" the man asked desperately.

"You can pick them up at my office tomorrow."

"But, *mein Herr!* I need them."

"I said, get out!"

The poor fellow stepped out of the taxi and remained standing in the middle of the road as Richard ordered the taxi to take him home. He glanced back and snickered at the lonely figure standing still as cars passed around him on both sides. Eventually it disappeared from view.

The little interlude had lifted his mood some, and by the time he reached his house, he was humming happily to himself. He recovered his briefcase and the flowers, paid both drivers, and scanned the neighborhood to see if he could find the hidden observer. There was nothing obvious, and he went inside looking forward to a good meal and a long discussion with his wife.

"Clearly your tail wasn't very experienced," Kasia observed as they discussed the day's events after dinner.

"What makes you say that?"

"Well, you spotted him so quickly."

"Hmm. Maybe I'm just good at spotting the bastards."

"Seriously, Ryszard. It sounds to me like this guy was told to follow you at the last minute. That would mean that Schindler is tailing you because of the American."

"I'm inclined to agree with you," Ryszard admitted as he held Piotr by his arms so that he could practice standing. He bounced up and down gleefully on Ryszard's legs and let a mass of milky substance drip from his mouth.

Kasia reached over and wiped the spittle from Piotr's mouth with a little cloth that she carried continuously. She had taken to letting the child nap for long periods in the afternoon and stay up late into the evening so that Ryszard could spend some time with him after work. She enjoyed watching the two interact. "I think the American is up to something. There's more to it than the arms shipments," she guessed.

"What makes you say that?"

"Well, for one thing, he was picked up in Calais. Why was he brought all the way to Berlin?"

"Don't know."

"And he gave in too easily."

"You think?"

"Yes. He's up to something else, he's protecting something to do with Schindler by giving up the shipments to you."

"Could be, but how am I going to find out what?"

"Let him go and follow him," Kasia suggested.

"Do you think it will be that easy?"

"From what you said, yes."

"And if he heads toward Schindler's territory?" Ryszard asked.

"We have a contact in London, make use of him."

38

*B*OTH BARBARA AND PETER looked up from their work when the officer entered the store. He walked directly toward the back with a manner that suggested he was not interested in asking after a book on gardening. The customers who stood in the queue backed away, some deciding to abandon the shop altogether.

"Herr Jäger?"

"Yes," Peter answered hesitantly.

The officer snapped open an identification and immediately snapped it shut again. "Your presence is requested at the district's security headquarters."

"Requested," Peter repeated quietly to reassure himself.

"Yes. You will accompany me."

Peter gave Barbara a quick glance; the blood had drained from her face. "Can you handle things here?" he asked.

She nodded slowly.

"Don't worry," he assured her as he kissed her good-bye, "I'm sure it's nothing."

The room was sufficiently nondescript that Peter could read nothing from its contents. A desk and chair, two other chairs facing the desk, bookshelves laden with files and loose papers. He had been offered a seat, and the officer who had escorted him had left him alone in the room.

He sat nervously waiting, not even bothering to check the door. He knew somebody was standing outside it and that it was pointless to try to leave. Ten minutes passed. He stopped drumming his fingers and tried rubbing his neck a bit. He stood up and paced the room, then reseated himself and began drumming his fingers again. His tongue wandered back to the tooth loaded with poison. It would be easy this time, he would not hesitate at all.

Another ten minutes passed. To pass the time, he was tempted to start nosing through the files, but he decided against such folly. With an effort he stopped drumming his fingers. He scratched through the material of his sleeve at the skin above and below the light cast he wore; underneath the cast it itched like hell, but there was nothing he could do about that. He pressed with his knuckles against the cast, but it was worthless. He stopped the useless scratching and began drumming his fingers again.

Finally the door behind him opened. He jumped up to greet whoever was entering.

"Sorry to have kept you waiting," Ryszard apologized brusquely, "I was unavoidably detained."

Containing his utter amazement, Peter nodded noncommittally.

Without offering his hand, Ryszard introduced himself, then said, "Have a seat," and gestured toward the chair.

Peter seated himself uneasily. Ryszard perched himself on the edge of the desk and lit a cigarette. He offered Peter one, but Peter refused. Ryszard smoked quietly for a moment and surveyed his guest in silence. Peter felt his heart pound in his chest. Had Ryszard finally gone off the deep end? Or was there something so terrible and important going on that he felt it necessary to sacrifice his brother-in-law? One life for many?

Finally Ryszard spoke. "I'm sure you're wondering why you are here."

"Yes, *mein Herr*," Peter's throat was dry and he cleared it.

"Ah, well, it seems we could use your help."

"My help?" he repeated pointlessly. *Helping police with their inquiries*—wasn't that the standard euphemism for being tortured?

"Yes, it seems the owner of your bookstore might be involved in an international drug-smuggling ring based in Göringstadt. We believe they use his stores as a way of moving the contraband throughout the Reich."

Peter blanched. Normal police practice would be to automatically assume his guilt.

"We were wondering if you could help us in our inquiries," Ryszard purred.

Would Ryszard see him killed without even letting him know why? He swallowed, then answered as any German would, "I am pleased to offer my full assistance, *mein Herr.*"

Ryszard smiled. "Good, good." Suddenly, he was all business. "Now, what we have determined so far, through the thorough investigations of my people back in Berlin, is that you and your wife are completely innocent of any involvement. Nevertheless, I'll need to question you at length to determine if you've observed anything useful, perhaps without being aware of the significance. After that, I'll need your active involvement in tracking these criminals down."

"I see," Peter sighed.

Ryszard paused and considered his surroundings. "This office is not very *gemütlich*, is it?"

"No." Peter shook his head. "Not *gemütlich*."

"Let's go out and get some fresh air. I think if we take a walk, you'll relax and be much more likely to remember useful information. It's brisk but at least it's not raining for once!"

"No, not raining," Peter rasped. Only now was his heartbeat beginning to return to normal.

"And perhaps we'll get a cup of coffee, or even a beer, somewhere," Ryszard suggested jovially. "Would you like that?" he asked, almost as if treating a child.

"Yes, coffee," Peter replied mechanically.

"Oh, yes," Ryszard interrupted himself, "but first, I think you should telephone your wife and let her know that you'll be home for dinner. We wouldn't want her to worry, now would we?"

Peter nodded, then shook his head. "No, no."

By the time they were walking along the street, Peter had recovered himself sufficiently to ask, "What the hell was that all about?"

"Ach, I need to speak with you."

"Obviously."

"Well, I can hardly waltz into your flat and say 'howdy,' " Ryszard snapped.

"You could have made it clearer from the first that I wasn't dead meat."

"I thought I was clear."

"You took your bloody time about it," Peter replied angrily.

"Did I?" Ryszard asked, unperturbed.

Peter sighed heavily; had his brother-in-law lost all touch with reality? "So what's up?"

"How's Zosia?" Ryszard asked incongruously.

"How would I know? She doesn't deign to communicate with my sort," Peter replied bitterly.

Ryszard looked at him, somewhat confused, but did not pursue the issue.

"Well, anyway," he began awkwardly as he led the way into a café, "here's what I know so far . . ." He described the encounter he had had with the American and the surveillance that had occurred shortly thereafter. "The agent was telling the truth, it was Schindler who stuck the tail on me. I gave him dire warnings about pulling any such stunt again, but frankly I didn't get much information out of him. He claimed to know nothing about the American and said he had just had his man follow me in order to give his agent practice. Try as I might, I couldn't cut through his crap, and since there was nothing I could threaten him with, I had to let it go at that."

"Is this the Schindler that the Vogels knew?" Peter asked. "The one directing that sterilization project?"

"The same. Anyway, my people followed the American here. Actually, to a town called Lewes. The American stayed in a place called the Bull's Head; he checked into a room, stayed a night, checked out, and left."

"That's it?"

"Yeah, flew to Geneva and presumably from there to the NAU." Ryszard rubbed his chin. "Didn't meet anyone, didn't do anything."

"Didn't leave the room?"

"They say not."

"Anything come in? Dinner, say?"

"No, he ate on the train and apparently nothing was exchanged."

"Anything leave the room, anything at all?"

"He put his boots out to be polished, picked them up in the morning."

"Ah, did your men go and check them out?"

"No, they were across the street, watching through the window, and they kept their distance."

"Shows a lack of initiative." Peter laughed.

"Initiative can get you shot. They followed orders and I wasn't there to countermand them. I have to keep them on a tight leash since they aren't ours."

"What did the boots look like?"

Ryszard glanced around the room. "See those boots on that young fellow over there? That's the style. Either somebody dropped something into the boots—"

"—or removed something from them," Peter finished the thought. "But that's not possible! Surely he was searched in Berlin?"

"They could have missed it."

"Something that obvious?" Peter was nonplussed.

"You have no idea of the incompetence . . ." Ryszard trailed off. He was embarrassed that he had stupidly assumed that Spengler's people had done an adequate job and so had not conducted an independent search.

"So you let the American go without questioning him?"

"My agents only managed to talk to me directly when the American was at the airport already. I had the border security pull him out of line and give him a full-body search."

"The whole thing?"

"Everything, including the bend over and cough bit." Ryszard snickered. "They didn't find anything, so I believe that something was removed from the boots, rather than put into them. Beyond that, I didn't have him detained. I didn't want to stomp on him since he might be working for our side, or at least our allies."

"What does Warszawa know about this?"

"Nothing so far. I'm on my own here. Until I get something concrete, the less they know the better."

"So if you don't ask, they can't say no."

"Something like that. Besides, the more people who know something, the more chances of betrayal."

"Which raises the question . . . ," Peter began.

". . . what do you have to do with all this?" Ryszard lit another cigarette. "I think the American was being used, could be his people in America were as well. They might have thought they were working with the English Underground and therefore were able to get the American Security Service to turn a blind eye to whatever they were doing."

"Agency."

"Huh?"

"It's the American Security *Agency*. If it were *Service* their acronym would be ASS."

"*Ass?*"

"That's the American spelling of *arse*." Peter was enjoying himself; it felt good to be involved in something without being in danger. Exhilarating even.

Ryszard shook his head in confusion. "Anyway, I have to tread lightly. If I go in and arrest everybody at the inn, I'll probably find out what's going on, but if it's Schindler, I'd have shown my hand for no good reason. I could hardly demand that he hand over whatever was exchanged; after all, we're both on the same side and I'm in his territory."

"And if the American really did meet up with the Underground—"

"—it'd be even worse for me to intervene. I'd blow their operation and cost them a few people."

"Do you think it was one of Schindler's agents working for the English? A double cross?"

"That's possible, too. Whoever it was, my hands are tied until I know more."

"And that's where I fit in," Peter guessed.

"Yes. I can't stay here long. What I'd like is for you to go to Lewes. Check out this place personally, see if you can find out anything. Do you have any contacts there?"

"I don't have any contacts anywhere," Peter reminded him.

Ryszard laughed. "Oh, yes, the man without a past."

They sat in silence for a few minutes. Ryszard hacked and coughed a bit, put out the cigarette he was smoking, and lit another. Peter sipped his coffee and stared out the window, thinking of his past.

"What's the problem?" Ryszard asked.

Peter looked down at the table and scratched absently with his thumbnail at a coffee stain. "I want to ask you a favor," he admitted reluctantly. He ignored the slight groan from Ryszard and explained how he had found his mother's diaries and her mention of the Pure German movement and her tentative contacts with the English Underground.

"And you don't know yet which one it was that got them arrested," Ryszard guessed.

"No."

"You know, the Underground might have turned them in to make you an orphan."

"I thought about that, but that's not their style."

Ryszard snorted. "You'd be surprised by what people will do for their cause."

"I'm already familiar with that phenomenon. Nevertheless, whether or not they'd think it was moral to *french* my parents, it was impractical. After all, they hadn't said no to the proposition yet, and I still had three years of schooling to go through. Even if the Underground had wanted me that badly, they would have waited until I was fifteen rather than burdening themselves with a thirteen-year-old."

"Fair point," Ryszard agreed. "So, you want me to see what political information I can dig up from that office around that time?"

"If you can. I realize that it's an unnecessary risk for what is nothing more than personal motives . . ."

"Not to mention against standing orders." Ryszard laughed. He leaned back and blew a stream of smoke into the air. "As if I could ever be buggered to follow them."

"So you'll do it?"

"Didn't the Council already look up these details for you?"

"They aren't fond of telling me anything, so I don't ask, but anyway, I don't think there would be much on current file. I was hoping you could look at material that has been archived in Berlin or here in London. You know, paper documents."

"Phew, dusty work! Why does it matter so much?"

Peter shook his head. "I don't know, it just does."

Ryszard grunted. "All right, I'll see if I can find anything, but it won't be a priority."

"I understand. Thanks."

"I'll send whatever I find to Szaflary, it's easier than trying to send it here. Presumably you'll be back there at some point."

"Yes, temporarily, for the birth," Peter answered in a muted voice.

"Temporarily? How long do they plan to keep you here?" Ryszard asked, somewhat incredulous.

Peter shook his head. "I guess until I learn my lesson, whatever it is." Regretting his words, he added quickly, "So, how's your family?"

Ryszard looked surprised by the question but did not hesitate to answer. "I always miss them when I'm away. I'm always afraid they won't be there when I get back."

"I know the feeling."

"And I miss the boys, too, now that Pawel and Andrzej have gone to Szaflary."

"What made you send them there?"

Ryszard gave him a sharp look as if Peter had blundered into sensitive territory, but then he said simply, "It was time."

"For Pawel, perhaps. But why Andrzej as well? He's so young."

Ryszard smoked in silence for a moment. Peter noticed how the tip of Ryszard's cigarette was shaking. As the extended silence grew uncomfortable, Peter glanced at the clock, then suggested, "The pubs should be open. You want a drink?"

Ryszard nodded. "Sure, why not."

39

AFTER LEAVING RYSZARD, Peter remembered that Geoff's family was from the Lewes area, and he asked Jenny if she could track down an address for him. She agreed on condition that she be allowed to accompany him on his fact-finding mission, and two days later she returned with an address.

"His official name was Georg," Jenny explained. "It took a while to connect that to Geoff."

"How in the world did his parents get Geoff from Georg?" Peter asked.

"I suspect, wanting to name their child Geoff, they went to the book and found the first name that began with the same three letters. How did your parents mangle Alan to make it official?"

"Oh, Alan is in the book, it's an officially acceptable first name," Peter explained truthfully, then confided, "But that's not the name my parents gave me in any case. They called me Niklaus Adolf, hoping somehow that would make me more Aryan."

"Klaus Adolf!" Jenny laughed. "You know, I would have thought they were nuts before I had kids of my own. Now I'm a bit more tolerant. I know what it's like to want the best for your kids, even if it's not ideologically sound."

Peter thought of Joanna and fell silent.

The next day they strode down the street where Geoff's family still lived. It was nothing like what Geoff had described, and Peter wondered if time had really altered it so much or if Geoff had wistfully been recalling a place that never existed. It was not even a separate village, rather an ugly concrete development tagged onto the southern edge of the town. The town itself, though showing the usual signs of decay, was quite nice, having escaped destruction during the siege. He and Jenny had toured it a bit and he had registered at the inn that the American had stayed at, but they had not been able to elicit any information or come up with any ideas other than to visit Geoff's family and hope they could offer help.

"Do you really think they'll be able to help?" Jenny echoed his thoughts.

"Hope so. We don't really have many other resources," Peter admitted. Ryszard had been loath to clue in the English Underground, and so they were on their own for now. "Here it is," Peter said, giving Jenny a hopeful smile as they turned into the dismal stairwell of an apartment block. They climbed three flights and he rapped on a door.

A moment later the door opened a crack and a woman peered out. "Who are you?"

"A friend of Geoff's," Peter answered. "We were in the labor camp together."

She pulled back slightly, tilting her head to examine him more closely. "That was a long time ago, young man."

"I know. This is the first chance I've had to come to you."

The door closed and a chain was removed, then it opened wide and the woman motioned them inside. "Come in. I'm his mother. You're Peter, aren't you?"

They drank their bitter tea with milk: Jenny because she preferred it that way and Peter because he did not want to raise any suspicions by having any un-English habits. The rest of the family was introduced, and a teenage boy, the woman's nephew, was sent to Geoff's widow's flat to fetch her so she could hear whatever Peter had to say.

"She remarried about six months after we heard," Geoff's mother explained. "She's a sweet kid and I can't blame her for not waiting longer. After all, she hadn't seen him in six years."

Peter nodded his understanding, remembering how often Geoff spoke of his wife and how much he missed her.

"You used to help him write his letters," Geoff's mother observed.

"Yes, anytime he needed help with some complicated concept."

Geoff's mother nodded. "Sometimes we had to get help reading what you wrote, but his wife appreciated all the beautiful phrases. I assume those were yours?"

"They were Geoff's thoughts. I was just sort of the camp translator."

"He described you in his letters," Geoff's father observed suspiciously, "but you don't look much like his description."

"I've dyed my hair. I'm on the lam. I'm traveling on German papers right now."

"So your sentence wasn't shortened?" Geoff's mother asked.

Peter shook his head. "No, I escaped. Please don't tell anyone I was here."

Geoff's parents exchanged a significant look, then the mother said, "We won't ask anything more about you then; the less we know the better. But can you tell us, what happened to our son?"

Peter surveyed his audience: the parents looked sorrowful, the aunt and her husband concerned, Jenny curious. "Yeah, I can tell you," he said quietly. "When his wife is here, I'll tell you all so I only have to say it once."

After Geoff's wife, Dora, arrived, Peter began telling them whatever he could remember of his friend. They were avid listeners, the wife and parents looking to recall something of their lost one, the aunt, uncle, and nephew more interested in what might lie in store for the boy when he was drafted. They asked a lot of questions, looking for memories in the details, and Peter provided them with every anecdote he could remember. The hours passed and still they did not come back to their original question; they seemed to be actively avoiding it as if hearing of Geoff's death would cause him to die all over again.

Peter was relieved by this and thought that he might be able to escape discussing those horrible last weeks in the camp, but eventually Geoff's mother left the room and returned with a bit of paper.

"This is all we have telling us what happened in the end," she said sadly. "Executed for murder. I don't understand, our boy was not violent, he was not a murderer. Why did this happen?"

Peter read the heartless words of the notification. It was written in *Beamtendeutsch*, the worst form of officialese, and he noticed that someone had penciled a few words and phrases in the margins as if struggling with the translation. "Can you read this?" he asked the family.

They shook their heads. Dora volunteered that a neighbor had attempted a translation, but they were not sure if it had been correct. All they knew for sure was that Geoff had been executed. Peter reread the document, then translated it for them as fluently as possible. The cold words revealed no more than they had already known, and when he had finished, he saw they were looking at him expectantly.

Seeing that Peter still hesitated, the father left the table and returned with a bottle of gin. They drank a round to Geoff, then without even bothering to ask, the father poured out a large tumblerful for Peter, saying, "Take your time, we've waited this long."

Peter sipped the gin. "I wasn't there when it occurred, but I will tell you what happened to me and maybe then you'll understand." He told them then of the *Kommandant* and his blackmailing the lads in the camp. He told them about approaching the *Kommandant* as camp leader and how he had demanded the abuse stop. He explained what had happened next, the *Kommandant*'s "deal" and all that went with it. He told them of his humiliation and how that had paralyzed him into inaction, and he explained how Geoff's nonjudgmental, levelheaded advice had rescued him from his isolated hell. "He organized the lads into getting information for me and kept providing me with support and advice as I worked my way into the *Kommandant*'s trust. Without him helping me . . ." Peter shook his head at the thought.

"Anyway," he continued, "we did finally find something with which we could blackmail him. I used it to arrange an escape but left the incriminating documents at the camp so that the *Kommandant* would be forced to remain on good behavior. We gave the stuff to one of the older lads because we didn't want it to be in Geoff's hands, figuring the *Kommandant* would assume he did have it and might search him and tear his barracks apart."

Peter chewed on his knuckle as he thought, yet again, of how he could have stayed until Geoff's term was up. The family watched him in silence, the father moving only to refill his glass. "I could have stayed," Peter said at last. "I had no idea. He only had about six weeks to go."

"Seven weeks and a day," Geoff's mother amended.

Peter looked over their heads at a painting on the far wall. An idealized country landscape. "Anyway, we didn't think the *Kommandant* was mad enough to do anything dangerous, except maybe to me. We figured he'd feel insulted by my presence there and so I left as soon as possible."

"That's why you're on the run now?" the boy asked.

Peter nodded noncommittally, casting a glance at Jenny, hoping she would not complicate his story. "Yeah. After a time, I heard about Geoff's execution. I heard that he hit the *Kommandant* with a candlestick and said it was self-defense. I assume the *Kommandant* attacked Geoff and it was indeed self-defense."

"Do you think it was the documents that he was seeking when he attacked our boy?" Geoff's father asked.

Peter hesitated, then decided to tell them what he thought. "The confrontation took place in the *Kommandant*'s private quarters, so I would guess not. I think the *Kommandant* intended your son to be his next victim." The words hung in the air, and he tried to soften them by adding, "But I don't know."

"What happened to the documents?" Jenny asked.

Peter shook his head. "I don't know. I suppose they were fairly useless after the *Kommandant*'s death."

Geoff's mother moved her lips as if praying under her breath, his father poured another round of drinks, then broke the silence by saying, "Thank you for coming here. Is there anything we can offer you in return?"

Peter paused only long enough to be polite, then answered, "Yes. Two things. First off, can my friend stay a night or two here with you? She has English papers, so I can't register her at the inn I'm at, and I don't want to try sneaking her into my room."

"Of course!" Geoff's mother answered immediately. "You should stay here, too. We have plenty of room." She gestured broadly to indicate the spacious two rooms of the apartment that she shared with her sister.

Peter shook his head. "No, thank you very much, but I want to stay at the inn.

I'm looking for information and I was wondering if you could in some way offer help."

"Information? How can we help?"

"I think an important package was passed from a guest of the inn to someone else. I was hoping someone at the inn might have seen something. Do you know anyone who works there?"

For a moment the family remained in silence, their brows furrowed in thought, then Geoff's uncle spoke up. "My mate's daughter used to work there. Maybe she's friends with one of the staff."

They went immediately to visit the girl. Despite her father's encouragement, she was loath to talk to Peter about anything, intuitively feeling that if information was wanted on one of her friends, then it could only mean trouble. It was difficult to convince her otherwise for, as she quickly pointed out, the connections to this stranger carrying German papers were incredibly tenuous: her father's friend's nephew's never-before-seen comrade from years ago? Wasn't it all just a bit suspicious? she asked. The three men looked at each other, stymied by her objections, but then Jenny took her by the arm and they went off into a corner and conversed in whispers. After a time the girl returned to say she did personally know one of the inn staff, and she would talk to her to try to get her help.

"What did you say to her?" Peter asked as they awaited the maid from the inn. He and Jenny sat in a tearoom not far from the inn, sipping their drinks, waiting nervously to see if the girl would appear.

Jenny laughed. "I told her you were my husband and I knew you were a good man. I gave her a sob story about how we rarely got to see each other because you were on the run from the authorities and how you were hoping to get some information that would let you come home."

"And why should she believe you?" Peter asked, astonished that it had been something so simple.

"I'm a mother," Jenny giggled. "I have that motherly, trustworthy glow about me."

"Ah, well, I guess you impressed her enough to even convince her friend, because there's the girl we're looking for."

A girl of about sixteen wearing a maid's uniform stood in the doorway, casting a look around the tearoom. Her eyes settled on Peter and Jenny and she approached their table. "Are you Jenny?"

"Yes, you must be Louise."

Peter stood to pull out a chair for Louise. She seemed surprised by the gesture and it took her a moment to gather herself enough to accept the seat.

"I know someone who was working that night," she began without preamble, "and I'll introduce you, but it's going to cost." She paused as if gathering her courage. "One thousand marks!"

Peter bit his lips to suppress a smile. He had never thought he could get off that cheaply. His hesitation confused the girl and she amended quickly, "We'll take eight hundred."

"If you really do have information," he said, "we'll pay a thousand. Can we go there now?"

The girl shook her head. "We'll come to your room tonight. After the day manager has left."

They spent the afternoon perusing the local bookstores, and Peter bought a crate of English-language books from a used-book shop for the store in London. He thought the books might sell well, and it also provided him with a good excuse for his journey in case anyone ever questioned him. That evening they ate a meal in a mixed-race pub, and then returned to the inn to await their visitors. Jenny nervously smoked one cigarette after another, while Peter stood impatiently by the window and watched as the street grew increasingly deserted.

There was a light tapping at the door, and when bidden, a young woman entered with Louise. She introduced herself as Tess and explained that she was the night manager, which meant she opened the door to late-returning guests and carried out some overnight chores such as polishing boots and removing room trays.

Peter asked if she remembered a Dutch guest, Wim van Wije.

"Let me see the money," Tess answered almost belligerently.

He pulled out twelve hundred marks and gave them to her. "I trust you. You can keep it."

Jenny's eyes opened wide with surprise, but Tess and Louise reacted exactly as he had expected. Their mouths dropped open, they glanced at each other, then they threw away their caution and relaxed. After that they were like trusted old conspirators. Tess explained how the night van Wije had stayed at the inn, there was another young man there, who had been registered for almost a week.

"Things were slow, so I did a round early that night to get started on the boots, and as I turned into the hallway with van Wije's room, I saw the other fellow fussing with his boots. I politely interrupted him and told him I was responsible for the guest's possessions and I could not allow them to be tampered with. I figured he was planning on stealing them, but I didn't want to say that. Anyway, he skulked off, and I took the boots downstairs to be polished, but I decided not to return them until morning. About five in the morning the same fellow showed up at my desk, put down three hundred marks, and asked about van Wije's boots. I said I could not return them to anyone but their owner. He put down another three and asked if he could just look at them for a few minutes. I refused. I figured he would have shown some government ID if he was with the police. Finally, he laid down another three and asked if I would do him a small favor."

"Did you?" Jenny asked.

"Yes. I was a bit afraid he would get violent if I didn't do as he asked."

"What did he want?" Peter prompted.

"He had me remove one of the clasps. He said the topmost one on the left side of the right boot would snap off easily, and inside I would find a small device which, he said, belonged to him. I should remove it, put the clasp back on, and bring him the device. I went into the back and did as he asked and gave him the object."

"What did it look like?"

"Small, gray, about this big." Tess held her fingers about a centimeter apart. "Really tiny. I couldn't figure out what it contained. It didn't rattle or anything, like it was solid."

"Did he say anything else?"

"No, except not to say a word to anyone—especially the guy who owned the boots."

Peter nodded. "Do you have his name?"

"Yeah, it's in the register. I can show you."

When they were at the desk, Tess pointed out the name. "He checked out the morning after."

"Schindler," Peter muttered, surprised to see that name. "Wolf-Dietrich Schindler. You said he was young?"

"Yes, well, not old anyway. His papers said he was from Berlin. His accent was consistent with that."

Peter and Jenny exchanged amused glances.

"Can you describe him?" Jenny asked.

"Of course," Tess agreed cheerily, and did just that in great detail.

The next morning they left their luggage at the inn and took a day trip to Dover just to see the ocean. They walked along the beach, totally alone in the bitter December wind. Peter stopped to stare from a safe distance at the western docks, where he had embarked so long ago into an unknown fate. Jenny huddled next to him and wrapped her arms tightly around his waist. She followed his gaze and then, leaning into him, asked, "What are you thinking?"

"Oh, I was thinking how my escape cost Geoff his life."

"You weren't to know."

"I know. Still, if I had told the truth at my interrogation, maybe that would have saved him."

"How so?"

"After my recapture, I lied about the extortion we had used against the *Kommandant*. I didn't want to get my accomplices in trouble, so I just made up a story that the *Kommandant* had freed me out of love, that he had planned to meet up with me after some time."

"But how does that change anything?"

"Well, when Geoff killed the *Kommandant*, he claimed it was self-defense. He claimed the *Kommandant* had attacked him. If I had admitted that the *Kommandant* had attacked me as well, maybe they would have believed him."

"He was hanged so soon after you left, your words couldn't have affected his trial."

"I only spent four days out of the Reich and, let's say, a day or two in transit. Geoff was hanged nine days after I left. There was plenty of time for me to corroborate his story. It might have saved him if they knew the *Kommandant* was a psychopath . . ."

Jenny shook her head. "You know better than that. We're *Nichtdeutsch,* the justice system doesn't work like that for us."

They padded along the heavy, damp sand in silence. The sea threw up dark waves onto the shore, then greedily sucked them back with a loud roaring sound through the pebbly beach. Clouds scudded across the sky, gathering on the horizon with a portent of rain. The wind whipped at them so much they had to lean into it to stay upright. Jenny huddled closer and Peter hugged her. "So much waste," he muttered at the sea.

"This trip?"

"Oh, no! I think we've got everything we could hope for, and that description was terrific."

"Yeah. She'd make a great recruit."

Peter nodded. "Thanks for your help. I couldn't have done it without you."

"My pleasure." Jenny sighed into the wind. "Anything for old times."

Upon returning to London, Peter relayed the information to Ryszard. Ryszard promised to call on him again if need be, but had pressing business in Berlin and had to abandon the hunt for the time being. He left Peter with strict instructions not to pursue anything on his own and then, upon seeing Peter's face, added, "I mean it!"

Despite the obvious temptation to spite Ryszard, Peter decided not to do anything so foolish as to play sleuth, and so he settled back into a routine with the bookstore and into preparing for the extra sales that were inevitable during the *Winterfest* season. For that he got little help from Barbara, for she and Mark threw themselves into the *Winterfest* activities that dominated the city. There were street markets and theater productions, sporting events and parades. The weather was uncooperative, but then, it always was, and nobody was surprised that they had to sip their *Glühwein* under the sodden awning of a street booth during the *Winterfestmarkt.*

Peter ventured out with them once or twice after closing up shop; the outings reminded him of some happy times in his youth, but even though the markets had grown richer and the entertainment was more elaborate, he found no real joy in the occasions. There was an ever-present fear that even in the huge, anonymous crowds he would be recognized from his wanted poster or by an old acquaintance, and though he told no one, he was also afraid of a bomb or other unforeseen event blowing his cover, the way it had done in Neu Sandez.

So he usually stayed at home in the evenings, enjoying his privacy and tending the books. He spent several evenings filling out the necessary papers to reapply for the bookstore's license to sell English-language books. The forms were tedious, requiring signatures and testimonials from several government offices, but since they had received approval in the past, it seemed likely they would be granted the license for another year.

Theirs was a dual-language store; that is, they sold both German and English books. The German books required no special license, but the English books did—ostensibly to prevent their shop from becoming a low-class establishment and thus destroying the character of the neighborhood. It was true that many of the shops that sold English books were located in the English parts of town and were therefore quite run-down, and it was this association that the Neighborhood Committee wanted to prevent. Peter knew, though, that it had little to do with the integrity of the neighborhood: the government simply wanted to keep an eye on all establishments that might become focal points for resistance. For that reason, they were careful to keep an extremely proper shop, and for that reason as well, he was careful to have all the forms filled out with due care and attention.

He tracked down signatures and testimonials during the day; assurances from the bank that they had credit, from neighbors that there had been no incidences, from the local police that there had been no complaints. The district security police certified that they had not been implicated in holding or selling any illegal books, the Neighborhood Committee confirmed that the shop window displays had been acceptable, and the Workers' Committee indicated that the bookstore had satisfactory hiring practices, though indeed there were no employees other than Barbara and Peter. In the evening, he collated the statements for paid taxes and bills, organized the list of books bought and sold throughout the year, indicated the typical customer profile, and included the necessary proof of his and Barbara's acceptable racial credentials and their approved marriage certificate.

When he had completed all the paperwork and bound the documents into a thick file, he hand-delivered them to the appropriate office with the appropriate, hefty fee and received a receipt. Once that was done, he happened to find an unmarked envelope stuffed with cash on the floor, laid it on the counter, and departed, trusting the clerks to find the rightful home for the money. Now, it was simply a matter of waiting. The license was important to the shop—it allowed nearly any type of customer to come and go without suspicion, and that was important to their work, but besides that, it was profitable as well. English books were somewhat difficult to find, almost always being located in the less salubrious districts of the city, and the shop managed a good trade amongst the middle-class English of their mixed suburb, as they timidly rediscovered their own culture.

New Year's Eve was celebrated in typical British fashion with everyone getting stinking drunk. Added to that were fireworks and every armed German shooting off his gun into the air. Early in the morning, the drunken revelers wandered back from the Central Square, or, as the locals called it, Trafalgar Square, singing their out-of-tune love songs in a mixture of obscene English and broken German.

Peter opened the door to Barbara and Mark as they stumbled in close to four in the morning and, taking pity on them, let them have the bed while he made a space for himself on the floor of the living room by putting the coffee table on the armchair. The next morning, after a peaceful night's sleep, he sat in relative comfort in the living room and took a unique pleasure in hearing one then the other of them stumble time and again to the toilet to empty their stomach. It felt good to be the healthiest one around!

Barbara tottered in some hours later and looked blearily at him. "What are you looking so cheerful about?" she asked with a surly scowl.

"Got permission last night to go home," he answered happily. "I leave in a week."

Barbara's face fell. She glanced back with a guilty expression toward the bedroom, then asked in Polish in a whisper, "You're leaving me?"

"It's only temporary," he answered gently. "Zosia will be giving birth soon. With luck, I'll get there before it happens."

"And then?"

He sighed. "Then I have to come back. That's the deal."

Barbara looked relieved, but said, "I'm sorry. I know you want to stay there."

"Oh, well, there's no point staying where you're not wanted. That's what my mother used to say." He laughed and added, "Just before she sent me off to that German school!"

Barbara forced a little laugh as well, then groaning and grabbing at her head, she rushed off toward the toilet.

40

"**O**H, WHAT THE HELL IS IT NOW?" the Führer demanded into the phone.

Stefi uncurled herself from his body and sat up on her knees. As she heard his tense answers, she began to massage his neck, pressing her head close to his in a gesture of affection, which quite coincidentally meant she could overhear both sides of the telephone conversation.

Schindler spoke angrily on the other end of the phone. The Führer listened, nodding his head in agreement. Stefi moved closer to him so that her bare breasts were pressed against the naked skin of his back. He arched his back in pleasure. "Look, look, I can't deal with this now. Haven't you any decency, Günter? What's wrong with you, calling me at home? Call me tomorrow, in the morning. I'll think about it and give you an answer then."

There was an angry diatribe. Stefi leaned forward and kissed the Führer along his neck; moving up to his ear, she inserted her tongue such that he gasped his surprise. "Oh, it's nothing!" he assured his listener. "Look, I said tomorrow. Got that? I told the secretary to pass on only emergency calls. Did you say this was an emergency? It isn't you know!" There was more muttering and the Führer added, "Yes, I know, but I'm busy. Go away!" He slammed the phone down on the receiver, then turning to the servant, who had stood impassively silent in the corner the entire time, he barked, "Go tell them no calls. Not even these so-called 'emergencies'!"

After the servant had left the bedroom, the Führer turned to Stefi. "Now where were we, *Schatz?*"

Stefi grabbed his hand and laid it on her breast. "Here," she breathed. As he tightened his hold on her, she asked, "Was that Günter bothering you again?"

"Yes, yes. He wants me to have your father investigated. Something about his poking his nose into affairs in England. I don't know exactly."

"Investigated? Oh, no! You can't do that!" she exclaimed, pulling away enough that he lost his hold on her.

"Huh? Don't worry! Your father's perfectly clean. If it will shut Günter up, why not?"

"Because he'll manufacture evidence against my father! Don't you know? Günter thinks my dad is having an affair with his wife!"

"Is he?"

"Rudi! I don't know! But does it matter to one as important as you? Are you going to involve yourself in Günter's petty vindictiveness?" Stefi asked pleadingly.

The Führer rolled onto his back and sighed expressively. "I don't know. I guess not."

Stefi leaned across him to kiss his chest. She worked her way downward, saying, "You're the Sun God king! I knew you would never involve yourself in such trivial mortal affairs. Um, what's this?" She stopped kissing and let her tongue begin exploring.

"Oh, you devilish little girl!" the Führer exclaimed excitedly.

"No, no!" Stefi admonished, reaching over to the side table for the riding crop. "I do believe you are the naughty little schoolboy!"

The Führer giggled excitedly. "Do you want to watch some of my tapes? Huh?"

Stefi shook her head. "No, I think you need some discipline right now! Your schoolmistress is very disappointed in you!" She swung the riding crop lightly at his chest.

"Ow!" he yelped. "Oh, you're right! But you know what?" he asked, suddenly quite serious. He grabbed her jaw and turned her face toward him. "I have a surprise for you. I'm going to show you just how tough I am!" He pressed a kiss onto her lips. "I'm going to go to war for you, my little goddess!"

41

*I*T WAS SO INCREDIBLY PEACEFUL. White on black, crowned by somber green. A bird took fright, its wings beating an urgent message into the stark solitude, and a plume of snow drifted down from the branch and spread into a crystalline shower over his head. His steps were muffled, and the approaching dusk cast an ethereal light that caused his steamy breath to glow. His long wool coat dusted along the snow as he stepped through a lightly packed region. His feet sank to the top of his tall leather boots, and he mentally congratulated himself on his foresight in having carted them all the way to London and back. Peter took another step and sank into the welcoming embrace of the snow-shrouded woods of his home.

At the large pine by the bend in the creek, he turned off his direct path and headed to the location of Joanna's memorial. He could not see the stone buried beneath the snow, but he knew it was there, and he knelt at the site and sent his love into the unknown, hoping she would hear him. He already keenly felt her absence, the lack of a snowball greeting, the haunting void where her laughter should have been, the sweaty wool of his scarf where her arms should have been hugging his neck. By the time he looked up, the last of the sunlight had disappeared, and he walked the rest of the distance in the dark.

"Welcome back, sir," the guard at the entrance said with a smile.

"Thank you," he replied, and entered the bunker. Zosia was nowhere in sight, but then she would not know the exact time of his return so there was no reason to expect her to wait at the entrance. He made his way to their apartment, greeting a few people along the way, thinking about her. He imagined what she would look like so near to her due date. He thought about the way he would hug her, and how he would tell her he loved her and was sorry he had not said so the day he had left. He would kiss her hands and her hair, and then, tenderly, he would kiss her lips. He would hold her and tell her how happy he was to be home, and then they would talk and touch and get to know each other again. He smiled as he walked through the corridors, his smile broadening into a grin as he reached the door of his home.

At the door he hesitated. Should he knock? It was his own apartment, but it would be polite not to just barge in and scare her. He glanced down at the boxes of tomato plants and herbs he had placed along the hallway; they looked well cared for and recently harvested. Probably Marysia. Actually, it was against the rules to block the hallways in any way, but he had constructed the boxes so that they were narrow and pressed against the walls and nobody had complained. The bunker had its own hothouses, but with his little indoor garden, using the perennially shining lights of the hallway, he was guaranteed a nonrationed supply of fresh vegetables and herbs. And the air was a bit fresher, too. He smiled and tapped on the door lightly; there was no response so he knocked a bit louder, waited a moment, and then turned the handle. The door was unlocked and he pushed it open, but it stuck halfway. He peered around the corner to see what the problem was and spotted a bunch of clothes lying in a heap on the floor.

Stepping into the room, he turned on the light and looked around. The place was a mess. Clothes and books and dirty dishes were everywhere. "Zosia?" he called out gently, but there was no answer. He made his way to the bedroom and peered in, but she was not there either.

He stood for a moment wondering what he should do, whether he should go looking for her. Then he looked up and noticed that the shelf of books he had left had been emptied and replaced with her stuff. He looked around again at the incredible mess wondering what it all meant, then sighing, he cleared a place for himself on the sofa and sat down. His right leg hurt from the long climb through the snow, and he leaned forward to massage the muscles.

"Dad?"

"What, honey?" he asked, looking up to confront the dim emptiness around him. He thought he heard a noise by one of the piles, like that of a little girl hiding, preparing to jump out and surprise him, but he knew nothing was there. He sat back and brought his hand up to brush away the tears from his eyes, and he scanned the room again, looking for something, not knowing what.

The bitter loneliness of the empty flat made him feel nervous, and he wished fervently that Zosia would return quickly. There was, though, no telling how long she would be away, no note, nothing. He got up and checked the kitchen cupboards, but they were essentially empty. He looked into the refrigerator and recoiled at the fuzzy green objects inside. He looked back in the cupboard; there was some barley in a jar he recognized from when he had left, a can of beans, some tinned herring, and a few bits of garlic shriveled in the corner. He turned to the cabinet and found the vodka, poured himself a stiff drink, walked over to the mirror, and tapped his glass against it. "Welcome home," he toasted, and downed the vodka in several gulps.

He took off his coat and cleared a space on one of the hooks by the door to hang it up. Then he removed his boots and went into the bedroom with his bag to unpack and change clothes. He had not brought much with him since he had left a reasonable amount of clothing behind, but when he looked in the closet, he found the space had been usurped. Exasperated, he buried his head in his hands and tried to remember where Zosia had stored Adam's stuff when she had brought it out for him. Some locker several levels down: it would take ages to find everything, if that's where it was.

On an impulse he went and checked Joanna's wardrobe. Everything was as she had left it the day they had gone into town. He stood stock-still staring sightlessly at the neat piles. Just like Anna's clothes, neatly stacked in her little cupboard, even after her death. He touched the cloth, stroking the fabric as if it were still cloaking Joanna's skin. Reluctantly he withdrew his hand, and then, as if dropping the blade on a guillotine, he shut the door.

He turned to Zosia's jewelry box and opened it. He knew what he would see: nestled there in the box was the necklace he had bought her, and beside it was the gold ring he had placed on her finger not even a year ago. In the back of his throat, spreading down his arms, he felt an old, familiar pain. His fingers ached with the sensation he knew so well. He did not try to stop the pain he felt coursing through his body; he had learned long ago how useless that was. He had learned to accept it as an almost daily fact of life. It was only a deep and abiding sense of being alone. Nothing more.

He showered and put back on the clothes he had worn up the mountain although they were still damp with sweat. He thought for a moment of visiting Marysia, or one of his friends, and getting something to eat, but then opted instead for the herrings, beans, and a lone tomato that he found on the vines. As he chewed his food, his mind strayed to the heaping quantities of meat that the Americans had served. Heaping quantities of everything, in fact. The volume of meat that he was expected to consume was particularly unappealing, and quite ironically the dinner conversation often turned around weight-loss programs as each person had shoveled more onto his or her plate. He laughed at the images as he carefully ran his finger around the sharp edge of the tin so he could collect the last of the oil clinging to the metal.

After eating, he cleaned some of the mess, stacking things into the corners so he could clear a path for walking. Then he sat and waited. After a while he decided to nap and finally fell asleep. It was late by the time Zosia returned. She came in yawning and squeaked her surprise when he sat up to greet her. She looked awkwardly large and carried herself uncomfortably, but still she was achingly beautiful to him.

"Oh my God, you scared me!" she gasped.

"But you knew I was coming back today."

She smacked her forehead. "Forgot!"

"Why were you out so late?" he asked without thinking. "You should be resting."

"Don't start telling me what to do!" she snapped angrily as she maneuvered herself through the room.

Stunned by her response, he almost snapped back at her, but managed to say, "Sorry. I didn't mean it that way. I was just getting worried."

She sighed. "Look, I'm tired, can we talk about this in the morning?"

"Talk about what?"

"Whatever . . ." She turned toward the bedroom.

"Zosiu."

"What?" she responded tiredly.

"Do I get a hello?"

"What? Oh, hello. Sorry about the mess, I kept thinking you were coming back tomorrow," she said between yawns.

"No problem," he lied.

"Did you get something to eat?"

"Yeah."

"Great. Good night, then. I'm exhausted." She yawned again. "Oh, I don't know if anyone told you, we're on alert. Make sure you carry your weapon whenever you're outside and follow strict procedure."

"Why?"

She turned back toward the bedroom. "Nothing special. Good night."

"Good night," he replied quietly as she disappeared into the bedroom. A moment later he called out, "Zosia?"

"What?"

"Do you want me . . . should I stay on the couch?"

"Wherever you're comfortable," she called out in reply. "Good night."

The next morning he cornered her long enough to find out where all his stuff had been stored, and then she was off to do whatever it was she spent the day doing. He tapped his fingers a bit, wondering at his penchant for setting himself useless, thankless tasks; then giving in to his inclinations, he spent the day cleaning their apartment and restocking their pantry. By seven in the evening he was exhausted but finished. There was still no sign of Zosia so he poured himself a cup of tea, picked up a volume of the cryptanalysis books that Alex had managed to send him, and had just begun to read when the door opened and Zosia came in.

He stood to greet her and was surprised to see Tadek follow her into the flat. Peter looked questioningly at her, but she was too busy looking around. She then turned to Tadek and said, "See! I told you it would be clean!" She turned back toward Peter and asked, "Did you cook anything for dinner?" as she tossed her files onto the coffee table and sat down heavily.

"No. I only just finished cleaning this place."

"But you were reading!"

"I said I only just finished. I haven't thought of preparing anything yet," he explained with exaggerated patience. He glanced meaningfully from her to Tadek and back again, but he could think of no clear way of expressing his feelings.

She nodded her understanding. "We can wait."

We? he mouthed, but Zosia did not notice as she was busy motioning Tadek into the room.

Tadek looked somewhat hesitant. "You didn't know I was coming?" he asked Peter.

Peter shook his head. "No, we haven't spoken about anything yet."

Tadek threw Zosia a rather annoyed glance and said, "I think we should do this some other time."

"No, don't go! I'm sure Peter will throw together something nice. Won't you?" she asked, turning her attention from one to the other. "Use the meat ration."

"We only got two pieces of rabbit for the entire week," Peter protested.

"I know. This rationing! Still, I'm sure you can make something nice. Come on, Tadek, pour us a drink, just water for me, okay? Then come and sit down!"

Tadek shrugged, moved past Peter into the kitchen, and began pouring drinks for the three of them.

Peter stood still, contemplating her, considering his options. He had wanted to be helpful, that was the stated reason for his return. He looked at the puffiness of her face, the bloated feet and hands. That must have been why she had removed her ring. She looked tired and there was a light sheen of sweat on her face even though it was quite cool in the room. And both she and Tadek had been working all day. Was it so unreasonable to make a meal for the three of them?

She interrupted his thoughts to ask, "So, any news?"

"At least one thing. I have a way of getting through the bad nights without drinking."

"Oh, that is good news. What do you do?" she asked, accepting the glass Tadek handed her.

"I write letters to you," he answered while walking to his satchel to pull out the stack of letters to show her.

"Goodness!" she exclaimed as if alarmed. "I'll never have time to read all that! You don't want me to read it all, do you?"

"No." He shook his head. "No, I didn't figure you would. I just wanted to show them to you."

"Vodka?" Tadek interrupted to ask. Peter nodded.

"Wasn't it dangerous carrying them with you?" Zosia asked as she struggled to get her shoes off.

Peter walked over and knelt down and removed them for her. "I didn't think so."

"Ah," she sighed happily, "thanks."

He went over to the cabinet, opened a drawer, and placed the stack of papers in it. "I made a space for them here. Don't throw them out. Please?"

"Oh, I'd never do that," she assured him, wiggling her toes, sounding relieved.

Tadek handed Peter a glass and he sipped the vodka, wondering if Zosia would remember her promise long enough to keep it. "And I found three diaries my mother wrote," he offered as his other major bit of news.

"Uh-huh." She picked up one of her papers. "This is the document that I think Katerina was referring to," she said to Tadek. "What she didn't tell you . . ." Zosia looked up at Peter. "What did you say?"

"I located some diaries my mother wrote."

"Oh! Goodness! How did you do that?" she said, finding the appropriate response like a coin under a sofa cushion.

"They were hidden in our old flat," he explained without feeling. "It was being torn down."

"Oh." She turned her attention to the papers. She paged through them as if trying to find something.

"I'm putting them in this drawer as well. They're very important to me. Don't throw them away."

"Sure. Here it is." She waved the document in Tadek's direction.

"Did you hear me?" Peter pressed.

"Yes, of course, don't throw them away. Of course I won't," she dutifully parroted. "Well, are you going to make dinner? I'm famished."

"Of course," he sighed, and went over to the kitchen. He boiled some beets and potatoes, fried some onions, and set aside some sour cream to make a borscht. Then as that cooked, he chopped up the rabbit, cooked it on the stovetop to speed things up, added some onions, potatoes, and carrots to try to give the pathetic bits of meat some substance, mixed up a wine sauce, threw that in, and tossed the concoction into the oven, rather indifferent to how it might taste. The entire time he cooked, Tadek and Zosia conversed about their day's work. They debated the merits of an appeal that had been filed by a district, requesting to have their taxation reorganized in recognition that they had not produced anything that autumn. The German authorities had already seized their seed corn for the spring, and they were facing possible starvation over the winter.

Tadek argued that the region had already been terribly hard hit by the recent upheavals and they should not be taxed, but Zosia countered that the Underground had to extort its fair share in order to avoid setting a terrible precedent.

"Why not collect the taxes," Peter suggested, "then give them a grant to see them through the winter. You could make the grant contingent upon their being discreet."

Zosia and Tadek both looked up at him in alarm. "Peter, I'm sorry," Zosia said. "You're not cleared for this. I didn't realize you were listening in!"

Listening in? This was exactly the sort of thing they had always talked about! How many times had he read and analyzed reports for her? How many times had he suggested solutions that she had later claimed as her own? Angry words leapt to his lips, but he glanced across the room at Tadek and let them die away unspoken. Listening in, she had said. In his own home. "I'm not," he finally assured her, and turned his back to finish the soup. "Could one of you set the table?"

As they ate the borscht, Peter told them about his time in London and what the city was like now. The conversation flowed smoothly, and though he had not planned to have a guest that evening, it was still quite enjoyable. After the soup, he got up to pull the casserole out of the oven and distribute it onto three plates. Zosia and Tadek began discussing Council business again, but as Peter returned to the table with the plates, Tadek gave Zosia a meaningful look.

"Oh, yes," she agreed, "we should discuss this later." She turned to Peter and smiled. "Maybe you could go for a walk or visit someone after dinner?"

Without answering, Peter set a plate in front of her, then the other in front of

Tadek. Zosia raised her eyebrows, waiting for an answer. He set his own plate in the center of the table. "I'll go now. There's really not enough food for three in any case, and I've been eating well recently. Go ahead and split my portion." He went to the door to pick up his boots, then sat down and began to pull them on.

"Peter! Don't go now, I said *after* dinner!" Zosia called out.

He ignored her and stood to pull on his coat.

Tadek stood. "Look, I'll go. We'll talk about this later, okay?"

"No, Tadek, don't run off so quickly! Stay a bit. Finish your meal!" Zosia pleaded. "Both of you! Stay!"

Tadek glanced at Peter, who stood silent and unmoving by the door, ready to leave. "I don't think so," Tadek answered.

"You must at least have a drink," she insisted.

"I think you two need to be alone right now," Tadek replied, obviously uneasy.

"Nonsense! Tell him, Peter."

"Nonsense," Peter repeated without inflection.

Zosia glared at him, turned helplessly back toward Tadek. "Please . . . ," she began, but did not know what to say.

"Thanks for the soup, it was delicious, but I really must go." Tadek headed toward the door.

"Tadek!" Zosia followed him to the door pleading, but he was already gone. She turned back toward Peter. "That was so damn rude! What the hell is your problem?"

"Why did you invite Tadek this evening?"

"Did I need your permission?" she asked pointedly.

"No," he answered carefully, "I just wanted to know why tonight, before we've even had a chance to be alone."

"We were in the middle of important discussions. I forgot you were back. But it shouldn't matter, I'm not going to ignore everyone just because you're here."

He stood there looking at her, feeling the same sensation down his right arm that he had felt the night before: the sudden shock of aloneness. Alone with another person, with a body that breathed air and said words but was not really there. Alone with a stranger.

Zosia shook her head at his silence. "I would think that with all your acting ability, you'd be able to act gracious to my guests!"

"I was myself," he answered, his heart aching with an undefinable sadness.

She shook her head. "For Christ's sake, what do you want from me? I have a life, there are important things going on!" she almost cried. "As soon as you're here, you want me to be something I'm not, and you sabotage every aspect of my life that isn't centered on you." She burst into tears. "Everything becomes so impossibly complicated!" she moaned between sobs. "It's you, you're impossible!"

"So I've heard," he replied as he removed his coat.

Later that night, he awoke to find her missing from their bed. By the time he walked into the living room, she was at the door.

"Been to the loo." She belched. "Oh, God, what I'd give for a night without all this indigestion. I'm so tired and my stomach is just churning!"

"Why don't you sleep in tomorrow and not go to work."

"Good idea. We can go for a walk. Would you like that?"

"You know I would."

"Great, it's a date," she said, yawning.

"Zosia?"

"Yeah?"

"I'm sorry about this evening."

She looked at him as if annoyed by his words. She said nothing though, just stared at him. He cocked his head, curious as to why she had not responded. Was he forgiven? Unforgiven? Did she understand her part in it all? He watched with growing hurt as she said nothing, then she shook her head and disappeared wordlessly into the bedroom.

No point in arguing, he thought. They were past that now—there was no point in arguing because there was nothing left to save. She was just biding her time in silence until he was gone again, until she could be rid of him. He stood staring into the gloom for a long time. Eventually she emerged from the bedroom and tugged at his arm. "Come to bed," she whispered. So he did.

42

THE NEXT MORNING he woke late after a good night's sleep. No dreams or nightmares or anything that he could remember. It left him feeling irrationally optimistic, and as he watched Zosia sleeping, he reviewed his interactions with her and decided that he had been somewhat harsh. She was tired, distracted, burdened with weight and water and hormones and expectations. She was not the excitable sort in any case, and if she had not fallen all over him in welcome, perhaps it meant nothing more than that her mind was on other things. It had been unfair of him to be so overly sensitive to her suggestion: business was business, his clearance wasn't as high as hers, and he should have taken that walk and left her to do her job. He had, after all, ostensibly returned to be helpful; he was not a guest, he was her husband and the father of their child.

Even as she slept, he could see the baby kick and squirm beneath her stomach. It looked crowded in there and he wondered if Zosia felt a lack of space and privacy. She was so independent, so self-contained. He mused about what it must feel like for her to be inextricably bound to another being for so long.

Inseparable. For months they were inseparable; if one hiccuped, the other knew about it.

Zosia's eyelids fluttered and she blinked awake. "Hi, there." She smiled at him.

"Hi, beautiful. How are you doing?"

She moaned and stretched and burped noisily. "Well enough. And how are you?"

"I had a dreamless night."

"Great!" She contemplated him as he sat there bent over her. She reached up, touching his unfamiliar dark brown hair, stroking some loose strands off his forehead, letting her hand stray across his face and then down along his back, her fingers skimming lightly over his scars. "Do you ever think of killing them?" she asked as she pulled her hand away.

He tilted his head in surprise at her question. "Not often," he answered at last.

"Why not?"

He shrugged. "That's the way I was programmed."

"You think they programmed you?"

"I know they did."

"But you always insisted—"

"I was wrong."

"But if you didn't even know they did it, how did they manage it?"

"Remember, I was a research project."

"Yes, I know."

"They probed for my weaknesses and went right for them."

"Which weaknesses?"

"Oh, things unique to me," he answered evasively. "They would have done something different to someone else, I guess. There were all those interviews, and I never credited their techniques, but I think they were rather clever—I think they learned exactly where to hit me. It wasn't the physical torture—that was fairly straightforward; it was the direction they pushed me in with that torture, and with the drugs. The words they used, the concepts they forced on me . . ." Worthless, he thought, unwanted, unimportant. Obliged to earn a right to live. He sniffed in amusement at how familiar it all was!

Zosia tilted her head at his sudden silence.

"I didn't even think about it until later, when I read my mother's diaries. I recognized some things about myself, and I realized, they did, too! They set it all up so that I fell right into my own personalized trap. And so, I became their tool."

"Was there any other option?" she asked as a counterpoint to his vague self-condemnation.

"Other than death? No, I guess not, but it's not pleasant to realize one has been so effectively manipulated."

"Was that what you felt with Frau Vogel?"

He turned his head away. "Can't we let that drop?"

"I just wanted to know," she pleaded.

He thought he heard something different in her tone, something less judgmental, so he risked answering, "Yes. She did not have to say one threatening word to me. I thought she had the right, and . . ."

"And?"

"And not only that, I wanted to please her as well." He paused. "You can hate me for that if you want. I certainly do."

She was silent, and he suddenly wished he had not said the last part, but it was too late. Now she knew, and she would always know that whatever else he had felt, buried deep within his instinct for survival had been a desire to please his masters because his life and the conditions of his life had so depended on them.

"How much do you think that still influences you?" she asked suddenly.

"Do you mean, am I a mental case?" he asked wryly. He was wary of giving her any more ammunition for later arguments. He had already supplied her with quite an arsenal.

"Don't be so negative," she chided.

"I'm sorry. It's hard to discuss things like this without even a cup of coffee to start the day."

"Don't duck the question."

"All right. How much does their 'reeducation' still influence me? I don't know. What I do know is, it took a lot of courage for me to speak out in America, more than either you or your father may have realized. I still had that horror of being punished for crossing them and for disobeying."

Zosia nodded in recognition. "Oh, yes, the psychiatrist warned us that it might push you to suicide. I knew that wasn't the case though."

"You knew," he repeated sadly. He hadn't known! How was it she was so sure that she had blithely risked his life?

"I knew the risk you were taking and I appreciated your courage," she praised, oblivious to his unease.

"I didn't escape their blackmail entirely," he admitted, deciding to ignore the issue. "I didn't tell you, but I had some of the worst nights of my life there, and the most awful memories. I won't tell you how many times, in the middle of the night, I held that bottle of sleeping pills you had given me and read the warning label. . . . Yet, I spoke out anyway, and I thought for sure I had finally defeated them, that there was nothing they could hold over me anymore. The trouble is . . ." He hesitated as he realized where his thoughts were leading.

"You've realized that their punishments can be worse than depriving you of your life."

"Yes. I should have known. They've always taken out retaliations on others, on associates, on innocent bystanders, on little . . . I should have known. I just didn't think . . ." His voice broke with the memory. Those little fingers clawing at those massive hands, struggling to get one last gasp of life, those trusting eyes pleading with him as they glazed with pain . . .

He tried to break the memory by looking at Zosia, but she had turned her face away. Deciding that enough was enough, he asked bluntly, "Zosia! What is it? Why can't you even look at me anymore? What have I done?"

"Nothing," she answered unconvincingly, fingering the edge of the down quilt.

"Do you blame me for Joanna's death?"

"Of course not. That would be stupid. It would play right into their hands," she replied mechanically.

"Then what is it?"

"Just a contraction, dear."

"A contraction?" he asked worriedly.

"Don't worry, just a practice one. They come all the time."

"You're not in labor?"

"No, don't worry. It's just that the contractions make me . . . They . . . I get distracted."

He nodded, relieved. Zosia did not blame him, everyone had assured him of that. He had assured himself of that hundreds of times. It was the contraction, that was all. He let Joanna's image slip from his mind and leaned over to kiss Zosia and then went to make some coffee.

Zosia kept her word to skip work, and they went for a long walk in the woods. The going was rough for both of them, and they took their time walking along the more level paths.

"I wanted to go to the waterfall, but I guess we shouldn't," Zosia commented. "It looks so beautiful in the winter."

"Ryszard tried to take me there last winter, but we never got to it," Peter reminisced. "I've only ever seen it in the summer."

"Oh, too bad! It really is quite different. Well, maybe before you go back, you'll get a chance to see it all icy and frozen."

Go back. His heart felt like lead. What had he done that was so unforgivable? Why this exile? To say something, he said, "It seems a favorite with all the kids here."

"Yeah, it's where they learn to smoke. The mist drowns out the fumes."

"Yeah, I know. It used to puzzle me how so many people, despite the rules, were smokers here."

"We find our way around the rules."

"You never took up the habit?"

"No, not really. I learned how, for masquerading purposes, but I never really enjoyed it. When did you start? At ten?"

"Yeah, on and off. Supply was always a problem. My father blamed Erich for the missing cigarettes, and I'd steal from shops sometimes. When Erich went off to the labor camp, I was in a bit of a quandary."

"What'd you do?"

"Stole them from my teachers at school. Over summer break, I ended up nicking some from my dad. Of course, he realized then that I had been doing it all along."

"Did he beat you?" Zosia asked as she picked up a handful of snow and sucked on it.

"Thirsty?"

"Yeah."

"No, he didn't hit me." Peter removed his sunglasses and cleaned them. "He wasn't that sort."

"What then?" Zosia asked, intrigued.

"Nothing really. He just seemed really disappointed that I would steal from him. He made me feel quite ashamed of myself. Up to that point, I had just thought of him as the enemy, and suddenly there he was my father, shaking his head at me, looking resigned, not saying much at all."

They continued their walk, enjoying the silence. Zosia lowered herself carefully to the ground and made a snow angel. Peter tried to pull her to her feet, but instead Zosia pulled him down into the snow next to her. They giggled and then lay there, side by side, for a few moments, staring up into the sky, looking at the black, barren branches of the trees as they traced a pattern of possible paths upward.

"Which one would you take?" she asked.

Somehow, he understood the gist of her question. "That one there." He pointed along a series of branches that led in a loop back home. He doubted she could tell where he was pointing, but it didn't matter. "What about you?"

"Over there." She pointed to the left. "See how the topmost branch touches that cloud?"

"Not from my angle."

"It does from here. I'd just leap off the end onto the cloud and then sprint across the sky and dive into the sun."

He laughed and rolled over to hug her. It wasn't easy but eventually they managed to embrace and kiss. He got onto his knees so he could lean over her and kiss her face and neck and hair and tell her over and over how beautiful she was. She looked up at him with that inimitable grin, her eyes sparkling, her entire face alight with joy. His heart felt as though it would burst with love for her.

As the snow began to melt and soak into their clothes, they decided to climb to their feet; again it was quite a job, and they congratulated each other on their nimbleness when they both managed to get up. They continued their walk, then stopped to eat the lunch they had packed and sip the mulled wine that Peter carried in a thermos. They talked of this and that and nothing at all, and every minute was unalloyed happiness.

As they were walking again, there was a natural break in their conversation and they listened enraptured to the sounds of silence, then suddenly Zosia asked, "What is it you believe?"

"Huh? What do you mean?"

"About God. What do you believe? Are you still an atheist?"

"Oh, I don't know if I would ever say I was an atheist." He wondered what had prompted the discussion.

"Why not?"

"That's a bit too active a denial of God for me. Up until recently, all I could say is I was raised without a religion and never cared to join one or formulate a sturdy belief structure on my own."

"Up until recently?" They had stopped walking and stood side by side on the path.

"Yes, thanks to events, I've thought a lot more about such things recently, and I guess I feel more sure that I believe in something. I'm just not sure what it is."

"How can you believe in it then?"

He shrugged. "Call it a spirit. Or the divine." He ran his hand along the bark of the nearest tree. "Maybe a tree god or some other pagan concept, except that doesn't quite work either. I feel it's more focused than that."

"So you're a theist?"

"I suppose."

"Then why not join an organized religion?"

"Oh, it's all the other crap that goes along with it that stops me. It's all so irrational and foolish."

"So," she asked quietly, "you think I'm foolish for having a religion?"

He fell silent, wondering if she had deliberately set a trap for him. "That's not what I meant," he answered finally. "I can understand what you do. If I had been raised with a religion, I'd almost certainly adhere to it, at least to the extent that you do. I miss not having a structure for my beliefs, I miss the community of fellow believers. I think I even feel the absence of ritual in my life. There's a great deal of power in . . ."

After a pause Zosia asked, "In what?"

"In belonging. I don't think I've ever really belonged anywhere." He paused and added wistfully, "No matter how hard I've tried." He thought of Joanna and how much she had made him feel as if he belonged, and a smile played across his lips, but he decided not to mention her, returning instead to a theoretical discussion. "Children seem to need that structure, that belonging. As do a lot of adults. It's clear whenever there's a vacuum in the belief structure, a new set of beliefs or mythologies or ideologies is invented to fill the gap, and it's usually these newer structures that are the most zealous and therefore the most dangerous."

"Like National Socialism?"

He nodded. "Among other things, yes."

"So, why not join something established then?"

"Joining as an adult is different from belonging since childhood: it looks like an act of approval of all that the religion entails. When something annoys you, you can shrug your shoulders and say that there's more than dogma involved. It's your tradition, your culture, your family, your past. It's not worth quitting about, or you hope it will change, or even, if you're really committed, you'll work to change it. But for me to join, say, your church, right now, would be a commitment to things I don't believe in."

"Like what?"

"Well, for one, the treatment of women. I should think that would bother you more than me, but you just ignore it."

"Ah, I assume it will change sooner or later."

"But you see my point? If I were to accept membership, I'd be approving that policy. I'd have to lie even as I was being baptized."

"No, you wouldn't. There's nothing in the statements about that! The status of women is traditionally screwed up, but it's not in the creed."

"There's enough in there to cause me to feel uneasy. In fact, most of it doesn't feel right. I find the whole Jesus thing problematic."

There was a long silence, and he was sure he had truly offended her. Finally she said, "Oh." After another long pause she asked, "Why is that?"

"I made the mistake of learning a bit of history. You know, the similar myths in prior religions, the timing of various bits of doctrine . . ." He hesitated as he tried to determine exactly the right words to convey his gut feelings.

Zosia stared off into the woods as if watching something. He looked to see if a deer or some other animal was in the distance, but he could discern nothing special in the direction she was staring. He continued, "I can accept a God who has awarded us free will and therefore cannot interfere; in fact, that's the only way I can believe there is a God, what with all that has happened in the past century. What I can't handle is the idea that there is some merit in suffering or that God in some way would encourage suffering."

"I think the idea of the crucifixion was that God understands our suffering."

"That strikes me as a convenient man-made fiction. It would serve well to tell the oppressed that they are doing something noble and see, look, your God did it as well!"

"Don't you think that's a bit cynical?"

He smiled without humor. "Forgive me if I don't believe in the basic good nature of all humans. I found absolutely no nobility or piety in suffering."

"But you wouldn't have, since you didn't believe."

"That's right, I don't believe. Not in that. But if I had believed, I don't think I would have found comfort in knowing that somebody else suffered. I didn't want anybody else to feel what I felt! And if I were to believe that Christ's suffering was voluntary, well, that I find utterly abhorrent." He shook his head. "It's all too medieval—this preoccupation with suffering and death."

"There's the resurrection."

He shook his head but did not elaborate. Gruesomely murder your own child to prove a point about suffering and acceptance and then resurrect him. What sort of God did that?

There was another long silence. Zosia still did not look away from that distant part of the woods. "It doesn't need to matter," she said at last in a quiet voice.

"But it does matter. I'll accept Jesus as historical, but divine? No! If I ever voiced such disbeliefs, they would be enough for me to be excommunicated."

"Call them *concerns,*" Zosia suggested. "No, not really. I imagine if you did it vociferously, you'd be excommunicated, but you don't need to do that. Nobody will mind what you think about the doctrine; it's not like being a priest or a theologian. Anyway, most of us don't believe in the leadership, so as far as we're concerned, they can't excommunicate anyone."

"If you feel that way, then what's the point? Why do you belong?"

"To belong. To have that structure there when I need it. To feel that I'm part of a community of people who believe in something beyond the mundane. To pass it on to my children. Because of tradition."

He nodded his understanding of her reasons.

"I want you to belong as well!" she implored. "Join us. You don't need to believe anything more than what you do. It's enough for me."

Peter bowed his head as he considered Zosia's request. Was this the reason for his exile? Did she feel he had rejected them by remaining aloof from their traditions? Was her rejection of him simply retaliation for that? His inability to participate in Joanna's requiem mass came to mind. He could have learned the words, could have recited them to comfort himself and to offer Zosia the solace of his company. Yet he had rejected all that, standing aloof and apart anytime they mourned a comrade or celebrated a wedding or baptized a child.

Would it be so difficult to have some water splashed on his forehead and recite a few words of consent? Was a piece of bread and a sip of wine so hard to swallow? If Paris was well worth a mass, wasn't Zosia? If entire kingdoms had converted for political convenience, couldn't he do it for love? Did he really believe deep down that the Vatican would take notice and would gleefully conclude that their patriarchal nonsense had triumphed over rationalism as the last recalcitrant Englishman gave in?

There was, he had to admit, something in the nationalism aspect to it all. It would be easier to consider the Church of England, though it held no greater theological attraction for him. He had all his life associated Catholicism with fanatics. Or the Irish. Same difference, his father would have said. In any case, it was something that he was not. Indeed, he recognized that such a perception was almost certainly propaganda from a bygone era, left over as a knee-jerk prejudice in the populace. If he had told his parents or friends that he had converted to Catholicism, they would have been horrified, yet if he mentioned that he had a Polish or French or Italian Catholic wife, they would have accepted the information with a shrug; just so long as it was not an Irish Catholic, or even worse, an English Catholic!

So, it was not so much a religion that Zosia was asking him to accept, rather, she was asking him to give up a lifetime perception of his place in the world with respect to that religion.

"Why are you asking this of me now?" he asked. "I understood before our marriage that you respected my beliefs, or lack thereof."

Zosia looked up at the sky as if searching for answers there. Then she lowered her head and said, "Two reasons. The first is that I was wrong. I thought it wouldn't be important to me, but it is. I want to have something we do together, something that makes us feel like a family. We do so little together. You're not fluent in my language, you won't dance with me when that is one of my passions, you don't go skiing with me—"

"You know the reason for all that," he interrupted bitterly. "I can't help—"

"—you reject my family—"

"They rejected me!" he retorted angrily.

"You don't want to hear me out, do you?" Zosia asked with exaggerated patience.

"I don't need a list of how we don't work well together."

"You think I work too much and am too committed to my cause. In fact"— she raised her voice to preempt another interruption—"I think you think I'm rather a fanatic."

"Oh, Zosiu," Peter moaned, "it's only when you judge me to be a failure. It's just self-defense: I can't live up to your standards! My past can't measure up to your expectations, and I'll never be as good as your ghosts."

She ignored that. In some ways, she seemed determined not to argue. It was as if she were informing a reporter of the difficulties she had with him, but saw no reason to engage herself emotionally in a debate. "The second reason," she stated dryly, "is the child."

"I have no intention of stopping you from raising the baby with your beliefs and traditions."

"How very helpful," she commented sarcastically.

"What do you want from me?"

"I want a father who can participate! Not someone standing smugly off to the side with a look of cynical superiority!"

"I won't do that!"

"You already do. And even if that were to change, your lack of participation will be enough of a statement. Can you imagine your child's important days, his first Holy Communion, say, with him asking you why you don't join in? I can just hear your answer: 'Oh, because I don't believe any of this crap your mother foists on you!' "

"You know I wouldn't say that!"

"I know it would be said without words. I've seen you at all our gatherings, the rationalist superhero! We can all see it on your face: the I'm-not-part-of-this-mumbo-jumbo look!"

"I don't do that! You're seeing things that aren't there." That was not what he thought, so why, he wondered, did she see that in his face? Was it what she wanted to see? Did she want to view him as different and alien? "There are all sorts of religions here. There are other nonbelievers here. I'm not the only one."

"But you are the only father of my child!"

"So, you don't really care what I believe or whether I'm part of your society. All you want is for me to put on a good show for the kids!"

Zosia did not respond. He saw the shadows pass across her face as she decided how to handle him. "I'm sorry," she said rather stiffly. "I really didn't mean that. It must just be the hormones talking. I feel sort of . . ."

"Are you okay?" he asked, though he knew the answer.

"Yes. I guess. Just a bit worn. I'm sorry. All I wanted to do was ask if you'd consider being baptized. For yourself, for me, for our children." She paused, then rather dramatically she added, "For us."

Peter looked down at the snow, disturbed by the tone of Zosia's request. Once again he knew he was disappointing her, once again he knew she was yearning for Adam. She and Adam were like two gingerbread men made from the same dough, with the same cutter, baked side by side in the same oven. With Adam everything had flowed naturally, but with him everything was a struggle.

If only he could say yes to her! Could he do it for love? For his children? Would it be so hard to lie about a few bits of trivial dogma? To lie for the rest of his life in front of his wife and his children? He shook his head. "I can't do it, Zosia," he replied without looking up at her. "I've had to lie too much in my life, I can't do it anymore."

"Have you ever lied on my behalf?" Zosia asked gently.

He looked up at her, appalled by the thought. "No," he swore adamantly, shaking his head. "You know what I'm talking about!"

"Yes, I know. You've lied a lot to survive, you've lived lies just to placate your enemies."

He dropped his head so that she could not see his expression, but she did not need to. "You told Elspeth you loved her, didn't you?"

He nodded.

"Over and over again, am I right?"

He nodded again.

"Was it true?"

"What do you think?" he asked bitterly.

"Was it true?" she insisted like some courtroom prosecutor.

He shook his head, mouthing the word *no*.

"So, you've lied about love. Can't you lie just once for love?"

Peter stared at the snow at his feet and thought for a moment. For Zosia, so she could feel he had accepted them. For himself, so he could feel he belonged. For his children, so they would not have awkward questions raised in their minds before the appropriate time. Sing a few songs, chant a few prayers, recite a creed, belong to a community, accept their values and traditions. "I wish I had been given something so sturdy as a religion when I was a child," he said at last, "and I'm glad you're going to pass on your traditions to our children."

Zosia's face fell as she recognized that a "however" was en route. "But?"

He shook his head. "It shouldn't be this way. Not like this, Zosia. Not like this," he pleaded quietly. "You're the only person I can be myself with. Please don't ask me to be something I'm not. Please."

She remained silent for a moment, then she conceded, "All right. I suppose you're right, it would be for all the wrong reasons."

He found the courage to look up at her then and give her one of those fleeting smiles with which she was so familiar. "Can you forgive me?" he asked quietly.

"Of course. I shouldn't have asked," she assured him, apparently distracted.

As he studied her face set in its hard lines of preoccupation, he wondered if, by his stubbornness, he had condemned himself to a permanent exile from the only place he thought of as home. Paris was well worth a mass. Wasn't Zosia?

43

*T*HEY CONTINUED THEIR WALK, sticking to less serious matters and stories about how they had spent their time over the months apart. Peter told Zosia about meeting up with Jenny, but decided not to give any details about his encounter with Barbara. As the sun set, Zosia decided she was too tired to continue, and they rested on a log before heading back to their home. She placed her head on his shoulder and purred like a cat to show how happy and comfortable she felt. He stroked her arm, enjoying the thought that beneath the heavy cloth was her soft skin.

"I'll work more on the language," he said abruptly but quietly, hoping that he could offer something in the way of strengthening their union.

"That would be nice," she murmured.

"And I think my legs have improved enough that I could try learning to dance again. If you could stand my clumsiness."

"You're not clumsy, you're very graceful, and I would love to dance with you."

"And I can come to mass with you, you know. There's no harm in my singing the songs, is there?"

"None at all, and I would like the company."

"You would?"

"Yes, I would." She wrapped her arm around him. He put his arm around her shoulders, and they held each other and watched as the sky turned orange and red and darkness crept across the forest floor.

As they walked back, he sang, "*Wmurowanej piwnicy, tancowali zbójnicy . . .*" *In an underground hideout, danced the mountain outlaws stout . . .* It was a traditional favorite that quite ironically fit them well. Zosia joined him on the refrain, her voice somewhat high and tinny. He stopped and let her continue alone, but she stopped as well.

"I'm sorry," she said chagrined, "did you mind?"

"No! Not at all, I just never heard you sing before."

"Oh, I don't do it much, I'm not very good at it. Though, I was much better than Adam. He couldn't sing a note!"

"Will you finish the song?"

"Only if you accompany me. I really am shy."

"All right." With that he began the tune again and they tromped back through the snow, holding hands and singing as they went. When they finished that song, he began another, and they managed to sing the entire way back, breaking into giggles now and then as they stumbled over or made up phrases for the bits they did not know.

When they arrived back, Zosia was immediately greeted by the entry guard's informing her that several people had been looking for her. As they walked down the hall, they saw Konrad, and he tried to pull Zosia away to confer with him, but she told him to bugger off. He chided her for not telling anyone where they had gone, and she responded breezily that she had forgotten.

"This is important!" Konrad insisted.

"It's always important," Zosia countered. "I'll hear it tomorrow!"

Back in their rooms, they peeled off their clothing and warmed themselves in bed under the feather quilt. They hugged and kissed and caressed, then Zosia decided to nap while Peter prepared a dinner for the two of them. He woke her an hour later to come and eat.

"This is great!" Zosia mumbled around a mouthful of food. "You wouldn't believe the crap they've been serving in the restaurant! Ever since all the supplies tightened up. How did you manage it?"

"Just a bit of creativity," he answered, pleased by the compliment. "Maybe you should learn how to cook a bit."

Surprisingly Zosia agreed. "Mmm, yeah, especially after you've gone back."

He bit his lip at that, but she didn't notice. She shoveled in another bite and continued, "Marysia hasn't been as helpful as last time."

"I haven't even seen her yet; she never seems to be around. What's she up to?"

"Oh, she's gotten busy since she took over some of Katerina's duties. Katerina has been feeling ill and I think she's winding down. Marysia's taking up the slack, so she never has time anymore." Zosia swallowed and added, "God, I've really missed you. This is great!"

"I do my best to be useful," he replied with a touch of irony.

"And you are!" she agreed enthusiastically, then exclaimed suddenly, "Oh!"

"What is it?" he asked worriedly.

"Just a contraction. It's nothing."

"Are you sure?"

"Yeah, they're just for practice. The real ones are quite different. God, though, my stomach feels harder than a rock!"

He stepped over to her and felt her abdomen. She was right, it felt rock solid. Then suddenly it eased and it felt like flesh again. He could feel their baby underneath, moving—always moving. With a look that asked for and received her permission, he explored her further, feeling the way her body accommodated its occupant, the miraculous swell of milk in her breasts, the way her nipples had magically changed in preparation for nursing. He perceived the months of changes he had missed during his absence and marveled at it all. He suggested she relocate to the couch while he cleaned up and made some tea. When he finished, he joined her and they drank their tea and then Zosia curled up against him and napped while he read a bit.

Late in the evening, she awoke. He poured her another cup of tea and poured himself a drink. "Is it all right for you to have one?" he asked, unsure of how important abstinence was at this stage.

"Don't know. But in any case, I have so much indigestion, I'll pass." She burped as if to prove her point. She giggled at the noise. "I really am quite a mess, aren't I?"

"My lovely, lovely little mess." He sat down next to her and kissed her. She seemed to enjoy the kiss, and he repeated it, working along her face and neck and the soft skin just over her breasts.

"Oh, I really did miss you," she moaned softly.

"Enough to let me stay?"

It was not what she had expected. "I'm, it's, well, you can't just abandon your position there," she answered rather too quickly.

"I see," he replied coldly, pulling away from her and reaching for his glass.

"Oh, don't be like that!" she moaned.

"Like what?" he asked testily.

"I said I missed you, isn't that enough?"

"What? As an offering? You're a lousy liar, Zosia."

"Don't call me a liar!"

"If you missed me, prove it! Get me reassigned back here."

"That's not my prerogative. It's out of my hands."

"Like hell it is!" He stood up to face her. "Look, you said it was dangerous for me here—maybe it was, but now I doubt they're even actively looking for me anymore. You said that I would need to get over what was done—well, I have, and I've done it without burdening you, unless you someday can be bothered to read what I wrote. You said you needed time without me; well, you've had it. You said you thought I was unhappy here—well, now you know my preferences. So, what's the excuse now?"

"They're not excuses."

"You really set it up, didn't you? Nice and convenient. You even set me up with Barbara!"

"She volunteered. There was no reason not to send her."

"You knew she'd try to detach me from you."

"I thought she might," Zosia agreed reluctantly.

"And you thought I'd go with her and conveniently get out of your life and take all the blame for a breakup that you stage-managed."

"No, I didn't think that."

He sputtered his derision.

"Have you had sex with her?" Zosia asked rather casually.

"Do you care?"

"Just curious."

"Not really. She was intimate with me. It took me a while to put a stop to it."

"But you did stop her?"

"Eventually."

"Did she take it well?"

"Rejection? No."

"Is she all right now?"

He sighed. "I think so. She's picked up an English boyfriend."

"Isn't that dangerous?"

He shrugged. "Assimilation is, at least officially, encouraged."

"What about adultery?"

"I suppose it'll give the next-door neighbors something to gossip about. She'd get thrown out of the N.S. Frauenschaften—if she belonged."

"No denunciations?"

"I can't see why anyone would bother. Remember, it's a crime to denounce a German without due cause. And what would they say, anyway? Pretty young wife cheating on husband? As if that's news?"

"But I thought the Germans in London maintained a higher standard of behavior."

He sputtered. "They maintain a higher level of hypocrisy! The only thing they're not allowed to do is be obvious in their depravity."

"But she is being obvious! It's an unnecessary risk. You should rein her in!"

"And how do you propose I do that? Chain her to the furniture?" Peter laughed grimly. "Now, at least, I know what all my commanding officers felt like when I acted like an impetuous fool."

"Me, too," Zosia agreed, resigned. "I hope she likes him and it's not just to spite you."

"So do I," he said, disappointed that Zosia's interest was only for Barbara's welfare. Zosia really didn't care about him or what he did. "They seem to get on together. He's like I was; you know, unattached due to his Underground connections. They both seem so young, though."

"We grow up fast here. Grow fast, die fast."

"I still think she's just reacting to circumstances. Rushing things. Why did you put her in such a position? You knew."

"I knew, but I didn't put her in it. She volunteered and she's an adult. I could hardly have objected on personal grounds; I don't have the right to make that sort of decision for her."

"But you do for me?"

"The Council wants you there. You need to go back," Zosia stated dryly.

"Why? What's the excuse this time?"

"They're not excuses."

"They sure as hell are. You know I'm way overqualified for that assignment. I'm sick of being pushed around. You either get me reassigned back here, or we're finished." He had not meant to give an ultimatum and he realized too late that he had. Once the words were said though, he felt obliged to stand by them, and that, he knew, was unfortunate, because she would not be blackmailed.

Zosia said nothing; her expression was pained. Finally she said, "I'm tired, I'm going to bed. I don't feel well, and I'd appreciate it if you slept out here so I can have the extra space."

"I'll do better than that," he replied bitterly, and pulling on his boots and grabbing his coat, he stalked out.

He walked a bit in the moonlight, looked at the stars, breathed the fresh air. Did he really want to come back? London was home. With an effort he could reestablish contacts there, make friends, and fit back in. He shook his head. It could never work like that. The meetings Jenny had set up for him had gone well enough as meetings, but he had felt no connection to the people he talked to. They had different experiences, different expectations; they lived in a different world. The people he cared about there were gone, and he could never be as free there as he was here. He could never walk without papers, without fear that his numbers would be discovered. He would be bound by curfews and restrictions, by police searches and patrols. He could never wander in the moonlight among pines and wildflowers; he would have to live a public life, surrounded by police who had his photo in their files, always looking over his shoulder. Even if he got an English identity, he could never truly melt back into the crowd.

He thought for a moment of going to America, but aside from the practical difficulties of travel and getting permission to enter the country as a permanent resident, his family and his friends were here. His son or daughter would grow up in these woods, there were people who welcomed him back, there were people he was glad to see. He belonged here. He had been misled by Zosia's behavior into thinking he did not belong, into thinking he had to defend himself against their rejection. It was she who had rejected him, and once that was clear, once that was made public, then he could establish his life among them independently. He could make their mountain fastness his home.

He thought about the ultimatum he had accidentally issued. Zosia had not answered him, she had put him off. She had not even tried to reason with him, to reassure him that even if he was not reassigned immediately, he would be back and welcomed back soon. He was tired of being pushed around at her behest. It was as much his fault as hers—it had been too easy to leave it to her to argue on his behalf, to arrange everything for him. He had been her project ever since he had arrived, partly out of necessity, partly out of inertia. He had come to her a mess of physical and mental injuries, and she, in her kindness and grief, had helped him, and he, in his gratitude, had fallen in love. Perhaps that was inevitable. But it was foolish to have married her before he had found himself. And it was foolish for her to have married so soon after Adam's death. It had all been a mistake.

He shook his head in sad recognition. It was time to undo their mistakes. Maybe later they could start again, when she no longer wanted him to be Adam, when he had something he could call his own. He turned and headed back toward the bunker and made his way to Marysia's. It was late and Marysia looked at him dubiously when he knocked on the door.

"Did you just get back?" she asked, yawning.

"No, I've been here since Thursday night. Didn't you know?"

"No. Zosia was unclear on the date. Why didn't you visit?"

"Didn't she even mention I was back?" he pressed, rather annoyed.

"No. What's up?"

"Where's Olek?"

"Guard duty."

"Good. Can we talk?"

Marysia nodded. "I missed you," she said, hugging and kissing him.

"I missed you, too," he replied, touched by her warmth.

"I assume you'll want some vodka?"

"Just exactly how," he began without preamble, "does one get one of these things annulled?"

Marysia's eyes widened; something in his tone warned her he was not joking.

"I've had enough, Marysia. I want out."

Marysia shook her head. "No, no, no—it's not that easy, Peter."

"Well, what do I have to do?"

"If you don't take these things seriously, you shouldn't have made the commitment in the first place."

"No morality lectures. We made a mistake, now how do we undo it?"

"All right, all right," she soothed. "First off, the child makes an annulment nearly impossible. You could, of course, file for a civil divorce, and for you that would be enough since you don't believe in anything anyway, but what's all this talk for?"

"I've had enough."

"Peter, this doesn't sound like you at all."

"Oh, it's me all right. I've been fucking used all my life and I'm fed up with it!"

"I don't understand. What's happened? You don't give up—that's not like you."

"Yeah, maybe I don't. And what fucking good has it done me? Huh?" he barked at her. "Tell me, what good has it done me? Maybe I've finally learned to get out while I still have something worth saving!"

"What about the child?"

"She wants to keep me away—she's going to argue for my staying in London forever. She can do it. She has all the rights, all the power. If by getting a divorce, I can prove she won't have to live with me, maybe she'll withdraw her objections to my being here. My hope is then I can convince the Council to reassign me back here and maybe get partial custody of the child—or at least visitation rights."

Marysia shook her head as if to indicate that she knew that would be unlikely, but she didn't comment on the technical details. Instead she asked in a conciliatory voice, "It's not that bad, is it? Zosia's just going through a bad patch. Joanna's death has made her unsteady. She's been terribly depressed. First Adam, then Joanna. Give her a chance."

"God damn it, I've given her chances! She doesn't want me around, and I refuse to beg. I'm fed up with begging. All I am is useful to her—that's all I am to her. Well, I've had enough of being used! Do you know . . ." He gritted his teeth as if controlling the torrent of words. "Do you know that I have worked every fucking day of my life since I was thirteen? Do you know that I have taken orders from somebody all my life? Do you know how much I have to show for it? Do you? Nothing! Not one goddamn thing! For a fucking lifetime of work! Do you know what it was like in America surrounded by people—younger than me!—with their families and all their things and their houses and cars and, and I have absolutely nothing to my name! God damn it, what am I going to live on?" He paused long enough to take a deep breath, tried to regain the original thread of his thoughts, and then continued his tirade. "She wants me gone, so poof!—the Council decides I need to leave! I'm not consulted, I have no rights; the apartment is hers, the kid is hers, where I'm posted is her decision."

"We thought you would want to go. We thought you were unhappy here."

"You didn't once think of asking *me!*"

"But you seemed so unsatisfied. And you both seemed to need time away from each other."

"I didn't! It was Zosia who wanted time away from me. That's all that mattered to you."

"No, really, we thought it was for the best."

"For the best? To throw me out of the only place in the world I might call home?"

"You didn't act like it was your home. After all, *you* were the one who called yourself a prisoner."

"So all of a sudden, all the concerns about my trustworthiness vanish and you all feel happy sending me off to London. Just like that, just because she demanded it."

"She didn't demand it. It was Katerina who pushed the idea," Marysia interjected, but he wasn't listening.

"I've worked too long and too hard to just be shunted around at someone else's discretion. I'm tired of being owned, I want my freedom, I want my life back!"

"Peter, it's not like that! This isn't like you. I know you, you don't just give up. Why are you giving up now?"

"It's not giving up. I've just had enough, and for the first time in my life, I have the right to walk away when I've had enough. For the very first time I'm not somebody's prisoner. And I'll be damned if I'm going to act like I'm hers just to preserve this farce of a marriage."

Marysia looked at him but did not say anything.

"And don't say 'I told you so'!" he almost yelled.

"That wasn't what I was thinking."

"Then what?"

"I was wondering why, if you were tired of taking orders, you didn't walk out of the Underground before your arrest. Nobody forced you to stay then, did they?"

He sighed as if obliged to consider his words more carefully. "I don't know. I knew a lot, they had a lot of effort invested in me; I don't know if they would have let me go that easily. In any case, I had nowhere to go."

"And where will you go now?"

"Presumably, my divorcing Zosia won't force me out of your organization? Or will it?"

"No, I'm sorry, I didn't mean to imply your position here was dependent on her." Marysia furrowed her brow.

He caught her look of doubt. "You don't know, do you?"

She shook her head. "No, I'm afraid I don't. You might be viewed as a liability if you are thought to be unstable."

"So blind loyalty to Zosia—no matter how she treats me—is the only way I can show stability?"

"No, don't deliberately misinterpret. It's a serious question and I'm trying to be honest with you. For Christ's sake, don't be difficult!"

"Difficult? Me? You can't even tell me if my divorcing Zosia would cause me to be a persona non grata here—and I know what that implies given what I know about you all—and you tell me *I'm* being difficult?"

"Well . . ."

"You're saying I could be shot!"

"I'm sure it wouldn't come to that."

"Then what? Tell me, Marysia, what would it come to?"

"The question has never been considered. But, Peter, before we embark on hypotheticals, can we please discuss this divorce idea of yours? Please—let's not argue about things that may not even happen."

Peter felt terribly disconcerted. He had not considered these possible consequences of asking for a divorce. Unstable, irrational, embittered: those labels could be deadly.

Marysia saw his look of dismay. She stroked his face with the back of her hand. His skin was still cold from the bitter night air. "It's not that bad. We're all interdependent. We all take orders from someone or some cause. None of us could survive without the others. Even in a free land, even in America, they must work jobs and pay bills and feed their children. No one is free. Not really. I know you've had no tangible rewards, I know you feel perpetually indebted to someone else for your life, but we all need each other. We depend on the guards outside to keep us safe, we depend on the sacrifices of those who planted our deterrents to keep us alive, we depend on hope of the future to give us a reason to live. None of us here has anything, Peter, none of us has anything to show for all we've done. Not gratitude, not even surety that we're doing the right thing. It could all be in vain. We could be destroyed in an hour and it would all be for nothing. You're one of us—homeless, dispossessed, dependent on those around you. Don't let a chimerical bid for freedom destroy what you have established here. Deal with your problems with Zosia. She's a good woman, she'll want to work it out. Tell me what the problems are and maybe we can sort something out."

"What problems aren't there?" Peter enunciated with exasperation. Did they get along on anything?

Marysia lifted an eyebrow, waited patiently.

"The most obvious thing is that she doesn't want me here. She has this idea that I'll be a drain on her, need her help like I've done in the past, and that she doesn't have the emotional energy to handle it. Not after . . ."

Marysia shook her head. "That's what she tells you."

"Yes!"

"That's not the real problem."

"What is, then?"

Marysia opened her mouth to say something, then stopped. She looked hard into Peter's eyes, then turned away from him and paced the room. When she returned to him, her expression had changed considerably, but he did not know what that meant. "The truth is difficult, Peter. Difficult and complicated and I can't—won't—explain everything, but there is one important fact you should know." She stopped, took a deep breath, then dove in. "She blames you for Joanna's death."

The bold assertion felt like a knife plunged into his flesh. Peter bowed his head. "So do I," he whispered. He had not expected that of Zosia; everyone had assured him that she was too competent, too experienced, to lay the blame on the victim. In fact, in the darkest hours of his nights, when he was trying to talk himself out of his guilt, he had depended on those assertions and used them to calm himself. "At least you don't blame me," he had written in his letters to her, "and if you don't, I shouldn't either."

"But you shouldn't and neither should she. She knows that."

Peter stared grimly at the floor.

"She also blames herself. All along she's been reckless with security on your account. She told me about your jaunt in Berlin, and there was the time she took you to see Ryszard without checking with anybody. She did it because she wanted to prove to you that you were trusted, and she wanted to prove you were trustworthy to everyone else. And it cost her Joanna."

"So why agree to my being sent away?"

Again Marysia paused. She licked her lips nervously. "I guess she didn't want you to see that she blamed you. She knew you'd see through her act, and she was afraid of what that would do to you."

"Rightly so." Without his realizing it, his hand reached impulsively toward the gun he carried inside his coat.

Marysia recognized something in his look. "Peter! Don't!"

He fingered the grip absently, stroked the rough surface as if seeking answers, then pointedly he brought out his hand and showed it palm up to Marysia. Empty. "I won't." Thinking of his unborn child, he added, "It's not even an option."

Marysia sighed her relief. "How about that drink I promised you?"

"No, thanks." He turned toward the door. "I have a lot to think about." It was not fair that Zosia blamed him, but it was understandable. If she thought she could not adequately hide her accusation, and if she felt that it would destroy him, then sending him away was not as cruel as it seemed. And now that he knew, there was no reason anymore for him to go. Was it that simple? Was it love that had motivated her cruel disregard for him? Was it love?

"Stay, Peter," Marysia pleaded.

"I'm not going to do anything stupid, Marysia, you don't have to worry about me."

"It's not that. I just think you should talk more."

"Why? You've told me what I need to know."

"You should discuss these things. Both of you keep too much inside. Let's go and get Zosia and clear the air."

He shook his head. "No, I need to be alone for a bit." He went out the door.

Marysia watched as he headed down the corridor past his own rooms and toward the exit. She stood undecided for a few minutes, then drawing her robe around herself, she went and knocked on Zosia's door.

"Come in." Zosia's soft voice sounded expectant. When she saw Marysia, she added, "Oh, it's you."

"We need to talk." Not even considering the possibility that Zosia would disagree, Marysia poured herself a drink and sat down next to her.

Peter spent about two hours walking around outside, trying to think. If what Marysia had said was true, then at least some of Zosia's behavior was explicable. But that wasn't everything. What about the fighting? The constant misunderstandings? The cold disregard she seemed to show him? Was it all his fault?

He shivered. He had not dressed adequately and the night was bitterly cold. Finally, near midnight, he decided it was stupidity to stay away like some runaway child. He had to face Zosia and their problems. Marysia was right, they needed to talk. He returned to the flat but it was empty. He went over to Marysia's and knocked on the door. She greeted him tiredly.

"Do you know where Zosia is?"

Suddenly Marysia looked worried. "She isn't with you?"

"No. I was outside."

"She said she was going to look for you."

"Oh, shit! I better find her. Did she head outdoors?"

"Yes. She said she had heard enough and she asked me to leave. She started to pull on her winter clothes as I was going out the door. And, Peter . . ."

"What?"

"She dressed heavily. Do likewise."

44

HE PUT ON SOME WARMER CLOTHES, then stopped at the bunker entrance before he headed out. The boy had not mentioned anything to him about Zosia when he had come in, but perhaps he had not made the connection between the two of them, or more likely he had thought it was none of his business to notice their comings and goings.

"Have you seen my wife?" Peter asked. The boy looked blank. "Colonel Król!" Peter amended angrily.

"The colonel took off in that direction." A young woman who was preparing to go out preempted the boy's answer and pointed to the right. "On skis."

"Shit," Peter swore. Zosia was an excellent skier; he would never catch up with her on foot. He, on the other hand, had never bothered to use them, and now they were his only hope of catching up with her. He stepped back inside the entrance, surveyed the row of skis.

"Can you help me?" he asked the young woman. What was her name? He knew it, but it had escaped him.

"Of course, Captain," she responded, indicating that she certainly knew him. She glanced at his boots, estimated his height, and selected a pair of skis off the wall. "Take these. The bindings will work with your boots." She then selected a set of poles. "These look about the right length." She handed them to him.

He stepped out with the equipment and thanked the woman as he pulled the skis on and fastened the bindings. He stood upright and gathered his balance, then began to move in the direction the young woman had indicated. It was not as difficult as he had expected, and within a few dozen meters he began to feel comfortable with his stride. Still, he was new at this and Zosia was expert—the only thing he could do was hope that her pregnancy would slow her down or that she would stop somewhere to rest.

As he put some distance between himself and the entrance, Zosia's tracks became clear in the snow. The terrain became more uneven as well, and he took several tumbles as he learned how to handle the gentle slopes and occasional turns that Zosia's tracks led him along. After the first fall, he glanced backward and was relieved to see he was already out of sight of the sentry at the entrance.

He skied for some time, picking up speed as he gained confidence. After about an hour, there was still no sign of Zosia. The tracks had not been broken— no falls, no rests—and he began to wonder if perhaps he had picked up the wrong trail. Was Zosia already back at the encampment wondering where the hell he had run off to this time? Still he kept going forward; if she was out there, he wanted to make sure he found her and brought her back.

Another twenty minutes or so passed, and then he spotted her in the distance. He was moving faster than she—either she was fatigued or simply awkward with all the ill-distributed extra weight that she carried. He put on a burst of speed and managed to catch up with her in another five minutes.

"Ow! Leave me alone," she greeted him. She made no effort to stop and talk. Clearly if she had gone out simply to locate him, she had changed her mind.

"What are you doing, are you nuts?"

"I said, leave me alone!" she yelled back, and skied steadily forward.

He had to struggle to keep up with her; the burst of speed had tired him and her anger had reinvigorated her. After several more minutes, he tried to speak.

"Zosiu—come back! At least stop. For heaven's sake, woman, let's talk back at home!"

"Talk!" she screamed back. "Why talk with me? Why not blather our troubles to everyone else instead!"

"What do you mean?"

"You went to Marysia and told her you wanted a divorce! You didn't even mention that to me—you just went behind my back and told her!"

Good Lord, what had Marysia been thinking? "I didn't think she'd . . ." He stopped that approach. What point was there in saying he didn't think she'd repeat what he had said. Maybe Marysia had hoped to impress Zosia with the seriousness of the situation. He chased after Zosia for a few more meters, then yelled over the sounds of her panting, "I'm sorry! Please, stop this nonsense and come back home. We can talk there!"

"Divorce!" she moaned.

"I'm sorry!" They were crossing a clearing and could ski side by side. The stars twinkled enticingly in the sky, the night was clear, cold, and dark. He kept pace with her, hoping that she would eventually agree to turn around; his other option would be force, and that, he knew, would be disastrous.

"What the hell were you thinking? Talking about us behind my back!" she accused after a few more minutes. He was making progress: she had not tried to outpace him this time.

"Me? What about you? You rearranged my whole life without consulting me!"

"That was official business!"

"Oh, Zosiu! Don't try that on with me. You've been running my life behind my back all along, and now you're going to go hysterical because I talk to Marysia about my concerns?" he responded furiously.

"Don't call me hysterical! Ow!" she yelped.

"What?"

"I said—"

"No, I meant, what's wrong?"

"You! Going to—"

"Not that! Why did you yelp?"

"Oh, that's just a contraction."

"A contraction! A fake one?"

"No, the real thing. Don't worry, they're not regular. And even when they are—I'll have hours."

"That's on a first birth! God knows how long you'll have once they're regular!"

"I don't care!" She skied forward.

He kept up with her and they argued back and forth. In between their mutual accusations, he pleaded with her to turn around and head back. She replied by increasing her pace and occasionally yelping with another pain.

Finally, when he was convinced she was gasping or otherwise indicating a pain far too frequently, he grew exasperated. Exhausted, he stopped dead and threw his poles down into the snow. "You're an idiot!" he yelled after her as she continued forward. "Come back now!"

Zosia stopped and turned to look at him. She looked livid, and he braced for her scathing reply, but all she did was whimper the Polish version of his name: "Piotr."

"What? What is it?"

"Piotr," she repeated over and over between sobs. He picked up his poles and approached. For once she did not turn and flee.

"Are you okay?" he asked, not knowing what to make of her sobbing or that she had called his name as if he were not there, as if she could not find him.

Looking as if she had only just begun to comprehend what she had done, she moaned, "It's too late. They've been coming more frequently. I'll never get back."

He glanced at his watch. Three in the morning. Had they really been skiing for three hours?

Zosia shook her head. "I'm exhausted, I'll never make it back." She continued to whimper and sob in a way that terrified him. He had never heard her sob like that, had never heard her express quite so much fear. She was so brave, so resolute, so rational! And now she was staring at him with wide, fear-crazed eyes. It was as if some animal spirit were possessing her.

"We've got to get you back!" He glanced around desperately. "We've got to get some help from a patrol!"

"There won't be anyone nearby," Zosia explained, her rational control reasserting itself. "We're out of the central sector. They're thin on the ground here and I imagine most have gone up to the front anyway."

"Front?"

Zosia groaned and doubled over.

"We've got to get you to some shelter." Could he possibly carry her, on skis, that sort of distance? It did not seem likely. Walking would be impossible, he would sink too deep into the snow even without her weight.

"We have to go forward," Zosia announced.

"Ahead? We have to get you to shelter!"

"The cabin is ahead."

"Which cabin?"

"The one we used on our honeymoon."

Ahead? They would be alone, without any supplies, and he had no knowledge about childbirth. What if something went wrong? As Zosia again bent forward in pain, his nascent urge to chide her for her stupidity evaporated. She was right, they would never make it all the way back. "Okay, ahead," he agreed.

Zosia straightened up, but she continued to cling to him. They turned in the direction they had been heading and set off. He wanted to try to help her along, but it was essentially impossible, so instead he let her lead the way, following and offering useless encouragement as they went.

They passed through a light stand of trees and across another small clearing. There was a downhill slope, a small stream, and then a rise that gave Zosia particular trouble. A few meters up the rise, the trees began again, and Zosia indicated that the cabin was in a tiny clearing through the trees. Peter marveled at her sense of direction and knowledge of the terrain—he would never have found the place and could not, even now, recognize this approach to it.

Once they had clambered to the top of the rise, Zosia turned to say something before she disappeared into the dark woods, but she was preempted by an ominous series of whistling noises. They both threw themselves down into the snow and covered their heads as the distant sky behind them lit up with the impact.

"Oh my God!" Peter whispered. The bombs were quite distant—probably at their borders, but the noise had not ceased with the first barrage. In between the aerial assaults they could hear the sound of distant gunfire.

"Oh my God," Zosia repeated. Peter clambered up the short distance to her. He helped her to her feet and they moved several yards until they were under the trees. There they stopped and looked backward to watch the assault upon the partisan encampments on their borders.

"I guess he finally decided that inaction against us is politically more risky than our threats of retaliations," Zosia commented. "We knew this was coming."

"It has happened before, hasn't it?" Maybe if they reiterated previous successes, then they might encourage success this time as well. It was just superstition—his answer to not being able to pray.

"Ahhh!" Zosia pressed herself into him. After a moment, she released her hold and replied, "Yes, frequently at first. We even lost the whole area in 1954. They had to evacuate over the mountains and scatter into the woods and towns. Lost a lot of good people then and it took all of 1955 to retake it. Since then we've moved underground, expanded the bunker, relocated some critical establishments, and never lost complete control. The last big attack was 1970. After that we established the protocols."

"Do you think they have a chance of taking the area?"

"I don't know. I guess it depends on what they decide to use and how much priority they're giving this operation. From what Ryszard's been saying, any action that isn't immediately successful will be politically impossible to sustain. Let's hope he's right and we can hold out long enough to get them to pull back. And I hope someone in Berlin has the sense to avoid going nuclear. If they blanket us with nuclear weapons, Peter, not only are we lost, but we *will* retaliate and . . ." She groaned again.

He held her as the pain buffeted her body. He did not even resent that he had been privy to none of the information she had just mentioned, but it did explain why everyone had been so tense.

"Ow! *Psia krew*," she swore. "My water broke!"

"How far is the cabin?"

"Just through the trees. About five minutes," she replied through gritted teeth.

"I'll just carry you." He bent down to remove his skis.

"No, no, I can make it. Come on." To prove her point, Zosia began skiing toward the cabin.

45

THE CABIN APPEARED THROUGH THE TREES, cold, dark, and empty. Zosia rested at the edge of the clearing while Peter went inside to check that it was unoccupied and safe. Once he had quickly inspected it, he skied back to Zosia and escorted her into their shelter.

It was dark and frigid; dawn was hours away. He found a candle and lit that, then helped Zosia to lie down on the straw mattress. She was breathing hard, barely cognizant of her surroundings. He covered her with a blanket and stroked her forehead as she gasped again in agony. He felt so helpless as he watched her suffer.

Once the pain had abated, he turned away to inspect the cabin and see what supplies they had, but Zosia cried out for him not to leave her.

"I'm right here. I just need to see what we have and make a fire."

"No!" Zosia exclaimed. "No, don't leave me!"

He sat on the edge of the bed and held her. Another contraction racked her body. He spoke soothingly to her as she gasped and clutched at him. When that one had passed, he said, "Zosiu, I must make a fire—it's freezing in here."

"No! They'll see us!" Zosia sounded near panic, not at all like herself.

"No, they won't. They're far away. We've got to use this chance to get this place warm. Maybe later we'll have to do without smoke—we've got to get this place warmed up!"

She was still gasping "No" as he gently detached her hands from his arm and went over to the fireplace. Thank God some wood was there. He stacked the kindling and logs hurriedly, assuring Zosia as she cried out to him that he would be at her side in just a moment. A few scraps of newspaper were stacked to the side, and he lit a page and ignited the kindling.

Just as the fire caught, he remembered the damper and reached up above the smoldering flames and into the chimney to open it. A rush of cold air met him and the fire leapt into life. A fireplace. How romantic. That's what he had thought a year ago. Now, all he could think was, too bad it's not a woodstove or a kerosene heater. Damn, it would be a cold few hours.

He removed his coat, set his gun and knife on the table, and threw his coat over Zosia. She was writhing again, twisting from side to side as if trying to escape her body. He scanned around, found another blanket, and brought that out as well, setting it at the base of the bed. There was no point putting it on her—she had already thrown off the other covers.

"Let's get you ready." He helped her to stand so that he could remove her coat and weapons and help her undress. He thought to put her gun and knife and stiletto on the table with his gun, but she insisted that they remain in the bed with her. He grimaced at the risk, but did not argue. They might well have to fight for their lives, and if she felt more secure with a pistol next to her as she gave birth, then so be it. He tucked the weapons into the bed and returned to peeling off the layers of sweaty clothing she wore.

When they had removed all the clothing that would be in the way, she was left with her long flannel shirt, an insulated cotton undershirt—both long enough to cover her thighs—and a pair of wool leggings and heavy wool socks, both soaked with sweat and amniotic fluid.

"Shall I put your boots back on?" he asked. They would be warmer, but it seemed they might also be in the way.

"I'll do without." She had sat back down on the edge of the bed, but decided she did not want to lie down for the moment. Another pain brought her to her feet, and she began to pace like a caged animal. He wrapped his arm around her and they paced together up and down, back and forth across the small room of the cabin. Every time she felt a contraction, she doubled up in agony and he supported her, fearing she might drop to the floor if he did not hold her up. As he held her, he comforted her, talked to her, and in between his words he scanned desperately for food, weapons, and fuel.

"Do you know if there's a rifle in here?" he asked her during a break in her pain. "A hidden cache of weapons?"

The break did not look particularly painless, and Zosia grimaced as she shook her head. "No, probably not. We don't have enough weapons to keep any in reserve. It's assumed that whoever takes refuge here—during a storm say—has been patrolling and is armed. There should be the basics for two to three days for two or three people. Maybe less now with all the shortages."

Without a rifle, they could hardly hope to defend their place against attack. Of course, with a rifle, all that would happen was that their deaths would take a few minutes longer. Peter tried to filter out the distant sounds of battle as he walked Zosia around and around the room. She clung to him as though he were her last contact with reality; she moaned and gasped and panted, and in between she whispered intense words to him. Words she had never said before, words she would probably never say again. "I love you," she murmured over and over into his ear, "I love you with all my heart."

"I love you, too," he replied again and again.

"I want you to stay here by my side," she whispered intensely.

For how long, he thought bitterly.

"Please don't go back to London," she pleaded as though it were something he had chosen. "I need you, please stay here with me."

"I'll stay," he replied, then to give her the out that she would inevitably need, he added, "As long as you want me to."

"Ow, ow, ow, ow, ow, ow! I think it's about time!"

He walked her over to the bed and helped her crawl in. He put the blankets over her top half, leaving her lower half exposed. Zosia grasped convulsively at the edge of the cloth and panted with the effort of controlling her pain.

"What should I do?" he asked.

"See if you can't find something to wash your hands and me with. I don't want an infection."

There was the snow—cold but probably clean. Still it was not likely to be very effective. He opened the cupboards and located a bottle of vodka. Thank God! Supplies for three days in a snowstorm—yes, vodka made sense. He rolled up his sleeves, washed his hands, then swabbed between Zosia's legs. "Hope that does it."

She giggled, then gasped a bit. After a moment she found the energy to tell him to look to see how large the opening to her uterus was. Indicating with her thumb and forefinger, she said, "It should be about this big."

Peter looked, probed with his hand. "I think so. I feel something behind— maybe it's the head?"

"Could be." Zosia sounded relieved.

As he helped her into a semi-sitting position and propped her up, she explained what he should look for. "I'm going to start pushing," she gasped around her pain. "If it's the head coming out, we're probably all right. If not, well . . . Ahhh."

After she had recovered herself, Peter felt the shape of the baby in her belly and reiterated that he thought the baby's head was in position. Sighing with relief, Zosia told him to check to see if the umbilical cord was out of the way and not wrapped around the baby's neck. "I think the head will slide out. Guide it out and then I'll pause and shove the rest out," she panted. "Tell me to stop if the cord is in the way, or if anything isn't going right. You might need to twist the shoulders a bit to guide them through."

He nodded, checking with his hands that all was going well. It did seem to be the head of the baby that he could see, and the color was good enough for him to suspect it was not being strangled.

Zosia seemed to lapse into confusion, so as he saw another pain overtake her, he commanded, "Push!" She did, and slowly the crown of a little head emerged. They worked for a while in this manner, and then with a great heave Zosia struggled to get the entire head out. It didn't work—the baby was adamantly stuck, the wrinkled pink skin of its head slowly turning blue.

Like a large, purple walnut, he thought.

They tried about fifteen minutes with Peter trying to gently guide the child out, but it remained stuck.

"Rest a bit," he advised as he whisked away some fecal pellets Zosia had expelled with all her efforts. He washed his hands again and Zosia rested, ignoring the urge to push on the next contraction. She raised herself up a bit to look down at the stuck head, then lay back and rested through another contraction. Peter went around to her and, lifting her up a bit farther, waited for the next wave. Her muscles tightened, the contraction shook her, and he ordered her to bear down. "Do it, this time!"

She did and, with an earth-shattering heave, expelled the child onto the mattress.

They both stared at the little thing lying like a rag doll on the blood-spattered mattress. "Shouldn't someone pick it up?" Zosia asked, her voice suddenly steady, her pain immediately relieved.

"Oh, God, yes!" Gently dropping Zosia back down, Peter went around to the child. "I thought you were just going to push out the head," he said stupidly.

"So did I." She smiled at the baby lying sprawled between her legs. Two legs, two arms, healthy pink beginning to replace the blue. Hands and feet looked normal and healthy. Sex organs red and swollen. It was a girl!

Tenderly Peter lifted the little bundle into his arms, remaining bent over Zosia's legs because of the length of cord that still tied the baby to her. He looked down at his daughter, gasping with the realization of what he held. The infant snatched at the air with tiny little sobs that developed into a hearty cry as he held her.

He cleaned a bit of mucus away from the baby's nose with his fingers and stroked some fluid out of her mouth. He wiped her face with a soft cloth, but it was insufficient to remove all the muck. He wanted to clean her face, but the vodka worried him. Would it be too rough? Without deciding anything, he instinctively bowed his head over her and, after kissing the tiny face, licked away the detritus that covered her face.

Zosia watched and nodded her approval. He finished cleaning the child's face, laid the baby gently on Zosia's abdomen, as far up as the cord would allow, then he turned to tend the fire as Zosia stroked the child's head. After pitching a log onto the fire, he returned to cut the cord. "Is it all right to do it now?" he asked. Still the sounds of fighting marred the morning silence.

"I think so," Zosia replied, desperate to hold her daughter.

There still seemed to be blood pulsing through the cord and Peter hesitated. Maybe they should wait? Then, because the baby could not reach her mother's breast, he grabbed a bit of the cord, twisted it to stop the blood, and sliced it with his knife. He held the ends for a moment, then picked up his daughter and handed her to Zosia to hold.

Zosia held her, crooned to her, sang her a little song as Peter fetched a towel to wrap the child. After a while, Zosia handed him the baby as she began to feel further contractions. It took a few minutes to deliver the placenta, then she took the baby back and, opening her shirts, tried to nurse it as he cleaned up what he could and then wrapped Zosia and the baby with blankets and his coat.

Once everything had been cleaned and the fire tended, he pulled a chair over to the bedside and sat down. He had not realized how exhausted he was. "Has she taken any milk?" he asked.

Zosia shook her head. "But that's not unusual."

He nodded. "Can I hold her a bit?"

Zosia handed the bundle to him. He beheld her as if she were pure magic. Their daughter, their little girl, the product of their love, their commitment to the future. That last thought made the fighting in the distance sound all too close. Was it closer? Did they have a future? He thought of Joanna as he held his daughter and wondered, why such madness?

The child slept obliviously in his arms, and after a long, long while he handed her back to Zosia and went to prepare breakfast.

Zosia held her daughter pressed against her, every now and then trying to convince her to take a nipple into her mouth. She was not interested. She sighed and squirmed and sobbed occasionally, but she did not try to feed. Zosia let her mind wander as she held the precious bundle. She felt tears streaming down her face as she contemplated their situation. They were farther from the northern border of their territory—the direction the attack had seemed to take, but they had moved closer to the eastern frontier. The terrain was more difficult in that direction and the boundary fluctuated more frequently due to the inability of either side to establish a firm hold. Was it possible that troops might come in from that direction? They could be overrun before the bunker, they could have troops marching through before the fighting even died down to the north.

She knew what would happen if they were discovered. Death was certain for her and Peter. Alone she might be able to construct an elaborate alibi, but since she was in his company, they would not believe it for even a minute. Only the child stood some tiny chance of survival. If someone took a liking to her, decided she could be adopted, then she might survive the journey down the mountains. She would grow up then, never knowing her parents, never knowing her heritage, never knowing what had been done to her.

Zosia started contemplating their options. She knew she should ask Peter to leave, but how could she say that to him? It would tear him apart. She examined another option: they could try keeping a lookout and defending the cabin against any troops that passed through. But with only the two of them and in her weakened state? And what sort of defense could they mount with two pistols and a couple of knives? Sit quietly and slaughter one or two soldiers as they stumbled in the door? Then what? Wait for bombardment or for the barrage of high-powered rifle shots through the walls or be burned to death? It was hopeless.

They could not flee either. There was nowhere to go except into the fighting. If the cabin was discovered, they could not hide in the woods, not even for a short while. Their tracks would be obvious. Maybe they could set off on their skis deeper into the mountains. But to where? Any other cabin would offer the same dangers; anything else would condemn them to freezing to death.

Maybe they should try to reach the bunker. Three or four hours on skis? A baby wrapped in their arms, slowly freezing, a trail of blood from between her legs. Did she have the energy to do that? And what would they find? Enemy soldiers? A smoldering ruin? Heavy fighting?

Peter asked her if she wanted breakfast. She shook her head. "I'm going to nap," she lied, and closed her eyes so she wouldn't have to talk to him, wouldn't have to tell him he should leave. She thought about her previous delivery, Joanna's birth. It had been so different then! The thought made her happier and she pursued the memories into dreams. Everything was so secure! Adam was home, had made a point of not going anywhere for weeks beforehand. Her mother and father were still living in the bunker, Marysia was nearby. The day had been beautiful, she and Adam had gone for a walk in the woods along a stream. He had stopped and pointed to the stream and suggested she remember it when her time came and she was in pain. She remembered staring at the brook, letting the rippling waters and the sparkling sunshine sink deep into her memory. Adam's arm was around her shoulders, his voice gently speaking to her.

Then there had been the delivery. He had held her throughout, had walked her up and down the narrow corridors. Her mother had held her hand and given her water to drink. Adam had whispered encouragement. Marysia, experienced Marysia, had assisted the birth. Zosia knew there was medical help nearby, but with her family and husband there, she felt sure it would all go well. Afterward she had looked at Joanna's tiny face and had hugged her tightly to her breast. Adam looked on with absolute adoration. He reached forward toward the child and stroked her head. "She's beautiful, isn't she?" she heard him say.

"Oh, Adam, she certainly is!" Her own voice woke her up and she opened her eyes in alarm. Something wasn't right. Adam stared down at her with a look of dismay, as though he was hurt but not at all surprised.

"Oh, God!" Zosia muttered as she realized her mistake.

Peter turned away and walked over to the fireplace. He stood with his back to her, staring into the flames for a long time. He watched as they leapt upward into the chimney. Too high probably, they were wasting fuel. The fire crackled, the warmth was reassuring. He wanted to throw his thoughts into the flames, to let them burn and rise through the chimney and be scattered in the wind. He wanted desperately to feel something other than what he did. He wanted to feel nothing, but instead he felt hurt and disappointed and trapped.

"Peter . . . ," Zosia said softly.

"We should put this thing out. Save fuel. It's warm enough for a while and we don't want them to see the smoke," he preempted her.

"Peter . . . ," she called again gently.

"I *don't* want to hear it," he snarled. Speaking quickly before she could say anything, he added in a calmer tone, "I should leave. You'll be safer without me here. If we're discovered, I'll be the death of us all. Without me, maybe you could convince them to take you prisoner or tell them you're German and concoct some story. If necessary, we can ransom you or spring you and the baby later."

"If you think that's best."

He turned to look at her. "Yes, I think it's best. There's enough food and fuel here for a few days. I don't know what you'll want to do about the fire; I'd advise keeping it going. If there are troops passing through, they'll probably notice our trail here whether or not there's smoke from the chimney. Do you think you'll be all right alone?"

She nodded, blinking repeatedly.

"I'll head toward the bunker. I'll tell anyone I find about you."

Tears gathered in the corners of her eyes.

"I'll come back for you both as soon as I can, I promise."

She began to cry.

"I'm sorry, Zosiu. I'm sorry I'm a liability. I'm really sorry." He resisted saying that he was sorry that he was not Adam, as he had once done, long ago. He walked over to the bed, picked up the infant, and held her in his arms. "Goodbye, little one. You're all I have in the world now, and I can't stay to take care of you. I'm sorry, little girl. Don't hate me."

He knew he should not tarry, but he did not want to let go. He held his daughter and quietly sang a little song to her. He held her and looked into the tiny face, trying to memorize its features. He held her and prayed to no one in particular to spare her life. He felt sure he would never see her again, so he pressed her close to him and kissed her forehead and whispered to her, "Remember, no matter what else happens in your life, I loved you—just as you are."

46

THE TWO SOLDIERS APPROACHED with trepidation. Next time they'd know enough to let the sergeant win at poker. God, how could they have been so stupid as to cheat him of all people! It had seemed a good idea at the time, but now as they invaded these mountains as if they were held by someone else, as if they had not been part of the Greater Reich for decades, now it seemed like the dumbest idea of their lives. The sergeant had not been able to prove they were cheating, so instead he was giving them every shit job available. "Check out that cabin," he had said. "Report to me if it's clear."

Clearly someone was living in the little hut. Why didn't they just blast it off the face of the earth? Could be one of ours inside. Could be useful stuff in there. Could be valuable prisoners. Could be the sergeant didn't care if they got their arses shot off. As they approached, each cringed in anticipation of the rifle shot that would end his life then and there, each urged the other to go first. Slowly, stealthily. Sneak up on them. But how across a snow-covered clearing?

They reached the edge of the trees and glanced back at their comrades who were supposed to cover them when the shooting started. Then they looked at each other; each took a deep breath, counted silently, and sprang into action, bounding across the open stretch like terrified rabbits.

Neufeld had his eyes closed, composing his eulogy as the imaginary bullets rained down on him. There was no response from the cabin. Nothing. They reached the door. Without bothering to clamber over the snow to look in the window, they simply kicked the door in and leapt inside, rifles at the ready.

A man, standing by a bedside holding a baby, turned to look at them; a woman, lying in the bed, looked at them as well. They seemed exhausted. Neither made a move toward the pistol that lay in a holster on a table a few feet away. The man could perhaps have leapt for the gun, but his arms were wrapped around the child and he did not attempt to move.

The soldiers held the pair in their sights; one of them motioned to their sergeant to come inside while the other poked around the room. The sergeant walked in and confronted the fugitive pair. What were they doing here? Peasants hiding? Partisans? Refugees en route to somewhere else?

Poor sods. He should shoot them immediately, he thought; it would save them a lot of pain and suffering. If they arrested the pair and the babe—obviously a newborn—then they would have to assign someone to hold them prisoner at the cabin or drag them around the mountain as they advanced. The baby would almost certainly die, the mother might collapse from loss of blood and exhaustion. If they survived their journey into town, the man would be hanged or shot out of hand, she would be sent to a camp, and probably, if she survived the train journey, she would be dead within a matter of days of her arrival.

The sergeant did not guess he was looking at officers of the Underground, wanted criminals; all he saw was a bewildered and exhausted couple who had inexplicably taken refuge in the mountains to have their baby. Poor choice of location, poor timing, poor decision. Perhaps it was the only one they could make. Perhaps it was *Rassenmischung*. Perhaps, out of love, one of them had sacrificed everything for the other. The woman looked pure Aryan: Was she a settler who had gotten herself tragically, illegally pregnant by some *Untermensch*? Had they fled the inevitable retribution of society to try to preserve the baby?

He walked over to the man who stood so silently holding his child. The officer reached for the man's left arm, twisted it around. There was no resistance to his action, the man just adjusted his hold on the child to make sure it remained secure in his arms. As the sergeant had suspected, there were numbers etched into his arm. An escapee. He glanced at the woman's arm. Nothing there. Maybe the woman had been a camp employee, or a daughter of someone associated with a camp. Or perhaps the man had worked in her house. Still the pair remained silent. Were they so terrorized they could not speak?

Then he noticed the man was wearing a wedding ring. The woman was as well. That was rather poignant—they would not have been allowed to marry; she could not legally marry him, and he could not legally marry at all. Yet, they had felt the need to have some pathetic marriage ceremony, probably carried out in hushed tones in front of a plastic statue in some back-garden shed. It was illegal, he told himself, immoral; it would weaken and corrupt their society, dilute the purity of their blood. He told himself what he was supposed to, rehearsed his catechism as he had been taught, but it was useless, for he felt, despite himself, that it was touching, romantic, and rather sad.

The sergeant looked down at the tiny baby. The man followed his glance down, and despite his terrible predicament, a smile flitted across the man's face as he contemplated the bundle of life he held. The sergeant continued to study the baby. Despite all his ideology and training, despite a lifetime of propaganda, he could see no evil in the child. It looked like a baby. Not an abomination, just a little baby. It made a face at him—sort of wrinkled its nose as if in amusement. A tiny baby, new to the world. So new. Like the one his wife had given birth to only two months ago.

The sergeant walked over to the table and removed the gun from its holster, tucking it into his belt; he left the knife where it lay. He then spun on his heel, walked toward the door, and announced to his men, "There's no one here.

Nothing worth taking. Let's move on." They left and pulled the broken door shut behind them.

Peter and Zosia let out their breath simultaneously.

"Was that a deliberately eloquent silence?" Zosia asked.

"No," Peter responded. "I just couldn't think of anything plausible to say."

"Me neither. Did you have a plan?"

"Only a vague hope we might take them hostage and bargain with the ones outside."

"Yeah, I put all my money on my gun here in bed with me, but with three of them and the baby in your hands, I wasn't sure when I'd get a chance."

"Me neither. I'm glad you waited."

"I wonder what he thought," Zosia mused. "I wonder why he let us go."

"Probably thought it would be a messy situation and it was better to ignore it."

"Did you get his name or his serial number off his uniform?"

"Afraid not." Peter had steady nerves, but not that steady!

"Ah, too bad, neither did I. I must be slipping. Getting old," Zosia fretted.

"You just gave birth, darling."

"We could have tracked him down and converted him later."

"You mean blackmail, don't you?" He marveled at her coolness.

"Whatever. If a system is so unjust that a soldier can't spare a baby's life without fear of demotion or imprisonment, then blackmailing him to betray that system is doing him a favor."

"That's pretty convoluted."

"It's a complex world, darling."

"Indeed." He went over to the window to check that they had really left. Their tracks led straight away from the cabin; there seemed no point in following them further. "I guess I should stay awhile."

"Yes, we need to make sure you don't stumble into them. They wouldn't give you a second chance."

"I'm worried about the trail though, it leads straight back to the bunker."

"Most trails do. It's inevitable. We're aware of that and our defenses are appropriately arranged."

"Will I have trouble getting back?"

Zosia fell silent.

"Well?"

"I don't know! I hadn't thought about that. Do you have an armband?"

"Yes." He reached into a deep coat pocket to pull it out. Technically he should wear it anytime he was out, but no one bothered with that under normal circumstances. "Will it be sufficient?"

"Should be."

He examined the cloth, wondering if he could bet his life on it, thinking that it would really stink to be shot by his own side. The thought made him laugh.

"What's so funny?" she asked.

"Oh, just the number of times I've been afraid of being shot by my own side. It's getting quite silly."

"One of life's little hazards, dear. It's nothing new."

"Nothing new," Peter repeated disconsolately.

He stayed several hours in the cabin. He helped Zosia use a bedpan and then buried the bloody urine as well as the afterbirth in the woods. Somebody had told Zosia that the placenta was edible, but neither he nor she knew how to prepare it, and the foodstores looked sufficient, so they decided to discard it. There wasn't much in the way of creature comforts in the cabin—the extras that had been there for their honeymoon had been removed—so he washed the blood out of the towels and cloths they had used and hung them by the fire to dry so that Zosia could use them later. Then he pumped some water and set it by the fire to warm so she would not have to use her muscles too soon. He looked around, tried to plan and do what he could so that she would not have to exert herself, but his efforts seemed inadequate.

He was worried about leaving her alone there. If there were no more incursions, she would do fine over the next several days; already the bleeding had abated and she looked much more energetic. The problem was, what then? If someone did not fetch her within a few days, she would be forced to make her way out on her own. And if no one had come within a few days, it would mean either he had not managed to convey her location to anyone or, even worse, that there was no one left who could come. Then she would be obliged to surrender with the baby and take her chances with the enemy. It was not a comforting prospect.

Still, if he stayed, he was not sure he would be much use. He could get fuel and probably food, but he would consume food as well. He might be able to defend them against the odd straggler, but Zosia was just as capable of shooting an intruder as he was. And if they were forced to surrender, he would only taint them with his presence.

"We could say you owned me," he suggested, trying to design some scenario where it would make sense for him to stay with her.

"What, you mean if we have to surrender?"

"Yeah, you ran off into the woods with an unwanted pregnancy, took me with you to help . . ."

"I hardly look like a teenager in trouble." Zosia laughed, then she added more seriously, "Besides, you don't have a manacle and neither of us have papers."

He grimaced. "Oh, yeah. I guess that'd make me a runaway."

"And that would make me an accomplice. Thanks, but no thanks."

His reason argued for him to go, his instinct pleaded with him to stay and defend his family. "Still . . ."

"Peter, give it up. If you survive the trip down the mountain, those numbers will tell them who you are! We don't want that, not after . . ."

They both fell silent.

He finished pulling some of the supplies down from a high shelf and placing them where they would be more accessible, and Zosia began again trying to get the baby to nurse. She sat in a chair holding the baby up to her breast as a milky fluid seeped out and splattered onto a towel she had placed on her stomach; still the little girl was uninterested.

"Do you think we're deep into enemy territory?" he asked in order to break the silence.

"I haven't a clue. Given those soldiers showing up at our door, I would guess so, but then again, did you notice there's been no fighting around here? Those boys could have marched up to this cabin without encountering anyone. The patrols might have simply missed them, or I imagine they might have gone forward to the front, leaving us essentially undefended. It'd be stupid and against orders, but not surprising. Most of them are just kids."

"What happens to the older ones? The ones who don't move into the bunker?"

"Oh, when they move off patrolling, they often become couriers or handle operations in the towns and villages: sabotage, theft, extortion, information, supplies. You name it. Sooner or later they get caught out. Not many make it to thirty." Zosia stroked the baby's cheek. The infant opened her mouth and Zosia guided her to the nipple. The baby latched on and began sucking.

"Look!" Zosia exclaimed.

Peter watched as the child finally took nourishment. He smiled at the peaceful image of the two of them, fascinated by the bond between mother and child. He walked to the window and looked out at the snow and sunshine. Incongruously beautiful. The noise of battle was still distantly discernible. Local artillery, probably in support of troop movements. It would be singularly ineffective against a guerrilla enemy concealed by the vast forests. No carpet bombing, nothing nuclear. Clearly, though determined to make a statement, they were still afraid of the deterrents, afraid of escalating retaliations. Yet, somebody had felt obliged to be seen to be doing something. Never mind if it was ineffective or costly; they were doing something: hacking at a thorn in their side with a machete. What would it take to make them stop?

"I should get going," he said at last.

"Be careful," Zosia replied from her seat. She was still absorbed in watching the child nurse.

He pulled on his coat, put his knife in its scabbard.

"Do you want my gun?" Zosia asked, looking up at last to contemplate what might be her last view of her husband.

He shook his head. "No, I'd rather you had it, but thanks for offering." He kissed her, kissed his child, and headed for the door. As he reached for the handle, Marysia's words came back to him and he returned to Zosia's side.

"What's up?" she asked. "Somebody outside?"

"No, not that," he answered uneasily. He swallowed as he tried to find the right words to say. He lowered himself to his knees, ostensibly so that he could reach out to the baby more easily, but it was really so that he would not have to look Zosia in the face as he spoke, and perhaps as well because kneeling seemed appropriate.

"I wanted you to know"—his voice quaked—"I want you to know how very sorry I am about Joanna."

"*What?*" Zosia's voice betrayed something close to anger. "Why are you talking about that now?"

"I never said I was sorry. I know deep down you blame me, there is no other realistic response to—"

"I don't blame you!" Zosia snapped angrily.

Peter stroked the baby's cheek and said carefully, "But if you were to blame me, I want you to know I think it's only natural, and I would understand, and we could deal with it together. I *am* sorry, Zosiu, the guilt is tearing me apart, and it would be a relief if you did blame me, because then I'd know you understand what I feel."

He leapt up, kissed her, and added, "I really must go. I love you, I love you both dearly. Take care." He was out the door before she could say a word.

47

*H*IS SKIS MADE A QUIET SHUSHING SOUND as he sped along in the direction of the bunker. The soldiers had been on foot and had marched along the compressed snow of his and Zosia's ski trails. That was a nuisance—he might well catch up with them; yet the alternative of leaving the trail to avoid them was not really possible as he did not know the terrain well enough to find his way back any other way.

He did indeed stumble across the German patrol; their bodies lay on the side of the trail. Three had managed to run some distance, the rest had fallen where they were. Each body had been stripped of its weapons—including Peter's gun—and other useful items including their coats and boots. The sergeant and another had only been injured in the initial ambush and had had to be executed at short range. All of them had been repositioned on their back with their eyes closed and their arms folded across their chest. Someone had taken valuable time to do that. Probably, Peter thought, somebody had said a prayer as well.

He looked at the sergeant and felt a sudden sorrow. He wondered if the sergeant had guessed he himself would so soon be dead when he had spared them their lives. Would that act of impulsive mercy weigh in his favor in the great beyond? Peter scanned the distance to see if he could find their killers, but there was no sign of them. Not two kilometers farther he met up with an AK patrol. They called for him to halt and skied out of the woods to inspect him. They were partisans who were unfamiliar with the bunker, but they knew his name and recognized him as one of their own. Peter noticed that several of them wore German army overcoats, their insignia still intact, blood and bullet holes defacing the wool. He told them about Zosia back in the cabin and asked them to return with him to help her travel to the bunker. The leader among them opined that she was safer where she was for the time being and promised to relay the information. "I'll send someone over to check on her as soon as possible," he promised.

"Can't we get her to the bunker?" Peter insisted. "I just need the help of one or two of you."

"We're not sure it's safe there. If she's in the cabin, she should stay put for now. Don't worry, she'll be all right. Besides," the leader added hesitantly, "we're not cleared for Central. We'd all risk court-martial—you for showing us the location, and us for going where we're not supposed to be."

Peter nodded his acceptance of their logic. Zosia would never tolerate such a breach of security and would under the circumstances refuse to move. He asked about the German positions, and they told him what they knew, wished him luck, and escorted him some of the distance toward the bunker before parting company.

Relieved that someone else knew about Zosia and the baby now, Peter continued toward the bunker along a slope. The trail was level, but the woods rose steeply to his left and dropped to his right. The surge of relief brought with it a matching surge of fatigue. The sleepless hours were beginning to catch up with him, and the brilliant sunshine on the snow was taking its toll on his eyes.

Abruptly he paused in his stride to take a rest—just long enough to close his eyes. A bullet whistled past his face. He immediately overcame his astonishment and leapt down the embankment to his right even as he heard a second shot. He tumbled out of control for a second, then rolled to a stop and clambered to his feet. His left ski had dutifully popped off, but the right was still attached to his boot, and he reached down and released it. He heard someone scrabbling down the other slope and crossing the trail as he scrambled to climb up the embankment under the cover of the trees.

The soldier skidded to a stop at the edge of the trail and pointed his rifle at his victim. Peter's eyes were level with the soldier's boots, and he lunged forward and threw his arms around them, bringing the man toppling down onto him as the rifle went off uselessly into the air. The rifle flew out of the soldier's hands and skidded down the slope out of reach of the two of them as they rolled together in an impassioned embrace of murderous intent.

The two were well matched: the strength of a terrified youth alone in hostile territory, intent on gaining clothes and skis that might see him safely back to the front, against the savage power of a new father determined to see his child again. They fought their battle of unequal goals with ferocity. The soldier freed a hand, pulled out his handgun, managed to point it at his adversary's face. Peter pushed the gun away, aware that he was in danger of losing his hand to it. They both struggled to control the weapon, each one's hand wrestling with the other in a contest of brute strength. Peter used his other hand and removed his knife and stabbed upward into what he hoped was the soldier's chest. The knife plunged into a soft belly. The soldier gasped in pain, realized what had happened, and in a surge of angry strength regained control of the gun. He brought it around to fire, but Peter had removed the knife and plunged it into the soldier's back. The blow sent the soldier forward onto him, and the gun fired harmlessly to the side.

Peter stabbed the soldier again. He could not reach upward with the weight of the soldier's body on top of him, but he managed to hit something crucial. The soldier gasped and choked and ceased to struggle. Still holding the knife, Peter shoved the body off himself, sat up, and spared a moment to catch his breath. The soldier was still alive but critically wounded; he tried to roll away to safety, but he was stuck against a fallen tree. He would freeze or bleed to death if left alone.

Grimacing at his lack of choices, Peter rose to his knees and plunged the knife up and into the boy's chest cavity, into his heart. Gasping for breath, he held the knife there as the body jerked convulsively, as the boy drew his last breath. When the movement stopped, Peter removed the knife. Panting with his exertion, he paused a moment, then checked to be sure the boy was dead. It was the first time he had looked at his enemy's face, and he realized the boy had been one of the two who had stormed into the cabin, a survivor of the massacre Peter had encountered earlier. He wiped away some clotting blood and read the boy's name: Neufeld.

Peter grabbed the pistol from where it had fallen and put it into his holster, then he washed the knife in the snow and stuck it back into its scabbard inside his coat. He moved a few feet away from the body and rested, breathing deeply, trying not to think about what had just happened. He wondered how Zosia was doing, thought of the little girl nuzzling her to get milk, and smiled at the thought. Then his eyes strayed to the wrecked body next to him. Poor sod must have been absolutely mad with terror.

Once Peter had regained his composure, he clambered down the incline and recovered the rifle. He slung it over his shoulder and climbed back up to the body. Keeping with what was apparently a tradition, he removed the soldier's identification and valuables, then arranged the body lying flat and folded the arms across the chest. He pushed the eyelids shut and placed small pebbles on them to keep them closed, then stood to climb back up to his skis, but somehow the ritual seemed incomplete. Groaning at the irrationality of it, but unable to restrain himself, he knelt on one knee by the soldier's body, made the sign of the cross, and said one of the short prayers Joanna had taught him. He finished with another sign of the cross, then stood, muttering to his nonexistent God, "I hope you're satisfied."

48

"**I** HOPE YOU'RE SATISFIED," the Führer sneered as he tapped angrily with his riding crop at the mapboard posted on the wall of his office. "Look at this mess! Just look at it!"

Schindler paused on the threshold, shifting uneasily from one leg to the other; he glanced at the roomful of men, sparing a scowl for Richard, then pulled the door shut behind himself.

"They were prepared, they're fighting back, they're well supplied, and we're taking losses!" the Führer fumed.

Composing himself, Schindler strode across the room to the map, studied it a moment, then pointing at a section, said, "We've pushed forward here and here."

"And lost territory here!" the Führer howled. "You said they'd never see it coming. You said we'd go through them like a hot knife through butter! Well, you were wrong!"

Schindler shrugged. "It's not my section of the country. Ask Traugutt. He's the one who is so knowledgeable about that area." He turned toward Richard. "Why have we allowed these criminals to gain such strength? Hmm? We don't have this sort of trouble in my sectors!"

"No, you just have Englishmen going on television in America," Richard replied snidely.

"I had nothing to do with that!"

"Can't control your own people?" Richard asked. "Maybe it's because you spend your time poking your nose into places where you have no knowledge, no expertise, and no business!"

Schindler turned abruptly away from Richard and said, "*Mein Führer,* the day is still young. We have hardly begun. Give our troops some time. You don't want to be precipitous. You must persist, otherwise you will be perceived as weak! You'll see, we'll send them scurrying like rats! We'll break these terrorists once and for all!"

The Führer stroked his chin. "Yes, yes, perhaps you are right."

"You will make your mark in history!" Schindler insisted. "Finally clearing this largest nest of rats!"

"And how do you think the Führer should publicize this great achievement?" Richard asked pointedly. "The populace is unaware that we have tolerated these isolated enclaves. Should we announce their existence before we trumpet our victory over them?"

Schindler groped for an answer but was saved by a knock at the door. A messenger was admitted to the office and personally handed the Führer a note. After he had left, the Führer looked around the room questioningly. "What's the meaning of this? A weapons laboratory in Breslau has been destroyed! We've been warned that another site in Berlin will go up within the hour!"

The men in the room looked at each other, some confused, some merely silent.

"Well?" the Führer demanded.

Richard lit a cigarette then stated coolly into the silence, "They are retaliations for our actions in the mountains, *mein Führer.* They will not stop until we do."

"Retaliations? Retaliations! We allow this?" Schindler screeched.

"We have no choice," Richard explained. "After our last unsuccessful attempt at an invasion, they claimed to have planted deterrents in our cities and military installations and vowed to use them if we ever again violated their borders. Apparently, they meant what they said."

"Then we'll just nuke them back to the Stone Age!" Schindler suggested. "Teach the bastards a thing or two!"

"No!" Richard barked. "They claim to have nuclear weapons planted in our cities! If you do that, none of us would be safe! Not even you!"

"Where in the world did they get the idea they could do that?" the Führer asked with surreal naïveté.

"They learned it from us." Richard laughed. "Though, since they have never yet struck against an innocent civilian population, I guess they have some way to go before they can compete with us in the terror stakes."

A number of surprised glances were thrown in Richard's direction, and he wished he had not said that last bit. It had been his anger speaking: Stefi, Pawel, and Andrzej were all under direct attack, and he not only felt helpless to defend them, he had to stand here and praise the means and methods of the Reich!

Fortunately, the Führer seemed too preoccupied to have noticed the gist of Richard's remarks. He was studying the map of the territory that had been pinned up on the wall, holding his riding crop behind his back. There was another knock at the door and another messenger was admitted. The Führer read the note. "Frauenfeld! What's the meaning of this?" he barked, turning toward the head of Communications security.

Frauenfeld read the message. "Our communications security has been breached."

"I can read the damn message!" the Führer spat. "What I want to know is why, how, and what do you plan to do about it!"

"*Mein Führer,*" Frauenfeld sighed, "I don't know why, but you can rest assured that there will be a thorough investigation and we will correct any flaws and punish those responsible. In the meanwhile, the corrupt lines will have to be abandoned and some orders to the front will have to be sent by courier."

"Better to send attachés," Schindler suggested. "That way we can be sure to maintain Party control over what the army does." He smiled. "This actually works to our advantage. Sometimes the army tries to get its head in these sorts of situations, better to keep them under a watchful eye as we run them through their paces."

The Führer nodded. "Günter, you stay, I want to discuss this some more. The rest of you, out of here!"

Richard scowled. It was the worst possible outcome. He would have to try to return later and turn the Führer's mind away from whatever nonsense Schindler had planted, but for now there was nothing to be done. For the next few hours at least, the fighting was sure to intensify, and the retaliations would be stepped up accordingly. He collected Stefan in the outer office, and together they made their way out of the Führer's residence.

"You may as well go home," Richard sighed once they were outside. "Try to enjoy the rest of your Sunday. We may be back later this evening, I'm afraid."

Stefan nodded. "Do you need a bodyguard?"

"No, go home now. I'll be careful about the route I take." After advising Stefan to stay away from obvious targets, Richard hailed a taxi and headed home. En route he thought about how he had mishandled the meeting. He should never have let Schindler take control of the Führer's attention! He had made a mistake and let his emotions speak for him, and after that, he had lost the initiative. Unforgivable!

He rapped on the door when he reached his house. Kasia herself opened it. From her expression, he knew instantly that something serious had happened, but he waited until she had closed the door before asking, "What's wrong?"

"It's Andrzej," she sobbed, wrapping her arms around him and burying her head in his coat. "He's dead."

"Andrzej? Dead? How?" he asked, too confused to feel any pain.

"We don't have all the details yet," Lodzia answered from where she stood a few feet away. Kasia continued to sob uncontrollably into his chest. "We're sorry, sir," Lodzia added, speaking for herself and her husband.

"Dead," Ryszard repeated, his mouth twitching. "Dead. Oh, dear God." Gently he pulled Kasia away from him and handed her to Lodzia. "I'm sorry, darling. I've got to go back before it's too late, before Schindler talks him into something even worse." He looked at Lodzia and ordered, "See that Stefi is sent back, whatever it takes. I need her here as soon as possible. I have to get access to him. I have to make him stop this madness. It has got to be brought to a halt!"

49

"**H**ALT!" THE VOICE COMMANDED.

Peter immediately stopped skiing and raised his hands in the air. "Don't shoot," he cried out.

They didn't. In fact, the leader of this patrol knew him personally, and after they had exchanged greetings and news, he was directed to a field camp. "You don't want to go back to the bunker right now," the patrol leader advised. "Konrad's at the field camp, he can bring you up-to-date."

Peter followed their instructions and arrived at the tent about an hour later.

"Oh-ho! Look what the cat dragged in!" Wojciech joked.

"Do you know where Zosia is?" Konrad asked, looking up from a map.

"You're covered in blood!" a young woman standing next to Konrad commented.

Peter explained where Zosia was, what had happened, and briefly recounted his return journey.

"What the hell were you two doing out there in the first place?" Wojciech asked.

Peter did not bother to answer. "We have to get her and the baby out of there."

"Don't worry, they're well inside our lines right now," Konrad assured him. "We'll get someone to fetch them as soon as we can." Turning to the young woman, he ordered, "Get someone to go and tell Marysia that both Peter and Zosia are okay and that she's a grandmother again." Konrad turned toward Peter and added, "Congratulations."

"Thanks. If Zosia is inside our borders, I can go back alone, I just need a sled or a horse, or something."

Konrad shook his head. "No way. We need you here. I'll send one of the kids to help out. She's better off there anyway."

"I promised her I'd return."

"You're not going back there," Wojciech interjected. "There's a battle on if you haven't noticed, and we don't have time for your and Król's theatrics right now."

"She's completely alone and she's just given birth!" Peter replied angrily.

"*That's an order!*" Wojciech snarled.

There was an awkward moment of silence as Peter scanned their faces. Konrad looked uncomfortable, but he made no move to disagree with Wojciech. Realizing there was no point in arguing further, Peter conceded, "All right, what do you want?"

"A number of things," Konrad answered with obvious relief. "I want you to broadcast to the British. We like to inform our allies of what's happening here."

"Fine."

"Here." Wojciech shoved a piece of paper at Peter. "Translate this to English and get Communications to fix you up to broadcast to England. Do one for the Americans as well."

Peter looked at the newsbrief; it was written in Polish. He frowned at the words and Wojciech laughed. "If you can't read it, get someone to translate it into German for you first."

"You're talking real-time broadcasts?" Peter asked.

"Of course," Konrad answered, distracted by a messenger.

"I'm not cleared for Communications," Peter reminded him bitterly.

"Oh." Konrad scribbled something for the messenger and sent him off before continuing, "That's right. Well, that's just an oversight. I'll clear you now."

Peter's look of disdain was wasted as Konrad turned to the young woman and told her to arrange a clearance. "Was there anything else?" Peter asked, preparing to leave.

"Yes!" Konrad motioned to him to wait as he read another message that was brought in. He relayed a command to the messenger, then turned to Wojciech. "Are those documents ready?"

Wojciech handed him a packet and Konrad handed them to Peter. "Work out some way to get these to the Germans."

"What are they?"

"Some maps and orders they'll be needing. We've intercepted their courier and have amended things to suit our purposes, so we want to make sure they get these before dawn."

"Why send me?" Peter asked, scanning the documents.

"Do you always question orders?" Wojciech returned with quick anger.

"No, sir," Peter replied in a tightly controlled voice.

Konrad glanced from one to the other while explaining, "You're the only fluent male speaker of the appropriate age who's available."

You mean expendable, Peter thought, but he did not interrupt.

"We were going to send Pawel, but he's too young. You're much better. Bolek's outside, he'll get you the uniform and explain what you need to do."

"Is the attaché known to them, or did he have any special passwords?" Peter asked.

Wojciech looked at Konrad. Konrad answered slowly, "We hope not."

"You *hope* not?"

"It's important these papers get through," Konrad stated dryly.

A gust of wind whistled through the flap of the tent, and the papers on Konrad's desk danced in the breeze. Peter was going to ask another question, but he had lost Konrad's attention to another messenger; so instead, he waved his hand in an approximation to a salute and turned to leave.

"Halifax! One last thing," Wojciech called out.

"And what would that be, sir?"

Ignoring the sarcastic tone, Wojciech turned to Konrad and waited. Konrad waved the messenger out of the tent and looked up questioningly. "Was there something else?" he asked Wojciech.

"I think his position should be clarified," Wojciech said.

Konrad grimaced. "I'm sure he's well aware . . ." He trailed off.

"Of what?" Peter prompted.

"You carry poison still?" Wojciech asked, then as Peter nodded, he advised, "Don't hesitate to use it."

Konrad hurriedly amended, "You know, if something happens, we can't—"

"I didn't expect that you would," Peter cut him off.

"It's not like that," Konrad insisted. "It's just that, with you, we know they would never—"

"Like I said," Peter reiterated, and left.

"How are your legs?" Bolek asked once he had been informed of Peter's assignment.

"Just fine."

"Good, you'll have to do the journey on foot—they're just on the other side of this pass. Our nearest people are A-seventeen located here." Bolek showed Peter a map. "Are you familiar with the area?"

"Not really. But that's well inside our territory, isn't it?"

"It was. Don't worry, we'll get it back. We're not doing that badly elsewhere." Bolek explained what little they knew about the attaché's destination and mission and then disappeared to get the man's uniform and papers.

While waiting for Bolek to return, Peter rested a few minutes on a log, listening to the news reports that filtered in, trying to determine the level of damage sustained so far and the seriousness of their attacker's intent. He caught the attention of a young lad he knew and asked if there had been any occasion to use their handheld missile launchers.

The lad nodded enthusiastically. "They tried some aerial incursions, but when they found out we were prepared, hah! Those things are great!" He swung his arm in a wide arc and imitated, "Blam, whoosh, boom!"

Basia overheard the discussion and added in passing, "I think they've really cut down on the bombing. I don't think they expected that. Thanks, Captain."

"Huh?" Peter responded, confused, but she was already gone. He rubbed his eyes and considered momentarily the feasibility of curling up in the snow and sleeping, but then Bolek returned to show him the uniform. "They got him in the head, so there are no holes in the uniform, but we had trouble getting his brains off the coat collar. It's still damp, but that's just water. It'll be dry by the time you finish your broadcasts."

Peter fingered the damp material. "How do I get out there without getting shot?"

"We're sending a courier up to A-seventeen. She'll escort you out that far, then they'll assign someone to take you the rest of the way."

"And how do I get back?"

"Ah, well, that is a little more problematic; we obviously can't inform everyone about you, and it is unlikely you'll be able to meet up with exactly the same group that sent you out since either you or they may have to move. If that's the case, make sure you approach where there is no fighting and make sure you wave your armband in the air. It won't be enough to wear it since they won't be looking for it if you're in German uniform, but we do have general orders not to shoot anyone surrendering without first checking them out."

"How reassuring." Peter got up to leave, then stopped. He pulled the blood-spattered personal effects of the soldier from his pocket and asked, "What do I do with these?"

"There's a collection point. Give them to me and I'll see that they're kept safe. Stick in a tag with your name on it if you want to keep any of it."

Peter shook his head: the unclaimed valuables could go into the general fund of supplies. In general, casualties would be buried where they fell and their names and serial numbers would be passed on to the German authorities, but proof of their deaths—their identification tags—would be held for personal delivery to the families. It was a dangerous business since the drop had to be made by hand to be sure it was not intercepted, so it would often take up to a year before the identifications would be sent back; nevertheless, this was the preferred method. It provided a useful counterpoint to the government's usual lies to the families about the circumstances of their loved one's death and presented the Underground with an opportunity to enclose a formal letter expressing their regret and explaining their cause.

Peter remembered the effect it had had on a friend of Frau Reusch's. According to the government, her son had died in a heroic battle against barbaric terrorists; a month later she received a polite and civilized explanation of her son's demise as he had taken part, under orders, in a reprisal involving the slaughter of an entire village. The reprisal had been preempted, their son had regretfully been killed, and his identification was enclosed as proof of his death. The family was assured his body had been treated respectfully and buried if possible, and enclosed in the letter was a ring he had worn that they thought might be an heirloom.

The calm tone of the letter, it's sorrowful explanation of circumstances, its brief and unfanatical exposition of their cause, the inclusion of the valuable ring, all served to convince Frau Reusch's friend overnight that her son had not died fighting murderous thieves in a glorious battle for peace, but had wasted his life in the service of a government that cared almost as little for its own people as it did for those it had conquered. Frau Reusch had confided the tale to Peter in hushed tones, not even daring to mention her friend's name, and Peter had gained some small measure of comfort from it, from the knowledge of a still-active Underground somewhere. But as there were no details to be had, it had remained no more than an incorporeal hope.

He was still thinking about that strange other life as he and Olek worked on translating the newsbrief that Wojciech had handed him. Peter did a fair amount of translating directly to English on his own and had to ask Olek's help on only a few phrases. After Peter finished the translation, the two of them exchanged news as Olek accompanied him to the radio room. Olek asked all about the birth, told him about Andrzej's death, then explained that Stefi had left to be smuggled back to Berlin for some reason. "She only just found out about her brother," he added sorrowfully.

Once Peter had completed the broadcasts, he bid Olek farewell and was already out of the room when Olek called out, "Captain?"

He turned back questioningly.

"Peter," Olek said as if making a brave decision.

"What is it?"

Olek came close and extended his hand. Reflexively Peter grasped it, and Olek wrapped his other hand around their clasped hands. "I know you English are uncomfortable with many of our gestures, so I won't do more than shake your hand." As Olek said that, he tightened his grip as if trying to convey a warm embrace through just his fingers. "Be careful, Peter. It's a dangerous job. I'd really miss you. You've been like a father to me. Please, be careful!"

Peter felt stunned by the intensity of Olek's emotion and only managed to stammer, "I'll do my best," as an obviously embarrassed Olek ducked back into the room.

As Peter changed into the attaché's uniform, he realized that he should have said much more, that he had not told Olek how much his friendship had meant to him, but there was no time to go back. He cursed his tiredness and finished dressing. He found his guide and together they set off toward the front. She took him down a well-trodden path, but as they continued farther and farther out, the path narrowed until there were only a few bootprints in the snow. Eventually even those turned off and he and his guide trod across a windswept clearing that bore no sign of having previously been crossed. Though the weather was wildly different, the lack of a trail brought up an eerie memory of when Marysia had first guided him back to the encampment. Then he had become convinced that she meant to kill him, and with that thought he glanced furtively at his guide.

Peter was startled when he realized the woman had stopped and was reaching for something, then he relaxed as he saw that she was putting on her snowshoes. Snowshoes! Of course! He had not been thinking. Snowshoes would have made a lot of sense, he thought, as he painstakingly lifted his legs time and again out of the snow to take the next arduous step. I'm an idiot, he thought, a tired idiot. I should have slept before leaving the cabin. I should have slept before leaving the camp. I'm an idiot.

Finally, after sunset, they reached their destination and he was handed off to the partisan leader. He had a brief discussion with him and was then handed over to his next guide—a short, skinny teenager with startlingly white skin and curly, jet-black hair. Under the cover of darkness, they left, diving into the woods toward enemy territory. It was arduous going through the snow, and his legs howled with pain as he and his guide clambered up an icy slope. Once they reached the top, he asked his guide to stop and the two of them rested on a log while Peter massaged his right knee, trying to snap the bones back into place.

The boy lit a cigarette. "You want one?"

Peter shook his head. It seemed pointless to say that they were near enemy troops and that the smoke from a cigarette could betray them.

"My father used to have problems walking," the youth volunteered.

"Oh, why's that?" Peter asked, feeling suddenly very old.

"It was his feet. He lost his toes. Fingers too."

"Gestapo?"

"No, no. He was deported to Siberia from Wilno."

"Why?"

The boy shrugged. "I guess they missed him in the first waves."

Peter frowned as he tried to work out what that meant, but before he could ask, the boy continued, "He spent nearly five years in a labor camp out there."

"That sounds rough. Is that where he got frostbite?"

"Not really. He said he was collapsing from hunger and exhaustion, so he decided to slice off some toes so he could get a few days' rest in the camp hospital. When they released him, he said he couldn't face the thought of going back into the mine, so he thought he'd head west and make for the Reich. He'd heard from some of the tradees—"

"The *what?*"

"The prisoners that the Nazis sold to the Soviets for slave labor, or usually 'traded' for raw materials," the boy answered as if it were the most natural thing in the world to sell prisoners. "He'd heard there was a free area in the mountains, so he just leapt onto a passing train and took his chances. That's when his fingers and the rest of his toes froze. He made it to the eastern reaches of these mountains, then hobbled across the border into our territory."

"On his own?" Peter asked in amazement. A brisk wind stirred the barren branches, and the clouds cleared long enough for the half-moon to shine its light on them. A wolf howled in the distance.

"I think he had help. Somebody here found him, they fixed him up, and . . ." The boy shrugged.

"When was this?"

"About twenty-five years ago. He met my mother, they married, and so on."

"How's he doing now?"

"Oh, he's been dead ten years now. One day he just walked off into the woods and shot himself."

"Shot himself," Peter repeated as he struggled to massage away his pain.

"Yeah, guess he had had enough."

"Shot himself," Peter whispered despondently.

"He was a coward," the boy asserted as he ground out his cigarette on the rough wood of the log.

*T*HE BOY LEFT HIM AT THE EDGE of a road a safe distance from his destination, and Peter made his way on foot, alone and deliberately obvious. As he approached the camp, a sentry challenged him and asked the password.

"Haven't a clue," Peter answered. "I was due here yesterday but some idiot shot my motorcycle out from under me. Banged up my legs. Had to hobble here on foot. I'm tired, I'm cold, I'm hungry, and I want to see your commanding officer now!"

It worked better than he had expected, and he was courteously led to the sub-commander's tent.

"Where's the commander?" Peter demanded.

"Sleeping, sir."

"Well, get him up!"

"It's four in the morning, sir!"

"I'm well aware of that!" Peter snapped. "I spent half the night trudging here. Your roads are inadequately patrolled, no one was sent out to find me, and I haven't slept, so I don't expect your commander will want to sleep either!"

His Berlin charm continued to work like magic, and the commander was roused and greeted him sleepily only fifteen minutes later. Peter upbraided him for sloppy security and for not sending out a search team for him.

"But you should have been seen, we checked that road earlier," the commander argued, his breath still heavy with alcohol.

"Obviously you didn't do a very good job. Here!" Peter slammed down the documents he was carrying. "You need these."

The commander sighed, scratched his head, and groaning, opened the packet. "Get Schweig," he told one of his men, then explained to Peter, "This is his department."

Peter and the man called Schweig seated themselves at a side table in the tent and consulted over the contents of the packet while the commander drank coffee and feigned activity at his desk. The sky lightened, the sun rose behind heavy clouds, and slowly the camp came to life.

Being an attaché rather than a courier had made it easier for Peter to bully his way into the camp, but it did leave him with the obvious problem of how he could discreetly leave. It would serve no purpose to stay past the time when the altered plans would be used—and that was scheduled for noon—nor would his cover last much beyond that time; nevertheless, they expected he would stay some days, and he was not sure how to get around that problem. He was just deciding to delay thinking about the logistics of leaving in order to solve the more immediate one of his hunger when he heard a familiar voice talking to the commander. While continuing his dialogue with Schweig, he listened to the urbane speaker to try to place him.

"What about it?" Schweig asked, indicating a point on a map where Peter's finger rested.

"Huh?"

"What about it?"

Peter fell silent again. That voice! Where in the world? "Do you think you could find some coffee for us?" Peter asked Schweig suddenly.

"Sure," Schweig answered agreeably, and left.

Peter remained hunched over the maps, his back to the speaker. The voice sent shudders through him. He listened to the words and realized they were talking about some prisoners.

"We've waited long enough! They must be interrogated," the voice demanded.

"We've already questioned them," the commander insisted wearily.

"You've got nothing out of them," the voice sneered. "Now it's my turn."

The commander sighed and Peter imagined he was scratching his head again. "Look, I know they sent you out here just for this sort of thing, but I don't really want that in my camp. I'm not all that comfortable—"

"Your level of comfort is not the point," the other interrupted in his well-bred and highly educated voice.

A chill of terror ran down Peter's spine. Shocks and burns and beatings. Drug-induced illness, hallucinations, mind games. Humiliation, indoctrination, the rantings of lunatics in power. Brutality and inhumanity too vicious to describe or even remember. And over it all, this little lord of terror lecturing him, convincing him that somehow it was all no more than he deserved. *How dare he!*

Peter leapt to his feet. "If you have prisoners here, they are the province of the RSHA, and I have first access to them and the right to determine their fate."

The speaker turned to face him and Peter confronted his erstwhile torturer. The tall, handsome young man was a little older than when he had overseen Peter's reeducation but was otherwise unchanged. "And who might you be?" the man asked with suave self-assurance.

The commander introduced Peter, explaining his presence, then introduced the officer to Peter as a Herr Lederman. As the two greeted each other, the commander slurped his coffee worriedly, unsure of what to do next.

Lederman spoke first. "I've come from Breslau explicitly to oversee the gathering of information . . ."

Peter was not listening. He stared into the face of his torturer. Though Peter had not seen him often, the man's features were seared into his brain. An unreal fear gripped him, and he felt himself detaching from the scene, rising above it as if floating out of harm's reach. He could not hear the words being said, could hardly see the faces of the others. Blackness hovered at the edges of his perception, his vision narrowing to a tunnel that was focused on that one face, that mouth, those words. His mouth was dry, and he nervously licked his lips, trying to feel the reality of his own body, the lack of chains or walls or even pain. He glanced down at his uniform and took comfort in the quality, the cleanliness, the imposing insignia. His hand strayed mindlessly to his gun, and as he felt the reassuring coldness of the metal, he regained his composure.

". . . haven't come all this way . . . ," Lederman continued lecturing.

"Enough!" Peter snarled with an anger that surprised the others and implied irrefutable authority. "You can have your chance after I'm through with them."

"I don't have time for—"

"Don't worry," Peter said calmly, "I won't take long. Then you can have your flies so you can pluck off their wings, if that's what you need to do to preserve your manhood. Such as it is."

The commander snickered. Lederman sputtered, but then the commander interceded, "It's my camp here and you'll obey my orders. Obviously, our comrade from Berlin has priority."

Schweig returned with the coffee even as Lederman harrumphed angrily and left.

"Who the hell is he?" Peter asked.

"Oh, somebody who's supposed to be an expert in breaking people."

"Hardly seems like something that takes expertise," Schweig commented. "We've got whole countries full of broken people."

The commander shrugged. "I heard he's supposed to be really very good at it, is able to spot fake information a mile off."

"I heard," Schweig interjected, "that he really screwed up with one of his subjects and still hasn't lived it down."

"Oh, how so?"

"Don't know. Just heard that it led to some sort of international embarrassment. God knows how. Must be just talk."

"Must be." Peter smiled, then returned the conversation to the business at hand. "I want to see to those prisoners now. Where are they?"

"Now?"

"Before he does something stupid," Peter explained.

"What about the orders? We're supposed to move soon," Schweig asked.

Peter brushed off his concerns. "Oh, you can handle it. They're self-explanatory." Indeed they were; he had only managed to explain their contents by reading a paragraph ahead as he had spoken to Schweig. "Where are the prisoners?"

The commander told one of the guards to take Peter to their prisoners. He found them, nine in all, sitting outside, huddled together against the cold. Their hands were bound behind them and a single guard kept watch. Peter scanned them but did not recognize anyone. He glanced around at their location and the proximity of other soldiers and decided there was nothing he could do for them at the moment. He thanked the soldier who had led him to the prisoners and made his way back to the commander's tent alone.

At the entrance to the tent, he stopped and debated what he should do next. He had taken an insane and unnecessary risk speaking directly to Lederman, and there was no way he could justify a further confrontation, yet the opportunity his presence in the camp afforded was unparalleled. Peter's mind worked frantically as he plotted one scenario after another trying to work out how he could carry out his mission, free the prisoners, and take some sort of revenge on his erstwhile torturer. Killing him was the most practical but least satisfactory option. Better yet would be to take him prisoner, hold him in the mountains and . . . There was a problem there. He would never be permitted to do what seemed most appropriate. So, keep his prisoner a secret, perhaps with a bit of help from one or two of Zosia's friends. Then what? Four months of torture was the obvious and rather unappealing answer.

Peter was not a torturer. As seductive as the idea of revenge was, there was no way he could do to someone else what had been done to him. It would be too humiliating. He was left with the option of killing the man. Given the circumstances, it would have to be a hasty execution with only the briefest of explanations possible: a swift murder as a ghostly reflection of the fury and hatred that motivated him. Would that suffice?

He sighed. He would have to jeopardize his mission and significantly lower the chances of freeing the nine prisoners in order to carry out an act of vengeance. If he failed, it would cost him and nine other people their lives, and it would ruin the very mission he had come here to fulfill. Even if he succeeded, he risked court-martial if anyone found out. He swore quietly and thought some more, but he could see no way around it: it was the opportunity of a lifetime and he would have to let it slip through his fingers.

He stood there in the dark and the cold, silently seething. Such a petty, banal man. A banal man in a banal uniform with a banal job and a banal name! The sort of man other officers made fun of. A nobody. For some reason Peter did not quite understand, he felt incredibly foolish. His torturer was nothing more than a tedious, insignificant officer, a nonentity who earned the scorn of his comrades. That his life had been in the hands of that nobody! Worse than that, his soul was still ravaged by what he had experienced at that man's hands. He felt humiliated, as if his god, which he had prayed to and offered sacrifices to for generations, had suddenly been shown to be nothing more than a bit of scrap metal dropped off a passing train.

The attaché had a pack of cigarettes, and on an impulse Peter lit one for himself. He looked at the gold lighter he had found in the coat pocket and read the inscription: *To Robert, with love always, Sybille.* Deeper in the pocket Peter found a small building block—the sort of thing a child gives a father as a present. At first it is carried as an indulgence, then a fond memory, and at last as a talisman. He pulled out the attaché's bulging wallet and opened it. A number of photographs were stuffed into it, and Peter leafed through them. He found one of Sybille, a pretty woman, or rather, widow. Children, too; at least five. The photos were of various ages—apparently Robert did not discard old photos even as the child grew. There was Hedwig at three and again at eight and again with her siblings when she was eleven. From the date, he guessed she had just turned thirteen recently. Just looking at her picture, Peter felt sure she would miss her father and would not understand why he had had to die.

He finished the cigarette and turned his thoughts to what he should do next. As he stood there, debating with himself, still trying to find a way to get his hands on his erstwhile torturer, he overheard the commander talking to Schweig, and intrigued, he listened.

". . . fucking sitting ducks, if you ask me," the commander was saying.

"I do wonder, sometimes, what they have on their minds in Berlin," Schweig agreed cautiously.

"All I want is someone to explain to me what the hell we're doing here, fighting some bandits over a bunch of useless rocks. Politics, if you ask me. Pure politics—and that makes bad strategy."

There was no response and Peter imagined Schweig was reduced to nodding.

"Have you seen the orders we've been getting?" the commander asked his friend. "First one plan, then another, then back to the first, like we're dealing with some sort of schizophrenic."

"Or too many bosses," Schweig agreed.

"For all the decisions I make," the commander sighed, "I could be a robot. The couriers are tripping over each other trying to get orders in here, then we get that clown from Breslau, and now this joker from Berlin . . ."

Peter smiled and entered the tent; they both glanced up at him guiltily. Before they could say anything, Peter said, "I want to take the prisoners to the nearest mountain stream. Where's that?"

"What? Whatever for?"

"In this weather, standing in a foot of water can be extremely painful," Peter explained without telling them he knew from personal experience. "It will make them more likely to talk," he finished, ignoring the commander's look of disgust.

Schweig walked to the entrance of the tent and pointed to the left. "About a half a kilometer, that way."

"I'm not sanctioning this sort of thing," the commander said with surprising courage.

Peter scratched his head. "That was an interesting conversation I interrupted, but I'm having trouble remembering it all."

The commander glared at him, then after a moment of silence conceded, "Fine. But just take one, we don't want you to have difficulties."

"There won't be any trouble," Peter assured him. "I want them all to witness everything: torture the weak if you want the strong to talk, that's what we always say back at home office."

"I can't spare more than two men," the commander said, trying a different objection.

"I don't need anyone."

The commander looked disappointed; he changed tack slightly. "They're my prisoners, they'll be watched by my soldiers, understand? Besides, as you so clearly pointed out, I'm responsible for your safety. You will have two soldiers accompanying you."

Peter rubbed the back of his neck. "Just the officer from Breslau. He's an expert, after all. He and I can handle them alone."

"I won't have interoffice rivalries played out in my camp. Lederman remains here and you will be accompanied by two of my men, otherwise you will be denied access to these prisoners. Understood?"

Peter hesitated, then deciding that he could push the commander no further, he gave up on revenge and gave in. "Fine. Two men. I'll take them now."

51

THE UNWIELDY DOZEN made their way out of the camp and to the stream. They stopped in a small woods near the banks of the stream, and there Peter singled out the strongest-looking captive, ordering the other eight to sit on the ground. He told one of the guards to remain with them, and then taking the selected prisoner and the other guard with him, they set off a short distance around a rocky outcrop and out of sight.

"Hold him for me," Peter ordered as he shoved the prisoner toward the guard. As the guard held the man from behind, Peter approached to face him. The man winced in expectation but said nothing. Suddenly Peter drew his gun and held it to the man's head. "I don't have time for any nonsense. Tell me everything you know."

"It's not me you want," the prisoner volunteered. "It's the other one—the short man with the black hair. He's a group leader, he's got information. Question him!"

Peter felt disgusted by this unexpected response, and for a moment it threw him off his stride. He backed away as if contemplating the information, then stepping behind the guard, he grabbed the barrel of his pistol and swung it with full force into the back of the guard's head. There was a sickening crunch, and as the man crumpled silently to the ground, Peter wondered if he had not hit him too hard.

"What the hell?" the prisoner stammered.

"I'm from Central," Peter said as he drew his knife and began cutting the man's bonds. "I want you to take me hostage, then we'll go back and free the others. Hold the gun on me and I'll order the other guard to drop his weapons, then place me behind him and I'll knock him out."

"Why not just shoot him?" the man asked, overcoming his surprise.

"They'll hear the shot."

"You have a knife." The man made a motion with his finger across his throat.

"No! I want to keep my cover; if they remain alive, they can corroborate that I was not involved in your escape. They'll think we were attacked by a partisan here, then when I disappear with you all, they'll think I was taken hostage." Peter chose not to add that he was loath to add another couple of corpses to the mangled body of the boy he had slain.

They disarmed and tied the unconscious guard and returned as Peter had planned. The other guard looked up questioningly as he saw the two approach, then in alarm as he realized what was happening. Before he could raise his gun, Peter ordered him to set down his weapons. When Peter saw his hesitation at obeying such dubious orders, he added, "We have their word they won't harm us."

"Their word?" the guard asked.

"Yes. Now do as I've commanded."

The guard set down his gun and Peter sighed his relief. The partisan who was holding him hostage ordered him to stand by the guard and he did so. The partisan began speaking, and as soon as the guard's back was to Peter, he struck him a hard blow across the back of the head. The two of them began hurriedly freeing their comrades, immediately detailing someone to keep an eye on each guard to make sure neither awakened and raised an alarm. There were quick explanations and a debate about the fate of the two guards. Peter was adamant that not only was it strategically important the two remain alive, but that he had also given his word, and eventually his argument prevailed over the bloodlust of several of the captives.

Or so he thought. However, just as they set out into the woods to make good their escape, he saw two of the freed captives circle back, and he guessed that they had decided to take matters into their own hands and "finish the job." He chose not to risk following the two, instead staying with the larger group so that they could provide cover for him and help him back into the mountains when his officer's uniform became a liability.

They trampled over the snow through the barren trees, heading away from the camp and toward the front. The two men who had initially veered off did not rejoin them, and over the next twenty minutes, as they made their way deeper into the disputed territory, he lost another three of his companions as they melted away to different destinations. The speed at which they chose to abandon the group worried him, and as yet another slipped off, he stopped to confront the remaining three.

"What's going on?" he demanded, but none of them answered. He had kept the sidearm of the attaché and one of the guard's semiautomatic rifles for himself, and now he noticed that all three remaining were weaponless and eyeing his guns. "We're not through the front yet, why is everyone splitting off? You're safer with me—if we meet up with a German patrol, I can pass you off as my prisoners."

"There would be safety in numbers," a slack-jawed woman agreed. "Don't you think you should share those weapons?"

On an instinct Peter shook his head. "What's the problem? I've just freed you, we're heading home, I'm unfamiliar with this territory, I assumed one of you would guide me back."

The three of them looked at each other guiltily, then finally a young lad spoke. "We can't, sir. We don't know who you are, and if we take you in, then we take responsibility. None of us wants to take that chance."

"Dammit! I took a hell of a chance for you. It's because of that little charade I'm not returning by the route I planned! The least you could do is get me back inside," Peter hissed angrily.

There was an uncomfortable silence. The slack-jawed woman shook her head. "Whoever you are, you're a sitting duck in that uniform, and I, for one, don't want to be anywhere near you when they start shooting." She turned and walked off. The other two shrugged and followed her. Peter watched them for a moment thinking that he could simply follow, but it would be difficult and there seemed no point.

He sat on a rock and closed his eyes, breathing deeply to try to rest. Fucking ingrates! He should have left them to their fate. He thought of how that boy Dennis had given him a shove in the direction of his home after he had been thrown out of his gang, then sighing, he stood, took his bearings, and started off again.

He followed an icy rivulet upstream. It ran through the middle of a combe, and the slopes on either side protected him from the wind and, he hoped, from snipers. As he progressed, the valley narrowed until there was only a few feet of space on either side of the water. The ground became slick with the icy spray from the stream, and soon he found himself constantly slipping on the rocks. His third fall hurt, and his foot slid into the water, wetting his boot but luckily not soaking through. He stopped to rest and reconsider his strategy.

Though there was ice forming on the water, it would never be enough to support his weight. Meanwhile the farther up he climbed, the narrower and steeper the valley became. It was getting nearly impassable, and in his present state he feared he might well injure himself and freeze to death before anyone found him. He would simply have to risk traveling along the top of the valley. He scaled the bank and emerged on the top of a narrow ridge. He glanced around nervously. There was no sign of anyone, and though he was not sure whether that was good news or bad, he breathed a sigh of relief.

He sat down and rested his head against a tree. God, but he had not realized how tired he was! Two nights without sleep and this almost constant movement. His muscles ached, his feet were sore, and his eyes burned. The wind was harsher up on the ridge, and he noticed how the side of his face that was exposed to it was growing hot. In fact, as he sat there, he felt flushed with warmth. He closed his eyes and thought about the paradoxical warmth, then he thought about Zosia and their tiny little baby. He hoped they were all right and imagined little Irena wrapped in warm blankets snuggling into her mother's arms, her face pressed against Zosia's warm, soft, tender breasts . . .

"Daddy?" Joanna called out to him. "Daddy, are you awake?"

He started awake. His hands and feet had grown numb. He wondered how long he had slept as he struggled to get to his feet. Only a light dusting of snow had accumulated on his windward side, and he guessed that he had not dozed for more than a minute or two. Nevertheless, that he had unintentionally fallen asleep scared him, and he began walking, stumbling on his numb feet until the blood and sensation returned, determined not to stop until he had reached some sort of safety.

He reached deep into his coat pocket and extracted his armband. Wave it, Bolek had said. At the time he had not thought to point out how impractical that was. He could mount it on the end of his rifle and wave that as he walked, or he could stick it on a branch, but it really wasn't much like a flag, and besides feeling ludicrous, it would prevent him from using his hands to help keep his balance when he was clambering over rocks and branches. He closed his fist around the cloth and decided he was still on the wrong side of the front to use it.

About twenty minutes later, the ridge path he had followed widened and joined a road. The mountain stream still burbled below him, though now the drop into the valley was rather precipitous and the area around the stream was too narrow to walk. Though he felt much more exposed on the road, he welcomed it nonetheless for the ease of walking, and also with the thought in mind that perhaps if he was spotted from far enough away, they would give him time to surrender and explain himself.

Thus, when he thought he heard a branch snapping, he immediately waved his arms to draw attention to himself and his armband. The grenade landed about three meters in front of him. It took a second for him to register its presence and decide what to do, and it exploded even as he threw himself over the edge of the road. He tumbled out of control down the slope and crashed through thin ice into the mountain stream. The bitterly cold water sent a shock of pain through his body and he scrambled desperately toward the bank. The stream was not deep—not more than two feet, but the bottom was slippery and as his muscles contracted in uncontrollable spasms, he slipped and stumbled back into the water. He crawled out, grasping at frozen tufts of grass to pull himself up the bank, then lay gasping on the snow-covered slope.

Seconds passed. It felt so good to lie still! His brain told him to move, quickly, but as he lay there, he could feel warmth spreading in a pulsing sensation through his body, almost as if a torch were being passed over him. Move, he told himself, but then again, whoever had thrown the grenade was likely to shoot at him if he moved. He knew he should stand and shake the excess water from his clothes before more seeped through, but still he lay motionless except for the shuddering of his entire body. Move and be shot or don't move and freeze, he debated. Move or don't move?

"Don't move!"

It took a moment before he realized someone had actually spoken. He could hear the sound of boots skidding down the bank toward him.

"It's not going to move, it's dead," a different, rather young voice opined, this time in Polish.

"Don't fool around, shoot it," a female voice advised. She also sounded quite young.

"It's dead already," the first voice answered. They were close now though he could not see them.

"Why don't you just shoot it anyway, to be sure?" the girl's voice asked.

"He doesn't want to ruin that pretty uniform," the second voice guessed.

Peter remained still as he listened. Both the boy and the girl had a slurred accent that made them difficult to understand.

"Kill it," the girl insisted.

"Shut up, you bloodthirsty little whore!" the first voice grated. "What the hell did you waste a grenade for like that!"

"Yeah, wasting grenades!" the other male voice joined in as an adolescent might.

"Fuck you," the girl responded angrily.

"You're supposed to use some common sense."

"Yeah, common sense," the boy's voice parroted, then asked, "What do we do now?"

"If he's who I think he is, you're in deep shit. Keep him covered, I want to look around, I thought I saw something," the first voice said.

"Look, he's alive, he's shivering," the girl said.

A foot prodded him in the back; he tried to speak but the words froze in his throat.

"Wait, look—there it is!" the first voice called out.

"Don't shoot," Peter finally managed to croak as he rolled over to face them. "I'm one of you."

A boy and a girl faced him, dirty, scruffy, poorly dressed, neither more than fourteen. The boy had an old-fashioned rifle, she a pistol and a couple of grenades slung on a belt. Both had their weapons pointed at him. The other speaker, a young man of about twenty, was a few yards away. He was armed with both a semiautomatic rifle and a pistol and was the only one of the three who seemed to be adequately dressed for the cold. He was holding a piece of cloth in his hands that Peter recognized as his armband. "This yours?" the young man asked, holding up the armband.

Peter nodded. "I was returning from a mission. I'm one of you."

"Not with that accent, you ain't," the lad sneered.

Peter pulled himself into a sitting position, waving angrily at the children to lower their weapons even as they poised themselves to respond to his action. "Put those things down!" he ordered. "You're under orders not to shoot if I'm carrying an armband. And there it is!"

"But you're not carrying it," the boy argued.

"I was, you idiot. Before you attacked me."

"Disarm him, tie his hands, in front, then you two get back to the road," the young man advised. "I'll take him up to my position and check him out."

The young pair did as they were told, relinquishing the captured weapons reluctantly to their older comrade, and then, as ordered, they returned to their posts.

"Kids," the young man sighed. "Just as well I got down here in time." He looked at the papers Peter carried. "Fakes?"

"Just the photo," Peter answered incautiously.

"Sorry about the ropes, sir, but I can't release you until you check out. Can you walk?"

Peter nodded and climbed to his feet. The warmth had turned into an itching sensation, and though he felt as if he were burning inside, his skin felt painfully icy. The young soldier indicated where to go, and Peter climbed wearily back up the embankment. They walked along the road for a bit and then cut off to clamber up a slope that became steeper and rockier as it headed toward a promontory. Fortunately, with his hands bound in front, Peter had no trouble with the climb; his legs did not even hurt, and he guessed they were too numb with cold to feel any pain. As they continued with their exertions, the water on his clothing froze providing some protection from the wind, and the wool of his coat kept him relatively warm despite being wet. He even began to sweat so that he felt the weird, uncomfortable sensation of being hot and damp under his coat while his extremities grew stiff and numb. They reached the top of the ridge, and the terrain suddenly flattened into a heavy pine woods. They walked along in silence, but as they emerged from the woods, they were greeted by a male voice.

"Captain Halifax—I thought you were in London. Where's my daughter?"

Peter located the speaker, sitting with his back to some rocks, eating a sandwich. It was Barbara's father, Ludwik.

"She's in London, safe and sound last I heard," Peter replied cautiously. "I'm here for the birth of my child."

"How's your wife doing? Heard she went missing. Do you know if she's okay?"

"Last I heard, she's fine. She's had the baby."

"Oh, congratulations! Hell of a birthday party, what?" Ludwik gestured toward the noise from the distant fighting. It had been reasonably quiet for a while, but now it sounded as if somebody was attempting an offensive.

Peter scanned the ridge, then looked back at Ludwik. "Thanks. Do you think you could get this gentleman to untie me?" Peter was shaking uncontrollably.

Ludwik smiled as though he was considering, at least momentarily, the idea of playing a joke, but then he turned to the young soldier and said, "He's all right. He's one of ours."

"You know him personally?" the young man asked.

"Yeah, my daughter works for him," Ludwik replied, then added almost gleefully, "Not only that, but his wife is a big shot. You harm a hair on his head and she'll have your balls!"

The young man hurriedly untied Peter's hands. "Sorry, sir. You know we can't be too careful."

"No problem," Peter lied, rubbing his wrists.

The young man fetched Peter some blankets, returned his weapons to him, and then went to join his companion on watch, leaving Peter alone with Barbara's father.

"What are you doing here?" Peter asked Ludwik while wrapping himself in the blankets. He used the edge of one of them to scrub the tiny bits of ice from his hair.

"I should be asking you that," Ludwik responded, but then answered, "They're down to two people up here so I was told to fill in. So, what happened to you?"

Peter explained.

"Yeah, someone back at the camp mentioned we had sent out an infiltrator and he might be back this way. They didn't say it was you, though. I thought I spotted a lone black uniform, so I sent the boy down to intercept you. Looks like he got there just in time."

"Just barely." Peter huddled into the blankets and shivered as sensation returned: pins and needles jabbed at his arms and legs and his skin itched with a vengeance. He clawed at his limbs through the fabric of his clothes, and though it felt as if he were drawing blood, it did relieve his itching some.

"When you get back, make sure you report that bit about the prisoner you questioned. I'm sure they'll be able to track down who it was and take appropriate measures."

"Like what? Extra duty?"

"I don't know. Rather serious, giving up his commanding officer. You're lucky he didn't blow you away, once he found out who you were. Maybe kneecaps."

"Ugh! You're not serious!"

Ludwik cocked his head at Peter. "They have kept you cosseted, haven't they? Of course I'm serious! If we don't keep these people in line, they'll go native and we'll have a hundred little gangs each with its own little chieftain bargaining independently with the Germans to get a separate peace for their own little fief. After all these years, the only thing that separates us from a bunch of outlaw mountain bandits is discipline and a sense of purpose."

"Is there really no other way?" Peter asked, aware of how much his own legs hurt thanks to Karl's sense of discipline and order.

"Got any suggestions?"

Peter pondered a moment, then shook his head. With so many innocents being hurt, why should he give a damn about one miscreant partisan?

"Here." Ludwik offered him a sandwich. "You look hungry, have you eaten?"

"Not really. Some buckwheat yesterday morning. Haven't slept either."

"Oops, this is not the time to fall asleep. We're expecting an attack anytime now."

"Don't worry. I've stayed awake longer than this before," Peter answered around a mouthful of sandwich.

"And is my daughter keeping you awake?" Ludwik asked slyly.

"Huh?" Peter responded, deliberately obtuse.

"She's hot for you."

"Was," he mumbled, trying not to spit food.

"Oh? Have you slept with her?" Ludwik asked in a studiously casual tone.

Peter wondered what in the world Ludwik thought he might say even if he had! Finally, aware that his silence might be misconstrued, he swallowed his food to reply, "No. Our relationship is entirely professional. She has a boyfriend in London, did you know?" Naturally, it was unfair to betray the privacy of Barbara's life, but it seemed a reasonable trade to get her father off his back. The man was, after all, armed, and accidents were known to happen.

"A boyfriend?" Ludwik sounded almost angry. "An Englishman?"

"Afraid so," Peter responded, his mouth full again. "They are fairly common in England."

"What the fuck!"

"They're behaving," Peter added hurriedly. "I've kept my eye on both of them." He hoped he sounded sufficiently serious and sincere, though he doubted that shoving food into his face as he spoke helped in that regard.

"You!" Ludwik squeaked his derision of the idea of Peter as chaperon, but then Ludwik seemed to bring himself under control. "Ah, well, yes, good. Thanks. She's precious to us. We appreciate your, uh, help."

"My pleasure," Peter responded with indiscernible sarcasm.

"I suppose, in any case, if he's anything like you, she'll have him whipped into shape in no time. Are all you English so henpecked?"

"My private life is none of your business," Peter replied somewhat too seriously. He should have laughed off the insult or returned with one of his own, but he was tired and in no mood.

"Well, it seems your life is your wife's business, isn't it?" Ludwik did not relent. "Of course, one would have expected that from her—they're all alike, think they can run everything."

"Who, women?"

"No, the nobility. Didn't you know—her great-grandmother was a Lubomirska."

"Ah, so it's in the blood, eh?" Peter attempted sarcasm; nevertheless, he was disturbed by Ludwik's comments. He did not even know the last names of most of his great-grandparents. How was it that not only Zosia knew her connection, but that he did and even Ludwik did? Was there a subtle message being sent?

"Indeed. Goddamned magnates. Still trying to push us around after all these years!"

"Who is us?" Peter asked, hoping to move the topic off his personal life.

"The workers! The peasants!"

"Are you a Communist?" Peter asked, thinking he could return the earlier insult.

"No, but my father was," Ludwik answered proudly. "He fled Lwów when the Soviets marched in."

"Fled the Soviets into German-held territory?" Peter asked in amazement.

"Yes, the GPU wanted to interview him. He felt his chances were better here."

"Better with the Nazis than with his fellow Communists?"

"He went into hiding here. He was known there."

"One would think he would have welcomed his fellow Communists with open arms." Peter liked using the phrase *fellow Communists.* It seemed to annoy Ludwik enormously.

"Yeah, well, those who did," Ludwik answered quite seriously, "disappeared into Siberia. The Russians are no less intent on our annihilation. If you look at the part of our country which they grabbed, you would guess that no Poles ever existed there. Compared to the Soviets, the Nazis are rank amateurs."

"Hey!" one of the two defenders called to them. "We need some firepower here! Both of you, quick!"

Peter grabbed his weapons and with Ludwik climbed the last bit to the precipice where the two young defenders were waiting. A young woman took automatic command and indicated where they should place themselves. The four of them then waited until the unit that had been spotted was in range.

Considering how awful he had felt about knifing the boy and the fuss he had made about not killing the two guards, Peter expected to feel a bit of hesitance at the idea of shooting, but as he saw the uniforms filter into view, he had no trouble placing one of them in his sights. He thought of Joanna and Allison and his murdered friends and his parents; he wondered how Zosia and his newborn daughter were doing. Then he thought of all those who were behind him, depending on him to defend them and preserve this last tiny vestige of their home and their independence. He waited for the others, and when they agreed they were ready, he picked off his target, ending a life, and readily lined up the next mother's son in his sights as the uniforms below broke formation and tried to scatter to safety.

They took cover rapidly, but they were in a lousy position. Ludwik and Peter and the other two picked them off one by one with virtually no danger to themselves. It was pathetic really, like one of those cheap video games he had seen in America; the soldiers should never have been sent into such a situation, but no doubt they were obediently following orders from someone who, by virtue of his brutality or his hair color or his uncle had won the right to command them.

As Peter thought of the strategy—or the complete lack of it—that the enemy so often exhibited, he wondered: Was it possible that their reputation for invincibility was no longer deserved? Were they a much softer target than anyone had assumed? Was it even possible that disaffection with the high level of corruption and nepotism in the hierarchy might lead to deliberate sabotage within the ranks, to desertion, maybe even to rebellion?

Had any of the advisers to the governments in exile noted this? Had the timid American security agencies overestimated the strength of the German war machine? They were notoriously reliant on dubious statistics, were hesitant to actually observe firsthand, were bound by politics to discover only that which was convenient to know. Were all the warnings about avoiding any direct conflict superfluous? Outdated? Misleading? Was Europe being held captive by a puppet regime with papier-mâché troops?

The American advisers, the governments in exile, the concerned opinions of the rest of the world, warned against outright war. They cautioned that a failed rebellion against the regime might lead to the annihilation of the subject peoples. But they were already being annihilated! True that some had a longer stay of execution than others, but they were all in the same queue for cultural annihilation if not actual physical liquidation. And it was interesting how concerned all the external onlookers became for the safety of the subject populations in this instance, but only in this instance. The concentration camps could still grind people to dust, the executions could still claim their numberless victims, malnutrition and starvation and disease could still destroy whole populations. None of that mattered enough to raise concern. Patience, they were told, have patience. All that mattered was avoiding the dangers of an outright war.

The most cynical explanation would be that too many people would lose power if a rebellion of the subject nations ever succeeded. The governments in exile, in particular, would lose all legitimacy. There was, however, a less cynical explanation: though no one dared say it, the Americans were terrified that a desperate Nazi regime might release its nuclear weapons in a nihilistic decision to destroy everything else as it collapsed. So, to lower their own risk, they allowed others to risk everything in futile and endless petty battles that did no more than slow the slaughter to an acceptable level of violence.

Peter rolled onto his back and reloaded his rifle. How many people had he killed already? Funny, but he had lost count. He rolled back onto his stomach and mindlessly searched the rocks below for a target as he let his thoughts return to politics and revolutions and the morality of risk. Had their governments given in to blackmail, accepting the eventual destruction of their nations for the guarantee of safety overseas? Was the chance for liberation worth the risk of nuclear reprisals? Of a Soviet invasion? Of civil war? Were their lives, after all these years of occupation, worth less than the lives of the people who lived in peace across the Atlantic? Patience, they were told, have patience. Was it possible for any of them to remain patient any longer?

The young partisan who had assumed command of the snipers glanced at her watch. "Time to move," she announced. They all slid out of position, down the slope. Once they were shielded by the cliff, the partisan pointed to a distant escarpment. "That's our next location," she said, and with her companion took off at a lope through the snow. Peter was exhausted and Ludwik looked fatigued, but they took off at a run as well. The next position was well planned. It looked onto a bit of valley that was farther along and would take the soldiers longer to reach than it took the defenders to move from one bit of cliff to the other. It was also distant enough and the rock face was directed such that they would probably be safe from an aerial bombardment of their first position.

When Peter and Ludwik reached the second position, the young partisan was alone. "Where's your companion?" Ludwik panted. Unlike the other two, neither he nor Peter had been trained for this particular assignment.

"He's waiting about halfway back to see if they'll use any aircraft against that spot. If so, he'll try and take it out. Once they organize a reply to us, we have to start moving fast."

"Is there another position after this one?" Peter asked, worried at both his and Ludwik's lack of direction.

She immediately understood his concern and took a few seconds to explain their next two locations and the planned time interval between each. "But to work! Let's see if we can't finish them off here and save ourselves running again," she concluded, and directed each of them to an optimal niche.

So, Peter lay down and prepared himself to kill again as the soldiers finally proceeded down the valley. They would proceed, he was sure of that. It had been ordered and they would follow their orders. He wondered if Geerd might be among them. Would it matter? He sort of liked the boy, and philosophically, it might have made a difference to him, but emotionally or physically or instinctively or whatever it was that governed his behavior then and there, he knew it was irrelevant. He was not a philosophical being at that point. He was defending his home and his loved ones against invasion, and he would kill whomever he had to in order to do that.

In the end, they did not have to move on from their second location. It had not even been necessary to move from the first. They destroyed the remnants of the enemy soldiers and waited for the next wave, but there was none. No more attempts, no assault from the air on their position. The four of them waited through the night and into the next day, sleeping in shifts, ever vigilant, but there was nothing. Radio communication with HQ had indicated that even though nothing more was currently expected, they should stay their ground until further orders, Peter included. So they stayed and watched and waited and chatted. But it was over. No one else came.

On the second day of their vigil, they were relieved by two more partisans.

The woman greeted a young man with hugs and kisses, and they pressed against each other intimately, unaware in their joy at seeing each other alive that the others were watching them bemusedly. The new arrivals had brought a tent and more supplies and told Ludwik and Peter that their presence was requested back at the encampment.

"We suppose you know where that is," one of them commented, perhaps sarcastically.

"The four of us will be staying here, guarding the gates," the other said, smiling at his girlfriend or wife. What did he care if he did not even know where the bunker was: he was at home wherever she was.

=== 52 ===

*P*ETER HEADED DOWN toward the bunker with Ludwik guiding the way. Once they were well out of earshot of the partisans, Peter asked, "What were the man and woman speaking to each other? It wasn't Polish, was it?"

Ludwik panted through a few steps before answering, "No, they're locals. Rusniaki."

"Is it a dialect of Polish?"

"I'd say not."

"Then what are they? Slovaks? Ukrainians?"

"They don't know what they are," Ludwik answered with something close to exasperation. Peter was not sure whether it was his questions or the Rusniaki that caused that response.

They moved on in silence for a bit, then Ludwik volunteered, "They moved into these mountains a few centuries ago, and they practice some sort of Orthodox religion, I think."

"You don't trust them?" Peter asked perceptively.

Ludwik gave Peter a sideways glance. "You do know that some of our Ukrainian buddies are pro-German?"

"Yes, or as they would put it, anti-Soviet."

"Whatever, they can make trouble for us, and we've had run-ins with them in these mountains. The Lemki—"

"Who?"

"These mountaineers, the Rusniaki."

"Oh."

"The Rusniaki"—Ludwik pronounced the term distinctly as if Peter were rather slow to follow—"on occasions have thought of themselves as Ukrainians, and I don't trust Ukrainians. Is that clear enough for you?"

"So, have you ever had any indication that the Rusniaki are disloyal?"

"No," Ludwik answered reluctantly. "Some of them join us, like those two. They're not conscripted, but all of them are taxed, naturally, as we are defending their way of life here. They're about the only people in this land who still live life the way they did before the invasion."

"How do they feel about a partisan army moving in on them?"

"I don't know, and I don't care. It's better than the fucking alternative, isn't it?"

"Yes," Peter agreed cheerfully. Ludwik was so easy to rile, and so much fun!

They trod wearily for a few minutes in silence, then Ludwik asked suddenly, "You think it's funny, don't you? My opinions, my history, my worries about my daughter? You think I'm overly sensitive, eh?"

"Well, yes!" Peter laughed. Even the serious tone of Ludwik's question was quite funny.

"Ah, you don't look in a mirror very often, do you?"

They were both tired and neither said anything more as they continued their journey until they parted company at the field camp. Peter retrieved and changed his clothes before reporting to Wojciech; there he requested and received permission to return to the bunker. Upon reaching his home, he entered, stripped off his equipment, and handed it all to a young man near the entrance who was tending to supplies. Peter wended his way through the halls and dropped the two levels to their abode. After all this time, home. It had been an eternity of four days. He had missed Zosia so much, had worried about her and the baby nearly every minute. His dreams had been filled with thoughts of her. Now he was back and could see her at last. He had already heard she and the baby were safe and sound, brought back by a team sent up to retrieve them the previous day, and he looked forward to holding them in his arms.

Maybe with Irena born, maybe this time, maybe they could finally get it all to come together. Perhaps Zosia had meant what she had said in the cabin—that she wanted him to stay. They could arrange a replacement for him, or even leave Barbara to handle the bookshop alone. She could do it—there was precious little to do there. They could start again, forget the bitterness, and build a life together.

He reached their door. It was open and he stepped inside without Zosia even noticing him. The baby was sleeping in a cradle on the table. Zosia had her back to him, and she was staring at something, holding it tenderly in her hands. She held it close, as though it were the most precious thing in the world. He knew what it was, and he was not surprised that as she turned and saw him, she pushed it even tighter against herself as if hiding it from him. There was an empty space where it usually hung on the wall—it was the wedding photo of her and Adam.

"Hello, Zosiu," he said quietly.

"You're back!"

He nodded. Was she elated or disappointed?

"What's all that? You look a fright!" She pointed at his coat, still clasping the picture with her other hand.

"Dried blood."

"Yours? Were you injured?"

"No. Someone tried to kill me after I left the cabin. I stabbed him to death."

"Oh."

He walked over to her. She threw a guilty glance downward but then looked quickly away toward the baby.

"What's that?" he asked, indicating the frame in her hands.

She bent it forward away from her body so he could see the photograph.

Gently, he removed it from her grasp, contemplated it for just a moment, then with sudden, furious violence he flung it against the far wall. Glass shattered and the bent frame clattered to the floor. Without looking at Zosia, he went over to where it lay and tore the picture out through the broken glass. A corner ripped on a shard and he cut his hand, but he did not care enough to even stop the blood from staining the photo. Without saying a word, he crumpled the photograph in his fist and threw it down onto the floor.

He turned then to look at her. Blood dripped from his hand onto the floor. She did not react at all, staring at him as though he were beneath contempt.

"I know you want your privacy. I'll leave for London tomorrow," he said, and left to go and wash his hands.

Once he had left, Zosia checked the baby. Blissfully asleep. Then she got a broom and dustpan and cleaned up the glass. She straightened the frame and smoothed the picture, wiping the blood off it as she did so. It was her only photo from her first wedding day, and she stood quietly contemplating it, wiping away a tear as she looked at the damage done to it.

In the bathroom, Peter stood before the sink and carefully removed the splinters of glass from his hand. What in God's name had he been thinking? Why did he always act so stupid and impulsive around Zosia? Did love destroy a person's rationality? The calm manner in which he had handled Barbara's outrage, the way he had viewed her explosion of emotion with pity and even mild contempt—she should see him now; she'd have a good laugh at him! If anyone knew how to make a fool of himself, he did.

He let the cool water run over his hand, hoping to wash out the shards and staunch the blood. His hand throbbed with pain, and it was the only thing that felt right. It was justified, unlike everything else he did. He was such an idiot! Such mindless violence was unforgivable! What had he been thinking? Where had that rage come from? It reminded him of the irrational surge of rage he had felt when Emma had slipped off her wristband. Then it had been jealousy at her relative freedom. And with Zosia? It was clear, embarrassingly so; it was simply jealousy of a long-dead husband. Truly beloved, truly missed. She had never said otherwise, and he had always known he would have to accept Adam's memory as an integral part of her. Yet, time and again he had been driven to ridiculous behavior by his jealousy. Time and again he had tried to come to terms with Adam's place in her heart. Time and again he had failed.

Marysia interrupted his thoughts as she came into the bathroom. "Did you hurt yourself?"

"Yeah, piece of glass." He backed away from the sink so she could use it and went to the cabinet to find some cloth to bandage his hand.

"Oh, don't let me interrupt, I'm just checking to see if the water's back on. . . . How did you like Zosia's surprise?"

"Her surprise?"

"The picture! You know, of your family?"

"What?"

"Oh. I'm sorry, she wanted to surprise you." Marysia sounded chagrined.

"Don't worry, I'll act surprised. What do you mean?"

Marysia sighed. "Promise you won't tell her I let the cat out of the bag."

"On my honor," Peter swore rather more solemnly than the joke he had intended. What honor? he thought.

"She said she was going to take down an old picture and use the frame to put up one of yours that she found in a drawer. By the way, I didn't know you had any—where'd it come from?"

Oh, God, it was worse than he had imagined. He really was beneath contempt! He quickly explained about the diaries he had found and promised to tell her all about them later. Then he made his excuses, and still trying to wrap the cloth around his hand, he left.

In the corridor he stopped. It was pointless. He had said he would return to London tomorrow and she would demand he keep that promise. How could he have said something so stupid? No matter how angry he had been, how could he have thought to leave her and his newborn child so quickly? He bowed his head and wondered how he could possibly undo the mess he had made, then gathering his courage, he opened the door and waited for her reprisal.

She looked up at him but did not say anything. She raised her eyebrows expectantly, almost welcomingly; a half-smile played across her lips. Clearly she would let him dive into his typical, abject apologies, let him truly debase himself, before she bothered to slam him down for his unforgivable behavior. He snorted at that; he wasn't going to give her that chance! Not again. Never again.

"I need to pack." He headed toward the bedroom. As he passed the baby, he felt a sudden regret. He stopped and looked at her. He really wanted to stay, if for no other reason than to see her for just a few days! But Zosia would make sure he kept his word about leaving, and she would have him ordered out if necessary. There was nothing he could do, and he would only humiliate himself, as he had done so many times before, if he begged her to change her mind or to forgive him. He bent down and kissed Irena and then went to pack.

When he emerged, Zosia still said nothing, just looked at him as if confused. But of course she was stymied, she was not getting her usual chance to rub his face in it! He snorted at the thought, then said, "I'll walk to a camp tonight. That way I can take my time getting out of the mountains tomorrow. I'll have them arrange everything from there. I imagine it will be complicated by all that has occurred."

Zosia nodded. "I imagine so," she said quietly.

He stopped to look at Irena again, gently stroking her face with his finger. In his heart he begged Zosia to ask him to stay, but she did not say a word, so finally he left. He did not get far. At the entrance he was told by the guard that there was no way he would be able to go into town and there was no point in his going to the edge. It was nothing personal, they were just in negotiations, and under current circumstances there were to be no border crossings. Orders.

He turned around and walked slowly back down the hallways. Damn! He would have to go back and face Zosia's wrath. He felt extraordinarily foolish, but deep down, he was also elated. He could not leave, and she could not make him leave, at least for a while. So, he would get some time to know his daughter! By the time he reached their door he was smiling, and despite his best efforts, he had not erased the smile from his face as he stepped back into the room.

"Borders shut?" Zosia asked as if she had known all along.

"Yeah." Peter hesitated, but could not bring himself to say more. He walked over to where Zosia had laid the crumpled photograph on the table. Gingerly he tried to smooth it. "Do you have another one?" he finally asked.

"No," she answered without inflection. Irena began to stir, made a little sobbing noise, and Zosia picked her up and went to the couch to nurse her.

Still intent on straightening one recalcitrant crease, he asked, "Negatives?"

"My mother might have it." Zosia was intent on getting the baby nicely positioned, getting a towel in place, a blanket over her own legs, a pillow under her own arm. Irena liked nursing at a leisurely pace, and Zosia liked to be truly comfortable before she started.

The other photo, the one from his mother's diary, was also on the table. Three smiling faces. Little Anna sitting on his lap, his brother standing behind the two of them. He labeled each of the innocent faces with a single word: dead, Nazi, and what? For himself he could not decide. Unwanted? Lost? Hopeless? Untouchable?

"What are you thinking?" Zosia asked as Irena snuggled and snuffled and sucked. The baby's tiny hands reached and pressed and pushed and grabbed at her breast and she smiled in response.

"Oh, just thinking about my brother and sister. What a mess our lives have been."

"Come here, *Kochany,*" she cajoled, patting the seat next to her on the couch.

He spun around at her use of an endearment. Was she being sarcastic?

"Oh, could you get me some water first? I get so thirsty as soon as she starts drinking!"

He got Zosia the water and came to sit down next to her. As he looked at her happy expression while she held and stroked Irena, he couldn't help but remember the look on her face only a few minutes ago when he had destroyed her only picture of Adam. He wished she would say whatever she was going to say and get it over with.

At long last Zosia looked up at him again. "I'm glad you couldn't leave," she whispered.

"You are?"

"I don't want you to go."

"But after . . ."

"Don't worry about the photograph. I was taking it down anyway."

"I know. Marysia told me. I'm sorry, Zosiu. I don't know what got into me. I didn't mean to destroy it. I don't do that sort of thing."

"I know it's not like you. Don't worry about it. We have a little one to care for; that's where your thoughts should be. Not on some stupid photograph."

"Can you forgive me?" he asked, confused by the ease of it all.

"Only if you can forgive me."

"For what?" Was there something he did not know about? Tadek leapt to mind. A confession finally. Or had she done something else? Reassigned him even farther away? Was that why she was being so kind? He felt a sudden panic.

"For putting you in such an impossible position."

"What position? What have you done?" he asked with barely controlled anger.

Zosia laughed as she suddenly recognized his misinterpretation of her words. "No, no, not like that! I haven't done anything! I was just talking about, you know, the way I've made things difficult for you in the past. Relax, I haven't found a diplomatic position for you in Antarctica!"

He felt relieved but could not join her laughter. It had come too close to the truth.

"I want to try and get you reassigned back here. Do you want to come home?"

"You know I do." Then he added somewhat less brusquely, "Yes, I want to come home. I want to be with both of you."

"Okay, next time the full Council meets, I'll suggest a rearrangement of assignments."

"When will that be?"

"I don't know. I'm afraid what with all that's happened, it may take some time before we can organize a return. They have other things on their minds right now."

"Yeah, I'm sure they do," he sighed.

Irena suddenly pulled her head back from Zosia, stretched, and yawned, a stream of milk dribbling from her mouth. "Do you want to hold her for a few minutes?" Zosia asked. "She'll take a break before she wants more."

He took the baby in his arms; it was the first time he had held her since she was born. She grabbed at one of his fingers, and holding it tightly in her tiny hand, she chewed on his fingertip with her toothless gums. The little eyes fluttered open for a few seconds, and a glimpse of deep blue greeted him, then disappeared again. She sucked contentedly on his finger as he studied her features:

the curves of her ear, the blotchy red patches on her incredibly smooth skin, the hint of downy eyebrows, the puffiness under her eyes, the broad little nose above full red lips. "She's beautiful, isn't she?" he asked.

Zosia glanced at his face but saw no accusation there. He was unaware that he had repeated what he had said in the cabin a lifetime ago. Carefully she replied, "Yes, Peter, we've made a beautiful little girl."

═══════════ 53 ═══════════

"**Y**OU LOOK TIRED," Ryszard said to his daughter as he greeted her at the train station.

"Oh, God, you wouldn't believe how long I've been traveling!" Stefi grumbled. "It took forever just to get to Krakau."

"I know exactly how long you've been traveling." Ryszard threw his arm around her shoulders. "I've been quite worried about you." He glanced back to see that Leszek had Stefi's luggage and then walked along the platform with his daughter.

Stefi did not mince words. "So what's so important that only I can handle it? I assume you'll want to tell me before I see Mother."

"Ah, little girl, you do know me well, don't you?" Ryszard steered his daughter toward a restaurant. "We'll stop to eat here and I can explain."

"What about him?" Stefi indicated Leszek with a toss of her head.

"Glad you reminded me." Ryszard dropped back, handed Leszek an official-looking card, then rejoined his daughter. "That will keep him out of trouble. He doesn't mind waiting. Come on, we've got some business to conduct."

Ryszard let his daughter enjoy her appetizer before beginning. He watched as she hungrily downed the thick, creamy soup and took large bites of the bread, which she had loaded with butter. "Didn't you eat on the train?"

"Yes, but I'm still hungry," she said around a mouthful. "God, this tastes good!"

"Haven't they been feeding you at Szaflary?"

She snorted, then took a few more spoonfuls of soup before answering. "Yeah, we eat. Cabbage, potatoes, potatoes and cabbage. It has been utterly miserable, especially for me and the boys. We're used to better than that."

Ryszard frowned at her words, thinking about Andrzej, but chose to ask instead, "And how is your aunt Zosia?"

"Big. Gigantic! She can hardly waddle down the corridors. Bitchy, too. But then, what's new?"

Ryszard laughed. "So the baby's not born?"

"Not as far as I heard."

"Is her husband back?"

"I heard he was there, but I didn't see him. Things have been hectic recently. I haven't had any news. What's happening over there?"

"You've heard about Andrzej," Ryszard stated, though he wasn't sure.

Stefi nodded. She did not look sad, rather distant, as if refusing to acknowledge any emotion whatsoever. "What else?" she asked brusquely.

"A truce was declared yesterday."

"So soon?"

"They've been convinced to back out before it became an embarrassment. As far as the public knows, it didn't even happen."

"Marvelous, we held them off!"

Ryszard pushed the remains of his pâté away. "This time."

Stefi finished the last spoonful of soup, sat back, and sighed her satisfaction. "God, that was good! Now, Dad, what's up?"

"I want you to get reacquainted with Wolf-Dietrich. He's back in Berlin, and he's lonely."

"I came all this way for a date," Stefi commented sardonically. She was going to say more, but fell silent as a waiter whisked their plates away.

"Exactly. The reason I called you back now was that I was desperate to get an end to this little war our Führer decided to throw for himself. I wanted you here as a bribe in case I couldn't get access. Obviously, that's not necessary now."

"So you were involved in getting the truce called?"

"Yeah, I kept nagging him that it would be an embarrassment. It finally worked. I even got myself a place on the negotiations team." Ryszard paused as their entrée arrived. "Nevertheless, I still need you. Schindler is becoming a genuine problem, that whole invasion was his doing. He's getting far too powerful as an adviser to the Führer, but especially as his own power base. I need to get something on him, and planted evidence isn't going to work. I need something real!"

"What do you have so far?"

Ryszard then explained to his daughter what he knew about the American, the device he was carrying, and the connection Wolf-Dietrich seemed to have with it all. "I'm guessing his father used him because this is all unofficial. I assume Wolf-Dietrich picked up the device from the American in Lewes, and now, either they have that device in Berlin or more likely somewhere in Hamburg. Trouble is, Schindler's authority is in England and the device was delivered there. Could be that was simply a matter of convenience, or it could be that whatever they're doing, they're keeping it over there, near London, well away from Berlin."

"And well away from where you can snoop easily," Stefi added.

"Exactly. That's where you fit in. Get reacquainted, find out what you can."

"Will I have to sleep with him?" Stefi asked with smooth innocence.

"Do what you have to, my dear. All I can say is, it's important to me."

"What about Olek?"

"What about him?" Ryszard asked.

"He's going to ask me to marry him."

"So?"

"Don't you think I owe him some loyalty?"

Ryszard's face was a mask. Carefully he asked, "Exactly where are your loyalties?"

Stefi did not hesitate to answer, "With the cause, Father."

"Fine. Then tell him only what you need to."

"And how much do I need to tell him?" Stefi asked plaintively.

Ryszard realized she was not looking for a clarification of her orders from a commanding officer, she was looking for fatherly advice, so he tempered his answer. "That depends on what sort of relationship you want to have with him. Just note two things: I tell your mother as little as possible about the less salubrious aspects of my work, and that seems to benefit both of us. Your aunt Zosia has toyed with"—he paused as he tried to find the right words—"with allowing her emotional life to mix with her professional life, and in my opinion it has led to nothing but turmoil for her. Olek is a soldier, he'll probably understand, but he's also a man. Don't underestimate his ability to be jealous and possessive."

54

"*I* THINK SHE'S GROWN JEALOUS of you!" Zosia commented as she lay in bed, cradling Irena in her arms and nursing her. The baby suckled at her mother's breast but firmly held on to his finger with her tiny hand. Peter felt pleased by her possessiveness, and as soon as Irena had finished her midnight supper, he pulled her back onto his chest, gently tapping her back so that she might burp before she fell asleep again. Her eyes fluttered open in the dim light of the night, and she stared up at him with the uncomprehending love of a newborn, happy in the warmth and security of someone's arms. A half-smile played across her lips, and he kissed her forehead and whispered to her, "For you, little one. If for no other reason, then for you."

In reply, she burbled up a mouthful of milk, which he wiped off his chest with a cloth they kept in the bed, then they both settled in to rest. Irena's hot little head fit naturally into the cradle of his hand, her soft cheek brushed against his skin, her little legs curled into the crook of his arm. She settled into the calm rhythm of his heartbeat, and he lost himself in the soft whisper of her breath. In her blissful unawareness of the care he lavished on her, he took comfort, and with the tiny sleepy bundle on his heart, he drifted into sleep, freed from his ghosts and contented in the darkness for the first time in years.

*   *   *

"Do you believe in ghosts?" Lucjan asked. He was the taller of the two, big and burly.

"That wouldn't be advisable, considering what we're doing to these fellows," Peter answered nonchalantly. While Lucjan put his heavy boot on the chest of the corpse, Peter grabbed its arm and wrenched it inward. Something snapped, but he could not tell whether it was ice or bone. Their companion, Staszek, swore loudly as he slipped in the snow while attempting to straighten a leg. Finally, with sufficient grunting, groaning, and swearing, the three of them managed to get the corpse down to a buriable size, and they stopped and panted heavy clouds of steam into the bitter air.

"This is shitwork," Staszek grumbled. "Why aren't we having the prisoners do it? Least they could do is bury their dead."

"I heard they are working. Just not here." Peter slipped off his coat and rolled up his sleeves as the other two had already done. "Besides, there aren't many of them who aren't injured." He took a sip of water. "What happens to them if we can't negotiate an exchange?"

Staszek shrugged.

"Maybe we'll convert a few," Lucjan suggested breathlessly, wiping sweat off his brow.

"Or we could make them into slave labor." Staszek laughed scornfully. His companion nudged him roughly and jerked his head at Peter. Staszek glanced at Peter's arm and clapped his hand over his mouth in embarrassment. "Oh, sorry," he breathed, then added as if in explanation, "I've heard about you."

"Nothing bad, I hope," Peter replied with a forgiving smile. "Are there many conversions?"

"It happens. Disgruntled ethnic Germans or Silesians or others with a mixed heritage. But not often, it's just too risky for most." Lucjan looked pensive and added, "More often, it goes in the other direction. Can't blame them really—after all, no one wants to see their own child go hungry."

"What I want to know," Staszek interjected as he picked up the mattock, "is why don't we at least wait until spring? This frozen ground is ridiculous."

"What the hell are you moaning about?" Lucjan chided. "If we wait till a thaw, we'll be doing this in the rain, hip deep in mud with their eyes pecked out and the smell of rotting flesh!"

"We could just leave them to rot naturally," Staszek suggested, perhaps humorously. "You know, compost."

"The children run around these woods," Peter answered seriously. "Besides, wouldn't you want a decent burial?"

"Naw, he couldn't care less," Lucjan answered for his friend. "Just as long as you left a liter of vodka by his side to help him into the next life!"

Staszek laughed, pulled out his hip flask, and passed it around.

Peter liked these two; they kept up a continuous friendly banter. It was the second day in a row he had ended up working with them. The previous day, when he had met them, they had told him their names and he had promptly forgotten. He spent the entire day stuck using *um* and *er* when he wanted to get the attention of one of them. Today, he had admitted his absentmindedness and asked them outright to tell him their names again. They had laughed heartily, joking to each other, "Clearly, he's an officer!"

They had found three bodies—one of theirs and two enemy in the small patch of woods located down a steep, rock-strewn slope. Peter glanced around, but there seemed no easy way out of the little hollow. He supposed they could do a big grave for the two Germans and a separate grave for the Pole, but the earth was so hard, that seemed foolish. Still, he did not want to trample on his companions' sensitivities.

"I wonder what happened." Staszek paused to look at the corpses.

"I'd say our guy got the other two, but was wounded. Then he died of exposure," Peter suggested.

"Looks that way to me as well," Lucjan agreed. He turned to Peter. "You're not bad at this for an officer. Done it before?"

"Never professionally." Peter wondered exactly what skill it was that he had supposedly exhibited. Perhaps not sitting on his arse and directing them to do all the work. They looked at him curiously and he explained, "We had some deaths over the years in the labor camp that I was in. I was usually detailed to the grave-digging since it was outside of normal work hours—overtime you might say— and I looked strong enough to do it without collapsing. Me and my friend Geoff. Dug the graves, then we usually carried out some sort of memorial service. It was funny, the first time I did it, I had to get one of the kids to teach me a few appropriate prayers. They seemed to take some comfort in it anyway."

"What'd they die of? Executions?"

"No, there weren't any done on-site while I was there. Troublemakers got shuffled off to prison, and I don't know what happened to them after that. Although I guess my friend was executed on-site shortly after I left." Peter paused, wondering who had dug the grave then. "No, they went out from disease, or sometimes an accident. There were some stabbings as well. It was hard to keep that many kids under control, especially at that age, especially without any females around. Card games, love triangles, idiotic risk-taking. Too much testosterone, tempers flared, you know, usual stuff."

The two of them nodded.

Peter contemplated the corpses again. Maybe Staszek's suggestion wasn't such a bad idea. The wolves would probably reduce them to bones soon enough. It had an odd appeal—do something useful even in death. He thought of the American woman who had tried to convince him that although Nazism had been catastrophic for the human inhabitants of Europe, it had given many of the other native species a respite from extinction. She had explained how the wolf population had exploded after hostilities had begun, and though she admitted it was rather gruesome, she pointed out that the bodies had not only fed the animals but the decline in human population had taken some of the pressure off their habitats.

Peter had surprised her by not taking offense at her deliberately provocative suggestions; instead he had agreed that all too often humanity saw everything only in terms of human costs, and he also, though hard-pressed by other problems, could lament the deplorable state of the environment and the cost to European wildlife. Nevertheless, he had disagreed with her thesis, pointing out that American society, by virtue of its freedom and concomitant wealth, was able to afford the luxury of caring about the environment, of setting aside preserves and of making laws to protect nature. On the other hand, the depredations of Nazi society had inevitably led to a poor, mismanaged, polluting economy that stripped the land of its resources and raped the countryside. "I'm afraid," he had concluded, "that no matter how noble an idea it would be for people to care for the earth, most people care about themselves first. We need to see that they have a just society before we can even hope that they might think about the land around them. With the pressure of population such as it is and technology as advanced as it is there, that is the only hope for what wilderness remains: that civilized people care about it."

She had then asked about the nature movements in the Reich about which she had heard so much.

There were such, he had admitted, but he had noted that true environmentalists were more likely to end up as wolf fodder than as leaders of these intermittent propaganda efforts.

"Are we going to put all three of them in this hole?" Lucjan asked suddenly, bringing Peter back to the present.

"I sure as hell ain't diggin' another hole," Staszek answered. "They'll do fine all together. We got their IDs and we can put up a separate marker for ours later, during the memorial service."

"That's fine with me," Peter agreed.

Lucjan glanced at the three bodies and was inspired to recite an old German poem. " 'They can no more revile each other, those who lie here hand in hand, their departed souls have gone together . . .' Something, something, something 'land.' "

"Very profound," his friend commented, and slammed his pick into the hard earth.

"Indeed, it is profound," Zosia commented, surprising them all. She stood at the crest of the hollow, wearing skis, Irena bundled on her chest.

"What are you doing here?" Peter asked as he climbed up to meet her. He reached instinctively toward Irena, but then withdrew his hand as he realized what he had just been doing.

"I thought I'd bring Irena out for some fresh air and keep you company. Am I intruding?"

"No, not at all! But how did you find us?"

"Oh, they said you'd be in this sector. After that it wasn't hard to follow your tracks and the smell of vodka."

Staszek guiltily tucked his flask away and slammed the mattock determinedly into the ground. "Here!" he announced. "This is where we'll put them."

Zosia removed a blanket from her pack, settled herself onto the ground, and after unwrapping layers of clothing, let Irena snuggle up against her breast to begin nursing. Lucjan turned his back and began work. Peter threw Zosia a kiss and rejoined the other two. He helped dig the grave, then when Irena had finished nursing, he took a break, sat himself nearby, and sang her a lullaby. Lucjan and Staszek decided to take a break as well, but they moved a few meters away, out of earshot.

"That line always bothered me," Zosia commented when Peter reached the end of his song.

"Which line?"

" 'The cradle will fall, and down will come baby, cradle and all.' "

"What about it, the violence?"

"No, the repetition of cradle. You've already said it will fall, so why say it again?"

"Hmm. Don't know. Maybe I got the words wrong."

"Yeah, maybe that's it." Zosia paused to rearrange Irena.

"Any word on Olek?" Only the day before Olek had stepped on a mine while working down near the front. He had survived but had been severely injured. Peter had been utterly stunned when he had first heard the news, but even more shocked to learn that, of all people, Olek had specifically requested Peter's presence as he was carried to the hospital. Peter had visited the boy again that morning, and he had looked much better, but once Olek had slipped into an anesthetized sleep, the surgeon had confided that there was not much hope for his legs.

"He wasn't awake when I left," Zosia answered.

"Is he going to keep his legs?"

"They've already removed both below the knee. He'll probably have the right taken off above the knee."

Peter covered his mouth as if trying to physically contain his dismay and bowed his head in sorrow.

"That'll be in the negotiations," Zosia said inexplicably.

"What?"

"Clearing the mines. They have the equipment and maybe even maps—although maybe not, the way they hightailed it out of there. In any case, we'll let them in to clear up the mess they left, and then they'll have to clear out."

"Will they do that?"

"Katerina will make sure of it. She was furious about that. She'll make sure of it."

"Who else is negotiating?"

"Konrad. He's in charge of defense. And someone to take the minutes."

"That's all?"

"Yeah, that'll probably be it." Zosia looked up at the trees overhead. They would probably be meeting about now, in the city, in Kraków, or as it was called now, Krakau. It would be warmer there, and they could sip tea as they debated the terms of a new peace.

Peace. What a word for it! If only.

55

"A<small>H</small>, F<small>RAU</small> K<small>ALISCHER</small>, so we meet again!" The elderly man stood and greeted Katerina, clicking his heels and bowing slightly.

Katerina nodded to him and to the assembled mass of negotiators and advisers, most of whom were already standing, but some of whom were too boorish and uncultured to know to stand for a lady. The man who had greeted her was Herr Kolisch. They had initially met during the negotiations after the 1970 invasion attempt. After that, she had encountered him infrequently as they had occasionally met to discuss topics of interest to both sides and to exchange information about prisoners and dead soldiers.

Katerina scanned the other faces in the room. There were some she did not know, and of those, many had a look of curiosity or contempt. So, this was the enemy! An old woman! How could they possible expect to negotiate seriously about military matters with a woman? She recognized but did not react to Ryszard's presence. Good! He was moving up in the world. A few more years and he would truly be well placed.

The negotiations were entirely political: Ryszard's attendance was an indication not of his position in the government, nor of his rank in the Party, but rather of a certain indefinable presence in the hierarchy of current and future policymakers and powers-that-be. If he plays his cards right and has a bit of luck, thought Katerina humorously, we might make him Führer yet. She wasn't sure of what use that would be, but that was a bridge that could be crossed after it was built. She made sure she was not looking at him as she allowed herself a short laugh of pleasure. She probably wouldn't live to see it, but it would be such a wonderful irony!

"Frau Kalischer, what do you find so amusing?" Herr Kolisch asked obsequiously.

"Just the number of negotiators you bring with you each time. So many brave men against one frail woman and her lone adviser. *Przeciwko kilku myslom . . . co nie nowe.*"

"What's that?" Herr Kolisch asked suspiciously.

"The last line of an old poem. Roughly it goes: 'Enormous armies, brave generals, secret police: Against whom are they ranged? Against a few ideas . . . which is nothing new.' "

Herr Kolisch scowled. "It shows how we honor you."

"Honor us with our land and our freedom," Katerina replied to put an end to the stupid pleasantries. They sat down and the Germans arranged themselves according to rank at the table. She and Konrad and their recording secretary on one side, a row of Nazis on the other, each with an adviser or two in tow. Ryszard sat behind a man who was only two places away from Herr Kolisch. Very, very good. And quite a fast move since his arrival in Berlin. But Ryszard was good at what he did; if he survived, he could go far. Maybe Führer wasn't out of the question.

Yes, he's good at his job, takes it seriously, not like that flighty sister of his, Katerina mused. Of Alex's six children, Ryszard and Zosia were the gems, shining brilliantly among a bright and brave group. Ryszard had applied himself steadily and patiently over the years to building up his position. Zosia had seemed to take an almost opposite approach, skittering from one job to the other, always doing excellent work, always on the verge of disaster. Perhaps it was frustration at being a woman in a man's world. She could never infiltrate the way Ryszard had done, could never have placed herself as anything more than someone's wife—and she would have none of that. So, she had followed in her mentor's footsteps and taken to assassinations. Would her next step be to chair the Council? Or run for a position in the government in exile? It would suit her well and she would do a good job. Katerina nodded to herself, yes, that should be Zosia's career path. But first she needed to settle down, needed to spend more time away from that husband who seemed to cause her so much emotional turmoil.

Marriage! That was the problem. Men expected so much of their wives, they never provided them with unquestioning support the way dutiful wives did, the way Kasia did for Ryszard or Anna had for Alex. Husbands rarely even managed to be a neutral influence; rather they were usually a hindrance—demanding of their wife's time, jealous of her commitments. No, a woman with an agenda simply could not marry. Look at herself! Look at what had happened with Marysia! Zosia should never have married, certainly should never have remarried. She had too much of a future to waste it on a man. Maybe, though, they could work around her marriage; keep those two separated. They needed to be apart, it was better for both of them, and he could be put to good use in England, where he was currently underutilized. He was at home there, he understood those soulless people—he'd be perfect for the job of fostering more cooperation. Besides, it would keep those two out of trouble with each other, give Zosia a chance to mature into a responsible position, give him a chance to find whatever it was he was so desperately seeking . . .

Katerina allowed her thoughts and plans to play in her head a few seconds longer as Konrad poured a glass of water for her, then she brusquely cast aside all secondary thoughts and turned to the business at hand.

56

As SOON AS PETER RETURNED to the encampment, he went to see Olek. He waited by his bedside until the boy awoke, and he was the one who broke the news to Olek about his legs.

"What about higher up?" Olek asked, glancing downward in fear.

"I've been told that's fine."

Olek laughed. "Hey, then it's all okay!" he joked nervously.

Peter recognized the bravado and responded appropriately. Each day thereafter, he made a point of visiting Olek frequently, waiting for the right moment to help him through the difficult realization of what had happened to him. After a few days Olek was moved back into Marysia's apartment, and again Peter visited. Olek was laid out on the couch, Peter sat in a chair, and they drank cups of tea and discussed work and the weather and the state of the world and how everybody in the encampment and the partisan camps were faring. Neither Peter nor Olek mentioned the pathetic stumps that hid beneath the sheet thrown over a metal frame, until at last Peter ventured to ask, "Are you going to keep working as the cipher clerk?"

"I don't think I have much choice," Olek admitted ruefully. "Just as well I learned a sit-down skill, eh?"

"Yeah. You'll make a valuable contribution." Peter glanced down at Irena, who slept in the crook of his arm, and it almost seemed he was speaking to her.

"Thanks for teaching me all that stuff."

"You're welcome. I guess I did too good a job though." Marysia's cat, Siwa, rubbed against his legs and then jumped onto his lap.

"How so?"

"Well, you stole my job." Peter laughed. He shifted Irena a bit to make more room for Siwa and absently began stroking the feline's fur. "Now they got me running errands in London."

"At least you can run," Olek said without bitterness. He paused and looked hard at Peter's legs. "Tell me the truth, did you ever envy my undamaged legs?"

Peter looked away, down at the floor. The truth, hmm, that was difficult. Finally he looked back at Olek and said, "Yes. Yours and everyone else's."

"Well, I guess the shoe is on the other foot now!" Olek laughed hoarsely at his own joke.

"I'm sorry about that," Peter said without specifying whether he was referring to his previous envy or to Olek's current predicament. Both, he supposed. Siwa purred noisily, Irena snored quietly.

"I was so sure I was going to come out of all this untouched," Olek said as if in confession.

So was I, Peter thought, but decided that was not much consolation. None of them felt vulnerable, otherwise they could never face the dawn.

"I have these horrible nightmares about it," Olek whispered as if embarrassed. "Do you still have those terrible dreams?"

Peter shook his head. "No. Nothing since Irena was born. I've even had some normal dreams, the sort I remember from years ago." He supposed he had Irena's birth to thank for the sudden shift, but he could not ignore the thought that her birth had coincided with his first killing, and he wondered if the stabbing of the boy and the shooting of the soldiers rather than the joyful birth of his child was what had brought him peace. Or possibly it was having seen his torturer in the flesh as a mere, and very petty, mortal. "I haven't told anyone yet—I guess out of superstition."

Olek snorted. "So, even that. Shit, I always thought you were the fucked-up one. Now look who's all messed up!" Olek's voice grew unsteady and he added softly, "I'm only twenty-two, what am I going to do?"

"You'll cope, Olek. You'll be an inspiration," Peter replied softly.

"An *inspiration*? Oh, jeez, Peter, I expected better than that from you!" Olek groaned. "Did you find any of your experiences inspiring?"

"I didn't mean it that way," Peter said apologetically.

"Do you think you're a better man for having suffered them?"

Peter shook his head. "No. I'm less than what I was. There was no value to my suffering, there never will be. It was pointless. As pointless as you losing your legs. I'm sorry, I shouldn't have resorted to idiotic platitudes."

"Or if you did feel the need to say something stupid, you should have said, 'Shit happens.' "

Peter laughed. "Yeah, that pretty much sums it all up." He continued to chuckle as he thought about all the people who had somehow implied that there had to be a point to it all. Not least, himself. And when he could find no redemption in the evil he had experienced, then he had looked for his own guilt. Something, anything, to explain it! But here was Olek, a lad of twenty-two, summing it up so nicely. Shit happens!

"I guess I'm off guard duty anyway," Olek said.

"Gives you more time for other things."

"I'll need it! Shit, when you left me alone in that office, I was swamped! I had no idea how much work was involved. You always made me feel so good about my abilities, I thought it would be trivial, but it wasn't!"

"I'm sorry. I didn't mean to mislead you."

Olek laughed. "The day you stop apologizing for being kind is the day I'll know you're okay again."

Peter bit his lip and looked away, embarrassed.

"You know what else?" Olek said. "When they give me my medal—I want you to have it."

"Why?"

"You deserve it more than me."

"No, I don't. I haven't done anything."

"Yes, you have, and it's about time someone tells you that. I haven't heard one person say they appreciated the sacrifices you made. Not one. Maybe because they can't see the injury, maybe we've just been at war too long and lost all semblance of civility. I don't know. But what I do know is that you gave up a lot, voluntarily. You chose to fight for what you thought was right and you paid a very high price, and I think someone ought to say thank you."

"Olek, I—"

"Don't insult me by saying no!" Olek ordered, then clearly determined to change the subject before Peter could object, he asked, "Do you think she'll still want me?"

"Stefi?"

"Yeah."

"Has she heard the news?"

"Yes, so I'm told, but I haven't talked to her directly. Do you think she'll want to tie herself down with a cripple?"

"I don't know," Peter replied honestly. "You're both very young. If it wasn't serious, then it won't last, no matter what happened or didn't happen."

"Oh, it's serious. I love her."

"Does she love you?"

"I think so. I'm going to ask her to marry me."

"Give her time before you do that. Make sure you've settled into your new life—you know, with all the changes your injuries will entail. You want to make sure that if she says yes, she says it for the right reasons."

"Why else would she say yes?" Olek asked with determined naïveté.

Peter fell silent as he tried to think of a polite way of phrasing things.

"Do you think," Olek preempted Peter's reply, "that your wife said yes for the wrong reasons?"

"Just possibly."

"Enough said!" Olek responded with humorous severity. "I'll heed your warning!"

Peter laughed at the thought that at least his marriage could serve as an example of how *not* to do it. His thoughts drifted to Zosia, and Joanna, and Irena. He scratched absentmindedly behind Siwa's ear, and she stretched and rolled luxuriously in response, falling off his lap as a consequence. She landed on her feet, looked arrogantly miffed, and walked off as if that had been her intent all along. Peter shifted Irena and stretched his arm to get the blood flowing again, then leaned forward and kissed Irena's forehead. Maybe he was wrong, he thought, maybe they had done it right.

"I'm going to ask her," Olek said suddenly.

"Ask what? Who?" Peter asked, having forgotten what they had even been talking about.

"Stefi. I'm going to ask her to marry me as soon as she returns from Berlin."

"So you're not going to take my advice."

"I don't want to wait. Besides, I was just thinking about you and my aunt, and even if she did say yes for the wrong reasons, I think it has worked out for you."

"You do?" Peter asked, amazed.

"Yeah." Olek smiled. "You obviously love each other. So you get on each other's nerves, who doesn't?"

"Obviously?" Peter asked, wondering at how the conversation was suddenly about his marriage.

"Yeah, obviously. Don't believe all that shit about things being perfect with my uncle Adam." Olek shook his head knowingly. "I think a bit of history got rewritten after his death."

"Really?" Peter asked, amused. He was afraid to pursue the subject for fear of appearing—what was the word, catty? But if Olek insisted on telling him these things . . .

Olek did. He spent nearly an hour tearing apart his uncle's personality, dissecting his aunt's previous marriage, and generally making Peter feel really quite good. "God, the noise they would make! I mean, you think you two argue? At least there's no hitting!"

"He hit her?"

"Oh, no! Never! But that didn't stop her from hitting him. Throwing things. My grandmother said she was a spoiled brat. But she doesn't do that anymore, does she?"

Peter shook his head. "No, not with me." He remembered the one time he had caught Zosia's hand in midair, angrily warning her that he would not be hit. The look on her face. Her denial that she was intending to strike him. "Not with me."

"Anyway," Olek concluded, his voice suddenly shifting from cheerfully confidential to serious, "now that I've told you all that, I want you to tell me something."

"What?" Peter asked cautiously.

"What do you know about what happened to my mother? And my father?"

"The day I first arrived, Zosia told me both your parents were dead . . ."

"Please, don't give me the old song and dance. I'm old enough to know."

"Have you asked your grandmother about this?"

Olek shook his head. "She won't talk about my mother. Not at all."

Peter sighed. He remembered what it had been like to remain in ignorance about his own parents, and with that in mind, he came to a decision. He told Olek everything he knew; he told him that there was no reason to suspect his father was dead, that nobody knew who he was, that his mother had kept it a close secret. He told Olek what they knew about his mother's disappearance and the details of the police report. "It looks like she blackmailed someone—perhaps your father—in order to get enough money to go to America, so you would be safe. After that, she either told someone about the money or the person she blackmailed decided to get it back. Maybe she increased her demands and that made him violent."

Olek looked stunned but said, "I thought it was something like that."

"You realize what this all means?"

Olek nodded. "Yeah, it might have been my father who killed my mother." His eyes drifted to the picture of her on the wall. "She was a good woman. Some people say some awful stuff about her, but she was really good to me. She really cared. If I ever find out who it was, Peter, would you kill him for me? I won't be able to, not now, not like this, but you could."

57

"**Y**OU HAVE SOME NEWS FOR ME?" Ryszard asked as he spread the pâté on his toast. Stefi sat opposite him smoking a cigarette and sipping her wine. The flame of the candle danced in the faint breeze caused by a passing waiter; its light cast shadows across Stefi's face, and for a moment she looked old and careworn. A father-daughter dinner: that's how they had presented it to Kasia; just a chance for Ryszard to spend time with his little girl. The waiters no doubt assumed otherwise, but they were well trained enough to maintain facial expressions of complete disinterest.

"Yes, Wolf-Dietrich is leaving for London in three days time, for that laboratory I mentioned earlier," Stefi answered. "I couldn't get any specifics out of him, he's very cautious nowadays, but he did mention the name of a scientist there: Shantler."

"First name?"

"Don't know. Just said something about having to talk to this chap." Stefi studied her empty wineglass and then scowled off into the distance searching for their waiter. Within seconds the young man dutifully approached the table and poured more wine for her. "Lousy service," she muttered after he had left.

Ryszard ignored her complaint. "Good job. How did you get him to give up that much?"

"Oh, when he said he'd be gone, I threw a fit and accused him of seeing another woman. That got the information about the lab out of him. When he received a phone call, another wave of hysteria on my part got Shantler's name."

"He really likes you?"

"He's hooked."

"What do you think of him?"

"He's a really nice guy. His father's a bastard, but I can't hold that against him," Stefi replied impishly.

Ryszard pushed away the remains of his appetizer and lit a cigarette. "Are you sleeping with him?" he asked as casually as he could manage.

Stefi stretched provocatively in her seat; there was something very catlike in her movement. She picked up her glass and sloshed the wine gently around, then sipping it, she moaned as if deeply satisfied. "The more I talk to him, the more I'm convinced that what I told you earlier in the week is true," she said, suddenly businesslike. "It seems like his father has some connection to information from the NAU. Whatever they're up to has something to do with the division of the Hamburg lab that was shut down, you know, the sterility program; that's why the son was brought into it, he worked in that lab and had some connections with the scientists there. I think Schindler senior is doing everything in London now because that's within his jurisdiction and nobody will question him on his orders."

Ryszard nodded and wondered if he should ask his question again. He decided against it and commented instead, "I guess I'll be heading out to London again."

"Be careful. Last time . . ."

"Yes, I remember. Don't worry, I won't stay long, but I have to try and get something on the man."

"Will Uncle Peter be there?"

Ryszard winced at the title. "Yes, Zosia's husband should be back there soon. That reminds me, I'm supposed to send him some files."

"There's one other thing," Stefi said as she peered at her reflection in the wineglass.

"What's that?"

"Wolf-Dietrich started bragging about a computer he had access to; he heaped scorn on the best we have in Berlin. I challenged him to put his money where his mouth was and he did."

"What do you mean?"

"I mean, he showed me a small, compact computer that was as good as the best I've seen in Szaflary."

"Which is that?"

"The one in the cryptography office. Olek's been using it, but he said it belonged to Uncle Peter and that it came from the NAU. This one looked just like that. Clearly American-made. Wolf-Dietrich said he'll be taking it with him to London to translate some information they have there. I assume that would be the device that was passed on from that American agent."

"I wonder why they've waited this long?" Ryszard mused.

"I think they only just got their hands on the computer they need. Wolf-Dietrich certainly acted like the proud father of a newborn with it."

Ryszard nodded, impressed by his daughter's efforts. "I'm glad you mentioned that. I'll see if I can't get permission from Katerina for Peter to take his computer back to London with him."

"So I lost the bet," Stefi concluded.

"Do you owe him money?" Ryszard asked, wondering how much he'd have to cough up.

"No. I just had to sleep with him!" Stefi laughed.

Ryszard coughed. Before he could say anything, a waiter came with their entrées. He sputtered silently for a moment, and by the time the waiter had left them alone again, he had regained his breath. Before he could ask anything, Stefi volunteered, "Don't worry, Dad. It wasn't a sacrifice. Like I said, he's really nice and a great lay."

"I'm not sure—"

"Don't be prudish."

"That's not what I was going to say," Ryszard bristled. "I'm just concerned that you may become attached to this man. He is, after all, the enemy."

"You needn't worry, Father," Stefi stated icily. "Remember, I liked Til, too."

"Ah, yes, Til. I'm sorry about that, little one. It was his own fault, he made it necessary."

"I know. I was just reminding you, I never forget where my loyalties lie."

Ryszard looked into his daughter's cold eyes; he did not doubt for a second that she was telling him the truth. "That's my little girl. I'm proud of you."

58

"*T*HIS ARRIVED FOR YOU." Zosia handed a pack of documents over to Peter. "It was labeled confidential, so although they opened it, nobody but the translator and the censor looked at it." She paused, then added, "Not even me."

"I appreciate that," Peter mumbled as he studied the resealed envelope. "Who the hell is sending me packages?"

"Ryszard apparently. I guess somehow he knew you were here, or didn't want to risk sending it to London."

"Yeah, I told him I'd be here."

"When did you talk to him?"

So Ryszard still had not told anyone about his jaunt to England! Peter smiled at Zosia. "Confidential information, darling." He had heard the phrase often enough, and it was an absolute pleasure using it on her for once.

Zosia's face fell but she did not ask more. "I'll leave you alone to read the papers then," she said rather huffily, and giving him a quick peck on the cheek, left the apartment.

Peter scanned the documents. Ryszard had gathered some internal reports on the politics of his father's office. The Pure German movement merited a separate file, and together the papers showed that it had been especially active in that region at that time. The regional leader, a man named Mentzer, had occasion to know of Charles Chase, and though there was no explicit connection between the two, Mentzer was implicated in some actions against other English Conciliators, though none amounted to murder.

Peter had to read between the lines to determine what sort of harassment was common since the reports themselves were rather cagey about offending any possible political power. From the transfers list and from a separate complaints report, it seemed that the movement used petty vandalism, bureaucratic obstinacy, and scare tactics until the targeted individual requested a reassignment. The transfers were almost always to positions of less importance and were, within a few years, often followed by early retirement or resignation from the service.

Charles was apparently on the same track to be driven out of any meaningful position. He had filed several complaints with the local police about mysterious vandalism; those stopped abruptly as he began filing his complaints with his employer directly and reporting to the new investigative office that had opened. There were also a series of citations for minor civil offenses and several instances of his being reprimanded at work for petty bureaucratic offenses, none of which Catherine had recorded in her diary. Peter guessed that his father had never intimated this particular form of harassment to Catherine. A transfer request was submitted in Charles's name and then withdrawn, the withdrawal claiming that the request had been bogus and filed by another party who remained unnamed or unknown. The special investigative office then noted his arrest and subsequent, unexpected demise.

There was an investigation into the death of a Party member at police hands. A young, inexperienced guard was assigned sole responsibility for having taken it upon himself to unofficially interrogate the English prisoner under his care. The short, slight boy apparently single-handedly entered the cell of the fully grown, well-built man and, without the aid of an accomplice or weapons or handcuffs, managed to pummel him to death. Under a plea bargain where he admitted his guilt and defended his actions as having been inspired by shock and outrage at the prisoner's alleged denunciations of the Führer in the dead of the night, he was demoted and reassigned to Scotland.

As for Catherine, she was held without charge for three days and eventually released for lack of evidence. Her release occurred just hours after her husband's death, and before she even exited the prison she was rearrested under charges of sedition and making inflammatory statements to other prisoners. She was tried several months later and sentenced to hard labor in a concentration camp for a period of ten years, sentence to be reviewed before release.

Ryszard had included a summary of Mentzer's career, and shortly after Charles's murder Mentzer was transferred to Holland without comment. Not long after his transfer to Holland he was transferred again with a demotion, then again and once again, until his unsolved disappearance several years later from a branch office in Sicily. Clearly, he had offended someone, somewhere, but the report did not draw that conclusion nor was he ever held accountable for his alleged actions.

The cover-ups were obvious, there was no reason for them not to be. The relevant parties were silenced, the political egos that had been offended by Mentzer's actions were assuaged. That was all that mattered. The murder of two apparently loyal subjects, the blackmail or bribery of a young guard, the destruction of a young boy's family—none of it mattered as long as everything was nicely tidied up on paper. The ground higher up had shifted, Mentzer had pushed that bit too far, he had been taught a lesson, case closed until the political power structure shifted yet again and another Mentzer took his place with support from above.

Peter grimaced. So now he knew the reason, if not the actual mechanism. Still, he could easily imagine what his father's last days had been like. His thoughts were mercifully interrupted by a knock on the door. A young sentry greeted him with a smile and handed him a note. He read the words without emotion and muttered, "No reply," to the waiting boy. The borders were to be opened soon and arrangements had been made for his return to London.

59

*B*ARBARA HANDED PETER A CUP OF TEA, then skirted around him to sit next to Mark on the couch. "Now, tell us all about what happened."

Peter hadn't been in the flat for more than ten minutes, but he understood her impatience. She had quickly passed on her news—the most relevant bit being that the license had been renewed. Now she and Mark waited eagerly to hear what he had to say. Everybody knew that something had happened, but nobody had the details; they had waited for his return to get news directly, and his delay in returning had only alarmed them further.

Despite receiving the succinct note that he was to return, he and Zosia applied to the Council to rearrange his assignment. The Council would hear nothing of it: there was too much going on for them to instigate any unnecessary disruptions, and he was finally told, politely but firmly, to leave. Any changes would have to be handled in due course.

Peter sipped the tea and wondered about Zosia's role in his leaving. She claimed that she wanted him to stay and was working toward that end, but when his case was finally called before the Council, it was dismissed within minutes with a warning not to waste their valuable time. Zosia had remained silent throughout, and he had left the Council room feeling humiliated and quite alone.

"Well?" Barbara pressed impatiently.

"Your family is okay," Peter assured her.

"And?"

"And I have a baby daughter. Her name is Irena," he announced with a surge of pride. The tiny face appeared in his mind's eye and he smiled at the memory. It had nearly broken his heart to part from her, but he had promised her and himself he would soon return, whatever it took.

"Congratulations," Barbara offered. "Now tell us what happened there!" She slapped the table in annoyance.

"All right," Peter agreed wearily. "Sharing my joy can wait."

He spent several hours telling them everything he knew about the invasion and its aftermath. He was even drawn into explaining what he was doing during the initial attack and in that way was able to celebrate the birth of his daughter. As he told them about their close encounter with the soldiers in the cabin, Barbara leaned forward, her eyes fixed on Peter's face. Her fingers dug into Mark's hand until he yelped and brusquely pulled his hand away.

"I thought we were all dead then," Peter continued, ignoring Mark's jealous look.

"What happened next?" Barbara asked, her voice nearly a whisper.

"He survived obviously," Mark pointed out sardonically.

Peter nodded and continued the tale. He described how the soldiers had left and how he later found them dead along the trail. Then he described the life-and-death encounter with the sole survivor of the ambush. Barbara leapt to her feet as though she could not stand sitting anymore and paced the small area near the couch.

"Oh, for Christ's sake!" Mark snapped. "Sit down, woman. It's only a story!"

Barbara spun around to face him, absolutely livid. "What the hell do you know about it!" she spat at him in English. "You and your cozy little Underground here! What could you possibly understand!" Her English faltered and she slipped into Polish, denouncing Mark in words he could not understand, though he could not fail to interpret the flinging of hands and the furious looks.

Peter listened to the torrent, gave Mark a small smile when the boy looked to him for a translation, and shook his head. As soon as there was a break in Barbara's temper, Peter concluded, "And that brings us up to the point where I've already told you about everything."

Barbara stopped her tirade, stared at both of them with a look of absolute embarrassment. Peter took the opportunity to refill his cup of tea, and as he poured the water from the kettle, he heard Barbara saying softly to Mark, "I'm so sorry. It's just that, sometimes I feel so far from home. And now, what with . . ."

Unable to procrastinate longer, Peter returned to the room. Barbara was already sitting next to Mark again, holding both his hands in hers. They gazed into each other's eyes with that sickly sweet intensity that only new lovers could manage. "We have something to tell you," Barbara cooed without looking up.

"What's that?"

"We're getting married," she whispered dreamily.

"No, you're not," Peter answered matter-of-factly.

That got their attention. "How can you say that!" Barbara scolded.

"You have no right!" Mark threatened.

Peter sipped his tea before answering, "Yes, I do."

It took several minutes for them to quiet down enough for him to continue. When he could finally speak uninterrupted, he explained, "As her commanding officer, I have every right to delay a marriage which would be disastrous for our mission. Besides that, she has to get clearance from the Council, and I don't doubt that you, Mark, have someone you have to answer to. I know things have changed since I was here, but they have not changed that much."

"It won't be a problem to our mission here," Barbara argued.

"I get to be the judge of that. Besides, have either of you considered the practicalities? How old are you both? Nineteen?"

"I've turned twenty!" Mark interjected with injured pride.

Peter ignored him. "What in heaven's name is the hurry?"

"I'm pregnant," Barbara announced triumphantly.

"God Almighty!" Peter howled. "You stupid, stupid children!" It was his turn to stand and pace a bit. "How far along are you?" he asked once he had gained control of his anger.

"Seven weeks," Barbara answered.

"You'll have to get rid of it."

"That would be murder!" Barbara shrieked.

"Don't be stupid, you have to get rid of it."

"I won't!"

Peter prevented himself from launching into a tirade of orders or threats. He could not force her, nor would he if he could. His mother's words about her second pregnancy came back to him and he felt suddenly quite ill. He lowered himself back into the chair and breathed deeply to fight back his nausea. "Will you love it?" he asked at last.

"Yes," Barbara and Mark both agreed enthusiastically.

"Whatever it is?"

Barbara furrowed her brow. "Of course!"

"We'll have to pretend it's mine," Peter whispered.

"But it's not!" Mark objected angrily.

"I know that, you stupid boy," Peter snapped in reply. He had, though, been around seven weeks ago, so he added rather more gently, "She's been faithful to you."

Mark flushed red but looked a bit happier nonetheless. Barbara leaned toward him and said softly into his ear, "Mark, it's like I said, he's never meant anything to me. He's too old! And married! You're the only man I've ever loved." Mark had turned to face her, so he could not see the way Barbara eyed Peter as she spoke.

Peter winced at Barbara's words, but continued in a businesslike tone, "The matter of your paternity is not in doubt, Mark; still, as far as the authorities are concerned, it will have to be mine. Or rather, Herr Jäger's."

"No! I won't have that!"

"Don't be stupid," Peter chided. "Barbara is supposedly a married German woman almost five years your senior. If she were to claim you as the father, she could face charges of adultery and God knows, with your pedigree, they might even push *Rassenmischung!*"

"My pedigree? I'm pure English!"

"You'd be surprised how inappropriate ancestors can be found when it is convenient for them."

"No, that's impossible! Both my parents have their documented bloodlines!"

Peter smiled at the naïveté. "You have an arrest record, don't you?" he guessed.

"Well, yes, a couple of misdemeanors, ages ago."

"I hardly had worse."

Mark looked confused.

"He's a condemned convict," Barbara explained reluctantly. "Numbers and all."

"They threw in an *Untermensch* classification, just for laughs," Peter added. "No blood proof, nothing!"

Barbara blushed with embarrassment, and well she might, since she took orders from him. She knew that the classification itself was enough to confirm an inferior status in almost everyone else's eyes—even the most committed revolutionaries had difficulty ignoring a lifetime of propaganda. Only in Szaflary, among the prewar generation and the untainted native-born, and in America, where such ideas of government classification generally had no currency, had Peter been free of the stigma that came with the official label.

Pursuing the advantage of Mark's fear, Peter clarified, "If you try and put your name on this child's birth certificate, the moral outrage of one bitter bureaucrat might be sufficient to destroy your life! You could be charged as an adulterer, or reclassified and charged with *Rassenmischung*. That's still a death sentence for the inferior male partner, you know."

Mark shifted uncomfortably.

"And what name would you use? How old are you supposed to be? Do you plan to stick with one identity for the rest of your life? Have you thought out any of the details?"

They both looked a bit sullen, but neither argued with him. Peter remembered being told to "grow up" at about the same age. He imagined he had that same look on his face at the time. The memory dissolved his anger a bit, and he added by way of explanation, "It would all be pointless. Barbara and Niklaus Jäger are supposed to be married, therefore, any child would be considered his—I mean, mine—no matter what any of us might say. That's the law. The only thing you would accomplish by advertising your paternity is that you'd be exposing yourself to an unnecessary risk. You don't want to do that. You don't want to give them any excuses to treat you the way I was treated."

Mark bit his lips.

"All right already!" Barbara objected. "We'll register Niklaus Jäger as the father. Maybe someday Mark can assume that identity. After you've returned to Szaflary."

"He'll have to age himself considerably and learn a fuck of a lot of German," Peter observed.

"Still, it doesn't matter what names are on the certificates," Barbara consoled herself and Mark. "At least we'll be married."

"Presumably you're talking about something not involving the authorities."

"Yes." Mark perked up a bit. "We have our own registry."

"What about your family? What about everyone back home?" Peter asked Barbara.

She shrugged. "I don't need their permission."

"I'm not so sure about that. In any case, don't you want them to be a part of your life anymore?"

"I'll make my life here."

"What sort of marriage is it going to be: not officially recognized, Mark living with his parents?"

"He'll live here!" Barbara protested.

"No, he won't," Peter disagreed.

"He has to! How will we raise our child together if he doesn't?"

"I don't know, you should have thought of that before."

"How can you possibly say no!" she nearly shouted.

"There's no room," he answered matter-of-factly.

"Mark and I will share the bedroom, you can sleep out here."

"No! The couch is too small and I will not sleep on the floor so that you can play house!"

"This place is bigger than my parents' flat," Mark interjected.

"I don't care." Peter remained adamant.

"Niklaus! Peter!" Barbara seemed confused. "You have to!"

"I said no."

"You're jealous!"

"Oh, little girl, if only it were that simple." Peter shook his head in exasperation. He did not bother to explain the complex motives behind his refusal; instead he said, "Whatever I'm willing to put up with is irrelevant: we are a proper German couple here and we cannot start living like the English. It would raise suspicions and I will not take that chance. That's my final word!"

"You're a horrid man!" Barbara seethed. She took a deep breath to arm herself and began, "You're—"

"Look," Peter interrupted. "If you work with me, maybe we can arrange something. I want out of here. You want to stay. If I can get Katerina to let me return, we can concoct some abandonment story. After the appropriate period, you can divorce me; then I don't think you'll be harassed if you strike up a relationship with an Englishman: after all, you'll be a lone woman with a child, and beggars can't be choosers."

"But it takes five years for a divorce based on abandonment! I want it quicker than that!"

"On what grounds?" Peter asked.

"Your adultery!"

"Too dangerous. You never know how they'll react to a social crime."

"You'll be long gone," Barbara reminded him.

Peter sighed. "I guess it will work. Trouble is, you'll need proof. With me gone, and without a woman to name, I don't know how you'll convince them."

"Photos. You and somebody else. We'll just make sure she can't be identified from the pictures," Barbara suggested.

"Photos," Peter groaned. He thought for a moment. "Not only would we have to hide the woman's face, but we'd have to keep my scars out of view as well. I wouldn't want them to link you to Halifax, after all."

"Oh, God, no!" Barbara blanched at the dangerous thought.

"Who's he?" Mark asked.

"Never mind," they answered him simultaneously. A dark look came over Mark's face, but he did not question them further.

"Perhaps," Peter suggested, "hotel room receipts, jewelry, flowers, restaurants, you know, that sort of thing would do better."

"I guess that would suffice."

"It will have to. Either that, or we can drop a stack of clothes at the beach and you can get Jäger declared dead. That might be quicker," Peter concluded while silently tabulating the number of times he had officially died.

Barbara nodded enthusiastically.

Peter ignored the irritation he felt at her response. "Of course, this is all contingent on my getting out of here. Until then, I want you both to behave. Don't arouse any suspicions!"

"We won't," Barbara moaned like a teenager to an overbearing parent.

"Barbara, have you thought about what to do if you're recalled? What is Mark going to do?"

"I'll request a permanent assignment here. They always have trouble filling this position due to the distance, I suppose. They'll be happy to give it to me."

"Do you want to be stuck with a German identity, in London, for the rest of your life? Don't you two realize the problems you'll have? You'll be completely isolated. The English will hate you and the Germans will hate him! You'll both be considered traitors."

Barbara shrugged. "It has been done before."

"Why make things hard on yourselves?" Peter asked with some concern. "There are enough problems in life without setting yourself into an awkward situation from the start."

"Awkward? Look who's talking!" she retorted.

"Huh? What do you mean?"

Barbara went to a drawer and removed a piece of paper with a scribbled note. It was in her handwriting. "I received this the day before you arrived. I guess she couldn't get the priority for voice communication or maybe didn't want to ask. She must have thought you'd be on the receiving end. I'm sorry, but I let her finish before I said it was me on this end." Barbara smiled awkwardly at him and explained, "I was curious." Then she bowed her head and whispered in Polish, "I'm not quite over you, you know. Sorry."

Peter took the note from Barbara's hand, held it without looking at it.

"She took some risk sending it here. I guess it was important to her," Barbara said as if he were unaware of such things.

"Before I read this," Peter said, "just listen to me for one more minute. All I want to do is suggest that you two get coincident IDs. Leave and come back as someone else. Either have them make you English, or better yet see if Mark can't get a German ID. That way you can at least move freely in one of the two societies."

"Won't work. I'll never pass for English—I just don't have enough fluency in the language. And you've heard Mark's German. It stinks."

"He can be *Volksdeutsch*. Have them find some relative and get him legitimized. He'll be more useful to them that way, and you two won't have to fight two cross-cultural battles."

Barbara looked hard at Peter, then switching to Polish again, said, "Okay, we'll consider it. After all, if anyone understands how to fuck up a marriage, I'm sure you do. We should at least listen to your advice."

"I thought we were past your snide attacks," he answered, also switching languages.

"No, as I said, I'm still not really over you," Barbara admitted with a rueful smile.

Mark looked in linguistic confusion from one to the other. "You're being rude, you know," he said to both of them. They both ignored him.

"Then do you think you should be getting married in the first place?" Peter asked.

"Yeah, I think it's the right thing to do. I won't be disillusioned. At least not more than I already have been," Barbara added in a whisper.

"You're being tough on me. You must have missed me."

Peter then retreated to the bedroom to read Zosia's missive in peace. It was odd seeing Barbara's handwriting conveying Zosia's words, but there was no mistaking his wife's style.

My dearest husband,

Bad news, I'm afraid. I went to Katerina directly about reorganizing your assignment and she was adamant that you stay put for a while. She won't even bring it to a vote! It seems there is a perception that I have been using my position too frequently for personal reasons. Katerina listed, among other things, my unilateral decision to interview you the night of your arrival (actually it was Marysia's idea, but that's neither here nor there), my getting a special hearing for your case after the vote went against you, that trip to Göringstadt, your Berlin outing—she had heard about it from somewhere—and the way I violated security to tell you about the Hamburg data. She also pointed out how she didn't want me to go to Ryszard's and I got to go anyway for Kasia's baby's birth. She even brought up the lax security on my part which led to, well, you know.

Her list went on, but I won't bore you. The upshot was, she thinks I've been meddling too much, and now, of all times, she's decided to draw the line. The old hag! Her ostensible reason is that she really is going to use you in a more active role with the British, once things have settled down here. Maybe she's telling the truth. Anyway, I talked to Marysia and she said there was no point my trying to get her overruled. Everybody thinks I've been mixing my work and my personal life too much—and unfortunately, that means anything to do with you. Sorry.

I'll let things cool down and try again later. A direct request for a transfer from you sent through a source other than me might help. Try Konrad—nobody will accuse him of anything if he presents your request. Or even Tadek. In the meanwhile, I have a lot to think about. Not to sound grumpy, but I'm fairly annoyed by their reaction. True, I have been involved in personal issues this past year, but I have otherwise given my entire life to my work. I should think they would cut me a bit of slack. Their lack of appreciation, blah, blah, blah. You get the point.

Irena's doing well. Her yawns are incredibly infectious. She stretches in the morning just like you! Sometimes in the night, she sobs a bit in her sleep and in my confusion I think it's you. Then I open my eyes and see her tiny little face. She has your eyes—those English eyes, you know, with as much eyelid below as above. Poor girl, maybe with luck she'll grow out of it. I hope you're sleeping better now. Rest well, darling. I'm sure we'll manage something soon. There is no need for an immediate reply.

Zosia

P.S. Ah, so you're not there yet! I'm sure your companion will be discreet in keeping our private affairs private. (Especially if she wants to keep her commission. I am willing to meddle at least once more!)

He reread the letter several times, then just sat and stared at it for a while. So, he was on his own and in exile for an indeterminate length of time. Ironic, he was back in London and still so far away from home.

60

A WEEK LATER, as they finished breakfast and Peter prepared to go down to open the store, Barbara stopped him. "Here." She shoved a small box at him. A ribbon was tied around it.

"What is it?" Peter asked as he took it in his hands. He was in a lousy mood. Despite their promises to be careful and discreet, Barbara and Mark had been spending an inordinate amount of time together. During the past week, they had taken up occupation of the bedroom for the first half of the night on four occasions. Each time Peter had had to throw Mark out in the middle of the night so that Peter could get some sleep, and two nights ago there had been a bit of a scene with a drunken Mark accusing Peter of trying to steal his woman.

"Open it, you'll see," Barbara replied elusively.

Peter untied the ribbon and removed the lid. Inside on a bed of cotton lay a solitary slip of paper. On it was written an address. "What is it?" he repeated warily.

"It's sort of an apology. Go to the address. You'll see."

He handed the box and paper back to her. "No," he answered simply. "I've had enough of your games." He turned to leave.

"No, wait! It's not a game. It's your brother's address!"

"My brother? Where'd you get it?"

"It took some finding," she said, not answering his question. "He's phoneticized his name."

"Huh?"

"Chase. He spells it T-s-c-h-e-j-s-s."

Peter made a noise of disgust, then asked again, "Where'd you get the information?"

"I had Mark ferret it out," Barbara responded proudly.

"So he's in on this, too? What else have you told him?" The other night, Mark had not failed to invoke Peter's subhuman classification as justification for his drunken accusations. It still irked that something Peter had revealed in an attempt to warn the boy away from danger had so quickly been used against him.

"Don't worry, nothing. I just had him get the address for you. Your brother's address!"

"Why would I want that?"

"Don't you want to see him?"

"No." Peter shook his head. He realized by the look on Barbara's face that she was serious and that her gesture had been well-intended. As he headed for the door, he added apologetically, "Thanks for letting me know he's okay. That's information enough."

"He has four children."

Despite himself, Peter stopped in the doorway. Erich had been married but childless the last time he had checked on him. Four children. Still he could not bring himself to ask.

"Two girls and two boys."

"How very loyal to the Reich," Peter replied sarcastically. It would be stupid to hope that somehow a family could make a difference. Pointless. Asking to be hurt. Stupid.

"Their names are Katerina, Anna, Karl, and"—Barbara paused dramatically—"Niklaus."

Peter remained silent, his back still toward Barbara.

"Don't you get it? He's named them all after his family, including you!"

"I can see that, I'm not an idiot."

"He wants to be forgiven."

Peter shook his head, but the motion was too slight for Barbara to notice. She grabbed his arm and turned him around. "Take it," she insisted, shoving the slip of paper back into his hand. "Take it and go see him."

He closed his fingers around the scrap as she pressed it into his palm.

Peter waited in a misting, cold rain outside the Technical Institute, where his brother worked. He wrapped his hand nervously around the identification wallet that he carried and scanned the workers as each left the building. When he saw his brother emerge, he approached him, snapped the official-looking identification open and shut in front of him, and said, "Herr Tschejss, may I have a word with you?"

Not surprisingly Erich blanched, but nodded his agreement.

"This may take a bit of time," Peter informed him. "We can talk over in that public house there."

"That's English," Erich cried as he followed Peter's gesture.

"Are you saying, Herr Tschejss, that we would not be welcome there?" Peter asked in his best obtuse, official accent.

"No, I, er . . ." Erich waved his hand randomly. "No, of course, we'd be welcome anywhere."

"Good, come with me," Peter ordered, and crossed the street in the direction of the pub.

They entered and Peter scanned the crowd. It was a popular place, noisy and large. When Peter spotted Barbara sitting at a corner table, he headed casually in that direction. She simultaneously chose to relocate to join her friend at a nearby table, nodding ever so slightly to reassure Peter that the surroundings had been checked. Jenny and her husband occupied a table close to theirs, and several of Mark's friends sat at the only other nearby table.

Peter and Erich took the vacated seats, and Peter waved peremptorily at the waitress who took the orders of customers who did not bother to order directly at the bar.

"May I ask what this is about?" Erich prompted after Peter had finished ordering beer for both of them.

"I assume you drink beer," Peter replied.

"Yes. Thanks. Now, could you tell me what this is about?"

"I've come from Berlin to pursue an investigation," Peter finally answered.

Erich fell silent at the name of that city.

Peter took the opportunity to look directly into his brother's face. He could easily discern the cocky sixteen-year-old he had known in the features of the man opposite him. "I have some questions concerning your family."

"My family? Is something wrong? Are they okay?"

"I'm talking about your parents, and"—Peter paused slightly—"your brother."

Erich stiffened. "That was all cleared up ages ago. I am completely loyal!"

"Ah, we feel there is further need for investigation. First I'd like you to tell me, what happened to your brother?"

"He ran away from home at twelve, or I guess thirteen. Drowned himself in the Temms."

"Suicide? Was he emotionally unstable?"

"I would say so. He was a spoiled brat, did nothing but make trouble for our parents."

"You named a son after him."

"He was my brother, even if he was troubled," Erich huffed.

"And your parents? What happened to them?" Peter asked somewhat disappointed that he had used his only edge so quickly and unwisely.

Erich stared gloomily into the crowd. "Certainly you must know, they were arrested. I never saw them after that."

"Why were they arrested?"

Their order arrived and they fell silent. Half of Erich's beer had already been spilled on the waitress's tray, and the glass that held Peter's beer was obviously dirty. Before she could place the sticky glasses on the table, Peter waved her away. "Get rid of those," he ordered, annoyed by the interruption. He stood and, telling Erich to stay put, went to the bar. He dove into the scrum, out of sight of his brother, and using English, ordered two pints of bitter from the bartender. He returned with clean, full glasses, set them down, and as he seated himself, repeated, "Why were they arrested?"

"I don't know."

"You don't?"

"No! I, um, there was . . ."

"There was a warrant for your brother, isn't that true?"

"Yes, so I've heard."

"You were the informant of record. You turned him in, didn't you?"

Erich did not look up from his beer. He sighed. "Why are you asking this?"

"Herr Tschejss, it is in your interest to cooperate."

"All right, yes! I mentioned to the *Kommandant* of the camp where I was interned that I thought my brother was engaged in some sort of illegal activities. I had worked my way up to a position of some authority in the camp and had the *Kommandant*'s trust."

"Ach. The *Kommandant* was your mentor?"

"I guess."

"Did you say your brother was in the Underground?" Peter studied his brother's face for a clue to his thoughts.

"Not exactly. I wasn't really sure. I just knew he was up to no good."

"Is that why your parents were arrested?" Peter asked, hoping to edge Erich into an act of contrition.

Erich misinterpreted. "Yes! I don't doubt he got them involved in something without their knowing it! He got them killed!" Erich snapped angrily, but somewhat unconvincingly.

Peter stared in silence across the room. He didn't really know where to go next with the conversation; it certainly wasn't going the way he had expected. Finally he said, "What if I were to tell you that your brother, at that time, was not involved in anything; that to the best of our knowledge neither was your mother or your father."

"Huh?"

"That's what this investigation is about, Herr Tschejss," Peter continued, ad-libbing. "You see, I'm from the Bureau of State Security and Oversight. We're trying to track what we believe is police misconduct which may have stemmed from political motivations. Your father may have been the victim of a vendetta, and you, with your petty denunciation, provided the flimsy excuse needed to carry out what was, to all intents and purposes, a political murder."

"A vendetta?"

"Do you know what happened to your parents after their arrest?"

"No." Erich shook his head slowly. He shifted uncomfortably.

"Your father died within days, under interrogation. He was beaten to death."

Peter saw how Erich's muscles tensed as he clenched his jaw, but his brother remained silent.

"Now that, for a prisoner of his status and considering that he was, at least officially, only a secondary arrest—that is, he was suspected of providing your brother with an escape and an alibi—that, as I was saying, is very unusual. Very unusual. Do you get what I'm saying?"

Erich shook his head in confusion.

Slowly, as if speaking to a moron, Peter explained, "Somebody killed him."

"I don't understand."

"Herr Tschejss, let me be blunt. Your father was a Party official taken into custody because of minor suspicions about his son. There is no reason for him to have been investigated that brutally; ergo, his death was not an accident."

Erich looked utterly blank.

"Don't you understand? He was murdered!"

"What happened to my mother?" Erich asked quietly, apparently unable to take it all in.

"She was sent to a labor camp, probably to keep her quiet. If they had released her, she would have doubtless made some noise and stirred things up. She was, by all accounts, a strong-willed woman."

"Yes, she was."

"So, she was left to die of disease or starvation or overwork. Officially, I believe it was typhus," Peter finished coldly.

"Just to keep her quiet," Erich repeated softly.

"Yes, that's what we believe."

"But why are you investigating all this now?" Erich asked plaintively.

"Well, the reason we think your father was murdered was not personal, or even really political. You see, there is a xenophobic movement among the upper echelons of the police, and they have a great resentment of any foreign involvement in the Party or in government. Your father was probably killed simply because he was English and making his way within the establishment."

The color drained from Erich's face.

"You can see where this could lead. We believe that this group has not been eradicated and that their activities have not ceased. Clearly from our point of view, we cannot afford to have loyal Party members removed simply because they have what might be called second-class blood. From your point of view, well, I think it's obvious."

Erich remained in stunned silence.

"I don't think you quite understand the danger you are in," Peter added, not sure of where he was heading. He had wanted to see if Erich was contrite, but all he was managing to do was scare him; it was hardly the right approach to getting an apology.

"But I have a German wife, my family—we're totally integrated. I, there's nothing English about me, nothing at all."

"There is your brother."

"What? What do you mean? I had nothing to do with him! He drowned ages ago!"

"Yes, the poor suicide, unable to cope with the stress. Interesting that it was you who had him declared dead. Do you know what really happened to him?"

Erich shook his head.

"A great deal. A great deal of unpleasantness," Peter replied tersely. He stopped himself from saying more and lit a cigarette, watching with a sort of detached disinterest as the smoke trembled heavenward. Joanna would have to forgive him this time, but he was having trouble keeping himself sufficiently calm and detached. Once he had regained his composure, he continued, "The upshot is, he managed to gain some fame, or rather infamy, for himself. He went to America and denounced the Fatherland and besmirched our good name!"

"Oh my God!" Erich exhaled. "I don't have anything to do with him. You know that! I thought he was dead! He's nothing to do with me!"

"No, of course not," Peter agreed. "But perhaps, after your three denials, a cock should crow?" he asked snidely, and ignoring Erich's blank look, he picked up the glasses and returned to the bar to have them refilled.

When he reseated himself, Erich asked, "What does all this have to do with me? I mean, if you know who murdered my father . . ."

"Well, we don't really know that. I was hoping you'd have some additional information that might clarify our case, a name that your father had mentioned, or something. But I guess you don't."

"I've told you everything I know. My father never mentioned any names. Look, what can I do about these people? You say they are still around. Is there something I can do to protect myself and my family?"

Peter leaned back and pensively tapped his fingers. "How do you feel, Herr Tschejss, about the Party?"

"The Party? I'm an associate member! I am utterly loyal."

"Only an associate?" Peter asked, noting the slight bitterness in his brother's tone.

"These things take time," Erich answered defensively.

"Ah. And what about the Party's involvement in the death of your parents and the subsequent cover-up? Doesn't that bother you?"

Erich stared at his beer. "Mistakes were made, I guess. My dad was loyal, just like me." Erich raised his head and scanned the room, then summoning up what seemed to be the last of his courage, he asked, "But why question my loyalty?"

"Oh, it's not me," Peter answered breezily. "It would be the xenophobes who might look for the slightest excuse to trap you. Like they did your father."

"But there is nothing they could say! I am completely loyal!" Erich protested somewhat loudly; he was already most of the way through his second pint.

Peter smiled and made a shushing motion. "You don't want to protest too much! After all, loyalty doesn't matter to the xenophobes, all they need is a reason to take you in."

Erich writhed in his seat. "I trust the Fatherland to do what is right."

At that point, Peter wondered if he was making any headway at all. He sighed, then said, "Perhaps you do have some information, but can't recall it. Maybe if we jog your memory a bit. Tell me about your family. What do you remember of them?"

Erich described his mother and father and even Anna. He recalled some incidents but avoided mentioning his brother at all.

Exasperated, Peter said, "You remember nothing of your brother?"

"No, not really. He was always in trouble. A real smart-arse. Too independent."

Almost to himself Peter whispered, "Yes, that fits in with his story."

"He told you this?"

"Weren't you listening? He told everyone of this! He told the Americans, our enemies!" Peter replied angrily.

"*The traitor!*"

"But it was the truth!"

"Still, he's a *Nest-Beschmutzer.*"

Peter paused and smiled tightly. "Herr Tschejss, you know English, don't you?"

"Yes, why?"

"I've never heard a good translation for that phrase. Perhaps you could give me one."

Erich thought a bit, then admitted, "I can't think of an exact equivalent."

"Isn't that interesting. Perhaps telling unpleasant truths isn't viewed so negatively among the English."

"Maybe. It's a loser culture given to whining, even against their own. They don't understand loyalty," Erich opined.

"Yes," Peter agreed sarcastically, "that must be our great strength: our unwillingness to criticize ourselves and our merciless revenge upon any who break that code. Your brother, for instance."

"Revenge?"

"Yes, we taught that bastard a lesson!" Peter laughed harshly. "Murdered his young daughter in front of his eyes! He's alive, all right, but he won't dare open his fucking mouth again!"

Erich's eyes wandered around the room. He looked thoughtful, or perhaps he was studiously avoiding listening. If he had not been relaxed by the beer, he might have wondered what this had to do with an official investigation of his father's death, but he did not state any such objection. Instead he asked, "You said he's alive? Is he in prison?"

"Alive, but not in prison. He escaped and is currently at large. He could be anywhere." Peter glanced dramatically around the room indicating the crowd. "In fact, since he was just a boy when you last saw him . . ."

Erich was staring at Peter, his eyes widening with realization.

". . . you could be looking right at him and you probably wouldn't even know it," Peter finished bitterly.

They stared at each other for a moment. "*Niklaus?*" Erich whispered.

Peter stared at him but did not respond.

"*Niklaus?*" Erich repeated, slightly louder.

"Do you know what it felt like to see Mom and Dad thrown into that Gestapo van? To be totally alone in the world with absolutely no one to turn to?" Peter hissed at him.

"*Niklaus?*"

"They killed our parents, Erich! How could you become one of them? How could you?"

"*Niklaus?*"

"They beat Dad to death! Do you know what it feels like to be beaten? I do! Mom probably starved to death! Do you have any idea what these people are like?" Peter slammed his fist into the table. "How could you become one of them?" At the look of surprise from his nearby companions, Peter stopped short and took a deep breath. In an attempt to goad Erich, all he had managed to do was provoke a flood of angry denunciations.

"So you're not from the Bureau of State Security and Oversight?" Erich asked as he began to perceive the deception.

"There is no such thing," Peter replied mordantly.

"How many other lies have you told me?"

"That was the only one. Oh, yeah, they don't know my real name either, so there's no link between me and you or your family. Niklaus Chase disappeared and drowned, just like you wanted."

"What do you call yourself?"

Peter made a dismissive gesture. "Lots of things. Doesn't matter."

"And your story about Father? Was that a lie as well?"

"No. It was the truth. I have friends who dug out the information for me."

Erich stood suddenly and without a word walked away. Peter watched in stunned silence as he disappeared into the crowd near the door. Barbara glanced over at him, looked worriedly in the direction Erich had gone, and then came over to the table.

"What happened?" she asked.

Peter shook his head. "I don't know. Nothing. He knows who I am, and he just walked away." No apology, no reconciliation, nothing. "Just walked away," Peter repeated quietly.

"Do you think he's gone to get the police?"

"Even he can't be that stupid."

"Maybe he just needs time to think," Barbara offered after a moment.

Mark made a hissing noise that drew their attention to Erich's return. Barbara went back to her seat before Erich had noticed her.

He came back with a bottle of whiskey and two glasses. "Can't stand English beer," he explained as he poured a glass for each of them. "They say they follow the *Reinheitsgebot,* but everyone knows they don't. We should have gone to a good German beer hall."

Peter nodded noncommittally.

"Now," Erich prompted, "tell me about these xenophobes. Do I have anything to worry about? What should I do? Is my family safe?"

Peter rubbed his forehead and laughed quietly to himself. He had been an idiot to expect anything else. With a prearranged gesture he indicated to his companions that they were no longer needed. He then spent the rest of the evening with Erich discussing Erich's life, Erich's family, and Erich's career.

At the end of the long evening, watching his brother stagger home to kith and kin, Peter contemplated the various choices they had each made and that had been made for them. He came to two definite conclusions: the first was that he needed to go home, and now there was no doubt in his mind where home was; the second was that he would give his brother's name to the Underground as somebody who could now be easily blackmailed.

61

*P*ETER LEFT THE BAR feeling a bit groggy with the devastating combination of beer and whiskey. It was drizzling, but he decided to walk home anyway. The fresh air would do him good, and besides, it would save money. This area of town was fairly well known to him, and he followed old paths without thinking as he mulled over the meeting he had had with his brother.

"Hey, there! Want a good time?" prostitutes called out as he walked along a narrow street. Just one question about how he was doing! But there had been nothing: Erich had wanted to talk about himself, about only himself. One of the prostitutes came close, started walking along with Peter, started to caress him. It was as though Erich had missed having someone to chat to, but made no connection between his brother's long absence and his own actions. It was as if he were still eleven years old in Erich's mind, incapable of having an independent life, there just to admire his elder brother's achievements and sympathize with his problems. As the prostitute stroked down Peter's chest, toward his wallet, he brusquely pushed her hand away. Even when he had handed Erich a selection of the photographs he had found, even then Erich could do nothing but talk about himself. He did not ask to see the diaries, did not ask if there were any other photos, did not thank his brother for the gift, he just sat there and smiled stupidly at his youthful image.

The prostitute finally gave up as Peter stepped over the sprawling legs of a drunk sleeping rough in a doorway. Just one attempt at an apology! He skirted around a young kid offering him drugs. He felt sorry for the kid: the boy would not get any of the profits; he did the selling because he was told to by his gang leaders, and if he did not sell enough that evening, then there would be trouble for him. Peter thought momentarily that maybe he should give the kid a break and buy something; some of the profits would almost surely end up in the coffers of the Underground and he could use a rush of some sort, but he was already well past the boy and did not feel like turning back. He recognized a shortcut and turned down an alley. Erich's continual blather about himself, his worried questions about the Pure German movement, not one question about what *his* life had been like! The two young men emerged from the shadows in front of him, and only then did Peter realize his mistake. He spun around to see that a third was approaching him from behind.

A lone, unarmed German in an English section of town! How could he have been so stupid as to leave the main road? Even as the men pulled out their knives, he reached into his coat and pulled out his wallet, holding it out as an offering as they approached. One of them grabbed it and began rifling through it while the other two held their knives threateningly close.

Knowing the severity of the penalties for physically injuring a German, Peter had decided not to fight in the hopes that the men would stick to a simple robbery, but as he smelled the alcohol on their breath and looked into their wild eyes, he began to doubt the wisdom of his decision.

"There's got to be more!" the one who had rifled through his wallet growled angrily.

"Let's cut him!" the second hissed, and flourished a knife in a hypnotic arc under Peter's face.

"Frisk him," the third suggested more practically.

"Kill him, then he'll be easy to search!" the second one insisted.

While the second one continued to swing his knife wildly in front of Peter, the first and third attempted to search him.

"How 'bout I take off an ear?" the second threatened, pressing the knife against the side of Peter's head.

"Don't do that . . ." Peter began in as conversational a tone as he could manage.

"What's this?" the first one howled as his fingers detected the cast. He pushed Peter's coat sleeve up, began cutting the material of his shirt.

"It's a cast," Peter explained hurriedly, trying to calm him down.

"Cut it off!" the second demanded. "He's hiding something!" The man made a wild stab at the material with his knife and tried to slice across it as the first one fumbled with the clasps.

"Hey, watch it! You almost got my finger!" the first one yelped angrily.

"Wait! Wait! I can remove it!" Peter struggled to remove the thing before the excitable one sliced up his arm.

As the cast dropped to the ground, the first one stooped to inspect it, the second returned to poking at him with his knife, while the third stared transfixed at Peter's numbers. "Bloody hell!" he exclaimed.

That alarmed the trio sufficiently to get all three of them pressing their knives against Peter to hold him at bay as they gazed in confusion at his arm. "He's a bloody escapee," the third one explained.

"Let's finish him and go!" the second one insisted.

"No! We can get money for him!" the first one argued.

As the second one raised his knife to stab Peter in any case, a sudden call of "What's going on here?" interrupted them. All of them turned to look at the officer who was rushing toward them down the alley. He was drawing his gun.

The three thugs froze in panic. Once the officer had drawn close, the first one shouted to him, "Look, look! He's an escapee!"

The third thug took the hint and thrust Peter's arm upward, waving the numbers under the officer's nose. As one, the three of them shoved him at the officer and fled in two different directions.

The officer spun his head first one way, then the other, but he was too afraid of losing his new prize to take the time to fire off a shot in either direction. "Vermin," he muttered as the trio disappeared into their rat holes. "But you"—he turned back toward his prisoner—"are worth some money, I expect." He held his gun pointed at Peter's face and reached down to inspect his arm.

"My identification is over there." Peter indicated his wallet with a nod of his head. As he had hoped, the officer stooped down and reached behind to pick it up, still holding the gun pointing at Peter.

Without a second's hesitation, he kicked the officer in the face, sending him sprawling backward. He then leapt forward and stomping on the wrist that was holding the gun, kicked the man in the jaw. As the officer lay stunned, Peter knelt on his chest, carefully extracted the gun from the man's hand, and wrapped his scarf around it. Then he placed it to the man's temple and fired. Despite being muffled, the noise sounded loud, but not surprisingly, it did not seem to draw any attention.

Peter did not waste time watching as the man's brain seeped into the mud of the alley. He left the gun next to his victim's head. The scarf had absorbed most of the back spray and he abandoned it as well. It was nondescript and would not lead anyone to him. He dunked his gloved hand into a puddle to remove the blood that had sprayed onto it, then wrapped his cast around his arm and pushed his coat sleeve back down over it. He quickly inspected himself for obvious signs of brain and blood spatters, running his hands over his face, neck, and hair, but could not detect anything. His coat looked passably unstained: something that looked like a bit of mud was on the cuff of his right sleeve, but it would not draw attention. He picked up his papers, scanned the ground and himself one more time, then with a calm stride, headed back to the main street. He paused only once, to inspect himself in a shop-window mirror. Satisfied that there were no telltale signs of the murder, he walked the rest of the way home along busy roads and well-patrolled paths.

That night Joanna visited him. It wasn't like usual: there was no bomb, no running away; nor was it the other versions—the one where he strangled her himself or where he saw every detail of her death played out in gory slow-motion. No blood, no screaming, no anguished cries for help. This time she just visited.

He perused her as she took off her wings and set them in a corner. She looked rather good for a ghost, he thought, and mercifully there were no signs of the injuries that had led to her death. "How are you doing?" he asked.

"Oh, okay." She plopped herself down on the edge of the bed. "How are you?"

"Fine, little one. I'm happy to see you." He wondered what else he should say. Could she read his mind? Did she know how much he loved her? How much he missed her? "I'm sorry about everything, you know, everything that happened."

"Oh, don't worry about that. You worry too much anyway."

"Do I?"

She nodded. Clearly, something was on her mind.

"What's up?"

"Oh," she sighed, "I just wanted to know why you killed that man this evening."

"Had to, honey."

"No, you didn't. You had him down, you could have just tried to knock him out."

Peter looked into her blue eyes. He saw clouds drifting past. Must be where she lives, he thought. "I guess I was afraid, baby. I had to act fast, decide quickly. . . . He saw my face, saw the type of identity papers I was carrying, he knew I was an escapee, he would have tracked me down sooner or later. I'm worth money, you know."

"Do you think he knew who you were?"

"Not then, no, but any escapee is worth a bounty, and once he had put my face together with my wanted poster, he'd know I was worth lots of money. I couldn't take that risk."

Joanna looked at him mournfully.

"Oh, little girl, I couldn't go through all that again. Look what happened last time!"

"I know," she said sadly. "Why didn't you tell Barbara about it when you came back? Were you ashamed?"

"I should have done. It does concern her. I will tomorrow." He was desperately searching for a way to placate her conscience. Her eyes grew ever more cloudy and he knew she was leaving him.

"Do you care that you've murdered someone in cold blood?" Joanna asked as her image began to fade.

He took his time answering, and by the time he opened his mouth to reply she was gone and he was staring into the darkness of his bedroom. He turned to look at Barbara, sleeping peacefully next to him. She would have been at risk, too, and anyone connected with the place, anyone who stopped in too frequently, such as Jenny or Mark. He thought of that officer, willing to let the thugs escape just to hold on to his unexpected prize; Peter could still see the lust for money in his eyes. He thought of Zosia and the baby, thought of all the people he had lost throughout his life, and he thought of all the people who had shielded him since his escape. They took upon themselves the responsibilities he now felt so keenly. They resisted. If there had been more of them in the beginning, perhaps millions of lives and untold misery could have been spared.

Funny that his subconscious had evoked Joanna to chide him; it did not fit her at all. Already at the tender age of five she was being trained to fight, and if anyone would have understood his action, it would have been she. Like her mother, she would have known there was a time to make peace and a time to fight. If anyone should have chided him, it should have been someone who had lived in determined ignorance and self-awarded piety.

Himself perhaps.

62

"**H**ERR JÄGER?"

Peter spun toward the figure of a man leaning casually against the wall near the door. He had one hand in his coat pocket, presumably holding a gun; the other held a cigarette. Without waiting for a reply the man motioned toward a car. "Come with me."

So soon? He was sure he had left no trace of his crime. He threw a glance back at the shop. "May I inform my wife? I told her I'd only be a few minutes." He was surprised that the man agreed. After telling Barbara that he was being escorted to an interview, he accompanied the man to the car. When the man opened the door for him, he realized that it must be something else—Ryszard perhaps.

The car made its way through the light morning traffic to the corner of Hyde Park that abutted Gestapo headquarters and the vast sprawl of Green Park prison. The man invited him to exit the car, and together they walked along the nearly frozen mud toward the restricted area around the Serpentine. A lonely sentry guarding the entrance to the exclusive park examined their credentials and let them pass without comment. Several meters from a disused bandstand, they found Ryszard contemplating the rotting woodwork and smoking a cigarette.

The man accompanying Peter led him to Ryszard and then waited expectantly.

"Any trouble?" Ryszard asked.

"No, sir," the serious young man replied. He glanced at Peter as if assessing him but said no more.

"This is Stefan." Ryszard gestured toward the man. "He's one of ours."

Peter nodded and waited to see if he would be introduced, but as Ryszard said nothing more, he guessed he was already well-known to the man or his true identity was considered inessential.

"We have an idea of where that device is," Ryszard began, but still he did not remove his gaze from the wooden filigree overhead. After a moment he seemed to gather his thoughts, and with a peremptory "Let's walk," he took off in the direction of the lake.

They walked in silence for a moment, Ryszard still consumed by his thoughts. Peter hesitated to break his reverie, but finally ventured to say, "I'm sorry about your son."

"Yes, so am I. One of those things. I thought I was protecting him, but I called it wrong." Ryszard paused, then added with some embarrassment, "I guess I never offered you my condolences for . . ."

"No, I don't think you did," Peter responded, trying to suppress any bitterness. Why should Ryszard have offered condolences on the death of his sister's daughter to an outsider? Into the silence of their footsteps he added under his breath, "We fight for our future while losing our children."

"We are the children. Who among our parents would have thought we would still be fighting this bloody war, even now?"

"Our entire lives," Peter muttered in sympathetic agreement.

Ryszard shrugged off their morbid commiserations and turned to business. "As you suspected, the Schindler name was not a fake; it was indeed the son of my colleague in Berlin."

"So it wasn't official business?"

"I don't think so. At least not admittedly so. Could be the Führer's office is trying to secretly resurrect the work done at that laboratory, but wants a handy scapegoat if things go wrong."

"Or Schindler is doing some independent research."

"Yes. In any case, I've learned that the son left Berlin for London and planned to meet up with a chap who works in that lab near here, the one that your little Underground group was keeping an eye on back in the good old days."

"Do you want me to contact the English Underground and find out what they know?" Peter asked, doubtful of his chances of success.

"No, I've already gone through channels and they don't know anything. Apparently they never got together a group to replace you and your buddies, and so all they get is intermittent reports from inside there."

"Hmm. Makes me feel like we were doing something really important," Peter commented sarcastically.

"I think you were, and besides, I think they realized that as well, but they just couldn't find the talent to keep up such a close surveillance. Your language fluency, scientific literacy, and cryptanalytic skills were hard to duplicate, not to mention your willingness to work in such danger."

"They should have thought of that before they used us as bait."

"Such decisions are rarely made by people who have a genuine grasp of reality," Ryszard answered quietly. "You guys should have elected your kings, the way we used to, then you wouldn't have all these messy politics protecting a deposed royal family from adverse publicity."

"We should have beheaded the lot, if you ask me," Peter grunted.

Ryszard laughed. "So, you don't feel loyalty in your blood?"

"Remember, I was in the English *Republican* Army!" Peter huffed.

"The same one that subordinates itself to the Monarchists?" Ryszard teased.

"Political expediency—you're familiar with that! Now, do you have any more details?" Peter asked brusquely.

"Yes, Wolf-Dietrich, the son that is, was supposed to meet a fellow named Shantler, but I couldn't find that name on any employee list. The closest I could find was Chandler."

"Yeah, that sounds like how they'd mangle it. What's this Chandler do?"

"Biochemist." They stopped at the edge of the lake and looked out over its cold, gray waters. After a moment Ryszard continued, "Schindler junior brought along a computer as slick as yours—"

"Ah, that explains Katerina's command," Peter interjected. "Did you tell her to order me to bring my computer?"

"Order? No. I asked her to let you bring it. I assumed you'd want it with you."

"Want it? Hell, no! Do you have any idea how suspicious it is for a normal working stiff to carry something like that around the countryside? I had to cross four internal border checkpoints with that in my luggage!"

"Well, no harm done," Ryszard commented, unconcerned.

Peter muttered under his breath.

"Anyway," Ryszard picked up the thread of his story, "he's supposed to use it to interpret some data. Presumably that device. I assume since you have the same type computer, you can—"

"I don't," Peter interrupted.

"What?"

"I don't have the same type."

"How do you know, you've not even seen his!" Ryszard snapped angrily.

"No, but I know that my computer could not read a microdisc."

"A what?"

"A microdisc. It's a device for storing information that's about the size of that device the American passed on," Peter explained. "It sounds like that's what we're dealing with. A woman I met in the NAU showed me it and the computers that can read it. It's a new technology, even in America, and my computer is too old and outdated."

"How old is it?"

"About two years old. They age fast."

"So you'd need a different computer?"

"No, I'd just need to upgrade what I have: add a bit of hardware, load the software to read it."

"I don't speak gibberish," Ryszard said, clearly irritated.

"The upshot, dear brother-in-law," Peter explained patiently, "is that, even if we had it, I couldn't read that device with my computer."

Ryszard swore under his breath.

"So, I risked my life carrying that machine here for nothing," Peter added.

"So it would seem," Ryszard agreed. "Well, maybe we can salvage the situation. I'll still need your help."

"What do you want me to do?"

"I want to go into the lab personally and see what we can find out. I need an excuse, and you're going to be it." Ryszard stooped down, picked up a flat stone, and flung it across the water. It skimmed nicely, skipping four times before sinking.

"How so?" Peter asked, picking up a stone and skimming that. Four skips.

"Well, I haven't a clue about science, but you can pass yourself off as an expert," Ryszard answered as he cast another stone across the water. Three skips.

"I *was* an expert, at one point, though now I'd be hard-pressed to know the current state of the art." Peter took his turn. Five! He grinned at Ryszard. It was like being a boy again, before the epidemic, before private school, back when he was carefree.

"Doesn't matter," Ryszard offered dryly, casting about for a worthy stone, "as long as you can spout a few phrases and nod at the appropriate points. I want to bring you in with me as an expert from Berlin. They'll be obsequious enough that no one will dare notice if you're not really all that up-to-date." Ryszard finally found the stone he wanted, and with a flourish he flicked it across the water. Four skips. He muttered to himself and began looking for the next stone.

"And once we're inside," Stefan spoke up from behind the two of them, "we'll get a chance to nose around and find out what the American passed on to them. They themselves might not know its significance." Stefan had quite clearly removed himself from any competition.

"How do you fit into this?" Peter asked Stefan, flinging another stone across the water. Five again!

"Officially, he's my aide," Ryszard answered; he kicked at the gravel with his boot, searching for the perfect stone.

"So you rate an aide now?" Peter asked, waiting for Ryszard.

"I have for years," Ryszard responded dryly. "Though this is the first time I've managed to have one I could trust." He finally found what he wanted.

"So I'll be essentially useless to this mission. Just backup," Stefan explained.

"In fact, I, too, will probably be useless other than as an entrée into the place." Ryszard squinted across the water. "It will be up to you to ferret out the relevant information. Neither Stefan nor I would have a hope of recognizing important information even if it was dropped on our heads."

"So I get to ask questions, nose around, and just see if I can find out what they're up to?"

"Yes, it's not ideal, but it's the best we can do. I can't find out anything in Berlin, which indicates that it must be important. Other than that, we're clueless," Ryszard answered distractedly. He positioned himself carefully, preparing to fling his stone.

"And our excuse for going inside?"

Ryszard finally released his missile. It arched too high but recovered on the first bounce and continued to bounce four more times, with the slightest hesitation on the last bounce. "Six!" Ryszard trumpeted. He turned away from the water's edge and began walking so that Peter had to follow in order to hear him. When they were a safe distance from the bank, Ryszard explained, "I've suggested a reorganization of laboratory work, and this is an inspection tour to see what exactly can be moved or consolidated or even abandoned altogether. So, asking questions will seem quite normal."

"Ah, clever of you," Peter said quite seriously, though it sounded somewhat sarcastic upon reflection. He was still wondering how in the world Ryszard had counted that last effort as six skips.

Ryszard shrugged. "At the least, I can probably cripple some of their science programs by doing an awful job."

"But how, without any expertise, did you manage to get this assignment?"

Ryszard laughed. "We're talking about National Socialist bureaucracy, what does expertise have to do with anything?"

The three men walked along and planned for some time, then before it got so late that Barbara became frantic, Stefan walked Peter back to the car and he was driven back to the shop.

63

*I*T WAS ODD BEING INSIDE the laboratory that had for so long been a target of his observations. So many hours of his life had been spent acquiring its secrets: purchasing documents, decoding their contents, filtering useless data, analyzing their results. Now, here it was all being presented to him with obsequious smiles and sly glances at his clothing.

Ryszard had forgone his usual nondescript suit and decked himself out well, aware that outside of Berlin and Göringstadt he might not be recognizably important without such plumage. The sharp black uniform with its medallions, ribbons, and insignia had the desired effect, turning heads and opening doors. Peter had chosen to wear something less imposing, hoping that once they had an entrée into the laboratory, he could win some confidences from the personnel by implying his credentials were much less terrifying than Ryszard's. Nevertheless his boots resounded ominously down the hall as they marched toward their next destination, and he found himself enjoying the sensation of power in the face of his adversaries.

"But what about something truly useful to the Reich?" Ryszard asked petulantly as they viewed yet another work station where the grinning, terrified laboratory technicians ran through their paces like rats in a maze.

The lead chemist was somewhat less intimidated. "All our work is useful, Herr

Traugutt. I know that it is difficult for one unfamiliar with the sciences to understand that a great deal of research must go into each discovery *before* the discovery is made, but that is the way of our craft."

The director, who had been leading the tour, stiffened at the interruption and eyed his subordinate balefully. Stefan pulled a file out of the case he was carrying and handed it to Ryszard, who perused it as the director blathered patriotic nonsense to try to cover the chemist's ill-tempered reply.

"Herr Niedermeier—oh, wait, I see here we've been misaddressing you. It's Niedermeier-Jones, isn't it?" Ryszard asked the chemist snidely. "How did you manage to get such an interesting name? Oh, wait, here it is, your wife's name is Niedermeier. So, you're really Herr Jones, or should I say, *Mister* Jones?"

The chemist's face reddened to match the color of his sparse hair. "It's Herr Doktor Jones, if you wish to be pedantic."

"An interesting bank balance you have here," Ryszard added, ignoring the reply and continuing to read the document Stefan had handed him.

"My group gets results!" Niedermeier-Jones snapped with angry fear.

"Indeed, many results. Many good results with chemical weapons," Ryszard acknowledged. "But these bank balances . . . Hmm. I don't know, I just don't know, Jones." Ryszard left the threat hanging in the air. It was a totally unnecessary act and not at all central to their mission, but Peter could see how much Ryszard was enjoying the man's discomfort. Earlier Ryszard had mentioned that he already planned to shut down this branch of the laboratory because Jones's group had indeed been producing good results and far too many of them. The fact that he, like most of his colleagues, had been taking his "fair share" of the research money for his personal needs only made Ryszard's job easier.

"Ah, gentlemen, I'm sure all this will be sorted out in due time. We should be moving on! There is so much to see," the director insisted before the confrontation could go further and destroy his job.

"Of course," Ryszard agreed pleasantly. "Now, what about this fellow, Chandler . . ."

"Chandler? Chandler? Who's he?" the director asked in confusion.

"A subordinate of mine," Niedermeier-Jones answered irritably. "I see no reason why you'd want to talk with him."

"No reason?" Ryszard asked, raising an eyebrow. "No reason?" he repeated ominously.

"Herr Traugutt . . . ," the director wheezed fearfully.

"Herr Traugutt," Niedermeier-Jones interjected, "I meant no disrespect. I was only surprised that the activities of a subordinate would interest you. He's not been very productive of late, but I can certainly show you to his laboratory."

"By all means," Ryszard replied.

Together they marched down the hall, toward the section containing Chandler's laboratory. As they passed by a large office containing a typing pool, Peter turned abruptly away from his colleagues and entered the office. He stood at the entrance scanning each of the women as they worked. The one nearest him looked up and asked, "Can I help you?"

"I thought I saw someone I know," Peter explained as he struggled to work his way through the myriad faces. During his days in the Underground, at least two of their regular informants had been young women whom he suspected were secretaries. All he knew about either of them was that they sold the information and were therefore involved in espionage for the money rather than any ideology. One, he guessed from the accents, was German, the other English. He tried to remember their faces and mentally added a dozen years to the images; then, as he continued to look, one woman glanced up at him and he recognized her.

"What are you doing?" the director asked, containing his annoyance with some effort.

"Oh, I thought I saw an acquaintance," Peter explained as he noted the nameplate on the woman's desk. She was staring at him as if flustered, but when she saw the director, she turned her attention back to the document she was typing.

"And did you?" the director asked. Ryszard and the others stood behind him in the hallway, obviously confused as to why they had retraced their steps.

"No," Peter sighed. He glanced at the director and winked. "An old flame, you see. I guess it was simply wishful thinking."

"Ah, yes. Well, if you want to join us now"—the director gestured toward the others—"we can continue."

"Of course, of course," Peter agreed cheerfully.

Eventually they reached Chandler's lab; it was in the old section of the building—the part that had once been someone's house. Here there was plaster on the walls, the ceilings were higher, and the windows were the old-fashioned sort that opened up and down. Though Chandler himself was not there, several of his subordinates were. They eagerly explained that their boss was away on business of a nature that they did not know and just as eagerly showed what they were doing. As the subordinates continued their antics, trying to impress Ryszard, Peter paced around the lab benches looking for something of interest. The subordinates were working on trivialities, and their answers to his questions had revealed nothing. As the minutes passed and their enthusiastic demonstrations reached an end, Peter realized that they were going to leave empty-handed. He glanced at the only separate office in the enclosure, taking in the plethora of files littering the floor and the outmoded computer on the desk, then he scanned the layout of the lab benches, and finally he wandered over to the windows to survey the grounds.

Ryszard and the others joined him there. "Shall we go?" Ryszard asked, unable to come up with any further excuses for staying.

"I feel ill, I need some air," Peter said, and suddenly reached for the window to open it.

"Don't do that!" one of the lab technicians nearly screamed. As everyone turned to him in surprise, he explained somewhat more calmly, "The windows are alarmed. If you open one like that, you'll have a half dozen soldiers running in here, waving their guns at us."

"Then how do I get air?" Peter rasped.

The other technician answered, "No problem," and reached over to a small plug that dangled from a wire. The wire led into a soldered seam that ran around the edge of the windowpane, almost like a decoration. "You see, there's a current around the edge of the window. If the current is disrupted, either by the window being opened or by the glass being shattered, then the alarm sounds. All we have to do is throw this switch over here"—the technician reached under a counter and threw a small switch—"and then unplug the wires here"—he pulled the small plug that led into the soldered wire—"and we can open the window for you." He finished triumphantly by lifting the window a few inches.

"Thank you," Peter responded, turning toward the window so he could breathe the fresh air and hide his smile.

<hr/>

64

"**W**HAT'S UP WITH YOU? You've been staring off into space and chewing your knuckles for days!" Barbara sounded exasperated.

"Huh?" Peter was surprised to see her. "I thought you were out with Mark."

"I've been back for two hours!" she replied angrily. "For heaven's sakes what are you mooning over? Are you in love?"

He was not provoked. "No, no, something else," he answered distantly, effortlessly dismissing her from his thoughts. There had to be some way into that laboratory, some way to get his hands on the files he knew must be in Chandler's section. The cursory look that he had been afforded with Ryszard had been insufficient to tell them anything; all that had become clear was that the director was probably unaware of Chandler's work with Schindler. Peter could not decide if that was an advantage or not. If Chandler's work had been part of the official laboratory routine, then the chances were that eventually someone would be willing to sell it. Of course, Peter could never come up with the sort of money that would be required, so he would, in that case, be excluded from acquiring it and it would be up to one of the Undergrounds to get their hands on the information.

That, however, was not the case. Chandler's work was apparently secret, even amongst his colleagues. So, the information would be more jealously guarded and less likely to be pilfered and sold. That was a disadvantage in the overall scheme of things, but a personal advantage for him, because he not only wanted to find out what the American had been carrying and what Schindler was up to, he wanted to personally acquire that information so he could use it to bribe the Szaflary Council into letting him return.

He considered the possibility of blackmailing the informant whom he had recognized into stealing the information for him. There were several problems with that, the most obvious being that neither he nor the informant knew what should be stolen. Another problem was that the informant could not be driven too far: his only advantage over the informant would be pure bluff, and if the informant discovered something truly valuable, she would doubtless sell it to the Underground and seek their protection from his extortion. The upshot of that would be that the Underground would gain the information without his help and might feel obliged to sanction him in some manner for his extracurricular activities.

So, he had to get inside the laboratory himself. He knew he could extort something trivial from the secretary, but first he had to find out where she lived and some way of contacting her. Where could he get that information? Once he talked to her, he could probably convince her to leave a window or something open for him, but that would not be enough, he needed to know the security routine for the installation. Who could tell him that? Plus he needed tools: something to get through the fences, something for locked doors and files and desks. Now where could he acquire the appropriate tools without raising suspicions? A bit of backup would help as well, someone to keep watch as he rooted around. Then afterward, how would he travel to Szaflary? All without official assistance . . .

". . . would consider it rude," Barbara finished huffily.

"What?"

"Ignoring me. Some people would consider it rude."

"Ignoring you? Ah, well, sorry," Peter apologized perfunctorily. "What were you saying?"

"I was suggesting that maybe if you talk about whatever's bothering you, it might help you to sort it out."

Peter rubbed his chin. "Sure, why not. I'm getting nowhere like this." He explained his situation to Barbara.

"Why not have Ryszard get you inside again?" she suggested.

"First, he doesn't have the authority to assign me to the place. Our one visit was the best he could manage, and even that took conniptions to set up. Second, for some reason, he couldn't stay here long. He had to return to Berlin to attend to business there, and I guess he can hardly be bothered to track down every loose thread that unwinds past him. He wants to hand it off and is only waiting because I asked him to. Finally, if he sets me up in there, he'll expect me to hand everything over to him, and I've already said I'm less interested in us getting the information than in my getting it."

"Rather selfish, aren't you?" Barbara asked almost innocently.

"I've learned from experts."

"That's no excuse!"

"I've been at this game a lot longer than you, little girl, and you will forgive me if my idealism is wearing a bit thin," Peter replied impatiently.

"What about the English Underground? You could have Jenny ask for their help."

"Same story. Once I tell them what's going on, they won't need me."

"Maybe they'd be sufficiently grateful—"

"Pff. They adhere to Stalin's view of gratitude."

"What's that?" Barbara asked.

"It's a dog's disease. No, I'm not letting this one out of my hands. The information is probably not all that important—just some boondoggle that Schindler has sunk his teeth into, but if I play it right, it should be sufficient to get me back home."

"You really miss the place, don't you?"

Peter stopped himself from replying angrily to what he presumed was sarcasm. "It's my home," he answered honestly. "It's where my child is. I love the mountains and the forests and the blessed free air, limited though it is. I miss the people and the work, and believe it or not, I even have a few friends. Marysia cares about me, Olek, Konrad, Kamil, Romek, even Tadek has come through for me. Hell, I even miss Katerina."

"*Her?*" Barbara's voice conveyed a complex mix of fear and awe.

"Yeah. I've finally realized why she was so determined to remind me that I was an outsider living on sufferance."

"Why?"

"Because she was, too. I would guess she never got over feeling terribly, terribly alone."

"I just thought the old bat had killed every emotion that wasn't deadly long ago."

Peter nodded noncommittally. "Anyway, I want to go back and I don't want to wait until the Council gets tired of holding me prisoner here. Trouble is, I can't figure out how to get into that damn lab."

"How about some help from your friends here?"

Peter snorted.

"No, I'm serious. You have Jenny and her connections, and me and Mark and all his friends."

"I don't think your boyfriend is all that fond of me."

"Perhaps not, but he'll be more than happy to help you leave this place. Besides, he'll do as he's told if he knows what's good for him."

Peter laughed. "Yes, I suppose I could use your help, if you're really offering it."

"I am," Barbara answered sincerely. "Between us, we can track down that informant for you. The tools shouldn't be much problem. As for the travel documents . . ."

"We can solve that later. There is one other thing though."

"What?"

"I need an expert. Chandler is a chemist. I suspect that whatever he has will be in that field, and I don't know enough to recognize useful information."

"Hmm. That is a problem, none of us have any expertise there. I doubt Mark knows anyone either—that's not what his group is into."

"I suppose I could just peruse what I find and trust my luck and intuition."

"Or you could recruit your brother," Barbara suggested.

"My brother!" Peter sputtered, but then he thought about it. His brother was trained in chemistry and worked in a government institute; he would almost certainly know enough to recognize something important and interpret it. A grin spread across Peter's face as he thought about forcing his brother to help him. He nodded to himself, pleased with the images that his thoughts provoked. "Yeah, I could do that. I'm sure he'd be more than willing to cooperate with me. Good idea, Barbara, great idea!"

Two weeks later Peter was at the door of his brother's flat. The dingy third-floor hallway belied the impressive rent the building almost certainly commanded. It was in a good location: not quite a gated community yet nevertheless a well-policed area with low crime and reliable utilities. Peter had walked uneasily through the streets, feeling, as he always had as a youth, that something in his clothes or demeanor would betray him as English and therefore unwelcome. Now at least, he carried appropriate papers and as Niklaus Jäger would not be challenged; nevertheless, he had felt ill at ease and had been glad that he could finally duck into the doorway of one of the monstrous apartment buildings that overlooked the river.

A modestly dressed, slightly overweight woman answered the door. Not surprisingly, she was not particularly attractive, and Peter did not expect that she would have a sparkling personality: her birth certificate alone would have been enough to lure his brother into marriage. Peter explained to her that he was a colleague of Erich's and asked if he might have a moment to talk to her husband about some unexpected work at the institute. She surprised him by inviting him in for a cup of tea, explaining that her husband had gone out but that he was expected back shortly. Peter accepted the invitation and sat down in their living room to await his brother's return.

As Erich's wife handed him some tea, he smiled pleasantly, then, to satisfy his curiosity, said, "Thank you, Frau . . . Oh, I'm sorry, do you use the name Chase?"

"No." She shook her head somewhat sadly. "I wanted to, but Erich wanted to use my family name, Schwarz, for our family. Turned out, it was almost impossible for him to change names, but not so difficult to use it for the children. So, he's the only one who uses that name. More's the pity."

"Why?"

"I think a wife should use her husband's name," she replied primly, then relaxing, she added, "But call me Gretchen! I like this new habit of using first names."

"Gretchen. What a lovely name."

She confided with a titter, "Oh, you have no idea how many people bought me the 'good-girl Gretchen' books when I was a child! What was worse was that my poor brother was named Hans, so he'd get the 'heroic Hans' series. The house was simply inundated!"

"Ah, yes." He nodded sympathetically. "Well, please call me Niklaus." That, as he had expected, reminded her to introduce her children, who had sat throughout in obedient silence, doing their schoolwork at the supper table, which was at the far end of the largish room. Upon her command, they lined up like little martinets and were introduced to him. He looked hard at each of his nieces and nephews; one of the girls had his mother's eyes, otherwise there was nothing to remind him of his parents. He asked them a little about themselves, what their plans were and how they were faring in school, and then, on a whim, he asked in English, "Do any of you speak the slightest bit of your father's native language and the language of the people who live all around you and serve your needs?"

They all stared at him blankly, recognizing the language but nothing more than that. Gretchen, also clearly unable to answer the question, frowned worriedly at what it could all mean. Peter smiled reassuringly and said in German, "Our department is trying to recruit students who speak English because we're beginning to increase our ties to the North American Union. You know," he added impishly, "one must know one's enemy!"

They nodded their understanding, and the children returned to their studies. He and Gretchen continued their pleasantries, killing time as they awaited Erich's return. While Peter chatted, he surveyed the room. There was the obligatory portrait of the Führer and another of Hitler, this time blessing little children who were bringing him flowers. A framed map was mounted over a bookshelf, and he got up from his seat to have a closer inspection of both. The map was of the Greater Reich, and he noted with some disdain that it did not show a "Carpathian Exclusion Zone" or any other unconquered territory in the region. A nice fiction, this total domination of the land and peoples of Europe! In the bookshelf he read the standard titles of a good German household. Nothing in English, nothing exceptional. Other than the fact that the bottom shelf was devoted to some texts on chemistry and biochemistry, there was nothing there that he would not have expected to find at the Vogels'.

As he was still perusing the titles, Erich returned. Peter waited until his brother was in the door and Gretchen had explained that a colleague had come to visit before he turned around. The smile of greeting slid from Erich's face and he stammered, "What are you doing here?" with something less than an acceptable level of courtesy.

"Erich!" his wife admonished.

"Unless you're into confiding everything to your family," Peter said in English to his brother, "you'll be clever enough to greet me as a colleague." He grinned a welcome.

Erich's face was absolutely white with fear. He glanced from his wife to his children and back again before mustering the wherewithal to say, in English, "What do you want from me?"

"Lots."

"Erich?" Gretchen asked, suddenly worried. "What's going on?"

"Ah, dear Frau Schwarz. Forgive me for playing a small joke on your husband!" Peter assured her. "We share a common childhood language and I like to tease my shy colleague into using it now and again. Do forgive me for being so terribly rude!" Peter leaned over and kissed her on the cheek. "I'm going to steal your husband for the evening. It's terribly important government business, you understand, and we appreciate your patriotism and loyalty, and I hope we don't inconvenience you too much with this unexpected requisition of his time. Please don't wait up, he'll be back quite late."

Gretchen was still touching her cheek where Peter had kissed it even as he grabbed his brother's arm and gently led him out the door.

65

"**W**E COULD BE HANGED FOR THIS," Erich reminded his brother yet again as they lay on the ground near the chain-link fence that surrounded the perimeter of the laboratory.

"If we're lucky," Peter agreed jovially. "Of course, since you're with me, they might prefer to torture you first." He looked up from cutting the lower links and grinned at his brother. "It'd be a great chance for you to learn about the government you serve."

Erich scowled. "Can't you do this without me? I'll wait outside and you can bring me the stuff. I'll stay here. I promise."

"Would you shut up already!" Mark growled, glancing around nervously.

Erich looked at Mark's angry face and then at Barbara as she sat nearly invisible in the darkness only a few feet away, casually holding her gun as if to suggest she would just as readily shoot him dead as not. He fell silent and listened to his heart thumping, trying not to think about the freezing dampness that was penetrating his clothes. "It's just that I have a wife and four children," he could not stop himself from saying.

"Gag him," Peter ordered. He was listening intently for the approach of any security patrols, and Erich's whining was an annoying distraction. Peter was also concentrating on not cutting the trip wire woven cleverly into the links of the fence. It was a fairly simple system, but still more than he had expected to encounter at the outer fence. As he carefully felt along each link to determine if there were any more alarm wires, he wondered at the sort of security they would face at the inner fence. Here they were relatively well shielded and could take their time, but inside, they would be exposed between the two fences and would have to move quickly. No dogs, no mines, nothing elaborate, he had been told. It had accorded with what he had known about the place years ago: just a government laboratory with the obligatory, minimal security. Consequently, the trip wires worried him. Had the security been tightened? Had they been fed false information?

Mark moved toward Erich intent on carrying out the order to gag him. "Don't, don't! I'll be quiet, I promise!" Erich pleaded in a whisper.

Peter motioned for Mark to stop. "Last chance," Peter warned Erich. He had not expected cooperation from his brother and had not even tried to get it from him. Once they had left Erich's flat, Peter had simply explained in no uncertain terms that Erich was going to help them or be turned in to the authorities. For what? Erich had demanded to know. Doesn't matter, Peter had replied, just as it had not mattered for their father. That threat had been sufficient; Peter had not needed to explain how he could manufacture evidence or how he could let it be known that Erich's brother was the notorious criminal who had earned the undying enmity of the Fatherland. No, it had been sufficient to allude to the Pure German movement—that had immediately won Erich's obedience.

"There, done it," Peter whispered. He lay flat on the ground and consulted his watch. When the time was right, he pulled apart the tear in the fence and motioned Barbara through. He motioned for Mark to stay put with his brother, then grabbing his bag, Peter hurried after Barbara. He joined her at the next fence and the two of them worked feverishly to inspect and cut the fence. Barbara swore quietly.

"Wires?" he asked, quite surprised.

"No. Lasers. Don't you see them?" She gestured to just the other side of the chain links.

He squinted in the direction she had indicated. After blinking and straining for some seconds, he finally saw the faint traces of horizontal red lines. "Yeah, I see them. Okay, time to dig; let's hope there's nothing buried." He pulled out a trowel. He glanced back at Mark and Erich and then at the height of the lowest laser beam and suggested, "Six inches down should do it."

The fence was buried to a depth of nine inches, and Peter and Barbara decided to clear a narrow trench that far down. He finished cutting the links, then Barbara pulled herself through the trench between the pieces of cut fence and under the lasers. She paused on the other side, and they waited to see if there was any reaction to her breach. After a tense few seconds, he decided that she had not set off any alarms and, pushing his bag through, lowered himself to the ground and scrabbled through the ditch. Barbara helped by pulling him so that he did not have to raise himself, and once he was safely through, he motioned to Mark to bring Erich through.

The two of them scurried through the first opening and across the open patch between the fences. As they arrived at the second fence, Peter could see that

Mark had resorted to holding a gun on Erich. Mark ordered Erich to the ground, and Barbara and Peter grabbed his arms and pulled him through. Then they pulled Mark through, and taking only a second to survey their circumstances, they bolted for the relative safety of the laboratory. They circled around until they were at the window that let into Chandler's section. The informant had agreed to disconnect the security wiring and unlock and open the window a few millimeters. Peter studied the three windows on that side: none of them looked open. He ran his fingers along the sills and determined that one was looser than the others—it was probably open though not visibly so to someone on the outside. He tried lifting the window using friction against the wood, but it was too stiff, so he and Barbara inserted screwdrivers on either side of the sill and together they managed to move it up an inch. Peter inserted his hands under the sill and pushed the window up the rest of the way with no resistance.

Barbara slipped inside, peered around, and then motioned the others in. Peter handed her his bag and went next, then he and Barbara pulled Erich in, and finally Mark tumbled in and quickly shut the window behind him. Barbara remained on watch by the windows as the others moved stealthily through the main laboratory area. Mark took up guard by the door, leaving Peter alone with his brother to carry out their inspection. Peter pulled Erich past the benches and over to the office area. Several desks were set up against the wall, but Peter ignored those, heading instead for the single desk that was enclosed behind glass partition walls. It was the only desk with a computer and obviously belonged to the section chief.

The door to the cubicle was locked. Peter glanced up at the height of the partitions and then, mumbling his disgruntlement, decided instead to pick the lock. His brother watched in silent fascination as Peter pulled out his elaborate lock-pick and began work on the door.

"What exactly are we looking for?" Erich whispered as he glanced nervously first at Mark and then Barbara.

"I don't know," Peter admitted. "Information of some sort. The information was received via computer, so it's either on that computer in there, or there is a printed copy of the information somewhere in that desk or in the lab."

"That doesn't narrow it down much," Erich commented sarcastically.

"Either you or I will recognize it," Peter assured him. He found the right key and soon they were inside the small, extremely untidy office. Peter flicked the switch to the computer and the screen slowly came to life.

Erich's eyes widened as he watched the screen flash information at them in a confusing jumble of words and images. "Do you know what this machine is doing?" he asked, his voice conveying wonder at the technology before him.

Peter snorted his derision. "This is an old piece of junk," he replied with a certain satisfaction. "Of course, I know what it's doing! Don't tell me you don't even have this level of technology in your laboratory?"

Erich was shaking his head but he did not answer.

"Shit!" Peter swore suddenly.

"What?" Erich asked. "What's wrong?"

"It wants a password," Peter groaned. He bit his tongue to keep from swearing and typed in a few likely tries, none of which worked.

"What now?"

"I'm thinking," Peter murmured, trying to recall what Zosia had said about passwords. He had not expected Chandler to have one, and so that implied that someone else had set up the security on Chandler's computer. Now, how would Chandler have handled that? He stood and inspected the back of the machine and under the desk, looking for a printed reminder of what the password might be. He did not find anything so he sat down and tried a few more simple ideas. Then he noticed the photograph hiding behind a stack of papers. It was a picture of the scientist with his wife and three children. Peter picked it up and removed the photograph from its frame. On the back of the picture the names and birth dates of each member of the family were noted in what looked like a tidy, feminine hand. Peter tried each name and date in turn without success.

"Guess we should go," Erich prodded.

"Shut up," Peter snapped. There was still the desk and file drawers. A printed document was likely to be somewhere. Plus he could try some clever tricks to get inside the machine if that failed. There were the other desks, too. Shit, there were hundreds of things they could spend hours looking at! Get in, grab the information, and get out, he had hoped; now that looked impossible. He glanced around the office again. What a pigsty! The implied laziness of its occupant was inspired. It gave him an idea and he called up the password screen again and tried simply hitting the enter key—it was the laziest possible password available to someone who did not even want security on his computer. To his utter astonishment, the trick worked, and the computer hummed into life, pulling up the last bits of software and preparing itself for use.

"What'd you do? What'd you do?" Erich asked, convinced that he had missed some magic trick.

"Telepathy," Peter answered sarcastically. "I thought the correct answer at it."

The screen presented a single prompt and Peter typed a command asking the machine to list its files. It took several variations, but he finally hit upon the appropriate operating language, and the file names were listed for the two of them to scan. They stared at the screen for a few moments, then Peter pointed out a file name and said, "I bet it's that one."

"What makes you say that?" Erich asked, shaking his head in confusion at the screen.

"Well, dear brother, the date, the file type, and—lo!—the file name is in English." Peter was hardly able to contain his laughter. He opened the file and read the first few lines; the text was in English as well. "I'll print it up, then we can have an easier time looking at it." He turned on the printer and typed in the appropriate command.

"How do you know how to do all this?" Erich asked. "I've never seen anything like this and I work in a government institute! You're not . . . Where have you . . . ?" he sputtered almost angrily.

Peter rolled his eyes, then almost gently he explained, "It should not surprise you that the Reich is a technological backwater compared to America. After all, we have a habit here of killing our best and brightest, or at least driving them into exile. Nor should it surprise you that even when we steal the relevant new technology from America, we are unable to duplicate it en masse since we have an utterly demoralized workforce which tends to indulge in sabotage either deliberately or through drunken carelessness. So, when our dear leaders finally do manage to organize something as simple as a decent computer, do you really expect that the few good specimens available are going to be wasted on a treacherous colonial backwater like London? Do you?"

"Well, then how does this laboratory have them?" Erich replied defensively.

"It's viewed as an adjunct to Berlin. Nearly everyone here comes from the old Reich and answers to their bosses there. Chandler is local talent, but he still answers to Berlin. Besides, this machine is definitely not state of the art. Believe me, if you want to see the good stuff, you have to go to Berlin."

"That still doesn't answer how you know all this!" Erich snapped angrily.

"No, it doesn't." Peter pulled the document out of the printer and began reading it, handing the pages to Erich as he finished each.

They read in silence, then Erich asked, "What does this word mean?"

Peter looked at the word. "Facilitate," he replied. "You mean you didn't know?"

"It's been a long time since I've spoken this language," Erich admitted sheepishly. "What about this word?"

"Inconspicuous."

"And this one?"

"Potable. Look, I'll peruse the document and when I have a question, I'll just ask you, okay?" Peter suggested, completely exasperated.

"But, but . . . ," Erich sputtered, somewhat confused. "I want to help," he whispered finally.

Peter was taken aback. "Really? Why?"

"I don't know, I just feel . . . I don't know, I feel put down, angry even. This machine, this lab . . . My language, I don't even know it!"

"All right, all right," Peter preempted Erich's soul-searching. "We don't have time for your thoughts on this right now. Just let me read what they've written and you can tell me if it makes sense or if I've stumbled upon somebody's idea of an April fool's joke."

The document was labeled "top secret" but was nonetheless written in the format of a completed, publishable research report. Peter read the abstract and introduction and then scanned the body of the paper. He read the conclusions carefully, then sat staring at the words, drumming his fingers nervously on the desk. Erich was studying one of the loose sheets, but when he saw his brother stop reading, he said, "It says in the abstract that this is a sterilization program. Is that what you were looking for?"

Peter nodded, perturbed by what he had read.

"Is it some sort of replacement for surgery?"

"Could be," Peter replied, still distracted by the conclusions he had read. "Maybe somebody wants to lower the obscene number of abortions we have in this country."

"So it's meant to be voluntary?" Erich asked hopefully.

"I doubt it. The conclusions emphasize the fact that the drug is potable and tasteless. I think you can read between the lines on that."

"What's wrong? I thought you knew what you were looking for?" Erich asked, perceiving Peter's grim mood.

"Not really. I mean, I expected it would be about this, I just didn't expect . . ." He didn't complete the thought. For some reason he felt an overpowering sadness, and all he could think of was Irena. He wondered what she looked like now and what she was doing.

"Didn't expect what?" Erich insisted in a harsh whisper.

"They've finished the research," Peter explained forlornly. "The fuckers took the information we gave them and finished the research."

"Who? What? What do you mean?"

"The Americans. This research was incomplete, heading nowhere, in fact, when we handed it over to them. And they went and finished it. With their high-tech analyses and their supercomputers and . . . If these conclusions can be believed, they completed it, they got the finished product." He stopped speaking. He could see Barbara glancing worriedly over at them. He lowered his head and rubbed the back of his neck as he tried to gain control of his anger. After a moment, he sighed deeply and looked up at Erich. "Look at the body of this report. Is there enough information in here for you to figure out what they've used?"

Peter sat in silence as Erich worked through the formulae. Occasionally Peter answered one of Erich's questions about the meaning of a word or phrase, but otherwise he did nothing. He knew he should sift through the mountains of files in the office or look through other files on the computer to find further information, but he could not bring himself to move. All he could think of was how he had felt when Barbara and Olek had shown him his number among the list of those tested. Now, with the research complete, would there be other numbers on a different list for Schindler to contemplate? He imagined the scenario: male prison laborers in a factory given the option of access to a brothel and all the doctored beer they could drink as a reward for exceeding some ridiculous quota. The poor bastards would work themselves to exhaustion, drink themselves into oblivious sterility, and then be allowed access to equally wretched women who would be watched to see if any of them got pregnant. "This society is sick," he muttered to himself.

"Huh?" Erich asked.

"I said, is there enough there for us to work out exactly what they've done?"

Erich glanced back at the document. "Er . . . It's hard for me to say, I'm not really familiar with what they're doing."

"Not many people are. Is there enough information for a nonspecialist?"

"I'd say no. We need more details, their laboratory books or something."

"Fine, we'll look for those." Peter turned his attention back to the computer. "I'll peruse what he has here, you get Barbara to help you unlock the lab table drawers and see what you can find out there."

"Look for handwritten notes," Erich suggested. "If it's at the stage where it can be entered into a computer document, then it'll be too condensed for our purposes."

Peter nodded noncommittally as he tapped some commands into the computer. Erich had no idea of the current state of computer software and was therefore unlikely to know how useful it could be; then again, Chandler was equally unlikely to be very up-to-date and would probably follow the same timeless routine that Erich used. After scanning the files for a few moments, Peter decided to follow Erich's advice and turned his attention to Chandler's office.

He ignored the mounds of paper moldering in the corners and tried the desk drawers. All but one opened easily, and each contained useful office equipment: paper clips, staples, rubber bands, writing paper, pens, pencils, and so on, all inextricably jumbled in heaps and piles. The locked drawer took only a few moments to open; it contained a bottle of single-malt Scotch, two glasses, a candle, matches, and some high-quality chocolate. Peter smiled, and wrapping the whiskey in a rag he found on a nearby table, he placed it and the chocolate in his bag.

He then went to the file cabinet and unlocked it. Labeled files were in each drawer and he quickly read the headings, hoping that Chandler had not been clever enough to indulge in disinformation. By the third drawer, the end of the alphabetical listing was reached, and a few unlabeled file folders were shoved in the back. He inspected these and found no papers, but there were several computer diskettes. Their size was the more compact form, common in the NAU but virtually unknown in all but the most advanced laboratories in the Reich. He glanced at Chandler's machine and saw that the diskettes were incompatible with it. Intrigued, he pulled out his computer and inserted the first diskette.

He felt a sudden shock of recognition as he examined the file list. He opened one of the files and checked it just to be sure, but he was not mistaken: they were his work. Every single one was a file that he and his team had decoded, translated, and sent on to the security agencies in the North American Union. This was not the muddled data they had stolen from the laboratory, this was no summary garnered from American press reports: what Chandler had was every detail that had been sent overseas in exactly the format Peter had sent it. Exactly. He scanned the file names and found the list that contained his entry, the list that

Barbara had tried to hide from him so long ago. He opened it and worked his way through until he found his own number. He sat stock-still staring at the entry as the burning sensation of having been betrayed spread through his limbs.

His brother came over to him holding several journals. "Look, it's all in here. We found them over there, and they even have the appropriate chemicals and equipment on the shelves nearby!" Erich waved excitedly toward a table that Barbara was still inspecting.

"What's it say?" Peter asked, his eyes still fixed on the words he himself had written months before.

"Hey, where'd that come from?" Erich gestured toward his computer. "Wow, that's small! Is it any good?"

"It's mine, and yes," Peter answered deadpan. "Now, what do you have there?"

Erich recognized something like anger in Peter's voice, and deciding not to ask any more impertinent questions, he opened one of the books and indicated the handwritten notes. "They've been duplicating the work in that paper, I guess they're checking the results. They refer to notes we haven't seen, but I don't think those will be necessary since it's all laid out in detail here."

"How far have they gotten?"

"Up to a few human trials. Nothing massive," Erich answered, obviously uncomfortable with his brother's inexplicable anger. "They must be volunteers, I mean, well, they have to be, don't they?"

"Volunteers," Peter muttered disdainfully.

"Look, I know you don't like this regime and have had your problems with them, but, seriously, they wouldn't do that sort of thing! I'm sure they're volunteers. It's easy enough to get people to agree to . . ." Erich stopped, confused by Peter's actions.

Peter had removed his jacket and had rolled up his left sleeve. There, on his arm, was what looked to Erich like a light cast. Peter carefully undid the clasps to reveal an undamaged arm underneath; he then rolled his arm under the light so that Erich could see the numbers printed there. "That was my name for some years. Now, check this list of 'volunteers' and you'll see that my number is on it."

Erich read the numbers on Peter's arm, and tracing down the screen with his finger, he located the appropriate entry. "You volunteered for this?" he asked, amazed and perhaps condescending.

"No!" Peter hissed with suppressed fury. "No, I did not! So much for your *volunteer* theory!"

"You were tested against your will?"

"I wasn't even told! The first I knew of it was seeing this list about a year ago."

Erich looked at him, his mouth open with realization. He ignored the implications of Peter's lack of cooperation and asked instead, "Then you've been sterilized?"

"No. Apparently not. Not if my wife's been faithful."

Erich looked confused.

"I guess they were testing a preliminary substance for something simple and obvious, such as toxicity," Peter explained patiently. "It was enough, I would suppose, to see if we dropped dead. I was injected and left alone; I guess it didn't have any adverse affects."

"You . . . You have a wife?" Erich asked stupidly.

"Illegally. And a daughter, also illegal."

"I have a niece?" Erich asked even more dreamily.

"Yeah, someday we'll have a family reunion. Now snap out of it. We've got to get out of here. Do we have enough information?"

Erich nodded, still obsessed by his new knowledge. "Yes, yes. That report, these books . . . It's enough."

Peter grabbed the books and tossed them in his bag along with the report. He tossed in the diskettes as well, having decided they were also useful for a different reason: they would prove the level of infiltration or betrayal involved. Information sent directly to the NAU security agencies had come right back to the Reich. That was proof of an extremely devastating leak and would be both useful and advantageous knowledge for the Undergrounds to possess.

Suddenly losing patience with the entire affair, Peter snapped at Barbara, "Anything else?" When she shook her head, he ordered, "Right, let's get out of here. We have enough." He packed away his computer, then turned his attention to Chandler's computer and typed in a series of commands that overrode the built-in protection and deleted all the files. As the machine cranked through the deletions, he went out into the main section and picked up a bottle of fluid. "Does this burn?" he asked Erich.

Erich read the label and nodded.

Peter picked up several more bottles of the fluid and began dousing the files in Chandler's office. He motioned for Barbara, Mark, and Erich to head for the window. "Take my bag, I'll meet you outside," Peter ordered, and continued to throw the fluid on the other desks and any other files he could find.

His three companions hoisted themselves through the window and disappeared into the night. Peter finished dousing the laboratory and laid a trail of fluid up to the window. He glanced out the window to be sure the coast was clear and that the others had already reached the first fence, then he lit a match, watched long enough to see the flame spread, and when the fire reached Chandler's office, climbed out and bolted for the first fence. As he scrambled on his belly under the inner fence, he could see his companions ahead of him, already at the outer fence.

As he emerged into the dead-man's zone, he rose to his feet and started to dash for the outer fence. He did not get even three steps before a lone guard called out to him, "Halt or I'll shoot!"

He stopped dead.

"Hands up!" the unseen voice ordered.

He complied, turning toward the voice as he did so. He could see out of the corner of his eye that Mark was already through the outer fence, Erich was just climbing to his feet, but that Barbara was still crawling on the ground. A small explosion emanated from the laboratory, and as the guard momentarily turned his attention in that direction, Peter began to reach for his own gun.

The guard caught Peter's action and turned to fire. Peter flinched as he heard the explosion of gunfire, expecting pain, but then he realized the noise had not been loud enough, as if the gun carried a silencer. The guard crumpled silently to the ground. Peter glanced at his companions and saw Barbara, on one knee, still holding her gun.

He ran toward his companions. They pulled him through the gap in the outer fence, and then they all disappeared into the night even as the sounds of an alarm were being raised in the darkness behind them. Once they were a safe distance away and all the incriminating evidence and weapons had been hidden, Barbara and Mark broke into the wild chatter that was a natural outlet for all their adrenaline. Erich seemed excited as well and soon joined in as if he were an old coconspirator.

Only Peter remained oddly silent, troubled by the information he had seen. He thanked Barbara for her well-aimed shot and patiently accepted Mark's profuse apologies for freezing.

"I didn't know what to do. I was afraid if I shot, it would draw attention to us. I'm sorry!" Mark continued to blather.

"I said it's all right," Peter repeated with growing irritation. Clearly nothing he said would matter, since Mark was waiting not for Peter's forgiveness, but for Barbara's.

"I've never shot anyone," Mark continued to plead. "I didn't want to . . . I wasn't sure it was the right thing to do."

Eventually Barbara had mercy on all of them, and grabbing Mark's hand, she pulled him around toward her and kissed him passionately. "You were great!" she praised. "Let's go celebrate!"

The two of them disappeared together and Peter continued to walk his brother to his flat. "Will your wife lie for you if the police come?"

"Yeah, she's not a bad sort. I'll tell her that story you suggested about undercover work for the government. She'll buy it," Erich responded, his earlier excitement completely dissipated. He sounded tired, almost sad. "Do you think they'll come looking for me?"

"I see no reason why they should. We've destroyed our gloves, it was a clean entry. Everything went well."

"That guy was going to shoot you!"

Peter shrugged. "No big deal. I've had so many guns shoved in my face over the years . . . Well, I'm sure one of these days that will be the very last thing that I see, but until then, there's no point fretting over something that didn't happen."

Erich shook his head, amazed by his brother's calm demeanor. They reached the entrance to Erich's building and stopped. "Niklaus?" Erich asked quietly.

"What?"

"I don't have a name, an address, anything!"

"I know."

"I don't even know you."

"You never did, Erich."

"Will I see you again?"

"I doubt it," Peter replied, surprised by Erich's tone. Peter bit his lip as he thought about Erich's comments during the evening, then said, "Look, if you're serious about what you said earlier, you know, about helping . . ."

"I am. I mean, I guess . . ." Erich sounded suddenly quite hesitant. Maybe it was the sight of his home and the thought of his family that brought doubts.

"You ought to know that both Mum and Dad, by the end of it all, were working for the Underground."

"They were?" Erich sounded stunned.

"Yes. So, if that's your inclination, I want you to know, it would have pleased them as well. It's a difficult decision, and you should take your time to think about it. Don't take it lightly, you'll be risking everything—your family included."

"What if I decide to join?"

"Some time from now, after you've had time to think, someone will contact you. She, or maybe he, will say, 'Greetings from Joanna.' They'll be a friend. If you want to join, listen to them. Okay?"

"And if I don't?"

"No harm done. No harm at all."

66

"**S**ORRY FOR HAVING YOU SUMMONED like that, but I don't have much time in London," Ryszard apologized quite uncharacteristically.

"Don't worry about it, I've grown used to your methods." Peter leaned back on the upholstered bench and rested his head on his hands.

Forced to lean across the table so that he could continue to keep his voice low, Ryszard scowled. The noise of the pub was sufficient to cover them, but he felt nervous anyway. "I'm here about that Schindler thing. There was sabotage there last week. Chandler's office was destroyed, a security guard critically wounded."

"Yes, I've heard." Peter's eyes wandered around the room, lighting on an attractive woman in intense conversation with a short, burly man. He tried to read her lips to work out which language she was speaking.

"There have been numerous arrests," Ryszard said, intruding into Peter's observations. "The police already have over a dozen confessions and three deaths in custody."

"Ah, really? So efficient, aren't they." English probably. There was something in her gestures.

"Retaliatory actions as well."

"Yes, I've heard the bulldozers were on the move." Her hair was dyed platinum blond. Still that was becoming depressingly common among Englishwomen. Ugh, what a horrible thing to do to hair!

Ryszard cocked his head and contemplated Peter. "Do you know anything about it?"

"Yes," Peter answered, without taking his attention from the odd couple.

"What? What did you have to do with it?"

Peter's eyes darted to Ryszard's face and then back to the blond woman. She looked angry now and her voice was louder, but still he could not make out any words. "Everything. I destroyed the lab so that I could wreck their research. Of course, there's no guarantee they don't have copies somewhere else, but it was my best shot."

"What the hell did you do that for? Now we'll never know what was going on!"

"Do you think I'm stupid?" *Verdammt.* Had she said that? German then.

Ryszard fell silent, unable to answer that. Finally he asked carefully, "What do you have?"

"Plenty," Peter answered brusquely. He felt fed up with Ryszard, with everyone for that matter.

"How did you get it?"

"The old-fashioned way. I stole it all. Me and a few friends broke into the lab and grabbed the results." Maybe English after all. *Verdammt* had probably worked its way into the vernacular.

"Why? That was risky." Ryszard sounded truly impressed. "Especially for you—you know what they'd do if they got their hands on you."

"I know; they would tear me limb from limb. But I wanted the information, so I got it."

"What did you find out?"

"Lots," Peter assured him, finally taking his attention off the woman. "We were right, Schindler was trying to resurrect his defunct sterilization program. My guess is he thought it would be useful to have his own 'secret weapon' in his political arsenal, though I can't fathom why."

"I can. They stopped that program not only because of the political heat it generated in the NAU, but also because it wasn't bearing results. Now, caving in to the Americans was unpopular, and if the program could be resurrected and made to work, then it would be a heroic salvaging of Nazi science from the weak capitulation of the Führer to the capitalists, and who knows, it could always be used against political enemies as well."

"Ah, that's the other point. It does now," Peter said.

"What do you mean?"

"The program, it works. Those formulae contained a final, potable, essentially tasteless agent for the sterilization of male humans."

Ryszard shuddered and instinctively glanced at the beer he had been drinking.

Peter caught his glance and nodded. "Fortunately, it would take more than that, so it would have to be in a water supply, or in a product that is drunk with some regularity, well, like beer. But essentially, you're right—that's all he'd have to do: have a lab mix it up and distribute it to some target population."

"How? The laboratory just got the documentation, how did they have time to complete it?"

"They didn't. The Americans did the job for them."

"*What!*"

"He wasn't using the American to ferry information within the Reich, he was using him to bring *new* information directly from the NAU. That's why it was on a microdisc and that's why Wolf-Dietrich had to acquire the computer that could read it. My guess is the courier knew that of his two missions, his appointment in Lewes was considered much more important."

"Do you think he knew what he was carrying or for whom?"

"Working for them and us at the same time?" Peter shrugged. "I don't know. My guess is he wasn't told more than that he should go to Lewes, check into that inn, and put his boots out to be polished. The arrest set him back a few days and he arrived on the wrong night—the wrong night manager was on duty, but they managed to work their way around that. Anyway, that's probably why he was so agreeable about the arms shipments with you. He was hoping to get away in time to make that second, more important date."

Ryszard nodded. "So you're saying the Americans completed the project begun in Hamburg using the data we sent them? How could they? It's been little over a year since you discovered that information. Don't such things take time, more time than that?"

"I would have thought so, but they have a lot of analysis tools which we could only dream of. Or maybe they had the information long before we sent it to them; after all, that lab was in operation for years before we infiltrated it. It wouldn't surprise me if the Americans knew about it all along."

"Those fucking—"

"That's only a conjecture on my part. In any case, they completed the research."

"That's immoral!"

"Don't be naive," Peter chided, "and give them credit; it may have been a pre-emptive strike, or they may have wanted to check to see that we weren't feeding them a load of bull. Once they started their research, I guess they just kept going."

"Did they go so far as to conduct human trials?"

"Nothing massive, just individuals. All volunteers," Peter added sarcastically. "Chandler and his crew were in the process of duplicating their formulae and testing the results. I guess they wanted to be sure the Americans weren't planting utter nonsense on them. They got as far as testing humans, and he seemed to be coming to the conclusion that it was effective. From his notebooks, it was still unclear to him if it was reversible or how long it lasted."

"So how did Schindler get this information?"

"I don't know, but I think the fact that he did get it, along with the technology that he had in hand, is almost more important than the information. They obviously have a huge security problem there, and we, worse luck for them, have proof of it. That computer, that microdisc, and the entire results from a top-secret research program . . ." Peter shook his head in mock dismay. "They even had the files I sent over there—exactly as I translated them. *Word for word!*"

Ryszard smiled. "Word for word?"

Peter nodded solemnly. "After all their pious shit about not sharing information with us, we have extremely embarrassing proof of a huge breach of their security. We can probably write a very long wish list of technology and cooperation, and they'll be more than happy to oblige us."

"Plus I have the goods on Schindler."

"How so?" Peter asked.

"Oh, you don't understand the politics, but he only did this to embarrass the Führer, and now I know about it. I can bring him down at my leisure or I can convince him to be a trusted lieutenant." Ryszard flicked a bit of dirt out from under a fingernail. "This is perfect. Just what I needed!"

"Blackmail Schindler, extort the ASA into cooperation, preempt any possibility of a nasty sterilization campaign . . ."

"Yes, good work," Ryszard praised condescendingly. "How do you want to give me the information? Did you bring it with you?"

"No." Peter shook his head. "I'm not giving it to you."

"What!" Ryszard calmed his voice immediately. "What the hell do you mean?"

"I want the opportunity to present whatever I find directly to the Szaflary Council. They can then do with it as they please."

"Why?"

"I want to make a deal with them: my findings for a chance to come home."

"I *need* that information," Ryszard hissed.

"Oh, you'll get it. I just want to be the one to hand it over."

"If all you want is to go back, I could have arranged that ages ago!"

Peter tilted his head as he thought about what Ryszard had said. "Would you have done that for me?"

"Of course, they'd have listened to me. I can get Katerina to do anything!"

"Hmm. Well, I was unaware of that, but never mind," Peter responded, politely disguising his disbelief that Ryszard would have helped him in that manner. "I want to do this myself. I'm too old for mentors, and if you had insisted on my return, all I would have done is trade one colonel's protection for another."

Ryszard looked confused and slightly insulted.

"I need to run my own life," Peter explained. "I can't have other people constantly doing me favors. If I get back to Szaflary, I want it to be on my terms, not yours."

Ryszard seemed ready to say something, but he stopped himself. He lit a cigarette and smoked in silence for a moment, then he shrugged. "Fair enough. If you plan on passing the information on, that's good enough; leave a copy with me or Barbara just to be safe, then go ahead and take it to them. I just want to make sure the organization gets it so they can use it to my advantage."

"Haven't you got that backward? Aren't you supposed to be working to our advantage?"

"Oh, it's essentially the same. I just need help promoting my career."

"To what end? You've been so busy promoting your career, I get the distinct impression you've forgotten that it is a revolution that you're supposed to be working toward."

"Have patience."

"When do you plan to do something useful?" Peter pressed.

"You mean something more useful than saving your wretched life, twice?"

"I mean something politically useful," Peter answered deadpan, refusing to rise to the bait.

"When the time is right."

"And when might that be?"

"When I'm Führer."

"You think you can pull it off?"

"With the organization I have behind me? I don't see why not." Ryszard gazed pensively at his cigarette. "I still have to shuffle some of the competition out of the way, then I have to deal with the current Führer."

"Assassination?"

Ryszard shook his head. "Probably not, more likely a setup that will get him to step down and name me as successor. Stefi's been working on that."

"Stefi? How can she . . . ?"

"Maybe a sex scandal. Top aide's daughter, depraved acts, blah, blah, blah."

"Your daughter?" Peter blanched.

Ryszard tilted his head at Peter. "She makes her own decisions," he stated calmly.

"So what do you plan to do once you achieve that vaunted position?" Peter asked as he recovered his composure.

"I'll be able to push forward some initiatives: cultural rights—"

"Initiatives?" Peter sputtered.

"—autonomy for various nationalities, maybe national assemblies with lim-

ited democratic representation. Abolish the camps, reform the penal code, introduce wages, and eventually outlaw slavery—"

"Eventually!"

"—enact education reforms, restructure the economy—"

"What about compensation for our suffering? What about all the murders?"

"—privatize industry, open up foreign policy, ease censorship—"

"What about justice? After all these years!"

Ryszard interrupted his list. "Too divisive."

"What about restoring our independence?"

"Impossible, at least in the near term. The complete scattering of peoples
around the Continent would lead to mayhem if we tried to divide things along
nationalistic lines. Millions would have to be relocated, land confiscated, nationalities assigned to people without one. It's a recipe for disaster. There's going to
have to be some sort of united Europe."

"You mean all mixed into one happy pan-European family?" Peter scoffed.

"Do you see any other way?" Ryszard asked calmly. "I've studied the demo-
graphics. If we start drawing lines on the map, we are guaranteeing border wars
and civil wars and genocide."

"And the lingua franca?"

"German. What else? If there is a sufficient concentration of speakers for
another tongue, then that region can be bilingual."

"So in your scheme, they win. It's that simple—a European Union under
German hegemony."

"Why not? All of North America speaks the language of one tiny, foggy, backwater island."

"That was done voluntarily—"

"Yes, so the American Indians say."

"—whereas everything we have here is based on force," Peter argued, ignoring
Ryszard's interjection, "and it must not be allowed to continue!"

"I'm dealing with reality, my dear brother-in-law. You can construct whatever
fantasy world you want, but the truth is they have had more than half a century
to leave their mark on this continent, and if we try to go back to the way things
were, we're asking for slaughter on a massive scale."

"So you're saying Joanna and Andrzej died for nothing?" Peter asked bitterly.

"Of course they died for nothing! I don't believe in causes which cost children
their lives! Do *you* think there was meaning in their deaths? Do you?"

Affronted by Ryszard's patronizing tone, Peter responded darkly, "I want this
regime toppled."

Ryszard blew a stream of smoke into the air, then eyed his brother-in-law
meaningfully. "Ah, yes, and *you* have been so effective in *your* efforts," he sneered.

Annoyed by the truth in Ryszard's words, Peter chose to ignore them. "What
you're suggesting—we could have had better than that by dealing with Hitler in
'39 without a war!"

"Yes, without a war *which we lost.*"

"So what you want is National Socialism with a human face," Peter sneered.

"That's one way of putting it," Ryszard replied, unruffled.

"What about the revolution?" Peter asked, exasperated.

"We can't afford such romantic nonsense. The system must be dismantled slowly, not overthrown—otherwise there'd be a power vacuum and a hundred, no, a thousand different groups vying for control."

"I think you enjoy being in this hierarchy and you don't want to dismantle it! You're power mad."

"And you're bloodthirsty. Do you want to change things for the better or do you just want revenge?"

Peter almost blurted *Revenge!* but then thought better of it. "Maybe," he answered carefully, "meting out justice is not inconsistent with establishing a just society."

"Do it on your own time. Once we're in a position to change things, we can't afford to lose the support of mainstream society."

"You mean the bastards who destroyed Europe in the first place."

"The criminals of that era are mostly dead. The children raised with this system cannot know what they are doing. What would you do, punish an entire population?"

Peter thought of Teresa. Was she guilty by birth? That was all too familiar a concept. "We could be selective."

"Assuming we're omnipotent and have nothing better to do with our time, yes. Otherwise, it's unrealistic and the alternative to a peaceful transition is civil war. Do you want a bloodbath?"

Peter fell silent. He felt rather perturbed because he had recognized something about himself in Ryszard's questions. He was no longer driven by the need for a just society, and indeed, if the Nazi leadership confessed its sins and righted its wrongs, that would no longer be enough: he wanted to see them hang. Peaceful evolution was not sufficient, the revolution had become a goal in and of itself. The righting of injustices, the restructuring of society, all took a backseat to his deep-seated need for vengeance, and when he closed his eyes and imagined the changes that would be wrought in the future, he no longer saw peace and prosperity and freedom, he saw Joanna's murderers swinging from gallows, he saw his tormentors on their knees begging in vain for mercy, he saw Berlin as leveled as Warsaw had been. He saw revenge.

"Just imagine that you get the world you want," Ryszard spoke into Peter's thoughts. "What do you think the economy would look like?"

Resenting the patronizing tone, Peter responded too quickly, "Who gives a fuck about economies?"

"Grow up!" Ryszard snarled. "Economic chaos means starvation and riots! You're asking for death and destruction as your idea of justice. Look at the numbers and think!"

"What are the current numbers?" Peter asked quietly.

"One hundred fifty million German or Germanic citizens. Of those, about two million are in prison or concentration camps and have been stripped of their citizenship."

Peter nodded, repeating, "Two million."

"Thirty or so million non-Germans who have obtained full Reich citizenship. Altogether, that's roughly one hundred eighty million people who have a vested interest in the current status quo and who would be the possible victims of any revolutionary terror. Then there are about eighty million subjects without citizenship. These are people who are governed by the Basic Law and the Minimum Guarantee of Rights. Of that number, about fifty million are in untied, paid employment and would have questionable loyalty to any revolution. The other thirty are in tied jobs. They receive minimal salaries and housing but must remain with their employer unless given permission to move. Even they would have a reason to fear abrupt change."

"And the rest?" Peter asked. "How many natural allies do we have?"

"There are about thirty million people in forced labor. About sixteen million of these are in conscription with a finite service length. The remaining fourteen million are either in indefinite or permanent forced labor. Eight million of those are living in camps, prisons, and industrial barracks and are completely cut off from the outside world. Of the remaining *Zwangsarbeiter,* about five million work in shops, restaurants, and other small businesses. The remaining million are in domestic employment, mostly in and around Berlin."

"Only a million?" The number did not match intuitively with Peter's own experience, but then he had been a resident of a wealthy and politically connected suburb. "Didn't the number used to be much higher?"

"Yes, in the forties it was, and the promise was that every German hausfrau, no matter how lowly, would one day own a servant, but that proved to be unworkable, and the Labor Ministry pulled back on the numbers."

"Why was it unworkable? Was there unrest?"

"No. Not unrest, fraternization," Ryszard explained. "You wouldn't believe the number of conspiracies between German women who wanted to skip the joy of eight pregnancies and the servant women who wanted to keep their babies. Even without sham adoptions and faked births, they found there were problems with children raised to speak fluent German. Once you get rid of the language differences, our people are indistinguishable."

Peter's thoughts turned to Josef and his wife, and he wondered if they were together with their child. He remembered Josef's vehement denial of paternity, Martin's sly look. "But that has always been true in Europe. What makes things different now?" Peter wondered aloud.

Ryszard shrugged. "I would guess, in the past, the strong combination of religion, malnutrition, and ignorance kept the lower orders in their place. Now, well, we still use malnutrition, but we're very weak at utilizing religion properly, the lower stratum is being educated by the Undergrounds, and . . ." He rubbed his chin as he thought.

"America," Peter suggested. "It's a thorn in their ideological side."

Ryszard nodded. "Yes. Proof positive that the mob can rule."

"So they cut back on domestic help."

"Yes, particularly women. You and your ilk are a genuine status symbol, held only by the most politically trustworthy. And even then . . ." Ryszard opened his hands, indicating his unwillingness to refer to Peter's affair with Elspeth.

"All right, so you think we're too mixed and confused to disentangle."

"Not only that, but the people with the greatest interest in revolution are those who have been brutalized for so long that we have no way of knowing how they would react to freedom. One could guess though that their vengeance could be terrible and not particularly well directed. Do you want that for Magdalena?"

Peter rubbed his forehead trying to erase the image of his innocent daughter being thrown onto a pyre of vengeance. "What do you suggest?"

"Clearly we need to restructure the system and establish some openness. Maybe when that's done, we can oversee letting the system gently collapse into a multinational Europe, but whatever we do, we can't afford a violent overthrow of everything. It's the only system we have and the alternative would be chaos!"

"You're assuming cooperation on the part of every revolutionary. That's a lot to ask." Could Peter pass his erstwhile torturers in the street day in and day out? Could they work side by side in some office in the interests of peace and prosperity?

"Yes, it's a lot to ask, but we'll cross that bridge if we get to it. I'm hoping, at that time, that you'll speak out as a voice of reason. With your experiences, your words could carry a lot of weight."

Peter's eyes strayed across the room to the woman and the burly man. He had his arm draped around her waist and they were intimately close, both drinking. "Fine. I'll do you a deal. You help me take the information directly to Szaflary, and later, I'll be your voice of reason. I'll say whatever you want."

"That was a rather quick change of heart," Ryszard noted suspiciously.

"Do we have a deal?"

"You have become rather usurious, haven't you?"

"Forgive me for having learned my lessons well. Is it a deal?"

Ryszard nodded. "Sure. Just don't waste this opportunity."

"What do you mean?"

"I mean, you can get a lot more than permission to come home out of this stuff. Ask for it."

"Ask for what?"

"A promotion, at least. Or a Council seat. You have the skills and experience—they should have chosen you by now." Ryszard lit another cigarette, then said into the silence, "The only reason you haven't been put forward is that you're a foreigner. Just like my dad. He had to fight for his place every step of the way. Even now he pretty much works alone."

"How could I get a Council seat? I thought the representatives were democratically elected."

Richard sputtered. "Believe what you want, but think about it. The elections must be conducted in absolute secrecy. Do you really think they're free and fair?"

"I was under that impression."

"Well, even if they are, how do you think the voters get the information on the candidates?"

"The Underground press."

"Which is?"

"Run by the Council," Peter concluded. A Council seat, that would be nice. That would shove all the shit they had doled out to him right back up their noses. As he thought of the possibilities, he began to smile. "Will you help me get there? I need papers and permits. Something impressive, so I won't be searched."

Ryszard thought for a moment. "Yeah, I can manage that for you. After all, I guess I owe you a favor."

"How so?"

Ryszard glanced into Peter's face, then waved away the question. "Just guarantee that our people will eventually get the information, no matter what."

"No problem."

"You know, my handlers are going to be very annoyed with me if it gets out that I'm doing this on the side."

"I thought you were in a position to tell them what to do."

"I am. That annoys them as well."

"Well, I've always felt that if your own side doesn't want to shoot you at some point in your career, you must be doing something wrong."

Ryszard laughed heartily. "So, I guess you've been doing things right all along!"

67

"Aren't you going to warn them you're coming?" Barbara asked rather worriedly. Only an hour ago, she had received a communiqué that indicated Szaflary was still ignorant of his plans.

"No, they'll just tell me to stay put," Peter responded. She looked concerned, so he added, "Don't worry, I'm sure when they hear what I have to say, they'll have much better things to be angry at me about."

"Be careful." She gave him a brief kiss.

"I will. And I hope you two have a good life."

"We will. Take care." Mark could barely hide his elation at Peter's departure, but he gave it a brave attempt.

Peter grabbed his bags, went down the steps, and climbed into the waiting taxi that would ferry him to the airport. Ryszard had decided the safest course was to fly Peter to Kraków himself. He said he had some business to conduct there in any case, and so he could carry the incriminating documents and computer, which in his possession would no longer be incriminating, and Peter could assume the role of his aide, using Stefan's papers. The English Underground had obligingly altered the photograph, and Stefan would get to spend the time holed up in Ryszard's hotel room with a bottle of whiskey and an amiable companion until his papers wended their way back to him.

In Kraków, Ryszard planned to make a quick visit to an office and then return to Berlin, while Peter planned to take local transit through to Neu Sandez and then on to the village. Local travel was usually unhindered, and Peter felt he could manage that part of the journey without help. Once he reached the village, he would contact one of the border entry guides and convince him or her to escort him in. He would explain he had been issued an urgent summons and would express surprise that they were not expecting him. They knew him, they would give him no trouble. The trouble would come later, with the Council, and for that he was well prepared.

"I can go it alone from here," Peter said to the woman who had walked him across the border. She had radioed their presence and made sure that he was not accidentally shot at. Once inside, they had managed to catch a ride most of the way, and now that the truck had to drop them off, he saw no reason for her to continue with him. "We're inside the internal borders and they know me personally here, so there shouldn't be any problem."

"Okay, but be careful," she warned. "After all, we weren't expecting you, so if there has been some miscommunication, they might not be expecting you here either."

"It's all right." He was touched by her concern and the extra effort she had gone through to see him all the way inside. "They're used to me walking around this area all the time. They won't shoot at me."

"Farewell then." She waved good-bye.

He sighed with relief. It had gone terribly smoothly, taking only two days to work his way from Kraków into the mountains, and his story had not been questioned at all. As he walked along, he thought that it should probably worry him that he had slipped in so easily while unexpected, even if they did know him, even if he was generally trusted. Border security clearly needed a bit of reorganizing.

Once he was sure his guide was well out of sight, he changed his direction toward Joanna's grave. When he reached it, he cleared away the snow and contemplated it for a few minutes, thinking of his happy little girl and how her brief life had been so cruelly destroyed. Then he smiled at her memory, and asking her forgiveness and blessing for what he was doing, he dug into the snow behind the stone and buried his treasure. It would be the obvious place for them to look, but he did not care. It would not go that far, but indeed, if anything untoward did happen, he wanted them to find the information. He had to admit, at least to himself and Joanna, that his entire presentation would be a bluff. If they did not give him what he wanted, if they arrested him, even if they shot him for treason, he still wanted them to have the information. They would find it here easily enough.

He said a casual hello to the guard at the entrance and went into the bunker, heading immediately to his apartment before talking to anybody else. He needed to discuss everything with Zosia, and besides, he did not want to draw attention to his presence until she knew what was going on.

The place was empty and neither Zosia nor Irena was in sight. It was also clean and organized. He walked through the room as though entering a stranger's house. On a bookshelf, Zosia's files had carefully been arranged using specially made dividers, each tagged with a subject and date. A thick blanket was spread on the floor, on top of a rug, to make a soft playing surface for the baby. Little toys and a mirror were heaped into a small pile at the corner of the blanket, ready for the baby's use. The refrigerator contained fresh food, the cupboards were well stocked. Suspiciously he looked at the dish-drying rack: one coffee cup, one dish, one set of silverware. If Zosia had acquired a roommate, he was marvelously discreet.

Peter went into the bedroom and scanned the clothes: his remained where he had left them, Zosia's filled the other spaces, and the drawers that had once been Joanna's now held Irena's tiny things. Nervously, he opened the small wooden box in which Zosia stored her jewelry. Neither her wedding ring nor the necklace he had given her was inside. Her stiletto and silver ring were also missing. He stared at the nearly empty box and felt both relieved and ashamed of himself for checking up on her. He returned to the main room and opened the cabinet drawer. The diaries and his letters were still there, though the letters had been bound with ribbon into a folder.

He picked up the folder and studied the neat handiwork. What could it mean? Apparently Zosia had overcome her depression after Joanna's death, but even so, where had she found the time, with a baby to care for, to do such things? It was so unlike her! As he stood there wondering, a bit of something sticking out from under the couch caught his eye. He set down the letters and went over to the couch. He reached underneath and pulled out a guitar case, then unfastened the locks and opened it. Inside was a guitar and an envelope addressed to him. He opened the envelope; inside was a note from Arieka.

I talked to your father-in-law (as I now know he is) and he told me about what had happened. I can't begin to express my sorrow. Even though I never met your little girl, I cried for days. When I learned you were still alive, I wanted to send you something. I remembered how much you liked playing my guitar that night after the show and I wanted to send it to you as a sort of remembrance, but I was advised that it would be better to send money and have one bought there. So, I'm hoping that is what happens. If my instructions are followed, you should get this letter along with an instrument. I've enclosed some instructions for various chords. I'm sure you'll be able to work out the rest.

Do take care, and maybe someday I'll visit (though I doubt I could blend into the crowd!).

Your friend, Arieka

He strummed his fingers along the strings and thought of that distant land. And of his friend there. He read the note again and then tucked it all away back under the couch. Somebody had carefully followed her instructions. He wondered if it had been Zosia.

He went to Marysia's door and knocked. Olek's voice yelled at him to come in.

"Where's Zosia?" Peter asked immediately.

"On an assignment. What are you doing here?"

"Ah, I'll explain eventually. Where's Irena?"

"With the colonel." Olek used his aunt's title, clearly indicating that she was at work.

"With Zosia?" Peter repeated, momentarily shocked to think of his child in such circumstances.

"Yeah, she's nursing, so she doesn't want to be away from Irena any longer than necessary. She took Stefi with her to watch Irena during the few hours that she's actually doing her job."

"Stefi's back from Berlin?"

"Yeah, said she needed a break and wanted to get on with her training with the colonel."

"Stefi's under Zosia's tutelage?" Peter asked, amazed.

"Yes. Been so for years," Olek answered proudly.

"That doesn't bother you?"

"Why should it?" Olek asked, genuinely confused.

"No reason." Peter shook his head at his own naïveté. He sometimes forgot that Olek, like Zosia and Barbara, had been raised from birth in this strange kill-or-be-killed world. Not his choice, not the choice of his parents, just the way it was.

"If our women want to do something other than stay here and be helpful," Olek volunteered, "they have very little option but to follow that route. They can't get well placed in Nazi society, except sometimes as the secretary of somebody important; so, they contribute in their own way, and that frees the men for other jobs."

"Yes, of course." Peter felt rather foolish that Olek needed to tutor him. It all made sense and Peter had long ago accepted the logic of it, but he still sometimes made snap judgments based upon his conventional upbringing, and on those occasions he realized that he looked rather provincial to people raised without such traditional prejudices.

"At least the able-bodied men," Olek added dejectedly.

Peter nodded in commiseration. "Where's your grandmother?"

"Oh, she's busy nowadays. You know, with the Council."

"More than before?"

"Oh, you probably haven't heard. Katerina resigned after the invasion. Said she had enough, said she kept thinking about her sister. Whatever that means. My grandmother was elected chair."

"Goodness! Well, congratulate her for me when you see her. Do you know when Zosia will be back?"

"I think Stefi said tomorrow morning. There's a full Council meeting at ten so she'll probably try to be back for that."

"Ten. Okay. I'll be back to chat, but I've got to arrange something." Peter waved and was out the door. There would be no time to consult with Zosia; maybe it would be for the best.

68

"A H, HERR TRAUGUTT, CONGRATULATIONS."

"Thank you." Richard nodded and smiled. Funny how many people knew him as soon as the promotion became public. It was a good promotion as well—one of the rare times the increased prestige was in accord with political reality. At the lower levels of the hierarchy, that was almost always true, but here, near the top, so much depended on posturing and allies and other intangibles that a promotion could often be interpreted as a move down or away from the core of power. Not this time: he was moving straight up in direct response to his increased political leverage. The Führer's personal adviser on internal security.

It was easy to smile at all the congratulations, and it was no wonder there were so many who went out of their way to remind him that they were friends. Not least of whom was Karl. He was waiting in Richard's outer office, suddenly timid about entering without permission. The boy from the provinces would soon be his boss.

"Richard! Can I still call you that?" Karl wheezed.

"But of course, Karl. Come on in," Richard soothed as he led Karl into his office.

Karl took a seat after Richard had sat down, and after offering Richard a cigarette, he lit one for himself, then plunged in. "Congratulations. Why didn't you tell me? I had to hear it from the boys!"

"Sorry. It was supposed to be completely hush-hush. But now you know."

"Yes, things just go from good to better with you," Karl moaned. "It was so fortunate how you broke up that disloyal ring working at *Die Zeit.*"

"More than working at," Richard corrected. "Actually running it."

"Yes, yes! So fortunate, too, that you brought the head of Krupps down for corruption."

"I like to think of it as good work rather than good fortune," Richard said with a hint of malice.

Karl was oblivious to the hint. "Burckhardt really liked that, since he was in line for the chairmanship. Did you know that?"

Did Richard know? He stifled a laugh. He had selected that sleazeball Rentschler with particular care. Of course he was corrupt, they all were. Of course he carried out dubious foreign deals, they all did. Of course he used slave labor and brutality in his factories, who didn't? The latter, at least, was not a crime. The corruption, however, under the right circumstances, was. And the right circumstances certainly existed with Burckhardt in line for the chairmanship. Had Richard known? Ha! It was the hard evidence that was difficult to find, and in the end Richard had had it planted.

Zosia herself had handled the majority of it, leaving a paper and computer trail that en route picked out a few others, targeted for one reason or another, before inexorably leading to Rentschler. She had done a masterly job and had mentioned to Richard that it was not only to promote his career, but was also a form of revenge for her husband's suffering as a Krupp slave.

Richard answered Karl briefly, "Yes, I heard something about that," without adding that not only had he known that the influential Burckhardt would appreciate Richard's efforts, but he also knew, quite coincidentally, that Burckhardt had a great deal of influence in selecting who would fill the vacancy for the Führer's personal adviser on internal security. Yes, it was all very, very fortuitous.

"You certainly impressed everyone with your advice about that invasion, too," Karl continued as if he had memorized a list. Things to do to get promoted? What had Richard done?

"How did you know about that?" Richard asked, genuinely appalled.

"Oh, just gossip. I know, I'm not supposed to be in that loop. I'm surprised you were and didn't tell me. I thought we were friends."

"Security," Richard answered tersely.

"Afterwards, the word was you were excellent in the negotiations. You seemed to understand exactly where they would cave and where they would hold fast."

Richard studied Karl intensely, but there were, as far as he could tell, no hidden implications, no subtle threats of blackmail. Still, it was worrying.

Karl seemed to understand Richard's look as a question. "Oh, I know I'm not supposed to know about that either—but, you know, people talk. They seemed quite proud of you there."

Richard nodded. He had not had time to let anyone know he would be at the negotiations, but as soon as Katerina had seen him, she had indicated she would be willing to make some meaningless concessions to promote his career. They had not rehearsed anything in advance, but they knew each other and the situation well enough to be able to ad-lib remarkably well. He had, during the meeting, gone from whispering into the ear of his superior to being encouraged to speak directly to the enemy as it was clear that what he had to say caused them to tremble and occasionally give ground. Despite the invasion's having been an utter fiasco, Richard's masterly handling of the old woman had even led to her conceding a bit of territory. Naturally, neither she nor Richard mentioned that the worthless bit of swampy borderland was essentially indefensible.

It seemed time to draw Karl's list to a close, so Richard stood, thanked him for his visit, and mentioned that he was quite busy. However, Karl remained seated and lit another cigarette. He did not even bother to offer Richard one. It could have been taken as a threat if only his face had not conveyed such a miserable hangdog expression.

"What is it?" Richard was driven to ask as he reseated himself on the edge of his desk. Was Karl planning to blackmail him?

"Oh, Richard," Karl moaned, "my friend, it's all going so well for you, but for me, it's just been terrible! Every move I made with that Halifax thing was a disaster! And now, they've removed me from that position and . . ."

"Well, it's probably just as well you're out of that job. After all, you're security, what do you know about propaganda?"

"But you said I should do it! You encouraged me!"

"At the time, I thought it would be good for your career."

"But I think they're going to investigate me! How did that tape get out in the first place? They might find out I viewed a copy of it. They might blame me!"

"You returned it to your source, didn't you?" Richard asked with concern.

"Right away. As soon as I got it back from you."

Still no hint of blackmail, but clearly Karl was not going to fail to mention Richard if he did get investigated. Richard was much better informed than Karl and knew that it would probably be worse than an investigation. The propaganda disaster had and was still causing far-reaching repercussions, and scapegoats were essential. One would be that fool torturer who had signed off on Halifax claiming he was no danger to society. Karl was the other obvious choice. He had screwed up so badly, he would be driven out, and it was doubtful that it would be a matter of simply resigning. If he did not end up shot or hanged, he would be expected to commit suicide. It was that bad.

Before that occurred, he would probably be interrogated. That was what worried Richard. Karl would give him up in a second, hoping to save his own skin by blaming Richard for his advice. It was a dangerous situation: one or two political enemies, one or two envious people, could see him made the scapegoat with or even instead of Karl. Richard could be shot for incompetence or hanged for having viewed the videotape unofficially. Even worse, if a plot was suspected, his entire cover could be blown and everyone in his family would be at risk.

It was time to cover his tracks. To that end, he decided to calm Karl down a bit and see precisely what his state of mind was, then Richard would decide on his exact plan of action. He drew up a concerned, reassuring voice and said, "Karl, dear friend, don't get too worried. Look, why don't we meet after work for a beer and discuss how things are shaping up? Say about six?"

Karl smiled weakly and agreed. He stubbed out his cigarette, reached into his jacket pocket, and felt the small knife he had carried since earning it as a boy in the Hitler Youth. "Six will be fine."

Karl was already at their club when Richard arrived. Richard spotted him in the public bar at the front and watched from a distance as Karl pawed at and whispered into the ear of a dark-haired woman sitting close to him. Richard grimaced with annoyance at the display and marched over to interrupt.

"Ah, is it six?" Karl asked as he wrapped a finger seductively around a lock of the woman's hair. "Let me introduce you to my friend here, uh . . ."

"That's quite all right," Richard assured Karl, and winking at the woman, he pulled Karl away toward the private lounge.

"What's the matter with you?" Karl asked, not yet sure if he had the option of being offended by his friend's abruptness.

"What did you say to her? Did you confide your troubles? Did you mention me?" Richard could not help himself from asking.

"Oh, I . . ." Karl looked to his friend, wondering what the right answer was. "Don't be jealous, I would have given you credit sooner or later," he finally said.

Richard sighed his relief and waved at the waiter to bring them two drinks. "Look, don't you realize those women can be trouble?" All he needed was Karl confiding in an informant!

"Oh, I can handle them," Karl assured him breezily. "I make sure they've been thoroughly vetted before I take a new one on. I was just toying with her."

"That's not what I meant," Richard snarled, but it was too late, Karl was on a roll.

"Bit cruel, I'll admit, getting her hopes up like that, but they're such avaricious creatures. . . . I don't have trouble with them, though, not since . . . And I handled that."

"How so?" Richard asked with an encouraging smile. He doubted Karl had any useful information in him, but it was a lifelong habit of his to listen to anything anyone had to say—the silly gossip and bragging stories of his comrades were often his best source of news and blackmail information.

"Oh, some bitch I had an affair with, years back. Pretty thing, long, straight black hair, dark eyes, tall . . ." Karl sighed as he remembered his long-ago passion.

"And?"

"Well, she got pregnant. I told her it wasn't my problem, and that was it, she just disappeared."

"When was this?"

"Hmm." Karl thought back. "Must have been twenty years ago, at least."

"Were you married then?" Richard asked, lighting a cigarette.

"Of course. Geerd was just born about that time, or was it Horst? One of them. Anyway, you know what wives are like when they're pregnant, or just after. Can't do a thing with them. This lady, she was, well, it was like fireworks, every time. Must have been Italian, although her name was German."

"What was her name?"

"Um. You know"—Karl sounded slightly nervous—"I'm not sure I remember."

"Doesn't matter. So, she just disappeared after getting pregnant?"

"Yeah, almost like she didn't care to trap me or try and get money. Just up and left. Left her job, everything, as far as I could tell."

"Did you try and trace her?"

"Why should I have?"

"No reason, just wondered."

"No, the last thing I wanted was a pregnant woman howling at me. God knows I had enough of that at home. Anyway, I thought I was done with it, but then, years later, back when I was in Paris for a few months, she just shows up. Just out of the blue."

Richard stared down at the table so that Karl would not see his expression, then took another drag off his cigarette. "Paris, you say?" he asked casually.

"Yeah. She shows up, still looking good, and she tells me I have a teenage son and she wants some money. First she asks nicely and I gave her some, quite a bit in fact, but she says it's not enough. She knows I have lots more and she needs it. Threatens to make trouble if I don't pay her. 'A lump sum,' she said. Pay her just once more and she would be out of my life forever."

"And did you pay her?"

"Hell no! I don't give in to that sort of shit."

"So did she make trouble for you?"

"No. I handled it," Karl announced proudly. "Had a bit of fun with her first, then, well, I shan't tell you how, but you could say, she's out of my life forever. For-ever."

"Glad to hear it." Richard had already made up his mind about his course of action.

69

PROMPTLY AT TEN the Council gathered. Peter waited in the hall, leaning casually against the wall, as they filtered into the room. Each looked at him with undisguised curiosity, but most did nothing more than nod a greeting in his direction. When he saw Marysia coming down the hall, he launched himself from the wall to greet her.

She hugged him. "Welcome back! Olek said you were here. But why?"

"I'll explain shortly." He kissed her hello.

Tadek joined them and interjected, "AWOL again, Captain?"

Marysia made an impatient gesture at Tadek, and together they left to go into the meeting. The door was closed and Peter waited with unusual patience. Only moments later, he was invited in. He entered the room and faced the curious, even hostile stares with equanimity.

"Now, Captain, why exactly are you here? You demanded to be heard by us first thing, and we have accommodated you. So?" Wojciech asked without patience.

Marysia glanced at Wojciech, clearly annoyed by his preempting her.

"I have important information to give you. Very important." Peter paced coolly in front of the assembled Council.

"And?" Marysia prompted, reasserting her authority.

"And I want something in return."

"What is your information?" Hania asked.

Before he could answer, Zosia came nearly breathless into the room. The front of her blouse was soaked with milk, and in her arms she held Irena tight against her breast as the baby nursed greedily. Zosia looked sweaty, tired, and irritable, as if her organized plans for peacefully feeding Irena had been hopelessly disrupted. When she saw Peter, a thousand miles from where he was supposed to be, she stopped dead and looked questioningly for an explanation.

"We don't know either," Marysia answered Zosia's look. "He just showed up last night and demanded to be heard by us today."

Zosia turned toward him. "What's going on? How did you get here?"

"I just walked in," he answered her last question first as he walked over and kissed her hello. He stroked Irena's head, marveling at how much she had grown. She looked so much more engaged in the world around her, as if, he thought bemusedly, someone had thrown a switch and her personality had turned on. Even as she sucked at Zosia's breast, her eyes turned upward to stare at him and wonder at the presence of this stranger. He felt his heart breaking with regret at the months they had lost, and he wanted to take her in his arms and hold her and teach her to know him, but all that would have to wait just a little longer. "I was going to tell you all about it last night," he added, "but you were out. Now you can hear it with everyone else."

Zosia's eyes widened slightly with worry or a warning, but he winked at her and she decided to settle in and listen. As she sat down, he poured her a glass of water, remembering what she had said about thirst and nursing, and then walked back to the center of the floor to face the Council.

"What is your information?" Hania repeated.

"I have in my possession the completed biochemical formulae for the sterility program which was abandoned after my visit to America. The information I have is proof of deep espionage within the American security agencies, a crippling embarrassment for a key political enemy of our most senior infiltrator, and useful blackmail of the Americans to force them into greater cooperation and trust. Not only that, but this information will be crucial in preventing the institution of any such program or in counteracting it, if it is instituted. My presentation of this information to you instead of Warszawa will also enhance your own political viability."

There was a murmur of surprise. Konrad was the first to overcome his astonishment, and ignoring Peter's strange presentation, he said, "Good work. Hand everything over and we'll see that it is treated appropriately."

"No."

There was a stunned silence at the bald refusal, and the Council members glared at him in confusion. Zosia adjusted Irena and sipped her water. Finally Tomek ventured, "Captain Halifax, what are you saying?"

"I'm saying, I'm not handing over anything until I get exactly what I want."

"You're blackmailing us?" Wojciech asked. "You do realize you could be court-martialed!"

" 'Dealing with you' might be more appropriate," Peter responded. "And if you court-martial me, you'll get absolutely nothing."

"But this is . . . You should pass it on to us immediately!" Wanda protested.

"When I get what I want."

"You got your life from us! That was enough, that's more than many people have. My sons . . . Now it's time to repay your debt!"

"I've *already* paid enough for something which should *always* have been mine!" Peter retorted. "Now I'll choose who gets my information. I'll give it to whomever shows as much loyalty to me as I have shown to them. Perhaps the English, perhaps an independent group. Perhaps the Communists."

"Peter!" Marysia could not contain herself. "How dare you treat us in this manner!"

"Oh, give it a rest. I'm fed up with being shunted around as if I were valueless. I'm proving my value, and I'm not going to let this opportunity go to waste. If you want diplomacy, rewrite the minutes, because I'm not going to waste our valuable time fucking around."

"What are your demands?" Tadek asked in his usual cool manner.

"First, that I am reassigned here. Immediately and permanently. No outside assignments that I don't personally approve. And by personally, I mean me, not my wife."

"We'll take that under consideration," Marysia intoned.

"You'll agree to it now, or there is no point in my proceeding."

They looked at each other, took a silent vote of nods, and agreed.

"We'll have to arrange something with your persona; it's not good to let them drop off the face of the earth like that," Hania commented. She held primary responsibility for the organization of the various identities used by their agents.

"Jäger is officially in London," Peter explained. "He can commit suicide at the beach at our convenience. Barbara already has some local talent lined up to replace him. She has a personal commitment to the lad and hence to London; so, not only will that solve your perpetual problem of finding someone to take that job, but you'll have an automatic link with the English Underground. Better than using me as a liaison since he's currently a member."

"Fine. We can untangle things later."

"What else?" Marysia prompted.

"I want access to the entire installation, especially Communications and anything which needs a security expert. I want free right of entry and exit to this place."

"That's impossible!"

"Let me make it possible. All I ask for is the rights of access that my wife has. Simple equality," Peter amended with a smile. Zosia had, as far as he knew, no limits on her rights, but if there were any, he would accept those as well.

"You exceed our patience!" Wanda glowered.

"Fuck your patience. I want your word!"

"Peter, you really are asking a lot," Marysia said in an obvious attempt to be conciliatory.

"I'm offering a lot in return. I could argue for these things, but you all know my record and you know my loyalty; these concessions are long overdue. Certain, uh, circumstances may have caused me to be treated as an honored spouse rather than an active member, but it's time that changes."

Zosia lowered her head, obviously embarrassed, or maybe just intent on Irena.

"All right," Marysia conceded. "If we grant that request, is that all?"

"No." He grinned.

"What else?" Tomek asked, incredulous.

"I want some sort of arrangements made to assist the *Zwangsarbeiter*. I want information disseminated to them, and I want there to be some way for escapees to seek assistance and transport to safe havens—something like the Americans' Underground Railroad."

There were several sputters at the near impossibility of that request, but Marysia was undeterred. Into the dismayed grunting of the various Council members she spoke. "I've been considering something along those lines for some time and have been in communication with the other Councils about it. You raised enough money in America that I think we can arrange a budget for you, if you are willing to take responsibility for organizing this so-called Underground Railroad."

"I'll do that," Peter agreed, pleased by Marysia's support.

"Indeed," Marysia added, glancing at the Council, "I've just learned that an anonymous American donor has promised us a substantial sum, but only if we get Peter's approval for how it is used." She looked back at Peter. "It seems you have a friend."

Peter thought of the guitar back in the room and nodded. Whatever gift she had sent though, there was nothing more valuable to him than her words, *I cried for days.*

"Now, is that all?" Marysia asked.

"No, I also want a promotion to colonel and a seat on the Council. Both permanent, and well advertised so that there is no reneging on your part."

"What!" Wanda screeched.

"You can't be serious!" Bogdan stormed.

"This is too much!" Wojciech protested.

Into the objections Peter inserted, "I'll accept the portfolios for dealing with the Americans, secure communications, and liaising with the English, among others. I can also work on negotiations, if you want, since I am already well-known to the Germans and they to me."

"You do presume!" Wanda complained.

"Who do you think you are?" Tomek asked.

The comments flew about Peter's head, some positive, some not. He noticed that the naysayers, though in the minority, were the loudest. He let them rant, remaining calm and quiet. Then, with her free hand, Zosia slid off her shoe and slammed it onto the table. The ensuing silence was deafening.

"He deserves it," she said simply. "He knows more about security than any of us, he has foreign experience beyond any of us, he certainly understands the English better than any of us could hope to"—this last she said with something bordering on dismay—"he knows the Germans and has lived among them, and he also handled the Americans marvelously—they know and trust him. And his loyalty is beyond reproach!"

"He hasn't been here long enough," Wanda objected.

"He doesn't know *us!*" Wojciech griped.

"He isn't fluent in our language yet," Tomek moaned.

"Fluency isn't necessary," Zosia responded as she played a game of tug-of-finger with Irena.

"He's not sponsored by a political party," Tadek noted rather pragmatically.

"He can join as an independent," Konrad suggested. "After all, we all know that's a farce."

"He doesn't meet the criteria," Wanda finally wailed.

Marysia nodded. "He meets all the formal criteria—what little there are. Besides, it might do us some good to get some new blood into this executive."

As the Council members continued their arguments, Peter felt that he had been excluded yet again. "Your arguments are irrelevant," he said undiplomatically into the fray. "You have no choice. You want what I have and I'm not giving it to you without a permanent seat."

"How would you trust us not to throw you off the Council as soon as we get what we want?" Tadek asked.

"I'll trust your word. You are people of honor, if not sensitivity."

"Very well," Tadek agreed, "you'll take our word. But if you get this seat, there will be too many from the same family—it's beginning to look like a royal family."

"Nonsense," Peter replied. "I am not related to any of you here. I am an outsider, as some of you have made abundantly clear on many an occasion. As for my marriage—my wife and I have divergent views on many issues and will not be in collusion or have a block vote."

"Besides," Marysia sighed, "it was worse when Adam was on the committee and nobody objected then."

"Have it your way." Tadek shrugged.

"Better yet," Zosia said, "give him my seat. I'm resigning."

"What!" the cry came from all sides.

"I've had enough. I'm cutting back on my workload so I can spend time with my family. If I resign now, there will be no charge of nepotism, and it is not unusual to award a vacant seat to a spouse so we can forgo the usual nonsense."

"That's usually for vacancies created by death," Tadek pointed out.

Zosia shrugged. "A vacancy is a vacancy."

"Zosiu," Peter whispered. He knew what her position meant to her. Was she acting the martyr to embarrass him into retracting his demands?

Zosia slipped her shoe back on and stood up. Gently she inserted a finger in Irena's mouth and detached her from the nipple. The baby seemed happy to suck her finger, obviously sated. Zosia handed the baby to Tadek, who, Peter noticed, took hold of her expertly. Then Zosia said, "Why don't you all discuss the merits of my suggestion while I have a private chat with my husband in the corridor?" She buttoned her blouse as she circled around the table, then looped her arm in Peter's and led him out the door.

70

ONCE THEY WERE OUT IN THE HALLWAY and the door was closed behind them, Zosia asked quietly, "Why did you do that to me? Why didn't you warn me?"

When have you ever warned me? Peter was tempted to say, but something in Zosia's tone sounded quite different, so instead he explained, "Given what you wrote in your message to me in London, I thought it better if you weren't involved, and this was the easiest way to do that. I just thought I'd show up and fill you in, but you weren't here last night."

"Makes sense." Zosia hardly seemed concerned and he suspected the question had been rhetorical.

"Now, what's this about you quitting?"

"I've read the letters you wrote," she said as if in reply.

"Oh."

"And your mother's diaries. I hope you don't mind."

"No, I had hoped you would. When did you ever find the time?" he asked, surprised by the sudden changes in priorities.

"I made time. I've made time to do the things you used to do for us." She smiled wanly. "It gave me a sense of their value."

He nodded but did not speak. She clearly had something more to say.

She bit her lip as if trying to decide something, then whispered, "And I've seen the tape of Joanna's murder."

"Oh?"

"Yes, I . . . You were very brave. I had no idea. I . . ." She was crying and he pulled her toward him. As she sobbed into his chest, he heard her mumble what sounded like an "I'm sorry."

He held her for a while, stroking her hair, hugging her to him, trying to steady her trembling frame. His questions about where and when and how were forgotten, and when she had calmed down a bit, he impetuously asked instead, "Do you want me to withdraw my demands? I mean, other than my coming back here?" As he said the words, he realized that he was making the same mistake he always made, making offers he did not really want to make; offerings that, if accepted, would cause him to resent her.

She shook her head. "No. I do think you deserve a seat. And I really do think it's time for me to retire, or at least take a sabbatical. I was going to discuss it with you before suggesting it to the Council."

"Oh, Zosiu! You love your work!"

"It has taken control of me, I need to get away from it. At least for a while."

"You're not just doing this for me?"

She shook her head. She seemed profoundly sad.

"What is it, Zosiu? This place has been running your life since birth, why quit now?"

She swallowed hard, turned away from him, and leaned back against him so that he could hold her, but could not see her expression. He stroked her beautiful hair and waited. After a moment she spoke, so low he could barely hear her. "I think Joanna didn't run away because I told her to watch out for you."

He stiffened. He did not trust himself to say anything so he remained silent.

"If they"—Zosia jerked her head toward the Council room—"had not been so worried about you and if I hadn't felt so loyal to my work, I don't think I would have said that."

"So you said *watch* rather than *watch out for?*" he asked as gently as he could manage.

"No. She would have never understood the idea of watching you, but she did understand that you might need help. I told her to take care of you, and especially, not to leave your side."

"It's not your fault that you were concerned about me. Or that she was." Nor did Zosia's confession relieve his guilt for not having told Joanna to run away. She would have listened to him, no matter what her mother had said.

"No, but I used her concern for you to assuage their concerns about you. So that you could go into town unescorted, I said Joanna would let us know if you did anything suspicious, and then I had a little chat with her about how important it was for her to stay with you at all times and . . ."

"And?"

"And to tell me everything you did."

"Everything we did," he repeated numbly.

"Yeah. I made it sound like I didn't want to miss out on the fun," Zosia moaned.

"Why did you do that? Didn't you trust me?"

"Yes! But I was being torn this way and that. My worries about your well-being on the one hand, their concerns on the other . . ."

"Their paranoia doesn't make sense, not after all the time I spent alone in America."

"You were watched anytime you weren't with one of us or someone we had vetted. The phone in the hotel was tapped, too. The one time you noticed someone, that was a bodyguard I had asked for. You never spotted the surveillance."

"Charming," he muttered. "Too bad they didn't bother to notice that photographer who got my picture with Joanna."

"Clearly their efforts were misdirected," Zosia agreed bitterly. "But you were with us then, so they probably weren't watching."

"God, I feel like a fool."

"It's not your fault, dear. They have extremely subtle techniques."

"How could I not have noticed?"

"They controlled your schedule and had direct access to your luggage and hotel room. I guess, most of the time you were wearing a device, and since they weren't actually trying to protect you, they could keep their distance. Your complete trust in them, in us, and lack of suspicion certainly helped."

Peter felt so disgusted he had an urge to push Zosia away from him. She was right, he had never inspected his clothing or his luggage or his room. He had not listened for any telltale signs of tapping on the telephone. He had trusted them. "They're sick," he finally said.

"No, darling, just worried. Security had a lot of difficulty with my father's suggestion; that's one reason he threw it out to the crowd the way he did. The only way he got permission to get you there was to accept these constraints."

"He didn't bother to mention any of this to me," Peter noted caustically.

"Of course not, he felt you would be offended."

"Well, he had that right. What about now? Am I shadowed in London, too?" he asked contemptuously.

"No. They've gotten over their concerns. The videotape said it all."

"This is why you want to leave?"

Zosia nodded. "I can't be a part of this sort of thing anymore. It's grown too big. It's . . ."

"It wasn't your fault."

"Nor was it yours. But does that make it any easier for you?"

"No."

"So, let me go. Let me deal with this in my own way. I really want a break."

"You won't regret this?"

She shook her head, but remained silent. He held her a moment, letting his cheek touch her hair as he thought about what she had said, all the things he had not known before. She felt warm and soft in his embrace, and he wanted to hold her forever, but there seemed to be a distance between them. He let his thoughts play through her words again, through the revelations of how he was watched in America, how Joanna was told to keep an eye on him, how Zosia always knew things after the fact, just at the right time.

"You've been using me all along, haven't you?" he said suddenly.

She was silent in his arms.

"You knew about your father's idea to send me to America, you knew from the first time he met me, didn't you?"

She shifted slightly but remained quiet.

They stood together in silence for a long time. He felt a sick twisting in his gut as his mind strayed back to that day they had first met. "I believe your story," she had said. "Not only that, but I think we can use it." *Think we can use it* repeated itself over and over in his mind. *Think we can use it* . . . From the very first day. The very first day.

Carefully he said, "It was *your* idea, wasn't it? From the day we met, you had it all mapped out, didn't you?"

Zosia remained silent.

"I was wrong all along," he whispered into her ear. "I wasn't replacing Adam in your heart, that was impossible. That was just a distraction to explain your coldness, wasn't it? You were using me, weren't you? You've been using me all along, prepping me to perform for you! I've been nothing more than your propaganda tool, isn't that right?"

Her silence was unbearable.

"*Answer me,* damn it!"

"Oh, Peter. It's not what you think. I'm not that unfeeling—"

"It wasn't love, was it? It was *never* love. It wasn't even compassion. Not even friendship! It was strategy," he stated coldly. "From the moment you walked into that tent, all friendly and alluring . . ." He swallowed. "I wasn't a human being in need, I was a piece of merchandise, up for sale, and you wanted to know if I was worth the price!"

She did not answer.

His mind moved forward to the night of the party, before their wedding, the night Zosia talked him into going to America to speak. As a wedding gift, she had suggested. As a *wedding gift*? He felt his stomach turning.

"You didn't love me, even when we married! Even marriage was part of the plan," he guessed. "You didn't love me when we made Irena together, I was just a physical substitute for Adam." He tightened his grip on her shoulders.

Still she maintained her maddening silence, as if she, herself, did not know the answer.

He took a deep, unsteady breath. "Have you *ever* loved me?" His heart was breaking with the weight of this sudden, horrible truth.

There was a terrible silence and he felt his world crumbling around him. All his efforts, all his senseless attempts to make their marriage work! All the inexplicable hurt, all the apologies, all the guilt at disappointing her. It had been worthless—she had never even given him a chance! There was nothing there, had always been nothing. Absolutely nothing. He closed his eyes tight as he realized what he had done to himself over the years. Could he really have been so blind?

Into the void Zosia whispered, "I love you now."

It was his turn to remain silent. Was there any reason at all to believe her? He did not want to believe her. He did not want ever again to be so susceptible to her lies, but still a stubborn part of him *did* want to believe. He did not know what to say, so he stood there holding her, until he realized that his fingers were clawing into her shoulders. He loosened his grip and asked, "And the rest of the time?"

"Believe what makes you happy. Believe whatever makes you happy." She pulled away from him, turned toward him, and threw her arms around him. "Just don't stop loving me now!" she moaned with a vulnerability he had never before detected in her voice.

Could he do that? Could he believe whatever would make him happy? His arms hung loosely around her as she embraced him so passionately. Somehow, he could not find the strength to hug her.

She recognized his rejection and pulled back to look up at him. "So, what goes around, comes around?" she asked sadly.

He shook his head. "No, it's not that." He felt horrendously confused. "Don't worry. I won't ever stop loving you. But . . ."

"But?" she asked worriedly.

"But it's not the answer."

"To which question?" she asked. He was staring down the hallway and she turned to look at what had caught his attention, but nothing was there.

The door to the Council chamber opened and Tomek motioned them back into the room. Zosia recovered Irena from Tadek just as she was beginning to fuss. Zosia returned to her seat, offering Irena the other breast, and waited to hear the Council's decision.

Marysia called for order. "We have come to our decision, Captain," she said quite formally. "If you can present us with everything you have promised, we will put your name forward for a seat on the Council with all the appropriate support." She glanced around at several of the gloomier faces. "It was not unanimous, but you have a majority. Until final approval comes through, you'll be awarded a temporary seat on my authority. As a member, you will have all the rights of a member including access to Communications. Your rights of entry and exit will have exactly the same restrictions as any other member of the Council. We'll award you the portfolios you asked for as well as several other committees that will be decided at a future date. As for the commission, that must go through channels. We'll apply for and recommend a promotion to major. Nothing more."

Peter paused as if considering the offer. Zosia mouthed encouragement at him, and finally he answered, "All right. I have your word?"

"You have our word," Marysia replied, then added, "If, and only if, the information you have offered us is all that you have claimed."

"Fair enough. I'll get it to you in a few hours."

"You don't have it with you?" Marysia asked.

"No. I . . ." He hesitated to elaborate.

"You thought we might forcibly take it from you?" Konrad asked, astonished.

Peter glanced at the four who had voted against him—it was easy to tell from their sour expressions: Tomek, Bogdan, Wojciech, and Wanda. The same crew as had voted for his death, except that, interestingly, Tadek was not among them. "Don't tell me," Peter responded to Konrad's indignation, "that it didn't at least occur to you."

The look of uncomfortable guilt on several of their faces was sufficient answer.

Marysia interrupted the uneasy silence and continued in a formal tone, "Now, on to Colonel Król's suggestion."

"Zosiu," Tadek took over from Marysia, appealing to his friend, "we've elected Peter to the Council independent of your offer of resignation. Nothing we've given him is contingent upon your leaving us. Please reconsider. My comment about royal families was uncalled for. Please stay."

Zosia shook her head. "No, I need a break."

"We need you," Hania added her voice to Tadek's appeal.

"No, no one is indispensable. I'll be around, but I just can't handle all the . . . I want some personal time. To see to my family." Zosia looked down and stroked her daughter's head. "To spend some time being a human"—her eyes strayed to Peter—"like someone dear to me has taught me. I'll sit through the rest of our business today, but I'd like my resignation to be effective immediately upon the close of this meeting."

"What about your other duties?" Marysia asked. She had not argued with Zosia, perhaps knowing better than anyone else the source of Zosia's decision.

"I'll still do assassinations—at my discretion, as per usual—and perhaps handle an advisory role for the new generation of computer experts we're training. Will that suffice?"

"Yes," Marysia answered without even bothering to consult the others. "Yes, that will be quite satisfactory." Marysia motioned to Peter to sit down. Peter started toward the stack of folding chairs, but Tadek preempted him, grabbing one and placing it between his chair and Zosia's. Peter thanked him for this simple gesture of welcome, and Marysia then continued, "Now, on to the other business at hand: we have a special request for an assassination. And soon."

"You mean a judicial execution?" Tadek asked.

"Not quite. That's why it's a special request forwarded to us from Warszawa. They received it late last night and passed it directly on to us. They're loath to handle it and they wondered if we might have any ideas."

"Who's it from?" Zosia asked as Irena kneaded and pulled and slurped noisily.

"Ryszard Przewalewski," Marysia answered. "As you know, he arranged for that Vogel fellow to be the government spokesman on everything to do with the repercussions of that video that was smuggled into the NAU—the one with . . ." She gestured helplessly toward Peter.

He greeted her questioning, sympathetic glance with one of wary confusion.

"You were aware of that, weren't you?" she asked. "That the film of you was played on American television?"

He shook his head slowly.

"Oh, I am sorry," she groaned, and rubbed her forehead, then somewhat nervously she began to shuffle some papers.

Tadek leaned over and explained the situation quickly and quietly into Peter's ear. He nodded as Tadek explained. Yes, it all made sense; yes, that must be why there had been that second surge of equipment; yes, that explained Ryszard's comment to him. A favor indeed! It had been an unadulterated exploitation of a terrible and tragic event; he ought to be offended that his suffering and Joanna's death had been prostituted so cynically. It was sacrilege, and that no one had told him about it indicated that they knew that was so.

He did not want to say any of these things though, and to keep silent, he imagined Joanna's smiling face. She was so brave! Such a strong spirit! Would she have been offended? He saw her laughing response. Of course not! Let the bastards pay for their crime! Let her death serve a purpose—better than having her life wasted for nothing at all. Yes, she would be laughing at her murderers; she would have her revenge.

That's the second habit of a lifetime you've managed to change, little one, he thought to her ghost. I've learned from you how not to immediately assume the worst of people's motives. And maybe somewhere therein *was* the answer. Trust in humanity. Or at least some of humanity.

When Tadek had finished his explanation, he ended with, "I'm sorry. You should have been consulted or at least told."

"It's all right," Peter whispered in response, and for once he meant it. He glanced up at Marysia and indicated that she should continue.

Marysia took a moment to recover the thread of her thoughts, then continued, "Ryszard, of course, advised Vogel and was very efficient at getting him to place the government in one embarrassing and difficult position after another. Naturally, after such a series of fiascoes and bad luck such as they have recently suffered, they felt the need to look tough. One of the results of that was the recent attempt at an invasion here. Another result is that Herr Vogel is certain to be investigated and removed. Almost certainly they'll find a reason to induce his suicide or to execute him.

"Now, we have no concern for this patsy's life or career in the normal sense, but Ryszard is afraid Vogel will point the finger at him during any investigation. They haven't got around to questioning him on where he got his inspiration from, and no one else is aware that Ryszard has been advising him, so if he can quickly be removed from the scene, before his own people get to him, then Ryszard stands a good chance of coming out in the clear."

"But if his death is anything other than accidental," Tadek interjected, "then we'll have violated the protocols and there will be massive retaliation."

"As well as a great deal of suspicion as to why we wanted to remove him," Marysia agreed. "If suspicion falls on us and if there is even the tiniest link between Vogel and Ryszard, it might be worse than doing nothing at all, both for us and for Ryszard."

"Has he done anything we can condemn him for?" Zosia asked.

"No. Nothing more than the usual. None of his actions have been directed against us. He's been based in Berlin for most of his career. It would look odd if we were to pick a quarrel with this man."

"Would any other group have a reason to assassinate him?" Konrad asked.

Marysia spread her hands. "Not that we know of. We could murder him and hint that it was someone else, but that would still lead to the death of hostages, though of course, not our own."

"What about his role as a spokesman? Defending the murder of one of our citizens?" Hania asked.

"Being a spokesman is not a capital offense!" Marysia replied, somewhat exasperated.

"How about contact through a prostitute?" Tomek asked. They all turned toward Peter for advice, but he seemed lost in thought.

"Peter?" Marysia prompted.

He looked up as if wrenching his thoughts back into the present. "Only on business trips, as far as I could tell. I think he had a regular mistress in Berlin, but if so, he didn't see her all that often."

"Street crime?" Konrad offered.

Peter shook his head. "He just didn't go out all that often. You'd have to wait a long time for a good opportunity."

"Can't we arrange an accident?" Wojciech asked.

"As you know, believable accidents, especially at that distance, are exceedingly difficult to arrange," Marysia answered. "It could be a last resort, but we were hoping for something less suspicious and quicker."

"Why not have him murdered by someone who has an even better motive than you do? You know, a simple criminal homicide. Would there be repercussions from that?" Peter asked.

"I don't think so," Marysia responded. "A criminal homicide in Berlin should not affect us. But what are you suggesting? A burglary gone bad?"

"Better." Peter smiled. "Let me kill him. I have a strong personal motive. Hatred and revenge are motives his superiors will understand. They won't even think of any other remote reasons."

"That's a good idea!" Konrad remarked.

"You'd like that, wouldn't you?" Wojciech commented sourly.

"They might associate you with us through Joanna," Hania observed.

Peter shook his head. "The story is I met Joanna's mother in America and her ties to this area are quite loose. Even if they do connect me with you, I can make it clear I'm acting from personal motives. They'll believe that, given all that's gone on in my life. You can disown any of my actions if necessary; they'll believe you since there is no obvious reason for you to bother with Vogel. After all, you guys should actually give him a medal for all that he's accidentally done for your cause."

"And what about you?" Konrad asked with concern.

"There's nothing they can do to me. They already have such a bit of nastiness lined up in my name that they can hardly improve on it for the murder of one idiot official. If they arrest me, I'm dead in any case. In fact, when I make it clear that I'm doing it all for personal reasons, I can add that in as well. I have nothing to lose and so I have a free hand. They'll understand that philosophy."

"It might work," Bogdan agreed.

"Oh, it will work," Peter assured them all. "I'm sure of that. I know the way they think. Ask Ryszard—he'll tell you it will work. They want to get rid of Vogel, but they're not sure how. Here comes his ex-slave and murders him for revenge.

I'll tell his wife why and she'll repeat it, and they'll believe it because it will be so damn convenient for them."

After a short discussion of the pros and cons, they agreed on the plan and turned to the details of how it could be carried out. Once that was decided, Marysia said, "We'll pass this on to Warszawa immediately. I'm sure they'll clear it and you'll be able to leave this afternoon."

"There is one request I wish to make," Peter added.

"What's that?"

"I'll carry out this murder on one condition."

"I thought you wanted to do it," Marysia asked, confused.

"No. I don't. I've only argued for its practicality, not for my desire. I want it made clear within our own organization that this is a professional execution done as a necessary part of our overall strategy."

"Confession might be easier," Zosia said behind her hand. "Why don't you just accept that you have religious scruples and get it over with?"

Besides Peter, only Tadek heard the remark, and he sputtered into his hand to hide his laughter.

"Is that your condition?" Marysia asked.

"No. It's just a statement of my moral position. My condition is that I be allowed to bring the youngest Vogel child back here as part of the same mission."

"Kidnap?" more than one voice called out in surprise.

"It's my child," Peter asserted quietly, "and I want to raise her here as part of our family."

"What do you mean by 'your child'?" Hania asked. "Do you mean that you feel responsible for her, or that you feel you have the right to a child since yours was murdered by them?"

Wanda shook her head as if answering for Peter.

"He means he is the biological father and that he is the only person in the world who has a genuine interest in that child's welfare," Zosia answered defensively. "I've heard the mother speak about her, and she has no concern for the child at all; we know the attitude of her husband is even more indifferent. You can talk to Ryszard's wife if you want confirmation of this. Magdalena is Peter's daughter, and he is her only true parent."

"He managed to leave that out of his original interrogation, didn't he?" Wanda commented bitterly.

"It wasn't relevant," Hania asserted.

"Wasn't it?"

Tadek leaned away from Peter to look at him with histrionic amazement. "You and Frau Vogel!" he giggled.

"Hilarious, isn't it," Peter agreed mordantly. He knew Tadek's coarse sense of humor and braced himself accordingly.

"Where are your standards, boy? What's next, sheep and cows? Or does that come before Nazi Party wives? Let's see, after sheep, we have . . ." Tadek continued to rib him, enumerating on his fingers a hierarchy of animals and objects that would be preferable to sleeping with a Nazi. As some of the other men joined in the teasing, Tadek came close to calling up memories of Peter's other unwanted sexual liaison, but Zosia, behind Peter's back, did a desperate slashing motion across her throat to shut him up just in time.

"Are German shepherds on the list?" Tadek asked as though genuinely perplexed. "Have you ever done anything with a German shepherd?"

Peter turned his attention to cleaning a bit of dirt out from under his thumbnail as he waited out the ritual humiliation that he had known would follow his revelation.

Wanda stood suddenly. Everyone looked at her in surprise. "*Kommandanten* and Nazi *Hausfrauen!* Is there anything you won't do?" she exclaimed bitterly. "Two sons! My two boys lie cold in their graves and a lying, Kraut-fucking, atheist coward lives among us. It's not right!"

There was a moment of leaden silence as Peter did a final swipe of his nail, then he slowly rose to his feet and, resting his hands on the table, leaned forward threateningly. "And who are you," he asked coldly, looking at Wanda, but addressing a multitude of people, present and absent, "to imply my life is something to be traded for *anyone else?*"

Wanda ignored his question. "You dare to lecture us the day you arrive, piously telling us how not to become what we hate; now we see, now we know what you meant!"

"You call me an atheist, but at least I don't try and play God with other people's lives. You have no right to judge me or my actions!" Peter spat in reply.

"You're a collaborator! Fucking a Nazi Party wife and now we award you a Council seat. I refuse to be on a Council that awards you membership. It's him or me!" Wanda declared.

There was an interminable silence, then Marysia calmly stated, "Wanda, ultimatums are unacceptable. If you wish to file an appeal of our decision, there are appropriate mechanisms, but ultimatums will not be accepted."

"We should have shot him when we had the chance!" Wanda yelled angrily. "It's him or me!"

"Wanda!" Marysia warned. "We do not accept ultimatums!"

"Then I resign!" Wanda screamed. Before anyone could answer, she had left the room.

The remaining Council members turned toward Peter, but all he could see was Joanna's trusting face. Trust, he thought. Open himself up, open those dark parts of his mind that they had created and he had so carefully shielded. Well, no one had said it would be easy. He breathed heavily trying to calm the pounding of his heart. He surveyed the faces staring at him. At one time he would have said they were laughing at him, but now he recognized other things: curiosity at what his reaction would be, sympathy, love . . . He settled back into his seat without saying anything. Zosia's fingers reached for his and her thumb gently caressed the burn scars on the back of his hand.

"Pff! She's finally lost it completely," Tadek commented, interrupting the uncomfortable silence. "It was a long time coming. Now," he continued in a businesslike tone, "we have a question before us. Does he get custody of his kid?"

Wanda's spell was broken. There was a quick discussion of the merits, the risks of setting a precedent, the special circumstances in this case. Finally, it was agreed that as long as it did not jeopardize the mission or destabilize the quid pro quo, they had no objection to welcoming the babe into their midst.

"It won't jeopardize the mission," Peter said, "in fact, it will make it look all the more plausible. A daughter lost, a daughter gained. As for the quid pro quo, I believe it's about time you start a tit for tat on the kidnaps. Maybe if they knew their precious babies were being raised in the Underground, they might hesitate to bomb or shoot at you. But in any case, I'll make it clear that I'm doing it on my own initiative and plan to go into hiding in England or America or somewhere else. The kidnapping won't reflect on you at all."

"Agreed," Marysia concluded. "As soon as we get clearance, we'll send you out. Will you need help?"

"I'd like to go along," Zosia volunteered. "And I request Stefi's help for Irena if I go."

"Fine," Marysia agreed. "Just clear it with Stefi."

Peter noticed he had not been consulted but decided not to comment.

71

"**O**KAY, ARE YOU GOING TO TELL ME what this is about?" Peter asked Zosia as they settled into the room Ryszard had provided.

"What are you talking about?"

"Why did you volunteer to help and why are we here for two nights?"

"We won't do Karl until tomorrow," Zosia answered as she rolled onto the bed next to Irena and stretched luxuriously.

He continued unpacking. "So what's up with tonight?"

"Business." She rolled into a sitting position and, picking up Irena, opened her blouse and offered dinner. Irena latched on enthusiastically. "Seemed like a good time to do it."

He was bent over the suitcase and could not see her face, but something in her voice gave him pause. He straightened and turned to look at her. Taking a wild guess, he said, "I know that's not true. What are you planning?"

Zosia sighed, stroking Irena's head distractedly. "Well, I didn't want to get you involved, but it would be nice to have your help."

"With what?"

Zosia explained about the men involved in his torture and Joanna's murder.

"You want to finish the job tonight? Do you have enough information?"

"Yes, I've gathered all sorts of details about the last man—the interrogator—thanks to Ryszard. He had him followed for a while, on some pretext. There's his dossier." She pointed toward a file in her luggage. "His name is Berger."

Peter picked up the file and opened it. The snotty voice of his tormentor played through his mind as he looked at the pathetic details. "Berger? That's a nice, simple name."

"It was changed in the thirties from something less acceptable," Zosia explained.

"You want to kill him?"

"Yes! Don't you? It's necessary to send a message, don't you think?"

"Maybe. I don't really care, I just want to kill him," he answered honestly. He felt that he should have gone through some crisis of conscience, examined the morality of revenge, or "preventative maintenance," as Zosia termed it, but he felt no inclination to do so. "I would have liked to have helped you with the others. Why didn't you at least tell me about them?"

Zosia repositioned Irena, mopped up some milk that had dribbled. "I thought you would call me a murderer."

"I'm sorry about that. I was wrong, I've already said that."

She shrugged. "I know what you said, but it still stuck with me. I've always valued your opinion and your sense of balance, and when you told me I was unbalanced..."

"You know I was just hurt and angry."

"I know. The problem is, it is a very fine line that I draw—the one between my being a murderer and my being a courageous freedom fighter. From my position, it's hard to know if I've misdrawn the line. In America, when I was able to get some untainted news of the world, and I would hear about some car bomb or assassination in some other part of the world, it always sounded like murder to me. I knew that whoever committed such crimes felt justified, but the perpetrators were labeled terrorists, and rightly so."

"Those other places are different from here. *Here* the terrorists are in power; just because they have given themselves the trappings of government doesn't make their murders any more acceptable. And you've never used random violence, not the way the Reich does, not the way some of those crazy organizations do. Your actions are as well directed as any responsible action can be. We *are* the side of right and justice, and if we weren't so weak, we wouldn't be driven to use such means! But inaction is even worse—it means we've handed everything over to them, and we've already seen what they do against powerless people. What we do is different, Zosiu. It really is and I should have never said what I did."

"We?"

"Yes," Peter sighed. "You know about the boy I had to knife, and all those soldiers I shot at and, no doubt, killed."

"Self-defense. Battle action. Perfectly legit."

"Then what about shooting an unconscious man in the head?"

Zosia's head snapped up from looking at Irena. "You what?"

He explained about the encounter in the alley and the fear that led him to "eliminate" a potential threat.

"What you did was right," she assured him.

"I know." He nodded. "More to the point, I didn't care whether it was right or not; it was convenient and that was sufficient. I've finally had enough, Zosiu. They finally got what they wanted: they've destroyed who I was completely and left an automaton in his place. Problem is, I'm the wrong sort of robot. Miswired, I'd guess they'd say."

Zosia smiled indulgently at him, shaking her head slowly. "We all feel like that the first time or so. You were the most gentle person I had ever met, and you still are. It's one of my reasons for loving you. Don't worry, you're far too human to ever be cut loose from your conscience."

Peter was unconvinced but did not say anything. It was not that he thought she was lying; it was simply that her words no longer carried such an overwhelming weight with him. Her revelations about what she had said to Joanna and the way she had let him carry the burden of guilt completely alone and unconsoled—it had hurt. At the time, he had been too overwhelmed by all that was occurring to understand exactly what her words had meant, but after having thought about it, he realized that this last straw, this minor cowardice on her part, had finally freed him. He still loved her, but he was at last free to love her not as the woman who had saved his life, not as the imposing political and military figure, not as the social and familial success story so in opposition to his own miserable failures, but as an equal. He was no longer in awe of her. He was free.

They walked together through the *Tierpark,* a loving couple intent on each other. Berger hardly took note of them as he walked his usual path home from the officers' club meeting. He was weighing up his earlier refusal to accompany his friends to a bar. The problem was, they always went out to pick up women, and if he didn't do likewise, he was left standing alone among strangers as each of his friends disappeared into the night. It had been months since he had left Neu Sandez, but he still felt nervous around strangers and was loath to walk off with a woman he did not know. Still, if he kept refusing his friends' invitations, he might well be thought a homosexual and that could be devastating! Perhaps he should take the chance to go out, maybe it was time to put his worries behind him.

His path led him across a narrow wooden bridge romantically arching over a small fishpond. He continued along despite the couple who had stopped to kiss right in front of him, almost blocking his way. Oddly, as he brushed past them, they swung into step with him, one on each side. Fear seized him as he felt something cold and hard pressed snugly against his ribs.

"Just a robbery," the woman intoned softly. "If you keep quiet and do as you're told, you'll be all right."

He looked at her and was stunned by her appearance. She was beautiful! Blond hair, fair skin, a true Aryan. Such women did not commit crimes! He was so taken by the woman that he barely noticed the silent, dark-haired man who strode along his other side, pressing the gun into his ribs.

"You can take my wallet," he offered worriedly. "It's right here." He started to reach for his breast pocket, but the woman intercepted his hand.

She clasped his hand warmly to her breast as if confiding to a friend. "No, no, you must come with us. Nobody carries all his money in his wallet. We are not fools." She gazed lovingly at her two companions as a patrolman passed them.

Berger was led to the edge of the zoo. The threesome stopped in front of a non-descript door cut into the surrounding wall, and Berger's abductors glanced casually around. Satisfied that they were unobserved, the man reached behind himself to turn the knob and together they slipped into the darkened room. The pair led him knowingly down a pitch-black corridor, then through another door. They shut the door behind them, and suddenly fluorescent lights blazed overhead.

Berger blinked against the brash lights, then took in his surroundings. It was a windowless storage room: shelves laden with packaged supplies, bales of hay or something stacked untidily against a far wall. In the small open area in front of them, against the outer wall, sat a single chair. He was escorted to the chair and pushed down into it. Before he realized what was going on, his wrists were locked behind his back and to the crosspiece of the chair. He looked in panic at the woman; she smiled sweetly in return. Finally he turned his eyes to the man who stood patiently in front of him. It took only a moment to get past the different hair color, then his mind went blank with fear.

The man opened a knife in front of his face. "I have to send a message to your comrades," his erstwhile prisoner explained, "and I'm afraid you're going to carry that message for me."

Berger collected himself. Ignoring the man, he turned to the woman. "Beautiful lady, whatever this man has told you, it's untrue! Don't listen to him! Help me, please. He's a madman, please, listen to me. Go get help."

The woman's smile gently faded from her face; otherwise she did not reply.

"You and I, sweet, noble Aryan lady, we're alike," he continued to plead, "we're superior to this scum. Please don't abandon me. You must help me. Whatever he's said to convince you to do this, it's untrue. He's an *Untermensch*, don't listen to him! He's a criminal—look at his arm, he's been condemned by a court! Please believe me, *don't listen to him!*"

"Shut up!" the man grated, slamming the knife down and into his captive's leg. Berger screamed, his head snapping down to look at the knife embedded in his flesh. He watched in horror as blood seeped into his trousers, looked up in shock as the man removed the blade and wiped it clean.

"Now that I have your attention," the man continued, "perhaps I could get you to look at the woman you've been imploring. Doesn't she remind you of someone? Hmm?"

Following the suggestion, Berger turned his attention back to the woman. There was a resemblance to someone. Someone in his dreams? He stared a moment longer, then began to quake with fear. The child! Oh, God, the child! Fighting against the pain in his leg, struggling to overcome his fear, he pleaded, "Don't. Please don't! I had to do it, I was following orders. It wasn't me. It was the others. I'm innocent. Don't! Please!"

He was so intent on the woman's impassive face that he barely noticed how the man moved in toward him. "I was just following orders," he repeated lamely.

"There are some orders which must not be obeyed," the woman reminded him softly as he felt the man's hands close in on his throat.

They left the body in a state similar to the others and walked away in silence. Zosia seemed relieved, a load removed from her shoulders; she had done what she could to avenge her daughter, and now it was time to move on. Peter accurately perceived her mood and wondered at it. A lifetime of being hunted, a lifetime of killing—it was no wonder she could settle a score and put the past behind her; if she had done anything other than that in her life, she would have been paralyzed by grief or fear.

As for himself, he felt no such release. The murder of the interrogator provided nothing more than another body to add to the count. He mentally listed his victims: self-defense, battle, fear of betrayal, and now, revenge. Each killing less defensible than the previous; yet, he could not claim that he really cared. They had achieved their original intent: he was now, at last, less than human.

===== **72** =====

"**D**ON'T TELL ZOSIA UNTIL AFTERWARDS," Ryszard said quietly, eyeing his sister as she sat nursing Irena on the other side of the room.

"Why not?" Peter asked.

"I don't trust her temper."

Peter nodded. He had a higher estimation of Zosia's professionalism than did her brother, but there was no need to betray Ryszard's confidence. Peter would wait until afterward to tell her. Both her and Olek.

"How did the rest of it go?" Ryszard asked.

Peter looked at him, mildly surprised. "You mean me with the Council?"

"Yes, did you get a seat?"

"Yes. I got exactly what I wanted. And without a patron."

Ryszard raised an eyebrow as if preparing to say something, but then he seemed to change his mind. His eyes returned to the little family tableau of Zosia handing Irena to Stefi as Zosia prepared to go. "Yes, without a patron," Ryszard echoed.

Together Peter and Zosia made their way on foot the mile or so to the Vogels' house. Even though they carried papers appropriate to being out late at night, they avoided the patrols, dodging into the darkness like cat burglars to avoid detection. The house was as it had always been, and it was easy to enter quietly— he knew all the tricks to the old place. They entered through the back and stood silently in the kitchen, listening to see if they had been detected. Zosia looked around, entranced, as she was finally able to put Peter's stories into a context. She tugged at his sleeve. "Show me the cellar," she whispered.

He agreed to the diversion and gave her a brief tour, even indicating where Karl had bound him to the overhead pipes. "I'll spare showing you the shovel in the garden shed," he joked quietly as Zosia looked up at the pipes, then down at the floor where the sweat and blood must have pooled. It all looked so ordinary! They returned to the ground floor, and he silently pointed out the piano, the sitting room furniture, Karl's walking stick in its stand. Nothing had changed.

Zosia shook her head; somehow, the physical reality of the cozy suburban house made the horror of his experiences seem less, rather than more, believable. It all looked so normal! Sheepishly, she confessed this thought to him, whispering it into his ear.

"I know," he whispered in reply, "that's what made it all so difficult."

As she took it all in, he left to disconnect the phone and unlock the doors. She walked along the hallway, ran her fingers over the wallpaper, the pretty floral print that could hide a multitude of sins. She turned and saw a small table; on the top was a cigarette box and a lighter, on the other shelves were sparkling-clean glass figurines. *Even in a room of pretty floral wallpaper and delicate glass figurines . . .*

They climbed the stairs silently to the first floor and found the child's room. They checked in on Magdalena, saw her sleeping soundly in a crib on her own. Zosia began sorting through the items in the room, packing anything that looked useful or might be special to the child. Peter left her to go check the rest of the house and looked to see if anyone was prowling around in a fit of sleeplessness. The children were sound asleep in their beds; the door to the attic was ajar. He peered in and saw a human form huddled under rags in a corner. He blinked into the darkness for a long moment, then resolutely turned his back on his unknown comrade and returned to Zosia.

She finished gathering the child's possessions, set the bag down in the child's room, and together they went out into the hall and over to the master bedroom door.

"I'll cover you," she whispered. "Good luck."

He kissed her and pressed on the door handle. It gave way and he slipped into the room. Both Karl and Elspeth were asleep. Peter watched them in silence for a moment, then he quietly cleared his throat.

"Who's there?" Elspeth's nervous voice asked into the darkness.

"Hello, Elspeth," Peter replied softly.

"Who is that?" She sounded as if she recognized his voice but would not believe it.

"Have you forgotten me so soon?"

"Peter?" There was complexity in the tone: fear, reproach, passion.

"Who else?"

"What are you doing here?" She sounded terrified but still she whispered; she was more afraid of waking Karl than of what Peter might do.

He could see she was sitting bolt upright in bed. He went and sat on the edge of Karl's side of the bed, his back against the headboard, his left side toward Elspeth with Karl in between them. He did not bother to point his gun at her or at Karl, just let it rest casually in his right hand on his lap. Karl snored away, clearly at ease with the world and his conscience. Peter casually brought his legs up onto the bed and crossed one over the other. He leaned his head back against the headboard as if resting after a long day's work. Even in the dim light he could tell the ceiling was still smoke-stained, still not scrubbed clean. The eagle, its talons wrapped around the swastika, still hovered over the bed.

"What do you want? Why are you addressing me familiarly? I haven't given you permission! Why are you doing that? What are you doing here?" Elspeth demanded in rapid succession.

"Oh, I just came to say hello to my old mistress." With his left hand Peter reached over Karl's prone form toward Elspeth. She tensed as if expecting him to hit her, but she did not pull away. He pushed a loose strand of her hair back into her night braid. It still felt like steel wool.

"Did you think I would hit you the way you hit me?" he asked.

"I don't know what to think. The way you abandoned me! After all I did for you!"

"Abandoned," he laughed. "Abandoned. Heh. Now there's a discussion point! But I'm afraid I don't have time to chat. I'm here to do you a favor."

"What's that?"

"Your husband has made a mess of things at work, hasn't he?"

"I don't know," she replied cautiously.

"Yes, you do. You're aware that he's in trouble, but you're probably not aware quite how deeply. He's a dead man. If they don't leave a pistol on his desk soon, they'll just arrest him for something. In any case, you'll be a disgraced widow. Impoverished."

"How do you know all this?"

"Abandoned," Peter repeated, and laughed again. "God, what a world you must live in! Anyway, I'm going to save you from all that."

"Save me?"

"Yes. I'm going to kill him for you. He'll be murdered by a disgruntled ex-slave; he'll be a martyr and you'll get to keep his pensions and honors and probably even the house and slave."

Elspeth studied him as if considering the implications. As she determined that he was serious, her expression altered and she weighed the consequences of his planned actions. Then she came to a decision. It was clear from her mien that she had decided to accept his offer and provide whatever assistance was necessary, but she was careful; first she asked, "Why would you do this for me?"

"Because of my undying love for you," he lied convincingly, then after a brief pause, he added, "And . . ."

She had expected that. "And what else?"

"My daughter. I'm taking her with me."

Again she hesitated. He could see her weighing his words and her own reaction: as a matter of form, she should argue for Magdalena—it would appear unmotherly not to do so, and she could gain some extra influence over him if he felt he were tearing her daughter away from her. Perhaps she should indulge in a bit of crying? But then again, there really was no time to fool around. He was right, Karl was already as good as dead, and she had to look to her future and her other children's futures. If she was to be a widow, a baby could be a burden, an impediment to a good marriage. And the sympathy factor after a kidnap could be enormous! He counted down mentally and reached one just as she compromised, "Will you give her a good home?"

"She'll be loved."

Elspeth nodded. "You always were kind to the children." She then added, almost as an admission, "No matter what we did to you."

He did not reply to that.

"Where will you take her?"

"Away from here. Overseas."

"All right, but promise me you'll tell her about me."

"I will," he replied without hesitation. He felt no compulsion at all to examine whether he was telling the truth. He would do what was best for Magdalena, independent of promises made to Elspeth.

"Do you dream of me?"

"Yes," he answered truthfully, choosing not to elaborate.

"Do you remember that night in Dresden?"

"Yes. I remember it well."

"I watched you sleep that night. I woke up in the middle of the night and sat up and just watched you sleep."

He smiled slightly. "I didn't know that." He wondered what else he was supposed to do with the information. Was it to show her kindness in contradistinction to the times she had kicked him awake when he so desperately needed to sleep?

"And do you remember that nice meal we had?"

"Yes, steak." He didn't add that he also remembered the time she would not give him the old bread that was to be thrown to the ducks. Even if she remembered, she would not understand his point.

"And the time we went to buy you some tea and a teacup?"

"Yes, the day you hit me in the plaza, in front of all those people."

"Did I? Oh, yes, that's right, you were so rude! I'm surprised you remember that," Elspeth pouted.

Peter realized he was straying from his plan and he amended his words accordingly. "Only because I felt so awful that I had offended you, my beautiful, merciful lady."

"So you still love me?"

"Of course, until the end of time. But I can't stay, I have to do this, then I must go."

"What am I going to say to the authorities?" she suddenly fretted. "I'll have to turn you in for my husband's murder. They'll hunt you down!"

"They're hunting me anyway. Their plans for me are sufficiently gruesome that there's nothing I can do that will make it worse."

"But you might betray me!"

"No, I won't. They wouldn't even ask about you. They'll be relieved to have him out of their hair. I'm doing them a favor as well."

"How do you know all this?"

"Frau Schindler." He winked at her. "But don't tell anyone."

"But . . . but how can I explain your taking Magdalena? I can't tell them she's your daughter!"

"No, but you can tell them that I said, 'An eye for an eye, a daughter for a daughter.' They'll understand."

"What do you mean?" she asked, unsatisfied with the quote.

"They'll understand."

"But I don't! What do you mean?"

He cocked his head to the side to study her. She was telling the truth—she didn't know. He considered a moment, then explained, "They murdered my daughter."

"What?"

"To punish me for speaking out, as I did in America, they took my five-year-old adopted daughter and they strangled her in front of me."

"No!" Elspeth hissed her denial.

"Yes," he asserted quietly.

"They wouldn't do that! Not to a child!"

"Oh, grow up!" he snapped. "Listen to your mother! Listen to your conscience! You've tied yourself in with a bunch of murderous thugs. What's one five-year-old to them?"

"I don't believe it."

"Ask him"—he nodded toward Karl—"he knows."

"What? How would he know?"

"Just ask. It doesn't matter what he hears since I'm going to kill him anyway."

Elspeth stared at Karl for a moment, utterly terrified at the thought of him waking up.

Peter decided to assist her and poked the gun into Karl's ribs. "Hey, you, wake up, sleepy."

"Hunh?" Karl tried to turn over. Elspeth waved her hands frantically for Peter to stop.

Peter jabbed Karl again. That didn't work, so he smacked him across the face. "I said, wake up, you fat moron!"

Karl jumped up onto his elbows. "What? What?" He turned to see Peter staring at him and his mouth dropped open. Despite his confusion, he had obviously noticed the gun.

"So you still recognize me? Even with brown hair? Even without my uniform?"

"You again! What are you doing here? Elspeth?" he snarled, looking to his wife for an explanation.

"Did you kill his daughter?" Elspeth asked immediately.

"Me? His daughter? No. No, I had nothing to do with it." Karl turned back toward Peter. "Honest, it wasn't my doing. I had nothing to do with that."

"So you knew about it," Elspeth concluded.

"Well, yes, but I didn't do it."

"I know," Peter assured him quietly.

"How did you know about it?" Elspeth insisted.

"There was a videotape," Karl explained, wondering why Peter was being more understanding than his wife. His situation was beginning to sink in.

"They taped the murder of a child?" Elspeth asked, aghast.

"No, no, no. Just his reaction," Karl tried to reassure her.

Somehow though she seemed even more appalled. "And you watched it?"

"Yeah, it was good for a la—" Karl realized his mistake. He looked at the gun Peter held and pleaded, "I didn't do it! It wasn't me!"

"I know," Peter repeated with such calm disinterest that it was not reassuring.

Karl stared trembling and sweating at the gun Peter held so indifferently.

Elspeth's face was like a stone. She looked at her husband as if judging all their years together: the uncontrolled rages, the way he had pummeled his sons, the brutal punishments he had meted out to the servants, the unending tension he had caused. "For laughs" he had watched a videotape of a child being murdered, he had reveled in the torture and deaths of prisoners in his charge, he had chosen to follow in his father's footsteps, knowing exactly what it meant.

"I'll tell them what you said," she told Peter.

Peter smiled enigmatically. He had never intended to get Elspeth's permission, and her consent was irrelevant to his intentions, but still it amused him.

Karl looked from one to the other in confused terror and growing anger.

Were they conspiring against him? His automatic mode of dealing with either of them was to issue commands, and without that option he was left helpless. Rage began to well up inside him, but then his eyes were drawn again to that gun sitting there. He was the master here! He was an *Übermensch!* The one was his wife, the other his chattel, but still he could not take his eyes off that gun. The natural order was disturbed, but he could not find the courage to demand the obedience and respect that was his due.

While Karl stared entranced at the gun, Peter reached into his jacket and removed his stiletto. He held it discreetly out of sight and whispered into Karl's ear, "By the way, do you remember Julia Hoffmeier? Her son sends his greetings."

Karl snapped his head away from the gun to look in horror at Peter. Karl was whiter than his sheets. "How, how . . . ?"

"Don't worry, old boy, I won't give your secret away." Peter casually swung his left arm around as if in a friendly gesture to give Karl a hug. The stiletto disappeared into Karl's fleshy neck even as he began to wonder at Peter's chumminess. He burbled incoherently and collapsed forward.

"Oh, dear," Elspeth muttered, looking at her dead husband.

Peter's hand was still on the knife and it was still deep in Karl's brain. He spent a moment in quiet admiration of the neat job he had done, then twisted the knife and sliced downward to make the opening bigger, more jagged, and less expert. Although it did not really matter given Elspeth's future testimony, there was no point in letting them see he was professionally trained. A coroner who really cared might work it out anyway, but he doubted the coroner would care or would be allowed to care.

He removed the knife, wiped the blade, and put it back into its scabbard inside his jacket. He grabbed a bit of Karl's hair and pulled him back until he was lying flat again. He looked sort of peaceful there albeit a bit surprised. Peter closed Karl's eyes and held them in place; then to be sure, he felt for a pulse at the neck. There was none, Karl was dead. It was that bloody simple. All those years and here the bastard was, a tiny stain of blood on his silk pajamas, dead. Peter missed the opportunity to have pummeled him a bit, to have inflicted just a taste of his own medicine, but Peter had promised himself he would do it professionally and as dispassionately as possible, and he congratulated himself on his success.

Other than that, though, he felt nothing: no thrill, no pleasure. The skies did not open up for him, his soul was not suddenly calmed. There was no great release from the burden of his past. As he looked at the body, Katerina's words of long ago returned to him: *Unjustly condemned, you are innocent of any blood in a time when innocence is in itself guilt. You will know no peace until you accept the guilt of war. You cannot stand idly by.* She was right, he thought, he could not stand idly by any longer, but she was also wrong, for even accepting the guilt of killing had provided him no solace. There was no peace in his land, and until there was, there was no peace to be had.

"Oh, dear," Elspeth repeated. "What should I do?"

"Wait about an hour, then call the police. Tell them it happened some indeterminate time ago, perhaps half an hour, and that you were too stunned and afraid to move. Say that I threatened that I would kill you if you moved."

"You'd never do that!" Elspeth admonished.

"You can say I said it," he assured her as he stood up. He had already disconnected the phone to slow Elspeth down a bit, but he saw no reason to tell her that. "Make it simple: you woke up, saw me, wanted to scream, but I threatened you. I killed your husband, told you 'an eye for an eye, a daughter for a daughter,' and then after telling you not to move, I left. Got that?"

She nodded.

"Repeat it to me. Everything that happened."

She did and, at his orders, repeated it several times and answered his questions.

From his point of view, it really did not matter what she said as long as it was clear he was driven by personal motives, but for the children, it was necessary that she not betray her collusion. Once he was satisfied that she knew what to do, he went over to her side of the bed and sat down by her. "Don't worry," he assured her, stroking back her loose hairs, "you'll do fine." He held her chin gently cupped in his hands and, turning her face upward, kissed her full on the lips.

As he walked toward the door, she stared after him in bewilderment.

At the door he stopped to say, "Remember, Elspeth, I'm already wanted. There's absolutely nothing more they can do to me so don't try to protect me, it will only get you arrested."

She shook her head. "I won't. I'll do exactly as you said."

"Exactly?"

She nodded.

He blew her a kiss and turned to leave.

"Peter?" Her voice quaked with emotion.

He turned back to look at her and smiled at the image—not a proper, subservient smile but rather a self-confident, almost happy grin. It was the smile of a man who, though perhaps not at peace, at least knew he was free. "*Gnädige Frau?*" he asked with good-humored sarcasm.

Elspeth hesitated, her expression intense, as a confession seemed poised on her lips. Then she apparently changed her mind and relaxed. As if only to fill the silence, she said, "Your behavior is totally inappropriate."

Peter laughed quietly. "Ah, yes, *gnä' Frau,* but you wouldn't have it any other way." And with that he went to collect his wife and his daughter.

Historical Notes

All the characters are fictional, but some are loosely based on historical or current (albeit generally anonymous) persons. The experiences of Katerina's sister were those of a real woman. Erich von dem Bach-Zelewski (Frau von dem Bach's unmentioned relative) did exist. He was responsible for the suppression of the Warsaw uprising, using such techniques as tying Warsaw civilians to German tanks. The retaliation visited upon Warsaw and the description of the resulting destruction is accurate.

The AK (Home Army) did exist and did establish an extensive Underground network including a university system and infiltration into German society. There was freed mountain territory during World War II. The British Underground did have extensive resistance plans ready for any occupation. The plans for the occupation of Poland and the actions of the occupiers as read by Peter are historical. In particular, there were plans for mass sterilizations. The plans laid out for Britain are also as documented. The occupation depicted is based upon these plans; the rather schizophrenic treatment of the English by the Germans is based upon the various writings of different Nazi officials and upon the existence of both a French Resistance and a collaborative French government.

Holocaust incidents (gas chambers, lime-laden railway cars, etc.) are genuine. There was a Warsaw ghetto created by the Nazi occupation, there was a Judenrat, there was a ghetto uprising, and the people of the ghetto were deported to their deaths. The emissary mentioned by Katerina did exist and did give early, detailed reports to the Allies and the American government. There was a council to aid the Jews sponsored by the Polish government in exile (the only such organization in occupied Europe). The execution for supplying a loaf of bread did occur.

Medical experiments were conducted on unwilling human subjects. Human hair was used as stuffing for furniture. Retaliation incidents mentioned for the World War II period are historical, in particular, the twenty thousand hostages of Bydgoszcz and the list that Peter read of persons murdered and villages destroyed. The incident with the pregnant woman recorded in Catherine's diary is taken from court testimony. The taking of hostages, the publication of their names, and their subsequent murder as retaliation for Underground action was standard. Retaliatory destruction of entire villages and their inhabitants was widespread. Manhunts (or "roundups") as described by Katerina occurred regularly. Killing children by slamming their heads against walls is a documented technique that was used to save bullets.

Nazi officials were required to document their bloodlines. Hitler did film the torture and execution of his own officers. *Nacht und Nebel* was a terror technique used mostly in the west. The SS Lebensborn did exist and did abduct children for adoption by German families. The quote from Himmler is historical. Ersatz pregnancies and deals between housewives and their servants are conjecture only.

Millions of slave laborers (of every nationality) were used in the Reich for industry, farms, and homes. Tattooing was used to identify prisoners in some (but not all) camps. (This included children and babies taken prisoner after the Warsaw uprising, but generally not the children and babies sent to immediate extermination.) Forced laborers were required to wear at all times identifying armbands with their number. Triangular badges of various colors were used to identify the various categories of prisoners, green being used for criminals.

Though select groups were ruthlessly persecuted, the variety and background of all victims were extremely diverse and no one was genuinely safe. Concentration camp inmates included an Italian princess, upstanding German religious people, and various Nazis who had somehow offended the regime. Even some American prisoners of war were worked to death.

The mass expulsion of the Polish population from conquered western Poland is historical. The de-Polonization of the territories that were incorporated into the Soviet Union did occur. Ludwik's Communist father's fleeing the Soviets into Nazi territory mirrors the experiences of a genuine Polish Communist leader. The Siberian experiences of the guide's father are those of a real man, though his escape and aftermath has been altered. There was a Nazi-Soviet pact that partitioned Poland, and the two great powers were allies until 1941. Polish officers, taken prisoner of war by the Soviets, were massacred, en masse, in the forest of Katyn and elsewhere. All prewar incidences are historical (the Statute of Kalisz, the Confederation of Warsaw, the partitions, Romuald Traugutt, the export of food from Ireland during the famine, the slaughter in the Belgian Congo, the Ukrainian terror-famine, etc.).

The concepts of *Nichtdeutsch, gemischt* (*Mischling* of various grades), *Volksdeutsch, Reichsdeutsch, Zwangsarbeiter,* and *Pflichtarbeiter* are all historical and had legal standing. The *Nur für Deutsche* signs existed. *Rassenmischung* (*Rassenschande*) was a crime with complicated gradations and various sanctions, as well as explanatory posters. There was a *Rassenamt* (Race Office), which tended to the technicalities of marriage and other race issues. The 1942 marriage law mentioned by Marysia was indeed enacted; *Nichtdeutsch* stepping into the gutter was legally required in at least some conquered territories. The playing of Chopin and the singing of certain songs were forbidden. At various times in various regions, passes were required for any travel by *Nichtdeutsch*. Food was rationed according to race. The Bund Deutsche Mädel and the N.S. Frauenschaften were genuine organizations. The Polish Underground did publish several newspapers allegedly from the German Underground.

The Norwegians did resist the German invasion, the British were termed *Volksverräter,* there was a Danish Resistance, a German Union movement is modern conjecture. There were also voluntary SS units formed from the erstwhile citizens of nearly every occupied country (though not Poland).

Most of the laws governing *Zwangsarbeiter* existed as stated. Use of public transit was forbidden, the workers had no right to free time and could not even give testimony in court. Sexual relations were legally forbidden. Forced labor was employed in households as domestics, nannies, etc. The conditions of *Zwangsarbeiter* varied considerably, all the way from those who were deliberately worked to death (usually in industry, usually resident in camps) to those who were forced to work but were not deliberately murdered (though they often starved or fell victim to disease and beatings). Currently these groups are most often separated by the terms *slave laborer* and *forced laborer,* though the vast number of possibilities in between is not well represented by such a stark division. The conditions under which the *Zwangsarbeiter* worked were completely dependent on the whim of his or her employer. In Reich law such persons literally had no rights.

Reeducation and psychiatry have been used as indicated. The techniques and incidents mentioned are not fictional; however, they derive from personal testimony, news reports, and recent history and do not date from the Third Reich—the Gestapo's techniques were much less refined in the 1940s. The level of sexual sadism in modern torture has been considerably downplayed here. The use of a drug that prevents suspects from breathing, banging buckets placed on suspects' heads, partial strangulation via wet sacks, and other methods have reportedly been used by *modern, democratic* states. American-made "prisoner control devices" are exported and used as weapons of torture worldwide. The quote from the author that Peter reads in the bookstore in New York is genuine, as is the author's history (except the manner of his release from Auschwitz) and eventual suicide.

Finally, though the setting of this fictional tale is the Third Reich, that is just a convenience. Many other societies have been used to construct this alternate reality, and the story is not a critique of German culture. None of the incidents derive from modern Germany, and indeed that country has an excellent human rights record.

Guide to Approximate Pronunciation

There is a slight rolling of the letter *r* in both Polish and German. The *ch* in German has variable (regional) pronunciations all the way from "sh" to "h" to "k." The accent on Polish words is on the penultimate syllable. The accent on German words varies.

Names

Andrzej: *Ahn*-jay
Elspeth: *Els*-pet
Firlej: *Feer*-lay
Genia: *Gen*-yah
Gisela: *Gee*-zel-lah
Irena: *Ee-reh*-na
Jan: *Yahn*
Joanna, Johanna—*Yo-an*-na, Yo-**han**-na
Julia: *Yu*-lia
Kasia, Kasiu: *Kah*-sha, **Kah**-shu
Król: *Kruhl*
Marysia: *Mah-ree*-sha
Pawel: *Pah*-vel
Piotr: *Pyoh*-ter
Przewalewski: *P'sheh-vah-lev*-skee ̣horse
Richard: *Rik*-hart
Ryszard: *Rih*-shart
Stefi: *Shteh*-fee (German), *Steh*-fee (Polish)
Tadek, Tadziu: *Tah*-dek, **Tah**-ju
Uwe: *U*-veh
Wanda: *Vahn*-da
Wojciech: *Voy*-cheh
Zosia, Zosiu: *Zoh*-sha, **Zoh**-shu

Other Words

Armia Krajowa: *Ahr*-mya Krai-yo-vah, the Home Army; the Polish Underground Resistance against the Nazi German occupation organized into an army of the people

Babcia/Babciu, Busia, Babusia/Babusiu: various endearing words for Grandmother and the vocative forms

Drang nach Ordnung: a drive/urge for order; a pun on *Drang nach Osten,* the (Germanic) pressure to expand eastward

Du: informal version of "you"

gemischt: (racially) mixed

Hakenkreuz: swastika

kochana, kochany: *ko-han*-na, ko-**han**-nee, beloved (f/m)

Kraków, Krakau: *Kra*-koof, **Kra**-kow, the city of Cracow (Pol./Ger.)

moja kochana: *moy*-ah ko-**han**-na, my beloved (f)

München: the city of Munich

Nichtdeutsch: literally, not German; legal classification given to non-Jewish, non-Germans

nur für Deutsche: literally, only for Germans; used for parks, shops, etc.

Ordnung: order, control, organization

Polska walczy: *Pol*-ska **Vahl**-chee, Poland fights—motto and insignia of the Home Army

Rassenmischung: race-mixing, of which German/non-German, Aryan/non-Aryan, Aryan/mixed-race were some of the myriad and continuously varying possibilities

Reichsdeutsch: German born within the Reich's pre-1939 boundaries or direct descendent of same

Reichssicherheitshauptamt (RSHA): the Reich's security service headquarters

Reinheitsgebot: purity law requiring that beer contain only the four basic ingredients

Sekt: *Zekt,* sparkling wine

Sie: *Zee,* formal version of "you"

Spree: *Shpray,* the river through Berlin

SS Lebensborn: division of the SS which abducted children and gave them to German families for adoption

Szlachta: *shlak*-ta, the Polish nobility and, during the period of the republic, electors of the king

Übermensch: super-human or superior being

Untermensch: sub-human or inferior being

Verräter: *Fehr-ray*-ter, traitor

Volksverräter: *Folks-fehr-ray*-ter, traitor of the Folk; term used against the English as betrayers of their Anglo-Saxon heritage

Volksdeutsch: of the German race; used for those who did not originally hold German citizenship but could claim some blood relation (often quite remote)

Warszawa, Warschau: *Vahr-sha*-vah, **Vahr**-shau, the city of Warsaw (Pol./Ger.)

Zwangsarbeiter/in: *Tsvangs*-ahr-bai-ter/in, forced laborer (m/f)